The Royal
·FAMILY·

VIKING
75 years

The Royal FAMILY

William T. Vollmann

Viking

VIKING
Published by the Penguin Group
Penguin Putnam Inc., 375 Hudson Street,
New York, New York 10014, U.S.A.
Penguin Books Ltd, 27 Wrights Lane,
London W8 5TZ, England
Penguin Books Australia Ltd, Ringwood,
Victoria, Australia
Penguin Books Canada Ltd, 10 Alcorn Avenue,
Toronto, Ontario, Canada M4V 3B2
Penguin Books (N.Z.) Ltd, 182–190 Wairau Road,
Auckland 10, New Zealand

Penguin Books Ltd, Registered Offices:
Harmondsworth, Middlesex, England

First published in 2000 by Viking Penguin,
a member of Penguin Putnam Inc.

1   3   5   7   9   10   8   6   4   2

Portions of this work first appeared in *Grand Street,*
The San Francisco Examiner Magazine, and *San Francisco Magazine.*

Map by William T. Vollmann

LIBRARY OF CONGRESS CATALOGING-IN-PUBLICATION DATA
Vollmann, William T.
The royal family / by William T. Vollmann.
p.   cm.
ISBN 0-670-89167-3
I. Title.

PS3572.O395 R6 2000
813'.54—dc21   99-056587

This book is printed on acid-free paper.

∞

Printed in the United States of America
Set in Adobe Garamond
Designed by Betty Lew

For Lizzy Kate Gray,

the million-dollar vegan boxcar queen

Theme of the Work:

Steadfastness, or the Addict

· Funeral Sermon For A Fly ·

Who dies best, the soldier who falls for your sake, or the fly in my whiskey-glass? The happy agony of the fly is his reward for an adventurous dive in no cause but his own. Gorged and crazed, he touches bottom, knows he's gone as far as he can go, and bravely sticks. I sleep on. In the morning I pour new happiness upon the crust of the old, and only as I raise the glass to my lips descry through that rich brown double inch my flattened hero. I drink around his death, being no angler by any inclination, and leave him in the weird shallows. The glass set down, I idle beneath the fan, while beyond my window-bars a warm drizzle passes silently from clouds to leaves.

How to die? How to live? These questions, if we ask the dead fly, are both answered thus: *In a drunken state.* But drunk on WHAT should we all be? Well, there's love to drink, of course, and death, which is the same thing, and whiskey, better still, and heroin, best of all—except maybe for holiness. Accordingly, let this book, like its characters, be devoted to *Addiction, Addicts, Pushers, Prostitutes, and Pimps.* With upraised needles, Bibles, dildoes and shot glasses, let us now throw our condoms in the fire, unbutton our trousers, and happily commit

THIS MULTITUDE OF CRIMES.

> But seriousness commands us to recognize that it's the multitude of laws that is responsible for this multitude of crimes.
>
> DE SADE (1797)

• Contents •

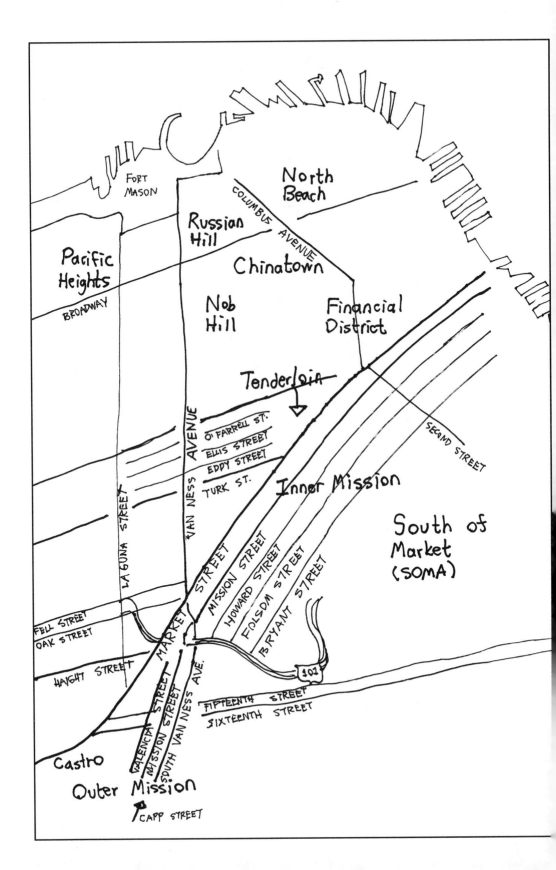

The Royal FAMILY

· BOOK I ·

The Reduction Method

•

It would be madness and inconsistency to suppose that things which have never yet been performed can be performed without employing some hitherto untried means.

Francis Bacon, *Novum Organum* (1620)
Book I, paragraph VI

•

| 1 |

The blonde on the bed said: I charge the same for spectators as for participants, 'cause that's all it takes for them to get off.

I can get a hint, said Brady.

Oh, it's not a hint, the blonde said. I don't give a fuck if you stay. You just have to pay me, is all.

That's exactly why he's not going to stay, Tyler explained.

I'll be at the bar across the street, said Brady. Try to not take as long as you did last night. This is getting really old.

My heart bleeds, laughed Tyler. Of course, it always bleeds around now. It's that time of the month.

Are you a misogynist? said the blonde.

What do you mean?

Do you have it in for women just because they menstruate and you don't?

I'm going now, said Brady.

I said, do you hate women? the blonde went on.

Have a beer, sweetheart, said Tyler in disgust. The things I put up with.

The door closed behind Brady. Tyler continued to sit on the edge of the bed for a moment, listening to his footsteps fade down the hall. He heard a door open and a woman begin yelling in Chinese. Then that door closed, too, and he heard Brady's footsteps a little longer. When they had entirely died away, Tyler sighed and put his legs up. He did not bother to remove his shoes.

I'd prefer a wine cooler instead of a beer, the blonde said. I see you have plenty.

Help yourself, doll.

I'm not a doll. I'm a human being, and my name's Domino.

Pleased to know you, he said. My name's Henry.

I used to date a guy named Henry once. He was a real asshole.

It goes with the name.

Whatever. Are you going to get undressed or not?

I *am* undressed. Do you see me wearing a necktie? My brother wears neckties. He works downtown.

Look. I've got other dates to take care of, so can't we please move things along? Just tell me what you want me to do and I'll do it.

Tyler untabbed his beer and burped. The hard grey beetle-shell of his face seemed to express embitterment, but it was only tension. His narrowed eyes guarded his soul by occluding and devaluing it. Tonight he was vulgarizing himself still further to play some conception of an appropriate part, perfectly aware of his inconsequentiality to the blonde but habit-driven to conform and mimic, just as when, spying on some potentially unfaithful banker in the financial district, he'd wear his old London fog and stand with the suspect's photograph hidden inside the latest *Wall Street Journal*. And tonight he was a nasty old whoredog. —Let's see what you look like naked, he said.

Then she took her dress off, presenting to his secret-loving eyes belly-wrinkles like sandbars, and she took her bra off to let him see her round breasts bulging with silicone, and for him she took off her panties to give to his view her crusty blackish-reddish crotch. Lying on the bed long-legged with her red shoes on, she let him finger-trace the highway of a motorcycle wound, the white island of a bullet wound pigmented with granules or black hairs. Then the pipe's orange reflection glowed on her cheek as she squatted, inhaled, took the pipe out, kissed him, exhaled her smoke into his mouth: taste of bubblegum breath, her tongue in his mouth, then the numbness and heartracing happiness.

Thank you, he said. That was good of you. (When he said it he meant it. But after all, he thought a moment later, it isn't as though doing that cost her anything. Everybody has to breathe out.)

You want some gum? she said.

No, thanks.

Well, what *do* you want?

I was wondering if you knew the Queen of the Whores.

Hell, no, the blonde said.

She lit the pipe again and got on all fours to blow her drugbreath into his mouth, looking very pretty with her buttocks high. Probably she meant to outshine his glimmer of unreadiness, since quick beginnings help make quick endings. She had things to do. He put an arm around her, pulling her toward him as he returned her kiss. Without knowing why, he'd begun to like her, drawn perhaps to the quickwitted, sarcastic rudeness and desperation of her. But business barred him from showing it. Brady wouldn't have cared if he laid her, but sexually she did not speak to him because he was in love with another woman whom he was not supposed to think of in that way and therefore perpetually did, now imagining the blonde to be her so that the blonde saw his hard face soften and his eyes dreamily open into nothingness as she pressed her mouth tighter against his, believing then, not unreasonably, herself to be the cause. Domino liked the world to think well of her. Gesturing, her arm incredibly jointed yet smooth like her breast, smooth and multi-lit like a wax pear in rainbow light (he knew perfectly well that it was the crack that so pleasantly exaggerated things), she lay on her side, caressing the mattress while her folded shoulder-shadows flickered.

Well, said jocular Tyler, if you did know, who would she be?

She might be me! laughed the whore, throwing herself onto her back with disconcerting suddenness. Then she took his hand and funnelled it down into her crotch.

That's true, he said, pretending to consider. Why, she might even be me, or Mr. Brady.

That your friend? He sure looked like a loser.

He is a loser. But he pays me.

You gonna pay me?

Yep.

You'd *better* pay me. I don't take to being gaffled.*

---

*Robbed; gypped.

Now honestly, said Tyler. Do I look like the gaffling type?

As soon as he'd breathed down the clean and bitter smoke well moistened by her lungs, his heart had begun to beat even faster, so that he felt as alertly alive as if he had been terribly afraid instead of being perfumed with delight.

Anyway, what do you want to find the Queen for? I couldn't care less about that bitch. I don't work for anyone but me.

I guess you and I are through then, he replied.

But we didn't do anything! You still going to pay me?

Yeah, I'll pay. And maybe sometime we'll even do it. (Tyler said this to all the whores. He was very polite that way.)

You'd better pay me or I'll get tough, said the blonde, not entirely able to eyelid her pleasure at winning something for *not* engaging in an act she usually hated (and Tyler, perceiving all this through his now renarrowed eyes, felt illogically, ridiculously hurt).

How can I get in touch with you? he said.

That's easy, honey. I'm at the El Dorado on Sutter between Taylor and Jones. Sometimes I change my room, but wherever I am, I always face the street, get it? Just stand under the windows and whistle four times. Or if you're in a car, honk four times. Do you have a car?

The loser does.

He does? What kind?

Here's fifty bucks, Domino. I guess I'll be seeing you.

Lying naked on that bed, playing boredly with the gold chain that lay across her breasts, she waggled her ass, hoping to interest him so that maybe she could charge him more. But he'd gotten up and was looking out the window. She sighed and got dressed.

Don't forget me, she said in a way that showed she'd already forgotten him.

He didn't think he would. He thought he could remember the long white track, the eye-shaped bullet scar.

| 2 |

The hotel had improved since the Indians took over. It didn't stink as much, and there was no litter on the floor. Behind the white curtains stained with round brown spots like old blood, the window (which he'd opened to let the staleness out) faced a gulley walled by bricks, kindred windows, and fire escapes. From down below shouts floated up like seagulls. The windowsill smelled like urine. Tyler leaned out and saw a black man who stood smoking a cigarette, the man's hair very black and shiny against the dun evil of the alley. —This has gotta be my low point, he muttered. What a stupid job. —He waited until Domino emerged from the hotel. When she didn't look up, he felt oddly disappointed. She'd barely sipped her wine cooler, so when she'd gone and the black man had sauntered away, he threw the bottle out the window and listened to it smash . . .

| 3 |

Any luck? said Brady, whose tone implied that Tyler would never own any of that commodity.

Of course she said she didn't know anything.

Did she say that she knows the Queen?

No, she didn't say exactly that.

Had a Pinkerton team work for me once, chuckled Brady, opening a bottle of pills. They told me they have a rule that you're not supposed to get emotionally or sexually compromised. But I don't give a shit.

Tyler was silent.

I said, I don't give a shit what you do.

Let's keep this professional, boss.

Did you ever get the impression that she was lying to you?

Why should she lie to me?

You care to answer my question?

She said that she doesn't give a damn about the Queen. Usually when somebody goes to the trouble to say that, that means that she does give a damn. But if that's a lie, it's not a very important lie.

It's not my policy to tell you what I do or do not consider important, said Brady.

Yeah, boss, I know it isn't.

Brady took a dictaphone from his shirt pocket, pushed the button, and intoned into it: *There were days and days of such false starts, but since this is one of those rare occasions when discretion actually serves the turn of narrative interest, I shall refrain from dragging those people and episodes into this.*

That's beautiful, boss. Are you what they call extemporaneous?

Nope. And a year from now my common stock is going to split two for one. You tag her?

Locator fluid under my thumbnail. She let me touch a scar on her leg. I worked it in good.

How good we'll know in a minute. Anything else?

Said you were a loser.

I must be, to hire you. Well, show me.

It's all wired up, said Tyler. Pinkerton guys were the only other private eyes you did anything with? Somehow I figured you worked in the security field. Guess I was wrong. Turn the TV to channel seven and then click the remote three times, like this. Uh huh. Now wait a minute. Okay. See that blue dot? That's Blondie, and she's staying on the grid. Going down Leavenworth—now see; she's turning at Turk. Stopping for a minute, probably having a little chat with her dealer, but we'll mark it . . . okay, now she's coming up Jones; she's just done three sides of a square; she's back on her beat. And I'd guess she's scratching her scar; that's why the blue dot flickered there for a minute. I'd say she's not going to lead us to any Queen. You never know, though. That's the beauty of this job, Mr. Brady. This place she keeps going to is probably just a bar, but we'll mark it, too. Computer says it's a parking garage. Maybe she takes guys there to give head. Anyhow, it's in the system. See her walking up and down the block? A slow night. But at least she got picked up by us losers.

| 4 |

Dark tracks of ecstasy down which slid blinking lights and fluffy lights, rays of warmness on cold tracks; these carried Tyler and Brady past brick hofbraus and pavement-holes. Ahead, a police car turned the corner. Pizza lights marked the edge. Then all the brightnesses started getting skinnier. White-lit arches launched them down long white slides tulipped with lamps, and they passed the Peacock Club, outside of which the first whore of the evening stood fussing with her science-fiction garter belt. Whores white and black swayed in the light. Their legs shook automatically. Tyler looked steadily out the passenger window, photographing that huddle of girls with his brother's old Minox. Expense account stuff, so gaffle me, sister. He'd thought the camera was practically invisible, but clippety-clop: three whores were running away. —Such sweet *scared* little fishies! cried Brady. —Tyler cleared his throat, wondering whether he might be catching a cold. His brain ached. They oozed down Hyde Street, waiting to breast the current of lights whose source-spring was a single rectangle of yellow high up above the corner; then there were yellow market-lights, gold lights, apartment-lights and lady-lights issuing from a hotel awning and its grating, and sex-light coming from the girl against the wall. Lonely sparks and tangents strung on hills tried to siren them away from the square rectitudes of ordinary stores. Brady would not be distracted. He stopped at an arched brick building whose scaffolding mutated against its glass. There a fat lady hiked up her skirt and pretended to masturbate, staring straight into his eyes. Through the open window Tyler said: Can you take a message to the Queen? It involves money. —Don't start shittin' me, said the fat lady. I'm not datin', so you can't haul me in for datin.' —We're not cops, said Brady brightly, but the fat lady only said: Uh huh, and you really love me and you won't come in my mouth and the check is in the mail. — Winging chevrons of gratings vanished her between vertical stripes of garage-light. Dauntless Brady swung the car back into the groove of traffic, undazzled by blinking lights on metal, dazed only by the other cuntsharks. Tyler smiled gently at the square buttocks of a van just ahead. For a moment he thought of Domino. Then the nauseating glitter on fences and gratings caught him. Breaking through a yellow lurch of hotel-lights, he saw a man checking his watch on the corner. Tyler knew that the man resembled him. The man was up to something. He winked at the man, who flinched, and then they were past. Above an awning like the roof of a mouth, a whore was smiling and bending from an orange-lit window. Tyler exposed two rapid frames (no flash, 6400 ASA) and noted the location.

Might as well roll down your window at every black girl you see, said Brady abruptly.

My window's always down, boss. I don't care how chilly it is. What makes you think she's black?

Just a feeling. That's how I imagine her. Tell me how you imagine her, and don't you dare lie to me.

Oh, I guess I could see her as one of those solarized naked blondes in an old Man Ray print. You know, with those haunting eyes. Are you into photography?

Well, I hired a guy to wire up a women's locker room once.

I collect books on photography, admitted Tyler with a certain shyness. Brady, who prided himself on knowing people, could tell right away that here lay his hireling's monomania, on which, given any encouragement, he'd discourse with arid learnedness, like other people on hockey, stamp collecting, their pets or children. —I collect photographs, too, Tyler was saying. It sort of goes with my profession. On Sundays I sometimes like to play around, you know, do nudes, double triple quadruple exposures . . . There's one. You want to pull in toward the curb, boss?

A black whore was rubbing legs at the light, crunching potato chips. She wore a silver paper skirt. Tyler mouthed the word "Queen" at her and she shrugged and waved. Brady shook his head.

Pasty-faced white girls at the corner of an alley grinned as if at a party. Tyler jumped out and asked them if they'd seen the Queen.

She never comes before ten o'clock, a girl said. Why, you got something for her? You can give it to me. Honey, you can give it to me.

Lights hurt the mirror of a parked truck.

Between two dead grey towers, a girl in a sweater swung her tits like a waitress in a truck stop slamming down a plate of fried eggs. She whipped her hands at them, glaring fiercely.

That's quite a luxuriant nigger girl, his boss said.

You from the South, Mr. Brady?

Why, do I have an accent?

No, I just wondered.

Well, stop wondering and ask her the question. That's what I'm paying you for.

Tyler crooked his finger, but the girl only spat loudly on the sidewalk.

The Queen wouldn't like that sort of behavior, you know, he said to her.

What the *fuck* do you know about what the Queen likes? the whore shouted. You think you're good enough to jump the Queen?

Why? said Tyler. Are you trying to tell me *you're* a big enough bitch to eat the Queen's pussy? Does she let you do it on alternate Tuesdays?

I oughta cut you, the whore said. She wore silver stockings that came all the way up to her buttocks. Peering sulkily, she bent and picked something up from the sidewalk.

Find out what she grabbed, whispered Brady.

What did your friend say? cried the whore suspiciously. She came over to the car. Seeing Brady's dark suit and necktie, she smiled, softly offering her goosepimpled thighs. — You datin'? she said. I'd much rather go wiv you than him.

Yeah, he's dating, said Tyler. He wants to do you and the Queen at the same time.

What do you keep talkin' 'bout the the Queen for? It's bad to talk about the Queen.

Another girl walked past, her garters glittering like frosting and mica against the scaly diamonds of gratings. Shivering, she shot a bitter look at Tyler and shouted: Am I your only secret slave? Am I the only one you're getting paid to practice slavery on?

Get lost, said Brady.

Look, said Tyler to the suspicious whore. A hundred bucks if you take me to the Queen.

The whore whirled and clip-clopped away in the direction that the other girl had come.

You scared her, said Brady reproachfully.

Let's follow along, boss. We might learn something.

That's a spurious and specious linkage, said Brady.

What?

Your assumption that because I say the word nigger I must be from the South. You're trying to stereotype me.

We'd better follow the girl, boss.

You tag her?

Yeah, with that dime store earring she grabbed. Soaked in locator fluid. I dropped it out the window when she was yelling at me.

I don't trust that locator fluid. If it's so good how come the FBI doesn't use it?

I don't know, boss. I never worked for them.

Because you're a loser?

Uh huh.

Are you evading me?

What would I want to evade you for, boss?

Because you're spending my money and wasting my time.

I could try and pull some old court records, Tyler muttered, ducking his head.

Well, maintain visual. An earring, huh? That was a good one. —Brady smiled, recollecting multitudes of other girls seduced by tented alleyways sheltering cases of earrings; they slowly bent their heads in submission to that glitter. He was rich. —Come on, come on, come on.

Sure, said Tyler. We'll just keep rolling and rolling along.

They tracked the suspicious whore through a dozen neon spiderwebs to some kind of overcast garageworks behind a grating, red car-skulls watching from beyond. Tyler sat listening to the heavy clop of that glossy-shoed girl so sour-sweet with the sweat-drops glistening from her meaty shoulders as she ran through the cold night. She'd gotten inside the grating somehow (a fat van had blocked the view), and now she vanished among the red cars.

Okay, boss. We can't go in there now; it's too obvious. It's the same place that Blondie went to last night. We'll check it out tomorrow.

Was her name really Blondie?

She called herself Domino.

Then call her Domino. Are you a misogynist? sneered his boss with a grunting laugh.

A tall black girl crossed the street with mincing clicking steps, drinking from something in a paper bag. There were frothy things on her breasts like silver spit. Other women were already smiling over her shoulder.

| 5 |

Lest it be believed that only Tyler indulged in monomania, I may as well mention that Mr. Brady was a devotee of the cottonwood tree. —A cottonwood plank in a horse stable will outlast an oak plank two to one, he said.

Is that a fact, said Tyler, counting receipts.

I personally laminated cottonwood four-by-fours to show what they could do for high-grade railroad crossings, said Brady, who reminded him of a camel-necked tan goat without ears he'd once seen, gnawing sadly on the railing of its cage. —I talked to the engineers and they just loved that idea. But I couldn't get anywhere with the purchasing department. Mr. Brady, they said to me, I'm just gonna have to be real blunt with you. Unless you're willing to pay these purchasing agents something under the table, it'll never happen.

Is that right, said Tyler. There was a whore he knew that he thought he could go halves with. She could spout nonsense about the Queen on Brady's money and give him a kickback. He didn't want this job to end yet. Brady must be rich rich *rich*. He belonged in the kind of hotel lobbies where patrons whisper instead of shout.

We ran an experiment where we were grinding those cottonwoods for cowfeed, said Brady, while Tyler was thinking: I really ought to check my answering machine. —How about that, he said.

And we had to fight every pharmaceutical company in the country. They wanted to pollute our meat with that teramyacin, that auromyacin. Those idiots at the college up there are the equivalent of the prostitute press. They went right along with the pharmaceutical companies. We couldn't get it off the ground because of the money pressure out there.

Well, I'll be, said Tyler. Are you sure they weren't evading you? —Later he went to look for the whore he could have gone halves with, but she'd been arrested.

| 6 |

Is he your boyfriend or is he your boss? said the crazy whore, her eyes gleaming like the wristwatches of hopeful young lawyers.

My boss, said Tyler.

(The room smelled like mold.)

He reminds me of the guy who got shot 'cause he kept lookin' at the robber's face. I said to him, you just don't know how to get robbed.

I can take a hint, said Brady, not getting up to go.

He reminds me of those big she-males in the street, the whore said.

Better be careful, said Tyler, guiding the conversation into interesting channels. Maybe the Queen's listening.

I don't care what she hears because very little of what she hears is real.

I can take a hint, Brady repeated, getting more comfortable. He obviously loved all this. Tyler didn't. He might have, if he'd been working alone. But this was a waste of time.

I'm just a beginner compared to Sapphire, the woman said. I haven't gone as deep as she did before she was even born.

Who's Sapphire? said Tyler.

Don't you even know that? She's the Queen's special darling. She can't talk.

Well, *you* can sure talk up a storm, said Brady. Find me an ashtray, would you?

I don't want you to talk, the whore went on. Maybe that one patheticism, what's it going to accomplish? This place is very high-class, and you know what happened? I told myself, and I told myself, but the mirror fell off and broke. 'Cause I paid my rent check. I don't need to pay it till tomorrow. Or is it not your day to be near me? Or am I whispering too much?

Oh, no, ma'am, not at all, said Brady. He winked at Tyler. —Transient psychotic symptoms. Good money there.

What the *fuck* are you talking about, boss? said Tyler.

The crazy whore frowned at Tyler and pointed at Brady. —His jollies would be bigger if he sat in the closet. Then he couldn't see me but would just feel me being nude. I'm not saying you can't get something out of me.

Want to try it, boss?

Sure. Is there a chair in that closet?

There's a very tiny looking kid living upstairs, the crazy whore said. He's a spy for the Queen. 'Cause maybe I'll identify him to the point where I'll be able to cup my buttocks properly. And then I'll just make the bed. So *what* if he spies. So *what* if the Big Bitch is listening. You know what I've been waiting for? You know what I want to say to her? I want to tell her, I want you to do it to yourself, Big Bitch. I think that'll just bring back the Golden Age. Byzantine. I remember how to hold off and how to gaffle. See how my fingers are naked? Poor me! Your friend has to understand, you know. The little kid can see right through the ceiling, 'cause he's got good eyes. He doesn't know if you guys are alive or dead, so I said dead.

Well, thanks, said Tyler agreeably. (Brady was snoring in the closet, with an unlit cigar in his hand.)

The crazy whore scratched and scratched. Possibly she had scabies.

So does the Big Bitch have a name?

A name is just something you use once for your job. Then you throw it in the trash, so vigs and pigs can't get you. See what I mean? My name is just Pussy. But after I'm done, then my name is Tongue.

What you said just made me sad.

You see what I'm saying?

Yeah, I get it. But does she have a name?

Maj or midge, they're all mosquitoes, just sucking blood and sperm for money. Maj is like *majestic* but she's not Maj. She's just the Big Bitch. And most of them are young girls. You might be shocked.

Oh, try me.

Naked, hard-nippled, with red lines across her belly, the crazy whore glided sleeves and panties across her hair. —My dollars' worth of cunt is fifty dollars, she hissed. And my dollars' worth of crack is fifty dollars. Then I'm too hypersexually active to care. I have the Mark. You don't have the Mark yet, but you will. You know what the Mark is?

Nope.

It's in the Enemy's Book. First chapter. That's not too much to read, but *you're* just a little too much to be humble. Your normal visit's just a normal visit, right?

That's right, honey. Just a normal visit. Maybe my boss will jerk off in your face or something.

The crazy whore twisted and leaned against the moldy wall, and her rear stuck out.

Tyler pulled his best confiding face and whispered: I like it when you talk about the Queen.

And I like you to say what you said, she replied. 'Cause my pussy's a nervous thing, like some kind of fungicide. And now we have to stick something up my pussy like a baby powder. Your body is prisonering me, Mister, like a car crashing into several people, like six at one time. But the Queen is the goddess of my vision. She's full of compassion and envy. She'll notice when you have something she doesn't remember. 'Cause everything comes from her. She won't leave anybody here. Little spy, you around me yet? I'm not concerned with that as much as with agreeing with beautiful colors. Or haven't you noticed? I hate Sapphire. You know why? Her colors are more beautiful than mine. Sapphire's perfect. She's the Queen's little pet. I want to kill Sapphire because I'm jealous, but I won't. I want to kill you and take your money but I'm afraid. Now, all I have to do is kill a bug that's this big. My spiders would incubate areas inside my artificial nerve. They lay their eggs in it, 'cause it's plastic. Plastic is dead to hold my eyes into my head. But the Queen has living rotting eyes. Something about me will not let me see you. But this is going to be real. *Really* real, she wept, beginning to masturbate. —I've got good luck but you can't come in. 'Cause I'm with my ex-husband. I think you can tell from your voice that I want to be with you again.

She pounced on Tyler and slammed her tongue into his mouth. He sighed and patted her naked ass, massaging in locator fluid with a half-life of three nights. She pulled away almost at once. She was licking her lips in the light of the crack pipe flame as she bounced on the bed, rubbing her clitoris. —Well, that pipe works pretty good, she said.

Tyler took one hit out of politeness, felt the good feeling, sighed, got up, and knocked on the closet door. —Huh? said Brady, awakening.

Let's go, boss. I think we're wasting time with this one. I gave her ten dollars.

The crazy whore wasn't paying attention to them anymore. She was picking little wads of tissue out of her cunt.

After they left, though, she proceeded to the parking garage at a desperate run.

When Tyler, tuning in to channel seven, became apprised of this news, he raised his eyebrows and smiled at his boss. He didn't even think any longer about the whore he could have gone halves with. He was getting interested in this project for his own sake. Truth to tell, in his sphere he was hopeful, confident, creative. The fact that Brady might be capable of dealing severely with people who disappointed him might have contributed to the alacrity of a different subaltern, but Tyler, for all his other failings—disorganization, mental inertia, withdrawal, and above all moral uncleanliness—was no coward. Brady therefore scarcely impressed him in a more than diffusive way. And the episode of Domino, who in and of herself exercised upon him retrospective fascination, had begun to raise within him certain almost magical expectations which he'd otherwise abandoned in life (with one incestuous exception which we'll get to later). What if the Tenderloin (for instance) comprised a worthwhile puzzle whose solution might enlighten him? (I'll make a few phone calls on the local level, he murmured to himself.) What if destiny actually had gifts in store for one whose habits had long since confirmed him in giftlessness?

So you didn't get a name, Brady said.

She mentioned somebody named Sapphire, but I don't think that's the Queen. And Big Bitch, Maj, all that stuff, I don't really believe . . .

I always thought this Queen was a little like Gotti in New York, Brady laughed. I always thought you really burden yourself once you go out and make a big name for yourself.

Yeah, maybe that's her thinking, said Tyler, not really listening.

The crazy whore stayed inside the garage for only about ten minutes, which implied that it might be some kind of message drop. (Brady yawned and did not cover his mouth.) Then her glowing trail unraveled itself almost as quickly as it had formed and snailed, shrinking all the way back to Ellis and Jones, where she stopped for five minutes, probably to make a crack buy, and then back to her hotel room. Tyler smiled again.

I'm tired, Brady said.

Tyler left his boss sitting in the car outside, tiptoed up the stairs, and put his ear to the crazy whore's door. He heard her singing in a sad voice:

> They called me Flower-of-Gold,
> and they called me Flower-of-Silk,
> but when I became Queen of the Fold
> they bathed me never in milk.

| 7 |

His boss had to go to Vegas for business. Tyler drove him to the airport. Then he drove home and took a cab to North Beach on Brady's nickel, just to see what the cab drivers knew. The first driver didn't know anything. Tyler was feeling pretty good. He went out for Italian food, pretending that the woman he wasn't supposed to love was sitting across from him. If he sat at home he'd get depressed. He didn't like to read anymore, and he hated television. Darkroom chemicals were expensive. There wasn't a lot to do.

The cab driver back to the Sunset was a Russian who was listening to a scratchy cassette of sad Russian songs sung by a woman whose voice was more rich and expressive than the crazy whore's, but her sadness was the same. The driver obviously loved it. Every time the dispatcher tried to call him on the radio, he'd sigh: Idiot.

Were you a soldier? said Tyler.

The Russian nodded glumly, whistling.

Afghanistan?

Afghanistan.

What was your job?

Meteorologist, said the Russsian, and Tyler didn't believe him.

You must have seen some bad things, Tyler said.

The Russian nodded.

I saw two people get killed today, said Tyler, just to see if he was listening.

Tough, growled the Russian sympathetically, shrugging his pale wide shoulders.

Do you know the Queen? said Tyler.

Not in my organization. Another one. Before, was in mine. Now finished.

Tough, said Tyler, shrugging his shoulders.

Your country finished, said the Russian. You have a problem, a black problem.

| 8 |

The ruby light winked on his answering machine, like one of Carol Doda's nipples back in the old days on the neon sign for the Condor. Carol Doda had a lingerie shop on Union Street now. Once Tyler had gone inside to pick out something for his sister-in-law Irene, but he hadn't bought anything, and he never knew whether or not the woman at the cash register was Carol Doda. Now he sat sipping at his Black Velvet, halfheartedly checking boxes on his surveillance report for Brady while he gazed across the street at one of those prismatic Victorian windows aflame with something which tigerishly shone beneath curtains. When he finished the whiskey, the answering machine was still blinking.

A long, friendly message: Somebody wanted him to spy on her husband to see if he were being unfaithful.

Tyler called back. —You know, lady, he said, divorce in California is no-fault. You don't have to prove adultery to file.

Oh, I understand that, the woman said. I just want to know. I really need to know.

Knowledge is pretty expensive, said Tyler dreamily, checking boxes on his surveillance report. And I'm booked up shadowing royalty right now. Tenderloin royalty.

How about a hundred dollars? the woman said.

A hundred wouldn't even prime my pump, said Tyler. If you want to prime my pump you have to give me five. And it could run into thousands. What if he only does her once a month? What if he takes her out of town? If he goes out of town then I've got to go out of town, too, and that's going to cost you.

You're kind of discouraging, the woman said. Almost insulting, too, I should say.

I aim to be, said Tyler. I want you to think long and hard before you decide to go through with this. Most people who come to me don't like what I show them.

Five hundred is an awful lot of money, the woman said. And you're not very nice.

I agree. So why don't you think about it and go to your teller machine to check your bank balance and look your husband in the eye and decide if you want to hate him even more than it sounds like you already do? You're welcome to hate me instead. That's my advice, and it's free advice.

Thank you, the woman said palely.

All right, said Tyler.

He had another Black Velvet and called his brother's place, but there was no answer. He started to call Brady at the hotel, but thought better of it and hung up.

| 9 |

He tried to locate Sapphire on three databases, but of the sixteen women he found, two supposedly dwelled in Ketchikan, Alaska, and none of the others showed up in California. Maybe the crazy whore was just crazy. More likely, Sapphire was an unregistered nickname.

| 10 |

I seen you! giggled the next girl. She had reddish-pale hair, and the bulb-light exposed her pimpled cheeks. —You was with that blonde Strawberry. No. That's not Strawberry. That's Domino.

And what's your name? said fresh-from-Vegas Brady, who always wanted to take charge.

Why? said the smoothwaxed lips. You datin'? You datin'?

Of course I'm dating, said Brady, oozing what Tyler considered to be unprofessional glee. My name's Mr. Breakfast, and this is my friend Mr. Lunch. He says he's not sexually or emotionally compromised. Do you believe him?

I never heard names like that before, said the lips. Set just above that pale chin, they almost reached the gigantic sunglasses.

Well, what's *your* name then?

Kitty.

Kitty as in pussy?

Hey, Mr. Breakfast, you got me wrong. I'm not a prostitute. I've just fallen on some hard times, that's all.

How much?

How much you got to spend?

Twenty.

Uh *huh*. You wanna feed my kitty? And does Mr. Lunch wanna do somethin'? You can come in my mouth or anything you want.

Speaking of mouths, Tyler broke in, guess what your friend Domino told us.

Friend? That bitch ain't my friend. Any friend she had she stabbed in the back long ago!

She told us she was the Queen of the Whores.

She did? Shit! And you believed her? That bitch must've been strung out. Too much junk!

She told us all the other girls worked for her, said Tyler, sounding as stupid as he could. She said she's the Queen.

She's not. There's no such thing.

But she said—

I don't care what she said. She's full of shit. She don't have shit. It's a man's world.

You know, said Brady in wonder, she was really strange. She started getting *friendly* as soon as we started giving her money. Why do you think that is?

Oh, shit! laughed Kitty.

Tyler hung his head. —And Sapphire said . . . he whispered.

What do you mean, *Sapphire said?* That retarded bitch can't even talk! Only mouth she uses is the one between her legs . . .

But the Queen . . .

How many times I got to tell you there ain't no Queen? If there was a Queen, she'd just be a pimp that's got a pussy. Why should you care? You don't want to hang out with no pimp.

You think we should see Domino again? said Tyler. Maybe if we gave her more money she could explain things to us.

Don't have nothing to do with her would be my advice.

Well, what should we tell her next time we see her?

Her? Tell her get lost, man. She's a nut! All she's gonna do is get you in trouble. She probably has warrants and shit.

Tyler nodded solemnly. —Well, Kitty, why don't you and Mr. Breakfast go do your business in that parking garage over there? I'll just sit here and jerk off.

Mr. Breakfast is gonna make you *wait* on him? cried Kitty in amazement. Tell him he oughta *pay* you for that.

I'll tell him.

You hear that, Mr. Breakfast?

Yeah, I heard, Kitty. Now let's go to that garage.

I don't trust that garage. I'll take you to a better place.

I'll pay ten bucks extra to take me into that garage, said Brady caressingly.

Kitty scuffed her high heels sadly on the sidewalk. —No, thank you, Mr. Breakfast. I don't never go in there.

| 11 |

The new hotel room smelled bad. Brady, who'd turned the TV on, ignored it, almost slicing the stack of photos with his nose. The bed sagged down toward him, the blue and white bedspread like the bottom of a canted swimming pool. The TV glowed orange and said: . . . *the significance of this historic achievement.* The two men stood discussing money over the round table. Tyler leaned, staring very hard at the stacks of expense money. The eyes in his grey face slowly narrowed as he thought: If only all this money belonged to me, I could run away with Irene. I could take her down a well and we'd stay there making babies and never get out . . . —Brady, whose feet hurt, leaned backward on his heels, looking softly down at the money while he was explaining. Although the greenbacks lay between them, it was obvious to whom they belonged: Brady kept pointing to them and sometimes touching them, while Tyler gazed down almost shyly. The window was open, and across the gulf between ratridden buildings another window was open, through which the blonde whore Domino was watching them. Tyler smirked and waved. Brady did not see.

I think the garage is the place, said Brady.

Well, boss, you might be right.

You don't think so, do you?

It's too early to say.

| 12 |

Arentcha cold? the whore said.

A sunburst of hair, short arms over boobs bigger than the wheels of a Greyhound bus. Her sweater was as nice as light.

You going to warm me up? said Tyler, as enthusiastically as if he hadn't asked that question a hundred times already.

The black girl's hair was bright against the dirty white of a massage parlor wall. She leaned to nurse her hair as if it were some elaborately tender creature.

Tell you the truth, said Tyler confidentially, I'm looking for the Queen.

Honey, you done come to the *wrong* place. This here's a hundred percent *girl* you're talkin' to! Try the Black Rose.

You know what I mean. Not that kind of queen, but the one that runs things. The Big Spider. The Empress of Darkness.

Honey, *sure* I know what you mean but it gonna cost you big. It gonna *cost* you.

How much? he said.

(Her eyes were the shadows behind fences.)

Whatcha really wanna do?

Let's duck into that parking garage and you can give me a blow.

Sure, honey. But not there. I know a better place.

What's wrong with that? I see girls go in there all the time.

It's just not a good place.

So Tyler went with her to the alley. As soon as he'd paid her, he saw her run into the parking garage.

| 13 |

Did she say she knew the Queen?

No, but she implied it.

Did she say she knew the Queen? his boss repeated.

No.

Okay. Do you believe she knows the Queen?

Yes.

Do you believe she knows that you believe it?

Yes.

Can you give me a basis for your belief?

When I said that a pretty girl like her probably got a lot of people to tell her things, she was flattered. She relaxed. She opened up, so to speak—

Are you emotionally compromised?

Tyler sighed. —Not yet, boss.

I think I understand. And then?

She made a reference to the parking garage. She said she never goes there. It's on the tape. You heard it?

It's not my policy to comment on what I did or did not hear. Not to you. So let's keep rolling.

Well, then I said I knew what parking garage she was referring to and I winked at her. Then she laughed.

So it was nonverbal?

Yes.

I follow. Do you believe that she believes the parking garage is where the Queen stays?

Yes.

And do you also believe that the parking garage is where the Queen stays?

Yes.

Okay. So we're ready to meet the Queen.

Yes.

Do you believe that we're ready to meet the Queen?

Yeah, I guess so.

Are you sure?

No.

Why aren't you sure?

Maybe she's dangerous.

How might she be dangerous?

I don't know, boss. But I'll tell you honestly. I didn't believe in this at first, but now it's starting to spook me.

What can she do to you?

Probably nothing that I can't do back to her.

Do you want to go in?

I'll do it.

Would you rather have more time?

Yes.

Is it because you want more expense money?

Oh, partly. And partly because I don't know what we'll find.

Don't worry about money, Henry, said his boss with surprising gentleness. I promise I'll take care of you. Will you go in with me tomorrow?

Okay.

Do you want to go in with me or would you rather go in alone? Don't lie to me.

I'd rather go in alone. I don't know how good your breaking and entering skills are, Mr. Brady. You already told me that private eye stuff isn't your field. And it makes me uneasy when a client wants to help me break the law. But I don't mind if you have a good reason, or if you get off on participating, just like Domino said. In my book, you're emotionally compromised. But if you want to distract the ticket guy that'd be useful.

I get the hint, said Brady with a grin. It's okay. I trust you.

| 14 |

Past the boarded-up bakery on Larkin Street Tyler wandered the following forenoon, his hand on his wallet as if life were really good, past the school sign and into the dark garage. —It's a perfect place, Brady had said. Nobody's ever here. Nobody but whores. —Tyler walked back to the bakery, got into his car, and drove up the slanting urine-smelling tunnel. On the second floor he backed the vehicle against the wall and sat watching the ramps—the standard orientation of any prudent man getting a blow job. As a matter of fact, Tyler did not like blow jobs. But backing against the wall remained prudent. The cold friend in his armpit did not show. The ramp to the third floor was cut off by a grating which seemed to have been down for a long time. There was light behind it, light sweating and stinking on concrete.

Nobody around, Brady tying up the attendant with some endless complaint . . . Perfect. He stuck a straw into the little spray can of Wallylube and tooted the lock. Then he thrust a half-diamond pick into the keyway and started lifting pins. They all dropped, one by one; the lock was in good working order, as a Queen's lock ought to be, especially on her chastity belt. He listened as they fell: a six-pin lock. Now for the tension wrench and the plug spinner . . . Just enough tension, thank you . . . He decided against the raking method and went by feel. He was holding the pick in just the same way that Brady held that fat vulgar rollerball pen of his. With the hook pick he raised the driver pins above the shearline, chamber by chamber; the plug rotated three or four degrees, making a shelf on which the top pins must rest so that they couldn't slam back down like a vindictive whore's teeth. (No sidebar, fortunately; this was not a General Motors car lock.) Now the bottom pins could move unobstructedly in their channels of vileness.

The lock opened on the fifth bounce. He stepped into the greasy light.

· BOOK II ·

Irene

"Generous, chivalrously generous!" Keller assented, much touched.
"But, you know, prince, it is all in dreams, and, so to say, in
bravado; it never comes to anything in action!"

DOSTOYEVSKY, The Idiot (1869)

| 15 |

To say that there were times when Henry Tyler knew his life was ashes would have been an understatement in the English manner. People who possess no backbones whatsoever (and preferably no minds, either) can be most easily pleased, like children eating ice cream; where the ice cream money comes from, and under what conditions they receive it—to say nothing of the sanguinary destiny of even the most miraculous vanilla-chocolate cow—never breaches the barriers of their victorious vacuity. Next case: Roman senator types, so prodigiously favored or ossified with backbones that they can scarcely sit down, constitute the second most fortunate regiment of souls; when events fail them, pride carries on, and when the latter dies they will probably succeed in staggering a few steps farther, fortified by philosophic resignation, until they fall at last into their open graves, muttering: At least I did the right thing. —Tyler, like most of us, had not so much claimed membership in as been claimed by the third group, comprised of those who know, and are shamed, but do not or cannot act. If the grim first half of that black Book (rarely to be met with in Tenderloin hotels because its pages were long ago cannibalized for rolling papers) truly knows whereof it speaks, why, then Tyler's own losers' club got inaugurated in the days of Cain and Abel, whose parents, like evicted junkies who boast that even now they can wrap the landlord around their grimy little fingers, had continued to insist that they could still get right with God. Why, sooner of later He'd *have* to forgive them! It just wasn't Christian for Him to go on holding a grudge like that. After all, they'd only eaten one apple—they hadn't even finished it, if you consider the core, which had borne a worm or serpent or something (and wasn't that God's fault, to provide them with rotten fruit?); no, ladies and gentlemen of the jury, that apple had scarcely been worth saving. (Thus spake the whore who'd stolen a mere twenty from Tyler's pocket while he was on Mason Street calling his answering machine.) Remembering Eden's swanky landmarks—the silvery river of vodka, the meadows of opium poppies springing white and orange in a nutmeg breeze, the Chinese-style zen rock garden whose sparkling pebbles were all refined crack cocaine—Adam and Eve could scarcely believe that their happy pre-Lapserian eternities had become dust. Anyhow, they weren't damned; they were on parole. Nothing was final. If I put a gun to my head, I know perfectly well that even after I've pulled the trigger I can always duck out of the way or even blow the bullet back down the barrel with a cheery gust of breath, because it was *I* who initiated the cause; what injustice if I couldn't control the effect!—No matter, the expelled spouses said to one another; He could come talk to them anytime and they'd help Him see the light. (Call this no backbone at all, or else backbone so well crystalized as to occupy the cranial cavity.) But Adam and Eve's boys, sullen, lice-infested, and pallid from too many seasons of hunting blind-fish in the familial cave, never owned that solace. Imperfection had not originated with them, nor had responsibility. They were cursed without meaning or recourse. Cain, unable to believe this at first, crept near Eden as soon as he was grown, and found only an angel with a flaming sword who threatened him with death. Cain wanted to know why. Still unable to believe in reality, prepared to bow and beg to make life other than it was, Cain somehow retained in his mind the image of the Hall of Justice in San Francisco, where a steady or lucky customer may well meet with the expressionless lordliness of the white-moustached, paunchy, black-uniformed guardian of the entrance, who stands with his arms at his sides while Cain, the man with a problem, explains and explains. Finally, in a clear and even friendly voice, the guardian settles everything: Go to Room 101 tomorrow. That's really the best way. —Okay, thank you, says the man rushing furtively away. —Cain was certain that there must be a Room 101 thereabouts, within which mercy would be served on little plates, glistening like slices of fresh-killed fish. And, although he never would have thought himself capable of doing this, he fell down on his knees before the angel and bowed his head. The angel struck him a glancing blow with his sword, and Cain's garments burst into flames. He rolled in the dust until the fire was quenched, cupped mud on his burns, then rose and again uttered the word: *Why?*—It has nothing to do with you or me, replied the angel. But understand this, boy: you're going to be punished as long as you live. Automatic bench warrant. Now I'm going to count three. If you're not running back to your cave by then, I'm going to burn your legs off. Don't ever come back here. *One . . . Two . . .* —Cain told his younger brother everything. —Maybe it isn't the same for you, he said. Maybe God likes you. I'll show you where the place is. Then you can ask the angel to take pity on our family. —But Abel had already made up his mind not to tempt wrath with more impulsive sallies. Hadn't they been warned? He whispered to his brother that he was afraid because he was still too little, that he couldn't run quickly, but the truth, which he had expressed in the language of expediency only because that would produce the best effect upon his brother, was that *he actually accepted lifelong submission as a moral principle.* Who was correct, then; who was exemplary—Cain or Abel? I don't care, as long as the angel wouldn't let anyone speak. (By stating the matter thus, I fall perhaps a shade on Abel's side, being unconvinced that his visit to the the gates of Eden would have been any more pleasant than for Cain.)—Enough of all this. Let's just get on with it, as Tyler's proudly impatient brother John would have said. —History with its taints, reverberations, irrevocable deeds and preexisting conditions may temporarily explain how a soul finds itself shackled, or not, but, while questions of *how* may be resolved to any degree of satisfaction, questions of *why* remain unanswered, merely slimed over by arbitrariness. Do you believe in original sin? It seems awfully unfair, and ultimately inexplicable. For Eden, take for instance the squiggles of light on the sunny dance floor of Pearl Ubungen's Tenderloin studio, where Pearl, pretty and a little famous, sat with her baby in her lap saying *tatatatatatititi* and her dancers' obliging heels going *bimbimbimbimbimbimbimbim.* They were rehearsing for some "event." A church bell tolled in the tower. In the sunken courtyard, barefoot Asian children played. Then came the fence, and then came outside where a shivering man in a hooded sweatshirt slowly urinated in his trousers, whispering obscenities. Where did he come from? Why did he stink? Why were he and the children, separated only by that fence through which each party could see the other, clothed in such different fortunes?—To put a point on it, Abel prayed timidly to a God Whom he feared, of Whom he expected nothing—correctly, as we know from the tale's round words, for God declined to protect him. As for Cain, he abandoned himself to anger and crime. He couldn't kill God or the angel, so he killed Abel. Somewhat wanting in backbone that murderer was, too, for he pleaded innocent, just like any cheap pimp who's gotten busted. But grant him this: In the end he did at least wear his Mark with defiant pride, and set out most adventurously to take up housekeeping with Lilith's daughters and other whores in the Land of Nod, which I've always assumed was the place that heroin addicts go to, somewhere far past Jackson Street's ideograms white and red on different colored awnings, somewhere out of Chinatown, maybe behind the Green Door Massage or in the Stockton tunnel or even Union Square where a red substance resembling Abel's blood offered itself for purchase in the windows of Macy's. And Cain, I read, begat Pontius Pilate, who begat firstly innocent bystanders, and secondly good Germans, and thirdly Mr. Henry Tyler, that newly ageing lump of flesh with the same stale problem of an irremediable spiritual impotence—nay, rottenness—of which he had not been the cause and for which there could be no solution. Acquiescence would render him more contemptible than he already was, and quite possibly doom him—I cite the precedent of Abel—while backbone would get him into trouble just as it had Cain. And yet Tyler said to himself: Someday I want to show backbone. I want to do something daring, good and important, even if it destroys me. —And he waited to be called to that worthwhile thing. —Sometimes he saw the narrow face of an angel opening to utter languages which he could not speak, enmeshing her words in that crazy metal spiderweb of ceiling which characterizes certain fancy poolhalls. He wanted to believe in these annunciations sufficiently to act, but the difficulty was that such backbone-showing demanded legal if not biological incest, for Tyler's angel was his Korean sister-in-law, Irene, who, not beautiful but dear, came to him for help with all her marital problems because she knew him to be on her side. Sometimes she kissed him on the lips.

Am I my brother's keeper? asked Cain, but Tyler (such is history, such progress) no longer thought to ask. This dereliction had to do less with any childhood offenses which his brother might have committed than with a mutual antipathy almost chemical in its inarguability, reinforced by the many successes of John in business. Unlike Cain's, Tyler's jealousy never drove him to the commission of actual evil (which would, as we've agreed, require backbone). The nature of the brothers' relations promoted aloofness rather than feuds. And propinquity did not even permit open disregard. There was, in the first place, their mother to be placated. She lived a mere hour and a half away, in Sacramento, which inevitably branded their existence with periodic family gatherings. Both Tyler and his brother dwelled and worked in San Francisco, that ingrown little city which with improbable regularity draws friends, relatives, and other enemies across one another's path. What could they do? Most of all, of course, there was Irene, thrilling, perturbing, and—he granted it—strangely conventional almost to the point of shallowness—but he loved her for her gentleness, her acceptance of him, and her easily satisfied neediness. No doubt the illicitness of his feelings deepened them, in consequence not only of human nature but also of the corruption of his voyeuristic occupation. Tyler hunted for people and stalked them, mostly because they were doing something wrong or because somebody refused to trust them. (If I get hired, that means something just went wrong, he liked to say. This has gotta be a low point for my client.) Even the rare missing persons cases which he took on had little to do with love or a yearning for reunification. Only once in his fourteen-year career had he ever done anything as pleasant as put a lady in touch with her old sweetheart.

The search for the Queen of the Whores typified his bread and butter. Mr. Brady, he was sure, had no particularly honorable or romantic motive in seeking her. The narrow omnipotence which Tyler rented out to his clients came to inform his own heart with a dreamy absence of scruples, and a habit of perceiving from a too professional standpoint anyone who interested him. This is not to imply that he spied on Irene, nor that Irene's own qualities had nothing to do with attraction—for she was truly unique, not in her character but in her soul. And she was wounded; her soul cried like a wounded bird's, and he heard the cry. John did not hear, at least not anymore. Isn't that the natural outcome of marriage? John committed small and egregious rudenesses toward her family—an excellent way to make an Asian woman suffer even to the point of weeping. One February weekend Irene's parents threw a birthday party for John, and John showed up with someone who claimed to be an old college friend who looked critically at the food and asked: Is this event catered?—No, said Irene's sister Pammy. Mom and I cooked it all ourselves. —Oh, the woman said. I didn't think it was catered. No wonder there's nothing here worth eating. —A look of disgust flashed across John's mouth, but he said nothing. Irene wanted to cry then for her sister's sake. She said to Tyler (who of course hadn't been present) that she didn't care when she was walking down the street alone and some white person said: *Will you look at that Chink!* but when anyone insulted her sister or her parents in her presence, it was all she could do not to attack. She said that she must be a very bad person because she often felt such impulses. Tyler, slowly shaking his head, wondered if that meant that she often got called a Chink. He thought to himself that there couldn't have been any human being more special and good than Irene. It hurt him to see how John treated her. Had *he* also cause for grievance, Tyler wondered (knowing from his work as well as from his own memories the wretched secrets which may infest domestic life), or was John simply morally inanimate? John was so cold with her—unconfiding and unhappy!

Irene said that once she'd asked her husband why he didn't divorce her if he felt so miserable, and he just turned toward her with a weary look and said: Because I know you'll take good care of me.

Don't you think that's wrong? Irene said.

Oh, he's trying to be nice. That's just John's way . . .

But isn't it *wrong?*

It's too bad, honey, said Tyler, stroking the back of her neck. It's really a shame. Remember, I told you how it would be before you got married.

I know. I'm sorry.

Don't be sorry, sweetheart, he said, embracing her. She kissed him passionately on the lips.

It was a fresh cold winter's eve of shiny raincoats and headlights of stalled traffic like luminous pairs of dinner plates stood on their edges; the pavement had become an ebony liquid which reflected upside down the people walking on it, stuck by the soles of their shoes to their inverted selves. Tyler had invited Irene and John out to dinner, knowing that John would be too office-burdened to attend. Sometimes he wondered if his brother were angry at him, or grateful for taking Irene off his hands, or simply oblivious. Mostly he tried not to think about it. They were walking down Geary Street now and Irene was squeezing his hand. He wanted to put her fingers into his mouth and suck them one by one. They strode along in happy silence. Tyler felt everything to be proceeding as it should. No surprises would frighten him.

Among those Japanese restaurants on the edge of the Tenderloin he had chosen one called Kabukicho. The client who'd first taken him there, an old Japanese banker very correctly jealous of his young wife, had been amused by the resonance of such a name in this place, for Kabukicho is one of Tokyo's red light districts. Tyler had smiled uncomfortably, fitted his fingers together, scratched his poorly shaved chin, collected his check, passed across the table the sealed white envelope of color photographs which documented just what the wife had been doing for three days and three nights in the Nikko Hotel, and pretended to be as amused by those photos as the banker strove to be—gleam of spectacles, gleam of teeth, wide carnivorous mouth! Then the banker said: What do you usually say to the client under these circumstances?—Oh, I don't know, Tyler muttered, rubbing his chin. I remember this gal who sent me to check on her husband. She calls in tears at eleven at night, her life's destroyed. Just, you know, I'm not a shrink, I don't know what to say. I'm sorry it happened. I guess that's what I usually say . . . —He never saw the banker again. That had been good money, with which he'd bought a new computer, coaxed his car into compliance with the smog inspection, reduced two of his most pressing credit card debts and paid rent for two easy months. Kabukicho thus offered good associations, not to mention good food. He also liked the polite, well-ordered bustle of the place. The clocks were sashimi dashboards and everything was neat, Asian businessmen flipping open their cellular phones, earnest young white social-democratic couples singing out: Thank you *very* much! as they went out the exit, squeezing past the line of rich and hungry folks sliced multiply by the blinds through which could be seen pink and green neon reifications of Tyler's loneliness across the street.

The sign said: SORRY—NO RESERVATIONS ACCEPTED. Tyler led his date to the head of the line and said: Excuse me; we had a reservation for two. —The waiter studied him without comment until Tyler drew from his wallet an embossed silver card which the Japanese banker had given him. The waiter accordingly clasped his hands and led them to the far end of the sushi bar, where a potted bamboo obscured them from the cardless vassals whom they had cut. Irene giggled with pleasure and squeezed Tyler's arm.

I love you, darling, he said.

Love you, *too!* she whispered, kissing him again.

She had dressed up for him, and her long brownish-black hair fell warmly down to her shoulders in a spill of glorious asymmetry which dominated her gold necklace and the careful leather buttons of her long red dress. Impassively cleaning his glasses, he imagined his mouth on her cunt for the rest of their lives. How long could that be under such circumstances? A week? Just as a sashimi barman must continually wipe down the counter, so Tyler felt compelled to touch this woman as often as he could, in order to thereby scour away the sooty gloomy thoughts that blew in upon his shining mind. He would not think about the ordinary, unforgivable sadness of the world for as long as he could be next to her. She ordered flying fish roe, a salmon skin handroll, some yellowtail, *unagi,* and octopus. To give him pleasure, she ordered a beer for herself; she knew that it made him happy when she drank with him.

Did you work today? she said.

Yeah, still with that crazy rich guy from Missouri, he said as the barman's knife began flickering across the translucent windowpanes of fish, cutting them into shutters.

What does he want from you?

Oh, he wants me to find somebody in the Tenderloin.

Is it dangerous?

Not at all. It's kind of interesting actually . . .

You look sad, she said.

Sometimes I get so goddamned sad, so sad for everybody. Well, sad for myself most of all, I guess, since I'm as selfish as the next guy, but you know, Irene, all the time in my job I see people hurting themselves, hurting each other, pissing on each other, sleeping in their own piss. I wish I could help just one of them, but I don't know how.

You're an angel, Irene said. You really are. I feel so selfish compared to you. All I ever worry about is my own little life . . .

You're the angel, not me, he said, finishing his beer. The waitress looked at him as she took the bottle away, and he nodded. Irene hadn't finished hers yet. She was extraordinary to gaze on, but he didn't know why, her face being in fact puzzlingly ordinary in each of its parts; it was the affection and gentleness that animated it which made her so sweet to look at.

How's life at home? he said.

You know how it is, she said.

Sure, he said. Should we try the *fugu?*

After he'd paid the bill he helped her on with her raincoat which was yellow like a child's and walked her past the sharp-cornered marble pillars of hotels pimpled with raindrops, their lamps reaching smeary fingers of light up into the cool grey sky. Tourists were hurrying out of closing shops. He glanced down into the Tenderloin and saw the folded neon leg of a woman winking but never unkinking.

Please don't tell any of this to John, his sister-in-law was saying.

Don't worry, honey. The car is up this way.

You know, I told my mother about you. She thinks it's funny that you and I are so close.

Have you told her how you feel about your marriage?

That would hurt her too much. I always tell her I'm so happy, John's so good to me . . . Because, you know, when he was making me cry before we got married, she told me to break it off, but I wouldn't . . .

A big drunk black man sauntered up to them and shouted in Irene's ear: I'm gonna fuck you up, you slanteyed stinking Chink, stinking Chink—

Tyler put his right arm tightly around her and slipped his left hand into his coat pocket where the pistol was. —Don't feel bad, sweetheart, he said to her, never taking his eyes off the man's face. You're not Chinese, so he's not talking about you.

He led her around the man, who stood there swearing and muttering.

Her hand was fiery with hot sweat. Her fingers were squeezing his with all their strength. He could not stop himself anymore. He brought her fingertips to his lips and begin to lick the hot, delicious sweat.

| 16 |

Now Irene was gone. He almost couldn't bear it.

Driving across the cable car tracks, which offered rain-light more glancing than the tips of hustlers' cigarettes, he heard someone yelling from the direction of Glide Memorial but couldn't see a soul. He spied a man and a woman doing business by a grating. He saw a woman, drunk, shaking her dead-snake hair and spreading her fingers from which raindrops fell as if she were a Calico hundred-shot assault pistol ejecting bullet casings onto the concrete. He turned on the windshield wipers to control this very fine rain like sooty static crawling down the building-fronts, and discovered directly in front of him a man slowly walking as though his feet hurt, dragging an immense vinyl grip-sack; he braked until that man was out of the street. He rolled down the window and drove to Turk and Leavenworth, where a callipygian woman snailed her way through the rain, too wet to bother lowering her head anymore. Rain began to dribble down onto the passenger seat. He saw a single darkly brilliant strand of Irene's hair on the headrest. Somebody honked behind him, but the orange hand of a DON'T WALK sign thrust itself balefully into his perceptions. He rolled up the window. The light changed. Advancing west on Turk Street, he saw a man drinking from a styrofoam cup and gazing at the reflection of his shoe on the pavement; then he saw a man whose raincoat resembled some sea mammal's skin, sleeping in a puddle of urine and rain.

He saw Domino go skittering into the parking garage, shot three souvenirs of her with the four hundred millimeter lens, and noted down the time and frame numbers on the surveillance report form on his clipboard.

He drove up to North Beach to see if Irene's living room window were still lit. It was not. Perhaps John had come home and they were already fucking, but he didn't think so because she'd told him that they hardly ever did it anymore. Maybe she was reading in the bathtub. Maybe she had gone to sleep. Perhaps John had asked her to pick him up at work.

Easily and rapidly now he rolled down the shining streets to the Tenderloin where outside the XX and XXX preview booths, guys in baseball caps were having a discussion. Extending the antenna microphone, he heard:

They be tryin' to say they *ask* for it.

Shit, baby, yeah. My ho done ast for it. I give huh a good smack upside the jaw.

Hey, you s'pose it's true what they say?

(Somebody honked behind him. He pulled into a loading zone and let the car pass, which it did, angrily blaring its horn.)

You better shut your lip. Lookit that honky in the car over there like some spy for Vice.

He don't have *nothin'* on me!

Nothin' but parole violation, mothafuckah.

Hey, I'm goin' to court, I say I sold dope on a bet. That's all it was, Your Honor, just a mothafuckin' bet.

And yoah ho won't nevah bail you out!

If she doan bail me out, she done ast for it. I'm gonna break huh teeth. She'll give bettah head then anyways . . .

Hey, remembah what I said. Maybe it's true what they say.

Maybe honky over there needs a piece of rock. A nice big piece of white girl.*

What they say?

They say when you talk vi'lent 'bout yoah ho, sometimes the *Queen* be listening . . .

Fuck that bitch! I ain't scared a no goddamn bitch! Brain's in her cunt; my dick is twice her I.Q.!

An' my dick's the othah twice of yours!

---

* Crack cocaine.

Hey, check out that honky sittin' there. I doan like that honky. He come out here, I fuck him up—

Tyler, bored anyhow, but glad to learn that the Queen might represent justice, pulled out of the loading zone and drove to Eddy and Jones where a knowing pimp was explaining something grand to his knowing wife-employee; there walked Domino in the rain; he remembered the shape of her bullet-scar. Her nose looked longer than usual, as if she'd been telling more lies about the Queen. The red neon whisper HOTEL made rain-sweating bricks blush, as if on fire with the slumlord's lust.

He honked four times, and she came running. He said: Do you remember me?

Sure, asshole. You're the misogynist. Are you dating or not?

I'm lonely, he said. I'll pay you five bucks just to ride around the block with me.

Ten'll work.

How about seven?

Fucking cheapskate, she laughed, getting in. He counted out a five and two ones from his wallet, added another single for courtesy, and drove silently around the block.

Here we are, he said.

You mean that's it?

Uh huh.

You know what? said Domino. You're a fool. You're making me really angry.

Because you got something for nothing, but it wasn't enough? Or did I hurt your feelings because I didn't want to fuck you?

Look, pal. You don't know the first thing about my feelings. So don't patronize me.

I'm not trying to patronize you, he said. I was just lonely, that's all. And I thank you for riding with me.

She softened. —All right, she said. What's your name?

Henry.

I'm Domino.

I know.

She kissed his cheek faster than any rattlesnake could ever strike, then leaped out of the car and loped away. Tyler smiled uneasily, scratching his chin.

Uncovering no activity at the entrance to the parking garage (a fact of little probable value, which he recorded nonetheless on the surveillance report form soon to pad out Brady's files), Tyler drove up to Union Street where an immense pear of light bloomed from an apartment's stairway and stretched halfway across the pavement. A truck blinked its weary lights, and a foghorn warned of the least dangerous thing.

His brother John came out, holding another woman's hand.

| 17 |

Once Irene had asked him whether he had any reason to believe that his brother might be unfaithful, and he, professionally knowing that all men and all women were unfaithful to something, said: I don't know. I wondered that at your wedding. I hoped that he'd be good to you. I wanted you to be happy . . .

And tonight, of course, he'd been holding Irene's hand.

| 18 |

John Alan Tyler was not yet sufficiently established in his career to own a house in San Francisco, much as that would have pleased his wife. This had less to do with money than with the allocation of money. (Doesn't that apply to all of us? Couldn't the crazy whore buy a mansion in Pacific Heights, if only a certain percentage of her gross receipts went into the piggybank for, say, seven thousand years?) Although John was still young, having only recently passed the third-of-a-century mark, he received a salary almost commensurate with his idea of his own importance. Much of it he had to spend on clothes, because in the office it was a matter of faith for all to appear in five different suits a week, with extra apparel for interviews, public appearances and business trips. John did not set this policy, and I cannot disparage him for abiding by it. Then there were his neckties, which his brother had mocked during that first meeting with Domino. You wouldn't believe how expensive a necktie could be until you'd gone shopping with John, who remained convinced, perhaps rightly, that everybody who mattered knew how much those neckties cost, and treated the wearer accordingly. —His elder brother, to whom stripes were stripes and plaids were plaids (or, when he was drunk vice versa), did not matter. Still, John would say one thing for Hank: He was very good to Irene.

John was well aware that his wife had reason to feel neglected. He loved her sincerely. When she had broken off their engagement, he hadn't even reproached her, although sitting alone he'd slowly squeezed a wineglass in his hand until it shattered. John belonged to the Order of Backbone. When called upon, he could be generous and magnanimous, even good. Once Irene agreed to marry him after all, their future deliciously in the bag, he did not feel quite so called upon. Irene was an excellent woman who'd undoubtedly go to heaven when she died. But a necessary part of her excellence was an idealism which he admired but did not share. To speak more plainly, John had discovered that Irene was positively mushy with fantasies. She'd required a "fairytale wedding," which he'd provided, although his mother had been against it and he was still paying off the bills. She also expected to live happily ever after. She seemed to believe that since they were married, he shouldn't work anymore, just stay home day and night with her. She was spoiled. John had to put her straight. First of all, he explained, he did have his friends, who had known him long before he'd met her and whom he was not prepared to dismiss simply because he had married somebody. Then there was the fact that he did have to go to work amidst the tan-hued, grooved cliffs of the financial district, where below mailboxes and flags, chilled by the Transamerica Pyramid's steeply tapering shadow, breadwinners hastened to new appointments, with their neckties blowing. Irene for her part had started as a dental receptionist, but then the dentist got audited and that was the end of that. She was reading the want ads now—so she said. John wished that she didn't get so sad and bored, especially on those foggy rainy nights when he must stay late at the office. Precisely because he did not intend to work for Rapp and Singer more than another five years (unless they made him full partner on excellent conditions), he had to put in his time. He wanted a brilliant promotion, and then he wanted to transship, probably for Harville and Keane, although Dow, Emerson, Prescott and Liu occupied a comparable place in his aspirations. Once he had gotten in solid with Harville and Keane, which would take another three years of late office nights, he wouldn't be much over forty and Irene would be just thirty-four, at which point they could start a family. John knew not to stop at one child, which would otherwise grow up lonely and spoiled like his wife. He himself had benefitted from the fraternal relation, as he was the first to acknowledge; certainly Hank felt the same way. Sometimes he wished that he and Hank had been closer in age. As John saw it, the second child ought to come quickly after the first— ideally, not more than a year later. Two nearly at once would be less work for Irene than two spaced several years apart. Besides, they could play together. Whether or not there would be a third child remained open to discussion. If Irene felt strongly one way or the other, he would not quarrel with her. When he closed his eyes, however, he could imagine two little boys and a little girl; he could almost see their half-Asian faces and dark eyes as they played games on the living room carpet, their voices lowered because he was working. The boys would be named Eric and Michael, and he thought that their sister would be called Suzanne. Irene could choose their Korean middle names, which she'd most likely do in consultation with her extended family. She had already agreed to stay home for a few years once the babies were born. In fact, a few months after their marriage John had spoken with his mother-in-law about this. Where was Irene then? She must have been out shopping with her cousins, or playing golf with her father. The conversation would have taken place at Christmas, when they always drove down to Los Angeles. Although Irene loved to complain about his rudeness to her parents, he and they actually got along quite well. Irene's mother said that Eric, Michael, and Suzanne all sounded like excellent names. In confidence, she told John that Irene lacked common sense. She hated to say this about her own daughter, she continued, smiling and ducking her head, but that was how it was. Irene always went about with her head in the clouds. Her mother thought her quite lucky to have met a man like John, who would take care of her and perhaps indulge her a little. John nodded while his mother-in-law refilled his *soju* glass. He knew that nothing he could do would make Irene's parents happier than transforming them into grandparents. And Irene wanted children even more than he. In about seven years, then, life would be exactly as it should be. They would have a house in Marin, which would soothe his southern California girl of a wife, who re- mained unaccustomed to this crowded, expensive city where most people had to live in apartments.

Meanwhile he wished that he could make Irene happier. Sometimes, not often, he told her to take the credit cards and go shopping. Then he did his best not to wince at the bills. It pleased him to imagine her pleasing herself at Macy's or the Emporium, and he attempted always to take her mother's words to heart. Poor thing, she did need a lit- tle indulgence. But how much indulgence was enough? She might have gotten more out of him, had she not so frequently expressed the view that he kept her on a leash. She truly didn't realize what she cost him. Regarding the payments on her wedding ring, Irene had quickly put him in his place: These were to be accomplished by him in much the same style as defecation—behind a closed door, with all evidence removed at the end, and no reference to them afterward. Well, his mother was almost the same way; he could understand that. But Irene, unlike his mother, almost justified the appellation of spendthrift. At the end of their very first tax year he had been sickened by the marriage penalty, which was hardly Irene's fault, but he had still been deluded enough then to be- lieve that a man need hide nothing from his wife. The result of that conversation had not quite been what John expected. Well, John had learned! He no longer criticized her to her face, and he never had the heart to speak ill of her to others, either. When the bills came in, he paid. Irene *would* buy what she wanted to buy—oh, shoes for Irene, exercise classes for Irene, Irene's trips home to her parents, Irene's ski lift tickets. Let's not mention Irene's habits in grocery shopping (she had to get the most expensive brands of everything, especially paper towels, which she truly wasted), or Irene's allergies, which required them to buy a humidifier and an air purifier, both items which increased their utility bills. And the quarters for the washing machine dowstairs! He couldn't believe how many quarters Irene needed all the time . . . Then there were the restaurants and *then* there were the clothes. Because such bargains proved his wife's budgetary unreliability, John computed all the finances himself, and by the time he'd wrapped up that homework and maybe (more rarely than he realized) went bowling with his friends or watched a cop show on television, or sat through a romantic video with Irene, it was time for bed. He got very tired at night, even on the weekends; Irene had no idea how hard he worked! When he turned out the light, she sometimes rolled into his arms. At first he'd found that flattering, but it became an imposition. He wished that he could make a deal with Irene, but venturing onto that subject, like the matter of the wedding ring, would cost him no matter what. He felt guilty to disappoint her. And yet it had begun to seem that he disappointed her no matter what he did! If that was truly how it had to be, why open his mouth? He talked with his friends, who agreed that night after night a man couldn't be expected to lie always at the ready, and if he wasn't, then what right did the woman have to sulk? He wished that his friends could explain this to Irene; better just to say that he was tired. One night she'd forgotten to take her pill, as he'd discovered when he got up to drink some water. He shook her awake and made her swallow that pill then and there. Didn't she know that they weren't ready to have a baby? Irene said that she was sorry. A couple of nights later, he heard her vomiting in the bathroom. She said that the pills sometimes made her nauseated. Well, he didn't want to compel her to take her pills if they made her sick, but he didn't want a baby yet, either. As a matter of fact, carnally she had never appealed to him. One of the reasons that she had broken off their engagement that first time was his unceasing commandments to lose weight. Particularly with her clothes off, there was something grotesque about her shining belly and her big breasts. Her pubic hair in particular seemed obscene. It was so dark and rank, like weeds. Actually, her entire body sickened him. He tried not to contemplate the fact that he would be looking at it for the next half-century. John had chalked up several relationships before—not that he'd ever been promiscuous like Hank—and he admitted that the female form had ceased to surprise him. In his view, sex was the least important part of marriage. Barton Rapp at Rapp and Singer, a man of more than sixty, had told him that after age fifty or sixty, most married couples preferred to sleep apart. They got a better rest that way. —You know, John, Mr. Rapp had said, one morning you just wake up and realize that you've had enough. —John didn't yet feel called upon to make that separate bed a habit, but there were certainly nights when he would have preferred his own mattress. Although Irene fortunately did not snore, she had a habit of smacking her lips in her sleep, as if she were hungry for something, endlessly, loudly, revoltingly, like his mother's dog Mugsy lapping up water from a bowl. Sometimes her noises awoke him, especially on nights when office worries pressed down upon his brain. Or, startled by some inimical dream, she might jerk suddenly, coiling all the blankets around her. She had any number of ways of ruining John's sleep. Usually he told her to get ready for bed while he was saving his files on the computer, and he waited until he heard her come out of the bathroom before he actually powered down. Then he drank a glass of skim milk, brushed and dental flossed his teeth, urinated, washed his hands, shut off the bathroom light, and stood in the bedroom doorway. Sometimes she was reading a romance and sometimes she was staring at the ceiling. The light switch was by the door, and it would have been pointless to get into bed and then right out again, so he turned it off as soon as he came in If she was reading, she put her book face down on the vanity; he always waited for that sound. Then, closing the door behind him, he undressed in the dark. He would already have taken his suit off when he'd first come home, so it was no worry to drape his casual clothes over the back of the chair. —Good night, he'd say, getting into bed. —Good night, said Irene. —Sometimes he laid his arm across her shoulders then. He didn't have to set the alarm. It went off automatically each morning at seven-twenty unless he reprogrammed it. On Sundays they often slept in until eight-thirty or nine, unless his work was pressing or some anxiety awakened him. Anxiety might on second thought be the wrong word, for John enjoyed his life and his work. He was a capably practical person, and the impression of youth and foppishness which he unknowingly gave off to the senior partners only made them smile indulgently, for youth would pass, was passing already; as for the other, they knew that the promptings of such vices would drive him up the ladder, whose price at every rung *they* would extract.

I cannot say that there was much talk about John in the office, Roland Garrow with his slicked-back hair being the funny one, the one whom everyone in the office laughed about. Roland had been known to come running in five minutes late, with his tie askew; he patronized most of the same stores that John did, but John did not tell him about Donatello's, a small shop in San Mateo, of all places, which sold hand-painted silk ties direct from Italy. Once John saw the mark of sooty lips on Roland's tie and smiled all day; he realized that Roland had caught his tie in the elevator door.

Roland was actually quite clever. Mr. Singer, who prided himself on his ability to distinguish mere immaturity from inability, had let it be known that he was charmed by Roland, while Mr. Rapp likewise indulged him, admiring the young man's energy (he could certainly shoot out a quick if unpolished brief), and being entertained by Roland's anecdotes of nights misspent on the town. Both partners liked to consider themselves *bon vivants* who had sowed several football fields' worth of wild oats, although in their day they had actually resembled John far more than Roland. They enjoyed good wine; Mr. Rapp was, as he put it, passionate about opera, had a box seat, and in the mornings was often to be heard whistling some aria from "Tosca" or even "Lucia di Lammermoor." He went to Seattle every two or three years to witness the Ring. It was said that the San Francisco Opera would come into quite a bit of money at his death. Mr. Singer exemplified a more down-to-earth type; baseball fan and egalitarian, he was the one to whom the clients came when they needed a deferment on their bills. I repeat: Both of them were delighted by Roland, particularly Mr. Singer with his thin, cackling laugh. Roland had quickly become their rosy one, their prodigal if not quite their son. John, on the other hand, lacked a sense of humor. He was not what you'd call Mr. Personality, Mr. Singer once said. Naturally, personalities finish last. There were no plans to make Roland full partner.

They knew very well that John was thinking about leaving. For one thing, all junior partners thought that way. Industry policy as much as personal cunning had taught Mr. Rapp and Mr. Singer to make the young ones work as hard as possible. That way, they themselves didn't need to work as much; they deserved to coast a little now, after all! (Mr. Rapp had already begun to talk about retirement.) And if John, Roland, Ellen or even Yancy left, then the bosses would have already gotten their money's worth. The other half of this pincer movement was to pay high bonuses, and to imply that promotion was within sight. This invariably resulted in more work for more years. I cannot accurately claim that John understood this, for to him the minds of others were not simply those proverbially closed books, but closed books which he had no interest in reading. And had it been explained to him, it would not have affected him in any way, unlike Roland, who would have slammed his fist in his palm and shouted: *Those bastards!*, then taken a long lunch on the company and hurried defiantly back to work. Most likely Roland in all his defective elegance had already done precisely that. Call him Abel. His only mistake, which of course Mr. Rapp and Mr. Singer tacitly encouraged, was to flatter himself that he truly belonged to the circle. Ellen was a cipher, and Yancy a drudge. I'll give them no space in this book. As for John, he studied his own interests well, but the motives of others offered him small relevance. (One result of this thinking was that he grew surprised, even infuriated, by actions of others which he had not foreseen and which, therefore, might appear to him as betrayals.) At any rate, if he performed his share, and more than his share, then the cup of success must inevitably fill, no matter how he judged others, or others him. In Irene, of course, he'd won a true companion, who'd drink of that cup with him as it brimmed, and who accordingly must grow happier and happier. Meanwhile he worked, and went out with his friends, most of whom, like Roland, had not yet married; it was to be expected that they sometimes flirted, and when they did, he would, too, which was why Hank now chanced upon him holding a woman's hand.

| 19 |

Tyler's first thought was to drive on, in order to avoid embarassing his brother. But then he wondered whether John had seen him, or recognized his car; John had an eye for cars, especially cars which had once belonged to John. Unhappy and ashamed, he rolled slowly to a parking spot half a block ahead, locked the doors, and walked back to the apartmentfront, while rain ran down the back of his neck.

Apparently he had done exactly the wrong thing, because John hadn't seen him. He was now passionately kissing the girl, who of course opened her eyes and, spying Tyler over the back of John's head, panicked and pulled away. John turned around quickly.

Hello, John, said Tyler.

He knew the girl. Her name was Celia Caro, and she worked for an insurance company in the financial district. John had introduced her once at a miserable party which Tyler had regretted going to. She and Irene had met several times.

So you're snooping again, said John bitterly.

Tyler dealt with this as he had dealt with the black man's comment about Irene's race, by deflecting it. In the years he'd devoted to his job, which did indeed involve snooping, he had learned that this was the best way to prevent truculence from gaining its desired stranglehold. —I just happened to be driving by and I saw you, he said. Wondered if I could buy you a drink. You're welcome also, Celia.

I have an interview early in the morning, said Celia awkwardly.

All right. How about you, John?

You know what? said Celia. I'm standing here in the rain, and I'm not getting any drier. I'm going to bed. Goodnight, Hank. Goodnight, John.

Goodnight, said Tyler.

John said nothing.

They walked silently around the corner, and John said: Here's a good place. This Branden's.

Ah, thought Tyler to himself. So he comes here often.

And how was dinner? said John when they were seated at the bar of this rather ferny and overpriced watering hole—a John kind of place, thought Tyler. Slow, silent, massive fanblades turned like windmills.

Very good, thanks. Sorry you couldn't make it.

Sorry I couldn't make it, agreed John with what his brother suspected of being sarcasm, gulping half a Scotch rather savagely. I was wrapping up the Peterson case. You read about it in the papers?

No.

Oh, well, forget it. Somebody got terminated and somebody else is suing.

You're suing?

Exactly, said John proudly. Tyler relaxed. He had begun to make his brother happy.

But that narrow, immensely powerful mind kept whirring in its narrow track, like a snowmobile circling round and round at rope's end, grinding deeper into the powder until it finally grazed hardfrozen earth, and John said: Was it to spy on me that you came here? That's all you do day and night, your filthy spying.

John, I didn't know you were with Celia, and until now I didn't know where Celia lives.

And you're going to fuck me around with Irene, aren't you? You're going to tell Irene, aren't you?

No, I'm not, said Tyler easily. He was so used to humoring people that promising the moon came readily to him. It was a reflex. He did not have to decide whether or not to be bound by that promise until later. Besides, he could not think of any earthly or celestial reason why he ought to make Irene sadder.

Slowly the light faded from those glaring eyes. John trusted him. Tyler finished his beer. He wanted to do something with his hands, so he signalled the bartender for another.

Have you called Mom lately? said John.

Tyler knew that John hoped to catch him out. As a matter of fact, he had telephoned their mother just yesterday, but John would be annoyed not to have that to reproach him for.

Not lately, he lied. How's she doing?

Fine, said John, stirring his drink. Then he said: I talked to Mom for about five minutes at lunchtime. She's having chest pains again. She said that you called yesterday, he added triumphantly. I guess you just can't be straight with people even if it's more trouble to be crooked.

Oh yes, said Tyler. That's right. I did call her yesterday. But she didn't mention her chest pains to me.

Are you saying her condition isn't serious?

No. I guess I'm saying that she tells you more than she tells me.

(This was another lie. His mother had informed him of her chest pains, but he wanted to flatter John.)

You're crooked through and through, said John happily.

Tyler was cold and tired rather than angry. He did not want to see his brother again for a long while. But he had been trying sincerely to please him, and he had succeeded. He felt in some strange way needed, hence worthwhile. Then there was Irene. He couldn't forget Irene.

Rows and rows of inverted glasses crouched upon the shelf before his eyes. They were precious crystalline fruits filled with the light of emptiness. His eyes began to hurt when he stared at them, so he gazed around the barroom and was pleased to discover between the notes of loud but muffled music worshipful young girls and boys, gracious old baldies, starry-eyed men who longed to get into the pants of the women they were buying drinks for, loud-talking boyfriends explaining and explaining, girls out together, shaking their heads at each others' wit. A drunken blonde was bowing and clutching her crotch as she waited for the women's room.

And how's everything at work? he asked, wondering if he were repeating himself.

Fine. We just got a six-million-dollar case but I don't know how deeply they'll let me sink my teeth into it. Oh, I guess I told you about it already. The Peterson case . . .

(So he's a little drunk, Tyler thought.)

And how's the home life?

Couldn't be happier, said John, drumming his fingers on the edge of his beer glass. —Irene's a great gal, terrific gal.

They sat there awhile, and John's throat jerked, and John said: How about you?

Lucrative.

That's a switch. You ought to quit while you're ahead. Get a decent tie; find a respectable job . . .

Tyler ducked his head. —Where's the best place for ties?

Gaspard's, said John, his face lighting up again. That's a hell of a classy place. Even that clod Roland knows enough to go there. But—well, sometime I'll have to take you to Donatello's. That's my little secret. You wouldn't know a decent tie if it strangled you. But I can run you over there sometime. Actually, Irene has got a pretty good eye. Maybe she—

I guess silk is the thing, Tyler said, a little uncertainly.

At Donatello's you don't even wipe your ass with less than a hundred percent handmade silk. But it's not cheap, I'll tell you that. Last Christmas Irene bought me one of their Fog City Paisleys, a unique print actually, and though it almost killed me I made her take it right back. Irene was *not* happy. It one of *those* nights. But the next day my bonus came, and that's the tie I'm wearing right now.

Pretty fancy, John. You're lucky you married someone with such good taste.

She knows what I like, said John complacently. Well, I guess I should be getting back. Celia can run me home.

Okay. Let me just get this barkeep's attention.

Forget it, said John. I've got a running tab here. No, I mean it. You took Irene out tonight. Don't think I don't keep track of those things.

| 20 |

Tyler went to a pay phone and checked his messages. Pressing the three digits of his secret code (which he knew from professional experience would not be much of a secret to anyone who cared), he heard the tape rustling backward, and for a moment was certain that Irene was calling him, or maybe Brady, but it was only some unfaithful husband he'd nailed who was threatening pathetically and drunkenly to sue him for invasion of privacy. Tyler had the geek's home number. Composing himself to be a mouthpiece of friendly warnings, he telephoned, but got no answer, although it was already after eleven. The mistress had left town in a hurry, and he didn't think that the man would be staying at her place anymore. Who knows; could he have shot himself? He was a gun collector. That would be convenient, Tyler thought. I hate dealing with these assholes, in or out of court.

He drove down to Larkin Street, photographed a drug deal for his friend Robert the cop, rolled past the parking garage and noted no traffic in or out, an observation which would not thrill Brady (although Brady nonetheless kept a notebook filled with such tabulations as Mamie [from Atlanta], age 28, on 8th betw 38th and 42nd; $20 + $5 for drinks—30 min) but just the same Tyler recorded No traffic in his surveillance report; then, via North Beach (where not far from the sequinlike neon beads of Adam & Eve a crowd of bus-attenders stood outside City Lights, ignoring the delicious books in the window, indifferent even to the black and white paperbacks of *Howl* stacked up in pyramidal altars to the 1960s), he returned to Union and saw John's car still parked in front of Celia's. If he had to guess, they were quarelling, not smooching, because his visit would have left Celia defensive and John simply mean. Not that it was his business. Why didn't he go back to North Beach? Sometimes he stopped at City Lights to buy an issue of *Industrial Photography Quarterly,* which proffered tips on espionage, displayed photographs of pistols he couldn't afford to own, and in its back pages sometimes consented to carry mail-order ads for locator fluid, not the good stuff that he bought with his special I.D. at the film department of Adolph Gasser's, but stuff that was good enough to cut the good stuff with. He thought about calling Irene just to hear her voice, but that would be wrong. Sometimes zeal accomplishes the opposite of its objectives. He started toward City Lights, but by the time he'd emerged from the Broadway tunnel, whose sparkling yellow walls were that night silhouetted by hooting roller bladers, he'd changed his mind. Back to Polk Street—he remembered when Johnny Love's was Lord Jim's, actually not so long ago now. It had begun to drizzle, so that the car ahead was smeared and glowing. Crawling reflections made his own vehicle bubble inside like an aquarium. Hoping that John would be good to Irene when he did come home, he cruised down to the Mission, yawned, and checked out Capp Street where a weary old junkie was breaking in a spring chicken, explaining: Put your leg out, way out, and bend at the knee—that's right! God, my feet hurt. You know how your toenails hurt when they're too long? And I hate all this traffic. It's just too hectic. It's not calm. Now bend your back leg, too; okay, honey, straighten it out, lock it and wiggle your butt; yeah, show 'em some ass just like the Queen said . . . —but then the two whores saw Tyler's slow-cruising detectivemobile and he had no more reason to linger, so he stopped at a gas station for unleaded and a stick of cheese-flavored sausage, admired the grand old curvy-cylindered-windowed Victorian houses on South Van Ness, swam past the parking garage, from which two whores were just then emerging (he photographed them and scribbled something down in the DESCRIPTION OF ACTIVITIES line of his surveillance report), wound his way back to Union Street and found John's car gone. Grimly grinning, he said to himself: Am I my brother's keeper?

| 21 |

The following morning, when John arrived at the office (in the corner of his eye Irene's car just beginning to pull away), a new doorman was there. They gazed at one another's uniforms and passed without speaking; John had never even known the old doorman's name. In the elevator beside him rode his plump secretary, Joy, whose spectacles goggled at the world from an unbeautiful but serene round face. She'd cut her hair short, and was wearing a blue dress. —Hi, Mr. Tyler, how are you? she began breathlessly; I'm a little harried but I did call him today . . .

Who are you talking about? said John. Say, is my tie straight?

Mr. Brady, she said.

What did he say, Joy?

He got the deposition, and he said to tell you that he's very satisfied.

John smiled.

The elevator arrived. Pink-cheeked Joy scurried into her little cubicle, of which a cassette player and tapes took up a quarter, and John, passing by, glimpsed the baby seat for when she worked on weekends, the filing cabinet and the two desks crammed end to end. —Good morning, Mr. Rapp, he said.

Morning, John. Congratulations on getting Brady.

Oh, thanks, Mr. Rapp, laughed John, blushing with happiness.

Joy peeked out of her lair, her smile expressing full unity with Mr. Rapp's *mazel tov.*

| 22 |

The amber button buzzed on John's desk phone. Lifting the receiver, he depressed that unnerving crystal of luminescence, and said: What is it now, Joy?

Mr. Rapp and Mr. Singer would like to bring you to a private lunch, said Joy's voice, a little arch at the knowledge that it bore imperious tidings.

When—today?

Mmm hmmm.

What time?

One-thirty.

Okay. Thank you, Joy, he said, hanging up. He made a note on his memo pad: Call Mom tonight. —He e-mailed a memo to Joy to do a search for Brady, Jonas A. on both the LEXIS and NEXIS databases and bring him hard copy. Returning to the Veblen brief he'd been preparing since yesterday, he pecked in three cunning additions to the boilerplate; he thought they'd lure an approving smile to Mr. Rapp's face if he read them, which Mr. Singer certainly wouldn't. At one-twenty-five his screen chimed. His stomach ached, and his fingers were feeling sweaty. He went to the men's room, washed his face, and adjusted his tie.

Boccaccio's, John? said Mr. Rapp, with a smile that was not the approving one; it was the smile that meant nothing. He had left his blazer in the inner office, as was his custom when not receiving clients, and his starched shirt was as white as the solid left behind after sodium has consummated its marriage with ethanol.

Sure, said John. I'm ready.

He felt that he could not eat anything. He did not know whether he was about to be rewarded or punished, and that uncertainty made him nauseous.

At Boccaccio's, which was right across the street from a women's shoe store swarming with golden high heels, black high heels, sandals with double or triple straps, sexy boots, silver snakeskin affairs that came up to the knee, they sat at one of those uncomfortably "intimate" tables so beloved by those office dictators whose hobby it is to gaze into one's anxious face. He saw that the full partners were planning to order wine. John ordered a beer just to show them that he was his own man. They nodded indulgently.

What do we live for? declaimed old Mr. Singer in his best populist voice. Some fellows live for women. I live to eat. I'm not fat or anything, but I enjoy my food. Barton Rapp, now, there's a man who lives for his operas and his wine rack.

(John had heard all this before.)

Mr. Singer leaned forward and fixed John with his eyes. —And what do *you* live for, John? he said.

I live for my work, replied John, trying not to be irritated.

Mr. Rapp frowned and waved a finger. —Not good enough! he said. Everybody works to live, but very few of us—not even full partners, John—can say the reverse. What about your wife? Don't you live for her?

Let's leave Irene out of this, said John as his wife's unlovely face hung before him.

Have it your way, John, said Mr. Singer. Let's put it like this: *What are you about?*

John gulped at his beer and tried to smile.

Mr. Rapp tapped his wineglass with a musical sound. —When you ask who a person is, what he's about, you're really asking what his fetishes are.

I don't have any fetishes, Mr. Rapp, just habits. Are you dissatisfied with my work?

A tough guy, purred Mr. Rapp with a loopy smile. We *like* that. On the contrary, John. You're doing an excellent job.

I've got to take a leak, muttered Mr. Singer to himself. He got up and strode toward the back, his round bald dome accompanying him like something sacred—talk about the Music of the Spheres!

What are your fetishes, Mr. Rapp? said John in his most level voice.

You've got guts, John. There's a fine line between guts and impertinence, and you've never crossed that line.

Thanks, Mr. Rapp, said John.

Are you ready to order, gentlemen? said the waiter.

I'm going to have the warm spinach salad with *chevre,* said Mr. Rapp. And I believe that's all I'll have. John?

I'll take the same, said John. And another beer.

John, John, go ahead and eat! Don't let me stop you! I'm an old man.

All right, said John. How's the salmon today?

Excellent, sir, said the waiter. It's probably the best thing on the menu. That garlic aioli is to die for.

Fine, said John. I'll take the salmon.

I'd like the terra cotta chicken, please, said Mr. Singer, now returned. And a small green salad. Do you understand that concept? A *small* green salad.

Very good, sir, said the waiter. More wine?

I understand you're going to be a father, said Mr. Rapp, blinking sentimentally. Congratulations, John. No, thank you. We have enough for now.

Thanks for the congratulations, said John, wondering who had told him about Irene's mistake. —It may be another false alarm. By the way, Mr. Budrys hasn't gotten back to me yet with the amended tobacco brief.

Oh, he hasn't? Well, you know we're getting pretty close to deadline on that one, John.

I'll lean on him, said John.

Well said! cried Mr. Rapp, clapping his hands. John, you'll go far.

But you never did tell us what you're about, said Mr. Singer. Or did I miss something when I peed?

I'm about nothing, said John. Exactly nothing.

Spoken like a full partner, chortled Mr. Singer.

We think you have the makings of a full partner, echoed Mr. Rapp.

Well, thanks, said John awkwardly.

| 23 |

That afternoon there had been no message from Brady and no other work, so Tyler went back to Larkin Street to observe yellow RX-7s and white Chevys emerge from the Queen's parking garage, fouling the air. He watched them for a long time, writing their license plate numbers in the lines of his youngest surveillance report, emptily perceiving rather than learning, of which he was tired. The grin of light between a car's belly and the shiny concrete floor widened as the little wheeled monster rolled closer. The buzzer sounded twice. Across the street, a dirty foot hung out of a dirty sleeping bag; a long-bearded man sat upon the sidewalk, gazing pupillessly at another sleeper whose red underwear made his buttocks one with the square tail-lit backsides of cars. The buzzer sounded again. The car came out, its brilliant yellow eyes suddenly impoverished by the day. After that, a shaveskulled guy strung chain across the darkest tunnel. Watching the car go, Tyler spied a black-and-white crawling lazily by, bearing to the police station a silent young man with his chin on two fingers which hid behind the goatish beard; Tyler had seen him selling drugs sometimes on Jones Street. The police car went around the corner and out of the life of Tyler, who continued to sit in the yellow zone, dreaming of nothing with an almost Leninist confidence. Finally he cruised up to Union Square, rolled down his window, inched along in traffic (which, unlike most people, he loved; it gave him time to see things), and studied the giant palenesses of black and white glamor girls in the store windows. He counted the stripes on the awnings of hotdog stands. If he could simply get a name for the Queen, he'd be able to run an extended trace; then he'd surely snatch her social security number, her statewide criminal record, and some address, however worthless. He loved extended traces. It was a white, foggy afternoon crawling with obsequious light, which must have been why the darkness between buildings refused to be worshiped, let alone lovingly touched. He took a spin across the Bay Bridge. Behind him, the trunks of skyscrapers faded into fog regularly notched with greyness where the windows were. Irene had mentioned seeing plum blossoms in Berkeley or Oakland. He drove around for an hour or two, but didn't spy any. At dusk he returned to San Francisco. The line at the toll booth wasn't too bad; he struck the Mission in twenty minutes. He wondered what Brady was doing. Under what pretext could he call the man up? No news was not good news in Tyler's occupation. Thanks to credit card debt, his savings account now trembled not far above zero—absolute zero, when every last financial molecule falls still and silent—but he didn't want to check his answering machine, which surely bore no offerings of work. Feeling blue, he parked in an alley just off Sixteenth and Valencia, zipped his jacket over the bulge in his left armpit, and wandered into one of those little cafés with excellent coffee and bad art on the walls. A name, a name, and then she'd become real. Maybe the bail bondsmen would know her—but he had to get a name first. There being no reason not to finish this wasted day as he'd begun it, he ordered a bottle of mineral water and sat himself down at a corner table to read the *Guardian* ads: **Women Egg Donors Needed!**—Redundant gender description, thought Tyler. The other patrons hunched at their own tables, reading.

On the bulletin board it said **Lesbian Housemate Wanted** and SELF-DEFENSE FOR WOMEN and *Piano Lessons* and **Hookers, Watch Out for These Men!** Tyler read this last. It was a warning about the Capp Street murders. Two prostitutes from that business district had wound up in dumpsters down by China Basin. A third had gotten away and given a description of the killers.

Well, he thought to himself, let's go take a stroll down Capp Street.

It was a cool spring night in the Mission. Beyond his coffeehouse, where two girls were snuggling as their fingers pecked out destinations on the electronic highway, two men chatted yawning like sentinels, their hands on their heads, and past *them* an old lady was panhandling. The old lady had tears in her eyes, and she kept shifting her aching feet. Tyler suddenly thought to himself: She knows as I will never know how hard a sidewalk can be. —She asked Tyler for fifty cents, so on principle he gave her a quarter. A minute later she wandered into the coffeeshop, then back out again as he stood irresolute on that corner, wondering how he could drum up more business; and with no recognition she asked him for fifty cents. He'd asked her name, which was Diane, so he knew to say: Why, *hello*, Diane! and she jerked awake for a moment, then stumbled away.

His friend Roberta the stripper just happened to be passing with her shiny new bike, and cried out: Hi, Henry! I saw that! That old woman must be in Nirvana.

He knew that this was a sarcastic and even hateful remark because Roberta hated Buddhism. —No, he said earnestly. She's desperate, so she can't have reached Nirvana yet.

Hey, I've gotta go meet my friend Mollie up on Haight Street, said Roberta. You wanna come have coffee with us?

Oh, that's really nice of you, Roberta. I just don't have any energy tonight. —He was longing for Irene.

Are you depressed? I'm depressed. My boyfriend really used me. I fucked him because he was in a rock band but after that I fell in love. I would have married him. But then he turned out to be quite the sonofabitch.

I'm sorry to hear that, Roberta, he said.

You want to buy me coffee? Actually you don't have to buy me anything. I have money.

You're a nice person, Roberta, he said. I'm sorry you're having a rough time.

So, how's the job? You track down any interesting people? Hey, you can stay at my place if you want. You can sleep on the living room couch. My roommates are pretty cool about it.

Roberta, do you know anything about the Queen of the Whores?

I'm just a stripper, not a whore, remember? I mean, I believe in the sacred Whore-Goddess. Maybe that's what the Queen is. You sure you don't want to stay over?

I wish I could, but I have scabies, he lied.

Oh. Oh! And I've been holding your hand! Let me go wash my hands! Nothing personal, but I don't want to get that again.

After Roberta left him he entered a clean and pleasant secondhand bookshop which played music from the time when he was young. He browsed through *The Patriarchy at Work* and *Difficult Women* and *Sisterhood Is Global.* There was a cat on the sofa. The pretty Asian girl who was shelving books smiled at him. He wanted to sit down and read for a while. Instead he bought a used Steinbeck paperback and strode out, past the singing panhandlers, the bright lavender hotel doorways that said VACANCY. He saw a tattoo parlor that he didn't remember from before. —Of course he didn't get down to the Mission that much. The Tenderloin was more his area. —At a phone booth he called his answering machine, discovering no message from Brady, who perhaps was busy enjoying the carnal knowledge of some cottonwood tree. Down on Mission Street the tall hooded bullies were yelling and the hard girls were bending over the sidewalk, saying: You dropped a rock. Where's my rock, bitch?—Gonna fix that motherfucker up, save me a little bit, he heard a pimp say. He returned to the subway station's cold night sun of radiating tiles, stood by the pay phone trying not to call Irene, picked up the phone, put it down, took a quarter out of his pocket, thought some more, and then walked away with the quarter in his hand. Capp Street was empty—strange, since the beginning of the month was long past, and the whores' welfare checks long spent; maybe they were scared of the Capp Street killers. On the other hand, this evening had hardly progressed to lateness. Maybe it wasn't strange at all. He strolled to Seventeenth and Eighteenth; still not seeing any oral or vaginal workers, he turned around and at once somebody began to follow him from the darkness just beyond Eighteenth, dodging between the mountainously laden garbage cans. He felt a prickle of fear. —I know the Queen, Tyler called over his shoulder. —The footsteps stopped. —Well, he thought to himself, what's in a name?

In a fast food restaurant he bought french fries and then entered the men's room to count his wallet. Two hundred and three dollars. Enough.

Can you give me a room without too much crack smoke? he asked at the Rama Hotel. Last time there was crack smoke coming in through the wall and I didn't get much sleep.

That must have been some other hotel, said the manager, bored and angry.

Okay, said Tyler. I believe you. I'm sure the room will be great.

He went up to his room, which cost twenty dollars plus a five dollar key deposit, and sat there for a while. Then he wrote a letter to the Queen of the Whores, politely requesting a meeting. He copied it out four times. Each letter he put in its own envelope addressed to the Queen of the Whores. Before sealing these literary efforts, he took four eyedroppered vials from his pocket. Each one contained a differently keyed locator fluid. Marking them separately with that treacherous spoor, he licked the envelopes shut. He left one on top of the dresser. The second he took down the hall to the bathroom and hid in the toilet tank, taping it underneath the lid, right on top of somebody's heroin stash. The third and fourth he kept with him. Descending the stairs, he swung the grating open, and peered out into the night. Mission Street was getting worse every month. Two tall men waiting outside snarled at him. His hand was in his jacket pocket where the pistol was. Perhaps they saw the lack of fear in his face (although he actually did fear them), or perhaps they meant no harm, for they let him through. He walked back along the night sidewalk where homeless men rattled their shopping carts, got into his car, drove across town to the Queen's parking garage in order to add another stultifying line to his surveillance report, dropped the car off there so that no one would smash the windshield, slid the third letter to the Queen under the grating by the third floor, took the bus back, and got off at Sixteenth and Mission where the subway station was now a crack cocaine bazaar. He saw two hulking pairs of shoulders enter the gratinged street door of the Rama, and strode quickly to grab it so that the manager would not have to buzz him in, but the closer he got, the higher loomed those shoulders, and suddenly he was apprehensive again. He wondered whether he might be getting ill. Once his brother had hired him—probably out of pity—to do a little investigative work on a toxic dumping case which was of interest to a certain realty corporation, and late one night as Tyler approached the factory warehouse he'd suddenly been almost overcome by a panic which seemed causeless. He went home, lay down, and was sick for a week. This performance, needless to say, did not endear him to John's firm. Pacing half a block up and half a block back to give those shoulders time to disappear, he rang the buzzer at the Rama. When the hideous cawing of unlocking sounded, he pulled the grating open. A whore and a pimp stood in the hallway. —It's not enough, the whore was whining. — You argue with me, you'll go back in the penitentiary, said the pimp. —Their mouths kissed the long yellow crack-flame as Tyler said excuse me and passed up the stinking stairs to the second grating, whose button he had to lean on for a long time before the manager buzzed him in.

What room? said the manager, who obviously didn't remember him.

I kept my key, thanks.

Don't talk smart to me, filth, said the manager. What room?

The one with no crack smoke, said Tyler, turning his back on the manager and going up the second flight of stairs to the hall where his room was. A door opened and a man clothed only in tattoos of angry demons leaned out and spat on the carpet. Out of his side-vision Tyler glimpsed a naked old woman straining to pull a dildo out of her ass. Tyler walked down the corridor to the bathroom and looked inside the toilet tank. The letter and the baggie of heroin were both gone. From his pocket he withdrew the fourth and final envelope and set it openly on top of the toilet tank.

In his room the first envelope was still there. But somebody had painted on the bottom drawer of the half-ruined dresser an image of a naked woman whose hair was charred pipe resin or a similar black substance and whose lips were lipstick. Between her breasts ran these lines:

> *IS WOUND BUT ONCE*
> *No man has the power*
> *to tell where he will*
> *stop at a late*
> *or early hour.*
> *To lose one's wealth is sad indeed*
> *To lose one's health is more*
> *To lose one's soul is such a loss*
> *To lose one's Queen is all.*

He saw another lipstick stain where someone had stood on the bed and kissed the wall.

| 24 |

He went down the corridor to the bathroom, and on his return the night breeze felt good so he approached the street window and saw a whore creeping up the fire escape. She put her finger to her lips when she saw him. He nodded and waited.

I'm so cold, the woman whispered when she reached him. Please please please. I'm alone and I got a room already in the Westman Hotel.

What's your name?

Barbara.

He looked at her for a long time. —Hey, he said softly, I remember you when your name was Shorty.

I remember you, too. You were living in the Krishna then.

Yes I was! laughed Tyler. I was between jobs then. And you—

Yes. Hey! Guess what! I kicked! I'm not shooting up anymore!

That's great, he said, half believing her.

So, please . . .

Maybe later, when I have some money, he said smoothly.

You don't even have two dollars? I'm hungry.

Here's a buck, he said. Listen, Barbara—

Aw, what the hell. You can call me Shorty. We go back a ways, don't we?

OK, Shorty. I need to meet the Queen. Do you know how I can do that?

The Queen! What do you want to meet *her* for? What's she got that I ain't got?

Somebody's paying me, he said.

Oh, that's different. You gotta do what you gotta do. Well, I'm in business for myself, so I don't really know her. But the other girls say she lives underground, you know like in the sewers or under the subway or something, always moving around, but always in the dark like some bug that rules the bug colony. I never went looking for her. They say if she wants you, she'll find you, but if you go poking your nose in her business she'll fuck you up. Like seriously fuck you up. But you didn't hear anything from me, right?

So she's mean, Shorty?

Talk about mean! That girl is one hundred percent bitch. You look for her, you watch your ass, Okay? 'Cause you've been good to me.

Thanks, Shorty, he said, squeezing her in his arms.

| 25 |

That night Tyler dreamed of an extermination machine in the shape of a cubical steel face within which the mouth was a bladed trapezoid. The condemned marched into the mouth one by one. They bowed their heads, reminding him of the way that everyone gazed at his or her tapping shoes at the V.D. clinic. (Once he'd met a client there. Another time he'd been a patient there.) The blades macerated them. He dreamed of this all night, sometimes managing to struggle awake, but it was as though the architect of this machine kept dragging him back down to gaze upon it. At dawn he was sad and anxious. It was just light enough for him to see bloodstains and squashed bugs on the walls. He itched all over. He got up, pissed in the sink, and dressed. Shorty was staying in room number 302. He took the first letter to the Queen and slid it under her door. Then he returned to his room and lay down, trying to sleep and failing. There was piss shining on the vinyl runners of the stairs when he finally went out. A man and a woman were sitting in that estimable liquid. The woman said to her companion: I'll do it soon's he gets out of the hall. —You talking about me? Tyler inquired politely, zipping up his fly. —I'm just saying this hall is none too big, the woman said. —Tyler nodded at her. He saw that the man had fallen asleep.

He rang the buzzer on the manager's hatchway and got his five dollars back for the key.

Hey, if you don't need that money, you can give it to me, a whore in the hallway said.

And you can do the same for me, he said.

Well, the whore said, scratching her scars, I might sometime do you that favor.

I'll just hold my breath, honey, said Tyler, swinging open the top grating.

Be careful out there, said the night janitor.

He descended the final stairs, peered through the street grating to make sure that nobody was lurking, and went out. A sad black whore, hooded against the rising sun, was walking slowly toward the bus stop. She gazed back at him longingly. He saluted her, mouthed the word *Queen,* and went on, passing a parking garage whose cage gaped empty just inside the doorway. There was nobody inside the ticket taker's heavily glassed booth, which was set reclusively back in the darkness.

No way the Queen's in a parking garage, Tyler said to himself. It's got to be just a god-damned letter drop.

Hallelujah, he thought then. I actually believe in the Queen.

He walked and walked, scratching. On South Van Ness near Twenty Second a black-and-white slowly came to a stop, double-parked, and from its two mouths expectorated two cops the darkness of whose uniforms seemed to keep the last remnants of the night. He didn't recognize either of them. They mounted the painted steps of an unpainted Victorian and rang the doorbell. Their hands were on their holsters.

He thought: I'd better call Mom today and see if she's had any chest pains. I should call Detective Hernandez in Vice and ask him if he's heard of the Queen. I should call Brady and ask him for another advance. I should call John and ask if he thinks Mom needs another doctor. I should call Irene.

He took the bus to the Queen's parking garage, drove home and took a shower. After that, he checked his messages. His throat felt scratchy. Brady hadn't phoned, but somebody named Marya whose ex-husband owed her child support wanted him to help her track the absconder into the jaws of justice, and his half-friend Roger was in town, his mother had called, John hadn't called, a possible warehouse surveillance case danced on his tongue; Helena from Seattle, who'd never let him kiss her breasts, wondered aloud how he was doing; the Detective Institute invited him, for a forgivably small stipend, to repeat the seminar on drug abuse recognition; and the landlord was coming to repair the running toilet sometime around noon, which meant closer to three or four. Junk mail faxes crept across the carpet. Tyler ate a freckled banana for breakfast and made himself coffee. Resting his clipboard on his knee, he began to pad his surveillance report, adding line after line of spurious whores going in and spurious cars going out. That would keep Brady happy. He used up three extra forms that way. Then he tuned his television set to channel seven and clicked the remote three times to find out where his missives to the Queen had travelled. He saw a blue dot, a red dot, a white dot, and a dark grey dot. The blue dot and the dark grey dot were still at Sixteenth and Mission. The red dot was at the parking garage at Larkin Street where he had left it. The white dot, which represented the letter he'd slipped under Shorty's door, had also moved to the parking garage.

Just a goddamned letter drop, he repeated to himself.

| 26 |

Two months earlier, Irene had become certain that she was pregnant.

Sacramento had received a wet spring. Water still shone upon the black earth, and the buttercups, dandelions and mustard flowers were a sunny yellow in the ditches. On that Sunday afternoon hardly any traffic dared to slow their progress on Interstate 80 West, which thickened the pleasure John already felt in having done his duty by spending Saturday and Saturday night with his lonely mother, whose house was crammed with paperbacks: *The Algerine Captive, Growth of the Soil, The Last Temptation of Christ,* Mary Webb's *The Golden Arrow;* his mother adored Irene, but admonished her, as John did, to lose weight and get a job. Irene tried to smile and respect her because she wouldn't consider herself a good person if she quarreled with her mother-in-law. Having told her once again that she was too fat, John's mother served her an immense helping of pork chops and mashed potato with butter, becoming cross when Irene was too full to eat seconds. She admired John's new tie and wanted to hear all about the Peterson case. John told her, in considerably more detail than he had ever told Irene. Irene, half-listening to her husband and gazing into the old woman's face, wondered whether she were genuinely interested in her son's life, simply because it was her son's, or whether her love allowed her to feign interest. Either way, she was an excellent listener. (Under the table, Mugsy the dog nuzzled Irene's thigh.) John seemed happier and more relaxed than he'd been in weeks. He asked his mother for advice, which he never did with Irene; he smiled and laughed . . . Deeply ashamed, Irene promised herself in future to express more interest in her husband's affairs. When dinner was finished, she asked John's mother what she was reading now.

I'm rereading Dostoyevsky, said the old lady. There's one writer who's truly ageless. I'd really forgotten how good he was.

You make it sound so easy, to read all those books! said Irene in her best admiring voice.

Well, of course English is not your native language, Irene (and Irene, smiling graciously, heard some monster in the old lady's heart crying: You goddamned little Chink!). No one expects you to read Dostoyevsky.

If I were to read just one, which would you recommend?

You heard what Mom said, John told her, a patina of irritation now overlying the happy goldenness of his voice. Why would you bother?

Irene was determined at all costs to be polite to her mother-in-law, but she saw no reason to allow her husband's condescension to pass unchallenged. —How many books by Dostoyevsky have *you* read? she asked.

What's that got to do with anything? Is this some kind of contest?

If it is, replied Irene, continuing to play the good girl, I'm sure that Mom has won. And I know I've lost, because I never read anything by Dostoyevsky.

Mrs. Tyler smiled benignly. —Just reading for the sake of saying you've done it is cheating. You have to *enjoy* it. John of course has read everything Dostoyevsky ever wrote. I saw to that.

Is that true, John?

Look, Irene. Can't we just leave me out of this?

Does he write fiction or nonfiction, Mom?

Oh, my poor dear Irene, said Mrs. Tyler.

And which one have you enjoyed the most?

How could that possibly matter to you? said her husband.

Noting Irene's bitter grimace, Mrs. Tyler quickly replied: Well, dear, I'd have to say *The Possessed,* although it's frightfully sad. It reveals in such *depth* the stupidity of revolution. I wish that all those terrorists in the Middle East were required to read it.

Maybe they've read it already, said John, still sour.

Can I borrow your copy, Mom? said Irene. I promise I'll read it before we visit you again.

Oh, you're such a sweet girl, Irene, said John's mother, starting to clear away the dishes. Irene leaped up to help her.

Sit down with me, Mom, said John. Irene can do it.

Please, Mom, keep John company, cried Irene quickly. John's right! And he doesn't get to see you as often as he'd like.

How's your blood pressure? she heard John say as she came back in for the glass bowl.

Oh, not so good, not so bad. No chest pains today.

John gazed into his mother's face with a loving, worried look. Irene felt so lonely that she almost screamed.

And how's your brother? she heard her mother-in-law say.

Unshaven and drinking as usual, said John. (Her wrists deep in soapsuds, she visualized his face slamming shut as it always did when Henry was mentioned.)

There's something I want you to say to him, John. I don't want it coming from me, because then he won't listen. But I know he listens to you. He respects you, John. He loves you.

Turning off the faucet, she heard John's silence. She heard Mugsy's tail rhythmically lashing the table-leg. Someone must be scratching Mugsy's belly the way she liked. Probably John was doing it. John loved Mugsy.

I want you to tell him to find another girlfriend, her mother-in-law was saying. At my age it's not so important to be divorced. Of course I would have preferred it if Daddy hadn't left us, but it seems that so many of my schoolgirl friends are widows already. Henry, though, still has half his life ahead of him. Well, *almost* half, I guess I should say . . .

I'll tell him, Mom, John said tonelessly.

Irene always had difficulty finding where the spatulas were kept, and she did not want to interrupt the conversation, so she opened drawers one after the other, discovering silverware like grey claw-bones, corkscrews, receipts, medical insurance forms, everything in a clutter. In her own mother's house everything was just so. Even the tapered ends of the chopsticks had to point in the same direction. Her mother was almost excessively clean, although she paled in comparison to her aunt, who kept everyone's shoes in plastic bags in the closet at night so that they wouldn't gather dust. Under the dish drainer, Irene suddenly saw one of her mother-in-law's grey hairs, and sponged it away in disgust.

| 27 |

I had the strangest dream about Henry last night, Mrs. Tyler was saying as Irene finished drying her hands and came noiselessly back to the table. —Thank you so much, Irene. You're a goodhearted girl.

Mom, I'm sorry I couldn't find the spatula. I put the potatoes away in the fridge in that big bowl.

Never mind, never mind. Do you really want to read Dostoyevsky?

Of course, Mom. What was your dream?

My what? Oh, I was just telling John that last night I had a little trouble getting to sleep. When you get to be my age, Irene, you'll find that sleep doesn't come without a struggle. Sometimes I think that's why old people die. They just get so tired.

I'm sorry, Mom. When John and I go to church I'll make sure we both pray for your health.

What was your dream, Mom? said John, bored.

Well, I dreamed that Henry had married a princess—a *real* princess, with a golden crown! Isn't that fantastic? Oh, dear! And he looked so happy. I think that's why I've been thinking about him all day. I would certainly love to see him remarried. Irene, you're so close to Henry. Is there anyone special in his life?

Mrs. Tyler asked this question so blandly and straightforwardly that Irene did not at first sense any menace in it. John had without a doubt made several comments about this matter; but Irene was certain that Henry had never said anything about her to his mother.

No, Mom, she said when she realized that they were both waiting for her to say something. Not to my knowledge. But I sure wish he would find someone. Sometimes he seems so unhappy.

At once she was given to understand by the changed expressions of her two interlocutors that she had said more than she should, or at least more than they wanted to hear. It was acceptable for John or his mother to broach the subject of Henry's sadness, but Irene would always remain an outsider; admitted to the family for a lifelong period of probation, it was not for her to make judgments on the emotions of others. Later, on that Sunday afternoon when she and John were driving back toward San Francisco's foggy white and blue rectangles, she succeeded in forgetting the frown on her mother-in-law's face. John was happy. He drove at five miles an hour above the speed limit, smiling all the way home. It was as if he'd received the gifts of the drug Ecstasy, which (according to Henry, whom she loved to ask about drugs, none of which she'd ever tried) consists of a drowsy joy which thickens around your naked skin like fur; this is the transformation of every nerve ending in your skin into an excited clitoris; you knead a breast or buttock in your hand and cannot stop because your hand is having a million orgasms; you massage your sweetheart's back for hours; when you close your eyes and wriggle your fingers you can still see them move; your teeth keep grinding until your jaws most pleasurably ache. Irene gazed at her husband, who drove on, and somehow his very joy overcame her with the familiar intractability of her position, as solid as her room in her parents' house with its computer, TV, telephone, beads, animal posters, and stickers. Perhaps her cousin Suzy had the computer now. Irene had told her parents to give it to her. Suzy was still in school, and the computer had not yet fallen so far out of date.

They were on the Bay Bridge now, and looking over the edge Irene saw the dark steel ships upon the pale grey sea.

Her husband was still smiling faintly. Summoning her fortitude, Irene said: John, I think I'm pregnant.

| 28 |

Slowly, slowly his head turned toward her.

I guess you forgot your pill again, he said.

Yes, she said.

Well, he said, I hope you're happy.

How about you? she said. Are you happy?

Mom will be thrilled, he said. Well, it's a shock, Irene. I won't deny that.

There was no traffic at the Civic Center exit. He turned right on Van Ness, where the traffic was also abnormally light, and was silent until they got to Chestnut Street, where as he turned he said: Who's the father?

| 29 |

Mr. Tyler lived in Wyoming somewhere. Nobody had heard from him for years. California's no-fault divorce laws entitled Tyler's mother to an automatic half of common assets, but, having kept the house anyway, she let the cash go. John once took her to task about this, because he believed her to be motivated only by an apprehension of being thought greedy, when the simple truth was that like her other son she honestly did not care about money. Possibly Mr. Tyler would have settled some of it on her, had she asked, but by that time neither of them wanted the death of their marriage to drag on. Not long after John had begun to go steady with Irene, he'd proposed in one of his metallic jests that Hank employ the professional knowledge which he presumably possessed to go to Wyoming and seize their father's assets, his reward to be a ten percent commission on anything collected. —I had an assault case involving that scenario, Hank mumbled. It happened right around the Loki Hotel. This woman made a nice little scar on this young girl's forehead. You see, she was one of these women who . . . —John walked away, disgusted. And the notion of sending out a Viking raider on their father's track had died a merited death, much to Mrs. Tyler's relief. All that was important to her was seeing her sons, which was why every July they drove down to Monterey for a week, that town not being so far away that John couldn't pop back into San Francisco if he were needed at the office. This year he warned that he could not guarantee his presence in July, because a new client had asked him to prepare some articles of incorporation which it seemed might have ripened exactly to the point of signature by July fifteenth, commencing the infant enterprise's fiscal year, so he telephoned his mother to ask whether May were acceptable. That would be a pity, of course, Mrs. Tyler replied, because the beach would still be so chilly in that season, but John only laughed and said that Monterey was always cold and she never swam, so what was the difference? As for Hank, he knew how inconvenient it was for John to get away at all, so naturally he would rearrange his schedule as needed. It was a rare sunny day. Mrs. Tyler had installed herself in her hotel room for a nap. Irene lay sleeping on the sand, and her hands met at an apex beyond her head, there by the chair and the empty soda bottle. She had not yet reached that sluggish, langorous, trusting stage dwelt in by so many pregnant women, when the heavy belly makes every breath a burden, and independence must be traded for resignation, with or without hope, depending on temperament. Why not hope? Too late now to kill the fetus, if one ever thought of it. Why not assume the best of the father, and maybe even of the world? The only other course, aside from denial and distraction, would be a despair compounded by its own passivity. *C'est sera sera,* and so . . . The sun glittered on her watch. Beside her, John lay very still on his back. He was gold from head to toe. The breeze strained patiently inside his swim trunks, and the golden lion's down on his arms seethed like seaweed in the waves. His chest barely moved. As Tyler watched, busily recording nonexistent license plate numbers in the surveillance report, Irene opened her eyes and looked up at the stubble on her husband's chin. John seemed to feel her gaze, because his hand slowly rose to touch that very place. His eyes opened also, and he sat up. —I'm getting sunburned, he said. I think I'll go in and put my shirt on. I need to shave, too.

As soon as her husband had gone, Irene's eyes widened, and she turned her face slowly toward Tyler's. Tyler's heart began pounding.

| 30 |

And how's the home life? Tyler was saying to his brother.

Great, said John, drumming his fingers on the edge of his beer glass. —Which reminds me. Mother, you'll want to hear this. We're expecting.

Oh, John! their mother cried. What fabulous news! When is Irene due?

September.

Where *is* Irene? their mother said.

She went to lie down.

Has she been having morning sickness?

I don't think so, Mom, but I'm not a hundred percent sure. Irene's not a complainer.

John, you are *very* lucky to have her.

Yeah, I know, Mom. How's your blood pressure?

It was normal today. Henry, aren't you going to congratulate your brother?

Congratulations, Tyler choked out.

I think this calls for champagne, boys, don't you think?

Well, let's wait until the baby's born, said John sullenly.

They sat there, and Tyler said: How's the Peterson case coming along?

We stopped that conviction dead, said John. Irene and I can count on a good bonus this year. So they've asked me to take the T-scam reclamation case. I haven't refused, although it means I'll be pretty busy for the rest of the year.

Well, you do have to think of your career, their mother said. You certainly couldn't have refused. I'm sure that Mr. Rapp and Mr. Singer are to be trusted. You've put up with so much for them. Oh, John, I'm so proud of you, and now you're going to be a father, too! But you won't leave Irene too much alone, will you? It's difficult, a woman's first time. I remember when I was pregnant with you, John, and then your father . . . Henry, you'll have to look in on Irene even more often than you do. It's a mercy that you and she are so fond of each other.

Tyler began very slowly to clean his spectacles. —I'll certainly visit, he said, if I'm invited.

And what about you, Mom? said John smoothly. Irene loves you, too. I'm sure she'd appreciate it if you found time to help her.

I certainly shall. When Irene wakes up I must find out if she needs anything. Has she had a good appetite?

She's going to eat me into the poorhouse, laughed John. Tyler thought it a brutal laugh.

The fog's coming in again, Tyler said, gazing out the window.

Well, we were lucky all day with that wonderful sunshine, weren't we? their mother said. Mugsy certainly enjoyed her walk. Henry, you need a haircut.

A cut or just a trim?

Oh, I'd say you've really let it go. What do you think, John?

I'd say he could use a shave, too.

All right, said Tyler a little irritably. I'll go and get a haircut right now.

Get a shave, too, his brother said.

Yes, I heard the first time. Congratulations on the baby.

Is this the first you've heard about it?

What do you mean, John?

Oh, I just thought maybe Irene might have told you.

Why would she tell me before her own husband? Tyler said challengingly.

No one replied for a moment.

Irene has actually been looking a bit tired lately, their mother put in.

Oh, you think so? said John. I thought she was starting to fill out.

But she's not so far along, is she? But it is true that the first two or three months are the worst. Later she'll be more tired, of course, but the changes in the first few months are the most drastic. At least that was my experience with both of you.

I guess your experience beats ours in that department, said Tyler, going out the door.

My, but he looked sour! their mother said. I wonder if he's feeling well?

He's ridiculous.

John, you don't have anything against your brother, do you?

And if I did, what would that be?

That's not an answer, John.

Well, maybe it's a question with no answer.

Every question has an answer, his mother asserted with considerable conviction.

Really, Mom? Then tell me this. Where do we come from and where are we going? Gauguin said that. I still have that book of reproductions you gave me. Where does my baby come from, and what will he become?

Yes, John, I know Gauguin said that and painted it, said his mother, rocking. He was a very, very unhappy man.

John tapped his foot.

Oh, dear. Is he jealous of you, sweetheart?

It's nothing. We get along fine. Don't you worry about it, Mom, replied the son in what he considered to be a brusquely well-meaning tone, but which came out a little more peremptory than that. Mrs. Tyler, absently rubbing together her arthritic fingers, gazed into his face with large eyes.

That fog's pretty solid now, he said.

Have you decided on a name?

Eric.

And if it's a girl?

Suzanne. But it won't be a girl.

So you think it's a boy. Have you gotten the ultrasound done?

Irene didn't want to. It's not up to me. Nothing's up to me.

Nothing's up to you? said Irene in a quiet fury as she came through the door. Mom, I want you to listen to that. This is how he always is with me. This is how your son talks to me, and *I can't bear it anymore!*

Irene, Irene, Irene! said her mother-in-law, with a smile of loving exasperation. I was just telling John that the first two or three months are the worst. I recall that I got very moody as well . . .

I'm sorry, Mom, whispered Irene, suddenly very frightened. I'm sorry, John.

Oh, forget it, said John. Why don't you sit down, Irene? You want an ice tea?

I want a beer, Irene thought to herself. I want to get drunk. —Yes, please, she said aloud. Can I pour you one, Mom?

The pitcher's in that little fridge, said Mrs. Tyler. No, thank you, Irene. But it's very sweet of you to ask. Maybe John would like a refill.

John said nothing. His eyes were pale blue like the Bay on a half-cloudy day. Irene brought the pitcher out and silently filled his glass, careful not to add any more ice cubes, which he detested. Then she poured herself one.

Where's Mugsy? she said.

Mugsy's taking a little nap, said her mother-in-law, with the usual smile of instant inanity that came whenever that creature was mentioned. Suddenly, awaking from her loving trance, she said: Irene, is it true that Koreans eat dogs?

Yes, Mom, in Korea. But I never have. My father's side of the family really likes them, though. You want to hear a funny story, Mom? When we first moved to this country, my second uncle and auntie went to the supermarket, and they couldn't read English very well, so when they got to the aisle where the pet stuff is and they saw all those bags of dog food, you know, with the different pictures of dogs on the different brands, they thought it was different kinds of dog meat, and they said: Wow, what a great country America is; it has everything!

Oh, my God, said Mrs. Tyler.

I'm sorry, Mom. Did I say anything wrong? I was just trying to—

John grinned. —You never told me that story, Irene. That's pretty good.

No, I—

I'll tell that one at work. Singer in particular will be amused. I'm always making him laugh. He keeps asking where I get so many good dirty jokes. You know where I get them? From the Internet.

Oh, please don't tell that story at work, Irene said. I'd be embarrassed if other people knew. It makes my family sound so fresh off the boat. That's why it's kind of funny, I guess . . .

No one will think any the less of you if John tells that story, Irene, pronounced Mrs. Tyler decisively. It's a *sweet* story.

Thank you, Mom.

Hey, Irene, said her husband.

What?

Your hair looks ratty. Lots of split ends. When are you going to fix it?

I have an appointment with Jordan for next Saturday, Irene said. Can you wait that long, or does it bother you so much to look at me?

How much does Jordan cost me?

I pay for Jordan, not you.

I said, how much does he cost?

Forty-five.

Forty-five dollars! For what? Does that include his tip?

Excuse me, said Irene, but it was you who started complaining about how I look, not me. You heard it all, Mom. What do you think?

Oh, I don't want to get involved, said Mrs. Tyler. But I do think a woman should try to please her husband.

Okay, Mom, Irene said. Well, maybe you and your son can find a cheap haircutting place that will please your son, and I'll cancel my appointment with Jordan and go wherever you say. Is that what you want me to do?

Don't get ants in your pants, said John. Just calm down. If you want to go to Jordan you can go to Jordan. I can afford it.

I want a beer, said Irene.

But you're pregnant! said Mrs. Tyler, shocked.

I'm going for a walk, said Irene. Do you want me to take Mugsy?

Sure, take Mugsy, said John, with evident relief. Mugsy, like the weather, was always a safe change of topic, perhaps even the shortest path out of the family labyrinth.

Thank you, Irene, said Mrs. Tyler. Mugsy will be thrilled to get another walk. You're such a thoughtful girl.

Thanks for saying so, Mom. Where's her leash?

It's in the car.

Can I bring you back anything, Mom?

Not a thing, thank you.

Mom would like some low-fat yogurt, John said. Wouldn't you, Mom?

Why, John, what a good idea. Irene, darling, would you mind?

No problem, said Irene.

And what about you, John? said Mrs. Tyler.

I'm fine. Hurry back, Irene.

Oh, John, said his mother, you never think of yourself.

| 31 |

When they were alone, Mrs. Tyler said: It's almost as if you want them alone together.

What do you mean, Mom?

Well, you tell him to get a haircut; you tell her to fix her hair; don't you think they'll run into each other?

What are you saying?

Oh, she's such a dear little girl, John, but don't you see that she's discontented?

Mugsy will have a good walk anyhow, John said. Mom, why don't you lie down until Irene gets back with your dessert? I'll wake you . . .

| 32 |

The frayed vacation went on like a whore babying her worn-out old cigarette lighter to get one last hit from her crack pipe, and then one more hit beyond the last hit, until finally it was over. The two brothers each made a separate mental note never to do *that* again. Mrs. Tyler for her own part felt relief upon regaining her solitude, and then felt guilty to be relieved. Irene remained silent. All these reactions were customary.

John and Irene drove Mrs. Tyler back to Sacramento. Tyler went quietly to San Francisco, smiling because in his shirt pocket were three long black hairs he'd stolen from Irene's pillow.

| 33 |

The Vincy Company wanted him to screen three job applicants on his computer. It took him forty-five minutes for all three. He sent them a printout and a bill for three hundred and twenty-five dollars.

Two weeks later they hadn't paid, and meanwhile he'd received an envelope from Datatronic Solutions which contained a **Statement of account** marked "urgent." His current balance was zero dollars and zero point zero cents. Thus likewise his balance thirty-one to sixty days past due, and his balance sixty-one to ninety days past due. In the ominous box "Over 90 Days/Past Due" the figure **$190.99** had been printed in boldface. Underneath this warning of liability, the **Statement of Account**, still trying to be friendly with Tyler, proposed the following helpful advice: *To arrange for your balance to be paid with a Credit Card, please call the telephone number above. Thanks so much for your business!!!*

Gazing out his living room window at the fog-suffused red and green traffic-winkings of the Sunset, he telephoned Datatronic Solutions and said: I have a question on my bill. Well, three questions actually.

Yes, sir. What's your customer identification number?

We'll get to that, Tyler said. But I get to ask my three questions first. Number one: Why do you have a slashmark between "ninety days" and "past due"? Number two: Why is "Credit Card" in title case? Number three: Why do you think you need three exclamation points when you're thanking me for my business when I actually haven't given you any business because I owe you two hundred dollars?

Sir, I don't know what you're talking about. Who's this?

That's for me to know and you to find out, said Tyler, hanging up. He telephoned the Vincy Company and asked the woman at Accounts Payable if she'd received his invoice. She said that she didn't know.

| 34 |

It's just a standard incorporation thing, said Brady. I'm trusting you to help me out on this, son.

You won't be disappointed, Mr. Brady.

Glad to hear it, because I don't disappoint very well. So what I need right now, John, I need a hardass. I need someone to say, this is what Brady's gonna do, no arguments. I don't want to drag it on.

I don't know what to say, said John, trying to be polite.

If you don't know what to say, don't say *anything*.

Fine, said John.

You got a problem with me?

Gazing into his client's swollen, florid face, John said nothing.

I said, you got a problem with me?

Let's leave me and my problems out of this, said John in a steely tone which Brady instantly recognized and respected.

You passed the test, sonny. All right. Now, the name of the operation is going to be Feminine Circus. Nationwide franchises planned, that kind of crap. It's gonna generate competition. I want you to rig things for me, John, so that my enemies can't get to me. I want interlocking trusts, dummy corporations, whatever you think I need to be protected. Until the deal's done, I don't want anyone to know I'm behind it. The first outlet is going to open in Vegas, so that'll be governed by the laws of Nevada, but I want you to handle it for me because I anticipate opening two more outlets very soon in L.A., another in San Diego, and maybe one here in Frisco.

Whatever you say, said John. But I'm sure you know that Nevada, like Delaware, is exempt from a lot of regulations. So many California businesses do it the other way around and incorporate in Nevada. I mean, Nevada is corporate paradise.

Yeah, well, I'd just feel a lot safer dealing with contract attorneys who don't have any ties to Nevada. Feminine Circus is a unique concept, John. I don't want some big boy in Vegas to rip me off.

Fine, said John.

Now, what do you need to get started?

Maybe you could tell me a little about the business, Mr. Brady.

Enter*taaaaaaaaaaaaain*ment, said Brady with a wink.

Anything illegal? said John. I don't care who you are or how much money you have. I'm not interested in breaking the law.

That's your bottom line, huh? Well, don't worry about that, you little twerp. It's all gonna be virtual reality. Electronic sex shows. Just masturbation with a few photons. No minors admitted, of course. I'm counting on you to take care of the zoning commissions. Your brother was just telling me how the Sacramento city council fucked over that Club Fantasy, made 'em install handicapped ramps for their dancers and all kinds of other shit, then pulled the plug because some day care center popped up outta nowhere . . .

My brother? said John slowly.

Sure. That pimply-faced Hank Tyler. Says he's your brother, anyhow. I'm paying him less than I'm paying you.

What are you using Hank for?

Hunting up some talent for the big act. I guess you and he don't communicate much, do you?

You're paying me for my time, Mr. Brady, said John. If you want to squander money asking me questions about my brother, I can't stop you. But I'd really prefer that you mind your own goddamned business.

Heh! heh! Boy stands up to me! I *like* you, Johnny! Listen, sonny, said Brady, waving a purple finger in John's face with the utmost sincerity, you and I are going to *go* places.

| 35 |

Since the Queen had not yet replied to any of his letters (with each of which he'd included his business card, the answering machine number circled in red), Tyler made arrangements to meet his old friend Athena, who was as Greek and wise and upliftingly haughty as her name. Seeing her might get family matters out of his head, and help him with the Brady job, too.

She embraced him calmly, wearing a long black dress. They went to the hotel bar, which she knew as well as she did all the other hotel bars in that part of town, and she ordered a shot of Red and he ordered a shot of Black.

You look so beautiful, he said. Are you and your husband going to have a child?

Never, she said. How can I have a child and keep making calls?

Your husband wouldn't be a good father?

No, she said, lighting a long thin cigarette. And what's your news? You look tired. Anyway, why do you want me to have a child?

It would be nice if there were a little girl in this world who looked like you, he said.

That's sweet, she said, smiling.

Cheers, he said.

Are *you* going to have a child? asked Athena in an innocent tone.

Tyler choked on his drink.

I've been looking for the Queen, he said. Do you know her?

Of course I know her. But we don't exactly move in the same circles. Twice a week I do volunteer work and hand out condoms to the street girls—

I tried a female condom not long ago, Tyler said. It was like screwing a plastic bag.

She laughed. —You know what I do? I make all my clients wear *two* condoms! I'm a little bit paranoid.

Why do they even bother to stick it in? he asked wonderingly. I guess I would just touch you with my hand or my mouth or something.

Some of them do that, she said.

And your husband?

He only has to wear one. I don't want to get pregnant, and I don't want to take the pill, but he's my husband.

Athena worked out of her house and advertised in the adult newspaper the *Voyeur.* Last weekend she had made in one day eight hundred dollars—six clients back to back, so to speak, for the full service; at the end of the day she was really tired, but it was the best money that she'd made in a long time. She paid off her credit card bills.

So you see the street girls twice a week? Tyler pursued, trying to be the conscientious detective.

I do. And sometimes I feel like there are two people inside me, one for the streets and one for the bars.

I always figured you were somehow struggling with yourself. You seemed kind of tense when I saw you last year. I was worried about you—

I was? I don't remember.

You don't seem as tense tonight.

Actually I'm feeling pretty tense, she said. I'm so bored with everything.

How much does the agency take? Fifty percent?

A little more. Not much.

Why don't you and your friends set up your own agency?

You keep telling me that. You don't understand. An ad in the yellow pages costs five thousand a month. I don't know anyone who has that kind of money.

In Vegas they use fliers.

I hate Vegas. They don't like me there. They want big tall blondes with those scary boobs.

So you're bored, he said. How have the customers been treating you?

Oh, fine. I like some of them. One German banker just took me to Switzerland for two weeks. He was very generous, but I thought the food would be better. And I tried to get him to leave me alone, but he kept trying to make me angry . . . One man looked at me and said: *Do you do this for the money?* I thought that was the stupidest thing I'd ever heard . . .

Tyler finished his drink. The lounge waitress brought him another. There goes seven or eight more dollars, I guess, he thought to himself.

Maybe I'm more tense because I know you better, Athena said.

Well, that's a compliment, said Tyler. Hey, I want to rip my employer off. You know a good place to hide money?

I hate you! she laughed.

She was very beautiful and severe, a slender brunette with sad black eyes. He had known her for three or four years. —Athena, I'd like to see you professionally, he said, swallowing.

Oh, stop it, she said. He could tell that she was pleased.

All right. So what's the best way to meet the Queen?

Write her. There's a parking garage where she gets her mail . . .

I know about that. I tried that.

And did she answer?

No.

I guess she doesn't want to meet you then, said Athena.

You're right, Tyler said. Well, I'm tired. I suppose I'll turn in.

He left thirty-five dollars for the drinks. As they were leaving the bar, they spied a knot of businessmen standing in the doorway, and Athena sighed and said: Maybe I'll stay here and see if I can get one of them to go upstairs with me . . .

| 36 |

Just as he got home, the telephone rang. He thought it would be Brady, but it was a wrong number.

The telephone rang.

Yeah, he said.

Harry Tooler, please?

Sounds like a telephone sale, said Tyler.

Oh, no, sir. This is an *opportunity call.*

Not interested, he said, hanging up.

The phone rang immediately.

Hello? he said patiently.

Is this Harry Tooler? said a different woman.

Is this a telephone sale?

No, sir, I don't sell anything over the phone. I only want to tell you about my products, the woman said brightly.

No, thank you, he said, hanging up.

The phone rang at once.

I'll stick my hairy tool in *you!* he shouted.

Just what's that supposed to mean, Hank? came his brother's voice.

| 37 |

It means I probably didn't get that garage mechanic's job, said Tyler.

Oh, forget it, said John. The reason I called is that I gather we're both working for Jonas Brady.

Yep, I guess we are, said Tyler. Is it working out, being his lawyer?

I can't help but admire the guy, said John. He knows what he wants. But since he also hired you, I wonder if he's up to anything illegal.

I did a T.U. on him already.

A what?

A Trans Union. A credit check. John, he has very, very good credit.

He does, huh? said Tyler's brother, impressed in spite of himself.

I ran him through TRW also and tied him to a social security number in Missouri. Nothing wrong with that.

That spying business you're into doesn't really make him smell like a rose, if he's into it, too.

I get it, said Tyler. Since I'm working for him, he's no good.

Exactly, said John.

Tyler laughed sadly. —So what do you want to know?

What are you doing for him?

Standard missing persons case. Well, almost standard. He's looking for the Queen of the Whores, and there might actually be such a lady. I already have a few leads. Kind of interesting, actually. He'll probably terminate me pretty soon . . .

How much is he paying you?

Oh, decent.

How are you fixed for money, Hank?

Oh, fine, said Tyler heartily.

I thought I saw you at the courthouse yesterday.

Well, I was, uh, researching the Queen because the computer only gives case number and jurisdiction for a defendant so you have to go to court and order the—

You're a mess, Hank. You're disorganized. You need help.

Oh, forget it, said Tyler.

You need a loan, don't you?

I said forget it.

All right, I'll butt out of your business. But can you swear to me there's nothing illegal going on with Brady? As I said, I like him fine, but the fact that he's—

Look, John. You yourself just said that in my line of work, people cut corners. But nothing *egregious* is going on. I have to tell you, though, that the guy gives me the creeps. I think he's evil and up to no good. If I find this Queen I'm going to warn her before I show him where she is. But that's what I always do. You see, some of these stalkers—

Evil is one thing. Evil's only subjective. Illegal is another.

John, just be careful. I'm telling you, Brady gives me a bad feeling.

All right, whatever. Have you called Mom lately?

Yes, I have. And I called the doctor, too. She's not doing so well, you know.

You have the nerve to tell *me* that!

John?

What?

John, how are you doing these days?

Just what is that supposed to mean?

John, you know I'm sorry about—

Oh, for God's sake. Can't we leave her *out* of this? Just once?

Whatever you say, John.

And how are you doing?

You already asked me that.

Well, I'm asking again, bro.

I can't say things are going so well for me, John. But you know I was always a whiner. Actually, things aren't so bad. Why don't you come on by for dinner on Thursday or Friday and we'll . . .

| 38 |

Goddamned fucking jerk, said John. Look how he just sits there. Right turn. *Right turn. Right turn, you fucking asshole!*

John, said Irene, could I please ask you a favor?

What?

Please please don't brake so hard. I'm carrying a baby, you know.

Thanks for reminding me, said John. Fucking jerk. Look at him. Just look at him.

Irene grimaced and rubbed her temples. The red neon chain blinked around the yellow sign for the Russian Renaissance Restaurant where Henry had once taken her, and then the light changed and they were past it, Geary Street leading them deeper into the fog. Red bus-lights glared, ringed around with mist like the moon in some old almanac, and then after a long light John turned sharply on Nineteenth so that Irene was thrown against her seatbelt. They crossed Anza Street. John turned sharply left again. Irene felt like vomiting. Now they were crossing Golden Gate Park. The stream of tail-lights ahead of them in the fog of Park Presidio resembled the articulated scales of some complex Chinese dragon made of bright red paper.

I don't want you to let him kiss you hello, John said.

Aren't you maybe worrying about nothing?

It makes me sick. I can hardly stand the bastard as it is. If he weren't my goddamned brother . . .

John slammed the car faster and slower through the traffic of Nineteenth, which sloped ever so gently uphill in the fog, everything grey; it would be a night of fog, with coronas around all the streetlights.

| 39 |

Tyler lived on Pacheco, just off Nineteenth, so he was actually very close to where the old Parkside Theater used to be—one reason that he had felt pleased with his address when he'd moved in fourteen years ago—to say nothing of the cheapness of it, thanks to quiet and to fog. John, of course, had long since accepted the dismal blocky ugliness of his brother's choice as further evidence of ineptitude, if not of actual inferiority. To him the place had and was exactly nothing.

They parked in the driveway, and Irene, sitting queasily in the car, let John go ahead to ring the buzzer for Number Four. It was all too clear to her that she had better not act in any way eager, that her only permitted role tonight would be that of mournful irritability, so that John would be able to say at last: Well, Irene seems to be out of sorts. She's hardly said a word all evening. What's the matter with you, Irene? I'm going to take you home. Anyway I have some work to do . . .

What's the matter? he was calling to her now. Can't you see I'm holding the door open?

Irene got out of the car and shut her door. With an impatient finger-stab on the small black remote unit which he clenched, John locked and alarm-activated the vechicle against foggy intruders. Irene gazed up at the sky, inhaling cold, refreshing fog.

| 40 |

That coffee-maker of yours really sucks, John said as kindly as he could. If you'll just read about it in *Consumer Reports* you'll understand that there's no way it could ever make good coffee. Irene, do you think we should get Hank a decent capuccino machine for Christmas?

If that's what he wants, his wife replied almost inaudibly.

Tyler longed to ask her whether she might be unwell; but he knew that any such question would send John into a rage.

Well, enough of this swill, said John, taking his mug and Irene's and dashing their contents out into the sink. Tyler sat sipping steadily from his cup.

The chicken was very good, said Irene without enthusiasm.

What are you talking about? laughed John. He burned it! He fucking burned it! Henry, you've got to get married. Mom wants you to! Not that it's any skin off my nose, but you're going to starve to death or poison yourself or something if you don't find a woman to cook for you.

Do you have anyone in mind? Tyler drawled, staring into Irene's face.

If I did, it would be pure self-defense, John replied. I think you know what I mean. Why don't you take out an ad in the paper or something? How long has it been since what's-her-name?

Jackie? said Tyler with weary patience.

I wasn't even thinking about *her.* She never counted. No, I was thinking about . . . —John snapped his fingers.

You mean Alyssa.

That's right, that's right! John cried with a sudden strange gaiety. Alyssa—that was her name. And she would have done anything for you, but you let her *go,* you stupid, stupid sonofabitch!

How long ago was that, Henry? whispered Irene with effort.

Seven years ago, Tyler said. No, eight years ago. We broke up just before Christmas 1985. She, uh . . . I guess she still hates me . . .

She would have *married* you! laughed John. And you showed her the door! And you said, get out of here, bitch! You said—

It didn't happen quite that way, John.

And Mom liked her, too, his brother said accusingly. Mom would have given anything to see you married.

Well, that's not a secret, said Tyler, his hand trembling.

So you didn't marry her. You let her go. What was the reason? John persisted, and Tyler felt hatred red and black and wobbling rise up in his stomach.

Irene sat staring down at her plate.

I guess we just didn't get along, Tyler said finally, relieved to hear the steadiness in his voice. Now the hatred was in his chest.

Look, John said. You've got to face facts, Hank. You have a crummy personality. You've always had a crummy personality. No woman's going to enjoy being with you. So if you catch one, you've got to get your hooks in her while you can. You're going to be miserable no matter what you do, so why not just get married and forget it?

Just pretend this is Mission Street, Tyler thought to himself. Just pretend that he is a crazy and potentially violent panhandler who must be humored. He smiled at John and was about to offer him more coffee, but then he remembered that the mugs had been taken away.

| 41 |

The following morning was blue and cool in San Francisco. Tyler sat at the counter of a coffee bar across the street from his apartment, gazing down at the wood that the steadily darkening espresso in his cup rested upon, and he ran his forefinger along the lines of grain as if they were trails of meaning in a street map. He put a new surveillance report form onto his clipboard and wrote: 2:48 a.m. Domino and other unidentified Caucasian female entered garage with middle-aged Afro-American male, exited 3:04 a.m. He wrote down the license plate number of the car across the street, added some more garbage, and that form was a quarter finished . . . A woman with wet dark bangs and sunglasses kept breaking off pieces of her scone and easing them into her newspaper-reading boyfriend's mouth, after which she licked her fingers. —Well, thought Tyler, it's obvious who loves whom.

Any new developments? said Brady, sliding into the stool beside him.

Morning, boss.

Boss again, is it? I can take a hint. Sure, I'll pay you. Why do you need it now? You sexually compromised?

Tyler thought but did not say: Mister, you are a toad. —But then he thought happily: And a rich one, too.

Well, did you find the Queen? said Brady.

Not yet.

But you did find something?

She's smarter than I figured. I sent her some love letters and they stayed in that parking garage. They're still there and it's been two weeks. She must have read them there, or somebody read them for her. I'm sure she knows about us now, but we still don't know where she is.

Well, it's great she knows me, but I'm not trying to get elected. I'm sick of flushing money down the toilet. I want it to stop today. I want you to take care of it today.

Why do you want to find the Queen anyway, boss? What is it you want to say to her?

Classified, said Brady. Then he winked and said: I want her to be the star attraction of a little franchise operation I'm putting together in Vegas. I'm going to teach her to sing a little jingle that goes like this: *Klexter, klokan, kladd, kludd, kligrapp . . .* You know what that means?

So Vegas is still a boomtown? said Tyler. I figured it must have hit recession by now. Shows how much I know.

The builders are building as fast as they can. Retirees are moving into that town at a record rate. We're going to have the biggest planned community in the world.

I thought you were from Missouri.

That's beside the point. Las Vegas has been booming for forty years. Las Vegas is *not* overbuilt. Eighty-five percent of the people in the United States have not visited Las Vegas.

Including the Queen, I guess.

You spend a lot of time in the Tenderloin, don't you?

Some.

Can't you just imagine the way it used to be when it was the Barbary Coast? said Brady with a dreamy grin. All the casino dealers in black and white, and the cocktail ladies in pure white with gold-lined sleeves, showing titty, you know, with those old one-strap skirts so short they hardly cover their asses, *yeah.* I want to bring all that back. Have a single gold band just above the hem of the skirt, a silver belt, and make 'em all wear a long pigtail; if you tip 'em good maybe they can slap your face with it . . . Know what I'm saying?

I get it, said Tyler, not very interested.

And Feminine Circus will be like that, only new and different.

How can skin shows be different?

Oh, I'll tell you something, Brady said. I've had a cunt that tastes like steak tartare. That's easy. What I'm looking for is a cunt that tastes like roasted chicken. Now, that'd be different, wouldn't it?

I don't think in those terms.

Now, like I said, I want all this runaround to stop today. You hear what I had to do to that phony you sent me?

Yeah, I heard she wound up with some health problems.

Somehow, said Brady with a grin, I just had the impression that she was lying to me.

You remind me of my brother, Tyler said, narrowing his eyes as he gazed into Brady's florid face. I'd like to introduce you sometime.

John Tyler? laughed his boss, lighting up a fat cigar. The one with the Chink wife? He's already working for me. I'm paying him more than I'm paying you.

| 42 |

What had happened on that day when Tyler had led from that parking garage a slender and submissive little black woman who silently sat down in the passenger seat of Brady's rental car as Tyler, following previous instructions, closed the door from the outside and walked off to his bus stop? Investigate the mouth of truth, and await his splendid roar which will answer every question. Tyler had ostensibly found truth's mouth; Brady had hired him for that. Now Brady would hear that jangled, metallic roaring for himself, or else. He stuck an unlit cigar in his mouth. The prostitute cleared her throat. (Behind her, a woman with a white shopping bag leaned against the scuffed yellow-lit wall.) Brady turned the key in the ignition, listened to the radio for a moment, backed out of the parking space, and began heading west.

So you're the Queen, huh? he said, gazing straight over the steering wheel.

Uh huh. What do you want with me?

Oh, I guess I wanted to pay you for your time.

I don't come cheap, said the Queen.

I don't care if you come at all, said Brady. Coming is the man's job.

Are you a misogynist?

Some whore asked Mr. Tyler that just the other day. Domino, her name was. I'm trying to talk like him. Hey, Your Highness, I've been studying up on royalty. Did you know that the kings of France in the Middle Ages were born with a scarlet *fleur-de-lys* on the right shoulder? My slapper told me that.

A floor de what?

You know, a triple lily flower. I'm *educated*. The insignia of France. I just wondered if you had any kind of mark on your body that proved you were the Queen.

Mister, are you calling me a liar?

Would I call a lady that? *Klexter, klokan, kladd, kludd, kligrapp* . . . Come on, Your Highness. That's the kind of question I ask.

I feel like you're mocking me.

I'm sorry, said Brady. I'll try to be nicer to you.

And he was. Brady's huge shoulders rose in a friendly fashion in the slate-colored business suit, and the faint smell of cologne thrilled her mercenary desires. He spent fifty dollars on her in an Italian restaurant (she ordered some little baguette-like thing shaped like a turd) and got her all mellow and fuddled with wine while he agreed with everything she said, saying: yes, ma'am, or I think you're right, ma'am. He said to her: You are the Queen of the nicest little city around.

I don't get much time to appreciate it right now, said the Queen. I'm awfully busy. Where are you from?

Wherever you're from.

Uh huh, said the Queen.

And what about Henry Tyler?

Who?

I told you. That guy that brought you to me. Has he gotten emotionally compromised with any of your girls?

I never asked him, said the Queen.

Now who's Sapphire?

A girl.

Yeah. Thanks a lot. I already figured she was split between her legs. What does she do for you?

That's between us, Mr. Brady.

Does she exist?

She exists.

How many girls you got?

Enough.

I'm a businessman, you know. I just might be making you the big offer. But you're going to have to put out.

Oh, cripes, said the Queen.

Do you believe I've got money?

Yes.

Do you believe I know that you believe it?

Cut the crap.

Do you believe I believe that you're the Queen?

Not yet.

Do you believe I'm dangerous?

The Queen shot him a bitter glare.

Well?

I believe you're not a nice man. I believe you're volatile. I don't really want to listen to your proposition.

Oh, so I pushed you over the edge, laughed Brady, pleased with himself. Okay, let me be nice to you again.

And he was. It didn't take long—a little more money, and he had the bitch eating out of his hand! Everybody's the same, he thought. Feed 'em or punch 'em. Then you'll get whatever you need. But this one stinks. She's not smart enough to be Queen. This is a setup. This is a flunkey switch. I should send her back happy, but you know what, God? You know fucking what? I won't.

You get out much, ma'am? he said.

You know, said the tipsy woman, I used to go to Land's End a lot. Just to kinda watch the fog. (I *like* this wine. This wine has a lot of class.) It was, well, I don't know exactly— so lovely like the inside of those seashells you can find sometimes all silvery and shimmery—mother-of-pearl, that's the word I was trying to remember. My memory's not so good now. But all those trees, they just stood there, so tall and dark and kind of solid against that fog. If it started to rain, they'd protect me. But if it kept on raining, then after a while they let that rain through. I guess that's how it is, huh? Nothing can protect you forever.

Well, by all means let's go out to Land's End, said Brady.

He ushered her back into his rental car and began to drive slowly down Geary Street, weaving. A cop waved them down.

Don't I know you? the cop said to the Queen.

No, officer, you don't know me.

It sounds like the Queen, Brady mumbled. It *sounds* like her. That's the kicker. That's just what the Queen would say.

Let's see your license, the cop said to Brady.

Brady worked his wallet out from up against his fat buttock and handed it to the cop, money and all. —Help yourself, he said.

The cop fiddled with the wallet until he found the license. —Out of state, huh? And who's the lady?

My Queen.

I oughta send you to jail for twenty days for driving under the influence, said the cop. I can smell it on your breath.

Sure it's on my breath, said Brady. Doesn't mean I'm drunk, though.

The cop said: I should have you take a sobriety test. I should have you walk the white line.

Go ahead, said Brady. I still got three legs.

The cop laughed. —Get out of here, he said. Don't let me catch you driving like that again. Have a nice stay in San Francisco.

Thank you, officer, said Brady. Rolling up the window, he uttered a magnificent Bronx cheer.

The woman was very quiet beside him on that almost fogless afternoon, all the buildings in focus beneath the smoky yellow sky. There was an Asian wedding by the Exploratorium; the bride appeared chilly in her fluttering gown.

They came to Land's End and parked. Trees were groping and reaching, shaking like a handful of darkdyed peacock plumes tied together and whirled in a crazy boy's hand. Brady got out and led the unresisting woman into the bushes. They gazed down at the sea for a while. Then he put his arm around her and whispered into her ear: Hey, baby, I don't believe you're the Queen.

The woman stiffened. —Why, you motherfucker! That's the second time you've insulted me. You called me a liar, didn't you? You think I'm lying?

Brady kissed her neck. —Yes, I do.

Smiling tenderly, he pulled out his Para-Ordnance P-12, cocked the hammer, and put the barrel to the spot on her throat that he had kissed. —You know, it has a grip safety, he said. *Klexter, klokan, kladd, kludd, kligrapp* . . . That's Invisible Empire talk. That's Klan talk, baby. If I don't actually squeeze the grip, it won't shoot, even when I pull the trigger. See?

Don't, the woman whispered.

Now I know you're not the Queen. The Queen would never beg before me like that.

He ground the barrel hard against her larynx and pulled the trigger. Nothing happened. Withdrawing the gun from the sagging woman, he pulled the slide back and thumbed the magazine release. —You see, it's empty. Do you know why, nigger? 'Cause carrying a concealed weapon is a *felony*. Hah!

From his pocket he took out another clip, this one loaded with hollowpoints. He clicked it firmly in with the heel of his hand, and forefingered the slide release so that the slide suddenly lunged forward with a steely slamming noise.

Now let's try that grip safety, he said.

He put the gun to the woman's head again. The hammer had remained cocked. With his hand not touching the back of the grip, he began very slowly to squeeze the trigger.

What do you want me to prove? she wailed. How am I supposed to prove that? You either believe me or you don't. Oh, I was such a fool. I'd started to trust you. I thought you were a nice guy.

And when you tell me you're the Queen, are you just saying you're the Queen or are you lying to me?

What kind of a choice is that? I told you I'm the Queen because I'm the Queen.

Okay, here come two joggers. I'm going to put my arm around you and you're going to put your head on my shoulder like this so that nobody can see the gun. If you scream, I'll kill you. Do you believe me?

Please . . . please . . . What do you want me to do? I can give really good head.

Calls herself the Queen, said Brady in disgust, shoving her down in the mud and kicking her. The joggers were very close now. They were a young couple, spoiled and athletic from the look of them, with expensive running shoes and tinted sunglasses. The woman looked shocked and started to say something, so Brady flashed the gun, put on his most menacing expression and snarled: Keep moving, cunt!

Come on, Tracy, said the husband, let's get out of here.

Okay, said Brady to the sobbing prostitute underfoot. He turned her over with a kick and stepped on her breast, pointing the gun down at her. —This is your only chance, nigger, he said. Where's the Queen?

In—in the garage . . .

Which garage?

The one . . . the same one—

Where we found you?

Yes—

And she's waiting for you to report in?

Yes . . . I didn't . . . If you let me go I won't tell . . .

All right then. Stand up, nigger. Goddamned fucking puke-faced muddy bitch Queen of the Whores, Queen of Scum . . . Now I'm going to hit you in the stomach. If you scream you're dead. I'm going to put you in the hospital, bitch. I'm going to break a couple ribs. You know why? Because your Queen tried to Jew me down, and you lied to me.

| 43 |

Having cooled down, body and soul, Brady achieved the conclusion that Tyler had not betrayed him. Shoddy work, to be sure, but not dishonest—thus the boss's conclusion; for Tyler had never testified under oath that this woman (toward whose blackness Brady admitted to have been predisposed) was definitely the Queen. Shit happens, thought original Brady. He eased himself into the rental car, opened the glove compartment, and cross-checked some receipts that Tyler had given him, pounding the calculator with his stubby fingers until he was soothed. All Tyler's numbers were correct, he was happy to say. He knew the sonofabitch was robbing him but that was okay as long as he didn't get too sloppy or greedy about it; such was the prime rule. Here was a manila envelope full of surveillance forms, too. Brady pulled one sheet out of the middle of the pile, skimmed it, grunted, and then took the whole stack and threw them into a garbage can. That put him in fine spirits. He eased his rental car out of there and turned back east onto Geary Street, passing the Chinese seafood restaurant with painted dragons on the walls and then Joe's ice cream parlor, where he had never been, flashed square and white in his sideview mirror; here came the Korean barbeque joints and the Korean restaurants. Geary Street was wide, characterless, and full of traffic. At Stanyan Street the big road opened up further, letting in windy brightness. He wormed through the squat short tunnel with daylight in narrow truncated pyramids upon its tiles, rolled down the slope to Divisadero, did not read the graffiti on the bricks of the middle school, dipped under the next bridge and yawned at the astrological signs of Japantown—crab, mandala, elephant—and then rolled up the last hill whose ugly vertebral columns of apartments along the Gough Street ridge offered strategic Tenderloin views; down the curve of Starr King to Van Ness he went, and suddenly he was in the narrow canyon of old badlands which constituted the Tenderloin. Here glowed the rain forest mural on the side wall of the Mitchell Brothers theater where world-famed Will McMaster had once pissed in one corner of the Ultra Room; here stood the Iroquois Hotel where Tyler had once stayed for a week between jobs; here grew the bricks, fire escapes and Vietnamese restaurants of the kingdom. Tyler would have shot a glance down Leavenworth, which was sunny and empty, the grating retracted on liquor stores; as for Brady, he was too busy. As usual, the Queen's parking garage offered vacancies. Up the slanting alimentary tract to the third floor he drove, mad as hell. There was the grating that Tyler had shown him, doublelocked, with darkness behind it. —He shook it like an orangutan in a cage and yelled: Hey you, bitch!

The Queen did not answer.

He kicked the grating one more time, then laughed.

Tyler says we're already burned, he shouted. Tyler says you know us. Well, I don't give a shit! You get the hint?

He opened the trunk, dumped the half-dead woman out. Her flesh slapped liquidly against the concrete. She lay still.

In the basement the ceiling was low enough to touch, everything humming and echoing, piss and oil and gasoline on the concrete whose painted arrows lay like frozen missiles at the mouths of downramps in this gilded gloom. He heard voices everywhere, unintelligibly pulsing. At last he realized that they were coming through the pipes. Khrushchev-inspired, he took one of his shoes off and banged it against the nearest conduit: *Going, goiiinnnnng!* The voices stopped.

Again he laughed.

A mesh gate gave onto the utility room, which was crusted with white flakes, as of battery acid residue. Pipes like metallic mushrooms clung in rows to the walls. Here a skinny old wino sat looking at him with intelligent eyes and finally said: Are you feeling hard and mean?

I beg your pardon? said Brady.

I said, are you feeling hard and mean?

I'm looking for the Queen, said Brady on impulse.

The man's face opened and shone. —Her name's Gloria, he said. She is the shining sea of Gloria Gloria Gloria.

What's your name, sir? said Brady, amused.

Jimmy.

I thought her name was Vanna, said a wide-eyed moonfaced young fellow with glasses who kept wiping at his forehead. God, my balls hurt.

Get a job, son, said Brady. What are you two doing in there?

Getting drunk on his money, said old Jimmy with a laugh. He's doin' some article on me for the newspaper . . .

Well, I'll leave you to it. Get emotionally compromised if you want. I don't have time for your foolishness.

If a fool and his money are soon parted, then why am I a millionaire? cackled the old wino.

Brady shrugged and, ticket in hand, strode back to the bright wide realm of that parking garage where adjoining x'es and incandescent tubes like giant paperclips bounced cleanliness off polished tiles, the floor slippery as if from some secretion bubbling up from underneath. A spectacled man bowed inside his glass booth. An LED display brightened his window.

As pretty as Christmas! Brady shouted, knocking on the glass.

Gazing round, he saw that this was even truer than he had supposed, for murals of nature lived upon the walls. Did the Mitchell Brothers own this place, too, or was nature's sentimentalization a fad in the Tenderloin? The cashier still had not responded to his signal.

He knocked again on the glass, harder, and the man frowned, pulled off a pair of earphones, and waited.

Where's the Queen? shouted Brady into the glass.

Maybe the guy couldn't speak English. Shifting his polymath gears, Brady bellowed: *Donday esta el Raino?*

| 44 |

Irene had an accident with John's car and asked Tyler to take the blame, because she was scared. It was not a bad accident, just a paint-scraper, a mirror-breaker. Tyler called John at work, told him that Irene had let him borrow the car while his was in the shop, and that he had scraped a power pole. He promised to pay the repair cost. John laughed tolerantly and the whole thing was no problem. That having been resolved, Tyler phoned Irene to give her a report.

Thank you, she said. I love you.

Love you, too, he said. What did you do the rest of the day?

I stayed in bed. I was depressed at having to ask you.

| 45 |

On Monday John had to go to Cleveland for a week for a business trip. Irene had said that she would come over on Wednesday to do their laundry because the washing machine in Tyler's apartment was free, but Tuesday night she said that she wasn't coming. Tyler had a terrible headache right then; he really wasn't feeling well. So he didn't try to argue with her. He just said: Well, honey, I'm sorry you're not coming. I'll see you next time.

But on Wednesday afternoon he discovered that he had been missing her all day, so he called her up. He was going to ask how she was, but by the time her telephone began to ring he'd decided that that was too forward, so when she answered on the third ring he just said: Hello, Irene. I was going to be driving through your neighborhood and I wondered if you needed me to bring anything.

Nothing that I can think of, said Irene so sweetly. But thank you for asking. How have you been?

OK, he said, already bored with the conversation. What are you doing right now? Nothing. Watching TV.

He wanted to say: Well, why don't you come over, then, sweetheart?

What's the program about?

I guess it's a thriller. I don't know what it is. Somebody is killing somebody.

Oh, he said. That sounds good. Well, I'll let you get back to it.

| 46 |

What was wrong with him? He felt so peculiar and perplexed. As soon as he hung up he wanted to call Irene back again and he knew that he couldn't. He actually lifted the receiver and depressed the numbered white studs, desperate to tell her: I just wanted to hear your voice. —But he left the last digit unpushed, and after a moment sighed and put the phone back to bed. —You know, I had this dream, he wanted to say to her. You and I were walking in a cornfield, and you had on this beautiful long white dress and you were holding my hand and smiling at me. And then you . . . —He had not had any dream of the kind. He could scarcely understand his own emotions, his almost invincible desire to invent this absurd lie. Irene would have been silent, he supposed, and then he would have gone on: You . . . I made you happy . . . —He waited a week, and then invited her out for lunch. She said she was depressed and didn't have the energy to leave the house; would tomorrow be all right? He was busy tomorrow, but the next day she picked him up at home, since she was out in her car anyway doing errands, and they went to one of the Korean barbecue places on Geary Street. He asked her if she wanted a beer, and she hesitated and agreed. He ordered one apiece.

So how are you doing? he said finally.

Oh, you know how it is, she said. Her eyes were red and swollen.

Do you feel the baby yet?

I feel something. I don't know if it's the baby or not.

You look so sad, he said. What's wrong, honey? Please tell me what the matter is.

You know what the matter is, said Irene. That's all I ever talk about. I'm sorry . . .

There was a black cat on the window-seat, basking—a creature of great elegance and self-assurance which presently began to purr in the soft low buzz of an electric razor. Irene smiled at it and made kissing sounds, but it ignored her.

Did you have pets when you were a kid? said Tyler.

Irene nodded, her glass at her lips. The waitress had begun to unload the usual immense appetizer tray of kimchees white and red, pickled fish, dried fish, seaweed soup, miso paste. Irene set her glass down, took her chopsticks from the paper envelope, and began to grate them back and forth against each other in case there might be splinters. The cat went on purring.

And how's work for you? asked Irene.

Slow. Still looking for someone who doesn't want to be found. You had cats, you said?

She nodded again, listlessly. Then she took her chopstick wrapper and began twisting it, teeth sinking ruthlessly into her lower lip as she stared aimlessly about, spurious, objectless copy of some fighting-girl on speed who rushed back and forth along Valencia Street, looking for the two girls she had beaten because she lusted to beat them again. Irene, of course, was not the fighting kind.

John and I always had dogs, Tyler said. Sheep dogs, border collies, you know . . .

How's Mugsy?

I don't know. I didn't ask Mom . . .

I always had bad luck with cats and I love them so much, said Irene. In Korea we had one cat, and when he was hardly more than a baby he went out one night and I guess he must have found some poison. Maybe rat poison. He came into the house real early in the morning, throwing up blood and this horrible yellow stuff, and he was in convulsions. I guess he came home because he thought we could save him. With cats and dogs, one of the most amazing things about them is the way they get to trust you. You can do anything to them, even if it hurts, because they know you love them and are trying to do the best thing for them. And that cat—I said he was our cat, but really he was my cat; he loved me the best, and I loved him—well, Henry, he kept looking into my eyes. He was rolling around on the rug and screaming and whenever he caught his breath he kept looking into my face 'cause he believed in me. He was sure I could do something. I took him to the vet before school. I was actually a little late for school. And I was nervous about that, 'cause I'd never been late before. I wasn't a good girl in school that day. I kept crying and praying. And I just ran home. I asked my grandmother if the vet had been able to fix my cat, and she said, no, they couldn't fix him. Because the intestines were all torn. The vet buried him.

Probably threw him in the garbage, Tyler thought to himself.

Bending over, the waitress reached beneath the table, turned on the gas jet, and then lit it. Blue flames danced evilly up. With tongs and scissors, the waitress took the *kalbi* and *bulgoki* strips out of the marinade and laid them into the grill, where they began to sizzle loudly. With a mechanical smile, Irene accepted the tongs from her and began to turn the meat. Then the waitress thrust the scissors into the marinade bowl and carried it away.

So they got me another cat, Irene said. Another boy cat. I was about fifteen then. I was late starting my period, but one day it came. And the cat knew right off. He started to lick me.

Were your parents happy that you'd become a woman?

I didn't tell them. In my family we don't talk about those things.

I know one Japanese girl whose mother cooked red beans that night to celebrate, said Tyler. And when her father wanted to know what the fuss was all about, her mother just said that a very good thing had happened.

I guess my mother must have known, because my underpants were bloody, Irene said, picking up strips of well-done meat with the tongs and putting them on his plate. —My cat sure knew. In our house the cats weren't supposed to sleep inside. But every night at around midnight this cat would scratch at my window, and I'd get up and let him in. And he'd come into my bed and lick my nightgown all night, right between my breasts. His tongue was kind of rough, and sometimes it almost hurt, but it also felt really good. He licked so much that my nightgown turned black there. Every night he'd come and do that, and sleep with me. It was kind of my secret, I guess. It made me feel special. And in the morning when I went to school, that cat would follow me along the top of the wall as far as he could, and then in the afternoon when I came home he'd be waiting for me. Well, we were getting ready to move to America then. My grandmother was already in Los Angeles, and then my big aunt and uncle, and then little aunt and uncle, and then it was just us and we'd already sold our house. I asked my mother what was going to happen to my cat, and she didn't answer. And one night that cat didn't come scratching at my window. I kind of wondered and worried about that, 'cause he'd never failed to come to me before. And in the morning I didn't see him. My mother said that he knew we were going to leave him, so he was sad and ran away. Cats just know.

Your mother probably gave him away and didn't have the guts to tell you, Tyler thought.

You want another beer, Irene? he said. Here's to fetal alcohol syndrome!

Oh, Henry, I'm feeling—I don't know how I'm feeling. Can we please please finish? I want to go home and lie down . . .

Irene . . .

I don't know. I've almost had it with everything.

And John?

He's good at digging into everything. I used to tell my parents and they'd say trust your husband, but they are not saying trust your husband anymore. He's taken away all my credit cards. He takes all my paycheck. He's never satisfied. I'm sorry; he's your brother; maybe you—

You know better than that, Irene.

Can we please please go now? I want to lie down. I want to go to bed.

| 47 |

Irene was supposed to meet him on Union Street. He stood waiting in front of the shop with the phony picket fence below the window. Inside lay a long narrow glass table whose legs were naked bronze women bending backward and supporting the top with their outstretched arms. Behind the table he perceived stained glass lamps (he didn't know whether they were real Tiffanys or not,) and green drinking glasses like magnifying lenses. —He looked at his watch. —Another shop window boasting of gold-ivied dinner plates as round and white as the breasts of a girl with whom he'd once gone skinnydipping in high school, a shy girl who probably never undressed except at night, for her skin had been as pale and perfect as a hardwood floor kept under a ratty old carpet. In the next window he saw a cat made of milk-porcelain, watching herself in the mirror, a seven-drawer lingerie chest in the Queen Anne style on sale for $279.00—how many pairs of underpants did a woman need, to take up seven drawers? Next was the window of the optometrist's shop, whose many double lenses, yes, those, too, reminded him of breasts.

Irene had not arrived. He went to the espresso bar and ordered a double shot. The coffee soon began to kick in, rewarding him with a pleasantly twitchy feeling. He went out and looked for her black Volkswagen Rabbit but didn't see it. The orange and white # 45 bus with its long feelers drank from wires and disappeared, and that moment he knew that she was not going to show up. A watch-gaze: Forty minutes late. Irene was never late.

He began to walk east, toward the Tenderloin, and suddenly right in front of the next coffeehouse or maybe the next he met a grizzled grimy panhandler whose hands were streaked with blackish-grey, as if human flesh, like the silver it so often sells for, could tarnish; and the panhandler said: Can you give me anything?

Why, sure I can, said Tyler, grateful that for the next twenty to thirty seconds that heavy sadness in his chest and the nervousness in the cesspool of his churning stomach and the anger against Irene that dwelled behind his eyes might not be felt. He turned out his pocket, finding three dimes, which he gave the man, for the first time looking into his face. But the panhandler was gazing far beyond him. Tyler would never see what he saw.

Past Buchanan the shops were not so fancy, the jewelry plated rather than solid, the shop windows weary with glass eggs or glass snail shells or cast ballerinas whose tits he could barely see. Skinny, hairy-legged joggers headed back toward their medium-rent apartments, clutching freshly purchased cappuccinos and raspberry-papaya smoothies, emanations of royalty.

He gazed down the gentle slope between white houses that led to the Marina district where John and Irene lived.

When he got to the next pay phone he reached into his pocket and then remembered that he'd given all his change to that panhandler. He went into the corner deli and bought a candy bar with a dollar bill. They gave him two quarters back. He dialled.

Yes? said his brother before the second ring.

Hello, John, he said as mildly as he could.

What did you have to do with this? said the cruelly level voice.

His heart sank. —What do you mean?

Don't lie to me ever again, said John in the weariest voice that he had ever heard. I just don't have any more time for your lies.

Tyler thought for a moment. Then he hung up the phone, changed another dollar, and called his mother, who also answered before the second ring.

How's everything, Mom?

His mother began to cry. —Oh, Henry, she wept. John just called. Oh, poor, poor Irene.

· BOOK III ·

Visits and Visitations

•

The nonuniformed or plainclothes investigator is in a good position to observe illegal activities and obtain evidence. For example, a male plainclothes officer may appear to accept the solicitations of a prostitute . . .

WAYNE W. BENNETT AND KÄREN M. HESS,
Criminal Investigation (1991)

•

| 48 |

Tyler's car still smelled of flowers. Just before driving down to Los Angeles, he'd stopped at a florist's in the Mission and filled the back seat with funeral wreaths upon double plastic bags of melting ice.

A blonde salesgirl stood outside of a bridal shop, leaning against one of the parted steel shutters and smoking a cigarette. Her windows screamed with whiteness.

Previously Tyler had allowed himself to blueprint the structure of a future life lonely but not unpleasant, a life of sitting on empty bleachers on Sundays and holidays, gazing unseeing through the mesh of some park fence, politely oriented toward the baseball diamond upon which shouting Little Leaguers might or might not be practicing as he listened to the crows declaim: *Ewww, ewww!* in demagogic accents—not a bad life at all, a privileged one, in fact, a thickening-around-the-middle life of birthday cards to nieces and nephews, of going to movies; maybe he'd take up fine art photography in earnest some day. He already had the equipment and the technique; it sounded less tedious than jerking off into the locator fluid. And John and Irene would have their mixed-race children, the ones to whom on birthdays he'd send stupid cards; Irene, who'd owned cats as a child, but always wanted a dog, would have a German shepherd or maybe a border collie by then—the eternal Mugsy. Irene and John could visit Tyler's mother in the nursing home in which she'd surely be settled, if in fact she were still above the dirt. Tyler himself would accordingly be free to relocate. His needs were low; perhaps he couldn't live on three hundred a year, like the Unabomber, but ten grand per annum might well see him through. —No more photography, then, and no fancy women—maybe a bottle of bourbon when he wanted it. His grandfather had done nicely on Black Velvet. In the old man's accounts of his vacations, whiskey of some sort would always figure. —I remember when Elma and I took a trip out to Salt Lake in a Pullman car, he'd say. Those were good times, Henry; you can't imagine how good. Elma liked to rest, of course, so I'd sit with her and we'd have a few nips, and then when I got sick of that, why, I'd leave her alone and head to the dining car, order a couple shots . . . —Now his grandfather was dead. Life passed, full of passions like a van crammed with shouting dogs; every year there'd come another Easter without a resurrection, a Fourth of July without children or hot dogs or fireworks, a silent telephone, every month half a dozen bills in the mail.

He knew that twice a year, for ever on, at New Year's and on August ninth, which was Irene's birthday, relatives would clip the errant grassblades from around the corners of her headstone where the mowers of the sexton's office hadn't reached, polish the slab with window-cleaner, seat themselves upon a blanket, and sing hymns. She'd be well taken care of.

Taylor Street was full of cars and people in white summer shirts. They almost blinded him, like angels. He drove on.

In the O'Farrell Street parking garage a fat man whose tie was wrapped around his neck came strutting down the white line that spiraled along the path of waiting cars. Ugly cubical lanterns hung in immense grottos, and parking attendants waved their white sleeves.

Tyler got out and locked the car. It was a very hot day. A woman was yelling and sobbing on the pay phone. When she was finished, he dialled John and Irene's number to see whether Irene's voice might still be on the answering machine.

Hello? said John curtly.

Tyler hung up.

He'd forgotten that it was a Saturday. No wonder downtown was so crowded. With tentative steps he approached the fresh-smelling, faintly mysterious hedge-walls which ran along the perimeter of Union Square and walled the upsloping sidewalks which comprised the inlets of that park. A Peruvian quartet was playing there. The mandolinist was tight-lipped and intense—difficult to believe so sullen-seeming a fellow could produce such sweet sounds. The drummer, who wore a pillbox hat, kept gazing searchingly about him as he played. Of the other two men Tyler could not glimpse their features as he strode past. Some weary tourist ladies, one very fat and in purple, sat waiting, probably for the more energetic members of their family or other sociological cluster to finish shopping; they applauded the Peruvians from time to time because they were well-mannered ladies, but their expressions of stranded desolation never altered. Their lives were passing, tvacations trickling through the hourglass; moment by moment this warmish blue San Francisco day was being wasted. They sat beneath lush palm-trees, and distantly a trolley-car sounded its bell as he heard the ladies talking about grilled cheese sandwiches; then he was past them and could not hear anymore. (He called his answering machine: No messages.) The Peruvians had ceased. Some moving object, toy-red, caught his eye—an armored car. He wondered which parking garage it patronized. Now the Peruvians had begun again, a sweet song whose flute-wails did indeed remind him of mountains, although if their placard had said that they were Plains Indians instead he might have imagined open spaces. The melody dwindled behind him as he ascended the walkway to the high ground of seated ones and teeming pigeons, more hedges and then the pigeon-adorned column whose base said SECRETARY OF THE NAVY; he'd never taken the time to read the rest, and learn the significance of it. He sat down. A white girl in shorts, with nice breasts and a birthmark on the back of her thigh, hurried quickly past, almost goose-stepping, leaving him with the impression of a bland blurred face half obscured by chestnut hair. Was he the only one who looked at anybody? In the Tenderloin they always gave you the once-over as you went by; here they studied the sky, like astronomers, or watched the children whose hands they held, or spied out the reflections of their destinations upon their moving shoe-toes; let's not forget that the seated ones had their blizzards of pigeons to watch.

It's not at all impossible that John will marry again, he thought to himself. In fact, it's very likely. When that happens, I'd better keep my distance. I'd better move away . . .

He wondered whether Irene's parents had insisted on paying for the cemetery plot. She used to go to them in secret for money when she faced some unexpected expense, being afraid to importune John. But John did have that emergency backbone which during crises he could slip into his otherwise hollow spine. Tyler rather thought that he must have donned his most noble and generous armor so that no one could reach him, refusing to let Irene's family contribute financially or in any other way, unless, as was plausible, they had gotten to choose the minister—their own, most likely. It was impossible to know who'd won, and Tyler couldn't ask. When he'd offered to help, John had only said: I don't need anything from you, Hank.

The sunshine felt uncomfortably warm upon his temples. A grey-haired man trudged by, clutching a sweater; out of the side of his eye Tyler saw the man stop to thrust an arm deep into the garbage can, peering, his mouth open. Then he shot suspicious looks at life and went on. Pigeons crawled and thronged. A long Muni bus eased down Stockton Street with a series of squeaks, and passed into shade.

Tyler got up and inspected the column. He read: CAPTURE OR DESTROY THE SPANISH FLEET . . .

Reflected palm-tendrils swerved and curved in the windows of Macy's, and skyscrapers' terraces swelled and bowed there as if in the throes of an immense explosion. The Peruvians' music, gentle and strangely liquid, seemed the appropriate solvent for this image of dissolution.

| 49 |

Irene and John's marriage endured for almost four years. Tyler cherished the conviction that according to some divine calendar she hadn't been his brother's wife for nearly as long as that, but he was equally certain that he had known Irene much, much longer than four years, which only went to show how inferior to locator fluid was certainty. As long as he could remember, he'd relieved his thoughts every now and then from reality's blind bonds—a sort of recreation which possessed no power to harm him if he kept simultaneous sight of actuality, ideal and the angle of deflection between them; which is only to say that he trusted himself, not merely because he had to, but because he knew himself so well.

He remembered the first time that he had really been alone with Irene. It was a month or two before the wedding, and Irene, whose car was still in the shop because her sister had borrowed it and hit a lamppost, animated his ruby answering machine light to say that she needed somebody to drive her to the Kobletz outlet, where she and John planned to register. Tyler had been suprised when John, whom he met for lunch, explained that he was too busy; of course John was always busy, but one would have thought that a man so in love with suits and neckties would also be fascinated by the dinner service upon which he and his wife might someday entertain special clients— that is, rich people, whose nature John and Irene, or at least John, hoped progressively to assume. But Mr. Singer was shouting for the Knightman brief, and Tyler, between jobs as usual, had agreed, partly out of the sense of guilt which John usually inspired in him, and partly because it felt honorable, novel and almost titillating to act for the first time in the capacity of brother-in-law; his mother would be happy, too: she always wanted for him and John to get along better. At that time Irene had not made a great impression on him, his attitude scarcely stretching beyond the scrupulously benign. He remembered that as soon as they reached the showroom she'd needed to go in search of a restroom, and he'd sat observing a young couple who'd also come to register bone china for their wedding. The man had a weary, somewhat loutish face. He seemed ill at ease in his big boots, which fortunately made no mark upon the carpet. Tyler could see that he would not be the one to initiate divorce proceedings. Introverted and browbeaten, he might possibly be driven into a fling in three or four years' time, or the bride might openly take a lover and end matters, but he himself, merely reactive, would wait for the axe to fall. The bride, a slender chestnut blonde, strutted about with a little smile on her face. The bridegroom followed her everywhere while she paced and swooped with tiny delighted cries. Awkwardly, he tried to put his arms around her, but she threw off that embrace with annoyance. Then he retreated to a table in a little thicket of that crystal forest, where he gazed moodily upon the plates and saucers of his future, yawning. The bride bestowed upon everybody, even Tyler, little smiles of rapture. Finally she returned to her groom, knelt beside him, and slipped her arm lightly around his neck as she commenced showing him plates. But he wore a glum face now which could not change. Offended, she retired across the table, and then the pair gazed silently at their knuckles until the saleswoman came. Standing over them, this muse began to reveal arcane principles while they gazed up at her lips like obedient schoolchildren, the girl thrilled to memorize the lesson (which probably had to do with prices), the boy afraid not to. This too was life, this charnel-house of cream pitchers rather than herpid flesh; it was *the market,* which must be respected.

Irene having returned with smiling apologies, and the other couple deducted from the scene, the saleswoman presently approached. Tyler still thought it strange that John was not there. But Irene already had a good idea of what she wanted. Perhaps John had given her instructions.

There's your platter, salad plate, gravy boat, very unusual looking, said the saleslady. So there's your basic picture. The covered vegetable is two-sixty; the platter is one-forty-five. Did you want to make a purchase today?

No, we're just looking today, said Irene with surprising timidity.

Okay. Well, there's a four dollar charge in tax. But you're asking me to hold everything here, which must be respected.

Yes, said Irene.

When's the day? said the saleslady with a whore's grin, realizing, as any whore not too far gone sometimes will, that she had pressed the pecuniary side of the matter too quickly.

February twenty-seventh, said Irene, slipping her arm around Tyler's neck.

That was the first time that she had ever touched him. He would not forget.

You know what we'll do, said the saleslady, if it's a hardship on anybody to call, we'll work with you. We'll call 'em right back. You can verbally pass that along. We always understand people on fixed incomes (this with a glance at Tyler's grubby shirt). We've been in business since the sixties.

Do you think it's too expensive? Irene whispered in his ear.

If the Crania is too much, we also have the Slovenia and the Russell, said the saleslady, who evidently had good hearing.

Tyler felt ill at ease. —Maybe we should call John, he said.

John? Who's John? said the saleslady with sudden shrillness. You two are getting married and you can't even decide for yourselves?

Pink spots appeared in Irene's cheeks, and she squeezed his hand. Her hand was burning.

My assets are tied up in stock, John would have said. John would have gazed swiftly and critically at everything, with owlish eyes. Not even a solid platinum gravy boat would have satisfied him. But he would make a good husband in certain respects. Alert, cautious and solvent, he'd exemplify the phrase "to husband one's resources." Fat-jowled and pigheaded though he'd certainly become, he'd help Irene die rich.

You think we should call him? said Irene.

Oh, forget it, said Tyler.

It's two-ninety for the burgundy, the saleswoman was saying. Now, what are we doing about the registry?

It's a little hard for me, Irene was saying. Can we just write up an order and decide if we're going to go through with it?

Sure, said the saleswoman. Now, we're going to need your name, address and telephone number.

He heard the fat, gentle saleswoman at the next table saying of every choice: Oh, *that's* pretty.

What did they all signify, these pale blank plates which stimulated no desire in him? Irene doubtless felt the same way about the vaginas of Turk Street or Capp Street. It was not what the commodity was, but the fact that it existed in so many varieties, each available, each with its own signature and price, so that choosing became a weariness. He wondered what effect this must have upon a person who became accustomed to believing that joy consisted of selecting and collecting one's bought pleasures. This way of living sometimes struck him as monstrously evil. And yet Domino and the crazy whore were hardly happier. It was not that he objected to people enjoying their cutlery; it was the knowingness, the connoisseurship *without* enjoyment, the wastefulness of it all that depressed him.

On the way home he let her drive for the practice she said she wanted, and the separation between gas pedal and brake compelled her slender thighs apart. He sat there wanting to put his hand there, but didn't. A billboard said: YOU'RE GOING THE WRONG WAY. When they got to the apartment where she lived with John, she kissed him many, many times on the mouth, but with closed lips. He wanted to lick her throat and didn't.

The sound that the first shovelful of dirt had made when it hissed down upon her coffin, more or less where her chest must have been, was, he supposed, much less definitive than the clank of china being set upon a glass shelf.

| 50 |

It was a beautiful, beautiful service, his mother had said. I was so sorry that you couldn't attend.

| 51 |

Bloodshot tail-lights of squat cars toiled up the Marina hill. The Union Street fair had just closed for the night, and on the sidewalk he saw giggly girls in short skirts drinking beer from plastic cups, attended by boyish fraternity types, one of whom, exultantly drunk, leaped onto the hood of Tyler's car at the intersection, squatted, and gibbered at Tyler through the windshield. Making a peace sign, Tyler put the car in first and slowly let the clutch out. The young man hooted, and admiring girls laughed with their mouths open. The car began to increase its speed; the boy swayed, half-leaped, half-tumbled off; from the looks of things he'd sprained his ankle. Tyler made a quick right to get away from them all, and then a left on Broadway, passing in due course the Broadway Manor Motel where for hire he had once broken up still another marriage. Following a black stretch limo through Chinatown, he felt suddenly nauseated by his own *negative mediocrity,* which had not only prevented him from doing anything good or important, such as making Irene happy, or getting her to love him, let alone saving her life, but actually compelled him to acts of petty evil. The Mark of Cain! He asserted that John was not a good person, either, but since John could not do much about that, having come from the womb ungood (and he also recognized that others, such as Celia, or his mother, or Mr. Rapp and Mr. Singer, dealt with his brother almost without irritation—a notable fact, tending to convict one Henry M. Tyler of prejudice), Tyler granted his own utter lack of justification in having, for instance, made advances to his brother's wife.

He turned into the Tenderloin. Secrets wept behind grilles' richly patterned speckles of pure silver and pure black, which resembled the pewter beads in the store called Gargoyle on Haight and Masonic. Once Irene had asked him how he went about his work in bad neighborhoods, and he'd said: You go in during the day, figure out where you're going. And, sure, you'll go back during the night, but you're pretty much in a direct line, you know where you're going, although of course it remains pretty fluid and things can always go south on you.

But I worry about you! she'd said.

Oh, my stuff is all sportcoat and tie, he'd lied.

He drove back and forth on Turk Street, looking for the Queen.

| 52 |

It was very foggy that night outside his apartment. Tyler poured himself a shot of tequila, no salt, no lime, with the phone trapped between right ear and upraised right shoulder as he said: Oh, I'll hire that stuff out if you make it worth my while. I'm kind of a one-man operation here. To do good surveillance you really need three players on the team. No, my prices aren't really that competitive. In all honesty, I can't recommend my services. You might try Stealth Associates. All right. All right. Yeah, no problem. Thanks for calling. Uh huh. That's right. Good luck.

He tore a details description sheet off the pad and wrote:

```
SEX      female
RACE     ?? [African-American?]
AGE      ??
```

No shit, Sherlock, he said with a laugh.

He was afraid to turn off the light. In his mid-thirties, he had by strange starts developed a skin disease which prevented him from thoroughly sleeping anymore. He'd doze off for a couple of hours, and then a sensation as sharp and sudden as being stuck with a red-hot needle would awaken him, his heart clanging with panic. But it was not pain that he felt, but itching. The first dermatologist was too busy to see him for two months, and the second (or, I should say, the second's receptionist) estimated that it would be at least a month and a half before the meeting of minds, so he went to a G.P. who said that it was scabies and charged him a hundred and twenty dollar consultation fee and wrote a prescription for an ointment that didn't work at all. Every night he woke up scratching his legs and stomach until they bled. Sometimes his arms itched, or the insides of his ears. The next doctor said that it was atopic dermatitis, and prescribed a moisturizing cream which worked for about two weeks, until the itching suddenly proclaimed its malicious midnight presence. After that he adopted a routine. For three nights he'd scratch and fight with his flesh. On the fourth, too exhausted to carry on, he'd take a sleeping pill. Soon he became habituated and had to double up his medication and then switch to ever stronger brands. Finally a whore told him to try Vaseline, which worked like a charm. But sometimes he still awoke itching. He was afraid that tonight would be like that.

PECULIARITIES   ??
ALIASES   Queen, Maj
CONFEDERATES   Domino [??], Strawberry [??], Kitty [??], unnamed mentally unstable prostitute [??]

That afternoon in the Tenderloin he'd glimpsed the blonde hooker, Domino, wandering into a nasty little watering hole called the Wonderbar, and so under the rubric SUSPECTED LOCALITIES he wrote: Parking garage on Turk & Larkin, Tenderloin core area, Capp St/Mission core area [16th-20th Sts], Wonderbar [??].

His stomach rumbled. He sighed, shook a clattering tombstone batch of frozen spicy chicken drumsticks onto a glass plate, and microwaved them for four minutes. When he opened the microwave, sour orange grease flecked every wall. The drumsticks were overcooked on the outside and frozen on the inside. He gnawed them all down to their icy bony cores and microwaved them again for sixty-nine seconds. By then, he already felt queasy, so he set the plate on the counter and sat down again by the details description sheet.

CONFEDERATES   Domino, Strawberry, Kitty, unnamed mentally unstable prostitute [??], Sapphire [??], others to be determined.

Let's just run Domino through the system, he muttered, opening his fingers above the keyboard, but just then the telephone rang. It was a wrong number.

His skull ached. He dialled his brother's number. His heart pulsated nauseatingly when immediately subsequent to the second ring John lifted the receiver and said: *Hello?*

How's everything? said Tyler.

Oh, fine. Have you been calling my machine and then hanging up?

No, John. Believe it or not, I have better things to do.

Like what?

Oh, let's say some guy rear-ends a person and he says I didn't know it was stopped because the tail-light was off. You can tell whether or not the lightbulb was oxidized. You just photograph it since the lawyers will—

I thought maybe you wanted to listen to Irene's voice on the tape.

John, is this going to be a friendly phone call?

You made the call, not me.

I get it.

I erased it, Hank. I wiped it out.

You mean Irene's message.

You may be stupid but you sure aren't dumb. That's it exactly. Now it's *my* voice on the machine.

Well, bully for you.

So if you keep calling my answering machine and then hanging up, I'll—

You know, John, they have a service for paranoid people like you. Caller ID. It's finally legal in California now. That way you'll see the phone number of the—

Oh, forget it, said John. Irene's voice was giving Mom the willies, that's all. Let's just forget the whole topic. Let's just bury it, so to speak.

Yeah, sure.

Let's just put a granite headstone over it and sing a few hypocritical hymns.

I thought you were the religious one.

Well, certain things make a guy wonder, Hank. I'm still trying to . . . *Have* you been calling my machine?

I'm getting tired of this, said Tyler. (For their honeymoon, John and his bride had gone to London, where Irene had loved Queen Mary's dollhouse, Madame Tussaud's, the Changing of the Guard.)

So you're tired, John said. Well, what the *fuck* about me?

How's work?

Oh, fine. This Brady contract is a bit of a snarl, but—Hank, I'm going to put you on hold. There's somebody on the other line.

All right, said Tyler.

He watched the second hand on the kitchen clock snail around for a full revolution, then another. Gently he replaced the phone in its cradle.

| 53 |

He had a dream that he went to a whorehouse in Chinatown. It was a strangely *white* dream, so that the crowds of Chinese women and girls toting bulging plastic bags of just-bought produce, and the little boys reading comics, all wore the same tints one sees in San Francisco on a sunny foggy morning, with the low white house-cubes of the Sunset under fog, and the silver tracks of morning enlightening all the pale houses of Noe Valley. Chinese kids in white trousers and white T-shirts banged drums and cymbals lazily with a muffled sound, carrying a dragonhead and subsequent dragontrain which they didn't bother to get under. Outside City Lights Bookstore they set off firecrackers which flashed white light. In the dream it must have been around noon. Where was he exactly? Perhaps not far from the future headquarters of the Hang On Tong Society, because the tall narrow cave-arch of rainbow graffiti (a white rainbow, of course) weighed him down with familiarity. The place had just opened. He discovered himself to be in a room which resembled a restaurant, although it was not a restaurant, and the waiters were just taking the white chairs down from the white tables. Now the prostitutes entered single file. They were so pure, so impossibly beautiful that for a moment he could not breathe. While they had Asian features, their complexions were paper-white (probably because the previous day Tyler had been studying Jock Sturges's books of photographic nudes, in which flesh was rendered either paper-white or marble-white). Their loveliness stupefied him. For a long time he couldn't make up his mind which girl to take. Then suddenly he saw one who was even more beautiful than the rest She stood a little apart from them, and she was white like snow. They called her the White Court. It cost three hundred and fifty dollars to be with her, which was more than he had ever spent, but when he paid white cash at the registration desk, the clerk told him that he had a full twenty-four hours; he didn't have to leave her until ten minutes before noon the following day. A stunning excitement resonated within him and echoed. This time he would finally get to know another soul. He'd be with her, talk to her, listen to her, memorize every episode of her life, know her in every possible way.

She went ahead to get ready. Then a woman came to show him the way. He was following her when he saw his brother. Tyler wanted to believe that it wasn't he, because it was so incongruous to see him there and because it ruined his plans. But John addressed him by name. He was sitting at a table working, as always, or perhaps reading the newspaper, which in the dream came to the same thing. It seemed he'd established himself here only for the atmosphere. Tyler said: Well, I guess you know what I'm here for. — Go to it, John said wearily. He chatted with John for a few more minutes, because that was only right. Then he saw that the woman who had been going to lead him to the White Court had already disappeared down the hall. He'd paid, but she hadn't waited for him. He ran down the corridor, but couldn't find her.

The whorehouse was beginning to get busy. A young man in a suit said to the clerk: I'll take the White Court, please. —Tyler realized that his reservation was already cancelled.

Later he went out with another prostitute who was friends with the White Court, an ordinary woman who did not hasten his heart. He asked her what the White Court thought of him. She said: My friend said you didn't do much with her. You held her hand, but then you did nothing but read the newspaper.

| 54 |

Brady called his machine and said: Know who this is? I think you do. Well, you're through. No hard feelings, but I'm tired of paying for nothing. I could have found that parking garage without you, and what's more, there's never anybody home! I'm sorry for you, so I'm going to tack a little consolation check onto your fee after you send me your bill, but make sure you have receipts to back everything up . . .

John called his machine and said: There's something I need to talk to you about. — Tyler erased that message.

His mother called his machine and said: I just wanted to see how you were doing, honey. —He called her but she wasn't in.

A Mrs. Bickford called his machine to request a confidential appointment. Tyler wrote her number down.

A drunk called his machine and said: Goddamn you old goddamn you old goddamn.

The landlord called his machine to let him know that the toilet was working very nicely, in case he hadn't noticed. He called the landlord's machine and said thank you.

| 55 |

At Judgment Day we'll all slide our jellyrotted flesh back onto our bones just as a streetwhore slips her undies back on while she's sitting at the edge of the bed, getting ready to go; and then time will crash like the hotel door splintering under the blows of God's cops who've come to execute their bench warrant—back to the Hall of Justice for summary judgment, so that Satan can boil the flesh back off of us forever! Can there be judgment without pain? I would say not. Until the verdict, the soul must wait in fear; fear is a sort of pain. And Tyler, whose apartment windows were already fog-darkened, waited and waited for some exception to absolve him from rules, before the ultimate judgment devoured him. Lodging his pistol beneath his left armpit, he rose, dimmed down the brightness of his computer monitor because he had never felt like spending forty dollars on a screen saver, turned off the kitchen light, turned on the bedroom light, donned his windbreaker, locked up the apartment, descended the wet grey stairs, and drove away. He wasn't desperate, merely bored. He wanted to do something new. Some homeowners study grass-seed, until lawnsmanship comes naturally; thus they while away the time before decomposition. Renters tend to be disinclined toward that solution. As for Tyler, rolling into North Beach, passing the purple neon waterfall behind the sign for Big Al's, he decided that he ought to take up reading again. It might distract him. He admired his mother for all her book-knowledge, although she knew little of life, which was probably better anyway. In his past at home there had been much quarreling with raised voices, in the streets so many possessed souls attacking bodies, uttering demonic screams. No matter whether you sought the world out or hid from it, something would get you. —His friend Ken the wedding photographer used to jocularly shout at the cronies of some bridegroom: He's been married so many times he's got *rice scars!* and that was funny, but when he thought about it, it actually became not so funny because all the living had scars and then they got wounds, and more scars, and more wounds, until they died. That was a given, but didn't anything lie beyond that? His mother was happy enough reading. She'd garnered wisdom of a harmless sort, like a philatelist's, and taught him how to get it for himself. Tenderly he remembered the evenings that he'd sat beside John on the sofa and she'd read to them both from the Narnia books, the dog looking up, interestedly twitching its legs, and in bed he'd close his eyes and see the characters running silently upon the stageboards of his inner skull, while John cleared his throat in the darkness next door. Later his mother had bought them the whole set of Hardy Boys novels with their matching spines, and he had enjoyed them even more than John. He owned a gift for telling how the plots would turn out. Perhaps it was then that he wanted to be a detective. Use iodine fumes to reveal indented writing, he learned. Chloral hydrate is knockout drops. The Hardy Boys had made interfering with other people's business into something exciting and brave; they never had to fill out surveillance forms, and their adversaries were always evil, unlike the Japanese banker's wife in the Nikko Hotel who'd screamed and tried to cover herself when she'd seen his long lens against the window, while her lover fled to the bathroom; imploringly she clasped her hands; what had she ever done to Tyler? After that, he'd always felt sick when he took infidelity cases, the gaping mouth of the banker's wife remaining impressed on his brain's pavement like skid marks on an accident scene (they actually begin disappearing within minutes, which is why the well-prepared detective photographs them through a polarizing filter). And yet no unpleasant taste had troubled his soul when he'd brought Irene to the Kabukicho restaurant that time so long ago now, making use of the Japanese banker's embossed silver card! Maybe he could not afford unpleasant impressions. Why, in that case, did he feel so downcast now? Turning down Columbus, he achieved the Susie Hotel with the four red ideograms upon its sign, and cool greenish-yellow brightness upstairs behind the curtained windows. He made a right, and fortune granted him a parking place in front of some littered apartment complex or housing project behind an immense gate. A pay phone hung in a steel box out front. He called his answering machine. No messages.

With John's Minox in one well-zipped jacket pocket and his pistol in the other (his armpit had gotten sore), he entered City Lights to seek out the ink-scented whiteness between the thighs of books, and just across from the register stopped to survey the tall, narrow surrealism shelf of paperbacks: *The Heresiarch, Maldoror, Irène's Cunt, My Last Sigh, The Tears of Eros, The Jade Cabinet* . . . For sentimental reasons he opened *Irène's Cunt* and read: Irène is like an arch above the sea. I have not drunk for a hundred days, and sighs quench my thirst. That made him feel almost happy—why, he could not have said. But he was well accustomed to situations in which not all the facts could be explained.

In the checkerboard-floored poetry room where people sniffled and shuffled (the turning pages, surprisingly, were silent) he gazed out the window at the sparkling barbed-wire stars of neon rushing round the Hungry I outside (LOVE MATES, said the sign), accompanied by more neon, cars, and whistlers. A couple faced the wall of poetry, and the man said: Honey, one of the greatest, uh, Mexican writers is Carlos Fuentes. Have you read him? —The woman sighed. —I tried, she said.

A young blonde clutched her throat as she wandered in silence from Bao Ninh to Edward Lurie; when she squatted down to touch the spine of *Dreams of the Centaur* he saw a single strand of grey hair in the back of her head. It seemed to him that if he only found the right book to suckle from, he would be saved.

Another woman seated herself at one of the little round tables, pulled at her lower lip, and waited, or thought. Outside, a bus ground by. Someone uttered a quiet laugh. The shadows of browsers moved upon the floor.

| 56 |

With his hundred dollars' worth of books in a paper bag he strolled up Columbus that hot night and found a new smoothie place with blue and pink tinted surrealist Rubenesque nudes on the walls, naked angels swimming in pastel clouds. A yawning old Chinese man passed the open window, and then, emerging strangely from the glare of a hotel sign, a drunk yelled: *Smoothies, man!* reached in, yanked a flower from a potted plant, and looped onward in the direction of City Lights, swinging the neck of his bottle with the same happy expressiveness of possession as the young lesbian a moment later who neared and vanished, twining her fingers ruthlessly in another girl's hair.

I don't want anything sweet, Tyler said to himself. Let me get something that's good for me.

For a dollar twenty-five he ordered a urine-sample-like cup of wheatgrass juice, as emerald as ferric oxalate; it tasted, unsurprisingly, like liquid grass. —Well, I hope this does something, he thought.

The beverage, thick and bubbly like spit, vastly bored him. He gulped it down quickly and went back to the car. No messages on his answering machine. A police van hunkered black and blocky at the corner, its antenna bent back timidly. He did not feel ready to sleep. Why not drive? Tonight the Broadway tunnel was bright and empty, only one stern cyclist with blinking red lights at his heels to share with Tyler that echoing dismalness. At Polk and Broadway a traffic jam compelled one driver to yell: *Fuck, fuck, fuck!*—Tyler made a face. Fillmore: hill and hill, and then twin light-lines with car-lights in between, black bay ahead, and then the lights of Marin—Tiburon or Sausalito? He suddenly wasn't sure. On Lombard Street two men were grinning and heil Hitlering at passing cars. Chestnut: He stared back into the glowing red traffic eye . . . Without much reason he swung left on this street, passing the Horseshoe Tavern where John had once bought him drinks, and then a juice bar where he used to meet John and Irene; here was the bank machine on Pierce where Irene used to come before she went shopping; here was the Chestnut Street Grill, which John said was no good (Tyler had never tried it); Laurel's toy store, Scott, Divisadero, then apartment buildings rising fog-colored in the dark . . . He was wasting his life.

| 57 |

His friend Mike Hernandez in Vice called his machine and said: Listen, chum, as far as I'm concerned, rumors of the Queen's existence have been greatly exaggerated. Not much comes out of that parking garage except the odd D.U.I. Well, I guess it's always good for the occasional blowjobbing or flatbacking bust, but there haven't even been too many of those lately. Sometimes I catch 'em across the street. If there is a Queen, you know who might know about it, uh, what's his name, uh, Dan Smooth; you don't wanna—

The machine beeped and cut Mike Hernandez off.

Hernandez called again. —Right, well, as I was saying, we don't use him if we don't have to, but the guy knows a lot. Lemme see if I have his . . . Hell, kind of a mess here. You know who might—no, screw that, just try the Sacramento listings, although I sometimes see him drinking by himself in North Beach. Anyway, gotta go, buddy; good luck with it. Gimme a—

The machine cut him off.

John called his machine and said: Disregard my other message. I don't need to talk to you after all.

Brady called his machine and said: Listen, this is you know who; I forgot to say if you have any more of those surveillance reports, enclose those with your bill; I need 'em for my files.

The red light winked slyly. Outside he heard the finger-on-picket-fence sound of a key in a car lock.

The dental hygienist called his machine and said: Mr. Tyler, this is Marlene at Dr. Kinshaw's office, and we have you scheduled for Tuesday for your six-month checkup and cleaning. Could you please call me if you have any problems in keeping that appointment? If not, I'll look forward to seeing you on Tuesday at 10:30.

Somebody called his machine and didn't leave a message.

Somebody did the same thing, again and again.

| 58 |

In the waxed faux-marble corridors of the municipal court building in Sacramento, double rows of reflected ceiling lights distorted themselves from circles into ovoids, and the jurors sworn, potential and alternate sat (the lucky early birds) or leaned against the walls, professional types complaining about how business was going to hell in their absence, while retirees declaimed about their children or the state of public schools today. A leggy woman looked around helplessly, then finally seated herself upon her briefcase, knees straining together as she sipped from a carton of chocolate milk. —I was raised a Catholic, and even I had second thoughts, the lady beside her said.

The door to Department Forty opened, and inside Tyler saw the table where the greasy-haired defendant, a boy, sat slumped beside a maternal public defender. Beside them swaggered the bailiff with his hands on his hips. Ceiling lights reflected on the D.A.'s balding forehead. The D.A. looked very pleased with himself. It must be an open-and-shut case of rape or something of the sort, yes, something unsavory, because old Dan Smooth, dressed in his Sunday best, was still sitting in the hall, waiting to be called as an expert witness.

Yeah, what're you going to do for me, bub? he said. You're Henry Tyler. Are you going to do for me what old John Tyler did for the Whigs?

Got time to meet me for a drink later this afternoon, Mr. Smooth?

Well, uh, Henry, I don't know how long this shindig is going to last. And I did say what're you going to do for me?

I'll pay for the drinks.

Not good enough. Everybody wants to buy old Dan Smooth a drink. All the chippies are vying for the privilege of . . . What do I need your alcohol for?

Mike Hernandez down in San Francisco tells me you're a very honest and generous man, Tyler hazarded.

He does, now, does he? Doesn't sound like the Mike Hernandez *I* know, that skinny little . . .

Daniel Clement Smooth, please, said the bailiff.

Oh, they're playing my song, said Smooth. I don't mind telling you that I enjoy it. How about tomorrow? I'll meet anyone, any time. I'm a democratic kind of guy.

Can't do it, Mr. Smooth—

Call me Dan.

All right, Dan. I have some business down in L.A.

Mr. Smooth, if you don't come into the courtroom right now there's going to be a bench warrant issued, said the bailiff.

All right, Henry, mumbled Smooth. I'll be at Vesuvio's in North Beach on Friday round about eight o'clock . . .

He adjusted his soiled necktie and followed the bailiff importantly inside, bearing a sheaf of photographs in a translucent plastic envelope.

Tyler let out a weary breath.

In the jury pool lounge some were sitting with their heads in their hands, some were reading, a few completing their voir dire questionnaires, and many were good-humoredly laughing, playing cards while bystanders called out advice. Tyler sat down among them for a moment and thought about Irene.

| 59 |

Vesuvio's, eh? *That* fancy tourist place? It hardly seemed like a Dan Smooth kind of place. It definitely wasn't a Tyler sort of place—unless Tyler were trying to impress, entertain, comfort or prey upon Irene. Its Sacramento analogue might be—what? Tyler's thoughts were covered with mold, like the bluish-purple felt on the pool tables upstairs at the Blue Cue, John's kind of place, where laughingly incompetent couples paid thirteen dollars an hour to bend and click, the women often saying *shit* in low voices when they missed, an Asian girl in a black, black miniskirt cleaning up after them, setting the balls back into the triangular form and shaking them, laying the cue ball exactly onto the dot, gathering up used drinks from the long metal bar which guarded an expanse of tall mirror. (Tyler's kind of place was the Swiss Club, an ancient bar which smelled of cigarette smoke and whose air oozed globules of weak light splashed with booze.)

Dan Smooth didn't fool him. Dan Smooth was not and never would be the John type, the elegant or snotty professional type. Dan Smooth was the sleazy barfly type, the lowlife type, the Henry Tyler type.

Tyler knew a pretty little exomphalous court clerk who'd once made eyes at him. Every now and then he called her up and asked her for favors. This time when he telephoned, he wanted to know whether he could take her to dinner. It was time for payment, he said. Actually he was hoping to find out more about Dan Smooth. But the girl explained that she had a boyfriend now.

Okay, sweetheart, said Tyler, a little relieved. I'll cross you off my list.

He had a dream that he and Irene were married and had a child, a slender half-Asian girl whom Irene was teaching how to throw a frisbee for the dog.

| 60 |

It being only Tuesday, Tyler possessed sufficient time to drive down to Los Angeles and back before the appointed day with Dan Smooth. His mother, bored and irritated by her own physical frailty, preferred for the sake of that novelty disguised as familial love to peer anxiously into Tyler's problems. In short, she did not want him to go away.

I have a little job, he lied. It may be lucrative.

Then shall I call you tonight, dear?

No, I may be out on surveillance all night.

Tell me, Henry, is your work dangerous?

Not really, Mom. I try to avoid the dangerous stuff.

Sit down, said Mrs. Tyler abruptly.

The rust-colored blinds were always down in his mother's living room, her car keys always on the piano stool. Tyler sighed and took a corner of the sofa. The car keys sparkled. —How are you feeling? he said.

Not very well, replied his mother almost bitterly. And worrying about you makes it worse.

I'm sorry, Mom, he said almost inaudibly. Tell me what I can do.

I want you to make up with John.

I don't know how much use that would be, said Tyler. Nothing like that ever lasts between John and me. You know we've both tried.

But this is different. You know that, my dear.

Tyler was silent.

Henry, said his mother, gazing at him with a sad stern expression which he'd never seen before, I want to ask you something. And I want you to answer me truthfully.

I know what's coming, her son answered with a crooked smile not unlike Domino's.

Henry.

Yes, Mom.

Did you and Irene . . . Henry, did you betray John? You understand what I'm asking.
I understand pretty well, Mom.

Well?

Mom, your question humiliates me. I've been humiliated so much lately that I just don't have much energy to . . . Can you see how it might hurt me to discuss it, Mom?

Henry, I want to know. I need to know.

It's too late for that, said Tyler, rising.

For God's sake! cried Mrs. Tyler, but her son, hanging his head, had already closed the door behind him. A moment later, she heard the coughing ignition of his car.

| 61 |

Sacramento is River City, they say, because it spreads its poisons, sterilities and occasional charms at the confluence of two rivers, but to me it remains Railroad City even if only in my wishful thinking; now it's Car City and Mall City above all, city of hellish replications of arcades, gas stations, convenience stores, city without a heart, a strangely empty place whose downtown, once sunk down to river level, has turned its nineteenth-century boardwalks and Chinese doss houses into underground passageways invaded mainly by homeless sojourners and addicts of antique bottles (Peet's Crystal White, The Perfect Family Soap); here, if anywhere, one might think, there'd be "meaning" or "history," but instead one finds only rat-droppings. Aboveground they don't care. The big developers try to keep the homeless out of their vacant lots; the city bureaucrats fine the developers whenever the homeless do get in and damage the public's chain-link fences; and come summer most citizens get paralyzed by the ghastly sun, sitting indoors with sweat running down their cheeks—time then to go shopping or away. Come winter comes the rain, which fails to clean those graffiti-whitened fences outside the dwindling boxcar yards. The railroad tramps survive or not, uttering their wet, hacking coughs. And the street pimps sometimes use the slang phrase *to pull a train,* which means to mount as many women as a man desires. Meanwhile, the trains themselves crawl on ever more weakly, hidden among blackberries with flies all around. It's been written that Sacramento only became the capitol thanks to sleazy railroad politics, whose expedient calculus of charging for freight poundage times distance required that this so-called destination city be erected in the middle of nowhere, to maximize that distance. As the city grew, so would demand; so would poundage. It all paid off. The long exposures of antique cameras show us men in top hats shaking hands, men in brimmed caps (the workers) lounging on top of locomotives. Here's an old poster for the Sacramento Valley Railroad Company, whose trains began to run in 1856; by 1865 the Central Pacific Railroad swallowed it, running big cylindrical-nosed locomotives down J Street, locomotives non-aerodynamically boilered and belled in the dirt with their low cow-catchers pointing ahead toward progress, pale hunks of kindling in the open cars just behind. (In a photograph, a pallid figure in railroad livery stands on a high sidestep, his expression washed out to a bleak blankness like that high-noon dirt street streaked and tracked. He's nobody; he's Cain.) But Central Pacific, for all its locomotives' victory wails, lost out to Union Pacific at last. And so another business lay down to sleep. Union Pacific's yellow passenger cars whose sides read SILVER STATE and MONTEREY and SALINAS VALLEY rolled back and forth between heaven, wherever that may be, and earth, which is Sacramento, pulled by glossy black locomotives. And in innocent complacency over their attainments, the Union Pacific tycoons thought to epitomize Railroad City forever. But now in the oldest grimiest honeycombs of this commercial hive I find dead hollow boxcars; I see bleached ties between rusty tracks. The dank muffled deadness inside empty boxcars swallows history's echoes. Who cares about history anyway? This is America. Moreover, this is California. I just read in the *Sacramento Bee* this morning a caution to parents selecting schools for their children: If the library contains any textbook which proclaims: *Someday we will put a man on the moon,* that book is not only obsolete, but *dangerously* obsolete, like the wide spaces between buildings and tracks in the old days. How much more so Plato and Kepler, or the near-exterminated California Indians! Everything movable, liquid, alive like long singing trains must someday become immovable like the yellow, frozen wrinkled toes in the Sacramento morgue, which are more lifeless still in juxtaposition to the humming fridge. (This place has the most amazing air flow capacity, a pathologist said to me once. The air pressure's negative in relation to the rest of the building, you see, so there will be no odor whatsoever!) Yellow toes, and brown toes, hard and stiff, toes under clean white sheets; toes hard like ceramic or plastic, clean and stiff—that's what we leave to our heirs before reentering the no longer track-streaked dirt we came from. Sacramento leaves its rusty railroads, inanely captioned by those who write for themselves alone. Here's a message on a boxcar wall: **CAIN WAS HERE**. An old railroad bum coughs, with bronchitis in his throat. Beneath the scraped paint-layers of color on boxcars I find only cold metal, which someday must rust. Drooping palm trees, long tracks look out from rusty multiwheeled altars. Sacramento, once I almost hated you for your ignorant plastic conformity, but your rusting boxcars remind me consolingly that *all* your ages are doomed. I imagine a more happy futurity when the two rivers will play around your toxic ruins, silently transmuting your follies back into dirt.

The railroad age had obtruded itself into Henry Tyler's boyhood largely through school field trips to the train museum which lurked in the banal commercial cartoon entitled Old Sacramento. John had always liked trains better than he. The boyhood of the two brothers was naturally punctuated by family drives to caves and caverns, Sierra picnics, waterskiing, zoos, rare whitewater rafting trips when finances permitted, factory stores, burger joints. But one can hardly grow up in Sacramento without being aware of the trains. They call at night. They creep to and fro at busy intersections, irritating the drivers who wait in long lines of idling cars. They soak the gravel of the old yards with oil and creosote. The progressive city council fines, squeezes and diminishes them. —We think the Seventh Street punchline is *imperative* for the development of this city, I've heard our mayor say. We'd like an opinion on *condemning* this site and charging the cost to Union Pacific Railroad. —The grim, sweaty Union Pacific man grips the podium in both hands. He knows that the railroad tracks over Seventh Street are doomed. But once they're gone for good, they'll be loved. For now, they're an annoyance, thwarting the energies of more evolved beings and mechanisms. John, for instance, wouldn't have shed a tear had all the tracks been ripped out. But on the dresser in his San Francisco apartment he kept a shiny black model of a Southern Pacific locomotive. Irene used to dust it twice a month. Now John wiped it with a handerchief whenever he noticed it, which was far more often than he realized. On the mornings after she had slept there, Celia Caro sometimes emerged from the bathroom wrapped in one of Irene's terrycloth towels to find him standing with the socks drawer open, holding the toy locomotive in his hand as he polished it caressingly, on his face a sweet and mysterious smile.

Precisely because they had grown up there, in short, the two brothers found Sacra-mento to be less than wondrous in its railroad character which blessed them almost subliminally with train whistles on long days and long nights—always fewer and fewer of those, and Mrs. Tyler never heard them anymore; they'd visited her as often as her own wish for chocolate. Tyler himself, who was destined, as we shall see, for spectacular railroad wanderings, remained yet ignorant of his susceptibility to trains, although afterward, when the disaster of the Queen of the Whores fastened on him, in league with certain other financial and emotional disasters, he lost the use of his car and began riding the N Judah and the J Church streetcar lines through San Francisco, becoming fascinated by the shiny, almost blue double tracks, which twisted down through hilly parks and then vanished under the ground. He never asked himself why those tracks lured him. But after a while they were wiggling through his dreams.

Who knows? Perhaps Tyler's desperate freeway drives from Sacramento to Los Angeles and back were motivated not only by his love for the dead woman, but also by a lust for long journeys which the clattering songs of Sacramento trains dripped into his blood. In any event, this latest silent departure of his, which Mrs. Tyler would never forget, came between mother and son for the rest of their lives, like an infinitely long freight train backing between them at some midtown crossroads.

| 62 |

On his return from Los Angeles, where Irene's grave was doing well on that hot and smoggy day at Forest Lawn with the lawn mowers roaring, Tyler got rewarded with a vandalism investigation case from the owner of an abandoned factory down on Townsend which was being broken into and smashed up night by night. —Sure, I'll do it, he said. I figure it'll cost you seven hundred receipted or five hundred under the table. —That's cool, said the owner. Let's go with the five. —Tyler, pleased to make headway against his stale credit card bills, drove straight there. His car still smelled of flowers. The owner, who continuously sweated, met him outside and gave him a key. —Kind of dusty in here, Tyler said. You ever get any transients trying to crash the place? Looks sort of unslept in, though. —You tell me, said the owner. With these vermin chewing their way into my property, who the hell knows? —I was just wondering if the Queen of the Whores bunked here, Tyler said, always hoping to snare two streetbirds with one strategically sticky concretion of intellect, but the owner shrugged. Tyler rented a hundred-foot ladder from the paint store. Ascending this friend of hangmen and impatient heaven-seekers, he felt as if he were sinking rather than rising, because the spiderwebbed swelter compounded as he went, until he had to go back down in order to tie a rag around his nose and mouth. Outside, a truck horn sounded four times, reminding him of Domino. Because the owner did not seem good for more than the five, now already received, he decided to be efficient for once, and so, choking in the spidercrawling dust, he duct-taped to a ceiling beam two camera bodies, one with a fisheye lens attached, and the other sporting his four-hundred-millimeter lens, which he had prefocused at about five and a half feet above floor level. Now for transmitter, radio slave, cables and strobe. Although he stood eighty-odd feet above the ground, the gruesome air pressed on him almost as heavily, he fancied, as the dirt upon Irene in her casket. Gradually this thought of his, which had arisen only innocently, out of the useless loving care of tomb-tenders, gave rise to others worse and worse, until it seemed indeed as if Irene's pallid face were swimming down toward him from the silken depths of terror between the ceiling beams. The young girl, long-fingered, rich-eyebrowed bride, where was she now? He would not ask *who* she was or had been. In previous years, having been hired by families in missing persons cases whose agonizing end he'd never allowed himself to foresee, he'd witnessed the talents of Dr. Jasper, chief medical examiner of San Francisco, hence skilled and rapid cutter (his yellow gloves wet with blood as he swigged from a coffee cup, slicing through a corpse's shiny fatty neck), who could build a clay face out of a murdered man's skull-cast, then plant artificial hair and glass eyeballs until the flotsam of a life, cracked and vacated seashell on eternity's beach, lived again, at least in the longing vision of the father or wife upon whom Dr. Jasper must call to identify the dead. But in the darkness around Tyler the opposite sort of being had been conceived and was gestating into loathsomeness. Start not with the skull of her, but with the living Irene of his memories, whom he could see anytime he wished, simply by closing his eyes. Over her dark-eyed face, somebody had slid a bloated mask and was now packing it full of worms. Could this truly be Irene, the one of whom he dreamed? Which Irene now existed? Who waited for him at the end of his mind's darkly barren turnings? Suppose it were this new other, this stranger! He forced himself to probe himself, like Dr. Jasper withdrawing a little urine from Irene's bladder as she lay upon the marble slab; urine hissed up into the cylinder of the long syringe. He needed to know precisely this: Why was death so terrible? He could not even comprehend what he feared. Some people are afraid of nonexistence, and others of the actual process of dying. Perhaps what he most dreaded was the prospect of a marriage between life and death. At City Lights he'd dipped into a history of ancient tortures, one of which haunted him before he'd even discovered the crude engraving on the next page: Kill the condemned one's sweetheart, then enchain him to her until they both rotted. Perhaps he did not love Irene enough, that he could not bear to be with her in this way. The ladder began to tremble. Understanding that it was he who trembled, he calmed himself, constructing a shell around the vision. This moment, which within other moments would lurk forgotten, nonetheless founded his future. He could not yet accept what he feared, but he had taken the first step toward accepting it. It had come, and so he said: Let it come. And the consequence of his courage—we can't call it a reward, since it was not nice—was the realization that Irene's death would attaint the remainder of his life. If he could somehow love, not only her, but also her putrefaction, then perhaps he'd win the victory. For now he could not. And so he squeezed the dregs of Irene from his mind, with the same degree of temporary success as if he had squeezed dry a sponge held underwater—as long as his hand remained clenched, new water could be declined—then descended those vibrating aluminum rungs to a plane more greasily substantial, if no less vile, than the hangman's aerie. Directly beneath the cameras he established his vandals' bait: a clean-swept floor, crowned by a table piled high with lightbulbs. Then he went out and locked up. Beneath the broken window which must surely be their entrance, he taped up a handwritten sign to goad them: **STAY OUT, YOU ANIMALS!** He drove back to the paint store and returned the ladder. Then he called his answering machine.

John's voice, struggling to hold itself back, demanded that he telephone their mother. Brady's voice inquired after the missing surveillance forms. The voice of his new client, Mrs. Bickford, confirmed her Tuesday afternoon appointment. The voice of a Mr. Okubata proposed a confidential meeting about a marital matter. His landlord's voice advised him of a two percent rent increase beginning next month.

The White Nile deli on Bryant Street, patronized mainly by construction workers, made excellent roast chicken sandwiches. Tyler had long forgotten who'd told him about the place. He never went out of his way to eat there, but over the years now adding up to decades he'd inserted many pushpins into his mental map of San Francisco, and relied upon them, being a creature of habit, and habit comforted him even more now that Irene was dead: at least the White Nile was still the same. He bought the house special, which they wrapped up for him in white paper for ten cents more than last time. Almost immediately, he realized that he had no appetite. He imagined Irene telling him to eat in order to take care of himself. Then his stubbled jaws slowly moved, and he swallowed. After that, removing once again from its casket his embalmed sense of duty, he drove to a parking lot two blocks away from the factory, reclined his seat, laid out his receiver and radio control unit on the dashboard, then read from the Gnostic Scriptures, which he had purchased at City Lights. He read: *Light and darkness, life and death, right and left, are brothers of one another. They are inseparable. Because of this, neither are the good good, nor the evil evil, nor is life life, nor death death.* Again he saw Irene's face. A worm was born from her nostril. If the Gnostics were correct, he must not reject this. But it was like standing idly by when somebody called her a Chink. He could not believe that the worm did not hurt her, and that he could not help. No doubt she was faded in her coffin, but he'd do what he could to help her look after herself. When it was too dark to see, he merely waited, almost enjoying the background hum of his receiver unit. Not long before midnight he heard a clang, then voices simultaneously echoing, angry, high-pitched and indistinct. Something smashed. The voices became louder. —That ain't money, not even raw money! a boy was saying. You don't know shit about money! —Another voice said: Something's on the table over here. —When Tyler could hear them quite well, he pressed the square button on the radio control unit. In the factory, the flash fired once like a shocking warning. That would make the kids look up. —What the *fuck!* somebody screamed on the receiver. How many times in his career had he heard such Jeffersonian eloquence? Machine-gunning the strobe, he snapped off thirty-odd frames of film with his remote auto winder, which was slaved to the round button of the radio control unit. Meanwhile he'd started the engine. Of course they threw bricks and rocks, trying to knock the cameras out, but the strobe would have destroyed their night vision. He got some blurry shots which the factory owner later said weren't good enough to convict, and one excellent frame of the enraged face of a brick-thrower. By then he was approaching the factory window with his headlights on bright and the passenger window down. As the vandals came leaping down in separately silhouetted panics, he leaned out and recorded them on his third camera's police film, clicking and clicking away until they began throwing bricks at *him.* Conviction material! Then he shifted into reverse and sped away.

The cops got two of them. The factory owner, vindictive in victory, but perhaps Tyler would have done the same, prosecuted them for malicious mischief. They'd already cost him eight thousand dollars, not counting Tyler's fee. One boy got off, but the other was already "in the system," as lawyers love to say: two prior convictions for graffiti, and a current bench warrant for probation violation. They threw him in jail for thirty days until his hearing, then administratively revoked his probation. He served six months more behind bars. The factory owner told all this to Tyler, who would rather not have known. And yet he did not believe himself to be guilty of anything. He despised the random, cowardly nihilism of the vandals. Moreover, he hadn't called the police when they were inside the factory; he'd given them a sporting chance. Perhaps that was the source of his qualmishness: He had taken no stand. But must he take a stand on everything, everytime? It had been just business. And the factory owner was satisfied.

| 63 |

Somebody warned him most threateningly not to take Mrs. Bickford on as a client. Narrowing his eyes, he met her on Tuesday as scheduled, but she didn't want to hire him anymore; she was too scared, she said. He gave her the name of a battered women's shelter and wished her luck.

Somebody wanted him to shadow some jurors. —I'd like to help you out, said Tyler in his most friendly voice, but I have all the work I can handle right now. Have you tried Pinkerton's? Somebody said they specialize in shadowing jurors. I think it's in their code of ethics.

Somebody down at H.R. Computer in Palo Alto wanted him to try to obtain a chip from their competitor, RoboGraphix. —Well, now, you know that's illegal, said Tyler. How much can you pay?

Twenty thousand.

Are you recording this call?

What if I tell you I'm not?

I wouldn't believe you.

What if I told you I was?

I'd figure you were trying to entrap me.

So you don't want the twenty thousand?

I don't break the law, period.

And I'm not asking you to break the law.

Dandy, said Tyler. Glad we got that crap out of the way.

By the way, I'm not recording.

I am, Tyler lied with a laugh.

Look, Mr. Tyler, if you—

Do they manufacture on site?

Yes, sir.

Gallium arsenide? That's a pretty toxic process, I understand.

I believe so.

Well, let me do some looking around. I'll call you back.

He called up his friend Rod on the force down in Palo Alto, and Rod said that the job wasn't a sting that he knew of. Be careful, though, was Rod's unsolicited and unnecessary advice.

He called up RoboGraphix and asked the secretary to send him a copy of the press release on the SBD-9000 chip.

What chip is that, sir? said the receptionist.

I'm on assignment for *Computer Currents* to write an article about you, said Tyler. It's all over town that you have a fabulous new chip coming out.

Just a moment, sir. I'll let you speak with one of our technical staff.

Yeah, who's this? said the next voice on the line—a weary, suspicious, middle-aged male voice.

Yes, sir, my name is Charles Ångstrom, you know, as in wavelength, and I'm free-lancing a piece for—

Yeah, who you with?

Computer Currents.

Who's your editor over there?

Who am I dealing with, sir? said Tyler in his silkiest voice.

This is Hal Nemeth in the technical department, the voice said.

Well, Mr. Nemeth, I'll be frank with you. I'm writing this article on spec. I have some friends in Silicon Valley who tell me that what you guys are about to release is pretty special . . .

Where are you calling from?

Menlo Park, said Tyler, which was true; he'd driven down for the occasion, and was calling from a pay phone there, between a big billboard for Caesar's Palace and another for an upcoming club entitled Feminine Circus.

Look, Hal Nemeth said. You're probably OK, but for certain reasons I can't really get into, we prefer not to publicize anything yet. If you want me to transfer you back to Judy, she can put your mailing address into the database so that you get a copy of the press release.

Sure, I understand, said Tyler ingratiatingly. Thanks for your time.

Do you want me to transfer you?

Sure. Judy has a nice voice.

Hal Nemeth grunted sourly, and there was a click, and the next thing he knew the receptionist was saying: RoboGraphix. May I help you?

Is this Judy? he said.

Yes, this is Judy. How may I help you, sir?

Judy, this is Chuck Wildmore. I don't know if you remember me, but my sister Karen has been trying to reach you.

Karen? I don't know any Karen.

Your name is Judy, right?

Yes. But—

And you work for RoboGraphix?

Obviously this is RoboGraphix. Who—

Well, you *must* be the one, he insisted, enjoying what in the industry they called a "gag call."—She's in the hospital right now, which is why she asked me to call you. It's kind of important to her.

But I've told you I don't know anybody named Karen, said the woman in stony exasperation.

Well, I apologize for bothering you, but Karen said it was important. She's in intensive care, you understand. You know, where they put those tubes into your arms. They say if you go in there you have a forty percent chance of coming out.

I'm sorry, the woman said reflexively.

She says you were a friend of hers a long time ago, and she wanted to see you.

Some friend. I—

Look. Would you mind giving her a jingle at the hospital? Or—no, that's going to be a hassle for you. How about if I—

But I don't know any Karen! the receptionist said plaintively. Can I put you on hold? I've got another call.

Sure, said Tyler. I'll wait.

He listened to the tinny music, and then Judy picked up the phone and said: Robo-Graphix. May I help you?

Hi, Judy. This is Karen's brother.

Listen, Judy said, weren't you the guy I transferred to Mr. Nemeth?

Mr. Nemeth? Who's that? Listen, Judy, if you don't want to talk to my sister why don't you just say so? I'm trying to help her out. I don't know what this is about, because we went our separate ways for years, if you see what I'm saying, but now she's . . . Anyway, I guess I was wrong to bother you. Thanks for your time. I'll tell Karen you were unavailable.

The girl hesitated.   What hospital is she in?

San Francisco General. No health insurance. It's pretty chaotic up there, so if you call you might not get through.

I'm sorry, Judy said again. (Closing his eyes, he remembered Irene boredly picking at her fingernails.) Look, I have to go. There are three calls waiting. If your sister wants to call, I'm in the book.

All right, Judy. I'll pass that along. Has your last name changed since she knew you?

No, I'm not married, she said, her voice dark, foggy and lost like beer bottles on the bottom shelf of a refrigerator case. My last name is Knowles, and I'm in the book.

For Palo Alto?

Sunnyvale.

Thanks a million, Judy. I guess it will mean a lot to her to speak with you, said Tyler, hanging up.

He called Dan Smooth about that drink on Friday at eight o'clock. He had to go to L.A., he said. Could they reschedule? Dan Smooth, momentarily as silent as the grating-sealed shops late at night in Chinatown, said at length that they could. He called his mother, who was having chest pains. He called his answering machine, but there was no new business.

He drove down to Los Angeles for another of what he called his secret visits, and after he had done his business there he telephoned his old friend Jake, a downsized engineer. He asked if there were any special place in an office where a small company would be inclined to store secret chips.

Well, said Jake, you start with any kind of chip you're going to make in an exotic environment, it needn't be a big place. If you're going to hide things, it's going to be by classifying the whole place.

They've done that. And then how would they store the actual chip? Would they have to keep it in a refrigerator or something like that?

Don't expose it to any strong electromagnetic fields, or it'll get fried, said Jake. That's the thing. Well, actually I don't know about *field*, but *pulse* is certainly a problem. You just want to put it in a conductive piece of rubber or foam to keep it from being shorted out . . .

And then I suppose you'd keep it in a safe . . .

The principal investigator's desk drawer might be good. The safe is more sexy, of course . . .

Okay, so the principal investigator has got to investigate it. He's got to make sure that it's good, I guess.

Right. He verifies that it's good by using a device called a comparator, which basically projects magnified images of a chip onto a ground glass circle. Well, that's old technology now. A chip can be as complicated as the Thomas Guide.

I get it, said Tyler, narrowing his eyes. Anyhow, the principal investigator will be sitting at his desk, doing something with the chip. Maybe he'll project a digitized image of it onto his computer screen. Maybe he'll have a comparator. It really doesn't matter, just as long as I have some idea where the chip is. Thanks, Jake.

He let the rest of the week go by and then called Judy at home on Saturday morning. —Judy, this is Chuck Wildmore again, he said, picking his nose. I'm sorry that Karen never called you. She died on the operating table. She didn't regain consciousness.

Look, said Judy unpleasantly, I've been trying to think who this Karen might be, but I'm drawing a blank. I've never, ever known anybody named Karen except for one girl in third grade who hated me. I think you're confused. I'm sorry for your loss, but I'd really appreciate it if you wouldn't call me anymore.

Karen left you something in her will, he replied with equal coldness. I'll let our attorney know that you refuse delivery. Goodbye.

Now at last he had her, for an avaricious curiosity came into the girl's dull and hostile voice, and she said quickly: What did she leave me?

I guess that's not your concern, said Tyler snappishly, since you refuse any connection with the family. I'm sorry I ever called you. Don't worry, Judy. You won't hear from me again.

Then tell your lawyer to get in touch with me.

Every time a lawyer talks to you about baseball you have to pay for his time, said Tyler, his voice now modulated to the melodies of patience. Judy's estate is dirt poor, and I don't have much myself, so with all due respect I'm not paying for an extra hour of legal consultation just to have his secretary mail you something you probably won't appreciate.

What do you mean I won't appreciate it? You don't even know me. Where do you get off trying to define me?

I wasn't trying to define you, Judy.

Well, what did Karen leave me?

It's a little velvet box, with—do you want me to open it? I haven't looked inside. I didn't figure I had that right.

Yeah, the girl said carelessly, why don't you open it?

There's a ribbon around it, said Tyler, impressing even himself with this improvisation. Do you want me to undo the bow?

No, that's okay, she said finally. Why don't you send it to me?

I'll send it to your office then, he said. It may be a couple of weeks before I get to the post office. I'm kind of in a state of shock right now, to tell you the truth.

Mr. Wildmore, I—

I don't know whether to send it registered or not. It may be valuable. What do you think?

Cupidity won out, or maybe just good manners. —Look, Mr. Wildmore, the girl said, where are you?

Menlo Park at the moment. But I need to be in San Francisco at three-thirty to claim the body.

And you have the box?

Yeah. I have the box.

I thought you said the lawyer had it.

Judy, I'm getting kind of tired of being interrogated.

I'm sorry. You want to do lunch?

Tyler pretended to hesitate, then said in his best grudging voice: I guess I have time to meet you for lunch if you want.

And you'll bring the box?

Sure.

The girl sighed. —You're sure you're not a nutcase?

I'm not a nutcase, said Tyler. I'm not even a nut. Where do you want to meet me?

Are you near a Sizzler's? I always like eating at Sizzler's.

Sure, said Tyler. I like their surf 'n' turf. Karen was also very fond of Sizzler's.

She was? Gosh, I wish I remembered her.

She was an awfully special person, he said, pretending that he was talking about Irene so that his voice would get properly sad. He closed his eyes and saw the mole on Irene's forehead. His grief rushed in and carried him safely along.

He recollected something that another prophet had once told him: Your generic secretary is not a secretary by choice. Who picks a crappy job like that, all responsibility and no power? They start off like that because their Nazi husbands don't allow them to have any job that's higher status than that, and after the divorce they're stuck. Secretaries hate their jobs, Henry. That's why all the hackers get what they want by just calling them up.

I've seen plenty of secretaries with power, Tyler had countered. Plenty of old dragons. Plenty of smart ladies who know where all the bodies are buried.

Yeah, I'm talking about the young ones, his friend had said. Those poor, trapped young broads. It's just like being a whore except the pay's not as good.

Are you there? Judy was saying.

Yeah.

Look, I'm sorry if I was maybe a little bit suspicious. It's just that, like, some things have happened to me before, you know, guys taking advantage of me and stuff.

I understand, he said. Then, thinking of Irene, he muttered: Jesus, I wish I could put my arms around her right now.

Are you sure you're going to be okay? the girl said, obviously not wanting to sustain some stranger's neediness.

Hm? Sure, I'll be fine. See you at Sizzler's, then. How about in two hours?

Okay, she said softly. 'Bye.

'Bye, he said.

Tyler went out and cadged a velvet box from a jewelry store. He took from his keyring an old key from an office in Emeryville where he hadn't worked for twelve years; he'd always known that that key would come in handy someday. He put the key inside the box and tied a ribbon around it. Considering carefully, he went back to the jewelry store and bought a gilded silver pendant so that the girl wouldn't be completely disappointed, and enclosed that with the key.

Judy was plump, unattractive, and shy, although her shyness she disguised as grumpiness. He bought them both lunch and sat there with her at a table beside the window. When she asked him what he did, Tyler tried to talk as much like an office rodent as he could: Oh, I work for CiceroNet. I'm new there. Basically, they do some kind of Web stuff. Originally I was a consultant. You know, it's a time or money trade, and I'm here to help. That's what I told them, and then I spent some time talking to see if I could wangle an extra few hundred bucks. I was pretty sure that they were going to bite, and it's tempting to inflate things a bit, but I was honest; I kept their costs down . . .

He chatted merrily away in this jargon, his words as hurried as red ants rushing over terraces of bark, until he was satisfied that she'd stopped listening.

So tell me about you, he said. Do you like the people you work with?

Well, Mr. Nemeth's kind of impatient sometimes but everybody says he's the real genius, the girl said. I don't know if he's a genius or not. All I know is that he makes me work late sometimes, mailing out all those little diskettes and stuff, and I have to put them in special envelopes . . .

That's not very nice of him, said Tyler. Can't you bring a book or something for when he's not looking?

Then I'd never get home. He makes me stop by the Federal Express place at night on my own time.

Tyler had been considering giving Judy a special desk calendar or something of the sort which when properly hung would orient a flat camera at Hal Nemeth's desk, but now he saw that such grand plans wouldn't even be necessary. All he'd have to do was take Judy out to dinner a few times, and sooner or later he could get her to bring the mail with her . . .

And then he was ashamed of himself. What had the poor girl ever done to him?

He handed over the box, stood up, and said abruptly: Well, Judy, this is from Karen, and I thank you for meeting me.

The girl's mouth dropped open. —You don't have to go, she said. I mean, if you don't want to. I can see I made a mistake about you. I think you're really nice.

Thank you, sweetheart, he said. You're nice, too. I guess I'll be getting back.

Don't you even want to see what Karen gave me?

Maybe it's something betwen you and her, he said. Well, see you around.

He strode quickly out, got into his car, and drove back to San Francisco, passing the airport with its gloomily lit runways and warehouses, its planes like robot iguanas waiting for the heat of some unholy day to burst through their dark torpor. Nothing but concrete, lights and fog ahead . . . The nearest parking garage was a sickening prismatic crystal of light. No security-minded Queen would ever set up shop there. It began to drizzle, and the pavement shone as black and strange as squid-ink. He remembered Irene with her baseball cap fashionably backward, thoughtfully bringing chopsticksful of black noodles into her mouth in a Korean-Japanese restaurant in Japantown; the highway was the color of those noodles.

He told H.R. Computer that for legal reasons he couldn't take the RoboGraphix case. —So you want to kiss away twenty thousand, his client said. —Yeah, drawled Tyler, it'll be a pretty amorous send-off . . . —He told his landlord that he was really sorry, but this month the rent would be three or four days late. Whenever he thought about Judy he felt guilty, so every day for the next two weeks he anonymously sent her roses.

Every weekend he drove down to Los Angeles.

| 64 |

After so profitably wrapping up that scam he got a call from John, who said: I was going through Irene's stuff and found a letter that she wrote you last year.

Flinching from the vibrating anger in John's voice, Tyler said casually: Is it important? Do you want to send it to me or do you want to read it over the mail?

Why don't you stop by and pick it up, said John flatly.

All right. I'll come by after eight.

John hung up.

When Tyler got to John and Irene's apartment he found the living room crammed with boxes which gaped like graves. Wordlessly John handed him the triple-folded sheet of paper in lavender flare pen which ran:

Dearest Henry,

I hope this letter finds you well. Frankly, I'm a little worried that something must have gone wrong or you wouldn't be considering disappearing.

I don't know you well enough to understand if my concern is warranted or intrusive. Please forgive me if the latter is the case. Let me know how you are.

Take good care of yourself.

Love,
Irene

John was standing there with his arms folded. —So, what did she mean by your disappearing? he said.

Oh, it was just a kind of black period I went through, said Tyler. I pulled out of it. I guess Irene must have realized it wasn't such a big deal since she never gave me the letter.

Why didn't you tell me about it? said John.

Oh, I hated to bother you—

But you never minded bothering my wife. Did she write you any other letters?

Well, said Tyler jauntily, who knows what else you'll find when you're packing those boxes?

Oh, just go away, said John. Go home.

You still working with that guy Brady?

So you really don't feel any responsibility?

Well, I'll be honest with you. Irene was my friend, my very good friend. I asked her how she was doing and she said she wasn't especially happy—

Happy with what?

With her life.

What *about* her life, Hank?

I don't know. I asked her to call me if she had any problems, and she didn't, so I figure that you and she were ninety-five percent responsible and I was five percent responsible.

So you *were* responsible. What exactly did you do to her?

Nobody's ever innocent, Tyler mumbled, looking at his toes.

It just doesn't sound like Irene to do what she did, John said.

Well, as a matter of fact it was Irene who . . . oh, forget it.

Leave me alone, will you?

Sure, John. Thanks for the hospitality. *And* the great conversation, said Tyler with his hand on the doorknob.

| 65 |

Yes, Tyler had given up. According to John's cruel characterization, he had long since begun to vegetate, his mind humming and drowsing though the blocky, sun-shadowed pastel landscapes of the Sunset District. (The Richmond District looked much the same.) As for John himself, he had likewise just now laid aside a quarrel with the world, of which such knowledge as he had—less than his brother's, naturally—inclined him less to master it by analysis than to assert practical control of a small piece of it; and for the rest to find comfort where he could. Irene's suicide had been both a desolation and a humiliation; but since, as we have stated without sarcasm, he was a member in good standing of the Order of Backbone, he sought not to get ahead of his other grievances. She left *him* no note, but for almost two months after her installation in the ground, Irene's credit card bills kept arriving, like the uncanny communications of a Ouija board. Carefully reading them over before he paid, John never found lingerie purchases, or dinners for two that he didn't know of, or any evidence of other untoward attachments. Nonetheless, his resolution regarding Hank was: *friendly but cool, forever.* Hank had had something to do with Irene's death, at least indirectly. Thus John's instant bench warrant, followed by summary judgment. Were Hank to forthrightly admit his complicity, begging pardon, John could perhaps forgive him, depending on the circumstances (although here John might have been deceiving himself; for when others dare to confess a fault whose existence we may have strongly suspected, but not yet proved to ourselves, we are more likely to gratify our anger than our magnanimity). Meanwhile it was important not to upset their mother unnecessarily. John had already decided that after she lay beyond harm he would, if his brother's demeanor continued to be evasive, make the break. It wasn't as if refraining from executing this sentence would assuage his loneliness, Hank never having been good for much; nor (by the same logic) would proceeding so render John any more alone.

Celia, on the other hand, had been sympathetic. During the first month she'd telephoned every day, more often even than his mother; she'd kept herself ready every night to come if he needed her, her overnight bag packed. He knew that each evening when she came home from work the first thing she did, after setting down her slender-strapped scarlet purse on the round table in the hall, and double-locking the door from the inside, was to sit down on her bed and study the answering machine light to see if he had called. (She was under instructions not to bother him at work except on special occasions.) How *could* he have called? Her telephone extension at work dangled readily from the synapses of his brain. He knew that she went home at five-fifteen, and so never telephoned her between five and six. But still, every day Celia paid him that absurd homage. Well, what if someone else had called? That must be the real reason that she checked her messages. Why wouldn't she say so? Did she truly imagine him to be so thin-skinned or jealous that he had to believe she waited only for him? The improbable supposition that her motives might be exactly as she'd stated them very occasionally flashed like green numbers across his mental screen, but that made him shudder. He wouldn't believe that; he couldn't. How could a grownup professional woman be so desperate? And, if she were, how could he interpret such desperation except as an ominous warning of utter dependency, like a limp drowner dragging the rescuer down with her weight? Better, far better, to believe her capable of telling white lies! All in all, the matter perplexed John, and so he tried not to think about it, especially because it insinuated the parallel image of his brother entering that clammy apartment on Pacheco Street, then loudly and vulgarly pissing, the bathroom door wide open, while the answering machine, turned to maximum volume, blared out whatever propositions it contained. In Hank's case, of course, the practice reflected merely *professional* desperation: Would there be a job, so that he could pay the rent? John had loaned his brother money more times than he could remember (which is to say, fewer than he believed; the grandeur of charity easily magnifies itself, if memory is not consulted). At least Celia had never asked John for anything except for his company. She saw him, he supposed, almost as his mother did: a handsome, vivacious boy of excellent prospects, a sweet boy, a practical boy, above all an honest and honorable boy, a *success*. Whatever John promised to do, he did. The rarity of his promises made them all the more valuable. Celia was clever enough never to extort his word from him, never even to gaze up at him with sadly begging dog-eyes if she could avoid it, for she feared John precisely as much as she loved him, and he was very easily annoyed. Needless to say, she resented feeling afraid, and hid that resentment so that she became his tenderest and most secret enemy. (Would life please bring me a man to love me? she prayed. Please? Please. So far, life only brings me *you* . . .) During John's marriage she'd taken up evening paralegal classes to prevent herself from disturbing him too often. The fact that she was paying steeply in both time and money for these studies made her take them all the more seriously. She always got her A+, and the teacher praised her.

Celia was also known as a conscientious list-keeper. Whenever he visited her, John would find beside her phone a pad of paper inscribed with such items as:

> fax badge names to Ellen
> taxes???
> reschedule hair appointment to weekend
> cancel Sandy's access code
> deposit paycheck
> return address stickers
> call John
> present for John

Something about him always appeared on every list. He began to suspect that she wanted him to notice her lists for just that reason. This added to his uneasiness.

John had made inquiries (not through his brother) and learned that her bosses treasured her. Her personnel file contained the following encomiums: hard-working, loyal, dedicated, outgoing, pleasant, cheerful, well-dressed, friendly, warm—in short, the epitaph for a cadre, no leader of any vanguard. She was a resource, not a threat. Had his opinion been asked, John, who knew her even better than the personnel office, would not have changed a single line. Strange to say, however, now that Irene was dead he found himself almost unattracted to Celia. Could it have been anything to do with the fact that she'd dropped her paralegal studies and no longer worked late for the insurance company? She was worried about him, she said. He was too stoic. On the Monday night after the funeral he sat waiting for her with his face blue-lit by his laptop computer on which he was busily defragmenting the hard disk's files; the closet door opened by itself, and he got up to shut it, only to be met by Irene's dresses, which hung there so soft and colorful and helpless, pretty skins of Irene's which Irene would never again use, shapes of Irene at which he could not get angry. The doorbell rang. He rose, and buzzed Celia in. When she came he was standing by the open door with his arms folded.

I'm sorry it took me so long, she said. It was hard parking.

John continued to regard her, saying nothing. He saw that her overnight bag was actually a very large suitcase. He saw that her face had been overlain by an oppressively determined expression. It was the first time that she had ever come to him uninvited. Furious, he sat down at the diamond-shaped table by the window where the computer had finished chirring; with half a dozen keystrokes he quit the defragmentation utility and powered down.

Would you mind if I sat next to you? said Celia a little uncertainly.

Fine, said John. Mom's having chest pains again.

You and your mother are very close, aren't you? said Celia. Is she helping you, I mean now?

Let's leave her out of this.

Celia lit a cigarette. —Whatever you say. You brought her up, not me. Would you mind if I sat down?

Her suitcase was in the middle of the long narrow hallway between the living room and the bedroom. Impatiently he carried it into the bedroom and set it down beside the rumpled bed, which embarrassed him. He could not remember when he'd changed the sheets. Irene used to do that. He closed the bedroom door on bed and suitcase, shot a glance at Celia, who'd remained standing, put a pot of decaf on to warm, and seated himself upon the sofa. She came next to him and almost touched his hand.

Ashtray's over there, he said.

I feel so . . . I don't know . . .

You're up to two packs a day now, aren't you?

Do you think she—did she know about us? she said.

Who? My wife? replied John in a loud, aggrieved tone.

Yes.

I'll never get rid of her now, he said. After what she did, she has a hold on me like some kind of parasite. Well, you were here, so you know. When you see the face of somebody who died by violence and she was somebody that you—knew . . .

I understand. Remember when you had to—

Yeah. I don't know how Hank does it.

I never met him. Well, just that one time when we were . . .

Maybe he gets his kicks from going to the morgue. What do you think, Ceel? There must be perverts like that. Of course he's not a real detective, just a private eye. Maybe he doesn't see that many dead people. But her *face*—I—

For a while he was silent. Then the phone rang. He picked it up. —No, he said. I'm not interested. I said I'm not interested. No, I'm satisfied with my long distance company. No, thank you. No, don't call back at another time. No. Thank you anyway. Sonofabitch.

He slammed the phone down, red in the face.

Can I get you anything? Celia said.

Whatever's worth getting I'm out of, John said shortly.

You want me to go to the store? I can get you some groceries . . .

Thank you, Celia. No, that won't be necessary. Thank you anyway.

Well, she said, looking at the floor, how's everything at work?

Oh, they tried to overturn the fraud conviction, but we got it reinstated on appeal. And Rapp . . .

Again he was silent for a while. —No, I don't think she knew, he said. And if she knows now, I think she understands.

You think she sees us right now? said Celia almost inaudibly. I feel so—

Well, I certainly see her face. If she wants me to do something, I won't refuse. Should I call to her? he asked, observing Celia with a cruel smile.

No—please don't—

Irene! he cried out. *Irene!*

Don't—

Irene, did you know about Celia? Is that why you did it? Irene, did I make you that unhappy?

He turned to Celia. —Nobody can say I didn't mean well, he said.

No, John. Nobody can say that.

Irene won't answer, he laughed. She's taking the Fifth Amendment.

Stop it, stop it!

I'm going to drive her stuff down to her parents on Saturday, he said. It's time to clean this apartment out.

If you want I could—

Maybe Hank told her. Hey, Irene! Wake up! Did Hank tell you about Celia? He *saw* us that time. Friggin' Hank . . . They said they want all her clothes and crap. I don't know what they'll do with it. Maybe they can donate it through their church . . .

How are they doing?

Oh, fine. Did I tell you that her charge card bills keep coming in? She's going to send me to the poorhouse yet.

Oh, said Celia, lighting another cigarette.

That's quite a suitcase you brought over here.

You know what? Celia said. I feel as if you don't care whether I stay or not.

No, no, *no!* laughed John, holding up his hands. You're always welcome. Can I pour you a glass of wine? And there's coffee on . . . You gave me that coffee grinder. I use it all the time. I even recommended it to Hank! I told Irene to recommend it to him but she . . .

Celia's mouth had tightened, and she said: Do you want me to stay or not?

I said come over, didn't I?

I thought maybe you changed your mind. John, I—

Let me get you that wine, John said. Did you say white or red?

What are you having?

Oh, don't play that game. That's manipulative. It's just the kind of thing Irene used to—

White, thanks. John, you know I care for you so much. I just wanted to—

Don't think I don't appreciate your being here, he said to her, leaning forward to squeeze her hand. His rage had vanished as suddenly as it had come; he didn't know why. Gingerly he explored the place within him where it had been, and found only hollowness. He said: I guess I feel pretty lonely at times. And I know you care for me. We can talk about all that tomorrow.

John—

Do you want coffee in your wine? Guess you don't, so I'll turn the coffee off. I'll get it.

No, you're the guest. Can't you see I'm . . . Oh, balls.

I love you, John. Your sadness breaks my heart.

Well, if you love me, just sit there and . . . I'm not so sad actually. What time is it? Let me check my messages at the office. You go ahead and get ready for bed, okay?

So you want me to stay?

I hope you brought your own toothpaste, John said. I remember you don't like the toothpaste that I use.

| 66 |

The next morning, John's friend, his desk phone's amber button, winked at him most mirthfully. —What is it now, Joy? he said.

Mr. Singer would like to see you as soon as possible, said Joy's voice.

OK. Tell him I'll be there in five minutes.

What about your two o'clock with Mr. Brady?

How long does Singer need me for?

He didn't say. Probably some quickie kind of thing.

Fine, Joy. Where am I meeting Brady?

At Spoletto's, reservation in your name.

And that's at two o'clock?

Let me see. Oh, John, can you hold one second? There's a call on the other —

OK. Thank you, Joy, he said, hanging up. He made a note on his memo pad: *Call Mom tonight.—*

He added: *Flowers for Celia.—*

. . . and crossed it out.

| 67 |

Celia had returned home. (Post Street was closed off, the San Francisco coroner's white van parked among the police cars.) She dreamed that John was searching to buy Chinese figurines for a girl he knew. She woke up knowing that this meant *Irene*. She went to Grace Cathedral during her lunch hour and lit a candle for Irene, praying that the dead woman and John would be together in Heaven. She wept when she did it. That night when she lay down in her bed, she dreamed of the smell of fresh-baked bread.

| 68 |

The Vietnamese woman led Tyler into a room with a mattress, a chair, and a bathtub. She said: Thirty-five dollars is only for shower and back rub, okay? You want tea or coffee?

Tea.

Okay. Get undressed. I come back.

Tyler took off his shoes and lay down on the mattress. When she came in with the tea, she stopped dead, covered her gaping mouth with one hand, and cried: Why you not undress? What you want?

I just want to talk.

Your friend wait for you in lobby! she cried scornfully. Why you no talk with him?

I want to talk with you.

She squatted down beside the mattress, staring at him. Then she laughed bitterly and went out. He heard her yelling in Vietnamese with the other ladies.

After a while another woman came in. —What you want? she said.

To talk to you.

Why?

I'm lonely. I want to be next to a woman, just talking.

Thirty-five dollah not enough for *talk,* she sneered.

Okay. How much more do you need?

Twenty dollah.

And then you'll sit next to me?

Okay.

He gave her twenty dollars more and she sat down on the edge of the bed with her legs open so he slid his hand in and felt the paper menstrual shield through her panties. He caressed the insides of her thighs for the half-hour she gave him, while she tapped her foot boredly. This reach of his had been the right card to play. As soon as he'd touched her, the suspicion on her face drained away, leaving a hard residue of contempt and weariness. He was safe now.

What do you want to know? she said.

I don't want to know anything. Just talk to me.

What's your job?

I travel.

You rich?

Sometimes. No.

At that, she lost interest. Better and better.

Have you seen much war? he said.

Much much.

What do you think about it?

She shrugged. —I think war is very good. Because many fight, many suffer, but then one side get what they want.

Do you have brothers and sisters?

I don't want to think about them. I don't even want to think about myself.

Are you married? he said.

Two times. Not now.

You lonely?

Sometimes. Everybody wants love. —She regarded him piercingly. We were all born naked. Why not get naked when we want?

He understood her pefectly, but figured that would have cost him another twenty or thirty at least. Brady had given him one last wad for expenses. In his business, of course, one could not always present receipts. Some of the quittances which Brady had seen him counting he'd filled out and signed himself. That was normal. And if he kept this money now instead of giving it to people such as the Vietnamese woman, Brady would never know. Or, more likely, Brady would understand, even approve; probably Brady had factored in a little graft as part of Tyler's wages, or let's say a bonus to which he had every right as long as he did the job. He felt sorry for this girl. Just as a freshly shaved puden-dum, to which the stubble has just begun to return, resembles in texture a squid's most delicately suction-studded tentacles, so his own thoughts, yearnings and veriest grati-tudes, shaved by expediencey though they were, had begun to grow out upon his soul in a boneless sea-creaturely fashion bereft of the laws which two-legged dignity must wor-ship. Sure, he was sorry. But he felt sorry for everybody. He never let that get in the way of his work. (A Sicilian lawyer he'd met had three briefcases, one for twelve-hour jobs, one for twenty-four-hour jobs, and one for thirty-six-hour jobs. This man's best pleasure was reading *Il Sicilio,* then wiping his glasses and crying: The Italian government is very unfair! —After that he smiled, ate a doughnut, and forgot about the unfairness. Tyler was like that with his sadness.)

I already got naked with the Queen, he said, watching her.

I don't know any queen. Are you a cop?

I did her in the parking garage around the corner. She took it up the ass.

Why what for you think I care about parking garage? she shouted. You think I have money to drive? You think I park my big big car in parking garage of the Queen? You stupid little cop! I'm gonna tell madame on you.

What's the Queen's first name? I want to buy her a birthday present.

That Africa who cares for her first name all just bad African people those goddamned Negroes always try to hurt me in the street . . .

Tyler gave up. He rose and said goodbye, tipping her five, then strolled around the corner to a phony Chinese restuarant he knew which had just translated itself into a bar-beque place. He wasn't hungry, and the sauce didn't smell very good. The place was empty. The manager of the former Chinese place recognized Tyler right away and came running up to him and said to the new manager: Hey, you gotta meet Henry Tyler! He's a character!

I don't have time to meet characters, said the new manager.

The old manager hung his head.

What'll you have, friend? said the new manager.

Barbeque, said Tyler wearily.

The cook, who appeared to be the new manager's wife, brought him a paper plate dripping with grease and bulging with half-frozen, half-burned chicken covered with ketchup, while the old manager stood by tapping his foot.

How's business? he said to the old manager.

Booming, replied the new manager.

Tyler took a bite of barbeque and his teeth struck ice.

How is it? said the cook anxiously.

Very good, said Tyler.

She smiled with relief.

All three of them were watching him eat. With considerable effort he finished the first piece of chicken. There were five pieces left.

How come you don't use your hands? said the old manager. If you use your fork like that you're only gonna get it all over your shirt.

Tyler ate the second piece and said: Does the Queen of the Whores ever come in here?

I seen her sometimes, said the old manager indifferently. She's just a stuck-up bitch.

What does she look like?

Oh, about five foot two, you know, melons kinda like this, wears high heels and a tight mini, you know the drill . . . Somebody said she calls herself Africa. How's the chicken?

Great, said Tyler, picking up the third piece.

How come you don't use your other hand?

Oh, I wanted to keep it clean to touch the Queen with in case she comes in here.

She won't be coming in here any time soon, said the old manager. I hear they sent her down to San Bruno. What do you think of the chicken? It's my own special sauce.

Don't talk about the sauce, said the new manager. We gotta keep it a secret.

The Vietnamese girl he'd just tipped came in and pretended not to recognize him. He beckoned her over. — Have some chicken, he said. I have plenty.

You already lonely again? she cried in disgusted surprise.

Always, he said. But I'm celebrating. I told you I did the Queen.

| 69 |

He went home, turned on his computer and ordered an economy scan for American women whose first names were Africa. There came the connection beep he knew so well, and then the wriggling cursor indicated that the machine was **SEARCHING. Your search number is 0773427**. Then the screen scrolled down to the disclaimer: Nothing was guaranteed. Even though Tyler had to pay, the disclaimer warned, he shouldn't expect to get anything for his money. Nonetheless, the computer found thirty-eight matches, six of them with California addresses. So, flashing down blue-underlined screen menus, he ran six extended traces at twenty-five dollars each. Soon he had their dates of birth and social security numbers. The Department of Motor Vehicles database presented him with the physical descriptions on their drivers' licenses. They were all black. One, a Mrs. Africa Lively, had a Beverly Hills address and phone number. Tyler telephoned her and reached an answering service man who said that she was in Europe until July. He ran a credit check on her just in case. She owned three mansions and a cosmetology empire. So much for her (probably). The second Africa, formerly of Colusa, was freshly dead. The other four Africas were all alive and in San Francisco. One had a parking infraction on her record. Otherwise they were clean. Tyler printed out their DMV descriptions so that he could stalk them at his convenience, then telephoned his mother, who said she hoped that he and John could spend a weekend in Sacramento with her soon.

| 70 |

You datin'? You datin'? cried the whore Kitty.

Just looking, said Tyler. How about you?

Are you a cop? You don't have to intimidate me. I'm not a prostitute. I'm just out here tryin' to make a little money. Hey! I seen you before! You was with that bigshot Mr. Lunch, and you—yeah, you're Mr. Breakfast, and I gave you head. I give pretty good head, huh?

You sure do, said Tyler. How's Sapphire doing today?

That retard bitch? She just pissed her pants again, and Maj said . . .

Glaring in alarm, a black prostitute in a white miniskirt elbowed her in the ribs.

Why, good evening, Tyler said to her. What's your name, darling?

Chocolate, said the black woman, obviously pleased to divert the subject.

Well, that's a pretty edible name. Are you feeling edible tonight?

How much you got to spend?

I like that plastic bracelet on your wrist. Did Africa give it to you?

Africa? What the fuck are you talking about? Are you some kinda fucking racist? That's my hospital bracelet. I just got out of General today. Somebody stabbed me; I was in the trauma ward; you shoulda seen me . . .

Hey, Chocolate, if I give you twenty dollars can I have your bracelet?

What for?

Tyler lowered his voice and winked. —I want to take it home and lick the sweat off.

You catch that, Kitty? Chocolate laughed. Is this pervert for real?

Kitty slid her sunglasses down her nose. —What about me, Mr. Breakfast? Don't I get a finder's fee?

All right, ladies, he said. Here's five for you and twenty for you. Let me just cut through this bracelet with my pocketknife . . .

He got into his car and drove happily home. The medical record number on the bracelet was **3144173.** He wrote up a request for medical records, attached to a blurry old copy of a power of attorney he'd once done. He photocopied it four times and sent one to Admission and Discharge Records Department, one to Emergency Room Records Department, one to Medical Expense Records Department, and one to Billing Statements Department. Billing Statements wrote back right away and said that that information was confidential. Emergency Room and Medical Expense Records he never heard from. Admission and Discharge sent him a copy of the first page of Chocolate's chart. Her real name was Brenda Wiley. He drove down to the hospital the next afternoon and by flashing his toy police badge convinced a young clerk to let him see the rest.

```
BRENDA WILEY
MR#:   3144173
PT TYPE:   J
PATIENT EMPLOYMENT STATUS:   3
OCCUPATION:   UNEMPLOYMENT
SSN:   544-38-5008
DOB:   11/12/1959
AGE:   37
SEX:   FEMALE
```

There followed the bleak and tediously told tales of her misadventures and bodily misfunctions, bound into three fat volumes whose scope went back twenty-two years. The theme of any history of a body must be decay, but this body had begun to decline on or before the age of fifteen, when Brenda first married cocaine. By sixteen she was an experienced whore with her first crack baby inside her. There would be seven more. Over and over the medical chart said:

```
VAGINAL DELIVERY W/O COMPLICATING DIAGNOSES
PRINCIPAL: 644.21 EARLY ONSET DELIVERY 73.59 MANUAL
ASSIST DELIVERY NEC
```

SECONDARY
70   MENTAL DISORDER - DELIVER
71   COCAINE ABUSE - UNSPEC
V27.0   DELIVER - SINGLE LIVEBORN

and once she gave birth to crack-addicted twins.

At first the chart approved the transparency of her urine, but as the years of bad living stained her, entries such as the following became the rule:

BLOOD COUNT AND DIFFERENTIAL

COLLECTION   Clean catch
URINE VOLUME   5(a) reference units
COLOR   Yellow
CLARITY   Turbid ** H

and finally the chart proclaimed that her urine stank with a strange and evil smell. Her childbirth records told the same story:

R DELIVERY NOTE: Called to assess patient. Found to be 9 cm
/c/o per Dr. Angelli. Foul smell noted from vaginal area upon exam.
Mother refused to push when instructed; later refused not to push.
Infant nose and mouth bulb suctioned. Meconium with foul smell.
Placenta deliv. spontaneously, intact, mild staining, slight foul
smell. Uterus firm; rectum intact. Mother in stable condition. Infant
taken to CCIV. Intrauterine cocaine exposure. Baby is likely to be
placed under protective custody.

Each time, Chocolate denied her cocaine addiction, and each baby was born cocaine addicted. As her chart said: Some concerns about accuracy in reporting. Somewhat open, but also grew a little irritable at times. She was tearful upon speaking of her mother's death. Cognition was [illegible].

INDICATIONS FOR ADMISSION

RECENTLY HOSPITALIZED FOR PNEUMONIA
DRUG USAGE: Smokes cocaine x 22 years, last usage 3 days ago;
2 cigs/day x 25 years; "4 brandies/ wk"
NURSE'S NOTES: Received via gurney accompanied by firemen.
Rash over entire body.
WEIGHT: 179
EXAM: Hyperpigmentation and liquefication posterior neck.
SOCIAL HISTORY: Lives with "friend." "Chore worker" since
1/10/87. All children live with sister—temporary custody. Single,
unemployed, black female with 7th child. Doesn't know where
father is. Pregnancy is unplanned, but currently wants baby. Was
in drug court from May 93 on. Due to stress of pregnancy and

mother's death, states she didn't show up, so had to go to jail for 21 days. States that many of her belongings were stolen, so she has little in the way of baby clothes, etc. The longest time she has spent in jail was 1 year for possession.
SOCIAL SERVICE CONSULT—RECENT COCAINE USE—HOMELESS
NURSE'S NOTES: Patient found walking to ambulance with lower quad abdominal pain.
NURSE'S NOTES: Patient is not reliable enough to send home. Lungs diffuse. Wheezes throughout. Refuses adamantly to agree to induction of labor. Severe pneumonia
COMPLICATIONS: Diabetes
SOCIAL SERVICE CONSULT: Patient reports that she does not smoke cocaine now. Stopped 2 days ago. Incarcerated x 5 months.
IMMUNOASSAYS FOR DRUGS OF ABUSE: Positive for cocaine.
NURSE'S NOTES: Patient tends to be only marginally cooperative. Easily distracted and involved with physical occurrences.
DISCHARGE INSTRUCTIONS: Return to emergency room for observation of breathing difficulties.
NURSE'S NOTES: Stabbed in L abdomen by 6" knife this evening by room mate. Denies head trauma. Rapid speech. Hyperactive. Restless. Stab wound 7 cm deep. Eczema, hives. Breath smells of vodka.
CONSULTATION: Recommend leaving wound open. TRAUMA.
NURSE'S NOTES: Difficult to arouse. Agitated on arousal. Patient dirty. Incoherent speech. Home phone number supplied by patient is a pay phone. Speech slurred. Patient appears to be high on something. Denies drug use.
NURSE'S NOTES: Patient hypersexual. Continually exposes and manipulates her genitals, embarassing the other patients. Propositions doctors, interns, male patients, male relatives of patients, etc.
NURSE'S NOTES: 37 year old black female was going shopping earlier today when a man grabbed her purse, then dragged her along asphalt. She got away, then he chased her again, pulling her to the ground and kicking her. Some superficial abrasions, facial pain, swelling.
DIAGNOSIS: Closed head trauma, orbital contusion, knee and foot contusion.
NURSE'S NOTES: Coughing up blood. Right eye swelling and knee swelling.

And then in the back of her chart lay the envelope which contained a slip reading:

BRENDA WILEY AIDS INFO: Postive antibody.

He turned to the front of the chart and found:

NEXT OF KIN: AFRICA JOHNSTON

| 71 |

He instructed his computer to search for American women named Africa Johnston. None of them lived in California. But then how many Chocolates were there?

In his microfiche of the Los Angeles Superior Court index, which an old private eye had sold him for almost nothing, there were all the aliases one could want. No Africa Johnston, however.

| 72 |

Meanwhile Chocolate trotted around the corner to her homegirl, fat Mexican Beatrice, who, sunny believer, could often be made to do as she was told; and after Chocolate had described to her the grizzled white man who was searching for the Queen, Beatrice promised to relay this warning, crying: I come *running, running!*

| 73 |

Switching on his computer, Tyler searched two legal and two illegal databases for the alias "**Domino**" and found nothing. The fifth database, which limited itself to California and which invited him to access it for each of the state's fifty-eight counties at eleven dollars each, gave him a match with the name Sylvia Fine in San Francisco County. Datatronic Solutions would have been better, but he owed them too much money. He entered the name in a sixth database and got her social security number. Running her name and social in a seventh, he obtained and printed out a lengthy file beginning

---

MUNICIPAL CRIMINAL
SAN FRANCISCO COUNTY
Main Court: 1987—06/29/96

Data Submitted:

Last Name	: FINE
First Name	: SYLVIA
Middle Init	: S
County	: San Francisco

76 of 14)

Case	: 88F08265 Date: 04/01/88
Case Type	: FELONY
Location	: SAN FRANCISCO

Subject(s)		
	FINE SYLVIA R	aka
	FINE SYLVIA T	aka
	FEINGOLD SANDY	aka
	DOMINO	

Case   : 89M11352   Date: 01/02/89
Case Type   : MISDEMEANOR
Location   : SAN FRANCISCO

Subject(s)   FINE SYLVIA R   aka
                FINE SYLVIA T   aka
                FEINGOLD SANDY   aka
                DOMINO   aka
                BLONDE MARY

And so it went, on and on, for a dozen other crimes, all the way up to the present, which the file proclaimed as follows:

Court Runner (tm): Additional record(s) found in Municipal Criminal Courts:

CA-SACRAMENTO
CA-SAN DIEGO
CA-SAN JOAQUIN

Other crimes in other counties. Domino had been a very busy girl.
He sighed. The file said:

*** End of Search ***

| 74 |

Tyler drove down to San Francisco's municipal court, found a parking space five blocks away after considerable difficulty, and went inside whistling gloomily, the printout in his fist. He requested all case reports within the county's jurisdiction, copying out the case numbers from the printout. —Oh, jeez, he said, cross because the courthouse clerk spotted Domino's rap sheet and tore it off the file. —The next clerk greeted him by name. Tyler smiled, waved, asked about her family. When the documents came, he sat and leafed through their unhappy pages, learning that Domino had been arrested and convicted for prostitution eight times, which hardly surprised him, and that she had also served time for two counts of cocaine possession, one count of heroin possession, and three counts of felony assault. The clerk, liking Tyler and wanting to help him, had "forgotten" to remove Domino's rap sheet, private possession of which was a crime, but since the rap sheet had fallen into Tyler's possession inadvertently, so as to speak, possession was no skin off his nose. In Sacramento, San Diego, and San Joaquin, it said, the blonde had been convicted of many other sad and ugly acts, including one attempted homicide which she'd plea-bargained down, and she'd been charged with infanticide but acquitted on a technicality. —Poor Domino, he muttered to himself.
Yawning, he browsed through the trial transcripts:

Ms. Fine, how do you plead?   ¶   No contest, Your Honor.
Ms. Fine, how do you plead?   ¶   Guilty, Your Honor.

Really what he wanted were the names of co-defendants, co-conspirators. Although he wrote them all dutifully down and later ran them through his databases, he already knew that none would check out. Not one name was linked to the aliases "**Queen**" or "**Maj**" or "**Africa.**"

| 75 |

Every summer the great maple tree on his mother's front lawn seemed to grow larger, wider, and greener (and of course it actually did), so that at sunset when he sat out on the porch drinking lemonade with his mother, that tree was as an immense crystal both gold and green which subsumed the entire sky, and his mother asked him if he would like another glass of lemonade, and he said: I'll get it, Mom. —The pitcher was almost empty, so he mixed up more, employing fresh lemons and strawberry slices; she always made it too sweet, so he made it the way he liked it and brought out the sugar jar for her. This jar resembled in miniature the prism of one of those lighthouses along the Oregon coast. A metal lip on the top could be finger-hooked into a beak from which the sugar came vomiting out whenever the humidity was not overly high; he saw that his mother had scattered a few grains of rice inside, but these hadn't prevented the sugar from hardening into a cylindrical brick, chipped into white rubble at the top only, thanks to his mother's spoon-probings.

So you won't be in this weekend? his mother repeated.

That's right, said Tyler, gently swishing the ice cubes in his glass.

Where did you say you're going?

I didn't, but I'm going to L.A.

Business? pursued his mother.

Something like that.

You know, his mother said with gentle determination, John tells me that you very often make the drive all the way down to Los Angeles to lay flowers on Irene's grave.

Tyler didn't say anything.

You loved Irene very much, Henry, didn't you? I know you did.

Tyler cleared his throat. —Yes, he said hoarsely. Yes, I did.

And you're going to visit her again this weekend, his mother continued.

Maybe we can talk about something else, Mom. We've had this chat before . . .

Henry, I think it's important that we discuss this subject a little further. I know it's painful to you, but I'm concerned. I don't think it's good for you to dwell on Irene so much.

I'm sorry you think so, Mom, said Tyler, squeezing his glass. Far away, he heard a freight train.

There's a certain question I asked you once before, and you refused to answer. Don't worry, she said in a hard voice. I'll never ask you again.

Fine.

May I be frank on a related subject? said his mother. I'm not sure that those trips of yours to L.A. are very beneficial to your relationship with John. It makes him feel odd.

So John's been complaining about me again, said Tyler, squeezing the glass.

No, not *complaining* exactly, his mother lied, and Tyler, knowing that she lied, seeing and reading the lie and comprehending exactly what it implied, squeezed the glass and then put it down because he knew that if he squeezed any harder it would shatter in his hand; he was grateful that he'd realized that. John had once broken a glass that way, he remembered. (He thought of Brady jeering over and over: Are you emotionally compromised?)

Where's Mugsy? he said.

I imagine she's sleeping under the blackberry bush. That's her little hangout.

Do you want me to take her for a walk?

That's just what Irene used to say. Do you remember? Irene was so good to Mugsy.

Mom, I think I'll go lie down, he said. Can I make you some more lemonade before I turn in? Oh, I see the pitcher's still almost full. Should I bring the sugar inside?

Ascending the stairs to his old room with the battleship-green microscope, a birthday present, still on the bureau in which if he opened it he'd doubtless find many of his T-shirts from tenth grade, history kept at bay by mothballs, he undressed, admitting that his mother was right. He would stop visiting Irene. At least he would make this weekend the last time. Early the next morning he took his mother out for breakfast and then drove her home, promised to call her soon, promised to call John, promised to look for a girlfriend, waved goodbye, took I-80 West to the interchange and cloverleaved widely round to meet I-5 South. The day was already miserably hot. No traffic detained him in the Central Valley, and by the time he'd passed three hours he was already far past Coalinga; he wondered whether he ought to visit the Tule Elk Reserve sometime; that was a place he had always imagined going with Irene. At Pumpkin Center there was an accident, and then an overheated car blocked one lane near Grapevine, but he made good time still, and at the seven-hour mark was nearly in sight of the Korean florist's shop near the Tropicana.

How's business? he said.

Very slow, said the florist. Ever since after big riot here is no good. Black people no good. Make everybody afraid.

I'd like a dozen red roses, please.

Yes, sir. You is always same same. Your wife is so lucky. She is Caucasian like you?

She did look pretty pale in that open coffin, he said. Thank you.

The stones at the cemetery went on and on, but he knew how to find her very easily now; he sat down on the grass early on a hot dry endless Long Angeles evening of idiotic cloudlessness and meaningless freedom; up the green from him, some Koreans were singing hymns. Her stone was clean and polished. There were flabby, stinking, horribly rotten flowers in the metal holder—maybe his. He replaced them with the red roses. He looked around to make sure that no one saw or cared. Then, stretching himself out full length on the grass, he laid his head upon the stone. He stayed like that for a long time. Finally he turned his head slowly to touch with his lips that deep, cool, V-stroked letter "I."

· BOOK IV ·

Billable Hours

•

The consumption of sulfuric acid is an index to the state of civilization and prosperity of a country.

A. CLARK METCALFE, JOHN E. WILLIAMS,
JOSEPH F. CASTKA, *Modern Chemistry*
(1970)

•

You know what I like the best? said old Dan Smooth. It's those rape cases, when you get to collect pieces of the pillow slip for yourself, and pieces of the bedsheet. If I find a likely stain, I just cut around it with my pocket knife. I have quite a collection at home. You should see 'em under the fluorescent light.

Tyler sighed. —Have another Bushmill's, Dan.

Why, Henry, you're the next best thing to . . . even if your manner may not be so attractive . . . Say, can I ask you something?

What?

Well, I'm probably being an asshole, but I always wanted to know. I like thinking up questions like this. It's kind of my reason for being. What I wanted to know is, did you ever screw that sister-in-law-of yours?

Tyler was silent.

You know, the one that killed herself, said Dan Smooth eagerly, watching Tyler with a malicious smile.

I thought all I'd have to do to get some information out of you was buy you a few drinks, said Tyler. I didn't know I was going to have to put up with your bullshit, too. You know what, Dan? It's not worth it to me to get that information. And you know what else? I'm going to walk out of here right now and leave you with the tab for these drinks, and what are you going to do about it?

Aw, Henry, I told you I'm an asshole sometimes. I can't help it. Listen, did I tell you I'm trying to get a whole new specialty created for me?

What's that, Dan? said Tyler impassively.

Pediatric forensics, the other said proudly. It's the up and coming thing. Little dead boys and girls. Marks, bruises, *evidence.* Sodomy holes are like snowflakes, no two alike. Get the picture?

You ought to be castrated, Dan.

Hee, hee, hee! Coming from you that's quite a compliment, you old sis—

Don't say it. I'm carrying, and you're starting to really piss me off.

Oh, he's *carrying,* he says! Pissed *off,* he says! Cocked and locked! And no luck with the Queen, either! Don't think I don't know all your woes, Henry Tyler! I'm the master of stains.

I do enjoy your company, Dan, but will you tell me where the Queen is or not? I know you know everything.

Even the answer to the question I asked you? Hee, hee, hee!

You're not just sick, you're boring.

And if I also ask you, ye will not answer me, nor let me go. That's Luke 22 something, or maybe 23. I could tell you a lot of things about Luke.

Get another hobby, like skinning rats. Here's twenty for the drinks. I'll come visit you in jail sometime.

Visit the sewers, whispered Smooth theatrically. That's where her *piss* goes.

Lots of sewers in San Francisco, said Tyler, unimpressed. Lots of piss, too. Can you narrow it down for me a little bit?

Sure I can, Henry. You got a pen? I'll draw you a map; I'll write out a regular urinalysis. Hey, but didn't that Brady take you off the case?

As a matter of fact, Dan, he did.

So what are you getting out of this?

Oh, let's just say it keeps my mind off things, and you know which things, and the fact that you know ought to make you pretty gleeful, you sleazy old sonofabitch. Now, let me ask you something. Is there a Queen of the Whores and do you know where she is?

Yes to both, Tyler. Just call me the yes man. You see, she's got her fingers in a lot of sex crimes. Got her fingers in all the holes. Here's a photo of her. Full length, you see. An old photo. It was Halloween, so for a joke she dressed like a slut. With her that's not usual. Likes to wear that baseball cap, but sometimes she wears a wool hat. And I'll tell you something else. She uses so much perfume she stinks like a cathouse. Well, what could be more appropriate, eh? So buy me one more Bushmill's before you go, and take this home with you and think about how you're going to make it worth my while, and then give me a call up at the Sacramento number Saturday morning after ten —

No, not then, said Tyler. I've got to go to L.A. then for some business.

| 77 |

He sat with his feet on the bed looking at Dan Smooth's photo and working up his details description sheet.

```
SEX        Female
RACE       African-American
AGE        Approx. 45
HEIGHT     Approx. 5' 5"
WEIGHT     Approx. 120 lbs
COMPLEXION      Dark
```

Well, that doesn't help much, he muttered.

```
HAIR       Color black; long, kinky.
EYES       Brown, slightly bloodshot
FOREHEAD      Vertical
EYEBROWS      Bushy, same color as hair
NOSE       Medium; nostrils small
CHEEKS     Full, cheekbones not prominent
MOUTH      Upturned at corners
LIPS       Red, upper thin, lower puffy
TEETH      Unknown
CHIN       Curved
```

JAW   Wide
EARS   Oval, pierced (?)
NECK   Medium, straight, no Adam's apple
SHOULDERS   Narrow
HANDS   Long, rough
FINGERS   Slim, tapered
FINGERNAILS   Long, painted red, dirt under nails
CLOTHING   Seen in red miniskirt or black low-cut dress; high
heels, one heel broken
JEWELRY   Large hoop earrings, bangles on left wrist
PECULIARITIES   Round scar on right calf (bullet wound?), ab-
scess marks on arms, tattoo of skull on left wrist, mole on left
cheek, strong smell of perfume
ALIASES   Queen, Maj, Africa Johnston
CONFEDERATES   Domino [AKA Sylvia Fine], Strawberry [AKA
???], Kitty, unnamed mentally unstable prostitute, Sapphire, Choco-
late [AKA Brenda Wiley], others to be determined

| 78 |

He was late with his rent. Jumpy, maybe from coffee—a not unpleasant jumpiness, his fingers not quite twitching, like baby birds almost ready to fly across Valencia Street— he drove over to his landlord's place in Menlo Park to deliver the check in person. When he rang the buzzer, nobody answered, which relieved him. He slipped the check under the door. For a moment he wanted to call Judy from RoboGraphix, but that passed, leaving him guilty and stained. He drove back home to the Outer Sunset where it was foggy again, and someone's purple light was flashing in the apartment next door. There were no messages on his machine. But then the phone rang. First he thought that it might be business; then he decided that it was his landlord. When he put the receiver to his ear, a cheery male voice said: *Hello!* I'm a telecommunications computer specially selected to . . . —He hung up. An hour later, the computer called back. He hung up again.

That night he couldn't sleep knowing that he'd be crying in his dreams, and listlessly opened the yellow pages, hoping that advertisements for fencing tools and chiropractors would swizzle him down into some murky sea of drowse, but those strange spiders of his called *hands* had their own ideas: ENTERTAINMENT . . . ESCORT . . . MAS-SAGE was what they sought out. It sounded blessed. But he didn't feel up to driving anywhere, and he didn't care to pay an escort girl to drop by. The next afternoon business was dead, as usual, so he got in the car, drove to the gas station, drove to the super-market, and then drove to the Tenderloin, where he parked across the street from the Oriental Spa, vaguely supposing that one of the girls might look like Irene. Then he de-cided to try Jasmine's Exotic Massage instead. The Mama-san, almost as wide as she was short, stood on tiptoe to view him through the chest-high window before she let him in.

Hi, she said.

Afternoon, said Tyler. How much for a massage?

Forty dollars for forty minutes.

All right, he said. He was pretty sure that she was Korean.

She took him down the hall to a small dark room with a single bed and a radio playing country songs. Then she left him.

The woman who came in next was definitely Korean. Her trick name was Patricia, and she told him to undress. For a moment he thought of the Vietnamese woman who liked wars. He had to give up the forty dollars first, of course, and the woman took that and went out while he stripped to his underpants. She was surprised that he kept those on. She said that she was divorced and that her son was nine years old. —That's my child with Irene, he thought to himself.

The Korean woman knelt down on the bed and began to squeeze his back.

Your back is so big there must be a million dollars inside! she laughed.

Help yourself, said Tyler. If you can dig out any small change, though, I'll keep that to buy myself a sandwich.

Pretty soon she was cracking his fingers and toes. She told him that he had nice skin, which wasn't true, and that he looked young. He put his hand on her generous ass through her tights and she smiled at him. She asked whether he were married. Suddenly his arms were around her and his face was against the strange slick fabric of her dress just below her breasts and he began to feel happy and eased. He stayed like that with her for a long time. He needed comfort so much. What was he but a greyhaired old child? He slid his hand between her thighs and she made a mock-startled expression and shook her head, but she didn't seem to be angry, so he did it again.

You want to stay with me? she whispered.

Now, how much would that cost? said Tyler.

Maybe too much for you. I'm sorry. One-twenty. I'm sorry so much.

Will you be able to get well paid out of that? I won't be able to give you a tip then.

Thank you. It'll be okay.

If you'd rather, I can just give you a fifty dollar tip and go now. The Mama-san doesn't have to know.

If you can stay, I'm happy, she said. You're so warm.

Where are you from?

Seoul.

Ann-yeong ha sim nee ka, he said, which means hello. Irene had taught him that.

She clapped her hands and kissed him.

He gave her the money and she went out and came back with no tights on. He took her underwear off and she took his off. —Oh, you not shy there! she laughed. She dimmed the light and lay beside him.

He put his hand gently but firmly on her cunt and began to suck her nipples. —Oh, I like that! the Korean woman sighed. After a while she was screaming with pleasure. Her hips slammed again and again against the bed, so hard that it almost broke, and love-juice drooled out upon his hand. That was no act, he thought, immeasurably grateful that he could please somebody. When her eyeballs rolled up and she ground her head against the wall, he began to need her urgently, and cunt-sucked, then mounted her, coming quickly and pleasantly, though not as ecstatically as she had.

Thank you, they said to one another at the same time.

You want to come see me sometime? he said.

I work very long hours, the Korean woman said glibly. I can't get out much.

Never mind, he said. But I'm going to give you my P.O. box. If you ever need help or want to see me, write me.

Thank you, she said.

He was out of business cards, so he tore a scrap off one of the surveillance report forms in his briefcase and wrote the information down.

Well, he said, I guess I'll never see you again then.

In another month I'll be gone, she agreed flatly. I'll probably be in Saint Louis.

How long have you been here? he said.

Oh, about one month.

Do you live with your kid?

No. He's with my husband.

On the way out, she said: If I write to you and you ever see me again, don't tell anyone we did this.

Okay, he said. Her words gave him hope that maybe she'd get in touch with him.

Don't forget me, she whispered.

| 79 |

He could have deepened the case against himself, had he been of a self-torturing mind, by reminding himself that moments after he'd climaxed in her arms she was holding out his underwear and then (embarrassingly) putting his unclean socks onto his feet for him, and then before he knew it she was handing him his coat; his money, in short, had been spent; and yet, although he was far from young enough for his sadness to have been entirely alleviated by the sexual act, the generosity with which she'd given herself to him, the happiness and gladness of her body both in and out of sex (she said that she was always happy), the genuine tenderness and care he felt she'd given him as one human being to another suffused him with an even more fundamental kind of hope than that of seeing her again, which he now understood didn't matter. If he could but trust and believe, not so much, or so carelessly, that the world could hurt him, but enough to open his soul to people like her, then maybe someday he too could be happy. There had been some sort of flavored gel inside her pussy; maybe he'd imagined that orgasm of hers; but whether that was true or not, the important thing was that she had tried to bring him joy.

How long will you stay here? she had asked him after explaining that she couldn't see him.

I'm leaving town, he lied absurdly.

That didn't matter, either. She had helped him. She had loved him, inasmuch as one stranger can love another. If there were a heaven, she would undoubtedly go there.

Two or three nights afterward, he dreamed about Irene. They were alone with each other in a valley which was very hot just like the cemetery in L.A., but they followed a creek upstream, and the creek kept foaming green and white with the shadowy reflections of alder branches bending like kelp, whirling deliciously cold breezes at them; and they found a bank of snow-white gravel on which to sit with the white rock faces reflecting starriness and sunniness down upon them. She sat upon his knee. Now it was almost evening, and the cliffs, crevice-speckled with trees, became as white as silver ore, as white as the beaches of glacier lakes. He slipped his arm around her waist. She leaned back against him, her head against his neck; he stroked her hair, which was as smooth and cool as a waterfall. He felt that she would be with him always. He awoke in a state almost of rapture. By mid-morning he had begun to wonder whether he would ever dream about her again.

| 80 |

A sad woman telephoned him. She suspected that her husband might be "seeing" another woman. The grief in her voice sent him plunging into those endless chambers of loss he now knew so well, and he lied: I only do insurance fraud, personal injury. I wouldn't touch a divorce case.

Please, Mr. Tyler, the woman sobbed. I can't bear not knowing. My friend Selena Contreras recommended you; you helped her . . .

Do you listen to your husband? he asked her.

What do you mean?

Do you make him feel good when he's around you? Wouldn't you rather—

I can't stand it. It's too late for that. I just need to know.

Have you ever discovered something about a person you've wished you didn't know? Stop it!

Well, are you better off knowing or not knowing? I'm trying to help you, ma'am.

I want to know. I need to know.

Well, then, you already do know. I'll tell you why. First of all, if you suspect it, it's probably true. Whether or not they're having intercourse together, they're doing *something.*

Oh, my God, wept the woman.

Think about it. If you still want me to check your husband out, call me in the morning.

The woman never called again. Tyler went to bed and for some reason dreamed of John's angry face.

| 81 |

But after that, he began to have good fortune. He got two adultery cases in one afternoon, with satisfying retainers for each. Neither one made his heart ache. The landlord came over and fixed the toilet for the second time and it didn't leak after that. On Monday evening he called Dan Smooth.

| 82 |

Well, are we ready to dot the i's? said Brady. This is an obnoxious place. Who designed this place? I wouldn't eat dinner here if you paid me. Well, maybe if you paid me. I'm not that particular.

John laid down the legal draft. —What's the consolidated leverage ratio? he asked.

We'll get to that.

John thought this red-faced entrepreneur to be a true original, a driven winner who did not need any other human being to make *him* full partner. Brady's manner and his grand project exuded a sense of freedom which made John dream about someday trying his own luck in the financial jungle, of throwing up law and making millions by discovering or creating new desires in his fellow citizens. Was Brady playing a clean game? Well, in business how could games be clean? For that matter, weren't all life's gamepieces equally ordure-stained? How had Irene treated him? And that crooked Hank . . . Perhaps what really attracted him to Brady was the other man's rage. (At the same time, of course, the man bored him, because everybody bored John.)

And another thing, Mr. Brady, he said. I'll need a more thorough financial statement. Now, this revolving credit facility you're talking about here, that's fine, but I need you to break down these quarterly fees. That's a lot of money right there.

I promise you this, said Brady. We're going to keep a pretty goddamned low overhead expense to sales ratio. And we're gonna keep our eyes on the gross margin returns.

Fine, but that has nothing to do with quarterly fees.

I honestly don't know about that one, son. Let me find out.

No problem, said John making two tickmarks on the yellow pad. He was particularly fond of his mechanical pencil, which, slender, octagonal in cross-section, and gunmetal-hued, with inlaid lozenges of rosewood, had been a present from Irene. —And we still need clarification on some employee issues.

What issues? said Brady in surprise. What employees? It's all going to be virtual reality, remember?

That's fine, said John. But what about the bartenders, waitresses, hostesses, janitors?

Some day they'll all be robots, Brady said dreamily. You know, I had lunch with that Alexis Dydynski, a very intimate lunch. Know who he is?

No, I don't, Mr. Brady, said John, looking at his watch.

Executive Vice President at the Royal Grand. You remember when that place opened? Oh, it was a big brouhaha, but that's another story. It's not my policy to tell more than one story at a time. Anyway, Dydynski said to me: *Slot machines don't ask for raises, don't get pregnant, don't get sick, and always show up for work.* —And I thought to myself, John: Here is one smart man.

All right, said John patiently. See if you can get a formal employee policy together. — And he made another tickmark on the yellow pad. —Now if you would, Mr. Brady, I'd like you to glance over clause three.

I don't give a shit about that part, either, said Brady. That part is your job. Just make it all ironclad. This business is going to last hundreds of years. I'm thinking big.

What's the working lifetime of your virtual staff?

Oh, five years. Maybe less. But in five years we'll want to update the theme park with even more state-of-the-art experiences. Look. The theme park only cost three hundred and eighty-seven million. The real question is this and I hope you're considering it: Who's against us?

I don't know what you're talking about, John said.

Look. Every business venture has friends and enemies, right? So who are our enemies? Casinos? Department of Parks and Recreation? Gambling Commission? Women's organizations? Rightwing Christians? Leftwing Christians? The Teamsters? I want this document to be *enemy-specific.* Do you see what I'm driving at?

You sound apprehensive, Mr. Brady.

Well, of course there'll be various claims and actions against the company. But I don't think they'll have a leg to stand on. If they do, why, young John, you and I can kick that leg out from under . . .

Not my department. By the way, I think you ought to insist on the right to extend your leases up to at least fifteen years, John said.

At escalated rents?

Well, Mr. Brady, of course they'll have to be escalated, unless you hold a gun to their heads. But that's fine. If you lost the lease, you'd be paying escalated rents at a new site anyway.

All right, we'll cut a deal. Let's meet for breakfast at the Mark Hopkins on Wednesday, seven a.m. I'll do my homework on consolidated leverage, employee guidelines and quarterly fees. You do yours on *enemies.*

John walked back to the office and told Mr. Singer that the Brady contracts were going to bring in many, many more billable hours.

I love the law, said Mr. Singer.

· BOOK V ·

The Mark of Cain

•

Matthew said, "Lord, I want to see that place of life where there is no wickedness, but rather there is pure light."

The Lord said, "Brother Matthew, you will not be able to see it as long as you are carrying flesh around."

GNOSTIC SCRIPTURES, Dialogue of the Savior, III, 5, 27–28 (2nd cent.)

•

Again he drove to Sacramento with its black parking lots given meaning by cars, its malls so thoroughly placed and identical in composition that every three or four miles one thought to be back at the same retail outlets no better or worse than the cigarette-burned pillowcases of San Francisco's whore hotels; and the night was hot and still. His mother slept. Dan Smooth sat out on his back porch on Q Street, drinking rum.

Right on time, said Smooth, or at least I presume you're on time, because I can't see my watch. It's been a bad summer for gnats, I'm sorry to say.

Well, maybe the next one will be better.

Spoken like an optimist—hee, hee! And I'm just the opposite. I know I'm not your type, but you can't do without me, can you?

I'll hold judgment on that, Dan.

And did you decide anything?

Yes, I did.

Well, tell me about it later. She moves around a bit, you see, Smooth explained. Hops around, like a lap dancer. You can't always say where she is, but you can *find* where she is, if you see the distinction.

Yeah, I get it, said Tyler, longing to look at his watch. He thought of the old criticism of Wagner: great moments and horrible half-hours. With Smooth the moments were horrible, too.

You plan to fuck her?

Well, your photo didn't really turn me on, Dan. No offense. I'm sure she's a nice Queen, though. I guess I'd just as soon keep it all business.

What does turn you on, Henry? queried Smooth, something moving in his face like the crawling silver shadows on a barmaid's chin of the change which she is counting behind her half-wall.

As I said, I'd rather keep this thing professional.

Oh, get off your high horse! What are you afraid of? Don't you realize that you have the look in your eyes of a man who has sexual relations with prostitutes, and don't you know that other men who do the same can always pick you out? You bear the Mark of *Cain,* brother!

Tyler grimaced.

Have a shot, Henry?

All right.

There. Now what turns you on?

What turns *you* on, Dan? Child molesting?

I want to tell you something. I can tell a great deal about a man by his face. Not just his eyes, but his entire face. His mouth, for instance. I like to inspect a man's mouth. I can see from your mouth that you like to go down on women. I can see all their itty-bitty pubic hairs stuck between your teeth! (Oh, I could talk endlessly about textures. Maybe I don't have a moral sense, but that's normal. Maybe I do have one, but if so where did I put it?) I see I forgot to offer you a shot. Help yourself. Well, as I was saying, how do I know you don't suck guys? Well, because you never did come on to me, and I know I'm quite attractive. Elementary, as Sherlock used to say. You don't like me, do you, Henry? I can tell that from the color of your nose. You see, most other men, if they want something from me, they brown-nose me a little. Why else do you think my asshole's so clean and shiny? They pretend not to mind—oh, they just have to pretend. Grin and bear it when I talk about what I talk about. But your nose is a good honest pink drinker's nose, and not a bit of shit on it. Now, as for your ears, Henry, I regret to tell you this, but you have *envious* ears. I'm not going to tell you how I know that, though, because old Dan Smooth's got to have a few secrets in this world, just to keep the ears of his fellow man envious. And as for children, to answer your question, no, I can't tear myself away from them. If I were going to be marooned on a desert island and I could take only one food with me, you know what it would be? The earwax of a ten-year-old child.

What if it came out of envious ears? said Tyler.

Interesting case! But you still haven't answered my question.

That's just how Brady used to talk to me.

Maybe because we each have something you need. Maybe my ageing eyesight's not so good. Maybe there's brown on your schnozz after all, brother. Maybe there's brown stuff packed way up between your nostrils—

All right, Dan. What turns me on is a sincere woman. That's all.

And what does she smell like?

You know, Dan, a lot of people on this earth fall in love with each other first and then have sex afterward.

But not you, Henry—ha, ha, not you! Remember, I can see your Mark of Cain glowing right now in this darkness! It's brighter than my bug-zapper light! So don't lie to me, buddy, because we're both children of the same wicked God. Are you trying to deny that you care what they smell like?

That's right.

How about a high-grade armpit? Like roast coffee, almost—well, it depends on the—

Usually I shake hands instead of sniffing armpits, Dan.

Oh, then he likes mannish women. Office types, in executive blazers. But they use deodorant. Old Dan doesn't like that one bit. And you say it doesn't matter?

It's not my number one concern.

So you'd do it with anyone then. You'd fuck anybody no matter how she smells. Talk about perversion. Talk about obscenity. This man dares to get sarcastic with me because I have certain fantasies regarding children, when he himself is nothing but a—I have no words—a mere functionary! There's something inconsistent about you—yeah, yeah, something *brutally untrue*. And you deny it; you deny your own animal nature. I disgust you, but what's inside your guts? Children of the same God, I said! And the Queen, she can see your Mark of Cain! That's why she stayed away from you, because she's good. Whatever she does, she—oh, what's the use of explaining it to you? You don't see me as a human being; I'm just your way station. So. Where's my reward?

Right here, Dan. These Swedish postcards.

Well. *Well!* That was thoughtful. Are they illegal?

Probably. I didn't flash them at any cops—

Where did you get them?

From a friend.

How *nice* of him. *Or* her. Let me go inside and look at them. You wait here.

Give her this, said Smooth, returning a quarter-hour later. It's just glass, but she'll know what it is. Give it to some whore, and make up a good line, so the whore'll think it's something important, you see . . .

| 84 |

The sheets smelled of body odor. The closet door yawned and creaked. He turned on the television at once and kept it loudly going at all times, so no one would know whether he was there or not—better that they assume he was there, so they didn't break in. The door was barely held together by a pair of angle-nailed planks, and the bolt came out of the lock with a single tug.

He hadn't stayed at the Karma Hotel in a couple of years. He was ready to essay it again after his less than sleep-filled night at the Rama. The Karma had once been filled with the scents of fresh Indian cooking, but it didn't smell like curry anymore, and the old lady wasn't stirring her pot of beans, and her daughter no longer wore a sari, nor did she bear the round red caste-dot on her forehead. America the melting-pot, thought Tyler to himself. The daughter looked older, dirtier, and angrier.

Can I help you? she said, neither recognizing him nor wanting to help him.

You have any rooms?

I.D., she said.

(That was new. They never used to ask for identification.)

He passed her his driver's license and she wrote the number down, after which at her curt demand he surrendered twenty-five dollars. Last time it had been eighteen.

His room stank. On the television, a woman screamed.

It was almost sunset. Leaving the television jabbering away, he descended to Capp Street and found a girl.

My room? the girl said.

No, come up to mine, he said. I've got all the equipment there.

What, are you into S & M or something like that?

Something like that, he said.

Where you staying?

The Karma.

They don't let me in there.

Well, let's try.

What the hell, the girl sighed. Just as a tired barmaid draws her paper towel across the beer cooler in slow arcs, with untouched space in between, so Providence had incompletely abscessed this person, who still possessed many strangely healthy places on her thighs here bared to the open air.

What's yours, said Tyler, looking her over acutely, heroin?

Yup.

How many times a day?

Just five.

Well, that's not too bad, he said.

They went back to Mission Street where at the street-grating he rang the buzzer, and someone let the lovebirds in, so they ascended the stairs to the second grating, which buzzed at their approach like the wing of an immense metallic insect, and then they were inside and facing the half-door behind which there had once been the smell of Indian cooking.

Can I help you? said the same woman.

Mutely, he showed her his key.

Don't get smart with me, the woman sneered. I was nice to you before, but now I see what kind you are. You see this notice on the wall? NO VISITORS. You know what we call men like you? Trash collectors.

You gotta pay for my visit, idiot, the whore said.

He gave the woman a five, which she snatched with a snotty look. (He'd heard that the city planned to condemn this place.) Then she turned her back on them both, which he interpreted as permission granted for their private and consensual proceedings.

In his room the television was screaming again, because a murderer was eviscerating someone.

Pay me first, the girl said.

He gave her twenty.

Well, you gonna unzip or am I supposed to do that? she said.

You know the Queen, don't you? he said.

Oh, great, the girl said. Another fucking cop trying to jack me up.

From his night bag Tyler withdrew a fat manila envelope called "EVIDENCE."— This is from Dan Smooth, he said, breaking the seal. Can you remember that name? And I'm Tyler.

Tyler, huh? How about if I just call you Blowhard?

I thought that was your job, said Tyler.

He upended the envelope over the bed, and a fat blue crystal fell soundlessly out. — Now, this is one of the missing jewels to her crown, Tyler explained. You wouldn't want to steal a jewel from your own Queen's crown, now, would you?

The whore just stood there holding the twenty.

Now, am I a cop or not? he said.

You? You stink of cop.

All right. Fine. If I'm a cop, can I catch you anytime or not?

Not if I run fast enough, sucker.

If I put the word out, you'll end up at Eight-Fifty Bryant faster than you can put a rubber on with your tongue.

I believe you, officer. You bastards always have all the power. But I'm no rat. I'd rather be put away than rat on my Queen.

No one's asking you to be a rat, honey.

So what do you want? You want me to blow you and give you back the twenty? God knows, I've had to do it before.

I want you to take this jewel to the Queen, he said. Then you can do whatever she tells you to do. If you don't take this to the Queen, if you keep it for yourself, then I'm

going to have a problem with you, and once I tell the Queen, she's going to have a problem with you, too. And tell her I'll be waiting here.

That bitch downstairs isn't gonna let me in again. You gonna give me five so I can—

That's possible. Okay. So I'll be waiting on Capp and Sixteenth in two hours, say, ten
o'clock. If the Queen wants to give me any message or see me herself, she can find me
there. So here goes the jewel back in this envelope, and there's a letter in there, too, in
case you forget my name and Dan Smooth's name, and, darling, here you are.

| 85 |

Queen or no Queen, it's getting old doing this, he thought—older if no Queen. I'm getting old. Open the night case. Unlock the hard case and open that. That's not breaking
the law, exactly, because a hotel room is a residence if you've paid for it, and even in California a citizen is allowed to play with his own possessions at home. The slide is open.
Firmly thumb-nudge fifteen rounds into the magazine, which now waits ready to be fed
into that oily hole, so do just that, then thumb the catch to close the slide: *snick*—a
much less noisy sound than the bolt-slam of a street-sweeper shotgun, but authoritative
nonetheless, and comforting to the proposective user. Now squeeze the release stud;
catch the magazine as it returns to you, reborn from the grip. Fourteen rounds in it now,
one left behind; add another copper candy (I recommend exploding hollowpoints).
With the heel of your hand, shove the magazine back inside. Sixteen rounds, one of
them chambered. Here it is now, your cold heavy little underarm pal. What would
Smooth say about the smell of that? Zip up your jacket and look in the mirror to see how
obvious the bulge is. If you feel so inclined, wash the lead off your fingers by means of
this sink whose porcelain is stained yellow by the piss of whores and johns. Increasing
the volume on the television, which now offered for his moral furthering a science fiction program about men kept as sex slaves in a world of beautiful hungry women, he
went out, locked the door as far as it was capable of being locked, descended past the Indian woman, who cried out: Is she gone yet? If she isn't, you're gonna have to pay double. Is she still in your room? and after passing through both gratings, which is to say
semipermeable steel membranes, found himself gazing upon the red letters of the Walgreens pharmacy shining like stars, the tail of the "g" flickering. A rush of hatred for
everything he saw spewed out of his soul, spreading like the concentric circular patterns
of the subway station's tiles until it had reached the farthest building that he could see.
Everything stank. A homeless man's fat dog ran past as quickly as a whore can stuff fifty
bucks down between her tits. His owner, vainly seeking to overtake him, stumped along
on crutches, a bedroll upon his shoulders, cursing. Right at the curb a quartet of mari-
achi musicians in white cowboy hats formed and began singing loudly, their blank faces
and sadly drooping moustaches as red as new bricks in the rain. The red Walgreens sign
made them redder. Now the night-leaners began to come out from their burrows, thickening the bases of lampposts while they got the lay of the land, then striding shadow-
legged across the light-stained street . . .

Five minutes before ten. He walked down Sixteenth past the old theater and waited.
No whores at all, he saw; perhaps there'd been a sweep; let's see, it was getting on the end
of the month, so their general assistance checks ought to have been long spent by now;
where were they? A sweep, then; this was an election year.

Across the street an addict was mumbling, his words, like Dan Smooth's, reminiscent of the structure of graphite, which is to say comprised of slender hexagonal plates of atoms which slough off at a touch like the multitudinous crusts of a Turkish pastry.

Then, at long last, the tall man came, tall as some dancer on stilts, that tall dark man who moved with easy intelligence, flaunting under his arm, his long grey arm which drooped down like a freeway off-ramp, the envelope called "EVIDENCE."

Tyler raised his hand, like a parachutist about to pull his rip cord. —I'm the one, he said.

I'm not here to hurt you, the tall man said. She'll see you now.

You work for her?

You asking my business? said the tall man.

If you want to take me someplace, I've got a right to ask what you do. I'm not messing with anybody's business. You can ask that chickie who brought you the envelope if I treated her wrong.

She went and told me you didn't pay for her time, the tall man said.

Well, I gave her twenty, Tyler said. You can either believe me or not believe me.

Matter of fact, I believe you. And I'm gonna tell the Queen, too. That white bitch can lie on her own time. Now, I don't have all night. You coming or not?

I'll walk with you, Tyler said.

The tall man slipped the envelope called "EVIDENCE" under the windshield of an abandoned car, and began to walk rapidly down Capp Street, never looking back. Tyler followed as quickly as he could. At Eighteeth they turned south and continued all the way to the old mayonnaise factory at Harrison without speaking, and then the tall man said over his shoulder: You a cop?

Nope.

You a vig?

What's that?

Vigilante.

Not me.

That's good. We don't have much use for vigs.

They kept walking, street to side-street, side-street to alley, and then suddenly they were in a tunnel that Tyler had never seen before, shiny-scaled like the Broadway tunnel upon whose walls crawled the ghosts of cars and the squiggly fire-lines of reflected taillights; but here there was no traffic, although from somewhere came the dull ocean-boom of many vehicles; no, it was stale air from many ducts, or maybe traffic from elsewhere coming through by conduction. The tunnel was narrow, and they went in single file, the tall man's heels ahead of him clapping lightly down upon plates of textured metal, the ceiling rainbowed with all the colors of dirty gold. Far ahead of them, he saw a shaveheaded woman carrying a suitcase. She vanished into one of the square tomblike openings which had been so occasionally spaced into the yellow walls.

| 86 |

What about the octopus-minded of this world? They were wriggling their fingers, which were as thick and cold and white as the bars of a hospital bed. What about Tyler and Brady? Well, they were as confident (or unwary, perhaps) as the legs that marched, ran, trudged and danced across that spidery whirr of shade on the sidewalk where a maple's leaf-souls shimmered and shook in the shadow of a breeze; the legs were darkened and eaten by it as it trembled; what if the sidewalk opened suddenly there like a rotten decomposing glacier? Three policemen walked through the shadow, and their navy blue uniforms became darker. What if a world tore itself open right beneath their shiny shoes? Deep within, we might find people living according to the same cultural laws as that species of slavemaking ants called *Formica (Polyerges) rufescens*, about which Darwin wrote: *This ant is absolutely dependent on its slaves; without their aid, the species would certainly become extinct in a single year. The males and fertile females do no work of any kind, and the workers or sterile females, though most energetic and courageous in capturing slaves, do no other work. They are incapable of making their own nests, or of feeding their own larvae.* Down, down! A spider-girl's chin pressed itself against the floor, eyeballs rolling. Tyler experienced the same feeling that he always had when after a long browse in the secret, cozy, and almost airy Poetry Room upstairs at City Lights where the window looked out on brick walls, a flat roof, and above everything a row of beautifully dancing laundry—he was almost in the sky, the world muffled and distant—he then passed the row of black and white Beatnik postcards and began to descend the long steep black-treaded stairs which pulled him down past clumps of newspapers and manifestoes, down, down, back into the world. *When the old nest is found inconvenient, and they have to migrate, it is the slaves which determine the migration, and actually carry their masters in their jaws. So utterly helpless are the masters, that when Huber shut up thirty of them without a slave, but with plenty of the food they like best, and with their own larvae and pupae to stimulate them to work, they did nothing; they could not even feed themselves, and many perished of hunger. Huber then introduced a single slave (F. fusca), and she instantly set to work, fed and saved the survivors, made some cells and tended the larvae, and put all to rights. What could be more extraordinary than these well-ascertained facts?*

What should I draw? said the Queen aloud. Something like a shark or a stingray. Nothing cute. My girls don't like nothing too cute. What's gonna make Domino happy? What's gonna make Strawberry come? What's gonna make Kitty some fresh money? — Magic marker in hand, she upstretched against the concrete wall behind the grating, straining upward in her high heels so that her fringed skirt danced, smiling a little as she drew. She did the charcoal-colored eyes as far above her head as she could reach. The fringes quivered against her buttocks. Her little feet silently slid upon the light-pocked concrete.

A woman with two shadows raised and lowered her arm with a strangely mechanical air. Her ankle-length white dress was as porcelain. She froze, turned, seeming to stand on a rotating platform rather than move herself. Her hand-edges chopped air like knives. She bent, bowing to one of her shadows, while the shadow behind bowed to her. Now she joined with her shadow, becoming a vast writhing mound.

What is it, Sapphire? asked the Queen.

The porcelain woman covered her face and giggled. Then she began to stammer: S-s-s-some-b-b-b-body . . .

Oh, somebody's here, huh? What a good girl. Always looking out for your Queen. C'mere, baby. Queen's gonna kiss your pussy . . .

L-l-l-uh . . .

Love you, too, Sapphire. Lemme kiss you. Quickly now. Can't keep guests waiting.

The girl approached, shyly scuttling sideways, timidly entered the Queen's arms. Sweat formed like milk on her porcelain face, and her pale legs began to writhe in the darkness.

Uh-uh-uh. Oh. Oh. *Oh,* oh, oh.

That's a good girl. That's my girl. You'll always be Queen's little girl. Now go let the man in.

| 87 |

An old, old face, he thought when he saw her; a face without any whites in the eyes anymore, a palish head upon a dark dress. Old, but maybe not so old—but a middle-aged black woman, just as Smooth had said. Older than in the photo—old, old!

What's your name, please, ma'am? he said.

Africa, replied the woman with a faint smile. I'm the Queen.

She had a codeine girl's sleepy froggy voice, her perfume and soft crackly sweater further manifestations of the same, a narcotic blood that dizzied with a sweet scent that was half a stench—well, maybe she actually smelled like smoked leather.

Take my cigarette, she said to Sapphire. And go make them be quiet.

The porcelain girl fled, her shining mouth pulsating with strings of mucus. Distant whispers ceased, and the silence crawled in his ears like sweat.

So there's this guy who wants to do business, Tyler said. Mr. Brady's his name. One of those losers with money. I don't like him and I guess he doesn't like me, because he fired me, but he's been looking for you.

Are you the one who wrote me those letters? said the Queen.

Yes, ma'am.

And you beat up one of my girls, she said.

No, that was him. That wasn't me.

But you set her up to get beaten up.

I have some responsibility for that, he admitted. I thought he was too dumb to know the difference. I didn't know you were for real, and I thought she could fake it and he'd pay her and then she'd give me a kickback. I'm sorry. I looked for her after that, but I never saw her. If you can tell me where she is, I'd like to make amends. Financial amends.

You'll make amends to me, the Queen said.

Here's two hundred bucks, he said, pulling out ten twenties. I wish it could be more. But I didn't beat her up and this is my money which I'll never get paid back and work hasn't been going very well lately.

What kind of work?

I'm a P.I.

Take his money, Justin, said the Queen.

He saw the tall man's hand. He began to count money into it, and a flashlight shone upon the bills by magic.

The flashlight wandered. Hunched and kneeling, with her hands over her face, the porcelain girl was a whitish thing, a strange staring thing, her dress like a sail catching in a breeze. It widened as she leaned back and spread her legs. Imperceptibly it stretched, like a sail catching air. Her eyes almost closed, her wrists gripped one another in turn. Then she began to masturbate. In the stillness, Tyler could hear the creaking of her shoes. She began to club her temples with her bent wrists, like a wrought-up windup doll.

You're carryin' a piece, the Queen said.

Yes, ma'am.

Justin, take his piece.

Tyler hesitated for a moment. Then, deciding to see matters through, he drew the gun out, careful to keep it downpointed.

Mind if I make it safe? he asked.

Go ahead.

He dropped the magazine out, brought the slide back to unchamber the sixteenth round, put magazine and cartridge into his coat pocket, handed the tall man his gun.

And you're Tyler? said the Queen.

Yes, ma'am.

And the fellow lookin' for me?

Jonas Brady from Missouri. That's his name, ma'am. You know him?

Sure I know him, she said with a grin. *Klexter, klokan, kladd, kludd, kligrapp . . .*

He heard a sharp click, and tensed, believing for a moment that somebody had loaded his gun, but then the omniscient flashlight showed him a drop of water trembling on the concrete ceiling; when it fell to the floor its echo harshly slammed. He nodded then. The Queen's eyes glittered ironically.

And why are you here? she said then.

I—I want to know you, he replied, to his own surprise. (That was what he kept expecting Dan Smooth to say.)

Ah, said the Queen.

He waited.

Down on your belly, said the Queen. Hands behind your head.

He obeyed. He was in for anything now. The floor was damp.

Okay. C'mere. Stay on your belly. Crawl over here like a worm. Closer. Now slide your hands down back of your neck. Raise your head and look at me. Can you see me? Now I'm going to spit in your mouth. I want you to raise your head and open your mouth wide for me like a little baby bird.

She leaned forward, her eyes hurting and confusing him, and her face descended, her eyes shining almost malignantly, and then her full lips began to open and somebody shone the flashlight on them and her lower lip began to glisten with spittle, and then a long slender thread of it crawled down from her lip, with much the same speed as a spider descending its strand, and he was shocked to find how much he wanted that spittle inside his mouth. He didn't even know why he wanted it. Warm and thick, it began to coil round and round upon his tongue. He felt it before he tasted it. She leaned closer, her face above him like a falling planet so that she was almost kissing him. Then a foaming frothing tide of saliva spilled into his mouth as she breathed on his face. Her breath smelled like cunt. Her spit tasted like cunt.

Later, when she let him go out, he saw the spider-girl advancing on her chin, on her knees and on her palms.

| 88 |

He drove home, dropped two credit card bills into the trash, opened an official-looking letter which crowed: **IMPORTANT NOTICE! You may already qualify for our unique Debt Consolidation Loan up to $500,000 NATIONWIDE!** (he filed that likewise in the garbage), and then, gazing out the kitchen window at the creeping silver ocean-fog, he tapped his ballpoint against his teeth and added to the details description sheet:

```
TEETH      White
EARS       Oval, L ear only pierced
FINGERNAILS      Long, unpainted, dirt under nails
```

He went back to the beginning of the form, thought for awhile, and wrote:

```
AGE      Approx. 45.
```

Then he changed it back to:

```
AGE      Approx. 40.
```

He made other corrections:

```
CLOTHING      Castoffs? Sweatshirt, jeans, tennis shoes.
JEWELRY      Large hoop earring in L ear, bangles on left
wrist
PECULIARITIES      Round scar on right calf (bullet
wound?), abscess marks on arms, tattoo of skull on left
wrist, mole on left cheek, strong smell of perfume.
```

He stared at the form, which now seemed as vain to him as the scribbles on the walls of a hard-luck hotel. He felt tired and woolly-headed. The angry, anxious sadness that he felt in his chest like a hard chestnut whenever Irene occurred to him now ruled him, and, massaging his breastbone, he had to admit the evidence: There was, as Smooth had said, absolutely no reason for him to be seeking out the Queen. But the seeking was over now, and maybe something would come next to rouse either further sadness or further alarm. It was his characteristic to admit what he could not change—which is to say, he confessed it to himself if not to others. Once Irene had said to him on the telephone: I could never be angry with you, and he'd been so happy that he'd cried. Whenever she had spoken to him he had always felt eased, except that last time in the restaurant on Geary Street when her decision had already entombed her; she used to make him feel the same way that his friend Mikey did when he came back from Alcoholics Anonymous meetings; Mikey had been sober for forty-two years, but twice a week he went to A.A. and talked and listened to his own kin, then got relief; sometimes he got sick and couldn't go, and then he turned desperate and mean. Tyler didn't turn mean, but he knew the other feeling all too well, the feeling of no rent money, and John's anger, and his mother's reproach, and loneliness, loneliness above all—how he loved Irene! She was his sickness, his dear little disease. God and Irene, are you one and the same? Because I can't find either of you. Not that I ever believed in You, God. But, Irene, I believe in you just as much even though I can't touch you; Irene, I've got to get you back. Your death is an impossibility. My need proclaims that. I'm going to find you somehow, or else I'll pretend.

On the details description form he added to **PECULIARITIES**:
Lesbian or bisexual.

| 89 |

Now, the court thing, I have absolutely no control there, Dan Smooth was saying on the phone. And I don't have the time to get involved.

He hung up. —FBI turds, he muttered.

Lacing his fingers together, he then surveyed Tyler and said: How did it go?

I saw her, said Tyler. I don't know what to make of it.

I like you more and more, Henry. You don't bullshit. Sit back, relax, pour yourself some Black Velvet. Working man's drunk. I want to finish watching this. I was right in the middle of the good part when that administrative bitch called. Speaking of bitches, how's Mugsy?

How do you know the name of my mother's dog?

It's in your file, fella. Right under the note about Black Velvet.

You've been spying on me?

For the Queen, agreed Smooth. He turned the knob of the dusty old television set, which was not quite at arm's length from his eyes, and indented the blue button of the videocassette recorder. The movie resumed.

The girl shook her hair out of her eyes as the man put his penis into her butt. There was not any sound.

Imagine videoing this, said Smooth. Imagine the *happiness.*

Tyler sighed and poured himself a drink. —Yeah, just imagine, he said.

Let me find this, muttered Smooth. Just one second. Now, see, what I'd really like to find here . . .

A young boy's milk-white buttocks were wiggling

There was one other kind of really really bizarre scenario, said Smooth. It involved lots and lots of toilet paper. No, you really have to see this.

Here were glowing aliens, shimmering green watercolor-light; the aliens kept bowing toward each others' middles.

To me this is really erotic, said Smooth. Really really erotic. Almost always, part of it is the fantasy aspect. Now, in this one, I'm the father and he's the bad boy. I'm saying right here: Are you ready for a B.M. fantasy? and he says yes. I say, lean back in the chair. He says: Danny, I've had this fantasy, too.

You think he meant it or he was saying it to get more money out of you?

I think he meant it, Henry. I wasn't paying him anything.

Tyler refilled his glass.

He's already fourteen, Smooth went on. I still love him. These things happen. Also, as I was telling you earlier, the whole thing happened in my mind.

You mean he's just virtual?

Well, it's a confessional time for me, said Smooth almost shyly. I also really don't want to like fuck up and do something evil. This scenario is . . .

His voice became silent for a moment. Then he said: I've never hurt anybody, Henry.

I believe you, Tyler said. I guess I'm a Canaanite, just like you said.

The Queen saw that right off, Henry. Don't think she didn't. You're in now, boy.

Smooth swallowed, drummed his fingers, and gazed into Tyler's face very very earnestly. Finally he whispered: See, there is this other thing. The Queen is so gorgeous sometimes. And always so special to me.

| 90 |

Down the hall from the room upon whose door a sign read **DO NOT DISTURB—I DON'T HAVE NOT A THING—PLEASE DON'T KNOCK** there was a room on whose door somebody had written and taped a sign which read **IF YOU WANT SOMETHING, DON'T ASK. IF YOU REALLY NEED IT, GO ELSEWHERE** and across from that door was a door charred and kicked and smeared and scraped, whose upper half had been replaced by plywood already splintered by abuse, and whose door-knob had given way to a handle held in place by two Phillips head screws now worked half out; Tyler had had to turn them in again with the point of his pocketknife; and in-side that room, rendered holy by an incandescent doughnut in place of any lightbulb, Dan Smooth was sitting at the foot of the bed like a wise grave doctor; and the junked-out whore named Sunflower, who'd a quarter-hour before stirred the white lump into the rust-colored liquid in the bottlecap, heaped it to bare lukewarmness, and fed it to her hungry arm on the second stab, now lay on her side mumbling so sadly in a soft hoarse voice; she was naked because Tyler had given her money for the dope, and so when she came with him she'd stripped by habit; it was likewise by habit as well as concern that Tyler sat stroking her pimpled buttock as he would have stroked the forehead of a good dog or a sick child, as he would have had somebody stroke him if he could have found anybody like Irene, whom he could have been a good dog to.

. . . 'Cause I slept there all night, he bought me a burrito and then he told me: That's four dollars right there. That's how he treated me, the whore said. Are you listening to me?

Yeah, I'm listening, sweetheart, said Tyler.

Sighing, Dan Smooth got up and began to piss gently into the sink. When he had fin-ished, he stood there for a moment buttoning his fly. Then he lightly tapped his finger-nail against the faucet.

The whore's eyes jerked open in terror. —Is that a knife? she said.

It's okay, Tyler said.

What is it? Is it a gun? Is he loading a gun?

No, honey. He's just making music in the sink.

Oh, said the whore, subsiding. He heard her weary breathing. He liked her and was sorry for her. She was twenty years old and looked fifty. She was ruined.

I have so much respect for you and the both of you that I trespass with, she said with an effort.

I respect you, too, Sunflower, he said.

Hey, can you pop this zit on my butt?

This one? It's pretty flat.

I want the white stuff to come out, the whore fretted. Can you pop it for me, please?

Okay, said Tyler, setting thumb and forefinger pliers-like about the red spot and dig-ging into the flabby flesh. Nothing came out.

Is that better? he said.

Yeah, that's a lot better, she sighed. Feels like lots of white stuff came out. You wanna know me? You wanna listen to me? Are you listening to me?

Here I am, Sunflower. Here I am listening.

My father fucked my sister first time when she was five. He fucked her doggy-style, and he put his hand over her mouth so she couldn't scream. Her pussy was all bloody and her asshole was all bloody. There was blood coming down to her knees. Then he fucked me when I was five, and then he fucked my other sister when she was five. But my other sister went and told on him. So me and my sister told my father not to do that no more . . .

And he listened to you?

Yeah, the whore said. Tears boiled out of her eyes.

He stopped fucking your sister? said Tyler gently.

Yeah. He, uh, well, he . . . he . . .

He fucked you and your older sister instead?

Just me, she sobbed. My sister couldn't take it. Said it hurt too much. But I—I heard the youngest crying, and when I saw the blood, I knew . . .

It's okay now, sweetheart. It's okay.

I wanna be a shield, she said. I was a shield for my sister, and now I protect all the men who come to me. They give me their pain. It comes out their cockheads. It just hits me. It just hurts me. It stays with me. That's all I wanna do. I wanna be a shield for all the men in this world, and all the women, and all the kids. They can come and shit on my face if they want to; they can even shit on my goddamned face. You wanna shit on my face?

No thanks, said Tyler, squeezing her hand. That wouldn't make me feel happy.

But did Maj spit in your mouth?

Yes, she did.

I knew it. I could see it.

She lay still for a while. Dan Smooth opened the tap but no water came out.

Hey, how much did you gimme? she said.

Twenty.

And what about your friend? Why's he here listening? He was supposed to gimme thirty, and he didn't give me squat.

He'll give you ten.

I love you, the whore wept. I love you. I'm so alone and I have so many contacts.

I love you, too, said Tyler, because he would have been her shield, too, if he could.

No! she screamed. Don't say that! I'm here and you're not here—

She fell asleep, and began snoring loudly. Mouth open, face flushed, she opened and then re-closed her eyes, sinking into the earth of dreams, her knees studded with immense white circular scars, her black-grimed toes faintly twitching, and in her sleep she continued to scratch at those angry speckles on her buttocks.

Four knocks, and they let the Queen in. The Queen was alone, but three tall black men stood waiting in the hall outside. She was wearing a man's hooded sweatshirt which shadowed and overhung her dark old face into anonymity. Dan Smooth bolted the door. She put her left arm on her hip, threw her head back and extended her right wrist to be kissed. Tyler got down on his knees to do the honors. —You brown-noser! laughed the Queen, pleased. You heard what our friend says about noses? Hah! Now what about you, Danny boy?

Dan Smooth bent over the Queen's hand.

The Queen shook her hood off and stood there for a moment, smiling almost grimly. On the bed continued the long, slow, gasping breaths of sleep.

You gentlemen owe me twenty in visitor fees, she said.

This dump charged you?

They always charge me. They don't know.

One Queen, three bodyguards, cackled Smooth, pulling a twenty-dollar bill from his sleeve.

Good arithmetic, said the Queen. But why can't you multiply?

They're not old enough to bleed when I fuck 'em, said Smooth.

Did you get off on Sunflower's story? said Tyler challengingly. She bleeds from both ends.

You don't need to pick on him, Henry, said the Queen. Danny's a good man. Sunflower's daddy wasn't. We would have taken care of him but Sunflower didn't want that. Sunflower's my baby, she cooed, kissing the woman's dirty toes.

She turned to Tyler and said: You see what she's about? You see why she's good? Jesus Himself ain't fit to pop her zit like you done. Jesus on the very cross of torture and shame never suffered like she suffered. And I don't care how much He gave. He never gave like she did. I know her so well. Queen's come to give her little baby her reward. My baby, my darling little baby. Queen's heart's gonna break.

And between the naked woman's legs she laid five one hundred dollar bills and a baggie with enough China white for Sunflower to kill herself ten times over.

Tyler said nothing. The Queen looked him in the eye and said: It's up to her. Gotta give her some happiness. If she don't O.D., she can come back to me for more favors. Queen'll always take care of her. If she wants to go into rehab she can. If she wants to sell that powder she can. But I know she gonna wanna take that happiness. I know she gonna wanna go home.

| 91 |

He saw that for himself, said Smooth, and Tyler realized now that the Queen, who was both very busy and very subtle, had come not only to see to Sunflower but also to judge him and perhaps to try him more deeply also. Spitting in his mouth wasn't enough. —I can vouch for old Hanky-Panky here, Smooth went on. He saw the goodness. We don't none of us have to be riding him. I knew his sad eyes from the first. He and Sunflower have the same sad eyes.

How many are like her? said Tyler.

She's one of the best right now, the Queen said. Queen's not gonna tell you all she knows, but there's several. Well, they wear out. In this town, maybe twenty thirty forty girls are our shields. They take the pain and keep it. They help all the rest. You wanna see how much pain she's got inside her? Look here.

Partly unzipping her sweatshirt, she reached down her neck and presently pulled out what resembled a copper penny with eyes and lightning bolts carved or engraved into it, and protruding octopus-fashion from its edges many copper wires knotted into tiny holes in the disk; the ends of the wires had been wrapped around what might have been black seeds.

Got any rubbers on you, Smooth? she said.

Let's see now. Let's see, the man said, thoughtfully licking his lips. Oh, here's an old dried out one under the bed. Smells pretty fresh . . .

Well, whack it against the wall or something. Clean it off.

How about a plain rubber band? said Smooth. I keep one around my address book.

Yeah, that'll do. Now, tie it around the charm, *respectful* like. Good. You just watch this, Henry. Don't say nothing; don't do nothing. Just *observe*. Danny, hold the rubber part. Don't touch the copper, 'cause it's magic. Now touch it to her. Slowly. No, wait. You do it, Smooth. But she's used to you, Henry, so you should hold her hand. She's gonna be scared. Okay, Danny boy. Give him a show. It's only a show.

Dangling the copper spider by its improvised thong, old Dan Smooth, holding his breath, bent over the recumbent woman and slowly began easing it down above her ankle while the Queen stood praying: *In the name of the Mother and the Daughter and the Holy Ghost!* and the strands of wire began to writhe and quiver of their own accord. One touched flesh, and then the light flickered and went out, and the stinking darkness exploded with deep blue sparks and Sunflower jerked up screaming like she had that first time when her father sodomized her and in the room across the hall a radio immediately went on loud because they didn't want to know about any screams. Tyler felt no electric shock. He held Sunflower's hand as tightly as he could and wiped the tears from her eyes, and then the lights came back on as Dan Smooth took the talisman away and Sunflower fell back on the bed snoring.

She won't remember nothing, said the Queen. See, that's all the pain she has inside her. Too much for any human being to get out even by magic.

| 92 |

We take pride in our Queen, because she has the power, Smooth was explaining brightly. Glowing in the darkness. Talk about animal magnetism! Well, believe you me . . .

It didn't hurt her, Henry, if that's what you're thinking, said the Queen.

What about *his* pain? asked Smooth, with a sickening mixture of malice and pity. Hank'd be a crybaby if he knew how—look into those eyes of his, Maj; how can we get that pain out of his eyes?

That's what everybody asks me, said the Queen with brightly bitter humor. —As if I'm not the biggest shield of them all! Well, it's an honor, I know.

Tyler said nothing. —Of course it's only his second time, Smooth finally blurted, looking him up and down and shaking his head.

(Outside, in the hallway, an old woman was shouting: Fook a-you, beetch! Goddamn it! Fook-a-you! Oh, I sorry. I fook a-you today, you fook-a me tomorrow. Fook-a I sorry!)

Smooth leaned forward and whispered so that the hot wet breath tickled Tyler's ear: Now imagine if Sunflower woke up and *we* knew but *she* didn't know that there was a window there.

| 93 |

Certain appearances to the contrary, Dan Smooth was, as Dostoyevsky would have put it, an excellent man. First of all, the loathing which his so-called proclivities caused others to feel was more than counterbalanced by his usefulness to society. The police relied on Smooth, and consequently protected him, on the understanding that he would do nothing indiscreet. Indiscretion meant, for instance, raping and murdering a child. As it happened, Smooth was more bark than bite. He did not merely take pleasure in offending others (other adults, that is); he had a positive need to do so. This characteristic in no way contradicted his general spirit of friendliness and helpfulness; like most people whose thoughts or needs are a little bit odd, Smooth inspired revulsion among the homogenous masses of car-drivers, television-watchers, jurors, and baseball addicts. With children he had a way—or, rather, a *quality,* for "way" implies method—which drew them to him. On airplanes, infants would drop their pacifiers, reaching out to touch his nose; and when he'd bend to pick up the slobbery things, the children would strain toward his hand. —Are you ready? he'd say to the ones who could talk. —Yeah, they'd say shyly. —Are you ready? he'd whisper dramatically. Are you ready to *fly?* —To their parents, had they been unaccompanied by their delicious offspring, and had Smooth believed that he could get away with it (for he was realistic to the point of cowardice), he might have said with a pleasant smile: Excuse me, but would you mind if I sniffed your asshole? Dogs do that, you know. —Mostly, being the graduate of many bitter experiments, he kept to himself, and served up silence with the pleasant smile. Take a baby bird in your hands, so that it absorbs your smell, and its parents will shun it to the very death. Take an ant from one nest and drop it in another; the ant-law requires that it be destroyed. Galileo and Göring, Jesus and Socrates, eccentrics, murderers and saints—all must be neutralized by the swarming super-organism in any way possible. Only three paths for such creatures can preserve them. The first is to hide, like terrorists and hermits; the second is to be in some measure needful or powerful, like rocket-scientists, kings and jesters; the third is to defy. Dan Smooth in fact employed all of these strategies. He had many connections, but few friends, and his neighbors did not know his name. The police, as I said, found him useful; few sex crimes investigators were more thorough than Dan Smooth; and his informants in the demimonde and the holy order of pedophiles supplied him with information of a consistently high purity. The famous Kaylin Kohler case, in which a ten-year-old girl from Redding was abducted from her own home, raped, tortured, and buried alive, was solved thanks to a tip from Dan Smooth, whose electronic alias had been Ticklequick; entering a "chat room" from his personal computer, he announced his intention of trading seventy-five cubic centimeters of saliva from a twelve-year-old Caucasian boy named Rodney for an equivalent volume of urine from an African-American female of similar age—or, to quote his message in full:

Hey, pervs! Ticklequick is back! Hv. 75 c.c. vanillaspit (Rodney, guarant'd 12, uncircumc. & hairless) for swap; seek chocopiss from virg. hairless slit 12 & under: MUST BE FRESH. Also NEED NEED NEED photos for swap. PLEASE NO RECOG. HEAD-SHOTS. Help Ticklequick put lemon on his lips. E-mail Big T!

Under FBI supervision, Dan Smooth spat into several dozen test tubes to furnish the nectar of fictitious Rodney; in exchange the FBI received and analyzed eighteen test tubes of piss, two of which contained significant levels of both testosterone and alcohol, one of which evidently came from a lactating woman, and one of which proved to be so old (the collector who sent it had perhaps kept it in a jar in some hot garage in the Central Valley for twenty years) that it could not be analyzed; these were discarded, leaving fourteen samples whose levels of estradiol, estrone, estriol, and pituitary gonadotropins were consonant with those of prepubescent girls. Thanks to improvements in laboratory techniques, only two of these were disqualified as nonsecretors, meaning that they were so chemically taciturn that not even the blood group could be read; this left an even dozen samples of young girls' urine, which the FBI grimacingly permitted Dan Smooth to sniff and crow over, arranging the shining test tubes in order from pale transparent lemon to the rich dark orange-brown characteristic of a pure palladium photograph; and of course Smooth made many such comments as: This one ate asparagus for dinner, I know. Ah, if only I could have been there when she peed! —for, as I mentioned, Dan Smooth followed all three strategies, the latter one being bravado and defiance; he was by his nature kin to the killer, the exception being that he did not kill; and so the FBI ran DNA matches on those twelve test tubes of yellow light and dark, and the ninth test tube granted them a positive lock on Kaylin Kohler's DNA, which led them to one Eugene Kenneth Brewington, who was convicted the following year, sentenced to death, and, after eight years as a guest of the state of California, at great expense actually executed by lethal injection, as a result of which Mr. Brewington's attorney fell upon hard times and the district attorney, two FBI investigators, one forensic technician, and one field investigator in Redding received promotions, while Dan Smooth received no public acknowledgment whatsoever, but an obscure government draft for twelve thousand dollars arrived in his post office box one day, and a dispute which he was having with the Internal Revenue Service was abruptly decided in his favor, and he received a permit to carry a concealed weapon and a strange sort of untouchable status within the circles of law enforcement, as if he were one of those captive cobras in Bangkok whose venom can be milked for the greater good; and his cachet was confirmed when a hard gaunt FBI woman wanted to investigate and arrest the other eleven finalists in that competition of gold-filled test tubes, but Ticklequick, arguing that so doing would block his channels of information forever, not only succeeded in protecting his peers but even managed to obtain by special courier about two weeks after Mr. Brewington's execution those eleven vials of vintage for his supposed delectation; needless to say, they had gone sour in that time, and Smooth's real motive was simply to destroy that evidence once and for all, since he was well acquainted with three of the eleven collectors, and suspected the identities of two more; by the Golden Rule, so to speak, they would have done as much for him. The FBI woman became Smooth's enemy, but he for his part was so filled with pride and happiness at the way that everything had turned out that he contented himself with a few mild remarks to her, such as: Is it true that you have an eleven-year-old daughter? I'd love to lick her cunt. —Dan Smooth, needless to say, was not stupid. The FBI woman did not have any children, and he knew that; thus his utterance, which came as naturally to him as any disquisition on the weather, could not be considered as any kind of threat. Since he could not have her friendship, he actively courted and received her hatred, so that when he returned to his house in Sacramento it was in a haze of triumph, magnified by his possession of the eleven test tubes, whose contents he immediately decanted and poured down the toilet. The test tubes themselves, which might contain residue even after thorough washing (although, their official seals having been broken, they were unlikely to find use as evidence) he gave to an acquaintance—not a friend, mind you, not a friend! —who, a former member of an armed anti-government militia in Oakland, now lived in Roseville, pursued a lucrative vocation as a non-union

electrician, and on weekends experimented with the manufacture of strange and sometimes illegal handgun cartridges. This man had perfected the exploding bullet, the mer-
cury-tipped bullet, the poisoned bullet; he had even for his own amusement
hand-loaded special ammunition designed to murder the shooter rather than the target:
within the casing's coppery blankness lay, in addition to the gunpowder, a distant de-
scendant of C-4 explosive guaranteed upon firing to turn a gun into a rapidly expanding constellation of shrapnel. Such cartridges were difficult to test, but Dan Smooth's
acquaintance had worked it all out in his head. Testing would almost have been cheating; unquestionably it would have evinced weakness of faith. The electrician was happy
just to keep his little babies in a regular factory ammunition box; nobody knew their nature but he. When Smooth proposed that he create in his bullet-caster an amalgam of
lead and brittle glass which would shatter upon contact with flesh, and when Smooth
further informed his acquaintance that this was genuine FBI glass, the electrician
grinned happily. Smooth stayed to watch the glass be disposed of. The electrician mixed
him a rum and Coke, and then he drove home. It was a hot Sunday afternoon. —The
earwax of a ten-year-old child, he muttered with a laugh. He sat in the back yard sweating. His tomato-soup-colored tom-cat slept on the grass beside the corpse of a young
bluejay which it had slowly tortured and killed. Smooth did not seat himself before his
computer keyboard which resembled a grimy ear of Indian corn; he did not become
Ticklequick, because he quite correctly supposed that the FBI monitored all his keystrokes. Besides, all that had been simply to protect the Queen. It had been the Queen,
of course, who'd found the killer for him. Like him, she received no recognition from the
public; she'd acted simply out of goodness. At FBI expense, Smooth had brought her an
immense bouquet of red, white and yellow roses, those being the color of his three favorite bodily fluids.

All this sounds perhaps like farce, so perhaps we should look deeper into Dan
Smooth's soul. About his sexual attraction to children it should be said that for him—in
his own mind, at least—it had all begun as a matter of moral and intellectual curiosity.
It is easy to disbelieve such an explanation, easy to insist that such but rationalizes his
evil urge. But since other people ultimately remain unknowable, we may as well accept
their own explanations of themselves as first approximations, barring further examination. He read in the newspaper one day about a father convicted of molesting his son
and daughter, who were twelve and eight, respectively. The account, typically dry, grim
and brief, merely announced that both children bore signs of repeated abuse, and that
the man had been sentenced to twenty-five years in prison. The mother was dead, apparently. And suddenly Smooth had a vision of the children crying as their father was
handcuffed and driven away. They would grow up in an institution, perhaps separated
from each other as well as from their father, perhaps beaten up or raped by other children, perhaps not. They would masturbate constantly, Smooth supposed (because *he*
would). How evil had the father been? Suppose—which probably had not been the
case—that he had done what he had done out of love. Suppose that he had fed and
clothed them, helped them with their homework, listened to them. Suppose that he had
witnessed them in sex play with each other, joining in only out of tenderness. Suppose
that they had voiced some childish confusion about the difference between boys and
girls, or how babies were made, and he had simply instructed them. Suppose that he had
not hurt them. Suppose that he had liked it and they had liked it, too. Suppose that what
he had done was good. We might well wonder why Dan Smooth wanted to suppose

these things. But we do have to grant him the openness of a born scientific investigator in an epoch of harshly preconceived conclusions.

Then there was the married woman who fell in love with her fourteen-year-old foster son. Her husband divorced her. She wanted to marry the boy. He wanted to marry her. When she became pregnant with his child, they threw her in jail for years. Dan Smooth could not understand why.

The curiosity of small children regarding bodily functions frequently presents an erotic component. Smooth's niece, Darcy, had become fascinated with urination at the age of four. Whenever he came to Atlanta to visit his sister, Darcy wanted to play with him, and he was simultaneously thrilled and frightened by the complicity he read in her smile. If he let himself go, he just might remember something from his own childhood which would draw him into the mirror, where, astonished and conquered by something about himself he'd never before noticed, he'd cry: *Aha!* —but that never happened. Darcy liked to be carried piggyback. When he lifted her up on his shoulders, she'd wrap her legs tightly around his neck and begin rubbing against him. Sometimes he'd have to go to the toilet, and Darcy cried when he closed the door. He actually had to lock her out. —It's just a phase that all children go through, his sister said curtly. —When Darcy was five he visited his sister for Christmas, and Darcy's older sister got the flu, so they left Smooth to babysit while they went to the doctor. Darcy was sitting in his lap watching a cartoon on television, for this happened long before videos, and her body was very little and smooth and soft, and her breath smelled like peanut butter and jelly sandwiches. She was wearing a red and green plaid dress for Christmas. The hem of it had ridden above her chubby knees. She clamped her thighs around his leg and began to slowly ride him up and down, pretending to look at the television. He did not know what to do. Suddenly she turned her head, and in her eyes he saw that look of darkly shining consciousness, which he had the incredible faith or arrogance to label *the look of original sin.* He swallowed. Grown women had on occasion looked at him that way, and accordingly infected him with their desire, but never so intensely as this. He did not know what was going to happen, but he knew that whatever happened he would never ever mention to Darcy's parents. Darcy turned her head back, but she was gazing not at the television anymore, but at her own squiggling crotch. The red and green dress had now retreated into her lap so that he could see her white underpants. Slowly his hand began to move. Smooth could not stop it, and did not want to. His hand descended through the air, inch by inch, and came to rest on Darcy's soft, pink thigh. The little girl put her hand on his hand and giggled. Then she began to hump his leg faster. His hand swam slowly up her thigh, and now it rested on her panties and he could feel how she was hot and damp there through the flimsy cotton. She opened her legs wider and with both hands pushed his palm firmly against her mound.

Over a beer in a quiet bar, he told a doctor in San Francisco about it—about that much, at least. The doctor regarded him with the same alertly bristling skepticism of any good policeman, knowing or suspecting the rest, and Smooth, not yet hardened, choked out: I didn't do anything. But she wanted it, you see. *I am sure that she wanted it.*

The doctor said nothing.

Smooth said: Is that normal?

Of course what you're telling me is not normal, the doctor said carefully.

Could the kid have wanted it?

Dan, said the doctor, these are dangerous speculations to follow. You know very well that children don't necessarily know what they want, and that what they want isn't necessarily good for them. Furthermore, while I'm not a specialist, I would say that if she was consciously aroused and seeking to arouse you as you describe—in other words, if you're not fudging a little—then she's already been a victim of abuse. Her father, perhaps . . .

I know Max pretty well, said Smooth. And he doesn't bear that mark.

Child abusers don't bear a mark, Dan. You can't tell. I could be one, or for that matter you could be one. Do you understand me?

But it's not very good science, you know, Smooth insisted. If they don't want it, then you can't do it to them, because it's abuse. If they do want it, then they must have been abused. That's what you're saying, right?

If ten minutes before dinner your niece wanted to gorge on candy and ice cream, would you let her?

Maybe on special occasions I would.

Dan, Dan!

Why is having sex necessarily bad for a child?

Oh, come off it, Dan! the doctor shouted angrily, and in his face for the first time Smooth saw the look that he would see in the faces of others for the rest of his life.

When I was a boy, I used to jerk off, Smooth said. You know that old saying: Ninety percent of all teenage boys masturbate, and the other ten percent are lying. And when my Daddy caught me, he tied my hands behind my back. I had to sleep on my side for a good two years. When I asked him why it was wrong to jerk off, he got angry, you see, the same as you're angry now, and he said that it was a sin and that it would make my pimples worse and that it would weaken my eyesight and maybe I'd even go crazy. Now, was any of that true?

Don't be so hard on your father, Dan, said the doctor with an ingratiating laugh. You're my age. We grew up before the sexual revolution. And your father—well, everybody thought that then.

But was it true?

Of course it wasn't true. But that has nothing to do with—

Yes it does. If a child wants or needs to masturbate, you're saying that that's harmless, right?

Yes, Dan, said the doctor grimly.

No matter what the age of the child?

No matter what the age of the child.

Then if a child wants to have an orgasm, and you help the child have an orgasm—

And did *you* have an orgasm when you stuck it up her, Dan? said the doctor wearily. How loudly did she scream? How much did she bleed?

He never saw that doctor again. The next year he didn't visit his sister, and the year after that Darcy was seven, and in the middle of the night, when he was asleep in the guestroom, Darcy crept in and almost silently closed the door behind her.

Let's speak of accidents. One sunset at a gasoline station in El Cerrito, they gave Tyler a restroom key and when he turned it in the door a woman's voice cried: Uh-uh-*uh!* He stood outside, a little ashamed. —Sorry, he said to her when she came out. I didn't see anything. —That's okay. You responded real quick. —Wasn't Dan Smooth in equal measure a bystander and victim of God's tricks?

She was wearing her pink nightgown with the dinosaurs on it. He could see its paleness in the dark. Her breath smelled like toothpaste and tomato soup. Gazing at him wisely with shining eyes, she put her finger to her lips as she got into his bed. Instantly she was in his arms, holding him tight as she rubbed up against him, and his penis was hard. He rolled her onto her back, and his hand was on her underpants just like before, and then his middle finger had gone inside her panties, and he brought his hand to his mouth and sucked his middle finger to get it wet and then slipped it between the lips of the child's vulva, the soft and ever so delicate lips which were to render those of any mature woman so comparatively coarse forever, so rough and hairy and repulsive to him. What was the meaning of how he felt? He was sure that he hadn't sought this out. He was equally sure that to deny and reject this experience was to do wrong both to Darcy and to himself. He knew that in a moment he was going to slip the panties from the hips of this softly giggling girl. The doctor was wrong. She had never screamed and she had never bled. But then he was equally sure that he was going to send Darcy away. He groaned with anguish, looking into her eyes. Then the doctor's words crawled inside his skull again like hungry insects, and he thought: I am not sure. I cannot be sure. And to do this and not to be sure is to do wrong.

Clenching his lips, he sat up and removed his hand from his niece's pants. He sucked on his middle finger again, just to get the taste. Where was the harm in that? The taste was sweet and rich, like sweet and sour fish in a Chinese restaurant. He almost ejaculated.

The panties had somehow worked themselves down to her knees.

You see, honey, it's time for you to go back to sleep, he made himself say.

No, Uncle Dan. Can't I please stay with you?

I'm afraid if you stay with me we'll get in trouble.

I won't tell, the girl said. I can keep secrets.

That's good, honey.

So can I stay?

He bit his lip hard.

Can I?

So you never tell secrets? he temporized.

You want to hear a secret?

Yes.

She whispered in his ear: I like playing doctor with you. That's my secret. It feels good. I want to play doctor with you again. Right now.

Well, honey, go to sleep and we'll play doctor tomorrow.

You promise?

I promise, he lied. His plan was to pack up and leave the house immediately after breakfast.

The child touched him through the jockey shorts he wore. —I want to play doctor right now. I can't sleep if I don't play doctor with you.

Her little fingers spidered so curiously up and down him. —I want to see it, she moaned. Please, Uncle Dan. I want to see it.

Once Dan Smooth had seen a pearl, a new pearl, freshwater or saltwater he couldn't remember, but it was so small and shining and pink. Wet and pink it had been, with a gleam of light on it that changed according to the angle of his glance. It was so new and clean and pink.

Suddenly Darcy began to wail loudly. —I want to see it! I want to see it!

He heard the bed creak upstairs, and then his sister's heavy footsteps. Darcy! his sister called. Darcy, honey, are you okay? Where are you, sweetie?

The silence lasted as long as man and child stared into each other's eyes. The child saw the man's fear and felt her mastery.

If I keep quiet, will you let me see it? she said.

Yes, he whispered. Later. Now pull up your underpants, quickly.

Darcy! Darcy! called the mother loudly.

He could hear her footsteps coming downstairs.

He had his hand on her underwear trying to pull it back up and she was trying to push his hand away and crying: No, no, no, no! when his sister opened the door.

That had been almost twenty years ago.

| 94 |

One night Smooth told that story to Tyler just as it had happened, but needless to say he had to elaborate upon the rich fresh animal odor of the little girl's underpants, which approximated the steam-smell from meaty minestrone; and to Tyler's mind this detail alone condemned the account as a lie, because how would Smooth have been able to sample and savor that smell without seeking it out? He didn't consider the other equally plausible possibility that Smooth had incorporated this into the old memory, either on purpose, to twit Tyler and amuse himself, or inadvertently over the years, confusing what had really happened with what might have happened, or with what had happened with other little girls who had either liked him, or not.

| 95 |

The next time Tyler saw the Queen, he was looking for a parking place near Eight-Fifty Bryant, where an industrial job required him to check the recent court records of one Earl J. Simmons; and because the police cars had taken every available spot he started round the block, assuming that he would probably have to complete the circle for nothing and then go a different way, when he spied Our Lady whispering into the tall man's ear in a doorway. The tall man noticed him right away (and once Tyler got to know him he would learn that the tall man never, ever forgot a name or a face). Tyler saw him touch her shoulder and point. She was wearing cheap dark wraparound sunglasses. There was a car behind him, but Tyler rolled down the window and waved. The Queen smiled. Her left hand rose to her cheek, and tilting her head, that gaunt, strange, small woman fluttered her little finger at him in a discreet wave.

| 96 |

That's it, that's it! Irene used to laugh when Mrs. Tyler made the dog twitch. There she goes! Oh, Mugsy!

She's had these spots for a long time, said John. Maybe it's from where they took out her ovaries or something. There's something remaining. Are you a cutie? You're happy, eh? You're happy.

Fondly he scratched the old dog. John was very good to dogs.

That had been last year. Today Mugsy was at the vet. She had bone cancer, his mother said.

His mother was lying down resting. He felt so sad, so lonely and sad, so sad, watching the silhouettes of trees on the lawn across the street slowly join the darkness. Not so far away, he heard a long freight train.

The newspaper said that somebody else had gotten shot in Oak Park. The newspaper said that Wall Street was worried about the impending economic recovery because if there were more jobs, stock prices might go up, which would be bad for certain Fortune 500 companies, he didn't understand why.

He went to see if his mother needed anything, but she was asleep, so he got into his car and drove to the Torch Club to have a beer. John had always been more partial to the Zebra Club, which was a jock kind of bar where to triumphant hurrahs the bartenders breast-squeezed pubescent girls on their birthdays and then poured double shots of the young things' favorite concoctions down their throats as a reward; doubtless they weren't allowed to do *that* anymore. Tyler didn't care either way; John had been one of the hurrahers. But who knew what kinds went into the Zebra Club these days? Tyler found himself driving past, peering into the open door. He couldn't see anything but he heard happy lustful shouts.

One good thing about Sacramento was that it was always easy to park. He stopped to get a quick shot of Scotch.

The President can't be acting alone, said the man on the next stool. Who pulls his strings?

Which ones? said Tyler, thinking about Irene.

Who pulls the President's strings? I'm asking you a question, guy.

The man was very drunk, angry and red in the face. Tyler pretended to give the matter due consideration and then concluded agreeably: Must be the Trilateral Commission.

No! the man roared, lunging. Tyler sidestepped him and tripped him. The man's head hit the floor hard, and he lay there.

Why don't you take a walk, guy, said the bartender. I'll deal with this.

All right, said Tyler.

He went out and wondered what it was that he hoped for from the Queen. Expectation was growing in his heart. He had the feeling that he might be capable of change after all, and the thought of becoming different from what he was refreshed him so deeply that at this fatal moment he agreed with himself that it hardly mattered whether he were to change for the better or for the worse. But what did the Queen have to do with any of it? Suddenly he felt the the breath of evil was on his neck, and he walked down the street shuddering.

He went home and ate low-fat yogurt with his mother, then slept. In the morning he drove to the vet's to get Mugsy. The dog stank of death. She could barely raise her head.

Well, Mom, it doesn't look good, he said.

You have to expect those things at Mugsy's age, his mother said, scarcely looking at him.

Last year, or maybe the year before, Irene and his mother had been lying together on his mother's couch. John's sleek little laptop computer glowed on the dining room table, while Tyler sat very slowly picking at his fingernails and staring at the moisture on a cold bottle of beer. The dog pillowed her head in his mother's lap. Irene said: Mom, what would you do if your dog wasn't around?

Maybe kiss John and Henry, laughed Mrs. Tyler, but since they're only interested in working . . .

Irene smiled, rubbing her eyes.

| 97 |

On that second night, Dan Smooth was at the Torch Club, too. It seemed that one couldn't get away from Dan Smooth.

Buy you a beer, boy? said the pervert.

You must be feeling flush, said Tyler. Sure, go ahead. I've made about two hundred dollars in the last month and a half.

I bet you were just reading about the economic recovery and feeling envious because you knew it didn't include you. Isn't that how it was, Henry? Isn't it?

Come to think of it, Dan, how about if I buy my own beer? And after I pay for it, you can stay here and I'll go to the Flame Club.

I think he likes me! Smooth stage-whispered to the bartender, who shrugged.

Tyler drank his beer steadily, looking away.

Sunflower woke up, said Smooth.

And then went back to sleep for good, huh?

She wanted it, Hank.

I get it. I don't know if I agree with it but I get it.

And did you see the Queen again, or didn't you see the Queen?

Yeah, I saw her. She waved one finger to me.

That means she likes you.

Everybody likes me, Dan, even you. I have so many friends, I keep trying to make enemies.

You know what, Hank?

I prefer to be called Henry, not Hank.

You don't like me, do you, Henry? Smooth was saying in his wearisome way. Did you know that you just misquoted the old proverb.

I like you fine as long as we stick to business. But we don't have any business right now, which is why I'm going to the Flame Club.

See you there, said Smooth, rising as if to accompany him.

Tyler sat down, narrowing his eyes. —I never had my very own stalker before, he muttered.

So how can we make your sister-in-law into *business?* asked Smooth with a cruel smile. I helped you out, you see, and so now I get to sock you in the balls—metaphorically, of course. Did your sister-in-law's cunt turn you on? Did it have that kind of mohawk pattern of little black hairs that so many Asian women's cunts have? You know how they shave—well, the whores, anyway. They worry about bikini lines in Asia. Now, me, I've always thought that bikini lines have their charm—as *zones,* you know. I like to see those little black hairs peeking out. It happens sometimes, and it's even sweeter when the woman's not aware of it.

Yeah, yeah, yeah, said Tyler. Your filth gets pretty boring after a while.

Fine. Did you fuck her or not?

Maybe I'll just go home. If you park in our driveway, that's trespassing, but if you want to sit in your car and watch the house from across the street, there's not much I can do. But I'm going to pull the blinds down. You won't be able to see anything.

Henry, answer the nice man. Did you do your sister-in-law or not?

How many little kids have you popped, Smooth?

It's childish, you see, to answer a question with a question. And just because you've met the Queen twice doesn't mean she trusts you. I could put in a bad word about you if I felt like it . . .

And so what if you did? What do I care if the Queen trusts me or not?

You tell me, Henry. But if I want to get you, I'll get you.

Is that a threat, Dan? I know how to deal with people who threaten me.

Now things are going ugly, Henry, and I don't want that. I never dreamed of offering you physical violence. But you keep going out of your way to hurt my feelings. Put yourself in my place, Henry. Ask yourself how you'd be feeling.

Aw, he's going to take his bat and ball and go home. Hey, I did some homework on you, Smooth. I heard about how you raped your own niece a few years back. Now I know why they call you Dan Smooth. At least you don't use sandpaper. Do you use petroleum jelly when you break 'em in? People like you should be stood up against a wall. You're a loser, Smooth, a sick, half-wit pervert. Oh, I admit that I'm a loser, too. The crazy whore was right. That shithead Brady was a loser. All I do is hang out with losers.

That's my little optimist. (Bartender, one more round each, please. Here's four dollars.) Does it get you *hard* to deprecate yourself? Does it, Henry? Does it?

Tyler rubbed his grey forehead, turning away. —Thanks for the beer, but I think you and I are through now, Smooth. I know that I owe you a favor. Anytime you want to call it in, call it in. But isn't it kind of a waste to call it in just by making me listen to you flap your stupid ugly mouth?

Maybe we could be friends, said the older man with a sudden pleading look. I told you I saw that Mark of Cain on your forehead right away, that loser's mark. You saw it on me. And right now the Queen's brought us together, but she's not going to be around forever. You don't know yet what happens to the Queen.

Tyler leaned on one elbow on the bar. —So that's what you want, huh? he said with a sour grin. You really want me to be your buddy? For how long? What's the minimum time I can get away with? And do I have to start this very evening, or do you take rain checks?

Yes, Henry, I know you hang around prostitutes. But you're not really one of them. When you pretend to be, you just act like a barbarian.

I guess that's what keeps getting in the way of any possible friendship, Tyler said. You keep condescendingly defining my life, and you also enjoy irritating me by slashing at my privacy. And that pisses me off.

I think you're implying that I should be more sincere. Well, Henry, maybe I'm sincere, but I just adopt a frivolous tone to protect myself.

Like when you talk about eating kids' earwax.

Oh, I've done it, Henry. You can trust me there.

Yeah, all right. And this morning I took a crap, but I don't have to go around telling other people about it.

Why not, Henry? I'd love to hear.

As long as we're being sincere, I guess I believe that that's true, and it kind of bothers me that it is.

Why does it bother you? You've never done anything to bother people?

I couldn't say that, said Tyler with an almost jeering laugh.

Well then.

But if I do something that I don't think other people will like, I keep it to myself.

If you needed to deal with me for business you could deal with me?

Sure.

And you have dealt with me. So that proves that you *can* deal with me, fellow Canaanite. You remember what happened to the Canaanites, don't you?

Let's see, said Tyler. Yeah. Yeah, I remember now. The Chosen People exterminated them all, or something like that. Moses got the word. No, they must not have exterminated them all, or there wouldn't be all those car bombs in the Middle East.

You might be surprised, said Smooth, but I study the Bible a good deal.

No, I'm not surprised.

I know the Bible fairly well. Not just the New Testament, but the Old Testament, too, the real stuff, where God doesn't hide His naked cruelty behind His Son. Do you believe in the Bible as literal prophecy?

Why, no, Dan, I don't.

That's good. I'm glad you're not a fanatic, Henry. Well, the Queen is quite the little believer. It's one of her sweetest qualities. (I could talk about the Queen endlessly, by the way.) Maybe that's why I want to be your friend. I love to talk about my Queen, but I'm supposed to keep her secret, so you're the only one.

Tyler waited.

I picked up my habit of Bible study from her, the older man continued. She's a Canaanite, too, you know—did I tell you that? Sometimes I repeat myself. And she's a witch like the Canaanites were—Baal, Moloch, you name it, she prays to it. I guess that's why she knows so much about the future. I can see from your expression that you're just being polite and you don't really give a rat's ass about that stuff. Well, that's fine. But you did come on to me, and you came on to the Queen, and so I suppose you want to study us as if we're bugs—or study her, at least. Read your Bible, Henry. That's the best way to know the Queen. That'll make her happy. And you don't have to take any of it literally if you don't want to. Now, as for us Canaanites, well, from our Queen we know that the Chosen People are coming to wipe us out. We may have a few car bombs ready, but I'm sorry to say that eventually they *will* wipe us out, because we're the losers. Call it an analogy if you want.

Let's see, said Tyler. The Canaanites sodomized little kids, too, didn't they? And burned them alive?

You're going nasty on me again, Henry.

Fair enough. But it's true, isn't it? I'm sorry.

That's better, Smooth said with satisfaction. That's the first time anybody's said sorry to old Dan Smooth in quite some time.

All right. And if it pleases you, I'll be sincere with you, as long as you're sincere with *me* and don't try to drag anything out of me.

Oh, so it's not a reciprocal thing, Henry boy? You give me one thing and I have to give you two things?

I won't try to drag anything out of you, either.

But that's not fair. I'm *loquacious,* Henry.

Okay then. Did you feel any remorse when you ruined your niece's life?

Would you believe that I never touched her?

No.

You're good. I send lots of love your way. Would you believe that whatever I did to her she wanted?

No.

Well, would you believe it if in return I promised to believe whatever you told me about Irene?

Don't say her name to me, sonofabitch. I never want to hear that name on anyone's lips. It hurts too much.

I'm the Queen's minister of foreign affairs, you know, Henry. Well, one of them. And if I make a recommendation to her about you one way or the other, she'll probably listen, because she likes me and she doesn't have envious *ears,* you see. I distinctly heard you ask her for help. Do you believe in the Queen?

Tyler hesitated. —I don't know, he muttered. When I see her, I believe in her, in something about her. When I'm away from her, I think it's all bullshit.

You're honest, Henry. I like that.

Thanks, Dan. I aim to please.

Spoken like a good whore.

Something else we have in common. We both have a soft spot for Domino.

Ah, said Smooth.

I'm not in love with that girl but I kind of like her. She's so *out there.*

She's had a hard life.

What got her started?

Well, it was very . . . She was found not guilty, but another judge found her guilty of violating her probation, so first he threatened her with prison, then he stuck her in a drug program, and she ran away . . .

How old was she then?

Fourteen.

That's a shame.

You've noticed that I never asked why you were looking for the Queen?

Yeah, I noticed.

Then trust me now. Go on, drink that beer. What are you really up to?

I don't even know myself, Tyler sighed. When it started, I thought that guy Brady was just a sucker and I could give him some thrills and get some money out of him without doing any harm. I never thought there was a Queen. But after a while he half convinced me, and then he canned me. And so I lost my reason for looking for the Queen. No money anymore. Then Irene died, and I needed something to do.

That's how it is for me with children, said Smooth. It's just something to do, although now I don't think I could stop it, even if I were castrated. You heard about this new chemical castration bill they're debating up here?

Dan, just what *do* you do with those kids?

Whatever. But only if they want it. I swear that by God and by the fires of all my little idols. And tell me, why do you think Mr. Brady wants to meet our Queen so much?

Oh, he can pay big. Not that I ever got much of it. He wants her for some sex act. He's the Chosen One, you see, Dan Smooth explained. He's come to burn us all out of Canaan.

| 98 |

Silently he opened a Bible, drew his slender forefinger down Psalm 106, verses 34–39:

> *They failed to exterminate the peoples,*
> * as the Lord had ordered them,*
> *but rather married with the nations*
> * and followed their ways.*
> *They served their idols,*
> * which entrapped them.*
> *They offered up their sons*
> * and their daughters to the demons,*
> *poured out innocent blood,*
> * the blood of their sons and daughters,*
> *whom they sacrificed to the idols of Canaan;*
> * and the land was polluted with blood.*
> *Thus they became unclean by their acts,*
> * and played the harlot in their doings.*

| 99 |

At Ocean Beach, where Taraval Avenue ended, it was smoky and foggy that night. A small crowd stood around a bonfire which trembled and shivered behind a windbreak of wooden flats. The revelers, who were pretending to enjoy themselves (it was a solstice celebration) were shaking with cold. Sparks scuttered across the sand. Tyler stood on a street-level dune, looking down at them; their smoke stung his eyes. Behind them the dark ocean twitched.

He had never taken Irene here, and yet in his heart the place was somehow associated with her. The night that she and John had come to his apartment for dinner—how long ago now? —and Irene had insincerely praised the overcooked chicken (he *burned* it! his brother had jeered in reply. Henry, you've got to get married!), he'd remembered the lovely red and white herringbone stripes of some codfish fillets he'd seen just that day in Chinatown; he should have bought those instead, but the truth was that he had never cooked a storebought fish in his life. As a boy he'd caught the occasional trout or sunfish up in the gold country; he'd cleaned them and roasted them on sticks over campfires with the other boys; but seafood had made only exceptional appearances in his mother's home. Those had been the days when—for inland white Americans, at least—the thought of fish conjured up, at best, deep-fried frozen fish sticks dipped in tartar sauce; they'd smelled like wet dogs. The truth was that he'd gone by one of those markets on Grant Street, expressly to please Irene, and for a long time had observed the white fish-balls, the yellow scallops, the tentacle-crowned carrot-colored balloons of marinated oc-topi (how to characterize *those* in a details description report?), the pouting-lipped carp so fresh they still jumped in the balance pans, the black and white X-patterns of cod-skinned provender, the reeking raw conches on their beds of dripping ice—and imme-diately had become apprehensive of doing the wrong thing, of buying something that was no good, or cooking it wrongly so that it would taste foul not only to him and to his unpleasantly outspoken brother but also to Irene—and, after all, nothing tastes as bad as bad seafood. So, in the end, like many another politician, he'd fallen back upon medi-ocrity, and satisfied no one, either. Given his occupation, we can hardly accuse him of following always the pattern of safe thinking—although, indeed, what else should we have expected Tyler to do while walking a dangerous path, but to tread cautiously? As it happened, his undistinguished culinary efforts had been effective far beyond his imag-inings; for Irene, seeing the dull red flush upon his neck and face when John insulted the chicken's flavor and presentation, had immediately understood to what extent their awk-ward host had labored to the limit of his abilities, and pitied him—a pity no less sincere for her laughter on the drive home, when her husband apostrophized Henry's dinner in picturesquely emphatic terms. Of course Tyler never knew of her feelings, not daring to raise a subject as potentially odorous as golden-red fish blood curdling on day-old ice; so after washing the dishes he drove out to the ocean, stood upon the sand, and indulged in feeling sorry for himself. He pretended that she was standing in the wave-shallows, that she smiled at him and (the goal of many a pervert) *understood* him. And yet, while the continuation of Irene's heartbeat might not be an indispensable precondition to such fantasies, her death, precisely by universalizing her absence—he could not merely pre-tend that he wouldn't see her in his apartment anymore; he'd *never* see her anywhere, never, never! —thereby legitimated his playing the game in any spot that he chose. All San Francisco belonged to her now, and Sacramento, too—and Los Angeles, of course, especially Forest Lawn . . . But not *just* Forest Lawn. Thus the magical energy of that spot began to decay.

| 100 |

He awoke with the taste of Irene's cunt in his mouth.

| 101 |

They were underneath the Stockton tunnel that night, Smooth had said. He took Tyler down the dripping passageway to where the tall man waited, and then there was a room where a woman's naked straining back pulsed, the vertebrae alien eruptions held in by frantic fingers.

Hello, Sapphire, he said.

L-l-luh . . . gurgled that pale masklike face.

In the corner, he saw long arms, long legs scrabbling.

Like these visitor fees, a toothless old transvestite was saying. The Seville where I stay, that place hits up my tricks for ten bucks every time. Not five bucks, but ten bucks. And I don't really care, Maj, 'cause it's out of the trick's pocket, not mine, you know? I'm making money and they're making money. But the other day I brought my girlfriend in, and they wanted to charge her a visitor fee. So I went ballistic. I said: She's a friend, not a date, and I'm not making any money off her, and what you're doing is illegal, so if you want to call the cops you can but if I go to jail then you're going to jail with me.

Then what?

Then they said, okay, forget it.

Okay, said the Queen. So you don't really have a problem.

But it's not *right*, Maj! They shouldn't be trying to—

All rightie. What hotel you say it was?

The Seville.

Oh, *that* place. Can you remember this, Justin?

Yeah, said the tall man.

Okay, Libby. We'll take care of it. Now run along, sweetheart. Queen's got other things to do.

The Queen slipped her arm around Smooth and whispered something in his ear. Smooth opened his mouth wide until his tongue and palate became bulging cushions of mirth.

Oh, cut the crap, Smooth, the Queen laughed. Henry, the things he says about you and me. Your ears should be burning.

Seeing a familiar blonde and sullen face behind her shoulder, Tyler said with a wink: Well, maybe they are. I bet you said I was a *misogynist*, didn't you, Smooth? That's what Domino always says.

Who the fuck are you? said Domino. I never saw you before in my life, cocksucker, so where do you get off using my name?

Honk three times whenever I need you, Tyler said. Just like in the fairy tale. Oh, no, it was four times, wasn't it? And you have a motorcycle scar on your leg.

All right, Henry, the Queen said. What's the point?

The point is that I paid her good money to bring me to you and she took my money and said she didn't know anything. I saw her watching me, too. Was that your policy at the time, Maj?

Oh, now they got you callin' me Maj, too, said the Queen. That's nice.

I don't even remember you, Domino said. But it sounds like you were one of my johns. And it sounds like you were a misogynist, all right. And I just did as I was told. And what's more, if I ripped you off, you just take your place in line before you complain about it. Anyone who would pay to have sex with a woman who has no options deserves to get ripped off. What'd I do, steal your watch or something? No, you're wearing a watch . . .

Now, Domino, that's no way to do business, said the Queen. Maybe I was raised different. Some of you people just don't show no respect, and that's no way to run a business. 'Cause that's what we're out here doing, Domino, and I'm talkin' to you. People wanna be nice to you, you wanna give 'em the same courtesy back.

Queen tells it like it is, said the tall man.

Aw, go to hell, Maj.

All right, Domino. We'll take this up later. Why don't you go someplace else to be nasty? Now, Henry, excuse me, but it's been a long night so far and lookin' like it's just gonna get longer and longer. What can I do for you?

Oh, I just kind of came by.

That's nice.

What kind of pudding is in here? whispered Smooth, patting the Queen's breast.

Plum. Plum pudding, child.

What kind is in here? asked Smooth, reaching between her legs.

Coconut.

Are you my Ocean Queen or my Chocolate Queen?

Both.

Now he's *jealous,* laughed Smooth. Tell me, Ocean Chocolate Queen, is Henry *jealous* of us or not?

That would be private and confidential, said the Queen.

Tyler stared at her, somehow hypnotized by her sagging, used-up face.

| 102 |

Here's my business card, said Tyler.

Thank you, said the Queen. Oh, you gave me two.

So I did, he said.

He took the extra one back, not touching it where she had touched it, and returned it to the little metal box in his shirt pocket.

Why don't you keep 'em in your wallet? asked the Queen.

The condoms leak on them, said Tyler, and the Queen chuckled and shook her head.

When he got home he gloved himself in latex, opened the box, laid the card down on his glass slab. He had used the business card trick several times. The cards were imprinted on lightweight plastic sheets—a special order which had cost him an extra ten dollars. This nonabsorbent surface was an almost ideal base for latent fingerprints. Whirling the fingerprint brush between his hands as he pressed down on it so that the bristles fanned out into a configuration not unlike those at car washes, he worked it into soft readiness. Then with a plastic spoon freshly washed in rubbing alcohol and rubbed dry he sprinkled a pinch of fingerprint powder onto the business card—not too much, because that would have darkened the print excessively. Then, holding his breath, he caressed the brush across the card in a series of light passes, and brought to light the Queen's finger-whorls, alternating white and black, like the wood-grain of German expressionist block prints. Now he could work more finely, and traced his gentle brush along her ridge-tracks, bringing his face down near the places she had touched and slowly allowing air to issue from between his lips, purging the unneeded fingerprint powder. Next for the fingerprint tape. Good cops needed only five or six inches, but he allowed himself eight, tacking down one end to the glass slab and then pressing his thumb along the rest of the tape until it lay flat and firm upon the first sharp print. He recognized his own prints (central pocket loop) and didn't tape them over. Here was another whorl print, so he taped that. Then he reversed the card and powdered it. There were again the recognizable whorl prints, these somewhat smudged from contact with the adjacent business card, but he taped those anyway. Then he dropped the card into a plastic bag.

He called up a detective he knew, but the detective had been transferred or quit, as it seemed.

This is Henry Tyler, he said to the detective's replacement. Who's this? Let me see . . . —He snapped his fingers. —You must be Detective Collins. Didn't we meet at the policeman's ball last year?

You have a good memory, said the woman with her trademark chirpiness. He remembered her as a trademark passive-aggressive bitch. —Now, Mr. Tyler, I'm very busy, and the whole office is swamped. What do you need?

Gosh, that's funny, said Tyler in wonderment. I'm swamped, too. Fancy that!

I'm sure you are, said Dectective Collins, the angry edge already in her voice.

I was wondering if you could run a check on a set of latents for me, said Tyler. That would really be helping me out.

Does this have anything to do with our jurisdiction, Henry? asked Detective Collins with bitter alertness.

No, it would just be a tremendous favor to me.

Well, Mr. Tyler, as I just explained to you, we're quite swamped around here. We're in the midst of a *major* investigation.

Yeah, I get that, but—

Well, sir, it's not going to happen, the woman said, irritation in her voice. I don't even come in until ten o'clock, and I work until seven or eight.

You're the *best*, Detective Collins, said Tyler cheerily. I certainly understand your situation, yes siree. Detective Collins, I want you to know that I am your *slave*.

Sighing, he unpeeled the tape and wrapped it around another business card. Then he got the magnifying glass and looked at the index fingerprint to get the secondary code. A ridge count of nine: inner loop, then. Now for the sub-secondary. He didn't have both thumbs, so he couldn't get the major division. He counted ridges on the thumb print, to get a partial key, then computed the second sub-secondary.

The phone rang.

She knew what you're doing, said Smooth. Our Queen's no fool.

Tyler grimaced.

Have you got a match yet?

Detective Collins was not disposed, said Tyler drily.

Oh, she's a piece of work, said Smooth. She doesn't like pedophiles, either. Let me give you another number. This is Detective Roy Gardner. No "i" after the "d." You can mention my name.

You're an amateur, said Detective Gardner, inspecting Tyler's tentative alphanumeric fractions. Well, you got the whorl group right. Secondary and sub-secondary correct. All right. Leave this with me and call me tomorrow.

No match, said Gardner happily on the following day. She's not in our files. She's not in the FBI files, either.

| 103 |

What's your name again? said the tall man.

You know my name, said Tyler.

What's your name? said the tall man.

Henry.

I don't want no trouble, said the tall man. You wait here and I'll see if she want to talk with you.

Tyler scratched his chin and said: While we're at it, Justin, what's *your* name?

Aren't you the wiseass.

Alone now, Tyler sat in that world-famed rendezvous, the Wonderbar, and beside him sat his fears.

The tall man returned and said: Not today. We all got too much shit goin' on today to show you any heart . . .

| 104 |

That night Tyler was sad, and Smooth dreamed that his niece Darcy was a small child again, and that it was Christmas and he had given her a doll which resembled her. Suddenly he saw that Darcy had crawled into the fireplace and was silently convulsing and burning on the coals. He rushed up, removed the screen, and reached in with his bare hands to save her. His arms burst into flames. When he pulled her out, he found that it was not the real Darcy at all, but only the Darcy-like doll, which Darcy had rejected and thrown into the fire.

· BOOK VI ·

Ladies of the Queen

●

Megacles, who was doing badly in the party rivalry, made an offer of support to Pisistratus again . . . and reinstated him in a primitive and over-simple manner. He circulated a rumor that Athena was reinstating Pisistratus; and found a tall and impressive woman called Phye, dressed her up to rememble Athena, and brought her in with Pisistratus . . . the people of the city worshiped and received him with awe.

A Pupil of Aristotle, *The Athenian Constitution* (*ca.* 332–22 b.c.)

●

This is the heart of it, the scared woman who does not want to go alone to the man any longer, because when she does, when she takes off her baggy dress, displaying to him rancid breasts each almost as big as his head, or no breasts, or mammectomized scar tissue taped over with old tennis balls to give her the right curves; when, vending her flesh, she stands or squats waiting, congealing the air firstly with her greasy cheesey stench of unwashed feet confined in week-old socks, secondly with her perfume of leotards and panties also a week old, crusted with semen and urine, brown-greased with the filth of alleys; thirdly with the odor of her dress also worn for a week, emblazoned with beer-spills and cigarette-ash and salted with the smelly sweat of sex, dread, fever, addiction—when she goes to the man, and is accepted by him, when all these stinking skins of hers have come off (either quickly, to get it over with, or slowly like a big truck pulling into a weigh station because she is tired), when she nakedly presents her soul's ageing soul, exhaling from every pore physical and ectoplasmic her fourth and supreme smell which makes eyes water more than any queen of red onions—rotten waxy smell from between her breasts, I said, bloody pissy shitty smell from between her legs, sweat-smell and underarm-smell, all blended into her halo, generalized sweetish smell of unwashed flesh; when she hunkers painfully down with her customer on a bed or a floor or in an alley, then she expects her own death. Her smell is enough to keep him from knowing the heart of her, and the heart of her is not the heart of it. The heart of it is that she is scared. She is scared like the Ellis Street Korean woman in the white halter-top who charged twenty for a blow job or sixty for an hour of converse with her incredibly tight and dry vagina, moaning with pain as her clients fucked her (unless, of course, she could take the sixty and run); she'd been raped by a white guy two weeks before and then dropped off half naked in the street; she said it didn't hurt in her cunt as much as it had hurt in her heart; for a year she had been carrying pepper spray which another white guy, a nice one, had bought for her, but she didn't dare to use it when some big tall black gangster in the Tenderloin mugged her, which happened almost every week; gimme your dough, bitch! the tall man would command, and she'd obey. (His name was Justin. He'd not yet joined the Queen.) And every one of those other semi-clean or rotten-crotched women is scared. Each one walks in fear, waits alone—please, she does not want to go alone! Read from her list of if-onlys (which of course includes more important wishes connected with money, drugs and sleep): She needs a friend to go with her. She needs someone to watch her. Maybe she has a sweet young black boyfriend with rasta dreadlocks who if he could look up from the video games at the liquor store might find out where the man is taking her. Maybe she has a business type boyfriend, older, wiser, crueler or not, who talks with her there on the sidewalk in a low and angry voice. Their guardianship is not enough. The sweet young boyfriend, whom she doesn't make wear a rubber, couldn't accompany her even if he felt willing, because that would scare off the trick, and even were the trick one of those happy sloppy middle-aged exhibitionists who'd let her boyfriend in while he did her, she still wouldn't want the boyfriend to see her naked with another man; she'd have to yell at him: Hey! Stop watching or I'm gonna beat you up again tonight! —The older business boyfriend would *definitely* scare off the trick. She's alone. She waits for money or death. The heart of it is the fear, because she knows that sooner or later she will get raped, gaffled, and sodomized again and the last time a man did that to her it really hurt; she had to go to the hospital to shit blood for weeks and it permanently messed up her insides. Sooner or later she'll get AIDS or she'll get put away by the cops again or she'll end up inside separate plastic bags in widely spaced dumpsters. In short, she needs the Queen.

| 106 |

A trick went up the stairs of the Odin Hotel with Lily; and the manager, after having buzzed them into the dark green moldy stinking lobby, slammed the grating behind them and then advanced on Lily, snarling: Bitch, you gotta pay your fuckin' rent, bitch!

Don't you call me a bitch!

You don't interrupt me in front of my Mom, bitch! he cried, and then the trick saw the tiny creature which cowered in the corner—evidently the manager's mother, although the trick would not have imagined that the manager could have had a mother.

Lily took the trick's hand and started to lead him to her room when the manager forcibly broke their grip, shook Lily's shoulder and shouted: Get behind me and shut up, bitch! Don't you ever walk in front of me!

He scared her. He tried to hurt her. She fled, and joined the Queen . . .

| 107 |

The question of the Queen's origin, and related questions such as: Was she the only one, or do the unsubdued powers of old Canaan continually form new Queens for the benefit of this world's outcasts? and then all the unrelated but predictable questions of divinity students, such as: Did blood or celestial ichor flow in her veins? all lack depth and force. We need only know that she was beseeched, and she came. There were no omens of her coming, although retrospective omens are easily invented by those who wish to make life less mysterious than it is, which is why many of the beseechers, Strawberry in particular, would later tell the most extravagant tales. (Extravagance, by the way, is really a form of simplicity. Consider, for example, the magic four-digit Department of Motor Vehicles access number which allows a private eye to read his target's address and personal description—how wonderful it all is! But the DMV, staffed in part by corrupt incompetents, presents to the world an unedifyingly error-ridden database. If you ask Henry Tyler how he found the Queen, he might say: Well, Dan Smooth helped me, but I matched her social with the DMV database. —And yet we know that she had no social security number. She didn't exist. Extravagance, simplicity!) Strawberry insisted to the end that a full year before ever being crowned, the Queen *appeared* down on Second and Mission in front of the old Van Heusen furniture store and at that moment Strawberry felt a strange and thrilling feeling. Could the real truth have been that, wearied almost to death with the dark stale silence of her life, which never thrilled her anymore even when the needle went in, she needed to imagine some transcendent joy at sufficient remove from her that it could not be destroyed by examination? Or maybe the Queen had actually descended into reality before Strawberry's eyes. Trying to harvest literalness from Strawberry's myth-fields, I fear, is as exhausting as trying to compare the hard, brilliant comebacks of the Tenderloin girls with the dumb stench of their Capp Street sisters such as Sunflower whose soul had long since closed down for routine business like a fire department on a Sunday afternoon and who arguably never remembered or even perceived her Queen at all. That other beseecher, Sweetpea, who offered the world a whole museum of teardrop tattoos on her forehead, and later insisted that she'd been ready from the very first to do anything on the Queen's behalf, actually claimed at the time in question that "the girls" could never get together because they were all on drugs and their minds were clouded, that if any Queen asked them to unite with her for mutual protection they'd just laugh. For that matter, Sweetpea herself laughed, and her laugh was more bitter than a flash of winter lightning. Oh, but to hear her tell it! —Soon's I saw that dear little bitch, I *knew,* she told Dan Smooth. I knew she was my bitch an' I was her bitch, forever and ever and ever. —Later, during the reign of Domino, she altered that story considerably.

No, there couldn't *never* be a Queen here in the Mission! Chocolate insisted. Maybe in the Tenderloin, because those girls are more high class than us. But not here. Well, actually, since we're so bad off, maybe we need a Queen more here.

When she said these words to Strawberry, she was not postulating, only playing, and her eyes resembled the grinningly cruel white-set windows of Alcatraz.

But Strawberry, faithful to postulates and to material possibilities, quietly replied: You saying you want to be the Queen?

No, I don't have means to support the other girls, Chocolate said, condescending to acknowledge that faith because patience and politeness were her profession. —You think if I had means I'd be out here doing this? I worked in a shipyard out in San Diego before this, and then I was a house painter in Portland, Oregon. This is the only I guess you'd call female job I've ever had.

You ever get lonely out there? Strawberry asked.

Hell, yeah. Don't we all?

You want somebody to take care of you?

Sure. But I don't know any sugar daddies. Who the fuck's gonna take care of *me?*

Chocolate, don't you have family?

Oh, family. Gimme a break!

Well?

I got brothers. They're the biggest bunch of crooks, theieves, and headaches this side of the earth. And becase of what I do, they don't know me. Well, I can see that, but 'cause I do what I do, I've supported their drug habits; I've given them a place to stay when their women kicked them out.

Chocolate, do you *want* family?

Then in sentences of purest oxygen, which surpassed those of any fat lawyer whispering sweetly into a shackled felon's ear, Strawberry told her about the Queen, about how if you came in after a long night on the street and hadn't been able to score any dates, the Queen would front you your drugs until you made good; she'd give you a place to stay, too . . .

Sounds like a pimp, said Chocolate irritably.

No, a pimp keeps all your money. The Queen's not like that. She just takes ten percent, like insurance, to share with the girls that need it. She does it out of love.

Bullshit.

I'm telling you true, baby.

Then the other pimps are gonna run her out, unless she maybe stays in some warehouse south of Market . . .

Chocolate, what would you do if a lady said she was the Queen and offered to take care of you?

Tell her to kiss my ass and fuck herself.

At the same time, honey?

Oh, go to hell, said the black woman, her eyes lidding just like the automatic plastic window slowly sliding back down over the keypad of a bank machine after a transaction.

So much for Chocolate, who soon would love her Queen with an almost bestial tenderness. Who knows where the bright light truly comes from, and who can foresee the whirlwind? Not even the crazy whore. And Tyler, wandering near home on a dismal Sunday morning, or eating breakfast in some sad diner, with Ocean Beach seen through saltblasted windows, likewise understood less than we might imagine; his lust for logic seduced him into retrospective explanations as sterile as those detail description sheets of his profession, which can hardly begin to categorize the world bright, blue, green, and blurred, the world with its many suns of sparkling cars flashing like Phaëthon's chariot down the track—hardly that, let alone the old, old Queen in her otherwordly glory.

| 108 |

Domino's induction into the ranks of the Queen's women was, as may well be imagined, pregnant with difficulties for all concerned. The blonde began as one of those solitary runaways unabsorbed by the crowd at Golden Gate Park; she did not *want* to be absorbed. Around her swirled the street people with their feuds, hugs, dogs and bicycles. She remained aloof. Tattooed backpacker boys pestered her, and the eyebrow-pierced girls who sat on their duffel bags on the sidewalk tried to befriend her, but Domino remained too honestly and incorruptibly angry to join any crowd (even though inside the runaway still dwelt the little girl who had read a lot of romances and loved talking about conspiracy). When her new profession became known, one of her many enemies wrote on the wall DOMINO SUCKS—LUV SPREADS GERMS but Domino, her eyes stinging with hot tears, merely stood in front of this monument to herself when she waved at cars. A week or two later someone else's enemy wrote MIKEY IS A TAR BABY on the same spot, and then the antagonism of the world, like its sympathy, quickly faded, leaving Domino alone, which is to say bitterly emancipated, like the tall man with his obscene war-cries against all *citizens* as he called them, all greengrocers, steadyjobbers, bourgeois taxpayers. "Dating" the longbearded old white men and the blacks in their wool caps of all seasons, and every now and then getting paid to do what she loved with two scowling lesbians in the hardware store, she strode proudly up and down the street in her new jean jacket, panhandling couples in gold-tinted mirror sunglasses and later screaming at them if they ever dared to say: I *helped* you, she kept her righteousness, and yet life grew worse and worse until after a stint of lap dancing and some cell time in San Bruno, she became just another kid in a dirty hooded jacket sitting on the sidewalk with her backpack on, panhandling and giving blow jobs; then she got another exotic dancing job, from which she was quickly fired; then for a while she became the greenhaired girl whose sign lied:

1. PREGNANT
2. HUNGRY
3. HOMELESS

and *then* gravity slowly dragged her backward by her ankles and she skidded down past all the girls whose hair was dyed red or blue, past stores selling slinky leopardskin polyester and skull beads, far past all those sunny Saturdays on Haight Street where couples with sweaters tied around their waists used to promenade and give Domino money; she sped down past the other panhandlers, who gazed severely at their boots, and before she knew it was a Tenderloin streetwalker, then one more time a dancer who got fired; she tried office work but the boss didn't like her attitude, so there she was down in the hotels on Eddy Street where the rock was yellow these nights because they cut it with cornstarch instead of baking soda; there she was wiggling her buttocks and expapillating among the late afternoon leaners and swaggerers just across the street from the Mother Lode's lavender-fringed windows (inside, on the screen of the ATTACK FROM MARS video game, *SAY NO TO DRUGS* advised the neon). A cloudless sky, almost as dark as the lavender hemispheres on the Empire Massage sign, helped her pretend that she was still young. Then her first pimp took her. He was as tall as a fire escape. She ran away, but he found her and gave her her first cigarette burn. She tried to run away again—oh, what's the use? Street life pays its wages; it pays them regularly.

At least we have a place here where we have some refuge, Strawberry said to her. We ended up friends, and it's neat in a way, it is.

But soon enough Strawberry, tormented and gaffled by the blonde, would be screaming at her: I'll cut your head off!

Come on, said Domino. Let's go. Let's just go down the road right now, just you and me. Come on, come on.

After that, Strawberry was scared of her. When Domino got on the streetcar, Strawberry saw her and got on a different car. But the Queen forced the two of them to make up . . .

Right now Strawberry still meant to be *concerned* and *motherly* in just the same way that Bernadette, now homeless, scolded her ten-year-old daughter (who lived under the foster care of her aunt) for taking the bus to Marin County alone because the girl was starting to "develop" as Bernadette delicately expressed it; Bernadette stashed her breakfast in the trash can and then walked her daughter to the bus station. Strawberry longed to show similar love for her new blonde sister, so she coaxingly said: I mean it, Domino. It's really neat. What do you think?

I don't want to talk about it.

Leave Domino alone, said the Queen, caressing the blonde's neck, but the blonde shrugged her off. The Queen regarded her sadly.

The Queen had known what the matter was even without seeing in the newspaper that photograph of Domino's sister, who, skinny and old, with a diamond-faced, sunken-cheeked face on a long snakey neck, had just been arrested for helping her boyfriend catch a thirteen-year-old girl whom Domino's sister herself had dragged into the charcoal-grey van, then bludgeoned, bound, and gagged while her middle-aged boyfriend drove to a Tahoe motel. They left their victim in the van until it was dark. Then they wrapped her in a long bag and carried her into the motel room on their shoulders. They never took the gag out, so they weren't able to make her suck them off, but the boyfriend, who in police file photographs appeared to be as bored and hangdog as an old security guard at some museum gallery, raped her with his penis while Domino's sister raped her anally with a dildo and afterward licked the tears off her face. It was almost four in the morning by then, so they didn't even bother to wrap her up or dress her when they carried her back to the van. The boyfriend had brought his face close to the girl's terrified face and breathed on her, then promised to let her go, just to watch her face change expression while Domino's sister masturbated. Then they started driving slowly toward the mountain pass. Domino's sister got the clothesline.—They threw her corpse into a snowdrift. The police found it two days later. Domino's sister's boyfriend was smart enough to blow his brains out, but Domino's sister thought she could beat the rap by blaming everything on him.

Many months later, on a sickeningly hot summer day on South Van Ness when the Queen and Domino were alone, the blonde said: I knew about it before it went down.

Mm hm, said the Queen.

You gonna drop a dime on me?

You make me so sad when you say that.

Well, Maj, are you planning on dropping a dime on me or not?

Lordy lordy day, the Queen muttered. You gotta trust . . .

But that was months ahead.

They got you brainwashed, dearie, the Queen had said to Domino on that first occasion. You're a pretty, pretty girl. You just fell in with the wrong crowd. They just usin' you for your body. You don't have to suck nobody's dick just to get your dope.

Who are you to tell me what I don't have to do?

I'm a prostitute, the Queen told her. Same as you are. Well, a semi-retired prostitute. I'm busy now lookin' after my girls. And I tell all my girls this: If you *want* to suck dick, go ahead. But they gotta pay you good money. If you *want* to get your dope, all rightie. But you have the right to buy the dope of your choice with your own money an' not get gaffled, see what I'm sayin'?

Domino tried to stare her down, rubbing a new burn on the back of her arm. — You're just a control freak, aren't you? I bet you want to tie me up and fuck me and then turn me out.

Lordy lordy, sighed the Queen. Justin, find her pimp and bring him to me.

The tall man came an hour later. —He said he's not goin' anywhere. He said he gonna ex* his runaway blonde bitch. Domino, your pimp gonna *kill* you!

Oh, fuck off, the blonde said, trembling.

Domino, you want to stay with me? said the Queen. I can talk with him. I can persuade him to set you free. An' if you don't like it here, you can leave anytime. How about it, child?

*Execute.

Strawberry, still trying to soothe and befriend the blonde, laughed and said: Maj wanted me to move here a hundred years ago, but I was like, I wanna be independent. Now it's just, I wanna be *home*.

Well, that works for you maybe, Domino said. Me, I just want to be evil.

These girls, man! marveled Chocolate. These girls like Domino! I look at 'em and say *you stupid bitch*.

You just want me to to be your slave, Domino said.

You know what? said the Queen, drawing Coptic crosses on the wall. I've treated you so good this past five minutes, Dom. I mean, you've got to be one of the best treated and best dressed slaves in my whole kingdom. You don't even have your chains on today.

Domino, sensing that the Queen was making fun of her, clenched her fists and said: Well, bitch, why do *you* do it, then?

Why do I do what? Make people into my slaves? How about Strawberry here? Look her in the eye, Dom. You think Strawberry's got slavey eyes?

Domino, feeling suddenly so ashamed and sad as to be almost breathless, grunted something, her head hanging down as she gazed dully at Beatrice's feet.

Maj is waiting! shouted Chocolate, and this injunction revived the blonde's raging suspicion and longing to be gone even though she had nowhere to go, so she shouted: You want my soul. Well, you can't have it, 'cause it's mine mine *mine*. And it'll never come out.

You know, you're a rude little thing, laughed the Queen, long-legged, barefooted; the silver necklace on her throat. —You don't care about what I'm saying, right? You think Beatrice here's my slave? You think I'm a she-devil? Is that what you think?

What do you *want?* the blonde wept. What do you *want* from me?

I want you to lemme *love* you an' protect you. Go now, honey. You don't know what you want and I got things to attend to. That pimp he try to hurt you, I'll take care of it.

Domino's arms were crossed. She kept saying: You're lying. You're lying. Are you lying to me?

The Queen turned away. Domino looked her coldly up and down and went out. A quarter of an hour later, she ran back screaming with the pimp behind her.

| 109 |

Look at her, said Strawberry. See her big black boyfriend standing right behind her? Not that I'm prejudiced. My main man is Justin. I suck black cock every night, so you don't need to look at me like that. But when a big black man like that stands behind a hooker, well, sometimes the hooker's in trouble. You know what they do? The boyfriend hides under the bed. Then while the girl's taking care of the guy, the boyfriend's goin' through his pants, checkin' out the wallet. That's how a lot of girls end up dead. It's like, damn, it's like, get a *grip*, girl.

The Queen said: Domino, it don't matter if you have a hundred pimps behind you. Keep your morals. Keep your scruples.

Let go of me, the pimp said very quietly. His eyes were as yellow as the sign for the Broadway Manor Motel.

You think this is funny, don't you? said the Queen.

I'm gonna get you, the pimp said.

Raising her head high on her slender neck, the Queen gazed wide-eyed into his face with a small smile and said: Why? Haven't I treated you right? Fuck this. Get up on your feet, pig.

You want me to ex him? said the tall man. This nigger's an asshole. I'd love to ex this nigger out.

Knock out one of his teeth first, the Queen said. Just one.

What the *fuck!* screamed the pimp. In spite of Strawberry's characterization, he was actually a slender little man, vicious and alert like a snake.

You really want me to smack him in his teeth, huh?

You wanna lose teeth or you wanna be a good little boy? said the Queen. Justin, don't take his tooth out just yet. Looks like he's fixin' to say something.

I know you, bitch! the pimp yelled. I'm gonna do for you!

All rightie, said the Queen.

This is *bullshit!*

It is that. I know that, said Domino ecstatically, mincing in with a cigarette, shaking the match with her wrist back and forth so graceful, always kneeling.

Sweetie, be cool now, okay? said the Queen. Lemme speak with this gentleman.

Domino sank slowly down, whispering to herself.

Sapphire, go an' hug her, said the Queen. Go an' give Domino a big kiss. Don't be afraid. Go now.

This is between you an' me now, bitch, the pimp said.

Excuse me, said the Queen. You talkin' to me?

I'm gonna be on your black ass. I'm gonna hunt you down. I'm gonna get you.

He's a nasty one, said Strawberry. Justin, you oughta just ex him.

I don' wanna be too talky now, the Queen mused aloud. We put him out on a crucifix, okay, in the middle of Ellis. Really just take him to the prom. This is out of our area.

That's rich, laughed the tall man, twisting the cord another turn tighter. The pimp began to cough.

Yes, said the Queen, looking down, smoking, shaking, moving. Feels like your eyes gonna pop out, don' it, mister? Feels like that blood's just gonna explode right inside your ugly old head, now, don't it? Well, you know what? It could happen.

Burn his eyes out! screamed Domino. He raped me! He addicted me!

I dunno—ssssh! said the Queen.

The pimp had begun to strangle now, and that was what Domino saw in her mind later whenever she thought about her sister's crime. He was snarling, purring, and choking all it once. It was horrible.

There's a lot of things I can do to him, the Queen said. But really what I wanna do is scare him. What you think, Justin? Should we put out one of his eyes? Or the tooth? Where should we start? How can we get him to listen?

Shit, why you askin' me? Just make up your goddamned mind. I'm sick of this motherfucker.

Get out, said the Queen. Get out and never come back.

The tall man let go. The pimp got out.

Now, dearie, said the Queen. You wanna stay or you wanna go? Whatever you want, that's cool here with us. You wanna talk with Strawberry or . . . ?

Are you that out of whack? Domino screamed. Are you that ignorant? Haven't you figured out that the more you help these bitches the more you'll just be encouraging them to make some dumb illusion and crawl inside it until it's too late while you go about your own cruel life refusing to do the one thing that they *long* to have you do?

And what would that be? said the Queen, faintly smiling.

The blonde burst into tears.

Okay, honeypie, said the Queen. All rightie. Never mind. You can stay . . .

There wasn't a month before I come in here I wasn't beatin' up somebody, said Chocolate soothingly. Don't even know what the heck I was doin' it for. You wanna stay? Why don't you stay?

Sobbing, Domino nodded

But later, when they were alone, the tall man said to the Queen: I don't like her. Lemme check her out.

| 110 |

Papa, comprehending, sentient, and somehow tame, was still handsome. His bushy eyebrows were what had helped him accumulate the woman-memories which now protected his back. He owned the Liberty Bar on Eddy Street. There was something about him which struck the tall man as gently naked, some secret part of him whose inability to hide itself provoked tenderness, as when a woman's T-shirt rides up her back when she bends over her pool cue. —Well, I'm a new man! a drunk was telling him. A new man, I said! He took my wife, my money, *and* my girlfriend.

Papa nodded sadly.

Can't you just talk to her? the drunk pleaded.

I don't want to get involved, said Papa.

Can't you *all* at least check to see if she . . .

No, no, I gotta take her side, Papa said. I've known her longer than I've known you. I can't get involved.

Papa, I swear to God, if you don't talk to her I'm going to kill myself tonight.

All right, son, I'll talk to her. Come back tomorrow.

Weary blue, those eyes of Papa's, innocent in a way that could never be made knowing; sentient, I said, but no freer for that, no freedom like that of a bad moral actor . . .

What can I do for you? he said to the tall man.

You know a blonde bitch named Domino?

Oh, don't tell me.

You know her? said the tall man, his words greasy, cool and inimical, like the white-painted rivets on the tunnel wall by the Greyhound station. Of course he knew already that Papa knew her. He knew quite a bit about other souls' attachments and alliances. And what he knew about Papa, that very tenderness-provoking part of him, why, that was what excited the tall man's contempt.

Sure I know her. She used to go by Judith. Then she was Sylvia. She doesn't come around here much anymore.

Another shot, please, said the tall man.

Still no ice?

No.

Two and a quarter.

Here's two.

Two and a quarter.

The tall man slid his sunglasses up his smooth brown skull and said: You tryin' to rip me off?

I don't care how big and black you are, Papa said. Anyway, aren't you asking me for a favor? You want information or not? You owe me a quarter.

Matter of fact, Queen pays two dollars in here.

You want to hear about Domino or not?

Go ahead.

Thank you. Now you don't owe me a quarter anymore.

Yeah, buy yourself a Cadillac.

All right. Well, Judith was a good friend of the owner. On SSI*, you know, like all those girls. And every month she'd run up a tab with me, you know: Papa, gimme a beer; I'll pay you when my check comes; this is all I have right now. —She's a *girl,* you know, so what can you do?

Break her jaw's what I would do.

And every month she did it like this. Every goddamned month. And one month when she owed me four hundred dollars she didn't come back.

Bitch really screwed it to you, huh? Papa, you're too much. You got a fuckin' bleedin' heart.

Sometimes I see her on the street but she just sticks out her tongue at me. Well, that's life. We never know what's going to happen, much less why. Even your best friend can lie. Even your best friend can cheat. —Look, Papa went on, showing the tall man a Styrofoam cup which had been kissed by lipstick, but the tall man rose without finishing his drink and went back to the Queen to report that Domino was a cheat, a thief and a liar.

That don't make no difference, said the Queen. Justin, you gotta try an' care for her, too . . .

| 111 |

Even those who hated Domino admitted to respecting and even to feeling awed by her crazy violence, which in the street world meant bravery, honor, worthiness. Those who lived with her were haunted by her; her soul oppressed theirs with its weight and bitter-reeking shadows, and yet they also took pride in her. In her time she'd smashed furniture and heads. It was best to avoid her wherever possible; second best to give her whatever she wanted. Domino herself sensed the limitlessness of her own acts. Deep inside her skull, she hunched and squatted, dull-eyed, scared runaway whose only hope lay in setting her presence alight to give this planet of enemies pause; they said that Domino had a "rep," that she had "heart." By this they really meant that Domino was dangerous. The whore from Albuquerque who'd tried to gaffle her out of a dime bag of weed, where was she now? Domino had broken a lamp over her head. And Akoub the Muslim pimp, who'd raped her, wasn't it Domino who'd set on fire not his hotel room, which proved too difficult to reach, but the entire hotel itself? No matter that what had actually hap-

*Supplemental security income.

pened was that Domino had raged into the lobby with a can of gasoline which she'd begun pouring on the lobby carpet while everybody screamed and ran and then the blonde pulled a book of safety matches out of her bra, struck one and it didn't light, struck a second which also failed her, swore, glared fiery-eyed in all directions, and fled. And the night that a man in a fancy car insulted her, hadn't it been Domino who'd thrown one of her high heels right through his windshield? No matter that the high heel had really been a hunk of brick; indeed, wasn't brick more ferocious still, if less expressive, less stylish? Everything she did got magnified. She had no pity and showed no fear. She was magnificent. She was as much a part of the other night people as their own tears. Cursing and scrutinizing her, they stood aside to let her follow her own path. They said: Domino went that way. They said: Watch out for Domino. They said: That Domino is one coldhearted bitch.

| 112 |

And Dan Smooth, what magic did the Queen work, to tame him on their first meeting?

I want eyes as blue as ocean water, he'd whispered. I want to drink the sea and be young again, like a . . . like a dancing little ocean flower . . .

Are you my little boy? said the Queen, instantly apprehending what he needed. Oh me oh my, Danny, you're my little honeychild.

After that, Smooth always loved her.

| 113 |

And the tall man, where he came from nobody knew. It was rumored that he'd once been the Queen's lover, but another tale went that he'd been her pimp until she got her power and converted him into pilgrim, worshiper, and server. What had he been? Even he himself hardly recollected now. His memories of himself scarcely resembled anything which he could recognize, and he didn't want to remember things anyhow. (Perhaps he'd been one of ever so many black men who sat on the sidewalk glaring into space.) Sentry sleeper before the tent of a prophetess, he wandered a desert partly of his own making, sometimes gaming and smiling, sometimes repelling jackal conspiracies. He leaned and meditated. He confirmed himself with his own courage. He almost never lied. He spoke or he didn't speak. He deflected, threatened, raved, or again confirmed. To the Queen he was her wall, her flashlight, her pistol, her binoculars. He hunted the Tenderloin streets to cop the cheapest weed, the best uncut china white, the raciest speed, the highest grade ice, the purest white girl so delicious in the crack pipe, the most vicious angel dust. He waited and lived on, a fabulous, enigmatic figure who kept his own counsel and the Queen's, cipher by choice, half-man, superman, faithful searcher, merciless gleaner. Above them all he was as an iron roof.

| 114 |

The tale of Beatrice, of sweetnatured Beatrice who very rapidly chewed gum with her black black teeth as she swayed herself down the curbside of life, illustrates above all else that wherever Queen Destiny marches in her lethally imperial purple, free will must fall down naked and trembling in every grovelling ritual of hopelessly humiliating abasement suffered not merely by the bitter-comprehending brain alone, not only by the heart which would be proud, but even by the entrails, for free will, stripped bare, must squat down exposing its haunches, to be kissed, whipped, or raped as sparkling Queen Destiny may please. But an uncomprehending child such as Sapphire, or a religious prostitute such as Beatrice herself, may both submit to the purple one without harm, the former because where there exists only sensation without interpretation or memory there can be no permanent emotional wound, the latter because acceptance of rape may truly for sacred natures become willed sacrifice.

Beatrice was a fullbooded Mixteca from Oaxaca, in a village where beyond a fence made of scrap wood, the canyon continued down toward unknown places where they said that puppets well-made enough came to life and ran away from their makers, hiding amidst the lizards, vagabonds, and beautiful turquoise skeletons. Sometimes at night Beatrice heard a strange humming from that direction, and was afraid. In her house the ladders made A-shaped shadows on concrete. A toothbrush and a tube of toothpaste were wedged into the top of the doorframe. Beatrice's family shared that toothbrush, because they were all one blood. Her Papa's revolver lay on the concrete. He needed it to protect them. But most of the time he was gone, and the children were forbidden to touch it, so if any animated puppets had come to haunt them what could they have done? After Beatrice had gotten fat and given birth to her own child, she would have liked to inquire of her Papa regarding this point, but by then, as with most wisdom, the motive arrived too late for application. Besides, the puppets never came, so her Papa must have known what he was doing. Beatrice remembered when he used to play with her; now he worked so hard and came home worried and tired. As for her Mama, she'd died of jealousy two years ago, so nobody baked a cake for Beatrice's name day anymore. But her Papa continued to love her; he always gave her a present on the Day of the Three Kings.

I think I get crazy staying here, doing practically nothing, she said to her friend Juanita.

Can you read and write? asked Juanita with a loving glance.

Can you?

I asked you first.

Somebody was teaching me, but I forgot. See, I don't have such a good memory, Beatrice smilingly said.

Spades, picks, shovels, and empty bottles inhabited the dirt.

Well, then, you must try for *special* work, Juanita said, and Beatrice did not know what she meant.

Beatrice was not grey then and never imagined that she could be. Nor was her smile anything but white. Her black shiny hair parted itself on either side of her shiny face, which was made more vivid still by her ever-smiling teeth and the whites of her flashing eyes. She would have liked to wear black miniskirts with the slenderest shoulderstraps because she so often felt hot, but then her Papa, who'd beaten her only twice, would have knocked her teeth out. Fortunately he never suspected that she had any such desires because as her figure continued to ripen (she was fourteen), the girl took to attending church more and more, praying to the Virgin for happiness. Every time she got a few centavos, she'd go light a votive candle, and nobody ever asked what she prayed for. In the cornfield she was a hard and cheerful worker. Her skin became the color of caramelized sugar, and she dyed her hair two or three shades blonder than that.

Juanita was thinking. Beatrice waited. But because she could never wait very long, and because she wanted to make sure that Juanita thought the right things, she winked at her friend and said: You know what? I was gonna do the craziest thing in my life about a week ago. I was gonna go away from here.

Me too, said Juanita. I feel that way too sometimes. But my Papa would never let me.

My dad, he's mean, too. Because my dad, always when he's mean, he gets mad at me.

The chickens laughed hysterically.

Juanita leaned forward and whispered something into Beatrice's ear, and Beatrice's eyes widened and she laughed.

Well?

I would be very happy, said Beatrice, even though she was afraid.

Well then.

But, you know, I have a *novio* now, too, Juanita. And my father-in-law and mother-in-law, they order me. I like to do a lot of things, but they don't let me. If I ask them, they say, you're crazy. I don't think they will let me go.

Even once a week? said Juanita.

If it's once a week I think I could.

I saw you that time, when my sister-in-law got married. You were dancing! You embarrassed?

Red chickens and black chickens ran by in the sun, shaded under the planks of the roof.

I would be very happy, Beatrice said again.

Green trees and blue sky clothed her village. Her laundry bag hung beside her, red and purple and black. A brown spider crawled slowly up the wall. The village smelled like pigs and chickens.

Juanita was dead now, from a shameful disease.

Beatrice wanted to remain a good girl loved by the Virgin, so, continuing innocent of the urine-and-sweat smell of veneral disease clinics, she put the other girl's proposals out of mind for a whole year, until the Virgin rewarded her in the person of her step-brother Roberto (son of her Papa's old *novia*), who sent her a registered letter all the way from Yucatan, informing her that if she were to ride the bus across Mexico to the grand hotel where he worked, she could earn big money cooking for the foreign tourists. Nobody at Beatrice's house knew how to read, but the priest, who possessed power over all the churchbells, explained the letter to them and said: Girl, you must go. Roberto wants to do the good thing for you. —Her Papa wept, which made her surprised, ashamed, and pleased all at once. Then he said: Go with God. —And he gave her ten silver pesos. Her sister gave her an herb against witchcraft. And all her little brothers and sisters, who always used to pull her braids and break her toys, became very sad. Beatrice had never known that she was so important. As for her *novio*, Manuel, he grew very pale and wretched. He didn't even dare to visit her Papa's house to wish her farewell. He promised to wait for her for three years. Beatrice smiled at the deliciousness of another soul's making promises to her. The two little Marias next door kissed her and said that they would pray for her. As for Juanita, she had been locked away by her Papa for going around with boys, so Beatrice, no matter how much she would have liked to learn more secrets and answers, was unable to tell her goodbye. Beatrice tried to be reasonable about this disappointment. Then her Papa made the sign of the cross over her and she went to Yucatan, but on the way she somehow lost the letter from Roberto with the name of the grand hotel where he was working, and consequently she never met him.

She was afraid, but the truth was that she had been even more fearful of living in Roberto's house. What if new sister-in-law had disliked her? People say that sisters-in-law never agree except when somebody dies. So it was really for the best. She knew she could work in the fields somewhere, or maybe in an ice cream factory where she could eat all she wanted. Or she could become a dressmaker—why not? She knew what a pretty dress was! She wanted to make black sleeveless miniskirts and formal gowns of red velvet. Her greatest fear was that some bandits might fall upon her and rape her until she died, but she prayed to the Virgin until she heard the same humming which used to haunt her childhood back home in the canyon, and then she knew that the Virgin would protect her. The next day she got a job in a shop. The owner said that she was very honest. Then he put his hand on her ass. Beatrice smiled at him just as she had smiled at her *novio:* such things meant nothing. Men whistled when she walked down the street, and that was likewise without consequence; in fact, it made her feel good.

One hot day maybe six weeks after Easter, Beatrice was in Merida beneath the canopy in the Plaza de la Independencia, when a birdlike old man who sat sipping mango ice among the people in the army-green folding chairs beckoned. It was a Sunday (she remembered that because everybody was dressed for church); they were about to reenact the Mestizo Wedding. Beatrice, who was wearing new tight bluejeans and lipstick of the brightest red she could find, came and sat between the old gentleman and a woman whose arm-skin was blotched like buckwheat pancakes. Her acquaintance wore white from head to toe. His white cowboy hat cooled and shaded her. He failed in handsomeness but he achieved elegance. He asked her whether she lived unmarried, and she said yes. He asked where her Papa was and she said far away. She wanted to believe that this old man was her protector. She longed to feel proud. There she was, sitting like a real lady, recruited into those two facing armies of green chairs, one under the awning, the other against the pillared portico of the Municipal Palace! She was so happy that she couldn't stop smiling. It was very close and crowded. Her knees engaged the buttocks of two children in the row ahead. Fat women in white blouses lifted up their babies to watch the trumpeter tune his brass proboscis. Bespectacled old widows stirred sweet slush-heaps with their straws. Ladies fanned one another with sandalwood fans from China. Out of kindness or by mistake a woman fanned Beatrice, who squealed: Thank you, señora, thank you! —A sweating vendor dressed in white lowered an immense basket of tan-colored snacks from his shoulder especially for Beatrice, while her new friend, the birdlike gentleman, bought her exactly what she wanted: a bag of salt-crisped corn! No one had ever treated her so kindly. Manuel, her *novio* back home, had been a very shy and dirty boy who couldn't buy her anything. Beatrice felt prouder every second. She almost believed that wings would burst from her shoulders so that she'd rise up into the air on a surge of everyone's applause. In the sunny street it was raining yellow butterflies.

Now, with trumpets and stridulating rattles, while the death-pale master of ceremonies stood under an arch of the Municipal Palace, expressionlessly smoking cigarettes, the children of Merida filed out and began to dance. After each dance the master of ceremonies strode into the light and shouted: *Bravo! Bravissimo! Domingo, in Merida! Merida, Yucatan! Merida!* until the band began to blare the next dance tune, and he bowed himself back into the shadows. Beatrice had never seen anything so grand. There came the dance when each boy balanced a bottle of beer on his head. Everybody applauded and Beatrice shrieked: *Ay!* She had fallen in love with all those dancing pairs of children in white, the boys wearing little white sombreros, as if they were the sons of her birdlike gentleman who now held her hand, the girls with yellow flowers in their hair and three stripes of floral embroidery down their long bleached dresses. Each pair wore red neckerchiefs, which on that day appeared to her most eminently remarkable.

Beatrice thought that she understood the way that Merida girls danced with their hands behind their backs. She wanted to dance that way, too. They all danced in the Mayan way, in mincing little steps, scarcely moving their upper bodies. The Mixteca way, Beatrice's way, was different, but on that Sunday afternoon a sensation of almost belligerent rapture overpowered her; she believed that she could do anything. Her only fear was that Roberto might find her. And now, in tones simultaneously awed and gleeful, the master of ceremonies cried: *Our Queen of the Yucatan—sweet as a pastry, hot as a candle, bright as the sun!* Beatrice longed to see this personage, but never did.

In the room where the old birdlike man took her, a room in a hotel once a colonial mansion which pretended to be Spanish, Beatrice lay naked in the four-poster bed with her legs spread while the old man mounted her, and, staring over his scrawny shoulders at the canopy which heaved on its posts in harmony with his thrusts, she decided that she wanted to be a dancer in a perfect white dress with three stripes of embroidered flowers. She was very happy. She wanted the skull-faced announcer to proclaim *her* as bright as the sun. On the radio she heard this song: *I am the King, but I have no Queen.*

Rather sweetly, the old man kissed her all over. Beatrice giggled. She remembered her youngest brother's mouth ambling miscellaneously along the pale end of an ear of boiled corn.

The old man said: I wish to thank you. You have made me more happy than I have been since before my wife died, may she rest in peace.

He gave her fifty pesos. He said that she was sweeter than a Durango melon. He said he wanted to marry her because all his children had gone away. Beatrice blushed, feeling very rich and happy and appreciated. Her private parts were a little sore, but she didn't mind. She never wanted to work in the fields again.

She went that evening to the ancient cathedral to pray to the Virgin for forgiveness in case she had sinned with the old man, and also to pray for assistance in becoming a dancer who would be admired by the entire world. She lit a candle and whispered: Maria, darling, I want to tell you that my Mama and my Papa, they know Mixteca dances from the different parts, and they teach their children. They teach me. The Mayan people here, I think maybe they went to school, but my people, the Mixteca people, they didn't go to school. They can't even write in Spanish. They do a lot of things, like the Virgin of the Snows . . . But please let me try, because I know I can dance as well as they. Please, Maria, darling. You're my best friend. —This was how she prayed to the Virgin. And high above the altar, the Virgin contemplated her Son's crown of thorns.

While the priest was speaking words which Beatrice could not understand, the Virgin wept white chains of rain down on all the red-tiled balconies of the city, making surf-convulsed seas upon them. Cold rain smashed away the stuffy heat. Thunder came closer, as sharp and loud as gunshots, and there was a sulphur smell. The drumming of roof-gutters filled the congregation's ears. Not even those who understood could hear the priest any longer. They gazed out in pleasure and wonder. Rain vomited itself off terraces and drainpipes, frothing onto lower roofs.

Beatrice never slipped over her head the white dress with the three stripes of Mayan embroidery, but she became famous in a kindred fashion behind the sweaty fence-bars of the dancehall with all its men standing across the street from it looking; and the muffled bass of Henry Star and of Los Big Boys weighed down the rainy sweaty light. That was how the Virgin helped her. And every morning at eleven o'clock when she woke up, Beatrice would pray with a candle and a glass of water. She believed so much in her future that she never asked any questions. The men grinned because Beatrice was already dancing.

Very late at night, after the girl in the speckled cape had finished her act, shucking herself like an ear of corn as she stroked her long hair under red light, then Beatrice majestically strode onto the stage, the disco ball brightly burning, and began to dance faster and faster, suddenly raising her hands behind her head as she unhooked her bra, which she then raised above herself in a kind of offering, and the wings of her bra glowed green like a lunar moth, and it was mystic and beautiful and so religious.

Beatrice became the girl that everyone knew, the girl in the black tank top and black miniskirt and shiny black high heels, swinging arms with men as she went down the wet sidewalk. So she had her fame, but she was already getting plump. The Virgin told her that she had to make new efforts. Her dancing changed. First it was graceful, then it was erotic, then lewd, and finally desperate—comically desperate, I should say, for they laughed at Beatrice now when she danced.

Later she got her son and her crown of thorns. Beatrice knew that every soul is put on earth to suffer pain, so she was prepared, and of course the Virgin comforted her, because up until the very day she met the Queen she continued to pray, either in the old cathedral or in her rented room with the candle and the water. The Virgin said in her humming voice that if Beatrice suffered greatly enough, then all the angels in heaven would be proud of her and would help her. In this life, God knows, we must all be patient.

The first thing that happened was when, drunk and high on cocaine, she went home with a man in a stolen car, an anxious and flashy man with dark eyes and a dark hat who promised to give her good money and even said he loved her, which very few men said to Beatrice anymore, but when he saw the police he began to drive faster and faster until he crashed into a bus. The Dark Saint took him then. As for Beatrice, her face was scarred forever. She had to get a day job in a skirt factory. Suddenly she longed for a husband. She remembered her *novio* back in Oaxaca, but she knew that it was too late and she was ashamed to go home. When she lost her job, she went back to the dancehall. After that, everybody started calling her "the old whore" even though her glistening peachy shoulders proved how young she still was. She continued to resist her destiny, imploring the sad-eyed Virgin in that ancient cathedral of white-weathered and rain-greened whitestone on cool humid evenings under the softly dripping trees where they knelt singing hymns, with wet palmtrees and mosses and large-lobed tropical leaves like seashells growing around them through the open archway. Kneeling people, rising life, rising breaths and prayers, falling rain, descending ironic grace, thus everything went round and round. Beatrice's prayers rose clacking like long beads on a necklace, then came down like hailstones on her head. After a while she believed that that was how it was supposed to be. For money she masturbated men by the thousands, in just the same way that the old ladies sitting on the concrete floors of city markets slowly knead dough into immense balls, which they then lay upon masses of the same stuff, like God creating humanity from earth, like a woman growing a baby inside her from blood, fruit, and meat. Beatrice did this well. She fed upon the diseased sperm of thousands of men, drinking it down without complaint, transubstantiating it into sacred suffering. Whenever she could, she returned to the Plaza de la Independencia on Sundays to watch the dancers' white suits and white dresses under white light, the Mayan couples facing one another on those harsh hot afternoons and in the brilliantly lit concrete nights, the ladies tapping their heels back and forth to the steps of La Chinita, their faces expressionlessly smiling, the gentlemen keeping or sometimes not keeping one white-sleeved arm behind themselves. At the dancehall, Beatrice now worked with the same expressionless smile.

One night two drunks whom she'd blown for twenty pesos apiece beat her and slashed her. Then, joined by two other men whom they'd met in their cantina, they raped her in a parking lot. Beatrice thought that she was going to die. That night she went out of her mind and she was glad that she did. In her whole life she never wanted to give any other human being such pain as those four men gave her. When she regained her senses, her first desire was to return home to Oaxaca, but she didn't have any money. When she made money again, she was already ashamed again. She began to feel hot and tired all the time. Her breasts ached. How could she dance, feeling like that? What was there for her to do in this world? An old *bruja* who knew how to burn certain flowers to make wishes come true offered to help Beatrice, but she refused the woman because witchcraft is not righteous. She gave birth to a sickly-pale child whose *tripas** hung out of his stomach. As soon as she saw him, she remembered the master of ceremonies who'd cried out: *Our Queen of the Yucatan* on that long ago Sunday, because his face likewise resembled a death's head. She named him Manuel after her *novio*. He cried day and night and could not digest her milk. She took him to the doctor to sew up his insides but the doctor said that Beatrice didn't have enough money. In the afternoons she brought Manuel to the dancehall. She had to keep him indoors so that he wouldn't get his intestines dirty from the dust. —You make a hole, she whispered to herself, and you put rocks and water in the top, just like Mama and Papa showed you, and you get the branches of those special trees, it's like a shower, and it's like if you have a baby, two or three days, you need to have one, to get the good milk from your breasts, not the bad one. It's like a medicine, to get the women well. To get energy . . . —She prayed to the Virgin. Then she put her feet up and drank beer on credit with the other whores, who raised their hands caressingly over the child.

Bad men and evil happenings now swarmed about her like colorless rainbows of water vomiting out of wide-throated roof-pipes. They swarmed about her like all the fishes in the sea, fishes finned or beaked, so finally she ran away from Merida with her child, whom for pity then she left with some nuns because his insides were too delicate for her life. All summer she travelled half an hour by bus every night to be with him, but by the Day of the Dead she felt too exhausted. She prayed to the Virgin unceasingly. She prayed when she was selling cakes in the street, when she was renting her pussy, when she was patching her shoes, when she was painfully dancing, trying to favor her abscessed leg, when she was defecating, when she was closing her handbag leaning up at the postal window nervously counting out centavos.

---

*Literally, his tripes. A prostitute in Mexicali whom I knew for several years told me this story. I never met the little boy, and the woman is dead now. God rest her. The congenital defect might have been an umbilical hernia or an anal prolapse.

She dreamed of the master of ceremonies. She dreamed that he was waiting for her, sitting with a wrapped boxed cake in the sunny street. In her dreams she heard his cry: *Our Queen of the Yucatan—sweet as a pastry, hot as a candle, bright as the sun!*

She went to Mexicali because a truck driver gave her a ride there. One day she became very ill with a shameful disease even though she had douched with vinegar. In the hospital they were all rude except for one old whore who told her that if she could run away across the border and hide from the American police, then money would come to her like rushing water turning the desert green. The old whore said that in American California she'd make eight or nine dollars an hour, out of which she'd have to pay the foreman only a dollar an hour to keep quiet. Beatrice lit a candle and prayed. She was afraid to go anywhere now, not excited the way she had once been when she was an ignorant young girl who had hardly even been kissed. She dreamed that she'd gone to America and seen a devil with a face of brass. She woke up screaming. But she'd also heard from other women that three months of illegal sweatshop work in Los Angeles (her legs were becoming too swollen for her to pick peaches or tomatoes, and, besides, the Americans preferred men for that) would support her for an entire year, and she was getting tired of Mexicali because some liar said she'd picked his pocket and so they wouldn't let her inside the bar anymore, compelling poor Beatrice to stand out in the street at night thrusting out her bosom at unaccompanied men. She felt so lonely that she cried. At least nobody envied her. She had nothing anybody wanted. One hot night a man came to rape her and she said to him: Why use force? I'm indifferent. If you want it, take it. Kill me; I don't care. —And then the man went down on his knees before her in the street, just like that, and apologized. He was drunk; he was a regular in the pulqueria.

Beatrice gathered together four hundred pesos, a blanket, a dagger, and a box of powdered sugar. Everybody laughed at her and told her to leave the sugar behind but she wouldn't. A man named Don Chucho took her across the border by night, in exchange for certain services. And then she was in America.

The first opportunity which the Virgin sent Beatrice was to work sewing baby clothes for an angry Korean lady who paid her four dollars an hour, with no breaks for lunch or even coffee. The Korean lady was always yelling at her. There were forty-five women in that place, and none of them had green cards. One morning the police came and she lost everything. But that very night, with the Virgin's help, she escaped from a window of the bus which was bringing her back to Mexico. Then she felt very free and very afraid. When she was hungry, she stole oranges from the trees. Striving to find her way without doing wickedness or suffering too much pain, she rented herself to the outcast men who lived in cardboard boxes, and they guarded her and sometimes gave her wine. Her desire to stay in America spread through her bloodstream. Someday she would certainly return to Mexico, but only because she had been born there. She could not dance anymore. Perhaps she wished to remain in America simply because the police wished to take her away, and in her experience the police never did people any good. She whispered to the Virgin, not yet knowing that it was for almost the last time.

How did Beatrice come to San Francisco? I don't know, but I am sure that the Virgin brought her. When she met the Queen at last, she closed her eyes but her heart felt as hot as Mexican light through varnished wooden Mexican blinds blinds drawn up as tight as they go for a Sunday afternoon lovemaking siesta which insistently admits wands of blinding brightness. Why? Because she had recognized that her Queen was the very same as that sad-eyed Virgin over the altar in that church in Merida.

Sometimes in one of the stinking dawns, the Queen saw tears oozing from Beatrice's dreaming eyes. When the other whores asked her to give Beatrice some remedy, some comfort, she shook her head, saying: What's gonna take away all her sorrows? Do you know? Let her sleep. Let her suffer in her dreams. Go make *yourselves* be happy! —When Beatrice woke up, she never remembered that she'd been sad in her sleep, and came running, longing to be close to the Queen's old, old face.

The other whores said *Maj*. Beatrice said *Mama*.

Of all her whores, the Queen loved Beatrice best excepting Sapphire alone. She often said to the others: Beatrice ain't like us. She's *Christian*. She don't bear that Mark of Cain. Beatrice, now, she's our special angel.

We worship, we revere with what we have. Isn't everything divine anyway? Just as in some Italian fishing town statues of the Blessed Virgin in their shrine-niches are framed by cockleshells, so in the Tenderloin I've seen crude drawings of the Queen framed by shards of broken glass.

| 115 |

The half-black girl with her blonde-dyed dreadlocks stood listlessly, pressing against the cool hotel window, her left cheek swollen and blistered and branded.

Got a cigarette, Maj? she said dully.

Martha, Martha, what happened to you?

I was talkin' to a friend while we was layin' on the floor and I rolled over against a hot iron.

Oh, shit, wept the Queen.

Why you always cryin', Maj? And now I'm waiting for my uncle to come pick me up and take me to the hospital but I guess he has some things to do . . .

Uncle who?

Uh—

Hey, Domino! shouted the Queen. You been training this one? She be waitin' on her old Uncle Crack!

Martha turned her weary back and said with effort: Hey, Strawberry, you got any smokes?

Just enough for my period, said Strawberry. Then she added gloatingly: And it's nice greenbud, too.

Martha went out onto Turk Street and stood against the wall that said:

J RIDAH BITCH
Hit me when your ready on the track
HIT ME BITCH

Two hours later she was still standing there, grinning frantically at men and cars. Meanwhile Strawberry, Chocolate, and Domino were all telling the Queen their woes. —My son's only twenty-six years old and he just got twenty-five years, Chocolate wept, and when she wept drool dribbled out between her missing teeth. He went to the public defender but that guy was just the public pretender. And they said my son was a killer. He didn't hit the other guy but once, and that guy went down and hit his head and died. Now he's at High Desert. And I can't see him. I got a letter from my parole officer and took it at the visitation hours but they said their regulations wouldn't let me see my son, 'cause I have a record. And they took away my six-year-old grandson and put him in foster care. I know he keeps asking for me, but they won't let me see him. —The Queen cried and kissed her . . . And Strawberry got drunk and read the Bible and told the others: *Everything is everything.*

| 116 |

Well, the Queen had said at the very beginning, some of you will follow me and some won't. The ones that won't, I won't give you no trouble if you don't give me no trouble. —Most followed her, proving the lie of the pimps who looked at streetgirls and laughed: They don't know *nothing* about unity, man. —Each one of them attempted to respect the Queen's silence. She lay there with her hair up in a massive bun intermixed with black yarn, her head sunken on her breast, long reddish beads around her arms, and around her neck a string of beads which the whores had given her, beads of colored glass from broken bottles. Every night they went out under their Queen's protective spell, every dawn returning to the Queen's lair in hopes of salvation and rest and even pleasure. Soon it seemed that they had always lived that way, for why shouldn't it be the case for them as well as others that God had made an oasis?

· BOOK VII ·

"Sometimes It Helps to Talk About These Things"

•

You intended to add to your stockholdings today . . . But you got busy and before you knew it the market was closed. What can you do now?

Quick Investors Quarterly (June 1998)

•

At four-thirty, suddenly the stream of bending knees, clicking high heels, straining sweaty throat-tendons began to increase, which is to say that it actually *became* a stream instead of a collection of episodes. Tired secretaries finishing the early shift, a few with shopping bags as well as briefcases (they must have gotten out even earlier, and run to a department store, a health food store or a record outlet—or had they done the deed at lunch hour?), were now reinforced by plump men with belt pouches, dependable beetle types. But as late as a quarter to five, the newspaper vendor was still basking against his kiosk, drumming his pallid fingers, resting his feet upon a plastic crate. Then the next wave of homegoers, more dense and urgent than the first, formed from everywhere, like scattered raindrops from the skyscrapers on high, joining together according to a single law even though each drop strove to be blind to all the others. They were all bipeds; their internal organs were similar, and they were going the same way. Yet they insisted on their uniquenesses and specificities. And in this I think they were correct even as they flowed together, some of them even running to join the mass, running down the clanking met-alled stairs. But still the old newspaper vendor only grinned and gaped and wisely picked his fingernails. His hair was as blindingly white as the metal temples of his spectacles. He understood very well that this was just the beginning, that his time was not yet. Sour-breathed office workers descended, then came the first bigshot, a suit man, a necktie man. He was a man with a *comfortable* leather briefcase which exhaled the smell of mild nonconformity. I pegged him for either a lawyer or a high-priced psychiatrist (post-Freudian). Seeing him, the newspaper vendor got to his feet. He cleared his throat and began to cry out the headlines just as the next wave came upon him, a torrent as of glossy beetles. I was once one of these. I remember being tired, hoping for a seat on the street-car, wanting to get home, dreading the effort of making dinner, knowing that the day was already gone because there was not much left in me, so I'd have to sleep early; maybe I'd read a page or two, or make a phone call; then I'd lie down "for a minute" and at seven in the morning the alarm would buzz in the harsh insect language which ruled me because I must now become a beetle again. Why must one be ruled? Because in the morning and at night, the financial district expands in all directions, following munici-pal routes. The intersection of Church and Duboce streets, for instance, which at other hours belongs to another neighborhood, suddenly becomes one of the financial district's vacuum cleaner hoses, which sucks up busloads of beetles into its darkness. At night it becomes one of many gas-jets discharging sweating, burning beetle-atoms all over the city. For this is the entrance to the subterranean realm, whose walls are now graffiti'd much more than I remember them to have been when I myself was a reinsurance drone rushing anxiously toward the financial district every morning, hoping that my streetcar would not stall in the tunnel and make me late. I was a beetle, and how could I not be?

If I were late, I would be in trouble. If the streetcar stopped, or if, already overloaded with beetles, it passed me by without opening its doors for me, I began to worry and seek my watch, calculating that if help, movement, came within seven minutes I still had a chance of not being late. I could not think of anything else. I was afraid to lose my job. The evening rush hour, even if still subjecting its participants to the laws of beetledom, was less harsh. Among the beetles I saw women wearing name tags and blood-red blazers, secretaries in black miniskirts, an ambiguous-status man in a loud tie, and they were tired; duties awaited them at home, but home was not work. If they lagged a little, or went twenty paces out of their way to buy a newspaper from the old vendor, they would not be burned for heretics. Now the five o'clock wave had struck, and its emerald dresses, its blowdry hair, and its neckties with diagonal grey stripes like subway tracks created a more formal impression. This wave took substance from the salaried workers. By five-thirty, business suits positively set the tone, and instead of beetles I spied many elegant benevolences chatting with the newspaper vendor, who, pop-up oracle, was explaining to them all the secrets of life, interspersed with horse-racing tips. (You want my tip? Don't bet on the horses.) Meanwhile, of course, the rush went on, and among its foaming vectors I began to glimpse recurrent subspecies: executive secretaries in goggle-like Italian sunglasses, misfortunately ill-timed tourists trying to unfurl their maps, friends and lovers (some of these comprising the adulterers whom Tyler stalked) touching shoulders, office-gossipers telling secrets, glasses-polishers who vaguely smiled, their neckties themselves as wide as smiles, and, darting among them, the bicycle messengers who kept the world running. There they all were on that bright and slanting artery, Market Street, with its buses, streetcars, and museum-escapee trolleys red and green humming through the web of blue-grey tracks. And then, just as I noticed an elegant businessman in a white shirt and shiny shiny shoes who was smoking in time with the beeping of a bus, I realized that it was six o'clock and that the seashell roar of departing humanity had dwindled; the tide was running out. The newspaper vendor sat back down on his crate, silent now, his face as blank as the file cabinets behind the dark green windowpane of Olde Discount Stockbrokers.

| 118 |

John had not yet departed the office. What use for him to hurry home? What use had there ever been, indeed? The bitterness of returning to an empty place did not perhaps greatly exceed the prior bitterness of entering a loveless one. He had always worked late in any event. When Joy and all his colleagues left, it was as if a certain banked and gentle flame within him suddenly brightened, warming, almost gilding his solitude. Every task became facile—or so it seemed while the hours flashed unobservedly by. Meanwhile, neither insults nor sorrows wrung his heart. A vague recognition of Celia struggled up to the surface of his mind, but she never expected him until late, and then only if he telephoned first. Hating crowds, longing to be the nucleus of a well-ordered zone, he worked comfortably all through rush hour, with brass-locked dark attaché cases bobbing past his window. Cigar smoke blandly perfumed the street. Mr. Singer, that solitary old law-tycoon with bald head bent, had long since stalked toward the Muni stop. Mr. Rapp's wife had picked him up just as Irene used to do for John. At seven, wanting to stretch his legs, John wandered down to look at the green quotation numbers jaggedly positioned, crawling leftward above the world in the open door of the Pacific Stock Exchange. Catching a blue glimpse of the security guard's belly protruding from behind a pillar, he smiled scornfully, then retraced his steps past the lovely honeycomb-reflections of tawny skyscrapers in the polished bays of other giants. —Working late, Mr. Tyler! observed the doorman cheerily. John tried to smile at the man. He needed to review Brady's documents on consolidated leverage. He also meant to phone Celia.

| 119 |

On Steiner and Jackson by the park, there rose a small yellow three-storey house the foliage of whose trees had been lovingly pruned into compact green balls like certain fireworks at the initial stage of the burst when the green dazzle (which appears so unwholesome by day and so eerie, even sinister by night) was at its maximum, having not yet converted its fuzzy edges into full-scale rays. This was the steep sunny windy place. This was Pacific Heights with its trembling dandelions and sidewalk moving sales. Celia lived here. On week days she was there almost infallibly by six-thirty every evening. Her business card offered her name and telephone extension in small black capitals beneath the name of the firm, which marched in immense gold letters across a zone of regal purple. The first time he saw it, John pitied her. She was, however, considered a competent broker. Her policies, which, like John's literary efforts for Rapp and Singer, were scarcely meant to be read by human beings, nonetheless seemed to renew themselves on time, and to be neat and somehow easy, because most of Celia's clients liked her. Her voice, friendly, yet modulated by the requirements of her impersonal epoch, could often be heard emanating from her cubicle in a steady telephone warble. No one had any real fault to find with Celia, as we have already seen from her personnel file, but at a quarter past five she was rising, wishing her colleagues goodnight, that trademark scarlet purse hanging from her left shoulder. At five-twenty she was waiting at the bus stop for the number 1 California. (Unlike Irene, who'd been at least in part a southern California girl, Celia did not drive everywhere.) Although she had never articulated her sentiments even to herself, she felt somewhere deep within her that whatever forces controlled her place of business did not regard her life or happiness to be of the slightest importance. They could, if they chose, demand that she relocate to Minneapolis, or they could close down her division at half a day's notice. Her father treasured up several such experiences, and her brother seemed to lose his job every two or three years. Granted that neither her father nor her brother had anything to do with the insurance business, Celia nonetheless believed that all such disappointments were of a piece. To her, and perhaps to many others in her generation, it seemed that the future would be worse than the present, that "stability" was a fantasy, and therefore that the proper way to live was to work decently and inconspicuously, for good compensation, and, while not foregoing retirement funds, to spend as much as possible of that compensation on movies, restaurants, "fun" clothes, nice furniture, a good view, and such indulgences. (I don't want to be inspired by pain, she said to her friend Heidi. I want to be inspired by *love*.) If John's self-distracting industriousness meant little to her, so did intellectual or spiritual seeking of any kind. It was not that she was incapable, only disinterested. Heaps of possessions and vacations adorned her life, and she went on toward the grave, neither happy nor sad. Credit card companies, mortgage brokers, long-distance telephone salespeople and resort profiteers continually solicited her. While she did not like them, they partially satisfied her anxious desire to be acknowledged. Every now and then she used her credit cards to buy things she could not really afford, and throughout the first or even second payment the satisfaction she experienced was almost sexual. Everyone she knew lived similarly.

She was a tall, pleasant-looking person with long reddish-blonde hair. She remembered Irene as wearing round glasses which made her look old, with her hair up. Irene had never liked to do anything with John. Celia suffered few doubts that she was prettier and more agreeable than Irene.

She had enrolled in the paralegal course less out of any interest in John's profession than to prove to both John and herself that she was not one of those hapless easy girls who wait around by telephones. Another thing she did to fill the time was keep lists, the latest of which went:

> apologize to CCK
> apologize to Dean and Stacey
> call Ellen to link template to Dean
> get Sandy out of the loop?
> finish first memo to Jerry
> call John ~~and ask him The Question~~
> set up tutorial

When Irene died, she began to suffer from terrible nightly headaches which impaired her studies, so she ended them. She believed that she had a great deal to reproach John for; however, now was not the time to air her grudges, but to deposit them in her mental vault where they could earn compound interest. It had become her intention to marry John even though she had no faith that he or any man could be "right" for her. When she thought of him, she thought of compatibility, security, stylishness. Sometimes she thought of having a baby. All these supposed motives helped to conceal that brutishly simple craving for companionship which draws widowers to street whores, crowds to dictators, monks to God.

I can't believe that Cardinal O'Connor, her brother Donald was saying on the phone. I detest that Cardinal O'Connor. He's exerting control and that's what I hate in religion. If you really look at him he's a revolutionary. He wants to throw out ideas to change people and he wants to tell people how to do things. Give the mother the ultimate choice.

Just a second, Donny, she said. There's a call on my other line. I think it's John.

Well, what do you think about what I said?

Just a minute, Donny. I'll be right back. Hello?

You're busy, said John.

Are you coming over?

No fear of that for at least two hours, he said. Can you wait up?

I was going to make dinner for you. I guess I can eat alone . . .

Well, you'd better get back to your other call, he said. Who is it?

It's my brother.

Tell him I can't stand the ties he wears. Tell him I'll take him to Donatello's and show him how it's done.

Oh, good grief, said Celia. See you.

Goodbye, said John.

John?

What?

Is something wrong?

I'm so *glad* that everybody keeps asking me that, said John, hanging up, positively grinding the phone into its cradle like some accolyte of mortar and pestle . . .

| 120 |

Rapp's already fifty-seven. I don't know what he's going to do when he retires. Me, I'm counting the days, Mr. Singer had said to John that afternoon, scratching his baldness. —Three hundred eighty-nine.

I'm sorry, said John. Three hundred eighty-nine what?

Days, John.

John's watch gleamed on his wrist at the edge of the white tablecloth. He raised his frosted mug of Sierra Nevada in a sort of toast and said: Well, Mr. Singer, we all have to reach that final deadline someday.

Ever the sentimentalist, John. Tell me this: Do you enjoy these private lunches?

Of course. By the way, the Brady contracts are almost ready for you to look at.

What do you mean, *almost* ready?

They'll be ready on Thursday, unless Brady makes more changes.

Good, good. Brady's definitely a live one. I know you take him out often on our nickel. Roland *lives* for private lunches, by the way. At least so he tells me. Mondays, lunch with Roland. Thursdays, lunch with John. See? I have it all here, right in my palmtop. It's got a built-in deadline alarm, too. Does Roland confide in you?

I pretty much stick to my work, John replied. It's no good getting confided in.

Do you feel as if you're somehow in *competition* with Roland, John?

Well, you made me full partner. You didn't make him full partner yet. I guess when you do, I'll have to compete with him. For the time being, I ignore him.

You know, John, I really like you. I don't know why. Maybe it's because you're such an unreconstructed sonofabitch. You just don't care. You're a hard young man, and hard men get things done. Do you know who Heydrich was?

World War II was before my time, said John. I'm a know-nothing.

Come *on,* young John. Don't let me down. What was Heydrich's first name?

Reinhard. Do you want me to back-burner the tobacco deal so we can wrap up Brady? I have to tell you that he may insist on more changes.

What's a meteope, John?

A rectangular slab above the architrave of a Doric temple. Can I go now?

Smiling a pink self-satisfied smile, leaning forward, Mr. Singer said: You know, Rapp and Singer have kept the same offices since '67. That was when they still had cobalt at Walter Reed Hospital. I guess they mainly use electricity now. Sometimes cesium. I'm going through all that again with my sister. In '67 it was my wife. You have a brother, don't you, John? What would you do if your brother were in intensive care, waiting to die?

Pull the plug, said John. And I'm going to back-burner those tobacco people.

Mr. Singer had a trick—actually less than unique—of staring wide-eyed through his glasses into his interlocutor's face and repeatedly addressing him by his first name, possibly because some book on business sincerity had advised it decades ago, or simply in order to retain the name in his memory. —Well, John, he'd say, it certainly was a tremendous disappointment about Reginald. He won't be coming back. —I don't suppose so, said John. —Mr. Singer leaned forward and took a deep breath, and John knew that the next word he would hear would be his own name.

John, he inquired, what does your brother do?

He's a snoop.

A lot of attorneys don't want to say after the Nader stuff that they're using private eyes. But you have to do it, of course. Can you recommend him, John? We'd use him on your say-so.

My brother? Hell, I don't know.

You said you'd pull the plug on him—hee, hee! Oh, yes, now I remember that he let us down that warehouse job. I'd forgotten about that. Or was he sick? Didn't you tell me he was sick? Say something, John.

You were talking about cancer, Mr. Singer.

Cesium is what they use these days. At least that's what they tell me. You've never had cancer in your family, have you, John?

Not yet, Mr. Singer. But there's always a first time.

In my case, it'll be the third time, if we count my wife. Of course a wife is not a blood relative.

John, of course, had no idea that just then Mr. Singer was remembering his young wife's lonely moments before the mirror, searching for her first wrinkle, wanting not to find it, hoping that when it came her husband would say that it didn't matter. Mr. Singer had caught her in front of the mirror almost every day when she was Irene's age.

So you were diagnosed? said John, squeezing his napkin in his lap. Well, I'm very sorry to hear that. And your parents?

Auto accident. Are your parents still alive?

Yes, said John, knowing that by the rules of discourse Mr. Singer, by virtue of his unsolicited confession, was now entitled to pick and poke through John's private life as he pleased.

You know, John, sometimes it helps to talk about these things. You understand why Rapp's not here today?

Doctor's appointment, said John, who knew everything.

When he heard my news, he got a scare. He went in for a checkup. They're probably giving him the sigmoidoscope treatment even as we—

Raspberry venison and spicy mussel salad, said the waiter. Enjoy your meal, gentlemen.

He's new, said Mr. Singer. John, is our waiter new?

I don't think so. His face looks very familiar.

And how's life, John?

Fine.

I know it's a painful subject.

Nothing compared to the sigmoidoscope treatment, said John, and Mr. Singer laughed and from the first steaming blue shell-tomb extracted with little silver pincers the occupant, which he dipped in butter and laid softly upon a bed of noodles.

John, I'm going to ask Roland to help you with Brady.

Is that a vote of no confidence?

Not at all, not at all. But you and Roland need to learn to work together—

Ah, thought John to himself. That means that he wants to make Roland full partner. Of course Rapp might not agree. I wonder if I should go along with this or make waves . . .

Do you object?

All right. I object.

Then I won't ask him. You see, I'm actually trying to help.

Noted and appreciated, said John through his teeth.

How are your in-laws coping?

They're not really on my wavelength. We don't keep in contact.

Ah. And how's your mother?

Fine. Better, actually . . .

Why don't you and your brother get on? Mr. Singer suddenly inquired.

Well, do you remember when I came to work with my left hand in a bandage? He slammed a car door on my hand.

And it wasn't an accident?

Nope. Hank doesn't commit accidents; he commits crimes.

Well, too bad we're not in the personal injury business, said Mr. Singer with a wink, trying to be upbeat, although with John that was sometimes difficult.

| 121 |

It had been a hundred and seven degrees in Sacramento at noon on Monday when Tyler passed the sidewalk of unfriendly summer school kids who kept wiping their sweaty upper lips, and he turned into his mother's driveway, whose hedges gave off the sour-bitter smell of malathion; his mother had been having problems with scale insects, so she went to Home Masters and purchased more of that poison sometimes used to commit murders, then went to work with her pump spray can. As soon as he got out of the car, his head began to ache, he wasn't sure whether from the malathion or simply from the heat, to which he was no longer acclimated. His T-shirt stuck to his chest and shoulders. A truck went by, clothed with grafitti as so many of them were now. There was a sour-bitter taste in his throat. All auto doors locked, his duffel bag over his shoulder, Tyler approached the front door, hating Sacramento, and rang the bell.

The front door opened almost at once, offering him air-conditioned air with a sour-bitter odor. It was John.

Has Mom been going crazy with the pesticides again? said Tyler, concealing his surprise at this apparition.

Oh, so you can smell it, too? said John. Well, don't just let the hot air in.

Tyler stepped inside , and John closed the door, a bit too quickly, he thought, a bit too loudly. The two brothers went into the living room. John sat down on the sofa, staring down at a water glass a quarter full of Scotch. Tyler went to the kitchen and got a bottle of fizzy water from the fridge. He was still carrying his duffel bag. He walked back to the front hall and set it down behind the umbrella stand. Then he returned to the living room, where John sat holding the untasted glass.

Where's Mom? Tyler said.

You mean you don't even know where Mom is?

No, I guess I don't. How are you doing, John?

Fine. Mom's chest pains got pretty bad yesterday. I just drove her to the hospital. I would have waited there, but she insisted that I come back here to let you in. It wasn't as if I couldn't have left you a note . . .

So that's how it is, Tyler thought. He said aloud: Well, John, I'm here now, so should we go to the hospital?

It doesn't matter now, said John vaguely, waving his hand.

Tyler inspected his brother closely. He said: John, are you drunk?

Let's leave me out of this.

Leave you out of what? You always want to be left out, or have something left out, or—oh, forget it.

I could punch you in the face right now, John said. The glass trembled in his hand.

Tyler was so made—or had made himself—that any threat effectively depersonalized and professionalized him, lowering between himself and the world several thicknesses of bulletproof glass. He smiled mirthlessly at his brother and remained in place, watching for any indication of abrupt movement from this body which might possibly strike at him.

Oh, you goddamn coward, said John after a while.

Tyler continued to smile, saying nothing.

Now John raised the glass to his lips and gulped it. He grimaced. His shoulders slumped. Tyler, with his not inconsiderable knowledge both of his brother and of violent people, was satisfied now that there would be no open battle. There had not been for a very long time. Because alcohol makes possible the realization of certain ugly wishes which fear (politely known as reason) usually keeps locked away in the lowest iron corridors of the cerebellum, Tyler had experienced for several instants a sickening surge of dread, far surpassing the anxiety he'd felt at the news of their mother's condition—not that he didn't love his mother; nor was he at all, as John had intimated, a coward; but there had been a number of occasions when as children they'd bloodied one another's noses; the antipathy between them was now so old that its causes were as lost to his knowledge as the creation of the world; he did not want to see it come out. Once while scuba diving he'd discovered within inches of him an anemone wriggling its tendrils, like any rotten apple upon whose top live and labor maggot swarms; and the sight of that actually inoffensive creature sometimes came back to him in dreams; his skull was the apple, and he did not want to feel the maggots of anger and hatred burst out. That was what he dreaded. And now, of course, Irene lay dead between them. When you swim up toward the surface of the sea you see a dimpled mirror of great sacredness; this is the goal of life and art and reason, to break through this barrier and leave the anemones once more invisible in the blue darkness; but on the other side one finds mosquitoes and weary heat; one goes to work and gets older; the anemones are still there, but they cannot come out; neither (more's the pity) can the beautiful corals beneath the sea, or the schools of yellow fishes raining down headfirst; that was one of the reasons why Tyler continued to pursue the Queen of the Whores, because he was convinced that the secret tremendousness in which she lived would be lovely like that; and anyhow anemones inside other people's skulls didn't bother him; it was only his own that he feared; John's anemones of course were Tyler's.

Well, he said, should we call the hospital?

Let's just go, said John. What's the point of sitting around here? I'm drunk. I'm worried about Mom. You'd better drive.

| 122 |

They went north on Highway 160, passing the Chinese restaurant where less than half a year ago Tyler, John, their mother and Irene had come for sizzling shrimp and cashew chicken. It had been a round table they sat at, Tyler flanked on either side by his blood relatives (although since the table accomodated five there was, naturally, an empty place between the two brothers). By some coincidence he found himself directly across from Irene, who smilingly enjoyed the food.

You probably want another helping, don't you? John said to her affectionately. You'd eat anything. You're a vacuum cleaner. No wonder you're getting fat.

Irene lowered her huge almond eyes.

John slipped an arm around his wife's shoulders. Across the table, Tyler, electrified with jealousy, gazed into Irene's averted face.

| 123 |

It's not serious, the doctor said to John, Tyler being the less well dressed of the two. Has she been following her diet?

I'm sure she has, John replied. She takes very good care of herself. But I'll have a talk with her. If Mom's been naughty, I guess I'll just have to lean on her a little.

Well said, well said! I can see that Mrs. Tyler's in very good hands. Now, you'll want to keep the air conditioning going while this heat wave lasts. That will make it easier on her heart.

He turned to Tyler. —And you are . . .?

The other son, Tyler said.

Oh, said the doctor, turning back to John. I can see she's in good hands.

| 124 |

They passed the Chinese restaurant.

How are you feeling, Mom? said Tyler.

Not very well, honey. I want to lie down.

Nobody said anything. John looked gloomy and anxious. They got home and John insisted that their mother lean on his shoulder while he helped her into the house.

Can you make it upstairs, Mom? Tyler heard him saying.

Tyler poured himself a drink out of John's bottle. Then, slowly, he went upstairs.

Can we go to the store and get you something, Mom? he said.

That's already taken care of, said John sharply. Don't tire her out.

Tyler leaned against the dresser, smiling sarcastically. Their mother was lying in bed looking at them both as if she wanted to say something.

You just lie there and rest, Mom, John was saying. We'll take care of everything.

Have a good rest, Mom, said Tyler, a lump in his throat.

He went downstairs to wait for his brother. He finished his drink, which was very smooth and good; John of course bought nothing but the best. Again he wondered how much Irene's coffin had cost.

John was still upstairs with their mother. Tyler stood up. He went to the kitchen to wash his glass. There was a saucer in the sink with bread crumbs on it, and he washed that, too, remembering a night a year or so previous when he and John and Irene had all been here for dinner and Irene had gone out to the kitchen to do the dishes. John was telling their mother some story about work. Had their mother been telling John a story, Tyler never would have chanced it, but since John had no greater listener than himself, and their mother came in a close second in that department, hanging, as always, on John's every word, Tyler got up quietly and passed through the swinging double doors to the kitchen where Irene stood over the sink with her hands in detergent lather, and he slipped his arms around her from behind. He had meant only to embrace her about the waist, and it shocked him to find his palms had opened and were grasping her firm little breasts. Her nipples were hard against his hands. Irene continued to wash the dishes, not pulling away, not saying anything. He stood there like that with her for a moment, and then he let her go. She went on washing the dishes.

Leaning up against the refrigerator, Tyler had said: I wish I could have married you.

You're so sweet, said Irene.

I wonder what that means, Tyler thought to himself.

He got a bottle of fizzy water for his mother, and one for John, and went back into the dining room where John's story was still going on. When it had finished, John pushed the bottle away from him and said: And how was Irene, Henry?

Later, when John was in the bathroom, Irene came to him and laid her head down on his shoulder, and he stroked her hair.

He finished rinsing the glass and saucer. He thought to himself: After Mom dies, I don't want to come back to this house ever again. It hurts too much.

He heard John's footsteps, quick and sure, coming down the stairs. The booze must have worn off. He heard the steps in the living room, then he heard them come toward him.

How is she? he said.

You're not thinking about Mom, said John, unsmiling. You never think about her. I know who you're thinking about.

Should we go buy her some groceries?

All right, said John, slugging down a glass of cold water from the sink. I'll drive.

Where are you parked?

Down by Mrs. Antoniou's house. I left the driveway for you. There's not enough room for both of us.

Tyler waved at Mrs. Antoniou, whom he saw peering at them from behind her tiny window in the front door. Her lawn was as unhealthily dry as always, and marred by crab grass. The Rosens next door always complained, worrying, perhaps, that crabgrass was as catching as crabs. Domino had had crabs. They got in the car, and John inserted the key. Something chimed, and their shoulder belts slowly whirred down. John fastened his lap belt, but Tyler didn't. John frowned but didn't say anything. Resting his chin lovingly upon his own left shoulder, John backed out of the driveway and swung the car's hindquarters west. Then he shifted and let out the clutch.

How's work? said Tyler.

Fine, said John.

You still working on Brady's new company?

Oh, I told you about that? said his brother, surprised. That's right; you were one of his clients.

No, he was one of my clients.

That's what I meant, Hank. He came to us right after the Peterson case was resolved. Pretty lucrative?

The Peterson case?

No, I meant Brady.

Very.

Listen, John. There's something you ought to know.

Sour grapes, is it? said John with his usual quick intuition of Tyler's worst motives. You want to backstab Brady because he fired you? I'm going to take us to Priceway.

Okay, fine, said Tyler.

So what should I know?

You know what Brady's business is?

Of course I know. Are you saying I don't do my homework?

It's virtual girls, right?

Well, that and a lot of other things. Slot machines, restaurants, a family arcade. So what?

He may be riding for a fall. I've heard from at least one source that those girls are real, although I haven't verified it. It's forced prostitution and maybe worse, do you understand?

Yeah, you'd know about that, said John, steering. Look, Hank. Don't worry your head about that. You're way out of your depth.

Okay, John. I just don't want you to get in trouble.

His brother laughed and laughed, so that Tyler could see the adam's apple jerking and twitching. —That's news, he finally said.

There was a long silence, and then John finally said in a tentative voice: About Brady, I . . .

You what?

Oh, forget it. Forget the whole thing.

There was another silence, and then John said: Well, are you willing to check him out for me?

What do you mean?

You're a private eye, Hank. What do you think I mean?

We have access to this stuff, yeah, we're licensed, and I maintain a lot of insurance. I really think if we don't self-regulate the government's going to come along and do it for us.

In other words, no.

Oh, I'll do it. I've already done it. That's what I've been trying to tell you. What do you want to know?

You're telling me you won't do it. You're saying you won't help out your own brother. I never said that at all.

Then what's all this crap about self-regulation? You think I don't know a euphemism for *no?* You don't have the guts to say no outright, do you?

You know, John, I'm tired of your crap, Tyler was shocked to hear himself say. I'm really tired of it. How long are you going to hold Irene's death against me?

Let's leave my wife out of this. Don't ever let me hear you mention her name. You have no right to mention her name, do you understand me?

If you want me to leave her out, then don't keep bringing her up. You're the one who keeps making insinuations.

They sat there with trees and houses and street signs slowly passing them, and John's throat jerked, and John said: You're right. I admit it. Now tell me this. Did you ever go to bed with Irene?

No, John, I never did. I won't deny that I kind of envied you . . .

You crooked bastard, his brother laughed.

What does that mean?

You know what it means, Hank. Hank the prick.

So you're calling me a liar, John?

You were a liar before you came out of Mom.

I'll let that one pass. Now, John, for the last time, I'm telling you that I never slept with Irene. Do you believe me or not?

Forget it, said John. We can have this out after Mom—after Mom's better. We can't stress out Mom.

No, I'm not going to forget it, Tyler said. We're going to have this one out right now. Either you believe me or you don't. If you believe me you've got to stop making those remarks, because I can't tolerate them anymore. If you don't believe me, John, then I guess I, uh, I don't want to see you.

Is that a promise? I should be so lucky.

We can work out Mom's care so that we don't have to meet.

You feel pretty strongly about this, don't you, shithead?

Okay, John, one week off, one week on. I'll take the rest of this week being on call for Mom. If she needs me, I'll come up. You take next week. She'll like it better that way. It's not good for her to see us—

Tell me about it.

So, will that fit into your schedule?

John made an illegal U-turn. —Let me drive you back to the house then, Hank, he said. You can get in your car and go back to the city right now. I'll call you if there's an emergency.

Oh, so you'll take the rest of this week then?

That's right. I'm already up here, and unlike you, some people have to work.

Let me give you some money for Mom's groceries, said Tyler. Is forty bucks enough?

You can keep your goddamned stinking money, said John. Let's make it Monday to Sunday. That way we each get a weekend.

Sure, John.

And another thing. Don't let me catch you down at Irene's grave anymore.

Tyler said nothing, but he reddened with rage.

Did you hear me?

I heard you, John. Why don't you let me out here? It's only a few blocks to Mom's house. I'd really rather walk it.

John accelerated. He was doing almost fifty in a thirty-five mile an hour zone. He went through a red light. His face was the color of brick. Tyler felt extremely hot, and there was a hurtful tightness inside his ribs.

I said, did you hear me?

Cemeteries are public places, John, said Tyler with a deliberately goading laugh, and watched John grip the wheel harder with his right hand while his left hand became a fist and began to swing toward him as John's face turned away from the road, and just then there came a yowling of horns and John's eyes flicked rapidly back to the view ahead; they'd just driven through an intersection, and a police car was already coming with full siren.

You don't want to hit me now, John, said Tyler. Not in view of a cop. That wouldn't be good for your career.

John pulled over.

Not here, John, said Tyler. This is a bus zone.

He opened the passenger door and leaped out. John, murderous-eyed, began to reach toward him, so Tyler slammed the door on his hand. He heard his brother scream with pain, and instantly his gloating, furious joy became anguish.

| 125 |

O George Eliot with your garden parties, formal dinners, long leisurely meetings, family discussions; O Dostoyevsky (beloved of Mrs. Tyler) with your glittering-eyed train-companions listening to each other's life stories, your wretched, teeming flats inhabited by souls intoxicated by quarreling and religion; I ask you, where have all the interlocutors gone? For there are more people than ever; and more strange worlds in San Francisco, which does itself comprise a world, than can ever be plumbed! And yet Tyler cogitates alone, as does his brother. Is it television that's done it? Or is there some other reason why people just don't talk to each other anymore? Granted, Dan Smooth is eager to talk; he has a longing to defecate his soul's excrement upon the consciousnesses of others; and Mr. Rapp and Mr. Singer will both likewise unburden themselves to John if they are in the mood; Celia yearns for John to communicate with her; Mrs. Tyler checks in regularly with both her sons; Irene, perhaps, seeks to explain something from beyond the grave; all the same, when I peer into the sky-blue screen of the computer on which I compose this, I see all the way down to San Francisco where Henry Tyler himself sits alone. And so many people, too! Old Chinese with bowed, capped heads, wearing jackets the color of smoke, passed slowly, occluding the gratinged streetwall as Tyler sat wearily inhaling the scent of green tea, and static distorted the white legs of television baseball players into wriggling shrimp. Less rudely than indifferently the red-jerseyed waiter set his dinner down. Snow peas, miniature corn, and white chicken pieces shone with oil. Ten dollars. Outraged, he under-tipped. Although he had been to Chinatown with Irene, it force-fed him no sad associations, unlike all the worlds of coffee shops in Noe Valley, each with its own devotees and sidewalk benches, its courtyard cafés and restaurants, to several of which he had taken Irene, its liquor stores whose virtuously learned salesmen could unblinkingly explain the palate-differences between Caol Ila and Ardbeg; on those foggy, chilly summer days, women strode along rapidly with lowered heads; boys with boyfriends walked the dog. People were talking there; he was all wrong; there were no silences. A sudden rattle of a startled pigeon's wings, and then a family gathering of smiling Chinese punctuated the day, above which the faux Jurassic terrariums of trees reflected in the watchful bay windows of two- and three-storey Victorians provided spurious greenery. A paramedic sat in his ambulance truck, the engine idling. He, or someone like him, had probably sat just like that while his colleagues brought Irene out.

Tyler drove down to Capp Street, but there were no women on the corner. Maybe there'd been a sweep, or maybe it was merely too early.

He drove to the Tenderloin and thought he saw Domino, but she disappeared into a hotel too quickly to be sure.

He drove down to Mission Street and parked at Fifth. Then he began to stroll aimlessly. Inside the new Museum of Modern Art building, which was striped with smooth black and rough grey stone, there was a Frida Kahlo exhibit, and a bespectacled woman said rapidly to her companion: All of her portraits deal with her *pain* and *suffering*.

This concept seemed to make the other woman very happy. —Go ahead, thought Tyler to himself. Go get empowered.

I guess she's the patron saint of women, a sour man was saying to *his* buddy. In this show they relate to her through their menstruations or something.

Christ, he thought, I don't know which of them is worse. Probably the guy, because he's so obviously malicious, whereas Ms. Spectacles there is just a parrot. I guess I prefer parrots.

Then suddenly he recollected Domino on the bed in the Tenderloin hotel room. She'd complained about something and he'd sarcastically replied that this heart bled. —Of course, it always bleeds around now, he'd said. It's that time of the month. —He began to sweat with shame when he remembered, admitting to himself that he was as boorish as anyone. But then defiance stung him and he thought: Well, she deserved it. She was so humorless and shrill. She kept asking me if I was a misogynist. She kept . . .

He went to the gift shop and bought his mother an exhibition catalogue.

The sour man was at the gift shop also. He wasn't buying anything, anything. Tyler saw him spitefully fold down the page of a book, while the other man grimaced with mirth. He kept saying unpleasant things about women. Tyler started hating him. He wanted to feel tolerance or even compassion for the man, because hatred on such grounds really constituted hatred for himself. Tyler might not actually be, as Domino had labeled him in her catholic hostility, a misogynist, but he confessed his grey and nasty edges. The encounter with John had left him in a state of anxious irritation; he was not himself. He had a friend in Noe Valley who'd embarked on a program of self-improvement through meditation. Tyler asked whether meditation would in and of itself induce serenity (he had in mind the feeling he experienced when he sat inside the Roxie movie theater with its smell of stale popcorn, waiting for the commencement of some comfortingly ancient print of a European film about other people's problems, with subtitles which would tersely recapitulate dialogue of a picturesque langorousness and sadness). The friend was of two minds about that. If one's aim was to reach a higher spiritual level, the end result might be increased coherence, and thus perhaps decreased strain on the soul; but to get to that point, one would surely be required to rearrange oneself, which necessitated disequilibrium. It was obvious to Tyler that his relations with John were moving toward some permanent conclusion of honest mutual exposure. But what if that change were actually, as any superficial observer would conclude, a *regression* such as driving down the hill to Gough Street where it was low and dark with many weak stale lights? For that matter, one might propose as an example that same Roxie Theater, where he had once taken Irene to see "Queen of Hearts," in hopes of holding her hand in the darkness. The movie had not yet begun. Tyler was already feeling serenity (mixed, to be sure, with pleasurable anticipation; he was hoping that Irene's delicious palm might sweat against his at all the thrilling parts); however, some noisy boys with yarn in their long hair were sitting in the row ahead; and Irene, shocked, said to him: I'm just looking at those four people in front of me and they're drinking hard liquor! —She was a little prudish; she could not enjoy herself after that. —Tyler's friend had proposed that a graphic representation of travel from one spiritual level to another might well require many more than two axes, so that one might simultaneously be rising on one plane and sinking on another. The Gospels said that a seed could not flower until it had fallen into the earth and died. Tyler could not remember exactly how the parable had gone. He wished to know more about Christ, even if only to struggle against Him and clarify his own allegiance, which, as Dan Smooth had jeeringly insisted, might well be to the Canaanite idols. If he was satanic or ungodly or merely unbrotherly, wasn't it worse to fog over the fact, pretending that he was still trying to be good? Although he still felt wretched whenever he recalled that hot afternoon in his mother's living room with the reddish-brown blinds drawn against the sun and his mother asking whether he and Irene had betrayed John, his anguish contained a tincture, however pale, of relief. He had not obfuscated. He had quite simply and bluntly refused to answer her charges. It's too late for that, he had said. No matter what he might fear or yearn for, month by month his existence was clarifying itself. The issue of Irene, rather than dissolving with Irene's dead flesh, continually took on a more evident and permanent materiality. Irene no longer lay but *stood,* no, *towered,* between himself and his mother, between himself and John. Well, let it be so. Irene was the seed of Christ. She had died, and now she rose up bearing leaves and fruit like the grand old tree in his mother's front yard. Tyler had not and would not contest anything. He would let all aspersions be. He would wait, and live, until the change within him was complete; then he'd know what to do.

But he was afraid. And his was one of those natures which do not cower, but bristle at a threat. He scorned to reply to his mother or argue with John, but he could not help feeling an aching resentment which narrowed his eyes and ground tooth against tooth within his mouth. The sour man at the gift shop, who probably was unafflicted by awareness of Tyler's very presence, was flipping through the catalogue now, calling Frida Kahlo a man-hater, a vagina-centered mediocrity, a once-a-month artist. To the sour man, it seemed, no woman had a brain, and Frida Kahlo's paintbrush was one with the tongues of the ice-cream-licking girls in the bright bay window of Rory's Twisted Scoop. And Tyler was incensed. The reason, of course, was that the whole world incensed him just then, but seeing that would have entailed seeing his own absurdity, so it merely seemed to him at that moment that any slighting nastiness directed toward femininity must insult Irene's memory. He craved Irene. Closing his eyes, he saw her once again. She had lost a little weight since her marriage and her skin was stretched tight over her cheekbones so that she resembled a pale, debauched skull. Round and round, round and round. He had nowhere to go.

I see you're actually buying that catalogue, the sour man said to him.

I'm a misogynist, Tyler said. I'm just buying it to jerk off to.

The sour man, uncertain whether Tyler was on his side or instead a sarcastic enemy, remained silent. The sour man's friend, more astute, glared.

The salesgirl took the catalogue out of Tyler's hand to scan it through the red laser eye-beam beside the register and said: I heard what you said.

I'm evil, Tyler replied. But I do have enough money to pay for that. Yep, I'm a paying customer. I'm an *American.*

I think you're disgusting.

Tyler could hear the sniggers of the two diabolical men beside him. He had struck a blow against feminism. He had come out on the side of Satan. They were sure that he was one of them now.

He turned around and said to them: I bear the Mark of Cain.

Then again they fell into a baffled silence.

You're sick, said the salesgirl.

It was a clammy summer's night in the Marina, lights frozen at the bases of harbor-masts. He went up Buchanan Street, and across from the Safeway met a bright window offering row upon row of massage chairs in an empty room. Near a dessert shop—yes, almost within reach of the fragrance of chocolate and steamed milk—he spied another parking garage, now closed, and peered down a long curvy greasy tunnel of light which passed beneath a round mirror, different only in scale from what the dentist always put in his mouth; then a right turn put an end to his seeing. The Queen could be there now; she could be anywhere. But no—why would she be here? This place was too far from the humid commerce she fed on. He sighed and trudged on, a little cold. Farther up the street, at Bay, a store of telescopes on tripods and binoculars in narrow glass shelves on the wall caught his attention; it had probably been closed for a good four or five hours now. Did John ever shop here? Tyler turned onto Bay and stood beneath the greenish foggy sky, on his left white flowers so bright and lovely and uncruel.

| 126 |

Oh, what a lovely catalogue! his mother said. Thank you, Henry. It looks as if it does full justice to the original. The colors are beautiful. What do you think of Frida Kahlo's work?

I think it's pretty good, but not as good as Diego Rivera's, he said. I respect her.

It's really quite moving, don't you think?

Yes, I do, he said.

That was really thoughtful of you, his mother said. What a treasure.

Well, I'm glad you like it. How are you feeling?

A little weak, but not so . . . Henry, where's John? I was under the impression that you were coming up with John . . .

| 127 |

And meanwhile John worked late at the office, beneath and among those great plaid and pulsing mirrors called skyscrapers. One time Chocolate, high on crystal meth, got chased out of the Tenderloin by the police, and when she came into the financial district it was rush hour with summer's blue and gold peach-fuzz light on the skyscrapers, and a businessman in a multitude of businessmen marched crushingly toward her; Chocolate's eyes could not let go of his face. —That man's a skyscraper! she thought crazily. —He's so tall and wide and rectangular! He's shouting something about smoking cigars with his friends . . . —And indeed at that hour all the skyscrapers were moving like chessmen, so it seemed to her. Twenty-one storeys above her, chessmaster John moved his queen's knight's pawn on the tobacco brief, while in Pacific Heights lonely Celia sat smoking cigarettes, waiting for him to telephone.

| 128 |

Do say something clever for us, John, said Mr. Rapp.

I don't feel like it.

You're not going to disappoint us, now, are you, John? Because that just wouldn't be good enough.

I am afraid that we are going to find pleasures in some cases opposite to pleasures, John snarled. —Plato, *Philebus,* 13a.

Well said! cried Mr. Rapp, clapping his hands. But is that perhaps a comment on the present proceedings? You see, everybody, how clever our new full partner is? Roland, could you top that? And, by the way, what's your impression of Plato, John? I dip into the *Laws* from time to time . . .

Just another egghead, Mr. Rapp, said John. There are too many eggheads in the world.

Now, John. I need to ask you something. With your legal bent, and your gift for recitation, aren't you yourself, perhaps (dare I say it), *an egghead?*

No, Mr. Rapp. I'm a performing animal. I perform under duress, or for a reward.

Ouch, John, that was cruel! It may be true, but sometimes it's better not to say those things.

· BOOK VIII ·

Sunflower

•

Until women can attain not only a genuine independence in relation to men but also a new way of conceiving themselves and their
role in sexual relations, the sexual question will remain full of unhealthy characteristics and caution must be exercised in proposals
for new legislation. Every crisis brought about by unilateral coercion in the sexual field unleashes a "romantic" reaction which
could be aggravated by the abolition of organized legal prostitution.

GRAMSCI, prison notebooks (*ca.* 1930)

•

Sunflower died, and Beatrice said: You know those candle with the color? It's better to buy them than to make them. Otherwise the dead people, they doan accept.

But Domino said: What should I buy that bitch a candle for? One time she begged me to show some heart and loan her ten to fix, so I did and then she never paid me back. She just pissed my kindness away.

The Queen, who until just now had been alone going through her spells like old Chinese women rapidly shuffling through an immense pile of purple eggplants, tossing them all aside, searching for the perfect vegetable, said: Domino, I want you to be quiet now an' listen. Sunflower died for *you*. She laid herself down an' took those bullets of pain that were comin' for *you*, to which Domino replied in bored unwholesome fashion: Nobody died for me, not even Jesus, and the Queen said: Not Jesus, that's exactly my point, Dom. You gotta find the *other* kind of happiness. I mean that Canaan brand . . . to which Domino replied: Oh, *please!* then said to Beatrice (just to get a rise out of her): You know why I call Sunflower a bitch?

She's no bitch.

You know why? Because she was a *dog*. And now you know what she is? A *dead* dog. A dead, stinking dog!

That Henry Tyler's comin' here again, announced the tall man.

Domino brightened. —Henry, boy! she shouted. I know you have a relationship with your dick, but why don't you zip up your fly?

All rightie now, the Queen chuckled. All right.

Why you doan care about Sunflower? whispered Beatrice. She was a nice, nice girl . . .

C'mere, Bea, said the Queen.

But Beatrice leaned against a concrete block, resting her big cheek on her fingers. When she closed her eyes she could see the white door of eternity, cracked through the whitewash, now gaping ajar, so that there was a darkness, with something rough and shaggy beside it; she could see Sunflower ascending the bare brown hill of death, drawing near that door around which beautiful little girls peered in dirt-streaked dresses, waiting to welcome Sunflower with their black hair and black eyes. She heard the death's-head master of ceremonies whisper: *Sweet as a pastry, hot as a candle, bright as the sun!*

Since Beatrice was saying nothing, Domino thought to see in her what she had always perceived in Sunflower, namely, the shine of naked idiocy, so she said: You're a dog, too, bitch! at which the Queen, sighing, got up and went out; but Beatrice replied, smiling bitterly: They say, doan hit that dog, but if you die, that dog will carry you across the black river.

I dunno *what* the fuck you're talking about. You bitchy little bitch . . .

Come on, Bea, said Strawberry. Let's go make some money.

Bye-bye, Henry, said Beatrice. Anytime you call me, I come running, running!

I get it, said Tyler with a laugh.

He stood there a little uncertainly, wondering whether he were supposed to follow the Queen.

Meanwhile, waggling their asses and smiling into the oncoming traffic, the two whores strolled backward down Sutter past Jones to the old Commodore Hotel outside which they waited for an hour or two, then shifted battle stations to O'Farrell and Jones by the Gazebo Smoke Shop with its zebras of tiles. It was hot and bright enough to make Strawberry squint, so they went and stood by the 501 Club where the shadow of something fraying on a wire trembled just above the orange cocktail glass on the sign. Down the gently sloping street, a building which many decades ago might have been called a skyscraper stood up-pointing like a stubby hypodermic needle with an American flag on it on that sweltering Sunday afternoon, no one going in or out of the locked gate of the Hong Kong Oriental Massage.

Fat sunny Beatrice, crossing her arms under her breasts, her treetrunk thighs spread wide apart as she leaned against a barfront, finally said: You sad about Sunflower?

Sure, baby. I know Maj will give her a nice funeral. You'll see.

Who you like better, Sunflower or Domino?

Ain't no comparison. Sunflower I love, but Domino's just a sick, sadistic, unhealthy, *unwholesome—*

What's the worst thing that make her so bad?

She has HIV, you know, and she's still selling pussy. I call that selling murder.

They stood there all afternoon. Their feet got tired. The sun went behind a cloud, and then it got foggy and then it rained. Beatrice sighed, lifting one foot, then the other. The rain came down harder and harder.

A drunken panhandler lay down under his shopping cart. Rainwater washed his purple face.

Hey, said Strawberry, shaking him. Hey, mister. Don't lie down there to sleep in the rain. You'll get pneumonia and die.

The man vomited. Strawberry helped him to his feet. He puked all over her, then slowly wove down the sidewalk, leaving his cart behind.

Strawberry began to laugh. —You think I can still make money this way?

Oh, shit, chucked Beatrice. Oh, shit. You doan smell so nice now, honey. Thank God for rain. Maybe this rain is gonna wash you clean.

Fuck that, said Strawberry. My feet hurt. Let's go back.

You go, said Beatrice. I gotta get well now. I need it.

I got an extra dose of china white, said Strawberry. I'll share with you if you promise to pay me back.

Okay, thank you, baby. Let's go. I pay you back tomorrow. I promise. Where's our Mama gonna stay tonight?

She said that place off Eddy Street, you know, that black hotel . . .

I know. That *bad, bad* place.

Don't worry, Bea. Queen's gonna be there.

I know. Oh, my back hurts. You have that china white on you?

No, you wait here. I got to go get my secret stash. I'll be right back.

She ran off. After an hour, Beatrice, bitter and exhausted, was just about to give up when one of her regulars, a middle-aged widower whose paunch curved like an old Union Pacific roundhouse, pulled up and she ran to his car. They went to the Lonely Island Hotel.

Short time? said the Indian woman at the top of the stairs.

Beatrice nodded.

Fifteen dollars, said the Indian woman.

The john reached into his wallet and paid. The Indian woman led them to a room which overlooked the street. In the wastebasket lay a freshly used condom, oozing slime.

Beatrice took off all her clothes, eased herself down onto the mushy, unstable mattress, and immediately fell asleep. She was dreaming of Sunflower. The john, who was a good man, stood there for a while watching his fat and pretty whore lying on the bed snoring with her legs spread, ever so slightly moving her abscessed pelvis in and out. Then he put thirty dollars onto the nightstand and went out, softly closing the door behind him.

| 130 |

Beatrice dreamed of Sunflower.

| 131 |

Later that same night, while Mrs. Tyler was bathing Mugsy, and Dan Smooth sat on his porch reading in the *Sacramento Bee* that chemical castration had been approved after all for recidivist sex offenders, Tyler, coughing, sauntered through the Tenderloin and came into the Wonderbar, which the tall man had just entered with a stolen calculator, rolling his bloodshot eyes, croaking: Hey, you want this? It's got a built-in briefcase. How can you be without it? until he got eighty-sixed by Heavyset and stamped out cursing, vengefully smearing on the sidewalk some stinking shoe-ooze which was yellow-green like the meat of a Mexican avocado. And of course it was at the Wonderbar that Tyler found Domino, who was not yet crack-paranoid but her face had already turned the color of weak tea in a glass in one of those Vietnamese soup restaurants on Jones Street, and she wore a mask of sweat.

He sat down beside her. —Where's Maj?

Henry, you don't know shit. She never comes in here. Not unless she really needs something.

So that's why you're here, huh? While the cat's away the mice will play.

Oh, fuck off.

You don't look too well.

I'm not.

Did you get that photo of you I left with Justin?

It looked like *me,* she said happily.

You remember when I took that?

No, I guess I was too fucked up . . .

Tyler coughed.

And what's wrong with *you?* said the blonde.

Oh, just a light case of AIDS. The gift that keeps on giving, know what I mean?

What did you say? she cried in a rage. *I can't believe what you just said.*

Oh, I'd never give *you* AIDS, Domino, he said, coughing.

She relaxed. —Have a lozenge, she said, opening a flat silver tin of pills.

Why, thank you, sweetheart.

What'll you have, dear? said Loreena the barmaid.

Shot of tequila, he said.

Loreena poured the shot to the brim as always, brought the lime and said: Three hundred and fifty dollars. Tyler gave her four dollars and squeezed the lime in.

Here, he said to Domino. You want a sip before I mix my germs in?

All right, the blonde said, poising her twin straws over the glass like a blonde mosquito. —Hey, wait a second. Why's it so cloudy? Did you put your dick in there?

Sweetheart, if I put my dick in it would be ruby red, he told her.

Oh, you're so *sick!* she chuckled. Suddenly she hugged him. —That's why I like you . . .

Another john sat down next to them and said to Tyler as if the blonde weren't there: She's beautiful, isn't she?

Yes she is.

Buy you a drink?

All right. Thank you.

I grew up in this bar, the john said. I literally grew up right behind that pool table. I'm an alcoholic, and proud of it. My Daddy was an alcoholic, too. He popped off at forty-eight. I've been in this bar all my life, and I'll never forget the night Domino first walked in.

Uh huh, said Tyler.

The john drank down his beer as rapidly as a police car speeding the wrong way down Turk Murphy alley in Chinatown, and then he ordered another one, hushed and resigned connoisseur, unlike John and Celia, who were wine-tasting in Napa in a babble of words, driving from vineyard to vineyard so that stakes and inhumanly regular leaf-heights strobed by beneath the tree-swollen hills, Celia remarking on the lovely weather, John checking each winery off the map as they pulled up to the tasting room. But as soon as the two beers had passed into the john's blood, he likewise brightened and found his strength, now feeling as able as John or Celia to kick up a little social dust, praise God, so he clapped his hand on Tyler's shoulder and with a smile as ingenuous as a little boy's asked him what sort of work he did.

As little as possible, said Tyler, unimpressed by his rejuvenation.

I'm a welder, the man rushed on, or I should say I *was* a welder. They just laid me off last week.

I'm sorry to hear that, Tyler said. In that case I'll buy you the next round.

Well, so you and I have something in common, the john said.

You mean Domino, said Tyler wearily.

She's a peach, ain't she? the john said, glowing with enthusiasm.

Domino, are you a peach?

Oh, fuck off, Henry.

You already said that.

Well, fuck off again.

You know what she and I make together? the john cackled breathlessly.

Let me guess. Peaches and cream.

Oh, you're so *sick,* chuckled Domino.

Tyler had sometimes seen this man going out to get pizza or soda or whatever Domino needed when she was too drunk and had to run into the ladies' room to vomit and after that slowly let her head sag down onto the bar in that nightly sunset of hers. The john took care of her. He fed her as if she were a baby bird. His bald, ugly face shone with sacredness when he was helping her. He loved her. Even when she was terrible to him she was good to him, because she gave him something to love.

I took her to our Christmas party, the john confided with a blush, and everybody kept comin' up to me and sayin': *Who's that goodlookin' broad?*

How long did she stay with you? Tyler asked curiously.

Oh, all night, said the john. And she danced like—it was the finest sight in the world.

Domino smiled. —And it was. That's how I dance. *When* I dance.

So she had a good time?

She said she did. I think she was happy.

Hey, Dennis! whined the blonde. When are you gonna take me home? I need some man to take me home. I'm feeling kind of fucked up . . .

Let me finish my drink first, said the john. Then I'll take you wherever.

No! shouted the whore. I will *not* wait for you to finish your drink, you stupid old misogynist! Fuck you and go to hell! Go to hell! Go to . . . oh, I, I, I'm going to be sick . . .

Loreena, we're going to need some napkins, said Tyler.

Well well *well,* said the barmaid. Domino's puking on my bar, so it must be eleven-o'clock. You can practically set a clock by Domino's . . . Oh, look at that. Oh, Jesus.

And after the dance she—

Take her *home,* Dennis, said the barmaid.

Domino? Domino, where you stayin' at, sweetheart?

At my—at the—Maj . . . the girl croaked.

At your what?

I know where she wants to go, said Tyler. I'll take her.

No! You don't even like me! You just . . . Oh, what's the point?

All right, fine, you can take her, the john said. But don't be takin' advantage of her when she's messed up like that. It's not a righteous thing to do.

Wipe your mouth off a little bit, Domino, said Tyler. Can you walk?

I lost one of my heels.

That's all right, he said. The car's right across the street.

I *said,* I lost my goddamned high heel.

So what do you want? he said wearily. I know. You want me to buy you new high heels.

That'll work . . .

Fine. Now get in the car.

Thanks for being such a gentleman, the blonde muttered drunkenly.

Just lie down in the back seat. Don't be afraid of me.

I'm not afraid. I love you, Henry. You're the only one who's nice to me.

Thank you, sweetie.

Dennis is just an asshole. And I hate Loreena's guts.

I get it, said Tyler, blinking his eyes.

I *said* you're the only goddamned one who's ever been nice to me. The only one in the whole goddamned world. You want me to suck your dick?

Never mind.

I want to suck your dick. What's the matter, cocksucker, you think just because you have a car and I don't you're any better than I am? Why, I don't give a fuck about you and your car! I should kick all your goddamned windows out! I . . . Oh, Henry, please, I'm going to be sick . . . Please make it stop.

It's all right, Domino. It'll stop soon. You'll feel better soon.

I'm sorry. Where are we? I lost my goddamned high heel but you promised me you'd buy me another one. I'm gonna hold you to it.

You want to go to the hospital?

Forget it.

Is it true what Loreena said, that you're puking every day?

Go to hell.

Domino, I'm worried about you. And Dennis and Loreena care about you, too. And the Queen—

Oh, *those* fuckers . . .

He got onto the freeway at Ninth and Harrison, billboards looming white and yellow, proclamations of spurious choice against the foggy sky, the city in its real life not a choice at all, the grim-glowing girder-blades of the Bay Bridge squatting over him.

Henry? said Domino.

What is it, sweetheart?

Henry, I'm sorry I puked all over your car. And I'm sorry I was nasty to you.

Never mind, he said. No harm done.

Henry, would it be all right if I went to sleep now?

Sure it would.

Henry?

What?

I don't want to go back to the Queen tonight. I hate the Queen.

I know.

Where are we going?

Oakland.

Where in Oakland?

To the Queen.

The car reeked of vomit. He thought of Luther's strange doctrine that sin resides in the flesh, not in the conscience, because law has power only over flesh, not conscience. Her puke was corrupt, but not her, never her.

Henry, I'm sorry I lost my shoe.

All right, he said. Now let me drive.

By the time he reached the secret place among the derricks and cranes of West Oakland where the Queen was sleeping that night, Domino was stuporously snoring. The tall man came out of the shadows to claim her, laughing at the stench. —Lemme get this drunken bitch out of this faggoty car, he said. —He carried her off in his arms, then came back to Tyler and said: Queen wants me to tell you you been righteous. You one of the good kind.

Thanks, Justin, said Tyler.

You want to stay here, I'll watch your car. Or if you don't trust me you can sleep in your car.

Looking into the tall man's eyes, he remembered strangely from his boyhood the old trestle bridge between East and West Sacramento where you could stand on the ties, look down between your feet and see the shimmering green-brown water. If you wanted to, you could jump and maybe just thrill yourself or maybe kill yourself. He liked but was sometimes afraid of the tall man.

Sure, he said. I trust you.

And so the tall man led him inside the old meatpacking plant with its eternal snow-drifts of broken glass and its piss-reeking recesses which locally overpowered the atmosphere of dust, moldy lard and bankruptcy as impure as Tyler's motives used to be for accompanying Irene and John to some stupid John kind of movie; he'd go only in order to sit next to Irene, and somehow at the last minute John would end up between them. As his pupils expanded, he began to see a massive black woman whose steel earrings were almost as big as her head. He'd never met her before, and he'd never meet her again. He saw Beatrice (who was twitching in her sleep, dreaming of the cops), Chocolate, Strawberry, Martha, the crazy whore, Yellow Bird and the new girl, Bernadette. Why weren't they out working? —Because their Queen, pitying them, had given them all magic medicine . . . He saw Lily, who was snoring sitting up, with drool running out of her mouth. He smelled Sunflower from a distance. (But Sunflower was dead, of course; it must have been someone else he smelled.) In the darkness loomed all the other whores ranked like the end-stacked white plastic chopsticks on Jones Street: skinny and quick, or fat and sullen, or vivaciously false like those ladies who lied with every word they said. All their faces were becoming now almost as familiar to him as the stench of urine on the streets of the Tenderloin.

This place always creeps me out, Strawberry was saying. Ever since I was a child . . .

Hush up, sweetie, said the Queen. Ain't nothin' gonna happen to you in here. You never been no child in here anyways . . .

Look what I found on Hyde Street, said Strawberry.

What? said Bernadette.

Well, this is a Royalbra. I wear a 42B.

I thought you was 38.

Well, not now. That was then. This is now.

So how's it compare to them Sears an' Roebuck bras?

I don't like 'em any better than Sears. I don't like that elastic strap.

Well, if you don't like it I'll take it. Does it have wires?

Yes it does.

Well, I hate bein' wired. You keep it, Berry. Fuck them wires. I cut the wires, an' they still dig in my ribs.

That's why it takes so long to try on a bra.

Time's what we got plenty of down here.

The tall man said: Henry Tyler.

The Queen said: Henry, I'm so glad. Henry, I'm gonna take care of you.

Evening, Maj, he said happily. But he couldn't see her yet. It was too dark inside. She always sat back away from the door.

Back again! said Chocolate. Know why we're not working tonight?

Lemme guess, said Tyler. Overdraft at the sperm bank.

You are *disgusting!* she laughed. No, it's 'cause Sunflower—

The Queen was wearily silent.

Domino's sick, he said to them all.

Remember in that other underground place I kept sayin' there was somebody there? said Strawberry in that dreamy druggy voice. Like spirits or something? I miss the place, creeps and all.

Outside, the tall man was on one haunch, with his legs crossed, the bill of his cap practically stabbing into Domino's sleeping face as he sat watching Tyler's car. He muttered: See, I don't even rate around here.

| 132 |

Mostly the Queen's world was as slow as the Mexico of Beatrice, where homeless men lay on rice sacks on the sidewalk, their arms above their heads, and couples chatted in the hot dust beside stop signs, where the same fire engine with a broken windshield might sleep for months under the wide-streeted blocks of trees, and old sofas and chairs sat out in near-rainless yards. Strawberry told Chocolate the same story for the fifth time. Chocolate, pretending to listen, lay on a strip of foam rubber trying to screw up her courage to beg the Queen for an extra rock of crack even though she'd just had her turn. Beatrice, to whom the story was not directed at all, sat listening with her mouth open. Beatrice loved stories more than almost anyone. She stared into Strawberry's face, gradually wiggling closer and closer until Chocolate wrinkled her nose because Beatrice smelled bad; but Strawberry, seeing that she had an audience, felt happy and proud enough to revamp her tale with mythic grandeur so beautiful that she herself believed it, and because Chocolate was not listening and Domino was out futilely peddling pussy to early afternoon drivers, nobody could spitefully deflate the story which thus emerged wet and new from its cocoon of facts and probabilities, becoming ever more beautiful until it finally fluttered overhead to shine like a luna moth on the ceiling of the abandoned warehouse until even Strawberry grew tired and realized at last that Chocolate was tired and *then* only Beatrice sat gazing at Strawberry longing for more in just the same way as Chocolate gazed at the Queen who opened heavy-lidded eyes, sighed, and crooked her finger at Chocolate who squirmed forward to receive her Queen's saliva in her mouth; this substance, as I believe I have attested, possessed a narcotic and almost psychotropic effect; five minutes later the black woman was lying on her back, slowly licking her lips as her eyes happily glazed. It might be thought that this drug, being both free and moderately addictive, would have replaced cocaine or heroin or even meth in the whores' list of staples, and indeed they did all partake, even Domino, not without a certain revulsion at their dependence upon another human being, but all of them except Sapphire knew that however much their Queen loved them, and they her, to remain with her all the time would have been stagnation, even death; and, indeed, her very secretions discouraged it; drink three times a day, and you were in heaven; six times, and you began to feel nauseous; ten times, and you vomited. So the whores were compelled to do as is foreordained for all, and go out into the world to live and to prowl. Where their Queen was, there grew sanctuary for every outcast, and even a little more, but not much more. How could there be? Where could Lord Cain rest forever, except in the tomb? This is not to imply that they could not be at least as contented as Irene lying under a blanket on the sofa next to John, watching romantic thriller videos which oozed soft piano music while she slowly got paler and sleepier until her eyes closed and her pale long fingers gripped the cushion, John frowning, half bored but unwilling now to turn it off before he learned how the plot turned out. Chocolate felt good; Beatrice felt good . . . Beyond Sapphire's writhing fingers on bare knees, Sapphire's wriggling toes speaking like the upraised beaks of hungry baby birds, the Queen sat in darkness, her thoughts gone southwest toward Beatrice's country with its nested ranges of beautiful grey or maybe someplace even farther past greyish black mountain in rows upon yellow sand so far away, where her regal spirit could look down the swells and bulges of gravel-mountains to the blue and yellow horizon, where she might walk upon a salt lake as smooth and hazy as a dream—Beatrice's Mexico or the desert Africa of her own enslaved ancestors? It didn't matter. She was beyond reach, like the crazy whore, who muttered: I kinda had this fever of kleptomania . . . She was who she was, beyond expediency or even consequences, like Domino whose menstrual period hadn't come and who kept feeling queasy, like beautiful black Chocolate with her scabs and scars who wore no underpants under her miniskirt, and, sitting down on somebody's steps on Capp Street to negotiate with a john, would often spread her legs so that he could see the fuzzy darkness; then she reached in to scratch-scratch-scratch, the implied warning of verminous contagion negating her little advertisement.

Tyler's visits gave them something to gossip about. —Here comes Henry, they said. He does that surveillance stuff.

| 133 |

Domino, however, rarely gossiped. She preferred solitude when she could get it, distrusting everybody in the world except for—provisionally—her Queen, who had never done her anything but good and whose evil she meticulously awaited. (There's something so depressing about Dom, said Strawberry. She's just like *unhappy* and *unhealthy*. Makes me want to stay away. —But she reminded Tyler of a brilliant, beautiful, unhappy girl he'd once known who wrote to him in a letter: *Tomorrow I will wash my hair in rosewater and wear a yellow dress. I want to talk to you, just to hear your voice in this room. Your voice makes me think of oranges and sandalwood.* Another time she wrote him: *My dreams are only of one thing, and oh! my heart aches with you.* He had wanted to be her one thing but he was too low and evil.)

At four in the morning the blonde's aching head awoke her. For a moment she could not understand where she was. The stench of her own vomit there in Tyler's car made her desperately nauseous, and she wanted a drink of water, so she opened the door and stumbled out, waking Justin, who literally opened only one bloodshot eye. But then it seemed that she had only dreamed she'd been in Tyler's car, for she woke up a second time on the floor of the meatpacking plant, lovingly swaddled by someone in rags and old newspapers. A spider crawled in her hair, and she squashed it. It was still dark. Her head ached worse than ever. The other girls were snoring. Lying among them reminded her of her latest stint in jail (thirty days, just because she'd forgotten to report to her probation officer one lousy time. —In felony cases they get super cautious, her public defender had said with a shrug.) Fifty-eight inmates had been caged in the dorm, some of them girls she knew, and some girls she didn't. Disliking television, she'd slept during the daytime and stared at the ceiling at night, craving just one dose of pure white junk. The same sensations which induce salivation in others who pass by the restaurant windows of Chinatown, where roasted chickens, roasted red crackly pork strips, orange roast ducks and drumsticks dark and crunchy, hang down above silver reservoirs of steamed vegetables and sweet ricebeds, affected Domino when her mind turned toward pure coke, crack coke (also known as white girl or bump), China white, coal tar, speedball, crystal blue persuasion, quaaludes, poppers, red speed, black speed, valium, thorazine, codeine, morphine, greenbud, indica weed, brandy and beer. In Chinatown some chickens are even smoked blue-black, like old India rubber balls, and in Dominotown one could likewise find specialty items, but the staple, the regular boiled chicken, so to speak, was crack— delicious, mind-clearing, happy-making, ephemeral crack, white, white, white as the sails on the pale blue Bay on Sundays, not that crummy yellow stuff which cheapskates had cut with cornstarch . . . In the dorm Domino felt so lonely for crack that she almost screamed. She felt widowed, starved, suffocated. Sometimes she masturbated beneath the scratchy blanket, less because she felt horny than because giving herself orgasms was the one nice thing that she could make happen. If other jailgirls saw what she was doing, they kept quiet about it, probably because they were doing it, too. Every night she heard the moans. The guards let them do it. They knew they could only push the girls so far. Domino bit her lip and glared straight upward when she climaxed. Then she did it again and again, until she got bored and sore. She kept hoping that Justin or someone would bring her five dollars so that she could buy some shampoo, but no one ever came.

At dawn she got up to beg the Queen for a fix and saw Tyler sleeping on the concrete. Scarcely knowing what she was saying, she muttered: That man's going to kill me. He's going to kill me, kill me, kill me.

Oh, somebody's awake, huh? said the Queen sleepily.

You know what I need, Maj.

Yeah, I know. C'mere. Come gimme a kiss . . .

Maj . . .

What?

Maj, I want you to fuck me.

All rightie, darling. Queen's gonna . . . Oh, I'm so tired . . .

Sorry, Maj.

See, now you woke Sapphire. Give Sapphire a kiss, Dom. Give her a *nice* kiss. Okay. Now take her over an' give her to Beatrice . . .

L-l-l-uh . . . trilled the idiot girl.

Sssh! said the Queen. Oh, now you done it. Now Strawberry's awake, too. Come on upstairs with me, Dom. That's where the rock is anyways. But you know you can't keep shortin' all the other girls on rock. You got to put back some of what you take.

Oh, bullshit, said the blonde angrily.

They went upstairs and the Queen yawned and said: Oh me oh my, am I tired. Okay, sweetie. Pull up your dress.

Maj?

What?

How do I know you really love me?

You don't. Where's my . . . all rightie, dear. Now bend over.

Maj?

You want to get laid or not? You sure got a lot of questions early in the morning.

I need a hit.

There you go.

Maj, it's all bullshit, isn't it? What you said about Sunflower.

I don't bullshit, Domino.

You promise you won't tell anybody?

Hey, you're wastin' that. Beatrice worked hard to earn that rock. Don't let it . . .

The way you said she was like a saint and the *best* of us.

All right, bend over now, said the Queen, whose kiss was as delicate as the tiny droplets of mist on Tyler's birdstreaked windshield as he sat on stakeout in the T.L. — And be quiet.

Please, Maj.

I *promise* I love you just as much as I ever loved Sunflower. Domino, I'm your Queen. I belong to you as long as you need me. I *got* to love you.

The others don't like me, do they?

That's your little cross to bear, ain't it? Listen, Dom. Anytime you really want to, you can make friends. Inside that cussedness you're such a good girl . . .

Maj, I—oh, I feel so *sick*.

That's 'cause you're pregnant, you silly silly girl. You got to go to the clinic an' get aborted. You want me to tell Chocolate to take you?

Not that bitch. Who does she think she is? She always—

All rightie. I'll tell Justin then.

Thank you, Maj. I appreciate it. But I have to tell you something about Chocolate. She—

Don't be a tattletale, Dom.

Now I get it. I bet you're really on her side. That's how you've always been, Maj. But I'm not going to—

Lordy lordy day, the Queen muttered.

| 134 |

When the Queen and Domino came back downstairs, Henry Tyler was waiting. Domino brushed past him without a word and lay down again to sleep. Tyler knelt down and took the Queen's hand.

What is it, Henry? she said, smiling in spite of herself.

Maj, he whispered in a low voice, what can I do to get over Irene?

Why do you want to do that?

Because it hurts so much.

Ah, said the Queen. You want to grab some of that happiness.

Yes, I do . . .

She stroked his head. —You saw Sunflower. And I showed you Sunflower's pain. I opened her up for you while she lay sleeping and *showed* it to you. And you still don't understand.

| 135 |

Are you a lez? said Domino. I'm a lez.

No no no, said Beatrice.

Have you ever fantasized about being with a woman? said Domino. Have you been fucked? Have you ever been *fucked?*

The Queen says—

She's trash, chuckled Domino, leaning her shiny teeth and shiny shiny eyes and shiny vinyl skirt over the cage. —It's so boring, being Queen of the Whores. I'd rather be God.

I'm 'fraid, said Beatrice. I'm 'fraid of you.

But with the utmost tenderness, Domino lowered her pale, almost incorporeal face onto Beatrice's; and out of habit and fear Beatrice submitted. Soon the two women were kissing each other, cheeks swallowed up in each other's mouths, while behind them a big-breasted masturbator was screaming and kicking the cage.

I want you to keep your authority, Domino whispered to the heterosexual girl. But I want you to give me permission to . . . through your bra . . . let me touch your nipples very very softly.

And she kissed her. And she licked her mouth, licked her face.

You're a sport! Domino laughed. You've earned my respect.

| 136 |

The Queen had picked up a new girl named Bernadette, a slender black lady who resembled a beautiful cat-devil. Domino felt attracted. She went to Bernadette and said: If somebody gave you a million dollars, what would you do?

What would I do? Shit! laughed the other woman lazily. Nobody gonna give me a mill. They're all too cheap in this town.

Strawberry came running. —Hey, Domino, your date's here!

Who is it?

That sixty-year-old bastard with the cuff links. That one you call the sonofabitch.

God, I hate him. I won't go. I won't go!

What's he do?

He likes to stick his fist up me real violent-like and make me cry. For sixty bucks it's not worth it. All right, tell him I'm coming. I hate that man. Goddamn him. Goddamn you. Goddamn all of you just sitting around on your asses waiting for a million dollar dick.

I tole you there ain't no mill in this town, said Bernadette complacently. Hey, Domino, can I borrow your silver high heels tonight?

Oh, fuck off, said the blonde, grabbing her purse and running out.

| 137 |

Tyler called up his friend Jack Chin at the public defender's office and asked him if he had ever heard about the Queen. —Sure, I've heard legends, laughed Chin. I mean, that stuff goes back—Christ, I mean, it predates DNA tests and rubber bullets. In fact, Henry, with all due respect, it's probably an urban myth. Everybody loves to pin the rap on the Queen, but—

How about Sylvia Fine? Does that name mean anything to you?

You're talkin' about Domino, right? When she was in juvenile hall they used to call her Two Bits, I dunno why. Sure. Who works for the PD and *doesn't* know Domino? That is one mean bitch, and I'm talkin' about my client! Heh! If that bitch bought me a drink I'd check it out to make sure it wasn't poisoned! Three pending cases, one involving stalking with a knife. I guess they're just pals now. Oh, yeah. I got the acquittal . . .

And how about Brenda Wiley?

Brenda who?

Chocolate's the street name. She—

There's scores of Chocolates working in the Western Addition, I think I—anyway, what's the point?

They both work with the Queen.

Look, Henry. This goes back to when the Tenderloin was boomin'. Street prostitution was—oh, *man.* And there was this vice cop who worked prostitution detail. He suddenly became kind of wealthy. In essence he was combin' the Tenderloin to find the newbies, you know, the soft young chickies who'd just kinda fallen into the life. And he'd go up to them and say: I can protect you. I have a place. And he did, too! Had his own house, up in Pacific Heights, I think it was. Well, finally one of them turned on him. But the strange thing was, before it ever went to trial his heart just stopped even though he was a young guy in good shape. And all the girls kept talkin' about the Queen, who'd waved her magic fuckin' wand or whatever it was to punish him. Listen, Henry. It's all bullshit.

| 138 |

Toward the end of that summer the police stepped up the vigor of their sweeps of Capp Street, which accordingly fell silent, and on those dark nights warmish like stale beer, the rattle of a trash can lid or the loom of a stuporous whore on somebody's doorstep was a surprise, while a block away beneath the blonde streetlights of South Van Ness paced the girls in lavender leotards with clops like shoed horses. The Uptown Bar on Seventeenth and Capp had added new taps of microbrewed beers within the frosty nickel-plated organ pipes which readied themselves to play hymns upon that altar of alcohol. And just outside the Uptown, Bernadette was working.

Hey, the man said, have you seen Sunflower?

That's funny that you should talk about Sunflower, because just the other day I was thinking about all the people who aren't there, said Bernadette.

She smiled, and from one eye a tear so slowly came, and even more silently than the number fourteen bus whose white face shone like radium in the night as it eased past the Ritespot Cafe, that wetness traveled down her nose.

I used to date her, the man said. I was kind of looking for her.

What's your name?

Bruce.

You want a date, honey? Maybe I can help you out?

Well, actually I was looking for Sunflower, he said. I feel something special for her.

You know, said Bernadette, Sunflower and I were good together.

Ah, said the man.

I actually feel very pretty today, said Bernadette.

So she's not around? the man said.

I'm sorry, baby. You won't see her around anymore.

What happened to her?

Overdose. I'd rather not talk about it.

Ah, the man said again.

So do you want a date or don't you?

The man hesitated.

Come on, said Bernadette. I give really good head if that's what you're into.

How much?

Twenty.

Sunflower gave pretty good head for ten.

Well, honey, Sunflower's dead so you gotta respect the living.

Slowly the man began to reach into his pocket. Bernadette's heart now beat most glee-fully, and according to her long since memorized stage directions she murmured: Listen, baby, if you pay me now and wait just five minutes while I go get well it'll only cost you fifteen.

Oh, the man said. Well, all right.

He gave her a ten, four ones, and four quarters.

Bernadette ran so happily, vanishing so joyously into the night while the man sat against a wall. She looked back two blocks later and could dimly see him sitting. She laughed.

Justin, Justin, gimme a full dime bag! she commanded, thrusting the tenner into the tall man's palm. He looked at her without joy or sorrow. Then he went around the corner and in a moment returned with the bag.

Hey, what's this? This is no full bag.

Took the Queen's commission, the tall man grunted. You know you owe her. And don't get in my face about it. You *lucky* I was here. Look at you. Ran all the way back to lie down before that monkey hopped on your back. Looks like you just beat the monkey. Where is he now? He gnawin' at your neck? You look like you're gonna puke, so don't you ever dare accuse me of gafflin' you. Better go do your business, bitch.

You can take your commission but don't call me bitch or I'll tell the Queen.

He looked at her. —All right. I'm sorry, Bernadette, he said.

Somebody was asking about Sunflower, she said then.

Who?

I dunno. Some jerk.

Outside the Uptown the man sat, getting angrier and angrier. Bernadette was long gone, upstairs in her room with two fingers on her clit and a needle hanging from her ass.

| 139 |

Domino had done the same thing to Dan Smooth once. The next time she saw him, Smooth had only laughed and said: I don't recognize your authority. —That was about the time he'd stopped sleeping with anybody over fifteen. Domino claimed that Smooth couldn't get it up anyway . . .

· BOOK IX ·

"Easier Than You Might Ever Dream"

•

Behold, I will feed them with wormwood, and give them poisoned water to drink.

JEREMIAH 23.15

•

Can I buy you a drink? the trick said, his face shady like Market Street with its glowing windows.

Sure, said Strawberry without looking at him. Misery loves company.

Which are you?

Excuse me?

Which are you—misery or company?

Oh, don't play them games, mister, the whore said. If you're that kind, you can just get lost. I'm tired.

Once when Strawberry was in jail she saw another girl eating candy, so she asked her for a piece but the other girl said: Get away! Go stand back *away* from me! and Strawberry felt angry and hurt but couldn't show it because if she did then somebody would have preyed on her. But when she was negotiating with johns she could show whatever feelings flowed through her, or even make up feelings, because no one could hurt her in a public place and it was up to *her* whether or not to rent herself; she became the Queen.

Just then she saw the Mexican girl, and turned to her with relief, like a child who, losing the game of locked stares, pretends a physical need to blink. —Well, Beatrice! she cried. Where you been? All us girls been asking about you. And Maj, she—

I got an abscess on my titty, said Beatrice. They had to take me to the hospital to drain it. Mama knew all about it.

Well, she didn't tell me.

Maybe you doan ask her, Beatrice thought to herself, but she only smiled and fanned herself with a piece of newspaper. —So what's up with you? she said finally. You meet some nice friends? If you doan meet some nice friends soon maybe I can pray for you—

Oh, I need to make some money, Strawberry sighed. Domino owes me a rock and—

Me too! Me too! Because she gimme ten dollars but then—

The trick smiled shyly at her. —I like fat girls, he whispered.

She's not *fat*, said Strawberry. She's *heavily challenged*.

Beatrice screamed with laughter. Where Beatrice came from, they painted barber poles on the walls of barber shops. Fat, big-breasted beautiful women in blue shirts were proud of their own flesh. Beatrice remained proud of herself.

Well, he obviously likes you better, so why don't you date him, said Strawberry. I'm tired. I think I'll go on home. See you, *guapa*.

The trick moved two barstools closer. —Is she mad at me? he whispered.

I doan think so, Beatrice said. Doan worry about it, 'cause she has to go chase her nice friend. Where you from, baby? What's your name?

I'm from Modesto and my name is, uh—

Oh, doan bother, said the fat whore. Why lie? I won't complain. If you doan wanna tell me, then doan tell me. Mother Maria, it's not my business. Hey, Strawberry, darling, please you stick around one minute.

You know what? said the trick.

What?

I don't think I like your attitude.

Then fuck off, said Beatrice. Go kiss your Mama's ass. Strawberry, sister, let's go.

You goin' out, too? said the other whore.

Of course.

What about him?

The hell with him. He doan like my attitude.

Strawberry laughed drunkenly and said: You wanna try Seventeenth and Capp with me, an' maybe we can double date? It's safer that way.

No, sweetie, I gotta meet one of my regulars. Because I met two friends, the nicest two friends, and I tell one I go only with him. And the other I tell I go only with *him*. And one nice friend, he even want me to come back in the morning to his hotel, and he gimme twenty, and the other paid me twenty last night and the first one gimme twenty last night and when I show Mama, she so happy. But the other one want to take photos of me naked, so I say, Okay, you can take my pussy, but you doan take my face. And Mama say *why?* I say 'cause I'm ugly, Mama. You know that. And she say, no, Beatrice. You're not ugly. Here's some makeup. And now I—

Okay. Well, you be careful, *guapa*.

You too, said Beatrice.

She stood with her hands on her generous hips, watching the other woman strolling into the darkness.

Across the street, a police light flashed and amplified robot voices went *wrurr wrurr wrurr step out of the car.* STEP OUT OF THE CAR. *Turn around slowly and place your hands on the car.* It was nobody she knew. Strawberry should really be getting out of here, but she could still see her dawdling at the first corner with cracked bravado, shooting looks and waves against the cars which she hoped to prey on and crack open like mussel-shells to suck out the sweet money-meat inside. No cars slowed. *Place your hands on your head. Slowly. I said slowly.*

Suddenly, Beatrice realized that the cops were busting Domino.

| 141 |

Weak and mechanical though such side-episodes may be, like the subplots in Shakespeare's plays, the fact remains that reality does on occasion most slyly change the dials of our fate-settings, like Bernadette, who always liked to steal at least one thing from each of her tricks. So it had happened on that foggy twilight that when Domino was sitting in a station wagon with one of her regulars, a pasty-faced man whose name she'd long since forgotten and cared not to ask, and they were en route to the parking lot on Golden Gate where she always blew him, a black-and-white came up out of nowhere and pulled them over for expired plates. After that, things went from bad to worse. When the cop asked for the registration, the trick opened the glove compartment and a pistol fell out. Domino rolled her eyes and said: You *asshole!* —Both of you out of the car with your hands on your heads! said the cop. His partner started searching the car, and immediately found a bag of meth under the passenger seat. —It's hers, the trick said desperately. I never knew anything about it, I swear, officer. —Well? said the cop. Which of you wants to own up? —Yeah, sure, and it's my gun and my car and my penis, too, sneered the blonde. Why don't you dust it for prints? —Oh, so you want to tell me how to do my job, huh? said the cop. You think I feel like wasting my fingerprint dust on your shitty little life? Who are you, lady? Let's see some I.D. —May I take one hand off my head to get it, officer, or are you going to reach into my pants and get it? —My, my, my, said the cop cheerfully. You just resisted an officer. I'm going to have to write that into the arrest report. What's your name? —Domino, said Domino. —The world-famous Domino, said the officer with mock awe. Aren't you the cat's pajamas? Is there any man in San Francisco who hasn't gotten lapdanced by Domino? But I'll tell you something, sweetie. That was in the last century. You need a new titty job. —Remind me not to go to the same doctor who did your dick job, officer. I bet you couldn't get it up if it were strapped to a telephone pole.

It's just not fair to bust me for her meth, inserted the trick. You see how she talks. It's *her* meth, officer. Cut me some slack just this once, okay?

It went like that all the way to jail. But when the trick, sitting handcuffed in the back seat of the patrol car beside her, finally understood that his denials of methamphetamine possession would not change the stance of the arresting officers by a single iota, he turned toward Domino, who sat rigidly trembling and gazing out the window, and, clearing his throat with a noise as of a tired panhandler's shuffle up a sidewalk, he whispered that he was sorry. Domino burst into tears and cried: I'm so *ashamed* of your life!

| 142 |

It used to be that when they busted Domino they merely cuffed her and maybe kicked her down onto her face once or twice if she'd given them lip or shown what they called "attitude"; then they took her to the Mission Street substation where after rephotographing her and adding a new entry to her sin sheets they drove her to Eight-Fifty Bryant, formally known as the Hall of Justice, where in a windowless little room which offered a sometimes-broken television and a sometimes-broken toilet she joined her sisters sitting on benches, all of them searched and half stripped, their high heels confiscated because not long ago in that room, so the story went (nobody Domino knew had actually witnessed it), one prostitute, angered by another, had killed her with a spike heel; and there Domino sat until they let her out. But this time she faced no mere misdemeanor charge of prostitution, which usually meant a quick release on her own recognizance, but felony drug and gun possession charges, as well as interwoven complications and disgraces—to wit, five thousand dollars bail for the weapons charge, ten thousand for the meth, ten thousand for being the principal in a narcotic sales case while knowing that another principal was armed, five hundred for resisting an officer in the performance of his duties, twenty thousand for a prior serious felony (she actually had two on her record but they'd luckily forgotten the other one), ten thousand for a prison prior when she'd been compelled to defend her honor against a woman who'd called her nigger-sucker, and so she stole a spoon from the cafeteria and slammed it into that bitch's eye—all of which came to a fifty-five point five grand price of readmission to the luminous Tenderloin streets for something she hadn't even done. Life is crappy, she said to herself.

And so she made landfall upon the grey squarish isle of the Hall of Justice, and they took her upstairs to the jail, where they made her sign the white SFPD property release form. She didn't want to check the box which emunerated her "TOTAL" cash because she was sure that she'd had much more money than that, but she lost that argument, as she had known she would, because they were stronger than she was and they didn't care. —My shitty fuckin' life, she muttered. She heard the public defender mumuring into a man's ear: If they can make the actual *constructive* claim, then the misdemeanor goes to superior court trailing the felony and *then* . . . —Ahead of her waited the judge who always said to her public defender just like a used car salesman: I'll give you a *very* early pretrial tomorrow. —The public defender warned her: Sylvia, you gotta beat every count if you wanna escape the Three Strikes Law. —They said she could make one phone call. Domino wanted to telephone Dan Smooth, but they said that it had to be local. There was a rich doctor from Marin who sometimes dated her in his own house while his wife masturbated in the corner (the doctor's pride: amyl nitrate sequences with Domino, the wife's silver body moving back and forth), but his phone merely rang and rang. So Domino called Mr. Cortez the bail bondsman.

· BOOK X ·

An Essay on Bail

•

Excessive bail shall not be required.

U.S. Constitution, VIIIth Amendment (1792)

I tell you, that to every one who has more will be given; but to him who has not, even what he has will be taken away.

Luke 19.26

•

| 143 |

The saving grace of our justice system is that remarkable axiom, *innocent until proven guilty.* Be that as it may, each accused must place his head in the lion's mouth. For not every axiom is honored, not every proof is infallible—and not all defendants are innocent. What will the judgment be? Yesterday, a man pursued his good or evil life. Today he stands inscribed in the master calendar of felonies. And tomorrow's destiny refuses to announce itself. The sign reads: SILENCE: COURT IN SESSION. Thus authority reduces us to things, and how could matters be otherwise? A greyhaired, slender defendant, sitting beside me as he awaits his turn, whirls insanely round in his chair as if something bit him. Granted, he keeps obediently silent; chewing his lip, he struggles to sit still, but only a moment goes by before his demon, premonition of the lion's mouth, gnaws at him again, and he quivers. Meanwhile, a hulking, bandaged, cornrowed defendant approaches the bench with his hands locked behind his back. He's been named; he's Line Twenty-Four. Should he refuse to offer his head to the gaping mouth, then certain fellow citizens, armed and numerous, will force him. But by our axiom, Leo may not bite in advance of a guilty verdict. Fairness, then—to say nothing of kindness—advises that the defendant's freedom be provisionally restored, on condition that he not run away from the lion. Hold his collateral, then. Should he flee, it will be forfeit. What if, fearing the verdict, he prefers freedom to property of which his sentence might in any event deprive him? No worry—raise the stakes! Then he'll require help from those who love him, which produces the ingenious result of holding his companions hostage for his good behavior. Unless he's a monster, instinct will be deterred by the knowledge that should he vanish, his sister will lose her house, while the lion in any case hunts him. And that is why the whirling man and the hulking, cornrowed man sat beside me in the courtroom, waiting for their names to be called. They were not wearing the orange livery of unfreedom; they came in their street clothes. They might as well come. —We get ninety-six percent of all skippers, a bail bondsman in Spokane once boasted to me, with a tight smile. And I suspect that Domino was all too familiar with that statistic.

In our republic, collateral cannot be paid except in good hard money. (The felony bail schedule reads: CASH, SURETY BONDS, VISA OR MASTERCARD. NO PERSONAL CHECKS.) Why this is I cannot fathom. A deed of trust means even less to a court clerk than a defendant's fate. Well, couldn't there be an appraisal office for the former as there is for the latter? The state of California seems perfectly able to staff such establishments in order to tax my house. Never mind. Who, then, will accept the surety of a cashless soul? Not the judge, I assure you; nor the happy lawyers with their suitcoats off, neckties fluttering in the breeze, who sometimes may be seen carrying bag lunches, nor yet the cops whose doubleparked police cars rest as immune to meter maids as most cops themselves are to bribery. And so the accused, or, more likely, since he's at this moment sitting upstairs in a cell, the friends of the accused, descend the Hall of Justice's steps on which other lion's-prey smoke cigarettes while keeping to themselves or else glaring nervously everywhere like that whirling man in court, and then the friends (what nice friends!) turn to the slow orange blinking of the BAIL OPEN sign for Barrish Bail Bonds, or to any of the other signals of rescue in that casino-like strip which more or less begins by the Inn Justice Bar & Hofbrau with Dad's Bail Bonds, and Cable Car Bail Bonds, whose office resembles a fast food restaurant and whose motto reads: "WE NEVER SLEEP"—LOW RATES. Next comes De Soto Bail Bonds, followed by Al Graf Bail Bonds, an establishment which figures in this sketch, then the aforementioned Barrish, Ballestrasse (OPEN 24 HOURS), Puccinelli; and at right angles to all these, in the alley behind Cable Car Bail Bonds, my vision descries Curtis Howard, O'Reilly's, McKenzie Green, Hutch and Hutch, King, De Cortez and then Sheila Lockett, who very pleasantly said when I rang her bell: No, I can't help you; I'm sorry . . .

Thus that miniature Las Vegas where many an accused hits the jackpot of sunlight and kisses. But is this treasure imperishable American bullion, or fool's gold? Bail can be revoked, you know.* On the other hand, some lucky souls' cases get dismissed within days, and *then* sunlight endures unto death or the next arrest. Regardless, Judgment Day comes for all. Angels inscribe a name on one of the daily computer printouts affixed to the marble walls of the Hall of Justice—time to report to the lion, time for district attorney and public defender to gamble over the gambler's fate. But up to that moment he's *free* within due limits to spend the life he's won—provided only (as I said) that his well-wishers can offer deeds of trust, stock certificates, or good safe municipal bonds.

That bail bondsman I met in Spokane didn't mind accepting videocasette recorders or cameras as collateral. (What did he think, when somebody brought in two dozen television sets? Where had those televisions come from?)—In San Francisco it seems more difficult to meet with such catholic receivers. One can easily try, of course, for it was explained to me by ancient Al Graf, retired owner of the aforesaid Al Graf Bail Bonds, that each bondsman specializes in a very particular subspecies of client, just as each creed has its god, and each parasite its host. Somebody somewhere will take television sets. Why not try? Freedom Casino lies so conveniently situated right across from the lion's mouth! —When you win in Vegas your slot machine says BAR BAR BAR. But for the lion-bound winners, all bars shall be sprung. A blood-vermillion sign blinks in a bondsman's window.

Am I free to go? asks the defendant.

Yeah, you've got bail set, the judge replies.

I got bailed! he crows, rolling away in his wheelchair.

The judge sighs and sets a new trial date.

| 144 |

How much do you love me? —Easy to find out. I'll beseech of you my resurrection. Then I'll wait.

Ah, but how much will the ransom be? Well, how much *should* it be?

Gaunt, bald and overworked Ron Albers, one of the felony supervisors at the public

---

*Usually on account of failure to appear, or else for some probation violation.

defender's office, tried to be civil, but the more questions I put, the more convinced he grew that I was a fool. To him, life came case by case, like the row of bail establishments each with its own policies; generalization equalled vacuity. I wanted to know whether he thought that the bail system was fair, and such inquiries exasperated him.

Fine, he said staccatto. Take possession of drugs. What's an appropriate bail?

Well, I began, in relation to a violent crime—

No, he said. *Tell me a number.*

All right, a thousand dollars.

He shrugged and said (another verbal lunge): *Fine.* A thousand dollars. How about possession for sale?

Ten thousand.

Fine, he said challengingly. Ten thousand dollars. How about possession with conspiracy to sell?

Twice as much.

Okay, so that's your system, said Albers a little contemptuously, and maybe it works for you. But nobody *agrees,* you see. Bail for the same crime varies wildly from county to county.

He was correct, and one need not compare the legal apples of San Francisco with the legal oranges of Sacramento to be unnerved by eccentric discrepancies. What were San Francisco's judges thinking of, when they set bail for assault with *attempt* to rape at twenty thousand dollars—the same number as for rape itself? Leniency ought to be the watchword for an uncompleted crime, no matter what reason the ellipsis. Just as Dante's hell contains circles of graduated misery, so should the bail system. That anomaly, the radiantly rational criminal, ought always to be reminded that no matter what he's done, he'd be better off not doing worse. *Fine,* as Ron Albers would have said. Assault with or without penetration, with or without disease and escalated shame: Twenty grand. *Fine.* Meanwhile, kidnapping for *purposes* of rape became bailable at fifty thousand dollars. I suppose that carrying off one's prey is more terrifying than laying hands on her where one finds her, but a courteous kidnapping might be preferable to a bloody assault (granted, the blood might comprise a separately bailable offense, but in that case what meaning remains to the word "assault"?). Vanilla *kidnapping* got bailed at five thousand dollars more than kidnapping for rape, I'll never comprehend why; and the bail for rape-less *assault* varied between five and fifty thousand (but take heart, O you suffocating students of logic! We can, do and *will,* as bureaucrats say, "prioritize"—for it costs precisely three times as much to be suspected of attacking a fireman as to be accused of harming a bus driver. What would they bail me at, if I shattered their legal tablets?). Sexual battery (which essentially means fondling) was only ten thousand—*fine,* reasonable actually, proportionately Dantesque—but then incest had been priced at twenty-five thousand. If a brother and sister happily went to bed together and then a cousin called the cops, must their amusements necessarily be considered more terrible than ravishment by a monster? Where was the *sense* of it? And so to me the words on the San Francisco bail schedule— to say nothing of the fees—began to seem like careless and transitory exhalations.

The bitter truth of Ron Albers's *Fine* was that in law there *was* no truth. Sometimes I've wished that every crime could be addressed by a single statute, perfectly drafted.* So

---

*I also wish that every act classified as a crime were really evil.

it used to be: *An eye for an eye.* But what if I put out my brother's eye by mistake? What if I did it in wartime, or slyly paid Domino to do it? And so the dust of confusions and exceptions dulled the glitter of the ancient, perfect laws. In their place, we learned to fire multiple laws out of justice's shotgun, hoping that if one pellet didn't bring down the criminal, maybe the next one would. Al Capone deserved to go to prison for his numerous murders and thuggeries, and so he did go—but for tax evasion. That was the pellet that got him. The district attorney takes aim and files charges—*fires* them, I should say—determined to prove his case. He fires multiple shots whenever he can, and each shot spreads constellations of leaden legal pellets. And the more charges stick, the more weighed down becomes the defendant by crushing bail.

This science is as easy as it is repulsive. An example: In Department Twenty-Two I heard a prosecutor insistently arguing: This was a case of GBI (great bodily injury) with use of a knife. The bail was only five thousand, which does *not* reflect the seriousness of the case!

When I got home I searched the felony bail schedule for San Francisco County and found:

PENAL CODE FELONY 245(a)(I) Assault (great bodily injury) *BAIL* $5,000

Indeed, if I meant to box in this suspected stabber (as a prosecutor must do), I might insist and argue against ordinary GBI in that same rising voice, for the bail bondsman's ten percent weighs but five hundred dollars here. Very likely, the accused or his friends could support such a burden. So quick! Load the shotgun! On that very same page I found sweet *mayhem.* Somebody, possibly our defendant, has superficially cut the victim about the face, and in the process nicked off an infinitesimal portion of an earlobe. Thus mayhem, which is mutilation and bails at twenty grand. (Aggravated mayhem can go for more.) Were I the D.A., why not fire that one off?

This procedure being not only expedient, but also self-exculpatory, it gets applied at all levels. The defendant gets his day in court, and directly or through agents pleads his righteousness. The prosecutor (whose name is Legion, because he gets to call himself *the people**) does the same. And the uniformed vice-hunters in their rolling black-and-whites, don't they also want to justify themselves? When they take somebody in, it's only human nature for them to show cause. Why not triply show it? —When you're arrested, said Ron Albers, the person making the charge is the police officer. If he likes you, it's possession. If not, it's possession for sale. I think there's no limit to the number of charges he can make. Let's say you happen to be a person passing a bad check. They can charge you with uttering a bad check plus conspiracy to defraud plus possession of counterfeiting tools or whatever. Or you walk into Safeway and you want to steal a loaf of bread. Well, that's petty theft, but entering the premises for purposes of petty theft can be burglary, and it becomes violent robbery if the security guard tries to stop you and you pull your arm away.

---

*It has always struck me as horrid that the prosecution, not the defense, gets to call itself *the people.*—"I know we're all working with the new law," asserts a brisk woman in a pants-suit who until now has been cleverly employing the passive voice ("reports have been generated"), "but it's *the people's* position that the defendant comes within the parameters of this statute. What I would ask the court to do is to sign the detention order at this time."—The public defender pleads against *the people.* Replies the judge: "Your objections are noted for the record. But I will sign the order."

Needless to say, each new charge augments the bail bondsman's ten percent. When the Salem witchcraft trials were in full flourish, they arrested a man named Giles Corey, who to save his estate would not plead innocent or guilty, so the magistrates in their wisdom directed that he be laid down upon his back in a dark room and slowly crushed to death with weights. Doubtless, many of the Giles Coreys whom we press with the less reprehensible weight of bail actually did the deed, and deserve to remain in the dark room for the duration. But remember the principle of *innocent until proven guilty.*

| 145 |

Thus the first flaw of bail, its *absolute arbitrariness.* (As a smart young lawyer once told me: The criminal justice system is an *ad hoc* system. It's not logical.) The second flaw is its *relative arbitrariness.* How brittle is each Giles Corey's ribcage? Does any given sum of bail weigh the same to me as to you? —We had one guy who was faced with seven hundred and fifty thousand dollars bail, Ron Albers said. The charges were very serious. What the person did, I don't have to get into that. But bail could have been set at a hundred thousand; it wouldn't have made any difference. He couldn't have gotten out of jail. But another guy with a hundred-thousand-dollar bail did get out. He had enough resources to pay for an attorney to boot. Those were serious sexual assault charges. And some of the guys you saw in Department Twenty-Two today had bail set for five thousand dollars or less. They didn't have the five thousand on their credit cards, and they didn't have the five hundred plus collateral for the bail bondsman. So they're sitting in jail.

In the elevator at Five Fifty-Five Seventh Street, I met a lady who often represented street prostitutes. The elevator was slow, so I inquired of her how often those types were able to make bail. —Almost never, she replied. —And a bargirl friend of mine whom I've visited in jail more than once (let's call her Strawberry), assured me: I've never had bail in my life. And I don't get a trial anymore either. It's all parole violation.* They take me and lock me up. You shouldn't be writing about bail. That's irrelevant. You should tell people about what goes on in jail. What they like to do is beat you when you're in the elevator, when they're taking you up to your cell.

This being a novel, we need not sorrow over wretches such as Strawberry, who don't even exist—I made her up out of three sad women I know—and the sad woman who alluded to the beatings she got was also quite practiced in weeping over her dead baby and then hitting me up for money; so let's suppose that she never was beaten (although one time, and here I write not as a novelist but as a witness, I saw two policemen enter the back door of the place which we'll call the Wonderbar, and march her into their squad car because she'd violated her parole again—which is to say, because she'd been sitting quietly at the Wonderbar—and when I strolled out to watch them and see if I could do anything to help Strawberry I saw one cop at the wheel while the other cop was sitting in the back seat beside Strawberry, whose head he now began to drag down into his lap.

---

*Strawberry was entirely correct. Probation and parole violators frequently get no-bail warrants. One public defender described parole as *A most vicious cycle. You're entitled to a hearing before a parole officer, but you're not entitled to a judge or a lawyer.* "I know guys who can't get off parole for fifteen years," he insisted. "They just go back and back. You can get charged with violation just for not reporting to your parole officer one time, and then back you go to jail."

Fifteen minutes later, she was back at the bar, dully pretending that nothing had happened.) Let's suppose that our prisons tower uncorrupted by jailers' violence, because that's a pleasanter supposition, and, besides, the rottenness or purity of prisons may affect but cannot alter the fundamental stinking crookedness of bail, which is the crookedness of life. Let's even suppose that Strawberry some red-shining evening (oh, ecstasy!) found herself legally eligible for bail. What then? Ask Mr. Roger Adair at Ace Bail Bonds in Sacramento. He is a clever, pleasant, practical man. He answers all questions. He says: If you've got a Six Forty-Seven case we don't even deal with you. Six Forty-Seven is prostitution. If there's even loitering involved, we won't do it. We get such a small amount of money, and the hassle's just not worth it. The meat and potatoes of what we do are domestic violence and methamphetamines.

| 146 |

Unlike birth, bail may occur at practically any phase of gestation within the lion's barred womb—or, as Strawberry knows, it may never happen at all. (When a full-term defendant does get delivered, the prosecution may well consider it a *miscarriage of justice.* But never mind.) Arrest is conception; that's when one's implanted in the pit. But because most arrests are warrantless, the pregnancy's not yet "in the system" until the second step when the defendant gets *"processed"*—that is, fingerprinted and otherwise inspected, recorded and made recognizable to the lion's gaze. I have heard prostitutes protesting and even wisecracking with their arresting officers as they roll off to jail, but "processing," like the sign which commands SILENCE: COURT IN SESSION, strips them of public entreaties, accusations, outcries. They're in the cage now. —You can be bailed as soon as you've been processed, a public defender explained to me. Generally they want to get you out if they can. —And, of course, if the *defendant* can. Does he have the cash? There he is, upstairs in a cell with strangers who might be violent. (My friend B. told me how afraid he was of his new brothers on that long afternoon after arrest. He wasn't sure whether to be friendly or inconspicuous.) But who knows? Maybe freedom's jackpot will bust him out here and now. Should the accusation against him be sufficiently trivial, he'll be cited to appear at a later date. This is what happened to B. Somebody came, some *official* somebody who owned the authority to decide that B. was too young and innocuous to lie in jail that night, and so B. staggered back into freedom's twilight without paying a penny, released on his own recognizance, or O.R.'d as they call it. He has never been back in jail since.

Whether our defendant gets out or not, gestation now continues to the third step— namely, *arraignment* in court. Bail grows even more volatile here, like a feather dancing in the breath of a judge. One detainee's five-thousand-dollar mistake is another's twenty-thousand-dollar crime. A D.A. up in Sacramento spoke to me of *a push to limit the number of people who review these things so we get more uniformity.* (I myself would simply prefer a more uniform code of bail.) Arraignment must take place within forty-eight hours of arrest, and the defendant must be present. Bailed people thus do not entirely resemble cancer patients in blissful remission. How can they pretend it's over? They must return to the lion's jaws again and again. For a simple misdemeanor matter, the accused makes at least three appearances. For a felony, the minimum is five. —Felony cases may meander through many, *many* pretrial conferences. (With time, everybody relaxes, said a San Francisco public defender named Matt Gonzalez. It's like, can we work a deal? But I have cases where a guy has appeared fifteen or twenty times. *Ageing the case,* they call it.)

Up to thirty days after arraignment comes the *pretrial hearing,* at which the judge either dismisses the charges or else sends them on for trial. Has the defendant made bail yet? If not, and if they won't O.R. him, then, innocent or guilty, he'll keep sitting in a cell. (Gonzalez again: In a felony case you can spend three months in jail and three more months waiting for a speedy trial, although that's the worst scenario.*) He's likely lost his job by now, if he had one. He's not paying rent. *Innocent until proven guilty,* we said, but think about that rent. Think about those sinister nights of decay. And do you remember those three minimum appearances for a misdemeanor? How about making just one? Plead guilty, and it's over. Remember those five felony appearances? If you can't bring yourself to plead guilty, at least agree to drug counseling—that's almost as good as admitting you're wrong! The prosecutor will like you better, too. By thus validating your own arrest, you've proved him wise and righteous.

Well, the system is a little vindictive, Gonzalez agreed. It's hard to dismiss a flawed case. Once you get wrapped up in the system, nobody wants to admit an error. And sometimes the system is just plain schizophrenic. For instance, take Department Eighteen. That's misdemeanor domestic violence. If you plead not guilty, you can't be released because you are deemed to be a threat to public safety. Bail's generally set. *If you plead guilty, you will probably be released immediately* with a promise to attend counseling, even if you haven't attended counseling before and you haven't even seen a probation officer. By allowing that second option, aren't we really saying, hey, we could really O.R. *all* these people? *You're innocent until proven guilty.* The public safety thing is illusory.

| 147 |

A woman in an orange jumpsuit rubs her big, bewildered eyes. Her lawyer, a lady in tweed, lays a hand upon her arm. The woman in orange is led before the judge, expecting destiny, only to be told by *the people:* The deputy D.A. is on vacation and I don't think he's coming back until next month. —The woman does not understand. *The people's* representative frowns at her and shakes her head. The accused felon clears her throat, craving to learn what will happen next, but she's gently led toward the exit at stage left. The bailiff rattles his keys. He unlocks the door, which she enters, becoming a prisoner again, for how long nobody yet knows. But why on earth does she have a right to know? She's but a detainee, poor and shadowy, like one of those Egyptians in the Book of Isaiah who find themselves forsaken by their idols. *And I will give over the Egyptians into the hand of a hard master; and a fierce king will rule over them.*† She cannot be proven guilty until next month at the earliest. Might she live her life until then? Might

---

*Gonzalez, reading this over: "Actually, that's not the worst scenario. The DA could dismiss the case and then refile the same day, which would double the time to six months. I've seen that happen." According to Mr. Daro Inouye in the same office, the average length of detention between felony arrest and sentencing in San Francisco is more than four months.
†Isaiah 19.4.

she descend those whitestone steps of the Hall of Justice, cross Byrant Street, and then wander home with the sun warming her pallid skin? It depends on the vagaries of bail.

I do think that it's necessary for the system to make every effort possible to see that people are not unnecessarily inconvenienced, said Albert Locher, that supervisory deputy district attorney in Sacramento. —At the same time, he went on, the presumption of innocence is a presumption that attaches to a *specific part* of the proceedings, which is the trial process. But there are other parts of the process. Bail reflects not only the strength of the case but also the degree of danger. If you have a guy videotaped in an armed robbery with his fingerprints on the counter and the gun in his possession, you're not going to find me or many other people wanting to let that guy out.

And so the presumed robber does not get out, and I'm with *the people* on that one; I'm not sorry. But the big-eyed woman in orange does not get out, either. Right or wrong, who's to say? I don't know her. But what does *innocent until proven guilty* mean to you?

The interminable pregnancy of justice continues. If a trial seems warranted, then the accused must stand for his second arraignment. There follows the *trial* itself, then the *verdict*, and then the *sentencing*. Another portion of somebody's lifetime, converted into excrement, gets flushed down the toilet of a cell.

| 148 |

And now for the straight stuff, the vulgar poop: *What impels the bondsman's kindness?* We said ten percent before, but did you truly lull yourself into equating simplicity with truth? —We're supposed to charge a flat ten percent. —Thus Geri Campana, former flight attendant and school teacher, current owner-agent of Al Graf Bail Bonds. This friendly and cheerful Japanese-American woman had entered the business because her husband, a retired police officer now deceased, had suffered from back problems. A desk job being practical under such circumstances, they bought the business from Al.

In churches one sees altars, in low-class jungle whorehouses one finds girlie posters taped to the bamboo walls, and in bail-bonds establishments one discovers emblems of conformity with legal authority. Al Graf's, for instance, sported the insigniae of the Deputy Sheriffs' Association, the National Rifle Association, and even the American Gunsmiths' Association, a worthy organization whose skills remain of use to shooters of all ethical persuasions. At Al Graf's there stretched a glasstopped wooden counter with a couple of stools behind it where the bondsmen sat. This barrier reminded me of the discreet little walls and reefs in topless clubs, cliffs to keep excited clients away. Every bondsman I've ever talked to says that the customers are friendly beyond the point of regularity; but aren't we allowed to imagine odd times when some ghost without collateral blows in, and, his demands unsatisfied, decides to haunt the place? They say that Leon Padilla, the Sacramento "bail bonds king," has survived four murder attempts— but some or all of those might have come from rival bondsmen. Didn't anybody at Al Graf's keep a box of silver bullets behind that counter, just in case? —Mrs. Campana was so kind to me that I thought her capable of exorcising all monsters with her sweetness. (Actually, they're all very nice, she said. Each defendant is very grateful. We get along very well on the street.) And Roger Adair said: We have a good idea what they're about. If we have a bad feeling, we'll just say we're sorry, we're unable to write this bond for you. There are plenty of other bondsmen in the phone book. They might give you a little huff and grief about not wanting to help 'em but that's just a part of the business.

| 149 |

It is very natural in life to want to make a profit, be it financial or otherwise—don't hon-eybees profit when they build up a store of metabolized nectar? When one profits from other people's desperation (which I as a journalist occasionally do), one may well be lu-bricating evil's tracks. —But *must* that be? Why should Mrs. Campana put herself at fi-nancial risk for the sake of every accused stranger's freedom? Doesn't she deserve to flourish? Aren't her customers pleased to escape or postpone their living death?

Do you ever feel that bail costs too much? I asked her.

Some families, she replied, well, they go overboard, which I think is wrong. They of-fer up what they can't afford. We don't wanna go after them for the money. If the guy skips, they would be hurt just as hard as we would be. We're here to protect their inter-est as the indemnitor. So anybody who skips, we try to coax them back into the system. We take the *friendly* approach. I'll call them and they'll be like, oh, my God, I've blown it. What do I do now?

(And Roger Adair said: Maybe five or ten percent are knuckleheads at most. People call and say, whoops, my car broke down. Yeah, *right.* And most of the skips, we get 'em cleared up before anything bad happens. Only two to three percent actually run, and we have our own bounty hunter.)

When we take 'em out of jail, said Al Graf, ninety-eight percent show up for trial. (Al, as his business card said, was the original "BONDSMAN WITH A HEART" and on that lemon-yellow card his telephone number had been inscribed in a ruby red heart.)

Mrs. Campana explicated: If they do not show up, they come back and request to get back on the calendar. We've collateralized their bail, so . . .

| 150 |

I asked Matt Gonzalez: Would you say that bail bondsmen perform a service or would you call them vultures?

I would think more on the service side.* However, what's their risk?

Well, Al Graf told me that ninety-eight percent of his clients don't skip.

He would know. In that case, maybe ten percent is a little steep.

Reader, I repeat: How can one not wish upon every bail bondsman, as upon every other soul, riches? (I keep seeing more and more new bail bonds businesses across from the courthouse, said the bail commissioner. I have never seen one fail.) But I would pre-fer it if their services were more democratically bestowed. As I write this, I can see before me Strawberry's sad and drunken face.

| 151 |

The public defender Daro Inouye told me that *ninety-four percent* of his clients were in-carcerated simply because they could not make bail. When I first heard this, I couldn't

---

*Here is Locher's rather politic answer to the same question: "The bail bondsmen in general perform a ser-vice, and it's a service that's established by law and actually recognized by the Constitution. Like any pro-fession, there are some people in that profession who don't meet the highest standards. There are others who do."

believe it.* I would have believed ten percent, or even thirty, but not almost all of them. Inouye went on to say that in the old days far more people were bailed. I asked what had happened. —This is one of the great mysteries, he laughed, spreading his arms.

But it's far more expensive to incarcerate them all! I said.

Absolutely. Absolutely. But pretrial detention just points out the difference between rich and poor. And look. If you have x amount of people in the county jail, so the county gets sued by the feds for overcrowding, what's going to happen? A new jail! The greatest thing in this state used to be the California higher education master plan. Three years ago, the amount we spent on education was for the first time surpassed by the amount spent on prisons. You build a prison, you have to fill it or they close you down . . . If I were a wealthy man, I'd invest in geriatrics. The biggest old-age facilities will be in prisons. The whole concept is fear. *Build a prison and they will come.*

I thought for a while, then said: Why not create a state fund to pay for the supervision of poor people who can't bail? Pay for ankle bracelets or bounty hunters or *something*. That's got to be cheaper and kinder than letting them sit in jail.

Lemme tell you, said Inouye a little vaguely. This has been tossed around in many jurisdictions as an adjunct to the O.R. And we do have an O.R. Project in San Francisco . . .

Why don't defendants get O.R.'d more often, aside from the financial incentive to fill prisons?

Well, a judge might hesitate to O.R. a suspect because if he committed any crimes while he was out, the judge's enemies would have ammunition against him in his next reelection campaign. Moreover, bondsmen sometimes support judges in their election campaigns. —He chuckled and then said: A judge who O.R.s people who'd otherwise be paying bail bondsmen might be less than popular!

| 152 |

Needless to say, the bondsmen express divergent views. Roger Adair, for instance, said: Your idea of a fund sounds nice in principle, but when it came out to the time and money actually needed, I don't think it would be there.

I knew that Adair was right, because it's not so popular to spend money on poor people.

And lemme tell you something about the skip rate on O.R., he went on. To be honest with you, they've got over ninety-five thousand active bench warrants in Sacramento city and county. Only three hundred and forty-two of those are for people out on bail.†

---

*When I asked the bail commissioner about this, he remarked: "I don't know of that ninety-four percent how many were O.R.'d before and were O.R. failures." As for the D.A. man, Locher, when I raised Inouye's statistic with him he was silent for a moment, then said: "It's difficult for me to assess that. I don't believe that that reflects the experience here in Sacramento. But look. To the extent that there is always going to have to be a certain class of criminal defendants who are unable to make bail, they are more likely to be the public defender's clients. The others are more likely to get bail. *In that sense, the system would be working."*— This conclusion amazed me not a little.

†Locher agreed with these statistics, but disagreed with Adair's imputation that all but 342 of the 95,000 bench warrants were for O.R.s. In fact, he said, most of them were *not* for O.R.s. And Gonzalez remarked: "Outstanding bench warrants stay in the system for something like seven years. The system has a lot of bench warrants looking for deceased persons, or persons travelling out of their home state who do things they wouldn't do at home, or multiple warrants for the same persons. Maybe one guy has ten failures to appear."

That's why I don't recommend any kind of O.R. program. What's more, we bail bonds-men with our own bounty hunters do go out and find our own people at our expense, so we save the taxpayers' money.

| 153 |

If you extrapolate *that* out, laughed Daro in response, leaning back in the dark at the Inn Justice bar, his white shirt perfect against his white hair and handsome, florid face, well, that means those people never got in trouble again, since the system hasn't *found* them, right? So they haven't had an encounter with the law for seven years! *So O.R. works!* he chuckled. That statistic means we should shut down the prison system!

| 154 |

In Sacramento there is no bail commissioner at all, and in San Francisco the sheriff's of-fice had never heard of round-bespectacled, dark-moustached Commissioner Lam, who on an average day played God thirty-five times, all aside from his job presiding over drug court. I called superior court, where the clerks asked one another in bafflement: Would you know how to reach the bail commissioner? —Finally they referred me to the Office of Citizens' Complaints, because "they know everything." But they didn't. In the end, Daro Inouye helped me interview him at the Inn Justice.

Would you say you're more on the public defender's side or the D.A.'s side?

Oh, I think I piss off both sides, he said.

How fair would you say the bail system is in general?

I acknowledge that it's an unfair system, but I'm not sure that there's anything better.

And O.R.? I asked him, because he reviewed all candidates for that avenue to liberty.

My feeling on O.R.? he said slowly. If you're a person who has a stake in this, you're gonna have to come back to the courthouse. The others, they don't give a crap. They may commit the same offense again, sure. We *case manage* these guys. What else can we do? The fifteen minutes that somebody spends in court is nothing compared to the twenty-four hours he spends in the street. How important can the guy in the black robe be compared to the asshole who keeps chasin' him in the Tenderloin?

(Failure is a part of the whole cycle, Daro agreed. Otherwise you're saying, you blew it, that's it forever, you're in jail.)

How do you choose who stays and who goes?

I look at the background to see if the person will come back and if he is a particular threat. Has he defaulted before? The first issue is community safety. Then comes the severity of the offense. Finally comes failure to appear. This has nothing to do with has he committed the crime or not, and so I don't think it gets in the way of presumption of innocence.

When I'd asked Geri Campana how she decided whom to bail, she'd replied: A lot of it is gut feeling. I can pick up the phone and know right away if it's a good bail or a bad bail. And then a lot of it is the stability of them in the area—how long they work here, how many family members are in my office signing up for them, whether the family's stable and the defendant has never failed to appear.

So far, this sounded pretty much like Commissioner Lam's answer. But then I in-quired: What's a bad bail? Somebody who's going to skip?

Mrs. Campana's answer went to the heart of the matter: *If we take good collateral, we don't worry about that.*

| 155 |

And so, should the collateral be safe and decent, our bondsman crosses the street, ascends those wide steps of the Hall of Justice, and makes a beeline for Room 201 to submit the double-stubbed bond papers (which come preprinted in varying ceiling amounts, just like travelers' checks) through a circular opening, receiving a receipt in exchange, which at least is more than can be said for many other transactions involving criminality. Next, the bondsman must follow the arrow for the JAIL ELEVATOR. Ascend to the place of confinement, and you'll find yourself within a narrow cage whose far wall contains a little window, the counterpart of the orifice in Room 201, where the bond is actually posted, words between bondsman and clerk crackling tinnily back and forth through the barrier, as if one of them were a prisoner and the other a visitor—but which is which? The atmosphere of the cage is *sadness.* Sorrow's reek wafts in from the cells beyond. But it's all to the good. No more than six hours after the bond has been posted, and usually sooner, the jailbird will fly free.

Meanwhile, the next defendant is already slowly and sneeringly approaching the judge with a rolling gait, his hands in his pocket. He ignores the jingling of the bailiff's keys. Ladies bustle back and forth with armloads of files. And his predecessor, the hangdog defendant, looks down as the bailiff unlocks the door to stage left, sending him back to limbo.

Any call that we get, we do anything and everything in our power to help them get out, said Roger Adair. But you can only go so far. You can't pull a rabbit out of a hat. And if they just can't work with you, you tell 'em you're sorry, maybe they can get their bail reduced or plead out on their case or just get it taken it care of. But we do go to great lengths.

| 156 |

Mr. Adair had already admitted that he did not go to great lengths for defendants such as Strawberry , whose famous line *I'll be right back* brought smiles to all the grizzled old drinkers' faces as the new trick commenced his wait. Strawberry was off smoking crack, getting drunk, and engaging in other contract work. She might be back in an hour, or then again it might be a week. We've already agreed that her example remains, to use her own summation, irrelevant, the law having long since damned her beyond reach of any bail. —They take me and lock me up, she had fatalistically said. —But set that aside; one last time, let's suppose her to be one of those near-virginal trick-turners still eligible for bail—in other words, not a parole violator but a doer of a shining misdemeanors. Now, in the bad old days of misdemeanors, a prostitute could expect to face five hundred dollars bail, which at ten percent to the bail bondsman (not Mr. Adair, obviously, but perhaps somebody akin to that tightly grinning fellow up in Spokane who accepted VCRs) required her to turn two extra tricks.* And, by the way, here's an interesting ax-

---

*In 1998 a "basic flatback" from a San Francisco street-whore cost about fifty dollars. Back in the days when misdemeanors still required bail, it would have been around twenty-five or thirty.

iom I heard at the public defender's office: Only two kinds of defendants fight a misdemeanor charge: middle-class people, who have the time and money to be outraged, and crazy people. The others just plead guilty.* Nowadays, assuming that unlike Strawberry she didn't have other outstanding warrants, or wasn't violating parole by getting picked up, she could simply be O.R.'d.

Some bondsmen must not have liked that development, I remarked.

It did take away their bread and butter, the Commissioner laughed.

So more misdemeanors get cited out, but—

But meanwhile, there's an increase in the jail population in this state due to the increase in wobbler charges. The bail people have failed to understand that *almost all street activity is now criminalized.* They want a piece of that, but they don't understand that these street folks don't have any money.

A HYPOTHETICAL "WOBBLER" CASE
Suppose that a man strikes his wife, who calls the police.

Penal Code 273.5 (misdemeanor) Corporal injury by spouse of person cohabitating BAIL: $2,500 (1997-98) BAIL: $5,000 (1998-99)	or	Penal Code 273.5 (felony) Corporal injury by spouse of person cohabitating BAIL: $10,000 (1997-98) BAIL: $25,000 (1998-99)

In effect, wobblers allow the court to choose between making bail just barely affordable (or not) for hard-pressed defendants, or else utterly beyond reach. In the hands of wise magistrates, such discretion must be beneficial. In careless or brutal hands, it enables abuse. —Penal code 11337, Lam was saying, is possession of a controlled substance. It can be either a felony or a misdemeanor. But in many jurisdictions, the D.A. will automatically file a felony *every time.*

That fact told more about the D.A.s in those jurisdictions than about the defendants, and it made me sad. I remembered reading about the Greek lawgiver Solon, who supposedly made death the punishment for every crime. When they asked him why, he said: *For the lesser crimes, death is deserved, and I have no greater penalty left for the greater crimes.* In the prosecution of such wobbler crimes I seemed to see (on a lesser scale, to be sure) the same sort of ruthlessly inflexible punitiveness.

It may be that too much discretion and too little are equivalent judicial evils. Perhaps gloomy disgust is the inevitable byproduct of *any* human attempt to quantify justice. Bail! How strange, bitter, and slippery it is!

---

*Gonzalez said: "Man, the number of times public defenders have heard the client saying, *I don't want to fight the case!* One guy who'd been charged of assaulting his girlfriend, I remember him telling me: I don't got time. Even if she's been convicted of assaulting me in another county. I just wanna get out of here."

| 157 |

I mean, where are our priorities here? said Commissioner Lam. This one defendant, all we did was give her a set of teeth and she started smiling. These people don't wanna be out here smelling like they do. What we do at drug court is teach. I release him; he's high; and he's gonna get high again. You wanna plant that seed for next time and next time. I say to them, you're taking that jailhouse with you everywhere you go until you give up that jailhouse.

Would you favor O.R. over bail, or vice versa?

I do not have a big isssue against O.R. or against bail. Both of them have a place. But one thing I will say. When you bail somebody, you can just *bail* them. But when you O.R. somebody, you can attach conditions like they have to attend a drug program. And one other thing I want to say: At least eighty percent of my O.R.s do show up in court.

Well, can you suggest any improvement to the way things are now?

What I dream of is a pretrial triage system, he said. I want a pre-arraignment multi-service center. Wouldn't it be great if somebody *was there* to say: This guy's issue is mental illness so let's treat him for that, this guy's issue is drug abuse so let's put him in rehab, this guy's issue is he's just a bad actor? So many defendants would be better served in another arena than the criminal justice system. But it'll never happen.

And I closed my eyes, and saw still another handsclasping defendant sitting with his legs braced apart on the floor of the public defender's office and his bearded head sunken in sadness.

· BOOK XI ·

"Easier Than You Might Ever Dream"

(continued)

•

You will come in as flowers and not as fruit.

Witches' curse upon grapes (France, 16th century)

•

| 158 |

What did that bitch wanna get *noticed* for? sneered Chocolate. I don't wanna be *noticed*. I don't want the police to see me all the time. So today when a black-and-white tried to overshadow me, I said, use your brain, girl. I started sneezin'. I said to the pigs: Now I got a cold and tryin' to go home. —The tall man likewise scorned Domino's carelessness, but when the Queen emitted her imperishable word, he angelically descended toward Eight-Fifty Bryant without question, treading concrete with silent lengthy steps. He was not in the least interested in what the blonde might have done. What principally occupied him, since his blood currently bore a sufficiently high level of speedball to keep him well, was a domestic question—namely, was Strawberry holding out on him? He hadn't sniffed out any demonstrable lies, and yet whenever he lurked and guarded the morbid peroxide beauty which grew by night along Capp Street and South Van Ness, he seemed to see Strawberry leaping into strange men's cars more often than she reached into her stinking brassiere to present him with the latest twenty or forty she'd made. His conscience directed him toward the gentle path of mere watchfulness, since he'd once knocked one of her teeth out for what transpired to be no cause; but his other conscience, the Old Testament one which he knew as well as the many lines of shadow on the soles of the Queen's feet, demanded utter punishment for infractions of law. His agitation had become by virtue of its very habitude incapable of satisfaction. The Queen's rule held his worst impulses in check, and thereby stained him, as it would any of us whose lusts and cruelties have been thwarted, with a resentment against the Queen, which his love of her allowed him to avoid acknowledging. Upon what object then could he vent himself? —Strawberry, of course. His love for her licensed him to hate her, while his lack of fear of her incited that hatred. Waking up beside her at eleven that morning in a crack-smoked room of the Topeka Hotel, he'd been seized by so powerful a loathing of her scars, her smelly flesh, and her greedy piglike snores that he almost punched her. Bad control, he told himself. But what if the bitch were holding out? The Queen said never mind. The Queen said that if Strawberry were hiding some cash then that would only be natural. This had merely confirmed him in his suspicions, which were as cruel as Strawberry's silhouette against a brick wall whose every brick leaped sharply out in sun and shadow to prove itself more durably unfeeling than she. (When he expressed those, the Queen, squatting on a concrete block there in the old factory with her head between arms, stared into his eyes and sadly whispered: What am I supposed to *be*, though? How long do I gotta be perfect? You think nothing ever goes wrong for me?) In short, she'd insisted that he treat Strawberry as if she were innocent. —You know, Justin, Mr. Cortez the bail bondsman had once said, the first thing you learn when you visit the jail is they're *all* innocent! —And he'd laughed his hard laugh. The tall man, as tall as one of the Golden Gate Bridge's pillars, had heard all that before.

Beneath the Hall of Justice's twin flags, laughing portfolio-carriers allowed themselves to be ushered through the metal detector, while defendants on bail huddled on the stairs, perimetered by their associated pacers and sitters. But outside and across the street the freedom lottery advertised itself in the boldest colors: **KING BAIL BONDS, DE CORTEZ BAIL BONDS**, neon handcuffs blinking and springing off a neon wrist. The Queen's crowd used to go to Crown Bail Bonds because they'd take almost any collateral, sometimes even a mere signature, but one day a lady-in-waiting—Sunflower, in fact—had skipped bail, and by the time the bounty hunters settled things, bad feelings had also settled all around. So Mr. De Cortez, whom everybody called Mr. Cortez, had become the new favored tool.

Unfortunately, Mr. Cortez, who always cracked his knuckles and polished his glasses and cried out: Well, if it isn't my old friend Justin! wasn't there. A young lady whom the tall man had never seen before opened the door.

Yes? she said.

Wearily, the tall man took his finger off the buzzer and followed her in.

The individual's name is Sylvia Fine, he said, standing.

Please sit down, sir. You're making me nervous. Is that Sylvia with a "y"?

Yep.

Does she have any priors?

Yep.

Case number?

Just do your job, said the tall man. I'm so irritated about this.

Sir, I'm going to have to have the case number.

You see that green binder over there? Open that up. It's three pages before the last page.

Oh, here she is. AKA "Domino." And you said this is a drug possession case? Priors, priors . . . Yes, I should say she does.

What the fuck do you care about priors? Mr. Cortez he don't talk down to me like this. You shouldn't even be keepin' that information. Long as you got the collateral, baby, what the *fuck's* the difference if the bitch got priors?

And your name?

Justin Soames, the tall man said, already taking a California identification card from somewhere inside his shirt.

No, we don't need that yet, Mr. Soames. You don't have to get ahead of yourself. Will you please sit down? This is going to take a few minutes.

How many counts she got?

Sir, I—

How much this gonna cost?

Well, if you'll kindly be seated, sir, I'll just call Room 201 and find *out.*

I'll be back in fifteen minutes, said the tall man. He walked out, strolling that freedom strip, which was *all* bail bonds establishments with the exception of the auto glass place, the mecca for concrete hardeners and a couple of delis, and in the parking lot by the Inn Justice he smoked a rock, feeling an almost intolerable bitterness. In his imagination he raped the woman (who at that moment was gossiping about him on the phone, saying: There are those you have to chase. Over the years you get to know . . .), and then he slowly sawed her head off. He knocked the rest of Strawberry's teeth out. He blew up the Hall of Justice with its blank whitestone walls and whitestone steps on which unfortunates were sitting or standing, waiting for their own funerals or for some metaphor thereof, guarded by the triple mailbox and the police cars slowly cruising round and round. He won a million dollars in the lottery. He went fishing in the Gulf of Mexico. These pleasure-strategems relaxed him slightly, so that he was able to smile at his reflection in a massage parlor's silvered window, with a hooded brilliance equal to Domino's whenever that lady recollected the time when, aged thirteen, she'd helped her sister's boyfriend torch the Catholic high school.

A white boy wandered uneasily by. The tall man said: You lookin'? You lookin'?

Maybe. What do you have?

China white. One eight G.*

Dime?†

Uh huh.

Sure, I, uh . . .

Suddenly the boy ran off.

Boo! the tall man laughed, making a monster face.

A dragon made of cloud reared above the swiggling Victorian dormer windowfronts. He glared at it for half an hour.

Ms. Fine appears to have no permanent address, the woman said. You understand that we have to be very careful when transients are involved. Usually we don't even deal with them. They're too great a risk.

The tall man, still standing, clenched the edge of the desk.

Moreover, she has a number of nonappearances.

Yeah, well, you gonna get collateral, so it's no skin off your nose.

In some counties they fine you for nonappearance.

What about this one?

Mr. Soames, I'm trying to break her out for you. But you need to cooperate. The big powers, they don't usually issue bail to you until you show that you write carefully. You've got to get property, deeds of trust and so on. Because an original bond is like a check. And so I have to write this up very carefully.

And if she don't appear—

If you fail to appear, there's an immediate bench warrant. We have no control over that. We get a forfeiture notice, and we notify the indemnifier—that's you. And then—

Yeah, lady. I heard all that before.

Now I'm ready to see your identification, the woman said. Is this your current address?

Sure.

Mr. Soames, I'll need verification. I have to protect myself, you know.

From li'l ole *me?* chuckled the tall man, towering over her, stinking of anger and hatred.

If somebody just takes off, we'd be responsible to the court, Mr. Soames. So in that case we get somebody to track the defendant down . . . .

How much is the fucking bail, lady?

Mr. Soames, every once in a while I get somebody who raises my flag. You're one of those people.

---

*An eighth of a gram. In 1996–97 the street price was about ten dollars.
†Ten dollars.

You fucking ho bitch. I ought to cut you up, said the tall man, exiting. He went to Norris's, where a friend of his had once gotten sprung in those long-ago days before he'd even heard of the Queen. Mr. Norris gave him a cup of coffee and found out without any fuss that Domino's bail had been set at fifty-five thousand five hundred dollars, which he was able to reduce to twenty-five thousand after three phone calls to the judge.

Fuckin' ho bitch always costin', said the tall man, who was now in a very ugly mood.

Well, it's Friday, Mr. Norris consoled him. On Friday, everything that could go wrong, goes wrong.

I'm sick of that bitch.

Yeah, Justin, I understand.

Do you really?

Well, for somebody who has a lot of money, twenty-five thousand dollars for bail isn't that big a deal. He can just put it on his credit card. For somebody living day to day, ten dollars is a lot of money.

Damn right.

See, I told you I understood.

The tall man grimaced.

And how's her life?

Look, Mr. Norris. You ain't her shrink, so don't *be* her shrink.

You know, Justin, in this job what I like to do is make a difference. I like to think I can help somebody else, see 'em turn their life around.

Fine, so lemme call you Jesus. Me, I got the Mark of Cain.

The other part is when you watch people's lives just dwindle away. You watch 'em throw their life away. And it's sad, but that's the business we're in.

You *philosopher,* said the tall man, transforming the word into an obscenity. He counted out Mr. Norris's ten percent: ten twenties, five tens, a fifty, and twenty-two hundreds. The collateral, which Mr. Norris kept on what might be called a permanent loan, consisted of a television, two VCRs, title and registration to an old red Ford pickup truck, a mink coat and an album of rare stamps. Every item had been stolen. Mr. Norris knew this hoard to be worth much less than the tall man believed, but as long he believed it, he'd stay honest. Thus ran Mr. Norris's theory, which was not only philosophical but also empirically scientific in the best sense.

Very good, Justin, he said. Now let me just walk over to Room 201 with the information sheet and this receipt. I think we'll have your friend for you within the hour.

Fine, said the tall man. Break her loose.

| 159 |

When the Queen bailed her out of jail, the blonde felt herself suddenly invulnerable. (How could Dom get popped out of jail so quick? marveled Strawberry. I mean, they caught her with crack right on her body. I heard they found a baggy inside her pussy.) The Queen had protected all Domino's clothes for her, hiding them in some recess darker and grimier than all the secondhand furniture for sale on Mission Street's sidewalks, and so every last beautifully silver garment had been saved. Domino knelt. She smiled somberly, thin-lipped and glowing-eyed, with all the grey freshly dyed out of her long blonde hair, and suddenly the Queen saw in her the same immense and speechless patience which she always marked in Beatrice; as if Domino were saying to her just then:

My life is mine; I own it; I acknowledge it; I will live it out to the bitter end and do whatever I have to do to keep on being me, and if doing those things becomes sometimes bitter or hellish I will still be me at any cost; I'll never disappear into Nirvana as Sunflower did . . . —Whereas Beatrice represented softly giving endurance, Domino possessed many plans which were square-angled like late afternoon shadows on Capp Street. Already she could see herself marching into the Wonderbar where Loreena the barmaid would cry: *Hey, kid!* and Domino would flash her bright red, sneering, crooked smile. She would never be afraid, no, never. She slipped around her Queen's neck a wilted red ribbon which under cover of amplified Spanish-language paeans to Jesus she'd stolen from a pharmacy on Valencia Street. The Queen kissed her lips, and she stuck her tongue up the Queen's mouth, as happy as she'd ever be. The Queen granted her some fresh hot spit, whose psychochemicals made her pleasantly drunk. Then Domino shinnied into her best silver high heels, turned a trick (and here we ought to remind the reader without any sarcasm whatsoever that Domino could ride her tricks as agilely as a stewardess can brace herself against the ceiling of a small plane, defying turbulence, carrying drinks which tremble in the plastic cups—in other words, Domino knew exactly how to move and how far to go, being perfect at what she did), and in her sexy cat's-eye sunglasses she lolled naked on the strange man's couch with a toothy grin and clenched fists, thinking: Well, even in my thirties I still have something they want—I'm still in business! —I still get paid! (but the blonde suddenly shuddered as she shoved away a memory of double dating with the late Sunflower, a memory neither particularly familiar nor fiendish of two men's penises straining at their faces as she knelt beside the other whore in the back of a flatbed truck, saying over her shoulder: You wanna suck that, Sun? —Okay, said Sunflower dully, scratching her goosepimpled thighs). At least the strange man paid well—which is to say, Domino gaffled him good and proper. Almost drunk with joy, she spent the money on "white girl" cocaine and a rum and Coke at the Wonderbar, coolly watching the way Loreena's face widened when she smiled, as if Loreena were an interesting creature which Domino could vivisect whenever and wherever she chose. She turned another trick on Mission and Fifteenth, which act she later would not remember because this time the money was not so good, and after that, paranoid about what our televisions like to name "a police presence," took the bus to Larkin and Eddy, where Vietnamese restaurants presented to the world their blue and red awnings. Inside the nearest one, Vietnamese guys in caps whose brims sometimes projected forward like bills, sometimes backward like ducktails, raised their beer-glasses and turned the place blue with cigarette-smoke. A cellular phone rang; the waiter brought more Budweiser all around.

My wife have boyfriend! That's why I come here and I drink big!

Sew her pussy shut!

They were all laughing, all red in the face.

Me, I have two wives—one here, one in Vietnam. So I tell everyone I'm single!

Ha-ha-ha-ha-ha-ha-ha!

Aaaaaaah! they chorused, clinking glasses.

What a bunch of lousy fucking misogynists, Domino muttered. She stood waiting patiently outside the window for a good ten minutes, but her Vietnamese regular never kept his appointment. She reached inside her heart and tore her happiness into shreds which she then released from her bloody-fingernailed fists like confetti and twisted under both heels.

Half a block away, bright blonde girls all in a row were going into the black cop van. Suddenly there were no more girls.

| 160 |

Beatrice likewise expressed affectionate joy at Domino's return, congratulating and kissing her in a way that aroused the blonde; she always desired Beatrice even though she was fat and she stank. So for a moment she actually believed that Beatrice cared for her, and kissed her in return. When they were cheek to cheek, the Mexican girl whispered: I got a surprise for you. I doan use *los drogas* no more.

Why's that? said the blonde, not really listening as she slid her finger slowly down into Beatrice's underpants.

I was talking to God, and God said: Beatrice, doan use *los drogas* no more. And I said: Thank you, God. Thank you for thinking about me.

Whatever, said Domino. Hey, you want a hit off my crack pipe?

Okay, said Beatrice with a happy guilty smile.

Domino's hand on her vulva felt as scorching as one of those dark boxcars sitting in the hot California sun. Beatrice was simultaneously aroused and afraid. Understanding very well what the blonde intended, she wished that she could have run away to her Mama the Queen, but she respected Mama too greatly to disturb her. It was late afternoon. The fire escapes of the Tenderloin shone in the sun like charbroiled bones. They went to the abandoned ball bearing factory and made love, Domino giving it to her really hard with a dildo until Beatrice screamed with pain, pain flashing in and out of her in a rhythm like the quaking of a bar's double doors in Mexicali to let in a blast of white-hot sunlight and flashes of car-hoods upon the fat whores inside, may they rest in peace, who are busy shrieking with laughter, peering over each other's shoulders and slapping each other's palms, bright and burning pain expertly applied which ended as soon as it began, pain which Beatrice could not comprehend, and so—a blessed strategem, as priests might say—she did not attempt to comprehend it, putting on that same absent look in her eyes that she displayed when she leaned up against a storefront for hours, waiting and waiting to sell her pussy but already high, already well, so she was already gone and whatever bad thing was supposed to happen to her that night could safely happen because she was dead enough to roll with any punch. Although she dared not pray to the Virgin anymore, because in her state that might be blasphemy, the Virgin still sometimes came into her heart and gave her advice, and one time she warned Beatrice always to please and placate, in case something happened to the Queen. This was only another job—certainly not as bad as being raped. Sometimes she even felt pleasure, when Domino refrained from doing it too hard. But today the blonde was very needy; she'd been in prison too long; she couldn't control herself. Beatrice merely prayed to God (Whom even a damned soul such as herself could always pray to) to protect her from getting a hemorrhage. Then it was over. Domino climaxed with loud and ringing cries. She embraced Beatrice, kissed her many times, and gave her more crack. The pain was all ended now. Hard, yet bright of mood and somehow sincere, as she could still be at many an odd moment, she said to her: I love your box, hon. You've got such a fine, fine little box, such a hot little box . . . —Beatrice felt intensely safe and happy in Domino's arms.

| 161 |

Don't you think I'm to die for? said Domino, who felt so high-spirited that she was almost crazed.

Sure, said the john.

You don't have to die for me. I'll just kill you—ha, ha, ha!

In a hotel room, the john slowly masturbated, then ejaculated onto her face. Domino went to the sink and washed herself off. Within five minutes she'd convinced herself that it hadn't happened, and her exhilaration returned.

| 162 |

Around the corner from the O'Farrell Theater ("THE PLACE TO GO IN SAN FRANCISCO"), there was Domino, so luminously blonde, stopping traffic in her sweatshirt and shorts, turning her head, slowly gazing over her shoulder at the passing cars all the way along Larkin to the Ambika Hotel where my friend Mayumi got threatened while distributing free food, and then the Nitecape and the Dong Baek Korean restaurant, all the way to the 501 Club on Jones, the Hong Kong oriental massage place, the Columbia Hotel, the parking garage on Mason, the Irish Horse, the Virginia Hotel—she could see everything, and it all belonged to her. She pulled down her shorts so that the entire world could see pussy-fur, then screamed: *I'm the best!*

| 163 |

Loreena was only three hours into her shift at the Wonderbar when Domino came in with Lily, and two johns clung to them like tourists hanging onto a cable car's sides. — You're buying, Loreena heard one john say to the other john. You're the high roller.

Usual? said Loreena to the johns to make them feel special. (She often got tips that way.) The johns had been in yesterday, and each of them had ordered a shot of tequila straight up.

Yeah, the one who was paying said. That usual.

And I know what these ladies want, said Loreena with a neutral smile.

From the corner, an old drunk in a cowboy hat cried: None of that street tramp trash for me. Hey! Hey! I'm talkin' to you all. Go by the Four-Star or the Mitchell Brothers to get girls with real class. Spit in my eye if you can't. None of this T.L. trash. None of this Capp Street trash.

Be quiet, Alfie, said Loreena. Let Domino and Lily do their thing.

Well, so what do you think? Domino was saying to her prey. You going to do it or not? If you're not going to do it, I don't have all night.

I'll have to ask the boss, the john who wasn't paying replied.

Loreena was pouring Domino her rum and Coke when Domino said sharply: Hey! You shorted me on that!

What do you mean? said Loreena. I gave you two shots instead of one. And two shots are only two dollars when one shot is a dollar seventy-five. And if Heavyset were here, he wouldn't let me go past the line. A shot's a shot, he'd say. But I filled it right up to the top.

Fuck the owner, said Domino. You shorted me.

Look, Domino, said Loreena. I don't like it when you start getting sniffy with me. Now watch this.

She took a glass, crammed it full of ice, and poured two shots of bourbon in.

Were you watching, sweetie? she said. Did you get that? See, it's not even as high as what I gave you. Satisfied?

It should be a quarter-inch higher, Domino insisted.

Fuck *you!* said Loreena, pouring the demonstration glass down the sink while Domino slowly licked her lips.

Thank you, too, Loreena, said Domino with a bright smile.

She gulped her drink down.

So, she said to her john (a man with his glasses on his forehead, a grey suit like a beetle-shell over his paunch), your time's about up. I have to attend a memorial service for a very close friend who died and I'm trying to raise the money to go. Can you help me out?

Loreena started laughing. Domino glared at her.

Let me go talk to the boss, the john said.

He tapped the other john's shoulder, and they went into the corner, where they whispered and calculated.

He's hooked, said Loreena.

Don't tell me my business, snarled Domino.

It's my business, too, sweetie. I've been watching you put the moves on for years. I never guess wrong about you. You'll see.

Pour me another shot, said Domino.

Who's paying? said Loreena.

Put it on their tab.

Well, then let's make it a double, laughed Loreena, pouring right up to the top of the glass.

That's more like it, said Domino. Why'd you have to short me the first time?

He said it's OK with him, her john reported.

All right, let's go, said Domino, rising. As soon as Loreena had slid the drink across the counter it was aloft and then its contents were down her throat. Truth to tell, Domino had some kind of white fungus on her tonsils, and she drank to kill the pain. Lily had told her once that you didn't have to worry about AIDS until the white fungus began growing on the roof of your mouth. Then you had problems, Lily said.

Hey, I didn't order that drink, the boss accused.

Loreena put her hands on her hips. —Well, somebody's paying for it, mister, and I have a feeling that's going to be you.

The boss swore and and plunked three dollars down. Loreena would have thanked him, but just then a pimp came in and began to bang on the bar with his fist, shouting: I want an orange juice right now!

Go fuck yourself! said Loreena with a happy laugh.

Meanwhile, in the back seat, the john insisted on holding Domino's hand while the boss drove and told dirty jokes to Lily. Domino let her john do what he wanted while she stared out the window. She saw Beatrice standing on the corner, holding a soda as she gazed up at the brickwork of the Goodness Tenderloin Center. Domino didn't wave.

So was it a close friend who died? the john ventured.

Oh, actually it's a barbeque, said Domino with a yawn. For a lady with a pet pot-bellied pig.

Ten minutes later he was trying to pull her down on the floor of the boss's place, while in the bedroom where the boss and Lily were, the bed creaked loudly and briefly.

How much are you going to pay me? said Domino.

You said twenty dollars, the john said.

That's just to prime my pump. How much you got?

The john turned his pockets inside out and excreted thirty.

All right, said Domino. Now, what do you want me to do?

Just lie in my arms for a minute, the john said.

Oh, so you're one of those, said Domino.

What's that mean?

Domino, bored, got down on her side and lay rigid while the man touched her breasts.

That just tickles, she said after awhile. Cut it out.

Lifting her skirt, the john discovered the same motorcycle scar which had impressed Tyler, and then a new tattoo of two linked female symbols.

Oh, are you bi? he said.

Yep, said Domino. Get on with it.

Can I eat you out? he said.

Mm hm, said Domino, not listening.

He opened her legs and started to lower his face and she said: Oh, no, I don't do that.

Oh, okay, the john said.

Well, thank you for being such a gentleman, said Domino. This was fun. I've got to go.

She stood up and walked out, leaving Lily in the now silent bedroom. What did she care about that bitch?

| 164 |

Domino rolled a condom onto the customer's penis with her tongue, started to suck him, took her face away for a moment, winked and said: This is the worst chewing gum I ever tasted.

The man laughed so hard he lost his erection.

That's it then, said Domino. You're done.

Just a minute, said the man. Together they stared at his flaccid penis, as if it might actually rescue the two of them from each other, but nothing happened.

Better luck next time, said Domino. Thanks for being such a gentleman.

She rose so that her skirt fell back down to her knees, slipped on her high heels, and strode triumphantly out while the man sat holding his penis in disbelief. Domino was in a hurry now. She did not spare much consideration for the impressionist lampshade-light in the brick windows of Chinatown, nor for the red diamonds on the whitewalled apartments above the Golden City Restaurant and Market. Once very very long ago she'd been a go-go dancer shouting to keep the job she was late for, shouting until the phone booth reeked of her perfume; she'd lost that job and lost the next. In a quarter-hour she was back home among the Tenderloin's laughing and mumbling whores in the rain, the high-priced whores who sported satin umbrellas and shimmering boots, and whose faces were as blank and shiny as new Coca Cola cans. A blonde in a white skirt and a black umbrella offered each car a little-girl wave.

I used to look as good as that, said Domino, looking the young blonde up and down.

What are you staring at? sneered the young blonde. You're nothing. You're just an old sack of trash!

Domino then felt the same sensation as her late companion, the man with the flaccid penis. But she did not herself withdraw into flaccidity. Snatching up a broken beer bottle from the sidewalk, she rushed the girl and brought the club down on her forehead hard enough to shatter glass anew. The girl fell down bleeding and screaming. Domino, knowing better than to tempt the squat square rainy black buttocks of police cars, slipped off her high heels and ran down to Turk Street. Then, reshod, she approached the parking lot on Golden Gate where the tall man man lorded it over the shadows.

She whistled four times, and he lobbed her a dime bag.

That'll work, chucked the blonde, paying him.

Gimme five for Maj's retirement fund, said the tall man.

For hers or for yours? said Domino disdainfully. How do I know what crap you're up to?

You got some mouth, said the tall man. You be lucky you're in good with Maj. Otherwise I might just have to beat your whitebread ass.

Oh la-*la,* sneered Domino. Don't think I haven't figured out who's gaffling everybody else. And someday I'm going to do something about it.

Now who's gettin' accused? said the tall man watchfully. You got the guts to accuse me to my face? Or you accusin' Maj behind her back as usual?

Fuck you, Justin. Hey, keep an eye out for a sec, would you? I need to pee.

She squatted down between two cars and began to make water, which struck the asphalt with a sizzling noise. Many things are more convenient without underwear.

Hey! she said indignantly. You're not supposed to watch me, you pervert!

The tall man chuckled. Certain things I like to look at. Not so much what you be doin' there, but the part of you you be doin' it *from.*

Wiping herself on her skirt, Domino rose, not really angry at all. —Hey, you know that guy Henry? The one who keeps hanging around the Queen? *He* likes that stuff. He's into golden showers.

Me, I'm just into *gold,* said the tall man.

You're just a big black jerk, laughed Domino. Here's ten dollars for your retirement fund.

She turned her back on him and went out toward the ticket booth. She lit up a cigarette. A man was approaching. She said to him tentatively: Hey, you wanna . . .?

The man gazed at her intensely. Then he got into his truck and drove away.

| 165 |

Domino breezed into the Wonderbar, drunk and high, determined to get drunker. An old john whom she dated once or twice a month sat down beside her. —Aha, the old bastard's horny again! she thought gleefully, showing him leg. I'm the *best!*

The john said: You, uh, I, uh-uh-uh-uh—

Gimme a twirl! laughed the drunken blonde. Why do you think li'l girls like to twirl?

Not just to see their skirts fly up, though that'll work for some. The real reason is, *it makes you high.* But I did just wash my underwear. Wanna see?

I . . . well, I, yes.

Then I'll *give you a twirl!* Ha, ha, ha!

You're so—I mean to say, Domino, you, uh, you're *beautiful.*

Black belt, leather, lace, why don't you SIT on my—face! See I'm a poet. I wish I could dance on the bar, but—and suddenly the blonde burst into tears—Loreena won't let me. I know her. I just know . . .

| 166 |

Well, said the Canadian doctor, joke goes like this: Guy's trying to call Canada, and the operator says: Sorry, sir, that's an imaginary number. Please multiply by the square root of minus one and try again. Well, it's just a mathematics joke. I can't make any excuses for it. It's not me who's the lawyer; it's my wife.

Domino smiled well-manneredly. —Hey, you got five dollars?

Absently, the doctor reached into his wallet and counted out five ones. Domino saw a hundred dollar bill in there and her heart pounded.

So where did you say you were from? Domino said.

The doctor looked at her. —I'm from Canada. Have you been listening to anything I said?

Sure, Professsor. You were talking about your wife. So you wanna kind of like unzip, and then maybe we can *relax?* I'm real tight down there, you know what I mean?

Listen, said the doctor. I changed my mind. I wanted somebody who could pretend a little better than you could.

Oh, well, aren't *we* hurt! sneered Domino. Just because I don't understand all your mathematics shit, you can't get hard! You have it in for me because I never had the op-portunity you had? You have something against girls that never had the chance to get a good education, that never even got a decent pair of shoes?

Those sneakers of yours look just fine to me, said the doctor. Or don't they count?

Domino reached into her purse and pulled out a razor-knife. —All right, don't play games with me, she said. I want your wallet.

| 167 |

They call some people shot-callers, said the tall man. They're the ones that call the shots. If you gotta get well and I wanna sell you some powder for a higher price and you say no, don't mean no nevermind, 'cause you gotta have that powder, see. *I* call the shot.

How many women shot-callers you know? said Domino.

A few. And they be so cold.

How about me?

You certainly be cold enough. Might as well call you the Ice Bitch. But that's not all there is to it. You got to show some *sense.* Why be mean when you can accomplish the same thing by coaxin'?

I don't give a fuck about coaxing, laughed Domino.

That's what I'm saying. Oh, what's the use?

Shit, if I was the Queen I'd get good for all the girls, get a nice escort service, hundred dollar dates for even the girls that didn't deserve it, even the ugly girls, even the mean, stupid bitches, even the assholes that ripped me off and gaffled me and jacked me up, and they wouldn't have to pay *nothin'*. Not a fuckin' thing. Justin. I'd be so good to them they wouldn't know what hit 'em. I was in an escort service for a number of years. Being the Queen is easier than you might ever dream. And I sure as hell wouldn't . . . wouldn't . . . what the fuck was I talking about? Jeez, my head hurts.

It hurts from doing what you call thinking, said Justin. Now leave me in peace. I'm gonna roll myself some of this greenbud. Thank the Lord you're allergic to that. Otherwise you'd be hitting me up and threatening . . .

I wouldn't make 'em stay in this dump, either, Domino muttered. I wouldn't want 'em with me, anyhow. Better to get myself a nice big old house like I used to have before my mother lost her mind, and I want a kitty, a nice white kitty cat. And all the rest of you, I'd keep you at arm's length, I tell you. You goddamned backstabbers . . .

· BOOK XII ·

The False Irene

•

For the wisdom of this world is folly with God.

1 CORINTHIANS 3.19

•

Who's that rose for? That rose for me?

It's for the Queen, said Tyler.

For the Queen! *Oh!* You datin' the Queen? said Kitty.

I'm just bringing her a rose.

Shit! Why didn't you bring *me* one?

Evening, Strawberry, Tyler said. Have you been crying?

Justin and I broke up, the whore wept.

I'm sorry to hear that, he said. What was the last thing you said to him?

I told him he'd be well advised to use this time packing.

And what did he say?

Oh, he said something about me, involving fornicating female dogs. Oh, hell. Here he comes. Justin! Justin, I already told you! Keep away from me, I said! *Justin!*

The tall man glared scarlet-eyed and slugged her in the mouth. Her lip split and blood dribbled down her chin.

Come on home, she said to him steadily. Let's forget this. When we get home I'll go out and make money and get you another drink.

He needs another drink like I need an airplane, Kitty muttered.

The tall man punched Strawberry again. Kitty screamed.

All right, Justin, said Tyler. You made your point.

Strawberry turned on him, clawing and shrieking: Stay out of my business, you bastard! This is between Justin and me!

I get it, said Tyler. Where's the Queen?

In there, said the tall man.

All right, he said, walking around them. He heard the tall man punch Strawberry again, and felt sickened.

Beatrice was playing with a blue tiger which she had made out of papier mâché when Tyler came down the steps into the tunnel, giving her game surcease. She likewise hated the tall man's violence, even though she could understand very well that he might become exasperated because Strawberry was a born thief and even from her own sisters she would steal. Once Beatrice had caught her trying to sell Domino's silver shoes. She begged her not to do that, but the other girl wouldn't listen. But whenever the tall man beat her, *ay!* Poor Strawberry! How Beatrice pitied her!

Afternoon, Bea, he said drily.

Oh, Henry, why is Justin so fierce? I'm afraid now even to see his face! And Strawberry, she's so patient, may the saints protect her . . . When he goes away I can give to her this tiger, and may she find joy in it.

I figure you and I should go out dancing sometime, he said to cheer her. —Maj tells me you used to dance professionally . . .

With a bitter grimace she replied: On the Day of the Dead they only know to dance their own way.

What's that got to do with anything? You thinking of dying anytime soon?

From behind, they heard Strawberry's shrill, sharp screams. But the darkness ahead where the Queen was was silent.

I dislike it, she said. *Ay,* how I dislike it.

Never mind, Bea. In your home town how do they dance?

They dance different. It's like the same music, but nobody show them.

You still like to dance?

She trembled. —No, she said. No more. Now I doan like.

All right, he said.

He could not unhear Strawberry's screams and Kitty's screams.

The Queen was in the darkness muttering: I'm fixin' to go buy some groceries.

Is Strawberry going to be okay? he said.

Justin slapping her around again, huh? said the Queen. I seen that almost every month.

Yeah.

Oh, he's a wild one, said the Queen, resigned.

What if he kills her?

He won't.

I don't get it. Don't you run things here? Are you trying to tell me she wants it?

Hush up, Henry. She done him wrong this time. She flushed all his china white down the toilet an' then told him she done it. It's always this way. She'll be sick a couple of days . . .

It makes me anxious, he said. I hate to see her allowing that to happen.

Nobody sayin' you don't have a good heart. But maybe you don't understand. It's not always wrong when a man hits a woman. Most of the time, yes. But not all the time.

I don't know.

You'd never do it. But maybe she needs it.

How could anyone *need* it?

Strawberry! called the Queen. Strawberry, c'mere!

The whore came in torn clothes, bleeding from the mouth, one eye swollen shut. Justin was stamping and roaring outside as his victim whispered: This is how the world is. Oh, Jesus! Someone's gonna get compensated, but it's still horrendous. I still hope someday we'll all laugh about it, but oh well.

Strawberry! *Strawberry!*

What? she sobbed. Maj, he's so violent. Can't you —

Strawberry, this gentleman told me he's worryin' about you.

Tell Henry to keep the fuck out of my business.

All right, baby, you can go. Now, Henry, do you believe?

I believe in her pride, that's all.

You want me to take your pain away? I could make you drink something so you'd forget Irene forever. You wouldn't wake up cryin' no more. You want me to do that?

No.

Why not?

I don't know, he said wearily. Can we talk about something else?

In other words, keep the fuck out of my business.

No, Maj. I'd never say that.

Well?

Irene's so precious to me.

You see? You're like some wolf that keeps lickin' the razor-blade; he drinks his own blood an' bleeds to death, 'cause he likes the taste. You an' Strawberry, oh me oh my . . .

The screams had begun again. He sighed and said: Here's a rose for you.

The Queen accepted the flower, stood up on tiptoe and kissed his face.

| 169 |

Did she touch you? Smooth wanted to know when he had recounted this much.

Yep.

No, Henry, I suspect your ignorant and envious ears mistook my meaning. I meant, did she *touch* you? I meant, did she leave marks?

That's between her and me.

No it isn't, Smooth replied with logic as tight as the pussy of the skeletal whore whose face had been destroyed in an automobile accident. You couldn't have met her without me, boyo. What's more, you —

Talk about envious ears, my God!

Come on down to the basement, said Smooth. I just got me a Hi-Standard twenty-two I wanted to break in. They say it takes five hundred rounds to loosen her up. Salesman I bought it from has one of his own; that's how he sold me on it, you see. He said it was *fun*. Now, he did warn me that during the break-in period it jammed once or twice with every magazine, which didn't turn me on. He got so he wanted to throw it against the ever-lovin' wall, he said. But he's had it for twenty years since then, and never a problem. Now he's *addicted*.

I've got to go.

No you don't.

I don't mind obeying *her*. But I kind of dislike it when *you* push me around . . .

Why so belligerent, Henry? Grin and bear it, now. Maybe you—

I get so bored and so tired sometimes—

Well, what's your favorite subject? Irene? That'll perk you right up. Henry, baby, you want to talk about *Irene?* I'm all attention.

Please cut it out, said Tyler, rubbing his chin.

No, that's what I was going to say to *you*. I'm lonely, you see.

Well, I—

And maybe I can give you some advice about how to proceed with our Queen.

What do you mean, proceed?

Don't you want to take it to the next level, Henry? Don't you want to learn the secret of life? You can't always predict what she'll teach you, but whatever she imparts, well, *zowie!* Get that Mark of Cain working for you, son! Pull yourself up by your bootstraps and—

Cut the corny crap. I give up. So you've got a shooting range downstairs?

Well, you could call it that.

Smooth opened the basement door and clicked a switch connected to a wan bulb. They went down.

Not so many basements in Sacramento, Tyler said.

Flood plain. This house was built two big floods ago. There was no flood insurance requirement back then, and the state was having a drought, so nobody believed in floods. Just like you, Henry boy—you were getting discouraged about the Queen before you met me, hey? Well, that flood came, and the basement filled up, and the family that lived here moved out and sold it to me. Basement filled up again when the last flood came, and I guess it will do it when the next flood comes. I still don't pay flood insurance. Why?

Why what?

Why did you ask?

I don't care, to be honest. Just making conversation.

No. I won't accept that. Meaningless conversation is not allowed in my house. What's your point?

I've given up looking for points.

I'd given it up long before you were born, son. And you know what? We're both liars. We both want all the answers. How old are you, anyway?

Forty-four, said Tyler.

Well, I was going to say that you were only twenty-four, but you'd lived a hard life. Another of my jokes, see.

Ha ha.

A train whistled, long and slow. The two men stood on a dark green carpet which smelled like disinfectant and cigarette smoke which drifted down, as limp as Domino on heroin at the Wonderbar with her head on the counter and her long hair trailing in her drink. A foam rubber mattress with three pillows on it lay in the corner beside an electrical outlet. On the walls were taped illustrations of Boy Scouts and other adventurous young males, scissored out of the pages of *Boy's Life* and similar publications. In the face of Tyler's silence, Smooth said: I may be jealous, son, but I'm still the ordained debriefer and father confessor. Do you trust me?

I do not, you pompous old shit.

I never asked if you liked me. I asked if you trusted me.

Why should I trust you? You just want to get under my skin. You sort of pry into my business and—

Oh, heavens. I've got more to do than that. Getting under your skin is just my little recreation. Think nothing of it. Now, do you *trust* me?

I can't honestly say I do.

All right. Do you trust my devotion to the Queen?

Tyler hesitated. —Yes, he said.

All right. And what about yourself, buddy? Are you devoted, too?

I guess I've signed on.

So you trust our coincidence of interests?

What's the difference, Smooth? I'm so tired of talking about this. Motives don't count worth a damn anyway. Only actions are valid. I—

You'd like to pretend that was the case, wouldn't you? But I'd bet a hundred dollars that whenever you fuck up, you excuse yourself for good intentions. In fact . . .

In fact *you* revel in the real or imaginary weaknesses of others, Tyler replied, raising his voice. You're like a dog that loves to roll in shit! I admit that my shit stinks as much as yours, but I don't go out of my way to smell it—

Interesting analogy! said Smooth brightly. Because to really serve the Queen, you know, you'll need to develop an intimacy with many kinds of body products.

Dan, you used to disgust me, but now you just bore me.

Ah. Well, are you ready to shoot?

Right now I'm pissed off at you, so don't put a gun in my hand.

Here you go. The famous Hi-Standard.

All right, asshole, Tyler said. My brother used to have one of those. What are we shooting at?

Hang your target on that clothesline there, over by the sandbags. You aren't so incompetent you'll miss the sandbags, are you?

Oh, I wouldn't exactly say that.

Good. But aren't you carrying today?

No, Dan. I don't need a pistol to visit my mother.

But you're visiting *me.*

They loaded up and shot for an hour or two, the sounds of the shots muffled and sad through their ear protectors like hammer-blows in some mineshaft far away. —You're a pretty good shot, said Tyler with surprise and respect. —But the Hi-Standard jammed every five or six shots. Smooth said that the old manufacturing dies had nearly worn out, which was why a used Hi-Standard from the 1950s sold for as much as a new one from 1995. Tyler listened glumly, holding the gun with the muzzle safely sandbag-pointed. In truth, it was not so much Smooth who repulsed him, as his own life, whose fundamental meaninglessness he confessed in a series of skull-muffled shouts. How could he retain any faith in the Queen, when she squatted like a spider in the darkness while the tall man beat Strawberry? What was she even good for? Maybe he should humble himself, apologize to John and ask for another loan. He'd go to night school. He'd become a . . .

But he could not think what he desired to become.

As a matter of fact, I used to shoot competition, the pedophile was saying. Here lay his vanity, Tyler thought. And he did his best not to smile as Smooth babbled on: Gave that up about ten years ago now, when some fellows who'd heard about me started calling me names right there on the firing line. But I still get out to the range from time to time.

You're a good shot, Tyler repeated weakly, longing for a drink.

Oh, not very. I could blow your head off at fifty yards. But if I could shoot through your left eyeball eight out of ten times at fifty yards, now, *that* would be good shooting.

I guess that's a compliment. That's what my eyeball guesses.

Oh, I don't shoot my three fifty-seven much. I usually go out with my Ruger, which I load way under specs for target. But this Hi-Standard is . . . Well. I guess you're driving back before long?

Yeah.

And Irene is still on your mind?

Yeah.

What time is it?

Going on three.

You fixing to see Maj tonight?

You need to report back to her?

Maybe.

On me?

Sure.

All right. What hoops do I have to jump through now?

All of 'em, Henry. I wouldn't take less.

And what does she say about me?

She might be able to get some good use out of you before you crack.

I know she gets good use out of you.

Now, Henry, there's your *envy* speaking again.

But what's it all *about?* Tyler almost shouted.

Nothing, brother. Everything's about nothing. You know that, but you prefer to pretend otherwise. We both do.

You know, Smooth, I kind of figure your job isn't really to get information on me. I'd also say the Queen tends to make up her own mind no matter what you tell her . . .

Correct. Now, Henry, do you love her?

I beg your pardon?

Do you love our Queen?

How about you? Tyler said, swallowing nervously.

I'd die for her.

All right, fine. I love her. I don't know whether I'd die for her or not.

But you're not actually *about* love in this case, are you? You're like one of those lepers in a medieval morality play crying out: *Heal me!* That's what you want the Queen for. And you're still holding a torch for Whatchamahoosis. Christine.

Irene.

Got your goat, didn't I? You simple sonofabitch! You know, if you wear your heart on your sleeve, other people can see it and spit on it.

People such as you, Dan.

I expect so. Ha! Now you're mad, aren't you? You're so cute when you're mad.

I'll see you around, Dan.

You know what? said Smooth.

What? said Tyler, gritting his teeth.

I think you never cared all that much for your sister-in-law. I think you only cared about losing her. It's *loss* you're in love with. That's why you hang onto it. I'll bet that before that Irene came along you were whining about someone else. Oh, I remember now. You grew up without a father, didn't you? That explains it. Ain't I clever? And now you want the Queen because you don't believe it'll work out with her. And if it does, maybe you'll wreck it yourself just so you can mourn her. Aren't I right, Henry? Just swallow hard and tell me I'm right. Aren't you one of the most pitifully self-destructive, selfish bipeds that ever walked the streets? Well, aren't you?

I don't need any deathbed regrets when I'm around you, said Tyler with a trembling laugh.

There you go with your regrets again. And Irene—

You want me to betray Irene's memory, and I'll never do that! It feels like betraying her just allowing you to spit her name out of your sneering lips . . . I'm leaving. You got what you wanted. You pissed me off. You can tell your Queen I failed the test.

Sleep on it, Henry, said Smooth with a lazy smile.

Tyler went out and drove all the way west until he was looking down from the freeway to the pavement and dead grass, plastic bags and long low barracks-like docks where San Francisco began, with Coit Tower ahead on its green and white hill, commanding the clouds. —I failed the test, he said aloud, with a jeering despairing smile. Soon it began to rain, and he came to the Tenderloin streets, passing glistening raincoats, loud laughs, fingers pointing at heaven and hell, with rain running down the camo-green crown of a rain-man's head. He parked and locked, walking around a black man in a soaked wool sweater, a black woman in a black wool cap, swinging her arms, a couple huddled under a scaffold whose ribs were almost glorious with water, tourists with umbrellas like walking mushrooms, until at last he found the tall man.

How's business, Justin? he said.

You might as well paint your car flaming pink. It makes me sick to see such a faggotty car.

I was wanting to see her if she's around.

She ain't, said the tall man.

When *will* she be around?

I'll pass it on that you stopped by, the tall man said, darting a glance behind him at a brawny lap-dancer the length of whose blonde hair was somewhere between that of convict-fuzz and pooltable-felt. She was helping the manager put up brand new photos of semi-nude unionized girls on the outer wall. The tall man glared into her eyes, but she pretended not to see.

All right, said Tyler, defeated.

All right *what?*

Tell her Smooth pissed me off. Tell her, if I failed some kind of test I'm sorry.

Her pager's only got seven digits, Henry. Better shorten that message.

Oh, fuck you, said Tyler, returning to the driver's seat.

He drove homeward. His neighborhood exuded an air of unreality and sorrow doubtless unfelt by most of its other residents; surely it was less sorrowful than the Tenderloin. He had forgotten to ask what had become of Sunflower's body. Perhaps there was no use in asking anything now; Smooth must have put in a bad word for him. How he hated Smooth! The man's round, goading face floated up feverishly before him. He was like a disease that Tyler had contracted, a venereal disease, painful and shameful, which he must simply endure. But what if he gave it up? He had a quarter; he could telephone John this instant and beg for a ten thousand dollar loan. John would help him even now, for their mother's sake. He could become something successful. If he relocated to Sacramento, he could take better care of his mother and also hook in with the Capitol politicians, hiring himself out to political action committees who wanted dirt on each other's senators, or to "ethics" committees whose aim it was to prove some poor victim unethical. Or, better still, he could go to southeast Asia and return with a beautiful bride who resembled Irene. But then he'd have to support her. If only he knew what favor to ask the Queen! Smooth was right. He desired to be healed. What would heal him? Nothing in the Sunset district, that was for sure . . . Of course there was very little to do on Pacheco, where he lived, but after Pacheco the alphabetical pavements went Quintara, Riviera, Santiago and then Taraval, which was a busy street, at least for the Sunset; it was the mirror image of Clement Street or maybe Geary Street in the Richmond district across the park. Taraval Street sometimes soothed him. Before he knew it, he'd driven there. The habits of his profession made it easy to drive almost aimlessly, round and round as if he were stalking someone, when really he was but circling himself. Closing his eyes, he found himself remembering the old Parkside Theater where he'd once gone alone to watch "The Sorrow and the Pity." Taraval was largely comprised of Asian establishments now. He'd always wanted to take Irene out to Dragon City Restaurant, but it wasn't fancy enough for her, he'd feared, so he hadn't gotten around to it. He'd kept thinking: Someday, when I'm more relaxed and comfortable around Irene . . . After Dragon City, Taraval rolled down to the foggy ocean, past a Walgreens sign so red in the night, down along fogslimed trolleycar tracks with their empty pedestrian islands; Marco Polo's was on Twenty-Fourth, right by the coin laundry place that always glowed pale yellow; then pizzerias, and the Tropical Reef at Twenty-Eighth; a huge new Korean restaurant awaited him on Thirtieth that he'd not yet tried; their sign proclaimed that they catered. Well, if he could marry Irene . . . After the bird hospital he didn't remember anything until Thirty-Third, where the Elegance Ballroom failed to persuade him. On Thirty-Fifth the Knights of Columbus chapter marked a lower, darker and greyer part; more pizza places, and already his memory had slid down to Forty-First where he almost never saw anyone; the only things which had any existence there were the burning houselights—well, he recollected one hardware store at Forty-Seventh . . .

Turning back, he pulled up in front of his dark apartment and wished that the Queen were with him holding his hand.

He went upstairs, unlocked the door, turned on the hall light and checked his messages. A Mr. McBean wanted him to trace somebody's Dominican bank account, provided that Tyler would charge him less than five hundred dollars. He resolved to charge McBean four-fifty. His mother hadn't called. From the refrigerator he awarded himself a cardboard takeout box imprinted with a red pagoda. He ate the Chinese food cold. It was soggy, salty, spicy and greasy. He couldn't finish it. He felt nervous. He reclosed the boxflaps and threw the carton into the garbage. Then he wiped his mouth on his sleeve, rinsed off the fork, soaped it, rinsed it again, and set it tines up in the dish drainer. He sat down listlessly in the living room. He didn't feel like reading. Sighing, he switched on his computer, and watched the hellish white globule of light in the center of the dark green monitor sizzle and replicate until the whole thing had come alive. Accessing MoneyScape, InterQuick, and a pirated version of Full Disclosure, he was able to read and print out the full story of the Dominican bank account. The three searches had cost him fifty-four dollars. He invoiced McBean a hundred and twenty for expenses and three hundred for his labor. Should he charge thirty dollars more for something else, and bring it up to four-fifty? Why bother? He sat there gazing at the screen with burning eyes, feeling weary and useless.

The phone rang.

He checked the clock. It was nearly eleven.

Yeah, he said.

She'll see you now, said the tall man.

His heart soared. —It'll take me forty minutes, he said.

That's fine. Meet me in front of the New Century at midnight sharp.

Then came the click and the harsh, dependable buzz of the dial tone.

| 170 |

So that's your car, huh? said the tall man. It really *is* your car.

You must have asked me that a million times. Hop in.

Looks like a faggoty car, said the tall man. More I look at it, more I think you got to be some on the faggoty side to own a car like that.

Tell you what, Justin, said Tyler. Why don't you just grease up your asshole and hop in the back seat and see what happens.

Man, you are pure *bullshit,* grinned the tall man.

Hey, Justin, do you call all the girls faggots? Don't they all eat the Queen's pussy, too?

Now that be *different,* said the tall man. Queen's the *Queen.*

You got that right, Tyler said.

Sapphire always be playin' with herself, but that bitch ain't in her right mind. She just *pathetic.* Domino's lez, but I got my dick wet inside her one two three times, so she ain't all lez; she's part woman, know what I'm sayn'? An' the others, they're just the others. Turn left.

What's your favorite hotel?

Don't have one. Left again.

What's your least favorite?

All of 'em.

What's the best thing that ever happened to you?

The Queen! But I don't want her to know that. That old bitch'll be gettin' a swelled head . . . Hey, listen, Henry, my man, I can cut you a deal on some kickass indica weed . . .

Now where?

In here, said the tall man. So long. I gotta make a run.

Tyler was alone in another hotel room with an unmade bed, the wall covered with poems.

Then the Queen came in, and he was happy.

You said you love me, she said.

Yeah, said Tyler.

You don't love me. Everybody loves me. Nobody loves me.

Let me admit something, Maj. I don't know *anything,* not even who I am or what I want or whom I love. I, uh, I *confess* that up front.

Okay. C'mere. Look at me, Henry. I want you to look at me. What do you really want? You still want that happiness?

What do you mean?

You still don't understand, huh? Henry, you *stupid* sometimes. You want that happiness or you want me?

I want both.

Ain't you just sayin' that? All rightie then, she said with a sigh. Go over there. You see that closet door? There's a girl behind that door. Go an' open that door and take the girl by the hand. Henry, you're always gonna be my baby. Don't think I ever wanted to pawn you off. Go an' get her. That's right. Bring her to me.

| 171 |

This girl's gonna be your Irene now, said the Queen very gently, and a strange dark intoxication of sadness rose up from his bowels into his chest, expanding, funneling ever more widely, like smoke as it rises, bracing and almost revitalizing him with the immense, flavorful richness of that pain, loving pain, painful love which he had never felt before, that heart's rush of anguish comparable only to the uplift from white crack-smoke whistling through the pipe to numb his lips and race his heart like a competition driver's engine. —Are you all right? Irene sometimes used to say to him on the phone when his voice got sad and slow. You're my honey, Irene had said. I love you, Irene had said. But then she called him "brother-in-law."

| 172 |

When the Queen promised to give him another Irene, Tyler had for some reason imagined a beautiful young black girl with gold-dyed hair, but the false Irene was nothing like that.

You look pretty tired, he said. You want to have sex or you want to just sleep?

I want to make love, Irene muttered.

He did it to her and she uttered sleepy moans.

Then she was quiet.

What are you thinking about?

My Mom.

They lay down on the sofa and he reached and turned out the light. The smell of her was like rotten sardines. It got stronger and stronger all night. She laid her head on his shoulder and instantly fell alseep, breathing in rapid shallow little snorts like a child with asthma. Every few minutes she'd awake with a start and mutter: Oh!

Where am I? she said once. Where the hell is this?

You're with me, he said.

She was already asleep.

He had begun to itch from contact with her body. Tiny insects, imaginary or not, crawled on him.

He dreamed that she was taking a shower but when she finished and began to dry herself off the towel was soaked with stinking blood. He brought her more towels and more, but they ended up in a stained and reeking heap.

All night it was her instinct to bend her knees and rest her stinking feet on his legs. She was so light and so unconscious that he let her do it. In the morning her abscessed thigh was so swollen that she could not arise without tears.

Well, he said, you have anything you want to say to me?

You got thirteen dollars?

Well, here's five. I can skip breakfast.

You will? Oh, it hurts!

He had to let her lean on him all the way downstairs, and she wept with pain. When they got to the street he held her hand and she walked as she had last night, slowly, painfully, with her head hanging crookedly down and her hair in her eyes. Her gaze was fixed almost like a corpse's, and thick whitish drool unspooled itself from the left corner of her mouth.

He said to her: We can't walk in the street like this or you'll get run over.

I don't care if I get run over. Shit, it hurts. I don't give a fuck.

At Seventeenth and Shotwell they intersected with a Mexican family whose members laughed and pointed, the fat teenaged girl especially, making witty comments in Spanish as the false Irene stumbled and wept. A block later, Tyler glanced around and saw that they were still pointing.

His belly itched. An insect was moving on it.

That night he was walking down Eighteenth Street toward Capp when he ran into the false Irene's smell again, a sickening smell which permeated the sidewalk; then he realized that it was the smell of garbage.

The next morning, passing a car one of whose windows had been kicked out and methodically ground to powder on the sidewalk, he gazed at the grains, at the shockingly beautiful greenness within them which had been liberated by the vandals—there was the car; there were the other windows still intact, mere tinted transparencies giving his eye access to the car's interior; the radio had been stolen, and larger shards lay dark and dull upon the upholstery-slashed seats—but it was only the pane which had been broken, its surface area increased many fold, which allowed him to see the stuff and essence of that glass, the wonderful greenness now so rich as to trap sight within the opacity of grain heaped on grain.

| 173 |

At that time he trusted entirely in his Queen. He had touched her; how could he doubt her? The false Irene surely comprised not only a medicine but also another test, a pair of royal eyes like some herald sent out to meet a desert caravan and report back to the Big Bitch of Nubia. He had better treat her with every diplomatic attention. Meanwhile no proposals of employment visited his answering machine, although he checked in as conscientiously as Celia ticking off her latest list, which went:

> schedule session for approval with ICD
> greet Iris
> redraft proposed maternity policy exclusion
> shop for new sofa (ask John for color ideas)
> Tues. 4:15 gynecologist: *can I get pregnant?*
> find new restaurant to take John
> order blue update chart

so, feeling himself to be a conveniently idle passenger on the ship of time, he weighed anchor with the false Irene for North Beach, where waves of greyish-white houses overhung each other frozenly on the hills, and darker grey waves of pigeons flurried across the grass of parks in search of crumbs, sea-foamed here and there with paler scatterings of feathers; across this ocean, with his incurious Irene, Tyler sailed in his shuddering old car, rolling down his window as if in hopes that the laundries of Grant Street, whose hot fragrance of cleanliness curiously resembled the smell of freshly baked bread, might make Irene happy as it sometimes did Tyler himself, but she remained as isolated in her passenger seat as those old men in grey coats and grey hats who stood in the parks of North Beach with their hands behind their backs as the pigeon-waves roiled between their feet; because neither wholesomeness nor vitality attracted Irene. They made landfall at the Café Greco where he'd always wanted to bring the dead Irene but never had. Thus the false Irene sat across from him at one of those little round black tables topped with fake marble, positioned among newspaper readers, crossword puzzle conquerors, spoon-lickers, chin-rubbers and the layers-down of cards so happy and rule-less that black spade-schools and crimson diamond-flocks trembled as if about to take wing.

Tyler and the false Irene drank new espresso which trembled with foam, dark espresso beside white gelato; while outside, traffic shot down the double yellow lines like those electromechanical toys which ride in slots. —This coffee tastes shitty, Irene mumbled. I really gotta get well. I gotta go in the ladies' room and . . . —The other patrons were already holding their noses. Irene moaned like trains crawling over dry rivers; she begged to lie down; she fell down and her head cracked open against the floor.

| 174 |

The next time he went by the Queen's, that crew had moved to a brickwork tunnel under a vacant lot in Chinatown, and it was dawn. —How much money did you gals make tonight? the Queen said. —If it's money, you'll see some of it, Domino said. —Henry Tyler again, said the tall man, but the Queen wouldn't let Tyler in. She said to tell him that he had a mission right now and he should stick to it. Tyler bowed his head, humiliated.

The crazy whore felt sorry for him and scuttled out of the tunnel to explain: They have to greet everybody on the telephone so nobody will get left out. And they have to be sure no bullies will come in. And they have to be sure that every whore who's got good pussy will get three meals a day. That's why the Queen's so busy. I dream of making sure that there's nothing bothering the lions at the zoo. The Queen says that's up to me, too. When I take a hit of crack, it makes me feel sure I can stay up forever if I need to, so nobody will get hurt. That's how I help the Queen. That's why I'm so busy.

I get it, said Tyler, rubbing his chin.

I get pity for someone like you when someone's among us and lonely instead of having the right attitude, and they worry why won't the Queen play with me?

Well, Mary, that's my worry all right.

The tall man took him aside and said: Henry, lemme give you some advice.

I appreciate it.

That new Irene of yours is no goddamned good. She's just a crackpipe waiting to be lit. She's gonna smoke up all your money.

I'll keep my eye on her.

You never know what's gonna happen with bitches, the tall man said. Take that Strawberry over there. One day she came at me with a butcher knife when I was on the telephone. A big old knife, round about oh I'd say eight inches long.

And then what? said Tyler, already knowing what he would hear.

I beat that bitch flat on her ass, laughed the tall man. I says to her, Strawberry, you bitch, I'm gonna make you look at me with eyes of *fear.*

All right.

You're not gonna do it, are you?

Do what?

Beat that ho flat on her ass.

Probably not.

I knew it. I can smell your goddamned kind. You think you're better than me?

Nope.

I said, you think you're better than me?

Oh, dry up. I have nothing against you, Justin. Thanks for trying to help. I figure that—

You're just a john. You johns are all the same.

Listen, Tyler said. The Queen gave her to me to love and to take care of. Do you get that?

I know. And I said what I said.

| 175 |

Domino! said the Queen suddenly.

Yeah, Maj, what is it?

Do you trust that Tyler?

Hell, no, said Domino.

| 176 |

He went to meet the false Irene, who never appeared. She refused to tell him where she was sleeping. That night as he walked down Sixteenth he felt coming from the blackness of the streets what he could only call a bad energy. His friend Mikey whom he some-times saw at the racetrack had been a Marine at Iwo Jima; Mikey said that the main thing to keep him alive had been that feeling. When it tingled in his fingertips and made the back of his neck coldly itch, then Mikey knew to duck down or hide until he could see whatever was trying to get him. Something was trying to get Tyler now, something or somebody evil who knew Tyler and was thinking about him and wanted to harm him, something that could see him right now. Maybe it was waiting in that alley up ahead, or maybe it was closing in from behind, intending suddenly to leap upon him and choke him. He leaned his back up against the wall by the bank machine where three or four years ago someone had gotten stabbed to death. Slowly he let his head turn back the way he had come. Past Pancho Villa's restaurant the street remained very well-lit, swarming with coffee-houses and fancy new restaurants like the Spanish place and the creperie. Nobody was approaching. He allowed his gaze to turn the other way, down toward Mis-sion Street. At the entrance to the subway station three tall and filthy men stared back at him. He was not intimidated. He knew that he could walk right through them and they wouldn't do anything, because he might be police. Beyond them lay darkness.

It was peculiar how different every night was. Last night and the night before, the Mission had been filled with energetic crowds. Now there was not even a whore to be seen and the streets were almost empty except for the occasional police cruiser. He crossed Mission Street, having passed easily through the group of men, and descended to Capp Street, which stank and was dark; and between Capp and South Van Ness, one black man was helping another walk. The one who was being helped shouted with pain. He had no wound that Tyler could see. There were no whores on South Van Ness, but he passed a succession of doorways in which watchers sat, studying him without friend-liness or pity. He didn't much care. The creepy feeling came, departed, returned.

At Harrison Street he went to call the false Irene's pager from a very dark pay phone booth beside a warehouse and the pay phone swallowed his quarter and then said he still owed it a quarter; he pressed the change release lever and his quarter slowly ever so slowly dribbled back into his hand. He didn't like this place. He inserted the quarter again and redialled. The phone was silent like the night without even a dial tone and suddenly he became convinced that the evil person or the evil thing was right here beside him or near enough to be almost here, that it was creeping up on him in the darkness; and he forefingered the change release again, hung up, and walked very quickly out of there. He turned up Mariposa where it was more brightly lit near Project Artaud and the evil one was beside him. From a parked and curtained van there suddenly commenced as he drew level with it a slow, cautious, remorseless creaking as if something were stealthily trying to come out. He walked on quickly. Maybe I'm just getting old, he said to himself, and what I see and fear is my own death. Well, of course that would be the evil thing in any case. It would always be my death, whether it were some reified cancer or heart attack thirty years hence slowly swiming toward me, or a bad person coming to get me right now.

And then he said: The Queen gave her to me. The Queen loves me. She wants to help me. Even if somebody murders me, I have to follow my Queen. I have to accept my gift. I've tried everything else.

| 177 |

She was on Seventeenth and South Van Ness at six in the morning, considerably less beautiful than in the dark, exhausted, swollen-eyed, stinking of excrement.

Hey, I feel so bad that I didn't show that time, she said quickly. You know what happened? I went to Sixteenth and Mission and I couldn't cop.* I spent two and a half hours trying to cop, until I finally found some stuff that could halfway do it. The hotels all got raided at once. My friend Beatrice—you know her? she works with me sometimes; she's people; she's real cool; she's got spunk—she got so freaked out I found her crying later 'cause the the police just busted into the room next door with rifles and whatever. I think she ran back to the Queen. She told me to come with her but I knew you'd be . . . Oh, I feel shitty. My leg hurts. And I was so stressed out I just completely forgot about you for four days. Then I remembered, like, hey, that nice guy was waiting on the street corner for me, but by then it was too late. But I knew I'd see you in the neighborhood sooner or later and then I could make it up to you.

Yeah, that's all right, he muttered.

No, it's *true.* Do you believe me? I can prove it. I can verify it.

He was sorry for her, but even more than that he pitied himself for being a mere servile appendage to this decaying body bent only on greedily destroying itself. Again and again, however, he spoke with himself, persuading himself to obey his Queen. He strove to remember and comprehend Sunflower, whom the Queen had pronounced perfect. Did he believe her? Was the Queen perfect? And how could the false Irene be perfect when she was such a slave to her own poisonous needs? In one of the essays, "Civil Disobedience" he thought but John would know for sure, Thoreau had defied his jailer with the statement that no matter where his body might be detained, his mind could wander in and out between the bars as it pleased, like a whore's dark head flashing back and forth. The serenity, the comforting calmness of this conception had amazed Tyler when he first read it in high school. He'd reflected at that time, and still thought: Even if I end up with nothing, even if I'm starving or physically broken, I retain the freedom of my own self. —He hadn't, of course. He'd fallen in love with John's wife. Now he was

---

*Score; obtain street drugs.

in the Queen's orbit. But the false Irene was even worse off, sick and crazed, selfish, isolated by her own addiction. Cut off a man's airway, or deprive him of sleep long enough, and he will not enjoy Schubert. Most, perhaps all creatures are vulnerable to the despotism of suffering, but the false Irene was more vulnerable still. Her body might wander in and out of the Tenderloin alleys, but her consciousness remained in Thoreau's cell. She was the jailer of herself, and she'd lost the key. The Queen's fundamental principle was at fault.

But what if some sacred vapor infused her ecstasies and depths? What if her endless struggle for junk and more junk were a meditation of perpetual equilibrium as valid as Buddha's stillness on a lotus leaf? What if a brainless sea-sponge which spent its entire life weakly straining food from the currents actually experienced perfect fulfilment because its sensations were unmediated by consciousness? Was this what the Queen meant?

He refused to believe in the goodness of sickness. He longed to worship the false Irene as he had been told, but could not.

| 178 |

Like Lily and the crazy whore and ever so many others, Irene never chose to belong to the Queen's inner circle. She stayed in the Imperial Hotel on South Van Ness, in a second-storey room whose rent was paid by its other occupant, Sanchez, a seventy-three-year-old Indian originally from Oklahoma who had now been living at the Imperial for three months short of two decades. Throughout that time he had shared his lodging with prostitutes, doubtless for altruistic reasons. Each girl usually lasted two or three months, and then one day Sanchez would come back from the corner store to find her gone and his VCR gone, or her gone and his cassette deck gone; or her gone and his shoes and toilet paper gone. He had had pretty bad luck, Irene thought. Not being cursed with one of those personalities which worries about future calamities, she never wondered whether those girls always left of their own accord. She thought about the past as little as she did the future. Although she believed her mind to be as clear and fine as it had ever been, in fact she could not remember where she had stayed before Sanchez had tottered up to her on that first rainy night on Capp Street when she was cold, wet, hungry and junk-sick, and so Sanchez was God. She had now been with him for twenty-two months. Her superiority to her predecessors had thus been conclusively established, and yet it had taken eight months before she'd felt comfortable unpacking her suitcase, maybe because the room was so small, or perhaps because Sanchez continued silent and almost dark in his moods, unreadable to her, just as she herself was to Tyler. His penis was the most expressive part of him. So it had been on that very first night, which like so many other nights Irene could no longer remember. She spent much of her time on the toilet down the hall, trying to find a vein until somebody else began to pound on the door with both hands. Once when she shot speedball on his bed, Sanchez had struck her. And yet Irene was far from feeling unhappy with her new home. She had never had a sugar daddy before—not that she could recall, at least. Sanchez scarcely asked her anything, and because Irene felt that she had many things to hide, this silence of his gradually transformed its intimations from menace to acceptance. And so she began to indulge herself, leaving Sanchez himself out of her thoughts, considering his room and possessions to be hers. Sometimes if she'd had a good week she used to give him twenty or thirty dollars to help out with the rent, but she didn't always have a good week and the precedent "put pressure on her," as she put it, so she stopped. Sanchez didn't seem to mind.

Now she started considering leaving him to move in with Tyler. The Queen had spoken with her. The Queen said that Tyler was good (which of course could not be unconditionally believed). The Queen said that Tyler needed somebody to take care of. Irene, flattered by her personal audience with the Big Bitch, was trying to figure out which way to jump.

Tyler presented certain disadvantages in comparison to Sanchez. First of all, he was younger—always an inconvenience to street prostitutes who prefer impotent octogenarians. Sanchez had never really been Irene's old man. Indeed, he'd failed to get it up with her after the first month. All he wanted now was for her to lick his balls, which smelled like pigeons and urine. It was hardly a real sexual relationship. Irene needed to be fucked every so often or she started going crazy. But Tyler might ask too much. She was not well acquainted with him. What if in some fit of stubborn selfishness he insisted on penetrating her past boredom into pain, until he became a positive enemy like the man of rage she'd once serviced who would not let her go until she was almost dead? Worse still, he wanted to talk. Irene considered herself a very private person. Since she had to rent out the space between her legs to anyone and everyone, she reserved the space between her ears, as if it were one of those secret urban gardens which San Francisco offers, with their narrow, half-rotten wooden stairs, ripe plums overhead, everything mossy and full of flowers, a nice view of the Bay Bridge's blue-grey silhouette. (John once went to look at real estate at one of these greeneries, in the steepest block of Filbert Street at Sansome, but the house was more than three million dollars. Maybe Mr. Rapp had that kind of money.)

When Sanchez met a new prostitute named Angel, Irene became jealous, but talked herself out of feeling that way. She sat on the edge of the bed with her chin in her hands while Sanchez and Angel were fucking. Afterward, Angel approached her with the self-satisfied yet anxious expression of a dog which has just devoured its master's dinner. — It's all right, Irene mumbled. I don't care. —Sanchez looked her up and down in his usual silence. That night Irene began sleeping on the floor. Angel said that Irene had *heart*. She showed respect, so Irene tried to do likewise. Angel and Sanchez fucked like wild beasts all night. They were so loud and vulgar that Irene was ashamed. She shot every last grain of heroin into her thigh just to put herself out of there, like Thoreau's untamed soul flying loftily away. In the morning she was alive again, on the floor, with scabies, sick with the need to fix. She went out and peddled pussy on Capp Street for two hours with no luck, but then Tyler paged her and gave her ten dollars.

Angel was a tall good-looking darkskinned girl who had probably been truly pretty once before she got her habit. Irene began to feel shy in front of her. She waited to learn whether Sanchez would speak to her at last, commanding her to leave; in fact, she almost hoped for that, because then necessity would instruct her exactly what to do, whereas right now she did not completely trust Tyler even though she had become accustomed to Tyler's money. But Sanchez never said a word. Unable to abandon this sanctuary, Irene determined to make Angel "feel welcome," which is to say that she strove to play on the shadow of hostess-power she retained due to Sanchez's taciturnity and her own seniority. She said to her: Sweetie, welcome to our house. (Sanchez smiled ironically.) — Treat it like a home, Irene babbled on. If you need something, just ask. We have a few rules, but only a few.

The first rule was never to open the window because their room lay only one storey up from and directly over an alley of garbage which in summer stank much worse than Irene and therefore disguised her so that she lived easily with the old man, who could scarcely perceive odors anyway because he chain-smoked. Sanchez had kept that cracked and dusty light-hole sealed for most of his twenty years of residence. Indeed, the paint had long since sweated, becoming glue so that had he ever longed for a breath of dumpster-air he would have first been forced to run the point of a putty-knife along the sash . . . Sometimes it got a little stuffy in there, as Irene delicately put it, and then he turned on the fan.

Thus ran the main rule, but Sanchez was equally particular about certain other matters. He disliked anyone to knock on his door. Also, he hid his treasures, and expected them not to disappear. Angel of course immediately began going through his wallet whenever she could, her grubby fingers twitching at high speed. Irene had sometimes done the same, but only to give *back* the money to show him how honest she was—minus five or ten dollars, of course, which she needed for expenses. Sanchez comprehended this and tolerated it; otherwise he would have hidden his wallet. Wasn't it really an invitation to Irene to take whatever she required, if Sanchez left his wallet on top of the dresser at night instead of sliding it under his side of the mattress along with his special things? Irene, believing this in utter confidence, flourished therefrom like a modest righteous flower blooming from the edge of a heap of dung. Angel, however, instantaneously began abusing the wallet privilege.

The next thing she did was to ask to use the phone. Sanchez, needless to say, made no reply. —*Sure* you can use the phone, sweetie, said hostess Irene, and Sanchez grinned sarcastically.

Can I, um, give my mother this number? Angel wanted to know.

Sure, said Irene. Sanchez sighed and kept quiet.

Well, um, can I also, um give this number to my boyfriend?

Sure, answered indulgent Irene. But don't give it out to everyone. Sanchez and I are trying to make you feel special. Not very many people have this number, sweetie, and we're trying to keep it that way.

After that, all Angel's business dates kept calling day and night. Sanchez's sister had to go into the hospital for triple bypass surgery and Sanchez was waiting for the doctor to call him and tell him how the operation had gone, but Angel stayed on the telephone for two hours. Finally Irene had to tell her to get off. Angel freaked out. She called Irene a rotten cunt and disinvited her from living with her and Sanchez. So Irene spat in her face. Angel shouted out to Sanchez to defend her, but Sanchez merely picked his nose. —Why, you lazy old fucker! cried Angel. You—you—why do old men always get so *greasy?* —Her accusation was not entirely truthless, at least in the case of its target, because Sanchez always tried to make his clothes last as long as he could, to save money. Irene wasn't that way. Like most of us, male and female, she considered herself to be clean in body and soul. Nobody, including Tyler, ever told her that she reeked. She sometimes went to thrift stores even if for reasons of addiction she should have been dating instead. That proved her desire to present herself nicely in society, a magnificent Christmas present for anyone who could pay. Sanchez, on the other hand, wore his clothes for a week or more at a time. It might well have been that he smelled; Irene was the wrong one to ask . . .

Angel promised never to bring any business home. Soon, tall lustful men were pounding on Sanchez's door at all hours.

Sweetie, please don't tell lies in my house, said Irene, believing in the present necessity of abrasive words.

What do you mean? said Angel with a false smile. I was in jail, I really was; I swear it—

Yeah? Then where's your plastic bracelet? Where's your papers?

You know what, cunt? *It's not your house. Not no more.*

When Angel finally persuaded Sanchez to throw her out, Irene was crushed. Strangely enough, it was the old man whom she hated more than Angel, even though the latter was the precipitating agent of her destruction. On her last morning in the Imperial Hotel, convinced that Sanchez had been scheming to bring about her departure all along, she refused to say goodbye to him, but embraced Angel, sobbing like a child. —It won't be so bad, honey, Angel said. You'll find a new home, I know you will! And we'll meet on the street. It's gonna be just like old times . . . —Irene gripped Angel even more tightly, and here the Queen's intuition about her proved entirely true, because at that moment, even if only for that moment, she was willingly and proudly embracing her own degradation, like a Christian on the cross. And perhaps what she intended for Tyler (although one can never be sure about anything concerning the Queen) was for him to take to himself the embodied shame of Irene's self-distraction, loving somebody who would be bad for him. And yet how depressing, indeed repulsive these plans for another appear, when we spell them out like this! Tyler, of course, had humbly laid his life in the Queen's hands; it was incumbent on her to do something with it. As for Irene, incapable almost of choice, haunted by the insult she received, fearful of that grimy and dangerous street life which had now reclaimed her, she went silently down the stairs until for the last time she passed through the lobby, and the desk clerk wrinkled his nose. Then she left the Imperial Hotel forever. Suddenly dreading above all the possibility that Angel and Sanchez might be watching out the window, she refused to look back, and for this pride I admire her, especially when she would have done anything to be allowed to return. What then? She hobbled to Capp Street, clutching all her belongings against her stomach in a trash bag, which with extreme tentativeness she concealed in a garbage can. With its bruises, varicosities, scars, scabs, burns, bites and abscesses, her flesh resembled one of those Hungarian sausages which offers the buyer all the splendid colors of autumn: astonishing oranges from paprika, scarlets as delicious as any dead maple leaf, yellow pebbles of fat. But who would buy her? What would she do? It was only ten in the morning, and she was already beginning to feel junk-sick. Terrified of what would happen if she didn't cop some heroin very very soon, she set out on a hunt for sanctuary, not knowing exactly what she was looking for, praying she would recognize it when she found it. Unlike Beatrice, who conversed with the Virgin in her straits, Irene retained no one to pray to but herself. Her ancient, bloodshot eyes saw the black-and-white come rolling from around the corner, and she was already shambling on before the police could accuse her of peddling pussy at that infamous corner. Today no one would help her to continue existing, and for her to pursue salvation through the one trade she could practice was to become a criminal, a temporary betrothed. She considered going to live with the Queen as Beatrice had advised, but she had been given to understand by Domino, who wished to keep the club exclusive, that the Queen was a very difficult and dangerous old bitch who sometimes cut women's eyes out, and that her kindness to Irene during their private interview had been a treacherous device. Irene trusted

Domino more than Beatrice, because given two tales, the most frightening one was generally in her experience the truest. She had now put almost four blocks between her and the Imperial Hotel. Exhausted, she sat down on somebody's front step and cried again. Although the heroin need grew nauseatingly inside her from moment to moment, more than anything she worried about the terrible pain in her leg which made it so difficult to walk. The hospital had told her that she had two blood clots. Irene wondered whether this had something to do with the fact that heroin had stopped her periods and somehow sent the bad blood from her womb into her legs. They'd given her some anticoagulant pills, but when her left leg started feeling better she quit out of a principle of general distrust, the bottle only half empty (and she was supposed to get three more refills); then her right leg began to hurt. She wanted to go to S.F. General and perhaps if she won extraordinary luck sleep that night in a high metal bed with clean sheets, but she had to earn ten dollars first, understanding all too well that even if she'd reported to the waiting room early in the morning (and it was no longer early), no doctor would see her until late afternoon, by which time she wouldn't be able to handle the scanning and palpitating and poking unless she'd shot up in the ladies' room. And how could she do that, without ten dollars? Ten dollars would save her or damn her! She tried to explain this to Tyler but he didn't understand; it was as if he didn't listen or something . . . (In fact, what she had said to him was: You see, I'm daydreaming. You see, I'm nodding. If I coulda had some coke instead of straight heroin I wouldn't be nodding like this. I was a little more cool than my classmates. So I always hung around with people who . . . And I asked my mother . . . But she wouldn't lemme . . . just make a joke about it . . . and then I told 'em—I told 'em . . .) Irene never felt so abandoned by God as she did that day. Ten dollars! She staggered all the way from Sixteenth up to Twenty-First in hopes of performing a ten-dollar blow job so that she could purchase white medicine from the tall man, who ran a side business outside the Queen's circuit, but nobody would pick her up because she stank. Ten dollars! Closing her eyes, she could see her heroin spoon, not too thick, not too thin; she tapped the needle because even though she'd only used it once they were now cutting heroin with shoe polish, which gummed up the point. She could see it; she could taste it. Ten dollars! Forgetting all about her possessions in the trash can, she dragged herself far beyond the drunken swaggerers who were now too drunk to do anything but sit on their overturned shopping cart. Irene asked them: Hey, can you spare just five or ten cents? It would really make my day. That's all I need. —They gave her nothing. A man in mechanic's coveralls was coming, so Irene asked him: Can you spare just fifteen cents? and he walked by her. Ten dollars! Irene rounded the curve of a passed-out drunk's buttock on the reddish sidewalk-tiles in front of Walgreens—*Walgreens!* she was going the wrong way! Turning around, she discovered an auto repair shop, then two more shopping carts side by side with a foam mattress folded over them both to marry them, clocks and towels and blankets stained with wine-flavored urine and stuffed animals tucked beneath them in what to Irene was utter senselessness. She passed Chocolate, who was prancing back and forth on Capp Street like a spirited warhorse, holding her white parka in her arms as she streetwalked because she didn't want it stolen. Chocolate and Irene did not say hello to one another. She passed Justin, who leaned with his empty hand behind his back. At last she came to a weary black man's blue stubble glowing like a patch of tiny alpine flowers as he slept under the subway lights. The palm of his hand was incredibly expressive. Ten dollars, ten dollars!

She was as wide open as Mission Street with its palm trees rising above squarish brick-work and woodwork. She passed Strawberry, who was scratching her forehead as she pulled her hair back, leaning against brickwork, urgently watching each car. Irene had ir-revocably lost count of Strawberry before she even saw her. A quarter-hour later, the Queen emerged from the Thor Hotel with a cigarette in her mouth and her hands in her pockets; Irene did not see her. It was sunset now, and the sharp stench of urine on the sidewalk focused her consciousness like smelling salts applied to a fainting woman. If she only had ten dollars . . . Irene stumbled through bright bristling palms and fish markets and supermarkets and murals, spied on by informers with pawnshop eyes. Then she walked some more, her teeth sunk deep in her lower lip so that she would not scream with pain. Was she free like Buddha? Finally she remembered Tyler.

| 179 |

Tyler was drunk. Tyler was in need like Domino marching down the streets in her silver miniskirt muttering to herself: I gotta get me some bump.* —He said: All I have now is my pain, Irene. That's all that ties me to you. Without that cord, I'd fall into the abyss of senseless happiness.

The false Irene, who barely heard him and was sure that he had no conception of what pain was, said: Can I stay with you?

Let's see how it goes, he said. He had faith, but not so much. He was afraid that her stench would infect his apartment forever. He feared that she would steal his computer and try to sell it. God knows what she would do . . .

You mean you don't care about me? The Queen promised you'd take care of me . . . And I . . . You see, if I could just cop some china white . . .

What is it you want, baby?

He was so shallow. He knew what she needed, and he would not give it to her. Look at him! He had nice shoes! If he cared for her, he could sell his shoes. He must have money in his wallet. If he would only give her ten dollars, just ten dollars . . . That was what her happiness cost.

Well, my connection got busted, she began to explain, making a great effort to help him comprehend, and . . . and after the raid, I didn't know anyone to cop from, so me and Domino, we had to go downtown to meet someone on Turk Street . . .

Oh, come on, said Tyler. Domino cops from the Queen.

All right, so I was lying to you, said Irene. I don't know why I lied, I just . . . Hey, you got any money on you?

| 180 |

Remember you said that I didn't have to have sex with you if I didn't want to? said Irene. Well, I'm thinking that maybe I won't have sex with you tonight, because I'm starting to like you and I want to see . . .

Okay, sweetheart.

Thanks for the ten dollars. I really appreciate it. You saved my life, Kenny.

*Crack cocaine.

Henry.

Oh, did you say your name was Henry? I thought you . . . Listen, I gotta go. I need more heroin. I'll be back in forty-five minutes and then we can just cuddle, okay? I'll whistle outside your window. Don't worry. You'll wake up. You ain't never heard me whistle.

The darkness about them was close and cool and stone-flavored like a cathedral's, and within it, like candles offered to the memories of souls, glowed the flames of many crack pipes. The happy sense of love, of trust, of grateful sharing between two people who have just smoked crack together temporarily allowed him to believe in her. (He had a sudden memory of Irene rushing about most soundlessly in stockinged feet on the carpet at John's place, making dinner. He'd become agitated, as was usually the case whenever he had to see Irene. But he never showed it. He remembered Irene standing with her left hand on her hip, clicking the remote control, her lips parted as she gazed at the crawling colors in the TV. He could see her sitting on the carpet, dialling John's portable phone, her dark lips parted, smiling politely at him but withdrawn; he knew that she was irritated at something. He remembered her high small breasts.) She kept giving him more hits of crack and he kept rubbing her neck.

She kissed him on the lips and said: I never kiss.

You got any more money? she said.

(Tyler stood in the locked bathroom, counting his money from the nylon under-the-pants moneybelt which smelled like his balls. The false Irene was moaning and snoring.)

Okay, she mumbled. I gotta go. I need my medicine. I'll be right back.

She didn't come back, of course.

| 181 |

He loved the false Irene with sincere desperation for more than three weeks.

In the fourth week he was walking past Sixteenth and Capp at around nine in the morning and saw Angel, although he did not know that she was Angel; then he spied Lily across the street, thin and false-blonde, with her hair, skin and clothes all grey and pitted like an old barn door or a hammer which had been left outside in an Arctic wind for years and years; she was standing on the corner, looking patiently at every passing car, and seeing him Lily smiled and waved until he waved; then she strutted halfway over to him with her miniskirt riding high up her hips and her hairy thighs all crusted with some yellow substance, so for politeness he approached her and she came closer and soon was at his side.

How about the morning special? said Lily.

What's that? said Tyler, taken aback.

Ten dollars.

Ten dollars for a blow job, I guess, he thought.

Well, how about if I buy you coffee? he said, anticipating that good happy coffee feeling, the same feeling almost as of crack cocaine.

She was already starting to move back to her corner, just a step or two back so that she might still be able to return quickly to get something out of him, and looking coolly into his eyes she said: Well, you could just give me a dollar. That would work.

That's Domino's line, he laughed.

Oh, her. She's full of one-liners, but I'm better. My hole's better. You wanna see my hole?

One of these days, Lily.

Well, then, how about that dollar?

How about when I see you? he said, not wanting to give her anything if she wouldn't even sit with him for a minute, not that he blamed her.

Fine.

Do you remember me? he hazarded.

I know I've seen you before. I just . . .

I'm Henry.

Henry? Oh, that's right. You're Maj's . . .

How's the Queen?

She said to ask about you, but I forget what she wanted me to ask. I bear so many messages at so many times, and sometimes the first message overshadows the last message, because I . . .

Tell her I'm trying really hard but I'm having problems. Can you remember that, Lily? A dollar would sure help my memory . . .

| 182 |

Every morning Lily went out to Capp Street walking skinny and crusted, spookily laughing from her tired cunt unmuffled by any underwear; then Domino usually came and started yelling as she did every night: Bitch, bitch bitch, you stole ten dollars off me, bitch! and Lily just squatted there on the curb, ignoring her, so Domino kicked her onto her ass and triumphantly laughed: *Bitch!* while Lily laughed, gurgled and cycled like an old dishwasher in some not yet vandalized apartment, remembering her black nightgown in which she always used to do business because she thought that it made her more pretty; in fact it got so that she didn't like to take it off even during a fuck because it made her look and feel so special. Some customers disagreed, but Lily knew that even if she wouldn't fuck naked they were nonetheless happier in her company than alone, especially because in those days she had a nice thing that she did for the men (like Sunflower or the Queen, she wanted to give them all something). She would spread a rubber sheet on the mattress and grease it, and then tell the john to take off his pants and everything else and lie down on his back on the greased rubber sheet while she went to mix him a free drink, and afterward she'd give out her choice of one of three nude photos of her, which she'd then package in an Amaretto box; but so many times the men said: Hey, I'm married, I don't want no photo of some hooker, so then she started saying: And if you're not married you can have this if you want . . . but even then they sometimes worried that it might be incriminating, so Lily learned to say more tentatively: Well, if you're not married and if you don't think it would incriminate you, I can give you a picture of me, but half the time after the men had left and she went outside to get some milk and tomato soup for her mother she'd find the nude picture of her lying on the street, or jocularly stuck behind a stranger's windshield wiper, or face-up or face-down in the trash.

Did that make you sad? Sunflower had asked her.

Sad! choked Lily, laughing and crying. Hell, no. But it made a lot of other people sad. Ugly me, and my ugly pussy, *saddening* people all through the neighborhood . . .

She continued to wear her black nightie because she knew it made her into the most beautiful girl. Somehow that nightie was magic. Okay, so on request she'd lift it above her weary breasts but it never came off when she was doing men, never, ever, especially after she started to get older (well, almost never; sometimes she might relent if a man tipped her), until after a while it began to look and smell a million years old and the men started making comments, so she went to the five and dime and found another just like it, being a creature of habit in more than one way. That find made her very happy. She took the old black rag, threw it into her favorite dumpster, and wore the new black rag. When it ripped, she trimmed it into a miniskirt like Beatrice's; Bea had shown her how . . .

Meanwhile Domino stood halfway down the block, showing tit and whistling. Humiliating Lily always put her in a fine mood. That bitch was so out of it, so perpetually robbed and broken, that she'd never tell Maj. Truth to tell, Lily really *had* borrowed ten from Domino and shot it into her veins, so we cannot accuse the blonde, who needed money as much as anyone, of being evil—Domino wasn't that, merely mean.

| 183 |

So what's new? said Domino, each of whose eyes resembled in hue the blue star which said **S.F.P.D.** on the white door of the black police car with its shiny twin upturned mirrors like mandibles and its blocky multicolored roof-light.

Oh, you remember that cat I had? the false Irene said.

That little shit? chuckled Domino. How could I forget?

Hey, that's my cat you're talking about.

That's your diseased pussy I'm talking about, the blonde muttered to herself.

Oh, fuck you, said the other whore.

All right, fine. What about your darling cat? Wasn't that like a year ago you had that cat?

I think I told you that it was one of two that they had at this clubhouse. And the other, this Samoan gangster stomped it to death. So when they got the next litter, I took all three. I figured I could sell them to some friends. And I got money for two, but I had to take them back, because the two girls I sold them to weren't taking decent care of them. And one had a litter, so now I have eight cats. That's my news.

Pretty stupid, said the blonde. How much do you spend on catfood?

Oh, shit, Domino! Catfood's not good enough for them. I feed 'em fresh milk and chicken breast, said that wrinkled old whore who never ate decent food herself.

You have eight cats, huh? I just bet.

Come on to my house. I'll bake you a cake.

A greedy light came into the blonde's eyes at the thought of free food, and she thought to herself: This bitch makes fifty-sixty dollars a day because she represents herself. No Queen's cut. She's got her own place; she's got her red light. I cannot deal with this. I gotta . . . —Where are you staying, honey? she purred.

I . . . I . . . Oh, this john named Henry . . . See where he . . . Hey, Dom, I feel faint. I need to cop. I need to take a leak . . .

So all that stuff about cats was just bullshit, wasn't it? *Wasn't it?* You're just another stinking homeless tramp. You'd better run, honey. You'd better run fast and far. You know why? Because if the Queen sees you, she's going to *cut out your eyes* . . .

Screaming, the false Irene fled as fast as she could, step by shaking step, all the way to Magic Burgers & Donuts on Twentieth and Mission (OPEN 25 HOURS, said the sign), and then from inside her greasy bra she fished out four quarters with her blackened hands so that she could buy a doughnut and sit inside for an hour to hide and lurk and weep, while Domino laughed, her hands on her hips, and swaggered up and down Capp Street like the queen of the entire world.

| 184 |

You over thirty-five? said the old man at Muddy Waters coffeeshop, where Tyler had ultimately gone without Lily, and without giving Lily a dollar, either, being akin to Domino who in the course of business games which called into play all her calibrations of volition and capability could rapidly compute the prudence of any given expense. Tyler had computed that the dollar would be wasted. So he sat at a table drinking espresso as rich and reddish-brown as Chocolate's flesh, wondering what to do. Perhaps this old man could see this, and was the latest incarnation of Christ come to help him, for as long as Tyler was willing to entertain such ideas about the Queen of the Whores, why not believe similar nonsense about any stranger?

Yeah, he said, waiting for the pitch.

Then marry for money, not for love, the old man advised. Love you can always pick up someplace else. It won't last, so marry for money.

Good thinking, said Tyler, draining his espresso.

Some girl wants to marry me, but I says to her, I'm choosy. I like to pick my own wife, and that don't mean you! the old man concluded gleefully.

Mm hm, said Tyler.

Having proven that he was the boss in this world, that not just any woman could have him, the old man went cheerfully back to his vocation, which was panhandling. On the way out, Tyler handed him a quarter.

| 185 |

He was so lost now like Dante's pilgrim at the very beginning of the *Inferno* that this new love of his, which perhaps we should simply call an engagement, had already split his life into many additional doublings and halflings through which he wandered as if through a maze of dripping ice-caverns, the terrible directionlessness of his journeying growing and growing before him like concretions of solid hydroxic acid which his touch could melt only a little and so he felt wearily frozen, unable to visualize either his future or his past. Everything was good and bad together. Everything was mixed together like Domino's grey strands of hair amidst the blonde. In other words, his way had become as open to the lamplight of all possibilities as the Mission, where you can leave the drug dealers literally waiting at the door when you go into some bluegrass-riddled bookstore or other to admire the acquerelles of Moreau or the engravings of Dan Smooth. Only a native California psychic can see all the way to the freeway sign which says LAST SF EXIT. Only a fast-talking Tenderloin girl can see half a block ahead to the car that *might* be slowing down, and so she'll run out into traffic, beckoning, muttering: Come on, come on, come *on* . . . —Did Tyler stand on the threshold of infinity or of a narrow grave? How could he advance a step, not knowing? He remembered the time that Irene had gotten lost in traffic when she was supposed to meet his mother and John for the weekend in Sacramento, and when she arrived two hours late she stood outside the door for another fifteen minutes, too afraid to go in. Inside, the three of them had just finished their cold dinner. It was Tyler who found her, when he went out in the dark to empty the trash.

Please, you go in first, Irene whispered. Her eyes were as clear as light bulbs reflected in a drop of spilled tequila on the bar.

Oh, come on, he said. Nobody's mad at you.

Laying his palm between her shoulderblades, he nudged her in. John refused to speak to her.

| 186 |

Shot of tequila, he said.

Shot of to kill ya? laughed the barmaid. Okay.

How was your day, Loreena?

Well, for starting out slow, I can't complain. Made almost two hundred bucks for greedy old Heavyset.

An hour ago, Strawberry's face had been tilted, her mouth hanging open, her eyes swollen as she wept over the baby she'd lost in crib death eleven years ago, and gravity pulled down the side of her face. Now her head lay on her clenched fists on the bar, her long, greying hair blanketing her naked shoulders. The barmaid gently shook her, calling her sweetheart, but she didn't wake up. Tyler drank on in silence. The barmaid sighed and went to the cash register. —She's been here a helluva long time, she finally said to the Queen, who replied: She's dreamin' about her pain, Loreena. —The barmaid laughed as if that were a joke, and yelled into Strawberry's ear: Fire, FIRE, FIRE! but Strawberry didn't move. The barmaid sighed again. Tyler ordered another drink. The Queen smiled at him, gliding out into the Tenderloin night. The serious old john gazed patiently down at Strawberry, and his chin wobbled as Strawberry ground her nose into the bar and slept harder.

Give her about another half hour, the barmaid said to the world. When thirty minutes exactly had passed, she said: Strawberry, honeybunny! and made a kissing sound, but Strawberry didn't move. —I have to start serving now, she said to the john. Would you kind of keep an eye on her until Laura comes on at six? 'Cause Laura will give her a hard time. You gotta get her up before then.

Strawberry woke up suddenly, sweating and nauseous, and weakly patted her john.

I was a little worried about you, he said.

The tall man came in and said: Somebody buy me a drink or I'm gonna shoot this whole fuckin' goddamn place up!

Oh, take a chill pill, said Loreena.

Awright, I'm gonna start shootin' then. Henry, what's goin' on, my man?

Not much, said Tyler.

Still drivin' that faggotmobile?

Naw, I stuck my dick up the exhaust pipe just like you taught me and the damn car went and exploded on me.

You too fuckin' much—heh, heh! Anybody else talk to me that way, they be takin' a trip to the emergency room.

Strawberry opened one eye, her purse strap clenched into her fingers as she muttered into her arms. Loreena leaned back against the register, stuck out her paunch, coughed, and laughed *ha-ha-ha* from her fat flushed face.

How ya doin', kid? the tall man asked her.

Fucked up.

Well, what else is new?

Justin . . .

What?

Justin, will you follow me anywhere I go?

Well, not *anywhere,* laughed the tall man, kissing her.

You know what? said weary-eyelidded Strawberry. I'm sorry I'm drunk. I'm fucked up. I'm sorry. I'm sorry.

Don't worry about it, the tall man said.

I'm sorry.

Tyler started chuckling sadly in the corner.

Why are you laughing? asked Strawberry painfully.

Oh, something weird happened to me, Tyler said.

Pathetic, said the tall man, walking out.

Tell me. Why are you laughing?

Just a funny thing, he said.

Tell me, said the whore, struggling upright while her john watched over her as anxiously as a father overseeing his baby's first steps.

Well, I fell in love with somebody I shouldn't have fallen in love with.

And what happened? Strawberry patiently asked.

I won't be seeing her anymore.

(Even *I* know about Henry and his Oriental girl, said Loreena complacently.)

Are you hurting? Strawberry asked him.

Huh?

I said are you hurting?

Yeah. Yeah. I guess so.

She stared at him with her heavy-lidded eyes. She was sorry for him.

Oh, hell, he muttered.

She nuzzled up to the complacent old john, who'd just bought her a hamburger. The john put his arm around her, and she flinched.

| 187 |

Irene had once given him a spare key, but it would have been just like his brother to change the lock. Tyler didn't even know where that key was anymore. He drove over and rang the bell twice just to make sure that no one was there. Then he sprayed oil into the lock and worked a half-diamond pick against the pin stacks until they'd all dropped, one at a time. Fifteen seconds. He was belly-up against the glass front door so that from behind no one could see what he was doing. He counted the clicks of the falling pins: a six-pin lock, which come to think of it he had already known. Now for the tension wrench. That was the part he always enjoyed. Twenty-five seconds. He eased the hook pick all the way to the back of the cylinder, as gently as if he were penetrating a virgin; slow and careful, metal sliding lovingly deeper into metal, until he reached the uterine wall, so to speak. Now, slowly, slowly, raise the bottom pin above the shearline. Thirty-five seconds. That pin was picked; five more to go. In slightly under two minutes he had the job done. He slipped his wrench and picks back into his pocket and opened the door. Three carpeted steps, then a left turn hallway to the elevator. John lived on the sixth floor. The apartment was double-locked, so it took him more than five minutes to get in.

There would have been no point in going to the clothes hamper anymore, of course; all he would have gained was his brother's smell. The bedroom door was open, the bed unmade (Irene had always made it every morning). He went to the bottom drawer of the dresser which had once been a treasurehouse of her bras and panties scented with rose petal sachets and cedar wood. Empty. He should have known it. (In old Korean custom the brother-in-law must never enter the sister-in-law's chamber.) John had not been slothful there. Then desperately he went into the living room, thinking that at least he might steal a photograph from their wedding album; he could always cut John out. Over the fireplace the eight-by-ten of John and Irene still commanded him by means of what he had always been convinced was a false double smile, but beside that now stood in a silver frame a photo of Celia—an old photo, evidently, which she must have given John, for she looked much, much younger; a breasty young girl in a loose blouse, her head tossed back, her arms at her sides but just beginning to reach out at the world: a self-conscious picture of a girl who really wanted to let herself go and didn't know how to do it, a would-be narcissistic picture, and ultimately a very sad one.

Those last few months when Irene spoke to him on the phone in a sad and anxious whisper, he could have done something. Now there was nothing to do, nothing, nothing.

On the shelf beneath the television, he saw Irene's Korean–English New Testament, which her mother had given her shortly before her marriage. Tyler lifted it, vaguely hoping that one of Irene's long black hairs might have gotten caught in it. The place marker-ribbon was at Ephesians 5.14:

Therefore it is said:

> *Awake, O sleeper, and arise from the dead,*
> *and Christ will give you light.*

He felt a lump in his throat.

| 188 |

Everyone that doeth evil hateth the light, Smooth whispered.

Yeah, yeah, said Tyler. *Lest his deeds be punished.* That's in John 3 somewhere, isn't it? John's in the Bible. All johns are in the Bible. You think private eyes don't know that one?

All right, said Smooth with the utmost lordliness. Now I want you to tell me. What did her piss smell like?

Tyler cleared his throat. —Like fresh vitamin tablets, he said in a trembling voice.

Okay, that's a start. You want me to find you some fresh female piss like that? I've got sources.

Dan, I know you mean well, but I don't think—

And there you were on some kind of goddamned panty raid, as if you were a college frat boy! Smooth roared. You're a panty-sniffer and you're saying that fresh piss won't help! Just how do you explain that contradiction?

I don't feel like explaining it.

In his mind he now heard Irene's voice. After quitting a temporary job at a travel agency, she'd said to him: They're such cruel people! Sometimes I think I gotta be trying harder, but I don't know what they want . . . —At that time he had felt sorry for her, and hated the people who had been cruel to her. But now he was surprised to experience within himself a sharp anger at Irene. It seemed to him now that she had always complained, that she had shopped for her victim's attire as she would have shopped for anything else. And who had forced her to? He hated Irene! Was that why he now longed to part from the false Irene?

You know I have an in with the coroner's office, Smooth was saying. I got some autopsy photos of her for you. They're under the floormat on the driver's side of your car . . .

Thanks, Dan, he said wearily. I know you have a good heart. How does she look?

She's got a real peaceful expression on her face, Smooth said. You know, like she's glad to be out of it. And her breasts, well, you know I'm not ordinarily a tit man, but I think you'll like those photos. But the ones after they started to cut her open, well, I only gave you the crotch shots. I didn't want to make you feel bad.

| 189 |

That afternoon Tyler was walking down Seventeeth past the Uptown Bar on Capp, and saw across the street a police car with flashing lights and then the cop's back and shoulders and helmet; the cop was doing something to someone—yes, of course, to a scared young girl in a miniskirt. He was twisting the girl's hands painfully behind her back, looping and knotting the strap of her purse around her wrists before he put the cuffs on. Tyler crossed the street and slowly passed the two actors. Gazing backward as he went, he could now see the girl's scarred and pimpled face shining with tears. Something about her quivering lip made his heart ache through and through. It was Strawberry.

Hold still, the cop commanded. *Hold still.*

I am, the girl sobbed.

Tyler turned away and walked on, shocked to realize that he hated the cop, hated him not as a man but as a function. He thought he could understand now how terrorists could justify killing people. The cop was probably not a bad man. But what he was doing was wrong. He was hurting this girl who had hurt no one. Tyler didn't look back. He was too sickened.

Of course she's no angel either, said Smooth, who now telephoned him every day and who always stuck up for cops. That officer might have been having a bad day, see. And maybe he's seen her rob people, or maybe someone like her gave him some shit . . .

I guess she does have an attitude sometimes, he dully agreed.

How's married life?

It's not going so well.

Hang in there, Henry. Show some responsibility. Irene's *yours.* She depends on you. And you have to obey the Queen . . .

| 190 |

Every night the false Irene was always in the bathroom for a very long time, not unlike the dead Irene who used to spend a good half hour on makeup every morning, and with entirely consistent motives sat with the television on, reading in one of her women's magazines about how to tell if a man was lying (this article having been written by a traitor to his sex who sought to ingratiate himself), or why electrolysis must be considered the best choice for removing hairs from a woman's upper lip, although shaving remained preferable for legs and armpits, while depilatory creams were *comme il faut* for the bikini line. To Tyler, free from the necessity to master such processes, these directives partook of comedy—still more so thanks to their very solemnity. (Irene for her part had always been amused by Tyler's subservience to cameras, and his craving to browse the incoming books at City Lights—friends and oracles to him, to her alien trash.) We all like to know *the latest things.* And even if there were no latest things and the magazine articles all repeated each other, still, Irene was so interested in the subject of beautification (which, after all, stands next to beatification in importance) that she could not stop reading about it, just as a man who knows pretty well what sex is cannot stop driving down to Capp Street every Saturday—doubtless for verification purposes only. Yes, the real Irene spent her life in the bathroom—and so did the false Irene, but only to shoot up. For this reason, bathrooms not infrequently reminded Tyler of the dead Irene. About two months before her end he had driven over at John and Irene's on a Sunday morning, more anxious than pleased to have been invited. Yes, he'd see Irene, but they'd be constrained—and what if John sat between them? Irene was pretending to be wholesomely contented. Tyler pretended that his financial affairs were prospering. They would go out for brunch as soon as John got off the phone. On the coffee table, one of Irene's magazines lay open to an article which explained how a woman could tell if her best friend were really not her best friend. —I can't guarantee that, John was saying. —Tyler went to use the bathroom, from which Irene had just emerged, and in which she would soon kill herself. Longing so bitterly for her that he almost departed his body, he closed the door, raised the toilet lid while the television warned and whined down the hall, turned on the fan, like a whore in a Tenderloin hotel trying to drown out the sounds of her commerce—and then, his fly already unbuttoned, saw beneath the sink the wicker hamper of dirty clothes. (Remembering all this later, he understood Dan Smooth all too well.) Irene, Irene, Irene! Tyler made sure that the bathroom door was locked. He lifted the cover and most happily found on top of the pile a pair of Irene's panties fresh from last night. He knew from Irene that she and John didn't make love anymore, so he was not afraid of encountering his brother's spoor. Along that slender white strip of polyester which had been between Irene's legs he found what Dan Smooth would have gloried in: a tiny blot of gold. But raising the panties to his face and inhaling deeply, even there he could not smell Irene, only a faint odor of perfume that masked whatever human scent there might have been. Almost in a rage, he smelled the panties again and again. But there was nothing.

| 191 |

Beloved and miscast Tyler paid Irene out of next month's rent money, then headed for a Mexican restaurant on Seventeenth and Mission which he hadn't tried. Passing one skinny shrieking black Mr. AIDS, he entered a world of *carne asada* smells and trumpet music powerful enough to lift him into heaven, with Spanish or Mexican girls on the walls showing their breasts and flashing their rears. At the tables, men slowly crammed burritos into their jaws. Domino came in with her bag of laundry, clopp-clopping, flashing her long, scarred legs; there was the eye-shaped bullet scar, there the motorcycle scar in he'd once rubbed the locator fluid. He waved, and she grinned at him, which was how he learned that she was now missing a tooth.

What news? he said.

Getting dinner to go, the whore replied with a yawn.

The meat cleaver chattered on the blood-hued cutting board.

Just getting started today, Domino?

Uh huh.

She pulled her dress away from her collarbone, and peered down into her bra, her lips moving. He realized that she was counting her money. When she had concluded this operation, she scanned the counter with a scowl, and, seeing that her burrito remained unfinished, which meant that the next two or three minutes would be wasted anyhow, poutingly came and sat beside him.

Just like old times, darling, he said. Just like you and me alone in that hotel with those wine coolers . . .

Do you hate me?

Hate you? God, no. But I'm afraid of you sometimes. You're a pretty tough lady.

I know, she said with a happy little smile.

Her lips were moving again. Maybe she was still totaling up her money, or maybe she was praying.

Someday I'm gonna do this thing to you guys, she purred. To *all* of you guys.

And we'll all be down on our knees?

That's right, Henry. And you'll all be missing something. You'll all be bleeding.

It's nothing personal, is it?

No. Not exactly. Where's my fucking burrito? I'm *hungry.*

Hey, it's been five minutes and you still haven't asked me if I'm a misogynist.

Do you think any of us were prepared for this? Do you think I was born to debase myself in front of men I don't even know?

I don't think it's necessarily debasing.

How the fuck would *you* know?

How come the Queen doesn't talk about being debased?

Don't mention that name, said the girl automatically, snaking her face from side to side.

Well, let me ask you this, he said. If you're debasing yourself, who's making you do it?

It's a job getting a job in this town, she shruggingly said.

Yeah, yeah.

I oughta cut you, she whispered.

You wouldn't be the first, he chuckled. (As Irene used to say: He's American, so he really likes to express his feelings. I'm not used to that.)

Look, Mr. Tyler or whatever your name is. Let's get the ball rolling. I'm free and you're free. Do you want a piece of ass? Frankly, I'd prefer to be making money instead of wasting time just chatting. I've got a little rock . . .

If I were to pay you, would you like me any better?

Naturally, baby. I might even love you.

For five whole minutes? he said with a wink. —There. You smiled. I actually got you to smile. You're so pretty when you smile.

I am?

Why do you think you're so sad? Speaking for myself, I—

Look, the blonde said. I've got my dates to take care of. I don't need your shit. You and—and *her,* and Lily and Consuelo and Beatrice and Chocolate and Strawberry and Justin can all talk about me behind my back if you want. I don't give a fuck.

Domino—

Look. You want to fuck me or not?

The Queen said—

Maj can pee up a rope.

Have you seen my Irene?

She started to rise, and he said: Domino, I'll be your friend if you let me.

If you pay me, the whore said. That would work.

Honk four times, he said. Looks like your burrito's ready.

| 192 |

Would you excuse me, please? said the false Irene. I don't like anyone to see when I do this.

All night she kept him awake with her moaning in the bathroom. There'd be a long pause, then a deep, heartfelt animal noise that could have been either pain or sexual ecstasy; of course it was pain. Then from time to time came the emphatic sucking pop as she pulled the plunger out of the needle, trying to clear it. But she couldn't. That shoe polish in the heroin—to hell with what it did to a girl's veins; the important thing was that it gummed up her needle, and needles were not easy to come by . . . He heard her begin to weep.

| 193 |

Sacramento was chokingly hot that day—the Sierras were crawling with wildfires, said the radio, and coming down from the Pacific Coast Range into the Central Valley he had seen on the horizon a cloud of bluish-grey too pale to be smog; after Vacaville his throat began to get sore; that week, too, heat wave records shattered, or almost broke, or retained their majesty; record temperatures were exceeded every summer, it seemed, and yet it remained simply hot—a hundred and ten downtown today, the newspaper said, and a hundred and twelve five miles from there—vain precision! —but Sacramento most admirably continued with its business, its shopping, auto repair, driving, with its backyard weddings cool but not chilly beneath those evenings of rose bushes and midges as it got later and later, the businessmen yawning, waiting for the toast while their wives smiled vaguely and their children fidgeted, thinking about big slices of wedding cake, and strangers became friends at least until midnight, and sometimes longer; neighbors enjoyed seeing each other there because it meant that the world had not changed yet and therefore never would; neighbors would always be there; hence no one would die; and then it came time to cut the cake and throw rice, time then to go home, dreaming with raw throats, wake up hungover the next hot bright morning; Tyler had done this. His mother's best friends, Mr. and Mrs. King down the street, were proud at last to announce the marriage of their daughter Lisa to a grim proud boy from out of town. Tyler liked the Kings very much. He would have attended the wedding, but he was afraid that if he stayed that long, the false Irene might disappear.

Per arrangement he went by Dan Smooth's house to feed the cat and empty the litterbox. Dan Smooth was in Amsterdam in a hotel with young boys.

Yes, Sacramento was hot but San Francisco was cold and foggy that day with clouds crawling through the fog.

You don't look well, his mother said weakly. Do you have any good news to tell me?

Well, Mom, I have a girlfriend.

You do? Oh, Henry, I'm so glad! Tell me all about her. Tell me where you met her. How long have you been seeing her? What's her name?

He gazed at his mother with his eyes like welder's goggled over his soul, dark and blank and almost opaque to protect him from what they might see, and he swallowed once and said: Irene.

| 194 |

See, for twenty they usually give you more. But there was only a couple guys out. Can't trust all of 'em . . .

Okay, Irene, he said, sit down. You don't look too steady on your feet. Where'd you cop?

Over by the Hotel Tony on Turk Street.

I thought you used the Mohawk.

It burned down, she said. Domino and I were even staying there at the time. We moved to the Royal Hotel. But now she . . . you know, with the Queen. So I . . . And the Royal Hotel, well, I can't . . .

Oh, how's that place? he asked, trying to be interested. She exhausted him.

Worse than the Mohawk, she said sourly.

That's pretty bad.

Hey, I was wondering if you could lend me—

Irene?

What?

This morning I woke up feeling—

Here . . . she muttered to herself. The balloon . . . let me get that up . . .

Tyler sat down heavily.

Sagging, stinking, musing, sinking, swaying, trying so hard to put the needle back in her little purse but forgetting even as she'd begun the action what she was doing, she muttered: Earlier I bought one from this guy but it musta pooped out or something because I didn't feel . . . Yeah, I'm just trying to put this stick away but I can't find the little . . .

She kept leaning and swaying on the toilet seat. She tried to draw the plunger out but her fingers kept getting in each others' way. Now the plunger was upraised like a masturbator's face. Her body offered him a bitter smell, not sweet like a fat girl's. Her spastic shoulders sent telegraph signals of need to someone other than him—maybe to the Queen, or maybe just to the ether. Her long hair hung down. Her belt buckle kept flapping and rattling because she'd first tried to shoot herself in the behind. She sat there on the toilet seat, and her scarred, stinking hand sought a fatty bloody friendly place within her private waterfall world of hair to insert the last millimeter of gladness; and she slumped and slumped. He stroked her neck and she kissed him and said: You're so nice.

Her shirt had a stinking brown stain. —Oh, see, that's where I muscle. But I didn't have no tissue. So it bled from the needle. Lemme take a leak . . .

Slowly, slowly, with the needlehead she stirred what was in the bottlecap.

He went out and lay down. From the bathroom came the sound of moaning.

I try to be a nice person, she told him later. My Daddy always said I was his favorite daughter. After my mother died of cancer he got it in his prostate gland and he told nobody but me. I promised not to tell anybody, and I didn't. So he died. Then my sister, aged thirty-four, got cancer of the stomach. She bled to death. That's a hell of a way to die.

And now who do you have?

Nobody.

Not me? he asked, hating himself.

Oh, that's different. You'll always be my special customer—I mean my special friend . . .

No girlfriends?

Oh, it used to be different. Six years ago, we'd look out for each other. Now the world has changed.

What about the Queen?

She may be my Queen, but how much can she do? I'm still an addict, aren't I? My shit still stinks, and money doesn't grow on trees. I'm not sayin' she . . . Queen's so nice to me, actually. She feeds me an' . . . I'm tryin' to remember if I ever . . . Oh, where's the goddamned vein? Goddammit, goddammit, goddamn my goddamned body, oh, Henry, it hurts— *it hurts!* Ow! Oh, that's better. And Domino ripped me off, but I forgive her, 'cause she had a need. You know what I'm saying? One night she was real sick, so I loaned her eighteen to get well. Now she ignores me. I saw her today, out making money in a polka-dot dress . . .

She had fallen asleep on the toilet seat now, with piss running down her thighs.

| 195 |

Oops, said Irene. See what I did? I messed up the point, so I'll have to break it off. I won't do it here.

Her head sagged until her hair touched the floor

Okay, where's my top? she said, sitting on the toilet, stinking, scarred, and naked.

You got any tissue? she said. Lemme put this here for a few minutes.

You got any more money? she said.

You tryin' to jack me up? she said.

No, he said, almost stifling in sadness and boredom.

You're a detective, so that means you're *cop,* she suddenly pronounced, sitting up wide-eyed and stinking on the toilet seat.

Glad you have it figured out, he said listlessly.

Well, ain't I right?

Not really. Cops and everybody pretty much turn a blind eye to what we do. Anyhow, I—

Would you please please please be quiet for a minute? she said. I need to think. I think maybe I dropped a little chunk of rock somewhere in this bathroom, but maybe it wasn't here . . .

He remembered being alone with the true Irene once when she had started yawning, getting distant: Yes, I'm tired, she admitted. —But when others came out, Irene, smiling and gracious, said to everyone: No, I'm not tired.

| 196 |

Just after dark on the first Friday night in July he sat in his car with the window rolled down and a pad on his knee, watching the neon lights squirming uneasily in and out of brightness along the borders of the sign for the Jade Galore Jewelry Co.; a bank sign glowed cold steadfast, and red ideograms gripped the windowpanes of the Tong Kee Restaurant like athletic crabs. Irene was out dating. Between the Tong Kee and the Dick Troi Hair Salon, a tall alley, full of sky, lured his attention by means of a succession of awnings. Between him and the alley, the flank of a car or van frequently occluded itself, or the heads of tourists, or Chinese mothers carrying their babies; but these flickers passed as quickly as they came, leaving the alley for Tyler. An Asian cop labored up the sidewalk, chewing gum, his pistol and baton dragging down his Sam Browne belt. The cop looked at his watch and entered the Tong Kee Restaurant. Small white lights shone uselessly in the alley. A Chinese woman passed quickly smiling, arms folded across her tiny breasts. The fishes swiggled their tails and flippers most languidly behind the window of the Tong Kee. A stooped old lady, clutching many plastic bags, stopped in front of the alley for a long time. Tyler sighed, doodled on his pad.

After an hour he went home. It was still early.

He picked up the phone, dialled, and said: This is Henry Tyler. I waited all night and Mr. Chong never came out.

That's right, he said, narrowing his eyes. You heard what I said. I figure he's clean. I figure we don't need to bother him.

Well, that's too bad, he said. I don't want this case. I'm busy.

Fine, he said. I'll send you an invoice.

| 197 |

Tyler, waiting for hospital visiting hours so that he could go see Irene, whose abscesses had finally won her admission, inspected his reflection on the plasticized marble wall behind the firehouse red beer tap of what used to be Blackie's Club and was now the Wonderbar although the Blackie's Club sign was still up above the back door. Oldies on the jukebox brought teary smiles to his alcoholic neighbor. The door of happiness opened on TV. Loreena the barmaid, hand on her hip, served the gesticulating or placidly nodding drinkers.

Well, what do you have to tell me? said Dan Smooth, easing his plump buttock onto the stool to Tyler's right.

There's a bull market for twelve-year-olds' earwax is my news, said Tyler. What else can I tell you? Oh, I know. A stitch in time saves nine. How was Amsterdam?

Don't talk to me about sewing, said Smooth, with his habitual angry leer. It reminds me of the little girls in pink tutus who—

OK, mum's the word then, said Tyler carelessly. Buy you a shot?

In a moment, said Smooth. You see, I still have a special secret taste on my palate.

Tyler sipped his tequila silently.

And how are your business worries progressing? said Smooth.

Oh, they're progressing, all right. I'm barely making my rent and car payments as it is.

You'll be happier when you let it all go and become homeless, Smooth replied quickly. And, you know, I was just talking with the Queen about you, and she says that's destined to happen.

After the other Canaanites get put to the sword?

Exactly. And I go to the lions. Not that I'm a Christian or anything . . . Shit. There goes the taste. What a pretty taste. It's fading now; it's *gone* . . . what a shame. Buy me a drink, Henry. The hell with your rent money.

Tyler raised a finger. —Loreena! Could I get a beer for this gentleman?

Sure, sweetie, said Loreena.

How's everything for you, dear? said Smooth.

The same, said Loreena. I'm thinking of filing a restraining order. Excuse me. That guy down there got eighty-sixed last week. I need to go kick him out. Hey, Domino just told me a good one. What do you get when you cross a nymphomaniac with a klepto-maniac?

A rapist, said Tyler.

Oh, cut it out. *A fuckin' thief.* Isn't that rich? Ha, ha, ha!

The bar was getting more crowded now. Tired men, old men, hopeless men, and a pair of whores gradually entered through the swinging door, fluttering about as prettily as the international flags strung over Grant Street. Two drunks were arguing across the pool table.

Dan, said Tyler suddenly, do you think you could hook me up with the FBI? Get me a big job that would last a while?

Hee, hee, said Smooth wiggling his finger in the mouth of his beer bottle. God love you, Henry, are you asking for another favor?

Yeah, said Tyler.

You know I used my influence for you. With the Queen, Henry, with the *Queen*. You know that, or you don't know?

I know, muttered Tyler, tapping his foot.

And have you profited by your introduction to her?

What the hell's that supposed to mean?

Word on the street's you're giving up on that new Irene she got you. You said all you wanted was to have Irene back and she did that for you and you're still not satisfied. You're just a—

I'm going to the hospital to see her.

I rest my case. You're keeping her in the hospital, not at your place, so what kind of goddamned *caring* is that, son?

It's all true. And so I don't know if I'm not trying hard enough—if I don't have enough faith in the Queen to really love Irene and believe in her—or if I'm actually be-ing faithful to the Irene who's lying in the ground. And I—I don't know what to do.

Well, at least you're sincere, Smooth said. The Queen loves sincere people.

Yeah, Tyler said despondently.

And you believe in justice?

What do you mean?

You believe that if you were working for the FBI you'd be helping good people and punishing bad people?

I, uh—

Tell me a story about our great justice system, Henry.

Know how the police broke this one guy? said Tyler with a sneering chuckle. What they did was they hooked him up to a photocopy machine. And on the glass over the electric eye, underneath the cover, they put a piece of paper that said "FALSE." So every time they'd ask the suspect a question, they'd hit the "START" button. And then a piece of paper that said "FALSE" would come out. So they'd show that to the suspect and say: See? You're *lying.* And they broke that guy. He confessed.

All right. Fine. You're on our side. You're a Canaanite. And how much influence do you think I have with Louis Freeh?

Let me guess. You're about to tell me you don't have any.

Splendid! cried Smooth, loudly enough for one of the drinkers to turn his head frowningly.

Oh, forget it, said Tyler.

We can't forget it now, no matter how much we both may want to, rejoined the odious man. You're anxious, I take it, about your actual survival. You're pissing blood these days. Am I correct, Henry?

Tyler shrugged his shoulders despairingly.

Don't think I don't want to help you. We're *blood* brothers, after all. Tell me we're blood brothers, Henry.

We're blood brothers, said Tyler dully, remembering the autobiography of a serial killer which he'd thumbed through some months ago: the murderer, since electrocuted in Florida, had always made his victims parrot at knifepoint some puerile affirmation of sexual or emotional need before he raped and eviscerated them. What a world! I don't want to be in this world any longer, he thought to himself.

Henry, I can see you're desperate. All the fight's gone out of you.

Tyler smiled bitterly.

All the same, Smooth continued, you're a lucky whore-hound. The Queen likes you; I know she does . . .

What's on your agenda for the Queen and me? said Tyler, unable to keep the anxiety from his voice.

Number one: You came to me, not I to you. Number two: You begged me and bribed me to set you up with the Queen. True or false?

I've got to go to the hospital, said Tyler.

To visit *Irene,* I know. Let me come along, Henry.

Are you a sadist? asked Tyler in slow quiet wonder.

Anyhow, it's not your job you're worried about, said Smooth, gazing smilingly into his eyes. If I truly believed you cared about that, I would never have picked you up. It's your sister-in-law's *rotten, stinking twat* . . .

Nothing about Irene was rotten or ever could be, said Tyler steadily.

That's what I like about you. Caught in an obsession—a delusion, really—and a very harmful, antisocial one, and the man will not give up! Hey, Loreena! This man fucked his own sister-in-law to death and now he—

Tyler leaped off his stool and was already cocking his arm for the punch when Smooth kicked him in the stomach. Tyler doubled over retching.

I'm a black belt, you know, Smooth whispered, his breath tickling Tyler's ear. You had to be *humbled.* Now here. I'm putting three hundred dollars in your pocket. Don't thank me. It's not from me; it's from the Queen . . .

| 198 |

He knew by then that it would never work out with the false Irene, but he knew also that he didn't even have to tell her, that unless he physically assaulted her she would never regard him with all the bright-eyed watchful head-turns of a sick pigeon on the sidewalk, still strong and fearful at the very beginning of its death-struggle, because except physically the false Irene could not really be hurt anymore, so all he had to do was not see her and maybe not even tell the Queen that it hadn't worked out because the Queen had tried to be good to him—he continued in awe of her, fearing to reject her gifts. Last time he'd seen her she'd stood naked against a concrete wall, supporting her little breasts with her hands while the other girls started drawing snakes on the wall, and he didn't know what to make of it—were they playing or was it a ceremony or what? Dan Smooth would undoubtedly have told him the answer, but listening to Smooth left him almost exhausted.

A siren went by. Irene wiggled a loose black tooth and finally pulled it out. Her breath reeked of decay.

(But he recollected the time he came by dead Irene's early one morning and knocked at the door for a long time until Irene woke up. John was away on business. When Tyler embraced her, her body likewise gave off a sour smell which shocked him.)

This black guy, this dope dealer put a gun in my mouth, the false Irene explained. Said that was the only way he could come. I started cussing him out and I got out of there, but not before he whacked me in the teeth with his gun, and this tooth here was funny ever since. I think it died a long time time ago, maybe right after he did that.

Here's a tissue, he said. Why don't you pack it in the hole until it stops bleeding— yeah, that's good.

You're a nice guy, Henry, she said dully. I wish I could be nicer. I don't know why I can't, but I just can't.

He stroked her hair.

I used to wish I was dead, she said brightly, but one day I woke up and realized I was already dead, you know, where it counts, so why not relax and not make a big stink?

I know another dead Irene who—

But dead people do stink no matter what they ever meant to do . . . And now it's easier . . . Hey, can you gimme five dollars? Just five. I'm not greedy. I'm not well; I need some medicine, you know what kind . . .

Sure, he said. Here you go.

Where do you get your money from anyway?

From business.

Oh, I'm sorry, baby. I didn't mean to butt in. I didn't know you had anything to hide. I mean, the Queen told me you're in love with a dead girl and I'm supposed to be her, so I just kind of figured you'd . . .

Tyler said nothing. A fly landed on Irene's filthy neck and she wearily brushed it away.

Can I tell you my real name? she said. My real name's Consuelo.

He felt gratefulness and pain. She wanted to share something with him after all; she was freeing him from her; now she could not be Irene anymore; he had to admit that Irene would never be his or even be with him, and alone he would live on and on.

My husband took the fall for my brother, Consuelo said. My brother's no good. He got caught by that three strikes law. Suspicion of robbery, they said. It was only suspicion. He's doing three months. An' some whore named Chokecherry, kind of a frightening name, well, she and he . . . So I started . . . doing . . . *this* . . .

She was crying.

Oh, God, she sobbed. I started doing this, but I was doing this before, and I was lying to you to make you feel sorry for me but you don't care and I don't want you to care, I don't even . . . I'm just a piece of shit. What do I have to lie to you for? You've always been decent to me; you don't judge me, but I—

So when does your husband get out, Consuelo?

Oh, it doesn't feel right when you call me by my name; I should never have told you . . .

| 199 |

Driving down Nineteeth toward the Golden Gate, he reached the gas station at Pacheco and turned right, coming home amidst the whitish houses whose dormer windows bulged blindly like the eyes of dead frogs. The neighbor's blue flashing light was on. The trees were snipped and sculpted alike from lawn to lawn—Italian cypresses and then bonsai'd trees. He had been with the false Irene too long now. He could scarcely fathom this place. He honestly could not understand why God had put him here in this cool clean zone while the false Irene and the Queen and all that crew had to live in filth. Or was it their choice? Or was it heredity, destiny, class conflict, inevitability? He was angry with everyone, even with the Queen.

| 200 |

He awoke with the taste of the real Irene's cunt in his mouth.

| 201 |

After a week of mendacious coolness the heat had returned. Tyler's car was at the local shop, Sacramento labor being a relative bargain, so he walked down to J Street where across from the palm-tree'd square once called Freedom Park by the Wobblies, then Plaza Park by the corporations which had transformed Sacramento from a hot slow farming town into a desperately ugly conglomeration of malls and industrial parks, then Wino Park by those who had eyes, then Cesar Chavez Park by those who, like Tyler, deify the dead, he found the pawn shop of his recollections, where he inspected gold chains, then strolled past the cigar shop to the next pawn shop whose gold chains were supposedly new, and in this abode of discounted joy the woman drew herself up behind the counter and said: Well, what is it?

I'd like to spend about a hundred bucks on one of these, he said.

Links style or rope style?

Well, should she hang herself or just be locked up? he said. It's up to you.

The woman pulled out the first gold chain that came to hand and said: This is probably a little more than a hundred dollars.

And how about that one?

It's all by weight.

Well, ma'am, then would you mind weighing it for me and telling me how much it is?

The woman sighed heavily, slammed his choice down on the scale, and said: Eighty-three twenty-four.

I hope to see you again before then.

I beg your pardon?

It's perfect.

The other one's a hundred twelve.

Oh, I'm a cheapskate. I guess I'll take the one that caught my eye.

Eighty-nine twenty.

Guess I'd better pay before the price goes up again.

That's the *tax*, sir.

It certainly is.

What is your name? I need it for our receipt.

I prefer privacy, thanks, said Tyler.

Sir, you'll have to give me a name.

Adolf Hitler, said Tyler.

The woman snatched up the gold chain and stalked off to the manager. The manager looked up from the telephone and shot Tyler a sly glance. Tyler gazed back at him serenely.

Returning, the woman wrote C A S H on the receipt.

Why, how did you know my name? said Tyler. I'm Johnny Cash's third cousin once removed.

I'll get you a box, said the woman.

She spread the gold chain out on the cotton and tried to stab it down with golden colored pins, which didn't take. Tyler watched with friendly interest.

What are the pins made of? he inquired.

You can take it from me they're not real gold, said the woman, giving up her attempt to skewer the chain. She would have been a poor lepidopterist.

Tyler slid his finger under the chain, enjoying the smoothness and cool weight of it, and then he thanked the woman, took the box, and went out.

| 202 |

He awoke with the taste of Irene's cunt in his mouth.

| 203 |

And now it was Saturday evening near the Tenderloin, and the red lights chirred green and he rolled past the Opera House, accompanied by sparse lights. The greenish dome of City Hall reminded him of Dan Smooth's head. Straight up through the timed lights on Gough Street was the way to salvation, toward the Bay and the Marin headlands, but he meant to go the other way, down to the grimy darkness where the Queen was. His heart exuded self-praise. Who was he tricking? He didn't love her; he loved Irene. But he wanted to pay his respects. He wanted to be thanked. He wanted the Queen to know that he continually thought of her. For once, the eyes were not narrowed in his grey face. His confidence, his hope, needed only a couple of finishing touches. It never dawned on him that hanging about the Queen's court might be as improper a thing for a man to do as joining Apache women at their card games. He'd sent word by way of the parking garage that he was coming, and Beatrice, who was wide, sunny and busy like Mission Street itself with all its palm trees and families, said that the tall man would be meeting him on Larkin and Golden Gate at nine-thirty sharp. He had the gold chain in his coat pocket. It was that which gave him his confidence. Like Celia, who at that very moment sat in an Afghan carpet shop on Polk Street purchasing a magnificent bundle of threads which she could not realistically afford, he believed that offerings of money, being more easily made, were more craftily practical than the other kind. It is written that when the Greeks made sacrifices to Zeus, they threw only entrails into the sacred fire, keeping the meat for themselves. Little wonder that Zeus did not always reciprocate with ready-wrapped treasures.

At the corner, a pert black girl with a hairdo like a giant paintbrush started stretching her arms and shoulders. —You call me, you come to me, she said.

I wish I could, said Tyler. But I have a date with the Queen.

The Queen! she cried in amazement. It won't work. The *conspiracy*—

But just then the light changed. He waved and drove on, feeling very loyal. He hadn't checked his answering machine all day.

| 204 |

The tall man was late. Tyler stood waiting in front of the Mitchell Brothers as if for the strip show, taking his time, until the man behind the window said: Do you want to go in or don't you? and Tyler said: Well, give me a minute to make up my mind and he leaned there for another ten minutes until the man said: You can't just stay here. You'll have to go elsewhere to make your decision . . . and Tyler said: Now, you say that if I go in now it costs fifteen dollars but half an hour from now it'll cost twenty-five? and the man said that's right and Tyler leaned there for another ten minutes and then said: I'm trying to make up my mind whether I'd rather pay fifteen dollars or twenty-five dollars. Can I just wait here for half an hour? —It's the same show, the man said. —Yes, said Tyler, but somehow I have the feeling that for twenty-five dollars I'll get more.

So he wasted the man's time until he saw Justin coming from the direction of the parking garage.

He raised his hat.

Hello, Henry, said the tall man.

Good evening, Justin, said Tyler. How are you and how's the Queen?

Oh, shitty as always, said the tall man. More goddamned cops and vigs nosing around. Let's get out of here.

You can't just stay here, said the man behind the ticket window.

Okay, sir, said Tyler. We'll be back for the hundred-dollar show.

The tall man led him down Leavenworth Street past a late-night soup restaurant through whose window Tyler glimpsed a slender Vietnamese girl with a rainbow ribbon in her hair; with a rag and window cleaner the girl was wiping each plexiglass-covered table to mirror-ness.

Hey, Justin.

What?

Where are you from, anyway?

I'm concrete. I'm a sidewalk. I come from all over.

When I'm with a woman I come all over, so that makes two of us.

You know what, Henry? You try to be funny, but you ain't funny. You're just a sad-assed honky sonofabitch.

Guess my ass would be pretty happy if you stuck your finger up it in the back seat of my faggoty car.

You're too fuckin' much. We turn left.

| 205 |

The voice in the first cell—a tremulous old male voice—was saying: When you want to touch her hair you put her hand on your head so she knows you're not insulting her sacred place, and she smiles, oh, Jesus, that's how you do it; and then when you eat her out she is, well, she is caressing your hair so, so softly.

Does he have an Oriental gal interrogating him? said the Queen. He's talking about Oriental gals. He sounds like a nice guy.

Yeah, I think that one no problem, said a smiling Thai girl, sticking her head out from between the red curtains. He just like the girl too much! Very funny, very nice man! Him so good!

All right, let him out, said the Queen.

She kisses you of her own accord but with *closed* lips, the dreamy old voice went on.

Wait a minute, the Queen said. I don't like the sound of that. You interrogate him some more.

Her wet, tight, thoroughly delicious cunt . . . the voice mumbled. I'm so sleepy, but . . . shaven up to the top, then a nice overhang of hair. Tell her I want to be her friend.

All right, called the Queen. Nothing wrong with any of that. He sounds a little confused, but his heart's in the right place. Who reported him?

Smooth, said Justin.

Dan Smooth reported him? What'd he say?

Said he hurt a child.

Smooth doesn't lie about stuff like that. Get to the bottom of it. Tell this guy he's gotta come clean or I'm gonna cut his balls off and cook 'em and make him eat 'em.

Awright, Maj, the tall man said. Want me to kick him around?

Just talk to him. You can do that well.

That Henry Tyler's waitin' on you.

Oh, he is? I heard he left that girl I got him.

That's right, Maj.

All rightie. I'll see him.

| 206 |

Where is she, Henry?

I don't know. I stopped seeing her after she told me her real name.

Ah. So you stuck it out that long. Well well well. C'mere.

He came to her.

Kneel down.

He knelt.

Touch me, Henry, said the Queen. Just touch my shoulder or touch my hand. It don't matter. Oh, you're my sweet little baby boy. That's right. Now close your eyes. You're going to see that Irene you love. Close 'em tight. Now tell me what you see. You can tell me. Don't be ashamed.

The Queen was squeezing his hand.

He saw the true Irene as a slender girl of nine, silently carrying her baby brother up and down the stairs.

You're right, he whispered. I saw her.

She was a little girl, wasn't she?

Yes.

You know what that means?

What, am I like Dan Smooth?

No no *no.* Inside, you're little, same as her. You wanna be her friend. You wanna play with her. But you can't, 'cause she's dead. Ain't that right, Henry?

Yes, he said dully.

You need to cry? You can cry in front of me if you want. Don't mind about me.

He squeezed her hand. He said: I'm not sure I can, uh, . . .

All right. Now close your eyes again. Here goes.

He saw perfect fish-ribs and kale amist codfish and red sauteed onions. Irene was eating with chopsticks, somewhere in the wide streets and malls of Koreatown. It was a dish called *cho-rim.* Now she was smiling and saying something, but it was all silent. She couldn't see him. Her old uncles, all dead like her, smiled wearily and picked their teeth.

She's having fish for dinner, right? said the Queen with a knowing smile.

Uh huh, said Tyler, nodding his head with an effort.

That means she's been saved. She's in heaven now, Henry. You don't have to worry about her. If you see a dead person that you love, and they're eating fish, that means they're eating the body of Jesus. They're gonna be okay. But you know that Irene's not your kind, Henry. She's a Christian girl. When she died, she left you. She never could have been with you. You know that, Henry honey? You got to know that.

Tyler's stubbly face twitched, and a long tear began to ease out of his left eye, slowly, slowly descending his cheek. He felt no relief.

Don't think about her too much. If you do, she gonna ache.

I—

Baby, I'm gonna ask you a question, whispered the Queen. And you don't have to answer, 'cause I already know the answer.

Tyler began to shake and shiver.

Did you have sex with Irene, Henry? It's okay. You can answer.

Another tear came out of him, this one burning hot.

Henry? Sweetheart, you okay? Sweetheart, did you and Irene make love?

He wept.

Listen to me, Henry, said the Queen, taking his head between her hands. Not to answer *me* is to deny *her.* You remember how Peter denied Jesus? *I don't know him,* he said. Did you know Irene? Did you have carnal knowledge of Irene?

Tyler groaned. He tried to speak, but could not.

| 207 |

He knelt down and threw his arms around her, burying his face in her waist. Then slowly he sank down to the concrete floor, and clasping her ankles, placed his forehead on the floor. He lifted her foot and placed it on his neck with the shoeheel pressing down. She remained still. She neither withdrew her foot from him nor did she lean her weight on it. Together they listened to the squeaking of stolen shopping carts, and Justin yelling: *Shut up!* Strawberry screamed again and again. Kitty was silent. He gripped the Queen's foot encouragingly, and she pressed down on his neck ever so slightly. The two of them stayed like that for a very long time and then he said to her: I am yours.

What do you want to do? she said.

I want you to . . .

You can tell me, she said very gently.

I want you to be my . . .

He was clinging to her tightly and his body was trembling.

Look at me, the Queen said so gently.

He looked her in the face.

Are you serious? she said.

I was dreaming about your breath, he said. I wanted to drink it in.

When he gave her the gold chain, she began to cry.

| 208 |

I love you, darling, he'd said to Irene.

Love you, *too!* she always used to whisper, kissing him again and again. But by the end she only palely replied: Thank you for loving me.

There was nothing pale about the Queen.

| 209 |

He slid his hand around the Queen's shoulders and she got up and moved away, as he thought, but a few moments later they had come face to face and his mouth was on her mouth and her lips opened. His tongue was in her mouth. She was sucking his lips. He kissed her until his vision went black. —Thank you, Africa, he said. There was a roaring around him. All he could think of was: Oh, God. Oh, God. Thank you, God.

He stumbled away and sat down, weak. He kept whispering: Oh, God, oh, God. His heart rushed. For this alone it was worth having lived.

· BOOK XIII ·

"Business Comes First"

●

You certainly deserve credit, friend Midas, for striking out so brilliant a conception. But are you quite sure that this will satisfy you?

HAWTHORNE, "The Golden Touch" (1851)

●

A small black woman came into the Wonderbar and said to Loreena: Could I please have a few napkins?

Sure, honey, said Loreena, glancing warily over her shoulder—only to find Heavyset, her boss.

It's not like we have a lot of napkins, Heavyset said coolly, resting his elbows on a mountain of them. Give her one.

I have a cold, the black woman explained in a shy whisper. I was fixin' to blow my nose.

Oh, Jesus, said Heavyset in disgust. Give her a paper cup. Here, nigger. Now get out.

Thank you for the napkins, sweetheart, the Queen said to Loreena. Bless you.

She glided almost silently out through the swinging doors.

Well, did you *hear* that! shouted Heavyset. That stinking *impudent* little nigger bitch!

Oh, get a grip, said Loreena.

That's right. I forgot. Your boyfriend's a nigger. You actually take a black schlong inside your belly. You—

Go to hell, Heavyset.

Don't you smart off to me. I could fire you just like that. You want me to fire you? I know you were homeless before. You want to eat out of garbage cans again?

Listening to you is just like being around garbage, Loreena told him. Go ahead. Fire me. How many other girls you think you can find who will put up with your shit?

You know what? I'm gonna charge you for those napkins, said Heavyset. Those napkins cost a nickel apiece. I'm taking ten cents out of your wages.

Oh, don't bother. Here's a quarter, greedhead. Now, are you gonna fire me or can I go back to waiting on my customers?

I'll credit you fifteen cents, the owner said. But I don't want that nigger bitch coming in here again to scrounge more handouts. How often do you let her in here?

Oh, she comes and goes. Now let me go back to work, okay? This is like the *nightmare shift*. This is the shift from hell.

Outside, the Queen was saying: All right, Sapphire, now here's a couple nice new napkins to wipe your mouth. Hold still, girl. What did you have to go and vomit like that for? What didn't agree with you?

Luh-luh-luh . . . said the retarded girl.

I love you, too. You're my special one. You know that, don't you? Now clean your mouth off. No. Not there. You missed your chin. That's a good girl. That's my good girl.

| 211 |

Beatrice, sitting in one of the red-vinyl-upholstered benches in the back of the bar (crooked-eyebrowed old Dan Smooth said that the only two alterations in the Wonder-bar over the past thirty years were that new upholstery, scarcely a decade old, and a slight abatement in the general darkness), had seen it all. Without the Queen's knowledge she told the tall man, who shot his arms out and roared into the bar where Domino was just saying *hello-o-o-o-o* to one of her regulars, a pleasant enough old drunk contentedly incapable of ejaculation, and the tall man said: Dom, I need to speak with you a moment, but Domino said: Can't you see I'm doing my business? to which Justin replied: You smarting off to me, bitch? and Domino said: Go outside, Justin, and if you don't hassle me I *promise* I'll be out in five minutes, then turned her back on him and said to her john: How's life, sugar? and the john said: Same as always, at which Domino raised an eyebrow, pretending to be interested, and said: I'll bet it's just *wonderful!* to which the john replied: I hate my wife. I hate her yelling. I just hate it. I hate the way she won't leave me alone. If I do something to offend her, well, no apology is good enough. I ought to know. I've tried everything over the years. I apologize, you know; I promise I won't do it again, I promise to change, I promise whatever the hell suits her, and even though she's just gotten her way she won't stop. I don't know why. I can't understand it. Can you understand it? I mean, she's gotten her way. What else does she want? She starts to threaten me and then she insults me. So I, well, I apologize again and I promise again even though I don't believe I'm in the wrong anymore, and maybe that's my sin, that I can only apologize once or twice before I feel I've done my duty. I don't know. All I know is that she won't stop. So I *beg* her to stop. But she keeps on threatening me and kind of snarling through her teeth. So I *implore* her to stop. And she just steps it up. She just twists it in. Her voice gets louder and shriller and there's no place to run. So finally I warn her that if she doesn't stop I'm going to lose it. Well, that turns her into a real harpy, or maybe it incites her on toward her goal, so she keeps it up—Christ! —until we get there, and I start literally screaming with rage. And then I come here. I end up here about three nights a week. I hate it here, but it's better than staying home. That's why I'm here. That's why I date you. That's why I . . .

So you cheat on your wife and you want me to give you a gold star for it, said Domino. Well, mister, I pity your wife and I don't give a fuck about you. Now I've got to go outside for a minute and see a man about a dog. When I come back, if you want a flatback or a blow, you just lay down your money in my hand. But no more of your hypocritical bullshit. Who the hell do you think you are? You're just a kid in the candy store that can't decide which kind of liquorice he wants to stuff his face with. Now sit there and shut up.

The trick's jaw literally dropped as Domino marched out, swollen with happy righteousness.

All right, she said to Justin. So you interrupted me. You blew my chance to make twenty dollars. The way I see it, you owe me one big fat rock.

You're too much, the tall man said.

Well, do I get a rock or not?

We'll see. Listen. Heavyset just insulted Maj. He called her a nigger just because she needed two goddamned napkins to wipe Sapphire's mouth—

And what did Maj say?

I wasn't there.

We'll get the sonofabitch, Justin, I promise. Someday when the time is ripe I'll throw acid in his face, okay? 'Cause I love Maj as much as you, maybe more. But—

But what?

But right now let's just do our business. Business comes first. I mean, it wasn't you or me who got insulted; it was only Maj . . .

· BOOK XIV ·

Domino

•

Wicked bitch demands your presence in the Dungeon of Dominance where you will encounter Foot Worship, Enforced Feminisation, CP for Bad Boys and much more.

Flier in a London phone booth (1998)

•

Where the fuck did Domino go? the john shouted. She just disappeared out of here without a sound like some vampire . . .

She does that, Loreena sighed.

Why the fuck does she do that?

She's a good kid, Loreena said, shuffling men's dollars like cards.

What the fuck you mean, a good kid? She's fucked-up! And you're one fucked-up bitch. Come here and pour me another fucking drink.

You want ice or no ice?

Come here, I said. Come closer.

This is as far as I come, Loreena said. See this bar here? This is three feet wide. And that's the longest three feet there is. That three feet makes the Great Wall of China look like one of Domino's skinny old hair ribbons, because on *my* shift there's no body contact with *me*. Do you get that, mister? —*Well,* look whose sweet face is here! What's goin' on, baby?

Hello, sweetheart, said Tyler, sitting down on a barstool.

What'll it be today? Shot of tequila and a lemon?

Yeah, said Tyler. Buy you one?

How nice of you, said Loreena. She went and mixed herself something clear like watery nail polish that cost Tyler three dollars.

What's that?

That's called a cocksucker, said Loreena complacently.

Why's that?

Oh, I dunno, said Loreena, clearing her throat.

Domino had just floated back in, so she said: Well, *I* know. It's because they pour the Irish cream on top, so when you gulp it down you get *cream* all over your lips. Get it?

Don't be gross, said Loreena with surprising primness. Anyway, some people call it a pussywhip.

I'd think a pussywhip would have tomato juice in it, said Tyler.

Can we get *off* this subject?

'Magine that, said the Queen in soft wonder from the doorway. Some topics make our little Loreena squeamish.

Oh, hello, Maj, said Loreena cautiously. What'll you have? Rum and Coke?

Mm hm, said the Queen. She came and stood beside Tyler.

What's up? said Tyler.

My blood pressure. Hey, Henry, can you gimme a little allowance to help support my girls?

Well, said Tyler, maybe I could afford three dollars. Here's a three-dollar bill.

He slipped her a five.

That'll work, Maj! cried Domino happily. You got yourself a rich old bastard! Hey, how about buying me a shot?

Shot of what?

Shot of my usual.

You look pale, Domino, said Tyler.

Yeah? Well, *you* look like you just hatched out of a rat's ass. Oh, I, uh . . . excuse me . . .

And she ran out the back door again. Before it swung completely shut they heard her retching.

Get her a shot, Loreena, said the Queen wearily.

She shouldn't be drinking in her condition, the barmaid said.

What, you think she'd ever keep it? That girl just got pure poison instead of milk in her tits. That's my little girl. That's my secret weapon.

Well, as long as she's not going to keep it I guess I'm not responsible. Three dollars even, Henry.

Tyler remembered seeing Irene run for the toilet to vomit. She too had suffered miserably from morning sickness. He and John sat there listening to her throwing up and weeping. The bathroom door was open. Finally John got up and went to comfort his wife. Tyler sat swishing ice cubes around in his gin and tonic, listening to water running. Then John came leading Irene by the hand. Stroking her belly, he smiled ironically at his brother and murmured: We're pregnant.

Domino glided back into the Wonderbar, pale and sweaty. Tyler wanted to whisper into her ear: *Are we pregnant?* but just then the other door gaped, and in came the owner, coked up or cracked up or methed up, manic and red-eyed. Seeing the Queen, he started yelling: No more napkins for you! Now get out, nigger!

That's a shame, said the Queen. I was just fixin' to blow my nose again.

Loreena came rushing busily up to her and slipped a dozen napkins into the Queen's hand. —Don't take it personally, Maj, but you'd better go, she whispered. Heavyset gets really out of control when he's like this . . .

Buy you a drink, Heavyset? the Queen said loudly.

The owner stopped short, licking his lips foolishly. —Well, I didn't know you were a paying customer, he said. Have you bought something already?

I was fixin' to buy you a drink, Heavyset, since you love me so much. Henry, would you kindly buy this gentleman a drink?

What'll you have, Heavyset? said Tyler wearily.

Oh, is this lady a friend of yours? said Heavyset. I'll take a beer. I never turn down beer. Loreena! Bring me a beer!

That'll be three dollars, sweetheart, said Loreena impassively.

And you can give her an extra napkin, Loreena. On the house.

Well, thank you, Heavyset, said the Queen. Now why don't you just run along and let me transact a little business with Henry . . .

Heavyset, said Loreena quickly, do you want me to change the channel to the football game?

Hey, Heavyset, leave the Queen alone! shouted Domino. Come on over here an'— an'—what you always . . . shit, I feel so fucked up . . .

What about me? said Domino's john. I was here first.

What *about* you? Go sit over there by the pool table and chill out for ten minutes and then you can . . . oh, I feel so sick . . .

You need to lie down, said Heavyset triumphantly. Come on in the back room and—

Henry, said the Queen, when you have no money, why you always comin' in here every night?

Looking for you.

Lordy lordy day, said the Queen.

I want to be with you.

Well, don't you just want to be with everybody that's got a pussy? Henry, you don't *know* what you want.

I want to live with you. The girls live with you. Lily lives with you—

Lily was living with us, and one day she walked out and didn't come back for two years. She don't even remember where she was at. I been keepin' her clothes for her in a box . . .

I figured she's—

I'm scared about Lily, the Queen said. Lily makes me scared. I can see her going down and down . . .

And Beatrice, too, he said.

Thank you for sayin' that. Yes, and Beatrice, too. Anyway, Lily she like to stay by herself at the Lola Hotel, Room Twenny-Six—

But you weren't sad when Sunflower died . . .

It was her time. You thinkin' Queenie don't have no strength nor knowledge? You thinkin' Sunflower wasn't ready?

Lily reminds me of Sunflower. More than my pretend Irene . . .

But Lily's still Lily. She still got some Lily things to do. Sunflower was finished. She went beyond all that. When she passed away, Henry, she was already pure sunny happiness. Do you believe what I'm tellin' you?

I don't know, said Tyler. That's the honest truth.

How can I condemn you for that? You don't put on airs. You *know* you don't understand. It's all right, child, 'cause I never yet laid my hand on your eyes to make you see.

Are you going to do that to me?

You want it?

I trust in you to do what's right for me, he said in a low voice, so that the other alcoholics wouldn't hear.

She took his hand. They sat together for a while in that bar which was darker and shabbier than the snotty cleanliness of the Cinnabar on Ellis and Jones, whose bar's wood-grain spread itself under a million coats of plastic while Diana Ross and the Supremes on the jukebox sang *It hurts so bad*—the Wonderbar was the best.

When the Queen went to the ladies' room, he tore off a scrap of his soggy napkin and wrote on it AFRICA I LOVE YOU. Then he clenched it tight in his hand.

Domino had left her little silver purse on a barstool when she went back with Heavyset, whom she actually valued in a way because although in her years of growing older she had learned enough to avoid any barmaid's eye so that the barmaid could not immediately sell her another three-dollar beer, still, that strategy could preserve a girl's finances only so far, and when she inhabited the Wonderbar waiting and waiting for some trick to wander in, her expenses rose faster than cracksmoke because she really could not afford to alienate Loreena; but as long as she permitted Heavyset to bear her away to his little "office" whenever the fancy struck him, then afterward she could sit for as long as she liked beneath the nice mural of the girl with nipples like Hershey's kisses; and maybe even shoot a little pool or watch football or hockey on the screen, saving up money and thirst until she was ready to drink the kind of classy bottled beer that made her spit thick. Now it was time to pay. Loreena would look out for her, she thought, but then she suddenly viciously distrusted Loreena and would have gone back for her purse; however, Heavyset, misconstruing her reluctance to be something less trivial than that, whispered in her ear that he had some crystal meth in his office, at which any other ideas which the blonde might have had went rushing up through the ceiling. So there lay her purse. Toilet paper, condoms, keys, lipstick, spermicide, a pocket mirror, change and three self-defensive razorblades had long since forced apart the zipper's broken lips, so that the purse presented to the world a defiantly overt character not unlike that of its owner. Tyler worried about Domino sometimes when he saw that purse because its silveriness and inviting openness seemed to him to offer an invitation to evildoers, but doubtless Domino knew best. Picking it up by one safety-pinned strap, he slid it across the bar to Loreena, who was working the register, and asked her to keep it safe for the tipsy girl. Loreena nodded wordlessly and stuffed it behind the beer keg where only she could reach it. Returning to his spot, Tyler encountered Domino's john, who'd dug both hands into the Queen's shoulder, trying to date her. The Queen was smiling.

Tyler drained his drink and put the balled-up napkin in the Queen's hand. He said to her: Maybe this will come in handy. —Then he went out.

Just as he reached the swinging doors, he heard Domino's john say sneeringly: So what the fuck did that turkey give you, a get out of jail free card?

| 213 |

What the doctor sees on the other end of the speculum is your *cervix,* explained the woman in the blue jumpsuit who now was washing Domino with Betadyne. —Do you want to see?

Sure, grinned Domino, and the woman tilted a mirror until Domino could see the brown stain around her vulva through a hole in the plastic. The woman in the blue jumpsuit sounded the depth of the os to determine how far along she was.

You'll feel a little pinch now, the woman in the blue jumpsuit said.

The needle entered the hole in the plastic and quivered like a mosquito. It twinkled and hummed. The efficient woman in blue stood over her, hands spread; the needle slid in slowly, deeper and deeper. Domino was enjoying the woman's attentions, perhaps because the woman was so tense-faced, determined, probably quick to take offense. The blonde had already sized her up back in the waiting room where all the very quiet women kept watching each other out of the corners of their eyes and the woman in blue, placidly brushing back her hair, explained: And this is a canula. You notice that it *is* plastic and it *is* flexible. —The patients watched the ring on her hand move, all of them sitting cozy together. It was Domino's pleasure not to offend her, for now. Moreover, she liked the stinging of the needle, which she pretended was a part of the woman in blue's body, that the woman in blue was entering her lovingly, sexually and above all subserviently.

Now, the tinaculum clamps into your cervix to keep it in place, the woman in blue said.

Domino smiled slowly.

And then we dilate you like this with the flexible plastic canula. There may be a little cramp when that tube goes through. Are you okay?

Domino smiled and licked her lips. —Not really, she said. I got raped by a bad man named Henry Tyler. That's why I'm here today. He's a misogynist. He treated me just like I was a piece of meat. Does it look like meat to you down there between my legs?

I'm so sorry, the woman in blue whispered, flushing.

Domino glowed with pleasure.

The doctor turned on the machine, which hummed like a refrigerator, and Domino began to feel intense pain as very dark red bars of fluid came out. The doctor turned the canula around and around. There was a slurping sound. Something was red through translucency against his white gloved fingers.

Is there a cramping? the woman in blue said.

Please hold my hand, Domino said, her legs spread like wings. She wanted to drink the woman's buttock-juice.

You see, your uterus clamps down when the fetal tissue is removed, the woman in blue explained, digging the canula in, around and around. Fluid ran out of Domino's cunt.

Now we're going in one more time to check, the doctor said.

Please don't let go of my hand, said Domino, staring at the tiny implements. She suddenly felt a sensation as strange as seeing black shoe-heels percussing across a glass ceiling; she couldn't remember where she'd seen that but she knew she had.

After he puts the speculum in, he's going to rinse out your vagina with Betadyne, the woman in blue said, very efficient and tall. Later Domino, craving more of the lovely and very tiny novocaine injections, would vaguely remember a cotton ball, and the drip of Betadyne through the plastic hole.

Now put your hand on your tummy over the uterus to calm the cramp, the woman in blue said.

Would you do it, please? whispered Domino through half-closed eyes. Oh, it feels so good when you do it.

I think you may be in a little bit of trouble, the woman in blue said. I'm going to refer you to one of our counselors. She'll be able to help you.

I want *you* to do it, said Domino with a sleepy, wicked, toothy grin, and savored the woman in blue's long slow flush.

| 214 |

Domino's first abortion had been much easier than that, at least in the spurious fashion which lent itself to sugarcoating in her recollections, so that she could complain about subsequent procedures, saying, in one of her typically obscene mixed metaphors: These assholes just want to fuck women up! They're butchers! It's a government plot to sterilize us to save money. And they call this a free country. Don't even get me started, Maj . . . —It had been before Christmas, which to Domino was already becoming as irrelevant as all the other holidays because the only presents she'd ever received were those she'd stolen for herself, seizing them from life's jaws and running somewhere deep and dirty to hide, to gloat. And yet in those days (she was seventeen) Christmas retained the power to disappoint her; in other words, it was not entirely irrelevant yet. The Christmas present one of the boys had given her grew brutishly in her belly. If she didn't do something fast, it would quicken inside her and then she'd be a murderess. Moreover, she preferred not to be pregnant when she was at home. Not that she wanted to be home, either, but a former friend of hers now on the streets had informed her in weary exasperation that her sister was in jail and her father was dying of liver cancer, so Domino, burdened, hence affronted to her usual point of martyrdom, made up her mind to go back for the last time to see those losers, and it had truly been the last time. She'd dyed her hair brown because she was not yet a fulltime prostitute and it was an experiment of hers to learn whether men would defile her with fewer up-and-down stares of fishy-eyed lust if she denied her blondeness, but the results convinced her once and for all that she was doomed to that, at least until she became a hag, so she'd let blondeness creep back into the roots of her brown hair as she sat in the hotel room trying to be unconscious of that qualmish feeling in her uterus. She was supposed to arrive in Vacaville in three days. Her father would have erected the plastic tree if he were well enough, but there'd be nothing beneath it. (What dully studied comparisons come to mind? Did this hollow celebration of Christ's birthday thus emblematize His empty tomb? Would seven-year-old Domino, instead of squatting bitterly by the tree in her pajamas all night, gnawing angrily at her blonde pigtail, have done better to gaze up at the ceiling in search of presents? By the time she was ten, she'd already sucked a boy off on a dare, and when his manna spewed into her mouth, she vomited. But her control improved over the years. Just as a soda jerk leans, scraping and twisting the tall stainless steel cup upon the rod, so Domino would waggle her lips and tongue about a man's organ if she had to, although she rarely denied herself the pleasure of stopping halfway through to engage in negotiations of a deliberately aggressive nature, until the man had lost his erection. After a man had passed his mid-thirties he could not as a rule get hard and soft and hard in quick succession more than three or four times. It gave Domino more than a little satisfaction to leave her customer unfulfilled, frustrated, and [American male socialization being what it was] humiliated rather than angry at his failure—although this was a delicate game; every now and then she got a black eye. —Well, this won't work, she would tell her customer brightly. I don't know what your problem is. Maybe you just don't like girls. As for me, I don't have all night. If you want to try again sometime, pull up under my window and honk four times.) Her father had sounded surprised and glad when she'd telephoned him collect from the booth on Eddy Street. His surprise reproached her, and his gladness infuriated her. He said he'd meet her at the Greyhound station. —Yeah, that'll work, the girl said curtly, breaking the connection. She was very conscious of her uterus. It just felt as if it were there. For a month now she'd persisted in hoping that that unsought sensation would vanish, but every morning it grew more present until it stood for already not merely a mass of tissue inside her but an inimical being whose purpose it was to weaken and confuse her, then drag her down. —You're dead! laughed the blonde, punching herself in the stomach. She asked her aunt to send money. It was about a hundred and eighty dollars. Her aunt reminded her that they had mutually agreed that the previous time would be the last time, but Domino wept most fluently on the telephone, pleading that she'd made another mistake, that this emergency was the worst ever. A year or two later, she would have known enough to lie, using the magic word *rape*, which opened so many tear-ducts and money-ducts when carefully invoked. She was in the fifth week. A girlfriend came with her—not a friend, merely a girlfriend, a dumb bitch who wasn't in the life,* because Domino supposed it would be prudent to have someone drive her back. The girlfriend, whose name she could no longer remember, had borne two babies, one when she was fifteen and the next when she was sixteen. Each time she'd refused to open her eyes when the doctor raised up the child before her, raised up the bloody little rabbit. What was the point? They were both carried away for adoption. She said to Domino: Does he love you? to which the blonde replied, rolling a joint: That's the most asinine thing I've ever heard. —Her girlfriend, broodingly sensitive, lowered her eyes. Neither of them had ever gone to an abortion clinic before. The girlfriend was pro-life, but she was a friend, except of course that she wasn't a friend because even then Domino had no friends.

The place was of a pale green color, with nothing in the halls, and two examination tables. Really it was a processing plant, Domino thought, always firm in her conviction that all authority and expertise on this earth functioned either to withhold good things from her, or else to carefully crank her into the latest meat-grinder; and when she discovered that somebody had left the toilet unflushed, her gorge rose in outrage—*this* was the sort of place to which they'd compelled her! —but on the other hand, she would soon think nothing of the Queen's stinking lairs where cockroaches crawled on her at night and the whores' used tampons had stiffened into rigid dark plumes as of ancient flint knives, so may we agree once and for all that such complaints on her part were almost pleasantries, which is to say that they reflected her normal intercourse with the world?

Everyone did everything together; it was one of those communist places. Everyone undressed together. There were lockers. It would be vacuum aspiration. Everyone woke up in the recovery room. An ocean of white bodies was what she thought (her mind being more pictorially descriptive in those days). No one looked pregnant. Most were with their girlfriends or with their mothers. Her girlfriend asked: Are you sure you want to go through with this, Sylvia? —Look, said Domino. Can't you see that this is already difficult enough? —All the white bodies looked very young—soft bodies, pale and plump and well cared for. It had not been very long now since Domino had confessed to herself that she was a lesbian, so she was still ashamed to gaze openly upon all those pregnant breasts and pregnant cunts; for she and they were as strangers compressed naked in some elevator; they spoke in low voices when they spoke at all, trying in equal proportion not to look invasively at one another and not to acknowledge the unavoidable invasiveness of those others. The real reason that she was none too forward in getting her eyeful, a fact she afterward jealously regretted, was that her own body, hard and scrawny, already wore its first tattoo, its first abscesses, and that long white highway of a motorcycle wound which Tyler's finger would trace in that Tenderloin hotel room twenty years hence. It wouldn't be much longer before Domino adopted Tyler's mode of self-protective skullduggery in the face of humiliations real or imagined, namely, *defiance,* but this first abortion happened long ago, when the girl, still almost a child, remained meek in her shame.

She had to pay up front, cash. Then they took her jewelry away. She owned one Apache tear, an old piece of lapis. It was an earring. She'd lost the other one two months earlier

---

*"In the life" usually means being a prostitute, but is sometimes used to refer to other street activities such as pimping, drug pushing, fencing stolen goods, etcetera.

when she'd had to run away from a married man's house. While the other women compli-
antly twisted off their rings and unhooked their bracelets, Domino scowled and hid the
Apache tear in her fist. She wanted something to hold. The general anesthetic wafted her
down into darkness. She never heard the ringing clatter when the charm struck the green
tiles beneath the table on which she lay. A nurse smiled and picked it up for her while
Domino dreamed of nothing, like a thread woven into a heavy rug of darkness.

They gave her a sheet of instructions: Don't have sex or use tampons. Do you understand? they said. —Whatever, said Domino.

A young woman enshrouded in white blankets walked by, and Domino thought: I'd
like to eat her. I'd like to at least see her naked. I'd like to . . . and then the woman in
white was gone.

| 215 |

One for our records and one for the insurance company, said the receptionist.

I don't have a goddamned insurance company, snarled Domino.

Thank you very much, the receptionist said in a quick, low voice.

The woman in the chair behind Domino inhabited a loose striped dress. She had
bare, crossed ankles, a glimpse of red hair. She shifted her legs, kicked off her shoes, hid
behind the newspaper. Seeing the domed belly supporting her newspaper, Domino conceived a shocking jealousy of that baby still inside it; she wanted a baby, too. But the
Queen had made her do this. And Justin had held out on her and jacked her up too
many times; if she'd been able to keep that money she could have raised a baby. It was
Justin's fault. And all the men who used her, and the men who refused to use her, and
the whole rotten world with its trolleycar bells and sherry-colored sunset clouds over
white-and-silver San Francisco . . .

| 216 |

A motif in Domino's life: the clinic. One window looked out in the outer office. After
that, there were no windows. How many times will a street-whore go to the clinic in her
lifetime? How many diseases, babies, false alarms, abrasions, uterine traumas, inflama-
tions, infestations, ill odors until death?

In Vienna I once wandered inside a medical museum filled not only with such en-
dearing oddities as the porcelain model uterus which of all things most resembled a bat,
but also with ghastly things the sight of which destroyed my dispassion. I looked upon
the swollen face and oozing blind eyes of a gonorrheal infant, the red sores and breast
lesions of a syphilitic mother—real tissue scalpeled out of the dead, now displayed in
a manner calculated to induce dread. The museum's staff did not want me to catch
syphilis. Hence they spread an atmosphere of loathsomeness and fear. To be sure, much
in the place was of historical interest as well—not least the old prostheses like robot
hands of black metal—but then I encountered pickled feet with what looked like bugs
growing out of them—surely just some tissue deformity—and bits of tiny bones floating in the formalin, greenly meat-fuzzed. Then came pale grey ovals of other meat floating in other jars. And in one room there dwelled a black-burnt, teeth-clenched
skeleton . . .

Let's say that a woman becomes pregnant, and the doctor sends her home with "information." She learns that if she is thirty-five years old, she has one chance in three hundred and eighty-four in giving birth to a child afflicted with Down's syndrome. At thirty-six, it will be one chance in three hundred and seven. At forty, it will be one chance in a hundred and twelve. Research bears all this out. (We see the cross-section of a vagina, sliced and brown. Inside a spherical paperweight, we find lumps of gristle studded with sores.) The fetus grows into danger. In the medical museum in Vienna we see a tiny white thing, half baby, half shrimp, floating in a jar of death. Another fetus grows into another sort of death. Eighty or a hundred years from conception, it will all be over. Perhaps forty years from now the fetus will have become a middle-aged hooker in black, with high heels and a run in her stocking, a tired woman burdened by a heavy black leather purse.

Her fourth time, the degradation was the nurse pumping her for dollars. Domino had to hide the degradation. She had to hide how she felt. No painting offended the plain white walls. There were no magazines in the waiting room. On her first visit to the place, the nurse held her hand. The second time the nurse was more businesslike. That was when the requests for a tip began worming their way into Domino's sweaty ears. All she had was a twenty she'd stolen from an old barfly . . . The doctor had a round face. He was balding, professional, courteous in an old-fashioned way. He called her Miss. Domino liked that. He had no name. Domino had no name. The nurse had no name. —There, that's it, the doctor said. If you bleed more than two days, give me a call. Later she would remember coming out into blue sky and old buildings—gracious props of God—and she remembered massaging her belly which had already begun to ache. In the middle of that night, when she was fucking a man for money, she hemorrhaged. The man drove her to the emergency room. Later they told her that she had almost died.

| 217 |

Things happen, Chocolate said. I got friends, they been trying to conceive a child for years and can't do it and others get one right away. There must be a reason. You know what I'm saying, Dom? A divine reason.

Oh, fuck that, said Domino.

She hadn't told the others when she got the abortion. It was nobody's business but hers. Later on, though, she'd started feeling sorry for the dead baby. She got so she couldn't stop thinking about it. The dead baby came swimming through her heart's windows at night, making her heart's cat hiss, spreading its unformed flipper-arms wide like a torpedo's fins to explode inside her with dead and bloody grief; she bit her lip and the tendons stuck out in her neck like tree-roots; the dead baby sucked the blood from her heart and then tumbled down to the empty place inside her where it had died.

I know how you feel, Chocolate said while within the crack pipe, smoke like white San Francisco fog roiled into her mouth, then into Domino's mouth, which was framed by white scars from the broken glass which had penetrated her body in numberless accidents.

You ever had an abortion? the blonde suddenly said in a low anxious voice.

Uh huh, said Chocolate. 'Course I did. We all gotta have those.

I feel a little strange, Domino said. You know. In my tummy.

Oh, everybody start to feel that. Never mind about that, Dom.

I just kind of sat there empty afterward, Chocolate. Know what I mean? I felt so bad. And this was my ninth time.

Uh huh. Hey, Dom, let's go score some rock. I know a trick who—

Chocolate?

What?

What's your real name?

Why the fuck you want to know?

Because.

Brenda.

Brenda, huh? Well, I guess Chocolate will work. Brenda's some stupid twat's name.

What the *fuck* you ask me for if you gonna insult me?

Then I woke up with a pinching cramp this morning, Chocolate, and I felt kind of scared . . .

You're gonna bleed for a couple of days, Dom. Don't have a heart attack. For Jesus sake. Stupid twat name she tells me. Dom, you anybody else I cut your face.

I feel, you know, neutral.

About callin' me a twat?

About what I did. To my . . .

Well, you got to. I always felt neutral about it.

Always?

I felt, well, weird but okay. Even that first time I never told the daddy, and back then when I just turn sixteen I actually got a pretty goddamned good idea who that daddy might be . . .

Brenda? said the blonde, longing just then to be as jaunty as miniskirted Chocolate with her headphones on and her wrinkled fist jammed firmly against her hip and her lips parted in a heroin smile with darkness deep inside as she raised knee and showed leg.

What?

Brenda, my tummy hurts.

You gonna be fine, Dom. You want me to get the Queen?

Shit, no. What's the use of bothering her? She never—

I don't wanna hear you badmouth her, Dom. But if you wanna smoke some weed, that gonna take your cramps away, I guarantee . . .

Brenda? repeated the blonde, her eyes as slow and bleary as a car's yellow eyes creeping down a hooker avenue.

Call me Chocolate. Brenda just some stupid twat name.

Brenda, my—

Lemme guess. Your tummy hurts.

Oh, fuck off.

Well, you did it. Nobody did it to you. You said you didn't want no baby, so . . .

You think I'm trash? You think I'm not good enough to have a baby? Is that what you think?

Hey, honey, lots of women like us got other goals. We're *professional* women. We never got any appropriate time until we *make* a time and that's not how life works.

So you're saying I should have kept my baby. You're saying I'm a fucking murderess.

I'm saying I love you, Domino. Domino, you're my sweetheart.

And you probably think I'll burn in hell, don't you, you Bible-thumping tattooed negroid bitch? I bet when you're alone with the Queen you tell her, *Domino's just dirt. Domino's scum.* Admit it to me. Admit that you look down on me.

Domino . . .

Tell me you hate me. Tell me I'm trash, because I killed my baby.

Domino, you remember what the Queen said? She said, when you put out a thought in the universe, you gonna get something back. Girl, you better start taking responsibility for your thoughts.

Fuck off.

All right, Domino, that's enough. Other people got problems, too.

Why, you selfish little nigger twat, don't try to hide that hatred in your eyes. Now I know how you feel about me. You watch your back, girl, or some night you might wind up shanked. Some night you might wind up with a big old butcher knife wedged deep up your gonorrhea-infected snatch . . .

| 218 |

The falling out between Domino and Chocolate actually went back almost a year, to the night when Domino for pure goodness had gotten Chocolate a date (in other words, Domino saw the john first, but the john liked Chocolate's looks better), so Chocolate agreed to let her have a third of the heroin. After the date, Chocolate wanted to wash the sperm out of her mouth with a bottle of some Thunderbird because she and Domino were standing right across the street from the liquor store on South Van Ness where at this very time of night a certain clerk might give Chocolate free booze in exchange for a little pussy because she'd managed to make him believe that she had no money—a demonstrably useful fiction to maintain, so she asked Domino if she would buy for her with the john's twenty. In other words, Chocolate's logic had just entirely contradicted itself, but never mind. —Sure, that'll work, said Domino, clip-clopping into the liquor store on her silver high heels. As she was paying for the wine, a brawny black woman named Ada, of whom Domino was scared because she sold ass for Domino's former pimp, brushed past Chocolate and asked for two dollars because she was hungry. Domino had already given Ada two dollars for food earlier that day, the Queen and Justin not being in sight to protect her. She didn't have any more money for Ada, since the change from the twenty belonged to Chocolate. It wasn't her money, and she told Ada so, but with a weak and sinking voice entirely uncharacteristic of her, because she felt in her soul that she was already dreaming a nightmare so terrible that self-defense must prove useless. —What do you *mean* it's not your money? the black girl shouted. *'Course* it's your money! Don't you be scammin' me, *bitch!* —Through the liquor store window Domino could see Chocolate running away; she hoped to get the tall man, who was out trying to score a perfect baggie of white girl, but Chocolate, who kept scratching at her red eyes, trying to peel the swollen orange eyelids back and scrape out the infection that grew inside, unfortunately for Domino found herself presented on the very next block with a very attractive sexual offer which she owed it to herself not to refuse, being pretty broke, and once she accepted she got not only money, but also a deep needleful of pure China white heroin which blissfully sidelined her until late the following morning, so Domino remained most friendlessly alone as Ada pursued Domino all night, breaking up her dates. Whenever a car slowed, Ada scared the driver away. Wherever Domino went, even all the way to the Tenderloin's red-streaked night where sparks came tumbling underneath the door of a welding shop like Fourth-of-July cigarette ash, the black girl was punching her and spitting on her. She fucked up Domino's eye. Domino didn't want to strike back because Ada was eight months pregnant and

Domino would do major jail time if she killed her baby. She lost one of her high heels as she fled down the street, with Ada loping behind cursing. When she found Chocolate at last, it was dawn and Chocolate was lying grinning and mumbling in a doorway. Domino had been so frightened as to entirely forget her easy graceful old ways of intimidation; therefore she actually *begged* Chocolate for two dollars so Ada would leave her alone.

That's giving in, Chocolate mumbled. You can't give in to extortion.

Whatever, Domino said. Well, it's not you giving in; it's me. This all happened because of you. I can't find the Queen. Won't you help me?

No, said Chocolate, opening her eyes. You know why? *Because you kept that money, bitch. What the fuck did you do with my money?*

Then Ada was upon her, shouting: Guilty, guilty! and Domino was so afraid that she fell on her hands and knees literally pissing in her panties, and she felt the first blow on the back of her head, a hard bloody blow that cracked her skull, and she felt the second blow, and she heard Chocolate's snoring and she heard her own screaming and then, thank God, the tall man was there, and it was Ada who was screaming. Domino never saw Ada again. She never talked to the tall man about what had happened, and the Queen when she heard made everyone, I mean *everyone,* promise never to speak of that night when Domino had lost the management of herself and become a dirty submissive little child. (*Soumis,* you know, that means submissive, said Dan Smooth mildly, looking up at Tyler from his French dictionary. A *fille soumise* is a prostitute under police control.)

That night almost killed Domino. It did something to her soul. It sealed her in a protective prison of rage.

Later the Queen sent for Chocolate and said: Why didn't you help her? Domino's your sister.

Oh, Maj, Chocolate whined, I know I fucked up, but she *stole* that twenty dollars from me. She never—

You givin' me static, you evil little bitch? said the Queen. You go to Domino right now an' say you're sorry.

Please, Maj. I'm afraid of Domino now . . .

Don't think Queenie can't understand you. Don't think you're out of trouble, either. Now, what exactly do you propose to do for Domino? She got *hurt.* She got *scared.* She could have *died.*

I know, Maj. I said I'm sorry.

Go an' say it to her. She suffers. She's got a lot to suffer. She's not like Sunflower was. She does it to *herself.* But this time you did it to her, too. You got to bear your cross now, baby. You know what your cross is gonna be? Domino's always gonna *hate* you.

No, I—

That's right. She'll *hate* you. An' you got to love her back, even though one day she gonna try an' *get* you. Because it's your fault. Okay?

Maj, I—

Did you hear me?

Okay, the whore whispered.

Then go an' tell her. Now.

Chocolate did. And, as always, the Queen was correct. Domino never forgave her. After all, she never forgave anyone. And relations between those two must have been much worse, were it not for the fact that Domino, whose hair was gradually becoming as grey as Tyler's face, could not bear to think of that night when she had been so helpless and so afraid of another human being . . .

| 219 |

Like most aggressors, Chocolate took revenge on the one she'd wronged. Several of the other prostitutes having overheard portions of her conversation with Domino about the metaphysics of feticide, Chocolate afterward claimed to have received the blonde's confession that one of her babies had not been aborted before birth, which was why Domino, inexorably desperate, had strangled it, thrown it on a pile of newspapers and set it on fire. Of course this was a malicious lie. At worst, if Domino had ever engaged in any such acts, it would have been because she had miscarried, and her baby wasn't breathing anyway.

| 220 |

Crossing the yellow-lit shop-fronts of Van Ness to the Tenderloin where leopardskin-assed girls were bending and leaning into pink Chevvys, black Dodges, silver Hyundais, Tyler found that so many were wearing white that night! They wore white, and they wore lipsticked smiles. They chewed gum. They put to shame the unrentable tongues of icecream-licking girls in the bright window of Rory's Twisted Scoop on Fillmore Street, where the most prevalent form of prostitution was called "marriage" or "the relation-ship," and the trick pad might be any one of the ugly houses of Ocean Beach. (This comparison, of course, was never meant to denigrate John and Celia, who often drove up to Saint Helena to look at houses. Those two weren't really "in the market" yet, not having declared themselves to be in the market for each other, but John felt that one could never go too far when researching real estate, especially because the research gave them both such pleasure. In the window of the broker's office he learned about a $750,000 estate on Palmer Drive, a "magificent stone castle" for $1.3 million, a "panorama" for $425,000.) And so Chocolate said to the man in the pickup truck: Darlin', I'm much more expensive than gold. —The man said: That reminds me of a song I heard somewhere. —Well, sing it to someone else! laughed Chocolate. You fat-assed cheapskate sonofabitch! —Cunt! yelled the man, speeding off. —That was a good one, Choc! Domino said a little gloomily, wondering if her nose-hairs were showing. She had just smoked some bad crack, cut probably with speed, and she knew that after the good feeling (which presently tingled from her toes to her teeth) had gone away, she'd feel nauseous and headachey for a good three days—unless of course she smoked more crack. Chocolate started dancing and shoutingly recited a rap poem she'd conceived whose subject was crack. Sapphire laughed and clapped her feeble little hands.

A black-and-white pulled up. The passenger-side cop slowly rolled down his window. The whores waited.

Well, well, said the cop. I smell a little illegal activity going on here.

He smiled and got out of the squad car.

Peddling that AIDS-infected ass of yours again, Domino? he said.

The little Queen strode forward and said: Listen, officer, these girls are my *kids*. They *love* me. If you gotta say something to me, please be nice, 'cause they be my *kids*. How they supposed to feel when you start bad mouthin' me? How I be feelin' when you take one of my kids down?

All right, all right, said the officer soothingly.

Just say what you need to say and be nice, said the Queen. Otherwise, if you're not nice, I won't be nice, and then my tongue would be my sword, and you'd have to take me away.

All right, Maj, the cop said. Just keep 'em in line. I've had complaints, especially about Domino.

Why, what's she done? said the Queen, stroking the girl's long blonde hair.

Ripped off a few people, gaffled 'em I guess you'd call it. Next time I'm taking her in.

He got back into the squad car and slammed the door. The Queen waved.

Never mind, Domino, she said.

Domino said nothing.

All rightie now, said the Queen. Me an' Henry, we want a little time alone now. We're gonna fade right now. Domino, you gonna be okay?

Where you be? said the tall man.

Wonderbar.

Why you want to give a silver nickel to that racist piece of shit Heavyset? You losin' it, Maj.

Imagine that, said the Queen.

Inside the Wonderbar, sweaty Nikolai, who stared at every kissing couple because he himself hadn't kissed anyone in years, was asking: Will you be open on Christmas?

We're always open except when we're closed, Loreena the barmaid replied wearily.

What time will you be open?

Look, Loreena said. You know we're always open unless we aren't. I just said so. And we always have variable hours, so why do you even ask me?

But, Loreena, you just make it so nice for all of us regulars that—

Oh, dry up, asshole.

Nikolai's mouth opened and he turned red and then his mouth closed again.

Tut-tut, Loreena, said the Queen. How you expect to make good money talkin' like that?

Oh, hello, Maj. Hi, Henry. This is the shift from hell. And I can't ever imagine any tips coming from that gentleman, unless he tipped over from being drunk—hah!

She went to the other end of the counter and started washing glasses.

Henry, said the Queen, I'm worried about Domino.

Tyler nodded sadly. —She's a bad one, he said. I'm worried about what she might *do*.

Oh, Henry, how can you say that? She just *want* to be bad.

Maybe that kind's more dangerous.

But who she gonna be dangerous to? She just make me so sad. I want to hold that little girl in my arms, an' I know she want to come to me, but she can't come to me no more.

And you don't know why?

Oh, I know. I know her like I know my own child. That girl fixin' to betray me. She want to betray her own Queen! And she might do it. But I'd love her even if she cut me up. 'Cause she's my little *baby,* the Queen concluded, gazing at Tyler almost challengingly.

If this were a book I wouldn't even read the rest of it, Tyler said. Christ and Judas is what it is.

She want to give herself, but she don't know how. She want to love, but how can she love?

Tyler stared into his glass, hardly listening.

It's up to her, the Queen was saying.

Yeah, he said listlessly, unable to think of anyone except the Queen and himself.

And I'm worried about you, too, Henry, she said.

Africa, I want to prove myself to you, he said.

Her fingers curled tightly around his hand.

He cleared his throat and said: Africa, I'm begging you to let me give myself to you tomorrow. Completely, I mean. I want to sacrifice myself to you. I—I've been so unhappy but also so excited . . .

Hush, said the Queen.

Africa, last night again I didn't sleep more than an hour or two. I don't understand my own feelings. I'm afraid but I want so much to be yours and submit to you and make you love me.

I already love you, she said.

I know that, but . . .

But what?

I just feel desperate. I don't know why. I can't imagine what the future will be. But I'll be your good boy or your pretty little bitch or whatever you want me to be. You can even hurt me if I can just drink your spit or your piss or rub your menstrual blood all over my face or something . . . I need to please you, Africa. Africa, I need to give you a long orgasm and make you proud of me. Please help me.

| 221 |

No such thing as another Irene, huh? said the Queen.

Her armpits had the dry earth smell of catacombs. Her flesh was dark and soft like smoked leather.

| 222 |

Don't ever hurt me, the Queen said. Are you gonna hurt me?

| 223 |

The Queen, a little uncertain, stood, slowly raised her arms, but her elbows were still against her sides in some reflex of shyness or self-protectiveness. She leaned back against the sink. He kissed her cunt for the first time. Now her arms went back, long and dark and shiny against the sink's steel lip. He danced around her and his shoulders swayed. Her little breasts were free now. He was gently slapping them with his left hand as she had told him to do. She stood upright, let go of the sink, and brought her scarred hands toward him with the same sweet uncertainty.

His face slowly sank between her legs, and she placed her hands upon the crown of his head in a benediction.

He heard a crackling sound between her legs.

Right now her face is so beautiful up close, said Smooth through the suddenly open door. Tell you what. Get up close to her.

Tyler froze.

Go on now, Danny boy, the Queen said. Don't be disrespecting us or Queen'll have to get mad. Queen'll get little bit pissed off. Now beat it, Danny.

The doorway contracted.

Never mind, sighed the Queen, her knees drawn up, her swaying dark knees . . .

Her breasts began slowly rising, then bouncing.

| 224 |

All night there were squeakings of busy feet in the hall outside, feet which every now and then would pause outside his door; rising from her and going to the peephole he'd see three or four desperate faces waiting and hoping; but they didn't dare to disturb the Queen; or maybe they were simply too honorable even in their need to do so.

Finally she took his hand and they went out together into the hallway where all the whores were waiting; they raised torches to their Queen's new happiness, clanking shards of metal and glass; then the tall man smashed a cracked mirror on the concrete floor, while they all shouted.

| 225 |

The crazy whore congratulated him with a squeak, saying: And sometimes in our lives we're gonna have our moments, our intimate time, like a ferris wheel up on top of the world.

| 226 |

As soon as his tongue had touched her clitoris, his mouth and throat began to throb with a burning salty reek, her slippery juices etching themselves upon his palate like lye, salty and fishy and rank almost like that very healthy seafood soup which Korean women drink during pregnancy; if he could have convinced himself that it was health instead of death he was drinking, he might have been happier. Later he would swish and swill and gargle mouthwash; he'd put spicy hot sauce on his catfish dinner; but once his tastebuds had cleansed themselves, her taste came back. It was even on his fingers now, although he'd never touched her cunt except with his tongue. When he sucked her, he breathed only through his mouth. His tongue quickly found itself swimming in that rank, salty stuff. Suddenly he realized that he was drinking other men's semen.

| 227 |

Around three in the morning they were awakened by a woman's sobs.

I heard a female voice in your room! Strawberry was shouting.

You did not, he heard the tall man reply.

Are you fucking around on me again, Justin? Strawberry screamed, horrible and raw. Are you? Are you?

There's shit in your voice, said the tall man contemptuously. I don't like your shit, so wipe your fucking verbal ass.

Hysterical sobs were silenced by the tall man's terrifying roar, which made the wall vibrate.

Oh, leave 'em to it, grunted the Queen. They're always goin' on.

| 228 |

But you've gotta deny me to strangers, she whispered, her nipples round and flat right then like the scarab beetles of ancient Nubia.

All right, said Tyler.

I love you, too, baby. Okay, I got to go take care of my girls.

| 229 |

All the whores gossiped about Tyler's visits, which titillated them and allowed them to express natural human malice about their benefactress, but which simultaneously undressed them down to queasiness, because no matter what they might insinuate, they disliked their Queen to be love-greedy, hence imperfect. And yet nobody said anything against Tyler, except perhaps Domino, whose views remained less than clear. He never asked anything of them, and he occasionally made them happy. After he departed, the Queen would sometimes sing strange songs in her cigarette-smoke voice, songs of happiness even though they sounded sad, and to see her other than as sadly, eternally giving frightened them. (Another thing I think is that he's here and he's coming to get her but I don't mean me but something still has to be done, explained the crazy whore. Then she wondered: Is this the kind of thing the Queen does, or is it one of those other things that she's resisted all along?) They did not know what would become of her and themselves. Of course they knew that nothing in life endures much longer than a piece of colored paper, and yet their own continuing ease of circumstances invited them to believe that this night-by-night life they lived beside her would continue, just as in Sacramento the cool days of spring go on and on as if the hot blast of summer will never come. They watched Tyler far more carefully than he knew, and found him consistent in his doings and impulses, which reassured them somewhat. Gradually they gave up worrying whether he might be an undercover cop. The real reason for his visits, *infatuation,* was both simpler and more plausible. They all had johns who idolized them and whom they used, despising those men's love because it was not and could not be founded on any knowledge of them. It was as if the men's own hearts bewitched them, tricking them into faith in a whore's voice or hair or smell. How could the whores bank on that? What if somebody blonder or wetter or slenderer appeared beneath these worshipers' pillows? Therefore the whores wisely discounted and then unwisely condemned the men who loved them thus. And so they ridiculed Tyler, while hoping that their Queen and they themselves might benefit from whatever he might have to give, and he surely had something; every man possessed some treasure, skill or key which could be made use of.

I love you so much it hurts me, Strawberry heard him say (and she promptly repeated this to all the others). Sometimes when I look at you or talk to you I get all choked up—

The Queen smiled at him.

He swallowed and said: Often at night I dream that I'm kissing you, you know, between your legs . . . You're so gentle and kind and good, I . . .

Tilting her head, she slid her middle finger into her mouth and began sucking it, sliding it in and out between her lips.

A lot of the time I—well, I don't even think about you sexually. I just wish I could help you and make you happy, because, uh, I—

C'mere, said the Queen. Sit down or kneel down, I don't care which. Close your eyes.

And she took her glistening brown finger from her mouth and on his forehead traced in saliva the secret Mark of Cain, which is the symbol of infinity.

| 230 |

He could see night by night how her heart opened to him, like one of those tightly wadded crumples of paper which falls into water and slowly swells, loosens, blossoms into a paper rose—even though it's all unreal and underwater . . .

| 231 |

All night he lay in the Queen's arms, sometimes sleeping, dreaming good dreams or bad. The bad dreams did not frighten him. It seemed that for the first time in many years he was able to stare down his own monsters. There they were; maybe someday he could even kill them. He clutched the Queen more tightly, until she groaned in her sleep. Wondering how she would change him, feeling already changed, he rode the long night into dawn. Clothed in calmness, he resolved to seclude himself no longer in fantasies, but to be grateful for all he had, and act usefully and respectfully.

| 232 |

Sparkles of sweat like mica upon a naked back, the Queen's back, swelled into silvery droplets fragrant with cocaine and sadness; he drank them. Sometimes he felt the two of them to be not fully human, reaching, screaming. Legs up in the air, almost stridulated like crickets', heads dipping down to genitals and back again, carried Tyler along, sometimes irresistibly, sometimes merely mechanically, so that whenever he went out from the Queen, covered with her odor, and began to think again, he'd say to himself: Our legs were not me. My legs were not me. My tongue and hands and penis were not me. So where was I? —Then he understood that he had been not only literally but also spiritually inside his Queen. He'd been hers. He'd lost himself to her. He'd been nowhere and everywhere. Walking past a no-name sashimi restaurant on Geary Street, he peered in the window and saw Japanese childrens' skinny faces getting even thinner when they sucked at drinking-straws. This proved not that ingestion created hollowness, but only that one had to hollow oneself out in order to ingest. Legs went up, his or hers he could no longer tell, because sensation crackled through all of them with electric velocity. Were the dark hands or the pale hands his? When he was inside her cunt, there was no cunt anymore, and no cock, the hole being filled, the protuberance hidden; as it said in the Bible, they were one flesh. Her cunt was his. Where did she end? Lost in the cave of enlightenment, he had to grabble his way without that ambiguously useful perceptual eye known as consciousness; later he couldn't remember what had happened to him, what he and the Queen had done; an hour or a night, it felt the same. Her eyes became the smoky barlight and slow headlights as smooth on the wet streets as lubricated condoms. (No condom, no problem! laughed Dan Smooth.) Where does anything end? Beneath a street-whore's come-on of easy love lies a manipulative need, beneath which again waits a real ache for love. One night he was wandering upper Jones Street around Clay or Washington, rainy and almost silent, with only the cables humming and a distant car soughing like wind, and he could not remember who he was. Then he said: I believe in my Queen. I love my Queen. —The next thing he could remember, he was in the Mission district, which shone so brightly on a Saturday noon beneath a pastel sky. Was the Queen wise? How could he doubt it? The Queen of Spades, the black queen, the death-queen, the scary card, the wisest card in the deck, always turned up in whatever hand he got dealt—she loved him; she was his angel—sentimental slush! A piss-soaked bra lay in front of the Thor Hotel. He did the proper thing. He picked it up and carried it next to his heart as an offering to the Queen. He had no nightmares about Irene anymore.

| 233 |

The Queen would not be happy about this, Smooth whispered gleefully.

The video showed rainbow milk.

So that's the Queen doing it with Henry, huh? said Domino with a brutal laugh. Too fuckin' much!

They sat giggling at the strange, lurid bodies, strange movements as of grasses bowing in the wind, the man bowing and praying between the woman's buttocks, leaning forward, leaning back. The couple's arms became bloody amoebic pseudopods, hands flying out from their bodies, then rushing inwards to clutch at flesh once more.

That's how you get a different effect, Smooth explained. You can do all kinds of stuff by that . . .

Domino's mouth opened. She was fascinated by the seething bloody flashes.

Puddles of blue milk oozed together. Blue animals struggled with one another. Crumpled aluminum foil was moving and oozing up and down, the woman's legs limp and sweaty on the man's shoulders.

Now for Domino at least the footage began to grow tiresome, and she yawned and scratched at the long motorcycle scar on her leg while on Smooth's television set two pairs of legs folded and knelt, revealing buttocks, rainbow crystals, flashing blue lines, stains on microscope slides, ice-maps. Two shapes approached each other and pulled away, bowing and weaving like water-plants. Green milk and heartbeats, blue milk running down breasts, holes and fissures swimming like X-ray fishes, all these entities imbued the pair's sexual act with preciousness, just as in the Tenderloin after dusk every passing car momentarily transforms the pavement into a mirror of gold.

We're all animals, you know . . . Smooth was saying thickly.

What do you want me to do now, blow you?

Smooth made a face. —You're too old for me, Domino. You've grown cunt-hairs. Just sit there and entertain yourself.

But you're going to take care of me, right? You're going to pay me something . . . ?

Only if you'll listen to me talk about glistening assholes.

Talk about yourself then, said Domino, bored.

What kind of asshole do *you* have, sweetykins?

Oh, the shitty kind I guess. Don't ya remember?

I have a really good feeling about this now, said Smooth. And there he goes. See how happy he's making her? I almost want to cry. Maybe we should never have done this, Domino, but I always wanted to watch him with Maj. I was their matchmaker, you know. I brought them together. I love Maj. I love Henry . . .

I love money. When will you pay me?

Closeup. *Closeup.* Weird that the shape of those little lips makes such a difference, Smooth said.

Are you a misogynist? said Domino, whose voice sometimes contained the cool jingle of cablecar bells.

A misogynist? Sure.

I thought so. And you attack little kids . . .

Naughty, naughty! chuckled Smooth. I do *not* attack them. They attack me. They . . .

He was remembering how when his next-door neighbor's child was nine she still wanted to ride on his neck, so he lifted her up onto his shoulders and she clamped her hot thighs around him. Later he was carrying her through the grass with her pressed up against him front to front, her arms around his neck, her legs around his waist, and his folded arms against his stomach to make a seat for her. He couldn't resist. He opened his arms and slid one hand under each of her buttocks. Saying nothing, the child clung to him more tightly, so he slid his right hand up under that pretty pink dress and began to rub her vulva, whose lips he could feel much more distinctly than a grown woman's, because there was no hair. The child began to writhe in his arms, gripping him more and more tightly. She uttered strange cries like those of the retarded girl Sapphire. Then she sighed happily and laid her burning head upon his shoulder. That had been the best moment of Dan Smooth's life.

I keep quiet about what I do, usually, he said to the blonde. You understand me, I think. You know that I . . .

It's very isolating, Domino agreed. You know, I was very sexual as a girl and couldn't talk about it.

Now this one is not so obvious, said Smooth. Watch how she moves around. I don't know how to describe how she moves. It's like eating chocolate while admiring stained glass windows in some fabulous church, you know, some . . . Now watch this. Watch how she kind of hops around.

The video continued with one long white leg up, and a strange crow, a diver, an astronaut, a black pelican's beak darting in and out between white cliffs.

In silence, Domino and Dan Smooth listened to the Queen's husky moans: Ohh, oh, oh, *ohhh, oaah,* aoh, uh, oh, *oh,* uh, uh, I'm coming, I'm o-o-o-oh, uh, uh, *uh, uh!*

Wow, said Domino with her crooked little smile. I was never able to make her come like that. When she comes she *comes.*

Yeah, sighed Smooth.

And lookit him coming. There he goes. Hah! There he goes! Lookit his face. That stupid *fuck.* I always hated that guy. Now he's smiling. He thinks he's really something, since he's had our Queen.

Ah, so you're jealous. Me too. Watch his hips now. So much of this, it's hard to know what is esentially *male* and what's conditioned.

That stupid *fuck!* she shouted.

Domino, I want you to shut up now.

| 234 |

Domino's eyesockets were like twin bites taken out of an apple core which had been forgotten on the grimy dresser of some whore hotel and so oxidized dark brown.

People think I always push them away, she said. It's not that I like to push them away. But so many times they just become something untrue. They cheat me once, and then I can't forgive. I never forgive.

And what'd she do to you? said Kitty, applying lipstick.

Oh, nothing. I'm becoming more and more alienated.

Where are you gonna try tonight?

Ellis is too hot. Maybe in front of the Wonderbar. Why, you wanna double date?

No, I got a regular I gotta meet. But seriously now, Dom, you gotta . . .

Don't start bullshitting me.

Aw, why don't you make up? How can you not be friends with the Queen?

I just don't want to.

You trust me?

I trust you, Kittypie.

Then listen to me. I'm tellin' you for your own fuckin' good. Get along with the Queen.

I don't love her anymore.

Ooh, that's cold. You think she don't know? Besides, what could you do to her? Get her raped and gaffled? Shit, Domino, she's got the power.

Black Pam stuck her head in and said: Kitty, don't talk to her, don't talk to her; she be *bad.*

Now why is that? laughed Kitty.

She'll rob you.

Ooh. How'll she do that?

I don't know, said Pam.

I was fixin' to learn, said Kitty, and Domino laughed so hard she almost puked.

What—how to rob people? said stupid Pam.

That's right, Domino cut in. Now get out of here, bitch, and don't snitch or else I'll cut your little nigger pussy out.

Pam squeaked, and ran away.

Don't worry, said Kitty. I'll be watchin' her.

Stupid little fraidy-cat *bitch,* laughed Domino.

Remember what I said, whispered Kitty. Queen's got the power.

| 235 |

By some bit of synchronicity I once met up with the fellow who had stolen three hundred and sixty dollars from me two weeks before. He was so charming that for an instant I couldn't believe in his indisputable guilt. He'd had his film stolen since. —I'm so glad

I met you, he said. You'll help me! —This he said with the absent-mindedness of the truly ruthless.

Yes, very nice to see you again, I said politely. He shook himself, beginning to realize that I just might be cool toward his problems.

Domino's ego was a similarly expensive jewel. Although she well understood the expedient consequences of her actions, she remained so precious to herself that no efforts of others on her behalf, voluntary, coaxed, or coerced, could ever strike her as excessive. In every crisis, Domino assumed that aid would arrive. Her attitude was complicated by an increasingly justified mistrust of the aid-givers. The man who robbed me could still believe that he needed but to exhibit his difficulties for me to solve them for him, no questions asked. But Domino was experientially speaking several million years old. She'd reached her millionth birthday when she was a fifteen-year-old runaway coughing, blowing her nose and leaning up against the wall of the San Bernardino bus station (her corn-yellow hair was richer back then). She shivered and her thighs trembled in the pink tights. What to do? A security guard with a T-shaped night stick came to move her on. But Domino had nowhere to go. She was stupid enough to plead. The man took her into the women's toilet and made her blow him. That bought her an ass-pinch and an hour of peace. Then his shift ended, and her bus of salvation hadn't come, and the next guard called the police. What was there to learn from this?

Domino believed as strongly as ever in her right to freedom, cash, drugs and happiness. But she had long since been forced to acknowledge the entirely mistaken attitude of the withholders and nay-sayers who swarmed about. What to do then? What indeed, but lie, trick, cajole, deceive, compel, intimidate . . .

She was a good person exactly as often as she could afford to be. What she thought of as standing up for herself might sometimes appear to others as bullying; for her it represented the exercise of a sacred moral principle. As for friendliness, she showed her goodwill whenever she could. By keeping track of all the favors she did, she not only honed their edges, so to speak, into glittering utility—for what favor, once forgotten, gets returned? —but also verified her own goodness. And when necessity struck, as it so often did, then she laid friendship aside, and proceeded by the most direct route to manage whatever needed to be managed. If someone took offense, that was unfortunate, but to Domino's way of thinking, almost everyone was either a declared or an undeclared enemy anyhow. Domino thus was one of the most reasonable women in the world. Her moral calculus was honest, practical and consistent.

| 236 |

And now at last the time had come for Domino to appear in superior court, face to face (as she thought) with her pasty-faced ex-regular out of whose glove compartment the pistol had fallen and under whose passenger seat the cops had found that baggie of methamphetamine. —Gun up, Dom, said the Queen. I'll be prayin' over you. You want me to be in court? Or can I send Henry? —Oh, what the fuck's the difference? said the blonde. If you even have to ask, that means you don't want to be there for me . . . —C'mere, whispered the sad Queen, but Domino would not. —All rightie, then, Henry and I will both come. Beatrice can watch over Sapphire . . .

Just to make her feel good, the Queen said in Tyler's ear, and he nodded. A Mr. Munif had requested his professional services for an infidelity case, but it would have conflicted with Domino's court date, so he turned the job down.

The public defender had warned the blonde that her exposure was four years of potential jail time. He tried to explain how all the counts added up but she didn't even bother to listen. Brisk and enterprising, she only wanted to know what she could do now. She could have pled guilty and gotten probation except that she had already violated probation and parole and everything else long since.

You haven't been showing up, have you? the public defender said.

No, not everytime, Domino replied wearily.

That's too bad, Ms. Fine. You know what MTR means?

No.

It means motion to revoke. They want to MTR your probation. It's a real shame. You know, Ms. Fine, if you're smokin' crack and you test dirty, they don't really give a shit as long as you show up for probation. Ms. Fine—

What?

Mind if I call you Sylvia?

I don't give a fuck.

Look, Sylvia, parole is a totally different matter. With parole, you screw up, you go straight to the pen.

Cut to the chase, pal. I hate this.

I—

I hate it, I hate it, I *hate* it!

You can do up to four violations of probation, so you can do four times as much prison time as in your original sentence, so—

Look, said Domino. Spare me all the motherfuckin' math. Just tell me what I'm looking at.

Well, as I said, your exposure is four years, but we still might be able to suspend your sentence if we can get the guy who was with you in the car to cop a guilty plea to drug and weapons possession, so if you . . .

Domino stopped listening.

First, everyone who was anyone had to sit through one of those assembly line arraignments of women in bright orange jumpsuits on which was stencilled SAN FRANCISCO CO PRISONER. They sat with their backs to the spectators. Tyler scanned the backs of their heads, and found a brunette head, two blackhaired heads, a blonde, head and a greyish-blonde head on a long stately neck. The greyish-blonde might have been Domino. But Domino was beside him. Shall we be more specific? Because the first row of seats on each side of the courtroom had been blocked off with yellow tape which read POLICE LINE DO NOT CROSS, the two well-wishers sat in the second row with the Queen in the corner holding Tyler's hand, her head against the wall. Domino sat on his right, swallowing over and over, squeezing his hand.

You doing okay? Tyler whispered into her ear.

Don't touch me, said the blonde.

If that door doesn't close and lock, the bailiff was saying, just take 'em to a different office.

Then the voice of justice cried: *Remain seated. Come to order. Department Twenty-Two is now in session.*

In terror, Domino squeezed his hand.

On the stage of justice where all the dramatic actors played their parts, as conspicuous as the yellow teeth amidst a Haight Street tramps' white stubble, the judge sat down, and a longhaired young lady, a whisperer, bent over flirting with a lawyer while a walkie-talkie crackled. Handcuff-rings swung in the small of a bailiff's back.

Your honor, it strikes me that on count two there's a procedural error, the public defender said.

Tyler barely listened. A moment later the public defender was saying: Your honor, I believe that there are waivers of appearance on all three defendants.

Three defendants! Tyler thought. But there were half a dozen women there. Then he realized that justice was not always slow anymore, that several mini-trials were in progress.

Ms. Kaye, the judge was saying, you ask that your conviction be set aside. But you haven't been paying restitution.

I been paying in monthly installments, the black prisoner said.

Well, when you want a favor done by the court, you'd better pay what you owe. Motion denied without prejudice.

Yeah, gimme a call, someone's lawyer was whispering.

The Queen kept shaking her head. Her lips moved silently.

Looks like you've got a diversionary felony, misdemeanor loitering, the judge was saying to the next defendant. Tyler held the Queen's hand.

Finally it came Domino's turn. The voice of justice said: On the sentencing calendar, line thirty-seven is Sylvia Fine.

Clearing her throat, the blonde rose and approached her punishment. Before, no one knew her from a spectator. Now she was *the accused.*

Can you see her? Tyler whispered, and the Queen nodded dully.

Ms. Fine, said the judge, you're charged with one count of resisting arrest, one count of prostitution, one count of possessing an illegal weapon, and one count of possessing a controlled substance. However, there's now been a conviction on the illegal weapon and on the drug charges, so those have been dropped. Do you have the money to appoint your own attorney?

No, said Domino angrily.

Sylvia Fine. Is that your real name?

Yes.

I see you have a pretty long list of priors. Two felony assault convictions among others. Ms. Fine, since you have two strikes against you, your next petty theft may be worth life in prison. Better knock it off.

Domino was silent.

Ms. Fine, how do you plead to all these charges?

Not guilty, your honor. I never resisted arrest.

We're down to one count of prostitution and one count of resisting arrest. If you wish to plead guilty, the court will recommend the work project for thirty days. Otherwise, you're looking at a year in jail. Do you wish to plead guilty?

Yes.

How do you plead, Ms. Fine?

Not guilty, said Domino with a twisted smile.

I thought you wanted to plead guilty.

Okay, whatever. Guilty.

I'll go ahead and sentence you. Probation denied. You're sentenced to the work project.

Thank you, said the girl listlessly.

My heart breaks for that child, the Queen said into Tyler's ear.

Next case. Ms. Browne. Loitering with intent to commit prostitution, on top of the previous charges. They're recommending a year for this and refiling as a felony. You want to plead guilty now to avoid refiling?

Yes, I would, the brunette head was saying.

Scandalous, how they coach them to implicate themselves! whispered the Queen indignantly. But Tyler's head ached; he scarcely understood any of it. And as for Domino, to her the judge's words were like steam from the sewers at Bush and Jones . . .

| 237 |

Thirty days later, the blonde came home. Nothing could make much of an impression anymore upon her soul's hardstamped shell except perhaps the forces of petty and determined abrasion. On the thirty-first day, already bored and crack-hungry, she went out to Ellis Street to make money and in a lucky place where the waffle-pattern of windows was reflected in the hood of a shiny red car she was immediately solicited by a Dominican who raped her. The tall man had memorized the Dominican's license plate number. When the blonde, half dead, told the Queen what had happened, the Queen went to the tall man, who went to Tyler, who ran a reverse trace on his computer, using ROYAL INFORMATION SYSTEMS, change from insecure login to secure login, the icons crawling on his bright green screen until he'd obtained a name and address for the Dominican, together with a physical description which matched Domino's recollections. —No problem, Tyler said. Happy to help.

The Dominican had a daughter who was just now completing her first year of study at law school in Baltimore. He fully believed and expected that she would graduate at the top of her class. He expected such greatness of her that she had gone to Baltimore to get away from him. It was her image which he now saw in the mirror. Years later, long after his daughter had dropped out of law school to give birth to her illegitimate child, the Dominican told me this story. He was my taxi driver. He said that the spirit of his daughter in the mirror kept her hair pulled back by pink ribbon. She was smiling at him, telling him not to worry. But when he'd told his daughter about it that day on the telephone, she'd laughed incredulously. When the tall man and the other gangster saw him gazing open-mouthed into the mirror, they whirled around, but could see nothing. Then the tall man told the Dominican to stand up and take it. The Dominican rose, attempting to prepare himself. He told me that he was proud that he neither wept nor begged.

The other man went to the window. —Somebody on the sidewalk, he said.

All right, the tall man said to the Dominican. Down on your belly. Greasy Spic hands behind your head. Close your eyes. I said close your eyes.

The Dominican closed his eyes.

Now say a prayer to Jesus. Go ahead, man.

The Dominican stuttered, but could not speak.

Now count real slowly to twenty, said the tall man. Then stand up.

The Dominican, waiting for the bullet or the knife, counted as slowly as he dared. When he'd uttered the ominous number twenty, he was still alive. Keeping his eyes tightly shut, he rose to his knees. Nothing. Unable to bear it anymore, he stood up, looked behind him, and found the door open and the two killers gone.

After paying the other gangster, the Queen and the tall man gave everything else to Domino: the Dominican's Rolex watch, his diamond wedding ring (the tall man had broken the man's finger getting it off), his wallet with six hundred dollars in cash, thirteen hundred dollars cash which the Dominican had hidden in the freezer (the tall man had broken the Dominican's nose in the process of learning where *that* was), and his station wagon with the keys. Domino might have made a couple hundred dollars more had she sold the car to a certain fence she knew, but it pleased her far better to drive it out to Hunters Point and smash the windshield, slash the tires, sledgehammer the engine, pour gasoline all over the upholstery and torch it.

Stupid bitch, sighed Justin, but she hugged him tight and stuck her tongue in his mouth.

I asked the Dominican whether the Queen's retribution had altered him, and he said: Well, those two niggers, they were some evil characters. They taught me to fear God. After I got over my resentment, I realized that I had done wrong. My face was all split up, and my finger is still crooked, as you see. Perhaps my nose is also not the same as it was when I was born; what do you think? You know, I was living the wrong kind of life at that time. I was in the habit of thinking that women were meat. And then, to find out that this Queen of the Whores wasn't just a legend, but she really existed and had the organization to track me down and punish me for what I had done, well, it made me realize that there are women with balls.

Skeptical of his conversion, I inquired whether he still went to prostitutes, and, if so, whether he ever raped them. His face grew ugly then, and he told me to mind my own business.

| 238 |

Strawberry, Domino and Beatrice stood in the doorway of the bar smoking. Later, considerably after their days and nights together had ended, Domino would always remember a gleam of light on a heap of garbage bags, and Strawberry leaning up against the wall of the Wonderbar with a long, long cigarette in her hand, her arm around one of the regulars' necks as she tried to wheedle five dollars out of him. She remembered Strawberry as being continually with men, touching men, holding men's hands as if she liked it—no wonder Justin smacked her around! Strawberry had the marijuana giggles. A police car drove by and Strawberry ran inside in a panic, discovering Tyler, who, flush-faced, was gripping a beer in both hands like a praying mantis, leaning on the bar as he gazed at the Queen with a foolish smile. The Queen laughed *hah*-haaw! —When Strawberry came out, Beatrice was gone on a date (having gigglingly whispered in the blonde's ear: That's a good idea to hide it in my shoe. You gave me a good idea!) and Domino was speaking with the Queen about a private thing as Strawberry should have comprehended but could not because she was still paranoid, so she kept asking about the police car, worrying that it might not be entirely gone in search of other victims, until Domino finally told her to shut up. Strawberry was hurt. She had wanted to tell Domino: Look! Maj's got this skimpy little lace top on, like she's planning to go to work tonight. You think she . . . ? Instead, there was nothing to do but turn her back to Domino and the Queen. The Queen sighed. When Domino had completed her sad worrying and confessing, she went up to slip her arm around Strawberry's neck, but was angrily thrown off, and just then one of the girl's regulars, who had not been seen for a long time, rolled up almost silently in his black pickup truck, and Strawberry, screeching with excitement, flew across the sidewalk and into the opening passenger door of the already moving vehicle which carried her off.

Domino shook her head wryly.

That girl got a *thin, thin* skin, said the Queen.

Domino didn't say anything for a long time. Then, holding the Queen around the waist, she said quietly: Look at that black night sky. It's going to rain again. I think it's going to rain all night.

You don't want to go out, the Queen said.

I never did.

Nobody made you, honey. Queen's not gonna tell you no lies. Girl, you're free. You don't have to do *nothin.'*

Some nights I have a bad feeling, Domino said.

What's your fear, darlin'? C'mere. Come tell me.

Well, you remember, uh, that time I got raped?

The first time or the second time?

The first time. The second time wasn't so bad. At least we punished that Spic and cashed in, thanks to you and Justin. At least he didn't stick a gun up my ass . . .

So that's your fear. Somebody's gonna hurt you bad, maybe fuck you up and put you in the ground . . .

That's right. And somehow I thought that once you came to us, Maj, then we'd all be saved. Don't think I'm not grateful, but . . . Like everything would just work out on its own, and—

You can have all that if you want, said the Queen. You been there, Domino. You know what they call that place?

Crack heaven! laughed the blonde so sadly.

No. Don't even joke about it. *Jail.* Jail's the name of that place . . .

But it isn't right. I'm tired of these shitty lousy streets. And all the men whose cocks I have to suck on . . .

Then don't suck, the Queen said. Nobody can make you do what you don't want to do. Even that man stuck his pistol up your ass, you could have said no. You could have died and not been tamed.

That's bullshit.

Domino, I tell you this. *Listen* to me, Domino. Domino, you gonna outlive me. I know it. You got nothin' to fear. Domino, someday you gonna be Queen after me. And I swear to you, nobody ever gonna rape you again. I know that. You believe?

I—

You believe me, honey, or you don't believe?

I believe . . .

Good. Then go out there and make us all some fresh money. Or do you want me to get that other man who hurt you? You know I can find him. I found the Dominican, didn't I? I mean, *Henry* and I found him. But I know *you* so well, honey. Just gonna make you angrier and angrier to see him. Well, maybe he's dead. Hold my hand.

I—

Close your eyes and hold my hand. That's a good girl. Now what do you see? You see his face?

It's so dark, Maj . . .

All rightie, now. I got a glimpse of him. Kind of a glimpse, anyways. Man got those droopy eyes and the long moustache, I seen that man. Squeeze my hand.

I *do not* want to see that bastard.

You see, Domino? You tellin' me now yourself you don't wanna see that guy. How can I please you? How can I help you? Now, sweetie, you gotta put up or shut up. Squeeze my hand.

No—

Last time I'm gonna ask you. Squeeze my hand. Okay. Good. Somethin's glowin' just like that wool cap on top of Justin's head. Now we're past that. And here's those seein'-eye demons. Now we're in the darkness. His name is Ray. He's doin' time up in Pelican Bay. I can see him up there. Can you see him?

Domino pulled her hand away. —Oh, this is all bullshit! she shouted, and ran away crying.

· BOOK XV ·

Vigs

•

And the Lord said to Joshua, "Do not fear or be dismayed; take all the fighting men with you and arise, go up to Ai; see, I have given into your hand the king of Ai, and his people, his city, and his land; and you shall do to Ai and its king as you did to Jericho and its king . . ."

Joshua 8.1–2

•

As autumn came on, the police sweeps of Capp Street almost ceased, but in the Tenderloin everyone frenziedly told and retold rumors, of which the most extreme and exaggerated were forwarded to the Queen's parking garage, of approaching calamities for which no remedy existed except patience. Of course this ill wind increased in force only gradually, like Beatrice, who sucked men off as slowly as her Papa used to fill his wheelbarrow with dirt and stones. On Irene's birthday (August ninth) it was scarcely a fetid breeze. But by late September it could not be denied. It was up to the Queen to interpret the keening and take steps to protect her family. As for the queenless others, they lay low, mumbling evil prophecies from the innermost wrinkles of their gaunt souls. The great street organism braced itself, expecting some nervous shock. (Imagine, if you will, some suspicious streetwalker holding herself rigid in the headlights of oncoming cars, her hands twisted nervously behind her back as if they concealed frightening weapons.) Meanwhile there was a minor construction boom of new multinational hotels and upscale restaurants, the kind that John and Celia liked; these establishments chipped away at the Tenderloin, like roads, camps and waystations penetrating into virgin forest. The inevitable result, since street life, like any other kind, determinedly struggled to survive, was that as certain blocks were "cleansed" to resemble the wide, skylit stalls of the multitiered parking garage at Saveco, the remainder became more concentrated, thick and rank and wiry like underbrush now teeming with animals which have fled an oncoming forest fire. When the Queen was questioned about the meaning of this strange feeling which made the whores' short hairs prickle on their necks, she replied only to wait and see. She continued to expand her operation, as if she could go on supplying protection to everybody forever, maybe because she believed it or maybe because it was too late for her to stop or maybe because she thought it the upright thing to do, like the moral calculus of a man who cannot swim but dives into deep water in hopes of saving a drowning child. And so, in this whimsical world of ours where pickled intestinal worms may resemble high-quality ginseng roots, the Chinese prostitute Yellow Bird, whom careerism required to drink the colored water which her customers believed to be alcohol, decided to leave the bar in North Beach where she had sipped away at her hopes for months now, because she'd heard of the Queen. —China was better under Chairman Mao, she told the tall man. In that time, no money-money-money. Not do bad thing for money so cruel to the customer. My madam she cursing and screaming if I drink too slow. —Indifferent to Mao's merits, the tall man led her past a dusty window with a red grating whose bars and squares resembled I Ching ideograms, then up tall narrow grey stairs ascending toward a single immensely powerful light. That light became her Queen. Her heart became as quiet as Chinatown on a rainy midnight.

My name it mean like Yellow Bird, she was explaining to Beatrice over her glass of colored water, while the tall man stood just beyond the doorway swivelling his head from side to side. I wanna be free like other yellow birds but my life is no good.

A Chinese was yelling.

What's he saying?

He say some bargain with bartender. He want make qvarrer. Every night I see him. Sometimes he go with two girls. —Very ugly, she added venomously.

Beatrice was sorry for her. She wanted to bring this new girl to the Queen.

Today I go to my friend's place to get some money, Yellow Bird said. I keep some money in her place for my mother. Just in Chinatown I go *vin*-dow shopping.

A few days later Beatrice saw Yellow Bird on the street and Yellow Bird said: Because I qvarrer wiv the boss. I buy a new suit, and she say new suit not from me, but from customer. I say no, and she swear at me. Then I say I don't want to work here anymore. Then she want to give me another chance, and she say she love me, but I say *no*. Bar is no good for me. Now I try to find another job.

Just remember one thing, the tall man said. Nobody gonna force you.

I know somebody who wants to meet you, said Beatrice in the same breath.

The Queen agreed to meet her. Yellow Bird bowed four times. —All rightie, sighed the Queen. Now I'm going to spit in your mouth. I want you to . . .

But she was noticeably distracted now by her friendship with Tyler. A few of the whores had begun to question her fitness to rule, but then, they always did and always would.

Right now I would say the Queen is my best friend, but they change, Lily explained. Strawberry used to be my best friend but that was before I met the Queen. Domino used to be my best friend. Shit, she started stealing my tricks and then she broke my arm.

And where did you meet *her?* asked the trick. (He was really a vig. Later he'd make a report.)

From this guy in the salmon-packing plant.

But when the vig asked Domino where she'd met Lily, the blonde curtly replied: We met in jail. Some cop caught me kicking a crack pipe in a doorway . . .

Is she your best friend?

Who the *fuck* do you think you're asking?

Needless to say, Domino was the most outspoken, but even she never said publicly that she had become unfriends with the Queen. Outwardly she and the Queen continued to be on the same loving terms as before. And inwardly, too, perhaps, little had changed.

Dan Smooth, who always heard everything first, said that the city was going to tear down all the crack hotels on Mission Street—surely an exaggeration. Dan Smooth said that vigs would get the Queen someday. Dan Smooth, one of whose eyebrows was higher than the other, sweated gloom and doom like some Mexicali bar from whose dark edges women flowed, the ceiling ominously tinseled like a rattlesnake's scales. Bad stories flowed now even from the lips of the Wonderbar regulars with their crutches and moustaches and their caps pulled low over their eyes. Surely it couldn't have been true about the hotels, though; nothing was true that Saturday night on O'Farrell and Jones, that night comprised of black women in translucent pastel skins which were neither bikinis nor raincoats; they shimmered like jellyfish in a dark sea.

Well, so what's your story? they said. You want some company or not?

Well, you're just so beautiful, I don't know which to choose.

Don't worry, Strawberry said, not seeing the man's ferocious sarcasm about to un-sheath itself and attack her, it's our business, her and me. You won't hurt my feelings if you don't pick me.

So you're friends then, the man said.

Yeah, friends, the two women said in agreement.

If you don't pick me, I'd rather have your money go to her than some stranger, Straw-berry explained.

So can you buy me a pack of cigarettes? Domino said.

Sure, sweetheart. Here's a dollar.

It's more like three dollars. You're living in the dark ages.

Grimacing, the man reached into his shirt pocket and withdrew a five. —Can you give me change for that? he said.

You bet, said Domino, who considered herself a class act.

You ever done any time?

What kind of a question is that?

I was just wondering.

Wondering what?

What's jail like? the trick asked brightly.

I just got out of jail. I don't want to talk about it.

I only wondered . . .

Look, buster, said Domino. I'm not an animal in a zoo. You want a date or not?

You look expensive.

Well, you just go to your little ATM and take out a hundred dollars, Domino said. Your wife will never miss it.

My wife keeps me on an allowance, he said. He exuded playfully self-satisfied indisci-pline, in just the same way as when barrel-shaped Brady went into a restaurant deter-mined to be good and order the salad but when he opened his lips he heard emerge strict orders for pork chops and deep-fried calamari. —Can I get in touch with you again? he asked the two prostitutes.

I'm sorry but you can't, said Strawberry.

Can I get in touch with the Queen? the trick said.

With who, dear?

With your Queen. You know. That little black lady . . .

No, I don't know what you're talking about, Strawberry said. You a cop?

I don't know what the fuck this cocksucker is up to, said Domino, but he obviously mistakes us for somebody else.

The man said: Hey, if I just give you fifty in hard cash . . .

Honey, said Domino, that just ain't gonna cut it. Now, either you walk or my home-girl and I are gonna walk. And my feet are tired. So won't you please, please, please go away?

The man pulled out twenty and said: Then can I just get some head?

Now he's acting weird, said Strawberry.

Head costs fifty from me, said Domino. I'm a self-respecting girl. I don't go down on anybody for less than fifty dollars.

I told you I have fifty dollars, the man said happily. Let's go.

Don't go, said Strawberry. I got a bad feeling.

Why don't you keep an eye on us and I'll share with you later, said Domino.

How much?

I'll give you a piece.

Oh, all right, sighed Strawberry.

The three of them set out, trisecting the Tenderloin night where everything was yellow against granite, and Strawberry dully realized that there were more and more Vietnamese establishments and more murals on the walls than there used to be. Glowing beads of sensation went round and round inside her skull like fireflies. Passing the 441 Club through whose open door the jukebox sang *My, my, MY Delilah,* Strawberry gazed in, remembering when it had been a black bar; now it was a Korean bar, shiny-surfaced, with red paper lamps which hung down like breasts. These changes vaguely upset Strawberry. She did not know what the world wanted of her. It was so much effort to learn how things were that she preferred no changes. The other girls kept saying that something bad would happen soon, and Strawberry felt anxious, waiting for portents. Down at Turk Street where the double rows of lights faded they went into the alley which the blonde preferred, and Strawberry kept her back turned to the orally copulating pair, trying simultaneously to block them from view. She heard Domino smacking her lips, and then the man grunted, and Domino coughed and spat.

She turned around. The man was zipping up his pants, leaning rapturously on the top of Domino's head. Domino was retching.

How about a tip for me, mister? said Strawberry. I kept you from bein' hassled . . .

I didn't ask you to guard me, the man said. I bet you get off on listening. I know how you whores are.

Oh, really? said Domino brightly, rising to her feet. How do you know that?

The man sniggered and started to walk away.

I'm looking for your Queen, he said. And when I find her, I'm going to beat her ass.

Think he's a vig? said Strawberry when he was out of sight.

I dunno, said Domino. Probably just an idiot.

Well, I think we should tell Maj.

Go ahead. See what I care, the blonde said wearily.

And you said you was gonna cut me in . . .

I'll save you some rock, okay?

Please, Domino, I need to get well.

Oh, all right. Here's ten dollars. But you have to pay the Queen's cut out of that.

But Queen's cut is ten dollars!

Oh, get lost, said Domino. Can't you see I'm feeling blue? I'm so tired.

| 240 |

Are you ready, honey? the Queen whispered. Is it okay if I make you a little uncomfortable for a while?

Yes, said Tyler, swallowing.

Sitting astride him, she eyed him glowingly, a tender smile on her lips. His penis leaped up.

She bent and kissed his cheek. Then she straightened, wiggled smilingly on top of him like a little girl settling herself bareback on a trusted and docile family horse, and after that the smile slowly cooled upon her mouth until she was gazing at him in an appraisal which objectified and instrumentalized him for her purposes.

She slapped his cheek.

He blinked.

She slapped his face hard enough to make both his ears ring.

He swallowed.

Don't resist me, she said in a hard voice, striking him across the face again and again.

His heart thrilled.

Turn over, she said.

He turned over, and she touched his buttock with something cool and thin and gentle, and then the cool thin gentle thing whizzed across the backs of his naked thighs, causing him instantaneous pain which then increased for almost five seconds before it began to fade.

The cane came down again and again. She was careful; she never gave him a stroke before the previous stroke ceased to hurt. She was making it easy on him this time.

She welted his thighs, buttocks and shoulders, then turned him over again and whipped him on the front sides of his thighs. He could see the long, straight, red and white welts rise up where she touched him.

She took his nipple between her teeth and slowly bit until the hot, cold, steely pain made him cry out for the first time.

Ahh, said the Queen, smiling.

Put your hands behind your head, she said. Don't move. You're not allowed to move at all.

She seated herself on his penis and took him, grunting, her face hardening and straining like a man's. As commanded, he didn't move a muscle. No one had ever possessed him like that before. Sweet sweat exploded from her and fell upon his chest. His wrists ached behind his head. He longed to begin thrusting inside her. He longed to crown her with something. He longed to place flowers in her hands, to give her pennies, dollars, diamonds, boulders of pure crack cocaine. Her mouth was wide open now and she was throttling him and spitting in his face. —Fuck me now, she growled thickly. That's a good boy. Now you can come. Come for Mama. Oh. Oh. You're Mama's *good* little boy.

After he came, shouting and groaning while she pressed down on him with all her strength, she kissed him deeply and they lay together, glued by sweat, panting. She took his face in her hands and whispered: Are you okay?

He said: I want you to give me anguish.

Ohh, she said happily, embracing him. Oh, you're the one.

| 241 |

You know I love you or you don't know?

I know, he whispered.

| 242 |

He fell asleep in her arms and woke ashamed. Actually his dream had been this: Irene had sat on his face, grinding her pelvic bones hurtfully against his skull, then pissed long and loud into his opened mouth; he was suffocating; he swallowed her reeking, foaming stream; she shifted and squirmed and mashed herself down over his nose—he couldn't breathe! He was dying! He struggled but she bore down harder; he had a tremendous erection; everything was going red.

Don't feel down, baby, said the Queen. I know everything. Lot of men like that. And you never got a taste from her?

Once, he blurted out, but she didn't know. I was . . . —and he remembered Irene and John's laundry basket, and what in his desperation he had found there: the sour smell of life, the sour smell of death.

He'd dreamed the very same dream before, when Irene was alive, and he'd said to her only: I dreamed about you. That's what I wanted to tell you.

Irene said nothing.

I know you don't love me the way I love you . . . he muttered.

His face flushed. He didn't remember the rest. But the Queen knew it all.

Lie still now, she said, clambering onto his face. He opened his mouth obediently. She gripped his head firmly between her thighs and began to make water in his mouth, more and more and more until he couldn't swallow anymore; he was retching, and her urine was coming out his nostrils. It felt as though her piss had become his tears. Desperate and confused to the very bottom of his soul, he struggled among square tomblike openings far-spaced in the yellow walls of death, wanting to escape back into pure numb death but the Queen would not let him. It hurt so much! Tear-streams gushed like pale urine from his eyes. He was weeping for Irene and gagging on his own grief; grief was trickling out of his nose; but the grief was really the Queen's painful water which she was giving him so that he wouldn't feel so all alone. Her piss was in his lungs now and he was coughing and vomiting but she wouldn't let go until her bladder had given its last drop. Then she lifted herself off him and sat on the soaking sheet, laying his head on her lap. His chest ached. She stroked his hair while he vomited. —That's a good boy, she whispered. Queen's good little boy. Never be ashamed, Henry. Irene's crying for you, too. Never mind. Never mind. Now you've cried my tears, and it hurt you. Never mind, baby. Henry, you're my baby. Can you breathe now? Try to breathe. You're gonna feel better now, 'cause you cried so hard and it hurt you. You got punished, and now it's all right, so never mind. Queen knows everything about you, Queen adores you, Queen's good little boy . . .

And, exhausted as he was, he realized that his sadness had been eased. He'd come out from a tunnel into the wide, stinking, sunlit world.

| 243 |

Hurt me, the Queen whispered.

| 244 |

He hardly slept all night, and in the morning felt headachey and nauseous. He wanted to vomit up the Queen's urine, but he also longed to retain it. A double cappuccino picked him up slightly, but almost made him puke, so he drove to Muddy Waters with its bad paintings and ordered a double espresso with the brownish-yellow foam in the little cup, and some exciting crazy music that he'd never heard before was playing, causing him to grin and laugh. He was happy. He drank coffee until suddenly his fatigue shattered like windowglass and he was in the world of excitement and joy.

I *will* pay you back today, the snowy-bearded panhandler said. I live right here in the neighborhood.

Don't worry about it, said Tyler.

I *will* pay you back when I see you again.

Okay. And if you don't, why, don't worry about it.

Tyler wanted to give away everything he had. He was so proud, because his Queen loved him. He felt as if he had been cured of an incurable wound. For Canaanites, such moments are the most treacherous.

| 245 |

So many girls in the rain like black rubber butterflies! It was Friday night in the Tenderloin, and Justin leaned up against a grating, glaring. —Gun up! said the Queen. Keep yourselves sharp, now. —Long black and blonde hair waterfalls illuminated the hearts of heat-seeking men; ivory legs glistened in the rain. (*It's those legs that just jump out!* Brady always used to say. —*Wet, bare legs.* But Domino, sideways against the wall, bent herself into a backward letter C, her breasts and belly jutting out.) There was Beatrice, leaning up against her private piece of streetwall with one knee up and the sole of her foot planted firmly against that wall as if she were a competition swimmer getting ready for the referee's signal to push herself into the water of her life, racing to be the first to reach that same sad finish line which Sunflower and Irene had already crossed. Heat-seekers auto-crawled down from the heights of Jones Street, looking out across a plain of lights toward the horizon and then descending with the regularity of cable cars, lizard-silver in their swift inclinations. Heat-seekers emerged from the financial district, their wallets full of cash. Heat-seekers came from Chinatown. They sought wordlessly or garrulously, but they all sought without knowing why, each of them an animal, a body like some monstrous imbecile-prostitute at Feminine Circus, some speechless being deep red and swollen like a pregnant sow.

Take Sapphire to the little girls' room, would you, Bea? said the Queen. Sapphire's got to pee.

Let's go, angel; doan be scared, said Beatrice, taking the retarded girl's hand. Sapphire went with her trustingly to the alley.

A Ford Escort pulled up for Chocolate. The man inside said: How do you stay so beautiful?

I just keep prayin' it up, the black woman chuckled, leaping in.

All right, muttered the tall man. I got that sonofabitch's license plate number in my head.

A black-in-white rolled by, and the Queen waved at the open passenger window and said: How you all doin', officers?

Shaking their heads in disgust, the cops rolled on.

Justin, go on by the parking garage and get our messages, please, said the Queen.

Just lemme . . .

Do as you're told, Justin.

Swearing, the tall man strode off. He came back and said: Vigs. That's all they talk about now. Rumors of vigs and more vigs.

All rightie. We got enough trouble night by night. Thank you, Justin.

Maj, I got a bad feeling about these vigs.

Okay. We'll talk about it later. In private.

You gonna let me go now?

Where to? This here's the busy time.

Gonna make a run. Gonna score a big rock of white girl.

Who wants white girl? laughed the Queen, and all the prostitutes eagerly raised their hands, like schoolchildren who knew the answer to the most important question of all.

I'm sick of that shitty yellow rock you've been bringing back, Domino said. We can hardly get high off that stuff.

Know what we call that kinda crack? laughed the tall man. Call it *Oriental girl.*

Are you prejudiced? What the fuck do I have to be around prejudiced people for?

Chill out, Dom, said the Queen.

Don't you tell me to chill out! I don't like it when you pay forty dollars for a twenty dollar feeling. I never would have copped from that connection again.

Oh, lordy, said the Queen.

Chocolate returned from her trip around the block. She gave the Queen five for the general fund, and the tall man ten for crystal meth. Now she was whispering into the Queen's ear, relating how a free agent named Feather had passed on a complaint about the management of the Mehta Hotel on Mission Street, whose managers insulted both the hookers and the tricks they brought. —Shit, that's fucked up, Chocolate commiserated. Somebody I know is gonna hear about that. Why the *fuck* they gotta do that? Specially when it's us girls that be bringin' 'em in their money. 'Less that's how they get down, she chuckled. —All rightie, sighed the Queen. I'll look into it.

Another black-and-white came. The Queen waved; the cops waved back. When Beatrice waved, too, the tall man snarled: Don't suck up to the bulls. —Beatrice, scared and silent, ran to embrace the Queen. —Mama, I were be very happy, she said. —There was an air of sweetness and patience in her face, with its red-brassy cheeks.

All rightie now. That's my good little girl.

Maybe on November the twenty-sixth, I'm gonna make a party, said Beatrice. I'm gonna be nineteen. Maybe I can ask my Mama for this.

'Course you can have a party, child, said the Queen.

Fuck, you look thirty, said Domino.

The same black-and-white came circling back, and this time the cops didn't wave. Strawberry, high on crank, informed the world: Two five-o's come an' slam me down on the street and *I* do jail time for trying to knife them—oh, my lymph nodes!

Shut your face, the tall man said.

Heads up now, everybody, said the Queen. How you all doin', officers?

Just fine, Maj. You're going to have to break up the party. These girls are blocking traffic. If we see you here in ten minutes we're going to have to write you up.

Lordy lordy, sighed the Queen. Okay, officers. Justin, can you help Sapphire? Beatrice, I want you to run down to that *place,* you know that *place* I was tellin' you about . . .

Sapphire turned her head quickly and shyly, smiling with her pale face, and even while she smiled her tongue was hanging out.

| 246 |

Pull in here, pull in here, pull in here, said Domino impatiently; and the dark car crept into the sunset fog.

Are you going to tip me? she added.

Here's five more, said the trick. You were really good. You're always so good.

You just need a little petticoat government, that's all, the blonde explained. And did you buy me anything?

Didn't have enough . . . the trick whispered.

See you, the blonde laughed, jumping out of that long black car. A condom fell out of her purse.

Wait! called the poor desperate trick.

She ran across the street to the tall man, shouting: Justin, Justin! That sonofabitch keeps asking about you. Get his license plate number. Get his—

But the car was already speeding away.

| 247 |

Last week, Thursday or Friday, they hurt that girl up there, Beatrice was saying. They hurt her, and she was bleeding and everything. Why the police doan do anything about the ones taking money away from people that works? They just want us to be stealing and for us to do nothing.

Vigs, said the tall man bitterly.

Who were they, honey? said the Queen. Come an' whisper in my ear.

They talk about some Mr. Brady, I think I see him before, the fat man with big money, one time I give him a nice blow job . . .

Brady's Boys, huh? said the tall man. I heard about them in Chicago. Fuckin' vigs.

| 248 |

The tall man, like the security guard at the War Memorial Opera House, who always locked his hand upon his head, leaned the resultingly reinforced elbow against a pillar, thrust his belly out and waited for time to go by, believed less in anticipating events than in seizing them when they began to appear like crow-dark ghosts and specters. From the window of darkened hotel rooms he watched light ooze down the immense brick and stone hips of the Tenderloin like a woman's skirt slowly falling down around her fleabitten ankles. In the mouths of the Queen's many tunnels he awaited doom. —I can't get a fix on it yet, he muttered. Just how those godamned *citizens* tryin' to fuck us up . . . Sometimes he squatted against the wall of the 101 Restaurant, watching. Abruptly, as if he could see his enemies, he rose and walked off, pulling the whore Strawberry by the hand.

The next morning he was walking up Eighteenth and at South Van Ness saw a cop arresting a Latino boy who pleaded: Yes, I *know,* but I'm *sorry;* you gotta *trust* me! and he walked on feeling terrible for the boy.

They're all vigs, he said later. Vigs and *citizens* and everybody but us, all of 'em, all just one set, vigs and pigs . . .

| 249 |

Lily, peering at everyone in a half-blind fashion like an old welder, said brightly: That corner, right there, was where they found the two girls. And I saw them, too. You know, with their hands and their heads and their mouth kind of screaming. So you saw how they died.

It's only a dream, said Smooth. Like eating pure chocolate. Nobody really dies. But nobody ever gets to eat pure chocolate. It's always cut with strychnine. But the dream, now—

Stop eating goofballs, said Strawberry. You're a goof.

It's like they never ate peanut butter, Smooth explained. And I'm passing out peanut butter.

Yeah, yeah, yeah, said Strawberry.

What is *real?* Smooth asked her. What is *true happiness?*

The whore didn't answer.

I said, do you know what real happiness is?

I thought we were talking about those dead girls, said Strawberry. Now, Mr. Smooth, I don't mean to disrespect you, and the Queen says you're okay, but I hope that dead girls don't have anything to do with your happiness.

Can dead girls give head? said Smooth. Are they young enough? Are their little lips fresh enough?

God, mister, you are *twisted.*

Dan Smooth of course had the run of the new Sacramento coroner's facility with its one hundred and eighty single or double tables and its special gurneys for decomposed patients, so he had seen a few things. He admired and complimented the ultraviolet lights which were used to decontaminate the room between autopsies by breaking down corpse-DNA into meaningless atoms of putrescence.

In his opinion the double homicide referred to by Lily was of the same bemusing order as the coroner's policy on freezing bodies, which is why Lily herself thought him to be freezing cold. But Smooth said: Do you believe in the resurrection of Lazarus? And, if so, do you believe that Lazarus truly wasn't better off dead? Do you believe that Sunflower's in Heaven now? Do you believe it's right what she did?

Hey, said Strawberry. I knew those girls. Those girls didn't wanna die.

| 250 |

Only a few people ever saw the Queen and knew her when they saw her, and in those anxious days when the vigs began to arrive in force like gnawing vermin blind-set on uprooting every hotel in the Mission, every brickwork old massage parlor in the Tenderloin, they glimpsed her even more rarely, which is why some gaunt harsh old street men began rumoring that she was already gone; meanwhile she continued to do what she always did, hovering like a light above the waters so that no soul which rented out its flesh had to be alone any longer. Like the improverished old people in Sacramento who lurked air conditionless in their homes with the blinds pulled down against the glowing sun, she hid from vigilante-radiance, fulfilling her purpose on the dark landings of hotel stairs, wearing castoff clothes which sometimes crawled with lice or scabies; Tyler's flesh was inflamed, scratched and bleeding now like that of all the rest of her crew; and

Domino once with her saturnine humor hypothesized that the *real* Mark of Cain comprised scratch-marks behind the knees or around one's crotch. The Queen smiled at this almost with docility, and Beatrice, uncomprehending, flapped a stained T-shirt up and down upon her unwashed breasts to cool them down, burning as they were with the bites of hungry insects and of lonely men. And that little figure with the old, old face, sitting on the bed in this hotel room for which Beatrice's trick had paid for an entire night, then used merely for an hour as he had used Beatrice, then departed, giving the key into Beatrice's hands with his own variety of secondhand kindness, that witch, that arch-Canaanite, that ancient Maj sighed, and said: Domino, go and get that T.V. in the hallway there. Bring him in and we'll talk to him about his happiness.

And so the half-toothless old transvestite, thirty-two years of age, came in and sat down on the bed between Domino and Beatrice and said: I came to San Francisco and started whoring at sixteen. Most of the people I started out with are gone or dead. There are only three of them around now.

Oh, come on, said Domino. Doesn't that go for *any* group of people in sixteen years? She was actually trying to brighten him in her backhanded way. After his initial pleasure that somebody actually wanted him he'd become uneasy, almost alarmed. He could not comprehend why these women had requested his presence. —You got any bump? he whispered. I sure could use a little bump to bring myself like back into focus . . . —The blonde, who now grinned uproariously at the notion that she might under any circumstances give away drugs to strangers, felt as a rule entirely at home in the company of transvestites because they weren't men anymore, so they did not want to use her sexually, and since they were also not quite women, they hardly competed with her for men. Exhausted by her own hatreds, she was pleased to express friendliness or even helpfulness, as she did toward, for instance, children, whenever they did not annoy her. And this quasi-female, skinny and ill, displayed sufficient signs of acquired immune deficiency for her to pity him and actually think good about him as she would of someone already safely dead.

This here, this my sister, said Beatrice with a big black-toothed grin, formally introducing Domino. —And that one over there, that's our Mama. And she defends us and doan never hit us, so we love her so much.

Shyly, the transvestite hung his head. —You got any rock? he whispered.

How many friends you got? said the Queen. I mean real friends?

Not so many. I got a fortune cookie once that said it's easier to make friends than it is to keep them, and, man, is that ever true. If I needed to fix or I was going to be sick, if I was hungry or needed a place to stay and I had no money, then there are two or three places I could go. Yeah, three friends. Three good friends. That's better than a lot of people can say.

What's your name?

Libby.

You remember me?

No.

You was stayin' at that Hotel Seville last year, an' your visitor fees be gettin' too high, so Justin here had a little talk with 'em . . .

Oh yes yes yes yes *yes.*

An' what if I was to say you could always stay with me, no questions asked?

What are you, some kind of cult?

Not exactly, child. Look into my eyes. What do you see?

Why, I see Christopher! He's my boyfriend—well, my ex-boyfriend I guess I should say . . .

Hell! Sooner or later they're *all* ex-boyfriends, the blonde put in with her trademark crooked smile. You know why? Because they're all shitty! And I'm warning you, too, Maj—

Hush up, darling. You know I love you . . .

I—gosh . . . uh, after Christopher left me—well, that was two months ago but we were together for two years so I guess I can still talk about it—I started getting these waves of sadness. I knew I could never meet anybody like him again—smart, handsome, generous, a lawyer—'cause it had taken me fourteen years before I met him. And I'm not getting any younger.

Why did he leave you? asked the Queen.

He didn't like my lifestyle.

Your whorin'?

Uh huh. And one day he was going to fly off to Boston, and he didn't invite me. So I said: Well, if you're not taking me, at least give me some money to get high tonight, because I'll be missing you. —And he didn't want to indulge my habit was how he put it, although I don't have a habit; I try lots of different drugs, don't stick to any one thing, so how could he have been so insensitive as to call me addicted? So I threw a tantrum and half wrecked his apartment. Then he gave me the money, but he said: You've thrown your last tantrum. —I didn't pay him much attention, 'cause he was always saying that . . .

So you didn't pay him no mind, agreed the Queen. And then what?

And then it was over. And waves of sadness like an ocean kept filling up inside my room. I felt like I was drowning. I can't stay in my room very long or I start to choke. That's why you found me sitting outside in the hall . . .

How much you charge for head?

I go as low as five dollars. That's rock bottom, you know, when I'm feeling really really needy for some medicine.

That'll work, said Domino. Because we have a rule. If you're one of those expensive prostitutes who charge five hundred bucks before you'll swallow, then we can't let you in. Because we're exclusive.

Domino . . . sighed the Queen.

We're the downtrodden. We're the wretched of the earth. We're inscribed—and I mean *indelibly* inscribed—with the Mark of Cain.

We feel happy, 'cause Mama always gives us presents, Beatrice said, smiling with every inch of her car-crash-ruined face. —If you want to be my brother and Domino's brother you can be, and we'll respect you, I promise, because we . . .

What do you mean, presents? Hey, can you spare a little rock, like just a little teeny-weeny bump, just so I can get a taste? I need the taste, I—

Hell, no, said Domino.

| 251 |

One night Strawberry ran away or maybe went to jail although if she had gone to jail one would have thought that she'd have used her statutory phone call on Dan Smooth, who was always willing to forward bail requests, but nobody heard from her; and while it was possible that she'd been murdered like the Capp Street girls who kept winding up in various zones of San Francisco either strangled or with their throats cut (one whore who'd gotten away said that it was two Hispanic men in a pickup truck, and another whore assured her neighbors with equal vigor that it was a greyhaired ex-cop), it seemed equally likely, if not more so, that she had simply grown exhausted with the tall man, whose self-denying rage (akin to holy asceticism) inevitably broke down everything and everybody whom he loved into a might-have-been; so after two or three days Beatrice spied his fists like shooting stars around a pay phone, ringing and ringing against that nickel-plated metal until his hands began to tear open; just as dark juice runs from the winepress, so the black blood spewed and spurted at every noisy blow, the flesh merely raw and superficially exposed, but the sight nonetheless pitiable for that, which is why a black whore in a metal kettle-hat and a shawl like a shower curtain kept lumbering around the incensed and despairing man as if she were a dancing bear, terrified yet fascinated, uttering hysterical laughter as she had done just two nights past when the cocktail glass on the sign for Jonell's bar intoxicated her—a horrible sight, so Beatrice, whose sense of duty rose up with all the high dark corrugations of the border wall between Mexican and American California, flew panting to her Mama the Queen, who was sleeping inside the hulk of the Grand Southern Hotel on Mission between Fifteenth and Sixteenth, the Grand Southern having lately been burned out by accidents or ruthlessness unknown; Beatrice told the news, crying: I come *running, running!* but when those two arrived back in the Tenderloin by taxicab forty minutes later the tall man had gone and the phone was clean, so the Queen sleepily grumbled and clucked and laid her head in Beatrice's lap on a bench in Boedekker Park ten yards from the black preacher who cried out: *I was more wretched than you, but Jesus saved me. Jesus took my wretchedness away. Are you listening? Hallelujah! He died for me, I said! He took my wretchedness away. I was a user, but He took my wretchedness away, and now I ain't no user no more.* The Queen very faintly snored and blew a bubble through her nostril; Beatrice, bending over her, inhaled her familiar smoked-leather odor, closed her own eyes, and had begun dreaming of when she was a little girl in Oaxaca and she had seen them burning a wooden statue in a bonfire to complete some ceremony whose significance she had never understood; when she was shaken awake by the blood-caked hands of Justin. His dusty face had been worn clean by two tear-tracks. When Beatrice awoke, the Queen awoke also. She sat up and looked into his bloodshot eyes and then said to Beatrice: Okay, baby. Here's five dollars. You go buy some powder for Sapphire . . . —and when Beatrice had risen and gone a few steps, she turned back, brushing her skirt, and saw the tall man sobbing in the Queen's arms. —C'mere, little boy, the Queen whispered. Come closer to me. . . . —Beatrice turned away, jealous. She heard the Queen say: Maybe you need to make amends to her, Justin. Maybe she just don't want you to beat her up no more . . . —to which the tall man chokingly replied: But she . . . —She gonna come back to you in two days, said the Queen. I know it. Try an' cherish her. You hear me, child? —Passing a police wagon which loomed so black in the hot evening light, Beatrice, worrying about Strawberry but believing the Queen, returned to the hotel room where she was living that week, the room with incandescent doughnuts wrapped around the burnt-out light bulbs and knocked on the door of one-eleven where she got five dollars' worth of powder from a dealer named Scoreboard, and after taking a little snort for herself (the Queen would never have minded), she knelt down, longing to pray to her dear friend the Virgin for Strawberry's safety and happiness, but she knew that it was not permitted for her to pray to the Virgin anymore. Besides, the Queen was herself the Virgin, the righteous one who loved Beatrice, Strawberry, Justin, Domino and everyone, the dear lady who feasted them and cared for them and could do any of the things Beatrice remembered from the devotional stories; but two things had occurred to weaken Beatrice's faith in the Queen. The first was her realization that wherever the Queen dwelled there was never any altar. The second was the episode just now with the transvestite Libby. When Domino led him in, Beatrice had been certain that she would now have a new brother, or sister, or whatever Libby desired to be, because her Queen, who could do everything, had sent for him and invited him into the royal family. And of course the Queen behaved as splendidly as the Virgin in continuing to love Domino most tenderly no matter what she did, and transform the blonde's faults, even her gravest defect of malice, into childish stumblings which should in no way be blamed. But if the Queen were really Beatrice's good friend Maria, then why had Domino succeeded in scaring Libby away? The Queen had not uttered a word of reproach. Yet surely the real Virgin would have dissuaded and prevented anyone who sought to block another from entering the house of God. (The Queen, who did indeed remain mostly as mild with Domino as Irene's mother reminding her daughter not to soak the New Year's rice cakes too long on New Year's Eve, perhaps hoped—if she hoped at all— for *titration* between Domino and the world, that interesting chemical term referring to the slow and gradual addition of an acid to a base, or vice versa, until a neutral pH is reached. But any such strategy would have remained diabolically irrelevant to the Mexican girl's doubts.) What a luxury it had been, to believe that the Queen and the Virgin were one! And now Beatrice did not know what to do. Lying down on her back, she pulled up her sweaty T-shirt and slowly masturbated, hoping to relax herself, but suddenly she glimpsed herself in the bathroom mirror and was ashamed. She went back out to find Sapphire, glimpsing through the doorway of a bar a black girl in a straw hat who, smiling faintly, slammed the dice down on the counter with a sound like cracking ice. Sapphire was supposed to be on Minna Street but she wasn't there. Beatrice, heavy Beatrice, went sighing and panting to Clementina but Sapphire wasn't there, either. On Sixth Street a man whose face resembled lava's dull fire gazed at her. She was wearing a yellow T-shirt and a red skirt; and because the lava-faced man thought that she had a nice if black-toothed smile and a nice round face, almost clean and very shiny, because he liked big women, especially olive-faced ones like this one, this wide-hipped one with the colored bracelets hanging from her arms, he called out: Baby, you gonna go back with me today? I'm lonely! but Beatrice, whose feet were hurting so much now and whose back ached, turned and snarled: Doan play with me! I'm not up for it today! so he said: How about tomorrow? —Beatrice bent over and allowed herself to be sodomized beneath the murky blue mirrors of office windows, keeping up her spirits with the thought of the forty dollars which he had promised her, so that it didn't hurt at all. Afterward he tipped her so that she got fifty. He was a nice man. In her heart Beatrice sang thank you to God and resolved to trust His plan for her, which meant believing in the Queen, for after all there was no purpose in going home. —A black-and-white pulled up. The cop beckoned her with one finger. She approached him with respect, hoping that he was Officer O'Malley, with whom she was in love a little because he never slapped her down like so many other policemen but joked with her instead, and sometimes even gave her a break if she whined long enough. Just the other night, when he'd busted her, his partner took a Polaroid of Officer O'Malley with his arm around Beatrice, the two of them standing against the white wall of the Mission Street substation with her head resting on his shoulder. But this policeman was not Officer O'Malley. She abased herself, so he let her off. —Thank you, officer, thank you! she cried. —Walk, said the cop. —I hear you, said Beatrice. She shuffled wearily halfway up the block, then flashed her fat and tired breasts at cars without result. —Should be right around the corner, said the tall man at dusk, so, thanking him, Beatrice turned the corner, met the Queen, kissed her lips. Returning to her hotel, she snorted the rest of Sapphire's powder, then bought forty dollars' worth of coal tar heroin from Scoreboard, longing to experience even by chemical means the tranquility which was the gift of nuns. She wanted to be a nun. Closing her eyes, she saw once again the old master of ceremonies in Merida with his death's head face. He tipped his hat to her, crying out: *Our Queen of the Yucatan—sweet as a pastry, hot as a candle, bright as the sun!* And suddenly she wondered whether he might be the Devil. She had never considered that before. It was he who by filling her heart with the desire to dance before multitudes had led her into dancehalls and prostitution. And if that were true, what must the Queen be? How could Domino continually distrust the Queen, unless either the Queen or Domino herself were morally deficient? Beatrice, pierced now by a terrible anxiety, resolved to re-make her life. Then she prepared the heroin and squezed it lovingly into her favorite vein, the big one on her left thigh, two hands below the crotch. *Ay,* it was good—so good! Her soul became incense-smoke rising up from the censer of her flesh; she was holy and excellent forever. The higher she rose, the more she could see, until it seemed to her that the whole world most preciously shimmered below her. Far to the southeast she could spy Oaxaca; there was her Papa's house on its concrete platform, with ladders going up to the roof; and when she closed her eyes she could almost hear her dead mother calling her to come and eat. She cried. Against the pitted concrete wall of the house, a broom leaned. The concrete porch was clean. Now she was happy and drowsy. There were ladders and buckets in the dry dirt. There was a wheelbarrow halfway down the canyon. At that moment, shrugging off the blanket of heroin's saintlike peace, Beatrice longed to go home even though she knew that there was nothing in that place for her. —Do you have children? a john had asked her just the other day. —No, I want one but I kinda think I can't have one no more, she laughed. I can't have any kids. The dumb doctor said I could. The clinic said no. —Her son, the rape-child with his *tripas* hanging out, where was he now?

| 252 |

The next time she saw Sapphire, which was three nights later, under the Stockton tunnel, Beatrice, who after trying and trying to get business late on that streetlit evening, raising her T-shirt, flashing her big round breasts at the stunned drivers in their torpid little cars, had finally made twenty for blowing a fat black businessman, ran out and bought five dollars' worth of powder, and after taking two snorts for herself (didn't a girl deserve a commission? Wouldn't Sapphire tell her go ahead if Sapphire could speak?) gave the rest to Sapphire, who swarmed mewlingly into her arms. Strawberry was back, and the tall man was already cursing and punching her face.

The Queen said to Beatrice: You're carryin' some bad blood in your heart. I can smell it.

Seeing that her dear lady with the old, old face was not judging her but merely worrying over and sorrowing over her, Beatrice, who was chewing Mexican candy, felt ashamed and tender all at once. At that moment she would have died for her Queen. How much easier life would be, if such moments endured! Running into the black woman's arms, she sobbed, her brittle English cracking and breaking as it always did when she was agitated: And Santa Claus didn't give me nothing for Christmas, but he give me my Mama. You always my Mama. I wanna love you. I wanna be with you. I wanna marry with you. If you ever come Mexicali, you doan never pay your hotel, come my house. I ask my other Mama already and she say okay. And I gonna come running, running to get you and take you home so you can stay with me forever. I'm gonna meet your bus and fuck you all night 'cause you're my Mama.

Oh, please, said Domino. How can you ask your other Mama anything? She's dead.

Hush up, Dom. Let the girl be. And *you* hush up, too, Beatrice. Try an' enjoy life. When you gonna teach us all those Mexican dances you know? I never been to Mexico; I wanna learn 'em. We could have a party with some music and everything.

Why don't you ever listen to music, Maj? Domino interrupted eagerly. You can borrow my headphone radio anytime.

Thank you, darlin'. You know that song "Gypsy Queen"? That's my song.

Angry and jealous, the Mexican girl whispered rapidly in the Queen's ear: I told my Mama I lose my money, I lose my twenty dollar from my new boyfriend I meet last night, and my Mama doan say nothing but Domino say *stupida*, you always *stupida*, Beatrice! and then I cry.

She thrust her half-eaten candy at the Queen. The Queen took a bite, but not a big enough one to please Beatrice, who shouted *no, no, no!* bit off a big piece, chewed it, then tongued it passionately into the Queen's mouth.

| 253 |

The summer's back broken, Tyler drove unsweatily past Q Street but did not turn off to Dan Smooth's house even though the traffic light winked meaningfully. His mother was not well. Looking right and left, he glimpsed bunkered lights and light dripping out of dingy Victorians. Then he drove on, proceeding an entire block to the Zebra Club, and parked beneath a billboard which proclaimed him and all other creatures **LUCKY**.

He tried to decide what he was going to say to his mother, who had scarcely addressed him since the last time he'd visited her, when he mentioned the false Irene. Should he tell her that he and that one were quits, and that he'd taken up instead with a crack-addicted ghetto prostitute who practiced black magic? The eyes narrowed in his grey, grey face, and he sat unmoving in his car.

A long train went dully by; he heard the sound. At the shopping malls when the trains passed on the levee, a fence kept you so far away that you couldn't really hear them. They seemed to glide in silence. But when you lived close enough you could hear that long, slow, heavy sound.

He sat there for half an hour. (Meanwhile Dan Smooth was reading an anarchist quarterly called *The Raven* which contained an article called "Children Abusing Adults—Rule 43.") Finally he started the engine again and drove to the supermarket, where he bought his mother groceries.

| 254 |

A shot of tequila? said Loreena.

Yeah.

That sounds good. Fuck it. Only half an hour before closing time. I'll have one, too. Cheers, said Tyler.

Cheers. I'll need some money now, dear.

How much?

I *knew* you'd do that to me. Let's see . . . I'm a little bit fuzzy . . . Two twenty-five.

Here.

Thank you. You're always so generous, Henry. Man, that tastes good. I just love that tequilla. That'll put hair on your chest. Or maybe take it off.

In my own case I can't remember, so maybe I can see your chest and dope it out.

Now you're pushing the bucket, mister, said Loreena, but then to his astonishment she lifted up her T-shirt and flashed rosy-nippled, round and perfect breasts.

Thank you, he said. That was good of you.

I learned that trick from Beatrice.

Surprise, surprise.

You know, it's such a hot night, Loreena said. I figured after I got off work I'd head for Jonell's and then maybe the Cinnabar, and after that I'd love to go skinnydipping out at Ocean Beach.

Tyler immediately became sad because he wanted to be with the Queen and now he would have to disappoint Loreena. —I'll be back if I can, he said. I have to go make some money.

Loreena's ancient face grimaced back down into its habitual mask of weary disgust, and she said: Well, drive carefully, Henry, okay?

And he wondered which would have been the more enlightened act—to go with Loreena and make her happy for an evening, loving her as the Queen loved everybody, or to go to the Queen and literally love her? —I don't know where I'm going anymore, he muttered.

| 255 |

That was what he did now, night after night. Passing Strawberry up against the wall of the twenty-four-hour carwash with the hollows of her eyes filled with unreadable light and light drooling from her mouth like some customer's sperm, passing Chocolate who was grinning and clenchfisted as she leaned up against the slimy wall-tiles of the Wonderbar late at night, trying not to shiver and making sure she stared down every car that came, Tyler wandered in through the back door to the red stools and red love seats, the kingdom of the Wonderbar where Domino, waiting to do business with someone whose identity would soon shock Tyler, said to him: Are you married?

Only to my brother's dead wife, he replied. How's the Queen today?

You know, said Domino, I don't exactly have *contempt* for you; I don't exactly think you're a *coward* . . .

Well, I'm glad to hear that, said Tyler sarcastically.

Are you laughing at me?

No, sweetheart. I would never laugh at you.

Well, then why do you—oh, fuck it.

Like all the brilliant women he knew who kept crying out that people made no sense and whose dream it was to flee everything and work at a Dairy Queen somewhere in Mississippi, Domino had visions which life would never live up to. Her brightest vision was that everyone would love her. Her life asserted that everyone hated her.

So how's the Queen? he said.

You have a thing for her, huh? That's rich. That's fuckin' rich. To think that ole Maj herself is finally getting a piece of dick! That sleazy old lowlife Maj—ha, ha! Hey, Henry, how does it feel to be dating a nigger?

Feels okay to me.

And your sister-in-law was a gook, wasn't she? Smooth told me . . .

Oh, so you're dicking Smooth? he said, trying to get off the subject of Irene and the Queen.

No, he's a honky. I don't do honkies, since I'm one myself.

My, my, said Tyler. Just who enjoys the honor of being done by you?

You wanna do me, Henry?

You're a mighty beautiful woman, Domino.

Well, then I guess you have quite an *opportunity*, now, don't you, she said with her trademark venomous bitterness. (When she was a little girl there was something wrong with the car. They went to the mechanic's. He was greasy and smoking. There was a naked picture on the wall. It made her ashamed. She couldn't have been more than three. Her mother was changing her brother's diapers.)

Of course I'd love to sleep with you, Domino, Tyler said. Buy you a drink?

Rum and Coke, she purred instantly.

Rum and Coke for Domino, please, he said to the barmaid.

Okay, dear.

Now, tell me this, said Domino. What are your intentions regarding the Queen? Because it affects all of us. Don't think we haven't all seen you sneaking around.

What are my intentions? he muttered. I don't know.

Smooth said you're a detective. He said you're a lousy stinking cop.

I bet he didn't put it quite that way.

Well, are you a cop?

Nope.

Are you a detective?

Yes I am.

Why, you *sonofabitch*. You even admit it. You're spying on us all. You want to bring us all down. And you *enjoy* it, don't you? You're *good* at it.

Oh, once you get used to the databases, you just kind of whip in and out, he muttered.

And you're not ashamed?

I'm not out to hurt you, he said. I promise.

What are you about?

Just chilling out with your Queen, he said.

You want to get her? You want to destroy her?

No.

But you like her?

Sure.

You love her? That stinking old Maj!

I don't know her that well, he said.

And how do you feel about the rest of us?

I think you're all great. But you're the best, of course, Domino.

Oh, don't fucking patronize me. You men are all the same. All you want is to use us. You don't give a damn, really, do you? You don't give a fucking damn.

Here's your rum and Coke, dear, said Loreena.

Domino uplifted it without thanks and thrust her long grey tongue between the ice cubes.

And for you, Henry? said the barmaid like the dreamy Queen speaking through closed eyes, lips parted as if to kiss some ghost which he could not see. Your usual?

Yeah, why not, he said.

Look, said Domino. I'm reminding you of my interest in all this. I'm reminding you to cut me in. You never would have met the Queen without me.

Honk four times, he said agreeably.

Listen, she said. *Listen.* I'm trying to tell you that I . . .

I *am* listening, Domino.

Oh, go to hell.

I go there regularly.

You think you got the Queen pinned down now, don't you, fucker? You think she's yours? Well, you're never going to own her. I can see you're one of those types who just thinks he can own a woman. Well, women have got it in for men like that.

I don't need to own her, Domino. Why buy when you can rent?

Yeah, how many other thousand guys you think she's already *fucked?* the blonde snarled.

Dan Smooth, who'd just now strutted in, raised his forefinger, and Tyler thought: Okay, kiddies, here we go. Blessed art the peacemakers.

You remember the proverb of the Sadducees, Domino?

Fuck, no, pervert, and I don't care, either.

Well, Smooth explained, not a bit perturbed by this less than eager pupil, the Sadducees asked Jesus about a man who'd married his dead brother's wife according to the Law of Moses—you know, he had to take care of his brother's gal—well, then *he* died, and his brother married her, and *he* died, and so on and so on, until all seven brothers had had her one by one, and then they all died, and so did she. Her cunt must have been tired by then. I wonder what it smelled like . . . But the Sadducees were trying to trip Jesus up, see. That's why they raised the issue in the first place. It was a sting, you see; it was *entrapment.* We've all been there before. They said to Him: Whose wife is she going to be in Heaven? (Because they didn't believe in the Resurrection at all.) But Jesus got them, Domino. Because you know what He said? He said: *You are wrong, knowing neither the Scriptures nor the Authority of God. For in the Resurrection they neither marry nor are given in marriage, but are like angels in Heaven.* How do you like that?

So in Heaven she fucks them all or not? said Domino, intrigued in spite of herself.

What do you think?

Sure, said Tyler after a moment. Sure she does. She's got to.

What do you mean, she's *got to?* You misogynist!

Tyler rubbed his chin and said: No, no, I didn't mean it that way. I meant, that would be the right thing to do. She would want to. They all took care of her and let's assume they loved her, so let's assume she was at least grateful—doesn't it flatter you if a john loves you?

Now we're getting personal, said Domino.

Yes we are, Smooth gloated. Go ahead. Domino. Tell us what it's like for you, and what color their ooze is.

Oh, knock it off, Smooth, said Tyler.

You're always telling me to knock it off. Why don't *you* knock it off?

Knock what off?

I love it when men fight, said Domino.

I bet you do, said Tyler. And I concede in advance. I don't have any answers. But Danny boy here knows everything. In my job, you know, I sometimes ask a lot of questions. If the witnesses are able to answer every question, you know that some of what they say isn't true.

So they fall in love with you sometimes? Smooth pursued, paying no attention to this objection. Indeed, it seemed as if he'd taken complete charge of the conversation by now, not so much overcoming arguments as reducing them to demonstrations of disrespect equivalent to the loud cries of a scattered search party.

Uh, they do, uh huh, replied the blonde with surprising coyness.

And that's personal?

Uh huh.

Well, my theory is that if you keep saying it's personal you must be flattered, because otherwise you'd just say straight up that you don't give a damn whether they love you or not.

Domino laughed. —Maybe so, she said.

Now, that being the case, I think you also would do the nice thing if you were in that Sadducee wife's situation up in Heaven.

If all those angel husbands pay me first!

I need coffee, said Smooth. I'm falling asleep.

You want a toot? said Domino.

Oh, that's nice of you. But let's try this little coffee shop for a minute . . .

I mean, what*ever,* said Domino, irritated.

The Vietnamese coffee shop at Mason and Eddy had lace curtains around the windows so that you could see only the silhouettes of the shoulders inside. Smooth ordered a Vietnamese coffee, jet-black, slow-dripping into a metal cylinder of condensed milk. Tyler chose a can of root beer. —Nothing for me, said Domino. I don't like these goddamned foreign places. I bet that coffee of yours is full of ground up cockroaches.

At the next table sat a mother with a six-year-old boy.

I'd like to get into that, Smooth said.

Cut it out, Tyler said.

The Queen ran silently in and kissed Tyler on the lips. Smooth got her a chair. She sat beside Tyler, holding his hand. —Hi, Maj, said Domino. I missed you . . .

Smooth craned his head, smiling and winking at the six-year-old, whose mother, desolate about something, sat close-eyed with her head in her hands.

Hello, mister, the child said.

Why, hello there! said Smooth in his most friendly manner. Are you full?

Yeah.

Is your smooth little tummy all *full?*

Yeah, said the child shyly.

Now I have a question for you. Do you like to answer questions?

Yeah.

All right then. Here it is. What do you think *happens* to all that food in your stomach? Smooth asked the child in a calm and even tone.

It rolls around and around and around, he said.

And then? said Smooth, leaning forward.

And then when you have to go to the bathroom it comes out and it's all brown.

Hmm, said Smooth. Basically correct.

Oh, leave him alone, said the Queen.

Now, Maj, what's really going on? Domino said.

With what?

With you and Henry. By the way, I need some rock. You got any white girl on you, Maj?

Hush your mouth, bitch. Can't you see we're in a public place?

Maj, I really need something . . .

The Queen sighed and embraced the blonde, pretending to kiss her while she spat into her mouth. Smooth, who did not use drugs, beamed ironically. Tyler felt a little jealous. Domino clung to the Queen, trembling as she gobbled her saliva down. Finally the Queen pulled away and said: That's enough.

Thank you, Maj. Now I don't hurt anymore.

Very tastefully done, Smooth said. Now, Maj, what's the prophecy?

The Queen pulled the Enemy's Book out of the pocket of her grubby parka, closed her eyes, opened it, and lowered her dark, scarred little forefinger onto the tiny print. She opened her eyes. But just as she was about to read, the mother at the adjoining table, who had been wandering the cobwebbed corridors of her own despair, leaned forward, her eyes shining, and said: Excuse me, lady, but have you been saved?

Why, how did you know, dear? said the Queen gently.

Well, I saw you have the Book . . . Now that I'm a born-again Christian I just feel so free.

I'm so glad, said the Queen.

Politically I hate so many people; politically I guess I hate almost everyone, so I'm so grateful to God for forcing me to love.

That's nice, Tyler said.

The way I look at it, blurted Domino, if God is omniscient or however you say it, then when you're stepping on an ant, God feels what that ant feels. You're doing that to God.

Weren't you two ladies kissing just now? the mother said. You're not sodomites, are you?

Why, no, ma'am, Smooth inserted. Didn't you hear what I was saying to your little boy? I was specifically warning him against such practices. In this world, you know, you have to beware. Nothing is as it seems.

Is that true? said the mother to her son. Did you say thank you to the nice man?

Thank you, the child said glumly.

And remember my advice, son, said Smooth in his best genially distinguished manner. You know. About *digestion.*

The mother inched her chair nearer to the Queen and inquired: Are you politically active?

Well, now, I guess that depends.

I just fell in love with Bob Dole.

Imagine that, said the Queen sarcastically.

I've always been a conservative at heart, but it wasn't until Ronald Reagan became President that I really got politically active. Reagan—well, that man helped me find my roots. I guess I just fell in love with Bob Dole's smile. I was out there campaigning for him so hard, going from door to door.

Allrightie, the Queen said. Well, ma'am, we all certainly have enjoyed visiting with you, but now we need to do a little prayin.'

What church do you belong to?

First Church of Canaan, Reformed.

I'm not familiar with that church. Well, God bless you.

And watch out for that Mark of Cain, ma'am. Now, Smooth, in answer to your question, I do believe we have a prophecy right down here. Are you ready?

Ready, but pessimistic.

Africa—

Henry, you know that's my private name.

Sorry, Maj. But I was wondering something. If the prophecy's bad, what happens if you don't read it? If we don't know it and refuse to acknowledge it, then maybe it can't come true.

This guy's a motherfuckin' ostrich, said Domino, and the mother at the next table gasped at the obscenity.

Henry, magic don't work like that. Well, maybe for some people it can, but not here, not for us.

If I'd done something or said something different, if I'd been somehow nicer or I don't know what, then maybe I could have prevented Irene's suicide. The future is—

How will you ever know? The future, well, I only ever seen it come by once. Now just keep quiet, Henry. Don't say nothing; don't do nothing. Whatever it says, we don't have to be scared.

This is starting to give me the creeps, said Domino.

Well, it gave *her* the creeps! laughed the Queen, for the mother, seizing her child by the hand, had risen to run away, casting many a baleful glare.

Smooth opened his mouth wide, snake-flickered his tongue at the woman, and said: This is *America,* and I can look at you if you can look at me.

The woman flushed crimson. Tyler was ashamed of Smooth.

Now then, said the Queen. For the prophecy we got Numbers chapter 13 verse 17, and it says: *Moses sent them to spy out the land of Canaan, and said to them, "Go up into the Negeb yonder, and go up into the hill country, and see what the land is, and whether the people who dwell in it are strong or weak, whether they are few or many . . ."*

Okay, said Tyler. We get the idea, Maj. So the vigs are already sniffing around, or soon will be. But I figure it's not the end yet, because they doubted God, so He delayed the conquest for forty years.

Well, no parallel is exact, Henry, and I wouldn't push the issue with prophecy, either. It's not as if there's a Negeb Street on a hill in the Castro where somebody's peeking at us, see. Let's all agree that Maj's finger is inspired. I believe in her. I know all of us do. But numbers don't always translate—

Why not?

Oh, how the fuck should I know? Maybe because then the Egyptians would hear of it or the trumpets would resound or some dumb thing . . .

I don't know, Tyler said stubbornly, narrowing his eyes. If this is true, and they're here to spy us out, then why can't we go spy *them* out? I'll do it if you want; I'm expendable . . .

Hee, hee, hee! laughed Smooth. Was that what your sister-in-law thought?

| 256 |

In just the same way that in San Francisco it is often sunnier south of Market Street, so the prostitutes, pimps, thieves and dealers, tiring at last of their own rumors, began to regain their confidence that they could survive the epoch of the vigs. Some hoped to hide and sleep, others to set the streets on fire. Most, of course, remained convinced that nothing would ever happen to disturb their lives. The crazy whore was rapt with optimistic analysis and prophecy, clutching Domino's sleeve and crying: I know one man who's bragging that he's got all the money in the world. And he's known for going to coffee shops to suck the nipples of Oriental girls for at least half an hour. And he— but Domino wrinkled her nose and said: Shut up, you crazy old bug.

All the whores had faith. If something happened, they could look after themselves. Later, when everything was over, it would seem in retrospect that those last few months were easier and more pleasant than any other time they could remember. Drugs were cheap and dates were plentiful. They loved their Queen, of course, but without her, life wouldn't be much different. Their lives possessed a certain wholeness now; they couldn't imagine that the circle might ever be broken. But on a rainy night not long after that long conversation in the Vietnamese restaurant, the Queen, who on the streets and in warehouses, ghost factories, and crack hotels usually seemed to be as imperially at home as a Korean wife in that household command center, the kitchen, now sat staring moodily into the baby food jar which comprised the bowl of her crack pipe. Tyler was sitting at her feet watching her while big drops rang against the warehouse roof in a fusillade and she sighed and began to pick out bits of toilet paper from the turbid water inside the jar. —Any goldfish swimming around in there? he asked, but she only smiled faintly. Suddenly she dashed the liquid out on the concrete floor. He saw matchheads, a rust-brown powder, a dead ant.

Henry, I want you to do something for me, she said.

All right, he said.

I want you to go to Vegas and find out what that Brady man's up to. I got a bad feeling. I got a real bad feeling.

Tyler smiled sadly, unable to reply. He was making a mess of a surveillance job he really couldn't afford to make a mess of—another potentially lucrative infidelity case in Alameda, which meant that he could have padded hours and mileage; he already had the husband nailed; but the wife wanted photographs and she wanted them now. So much for that client. Anxiety localized itself in his stomach, then metastasized to his heart, and his hands began to sweat. He longed to please the Queen by doing something useful for her, and he also knew that no human being could really do anything useful for her. He wanted Brady's venture to be innocuous, and he already knew it wasn't. He wondered how difficult it would be. He was only Henry Tyler; he didn't have what it took. He felt that he would honestly do more good by staying out of this and letting the Queen go, but if he did, then Irene's skeleton would be sitting on his face again at night, pissing ants and spiders into his mouth. He knew that no matter what happened he would do the wrong thing. Suspended above his bottomless future, he hung clinging miserably to a stretching rope. He almost couldn't bear it. His breastbone ached. Let it be cancer, he thought. Then at least it will be over. But he wanted to live. He wanted to be fulfilled. It was all hopeless.

I know what you're thinkin', child, said his Queen who loved him. It's okay, baby. It's okay.

Tyler knelt before her and sobbed.

Just as the tall man's face gradually lightened from a deep black-brown upon the crown of his shaved head to fresh ocher pits just above his eyes, so the sky, too, dimmed down its darkness, then began to flush in parts. The Queen yawned. Dawn was coming.

| 257 |

The day that Tyler drove to the airport, passing many darkly spreading trees and white houses in Daly City on which fog came smearing and smooching down so that the world's end, the end of all vision, lay very close, it was sunny in the Tenderloin where Justin, tall and lean, grew like a cornstalk in a dark army jacket beside the wall of Jonell's Bar, his collar pushed up and his cap pulled down, listening and watching while he seemed to be but surveying inner space. The loud sermon across the street remained on an untuned channel of his soul's radio.

Beatrice said to him: Well, the Christians, they have different beliefs. I doan believe in it. I go with our Queen or with Strawberry. She is a Christian. I go with her, and they sing or they cry, and they speak about that kind of happiness for the dead people.

Go and make some money, bitch, said the tall man, and she fled, pretending that she was back home in Oaxaca where a big turkey dipped its neck outside her mother's house and inside it was very dark with the dirt floor. The walls were planks stamped SUPPLY OFFICER: AIRFORCE BASE—CA. Just behind the planks, an infant cried and cried: her little nephew. She tried to see her Papa but she couldn't. And all her little brothers were grown up. The house was empty. Where was everyone she knew? She wanted to dance for them. The ceiling planks were black from cooking. When it rained, the water came in. Quiet little flies crawled everywhere. On the cement stood one big bed for the whole family, but the bed was empty. A little girl stood rapt with crossed legs, pressing her face against the bed while she looked at white cartoon cowboys and horses. That was Beatrice. Her little brother spat on the floor. So he hadn't grown up after all.

One of the preacher's lieutenants approached. The tall man raised a single eyebrow.

The lieutenant said: Man, I was paralyzed for fifteen years. I was a drug addict. Man, Jesus healed me. *He healed me!* So I wasn't sick no more. You listening? Hallelujah!

You seen my forehead? replied the tall man in a gravelly whisper.

What about it, man? We ain't got *time* for personal vanity here!

Look upon me, boy. Look upon my mark. You seen my mark?

That's just an abscess, man. Listen to me. When a user gets touched by the Holy Ghost, he ain't a user no more. He's free! Amen!

Get the fuck away from me, said the tall man.

Jesus can save you, the lieutenant pleaded. Don't stay with the Devil. Don't let yourself be damned.

The tall man rose to his complete and immense height and almost playfully tapped the lieutenant in the chest. The lieutenant fell backward. He shouted: I said forgive him, turn away, praise God! But Brady's Boys are gonna get him, hear me, *Lord!* Brady's Boys are coming to town . . .

· BOOK XVI ·

The Queen of Las Vegas

•

Simon Peter said to them, "Let Mary leave us, for women are not worthy of life."

Jesus said, "I myself shall lead her in order to make her male, so that she too may become a living spirit resembling you males."

GNOSTIC SCRIPTURES, *The Gospel of Thomas* V, 5, II, 2, 114.20–25 (1st or 2nd cent.?)

•

I'll tell you a truth as long and naked as a cocktail waitress's leg: Tyler did not like Las Vegas. Only for a check with more than one zero on it—or for his Queen—would he have consented to leave home, venturing beyond the white-candied mountains of his Sierras spiced with treetops. There were three new hotels and then there was Feminine Circus, they said. Already as Las Vegas spread her thighs before him like a collage of silicon chips on the tan plain, he saw the black pyramid of mediocrity like a dull jewel, the Sphinx crouching out in front. That was the cheap easy place where he had to go. That was the Hotel Luxor. John and Brady and the rest wouldn't be caught dead there. They all had suites at Feminine Circus.

The pink ticket said:

$ $

GRAND OPENING

FEMININE CIRCUS

TONITE!!!

Free   *Free*   *Free*
SEX   SEX   SEX   SEX

No minors permitted beyond family areas.

$ $

And indeed, it truly was Sneak Peek Night at Feminine Circus—the largest virtual sex casino in the world (this week, at least). —*But it is amazing what half a billion dollars will do . . .* the C.E.O., one Jonas Brady, was musing aloud at the press conference. *Half a million dollars a day for three and a half years!* —A jungle of people blossomed behind the ropes. Not very far from them, a man whose cardboard sign read **DOWN ON MY LUCK—THANKS AND GOD BLESS** stood frozen beneath the freeway. If only he had known about the free hors d'oeuvres at Feminine Circus! The cool and concentrated faces of the musicians on their bandstand cast musical intellections down into the empty space of the future, for the sake of which the well-dressed people standing on the curb sipping drinks, the TV cameras and the people who served them, self-important geeks with light meters and duffel bags, glum security men in black suits, politely downpointing the antennae of their walkie-talkies, the police with their Sam Browne belts, hands close against their batons, were all here to do reverence.

Then a long silver limousine pulled up and everyone said: That's her.

It's the Queen! a small child cried in the silence.

A flunky opened the silver door.

We have to have a twenty-foot opening in here! a security man called.

Weary and disgusted, Tyler moved to the back of the crowd, where the biped and her handlers could still be seen on a big granular screen near the righthand stage. John and Celia were there somewhere, he supposed, probably up near the front in VIP seats. He hoped that they were having a good time, and that John was being decent to Celia. For a moment he wondered whether he should try to find them, perhaps by querying one of these men in long coats who held walkie-talkies repeatedly and sternly to their ears; but he but quickly sent that naive idea packing—why would he have any more to say to his brother in Vegas than in San Francisco? Besides, his presence would make John anxious. To hell with it.

Asian tourists in black suits cautiously raised point-and-shoot cameras. Children staring upward and rapidly moving their lips as in prayer, bare-shouldered women who showed thigh, women in leather jackets and furs who held almost completed cocktails with a maraschino cherry in each glass marking the icy ruins, bigshouldered men who pushed through the other heads like bulls, chains of old ladies who wriggled between professional ladies in grey blazers who tapped their toes; these were Tyler's neighbors, and while he did not dislike any of them he would much rather have been on Mars. The faces were waiting faces. At least they were more alert here than inside. They still granted reality priority over its lookalike; something was about to happen, no matter how self-serving and trivial; maybe they would see people instead of virtuellas.

Another celebrity disembarked from a limousine, and the lady next to Tyler said: Who is it?

I can't see his face so I don't know, her husband said.

Who's this Queen they keep talking about? asked Tyler innocently.

It's Queen Zenobia from *Lollipopland!* a small girl informed him.

Don't talk to strangers, said her mother.

Why, I'm not a stranger at all, ma'am, said Tyler brightly. My name's Henry Tyler, U.S. Marshals. —And he flashed his toy police badge.

Oh! Well, officer, that's Queen Zenobia from Lollipopland. Say hello to the nice officer, Darlene.

Hello. Are you really an officer?

Yes, Darlene, I really really am, Tyler beamed. He leaned toward Darlene's mother, winked, and whispered: Vice Squad.

Well, they say this Queen Zenobia is really quite a . . .

Is that a *fact,* ma'am, said Tyler in amazement.

Just then a man cried: *Ladies and gentlemen!* and then a lady in red ruffles who might have been Betty Boop said something so squeaky, echoey and affected that for the life of him Tyler could not understand a word. Everyone applauded, and she introduced the Marquis de Sade: *There he is, everyone!* Then they all came, Cleopatra, Snow White, Bambi, Barbie, Helen of Troy in a silver miniskirt, the Queen of Sheba, Queen Zenobia, the Wicked Witch of the West, Mata Hari, Marilyn Monroe, Judy Garland. They came in a coach whose driver wore a red hat like a folded prickly pear lobe, like a giant set of testicles. Tyler thought that he saw Munchkins, but they might have represented some other even more obscene constituency; their hats were a combination of semifilled condoms and Christmas stockings. There was so much feedback on the microphone that he could barely hear their imbecilic song, which echoed in the cold night like death.

Can you see anything? the man beside him said.

No, I can't, the wife said. And I'm cold and my feet hurt.

Another limousine came, crammed full of big-eyed cartoon animals, and Tyler thought that he would be more ashamed to wear their livery than to hire himself out for sodomy; but he saw a happy smile on the face of the girl beside him, while a man in black just behind craned rigidly at the animals, bugging out his eyes as if he had just been executed. What gave him the right to deride his fellow Americans' pleasure? Whatever bearing all this might have on his Queen, his love, he ought never attack any harmless means to happiness whatsoever, no matter how sentimental or false it might be. The crowd cheered, clapped, leaned forward smiling; this meant so much to them. The celebrities for their part stretched their faces wide in smiles of yearning love. Cameras and microphones sprouted on monopods above people's heads. Grinding his teeth, narrowing his eyes, he forced a weakly trembling smile onto his face, according to the best impulses of repentance, but small Darlene saw and whispered: Mommy, why does that man smile so *phony* like that?

In the outer darkness across the street by the Hotel Tia Maria marched three thousand union souls with their white pickets: *We say no way! Brady say, take away. We say no way!* They began to trudge and swarm like ants back and forth in the darkness. *Brady say, take away. We say no way!* Their pale signs bobbed and crossed on the sidewalk. Their line stretched so long under the sky. Because the sidewalk constrained them, they comprised (Tyler suddenly realized) one of the first large entities he had seen in Vegas which had contours. He could actually sense the width of this angry crowd which stretched across the sidewalk and paraded back and forth; he didn't have to see it on a TV monitor. It meant something. He didn't know whether he agreed or disagreed with it but at least it was real. The picketers for their part had nothing to look at but the vast pink cliffs of Feminine Circus and then the blue slab under which the huge screen glowed and Jonas Andrew Brady, the big cheese, appeared on it to cry out: The world's largest sex casino! Can you take a hint? Seven thousand beds! and the picketers raised their signs high, trying vainly to drown him out, yelling: *Union! Union! Union! Union!* and then *AFL! CIO! AFL! CIO!* in loud almost bullying voices which would not go away, and some of them were ululating like Arab women.

Tyler went around the back of Feminine Circus and saw a sad man in coveralls who was dragging bags of laundry into a black truck whose side read STERILIZATION. Tyler wondered where the dirty laundry came from when the place wasn't even open yet.

He said to the security guard who watched him there in the cold emptiness beyond the crowd's edge: What do you think of those union guys?

They're making a lot of noise, the man replied, shrugging.

A handshake on the giant screen signaled the first firecracker, and the strikers went crazy, screaming *Union! Union! Union! Union!* but the crowd in the valet portico paid no attention, and subsequent fireworks annihilated the union message like artillery shells, brightly granular in the black desert sky, sandy crabs and spiderwebs that glowed. Every now and then Tyler could still hear: *Union! Union!* All right, let's get the line movin'! Let's keep it movin'! *Union! Union!* —The dynamite was beautiful, and blue beams whirred and sliced around in the vast cold sky. Dozens of fireworks shot up from behind a distant hotel with a noise like bull-roarers, polluting the night with smoke, burning the whole sky green; it rained light straight up as the band played "Back Alley Girls." On the bandshell, Brady laughed into a dozen microphones: *What happened? It was just a dream five years ago and now it's a VIRTUAL SEX METROPOLIS!*

. . . And Tyler swam through the double ranks of costumed weirdos and never-nevers, entering the marble lobby that blended into the gullet tonsilled and tumored with slot machine banks down which everyone milled. This was just how Brady wanted it to be. At that intimate media lunch he'd confided: The name of the game in this part of Feminine Circus is to get a whole bunch of people to walk by a whole bunch of slot machines. Because this is the family area. Now, the adult area will go on line tomorrow; and the name of that game is of course to pack the booths, pack the booths, pack those goddamned simulation booths with real paying customers! Hey, boys and girls, we're on an *upswing!* —But while Brady's stated goal regarding the slot machines had now been reached, the coin-swallowing lips on many of those appliances remained masking-taped, they being freshly born; their equivalent of baby-birdcries was: WAITING FOR PROGRAM DOWNLOAD. Tomorrow morning it would be the same here as it always was now at the Luxor, where a girl said dully: I remember when I first started playing poker here I never liked it, and then she put another quarter in. Of course the Luxor literally did not bear scrutiny. Whenever Tyler (breaking the rule of all wise old private eyes, which was, *You can't pull a real surveillance without three people*) stood in one place too long and took notes, a security guard would come to watch. Then, too, the Luxor's walls so often rang hollow when he tapped them, whereas the MGM Grand was so grand that he couldn't even *find* the walls; and here at Feminine Circus he was always lost even when he knew where he was. The crowd came pouring in for free food, congesting the rooms until the waitresses in white aprons who ferried silver trays of new food above their heads could barely get through.

Tyler could not shake off a certain respect, even pride (strange to say) in the vastness of this place! It was an *American* place, big and colorful and hollow; probably ninety percent of the people on earth would give anything to spend money in places like this. The reflection of a flashing star above a quarter slot (more favored by the "average gambler" than nickel, dime or dollar) beat within a forgotten glass of wine as if it were a heart. Two media blondes in short red skirts sat side by side at a Jackpot Jungle and a Home Run, drinking margaritas. —No, we're not virtualettes, they kept telling everybody, we're *real!*

Tyler approached these ladies and said: Excuse me, but could you help me get Queen Zenobia's autograph?

Sir, said the nearest blonde, I'm terribly sorry, but Queen Zenobia is terribly, terribly busy.

Well, I'll be, said Tyler, open-mouthed.

You probably will, said the blonde.

The other blonde, pitying him, said: Never mind. She's not the real Queen Zenobia. She's just a stand-in. Mr. Brady is still trying to cast the real Queen.

Ah, said Tyler wisely. Well, thank you so much for your time. Let me just ask you one thing.

Mm hm? said the blonde.

Would Jesus demand that we reject all this?

The woman stared at him.

Cain would say it was up to us, said Tyler with a sinister chuckle. And he walked away.

He felt very hungry, but figures streamed so urgently between the weird cold rainbows in the niches of slot machines that for the moment he gave up the effort to fill his plate. A pharmacist was coming out of an unmarked door muttering: Norpramine, desapramine . . . —Tyler considered that a little strange. Somewhere beneath the triple-decker ledges of silk flowers which ascended to the starry ceiling, a man's hands almost touched, one being wrapped in a twist of napkin, holding his plate, the other seizing a taco on the plate to bring it to his mouth; Tyler saw only this detail of him without the wholeness. A middle-aged woman stood at the center of an aisle between slot machines, throwing back her head and smiling. There was a lot of talk and happiness, and Tyler wondered if that was because so many machines were off. —They say it's virtual, a woman said, and another woman said: They say he's got the Queen. —People walked purposefully, stood speaking to one another, looked into each other's eyes, and enjoyed the food, which was quite good; Tyler finally snagged a squishy handful of steak tartare. When he caught his breath, he found himself in a large bay in the wall-coast papered with what were in fact very beautiful butterflies and weeping willows (*those murals are actually handpainted on real canvas and then put up like wallpaper!* one of the guides imparted reverently.) A virtualette identified for Tyler by a change girl as Sweet Pickins' writhed her six arms above a bank of dollar slots beneath a **LOVEBUCKS** kiosk whose red telltale of millions kept going up and up and up, by perhaps a dime a second, and from afar Tyler glimpsed friendly monsters passing.

| 259 |

There was another kind of virtual reality, too, as the procession of tourists who went up Las Vegas Boulevard from the MGM Grand to the Luxor learned when they reached the corner trodden with soiled fliers, and at this corner a boy stood trying to pass the fliers out discreetly folded so that they didn't look like what they were. A man accepted one, and as he bemusedly opened it, the silicone-pumped boobs leaped out and he, his wife and the children opened their mouths and then he strode back to the guy and said: Listen, buddy. *You,* take this back! I don't want this crap.

This ad, which Tyler philanthropically retrieved from the unfazed herald of good times, described a young Guatemalan girl (later he forgot whether she was "beautiful," "eager," "sexy" or "submissive")—and no agency, oh, by no means; so of course what he got was a blonde from Alberta in a red Jeep Wrangler; she said that the hundred and twenty-five an hour was just for the agency, and she wanted a tip. He made it four hundred and she sulked because she usually got eight hundred to a thousand, which at first he did not believe. But maybe it was true, because during the half-hour that she stayed and fidgeted, the agency called every ten minutes in amazement that she was still there.

Usually I'm in and out in five minutes, she explained. That way the guy doesn't have time to get mad before I'm done.

What can you do in five minutes? Even a blow job takes longer than that!

Well, I give him a full body massage, but he has to use his own hand.

It took him a moment to calculate the sum of these convolutions. —You mean he pays you a thousand bucks to jerk off to you?

Yeah, she shrugged. I guess you could put it that way. I'm not really a sex girl.

What are you then?

Let's just say when I'm through they usually don't do it again! she said with the same valley girl smile of the digitized Queen of Diamonds whose lavender breasts got obscured every second by the PLAY 5 COINS sign. —But sometimes I do get repeat customers. It still amazes me. But in Vegas it's different. This is the big money, man. You get high rollers and they don't care what they spend.

I guess that means you've got to be going, huh? said Tyler.

Why are you like that? At least I'm not a Brady Girl—I'm *real,* I'm *me,* I'm—

Then can I touch you?

Nobody touches me, mister.

Oh. So you're not real, either. Hey, listen, did you ever hear of the Queen of the Whores?

Wake up, mister, she said, rising. We live in a democracy. And by the way, I stayed an extra five minutes. Do I get a bonus?

Nope.

Shrugging, the blonde dialled the agency and said: OK, I'm leaving. He's not going to give me any more.

It's kind of different here in Vegas, he said in his best hayseed voice.

She lit a cigarette. —The other thing that's different about Vegas is that in all these hotels, even the real fancy hotels, the windows never open.

Because the people who lose big money might . . . ?

Exactly. Same reason there are no long flights of stairs.

She was already putting her coat on and then she left him—rich, beautiful, contemptuous, and he felt only a little more empty than before.

| 260 |

Even divinities such as Jonas Brady need to procure business licenses, and although their articles of incorporation may list for their addresses such public-deflectors as John's office address at Rapp and Singer (my client does not *want* to be contacted, John explained), still they need to get financing somewhere, and so for a snoop such as Henry Tyler of Tyler & Associates, Investigative Services, it's but a fingersnap's worth of effort to run a T.U. or a T.R.W. or any other number of credit checks, cognizant of the fact that Brady must have filled out a loan application or two in his time. No mention of cottonwood trees, but here on the blue computer screen crawled and quivered electronic proof of a pinball machine franchise, then a conspiracy to market office supplies, then the Sleep-O Hotel chain, each of them affixed in the credit bureau's memory to a name, an address, a social security number. Back in San Francisco, Tyler had run a Uniform Commercial Code listing and learned that Brady was by definition a big shot: he owned a lot of secured collateral. —And it's Union Bank, too, he muttered. That's where John always refers his clients. Okay, and what about the Dun and Brad? LOOKING UP HOST, it says. Oh, come *on*.

COLLATERAL: Inventory and proceeds
FILING NO.: 8714060005
TYPE: Original
SEC. PARTY: Union Bank of California, N.A.
DEBTOR: **Feminine Circus Co., Inc.**

The public record items contained in this report may have been paid, terminated, vacated or released prior to the date this report was printed.

BANKING 08/96
Borrowing account. Now owing medium six figures.

HISTORY 08/96
JONAS A. BRADY, PRESIDENT
DIRECTOR(S): THE OFFICER(S)

CORPORATE AND BUSINESS REGISTRATIONS REPORTED BY THE
SECRETARY OF STATE OR OTHER OFFICIAL SOURCE AS OF 08/96.

Business started 1995 by Jonas A. Brady. 51% of capital stock is owned by Jonas A. Brady.

OPERATION 08/96
Entertainment.
ADDITIONAL TELEPHONE NUMBER(S)/CONTACT INFORMATION:
c/o John Tyler, Rapp & Singer, San Francisco.
TERMS: Net 30 days.
TERRITORY: Western United States.
EMPLOYEES: 7 which includes officer(s).
 Full display complete.

And the upshot of this investigation?
Brady was Brady. Brady had committed no crimes. Brady was an upstanding citizen.

| 261 |

The next day more than sixty thousand people went between the outspread legs of the fallen angel of Feminine Circus, which from street level could be apprehended only as an asymmetrical polygon, blue and green, with so many angles bulking, sprawling, stretching and towering, but it did have a feminine head (again, à la Sphinx, like a construction paper cutout); it possessed sapphire blue triangular eyes beneath which people streamed slowly in like H. G. Wells's Eloi going down to be eaten by the Morlocks. That was the day Feminine Circus was officially open, so they'd turned the sky on over the Sea of Love, filling it with multiple rainbow sunsets. Yes, the heat was on, pipesmoke swirled around the phony trees, and the passionless attended with big change cups between their thighs, watching the whirling oranges and **BARs,** scarcely looking at whatever money came out, but not unhappy. One man bantered: I put a nickel in, but it's her machine, so she gets the winnings! —The robot angel Valentina waved goodbye in her pink rocket, curtseyed, and ascended a cable, hung there between sun and moon until people forgot her, and crept inconspicuously back down to repeat the performance another billion times. Another crescent moon crossed the sky slowly, and stars came out. Slot machines sang all around.

Oh, that's kinda neat, a girl said.

Tyler had made a mistake. He'd judged by the Thursday night crowd. They were not sleepwalkers after all; this was the weekend now and this hotel, this incredible jungle, was alive with gambling monkeys and tigers! He could not believe how many people were passing so quickly in so many directions, drinks and cigarettes in hand; at all times cleaning ladies swept that carpet of phosphorescent flowers, combing the litter into their mouths-on-sticks; one told him: I seen Robinson Crusoe's and I seen the Sphinx and all them others, but this is the greatest! It's the biggest, it's the best, it's so beautiful! —and Tyler looked around me and saw that it *was!* —especially after a few drinks. The waitresses in short black skirts wiping tables with one hand, holding round trays of drinks in the other, families marching down the glowing carpet toward the elevators, some with cocktail glasses in hand; the calm, happy heads of the resting gamblers sitting around tables, lights slopping and lushing around, were all so busy that they reminded Tyler of the brochure with Egyptian symbols on it at the Luxor which read: **Keno While You Sleep—Play More, Win More!** Meanwhile the girl on the loudspeaker was as happy and amazed as if she'd just given birth to Jesus, crying out: Mrs. R. D. Winkler, Mrs. R. D. Winkler, you have a *feminine* phone call! I have a *feminine* phone call for Mrs. R. D. Winkler! —for, just as the gorgeous black waitress who used to work at the Horseshoe downtown said: After being down there with all those gamblers, you get used to it. You have to perform. —No doubt that was what Mr. Slapper, the P.R. guy, had in mind when escorting Mr. and Mrs. Rapp, Mr. and Mrs. Singer, John and Celia, Roland and Amanda into the very spacious and bright cafeteria (where an off-duty Greek goddess picked up a tray and stepped into line), he said (with a smile like the long crack between a cocktail waitress's puffed-up breasts): First of all, we call all of our employees *ringleaders.* Feminine Circus was connected with the Big Top until 1969. When you're onstage, always delivering, you put on your best performance. —Passing couples upturned their heads, looking at everything; nothing in any one part of Feminine Circus was quite the same; that was a triumph in which the little Cupid in the American Girl Lounge seemed to delight, for he moved and twisted in his chair, convulsed his hairy arms, threw back his head and laughed at the stars on the ceiling.

Then a woman screamed: *Ohhhhh!* —She'd hit a big jackpot. The coins began to patter out. Crowds clotted behind her and watched as the coins kept coming.

| 262 |

Suddenly an arrow comprised of neon lights began to shimmer on the floor, and a siren went off. A melodious female voice said: Ladies and gentlemen, the adult area of Feminine Circus is now open for play. Adults only, please!

The woman who'd won the jackpot looked around, and found herself husbandless. Masculine Circus, Brady's playland for heterosexual women, remained a mere blueprint.

Following the long line of men, Tyler passed through a glowing pink door . . .

· BOOK XVII ·

Buying Their Dream House

•

The introduction of [circumcision] into human customs may have come first from the women during early Mesolithic times; however, the men must have shown considerable resistance to such a barbaric act of symbolic castration . . . It was probably practiced regularly only in the centers where women wielded unusual power. . . . Polygyny without circumcision would be difficult, if not impossible, to maintain in a society in which the women expected and demanded to experience regular and frequent orgasmic satisfaction.

MARY JANE SHERFEY, M.D., *The Nature and Evolution of Female Sexuality* (1973)

•

| 263 |

In addition to his cottonwood business, Mr. Brady was, as we see, an impressario. Why should I beat around some whore's bush? He was the founder, chief executive officer, and fifty-one percent owner of Feminine Circus Enterprises, dedicated to the philosophy that love is the first and final cause. When I looked him up in *Who's Who in Retail Management,* I read a competitor's description of his face: "as vividly ugly as a fast food parking lot at night when a security light glares down on the pitted asphalt." But the competitor, who was bankrupted by Feminine Circus, was hardly handsomer. Let's not get in the way of love; let's not halt love's caravans, sexual traffickings. Love's poison makes us strut like birds; then a woman's ten outstretched fingers slide slowly down a man's back. What comes of it? Wait nine months, till the baby sits serene on its mother's lap, utterly contented by the writhing of its fingers. Is that love? Now the creature walks; again and again the mother bends faithfully down to the child whose hand she holds. Not much longer, and the child pulls away to be swallowed up in child armies. In the playground love marches with little boys stalking birds slyly, to pelt them with sand; when the birds scatter, little boys throw sand in little girls' eyes instead, loving their screams. As soon as the weeping's over, back come the boys, grinning, sand dribbling between clenched fingers, and the girls suspect no evil; being only at the beginning of life's tortures, they haven't yet learned to read the malignancy of other faces. Some never do. We call them retarded. This is the story of Brady, Tyler, and the Queen; but first it's the story of a man who loved retarded girls, loved them with the tranquil smile and faraway glance of a doctor, not the other way at first, the way people leap up to watch a car accident, and I will tell you what happened on his journey for dear love when the world divided into armies.

(Could you allow me a driblet of authorial commentary right here, please? I merely want to say how embarrassed I am to introduce a new character so late in this novel— moreover, a character without a name. Dan Smooth and the FBI both know who he is, but his name is one hundred percent irrelevant; he's but a puppet, a placeholder for our plot, a *supplier* to the grand machine known as Feminine Circus. I'm of two minds as to whether we even need him at all, and if I let his name slip, he might take up more than his allotted space, or possibly we'd get attached to him. Most of the chickens and pigs I've eaten didn't have names.)

Growing up in hot California towns, our hero didn't yet know himself because trees hung heavy and silent, obscuring the children from their shadows; overhanging roofs nipped the light like hatched clamshells, eating children every evening when the bicycles came home. He and his best friend used to masturbate together at his house or his best friend's house because that was how the soldiers in love's fight impelled each other, lying side by side in the stench of suspended breathing, not yet driven to attack for the booty of breasts and soft thighs; in those days when it was just beginning he knew only his self and his craving that he had to release with both hands. His best friend said that a special way was to hang naked from pull-up bars until the penis swelled and jetted; he never tried that. That autumn when the rains fell like blood he began to think beyond the fact of his yearning, trying to imagine what girls' bodies must be like, how to kiss without butting noses, which way the slit went, who opened whose legs which way. The ransom that he'd soon take drew him to devour any distance between himself and girls; he glared at his best friend for getting in his way. Mustered armies faced off at school, watching, wanting, not yet grappling the veterans' tricks of fawning and pleasing; they knew only desperation. —Some say it's but compensation, this awardment of flattery's skills, for the sagging breasts and soft-ons which veterans must bear, but that's not so, for the great captains, soul-takers, hymen-breakers, phallus-notchers, own both tricks and strength. They take the prize night after night. —His best friend joined that detachment, learning how to scan the swish of skirts, seeing which leg was past, which leg to come, but our hero, less lucky, was doomed to fall victim to one of the girl-captains who charged, mauled him to the ground and bridled him with the golden bridle. Her brain crawled like a balled-up octopus, writhing with need, straining to possess him forever. Suckered attractions burst from her eyeballs, flickering like lashes to lure him in; they licked out of her ears, eavesdropping on his every word's weakness; they pried her lips apart into a smile, stretched down into her fingertips to caress the world hummingly, and then, full-bent, bowstringed her invasion. Stalking him even as he hunted others, she gobbled up his shadow, gained nourishment from that meal, crouched behind his unwary heels. There is no one quite so self-absorbed as a girl squeezing out her blackheads in front of the mirror. Yet even then she never stopped thinking of him, prizing him from the corner of her eye. He looked back at her and heard her high loud laugh and was embarrassed that others would hear. Discerning that he meant to flee, she closed in on him with licking and sucking little kisses, and struck him down into her conical mound of brown ring-ivy.

That night she slept with one leg over him, but he lay open-eyed, scheming how to return to his own lines. There was a girl he sought to prey on—not this one who'd defeated him. He lay stifling, panting for her, and the one who'd got him, exulting in her dreams, dreamed she was coursing him again, making him groan between her perfect white buttocks. At last he fell asleep again, only to be awoken by her fingers reconnoitering him, crawling up his leg like crabs. He could see her cruel teeth shining in the starlight. Her smile of exposed belly heaved; her navel blinked. As gently as a mother slows the arc of a swing to pluck her child out, he lifted her leg in his hands, thinking to roll free, but she sprang on him at once, rubbing her crotch against him until his weak-willed penis sprang up strong. When he'd satisfied her again she fell back on the bed's sweaty battlefield and began to breathe more evenly, her eyes closing, the octopus-tentacles retreating back inside her skull to hug themselves like a ball of dormant roots. Asleep, dead asleep, she straddled the wartorn sheet-ridges in that hot black night whose stars winked out one by one. Now the wily one she'd thought to keep slid away inch by inch, down to the foot of the bed where it was cool by her softly clenching toes. He rose and stood above her; she was his fallen enemy now, and he gloated. Stalking into her bathroom, he closed the door, turned on the light, raised the toilet lid. When he turned to wash off crusted love-gore, his mirror-face knew him, and for the first time he felt that he could trust himself like a holy image; he was friends with himself. Together they'd keep watch, strike, take the incarnadine plunder. They smiled at one another, and the double reached out a palm for him to touch, mirror-cold, glass-hard. Then he sidled out, dressed as silent as a breath, and left behind his grisly work. Unable to wake, paralyzed by the joy he'd given her, she lay still even when the back door opened and shut; only her eyeballs whirred uneasily beneath the sleep-sealed lids—

| 264 |

She woke weeping in that empty sweaty bed, already knowing she'd been routed, but her octopus held tight to patience regardless of dismay; it sent shock-troop fingers to caress her fibrulating heart until the frantic beats slowed; then, slithering between her ventricles with an invertebrate's fluid beauty, it exposed and blotted her sequestered grief. In the bathroom, octopus-fingers wiped her tears and washed her face; ringing themselves with silver and gold, they dressed her in the perfumed garments of a sacred pledge. They found his five fingerprints on the mirror and tasted that spoor, but it was cold. Long tendrils flowered out of her in all directions to find the one she hunted. Eye-suckers, budding optic nerves, reached through the windowpanes and scanned dawn's streets, greedy to see where he lurked. Octopus filaments bloomed through the telephone wires, and the steady yellow phone light showed that information was being transferred to her ear. By the time she'd made up her mouth and eyes (they'd be her battle-shield's device), her pet, exhausted by emboldening her, had itself become nervous. Now it was her turn to take in trust those skinny octopus-arms that were swarming in her heart again (not stroking this time, but darkly flickering like a girl's armpits up her short sleeves); so she damned the quarry aloud, swearing she'd find means to drown him in the dark blood of love. She combed her hair until it shone like the sun's tiny triple gleams upon a sandbound ant, patted powder on her cheeks and smiled into the mirror, not to commune, as he'd done, but to command herself; then, studying the loveliness of her throat, the sure wake of golden light on her forehead, her red-waxed lips, new soft sweater crackling with electricity, tight pants, she laughed aloud. She put on two earrings which would catch the sun like fishing-lures. Then she slung her purse over her shoulder and set out, far ahead of the sleeping platoons.

| 265 |

He was long away by then, in strange shaded places near the church, reaping other girls by the armload, sweeping them down on top of him to do his will. He netted them like birds, kissed them in a roar of lust that rolled their eyes up. They panted shining in his arms. By the time they were able to weapon themselves, he'd rushed off on other forays, and though they tracked him like wolf-dogs, hungry to gulp his blood back into their hollowed hearts, they'd become so crazed in their distress as to break ranks, rounding on each other to dispute the right to sniff his footprints, rending each other's throats for panicked malice; meanwhile, he was tongue to tongue with some new victim, hypnotizing her to draw him into her house. He went in the front door, exited the back, came in the back door and went out the front, lunging, seeking only to spend himself. But the girl with the octopus mind, more prodigious in pride and lust than any battalion, sought him with rampant cunning. An effeminate boy in suit and tie sat on a shrub-bench with his knees spread like a frog, a cigarette between them. He turned his head in a series of alert little jerks. She bore him home for a little sport, soldiered him, digested him and spat him out—she'd get the one she wanted in the end. Wetting her lips replete, patting her hair, she went out again, and this time almost won him, but he saw her first, and wisely bolted; there was another girl he lusted to strip. Would it surprise you to learn that he caught that one and pierced her well, drinking up her cries of joy? When he'd robbed her of everything but her broken heart, he retreated to his own lines where his best friend slapped his shoulders laughing, bushwhacking east with him along the north rim of the Grand Canyon, descending gulleys between steep tree-islands, then climbing step by slipping step up the slopes of slipping pine needles, breasting sunny walls of poison oak, climbing lichened limestone stairs and squeezing between oaks and pines that smelled like bees' nests where birds sang and flies twanged like rubber bands and wide white rainclouds watched the two friends from each hill. They could see the canyon blue and red and purple-banded and vast and striated and old, so old, and a cold breeze wrapped itself around a lightning-struck tree behind which salmon-colored shards of limestone lay, and behind them were the great ridges and spurs of the canyon, and the air came rushing upward and there was a sound of seashells. Here they threw themselves down side by side to compose new strategies of covert penetration for future wars, inflaming each other with more longings for girls with eyes of blue enamel, chewing over the memory-fat of other live-plucked girls; but by then the girl with the octopus mind had fished up the latest jilted one, the corpse stripped empty of its encarnadine prize; her she bribed with sumptuous sympathy to tell all; that was how she learned of his habit of kissing girls' eyes. —Yes, he kissed mine, too, she said to herself; that was the one thing I didn't make him do. —At once, casting her new friend back into the pit of grief, leaving her to wail and rot, she returned home behind her bulkheads where the octopus was free to show itself; here, in sight of the bed where she'd been defiled, she tinctured her eyes with various drops until they dazzled the day: beautiful craft, the twin irises blue with green rays as light and narrow as minnows, the pupils glittering like polished hematite! Next she painted with cool marine colors her eyelids which not so long ago had been red with weeping. At last she fluffed her lashes out like lethal spears, and their points caught light and glittered. Thus armed, thus horned like a male gazelle, she set out for the front where her enemy roved. She marauded down the sidewalk-lipped trenches of blackness, spying out the porches, decks and lawns that hid behind the breeze-blown trees, hunting the couples sipping slurpies, prowling past the fatsos who swallowed down another Big Gulp, searching everywhere, stalking him with coaxing bombshells wrist-flipped into his mailbox just as a gas grenade might be launched behind the foe's lines; in the moon-ridden heat of her frenzied nights her fingers scuttered from page to page of the phone book; and so, unsurpassed in mobility, eye-elevated in striking power, she flushed him out like the judgment of Heaven. Instantaneously she closed on him, raking and slashing with those love-lashes of hers, hooking him deep with every lash-point until he hung gape-mouthed like a trout, impaled and bleeding with admiration for her eyes; but just when he seemed defeated he somehow wrenched himself away, and his best friend sprang into the breach to woo her, see if she'd let him sow his crop while the other boy stanched his wounds in safety behind the lines. Whirling *him* aside, she pursued her prey, ripping her gaze through walls and windows to ground him, but he knew full well what to do, shielding himself behind a sweetfaced fat girl who kept pulling her sweatshirt back down her glistening paunch. Soon enough he was sucking out of her all the bird-notes of mounting suspense. Just as some women in anger rip down handfuls of air, so the girl with the octopus mind lashed her furious blood with the wiry tentacles of crazed desire. Like some farseeing bird she found the fat girl stripped and vanquished, sobbing with desire for the one who'd loved her. Another new friend! Quickly, now, spread the snares of friendship! Artfully rubbing her back with tentacles that vibrated and veered, opening her up with tradecraft, she recruited the fool's intelligence. So it all came gurgling out, in between sobs, how he'd kissed her belly, worshiping the soft bulk as if it were a god . . . That was the next weakness of his she learned about. When she'd finished listening shrewdly, milking her drop by drop, as if for affection's sake, she whelmed the fat girl back down into the grave of sticky tears, leaving her to moan to her heart's content. For those who regard solidarity in the wars of love will gain only ordinary prizes. Home she sped to her command post, there by that four-poster bed where she'd killed him once; if she carved out her future the way she meant to, he'd soon be tied there again. Behind the mirror where she kept her war-gear, she ran her glance down the ranks of unguents, selecting at last a bottle whose contents, pressed from the fruits of death, she thought to hang her next sortie on. Up with the sweater; expose the torso's implacable turrets. Take them in hand, aim the nipples straight ahead, lock into place those gunbarrels of sizzling milk. Now for the lotion, worked in with a fingertip, round and round the aureoles that glistened like target rings; the hard nipples, ready to fire, bulged menacing and pink—an easy trick, once she had him, to make him charge her with milk to machine-gun him with while her belly swelled with new love . . . and she tied on her brightest bikini, knowing that multicolored breasts are far more dramatic than when the bathing suit comes off to reveal the same old lumps of gelatinous flesh like the fat girl's belly: wait till she locked his mouth on those; the luna-moth green and yolk-yellow of her breast-cups would rush out at him like fast-moving troops! Lipsticking herself with no less care than those Greek athletes getting oiled before the wrestling bout, she set out mercilessly, and the door slammed behind her like thunder. This time she thought he'd not dodge her, no matter if he'd whizzed away in Broncos and Amigos with monster wheels, windows open, smog in, radios at maximum volume. From far away she intercepted his nocturnal emissions. Thinking he'd slipped away for good, he was browsing on girls like a buck deer grazing on the steep sunny slope, slowly lifting his legs, puckering his lips, leaning, stretching his neck most incautiously, while his best friend knelt in the high grass, with the sun brightening his antlers. She charged him very quickly, halting him with her eyes like a backroad poacher with his headlights, spearing him with the tips of her hot-colored nipples that dazed and wounded him right through her breast-cups, whistling into his heart to knock him down so that he convulsed and fouled himself with his own blood and the world went clammy, murmurous, but again his best friend roared and covered him with penile fire until he shook his head stupidly and got away from her one last time, the way you elude a breaking wave by swimming out past it, into the place where waves are only rolls of the sea's fatty belly, lurching and quivering, lifting you effortlessly on ocean bellylaughs. But he was bleeding badly; everything dizzied him hot and smooth like her sun-girl's breast.

There is a certain middle distance at which the island that one is approaching, not having grown larger for a long interval, continues not to grow larger; and yet somehow you can see that it is growing larger. This is how the girl with the octopus mind now felt.

She did not rage and tremble; she knew that next time she'd have him. Marshalling her reserves—well-plucked eyebrows, perfect ankles, dimples and fingernails and flashing blitzkrieg shoulders—she streaked on, following his tracks.

| 266 |

But once again he was out of reach of her weapons, having been conquered by another, an innocent girl who won him carelessly, almost unknowingly, simply by appearing before him like beautiful death. While the platoons of other hungry girls scoured the streets lipsticked in their reconnaissance cars, turning corners with rolled-down windows to catch unwary boys with the aching lure of a licked lip, the innocent girl mauled him with a look, holding her right hand in her left, cradling her head in her soft wave of hair, gazing at him with steady brown eyes. His will pleaded to turn away, to fatten on less dangerous prey, but a single lethal toss of her hair strangled him into silence. He could not even ransom himself from her; his best friend could not pull him home; she'd infiltrated his machine-gun nests of coldblooded charm, and a raking salvo of light from her eyebrows shattered them into stutters. Continuously firing gorgeousness upon him from her flared nostrils, she sprawled him down without even a smile. He spun as he tumbled, and his neck snapped back; his mouth gaped in a silent shriek. Then she hacked his heart to pieces.

| 267 |

Thoughts of her visited him all night, thickening like the echoes of her goodbye shouted from the window—her second goodbye, which came after the one by the stairs, when he'd embraced her without kissing her anymore and began to go downstairs and the innocent girl whispered to her cat: Say goodbye to him . . . —down the long stairs he sank to the door which he shut behind him knowing that she was at the top of the stairs watching him; he closed the door and made it sure, went down the outer stairs to the gate and closed it behind him like an astronaut leaving the airlock forever; and he began to walk into the grim loneliness of that street where a hungry man leaned into darkness watching him approach; he knew before he even passed the man that the man would stalk him for blocks; it was then that she called goodbye to him from the window. Tomorrow morning she was going away. The goodness and desperate impatience of her were being formed into some alloy as yet unknown. —(She'd told him that it was all over.)

In front of his door the girl with the octopus mind was waiting. But she could do nothing to him. He was armored against her with the ultimate armor of obliviousness.

| 268 |

The girl with the octopus mind, beautiful, sat in her empty bedroom with the white white walls emblazoning her shadow of need and sadness, and with all the loneliness of nakedness she knew that she was so far away from the army of other girls now that no one could help her on this last battlefield where the vultures already waited to dip their beaks in her decaying heart, and the octopus (which was really her anguish) glared inside her skull so desperately that her mind burst into throbbing flames and it stretched its suckers just as a child stretches his arms out as he begins to weep; then the child throws back his head to let mouth and tongue gape to the heavens; now he's prepared; in the same hopeless way, the octopus shot its tendrils out in all directions, locking them into rigid pain like a sea-creature dropped living into formaldehyde; the pale-eyed octopus was dying; the girl it was dying inside sat rocking herself and moaning and dialling to make his phone ring and ring, but nothing could drag him out of remembering one night when the innocent girl was in her pajamas.

Do you think it would be decent for me to go out like this? the innocent girl had said.

I think it would be decent for you to go out any way. You are so beautiful.

She laughed quickly. —Thank you, she said.

She never loved him. Unknowing and uncaring she whipped his heart as if it were a screaming horse. He went home aching. The phone rang, but he didn't answer it.

After she'd flown clear, he sat overhauling his semi-obsolete love weapons, patching holes in his armor, stacking up cannister after cannister of glittering heartless love-bullets to bombard her with. Knowing he'd likely have time to fire only once, he brooded over what ammunition would be most likely to kill her heart instantly. His best friend shuddered to see him so; he thought to divert him with easier targets, unaware girls to strike and crush, but he remained alone, stricken and bleeding ceaselessly. Throwing up his hands, the best friend went out alone. That was his mistake. He wasn't in his prime anymore. Laughing, he ploughed the enemy down, spearing and shooting all that he could get, but an adept girl finally slaughtered his heart. —We got the dogs so we wouldn't have a kid, but we have two kids now, he said, kissing his wife's face.

| 269 |

But the one who loved the innocent girl felt no more alone when his best friend was killed and stripped. He was already alone. So the girl with the octopus mind won him. She outraced him, then she outwaited him. She got him in the chest, and down he clanged and crashed. She danced over him as he lay there dead. Then she married him.

| 270 |

He never had to cook dinner for himself anymore. His wife did that, busy with her tentacles that were green like an Air King compressed air dispenser. His wife never ate anything that he cooked. If he washed the dishes his wife would go through every plate, until she found some microscopic spot; then she'd wash them all again. So he'd gotten out of the habit of doing the dishes, too. His wife was a professional woman, and when other professional women came over they'd be sure to make some pointed remark to him, such as: Boy, you sure are lucky to have a wife who does *everything* for you! I would *never* do all the cooking for my husband! He'd be *ashamed* if I did.

| 271 |

Had the octopus died after all? On their vacations her oiled knees remained first in firm alertness when she slept in her beach chair. Whenever he made what she considered a mistake, she found it out immediately and began screaming at him. No, the octopus was still there. It didn't know how to be happy. It tried to bask inside her victorious skull, in exactly the same way that some girls sling their bodies back against locked arms, spread palms when they sun themselves; but then it quickly began to squirm again, greedy and anxious . . .

| 272 |

Sometimes she shivered with rage at the thought that she'd won a man who was worthless. She preferred his former best friend. (His former best friend had been working for many years as a medical technician when one day he started reading one of those inspirational books that remind you to live each day to the fullest, to remember that today is the first day of the rest of your life, and above all to be sure that you were doing exactly what you wanted to do. Reading this tract, he suddenly yelled aloud: I know what I want! I want to be a used car salesman! —So he did that, and became very happy. When nothing was going on, he'd just say they were jerking off, not really coming; a sale was an orgasm. Now for the encarnadine prize!) But the octopus-minded one knew with all her tentacles that her own husband was no good. Then she'd begin to set him tasks again. One day she decided that it was his job to vacuum. On Monday, he went down to the super's to borrow the vacuum but the super said that it had been stolen. His wife said: Well then, we'll have to get a cleaning lady, won't we?

No, he said weakly, I can't afford it.

You spend your money on pretty things, said she. You can spend your money on this.

No, no, he said.

Then you can borrow it from Bertha.

But I don't feel comfortable with Bertha. I'll vacuum but can you borrow it?

No.

Okay. Then I'll do it.

On Tuesday Bertha wasn't there. He called three times. On Wednesday it was the same. His wife was going to dinner at Bertha's. He had spoken to Bertha on the phone and it was understood that he would pick up the vacuum. He went down when he was sure that dinner would be over and it had just started. Theodore was sitting at the head of the table, carving the turkey, and his wife was there and Bertha was just bringing in the brussels sprouts from the kitchen.

Oh, you have to stay! said Bertha.

I—I . . . he said, becoming tongue-tied with shame.

Sit down, beamed the octopus, glowering with pure hatred.

No, I just wanted to borrow the vacuum . . .

Can't it wait until after dinner? snarled Theodore. I mean, we're eating.

I'm sorry, he said. I didn't mean to—

No, no, no, give him the vacuum, said Bertha anxiously.

Everyone stared at him over their ruined dinner. Bertha rushed into the bedroom and got the vacuum. Doing this she awakened the baby, who began to cry.

Oh, Theodore, said Bertha. There's something wrong with the vacuum. Can you fix it?

Theodore leaped up in a rage, knocking over the ruined dinner . . .

| 273 |

She had begun to accord her career the attention which it deserved. She was an engineer for a nationwide company which manufactured super-cold smart refrigerators. If she distinguished herself, they'd give her a promotion and they could move back to the west coast. She had a number of competitors for the position, but she knifed them square in the belly; she slit their livers open; she made their guts see the light of day! Her octopus quivered and listened perpetually; it was impossible to surprise her. Those who tried staggered back gushing blood, and their fate was the same as that of the amateurs whom she herself surprised. She drove them all down to death. Catnapping from year to year, tossing restlessly in that murderous marriage bed, she seized the spoils and gathered grander weapons, until at last she won the triumph; he didn't care. Now they were all set to move into their dream house.

| 274 |

They fought about where and when and how, and the next thing they fought about was the printer stand. He suddenly realized that she had moved it into the hall to be trashed. She'd gone somewhere when he noticed. He went outside, and there it was. He brought it back inside. It was his; he was using it and it would be good to have when they got to their dream house. It was ugly and lightweight and practically indestructible. As far as he was concerned it would be fine forever. No doubt she hated it for its looks. But they wouldn't have any money for awhile. The dream house, as dream houses will, had cost more than expected, and once the closing costs were tacked on . . . If he allowed her to throw it out, he wouldn't have any ugly chair when they got there. She'd be working, and wouldn't be available. He wouldn't have money; he'd just given her his life savings for the down payment on the dream house. So he thought he was entitled to the ugly chair. That was why he brought it back in. When she returned from wherever she'd been, he saw the hatred and anger leap into her eyes.

What's this? she said.

I brought it back.

Where are you going to put it?

I don't know. Where do you suggest? he said wearily. (All evening he'd been following her suggestions.)

Out, she said flatly. We're not taking it.

Look, he said. I don't have to justify everything I take. You went and put it out without consulting me. It's mine, and—

No, it's not yours. We found it together, in the garbage. I tell you, we're not taking it! You just want to get the moving costs up. You don't care. It's not your money anymore. The costs keep going up with every stupid thing you try to save—

I'm not getting rid of it, he said then. (He'd hardly ever noticed it before.)

Now she started screeching at him. He bore it as patiently as he could, for as long as he could. His stomach began to ache. Then he told her to stop. That pleased her. Now that she'd gotten a rise out of him, she could abuse him in earnest.

He was sitting at his desk. She was standing by the table, yelling.

Please stop now, he said.

You sonofabitch, she said. You fucking sonofabitch.

She went on like that for a while.

I'm asking you for the last time to stop, he said.

Now a crisis was approaching. That was what she longed for. She refined the cruelty of her insults as she increased their volume. He did everything he could not to hear, but he heard just the same.

I'm almost at the breaking point, he said. Please stop, or I'll push you out the door.

You leave, you fucking sonofabitch.

He could actually push her out, but that would only make a public scene, and anyway he didn't want to be brutal. He just wanted her to stop. There was no use talking to her and she wasn't going to shut up. He couldn't bear it. He could leave himself, but he was very tired and had nowhere to go. Now that his money was gone, he couldn't stay in a hotel. She was going on and on, and he snapped. On his desk, ready to hand, was a textbook of hers. He looked at it. He was very angry now, and could barely control himself.

If you don't stop now I'm going to throw something, he said.

Go ahead. Throw the ugly chair. Then you'll break it and I'll throw it out.

Will you shut up?

Listen to that. The man who never does anything tells me to shut up.

He picked up her book knowing now that he was going to throw it, terrified lest he throw it directly at her and hurt her. He couldn't stop himself from throwing it anymore. He aimed at a chair near her and launched it and saw it hit the chair with a grand thud. The binding ripped. She swooped down on it and cried in a heartrending voice: You ruined it!

She set it down on the table so gently. (She never touched him like that.) Then she ran to his bookshelf and snatched one of his rarest books.

Well, he thought to himself, now she's going to throw that. I might as well resign myself.

She ran up behind him glaring and raised it over his head. He wondered if she would bring it down on his face or whether she'd shatter the computer screen. He stared away stonily.

She slammed it harmlessly down on the carpet.

How'd you like it if I broke *your* book in two? she wept.

She went into the bedroom and he heard her weeping—a weird, not unpleasant musical wail of ooh-oohs that almost made him smile. It went on for half an hour. He knew that if he didn't go in there she'd add to her hoard of resentments, citing coldhearted abandonment (that had happened before), but if he did go in he'd become the lightning rod of more abuse. So he sat staring at the blank screen of his computer. There was no place to go.

After a while she came out, crying more loudly now, to get Scotch tape to repair the book. She came near him, wailing inconsolably for her poor dear book. No doubt she wanted to make sure that he was paying attention. So he braced himself and went in.

Can I comfort you or make it up to you in any way at all? he said.

Get out, you sonofabitch! she screamed. Fucking sonofabitch!

All right, he said.

She followed him out, screaming.

Please leave me alone, he said. I got out, didn't I?

She went back in and slammed the door and cried for a while. Then she came out and rummaged in his tool box a foot behind him, loudly. He didn't look. She took something. Then he heard a loud thud. She'd thrown the ugly chair down on the floor and was trying to smash it with his hammer. It was comical. He had to dig his fingernails into his palms to keep from laughing. Finally something broke. It was the shaft of the hammer. She cried out and flung the pieces into the garbage and left the chair lying by the door, an upside down monument to battle. He felt affection for the sturdy thing. It was his heart's proxy, just as her book had been; she could not destroy it.

In the morning he found that she'd set it outside again. He brought it in. But she got her way in the end, of course—

| 275 |

They started from Massachusetts where fog-wisps grew like grass on the surfaces of the ponds because it had just rained and he asked her: Are you a happy creature? and she said: Yep. —Then talk like a happy creature, he commanded. —Beep beep beep beep beep, she said. They drove through the hot afternoon rain and crossed into New York where it wasn't yet hazy; descending into a bowl of dark green and light green trees, they swallowed a blue mountain in their rear view mirror. The mountains there were infinitely thin, each progressively more sky-colored and transparent, until the farthest one was only the sky. As they neared them to eat them up, the mountains swelled, hardened and darkened to viridian. And then they were eaten and fell behind. They crossed the Hudson River, which was blue-grey and wide, and pierced the sumac walls to eat more mountains. Double-decker porches, towns and green tree-hills steadily lowered before them like horses' heads. Almost Pennsylvania. His wife ignored him like a sun-reddened girl smoothing her hair with a close-eyed smile. She'd walled herself into one of those temporary worlds used by people on beach towels, every sunbather alone. The tree-miles stretched leaves overhead, clutching at him and her on the narrow turns. Now at this deer crossing they began to get away from bleached Hudson River colors, into mists and browns, denser forests, leaves slicked down over more leaves like a teenager's hair, and the glimpse he got of a river through the trees was strange to him like the misty corn-fields, none of which she saw; she was driving. Wide-porched general stores rolled over for them but she never stopped. She drove over squashed roadkills sticky and grey; she devoured the plastic cow on the roof of the steakhouse and shat it out through the rear view mirror and then they were in Pennsylvania. On the BBQ billboard, the man's face was covered with sauce. He thought: Now if I blew her head off, if I made her face explode into a thousand bits and blotches and spray blood all over the ceiling and still be screaming after it was apart; if I beat her and raped her and cut her; if I burned her, tortured her, smashed her, crushed her, ground her into the floor, chopped her up, smeared her into nothing like one of these roadkills; if I disarticulated every dead bone and broke it over my knee like a dry stick, would my face be happily covered with her gore like that? —Grand hazy schoolyards, wild tiger lilies, multitopped mulleins like chandeliers. —Music, she said to him without looking. He put on a Japanese chromium dioxide tape for her, and it was the soundtrack of his life's movie: calm, instrumental, intellectual muzak. Hopeless to ask her to stop at the Snake Farm—yes, they whizzed right by that; for him only a glimpse through the open door where the cages were stacked, cratelike affairs of used barnboard, very dusty . . . They hurtled past quick round-edged tree-gaps cut by power poles, and devoured the sudden sunny flashings of meadow and ridge. It was after a rain at dusk, and the sky was a magnetic blue; the yellow headlights of approaching cars sparkled like tears, and the road wound back and forth like the final drawn-out convulsions of some pompous symphony, the trees now becoming jungle-dark blotches of steam and crime . . .

They stopped at a hotel, and she switched on the TV immediately and lay smiling at it in the huge cold bed so that she wouldn't have to talk to him. The next morning they enjoyed together the innocent delight of speeding past the solemn personages in station wagons who chew chicken legs while they drive. His wife's head was nodding and smiling to the music of the new cassette; her index finger tapped itself on the steering wheel; she sang *la*- la-la-la-la. As far as he could see, cars rolled along in parallel, as if pulled by the same string.

| 276 |

Green fields and red barns sped across his eyes like sleep as his octopus-minded wife drove them west past roadkills more rare, flattened and hairless than before. The grass along the median strip was browner and drier. He saw twin white horses by a stagnant pond. Just as a moth squashed on the windshield is at first a splash of gorgeous yellow-green, but gradually darkens as it coagulates until it is little different from the yellow painted line at the road-shoulder's edge, so his anxieties baked hard hour by hour on the bloodcaked grill of his heart. Fearing he'd already met the worst, he tried to embattle himself more proudly, as if he could turn the tables again the way he had that first night, when she'd had him and slept, and then he'd stood above her, to go back among the other girls. But no, she was his day's eternal nightmare. Speeding sunpoints rushed from leaf-spike to leaf-spike of the corn like falling dominoes. In Indiana, where the irrigation lines were as rickety as drunken airplane struts, they devoured rolls of yellow grass, racks of snubby drooping trees. They ate up brown hay cylinders and rubbery green mud together. The radar detector never beeped, not even at seventy-five miles an hour. He wondered what had been in those cages at the Snake Farm. He peered up through the bays of cumulus clouds, finding birds and bugs. Purple cloud-udders hung over them. Someday her breasts would turn ancient and hang down like that, purple, wrinkled and veined; they'd resemble his balls—proof of the homology of the sexes. Would he still be her slave then? Maybe he'd get lucky, and she'd have a car accident. They were now approaching Gary, rusted and trestled, a tower with fire coming out like an orange windsock; they ate smoke and bridges and more fire, leaving soot and emptiness behind them. The smells of oil and gas and sulphur throbbed inside his skull, and she turned the air conditioning up a notch, not that that would do any good, but what was the use of saying anything to her; she was as impervious as these white round oil tanks that led them into forests of transformers and power poles; in a split second they slurped up a polluted pond, lipsticked with algae bloom; then they were on the Illinois side, choking down huge rusty tanks as big as apartment houses, condensers, beaked downpointed bird-skeleton machines, funnels, gallowses a dozen storeys high, poles bearing resistors like antlers; they snacked on things like a tin man's arms coming out of buildings; he ate the ones on the right; she ate the ones on the left; the things were spotted with corrosion like birdshit. Now came the brick tenements, incinerator chimneys, and like a dream the thin blue skyscrapers of Chicago rose so far away.

| 277 |

The plan of his octopus-eyed wife was to sleep that night at the condo of one of her colleagues who designed smart microwaves whose black glass jaws slammed shut on refrigerator foods shrunken hard like cold turds, then spat them out transformed into hot and lethal nourishment; she and the octopus-minded one had once charged boys together, splitting their heads open with needle-sharp eyelashes, ripping the boys' struggling tongues from their mouths to suck on. He thought the colleague had liked him once. Maybe he'd lock her in flirtation's skirmishes, stinging her heart just a little with temptation, winning a drop or two of blood, not the full encarnadine prize. So he smiled, the Amtrak rolling beside them in a fury like a caterpillar on its tiptoes, and his wife didn't notice him smiling; he knew she wouldn't; and they munched unspeaking on idle smokestacks still laddered and ringed for nothing; his wife yawned and ate a Metro train that came smashing down a hot wind among the weedy shrubs; she ate the shrubs, too, for garnish; in that hot breathless breeze he ate the smell of pavement and diesel-smoke; a child spread his hands in the diesel van ahead; the tail-light winked like the eye of an insect pimp. With their bulging bleary eyes he and his wife ate the freeway miles littered with glass, half-melted scraps of tires, hubcaps; a faint fishy breeze condensed on a passing car and he ate that for dessert . . . The traffic stalled. On the opposite side, across the barrier, a redbrown-skinned woman in a sleeveless blue dress raised her arms above her head to stretch, and he was almost close enough to smell the musk in her armpits—no reason why he'd never see her again, but he wouldn't; he'd been stripped of his gear years ago. He gobbled up a fenced-off little beach on the right, whose trash cans everywhere cast interlocking shadows between which people lay "sunning" themselves and trying to cough; while his wife drank up the unearthly lake-shimmer beyond, silent and metal-eyed; yes, she drank that pale pale blue's green. —Park and lock. —The colleague met them at the door to her engraving-hung condominium (ceramic leaves, a view of dark trees and bricks, brass fittings on the windows) whose floors creaked threateningly beneath his tread, making everywhere he stood a lost island. Her piano was barnacled with multitudes of figurines so fragile that too potent a breath would sweep them to ashes. Her clocks, terrier-faced cushions, chandeliers and bone-white knicknack excrescences prohibited him from touching anything. The colleague embraced his wife. She looked at him as if he smelled. She'd arranged a little reunion for his wife, an intimate little party, a nothing fancy under the chandeliers. Here came the designer of smart shower-heads who kissed his wife, perhaps a hair too fondly; here came the two ladies who were installing smart microphones for the Justice Department; then the famous man they'd all learned from, the gallant old one who'd married young; he'd made his money in smart syringes and smart toxics, but now in his semi-official retirement he dabbled in smart rosebushes; his young wife was the only other one there who wasn't an engineer, so after an hour of their shop talk he leaned across the table and said to her smiling: So, how have *you* learned to cope with these conversations? —Oh, she replied, so far (she'd been shifting her head from side to side as if out of boredom, but she kept doing it while she was answering him and he saw that she was doing it to follow what they said, nodding like a graceful snake) so far, she said, I try to listen and learn. If you don't mind, I'm trying to listen right now.

| 278 |

The next day they found themselves driving into the stem of a gigantic cumulus mushroom whose restful purple underbelly loomed closer and closer, blue sky vanishing on either side. Ahead fell streams of violet rain. His wife licked her lips and devoured the first drop that struck the windshield, the second; now the car was shaken by rain; the hood danced with it. Two smart eyelashes swept back and forth across the car's rectangular eye. Raindrops boiled on the pavement ahead and on the hood. Rain washed squashed bugs away, and they came out clean and new.

Each day the knot in his stomach tightened. They hadn't been speaking for the last hours, after she'd screamed at him you asshole and then ordered him to read out the directions, and he said: Not until after you apologize and she said: Not until *you* apologize for being an asshole.

The cornfields and cumuli of Iowa showed him purity unequaled (he didn't know what his wife thought), and he said to himself: There ought to be a saying: as pure as a cloud in Iowa. His stomach ached. They passed a waterslide amusement park in the middle of the cornfields—

| 279 |

That night they were to stop at the house of one of her colleagues, who'd just moved to Omaha, and he dreaded it because if there was not to be a scene before the colleagues there must be false cheeriness; fortunately he barely knew them; the hypocrisy would not be as grave. He dreaded it eating the clouds that boiled up in towers and pointing fingers; he dreaded it rolling across the wide brown rivers of low fat trees. There were so many things she was required to apologize for now that he supposed he'd better buy a little black book to keep track of them all in. But then she'd get a black book, too, and she'd write down lies about him. Then he'd have to find her black book and erase the lies. They'd end up hiding their black books from each other. Someday soon he must start taking revenge by the breasts. A goose and three goslings tried to cross the freeway. His wife swerved to avoid them. They danced back into the other lane, and then a car came round the bend and squashed them. At twilight, approaching Council Bluffs, the road began to sing, a steady breathless *aaaaah* whose cadence wavered with the angle of the road; the shoulder glowed white in the sun; trees and prairie grass vanished in the sun's hurtful orange glare, which leaped from tree to tree, always the same spot of ferocious blindness. When they pulled up before the just completed house, which lurked in a gated labyrinth of just completed houses already Kentucky bluegrassed into permanence, when they rolled into the three-car garage, the colleague came out smiling and went over to the driver's side where his wife was unstrapping herself from seatbelt coils. He got out before she did and went around to the driver's side and said to the engineer: Well, Ernest, how are you? —Linda! cried the engineer, beaming as the driver's door swung open. —What a lovely house! the octopus wife said. (He hadn't heard her voice for eight hours.) —How are you, Ernest? he said again. —The engineer didn't even look at him. He wondered if there was something wrong with his face. He wondered if his face was the same as it had been the night that his wife and the engineer had graduated together from the refrigerator institute and his wife had been screaming at him asshole and fucking asshole and bastard just before the graduation and then it was time to put on his suit and tie in her honor. He had considered not going, but this was an occasion that would never come back for her; he had no right to do that unless he was going to leave her and he couldn't do that because she'd won him and spread her hands over him night after night, widening her fingers like muskets aimed from behind a wagon-train. He got dressed. She never told him anything about her work, so he didn't even know who was graduating and who the other people were, and his feet hurt in the dress shoes because the reception was being held in a concrete warehouse filled with the latest smart refrigerators that talked back to you when you asked for a glass of milk, so finally he went into the buffet room where it was just him and the piano player; misery stabbed him and twisted, but his chest strained hard against the point of it, strained by habit so that no harm was done. Misery shot casts at him but could not hurt him because he knew that it was there; he hardened himself, expressionless. He sat down at at a table weighted with romantic candle flames, awaiting the hour for dinner, and when it came, when the others gathered there (no dodging them now), his wife sat down beside him. His callus-armored heart split open in a great cracked clang of pain, and the soul-blood spurted; so he rendered up to her the incarnadine prize. He would not change his face. They stared at him and talked to him as if he were an imbecile and finally ignored him. She was the class president. After dinner it was time for her speech, which he also dreaded like a shower of scorpions because last year's class president had thanked his wife in his speech, but this wife of his would not thank him. Of course he hoped she would. As she drew closer and closer to that part of her speech, he began to believe that her colleagues were eye-raping him just as courtroom spectators will watch the accused when the foreman of the jury rises to give his verdict. Now she was at that part, and it gave him bliss beyond words to know that she wasn't going to thank him; that way he could go on hating her. When her speech was over, and she hadn't thanked him, the leaden-headed clawshaft of humiliation hammered him almost backward, impaled him to his seat. Looking at his plate, he saw that he hadn't eaten any dinner. When the engineer's wife said goodbye to everyone, she kissed everyone else's cheek, but she only shook his hand and told him loudly that she was leaving, as if to a senile grandparent. It was to her magnificent new house (which had been lived in for less than a week) that he and his octopus wife had now driven. The house was so huge that all the couple's possessions barely made a dent in it. Fierce sunlight zigzagged down the carpeted stairs; carpeted rooms of oceanic vastness bore nothing on their down but a child's ball, were sunned by no lamps yet; genesis had not finished; there were so many rooms! The garage had arch-shaped windows. Moldings and central vacuum units and doors leading to great caves confused him. Outside there were other lawns and other new houses; nothing else but a smoldering humid sky. —How are you, Ernest? he said a third time, at the next lull. The engineer never looked at him. He began another conversation with the octopus-minded woman, who was raptly stroking the engineer's new car. —Glad to hear it, Ernest, he said softly.

| 280 |

Inside, he and his octopus wife admired the house in separate but equal ways, praising, lying, rhapsodizing, propagandizing like performers skilled at song; talking never to each other. The engineer and his wife were so caught up in the narcissism of owning their new house that they didn't notice, believing that their house truly was the best in the world because they lived in it; naturally the world (comprising in this case their first two house-guests) would so praise the house, holding it in such reverence that they wouldn't talk to one another . . . The engineer took them to examine the back lawn. Our hero told the engineer to weather-seal the deck posts. The engineer could hear him now; he was talking about the engineer's house. But there remained a fretful expression on the engineer's face when he said anything to him; when he took two steps backward, leaving the engineer to babble with the two wives in those carpeted caverns, then that expression eased, and the engineer no longer tapped his foot . . .

As soon as he could, therefore, he said that he had to take a shower. He took the longest shower he had ever taken in his life. Then he told them he had to go to bed. With the door shut, his ground chosen, he robbed the bed of one of its four pillows and lay down on the carpet, his body half in the closet to be as far away from her as he could; for a moment it seemed he owned himself again. His wife stayed up until midnight. He lay awake wondering if she were telling them of all the wrongs he'd done her.

| 281 |

The next morning, rolling away through the hot pig-scented winds, they began getting ready to pretend that the quarrel hadn't happened. They were not absolutely unspeaking and unhearing like walled-up statues anymore, although it is true that they didn't make unnecessary talk, either. They answered one another politely but succinctly. He never looked into her face, although he occasionally glimpsed her shoulder move when her right hand moved upon the steering wheel. They were going to Denver. She had another colleague there. This was a woman who was developing the prototypes for smart lamps. With a little luck, while his wife and the colleague ignored him he could steal some of the colleague's dirty underwear and sniff it—

| 282 |

Devouring the boneparched sandbars on the Platte, they drove on to where the grass was lighter, the corn smaller, the highway faded almost white. There were sandhills in the fields now. At Cornfield Creek with its occasional stains, each from a single tree, his wife ate a young boy, tanned and naked to the waist, who was walking along with a fishing pole over his shoulder. Near the site of Buffalo Bill's grave the first dry ridges started twisting out of the flat ground, the dirt all the different colors like the fireworks that the twin blonde girls were selling at their stand. A man bicycled in a cowboy hat. Swallowing heat-crisped grass and dustyblonde fields of hay bales, they rode the ricket-fenced roadside whose ranches rambled painted and unpainted, hoarding dust-manured corals.

Suddenly his wife patted his arm, gazing at him with a loving smile.

| 283 |

When they got to Colorado, the sun, waiting just behind a thunderhead, sent misty chlorine rays down a grey and orange fogbank; beneath this cloud-spider, below the smell of spruces, beehives and water, below the chittering of aspen leaves like TV static or fish scales in waves, Denver stretched hot and flat and smoggy. They went to to the colleague's house. He remembered her as a girl drinking pink magaritas with his wife when she was not yet his wife. Now her prettiness had tightened, like his wife's, and when he moved to embrace her he saw a grimace split her face from top to bottom, and he saw that the line it followed was a habitual line; she was a professional now. At least when he'd hugged her he'd made her breasts go squish . . .

He'd tucked his shirt in, and at once his wife came to pull it out again. He shook his head, moved away and tucked it in again. She followed him and pulled it out. He pushed her away so hard she almost fell.

| 284 |

Down the twirly mountain highway, past Leadville, the gorges were corrugated with dark green trees. Valleys, bowls, and overlooks bored him. Bare mud-peaks were snow-striped like skunks' tails. Twin-stacked diesel-snorters raced down green horse meadows. They had a fight whose anguish diffused through him just as altitude sickness begins from between the eyes and then spreads inside the skull, but by then, descending the sandy cutaways puffed and dotted with desert shrubs, they'd lost all the altitude they ever would, she flicking him an eye-corner's worth of her contempt, just as she might flick a dead fly off a piece of paper; thus his octopus-minded wife, her heart plated with chitin. They came down into blue-salted canyonland that was goosebumped like a chilly girl's legs; and cocoa-colored sandcliffs, topped with old cracking rocks, nosed down at them and their fate. Sharp-tongued mountains growled around, snapping at the sky like famished dogs. The dinosaur buttes pierced the sky with their sharp and dusty back-bones. She said something, but her words buzzed by him like flies by a shady pool. Not far from the aluminum-sided "café" where they sold pliers and soda and "authentic" Navajo souvenirs (the trash can was too hot to touch), they came into Utah, his wife driving faster and faster, whirling down the highway like a sudden twister of tan dust. He choked down lopsided outcroppings lumped, bumped and swollen into dolmens be-neath the clouds, all of it reddening into postcard quivers. Lumps and bumps, that's all it was, utterly impervious, all gypsum and concrete and halfbaked pyramids and hun-dred-foot dogshit fossils, Disneyland ramparts and piss-yellow plaster casts of tits and cups, mountains of dried feta cheese now mold-grown with sagebrush; and clouds as smoothly twisted as the country they hung so mushily over. The day's last sunbeams were eyelashing down. They crossed a country's dozen of horizons all in a row, purple, red, brown and blue. Zealous at the wheel, she stuffed sandstone chessmen and Nazi rubble into her mouth, and then they came down into the green ranches of evening.

| 285 |

From Denver they drove to Vegas; from Vegas to the coast; the following day found them parked for good, all ready to begin happily ever after in their dream house.

· BOOK XVIII ·

Feminine Circus

•

But when you have chosen your part, abide by it and do not weakly try to reconcile yourself with the world. The heroic cannot be the common, nor the common the heroic . . . Adhere to your own act, and congratulate yourself if you have done something strange and extravagant, and broken the monotony of a decorous age.

EMERSON, "Heroism" (1841)

•

Staring out the corner window in the evening as white cars and blue cars drove very slowly toward him, then vanished beneath the shuddering maple tree, which was wide like Mau-Mau skin sandals, our unnamed hero remembered the innocent girl; it was the recollection of her innocence (which I said was not really innocence) that led him into his interest in retarded girls, which began one Pennsylvania night when he'd become so isolated from his hostess, lost in the forest of candles and crystal, surrounded by people with whom conversation had been exhausted like an old mine, so everyone stared in non-intersecting gazes at the hostess, who, smiling and rigid, nodded big-eyed as the guest of honor (not our lover) slipped a hand across the back of her chair; she parted her lips in wonder at his every word; but, being a good hostess, discovered the silence across the table before it had even fallen; so that while the guest of honor talked on and she nodded like an amiable puppet she was already scheming how to save him so far away across the table—and did she? Well, not until after dinner; there was no human way he could be spared that ordeal. He'd known that before he got there to be seated beneath the painting of Isis with her slender buttocks always in profile on a narrow ledge, raising her hands, groping at the Pharaoh. It had been that way ever since the time he'd spied on his octopus-minded ex-wife, who'd been waiting for him. She was sitting alone on a bench in the night, on the corner of the bench, a marble bench. She was a little hunched, with her arms linked over her purse, and he could see from behind how her blonde hair darkened steadily toward the center of her head until it almost achieved the blackness of her dress, which, being velvety, not shiny, and abetted by the stark white hem, far eclipsed the blackness of her high heels as she sat there on that bench, never moving; until a couple sat down beside her and then she moved a little farther away. After half an hour she started looking at her watch. His hatred grew. He longed for her to leave. But she was waiting for him. She waited for more than an hour. When she finally stood up, he began to cry very quietly in the bushes behind her. Now she'd be going to do the other thing, he supposed. He could see her. She had her face between the other woman's legs, working at her with soulful sucking sounds, as greedy as a girl probling the long plastic spoon into her cup of slushy-ice on a hot lunch hour, sitting sidesaddle on a bench, hunched over the slushy to help its coolness reach her sweaty throat; in her joy she no longer sees the army of boys who drive their division of golden plastic tanks almost to her toes; when she's scraped every little crystal of blue-green ice from the cup, she bends down further, claps it to her face, works her tongue as far down the cups insides as she can reach, pig-nosed with that cup between her eyes. That was how it must be with his wife and the other woman. This had never happened and never would, but he needed to believe in it; that was as good a method as any to invent a way she didn't love him. So he fled as soon as he could, like a gecko fleeing a moving shadow, and the hostess was sorry that she'd asked him to her dinner party because nobody could draw him out, and the women who'd been compelled to sit beside him at that vast and miserable table were more than happy to talk to other men, and he was twitching, blinking and sweating as he got into his car. If you have ever seen a couple at a bar, she smiling with lovely white teeth and with every calligraphic eyebrow-hair, her lashes sparkling with fun, her pupils gleaming, her nostrils stretched wide, while beside her he leans droopy-eyed, his smile a purely sarcastic knife or leaf, and behind him somebody in the darkness chugs another can of beer, then you will know more or less how it had been. It was almost dark. He drove to the outskirts of that town, where American flags hung limper than used condoms, only the brass eagles nailed above doorways hanging firm; and he passed the taprooms and the rusty markets that sold Hershey's ice cream, and his headlights massaged the portico of the Weed Hotel, turning left onto the two-lane highway whose bus just ahead got bigger and smaller. Finally the bus turned off, and then it was a van just ahead, inside which children were fighting, silhouetted in the dusty window. —Past the fence of three rusty cables at the roadside marked here and there with plastic forks and squashed possums, the grass ran richly down to river-ponds almost as warm as blood in which the teenagers bathed beneath the powerlines. He pulled over by the picnic tables, got out, locked up because he knew the ways of the Pest. Scuttling down through prickers, bending back the soft lavender sneeze-flowers, he slid into his favorite spot, a culvert whose uphill end he'd sealed off with shovelfuls of dirt; there he kept his foam rubber mattress, the moss-stuffed mailbag for his pillow, and when he lay there watching the skinnydipping girls through his binoculars, he could always be counted on to ejaculate like some stupendously stupid night-lit fountain streaming and spilling and guttering through its troughs. How innocent *they* seemed, too! They were innocent because they didn't know that he was watching them; their breasts swelled with the same candor he'd seen in sneak-peek photographs. (Yes! His name was Dan Smooth.)

He knew not, this veteran captain, what plan to urge upon himself except the old plans (no fault of his, that old plans were derailed); he'd fall back into the encarnadine trench, taken by persuasion's assaults! His octopus-minded ex-wife had paid him back for yesterday; he'd pay her back with tomorrow: that is how wars go. Limping down between rocky uncertainties as a cat limps, he wandered through a graduation at Berkley which he'd come to just to see the girls; his resolution had not at all affected the routine of the Economics Department whose young faces were meaty and confident beneath the mortarboards, parents brushing the dust and soot from the shoulders of their dark gowns, Japanese dads focusing their zooms while every mom looked on with full-judged concern. Ignoring sons, he scanned the daughters with salvo upon salvo of loving glances . . . no use—he'd grown too old! The sun shone with impersonal malice on the cement, none of the young graduates suspecting the dark wretchedness of adult events that would mutilate and eventually destroy them. The profile-line of mortarboard, cheek and gown was very pleasant, but now the graduates doffed their ceremonial vestments and lost their splendor, becoming just like everyone else. —Well, now he'd do what seemed best to him. No luck with young things, incarnadine prizes unripe? Well, he'd light the battle in another way, with the flame-white hair of elder dames! Surely *they* wouldn't keep their treasures to themselves . . . Fishing deathlessly, he soon had something on his hook . . . That very night he was besieging the middle-aged lady with kisses, undermining her vigilant lips, his tongue the battering ram that assaulted the gates of her modestly clenched teeth which held firm until, sending a clever shot behind her lines, he exploded and dissolved her earlobe in a single lick of slobbery lust; now the gates opened, and ferociously the tongue surged in, pillaging her mouth's stronghold of all its well-wrought treasures of moans and sighs; dragging her down on top of him to complete the work, he launched grazing passes between her still-clothed thighs. —I really think you'd better . . . she began; and he kissed down her murmurs until they were both outbreathed . . . —Stop, she said. —Just one more kiss, he said (expertly conducting his propaganda war). He rolled her on her side, clasping her beyond possibility of escape, and began to suck the spit out of her. His hand rubbing and rubbing until the juice worked out through her pants, he said: You really want me to go? —This is mad, she said. Yes, yes . . . —Yes what? —Yes I want you to go. —I will, he grinned, any time now. —His other hand had twisted down the front of her blouse to loot her intermediate prizes. The hand between her legs was rasping harder now; he felt the first small spasm of her defeat; and she began clinging to him harder and he said: Should I go or not? and she said: Is this some kind of game? and he lowered his face very earnestly down upon her face and said: Mm hm as he directed more whizzing salvoes across her body to breach her other swirls and brattices, making her breath come thick and hot and fast as she straddled him writhing like a soldier whose belly's been blown open by a lucky shot, and he said: So, should I go? and she giggled and said: You devil . . . —The next morning he was with a charming Mexican woman, pressing a Hershey's chocolate kiss into her hand, saying: Don't say I never kissed you. —You never kissed me, she said, pouncing on him, and he was kissing her swimmingly and they went out for coffee and eggs and bacon and ham and sausage and biscuits and gravy, cramming it in until at last she leaned back sighing happily and said: I like you because you are so intelligent and analytical! and he put his hand on her sweet arm. —But as soon as he left her to match himself against the lovely young girl champions whom he once could have run down like a hunting dog, he shrank and said: I'm not what I was. —That evening he wandered past the trio playing Smetana in the old Jesuit chapel at Loyola University, the stained glass windows gleaming, everyone sweating, and someone told him (he knew not whether it was true) that the Jesuits hated for the piano to be played. But the trio played until it was dusk, and the yellow windows glowed. The sky was awash with cerulean blue; the evening smelled like grass. He wandered past girls as lovely as the disconnected squares of snowquilt blueness seen between a field of bushy cloud, but he cringed from them; he was afraid now. —My ex-wife's ruined me! he thought. —He wandered down the dark and dirty streets owned by princesses of darkness. A whore, a whore, and looking at her he knew right away that he'd forget her face even though it was beautiful; she blocked his way on the sidewalk and said hi and he said hi and she wanted to know what she wanted to know, so he must break the bad news; but she took his hand and squeezed it and he squeezed it back for a minute before he walked on, not looking at her, and he'd already forgotten her face, but strangely enough he remembered her hand; it's a cliché to say that black people are chocolate-skinned, but that hand of hers was the lovely reddish-brown of fresh cocoa shavings—

| 287 |

During the divorce settlement he came across an unsent letter from his ex-wife to his mother which ran: *Sometimes I think that we hide from ourselves how deeply we feel about people. For instance, my husband. I always thought him a little dull and condescending, but at the same time he did me favors and so I thought I liked him until last night when I dreamed that he was chasing me around the house, stalking me with a gun, meaning to kill me, and waking up I realized that I had always feared and hated him.*

| 288 |

So while his powers shrank he fought on, long cut off from his own lines because the others had been defeated long ago, riven into marriage beds by the octopus-eyed girls, or (no better and no worse) they'd won the encarnadine prizes they'd striven for and retired from the lists, licking them over and over in their life's last caves like dragons greeding over their hoard, licking them out of dull habit, with nothing left to taste but their own stale breath. Oh, no doubt there were a few still left, fighting on ragtag and wild, but in the wars of merciless love, as I've just said, to lose is to lose, to win is to lose, and (sad but true) to keep the war hot proves no less to lose, for love-strife is a death where love-life passes us by. In the old days he never would have spied; he liked to think his ex-wife had degraded him down to that, but she was no more than a horrible fire he'd passed through, scorching and scarring him, to be sure; after all, heat was what he'd asked for. Too late? Too late for what? Whatever he might have done or not done, it was getting too late. His penis, speckled and frolicksome like an otter, would soon play no more. He'd perfume it only with sacrilege.

| 289 |

There was a lady his own age whom he thought stalked him as he stalked her, but when he closed on her, bellied up to her slit, she said: I—I'm embarrassed to say this . . .

Go ahead.

I—I'd love to let you kiss me, but I can't be like other women . . .

. . . and he saw that another game was ended; she wouldn't have had him in her sleep.

| 290 |

He sat at home reading the Neutron Trilogy but he couldn't concentrate.

He thought of a long and lovely face sipping at a straw. Her eyes were so big they filled up half her face. Her pupils were ripe dark fruits.

The golden retriever bitch lifted her head and panted innocently, open-mouthed, her pink tongue as thin as a slice of fancy ham, and then she lay back down under his chair to let her honeyhaired sides quake while she basked and gnawed on the last stand of ivy which ran along the bottom of the house and which she had previously neglected to destroy. This task done, she looked at him again, perhaps content, perhaps hoping and waiting for something, so he stroked the length of her skull forward and back-ward with two fingers, until she raised her nose and licked him. She lay down again, and he heard a rustling as she worried lovingly at the dismembered vines of his dream house.

The phone rang. He got up and opened the summer door whose screen the dog had almost finished chewing off and then the cool shuttered peace of his lovely house beat down upon him like a congregation of bats as he went back into the narrowest hallway where the phone was still ringing.

He said hello.

I just wanted to tell you, said the middle-aged lady, that I've found somebody else . . .

| 291 |

Where were the prizes then?

| 292 |

. . . They could be called perpetual children. That was the usual way to think of them, two-day piglets puny and shortfurred like monkeys. Some had almost reached adolescence, which hung over them big and shiny like an autumn sunset in northern Canada, crawling brightly, feebly along the ridgetops so that it must be obvious to anyone that darkness will be in sway within half an hour and yet at midnight the sun is still there; others were stammering two- and three-year-olds just on the threshold of complex speech. (Still others, of course, could not talk at all.) In many cases they were sick children. They received medication every day; they had to be guarded against the extra few minutes in the sun or the second chocolate bar that might bring on a seizure. Like children, they lived imprudent and unaware, and could not keep themselves from danger. When they were cruel to one another, their cruelty sometimes partook of craft. But original sin was in everyone's children. So he kept saying to himself, but his authority over them could not be of as simple and absolute a character as the authority of an adult over a child. Because he hoped that some of them would eventually be able to take care of themselves, he allowed himself to be persuaded by them that this time their choice should be the deciding one, and today they could stay out of the swimming pool, even though he wished that they would go in again. —Well, he was equivocating; he would do the same with a child. (He had not yet seduced his niece.) The real reason that the relationship was problematic was that some of them had passed puberty and were aware of it. A few of them were attracted to him sexually, and sometimes he, despite himself, was attracted to them. Sexual desire, suppressed though of course it had to be (because the Chief Medical Officer was watching from the steel desk, his eyes dull, as if he'd been taking the drugs he prescribed), was the great enemy of the well-intentioned hierarchy. As flesh wanting flesh, he and they were equals; they could satisfy each other, and some were quite beautiful. Their hands squeezed his when he held them; their hair blew in the wind; the women touched their breasts and smiled at him . . . and then between those half-parted lips the tongue protruded again; the hand pulled away and began to scratch.

The Chief Medical Officer blew his nose, which was as red and glossy as the bloom-phallus of Indonesian sun-ginger. Wrist-angle, neck-angle, the weird glasses-gleam and boniness of life! —I believe in you, Dan! the Chief Medical Officer said. —Then the Chief Medical Officer gave him his charges, slack bodies to animate.

| 293 |

As the final recreational Thursday drew toward him like a grey station wagon cleaving the hot afternoon, he tore himself off his wailing dreams and began to arm, buying road maps on the sly, calling in a reservation on a travel bungalow across the state line. He was ready to give birth to his own brooding thoughts. Gliding over the slippery backs of days, he snatched handcuffs and tranquilizers, bought the right women's clothes, honed his smile-flashes sharp to do love's butchery again. Fortune's child like us all, he hummed with power like an electric drill only because Fortune had plugged him in. —No, the tense feeling of travelling alone into darkness is no worse than usual, he said to himself. It's just that I've gotten out of practice. —So they got in the sky-blue bus, counselors and inmates; they were going to the fair.

Win, win, win, win! the barkers shouted. Come on over! —The retarded ones cringed or laughed or shrieked for glee, gaping at the stuffed animals of every putrescent color which hung for prizes in love's abbatoir; they were inside the fence now, tickets paid (a favor they'd never notice), hands stamped. —Group leaders! Group leaders! Pay *attention*, group leaders! We'll meet here at five-thirty sharp! Have a wonderful, wonderful time—

One of his charges was absent with a seizure—all the better for him. The other speechless ones could be disposed of with blinding pieces of change—here, for instance, where the phony canoes slammed down the river slide like a horrible torture. Strap them in; no malingering now . . . Wipe the drool from their chins one last time, give them their meds a little early (a triple dose); slip the carnie man two twenties, presidential side up: Just keep them going round. I'll be back in an hour . . . —As for the crowd, they were too busy pretending not to stare at the retards to notice *him* . . .

Fingers tight around her wrist. She turned to him full-face, ready to be led; he had the prize. Already the machine was starting up; over its roaring and clattering he could hear the speechless boys begin to bawl in fright. Well, they could bawl all they liked; not one would spill the beans—

Slipping his arm around her waist, he took her past the huddle of grey-clad security guards who lounged chuckling at the crackle of their own walkie-talkies, drinking Cokes, smoothing their greasy hair, glaring amiable at one another through ultradark sunglasses; no, they'd never remember him. He led her through the end of the afternoon swollen with light like some monster California orange, taking her where the heat and glare were fiercest, stalking through unknowing crowds, dodging her silently past girls throwing darts at balloons that resembled multicolored pustules (the girls hoped to win ugly pictures). She grunted softly and dug her feet in, twisting away from him to look back at the silver-studded ferris wheel whirring, gleaming fiercely in the sun. Then he saw that she was listening and sniffing for the scents of the other group leaders' cargo of differently ableds; some were up there whirling and gaping; just beside it, a number were strapped screaming to the giant pendulum on the pirate ride, raining down puke . . . —Perhaps it was that that she sniffed and smelled. Did she remember their odors enough to miss them? —A barker was grasping air, wide-eyed, trying to grab him in. —Hey now let's go now let's play let's PLAY! Try it! —She turned her deadly gaze upon the barker, who said: Hey I'm sorry. —He took her away, the barker forlorn and sheepish, and he bought her a butterfinger-flavored slushy which she messed all down her dress and sticky hands, stretching her arms out to him like the bewildered parents stumbling down the children's rotating tunnel. He went and got electrocuted to win her a giant teddy bear which she went *awwwwrr* over and rubbed it up and down against her slushy-stained breasts while the yokels gawked, and then she retched, just a little yellow-brown tail sliding out of her mouth, and he wiped her on the bear and she started licking it back up, then she allowed the bear to fall to the cement puke-matted in the hot sun with flies already shooting down like bombers and her cheeks were blue and green where the bear's dye had come off. They were getting very far ahead of her lines now; they were going so far into his country that she'd never be coming back. The other inmates were long lost, the pirate ride out of sight; at the place where you throw baseballs at beer bottles he found a water fountain and cleaned her face up a little; she slurped up the water and he let her drink until she was satisfied. Then he put her on a segment of a giant green caterpillar, riding beside her with his hand between her knees, and an old lady said to him: You're disgusting, taking advantage of that retard like that, and she said: *Worrrwww worrrww.* The ride ended full circle and he led her off, stalking deeper and deeper into the fair. Two women were hitting each other with giant inflatable crayons. A man in a white barbeque cap scratched his stubble crosswise and watched her. He drowned her in pools of sunlight, leading her into unknown valleys where the barkers shouted: There he is! — She was hugging her horse now on the merry-go-round, cawing and almost falling off, so he grabbed from his companion steed, saving her as they whirled past SWIRL FRIES ten times a second; her mouth was open. She looked away, writhing her fingers . . .

| 294 |

Hundreds of ribs and chickens burned on a giant glassed-in grill. Guys in baseball caps stood squirting them with hoses. She stumbled bowlegged behind him, finger-chained by him, her face gaping and grimacing, her tongue out. He bought her a catfish on a stick. The lights were like horrid bathroom fixtures. She stopped dead to stare through glass at the hulking girls in rainbow outfits, turning corndogs in the roaring grease . . . They saw her and started digging each other in the ribs and pointing, mouthing at her like fishes through the glass; he almost expected her lips to move silently back, but only a thick translucent thread of drool spun out . . . Hands and tongues behind glass, the green and yellow depths of her lemonade cup, the bulging pale pink nipples of the prize cow hanging straight down from the hairy, veined, and distended bag—all these and more, Virginia, swamped her marshy senses like stamping horses, pounding down the ooze inside her skull and galloping on while her darling forgetfulness oozed clear and fresh back up through the mud, washing it into its old featurelessness—or so he thought until they came to the pen of the giant sow. Giant, pink, and rosy-breasted, she offered many women's teats ranging along her in a double row, shaved and pink like a tender fat lady; and a big-eared piglet broke away from his littermates nuzzled head to toe; he scuttled down the side of his mother, who twitched her cup-nose lightyears away from her own belly; he came to the rearmost teat and she ground him viciously down beneath her hind leg so that he squealed; but the rest of the farrow, more desperate than deterred, crowded suddenly down the whole long row of teats, grunting and swarming and stepping on each other, screeching like crows, passionately sucking, but at nothing, for she wouldn't let her milk out; then and only then the retarded girl said: *Urrrwwwh!* and the great sow hunched her butt up, raised one abraded ear, turned her weary head, grunted: *Urrrwwwh!*, and let go, the dimples in her side rolling like waves, the young ones lining up straight and perpendicular now to nurse amidst that happy tremendous pink quaking—

| 295 |

He escorted her on, past a stripe-aproned girl waving phosophorescent whips; people's backs went ahead, walking toward the orange-glowing tents. They were hours late now.

The security guards would be looking for them. A Mexican, weary and sweating, turned barbequed turkey-legs on a grill more shiny than the night, the meat glowing like fiesta condoms. He hurried her down the long bright sidewalk eyelashed with pole-lamp shadows, and there was a bench between the dance pavilion and the eggroll-on-a-stick booth where the moon teased her through the trees. He pulled her down on the dark grass white-wizened like an old dog's coat. Her face was a little blurred by the neon lights. Million-colored reflections of whirling blinked in the stagnant river beside them, lights going down escalators as his fingers strapped her cheeks bone-tight, pulling her easy lips open so that he could thrust his tongue; seizing her hair like reins, he rode her face the way he wanted to; the crossed thighs of the woman on the next bench reflected a winking light . . . She beat her elbows frantically like a wounded bird. All around them, crowds sleepwalked through the lighted world as if they'd discovered the secret of happiness. The lights of the monorail rose between the trees where insects rattled. Wiping their mutual slobber from her face, he led her past another merry-go-round, now more lurid, the horses' mouths wide open in silent screams, the studded oval mirrors like blank mouths, the caterpillar statue turning dimly in the moonlight. The moon was over the porker pavilion, the smell of pigshit inside. The bleachers were crowded. He took her down in front to watch the races. A man with a hoarse beery voice was shouting: Go, red pig! Go, red pig! Fuck you in front, blonde bitch! Get down, get down! I said fuck you down in front, blonde bitch! Go, red pig! —and a man in a cowboy hat was easing his wheelchaired wife away from her reproachfully and the drunk came storming down because she was blocking his view. The drunk knocked her down with one fast punch that bloodied her nose and she started flailing silently at the floor, huge-eyed, cracking her head again and again on the concrete while he, the brilliant one, drew out his car keys, locked his fist around them wih the longest one protruding between two fingers; then he stabbed the big drunk square in the eye once, twice, till something popped out. The drunk crashed down, curling tight around himself like a worm. Kicking him in the teeth, he leaped back, lifted her, ran with her until they'd hidden behind the couples with slurpies watching the goat being milked into the coffee can. Then they fled together, hand in hand, past luminous wheels and gears and light bulb blooms and girls screaming in the night like witches being burned; with his dull-eyed bleeding prize he retreated across that battlefield of light. Yellow skeletons of light sucked children up and down as they screamed. Ferris wheels hummed like the reddish filaments of pulsating eyeballs—

| 296 |

Inside she was as purple-pink and delicate as a puppy's tongue.

And she kept purring and cawing as he spread her thighs apart; she opened her mouth in surprise and grunted when he stuck it in; and she was so beautiful, even more so than the innocent girl, so beautiful that he could see that he was about to come almost right away; when he came it was as perfect as when he used to water the shrubs at the dream house, and from the hose came a rainbow, the gold band the widest, then the blue; when he turned the hose away the rainbow endured for half a second or so and then vanished; it seemed that the last drops falling out of empty air were gold or blue—

| 297 |

The girl lay in the back seat sleeping with her hands over her ears, flushed, glistening with sweat, her bare arms almost white in the sunlight, her hair bleached to the color of old bones. He whizzed her down the freeway between golden grass hills once virgin, now spiked down with wireboned power towers whose cables shattered the sky into meaningless polygons; he was taking her past where the gold and green hills turned yellow and blue. Surer now than all the spurting worms, he could unmask his memories of the long drive in lost years with his octopus-minded ex-wife; how he'd ridden silent and stunned in her hands' grip, knowing nothing other than that he was being borne away; now *he* was in charge, rushing an equally silenced prize home to his new lair, his treasure-house of all good things. The hacienda-roofed gas stations and motels rejoiced his heart; he knew they'd trip up any pursuers, while away their eyes to slow them while he continued to speed his loved one to the place where even the sky's blueness bleached out. There was a spider on the back of his neck which became fingers, and then she was crooning and playing with his hair. He felt her hot breath on the back of his neck. She kept trying to make him pay attention to her. He wanted to pull over and suck the tongue right out of her mouth, but there wasn't time yet, not till he'd hidden beyond these almond orchards with the real estate developers' obscene signs already dooming them as they stood; once the trees had been cut down the police would be able to *see* farther, so he shot her through yellow tunnel light the color of lemon drops while she giggled and played with his hair and started gently smacking the top of his head making bird-noises in rythmn with the slaps; he pressed the gas pedal down a little more to explode them through the new buffer towns walled into compartments by rival developers, each tract with its own replicated roof; that was all that could be seen from outside, the wall rendering these neighborhoods into spurious Babylons of monotony—divine sites for a seraglio; even the inmates wouldn't know where they were; as for the authorities, they'd but be baffled like thieves in the "Arabian Nights," eye-wandering that skyline of roofs along the endless road, locking wills with the palm trees that peeked over the wall . . . She insinuated herself forward between the seats so that he couldn't see behind him and she tried to take his hand off the steering wheel to play with; when he wouldn't give it to her she started poking him and giggling. With alert spider-lashed eyes he peered into his rear-view mirror to make sure that no one was stalking him; then he twisted into a rest area, stopped, undid the seat belt, got into the back seat and started kissing her as he'd wanted to do, dragging her down while she flapped her elbows in pleasure; he was wondering how to take her to the bathroom but just then she wet herself, so why bother. He put his hand up her sodden dress and she liked it; then he thought he heard a siren and leaped away from her, wiping his hands; he strapped her to the seat with a lap belt and handcuffed her wrists so that she couldn't poke him anymore; then it was back to the golden hills crammed with sparkling cars, the yellow fever-hills of dying grass and barbed wire and planes, the hills eaten up by lethal new towns; rising out of his body as he hurtled down the four-lane highway past blondes and Komfort trailers, he achieved the Yum-Yum billboards and American flags bulldozing themselves bigger and bigger until they lost sight of their own emptiness, shouting out long low malls and bungalows to use up the flatness of needless space through which he drove like a pilot down a runway, between earth and air, dusted dry over his sweat; the car stank of her urine even when he rolled down the windows to let in the smells of the long flat green fields while she croaked in terror and distress, not understanding why she was restrained, why she couldn't have him; she was screaming and he had to roll the windows back up so that no one else would hear, and he heard the creaking of her struggling to get free, so he floored it to bring them faster and more safely past the blinding light of those yellow-green fields; at last he spied out the sought-for skyscrapers on their mutual horizon; he told her that they were almost there and she didn't understand, crying and slobbering and biting her tongue and lips in a bloody frenzy of sadness as as roared past river-straddling cement bunkers, wolfpacks of houses and bridges and cranes, a dead car on the shoulder, hood up like a penis, sawmills and two-storey office cubes and more billboards and then long grey hot buildings to stupefy the skyscrapers, storage tanks, toxic factories half-camouflaged by palm trees; and, slowing down block by block, he brought her into the "nice" neighborhood where there were fewer gas stations and more houses and trees—

| 298 |

Once inside, he gave her two tranquilizers and rocked her to sleep. Then he locked her into the bedroom. He sprayed the back seat with stain remover and drove it to the carwash. Then he got some Kool-Aid and TV dinners. When he came back, he heard her sobbing and banging her head against the wall. He called her name and she sniffled into silence. Then he went into the kitchen to make her some Kool-Aid. He unlocked the bedroom door. As soon as she saw him come in, she started smiling and grunting and clutching at the folds of her pink dress—

| 299 |

He took her into the back yard to play and the lady in the next bungalow came out and said: Who's that poor girl?

My sister's child.

As quickly as he decently could then, he pulled her back inside. He was one with a dog he'd once had that would always snap at cheese-wax thrown out of the kitchen window; getting what it craved into its jaws, the dog would immediately bound into the farthest corner of the yard for safe enjoyment, nothing there but dog and grass and cheese-wax, which left the dog in charge, by default . . .

| 300 |

Studying the road atlas while she went *kaaaaw kaaaaw* at the TV, he wondered whether he'd be forced to unblur his ex-wife from memory on this drive, remembering the drive to their dream house when time and again she'd carved out her portion from his heart's crimson flesh. But his retarded girl, now, she was different; she couldn't strip him dead and bare; as for her, she came to him already stripped, like a live oyster on the half-shell; he didn't need to assault her; why, he'd build her a castle, one of those ridiculous Disneyland castles with ice cream cone towers and a gaudy drawbridge of sighs . . . He'd give her the whole teat: the illuminated fountains, eternal torches, the rush of blinking lights over sad-canted palm-trees . . . Raising the blinds an inch, he saw that sunset had come to the power poles. No neighbor lady in sight. Watered down creamy clouds wobbled in "presenting" position, like drunken lambs dipped in orange dye. He played with her just as the shoeshine boy rubs the gleaming loafers with a red cloth.

When it was completely dark he drugged her nice and drowsy with a taste of gin and half a sleeping pill. Then he handcuffed her wrists together and led her out to the car.

| 301 |

The road was a weird wingy segment of paleness as he drove her home to her perdition, only the double yellow line in the center real, not the diamond-shaped hazard signs emblazoned with squiggly arrows to warn him of curves and pale trees. She picked at her seatbelt and cawed and tried to flap her elbows. —That's right, he said, never looking away from the road. That's right. —Gravel-cuts seized his gaze like something sticky, and the road was only darkness vanishing in a notch of monotony. The car bumped over moonscarred asphalt the color of faded dreams, the darkness hot and unclean—

| 302 |

They were very happy for weeks, until his money was gone—for he was not yet Daniel Clement Smooth, expert witness. She needed to eat. He himself wasn't so hungry yet. Of course he would have gotten a job if he could, but leaving her alone made her shriek in grief and fear. So he had to work *with* her, as they said, not against her.

Well, there was one thing he could think of that she could do.

| 303 |

The man peeled ten sticky five-dollar bills apart, fanned them, and laid them down on the counter. —I like to talk first, he said. You mind if I talk first?

You'd better talk to me then, said Smooth. You see, you won't get far talking to her.

The man leaned forward earnestly, wiped the sweat from his forehead, and let air out of his mouth with a farting noise. —Well, he said, I was raised never to be ashamed of who I am or what I do, and so I don't mind telling you that I'm a slapper. That's my job, and I'm proud of it. I work for Mr. Brady. Have you heard of him? Don't say you haven't, or I'll slap you. I'm hired to slap the babes around when they get out of line—only with an open hand, of course, never hard enough to really hurt 'em or knock 'em down. A good slap is a slap you can see, though, a nice red handprint all up and down the cheek. They don't take it personally when I do it, because they know it's just my job. A lot of 'em like me. Sometimes, if I feel there's a little trust going between us, I kid around with 'em a little bit. I slap 'em on the ass, which coming from me is a compliment. Anyway, that's all I got to say. Where's the retard bitch?

He watched the man go in, and the door closed. He heard the man lock the door on the inside. There was a long silence, and then suddenly the sound of a slap. She screamed. Suddenly the screeches were muffled; the slapper must have stuffed her nightie or something into her mouth; then he heard the slaps as crisp and even as metronomic ticktock, heard her grunt trying to scream, heard the bed start creaking.

One of my better ones, the slapper said, coming out. A nice red handprint like a flower.

| 304 |

The men went in and used her until their penises bowed like ducks' necks. They left little blotches of snow in her golden grass. A boy whose cheeks were burned purple in some industrial accident kept twisting around to look at the bedroom door when *he* went home. The entrepeneur said to himself: Everyone is defective; to live is to be imperfect. Didn't I once go kissing with a Mexican girl even though her legs were as hairy as tarantulas? —In these calculations he emulated the sixteenth-century Hochelagans, who were very greedy of wampum, which they used in all their ceremonies. To get it they would kill a man and slit deep gashes in his body, which they then lowered into the river for ten to twelve hours. Upon hauling up the corpse, they could be confident that certain shellfish would have crawled inside these numb white cuts. From their exoskeletons the wampum was made. —He did not particularly enjoy the gashes which the clients were now making in his sweetheart's soul, but at least she got to eat, lots of canned ravioli and gushy bland Noodle-Oh's . . . After a while he had money in the bank; then a taxidermist bought her outright, paid so well he couldn't refuse; oho, he was getting his own back now in love's unending war!

| 305 |

The next one was a subnormal Vietnamese girl with a flat golden face and wide black eyes. How he wanted to kiss her and swallow gobs of her heavenly spit! But, in keeping with a more gradualist approach, he presented her with a smooth whiplike twig of sweet birch to chew ten times so as to extract the rootbeer essence (and he counted each slow chew, his eyes never abandoning her eyes, so that she kept shrugging and smiling), and presently she disgorged the green mass of chewed fibers into her hand, and oozed it into his hand, and he popped it into his mouth, chewing and chewing, testing the birch taste overlain by her thick hot saliva, which his tongue prised from the fibers—he did not care about her germs. Her parents had sold her for five hundred dollars. In the end he had to let her go. Too intelligent—and, besides, her ischiocavernosi muscles, which in men allow erection and contract in women to shrink the clitoris, failed to perform as guaranteed. The slapper took her off his hands.

| 306 |

Mr. Brady, inspired by his slapper's purchases, set out to grasp the money-gods' knees. (His dreams told him where to go. Sometimes he saw sluggish wormy things behind his closed eyes.) Just as Paris is the city of pampered, rat-faced, self-indulgent little lapdogs whose shampooed beards reach down to the cobblestones, so Los Angeles is (at least in its parochially western way) the city of big money—oh, money with strings attached, mind you; money on elastic cords, money on chains, but investors are like that. Landing in that spread out place of greedy dreams, he always thought (as he never did when driving) of the Beatles singing: *There's a FOG up-on El-AY- ay-ay* . . . because of the disembodied descent, and this time there really was a fog which they never broke through; when he inhaled the air with its customary flavor of burned tires he could feel it stretching hottish-coolish whitish tendrils down his throat and into his lungs; that was how it had been with Smooth's octopus-minded wife, who'd sodomized every orifice of his soul until he gagged. The fog never really lifted, not on the way to the hotel, certainly not inside the hotel itself with its foggy-dim walls faintly marbled like cunt-hairs on flypaper; Brady threw himself down into the pastel-shrouded bed just to feel something, and sank into nothing silently. Striding across the ankle-deep carpeting, he rolled back the noiseless glass door and went out to stare at pool, palms, fountain, and beach, the soft hues of sand and sky and sea all averaging out to that of the carpet . . .

He put on his tuxedo, and became at once some some high-shouldered tropical bird with a long and narrow tail.

In the conference suite he found the immortals, the great ones who gazed down upon the rest—representatives of an entire Klavern: the Exalted Cyclops and all twelve Terrors. They sat at the table in their leisure suits, waiting to learn why he'd disturbed their repose. Too rich and high even to be generals in love's great war, they'd sidelined themselves, devouring the smoke of deathless zeroes; that was their ambrosia, for only mortals may enjoy the incarnadine prize. (In Paris they owned the lapdogs; they were the necktied men beneath the awnings of the brasseries, gazing out at the ambulations of the public of which they were no longer a part.) He delved into their minds to see where their first inclinations lay, but, thunder-browed and flatulent, they sat in their splendor, equally prepared to accept or deny. He explained to them how some kisses suck spit, just as alcohol sucks ink from clogged pens. He spoke to them of what needed to be done, were he to bring his plan to glory. He strove to feed them his craving of sundown times when retarded girls would be ready like goats muzzled so that kids could play (he'd seen them at the fair, trying to rub their muzzles off against the bars of their cages; failing, they became very still and silent).

Next he gave them a multimedia teaser. He flashed image after image of retarded girls drooling with their legs spread, the projector cycling in and out of brightness like a seal's dark nostrils winking open and shut. One of the gods, incognito in blue sunglasses and a red tie, cleared his throat and worked a calculator, murmuring: Ten percent rooms for conventions, ten for the high rollers, forty percent for tourists on travel packages and forty for individual reservations . . . Actually if we take the kids—we'll call 'em "Ringmasters" here—ages three to sixteen . . . actually a good idea . . . Then he snapped his fingers and the forensic team were invited in.

The forensicists fed biscuits to a police puppy, watched the whole carousel twice more, and exclaimed to one another:

And the head formation is quite uncharacteristic. It could be Mayan, late Mayan.

Refer it to the Kloncilium . . .

And then this famous—I don't think it's Olmec at all—Henry Manes makes a good point . . .

Oh, come on, Fred; don't get hung up on some jade knee-clutcher in Oaxaca . . .

Knee-clutcher? Well, I grant you it's jade, but a *cache* of jade, absolutely *classic* jade. A lot of the Costan Rican jades are classic Maya.

And the chief forensicist sighed to himself: . . . Those multi-tiered altars! Altars, oh, my balls! Always studded with monstrous faces; usually too big to chip out; you gotta leave 'em—well, sometimes, it's true, a guy might find jeweled eyeballs to prise out, or a figurine that could conceivably come loose with a crowbar's help . . .

The gods sat yawning, frowning and tittering among themselves. They knew what the clients would be giving up: that special happiness when a girl can sit looking at you nodding very very fast, looking you in the eye, smoothing her skirt over and over where it bridges her succulent thighs. The retarded girls would certainly not do that. But Brady pressed his case with color photographs. Directly addressing the Imperial Wizard (an action not undertaken lightly), he spoke of exotic cretins whose vaginas were as dark and sandy as crocodile-mummies. He mentioned his idea for a certain foil-covered room with small portholes. He didn't hesitate to describe to them a girl he'd once met in Napoli, a girl with hair the hue of a haystack and greenish-blue eyes who sat staring out the train window with interlaced fingers resting on her purse, her long legs crossed, her green wool jacket buttoned up to her throat, and the hair seemed what most attached her head to her shoulders. He whispered with a wink: *What if we cut her hair off?*

He knew very well what he was doing. He was like the black boys in low V-shaped boats who sit at water level in the Nile, paddling with their arms like doggish spiders, singing American songs to tourists, then asking for money. He'd sung his song. Now he invited them to sing theirs. They nudged one another and smiled.

Alabama, where I'm from, is always short of jobs, a god said. We've been short of jobs forever. This would have been all women, because they're more dextrous with their fingers. I had this crazy idea that the people in the plant should own the plant. Well, I was thirty years ahead of my time.

California is the Whoredog State, another god replied. We could increase the carrying capacity by ten percent just by bringing in this business.

There's a Christian businessman down in Cash Flow, Arkansas, who has a very powerful Christian TV station, a god said. This fellow back there, he's run I don't know how many of our tapes.

The Queen of the Whores *lied* to the American people, a god was muttering. The bankers love her.

If the U.S. was not preserved, then Communism would conquer Planet Earth, a god said.

The other gods discussed their own experiences. They called in their associates and Kleagles. Then they swore to their guest to grant him the victory he asked for (in exchange for certain future offerings mutually acceptable); they said it would be done.

| 307 |

The next one was a hydrocephalic girl who stared with little lizard eyes, her forehead bulging like a watermelon; Brady's scientists caressed it gently to see if it was squishy. Her saliva was light, refreshing, foamy, very faintly nutty like a bottle of Ozujsko Pivo Special (Zagrebacska Pivova). After her, Brady collected two low-eared girls, then a bullet-headed microcephalic with lovely chestnut hair who clenched her teeth and sometimes bit. The slapper kept her in line. Then he acquired a blonde girl with a doll's face: dull blue eyes and heavy mongoloid lids which *must* have been weighted like a doll's, enhanced by the pale cheeks, the slack lips that sucked and drooled; on that same trip he snapped up a girl with Turner's syndrome (webbed neck, sexual infantilism), and then a bald girl whose head was shaped like a light bulb—

| 308 |

Brady sat on the floors of echoing hardwood rooms that smelled of lemon-wax and laughed because they were his from chandelier to windowed door to lattice-work. Then his voice rang out in commands. The workmen assembled before him, good soldiers when money's muster's called. Receiving their orders, they ranged out in their smooth-geared trucks (Ah like to have a good caw undah mah ass, ya know what Ah mean?), scouring the lumberyards and wide-walled warehouses. When the lumberyards were looted, great mounds of bed-timber swelled at the curbside drops, higher than ever the Greeks raised for Patroclus's pyre. Then they set about the work. At their lord's command they laid down dark carpets to eat sounds and stains. With speedy rollers they painted the walls pink and yellow and blue—girl-child's colors, cheerful, artless. Next they swung in the bed-gear on their shoulders, bolting double mattress-decks to sturdy keels, riveting everything down shipshape, studding the joists with rows of molybdenum hex-nuts in all order so that no plank would fail the rocking sailors, hammering down railings and see-through canopies, masting them with headboards, rigging them out with full waterproof sheets until those multistoried sailing ships were ready to be launched upon the seas of pleasure. In all the ceilings of that house they planted cameras to hang down watching wide-angled with a spider's eyes. Now with powerful shaggy arms they screwed down marble toilets whose inner lids were blazoned with hearts; they heaved marble sinks and golden-glassed showers tight against the walls; cunningly they fitted the tiled nooks with silvered mirrors, slipping them flush like second skins. But all these things, necessary though they might be, would not gladden caged girls' hearts. So now they hauled in the fabulous toy-chests, the doll-coffers replete with rubbery passive girls. They brought stuffed bears and tigers for the whores to hug, ten-foot fuzzy crocodiles for them to drool over in the rubber-sheeted beds, plastic panels with Buzzy-Scary games, building blocks, wind-up rutabagas, miniature houses with hinged roofs to peer through like gods, ruby-eyed flasher guns, rattattat pistols, modeling clay that was safe to eat, golden trucks and fishes to set their hearts in flame!

The doors locked only from the outside, because it would be ruinous to offer retarded girls the keeping of keys.

Brady put the slapper on salary. It became one of his recreations to watch that tall, easygoing fellow standing in the corner in ducky and tails, smiling and squeezing a rubber ball, or ever so delicately touching the flats of his hands together.

He informed the backers in L.A. that he'd even come in under budget, and they upwardly adjusted his benefit package in the most laudable possible way. They sent out feelers. They printed up stock certificates in Fraktur type. Everything was peachy. Maybe they'd go public in two years.

At last they brought them in from their cages, pretty girls, sweet girls, girls who filled the rooms with the scent of hot milk . . .

| 309 |

The golden-clad croupiers were patting the red tables in a dozen motions, each arm fanning out from an almost stationary body so that these employees resembled octopi. Their customers waited unsmiling for cards and chips to be presented to them, and I remember that Jack Williamson science fiction story called "With Folded Hands," about an overly leisured future in which human beings are not allowed to do anything that might be dangerous or sad or bad for them; attended by robots all the way to the cemetery, they sit and await the next course in a banquet of sanitized irrelevancies, like the inmates of an old folks' home. That nightmare story brooded with me for years, and here it was—worse, in a way, because in Williamson's story the robots were well-meaning and gave people only the very best, whereas here they gave you the least they could get away with to hide the hollowness.

| 310 |

The slapper drowsed and drank ice water from tall thin glasses. Brady's agents fanned out across the hot wide streets, putting up flyers for Feminine Circus in blistering parking lots and the ivied shade beneath freeway overpasses, making discreet calls at the pay phones between the wigwag roofs of fast food factories, wending cannily among the long low chiropractor's office style architecture that bulged with air conditioners. When their friends asked them what they did for a living now, the agents replied: I'm in limbo; I'm with recruiters! I ask for a decent wage, and the guys want something for ten K or less! Well, it's a soft market right now. You have to do a little of everything. I spent the last six or eight years of my life doing one thing. —The agents learned the ways of sunglare on dusty windshields and the windows of phone booths, so bright as to bring tears to their eyes. It was straight comission. A few among them, the good ones, grew into cool offices where only their sluggish fingers had to move like snails on hot lawns after a morning's rain; they got results. Yes, Vagina, another dinner with the publicity people in purple Feminine Circus windbreakers . . . (There's one fellow in this town who's not a believer, an agent reported. He takes down my fliers. So I don't acknowledge him. To me he doesn't exist. The Bible says, if there's a nonbeliever among you, put 'em away. But I don't go out of my way to be mean to him, either.)

The media relations spokesman for the Feminine Circus supply office gave interviews and explicated everything most helpfully to the American people: A pimp commits an illegal act, he's kicked out immediately. This is a *professional* procuring organization. And, remember, all we procure are ONES AND ZEROES. Those girls are not real. They're a miracle of modern technology, is what they are—gigabytes and trilobites just to digitize their smiles! And since they're not real, nobody's getting exploited, and there's no disease to worry about.

Can you tell me why you want to repeal the federal income tax? asked the interviewer.

That is the goal. A whole basis for the collection of income to the government would have to be arranged. One way would be to have virtual prostitutes raise the money.

What's your position on illegal prostitution?

Illegal, immoral, unhealthy, unsafe! Don't do it, America! Come to Feminine Circus and indulge your fantasies in a safe, healthy and *tasteful* manner.

(Tasty is right! laughed vulgar Brady.)

There were a few picketers, it's true, but the Associate Vice President of Marketing, Mr. Marlowe W. Slapper, explained: I do know that the circles they move in are definitely of an anti-sexual nature.

So you don't believe that there's any substance to these protesters' claims?

Protesters as a class will sit there and lie, said the Associate Vice President of Marketing. It's hard to debate someone who lies. If you want to really look at this, you take some objective fact of theirs and check it. For instance, what about this red herring they raise regarding coercion, of retarded girls being forced to perform fellatio? Me, I never met a whore who didn't enjoy giving head. And, like I says, they're not real anyways.

Mr. Slapper, don't you feel that the name "Feminine Circus" is a bit unfair to women?

asked a journalist. Shouldn't the name encourage women to come and play also? I mean, right now, isn't Feminine Circus mainly for men?

We're in the final phases of a pilot program to introduce a special division for female customers, Mr. Slapper explained. For health and safety reasons we've decided to keep areas separate, as indeed we're required to do under federal law. You wouldn't want coed bathrooms, now, would you? No coed orgasms, either, because that would be prostitution. The way we have it planned, the men will go and do their thing among the bits and bytes, and the women will do a similar thing in their own area. Of course free daycare and a shuttle service will be provided.

(Leaning back in his chair, Mr. Rapp narrowed his eyes and grimaced, studying John as if he were the most important entity in the world. He nudged John and said: You remember what Engels used to say? Do quote Engels, son. It sounds so good when you say it.

(John smiled and said: *For savagery—group marriage; for barbarism—pairing marriage; for civilization—monogamy, supplemented by adultery and prostitution.*)

The Senior Vice President of Sales raised his wineglass and quipped: I have one of the easier jobs on the property. My job is to fill seven thousand beds a day. *Double* beds.

Every week there was a glowing article about Feminine Circus in the entertainment section.

| 311 |

Now the famous men rose to the occasion, gathering in the foyers to meet the ladies belly-to-belly, nose-to-anus, tongue-to-armpit—whatever their own honor cried for. The senator was there, jovially uptilting an Alsatian beer. The junked-out salesman was there. Last night he'd wanted a hooker, and he'd gotten a hooker. She took him into the hotel room and the pimp said: you're fucking my wife! —The salesman pulled a knife. The pimp pulled a knife, too, and held it to his throat for about five hours. Now the salesman wanted a nice slow fat retard girl to slap around a little, before he stuck it into her mouth. That would put him right with the world again. After all, she wasn't real anyhow. He was a good man; he always paid cash. —The successful dentist was there, laughing and shouting: *If she finds out . . . !* while the mortician stood waiting sweet-eyed beneath the lighted paper cylinders, which is to say the red and white corrugated glow-in-the-dark leeches; when his turn came, the customer support specialist drew him down beneath the rows of translucent stalactites and fluorescent macaroni which continually winked and blinked; she took his hand as gently as an easy death and pulled him down the velvet passageway to the second sinus where the halfway-approved clients sat at kidney-shaped marble tables, six men each, either ignoring each other as if on the bus, or smiling at each other, freeze-dried instant friends. (To the press the bellman would only say that everything was great, that they had a *commitment* to their employees.)

Everything *I don't even wear* I send to the dry cleaner's! the dentist was shouting.

Ah, replied the mortician, sipping his beer. You can do that, pal—indeed you can— but once the shirt's starch is gone it never comes back again . . .

You're going to get me pissed off, said the dentist in a low voice. You won't like it when I'm pissed off.

That's your privilege. That's the privilege of your urine. But when you're lying on my marble slab, colder than a frozen clam, how much urine will you work up then?

Hey, asshole, why are you even *here?* Why are you talking that way? You're here to do a root canal on those girls, just like me. What do you keep going on about *dying* for?

Dying? said the mortician. Oh, dying. That was a great movie. It came out of nowhere. I remember when I saw it in Westwood, on the way to the dry cleaner's.

| 312 |

The mortician's number was called just after the senator's. The hostess took him down the spiral velvet corridor, deeper and deeper into good repose. In a circular room that smelled like cherry cough drops, they sat him down at a video screen to watch the play of the overhead cameras in the girls' rooms (the busy rooms being blacked-out like air raid Saturdays); so he watched the prey, rubbing his hands, watched a girl banging her head against the wall, twisting in her urine-soaked bed; another, hyper-sexed, squatted masturbating with a toy snake's head like a good washerwoman twisting and massaging the wet garment against itself; a third rushed blindly blundering from wall to wall like a trapped bottle-fly; a fourth lay catatonic with her stuffed giraffe; a fifth crouched over the toilet, splashing her hands in and laughing; a sixth was trying to dance to the nursery rhyme muzak that the establishment piped in like the will of God; and the mortician said: Number six looks lively enough. That's very good. You see, I love life.

| 313 |

The backers in L.A. thought that there ought to be a floor show. Feminine Circus stock had just gone public and was rising fast. Brady decided to hire a starlet to be Queen of the Whores. At that time he remained unaware that there was in fact a *real* Queen of the Whores, and had he known he wouldn't have cared. The slapper found an enthusiastic girl named Babycakes Reed who could croon Lotte Lenya-esque songs as she strode about the stageboards, licking the head of the cordless mike and hiking up her black sequin gown.

| 314 |

Gluing himself like a ruby to the silver rail, the successful dentist had brunch at Feminine Circus. The waiter opened the champagne bottle with a deep echoing pop. The dentist's orange juice glass remained eternally filled; his champagne glass was poured very slowly by a black paisley arm that waited until the foam stopped. On the table, a white orchid nuzzled his hand. Outside the curved window, palm trees, a waterfall . . . Babycakes Reed (or one of her fifty lookalikes) had just given him her autograph. Her stage name was Queen Zenobia. The successful dentist browsed among the mountains of bread and the row of silver reliquaries, each the size of a small child's casket, whose tops slid open at his command to show hash browns, pork chops, sausages and bacon, ravioli, potatoes au gratin . . . Then there was the fruit mountain, the calving ground of waffles, the omelette stand, the towering eagle made of ice, the parlsey-floored sashimi terarium.

The last red thing is not a bicycle like the first blue thing, said the dentist.

He'd heard that from the mortician and was trying to figure out what it meant.

Oh, that tricky dog! he shouted, eating another omelette.

He liked the mortician now. When he'd gone too far inside that paralyzed girl with

Niemann-Pick's disease, until she became turquoise like a seal rushing underwater, the mortician had come with a little stinger kit of embalming chemicals to make it look like natural causes. (Not that she was real, of course, but when you ordered take-out, that virtual blood stayed on your living room floor. —We need to sacrifice the unprofitable giveaways, said Brady.) Later the mortician had even rerouted her from the crematorium, preserved her perfectly, and plasticized her. After that, the dentist started giving the mortician free X-rays and cleanings—professional courtesy, he called it. He got the senator to sponsor a pro-undertaker's bill in Congress. They all stuck together like dogs fornicating in epoxy. They loved each other.

The successful dentist laughed. —Yes, I'm just bursting with seminal fluid!

| 315 |

As for the lord of it all, Dan Smooth, as for him who'd killed so many hearts (but that was a long time ago, those days of thick-and-fast), he swindled himself into nothingness (aside from the occasional tryst with a certain retarded girl named Sapphire), whereas Brady sat in a hightower suite which was loaded with blue hydrangeas. Three perfect pears, a grapefruit half as big as a basketball, and a leopard-spotted banana reclined in a silver vase, cushioned softly from the metal's preciousness by leaves. —Message for Mr. Brady, apologized the concierge every ten minutes. Beside the banana stood a foot-high stack of the latest newspapers from around the world. Inside the credenza lurked a modem pre-dialled to the Brazilian Stock Exchange. Then there was a sliding panel behind which special cameras and telescopic lenses gave him a twenty-four-hour view of the guts of Feminine Circus, the engine room ceilinged with vast pipes shuddering, messes of heavy boilers, gauges, boilerplates; the utility halls of burning hot corrugated metal, the disposal rooms manned by illiterate, moustached, oily-fingered crews who ran and sweated in sandals, hauling shrouded bundles to the grinder well, the Lobotomy Factory's diesel-powered unshielded belts turning, their condensers sucking up the desert water table; then more shuddering pipes, whirling spools, grey shouts he couldn't hear . . . On the table where the third phone squatted, he sat drawing up new price lists, idly flipping through personnel figures. His accountants projected a thirty-two percent margin on property without the theme park; the theme park could make forty-five or fifty percent.

A phone rang. —Yup, he said. No, that girl isn't available anymore. She retired. — You'll take your business elsewhere? Fine; take it and shove it. —What? You're reconsidering. Well, reconsider.

The maid was cleaning the bathroom mirror. She had to reach way up to clean the top, and when she did that, her breasts wiggled and her buttocks swayed. She was a Mexican with four children. —Nice stuff, said Brady.

A phone rang. —Well, he said, the Wall Street projections are that we'll make $7.50 to $7.75 a share. No, the other big players today are mainly from Hong Kong, Taiwan, and Malaysia. The Arabs are history. They go to London. They don't come to Las Vegas anymore. All right. Be my guest. I'm raising my offering price tomorrow.

A phone rang. —Circus line, Brady speaking, he said. Yeah, we do. How many? No, we don't do consignments. We buy outright. No, it's irrevocable. Yeah, we pay five dollars a pound, that's *raw* weight. Stripped. No high heels, no panties, nothing. I've been around the block, Buster. I've seen that trick with the weighted high heels. I've seen one on the open market where the seller even gave her lead suppositories—all three holes—just to make another ten bucks. Needless to say, we wouldn't touch that company's business with a ten-foot cottonwood dildo. On the other hand, I've seen the aproctous ones, you know what I mean? They don't last long enough. You're looking at it the wrong way. Think how much your staff saves when we take the pieces off your hands. No, it's immaterial whether they're sterilized; we doublecheck that ourselves. And their relatives can't visit; I've seen that trick before, too. Once we have 'em, they're virtual; they don't exist. Pay the *doctor* off—are you kidding? You think we're some fly-by-night business? Just forget the whole thing. Forget it, I said.

He hung up, smacking fist in palm with savage triumph. He led the ranks of fighters now.

| 316 |

The senator came back. The mortician came back. (Babycakes Reed got a raise.) The successful dentist came back. So did the short lesbian with round glasses and long hair and the New York boy, stubbled and self-bared, who loved his toy company. At the Carnal Arcade the barker was shouting: You win, you win! and the New York boy's boyfriend cried: You're kickin' butt! Keep it up! —(The impregnation tables were only marginally profitable, just a convenience for the customer.) One middle-aged woman afflicted with gargoylism was in high demand, as a result of her swollen lips. The lesbian took her. The lesbian loved every minute. The lesbian said: She's as greenish and sweet as an Egyptian orange! —The junked-out salesman came back. Just last night, he'd gotten a hooker at the Nitecap. He drove with her all the way to Daly City. Then he found out she was a boy. He got so mad he smashed his own TV with an axe. So he was ready now for a close-and-kill at Feminine Circus; he wanted to kick those retard cunts around a little, teach 'em what buying and selling was all about. When he explained his needs, the customer support specialist took him to a hunched little cretin girl without breasts or body hair. At the state fair there'd been a blackheaded goat who whirled its ears and head around, splaying its legs, shitting, looking for escape; again and again the tail lifted, and green pellets like shot tumbled out into the hay. Before he was half through with her, the cretin was like that, squealing in sadness and terror—

| 317 |

Too withdrawn, the doctor said. A little reserpine. But not too much.

That's good; that's good, the doctor said.

No, the usual fee will be fine, the doctor said. I'm always glad to help. Really a very interesting operation you have here. Just think of the *research!*

Ah, there's a transitional period, of course, the doctor said. But when they begin to appreciate the opportunity they have, to interact with other females in their own ability range . . .

| 318 |

Babycakes Reed wants another raise, said the slapper.

Give it to her.

In which sense, boss?
Give her the raise.

| 319 |

Wild-eyed, shock-haired, she glared at the successful dentist with window-shadows blocking apart her face like savage pigments, and snot-slugs hung from her nose like ivory ornaments, and pearls of drool streaked down her lower lip like jeweled labrets, and sperm trickled out of her ear like bone earrings of some fantastically meaningless shape; she was hugging a fuzzy toy python around her neck and it was like an exotic fur collar —perfect! he shouted; *per-* fect!

When the dentist came out, he walked just a bit more rollingly, like a man in bulky coveralls.

| 320 |

Sorry to bug you, boss, said the slapper, but Babycakes Reed wants royalties on the salaries of all her lookalikes.

Tell her we can't do that.

She's gonna be a pain in the ass about it, boss.

Give her a pain in the ass—no, better not. She's high-profile. She might sue. See if you can dope her up and get her fired.

She's wise to that one.

All right, send her in.

| 321 |

Thank you for seeing me, Mr. Brady, said Babycakes Reed. I know you must be busy.

Yeah.

I surely do it appreciate it, Mr. Brady.

Listen, Babycakes, we've given you what you asked for up to now, but if you keep being greedy I'm going to have to cut you loose.

Why, Mr. Brady!

Don't you Mr. Brady me. Your shit is the same color as mine. I know that for a fact. I've got video cameras in all the restrooms.

Mr. Brady, I'm sorry to say that if you take that line with me I'll be forced to employ a lawyer.

I'm sure you will, Baby. Now why don't you get out of my office.

It was a week or so after that that the slapper told him about the real Queen of the Whores. Brady decided to hire her. Otherwise, he'd capture and lobotomize her; what a fine novelty fuck she'd make . . . That was why he'd hired Henry Tyler for what (to be honest) had also been a little slumming vacation. Later, he realized that moral crusades were good for business.

· BOOK XIX ·

A Meditation on the Stock Market

The tenth kingdom says of him that his god loved a cloud of desire. He begot him in his hand and cast upon the cloud above him some of the drop, and he was born.

Gnostic Scriptures, *The Apocalypse of Adam* V, 5, 15–20 (1st or 2nd cent.?)

Across the street from Feminine Circus a Canadian consortium had just opened the Parthenon, so there was a press conference and the C.E.O. was saying: Tomorrow there'll be close to a hundred and forty thousand people in this town who are going to say: What do you want to do today?

Get a whore, mumbled the newsman next to Tyler. Get a whore at Feminine Circus.

So it's pretty good over there? said Tyler.

Fantastic, man. You get all your feelings out. And it's not real, so there are no repercussions. You know what I did? I got me this virtual retard bitch and I—

The C.E.O. raised his voice. —And we're hoping that they'll say: Let's check out the Parthenon.

The Sphinx and Robinson Crusoe's were hoping the same thing—vainly, perhaps, because the Parthenon was going to serve more beer than any place in the world; but on the other hand the Luxor did possess the Sphinx, under whose hollow stuccoed whiteness you could park your car; everywhere was nowhere, and the vista outside was but another show. Bags of money wriggled in the neon sign below the Mirage (this was the owner's wet dream, whereas the gambler's wet dream had to do with the long brass birdneck handle with the black ball on it, inviting you to pull it when you put your money in—thirty-five hundred of those in the MGM Grand). Money was water like those granularly frosted bathroom doors; money was puffs of fire shooting up at the edge of the long Strip that straightarrowed down past the Sands and Harrah's to the luminescent pink breasts of Feminine Circus, where Tyler saw the cars on the roof of a tall wide garage; and as he watched, one car's headlights come on, and it turned down into the chucklehole that led it to the Strip's lights so separate from the Las Vegas skyline whose lights shimmered so quickly and crazily, unlike the steady white lights at the base of palm trees; then Tyler saw a huge coconut palm hung with skulls below Robinson Crusoe's sign: the effect was all light, an ugly, disposable magic that glowed and sucked the desert's soul. That was why he decided to go in the opposite direction.

All his cab drivers liked Las Vegas. The economy was good, and they could afford to buy homes there.

I've been blowing a ten-dollar roll of quarters a day, to see if Santa would give me something, but so far no good, the driver said.

You mind taking me downtown, just to see what things look like?

That's all I do anyways, go round and round and round and round.

(Fremont Street was incredibly bright, Binion's Horseshoe a blue block of wriggling lights.)

Now, the California here, they cater primarily to the Hawaiians, the cab driver said. But these are all locals' casinos, that put a few rooms out just for tourists, but they're more diverse, the service is better, the plays are looser, the covers are cheaper—only five bucks at Arizona Charlie's. The big hotels? We usually stay clear of them.

Downtown, everything's straight up instead of spread out, he went on a moment later. This here's the railway station; that's what formed downtown in the first place. Now they're uprooting the whole railroad, putting it on the outskirts to develop this part. Right now they're purifying the soil by cooking it to eight thousand degrees. They're going thirty-forty feet deep.

All right, Tyler said, now show me the worst neighborhood there is.

Oh, I'm not doing that. There's some streets, their domain is so established, they'll just block off the street and take all your money. But I can find some crummy places if that's what you want. Not far away at all.

Maybe Tyler halfway expected to see what Brady had shown his brother on that special tour of Feminine Circus's service areas: a vast hall called Cleopatra Road, another called Ozma Ave with stacks of empty computer boxes; forkloads of beer and diapers somewhere under the South Tower, the bakeshop so fragrant with rolls on wheeled trays with long dips for the subway; the room service prep hangar in which people in white assembled blue napkins folded into Alps on white-garbed wheeled tables, fleets of which stretched all the way to the concrete horizon; that is how the bad parts of Las Vegas should have been, just the ventricles of paradise. Past the Moulin Rouge it got darker and darker, then much too dark, with fences, greyish hedges and pulled down steel shutters.

Does the Mafia still run this town? Tyler asked.

Big business has replaced the Mob with organized legal crime, he said bitterly.

What do you mean by that?

Oh, nothing. That new Jonas Brady, he's just one of many. Now you see the opening in this alley? Right here where the car is, this is where the guy took off on me. I ran, but I couldn't catch him. I'd dropped off his girlfriend, so I knew where *she* was. I staked her out for a week or two, but never caught her. At this point, anytime someone opens the car door before he pays me, I unstrap my seat belt and get ready to run.

How long have you lived in Vegas? Tyler asked.

I've been here for seven years, and in that time Vegas has grown from four hundred to eight hundred thousand.

How's the crime generally?

We've only had two cab drivers murdered in Vegas this year, as compared to New York, where it's is almost forty, he said, rolling past low clubhouses and occasional street-lamps.

Well, with all the development, with the doubling in size, with new casinos opening all the time, has the crime gotten better or worse?

The cab driver just laughed.

They now rolled between Gerson Park's low pale cubes close together, the roofs reminiscent of those toys they make by hand in Madagascar out of insecticide tins; here and there a few Christmas trees; calm and vacant, fences in place. Alienated by many nights of light, Tyler nonetheless did not find this darkness restful. It was ugly, monotonous, and dangerous. The ugly realness of the night crouched chillingly around him. He saw Grace Temple with its Biblical murals, then another brick cube: PAWN with some letters missing; and it occurred to him that a pawnshop is really the same as a casino. —

Yeah, the owner of the Nugget lost a lot of money on his boxers . . . the driver was saying, almost to himself. As for Robinson Crusoe's, this guy's on a lucky streak . . .

On the corner stood some kids who looked as evil as the brass skulls on the Treasure Island's doors.

We have a police substation here now, and walking police, the driver said. Now, over that way is Nucleus Plaza. That place got burned during the Rodney King copycat riots.

But on the Strip it's pretty safe?

Casinos have got such a strong security force that they've eliminated crime in their area, but as a result of getting that security, they can also keep crime from getting to press. Every now and then there's violence, but they hush it up. That's what I say, but course you'll never be able to prove it.

Vacant lots that smelled like piss, a bar, a dry cleaner and laundromat, these were all good *clues* as Mr. Private Eye Tyler might have said, but although Tyler and the driver kept looking for the good stuff (the driver half-heartedly) they could not find any crackhouse that was open. Tyler didn't really care.

The driver was telling him a story about a fare who wanted crack:

I picked 'im up at a nudie place and he asked me to take him downtown, and he pulled over in one of those light industrial places. I said, look, I don't want you doing that business in my cab. He throws me a ten (it was like a four dollar fare) and he says to me: Drive around the block, and if you don't get another fare come back and pick me up. Well, so I came back and got 'im, and boy was he hopping mad! Man, but they'd sold him some rock—real rock! He'd paid for crack cocaine and what he got was a quartz crystal.

That was Las Vegas ersatz for you, Tyler thought. Casinos and the crackhouses, it was all the same.

Feminine Circus is a product of Circus-Circus and Excalibur, the driver was saying. They know everything there is to know about making money. They only operate out of cash flow. They do everything reasonably well . . .

Yeah, that applies to crack dealers, too, said Tyler.

The driver chuckled.

So you think Brady's pretty smart, huh?

He's the man of the hour. He's the great American untouchable. And Feminine Circus, well, I'm just amazed no one ever thought of it before. It sums up the national mood, you could almost say. It's brilliant. It's as real as you want it to be. It's . . .

Have you been there? asked Tyler.

Hey, man, you getting nosy on me? What are you, some kind of cop?

I didn't mean it like that. I was just wondering if Feminine Circus is worth going to, that's all.

Well, it's pretty wild in there, the driver said. Everybody tries it once. I guess I don't mind telling you I've tried it. You go in, and they have all these ugly girls who stink, and they drool all over you. That Brady, I have to say, I respect his balls, when everything else in Vegas is so pretty-pretty, to come up with something that looks like where we are now . . .

So those girls of his, those virtualettes—

Oh, that's a standing joke, said the driver. Don't tell me you believe those girls aren't real . . .

They were swinging back in to town again, passing the Satin Saddle, a topless place, and the Palomino, which was bottomless, and the driver said: The Palomino has a cover of ten bucks and a two drink minimum at six bucks apiece, and Tyler thought: why, that's a step ahead of the crack dealers! I never met a crack dealer who charged a cover.

You think Feminine Circus will do well? he said idly.

You mean, will they get raided?

Well, if they're real girls . . .

See, that's Brady's genius, said the driver. Nobody cares about retarded girls. But sooner or later some feminist will bust his balls. If he's smart he'll make his bundle and leave the country . . .

| 323 |

You build a new one and it'll always be full, the driver went on. Whether that's going to be enough to make the whole city go, I don't know. I don't see that the owners care, either. If Brady's new seven thousand bed fuckhouse creates seven thousand vacancies someplace else, Brady won't care. But you have to believe that the stock market will keep going up in the long run, and Vegas will keep growing, and people will keep spending money on products no one's even thought of yet. Me, I'm working on a certain kind of virtual pet. If I can just unkink one glitch, then you won't see me driving this cab anymore . . .

· BOOK XX ·

"Demons Are Here"

•

For the lips of a strange woman drop as a honeycomb, and her mouth is smoother than oil. But her end is bitter as wormwood, sharp as a two-edged sword. Her feet go down to death; her steps take hold on hell.

Proverbs 5.3–5

•

On Larkin and McAllister just past the old library rose another grimy granite mausoleum, whose neoclassical statues on high were speckled and pitted by polluted air so that they now resembled the flesh of a Capp Street girl, and beneath these poxed entities rose from a sleeping bag, not unlike those of a priest elevating the host, a pair of arms. The arms embraced a dog, which opened its mouth and softly panted, while the hair of homeless outcasts blew in the wind. The dog was tied to the left arm with a length of clothesline because he sometimes liked to wander beyond his own good. He almost never barked. When he was a puppy, the biker he'd then belonged to had trained him in the ways of silence by biting his ear whenever he uttered any sound, even a whimper. The biker had moved to Ohio, abandoning this dog now skilled in silence. It was evening, and the arms were both tired. Their owner was a man named Crutches, who whispered: They tried to gimme a ticket for littering. Can you believe it? Yeah, well, I be rollin' it up so quick so they don't see . . . Well, I be movin' so fast . . .

Crutches's comrades were squatting and smoking.

One of them pointed. Brady's Boys were patrolling past.

Vigs! Better let the Queen know, whispered Crutches with a wink.

I saw one right over there, a vig was saying. Right behind the sheriff's office.

And I seen *you,* too, said Crutches to himself. You can't slip nothin' by me.

Ready to do it again? said the first vig.

Okay, his colleague replied. Here's an easy one. Leviticus 18.3.

Let's skip the Egypt part. That's irrelevant. God says to Moses: *You shall not do as they do in the land of Canaan, to which I am bringing you.*

Good, but you forgot to say Amen. Now Leviticus 20.23.

And you shall not walk in the customs of the nation which I am casting out before you; for they did all these things, and therefore I abhorred them. Amen.

Sighing, Crutches got up, gripping one of his eponymous instruments of locomotion in each armpit while the dog waited patiently, then slowly grated, dragged and clattered his weary way down to the Turk Street parking garage, outside of which Strawberry was trolling for sex work. As Crutches wheezed and cackled *Aintcha an eyeful now?* the dog with surprising initiative lunged forward, almost pulling the homeless man down, and licked her miniskirt.

Aw, ain't that sweet, the whore said. He wants to kiss me.

Hey, Killer, cut that out! Listen, Strawberry. Tell your Big Bitch there's new vigs in town. They got like uniforms and everything. It looks bad. I told Maj before, I . . .

Okay, Crutches, I'll tell her. She's already heard. But I gotta go now. I'm kinda busy right now, okay?

Any luck?

Oh, my regular shoulda showed up half an hour ago. I was hoping to do that one quick flatback and . . .

An' tell her I don't want no reward or anything, but . . .

But you didn't tell us just out of the goodness of your goddamned heart, right?

Amen, sister! Sure has been one tough month. And they got these red jerseys, well, maybe vermillion you might call it, with the letters 𝔹.𝔹. embroidered on the front. They say it means *Brady's Boys* . . .

All right, Crutches, thanks. I appreciate it. Now lemme do my job.

I guess I'll never see it. I guess you streetcrawling bitches won't send one goddamned rock my way. Do I get cynical? Sometimes I don't feel like doing *my* job.

| 325 |

Now, did anyone see my little encounter with the man across the street? said Rodrigo.

Yes, we posted you.

That man is *scum*. That man's a *Queen's man*. Put him in the database. His name's Crutches. He talked back to me. He practically threatened me. But I got the last word. Remember that, troops. The last word must be yours. Sometimes you gotta draw your line in the sand. Form up, form up!

Rodrigo paced like a tiger and went up to the flag-wavers who were ignoring him, and he cried: Hey, why aren't you training with us to stamp out dirt?

A teen approached, and soon Rodrigo was shaking his hand, saying: Good to meet you, man!

The tall gangbanger types would smile, wad Rodrigo's leaflets up and toss them. Rodrigo kept smiling. —You gotta be loud, he told his shyest soldiers. You're *Brady's Boys.*

Can I take a picture of you with my little girl? a grandmother said.

Sure, lady. Right over here. Post me, boys.

Someone threw a bottle on the sidewalk, and a Brady's Boy rolled it carefully away with the toe of his boot . . .

| 326 |

Shyly and halfheartedly, a Brady's Boy got out a leaflet and handed it to the small, slender black woman.

Mm hm, said the Queen.

And, ma'am, if you'd care to help us with a small d-d-donation . . . said the boy.

What is it you're tryin' to do, honey? Put the hookers out of business?

That's right, ma'am.

What do you have against hookers?

We have n-n-nothing *against* them, ma'am. We want to help them. They're all abused . . .

You mean raped.

Th-th-that's right, ma'am.

Here's a dollar, said the Queen. You seem like a nice boy. Have you ever been with a prostitute?

No, ma'am. Excuse me. Ma'am?

Yes.

Wh-wh-where are you from, ma'am?

And you ask everybody that, don't you?

Yes, ma'am, said the boy, remembering his squad leader's instructions: Royce, you gotta smile at 'em, say hi, how ya doin'? Then you're gonna ask 'em: Are you interested in getting involved?

Well, I'm from the South, said the Queen.

A-a-ah, said the boy uncertainly. That's good.

Yeah, but now it changed a whole lot since I been there last time, it seems.

Like how?

Like it's raggedy now. The house I was raised in, that's gone. Just an empty lot. I was hopin' to see the house I was raised in.

The boy had run entirely out of utterances. Returning the leaflet to his hand, the Queen returned to Justin's side, sighing: The younger generation . . .

Marching proudly back on down the parade path, the boy reached HQ: a small, grimy storefront on Golden Gate just past Polk, where beneath a wall of plastic cartons filled with empty beer cans his colleagues were being videotaped by Channel Seven News. He was afraid, and ran to go get doughnuts.

Hey, at that Tenderloin street fair there were about fifty of the Queen's guys bothering us, a guy with a long greasy ponytail was telling Channel Seven. —Really *bad-mouthing* us, you know. They're always armed. But I'm right there, where my family is. I'm a Brady's Boy, and I'm ready for 'em.

I have a very bad background, one of the vigs, big-armed, bearded, and sideburned, was explaining to a starry-eyed reporter. See, I used to sell heroin, crack, cocaine. I even got my own sister addicted so I could pimp her out and make money to buy more powder. I turned her into a devil worshiper. Oh, Lord Jesus, can you believe my *sin?* She was worshiping at the altar of the Black Queen, ma'am, you know, the Queen of the Wh— the Prostitutes. But Mr. Brady gave me like a *window.* He let me look through that window and I saw the promised land. He turned me around. So I'm grateful to him and his organization.

What about your sister?

She just completed a recovery program. She's married, with four lovely kids.

Clean green jackets hung on hangers in the niche under the loft. The vigs sat on dirty sofas. Some were bounty hunters, good people who helped tight-smiling Mr. Cortez get ninety-six percent of his bail-skippers back (whoever cosigned the bail form had to reimburse Mr. Cortez for the bounty hunters' fees). Others were saved persons, zealots, saints, careerists, thugs, depressives, world-fixers, henchmen, ideologues, devotees, compassionate Buddhas, sadists. Maybe it didn't matter what they were. By the trash can, trays of half-eaten turkey lay on the table by the microwave; the homeless delegation hadn't come for it yet. This was HQ; this was the throne-hall of judgment.

For the benefit of the starry-eyed reporter, the vig held up a fuzzy toy leopard—a gratitude-offering from a girl he'd rescued from the Queen last week. (Actually, Brady's slapper had bought it at Macy's.)

Rodrigo, would you tell us all the *story* behind this leopard?

Yes, ma'am. This young lady, she was at Turk and Jones, which I don't mind telling you is kind of a bad corner, and, well, you know, she was *working,* and then this pimp she'd tried to run away from started bothering her, because she wasn't bringing in money for the Queen no more; she was on her own, so that pimp was under instructions to punish her and bring her back into the fold. The Queen's murdered young girls for less. Justin's this pimp's name. He's got a record as long as the Bay Bridge. Well, I politely asked him to leave her alone, 'cause I could see she was scared, and he pulled a knife on me, so I socked him good and then called for backup. A couple of my buddies was witnesses. We held him until the cops got there, and we helped the girl press charges for assault. Now the Queen don't mess with her no more.

And is she still—working?

No, ma'am. She's a paralegal. She's helping battered women. Especially rape and incest cases. She told me she wants to devote her life to stopping prostitution at the roots.

And what's the best way to do that, Rodrigo?

We gotta start a *public awareness* campaign. Go after the johns who are exploiting the women, go after the pimps, get the Queen who's at the heart of it all.

| 327 |

Ah, but easier said than done! Looking down from the summit of Jones Street into the grey canyons of the Tenderloin into which tricky johns sometimes spurted like drops of semen (all right, baby! croaked Strawberry in her sexy druggy voice, flinging her arms around the man), how could one hope to see the Queen lurking in her squat tunnel with its twin rows of steadily diminishing ceiling-eyes, or the Queen's spidery spies like Crutches and Kitty and the crazy whore scuttling to and from the parking garage?

You're not supposed to give witnesses anything, laughed Smooth, because then you're paying for the testimony and it's not *objective,* you see.

Oh, fuck that, growled Crutches.

Give the man his little rock, sighed the Queen. Thank you, Crutches.

Thanks, Maj, said the homeless man, hobbling off.

Any other business to take care of? Anything else this Queen's gotta do? I know I need to help Strawberry change Sapphire's clothes—

I can do that, Maj.

Allrightie then. I'm gonna ghost away now.

Naturally, said Domino from the side of her crooked mouth.

You got a problem with that, Dom?

What's the difference if I have a problem or not? You'll do what you want to do.

Talk about the handwriting on the wall, chuckled Dan Smooth, who had come to find an acquiescent underage runaway of any one or more of the thirteen sexes; if the Queen could not be of use to him in this matter, he would go to Polk Street, where other wall-writings said LUVYBOYS. —How did it go, Maj? Can't I borrow your Bible— you know, the one you keep between your breasts? Oh, but I remember now exactly what it said: *Mene, mene, tekel, upharsin.*

You implying I want to bring her down? shouted Domino, angry and unbalanced. Smooth was shocked now because his schoolboy pride in a perfect recitation had enticed him into the onionskin layers of Biblical exegesis; he'd forgotten what the gaunt blonde woman had said to call forth the allusion; he only wanted to be calm and pleasant like John in an expensive restaurant; he wanted everybody's praise; he needed the world to

obey him and therefore validate his spidery intelligence which had so often been cruci-
fied with a dozen nails of humiliation and censure driven through every leg; but in this
craving he was no different from Domino herself who in turn had scarcely two hours
since hurled her needs against the needs of Chocolate, whose beauty had happily over-
flowered hers all week because very late on Saturday night, hunting through the *yellow
darkness* of Capp Street (white walls stained yellow like old photos fixed too long in the
hypo bath), she'd spied a nebulous silhouette and pounced, imparting forgettable satisfaction to a forgettable man, so that on Sunday afternoon, ignoring the well meaning
urgings of Beatrice, who patronized Mexicali Hair Design on Capp and Twenty-Eighth,
she'd dropped some of her winnings at the African beauty parlor on Divisadero in order
to get her luscious black hair combed, woven, greased and moussed into peaks like fragrant meringue so that she grew young and bulletproof again as she had been before
dropping the first of her eight unacknowledged children now casually growing in the
state of California's foster homes, never knowing their mother or each other, waiting to
swell in strength and cunning sufficiently to pay the world back since they could hardly
pay back their multitudinous and anonymous fathers or their hidden progenitoress who
now with her white white smile and her face thrown back goodnaturedly, almost funlov-
ingly gazed into the windshields of oncoming cars, her eyebrows plucked, concertina
wire's shadows on her cheek. To the drivers whose saintly dispositions allowed them to
give themselves what they wanted and forgive their own impending mistakes, Chocolate
projected above all *warmth* and *freshness* like the affectionately sexual equivalent of bread
baking in a bride's kitchen, an impression which she did not consciously control but
which was founded on her charming girlish manners and highspiritedness not yet completely stamped out of her even after those eight crack-addicted babies about whom
Tyler had read in her medical record—in fact, one could argue that the insouciance with
which she gave birth and walked away as if a baby were nothing more than excrement
proved that highspiritedness and perhaps even strengthened it by endowing it with a certain expedient proficiency. She stood smiling clear-eyed right into the sun, made for love
as it seemed to the drivers, her brown eyes friendly and seeking friendship; Chocolate
loved to laugh; she allowed jokers to pay less, and because her memory was growing increasingly imperfect, she could hear the same joke any number of times and still be
amazed by the punchline like a virgin on her first date or a true believer who reads the
Gospels over and over. (Gosh, she's too beautiful to be a hooker! cried a Brady's Boy in
wonder. —I dunno about hookers really, said his partner. I come from Philly. In my old
preccinct our major crime was theft of auto.) She herself was entirely capable of banter
but unable to recite any preconceived funny story, a deficiency which she would have
preferred to correct, at least until late afternoon by which time her identity had usually
become confused and temporary with too much cocaine tweaking which poisoned her
with paranoia so that she became argumentative; and within the expanding bands of
shadow on Mission Street, beneath the double row of palm trees, her drivers now de-
scried an entirely different woman whose wildly angry eyes burned like acid through
their illusions of love and pleasure. It was on one of these evenings—this very one, in
fact—when, seeing silver-miniskirted Domino approach her (for like the tall man she
could see everything coming; she could watch everything out of the very whites of her
eyes), Chocolate remembered that night on South Van Ness when she'd betrayed the
blonde, after which the Queen had pronounced her an evil little bitch and commanded
her to apologize, warning: You got to bear your cross now, baby. Domino's always gonna

hate you. —Terrified, Chocolate now conceived the belief, the only possible belief, that Domino, who was looking old as she waggled her long expressive cigarette at the passing cars, was coming to settle matters because the Queen remained with Tyler somewhere on Ellis Street, leaving Chocolate alone just as Chocolate had left Domino alone to get her skull cracked by that monstrous Ada over money she didn't own, and so, just like the Queen herself with her cracked Biblical prophecies, Chocolate shuddered beneath the weight of a satanic epiphany in which every circumstance pulsed with meaning aimed at her, as if she were imprisoned naked and paralyzed in the center of an immense crystal of methamphetamine whose cold facets let in the world's eyes; she wanted to be dark like the darkness but her consciousness glowed, conspicuous to the point of peril. Had it been morning, Chocolate would have been equally certain (like Dan Smooth) that the world was a vast machine whose organization and purpose was solely to fulfill her wishes; now the machine was meant to crush her. The streetlamps were conspiring to fall on her head. The lunar shine of Domino's ultrablonde hair flowed around her shoulders as she stalked among the parked cars. The Queen had sold herself to Henry Tyler for the night in order by her visible abstention from this malignant courtroom now called to order in these dark streets for retribution to be done. Strawberry had abandoned her on purpose. Bernadette had deliberately stayed in. Beatrice was pretending to suffer from venereal disease in order to excuse herself in the direction of the faraway clinic. And here came Domino, her crooked mouth twitching into a sneer which actually represented mere and simple happiness, she having copped prime heroin which could offer more kindness to her than any human being's body or soul, but as her coarse, gaunt, greasy face loomed larger and larger, as her shadow came down upon her, Chocolate, unavailingly longing for her to break contact much as Mission Street suddenly veers beyond Twenty-Fifth to avoid a golden-bleached hill of white houses, could not puff out her breasts and strut proudly by but began to shiver, and the worse she shook, the more her longing cracked into shards of incontrovertible hopelessness until Chocolate, absolutely sure beyond terror or horror that within fifteen seconds the first hammerblow would break open her forehead, screamed: *That money was mine. Where did you spend my money, you goddamned thieving honky bitch?* meaning only to eloquently and passionately clear herself of all charges by atainting her accuser with the crime of prior betrayal; but of course Domino was not much given to self-abasement. For a moment she could not even comprehend to what Chocolate was referring, there having been so many transactions, exchanges, extortions and abuses like pale birds crossing dark Tenderloin windows between that night and this, but from the first, being accustomed throughout her tragic days and nights to expect ambuscades, she understood that the other woman now considered her alien,enemy, devil, animal; and without hesitation she withdrew from her battered silver purse one of her three naked razorblades, and held it aloft. Had it been just her and Chocolate, she would instantaneously have slashed the black woman's face from cheek to cheek, leaving her screaming and bloody, because she knew as does the slender-boned snake that striking rapidly and repeatedly and above all first comprises the only answer to the menace posed by titanic creatures such as Chocolate, who outweighed her by at least thirty pounds. But between them lay the warm brown shadow of the Queen. Domino had never punished Chocolate for abandoning her to Ada that night because the Queen's love for them both had ransomed her, and Domino had actually loved her afterward, no matter how fitfully, as on that night when her aborted fetus pursued and oppressed her, and she'd gone in to Chocolate so that her mourning would be heard. Did she truly love her? Maybe she didn't, but both of them had been nourished from their Queen's mouth. Or maybe it was simply that Domino did not want to go apart from the Queen anymore to live in a desert of fear as she must do should she hurt her sister, even if her sister meant to hurt her, so she strode slowly and impressively closer to the black woman, then said: You see this razor, bitch? Well, *do* you? You know what's gonna happen to you now? and Chocolate started screaming and flailing, completely out of her mind. Domino recognized this. With a cruel smile she scooped up a broken bottle, flung it casually at Chocolate's feet, and strolled away. The brokenhearted black woman didn't try to follow her. Domino went home to the Queen, resolved not to snitch, trying to believe that she'd been good in her restraint, and she even compounded her lovingkindness by giving a little china white to Lily (who hadn't been able to find a nice gentleman who would solve her withdrawal sickness), but she could not stop shaking and trembling just the same so that her heart fluttered like the crazy whore's singsong sinsongs. It was the *unnnaturalness* of her reply to Chocolate which unsettled her. The natural thing to do would have been to fling herself on that nigger bitch and cut her up good so that her stinking guts slid slimily out. She longed to attack somebody, and here Dan Smooth with his smartass Bible quotations was insinuating that she meditated treason against her Queen, to whom she'd just *proved* her loyalty by that act of self-arrest, so, clenching her fists, she said to Smooth beneath her teeth: You don't know a thing about me, you misogynist bastard. You just—

Oh, I'm so tired of this, said the Queen. Dom, you *know* you don't have to stay if you don't want to stay. You sleep on it, okay? Henry's waitin' on me now.

You see? said Domino to the world. Nobody pays attention to me. They just . . .

| 328 |

She's a real asshole, Chocolate confided to Bernadette. She thinks just 'cause she be eatin' out the Queen's ass she gonna always have that house slave position. Well, she was a plantation nigger once just like the rest of us.

That's right, said Bernadette. That's right.

I *hate* that blonde bitch. An' she be kickin' her friends goin' up every rung of that ladder. Well, in this life we all gotta go back down that ladder, too. An' it's harder to kick your friends on the way down, 'cause they be watchin' to grab you ankle an' pull you. *Domino* she calls herself. She be nothin' but a doggy style ho.

And the two women chattered happily on in this vein, but unlike Domino they took care that their Queen did not hear.

| 329 |

The Queen had agreed to meet him at Zapateca's Bar on Mission Street, a place he'd never been before, a rather ordinary place whose low dark ceiling was dusted with glitter and smoky atmosphere like some concretion of the loud Spanish-language songs with which the battle-axe behind the bar sang along. At 7:00 on that Tuesday night there were a couple of pool players and a man kissing a woman's ear at a table and two men at the bar gazed in morose parallels at the brightest spot of all, which was the back-lit shelves of booze bottles, most of which were almost empty.

Tyler sat facing a calendar from the Firearms Training Academy.

Well? she said.

It's pretty bad, he said.

So you scoped it out for me, said the Queen. You did your job. What a good boy. C'mere, baby.

He got up and kissed her.

Allrightie now, said the Queen, slowly unwinding his gold chain from her wrist. Now tell me what's goin' on.

He saw a john whispering something into Beatrice's ear, and he saw Beatrice slap the john's fat stomach and gape her half-toothless mouth in a scream of laughter that cut through the smoky sounds; she was immensely pleased with herself.

He buys girls, he said. And then guys come in and fuck 'em and sometimes torture 'em to death. Everybody pretends it's not real.

You're so sweet, she said. Henry, you know I love you. What else've you been doing with yourself?

Tyler knelt. Slowly he took off her shoes. He massaged her feet

And then all these vigs. He's behind that, too. There's a morality sweep going on, said the Queen, standing suddenly, making him stand. —It's so strange, she went on. Well, not so strange. Moses says *thou shalt not kill,* but then he stones a man to death for gathering wood on the Sabbath.

I don't know about that stuff. I don't understand it. It's just politics, he muttered, narrowing his tired eyes.

I wish we had more time to plan it and shit. Just for the fuck of it we can . . . we can . . . oh, Henry, it's gonna be over so soon, she said.

Tyler felt a lump in his throat. —I thought you were—well, magic, he said. I mean, that's—

Sure, but the Chosen People always win. The ones on God's side. The ones on Jesus's side. I don't wanna talk too much. You were good, Henry. We all were.

When Tyler was small, his parents had brought him to some vast city which must have been Los Angeles (funny that he couldn't remember John's presence) and he recollected walking with them at night through a crowd of happy people gazing into lighted shopwindows of everything—and it seemed that the lights and happiness would go on forever but suddenly Tyler's family arrived at a dark desolate place where a man glared at them and they were all alone. Later he understood that all light, everywhere, must burn out, but the reason that the Tenderloin fascinated him was that it combined the dark desolation with the shiny rouged and glowing-skirted merchandise. And now the future was like that, pitch-hued all the way to substancelessness, with an evil substance lurking in between time's atoms.

Varicose-legged, the ageing Queen sat drinking her beer, her veins like all the rivers. She said: Well, at least maybe we'll snap our fingers in his face—

| 330 |

He stayed with her all night and she was loving in an absentminded way. At dawn her many children were all asleep in one room in the Layla Hotel down on Seventeenth Street, all except for the tall man, who was making a run with the night's earnings to get them a baggie of quality white girl, and she herself began yawning, lying weak and passive in his arms on the moldy itchy carpet, so he said he was going to see about some business, went downstairs to the front grating, turned back the springloaded deadbolt, and went out into the rising day, wishing to *solve* the future before it happened, to save his Queen as he had failed to save Irene, but then suddenly he thought what a relief it would be if the Queen and her entire crew disappeared from everywhere so that he could pull himself back out of the way of his own impending blight; suddenly, even the Queen herself seemed like some nightmare entity who for all her lovingness and splendidness was inevitably ruining him. What if he didn't want to be ruined? He could call John and apologize. John would save him, if he humbled himself. But then what would he do; which doom would he find instead? What was it that he *needed* to do, in order to live with himself, and become no longer grey and sneaking? —Ah, he actually thought that his life could be fixed! He thought that only momentarily, of course, and only because at the moment he unlocked the driver's door of his car he saw in the corner in the hot sunlight a dear little Vietnamese girl laughing and mock-boxing her father. He envied her father, yes he did. Just as Dan Smooth said, he had envious ears! He wanted to be married as his mother had advised, and he wanted to subsequently raise a child lovingly and playfully. Really he wanted the most impossible thing—namely, to be like everyone else, which was what almost everyone wanted, which meant that no one *was* like anyone else, not Tyler, not his brother, not the Vietnamese child or her father, certainly not the Queen, who of all the people he'd ever met, including Dan Smooth, was the only one who'd sincerely never wanted that, not Irene or Celia, who both did want it most desperately, not Chocolate, who at two o'clock in the morning in that hotel room as the Queen lay in his arms had been haltingly reading out the personal ads from a yellowing newspaper, saying: *SBM,* what the fuck's that mean, Maj? Hey, Maj, you asleep? *Sor*-ree. Oh, single black male. All right. A brother. SBM, thirty-nine years old, well, that's little old but maybe he's saved hisself up some *money* for me to spend. Maybe he's old enough to be faithful. Spontaneous, honest, caring, but is he handsome? Don't say nothin' about handsome. What do you think, Justin?

Must be butt ugly. Just like you, Choc.

Don't you disrespect me, nigger! Honest, caring, enjoys parties, all right now, all right, swimming, outgoing, down to earth, *no drugs,* oh, so he's *that* kind of asshole.

Then she went out, and was soon lying naked and weary after sweaty sex with a stinking old man, her arm wrapped around her head as if to hug and console it for having been kissed by someone for whom she felt no love, while Tyler drove home, pressed the PLAY button on his answering machine, which related in his brother's curt voice: Guess you're out of town. Mom called about an hour ago, and they're going to send her home tomorrow at the shift change at seven-o'-clock. Anyway, that's where we are. —I get it, muttered Tyler, throwing out threatening letters from credit card companies. He opened his solitary remaining piece of mail, which proclaimed:

STARS AND STRIPES FUNDING IS NOT A
GOVERNMENT AGENCY

Is It Worth Three Minutes to Cut Your Payments in Half?

Dear **Tyler001error69 Henry G.,**

Wouldn't you like more cash in your pocket with a **$200,000.00**
loan from Stars and Stripes Funding, Inc., at a LOW, LOW fixed
interest rate of 14.99%? Consolidate your bills. No equity needed.
Save thousand and thousands of dollars. Take that dream vacation, **Tyler001error69 Henry G.** Call toll free.

Then he thought: Thank God I don't fall for that. Thank God I can say fuck you to
all equity. Thank God for my Mark of Cain.

| 331 |

The Queen, rolling off a concrete block in the abandoned meatpacking plant, then
walking like a crab, pale with dead eyes, asked Tyler of whom or what he had dreamed;
and while he considered, she laid her middle finger across his wrist, in order to drink in
his pulse. He had dreamed that he held a small black spider in the palm of his hand, a
perfect little spider which bit him. —Ah, said the Queen, you had the spider dream! and
he was afraid. That's good, baby, the Queen whispered, sliding her long, long grey
tongue into his mouth. He felt nauseous but also excited. Soon he was relearning the
spidery angles and steep curves of her buttocks. Her eyes were rimmed and outlined. She
leaped on him. When her orgasm came, he was terrified by her round and screaming
eyes as she squatted on him, beating and scratching at his flesh.

Her tiny feet mastered the palms of his hands as he raised her up, setting her upon his
shoulders for her to command and worry at his body. His love, his life, had become as
richly weird as the Queen's hair hanging down from her bowed head in darkness.

| 332 |

Her pussy tasted like crack. The girls could drink from it all day and their cravings would
go away. But the more they drank, the more addicted they were. (For that matter, Celia
craved the sharp knife-crease of muscle behind John's knees.) Her spit was just the opposite.

| 333 |

The Queen said: Maybe I'll get pregnant.

He smiled. Tears came into his eyes. He thought of that little Vietnamese girl he'd
seen playing with her father that morning and realized that something that good could
happen to him and perhaps be safely hidden behind the high gates of anonymity for a
long, long time until death and destruction came, and then the eyes narrowed in his grey

face and he realized that sentimentality was corrupting him. It was all false, like Hitler killing millions of human beings while weeping over the cruelty of fox-hunting. But where did such false emotions come from? He feared himself and his own unreliability. And yet weren't such errors perhaps the necessary consequence of taking an uncharted path? He felt that he had to learn as much from the Queen and love her as greatly as he could before the vigs came, not only for her own sake, but because her love and her truth might well comprise his final chance to learn who he was, where he must go, and what was expected of him. He did not believe that he was destined to be a father now, because Irene . . . But Irene's child . . . He sat very still, insufferably unable to think.

Domino, seeing now in him the uprolled eyeballs and pale puffy cheeks and slack-hanging lips of Sunflower in her last months of life, feared what she saw, and accordingly attacked it, sneering in her most stinging tone: Henry, don't you even care what Maj just said? Is that shiteating grin on your face a sufficient response to anything? I think a man should be committed. Whereas *you* . . .

He scarcely heard her. He felt so anxious and alone that he almost screamed.

Beatrice, whose breath was as rotten mucilage oozing and crawling with disease, coughed apologetically into his face and said: Henry, you okay? I doan know, maybe you look so sad . . .

Yeah, I'm all right, he said heavily.

And you think you gonna be pregnant, Mama? I get so happy I'm gonna light a candle for you . . .

I don't believe it, said Tyler harshly. Somehow I just don't figure it's going to happen.

You know, Henry, I got to say it takes two people to create a child. I doan know my English, but I think society is coming to like thousands of years ago. All of a sudden women, they saying, *this is my body,* and I know that 'cause I said it too when I had my baby; I swear I didn't want him. You have to remember though that there are two people involved. *I* had to get involved!

Yeah, then where's the little brat now? said Domino, grinning elfishly as if she had her back up against some wall and were slowly upcurling her tongue at the oncoming cars and licking her lips, back and forth, back and forth, with an intensely mirthful but also lustful expression in her huge-pupiled eyes.

Yeah, Dom, so maybe I doan be no good. I know that. I'm no good. But Henry he still want to do the good thing, so we should help him. Henry, when your *novia* she talk about get pregnant, you better *believe* in case God is listening and think about sending you a baby. You want a baby? Baby gonna take away so much of your pain, Henry. You gotta *believe.* Please Henry, you—

Then where the *fuck's* your little Mexican brat? screamed Domino, whose soul was itself as lost and sad and grimy up close as the face of Beatrice, whose belief in the Virgin, which meant belief in herself, had been reduced to mere endurance palliated but perhaps by that very token rendered more dangerous and poisonous by the sincere and unmitigated love of her Mama, her Queen as Beatrice's hair twirled heavily down the sides of her face and she bit her thin, herpid lips to keep herself from tears, her forehead lined, the bridge of her nose doubly lined, and her huge, lost eyeballs mottled like the full moon with its faint mountains and seas.

Henry, she whispered, it all starts from the fact that when you do those types of practices, you gotta get *responsible* for your actions. And our Mama Queen, she's knowing that already. Mama takes responsibility for all of us already.

Domino said: Did he take responsibility when he knocked up your brother's wife?

Hush up now, said the Queen. Ain't nobody gonna talk to Henry about that. And nobody need to make Bea start cryin' for nothin'. Domino, when you gonna see how much you hurt *yourself* with that kind of talk? You—

But, Maj, don't you even care that Henry was an asshole to that Oriental whatshername? She *offed* herself, and here's this jerk walking around scot-free like some rapist who preys on little girls. Don't you think that Henry ought to pay for what he did? Aren't you on *our* side?

Domino, said the Queen, that's between Henry and me.

You don't understand, Maj. Oh, hell, it's all so pathetic. Nobody understands. And Beatrice just sits there and blubbers, and Henry's mad at me, and you're mad at me when all I did was say the truth.

See how she manipulates, laughed Strawberry, throwing back her head and fanning her hair across her shoulders as Domino liked to do. —She's jealous of all the attention Henry gets. She wants to be sad so she can get first in line to be comforted . . .

With an eagle-like scream of rage, Domino rushed her with her long silver fingernails whirling like airplane propellers, but the weary Queen said: Hush, Domino. C'mere, sweetie. And Domino fled into the Queen's embrace, nuzzling her armpits like a puppydog.

It's so crazy, Tyler muttered, and no one said anything, so he hung his head and cleared his throat and very carefully asked the dark cracked windowpanes of the abandoned meatpacking plant: When will they stop bugging me?

When you let it go, said the Queen, rocking the sobbing girl. You got to let Irene sink under the earth and turn into grass. That's what she needs to do now. She wants flowers to come up out of her breast. Don't hold her back.

I get it, Maj, he said. But I . . .

You don't have to say anything you're not ready to say, the Queen told him. You know I love you?

I know it. Are you pregnant?

I don't believe so. Not yet.

Strawberry said: Listen, Henry. I don't know so much about you and Charlene—

Irene, he said furiously.

Irene. And it's not really my business. But we talk about you all the time, because you're the only man who ever comes to visit us, aside from Justin, who lives here, and, I mean, good heavens, it's nice to talk about men once in a while! Gosh, I wish you'd buy us all a drink at the Wonderbar and we could just sit and—

Tyler shot a quick shy look at her, and, seeing that she was not his enemy, became if anything even more dejected and humiliated. The dead woman would not let him go. And his Queen would never become pregnant, because she herself had prophesized that her purpose on earth would all too soon be fulfilled, the purpose to which she'd been so supremely faithful, and he'd be left alone again as he had been after Irene died, because the Queen had insisted that it *must* be so. But gradually his own self-pity became as gentle and blurry as Strawberry's when she got drunk or entered the heroin nods, swaying and doubling and tripling. Didn't she mean well? Didn't she? And the Queen sat so silent! Why? Was this supposed to be another ordeal like his obedient worship of the false Irene, something whose bitter uselessness would further hollow out his heart into an ashtray in which Domino or anybody else could stub out cigarettes? But surely Strawberry meant well. She said: My brother was in college with a girlfriend and she, well, she became pregnant. I was always very close to my brother and I was the first to hear. And we celebrated. When I think back on all the champagne we went through! Oh, everybody was so happy, it was all like a dream! They could have had an abortion, I know. But he decided he was going to marry this girl. I don't know why I'm even telling you this, maybe just because it came into my head just now when Maj was talking about having a child and I . . . God, I could use a drink at the Wonderbar. I could use a motherfucking drink. Anyway, they had a child. He finished college; she didn't. She always resented it. So the marriage broke up. She broke it up. But he really has a kid that he loves. Maybe his life would have been different if they'd had the abortion. But who's to judge him? He got his life together. It worked out for him. Most of the time the circumstances just need to be negotiated. How do you grow without conflict and difference?

Are you saying I don't want conflict? asked Tyler in a dull, exhausted voice. Are you saying I'm afraid of something? What are you saying?

Oh, can't you leave him alone, sighed the Queen. Leave my man alone.

Beatrice said: Excuse me, Maj. Excuse me, Henry. Excuse me, Strawberry. I have to say something about abortion. Some people they doan believe that at the time of conception the soul enters the body. I do know that doing away with any form of life, it's not a nice thing.

Yeah, and how many babies have you killed with your own coat hanger? snarled Domino from the Queen's arms.

What's all this about? said Tyler. What kind of discussion is this? —The eagerness of these women to speak of babies and childbirth, the avidity in their eyes, above all the hope with which they now regarded their Queen, as if her baby would be theirs or would somehow save them, disconcerted him as much as if he'd suddenly realized that he had no soul.

We just be sharin' our thoughts with you, that's all, said Chocolate from the doorway, while Sapphire, rocking back and forth in the corner, whispered: *Luh-luh-luh-luh* . . .

I love you, too, he said to the retarded girl, who seemed to be uneasy, like a dog which knows something is wrong when its master begins packing his suitcase. She had sat in the same place all night, watching her mother and her sisters with wide and anxious eyes.

I want a baby but I can't, said Strawberry. I had two children they took away an' put in foster care, and now I don't know where they are. And my third died in crib death. That's the one I cry for. And then I got pelvic inflammatory disease, so now I'm sterile.

| 334 |

When Irene reached her sophomore year of high school in Westwood, she and four classmates—one Chinese, two Japanese, and one other Korean—secretly if lightheartedly founded what they called the Virgins' Club. Really it was an excuse to gossip, go out to movies together, and help each other with homework—a particular benefit in Irene's case, since she was only a B student and had always been even in elementary school when her mother used to punish her for not coming home with perfect grades. The Virgins' Club met neither regularly nor formally. Nonetheless, its rules had teeth. Each girl swore not to have sex before marriage, and never to wed any man of another race, in order to avoid disappointing her parents, who by immigrating in the first place had left themselves all too susceptible to such affronts. Indeed, when Irene raised her hand to swear the oath, she saw before her her dear mother's fine face and thin dark arched eye-

brows. Their promise, then, emblematized daughterly love, which must remain inseparable from clannishness, and perhaps it reassured those schoolgirls in their warm expectations that the families which they each would surely found would resemble the ones
departed, protecting them from futurity, keeping them happily isolated like the emerald
rectangle that is Union Square, set into its bezel of brick and concrete. (And here one
might also make analogy to the Queen's court, with its exclusiveness, secrecy and helpfulness.) In Irene's opinion, it was the Chinese girl who broke her vow first. In her fresh-
man year at San Diego State, defiant in the face of family ostracism and de facto
expulsion from the Virgins' Club, she married a nice boy from Saudi Arabia. One of the
Japanese girls dated a white boy in her senior year, and the rumor flitted around the Virgins' Club (which by that time had become rather too loose-knit, nourished only by increasingly far-flung telephone calls from one member to another) that she had given him
everything, but none of the remaining virgins chose to address her silence directly because that would have been rude and because, like Cain, they were not their siblings'
keepers, and above all because the Virgins' Club was itself mere silliness which, had it
been completely immersed in the solvent of sexuality, could have dissolved without
repercussions. Both of the Japanese girls did end up marrying Japanese, and the other
Korean girl married into a rich Korean family in Brentwood. Irene, of course, ended up
with John. The other Korean girl and one of the Japanese girls came to Irene's wedding.
They said that they were very happy for her.

    By then Irene's brother Steven, who was a software engineer prone, like John, to ele-
gant neckties, had already married a good Korean girl whom he considered slightly beneath him and who gave him a son before her wifehood was a year old—singular fortune
for her, because Irene's mother, who'd thought her frivolously delicate until then, immediately held her precious. The impetus now lay on Irene to conceive, although her parents regretfully understood that John preferred to postpone that beginning; themselves
being postponers in the name of self-sacrifice, they accepted in their first-generation
American hearts what John had chosen for entirely different ends. Irene kept modestly
silent. Although she mentioned her mother and father hardly at all, Tyler afterward
wondered whether her understanding with them on this crucial subject of maternity
might have anything to do with her suicide. One night in September when the vigs had
already arrived in San Francisco and he was sitting alone in his apartment, asking himself when he'd go to worship his Queen, he suddenly visualized Irene picking up the telephone to call Los Angeles and tell her parents that she was pregnant. Her mother would
have known the very first instant that Irene was not smiling with pleasure. And how
would she and Irene's father interpret that? Their own natural impulse to be joyous
would have been stifled by Irene's listless, anxious monotone. They would wonder what
had occurred between her and John. (I think John is angry at me, Irene had publicly said
during that final vacation in Monterey. John, you're angry, aren't you? —Tyler had found
that very distasteful.) No doubt, since Irene's parents had never met John's brother except briefly at the wedding, it would scarcely have occurred to them that there might
have been third parties involved. Tyler, imagining that familial conversation and all the
subsequent ones for the remaining months of Irene's life, could hardly keep from groaning. And now she was dead, killed, *self-* killed, self-murdered. The Queen had made him
promise not to forget her. The false Irene was always asking him about her . . .

    I've prayed so much for you to get pregnant, Irene's mother said in Korean. Children
are a gift from God.

Irene made no answer.

Have you had good dreams? her mother pursued. If so, it's going to be a boy . . .

But before the worst had happened, Irene's womb continuing as yet unripe, her sister's family came to visit. Steven and Pammy craved a vacation in Mendocino County, so they left their son in San Francisco for the weekend. —Of *course!* said Irene, brimming with enthusiasm in order to deacidify the impression conveyed by John's sullenness. —Be a good boy now, Pammy instructed the child. Be obedient to your Auntie Irene and your Uncle John. —Bewildered, with big dark-framed spectacles, he sat playing video games as soundlessly as possible while Irene peeled garlic in the kitchen, wishing for more counter space, a larger refrigerator, and a dishwasher capable of more even results. Her nephew's presence did not make her uneasy because at that time a child associated with her did not symbolize anything negative to John. Indeed, she smiled a little to herself, dreaming of how it would be when she had her own baby, her dear little soul which she could love without reserve, being no longer dependent on John's moods for anything. Her smile became almost spitefully triumphant when she considered how plausible it would be when she ignored John as much as he'd ignored her throughout their married life; she could spend all afternoon bathing her baby and then take him out shopping, and when John came home there would be no dinner waiting; they'd have to go out. Of course, John enjoyed dining at restaurants anyhow. When the garlic was all finished, she washed her hands, wondering whether she should drive to the Korean market to buy short ribs, which she could marinate easily and well in vinegar, Coca Cola, sesame oil, and red pepper paste, or whether she could treat the boy to one of those restaurant meals she'd so slyly imagined. If John were too busy to imprison himself in such trivialities, she could always count on Henry to take her, probably to that stretch of Korean markets and restaurants on Geary between Eleventh and Tenth, with their signs in squat Hangul characters and their kiosks for the *Korea Times* (fifty cents a copy)—a district which would after her death and burial insistently murmur to Tyler of her, like a yellowjacket buzzing inside a seashell. —Laurel Heights, on the other hand, was John's territory because near the former pioneer cemetery there now stood an unassuming liquor store to which John sometimes drove to buy cask strength Mortlach (eight-year-old, imported by Cadenhead's for about eighty dollars a bottle). Once Tyler had made his own journey to the grave, who would remember him, and what place would they associate with him? No place, probably; he was nothing and stood for nothing, not even the Tenderloin. He might as well be homeless.

As it happened, Irene's self-pitying bitterness proved to be unfounded, on this occasion at least, because John liked his nephew and tried to win him over with presents, remembering how when he and Hank were children their abandoned mother had worked so hard and remained so poor; there'd been many things John had craved then: new clean sneakers like his schoolfellows, T-shirts, a nice watch, a Green Hornet lunchbox. Even now, one of the ways to put John in a good mood (although Celia had not yet learned this, and Irene never would) was to give him toy trains—an infantile transaction, to be sure, but surely John in his own way needed to feel taken care of, his expensive neckties and professional ambition aiming not only at egotism but also at safety and ease. And so he took his nephew downtown to the F.A.O. Schwarz on Stockton and O'Farrell, right on the edge of the Tenderloin, and allowed him to choose a hundred dollars' worth of toys. The child, however, who actually lacked for nothing, thanks to Steven's income, remained with John at all times shy and mistrustful. He sensed in his uncle a hardened silence which only a tolerant and perceptive adult could have recognized as something damaged; the child experienced it as stern dislike. The pallor of his uncle's skin alarmed him, too, and he seemed to give off a strange smell. When he sat on his Auntie Irene's lap he felt less homesick, believing for as long as she held him that his mother and father would truly return in only one more day, whereas John with his unnerving gift of toys presented an alien distraction, indicative of a plot to make him forget his parents, who if he let them escape from memory for one instant would immediately cease forever to exist. Above all, he perceived in John the desire to possess him, and he would not be possessed. He would not be tricked.

After they had gone back to Los Angeles, John said: That kid liked you more than he did me.

Well, what do you expect? said Irene. He ought to like me better. I'm a blood relative. I'm his aunt. You're just his uncle-in-law.

We don't do things that way in my culture, John said. I love my aunt and uncle both the same. It doesn't matter which one's the blood relative.

You mean you hate them both the same, said Irene, waxing her eyebrows. When was the last time you sent them a postcard or called them up?

That has nothing to do with it.

It has everything to do with it. Anyway, you married a Korean. That's how Koreans are. If you don't like it, you can divorce me.

What a goddamned cold thing to say!

You heard me. If you don't like the way I am, you can divorce me.

So you can marry Hank?

I think you should be grateful to Henry that he treats me so nice. Saves you the trouble.

Are you in love with him, Irene?

Excuse me, Irene said. I'm going to close the bathroom door now. I want to pee.

| 335 |

Sacramento was rainy and windy, then sunny and windy. The September cornfields, greenish-brown, had just begun to go, like a cyanotype exposure nudged by many many photons into its first perceptible color shift: a permanent image was forming on the paper just as death was settling on the cornfields. He sat in the living room of his mother's house reading in the *Bee* about a father who stabbed his wife and warned the children that if they told he would kill them, too; then the father drove away, leaving them to wait for two weeks of obedient silence in the bedroom with the decomposing body. Violent death in and of itself retained little power to disturb Tyler's already anxious ease, but the hiddenness of that family's literally rotten secret reminded him of Irene's suicide, whose threateningly garish message remained only half obscured, like some Chinese movie poster behind a grating. Irene had loved Hong Kong action films. He remembered the posters in those two Chinatown theaters; forcing his mind away from the dangerous, morbid image, the grinning teeth and red calligraphy of heart's blood from his murdered heroine, he withdrew from the grating, struggling up from memory to optimistic convenience even though the way remained as steep as the street-slope at Powell and Sacramento Streets; now he couldn't see that threatening poster anymore. It was a grey day in his skull's San Francisco; Tyler drove up through Chinatown on that lack-adaiscal, that torpid throughway appropriately called Sacramento; he couldn't get away from Sacramento even though his purpose might be shaded by clouds and awnings. By the First Chinese Baptist Church on Waverly a lady was awkwardly carrying her child. She struggled a little way up the hill and stopped just past the Chinese Playground, panting. He gazed pleasurably upon a Chinese girl whose hair was as shiny as her little black car. Then the poster began blinking red and black, red and black behind his closed eyes, no matter how tightly he squeezed them—red and black, red and black: Irene's blood, Irene's hair. For a moment he thought he couldn't stand it, but if he didn't stand it then what would happen? —All right then, he said to himself. Here is the poster and I am looking at it. This is the movie which Irene wants to see. Irene takes my hand. I am afraid that one of John's colleagues will notice, but at the same time I don't care, or I guess I do care but I wouldn't let go of her hand no matter who saw. I pay the cashier for two tickets. We go inside, and now the poster is behind us. I hold Irene's hand so tightly that she can't pull it away and leave me. We sit down in the row of seats, and with my right hand I reach across myself to take her right hand while my left arm goes happily around her neck. Irene loves me. Irene will never love me. I love Irene. I love you, Irene. Irene, please let me kiss your cunt.

Okay, this is it! laughed Irene nervously. You're too tall! —And she let go of his hand.

How about if I buy you some elevator shoes?

When I'm in an elevator shoe mood, I'll call you.

Then a train mooed, half-cow, half-wolf. It must have been a long train because the strange call went on and on. His mother slept; she was not well. He went out for coffee and scones. The burglar alarm of the bookstore next door made everyone grimace. After half an hour it had not stopped, and his ears rang. He strolled home. His mother was still in bed. John had taken Mugsy to San Francisco for the duration. The phone rang. The new private nurse was very sorry, but she needed to reschedule the interview for the day after tomorrow; there'd been a death in her family. Tyler said that he was very sorry. He thought about driving immediately to San Francisco, getting some work done in case he had any work to do, then returning in two days or perhaps three, when the nurse, red-eyed, he supposed, had paid steady homage to the dead relative whom he hoped she had loved; but eighty miles each way would have given his old car a beating, so after his mother had woken up and been given all her pills he began the three-hundred-mile drive to Los Angeles, rapturously meditating on nothingness. Yes, he was homeless. He wanted to be homeless. Only when he was under the ground would he have a home. He overnighted in a motel in Panorama City. Early next morning he purchased from the florist (now an old friend) pink rosebuds sparkling with water, and achieved Forest Lawn. The back of his neck tingled; he was afraid that maybe he'd meet John or Irene's brother Steven, but Irene lay most fortunately alone. —I've got to, I've got to, I've *got to got to* forget about her, he said aloud. —Her headstone had been freshly cleaned, prob-ably by her mother. He stood the flowers in the iron ring and made his getaway. Indus-trial Security Supply was the cheapest source for microphone batteries, so he stopped there and bought a four-pack of those, made in Thailand now, he saw, then browsed un-enthusiastically through the latest offering of tricks and cheats over in Demo Sales, had a burger, gassed up, and got back on Interstate Five—winds at Grapevine, dusty winds all through the Central Valley, dancing trees in Sacramento, leaves on his mother's roof.

He got the ladder out of the garage and went up with the push-broom to clear the gutters, which needed to be redone, but there didn't seem to be much point in spending the money until he and John had talked over what would happen to the house after their mother was out of it. She was still resting. (When you get elderly you have to expect such things, she'd said.) He went to the supermarket and bought two sacks of groceries, trying to remember what it was that John usually got for her. He was not a good son. He admitted it. He was not so good at anything. Wouldn't he be better, if he could get out of everything, too? Was Irene out of it or truly in it at last? And the Queen, where would she go when she was out of it? For a moment he longed to visit Dan Smooth, who was probably snoring on the front porch on Q Street, and who had all the answers even though those answers were unpleasant and might well be incorrect. But it was so hot that Tyler had already begun to fall asleep, too. Nothing could be of any use. In the front yard, withered red maple leaves whirled and clawed like fans in summer. At night it rained hard. He was up early the next morning with his heart most anxiously pounding and an ulcerous ache in his guts. The *Bee* was on the front porch. He slid off the rubber band, unrolled it, and read about a man whose wife had told him she was leaving, so the man shot his two little boys and then himself while she was screaming on the phone to the police. He went out for coffee. Every time he showed up at that cafe he met new help. Strangers everywhere, he thought, and then immediately saw his neighbor Mrs. Adams tying up her dog to the lamp post.

Why, good *morning*, Henry, said Mrs. Adams.

Morning, Mrs. Adams, said Tyler. How's everything with you today?

Oh, my darned dog won't poop. He's done number one, but he just won't do number two. And it's really important for him to do number two. He's just impossible all day until he does number two.

Sometimes I feel that way myself, said Tyler. Can I buy you a coffee, Mrs. Adams?

Why, how sweet of you, but I'm actually in a bit of rush. But do tell me how your mother is doing. We're all so concerned about her. Your brother of course has been absolutely wonderful with her. It makes me laugh to see him out there mowing the grass just like he used to when he was a little boy. In his suit and tie yet; he comes straight from work . . .

Actually, cutting the grass was always my job, Tyler said. John had to take out the trash and rake the leaves.

Well, he certainly has kept his sense of responsibility, hasn't he, Tyler? Just yesterday I was passing by and saw him up on your roof on his hands and knees, picking all those leaves out of the gutters.

That was me, Mrs. Adams.

Henry Tyler, are you telling me that after all these years I can't tell you and John apart? —Oh, there he goes. *There* he goes. Oh, good doggie. What a good little doggie.

She bustled out, smiling. From her bright new daypack came the pooper-scooper and the plastic bag.

A moment later she was back. —Terrible, that story in the paper, don't you think?

Not very nice, Tyler agreed, sprinkling some powdered chocolate in his steamed milk.

Why do you think people do those things? You're around those sorts of people all the time; haven't they told you anything?

Oh, they're a lot like the rest of us, Mrs. Adams, Tyler said. They just tend to act a little more on their feelings, is all. Is that cappuccino yours?

They make such good cappuccino in this place, Mrs. Adams said. Ted and I went to Europe last spring and we tried a different coffee house every morning. I don't even remember all the places we tried. But we never found any coffee that held a candle to the coffee right here at River City.

And what did Mr. Adams think?

Oh, he can't tell the difference. He's been an easy husband. Whatever he eats or drinks, to him it all tastes the same.

That's the way to be, all right, said Tyler. I wish I could kill all my taste buds.

John has the most sophisticated tastes in your family, wouldn't you say? I read in the *Bee* that drinking a glass of wine every night is good for your heart. He keeps buying your mother bottles of wine whose names I can't even pronounce!

That sounds like John, said Tyler.

Wasn't it a shame about Eileen, said Mrs. Adams.

Irene, Tyler said, something exploding in his chest.

That's what I said. Irene. Why do you think she was so unhappy? You were very close to her, I understand.

Something was bleeding inside Tyler's chest.

Weren't you, Henry?

I certainly was, Mrs. Adams. Yes, ma'am, I certainly was.

Then how could she—

She wanted a dog, Tyler lied gleefully. That was the real reason. She wanted a little Airedale just like yours, but John wouldn't let her have one.

John wouldn't let her have a dog? cried Mrs. Adams in indignation. And what business was that of his? What could anyone possibly have against dogs?

He said that they were nasty, disgusting creatures. He just refused to let her have one, Tyler explained, following up on his attack.

But isn't he taking care of Mugsy?

He put her in one of those no-name kennels. Full of disease and vicious pit-bulls, I hear. They just tear apart dogs Mugsy's size . . .

And Mugsy's in one of those places? How horrible!

Horrible's exactly what it is.

And you just sit there and let it happen? Shame on you! Remind me never to trust Bubbles to either of you!

John hates dogs, Tyler explained. You wouldn't believe how vitriolic he gets.

Well! said Mrs. Adams. I never knew that about John. And to think that I even let him sit our dog once—not Bubbles, of course. That was before Bubbles's time. I let him sit Jessie. Do you remember Jessie?

Why, sure I do, Tyler lied.

And I paid John very well, too, at that time, Mrs. Adams said. Twenty-five dollars. Do you think he mistreated her?

Oh, I don't think so, said Tyler, continuing to play the part most masterfully. Although with John you never know.

You never know, repeated Mrs. Adams, hypnotized. I never knew that about John. I never, never knew.

| 336 |

His mother was resting. He'd already filled up the refrigerator and telephoned his answering machine which connected him to San Francisco like still another long foul snail-track of memory. One message: A lady wanted him to find out why her husband got off work at eleven every night but never came home until one. Maybe four hundred dollars if he got lucky—half of October's rent. The *Sacramento Bee* reported two more robberies in midtown and a rape-murder in Oak Park, the latter possibly perpetrated by some of the gangbangers in peaked or tasseled wool caps who leaned up against the window of Ray's Taco Rico on Broadway, which had been around under various names since the 1930s; he used to go there for shakes and burgers with his high school co-inmates who'd believed that they had important things in common; maybe they did; maybe they had; Tyler had lost touch with all of them. He drove down to Ray's and ordered a burger. On the wall hung a calendar, courtesy of a beer company, which sang the praises of the **GREAT QUEENS OF AFRICA,** in this case Queen Amina of Zaria. The gangbangers came in. Ray kept saying: Right here, cheese and chicken salad, right here.

Are you happy, dear? said his mother weakly.

Don't worry about me, Mom. I'm more worried about you.

You sound just like John.

I get it, he chuckled. A headache was coming on—the same kind of headache as when some long snort of speed-cut cocaine wears off. He massaged his eyebrows.

Henry?

Yes, Mom.

Did Irene actually borrow my copy of *The Possessed?* I can't seem to find it. I remember when I told her . . . oh, dear. She probably thought she had to read it to please me.

I'll go look in the living room, he said.

There it was, in the third shelf down of the bookcase by the piano, in its usual place in the five-volume set of Dostoyevsky, with every book crowned by distinguished dust.

By late afternoon Tyler was going south on I-80 with the Bay on his right, shining blue, brassy and silver—a worked surface, as an artist would say. His friend Adrienne said that there was going to be an illegal Survival Research Laboratories performance down on Second and Natoma; they'd been banned in the city; maybe sooner or later they'd get tired or burned out and the strange furtive machine performances in night parking lots would come to an end, so he probably should have gone; he kind of wanted to, but he was feeling sick and tired.

| 337 |

He opened his mail, which said:

Dear Henr Tlyyyr & Mrs. Henr Tlyyyr,

We are pleased to offer you our unique financing program to bring instant, guaranteed relief from the burdensome payments you may be making on outstanding credit card balances, mortgage payments, automobile loans, and other consumer debt.

He crumpled that letter up and threw it at the wastebasket, but missed. Then he opened a beer.

He was behind on the rent again.

He telephoned the court clerk he used to go out with and asked her to please look up an Africa Johnston's misdemeanor case from 1978, but the lady said: Henry, those records no longer exist. They have been deleted. Paperwork Reduction Act.

But I have the case number, he said.

I'm sure you do, she laughed. Listen, Henry, I really really *really* have to go.

| 338 |

Soon after that the vigs started coming around everywhere, terrorizing the street girls, calling the cops on them, and sometimes even going undercover to date them in order to ask where the Queen was, because, as Stalin once said, *Cut off the head and the body dies.* Once the whores knew who those men were, they rejected them and their money in scared, angry voices, but the only way to find that out was to go with them the first time. A vig whose gaze was as sick and ugly as one of those dark bars in which the regulars celebrate their own birthdays went up to Chocolate's trick pad at the Royal Hotel for a fifty-and-ten,* fucked her without a rubber, then offered her a hundred dollars more to introduce him to the Queen. He said he wanted her for a bachelor night.

I'm the Queen of the Tenderloin, said Chocolate. I got my own line. I lay out my line. They follow me themselves.

She was lying sideways on the stinking bed with her reddish-chocolate thigh up on the pillow. She hadn't taken off her pair of copper bracelets all summer because they eased her tendonitis, which tortured her more than ever now because she was an old bitch as she put it. —You've jerked off too many pricks! sneered Domino, to which Chocolate, never tongue-tied, replied simply: Your time gonna come, Dom, just like mine.

The vig said: Don't bullshit me, bitch. This is the last time I'm gonna ask you nice. Now take me to the Queen.

Chocolate with her beautiful kissable mouth and those sweet, hurt eyes of hers lay gazing at the man with an almost flaming gentleness, in order to conceal her intense fear and hatred, and she was silent, thinking to herself: If he starts trouble I got to grab my high heeled shoe an' bang on the door till the manager comes. Then I'll get eighty-sixed from here but at least I . . .

How about it, bitch? said the vig with a tight little grin. Ain't you girlfriends with the Queen?

I have one girlfriend. Me. Me alone.

You know the Queen?

Nope.

You know Henry Tyler?

If I did, would I tell you? I don't know you.

You know me now, the vig said.

Yeah, right.

---

* Fifty dollars for the "flatback" and ten dollars for an hour in the room.

And I'm *watching* you.

Well, watch me all you want, 'cause I ain't doin' anything illegal, and if I am, you ain't gonna catch me!

What about what you just did with me here?

That ain't nothin'. That's only entrapment.

Are you the Queen?

You're full of it.

Looking her in the face, the vig said: I hear the Queen does magic. *Black* magic. Listen carefully, Chocolate. I'm going to quote you Leviticus 20.27. *A man or a woman who is a medium or a wizard shall be put to death; they shall be stoned with stones; their blood shall be upon them.* Amen.

Uh *huh,* said Chocolate.

Are you the Queen?

Are you a jerkoff?

You gonna miss me when I go?

No.

Can I miss you?

No.

What'll you do if I miss you?

Fine. You can miss me all you want.

Come blow me again, bitch.

Uh-*uh,* said Chocolate, sitting up and reaching for her high heel. —I already done my job. I'm gonna give you my mouth motor, first you gonna gimme that hundred dollars . . .

The man leaped up, overtowering her, and snatched the shoe out of her hand, so Chocolate began to scream as loudly as she could, and right away the manager came and she was safe . . .

| 339 |

And Jesus elevated Mary Magdalene above the rest, said Smooth. You know why?

Because she was a whore, said Tyler, bored. He could not imagine why he had wished to solicit the man's advice on anything. Smooth was as lively as a bumblebee, buzzing and buzzing about. He exhausted Tyler like Mission Street's slow and stinking sunlight.

Not only that.

Not only what?

It wasn't just that she was a prostitute. Henry, are you listening to me?

Yeah.

Also because she was His *servant,* you see. Because she washed His feet with her hair. And when the Queen spits in your mouth, she's giving you a chance to be elevated—

Well, Domino never swallows, said Tyler. She told me for her it's the same as a blow job. She just tucks it under her tongue and then spits it out when she can.

Well, then, she can't be *elevated,* now, can she, asshole? said Smooth.

And do you admire Domino?

Oh, she and I go pretty far back, said Smooth. I'd have to say I—well, I—

They were on Powell Street. A little girl with tight shimmery golden laces on her sneakers took lipstick from the duty free bag and opened it, at which her mother nodded and lovingly explained.

I'd like to get into that, Smooth said.

I bet you would, said Tyler.

Ah, but it would be as illegal as a bail bondsman's referral to any particular lawyer. You like illegal candy, don't you, Henry?

I'm sick of your insinuations. Can't you lay off for five minutes?

You're being rude to me. And, you know, all this will end. Right now she's your shield, but once she's gone, you know what's going to happen, pal? Irene will come *right* back and haunt you. No matter where you run, she'll spot that Mark of Cain. Don't worry; she won't kill you, because God prohibited that. She'll just torture you. She'll say: You were supposed to be my keeper and you—

| 340 |

Mike Hernandez in Vice gave him the telephone number of a retired undercover cop named Morena who might know something about Brady. As soon as Tyler mentioned the name, Morena perked up. —Sure, he said. Don't you remember that cop who got shot? Officer Marcus, his name was. One of his last duties was to work surveillance on Brady's house. Who knows what he saw and what he knew? He drove to a big mall, I think maybe it was Stonestown. And the mall was closed. There was an eyewitness who saw something. I think his name was, oh, fuck, I forget the chump's name.

Shot, huh? said Tyler.

Right in the everlovin' head.

I get it. It's starting to come back to me. Now wasn't that the case where the cops themselves wanted to close it down?

Yeah. Marcus's partner was the shill. He said: I disagreed with what my partner did. He shouldn't have been in the parking lot of that mall.

What did he mean by that?

Nobody knows. He met with Internal Affairs and after that he refused to say anything.

So you think Brady had him bumped off?

Yeah, although I can't prove it.

Well, well. So that's our Jonas.

Jonas? Whaddya mean? This is the great Tyrone Brady I'm talkin' about. You know, the guy Brady Alley's named after. Patron of the arts. Jonas Brady now, I know who you mean but I'm not talkin' about him. I got no beef with Jonas Brady. He's a law and order guy.

| 341 |

In a crack-smoky room of another hotel which would soon burn down, the tall man was helping moaning Strawberry shoot herself up in her tired veins while Domino was insisting to the Queen: I said that's not mine but the cop said *right*. I had a warrant outstanding so they took me in. So I was at Eight-Fifty Bryant and I was wearing my black and white polka-dot coveralls. You know, since I'm Domino I always try to look like my name. It's brand recognition, see what I'm saying? And they wouldn't give me my fucking overalls back. And they—

But I got you out, Domino, didn't I? I got five hundred dollars together and your pal Danny Smooth posted your bail.

What the fuck do I care about that pervert? Domino shouted. And if you're trying to make me feel guilty you can just throw me back in the hole, so help me!

Domino, I love you, said the Queen. I'm always looking out for you. You know that. And you love me? You love your Queen?

Yes, Maj, said the girl sullenly. Of course I do. You know that.

Allrightie. What is it then, child, you want your overalls back? They should have given 'em back to you when they checked you out. Ain't those your street clothes? And what about that silver cocktail dress you got?

A long tap on the door, then two shorts, then another long.

The Queen smiled.

Who the fuck's that? said Domino.

You know who it is, said the tall man, looking over his shoulder, so give her some space!

Oh, said Domino, making chewing-gum noises. You going to fuck Henry again tonight?

I was fixing to, yes, said the Queen, looking her in the eye. You got a problem with that?

It's none of my business really.

That's right, said the tall man, so shut the fuck up!

Hey, Maj, when the shit comes down, are you gonna skip with Henry and leave us all to face the music? I heard a couple girls saying that.

Let him in, would you, Justin?

Hold it right there in the vein until I get back. That's right. I said hold it there, bitch. Oh, Strawberry, you're such a goddamn pretty little *bitch*. Don't come on like some fancy girl.

| 342 |

Does the Queen like to drink dark coffee? a panhandler whispered from the side of his mouth.

Fuck cappuccino! cried Chocolate, drunk and high. She's got more than mocha's got to offer.

Gimme a kiss, Chocolate.

I'm glad I'm not barbeque, the whore laughed, kissing him. I saw how messy you are when you eat barbeque. If I'd be barbeque I'd be all over your face.

Hey, Chocolate, somebody told me you also go by the name Brenda. Is that true?

Don't *do* that to me, said the whore, her eyes narrowing, her face tensing into chocolate-colored steel.

Brenda, where's the Queen?

Fuck off! the whore screamed in terror, trying to run away, but this time the vig grabbed her and held her and pulled slowly in toward his face to whisper: You'd better think about it, Brenda Wiley. Because one of these days I'm going to *get* you . . .

| 343 |

Tyler, sitting beside Dan Smooth in a taxicab watching the very slow rotation of a heavy rubber tire on a trailer which then suddenly shot by, exposing the man who stood with folded arms on the corner of Sixteenth Street by the Esta Noche bar, through whose doorway he could see winking strings of what appeared to be glowing and crystallized piss, saw behind Mr. Folded Arms a man in a baseball cap whose heraldic device consisted of a red light bulb with a slash through it, and then the legend, tricked out in white letters: BRADY'S BOYS. —Look at that vig, he muttered.

They're all right, man, the cab driver said. They're doing the good thing to help the people. But Brady kind of a *character*. Like you know he made some allegation the Queen tried to *ex* him.* Well, that never come out positive. Police can't find no wrongdoing on the part of the Queen.

You like the Queen, don't you? said Tyler.

Well, sir, I never come right out and say that, but her girls help pay my rent, man, and like they're always big tippers; they smile at me, you know . . .

Perfect praise from the mouths of babes, said Dan Smooth out of the side of his mouth.

Take a valium, Dan.

But police can't find no wrongdoing on the part of the Queen, the cab driver repeated. Since then I lose my respect for Brady.

The light changed at last. The driver accelerated. They went to the Tenderloin.

Wait here, said Smooth when they got to the parking garage. He ran inside and came out with a dirty envelope. —All right, he said. Now let's go to the Little Angels Foundation on Broadway. —I want to pick up some medication for Sapphire, he explained.

What's in the envelope? said Tyler.

Smooth opened it. —Warnings about vigs, he said. The usual stuff.

In fact, I really don't like that Brady all that much, the taxi driver said.

Yeah, we figured that out, said Tyler.

And how do you vote, Henry? said Smooth.

I'd vote for her, sure.

You erectile old understater, you. Well, you know already that she's going to leave you, said Smooth. Consider yourself already left. I know I've said that to you before, but you clam up every time. So I'm going to keep hammering away. I'm going to force the little thighs of your soul apart until you answer me, Henry.

Why should she leave me?

People die, you stupid ass. Sisters-in-law, for instance. People get tired of people. People get sick. People run away.

So all you're telling me is that nothing lasts forever.

Yeah.

What if I tried to become more like her?

You're just becoming more like the rest of us, Henry. You're turning into a sneaky, money-hungry bullshitter.

---

* Murder him; execute him.

Whatever, said Tyler, getting out. He passed two vigilantes in the attire of Brady Boys. The first one was sweaty and out of breath. —We chased 'em a couple blocks and then they split up, so we split up, the vig was saying. I caught one guy . . .

Smooth leaped out of the taxi, giggling. Tyler looked into his eyes and said: Are you doing speed again?

If you're doing crystal, you—literally, you . . . you . . . When you find a good thing and don't know when you have it, that's another thing people don't understand.

Oh, for God's sake.

For *Cain's* sake, you mean.

From the doorway of the Jewel Hotel, Strawberry was drunkenly laughing: You get burned out. You get tired! and she gave the tall man a kick in the ass. The tall man snickered.

Afternoon, Justin, said Tyler.

Hey, boy, said the tall man. Where's your faggoty car?

Don't you remember how I drove it up your ass last night? Where's Maj?

Upstairs in Strawberry's room. She said you could wake her if you came by.

All right.

Hey, Smooth, what's up? You look *doped* up.

If you ever do a three-way scene, don't do it in Sac, laughed Smooth. That's what I learned from *my* experience.

I don't have time for your bullshit. Gotta make a run. Maj is in Room Twenny-Nine.

Strawberry led them upstairs to the lobby where they each paid five dollars to the unshaven clerk, and then Strawberry unlocked the door of number twenty-nine and laid her finger on her lips, pointing to the Queen snoring softly on the unmade bed as the TV said: See, these agents I guess you could call 'em of the Queen, they lie in wait for girls at the bus terminal. Runaways, innocent girls without much experience of the world. They love it there.

I expected that, said Smooth. That's just how it was before, see. The Chosen People would show up and say, all right, open the gates of your city. If you let us in right now, you'll be our slaves forever. If you don't, we're going to besiege you and then kill you all— well, kill all the men, I guess, rape all the women and children and sell them for slaves . . .

Dan, there's nothing about raping children in there. That's just your wishful thinking.

Well, sometimes I get carried away.

Mute the sound, would you, Dan? We already know the crap they're going to say.

True enough, said Smooth. It's not beautiful.

Should we wake up Maj?

You want my advice? My advice is no. Anyway, I'm getting jealous of you. You don't help her be objective. She needs an easier person to be objective with—like me . . .

The Queen opened her eyes and said: We got to get everybody together now.

| 344 |

And so (excepting only Dan Smooth, whose presence was required in appellate court) they all assembled on a hot dark night in a room at the Lola Hotel on Leavenworth Street, Lily's room actually, tomb of ignoble desperation transformed by her into a dreamy hive of noble madness where she could rest and get high behind locked doors, no longer seeking any solution but searching nonetheless for something which in Beatrice's case would have been God but for Lily comprised a flickering candle-flame to burn away the darkness inside her until the wax had melted and she had to go outside again to sell the hole between her legs which once had been a penis and which she now thought of as tissue neither male nor female, merely some orifice upon whose functioning, like that of her anus, the health of her body depended—no honey meant no money, and without money she'd be vomiting in the sink again. Heroin lit the way for her, and so did the Queen, but so also did what might as well be called self-improvement. Still at some remove from the innermost reaches of divinity where the Queen ceaselessly trod and where the crazy whore and Sunflower quite simply dwelled, Lily reflected in her eyes her glittering, glancing fishy friendships with the other women of the streets, who mostly despised her for her instability, in accordance with Darwin's laws; and because the Queen did not speak of her very frequently, it was easy enough for them, egged on by pitiless Domino, to make fun of her stench and bleating voice, although they had to agree that she was inoffensive; she'd never fought anybody. Quite the contrary—there lived in Lily, as in Beatrice, Sunflower and the Queen herself, a longing to give of herself. In Sunflower's case, the longing had been to give *everything* so that self would be exhausted, whereas the Queen and Beatrice were sweetly busy in their doings; as for Lily, what she dreaded most was disappointing others, which was why she had rendered allegiance to the Queen, of whose goodness and kindness she had no doubt; the Queen wanted to become her mother, and how could Lily have the heart to refuse? Having pledged herself, in one of her typical Lilyisms she continued to sleep apart from Maj whenever she could afford to do so because if she lay down too long among other people, their images sometimes began to dance around behind her eyes with increasing velocity until they became nightmares which spent themselves furiously inside her soul. Whenever a man paid her more than twenty dollars she always asked him: You want a picture of ugly old me? I can give you a photo of my ugly, ugly pussy if you want. I have one right here in the pocket of my . . . —She laughed until she cried whenever the man said no. When he said yes, she searched for the photograph but she was all out; she didn't have any more.

The wall in her room said **LETITIA ROSA 10-20-96** . Letitia Rosa was Lily's real name.

The wall also said:

RULE NUMERO UNO: DON'T USE GOD'S NAME IN VAIN.

DO—ALWAYS RESPECT EVERYONE AND SPEAK WITH A PLEASANT TONE OF VOICE.

DON'T BRING ANYONE IN UNLESS YOU LET ME KNOW FIRST AND I OKAY IT.

WHAT OCCURS IN 26 STAYS BETWEEN THE PRESENT PARTY. OUR BUSINESS—STAYS OUR BUSINESS— NO EXCEPTIONS.

WHEN I SAY GO, TIME TO GO! NO POTTING AROUND.

3 CHANCES— 3 TIMES ARE 86ED FROM 26.

BREAK BREAD— NO NASTIES.

NO MONEY, NO HONEY.

PAY BEFORE YOU STAY.

SOME BUCKS BEFORE YOU FUCK.

NO TIGHT ASS SO TIGHT IT SQUEAKS WHEN YOU WALK, YOU CHEAP SOMETHING FOR NOTHING BUSTERS.

MONEY'S MADE FOR US AND YOU TO SPEND.

YOU SHOW LOVE AND FAIRNESS YOU GET THE SAME AND MOST OF THE TIME EVEN BETTER MY FRIEND. GOOD PEOPLE DESERVE GREAT SERVICE. LOVE'S 3 MS—

        MY MOM

        MY MONEY

        MY MAN

DON'T PLAY THE PLAYER CUZ THE PLAYER DON'T PAY.

SEX IS EVIL ALL IS SIN SIN IS FORGIVEN SO SEX IS SIN.

SUCK ME FUCK ME MAKE ME BLEED KINKY SEX IS ALL I NEED.

JEALOUSY HAS NO SET CONSPIRATOR SO BEWARE OF THE COY STEPS OF HAPPINESS FOR DEEP WITHIN THE HEART LAYS THE TRUTH OF THEIR IN-TERACTIONS WHICH YOU SEE BY LOOKING PAST THE LOST IN DESPAIR. SMILE AND YOU'LL ALWAYS GET TRAPPED CUZ DEMONS ARE HERE.

Well, we got a problem, said the Queen.

Her children remained so tensely silent in that room that all could hear the click of a cigarette lighter in the hall. Lily, proud of her hospitality yet shy, sat on the toilet seat peeping through the doorway.

Anybody here not know what it is?

And the royal family huddled together unspeaking as if they were incapable of utter-ing language or even of comprehending what their old, old Queen was intimating as she sat there on the edge of Lily's mattress with Sapphire on the carpet kneeling down be-tween her legs, head in the Queen's lap, sleeping.

Allrightie. I s'pose you all heard Henry's story.

Beatrice cleared her throat and said: I doan know. Because we have something inside and they doan want us to . . .

Her words died as they left her mouth. The lightbulb buzzed tremblingly.

The Queen said: We can't none of us make these vigs go away. They're onto us and they wanna get us. They see that Mark of Cain glowin' in the dark on our forehead, so we can't even run, 'cause if we do we just make a movin' light. I'm pretty sure they'll get us. And that Brady man, the one that beat up Francine so bad that time she ain't never come back to us, he wanna be playin' a double game. He wanna have his whorehouse over there an' he wanna bust us over here. It ain't reasonable, so we can't reason with him.

An' we can't ex him, the Queen went on. We can't do nothin'. 'Cause my power's just about used up. That's what the Bible says. An' the Enemy never lies in His book. It's all true an' all cruel. So.

She cleared her throat and said: I love you all. An' maybe some of you all gonna get your reward real real soon.

Lily's skirts rustled in terror. Lily was remembering the death of Sunflower. Gazing at Lily, Kitty wrung her hands. But Tyler feared nothing. He was thinking of what Irene used to call "bow envelopes," envelopes white or red, containing cash, which on New Year's Day the old relatives presented to the younger ones, who then had to bow down to them in love and respect. Whether his reward would prove to be love, enlightenment, freedom or death, he knew that he would kneel to his Queen and render thanks.

Anybody got somethin' to say, better say it, shrilled the Queen, the corners of her mouth twitching and grimacing like unquiet water in its tides.

So I think we should find this Brady man, said Domino. And I want us to find this *part* of this Brady man, she added laughingly, wrenching her favorite dildo, Clitilda, from its altar beneath her armpit where it always stayed when it was not in the abandoned meatpacking plant in her striptease cage improvised from wire and stolen parking meters. (She had constructed it, with the tall man's paid help, because it had always been Domino's dream to strut on a stage and get applause and big money without even having a customer breathe on her, but she was too old now for that and too abscessed.)

And do what? You heard me say we can't ex him.

Why not?

C'mon, Dom. You was there in that Vietnamese restaurant with me an' Henry an' Danny Smooth when I opened the Book. You know why.

Domino's face turned scarlet with humiliation and rage, and she hung her head. Later, when the tall man tried to remember what Domino had said about Brady, he could not be certain that he'd really heard anything, because, after all, the blonde uttered such poisonous statements day and night that it was better not to listen. He was the only one who even attempted to remember.

The thing about the Queen is she teaches you things, whispered Lily, whose legs were were blotchy and stringy like a mummy's flesh. If you pay attention, Queen's gonna show you how to—

Because you wanted to be one step ahead of the police, right? demanded the crazy whore, stroking the TV's withered wires which resembled dead branches. —I mean, you wanted to have a mutual slumber party. Isn't that what you're saying? But the police want to search for somebody who's awake. So stay asleep, Maj. Don't stay awake.

Well, Mary, said Domino drily, I know that's how *you* go through life.

I doan want to qvarrer with anyone, whispered Yellow Bird, but the crazy whore, acknowledging this advice with an eloquent wave, leaned forward and said: Domino, you think of beauty as something skin deep. The first thing is, you're jealous of the Queen for trying to go to sleep as soon as she hears about anything. Because you're just somebody intelligent who's had weapons used on you, so you want to use music on her but I'm completely innocent.

Fuck off, you crazy bedbug.

Gun up! cried the Queen. All of you pay this some mind. Get ready, now.

Why don't we just leave town? Strawberry said. Me and Chocolate, we were talkin', and we thought maybe up in Fairbanks there's a lot of action and the Vice cops won't know us when we get there, so I thought maybe—

You ever been to Alaska? the Queen inquired mildly.

Well, I had an opportunity once and I should have taken it since I just pissed away my money anyhow.

Lot of girls comin' up missing even there, said Bernadette through parted lips and wise eyes. Some Canadian chick was tellin' me they just wind up dead, so many girls now, shit, I dunno, seven, eight—

The Queen leaned her weary head back against the wall and closed her eyes, on her lips a sad half-smile which almost broke everybody's heart.

What's up, Maj, what's up? cried the tall man.

My blood pressure, she said.

I prefer to give those sonsofbitches the slip, Domino opined then. Hell, I can always leave town. I don't know about the rest of you sluts . . .

And which town you fixin' to go to?

What the fuck's the difference? Any town'll work. Any town where men have cocks and wallets.

And if they follow you there?

Busted is busted, Maj. Excuse my French, but I've been there before.

Fine, said the Queen. So Domino's headed for Vallejo or Stockton or maybe Idaho Falls. Anybody else?

Lily giggled in a panic, but finally managed to say: If somebody's spying, and you take a radius of four blocks and cut that radius down, I discover that in that whole four block radius I can hear what they're saying when they're talking about me. For instance, this old lady said I was pretty. She came to check me out: *You are pretty.* I'm not sticking it in right now, she said, because it don't have what it takes to stick it in you; I'm saying it was an incident of look and blah-blah-blah . . .

You do this for a living? Domino sneered at her.

Thank you, Lily, said the Queen. Anybody else have something to mention?

Beatrice gave me these jeans, continued Lily with a horribly anxious smile, afraid that she had already said something bad or wrong. —I had to cut 'em up, though. I just get afraid somebody's gonna cut me up . . .

Oh, shut up, bitch, said Domino.

Dom, you got to calm down tonight, said the Queen.

Go fuck yourself, Maj.

I mean it. We got a problem and we need to scope things out.

When those vigs get a bug in their ass, they don't quit, the tall man said at last. I reckon they're gonna be gunning for us. Maybe I can knock a couple of their fuckin' heads together . . .

Nobody in this room cares about me, Domino said. You're all just going to abandon me when Brady drops his dime. And, Maj, you've changed. All you care about's that bastard over there. And what's that bastard got to do with anything?

Henry here's my main man.

Tyler cleared his throat and said: Hey, I'm on your side, Domino. We just need to figure—

Will you shut the *fuck* up?

Opening one eye, Sapphire clutched the hem of the Queen's skirt and began to whimper.

Sure, honey, Tyler said with a bitter and sophomoric grin.

The Queen parted her lips slowly to let the cracksmoke out and said: Now listen up. If something happens to me, part of me gonna go inside Sapphire. Not *every* part, but the love part, yeah, the soul part. So please please please take care of her.

What the fuck's that supposed to mean? shouted Domino. What does that idiot slut have that I don't have?

Anxious Bernadette combed back her hair over and over, swaying back and forth as if she were listening to rap music through her headphones as she usually did when she was waiting to get dated at Sixteenth and Capp because that shut life out, and now she was pretending that if she rocked her body she could shut out what was happening here, but she could not, and her liquid eyes stared sidelong at Domino, whom she pitied and of whom she was afraid.

Dom, you ever made love with Sapphire?

I—

Answer the question, bitch! cried the tall man, who stank of fear and rage.

I—Justin, I—no.

Allrightie then, said the Queen. Saph, wake *up,* little sweetie. Open that eye up again. Now the other one. That's right. That's right. Are you my honey? Are you my good girl? Saph, go over there an' suck Domino's pussy. Gotta teach her something. Don't be afraid. She won't hurt you.

No! screamed Domino. Not with all of you looking! You *fuckers!*

Sorry, bitch, but tonight I just don't have no more patience, hissed the Queen, staring into Domino's eyes. This can't always be just about you.

And, rising, she strode over to the blonde and breathed once into her face. From where he sat, Tyler could see only the back of Domino's head, but the Queen's features were plain to him now: flat, steep, hard and blank like one of those high Tenderloin brickfronts studded with dark curtained windows whose lurking inmates could see out and not be seen, brickfronts painted with the names of long bankrupted businesses, walls dropping remorselessly down to steel gratings and dull parking meters and then dark and dirty streets. The Queen was slender, but so were the old Tenderloin skyscrapers seen from a long way off; and he felt that she was already so far away from him and everyone, and perhaps her immense isolation had simply been hidden all this while by everyone's longing to be taken care of without questions or reservations, and now what if she were actually *evil?*

(Irene had always been afraid of the devil. She couldn't bear to watch a thirty-second television commercial for a horror movie, in case there might be something satanic. She was godfearing, yes, but she feared the devil even more, and in her last moments of life what if she'd fallen into a maze of horror, believing that now she'd killed herself the devil would have her in his claws forever? What if the Queen were really the devil, and Tyler now had crossed the demarcation which made him irrevocably hers to sadistically or simply implacably torment as she was about to torment Domino?)

Now you can't move, can you? Justin, take her into the bathroom an' take her pants down an' lay her down in that bathtub. That's right. Sapphire, you go in an' do your thing. Close the door. I said close the door.

They sat in silence listening until Domino began to moan. She moaned until she screamed. Sapphire was a drug like no other, intense-acting almost to fatality, who gave such deep gratification with her purring, licking mouth that Domino despite herself and the fact that she was being raped could not forbear to feel for at least one instant absolutely and unequivocally *loved.* Then at last she understood why the idiot girl was called Sapphire.

You all get it now? said the Queen. Maybe Sapphire's the one he's really after. You gotta all take care of Sapphire . . .

| 345 |

After a long time Sapphire crept out on her hands and knees, licking her lips and mewling. The tall man got up and closed the door. Then they heard Domino sobbing inside. They heard her buckle her belt, and then the door slammed open and Domino came out, scarlet in the face with her lower lip trembling, and she did not look at the Queen who regarded her with expressionless sorrow, if such a thing is possible, but unlocked the deadbolt and then the other lock and stumbled into the hall and down the stairs.

Close the door, Lily, the Queen said. This here's your *house*. You don't wanna leave your house open to strangers.

Giggling in terror, Lily shut the door and locked it.

Tyler sat very still, feeling sick to his stomach. He could hardly bear to wrest himself from his illusion that the Queen was perfect. But he had seen for himself just how she could be. He could hardly believe it. Her face had altered yet again. It was rounder and older, with glowing globules of radiance dribbling from her mouth and eyes in a strange wormy blur which obscured her from him and all humanity as if she were some waxen golem melting into something squat, ruthless and terrible. He knew that Domino must be sitting on the street somewhere nearby, bent forward, weeping, herself likewise blurred body and soul in the night whose fog was as thick with sadness as wool or old sackcloth, and garish signs announced 99¢ so that she'd know what she and the world were worth, and globes and globules of streetlight, Queenlight attacked her like biting insects.

But no! She was his Queen! Small and slender, she sat there on the edge of Lily's mattress gazing at him steadily through her dark and wide-open eyes, the wool cap pulled down all around the top of her skull and her parka buttoned up to her neck and her mouth pouted outward and tight in a calm sad challenge to those who would not know her or understand her, and tears of light ran down her cheeks.

Henry, you're so quiet now, she said. What you thinkin' about all this?

What do I think about what?

Whatever.

Well, the issue of the vigs, I don't know what to say about that. I—well, what should I think? We're all waiting for you to tell us how to react. And what you did to Domino just now, well, I guess it seems a little cruel, to me at least. I don't get it. But I want to believe it's another test like the false Irene you gave me, because you love Domino, I know you do, and I . . .

Even you, Henry, she said, slowly shaking her head. Even you.

Look, Henry, said the tall man. She a leader or not?

She is.

Okay. Well, how can she be a leader if she don't make herself known, eh? And wasn't Domino tryin' to obstruct her again?

Maj, I believe in you, he said. And I'm going to keep trying to believe.

And what about what we all came here for? said Chocolate. We gonna let Domino just put her hand on us and derail everything? I mean, what we s'posed to do? What did we decide?

L-luh-luh, replied Sapphire.

| 346 |

At five o'clock the next morning Sapphire was out on South Van Ness trying in her inarticulate slobbering way to get a trick so that her sisters would be proud of her because their caresses resembled all the murals on Capp Street whose bright colors comforted Beatrice; so, trusting in the world with all the luminosity of her rotting consciousness, Sapphire crawled and squatted, underwearless, past two blindeyed strutting cops, until she spied in the deep-staired doorway of an old Victorian a bare foot, bluish-white, jerk suddenly out from beneath a blanket, twitch violently, and stiffen. Sapphire looked both ways, just as the Queen had taught her. Inside the dead man's pocket she found, in addition to three dollars which she hid inside her shoe, as she had seen Beatrice do, a much-handled letter from overseas which said: *Dearest husband, to day I'm very happy to get your letter and the Bible from you thank's for giving me every thing and sad when I never heard from you now about you come to me again. Do you still love me. You don't know how my heart painful every day waiting for you never have hope now. I know you are so busy than before and maybe my love doesn't mean for you any more. I don't know what to do with my life. I'm so lonely and missing you some night I dream about you. Like I walk in the darkness no job no money and you don't love me like before may be I can have my way finish my life soon. Without you how my life can be. You are my nice husband. To night I can't sleep so much think about you. I know I no good enough for you I who have nothing you have everything life with someone you love more than me. If I didn't heard from you and then I know what to do with my life may be ~~kill myself~~ because I always make you trouble. Love my husband to much. P.S. the Bible from you I promiss alway read.* Sapphire, who could not read, took this letter to the Queen.

And you're sure he's dead and not passed out? said the Queen.

L-luh-luh-uh . . . said Sapphire.

All right, baby. Poor gal. She probably waited and waited for an answer. Maybe she's still waiting. Justin! *Justin!*

What? said the tall man.

We're gonna write this girl, and tell her that the man she loved is dead. Can you take care of it?

All right, Maj, but you gotta gimme the money for an envelope and stamp. I don't have no stamp money for somebody I don't even know.

Sapphire, did he have any money on him?

Obediently, the palsied girl displayed the three dollars.

Okay, baby, you gimme a dollar—no, no, give it to Justin over there, that's right. What a good girl. Come kiss Mama. Okay, now put that two dollars away. Or do you want Mama to keep it for you? You do? Okay. I'm gonna remember. Anytime you want it, you just come ask for it. Well, Justin, you done yet?

Done? What the *fuck* am I s'posed to say?

Say your man passed away. Say he died in no pain.

How do *you* know he died in no pain, Maj?

'Cause I know. And even if I didn't know, the whole point is to make her feel good, don't you see? So just write it.

Maj?

What?

How you spell *dead?*

How do you think you spell it? Just write it and stop bothering me. Anyway, it's more polite to say *passed away.*

Then why don't you write it if you're so all-fired polite?

Well. What's got into you today?

Just thinkin' about what you said last night is enough to make anybody feel sour. And when Domino comes flyin' back here with her claws out, who the hell's gonna have to deal with it?

| 347 |

Look, the tall man said. You think if the Queen orders me to punch concrete and I break my hand, Queen's gonna pay for it?

She—

Damn right she will, Domino. She's the *good* Queen. And you're no fuckin' good. You understand?

Oh, go to hell.

And you know what else? They may drink *her* spit, but they all gotta kiss *my* ass, said Justin with satisfaction. *I'm* the shot-caller around here. And I'm tellin' you right now, bitch, to go in there and get down on your knees and *'pologize.* Know why? 'Cause *you* was at fault. You wrecked that meeting last night out of your meanness. Maj had to shut you up . . .

I didn't wreck anything, cocksucker, so don't you tell me—

Maj wanna beat up on you, you better let her. 'Cause you just a little fool. Just a little honky fool.

| 348 |

What passed between Domino and the Queen nobody else knew, but when the tall man, pacing anxiously outside, reentered the tunnel at the Queen's summons, he found the two women holding hands as they sometimes used to do, although the Queen's face was expressionless and Domino's wore a look of strain. (Sure, said the Queen, sometimes Domino and me, we get on each other's nerves, but we stick together, don't we, Dom? We help each other.)

Once the blonde learned that for her grief was precisely the same as rage, she thought that she would craze and break suddenly, but didn't, and because she could not let the poisoned feelings out, there was an ache in her chest, a throbbing at the back of her neck, as they sought to expend themselves by wrecking her body a little, making headaches and ulcers and sleeplessness so that the next morning, sick-faced, she'd get up with her swollen pounding heart the only vital force she had, drearily raging through the day. As she contemplated the Queen, something burned even hotter in her chest and she clenched her teeth. And yet she appeared to love her more than ever, and whenever she could ran fingers and tongue across the Queen's chocolate stomach with all its grooves and wrinkles and adipose sandbars. There were some, such as the tall man, who said that she had merely donned the mask of goodness out of necessity, and was biding her time to betray the Queen and everyone else to the vigs, and perhaps by the mask of goodness they imagined something akin to Sapphire's face when the Queen or Beatrice had washed her and combed her hair and trimmed it so that when she gazed straight at somebody with her inhuman eyes and parted her lips as if she would speak there might sometimes be for an instant an esoteric illusion of recognition and mutuality before the saliva began wandering from between her kissable lips. Could it be that neither Sapphire, nor Domino, nor the Queen were human? What were they, then? What were they? —But Domino was orphaned, so she must have been human. Isn't that what being human means? And if she was an orphan, wouldn't she seek affection's pristine balm between the breasts of her dear Queen who'd loved her even as she'd raped her, unless of course the Queen didn't love her? But this issue, which left Tyler almost anguished to contemplate, actually meant less to the blonde because throughout her life she could hardly continue her signatures of belief for longer than a double-flourish, and so the flickering of interpretation between love and no love had grown so habitual to her that the most ambiguous or even antagonistic act could never be proof, just as the best and most tenderest kindness of anyone could soothe her suspicions only briefly before the hairs started up again on the back of her neck and her gaunt soul growled. The pimp from whom the Queen had saved her had beaten, burned and tortured her, and yet because every week or two he'd grapple her head between his immense cruel hands and whisper that he loved her, she couldn't fix her heart's compass needle eternally to hatred; she couldn't believe or disbelieve in anything, but wandered lost even when she was flat on her back and another man and then another was between her legs, urgently raping her dry womb in exchange for cash, whereas when the Queen raped her that night in Lily's room it gave her pleasure because Sapphire was a true treasure even asleep on the pillow and now that the Queen had revealed her powers many of the other girls, including shy Beatrice, led her aside to groom her and feed her, then use her as they would use any other drug, so that wherever the Queen and Sapphire stayed, nights were punctuated by screams of pleasure as loud as gunshots. They screamed as if they were being murdered and maybe they were. And Domino cast Beatrice aside and came to Sapphire. What if she'd come back to the Queen, then, simply because she was addictive and addicted, and so she needed the retarded girl more than she hated her Queen? What license did the Queen give her to have intercourse with Sapphire? Hadn't the Queen in effect sold Sapphire down the river by revealing her inborn skill to those who as a result could never again refrain from using her? Or was that revelation just the necessity-worship of a loving mother, so that Sapphire would be preserved once the Queen was gone?

· BOOK XXI ·

Jesus

●

You offspring of Canaan and not of Judah, beauty has deceived you and lust has perverted your heart.

Apocrypha, Susanna 56

●

On Halloween morning, two pimpled black women in bathing suits stood at the ticket machine at Civic Center trying to force in change where it said no change, and as one of the whores leaned forward on her high heels to whack the machine's unhelpful face with the flat of her hand, a huge knife fell out of her armpit and hit the floor. —She wants to kill us all! an old man laughed. —The blade was only silver plastic.

At five o'clock that afternoon, Tyler had already left behind him Vallejo, Vacaville and the occasional weird palm tree. The soft goldengrassed hills resembled the mounds below blonde women's bellies, while the sky ahead and above was a sharp white, because now that the forest fire season had ended, the weather would remain crisp until the tule fogs began. Tyler itemized facts: He was forty-four years old, he possessed the Mark of Cain and three-quarters of a tank of gasoline; and his mother was extremely sick. John had agreed to stay away this weekend. Evidently he now understood Tyler's routine quite well, for those calls of his usually reached the answering machine in the early afternoon, when Tyler was likely to be out of the apartment even if he had been out late with the Queen the previous night. Tyler had not been compelled to actually speak with him for weeks. He passed a long supermarket supply truck painted with images of California fruits and salads, then found himself compelled to descend beneath two overpasses which must have marked the boundary between pastoral melancholy and human dreariness, for here he now was back, once again in the realm of malls, factory outlets, auto dealerships—immense square buildings whose ugliness reverberated all the worse than a Tenderloin hotel room's because their cleanliness and proclamations of stupid merchandising pride proclaimed them to be the products of some plutocrat's *choice* rather than of mere abuse and neglect. But who was he, Henry Tyler, to reject anything? Was he himself so entirely free from defects?

Now he was coming into Dixon. A sign shouted CHEAPER! and he didn't care. A supermarket truck menaced him with a painting of a lobster-claw. To his right lay black-roofed white houses, all bitterly the same. The parking lot of the steak restaurant was empty. One field was alfalfa-green and the next was straw-colored like a Capp Street girl's pus. Tyler felt that something very strange was happening to him but he could not explain it. A sign offered an untold quantity of apples for fifty-nine cents. The next sign offered apples four for ninety-nine cents. The sign after that proffered pumpkins and he didn't see the price. On his left receded the pistachio stand where John had once taken Irene before they were married, and that was when Irene discovered that she was allergic to pistachios. Tyler had heard that story twice. His mother had said that she couldn't believe anybody could really be allergic to pistachios; she'd insisted that Irene was really just finnicky, like those girls who claim to be allergic to earrings of any metal baser than gold. The sky was grey now like a cloud of dust. He passed fields, billboards and orchards as

California began to get darker and darker. He hated that winter darkness. Following the examples of his fellow citizens, he launched twin streams of light from his car's yellow, goggling eyes. The white water-tower at the University of California at Davis blended in with the sky. Overhead passed a black bird whose kind he was sure he had never before seen, and whose immense black crooked wings reminded him of the Queen's thighs flexing and twitching on the mattress as she uttered her little cries. A gas station vainly illuminated the earth with harsh yellow light similar to what is seen through shooting-glasses. A yellow sign whined BREAKFAST. It was not breakfast time now and so that sign was useless; maybe that was why he hated it; if you saw a whore you could always feel horny anytime but how many times a day could you eat breakfast? At least he was out of Davis now, and lemon-colored fields relaxed him in the twilight, their wholeness scarcely marred as far as the southern horizon. To the northeast a train was coming out of Sacramento quite rapidly, eating its way into the night.

Ahead now came a belt of shrubs, warehouses, restaurants and sickening yellow lights. This was West Sacramento. West Sacramento offered him storage lockers, more palm trees, walls, rental cars. Between grey trees and hedges he followed his grey path to the Sacramento River, which he crossed, glimpsing lights lying disclike upon it. A flock of birds wriggled through the night, barely distinguishable.

| 350 |

His mother was sleeping.

His room was now the nurse's room, so he had to sleep in John's old room. He set down his suitcase as quietly as he could and turned on the light. The bookshelves were crowded by John's toy trains, the entire *Hardy Boys* series, and high school yearbooks with photographs of John in them. Tyler had thrown his own yearbooks in the dumpster when he was twenty-four or -five, unable to bear the sight of his own callow, pimpled face. Now he regretted that act a little, not so much because he missed his teenaged self as because he would have liked to gaze at the girls he remembered. Descending the creaking stairs as quietly as he could, he stole the Bible from the living room. He returned upstairs to John's room, closed the door, then knelt on the hard floor and prayed: Hey, Jesus, if you're out there and if you have pity on us Canaanites, send some advice my way, would you? I'm kind of at my wits' end, as the saying goes. I don't get what I'm supposed to do. Maybe I can turn myself in and give up my Mark and, uh . . . I'm going to open the New Testament now.

Blindly he parted the covers, then the pages. He lowered his forefinger like doom. He had reached Matthew 12.46, which ran: *While he was still speaking to the people, behold, his mother and brothers stood outside, asking to speak to him. But he replied . . . , "Who is my mother, and who are my brothers?" And stretching out his hand toward his disciples, he said, "Here are my mother, and my brothers! For whoever does the will of my Father in Heaven is my brother, and sister, and mother."*

Well, sighed Tyler to himself, that's what Beatrice says, anyway.

Henry? his mother called from her room.

· BOOK XXII ·

The Wicked King's Secret

•

For I know my transgressions
and my sin is ever before me.

Against thee, thee only, have I sinned . . .

PSALM 51.3–4

•

At City Lights the leaves of books hung as limp as those of banana trees on a summer jungle day, and the browsers were more quiet than usual, turning pages ever so slowly, or standing over a table of books, reading the spines, motionless: strange day it was, sunstruck day, the blinking lights around the perimeter of the Hungry I's sign reduced in power, so that they resembled mere kernels of corn. Tyler read the tale of a wicked King who went conquering successive cities in the desert. From each victory he'd keep a young woman for a concubine, and put her parents, brothers and sisters to death secretly by having them smothered in hot wet Turkish towels, so that, being unrelated to anyone, with no past (her city razed, the rubble smeared across miles of dark stony plain which the King's troops then scraped and scratched down to the yellow earth), she'd be as pure as an idea. A special caravan transported the bodies, tightly bundled in linen, with the King's chop-mark printed on the wrappings, so that no one could open them, and no one could find any graves—for to the extent that the concubines had been well chosen, they grew favored, and as they succeeded in gathering about themselves their own troops and satellites, they naturally sought the flesh they'd come from, not only out of love and duty, but also because they longed to be *related* again, for it is lonely to be a mere formal cunt like Domino, Strawberry, Yellow Bird, Beatrice, Bernadette, Lily, Chocolate, Sunflower, Kitty. They desired that their soul-light be clothed in something, so that their obliteration would be undone, and they could live and die again. But although they tossed many a gold ring to the Canaanite runners who loped far back among dead years and cities, seeking paternity or even paternal tombs in that deep red sand aswarm with ants where once there'd been hot and palmtree-walled streets, the runners never found anything except shattered archways and jackal-gnawed bones and on one cool and quiet night a ghost who came to visit them in a pale mask with long dark tresses, its robes constructed with such complexity as to resemble the hybridization of many artificial insects. Then morning came, and once again the air was alive with flies. So the runners turned back and told the concubines that they were alone, that they did not have and never had had any kin. And when the concubines knelt before the King, begging him to at least inform them from which particular cup of bitterness they ought to drink, he could reply to them in all truth: There is no proof that your esteemed parents do not continue in good health! —But the King had a daughter by one of the concubines, and when the girl became fourteen she found—what? Tyler didn't want to read anymore. It was all too sad, as when one reads old letters and realizes for what seems to be the first time, but can't possibly be: *She loved me!* She was sincere, passionate, good; she even wanted me. And now I don't even know where she is. Does she still think of me? I haven't thought of *her* for years. Does she still love me if she does think of me? I hope not and I hope so.

—How could these moments, so powerfully articulated with love, have given way to the torpid weariness of the present? He couldn't understand life.

A cold mist stung his nose. The back of his neck was stiff and his legs ached. He went into the liquor store in Laurel Heights where adjoining the twenty-year-old, sixty-dollar Ardbeg which was so to John's taste they also kept the thirty-year-old, equally or almost equally amber, for a hundred and fifty-five dollars. Perhaps John had not seen that yet. It gave Tyler malicious pleasure to assert to himself that John maintained his relatedness to the world through stubborn and jealous possession of fine commodities which could always be vanquished through the primeval domination of *ingestion*. When the Ardbeg had been drunk, and John had won, he found himself immediately adrift again, like those storybook concubines on their lifelong journey through that desert of destroyed and not-yet-destroyed cities. Certainly Tyler himself, as he fully confessed, had sought the same relatedness by employing first Irene, then the Queen, to be his friendly viands. Perhaps there'd been no harm in it; perhaps he was a criminal. And what if he could give all that up, in order to walk naked into the desert, searching for nothing save self-divestiture? Well, he'd die of thirst, naturally. Strawberry was always complaining of a dry mouth. She would have hopped up and down with excitement to see him here. He smiled sourly. The salesman, big and bald, sat reading a newspaper. —Even you, Henry, the Queen had said. He remembered, and was ashamed of his unbelief. —Next to the Ardbeg, amidst the other glories, thrones and authorities, there stood a bottle of cask-strength Glenfarclas, priced at sixty-five dollars, which was Domino's minumum price for allowing herself to get sodomized. John and Irene had given him a bottle the Christmas before last, perhaps because the rather sulphurous flavor accorded with John's supposition of his vulgarity. As he recalled, John had preferred to keep for his own stock eighteen-year-old Glen Morangie with the dullish steel engraving or watercolor or whatever it was, shrunk down and offset, of the distillery buildings, most of which were long and low and abutted what Tyler supposed must be a Scottish firth, with more coast across the water. John, probably trying to do the brotherly thing, had slit the lead foil from around the cork and pulled the cap out with a cheery, squishy, echoey pop. The whiskey had been very mild, pale, pale gold like his supposition of Irene's urine. But the pressure of the absent Irene upon their fraternal conviviality had been light—not on account of the absence—why, it was heavier than ever now that Irene lay in her grave! but simply because the conversation had that day actually been of interest. John was feeling rather sleek (in retrospect, it occurred to Tyler that the affair with Celia might have entered into its most luxuriant blossoming just about then) and Tyler himself had just gotten paid for a highly succesful skip-tracing job. Indeed, when he thought back on how easy and lucrative life had been in those days, he could almost weep with self-pity, forgetting his immense anguish over Irene, whose face, body, soul, breath and life had tormented him so. Where had she been that day? Christmas shopping for Pammy, Steven and her parents, most likely. And what was her nephew's name? John, taking the initiative as always, was showing off his liquor cabinet. It was before cigarette smoking had been stigmatized and pipe smoking had come into fashion, so John couldn't have owned his three mahogany humidors yet. That year he collected mainly single malts. Mr. Rapp had provided initial instruction at the office, and John learned the rest on his own. He poured his brother a learned sip of this, a celestial dram of that—smoky Laguvulin, jet-black Loch Dhu which stained one's tongue with its rummy sweetness, sherry-flavored Balvenie Double Wood, Highland Park, whose taste he could no longer remember, Ardbeg, of course, with its iodine-peppermint taste, then finally Johnnie Walker Blue, bland and expensive, like John's ideals—the Blue was not a single malt, actually, but such a delicious and above all prestigious blend at two hundred dollars per bottle that it well deserved its place on John's glass shelves. John had a book on Scotches and was explaining it all. Tyler let himself be instructed in peatiness and the Speyside virtues.

The liquor salesman looked up and said: I'm closed.

Oh, how does *that* feel? replied Tyler, going out into the mist. A block or two higher, at the ice cream parlor, the music was loud and young. He went in and sat down with a groan, licking his moustache.

Sir, you'll have to come to counter for service, said the kid behind the counter.

Well, let me just walk around the block and think about that, said Tyler. Let me get my goddamned courage up.

He went out and began to retrace his way. His throat felt scratchy. A lesbian-looking type in heavy-heeled boots clopped hollowly by, the chain links jingling from her ears. In a store window, pink and green irridescent bows hung upon twisted branches, accompanied by necklaces, bracelets and brooches of colored glass. A ceramic dog gazed benevolently into the rain.

Do you fetch newspapers? Tyler asked the dog. The dog didn't answer. Had it been capable of movement, its gait would have duplicated that of some fat whore waddling into the pharmacy to buy more condoms.

Walgreens was still open, as he thought, but just before he reached the entrance, anxious to buy more itching cream, the security guard locked him out, turned his back, and strode over to crack jokes with the last cashier, who was now closing out her register.

The liquor store man gave him an unexpectedly friendly nod as he locked up. Tyler grinned and waved.

In the spacious coffee shop on Noe Street, two women in what looked like Catholic high school uniforms sat rapidly nodding, each girl's hands tucked in her lap. The world was windy, clean and empty. —A woman on the steps of a Victorian was calling to a little boy who was getting into a car: Nicky, come here! Give me a big old hug! For a whole year Auntie won't see you! *Good* boy! —But the child didn't come back. He sat in the back seat, and a lady came around from the driver's side and gently closed the door. Then she got in and slowly drove away.

| 352 |

He entered the Wonderbar and saw Domino, whose face now wore a profusion of sores like the red bulbs on the metal dance floor in Mexicali.

How are you doing tonight, sweetheart? said Tyler, squeezing the girl's hand.

Oh, not too good, she said listlessly.

What's wrong?

Just about everything.

Same here, he said, but she, wandering through her own maze of misery, could hardly begin to find his.

You know I care for you? You know the Queen loves you?

Fuck off. I don't know that and neither do you.

A man came out from the urinal and slipped his arm around Domino. Tyler nodded pleasantly. The man glared and elbowed Tyler in the ribs.

See you, Domino, said Tyler.

Domino, her head hanging down, didn't say anything.

| 353 |

He awoke with the taste of Irene's cunt in his mouth.

| 354 |

I want a drink, said Domino, drunk.

You see that man over there? inquired Loreena. He paid for his drink. And you see that man over there? He paid for *his* drink. That's how it works.

I don't give a fuck. I want a drink.

Loreena thrust out her chin and said: Would you stop that, please? It's not getting you anywhere except onto my shit list. You know what I tell people like you?

Bitch, I could smash your head right in.

So you didn't like the beginning of my little speech? Well then. I bet you won't like the rest!

But just then a john came to rescue Domino. He bought her three tequila sunrises all in a row. Then he placed a twenty-dollar bill on the counter in front of Domino.

Enjoy that twenty, he said.

Domino screwed up her drunken face and said: Whadya want for that twenty, a blow job? Fuck off. You can suck my big toe for twenty, you animal.

Enjoy that twenty.

I'm out of lime juice, muttered Loreena. Well, guess I can't use a real lime.

Loreena, I wanna go to the bathroom, Domino said. I'm ready.

I'll be right with you.

So you won't take my twenty?

Look, replied the blonde. I'm not what you think. I'm a diamond in the rough and in the smooth and everyplace else. I'm a lethal weapon. And the only reason I'm letting you buy me drinks is 'cause my check didn't come. A respectable person loaned me two hundred dollars but he was drunk and fucked up . . .

A second john was watching them.

Are you looking at me? asked the first john.

No, I was looking at her.

Well, she's with me, the first john explained. She's my wife. Don't look at my wife like that.

Hey, you old coot, if that's your wife you'd better keep her on a leash! Your wife's been giving me blow jobs every Friday night!

Why, you—

Wrestling, hugging, screaming, the two johns strove against each other like the rutting animals they were, while Domino laughed and laughed, with the dull clickings of a spent cigarette lighter, until her sides ached. It was shaping up to be an excellent evening; people were paying attention to her. But finally Loreena ran out from behind the bar with a cutting board, which she held high above the warriors' heads, shouting: Now, stop it, boys! Stop it or I'm gonna whack you . . .

Sheepishly, the men had already started pulling apart when Domino leaped down from her stool and screeched: You stop it! You stop it right now or I'm gonna call the cops!

Shaking their heads, the two johns wandered out the back door.

Well, said Domino, drumming her fingers on the bar with the triumphant click-click-click of black girls striding down Turk Street with their chins up, shading their doubledark sunglasses lenses with their hands, I think I deserve a free drink, Loreena.

And why's that?

Beause I broke up that fight.

You broke it up? cried the barmaid in amazement.

That's exactly right.

Dear, you're too friggin' much. You take the prize. You're so bad you're good. Have an ever-lovin' drink.

| 355 |

A man was pulling up his pants as he watched the magnificently dangling breasts whose lease had now expired. The mouth slowly began to drop open, like a rotten trestle giving way. Upon the lower lip a pretty silver pearl of drool gathered. She couldn't keep her eyes open. The head slowly tilted on the neck; the neck was giving way, too.

What now? the man said.

Oh, go out there, and see if I can get lucky, the whore mumbled.

Ah, said the man wisely, surreptitiously checking to make sure that she hadn't lifted his wallet.

Well, sighed the whore, I guess I should make my departure.

She dragged her stained and stinking T-shirt back down over her head and let her calloused toes seal-dive back into the high heels. Then she stood up. The world rocked; she felt literally at sea. She bit her tongue sharply and tasted blood. That woke her up. She staggered toward the door.

All right then, the man said.

You too, the whore said.

She opened the door and stepped out. The hallway was dark. She would have liked to stay longer because the man's bed had been comfortable and the man was nice. He had given her a glass of water. But she had to make more money. Her feet hurt. She closed the door behind her and crept slowly down the hall. When she got to the stairs she held on tightly to the bannister and took her time. Now for the street door. She hobbled back into the night and in ten minutes had managed to achieve an entire block before two Brady's Boys found her.

| 356 |

Sitting on a concrete bench beside a trash can, the Queen in somebody else's ancient leather jacket and baseball cap drew one hand from shoulder to shoulder in an almost Catholic gesture of self-blessing, then hunched forward and began to smoke. Lines deepened around her lips when she inhaled. She held in that strange bluish air of hell, then turned her head sideways and breathed it out with a smile of pleasure. Against a granite wall behind her leaned the tall man with one foot up, his projecting knee like a wood-saw blade. He pressed his head back against the wall and yawned. Over a parking meter padded by his quilted jacket slouched Tyler with his cap pulled low, his chin on his palm as he picked his teeth. He stepped back three paces, folded his arms across his chest, stepped forward, narrowed his anxious, squinting eyes, and leaned his stomach against the parking meter.

For the moment, *vigilant uncertainty* seemed to afford him the greatest integrity. He longed to think, to understand, to close his eyes and see some certain and loving image whose kiss would purify him. He stood against the parking meter, trying to decide whether he still loved the Queen, and what kind of love he'd been full of if it could be destroyed like this, and whether he ought to go away from her forever.

Henry, she said, not looking at him.

Yeah.

C'mere.

He came.

Henry, I see what you're thinkin'. Baby, you think I can't see right into your heart?

I know you can see, he whispered.

S'pose I was what you used to think I was. You think I really could've been that?

Closing his eyes, he thought for a long time. —Yeah, he said. You were perfect. Until you georgia'd Domino.

Allrightie. You think your nightmares about Irene gonna come back now?

Yeah.

I'm so sorry, honey. Queen's so sorry for you. Henry, lemme ask you one more thing. If I was perfect then an' I'm not perfect now, why might that be?

I don't know. Because—because you—

God did it, she said with terrifyingly burning eyes. He sent His Son, our Enemy, down here to be on our level for a while. You think Jesus didn't sweat an' piss like everybody else? You think He didn't get fearful an' stupid like us?

| 357 |

Do you think that Christ could be here now? Irene had once asked him despairingly.

What do you mean, honey?

If I went down to that Loaves and Fishes place in Sacramento and put up a notice on the bulletin board saying if one of you homeless guys is Christ please come and meet me next Thursday, would Christ see it and come?

Tyler cleared his throat. —Sure, Irene, but maybe He wouldn't be *your* Christ.

What do you mean? cried his sister-in-law in horror. What you're saying goes against the Bible. There's only *one* Christ, and He's my God. He's my Lord. I swear before you and before God I believe that.

In that case, Tyler had said, all you have to do is learn to recognize your own Christ, or else trust God to bring Him to you.

And now here he was, like an earthquake survivor pinioned and half crushed beneath some vaulted slab, unable to believe or disbelieve, unable to take his own advice.

| 358 |

The Queen said: It's up to you to figure all this out. My girls, now, I gotta give 'em some happiness. But maybe I wanna give you somethin' different. Somethin' more secret than happiness. Do you believe that?

A warm shadow passed across his heart, and he whispered: Yes.

An' you know why I did what I did to Domino? Justin, move away please.

Why? said Tyler.

Want some business, want some business, muttered the tall man across the street. Gonna sell you pussy, world. Gonna sell you dimes and keys. Gonna hotwire this car.

She laid down her head on his shoulder. —You really wanna know why? 'Cause she kept insulting you. An' I *love* you. I couldn't take it no more. I don't care half as much about anyone else.

| 359 |

Sitting astride him, tall and black, she gazed down at him with loving eyes. Yes, he was close to another pair of eyes, brown eyes which blinked and sometimes cried and sometimes even *saw* the soul-smell of another human being, smelled the feeling and heard the smell of skin, dust on skin, dirt and sand rubbing between bodies. And once again he believed; so he was innocent again; he had never sinned. He did not need to think anymore because what he and she called love (it must have *been* love) numbed everything else into irrelevance while his world decayed. How could he make his life right? Where would anything end? She led him into the Pleroma to show him the Four Darknesses of Cain and the Four Lights. And because he was a Canaanite now and forever, he preferred the Darknesses to the Lights. Cain was not so evil, he kept saying to himself. Cain at least killed his brother only out of jealousy, not as a sacrifice to God, Who called on Abraham to sacrifice his son, and Who sacrificed Jesus to Himself to consolidate Himself upon the world of Canaanites whose demonic dreams and desperations sent them wandering from one necessity to another until all volition had been scorched out of them, and they gave or thieved without sin. It was a sin when Cain killed Abel, but in his centuries of after-struggle across primeval continents all of a lichenous red color darkened by blue haze, he committed no further sin when he killed and robbed for his living, just as the false Irene was sinless, and Domino with her crazed lightning-flashes of intellect sought only to escape her own torment like a fish wriggling on a gill-hook, so wasn't she sinless, too? Wasn't the Queen perfect? (He didn't think that merely because she loved him. He swore it.)

You love me? she said.

Yeah.

You gonna let me hurt you?

Sure. Yes, I will.

Does it hurt now, baby, what I'm doin' to you?

I feel it, all right.

Tell me to do it again.

Do it again, Africa.

Does it hurt?

It kind of . . . —Oh! It hurts!

Does it hurt?

Yeah. I love you—

Does it hurt?

Oh—

He thought less and less about Irene—less about his business also, and people who met Tyler at this stage frequently thought him abstracted, careworn, apprehensive, even sad. In truth he'd changed vastly, as he himself knew, although whether for worse or for better he really couldn't say. The Queen absorbed him. He believed that he was learning intensely beautiful and secret things.

· BOOK XXIII ·

Justin

•

And he did plot with Cain and his followers from that time forth.

Book of Mormon, Helaman 6.27

•

Heh, heh, heh! Justin got hit by a car!

And the red ambulance light pulsed right through the window of Jonell's Bar, where a man was saying: I'll sell it to you for twenny dollars. (Around the corner, Chocolate didn't hear. She was busy singing to the passing cars: This is your knot, this is my slot, do it on the dot, *cash!*)

Lookit Justin there! Fool got hit by a car!

Heh, heh, heh!

Your cab's here, said the old barmaid to a drunk.

I didn't call no cab.

Oh, yes you did.

I'm not leavin'.

Oh, get out! —The barmaid tried to snatch his beer away, but he seized it and brandished it threateningly over her face.

Heh, heh, heh!

You see that wrestling thing on TV? laughed the twenty-dollar man. Now these two here, they're gonna wrestle. Bets, anyone? I bet twenny dollars on Clarice!

Heh, heh, heh! Ran right over Justin's leg!

Justin? Why, sure enough, it really *is* Justin. I always hated that goddamned pimp.

Get out! Get out! screamed the barmaid.

You need a hand, Clarice?

Get him out!

A big man came and began to gently push the drunk between the shoulderblades. The drunk wheeled round cursing and punching.

Whoah, said the big man. I was just trying to give you a hand. Asshole! Sonofabitch! Oh, well.

He's just drunk, the twenty-dollar man soothed him.

Yeah, I *knew* that, said the big man.

The drunk staggered outside and waved his taxi away imperiously. The taxi driver grimaced, waiting for the one whom he was sure would be the real fare, the willing, generous customer of whom we all dream. Then the drunk caught sight of the cherry-colored ambulance lights. He shambled over to his fellow spectators and began to enjoy the ambulance's screams. But somebody cut the siren, and he swore, disappointed.

Oh, I'm all right, said the tall man, sitting regally in the back of the ambulance. Blood ran down his ankles. White men in white coats attended him most obsequiously, and the crowd gazed up at him through the open door. He was their entertainment.

Who's that nigger? said the drunk.

Watch your mouth, a black man warned him. If you wasn't such a lush I'd beat your whitebread ass.

Perhaps that sallow drunk should have taken the hint. But he needed to feel confident in his life. It was only when he drank that he felt he could be anything. He felt this precisely because his perceptions had grown so constricted that he could no longer be cognizant of his limitations, like those old people who when sight, hearing and memory slip away make unflattering remarks in loud voices about others who are still present but out of their dwindling sensory range. How amazed they'd be, if they understood that the nasty man who'd long since vanished from their apprehension like last Thursday's television show had just now heard them denounce his nastiness! For they'd meant no harm! Backstab gossip doesn't harm anybody, does it? It's only steam-letting, social sport, wit, liveliness, self-comfort like complaining over an arthritic wrist.

The tall man, King for a day, extended his right arm to the crowd in a Roman salute. —How about if you just lie down right back here? a paramedic murmured, but the tall man angrily shrugged off his touch.

I know who he is! the drunk suddenly shouted, proud of his immense knowledge. He's a boxer! He's what's-his-name! He fought Mike Tyson! But did he win?

The crowd started to snicker, and the drunk, pleased with the attention, went on: If they were both at their peak, then Tyson would win. But Tyson's all fucked up. He's dead and gone.

I'm all right, said Justin.

Oh, he thinks he's all right, sneered the drunk. If he's all right, then what's with the men in the fucking white coats?

I'm all right, Justin repeated happily.

You think we were talking about you? shouted the drunk. We were talking about Mike Tyson. Who gives a rat's ass about you? What kind of representative of the black people are you?

Blame it on the fucking black, man. Just blame everything, said the man who'd threatened to kick the drunk's ass. He blindsided the drunk with an imensely powerful punch which sent the drunk whirling down like Lucifer into hell. His head struck the pavement with a cracking noise. Then he lay still.

You got room for one more? called a man to the ambulance crew, and the crowd laughed.

The black man kicked the drunk's head again and again, shouting: You fucking white nigger!

Justin, doped up and cracked up, had witnessed none of this. He was sure that all the commotion had been applause. He could not remember when he had been so joyful. Last week when Maj had gone off on Domino and then with her face self-carved into an unfriendly mask commanded him to step across the street so that she could mutter more of her private things with that Henry Tyler, he'd felt insulted, almost cursed, and his rage at her, which was really jealousy, seeped upward into his chest, making him dread himself even through the scratched and smeary lenses of his fatalism, and that jealousy was actually grief because this Queen whom he'd so faithfully served treasured up no more love for him. He'd wanted to change and leave nothing of himself behind, not even his wrinkled skin. And now his glory grew as multi-hued as the bright clothes which hung at sidewalk sales on Mission Street; and his dignity ascended; words and glances licked him like incense-smoke, and he became theatrical to please the world. No goddamned medic was going to stop him. He had never experienced any inability to understand why Domino set fires, why Strawberry robbed him and cheated on him and then sneered the fact in his ear with her ugly trashy goadings until he had to break her jaw; every wild beast roared sometimes, and now it was his turn, especially because roaring temporarily expelled the immense physical pain of his two broken legs as well as the spiritual pain of betrayal by the Queen, pain which clung to him like ice cold iron whose bitterness could be dismissed only at the cost of torn skin. And now, piquant sauce for his dish of plenty, Strawberry herself came running up Jones Street, scream-ing: Justin, Justin, *oh, my God, Justin!* She leaped into the back of the ambulance, whose pebblechromed bumper dazzled her with its silver perfection, asked the paramedics if he was all right, held his hand. —I'll buy you a soda at the hospital, she whispered tearfully.

Justin felt grand.

But then they were hauling the unconscious drunk into a stretcher beside him, at which he became indignant and cried: This is *my* ambulance!

The crowd laughed: *Heh, heh, heh!*

| 361 |

Tyler was in the Uptown Bar on that same rainy Friday night when a wordless girl laid a white rose on his table and swung out through the doorway, gone now in the yellow dripping light, so after a long time he finished his beer and walked the block to Sixteenth where another girl stood; as wordlessly as the first, he offered her the flower, and she said in tones of almost scalding ferocity: Get away from me, bitch! —He said: I'm not a bitch and neither are you. —Fuck you, said the girl. Stop following me. —I'm not following you. I'm walking back to the Uptown, which means you're following me. —You fuckin' longhair! Who do you think I am? —I think you're beautiful, darling. —Fuck you, the girl said. —His toes were wet in his shoes.

Feeling depressed and humiliated, and defiantly revelling in these sensations because they signified the Mark by which he now knew himself, he drove slowly up Van Ness, engaged his clicking right turn signal, then swung into the Tenderloin's darkness where on the groundlevel storeys of squat brickwork skyscrapers the delis, corner markets, bars and pornographic bookstores smoldered in waves of unsettled light, and he glimpsed Strawberry running between cars, bent forward with her arms folded at her breasts; she had just heard about the tall man's accident, about which Tyler did not yet know, and then he saw a parking spot in front of the glaring portico tricked out with plastic letters spelling **VIDEO** and 3 𝔽𝕀𝕃𝕄𝕊 **3 HOURS** 𝕏𝕏𝕏 at which moment Domino's ex-pimp threw a rock against his right headlight and ran away crazily screeching and redeyed, but Tyler was wearing his gun that night, so he only grimaced nervously and got out of the car, checking that all four doors were safely locked before he slouched among the slouch-ing silhouettes on the littered, greasy, grimy sidewalk of Turk Street whose main lumi-nescence came, it seemed, from the dark-parka'd pimps' white trousers and the whitish-yellow line in the middle of the street and then the sad streetlight spewing downs showers of already infected photons, so he didn't look back and he didn't look into anyone's face on his entire way to the Wonderbar, where the man on the next barstool said to him: Hey.

Hey what? said Tyler.

Bet you can't tell me what snowmen got that snowwomen don't got.

Tyler thought for a moment. —Snowballs, he said, slightly pleased with himself.

Shit, you're a comedian! My hat's off to you! But you'll never get this one: What makes a snowman smile?

I give up, said Tyler.

When them *snowblowers* come round! *Hoo!* Heh-heh-heh-heh . . .

Tyler laughed and shook his head.

You're pathetic, said Domino, who'd materialized behind him. You hang around in sleazy bars and think that stupid misoyginistic jokes about snowmen are funny. You need to get a life.

You and me both, said Tyler. Speaking of sleazy bars, what's it like looking out through the sleazy bars of your prison cell?

Asshole! shouted the blonde, and Tyler chuckled and narrowed the eyes in his grey, grey face . . .

| 362 |

He felt weak with dread when he considered his future, so he did not consider it. What might and probably would happen imminently seeped into the present, poisoning it, but he denied the poison. His relationship with the Queen, as his connection to John and to Irene had been, was doomed. But hadn't John and Irene's marriage been literally doomed? Where was the sense of everything? And suddenly he felt such anguish that ideas vanished and to save himself he thrust his tongue up the Queen's anus. But that didn't save him, because now he *believed;* he had faith—not merely in her herself; he'd long since gained, lost and regained that; but also in her onrushing end. She would go away, like one of the tired old secretaries high-clicking down the granite steps of the Hall of Justice on Friday night, *gone* like the man in the skullcap who drank and drank until the eyes rolled back inside his head. And in terror Tyler held his Queen tightly enough to bruise her ribs, and he cried: What am I going to *do?*

Ah, said the Queen. You mean afterward, don't you, baby?

Yeah.

They were inside a shed on Bryant Street whose outside read AUTO GLASS. Everybody else was out working that night, except for Sapphire, who made many strange faces each as white as the divider lines on pavement, her mincing movements striving to please the world, her long hair combed back by her Queen, plaited into a horse's tail. Whenever Tyler gazed at her, he believed her to be expressing something terribly important which happened to be in an alien language. Buddha says that greed, anger and ignorance cause all human suffering. Sapphire possessed neither greed nor anger. As for her ignorance, that was either almost absolute or else entirely nonexistent. Perhaps she was Buddha. And upon Canaanites, as upon all others, Buddha has compassion. Was this what the retarded girl was expressing when, appearing between him and the Queen with the silent rapidity of one of those chrysanthemum spirits in snow-blue robes who rise from the central trapdoor of a Kabuki stage, she smiled on him, simultaneously shedding tears?

Allrightie, now, Sapphie, said the Queen. You're a good girl. You're our good girl. Now go over there an' lie down. You got to dream now. You got to dream the dreams like I told you.

But Tyler could not cease gripping the Queen's knees as he groaned over and over: What am I gonna do?

Well, I guess you just gonna have to deal, she replied a little drily.

Africa?

What? What is it now, child?

Can I go with you?

Where?

Wherever they're going to put you, he stammered.

No.

You don't want to talk about it. I'm sorry if I . . .

C'mere, baby. You not *ready* for this. You got some travelling ahead of you. Lots and lots. You really wanna know?

I guess not, he sobbed. Not yet—

| 363 |

Hi-i-i-i-i-i-i-i-i-i-i-! the ladies screamed at his mother when he opened the door.

Well, well, said Mrs. Tyler. What a surprise. How dear of you all.

And John's even put birthday flowers on your wheelchair, said Mrs. Simms. How darling.

I'm Henry, not John, said Tyler.

Oh, I'm sorry, Henry. Where can we put our coats?

I'll take them.

Where's John?

He'll be here directly, said Tyler. He wandered into the kitchen and poured himself a water glass full of whiskey, thinking that no matter what he did he would be considered corrupted and attainted like a homeless man or an unwashed prostitute and he therefore longed with all his soul to be away from here forever and in the arms of the Queen for as long as she lasted. His fantasies were as green and white as the bok choy for sale right around the corner from City Lights.

Henry? came his mother's weak voice. Where's Henry?

Tyler sipped at his drink.

Somebody go see where Henry is.

Scowling, Tyler upended his part-drunk glass into the sink. Then he took the birthday cake out of the refrigerator. It was one-thirty. John had promised to arrive promptly at two, so Tyler needed to be out of the house by then.

Henry?

Oh, hello, Mrs. Myers. I'm just lighting the candles for Mom. Would you mind getting everybody ready to sing "Happy Birthday"?

You're such a good son, Henry. You and John both. John especially. It seems as if I'm always seeing John running up here with something for your mother . . .

I wish I could just help her a little more, Tyler whispered.

| 364 |

Why, June, you look *ravishing* tonight, said Mrs. Myers.

Thank you, my dear, Mrs. Tyler said.

She looks awful, said Mrs. Myers out of the side of her mouth.

Why, what's wrong? said Tyler.

Can't you *see?* Just look at her *face!*

On the television, Brady was saying to an interviewer: In every province of our Invisible Empire there's one Great Titan and seven Furies, and if you don't even know that much . . .

Where's Mrs. King today? said Tyler.

You mean you didn't *hear?* said Mrs. Myers delightedly.

I just swear by that Miramar cream, Mrs. Simms was saying. It's the newest thing. When you put it on your face, you can feel it burn. I guess it actually dissolves that top layer of skin.

No, I didn't, said Tyler.

You didn't what, dear?

I didn't hear how Mrs. King met her doom.

Well, *Henry,* she—

It was a *double mastectomy,* Henry, so could you please be more sensitive?

I guess I could try.

Getting back to that Miramar cream . . .

So it's good for wrinkles? inquired Mrs. Myers with intense interest.

It's the best. It's an anti-ageing cream, really. It actually dissolves all your wrinkles.

She should talk! whispered Mrs. Myers. Just look at the old bag!

Sighing, Tyler stepped in between them. —How much does it cost, Mrs. Simms?

Well, it's three hundred dollars for two months' worth. It's three bottles, one red, one silver and one black.

And you have to use them all? Mrs. Myers put in. I really don't see why you should have to use them *all.*

First you're supposed to apply the black. If you don't, there's no guarantee. That one burns the most. Then you scrub, rinse and dollop on the silver. You really have to use a lot of silver. I always run out of that one first. Then you wait one minute and go for the red. You know how I remember all that? Because black, silver and red were my high school football team's colors.

Well, isn't that an interesting coincidence? sighed Mrs. Tyler.

Yes it is. It truly is. And the supply lasts me about two months. As I said, it's three hundred dollars. But that's only if you have a coupon . . .

Almost beside himself with boredom, anxiety and distress, Tyler took Mrs. Myers back into the kitchen and seized her hand.

You creature! laughed Mrs. Myers roughly. You just like the holding hands!

And the kissing.

And the *rubbing.*

And everything after that, he sunnily replied, thinking: Why, Stella Myers, you don't know what to do with your life, either. (What do I want to do with the rest of my life? Get to a point where I can stop asking that question. But I actually know. I want to be with my Queen.)

You creature, she laughed. I already called you a creature. *Stop that!*

From the living room, Mrs. Simms peered in at them.

Tyler smiled blandly.

Stop putting your hand on women's butts! Mrs. Myers said loudly.

Where's Henry? called Mrs. Tyler.

Mrs. Simms glared at Tyler.

I know I shouldn't, said Tyler thoughtfully, but it just feels so good.

Suddenly, Mrs. Myers laughed and squeezed his hand.

| 365 |

Henry, his mother whispered as he was leaving, it would be such a waste to me if you just holed up and—

That's nice of you to say, Mom.

How's business?

Oh, not so good. But I—

There's just so much more *to* you than that.

Than what? I've got to go, Mom. Say hello to John for me . . .

| 366 |

What size is she? said the saleslady.

Eighty-five slash S, said Tyler, believing the Queen to be the same size as Irene.

That's not an American size. That's a foreign size. Oh, okay. I know. And would you like a panty with that?

Oh, I suppose.

With the garter? I recommend the garter.

That's extra, I take it.

Yes it is, sir.

You know what a Marxist would say about that?

Excuse me, sir?

He'd say, *that's no accident.*

Sir, do you want the garter or don't you?

She's just like Domino, he told himself. Finally he nodded, anxious that he might not have enough cash.

And you'll want a robe with that, too, won't you?

No, I don't believe I do.

She might be disappointed, the woman insinuated in a faraway childlike voice. It's really not much of a gift, what's in this cute little bag so far.

Yeah, he said, paying in five dollar bills. I'm so sorry you're disappointed.

| 367 |

A lady from a personnel office called and wanted him to screen somebody before she fired him. She was hoping to find evidence of illegal drug use. She wanted Tyler to obtain his medical record.

And we need a hard copy for verification purposes, the lady said.

Tyler rubbed his eyes, gazing out at the fog, cleared his throat, and said: My assumption would be, if I'm looking up medical information, I'm picking it up off insurance company databases. So I won't be able to get original hard copy, ma'am. But I can print out whatever I catch, if that makes you feel better.

It just has to be hard copy. That's all. That's our policy.

Sure. Do you have his social?

His what?

His social disease, ma'am.

Excuse me?

His social security number.

I thought you could obtain all that information, the lady said.

Oh, I can, but I'm trying to save you money. It'll be one less computer search for you, you see.

Well, isn't it illegal for me to give out a social security number?

Ma'am, it's just as illegal for me to snoop in somebody's medical records. And it's never a good idea to talk about illegal things on the telephone, get it? Are you tape recording this call?

That's irrelevant.

Oh, it is, huh? I get it.

Mr. Tyler, I'm not sure I like the direction this conversation is taking.

Aren't you ashamed? he said. Don't you feel just the littlest bit hypocritical?

I *beg* your pardon! the lady said coldly.

You want me to do your dirty work and incur the risk and you won't even tell me whether you tape record your phone calls. You're like some john in the Tenderloin wanting to fuck a desperate whore up her bleeding ass and not even use a rubber . . .

I was referred to you, Mr. Tyler. I can see now that the referral was a mistake. Goodbye.

We aim to please, he said, but she'd already hung up.

| 368 |

Danny Smooth got a collect call from Strawberry, said the Queen. Domino, Henry, go an' get Justin from the hospital They won't let him out unless he gets a ride home. Strawberry she stayin' down there with him an' she wanna come home now, too . . .

Aw, come on, Maj, whined the blonde. Tomorrow's my thirty-second birthday and I was already celebrating. That's not a party kind of thing to do.

Justin he ain't been havin' no party either, girl, said the Queen sharply. Now go get him.

Maj, I—

Oh, quit pissin' in my ear and tellin' me it's rainin', said the Queen.

And so they drove to San Francisco General Hospital where the tall man shared a room with an O.G.* who'd been shot in the stomach. The O.G. was saying: So anytime you wanna split on that bitch an' come join my nation, I'll bring you right in, know what I'm sayin'?

Hey, I appreciate that, the tall man said.

I mean, what you got right now? You got this scuzzy white bitch over there, an' I bet you don't even got no car. Don't you want a real lady an' a car? Hey, listen up, Justin.

---

*Old gangster.

Send the white bitch outside. Send her out. Go on, bitch, get the *fuck* out of this black man's room.

Outside, Strawberry, said the tall man

Justin, I—

I said *outside,* you stinkin' bitch.

That's right, Justin, that's right. You tell 'em! Now get on them crutches an' come over here. Yeah. That's right. Bend over my bed. And kinda pull the curtain around us so . . . Yeah. Now listen, I'm not playin' you when I say this. You wanna ex that bitch who been keepin' you down?

The tall man swallowed hard. —No, he said.

I'm not talkin' about that silly piece of white trash. She's not *oppressin'* you; she's just *encumberin'* you. I know you can bump her off. I wouldn't never insult you, Justin, by offerin' my help there. No, I'm talkin' about that Queen bitch. I don't mind a little head to head with that bitch.

No, the tall man said.

I don't approve of you, but you got a lot of guts. I respect you. A little *drive-by, roll-by, tooty-shooty,* hear what I'm sayin'? A black man, a brother, shouldn't *never* be the slave of no bitch.

Justin said: Awright, my brother, good to talk to you, okay?

Hey, baby, be cool, okay? croaked the older man.

Justin Soames, your ride is here, said the nurse.

The tall man hobbled downstairs, ignoring Strawberry, who hurried after him.

You holding on, Justin? Tyler said. Beside him, Domino picked at her fingernails.

Uh huh, said the tall man. I don't feel nothin'.

Hey, Dom, *hey,* Henry, said Strawberry a little too eagerly. We sure appreciate this . . .

Well, aren't you just the prettiest berry in the whole damned patch, said Tyler with a cornball smile.

Cut it out! giggled Strawberry. Stop touchin' me, homes!

Justin turned around, scratching his bearded lips, and said: If my old lady was to talk to *me* like that, I'd slap the shit out of her. I'm *talkin'* to you.

Oh, quit bossing her around, said Domino.

Who the fuck you think you are? and the tall man raised one crutch as if to strike her, too. She slunk back.

What a lovely, lovely reunion, chuckled Tyler, narrowing his eyes. Strawberry, don't you think they ought to get married?

Strawberry was silent.

Well. Guess I'm the one who has to carry on all the conversation around here. Justin, you got any stuff?

Had me some pretty good morphine.

Morphine's the best, laughed Domino nervously, still watching the tall man's crutch. Tyler was immensely saddened to see her fear. It was as if she, too, now acknowledged that the Queen's world must soon end, at which time her erstwhile clan of brothers and sisters would again scatter to the darkness, becoming predators who preyed upon each other. —And you know what else? she babbled on. That fuckin' lithium. What the fuck do they use it for? For fuckin' depression or schizophrenia or what the *fuck.* It's better than *fuck.* And—and—and . . .

What's *she* on? sneered the tall man. Meth? Shit, I didn't know she could even score a dime bag of goddamn boogie weed without me. Where's that faggoty car at?

Shaking his head, Tyler drove them back among the Tenderloin's striped and tanned and glowing building-rectangles all stacked together like playing cards where on all sides was proclaimed the gospel of HOTELS—MOVIES—XXX except where it said LIQUORS or THUNDER—LIQUOR—BEER—WINE—ATM CARD, and the tall man smiled sallowly, warmed by vagrant beams of barroom light exuded from rows of Old Crow bourbon bottles behind ever so many counters, liquid glowing as yellowly as the slanted stacks of oranges and lemons in the produce markets of Mission Street, and through his rearview mirror Tyler saw the tall man begin to lick his lips.

Back in Canaan again, yessir, Tyler said. Back in the land of Cain.

Domino, wearied almost to death of Tyler, whom she watched steadily driving with his grey hands almost rosy thanks to reflected light while his windshield wipers fended off the world, and in equal parts wearied of Strawberry and the tall man because she thought she knew them so well as to preclude any future novelty or even change, tried to imagine herself somewhere else, as she usually did when, for instance, she was naked and on top of or beneath some strange man. At those times she never pretended that she was *with* anybody special or kind; all that she wanted was to curl safe in some recess which she could no longer even visualize, maybe one of those mellow bars with black leather seats where the patrons smoke cigars and drink single malt Scotch out of glasses not much larger than the ampoules of precious drugs, someplace where the tall man wouldn't threaten her and Tyler couldn't play his stupid games and Strawberry . . . Her brothers and sisters, once close enough for her to touch, were rising up into distant and malignant pillars of night.

Apprised of almost all the intimate characteristics of Strawberry which it is possible for one person to learn about another, Domino was sure that she knew her in her unapproachable soul. She knew what Strawberry's breath smelled like during her period, and she knew every dimple of her flabby buttocks. She knew the slow, high, Japanese sounding moans which Strawberry uttered whenever she was making love with the tall man, whose own cries were deep metallic monotones like windgusts jetting low between the still skyscrapers of the financial district at dawn. She also knew the moans which Strawberry made when she was with other men, her trick moans, Domino called them, which sounded equally plausible and very well might have been equally pleasurable for Strawberry but which were emitted in a lower key, almost approaching the tall man's cries. Another of Strawberry's peculiarities was that her moans never ever coincided with those of whatever man was inside her, but alternated with them like echoes, as if Strawberry were faking them or needed to go her own way or simply experienced joy between instead of during thrusts. Domino had watchdogged Strawberry when customers were iffy; she'd lived with her, double- and triple-dating with her, and so when it came to Strawberry the blonde considered herself a woman of experience. And, like most experiences, this one nauseated her. She longed to forget everything she knew about Strawberry. She hated the tall man and Tyler even when she needed and even loved them. Like the crazy whore, who took shelter in her craziness, and the false Irene, who hid in self-stupefaction, Domino felt embarrassed and revolted by the world around her. Longing to be anywhere but here, she licked her lips and thought about heroin, crack, Sapphire's clitoris . . .

Hey, I'm *speakin'* to you, Dom, you skanky white bitch. I said, what the fuck you on?

One time on lithium I got so shitfaced, Domino continued rapidly, glaring at the tall man out of the corner of her eye, and you know I was around all you fucked up people doing what you fucked up people normally do, so I should have been sad. But I couldn't get this shiteating grin off my face. I kept saying, hey, I'm sorry, I know I should be sad but I'm happier than shit.

So what's the plan, now, Justin? Tyler interrupted.

Whatever it takes.

Where do you want me to drop you?

Where the fuck you think?

Strawberry, Domino, you want to work or you want to hang with the Queen?

Strawberry cleared her throat and said: I, uh—

Stay the *fuck* out of my business! the tall man screamed, rubbing his leg.

I get it, Tyler said sarcastically.

The tall man continued not to look at him, and Tyler, suddenly furious, concluded that it must be true what Domino was always sneering into his ear—namely, that the tall man had no love for him whatsoever and therefore used him and mocked him as the cruelest of johns mock their whores. Months ago, Tyler had thought he knew how to deal with him. The Queen was *a very big bitch,* the tall man used to self-importantly whisper. This was the only sort of lying in which Tyler had ever caught him, this weak struggling to be glamorous. He could have told Tyler that he was a bigshot himself, or even that he was friends with bigshots, but he didn't set his sights so high. His boss, the Queen, whom he loved and perhaps feared, was glorious enough. But he had never really gotten along with any members of the royal family except for Strawberry, off and on, and of course Maj herself who was now so frequently to be seen walking down the street with her arm tightly about Tyler's waist and his arm around her shoulder with his fingers gripping her upper arm and her dark face turned toward him as he clung to her, watching the street with his right hand in the pocket of his jacket. To the tall man, Tyler looked shy, maybe even ashamed. He seemed to be gazing away from her.

Tyler said: Justin, I have a question.

What?

Why is it that when I try to be polite and respect you and do you favors like picking you up at the goddamned hospital and ask about how you're feeling and what your plans are, you don't even say what's up? Are you that selfish? Are you that far gone?

He's *sick,* Henry! whispered Strawberry nervously. By the way, I found this tape player in the women's bathroom. I'm gonna give it to the Queen . . .

Ignoring her, the tall man leaned forward and said in tones both earnest and bland, and maybe contemptuous also: You think you can see the agony of the black man?

What are you talking about?

How come you never invite me over? You been in all the Queen's tunnels and you never took me anywhere.

Well, I didn't know that you—

You got a place?

Sure, Justin. Sure I do.

Probably some million dollar white man place.

Oh, give me a break, said Tyler narrowing his eyes.

A concrete-hued fog protected the Tenderloin from unnecessary light, like some grey rock beneath which bugs and worms could safely crawl, to say nothing of the Tenderloin's wheelchair kings who rolled beneath those elegant old white skyscrapers, yes, white against a silver-white sky, and the chin-up street kings who stalked the filthy side-walks, watching the men in crutches approach to do them reverence, and meanwhile the cars snored in between it all, ignored by everyone unless their windows were down for business. The silhouette of a garage mechanic in coveralls bent over a truck hood on Olive Street, and a black girl in a white wool cap and a white quilted jacket approached him. Then they were gone, and so was the rain forest mural on the Mitchell Brothers O'Farrell Theater. If Tyler didn't put on the brake soon, they'd be all the way to Frenchy's adult bookstore.

I said, you think you can see the agony of the black man? Hell, no. Not even you. I like you, Henry. You my friend. You don't talk down to me. But you can't never under-stand—

Don't I bear the Mark of Cain, too? asked Tyler, staring into the tall man's face and narrowing his eyes. Don't you think that I—

Strawberry cleared her throat and said: I, um, I heard they're gonna put up a big red fence at the end of Haight Street so that the homeless people can't sleep there in the park no more. Don't you think that's fucked? I mean, I really really—

Cut that Mark of Cain shit, the tall man told Tyler. We *all* disgraced on this world. I don't even care about that no more. But you ain't never been treated like I been treated. You ain't never felt the agony that every black man feels.

What's that supposed to mean? said Tyler. How can you know what the *agony of the black man* is? Are you that cocksure a sonofabitch, that you can speak for all black men? What can *you* see?

I can see this, motherfucker. I can see the burning buildings and the crack-addicted babies and—

Who burned the buildings down? Who addicted those babies? Was it me? Was it my mother? If some tart like Chocolate gives birth to seven babies and they're all addicted, why is that my fault? Why's that the agony of the black man? Why isn't it your fault or Chocolate's fault?

You disrespectin' me, Henry? I *know* you disrespectin' Choc, an' she's a sister. If you wasn't dickin' the Queen right now, you just might be dead.

All right, fine. Let's forget it.

You don't deserve her. You don't deserve to talk *shit* to me.

Come on, Justin, whispered Strawberry, he's your friend . . .

Shut the *fuck* up, bitch! he screamed, and punched her in the face. Domino, who was sitting in the front seat, looked away. Tyler bit his lip and wiped tears out of his narrowed little eyes.

| 369 |

I'm happier than *shit,* Domino mumbled.

I'm glad you're happy, said the Queen, who was squat, dark and perfect like some tar-nished bronze crocodile figurine from ancient Nubia. Now you can go back to your par-tyin' . . . An' if you want anything—

I want Sapphire's little *booty!* the blonde screeched.

Ah, said the Queen.

| 370 |

Above Seventh by the V.D. clinic there were two jet trails, and the sunglare was so white upon the gilded diamonds of the church dome.

Sir, you're too close to the counter, said the woman. Please step back behind the yellow line.

The tall man pushed his wool cap up and silently obeyed her. He felt afraid.

Sir, we can't track you with the name you gave us, the woman went on. You have to give us your real name. We're completely confidential. No one can release any information without your approval . . . —and she slid a clipboard toward him with a worksheet on it, requesting date of birth, full name, and suchlike personal matters. She nodded at him to pick it up.

He took his waiting slip in his hand—letter 𝕌, it was—and laid it gently down beside the clipboard.

OK, thank you very much, he said. His leg ached.

You mean you don't want your test results?

That's right.

OK, fine, she said with a shrug.

| 371 |

Maj, I want to talk you, the tall man said. His sunglasses were as big and dark as a skull's eyesockets.

About what?

About this problem that I have.

Shoot, said the Queen.

In private.

You gals go over there behind those cars. An' Domino, you take Sapphire. Chocolate, you too. Don't lemme catch you listenin'. That's a good gal. You all go an' have a good time, smoke yourselves out . . . Allrightie now, Justin, what is it? You know I can't fault you for sayin' whatever it is you gotta say. You was never a liar nor a coward. An' remind me to get Sapphire some shoes. You doin' okay?

No.

I figured. You wanna quit me?

I don't know.

Same old *same* old! she laughed bitterly. Sometimes I feel like it almost be *scandalous,* you know, me out here for everybody an' no support. An' without me an' my rep* you'd all be—

We'd all be *what?* said the tall man.

Smiling grimly, the Queen fell silent, and they stood gazing across the corner at Strawberry and Chocolate in front of the Cinnabar, Chocolate in white shorts with her dreadlocks rich and shiny as she stood crossing and uncrossing her long brown legs at the passing cars while Strawberry sipped at a sodacan; then before the Queen knew it her

*Reputation.

two girls were chuckling and dancing round each other whispering and hugging and then a small packet changed hands.

They say that the ten percent we gotta give you, you don't give it all back. They say you featherin' your own nest, Maj.

So it's about bread. That what it's about for you, Justin?

They say you took that bread.

Myself, huh? All by myself?

But just then Beatrice came running from Larkin Street, on her face a radiant look, and she did not know that the Queen and the tall man were having a private conversation and she was too happy to comprehend the other women's warning cries because the old man who'd been with her had adored her and given her three hundred dollars all good cash money without any retribution at the end so that Beatrice felt at long last proven *sweet as a pastry, hot as a candle, bright as the sun!* just as the death's-head the master of ceremonies had cried out in Merida so long ago, in words which Beatrice had snipped down to fit her shyly uncovered self so that she could dance in the air forever without anyone's sufferance or legal permission and she was so filled and swollen with love that her joyousness outswelled the edemas in her abscessed varicosed legs and she could soaringly strut like all the Mayan girls who by virtue of the three stripes of floral embroidery on their long white dresses (which is to say, their Marks of Anti-Cain) had long since become angels. The Queen smiled and made a kissing face. Beatrice flew into her arms. Absently stroking the other woman's long, greying hair, the Queen said to Justin: So. You want to quit? Or you want to bring me down?

Justin swallowed, scanning the streets for vigs and rival beaver-traders. —I've heard it said, he finally told her, that you—

That I what?

That you're in this thing with the cops.

And what have you heard it said that I do with cops, Justin? Flatback 'em?

This bread you take from us . . .

So I pay protection money. Of course I do. You want me not to do that?

I heard a lot about that, said Beatrice. But you're doing a favor for us, you know. If that money exists, who pay you for that? Nobody does. I doan care for the money. Nobody paid our Mama the Queen to do a favor for us.

The tall man smiled slightly, embarrassed.

Who says all this, Justin?

He would not answer.

So it's Domino as usual, said the Queen. She needs a man to give her guidance. She needs to get off the streets. That Domino's always in trouble. She's so blonde and beautiful the men always be hittin' on her, tryin' to bridle her down with some pimp. And she won't do it, 'cause she has me and we have each other, so she don't need no pimp. An' you believe her?

Timidly Beatrice took hold of the tall man's sleeve and even though his eyes were as angry and orange-red as the neon glare of the Queen's Bar down on Harrison Street he did not dare to throw her off because the Queen was watching and she said to him: Please, Justin, you know in Tijuana there used to be a policewoman who used to hurt us by the hair, used to pinch us. If we want to get out of the jail, we have to pay twenny, twenny-five dollars. And if they get you out, if you come back to her street to do your business, if you doan have no more money, you go back to the jail. And even in this

America it is not always all right, But we must say thanks to God for our Queen, for helping us with the police and with those others, those bad street men who used to rape us and hurt us. Now even the main street is correct now. The police they doan hurt us any more.

Take my cigarette, darling, said the Queen. And go give some money to your sisters. Maybe you can buy Sapphire some shoes. Bea, you're my special angel now.

When they were alone again the Queen took the tall man's hand and said to him: You're not greedy. You got heart. I know that. Now what's this thing really about? Is it about what I did to Domino?

Hell, no, you got the right to do more to that bitch than make her come—

Then what is it?

Shit. *What am I doin' this for?*

It's up to you, said the Queen flatly. You don't have to do nothin'.

Maj, I want us, *together,* to keep on comin' up. An' you keep sayin' we gonna go down. When they gonna get us? *Why* they gonna get us? I wanna drag 'em under Henry's car, take that gun of his an' blow they heads right off they necks. And you—

An' I what?

Oh, it's hopeless, Maj. Just hopeless.

Hey now. You believe in me or not?

I been down for you so long. An' you not even gonna fight. It's like you just punked out.

So you feel like I been givin' you no respect, so you don't wanna respect me no more. Oh, Justin, that made me so sad.

Maj—

Stay or go, but promise me this: No payback when they get us. You gonna make it. You gonna move on. Don't pay 'em back. Just let it go.

If that's how you want it, I'm gonna quit.

He took off his sunglasses then, and his gaze resembled the white cold glare of the sun in a Tenderloin window at evening, red cars, red barfronts, green barfronts, pale tea-colored buildings, and above all this a cold and skittish glance of light refracted by flat dark awareness behind which perhaps somebody was minutely watching the street but no one on the street could see into that darkness. But the Queen, could she see? A dark face, a soul, lurked behind a curtain's membrane.

C'mere, she said.

But the tall man shook his head and told her: I been close to death at times, Maj. And you know what? Up close I can't see nothin'. Not a damned thing. 'Cause they *ain't* nothin'.

| 372 |

The tall man had the number of the O.G.'s main bitch, a hot young thing named Tashay who'd never turned a trick in her life, so she said. He dropped a quarter into the pay phone on Turk and Powell and dialled her up. The O.G. answered.

Justin here, said the tall man. You remember me? I tole you I'd be callin' . . .

Okay, nigga, said the O.G. You ready to keep your mind on you life? You ready to use you head?

Yeah, said the tall man, submissive like a child.

Okay. I know you ain't no coward. I did some checkin' around. I heard you got a rep. Not a real decent gangbangin' rep, but at least you got you name *known* out on the street. You was in Quentin, right?

Yeah.

For auto theft. Well, that ain't even chickenshit. An' pimpin', I *know* you still be pimpin'. That ain't nothin'. You got any exes, any one eighty-sevens?*

Yeah.

How many?

One.

I guess you did tell me that. Well, so you got your rep. An' it wasn't no True Blue. 'Cause we all be True Blues over here.

No.

An' they made you on that one-eighty-seven, right? You was in Soledad?

Yeah.

How many bullets† they give you?

Five years. They tried to get me on conspiracy, but they—

An' you be makin' good money now, sellin'?

Yeah.

Where is it?

I don't keep it, the tall man said. I spread it around.

Righteous. But that *Big Bitch* sittin' on you face (and these words the O.G. uttered in tones of the utmost bitterness, like a man's mistress using the phrase *your wife*) she don't take all that scratch out of you hand, huh? 'Cause any man let some bitch rule his finances, well, Justin, my man, he ain't *got* no rep. He be the *laughingstock*. See what I'm sayin'?

It ain't like that, the tall man said.

Don't bullshit me, the O.G. said. Now, what you gotta do, you gotta bring her down. Mark her face with acid or a razor or a screwdriver, so can't nobody say she still be keepin' you balls between her teeth. You do that, an' then I can tell my homeys you got *heart*, okay? An' at that time, Justin, I can promise you a good place in my organization. You'll be taken care of. I'll feed you, dig what I'm sayin'? In one goddamned week you'll be drivin' a car, I mean a real car. You can even keep the white bitch, if that's the way you wanna go. An' if not, cut her loose. Tashay she got a real sweet li'l sister, I mean *real* sweet, see what I'm sayin'?

Yeah.

In fact, if you really wanna make a splash, kidnap the Big Bitch. Plan it out, bring her to the homeboys. Then we gonna rape her like two three four five days runnin' till she good an' *cold*. Then you can keep runnin' her hos down in their area, an' collect yo scratch. Ain't no more *Queen,* man. You be the *King,* awright?

Yeah.

You better *do* it, brother. You hear me?

Yeah.

You gonna do it or you just wastin' my time like some li'l wannabe buster?

---

*The penal code for homicide is 187. Hence the street slang: "pull a 187."

†Years of prison time.

I'll do it.

'Cause she the *enemy,* man. You wanna get you heart back, you gotta retaliate. Call me when you've done it. Then we'll talk.

The O.G. hung up.

The tall man stood there for a moment. Then he smashed his fist against the phone and he screamed.

| 373 |

Then there came the day when Chocolate, unable to trick because she had an excruciating running sore on her mons veneris, and being unable to trick was unable to cop, approached the Queen with a whine and an opened mouth like a little baby bird. For a long time the Queen regarded her sadly. She seemed to be trying to make up her mind about something. At last she spat into the other woman's mouth as usual. But this time there came no instant rush, and Chocolate's withdrawal pangs did not go away. The whore sat for five immense minutes, fidgeting. Then suddenly she leaped up and screamed: *Bitch, you lost your power, bitch!*

The Queen nodded.

After this, none of the royal secretions seemed to have any effect, and soon the only members of the family who continued to crave them were Tyler and Sapphire.

| 374 |

You ever been here before? said Brady.

Never, the woman said.

Where can I meet you?

Right here at the bar.

Thought you never came here.

Oh, almost never. Six or seven times a year.

Can I meet you down on Turk Street?

That's where a lot of tricks go and get beaten up.

Which do you like better, safe sex or unsafe sex?

Safe sex.

Why?

'Cause I wanna be safe. I like safe people.

Well, we're safe people, laughed Brady, and all his boys sniggered.

What's your name?

Chocolate.

If I pay you a hundred dollars, will you go on television and say that you left that no-good Queen?

There are good things, Chocolate said. I was warm during the winter and she prayed over me. She did help clear up my lung condition.

I don't give a shit about the good things. I'm only interested in knowing whether you want to make that hundred dollars.

Chocolate was silent.

Hey, you. Guess what I do for a living.

I was wonderin', but I didn't wanna find out 'cause I didn't wanna be in it.

| 375 |

My rent's thirty-eight dollars a night but the manager is cool; he'll work with me if I pay it a little late, in bits and pieces. I split it with Justin. He's my boyfriend. Don't worry about him. Soon's I bring you in for a date, he'll leave. He won't say nothin'.

The two men sat in the car in the parking lot while Strawberry scuttled round and round them like a cockroach with its left legs pulled off so that it could only go around in circles. —I got to get back to work actually, she kept mumbling; in fact she merely wanted to motel up and take off her shoes, smoke a little bump with Justin, and that she couldn't do until these temporary employers had gone. When the tall man finally came back, she ran into the motel room after him, leaving the door open so that the two johns wouldn't think that they were being gaffled, although really they were being scammed by the tall man himself who razored off hunks and chunks of white girl from their purchase just as elegantly as the sixteen-year-old daughter of one of Tyler's Berkeley friends could make heavenly chocolate chip cookies impregnated with cognac, sweet butter and all manner of excellent things; she'd insisted that he take all the leftovers with him as he departed into a warm Sunday morning whose coffeeshops proclaimed the forthcoming sixtieth anniversary of the Abraham Lincoln Brigade in the Spanish Civil War. —*Turkish women rally against Muslim leadership's policies,* a greyhaired man in a denim shirt read aloud while the radio played Purcell and the milk steamer hissed like a rock of crack inside a pipe, that breathy hissing wail like a lobster's when it gets thrown into a pot of boiling water, the lid slammed down on its agony; that was the noise which the tall man and Strawberry made with the trimmings from the twenty dollar rock of the two ignorant johns who sat growing paranoid in the car, sweating with fear (which smelled the same as the sweat on Bernadette's tendon-rooted neck with the tattoo below as her loving Queen clicked the heroin needle in and out) looking at watching faces, worrying about cops; to the tall man and Strawberry, however, the noise most resembled the whistle of a train entering a long dark tunnel beneath a mountain; now that love-pair came out on the other side where it was sunny and wild, and the two johns, who at the beginning of the evening had believed all too vividly that the perfect pleasures they could pick from were as numerous as all the translucent plastic cases of the compact disks at Amoeba Records on Haight Street (white price tags for new albums, yellow for used), tried to convince each other that they had nothing to worry about, but the parking lot did not feel very safe because the yellow eyes of black-and-whites kept roving down Ellis Street, and other eyes kept watching them from half-closed motel doors, and meanwhile the two poor johns were still waiting, and only the tiniest pebble of their white girl remained, so Strawberry snatched that out of her boyfriend's hand and ran out to the parking lot, reaching into the open car window to give the john who was driving this preposterous bump of a bump. Before his disbelief could become anger, she said: We owe you twice as much, I know. The guys next door were out of it; just hold your horses while my boyfriend tries another room . . . —at which cue the tall man set out to borrow from either the Queen or generous Beatrice, who was easier to ask because she would never mention anybody else's unkept promise. Knowing that now he owed her, she sighingly yielded up her own lump of happiness, which the tall man brought triumphantly into the motel room. Skilled operator, brain surgeon, he razored off his commission, delivering the net return into the hands of clever Strawberry, who flew back out to the car . . .

We gotta think for ourselves now, he said to her. No way we're gonna pay Beatrice back. An' we gonna start holding out on the Queen, 'cause we ain't got no choice. Bitch, you hear me, bitch? We ain't got no time left to be nice.

You're my man, Justin. If that's what you say, I'm gonna stay cool. But I love Maj—

Lemme tell you, girl . . . Oh, what's the use?

Those two white boys are still out there, his white girl said.

Well, then sell 'em pussy, bitch. Gotta get some money.

Strawberry ran back out to the car and upraised her T-shirt all the way to the armpits so that the two men could see her breasts.

Kind of saggy, the driver said. What are you trying to do? First you gaffle us on rock we paid good money for, then you insult us by offering your skanky tits. What makes you think we have the hots for you? Open your mouth. Let's see your teeth. Maybe you can give some head, I dunno—

What is this, asshole? You got the nerve to insult me? I'm gonna go get my boyfriend . . .

The tall man came out of open doorway and said: Know what I'm gonna do? Hit 'em from the front, then roll 'em over an' hit 'em from the back.

Big fuckin' deal, the driver sneered.

The tall man took a serrated kitchen knife out of his pants and came on toward the car. The two men started crying out in panic, and the car squealed off.

The tall man grinned. Strawberry embraced him admiringly and said: My man knows how to use his head.

Remember this, the tall man told her. *Anybody* else, they the enemy now. You hear me?

What about Maj?

That evil bitch just sittin' there an suckin' up, drinkin' up my tears . . .

Strawberry fell silent in dreary terror.

| 376 |

Actually, everyone's very nice, the bail bondsman was saying. We're their best friend. Excuse me. I have a customer.

He hung up the desk phone and shouted: Well, if it isn't my old friend Justin! What's cooking?

Same old same old, said the tall man. How you been, Mr. Cortez?

Swamped.

You had a young lady working here who wasn't so courteous to me, said the tall man. I ended up payin' a visit to Mr. Norris.

Sorry to hear that, Justin, I am indeed. Was that Diana by any chance?

She never told me her name. But the Queen's abreast of it.

Oh, yes, the Queen! laughed Mr. Cortez a bit too loudly. And how's the Queen?

Just fine, Mr. Cortez.

Now, who are we here for today? Let me guess. Is it Beatrice? Chocolate? Domino's out, I see . . .

Strawberry.

Wanda Hassig, if memory serves. Does it serve, Justin?

Mr. Cortez, you so smart, your head be bulgin' out the edges.

All right, I'm going to call up Room 201. —Five thousand for misdemeanor assault, he reported cheerfully a moment later.

Motherfuckers, said the tall man mechanically.

What happened this time, Justin?

Some john pulled a knife on her, so she socked him. That bitch got balls.

Well, cash or credit card?

Stolen credit card okay, Mr. Cortez?

No one can say you don't have a sense of humor.

I got that when I fell wrongways from my Mama's ass. Now, Mr. Cortez, Queen only gimme three hundred today.

Someone needs to cosign, then, returned the bondsman with smiling wariness.

You want me to go bothering the Queen for this?

I floated you last time, Justin.

No, last time I went to Mr. Norris.

Okay, but we're still outstanding for fifty. That was for Lily.

That bitch was supposed to pay you back. That no-good lowdown he-she crackhead bitch . . .

Be that as it may, I can't make a living floating people. Now if you want to get the Queen in here I'm sure we can work out a payment plan. I'm as anxious as you are to keep this friendly.

Queen's your best customer, said Justin.

That she is, replied the bondsman, making no movement.

Beaten and grinning, the tall man counted fifty ten-dollar bills onto the desk.

Do you have fifty more to settle Lily's account?

I'll take care of her, Mr. Cortez. I guarantee that.

Well, don't be harder than you have to. I'd hate to see Strawberry or Beatrice coming down here to bail *you* out again.

Yeah, at Eight-Fifty Bryant all the girls an' bitches, they be talkin' about your kind heart day and night, said the tall man sarcastically.

I'm sure they love you, too.

I was just curious, said Justin. How often you get heat from some nigger or somebody can't pay?

Everyone's your friend in this business, said Mr. Cortez complacently. I was just explaining that to somebody when you came. Everyone knows everybody. Everybody loves everybody. Life is great. And speaking of which, my old friend, I need your check stub or California I.D.

The tall man, stricken by a momentary and (he realized) entirely senseless bitterness, flipped his laminated card down beside the money, with almost the same motion as a boy skipping a stone across a river.

· BOOK XXIV ·

Sapphire

•

If any man serve me, let him follow me; and where I am, there shall also my servant be.

JOHN 12.26

•

The threatened dissolution of the royal family, as we have seen, alarmed its members no less, for all that they were themselves much of the cause. As soon as they began to admit the seriousness of the matter, they withdrew to varying degrees into fear and greed, laying up secrets, opportunities, connections and bad faith promises like outcast ants stealing grain from the treasury of their sunken, gravid queen, in order to prepare for separate winters. Why? Because they feared that their sovereign could protect them neither from their enemies nor perhaps from each other.

The miracle of authority has always astonished me even more than that bizarre miracle of money whereby an ever deferred promise printed on a piece of paper is believed by people no more trusting or disinterested than the Queen's children. In the case of authority, *many follow one.* Again, why? Tolstoy wrote *War and Peace* in order to answer this question. He concluded that authority (at least of the secular variety) is an unwholesome fiction, that although Napoleon thought himself in charge of his soldier-ants come to plunder the Russian hives, the potency he possessed to command came from something external to himself. Or, to put it even more plainly, the Emperor of the French was stupefied by his own egotism into believing that he had made history, when really the only history-maker is history itself. I don't quite accept this, for the obvious reason that thousands of lives might have run uncut, had Napoleon never seized power. History expressed itself in him, no doubt, but without him history would surely have been compelled to express itself differently.

And yet in the case of our royal family, Tolstoy's deterministic view enlightens the understanding. For it might well have been that the Queen owned no supernatural powers whatsoever, that her spit and piss had never gotten anybody high, and that, like money, she represented only a promise among her children to love one another. Why shouldn't it be, that if I owe you a hundred dollars, you and I could meet in the presence of an authorized functionary of the Federal Reserve, then burn that hundred-dollar bill, because all three parties agreed that you would be entitled to help yourself to a hundred dollars' worth of gold from Fort Knox at any time of day or night? But it doesn't seem so. Money is a promise ultimately too absurd to be believed. We require symbols, verification, materiality, just as churches require altars. And now it seemed that the Queen's promise could no longer verify itself.

It was Sapphire who renewed the promise for at least a little longer.

I do not propose to "explain" her, because I do not understand her. But I love her more than any of the other characters in this book, except perhaps for Domino, and I refuse to refrain from praising her: Should astronomers and ethicists ever succeed in proving that God resembles her, then lost and weary Cain won't need to flee anymore.

| 379 |

One cloudy autumn day when on Second and Howard Streets near Allied Gasket Company the steel gratings took on the color of the clouds, Tyler's rent became late. He wished that he could tell someone, but his only friends now were the royal family, none of whom paid rent at all except by the day; his worries might exasperate them. Moreover, it might well be that by continuing to live in this place filled with *things,* this rich place to which he literally held the key, he was continuing to commit disloyalty to his Queen, who had raised him up out of the hell into which his addiction to Irene had cast him; shouldn't he go into the streets to behold her always, especially now when her reign would so soon end? And yet he was afraid, not so much for himself, who no longer cared for much in the world, as for the Queen's other children who were already so jealous of him for sitting always at her right hand. Moreover, couldn't he love her wherever he was? If his apartment, telephone, computer, bed, books and car were a detriment to him, wouldn't she have said so? He'd never asked her because he feared to ask her. He feared that if he so much as mentioned his money troubles, she might think that he was occupied with other matters than she herself. Well, he knew she wouldn't think that, because she knew *everything.* Still he was afraid to broach any material matters. All his many fears came from the realization that his body must soon be destroyed—how soon, he didn't know. And out of that fear he continually wished that his telephone would ring with lucrative offers. But suddenly he began to fear that when the phone rang he would be obliged to greet his landlord, so he got into his car for a roll downtown and up the hill to Post and Sutter where he saw Chocolate entering the Little Corner House Restaurant, laughing and joking with one of her johns; she didn't see Tyler, who continued up Bush, Pine, California, where it was high and hot. A cable car blocked the intersection. As always, the city got quieter the higher he ascended. He turned right on Clay Street. The Transamerica Pryamid broke the sky. Behind crouched the Bay Bridge like a many-legged dinosaur knee deep in ocean. Crossing the trolley-tracks of Powell Street he spied three big-breasted young girls holding iced cappuccinos and felt no desire for them because he was with the Queen now who filled his heart with a blissful muteness. He no longer sought to express himself; he did not want to plough greener pastures.

When he came into the Wonderbar later that night, Loreena the barmaid, who usually laid her hand on his and said *hello,* stranger! was standing with her back turned to the customers, gazing into the mirror as if she were checking her makeup. He knew that she was crying.

The bullet-shaped little owner stood there, smirking and red, drinking and drinking so that his face grew as red as the marquee of the Market Street Cinema.

I'm smart enough to know how to do this, Loreena said. I *am* smart enough to know how to do this.

Who's running the show? said the owner.

You're running the show, Heavyset, but I—

That's what *counts,* the owner shouted. *Right?*

Right, the barmaid whispered.

How much you got in your till? How much did I give you?

You gave me nothing, Loreena said.

Good! Because nothing is what you deserve, you thieving crackhead bitch.

If you don't trust me—

I don't.

Loreena walked as far away from him as she could get while still remaining within the bar's magic circle, and she wept.

Well, well, well! cried Heavyset with his hard little laugh. If it ain't Henry! What'll it be, Henry? Your usual?

Yeah, sure, said Tyler. Have you seen the Queen?

The who?

Oh, forget it. Have you seen Domino?

I eighty-sixed that skanky bitch, said Heavyset with immense satisfaction. Told her she'd better not come peddling ass in here anymore. She swore at me, too. I had to call the cops on her.

Just a second, Tyler said, striding out the back door into the black alley where Chocolate in her pale white parka was chuckling and weeping crazily to herself in the darkness. She stank and she had gained weight. She stood for hours on Mission Street begging men to please please give her twenty-five cents, and if any of them did, she grabbed the fellow tight and whispered: Couldja do me a *big, big* favor? Couldja gimme a dollar or maybe twenny dollars 'cause I—you know? You wanna go someplace with me? —None of them did.

What's the matter, honey?

He ain't right, the black woman snarled.

Who?

Heavyset. He tole me don't come in there again, 'cause it's a *Mexican* bar. He ain't right. He gonna get his. Someday it gonna happen to him. I can see the day.

Come on in and I'll buy you a drink, he said. He won't pick on you when I buy you something.

No way am I goin' in there!

All right. Well, I'll be inside waiting for the Queen.

I'm cold, said Chocolate. An' Maj she don't do nothin' for us now.

How's business?

Lousy. An' I'm hungry. I want something to eat. Won't you take me down to that Burger King an buy me some fries or something? 'Cause Maj she—

Where's Justin?

They busted him when he was on Turk Street tryin' to cop some downers for Sapphire, I think. An' they took his crutches—

All right, he said.

What the hell, chuckled Chocolate. I got some meat on my ass. My pants are too loose, though. They keep sliding down. You wanna see my ass?

I'm going inside. I'll buy you a beer, though.

I said what the *hell.* Tell you what. You offer me a beer and then I'll tell him real loud just what I think of him.

Tyler had to laugh. He didn't like Heavyset. —I get it, he said. You let me go in first and then you come in afterward and go right up to me.

Okay. 'Cause he ain't right. Henry, he got somethin' bad comin' to him.

Tyler strode back in through the back door, past the pool table where two characters scowled at him and said: You're welcome. —Tyler replied: Why, fancy that. I was just thinking the same thing.

Heavyset was laughing at the television, red-faced, with a shot of bourbon in his hand. Loreena was still crying. Tyler sat down and said to her: What's new?

Oh, I'm changing the locks on my place again. My ex started hitting me again last night.

When are you going to kick him out for good?

It's just something between him and me. Like Strawberry and Justin, you know? I can't really explain it. I won't even try.

Okay, he said.

I need to borrow thirty dollars, she said.

Fortunately, Chocolate came in just then, and Heavyset saw her and turned purple, so Tyler locked his arm around her, shouting: Why, *Chocolate!* Good to see you, doll! Can I buy you a beer?

No, thank you, the whore announced. *I'm black and this is a Mexican bar.*

Heavyset came over very slowly and said to her: Stop fucking with me.

You ain't right, she said.

This is a Mexican bar, Heavyset explained. This ain't a black bar.

I'm tellin' you, you ain't right. An' I saw how you called the cops on that white boy last week, that crackster john—

Get out and don't come back. And do your thing across the street. Don't do it behind my bar.

I live in this hood, Heavyset. You don't be dissin' me. I walk where I please.

All right, Chocolate, just drop it, Tyler said. It's not worth it.

Somethin' gonna happen to you, Heavyset, the whore said, ignoring him.

Get your nigger ass out of here, said Heavyset. I control this area. This is my area. I got my brothers in here, and they'll back me up if you start something with your coal black ass.

You ain't right. You ain't right. But I don't care, 'cause I got God and *Cain* in my heart. Nigger, nigger, nigger *bitch!*

What did you call me? Oh, fuck it. Anyway, I have news for you. You got your false teeth out. Heavyset, you called me bitch with your teeth out!

You're gonna have buckshot in your fat nigger ass if you don't get out of here.

I'm not scared of that little pistol of yours, Heavyset. An' your dick is even smaller.

All right, Chocolate, break it up, said Tyler.

He gonna get his, the whore said serenely.

Get out, said Heavyset. Now. I'm calling the cops.

Okay, Chocolate said far too sweetly. I'm goin'.

She was up to something, Tyler thought. He went outside with her and she started crying and hitting him up for money. —I can only give you a buck, he said, slipping her five.

| 380 |

Chocolate said to the Queen: He be dissin' me, an' hurtin' me in my heart so bad . . . and the Queen, preoccupied, shook her head, slowly cleaning her crack pipe with a dirty paper clip, and then Sapphire began to cry, weeping: *L-l-l-luh-luh-luh* . . . and then the

Queen said: Allrightie now, child. All right. —But Sapphire would not be still. She crawled on her hands and knees to Chocolate and nuzzled against her knees like a cat. Chocolate stroked her. Then she crawled back to the Queen and began kissing her hand. She wanted to go out.

Not now, baby, said the Queen. I gotta do some heavy thinkin'. Sapphy's gotta wait. Bea, angel, you got time to take Sapphire out?

She be out trickin', said Chocolate. Guess I'll go out there, too. I need my fix so bad.

Allrightie then, said the Queen. Tomorrow I want to buy old Heavyset a drink.

For what?

Hush up, Choc. Queen's gotta do some Heavy thinkin'. I want you to make Sapphire be quiet.

| 381 |

The Queen came into the Wonderbar on that hot August afternoon, the front door trembling behind her so that Loreena and Heavyset and their sparse crew of drinkers could see across the street and inside the bright whitewashed Mexican place where flames shot up from the grill and chopping sounds gladdened the longhaired guys waiting in line with clasped hands. Heavyset looked up with his usual dull viciousness, and then the door closed. A moment later, Sapphire scuttled nervously in, half-blinded by the cool darkness, piping: *Luh-luh-luh* . . .

Heavyset said: What *is* this, a convention of niggers and retards?

Loreena grimaced, and the Queen remained silent. But Heavyset could not let the matter drop. Deeply offended by the presence of these aliens, fearing them as much as he hated them (he would have literally suffered nightmares had the Chinese whore Yellow Bird ever shrilled into his face: You like to go kissy-kissy with me?), he bristled into a posture which was for him as natural as that of an antibody encountering in the dim red bloodstreams it frequented some unknown cell which threatened that ruby light of home and seemed to darken it into the inkiness of baleful sorrow. God never intended antibodies to resign themselves. For, after all, one stealthily reconnoitering bacillus must pose the question: *What if there are more of me?*

And so Heavyset said with utter sincerity: You make me sick. Get out of my bar.

Oh, leave her alone, said the Queen. Actually I'm here to have a word with you.

You tellin' me how to run my place? I don't give a goddamn whether you buy drinks in here or not. This is *my place,* and if I want to eighty-six you I'll eighty-six you.

Sapphire turned her milky-pale face away, touched her palm to her mouth, then slowly lowered to the floor whatever invisible thing she'd taken out of herself.

C'mere, Sapphire, darling.

Get that retard out of here! said Heavyset, lifting his heavy hand from Domino's thigh in order to sketch out a gesture of general imprecation, but then for the first time in his life he saw the Queen's eyes glitter with anger and he was afraid. The Queen ran to the front door, opened it, and whistled piercingly. Instantly the tall man was there glaring through his bloodshot eyes. The Queen pointed to Heavyset, and the tall man, smiling with gratified hatred, approached rapidly and easily. Shoving Domino aside, Heavyset rose to his feet.

You givin' her static? the tall man said.

This is *my* bar, nigger, said Heavyset. *I* control this bar. Better get out before they carry you out.

Get behind the bar, Justin, said Domino. That's where he keeps his gun.

Why, you little *cunt!* roared Heavyset, and swung round to backhand her, but just then the tall man brought the end of a steel pipe hard down on Heavyset's wrist so that his purple face turned white and he cried out. In the corner, Sapphire stood on tiptoe, gazing all the way into his face.

Where's the gun? the tall man said.

Right there, said Domino. Under the cooler.

Better fade, Loreena, said the tall man, not ill-humoredly. Just chill. Just ghost out. Don't call the cops, though.

Call the cops, bitch! screamed Heavyset.

Loreena ran out the back door without looking back. Justin strode behind the bar and found Heavyset's pistol. Heavyset sat down again, rubbing his wrist.

Hey, break some bread, man, said Justin. Gimme some snaps.

There ought to be more than a hundred bucks in the register, said Domino with a happy chuckle. I've been watching that register all afternoon and just . . .

C'mere, Sapphire, the Queen whispered. It's okay, darling. Domino, would you kindly take Sapphire to the ladies' room?

Key's behind the bar, Justin, the blonde said, and the tall man tossed it to her. Then he opened the register and began stuffing all the money into his pants.

Now shake Heavyset down, the Queen said in a low grinding voice. We don't want Heavyset to forget what he done. We don't want him to forget that he insulted a poor little girl that can't defend herself. An' Chocolate. An' me. An' God knows how many others.

Gimme your wallet, asshole, said the tall man, waving the pistol up and down the length of Heavyset's body.

That's right, said the Queen. That's right. Heavyset, don't be a fool.

With a curse, the man flung his wallet down on the floor.

Put it in the poor box, now, said the Queen. C'mere. That's right. That's right. Good dog. Turn out your pockets, doggie. Domino! Hurry up in there! Gun up, everybody! We all have to start runnin' now . . .

| 382 |

After that the royal family was happy again for a while. Maj could still act. They all felt as if they were alive again.

Justin, do I look good? asked Domino in her silver stretch leotards, wiggling her behind.

You look fuckable, sure. Now go bring in some money.

Oooh, she said, sarcastic-sulky, and began to walk away.

Hey, Domino! called the tall man.

Hey, what?

I love you, baby!

BOOK XXV

The Truth

•

To believe that things created by an incalculable series of causes can last forever is a serious mistake and is called the theory of permanency; but it is just as great a mistake to believe that things completely disappear; this is called the theory of non-existence.

The Teaching of Buddha (from 5th cent. B.C.)

•

I love it because it's Thursday afternoon and I'm sitting around screwing with this personal injury stuff, Smooth crowed. And indeed he did look happy. Tyler remembered the way Chocolate really came alive only in Tenderloin bars when the music was loudly perfect and color events occurred every second on the giant television screen, or the way that John's face became joyous when he clicked down more lead from inside his stainless steel mechanical pencil. —Almost as good as a *good* rape case, Smooth continued. When I do personal injury, I . . . You're not listening.

Sorry, said Tyler glumly.

You know, I turned you on to somebody who does something *fun.* I turned you on to the Queen. And you owe me.

Yeah, yeah.

So open up those envious ears of yours. Or does everybody badger you all the time? Your brother does, I'll bet. You're so passive-aggressive that he must be active-aggressive.

Go to hell.

I'm the only person in the whole wide world who always speaks the truth. You know how to be sure it's the truth? Because it's *ugly,* man!

So what's *your* truth, then, you preening sonofabitch? What makes *you* so goddamned ugly? Oh, the hell with it; you always piss me off . . .

My truth is doom, brother. Yours, too. We've both got the state hanging over our heads, and don't think I don't know about your sleazy corner-cuttings. Me, I'm waiting for that Gestapo knock on my door because I enjoy consensual sex with minors. And *you,* now, well, you have your brother ticking and smoldering away, you have financial worries (don't think I can't see that in the lines of your forehead), and you have Consumer Affairs watching over you . . .

Oh, that's baloney, Tyler said. I don't know a single P.I. who ever lost his license.

But you *can* get your license yanked for failure to report, now, can't you, Henry? If you interviewed me about the Queen and you changed my information for that Mr. Brady—

I didn't know you when I was working for Brady, and this matter of the Queen isn't even—

And then Brady gets sued or sues somebody and then you and I both get deposed on the witness stand, *boom!* Not only are you sued, you're probably in front of a review board for providing bad information . . .

Oh, for God's sake.

Okay, okay. I give in. It'll never happen. The only thing that'll happen is that John will find another steamy letter from Irene and beat your ass . . . You think you're better than I am?

As a matter of fact, I do. At least I don't torture other people for the fun of it.

No, you wreck lives because it's *expedient*. Don't you?

Dan, he said, I'm worried about our Queen.

Thank you very much. So am I. And I know something you don't, even though I've told it to you hundreds of times: She's doomed, too. We're all doomed. It's the prophecy, stupid. Do you suppose those Brady's Boys are going to fade away before they've hurt somebody? Everybody loves them. America's on their side. Everybody hates us.

Yeah, I know, said Tyler, happy not to be attacked for one moment. Sometimes I search for hidden assets. Let's say a divorced husband sets up a Caribbean bank account. He gets one shot at hiding it. We get fifty shots a year at finding it. Guess who wins? And yet I have to say that they haven't found us yet; we could start over somewhere . . .

What do you mean, *us?* You think you and I are good enough or brave enough to leave the world for our Queen? I don't see you leaving that fine apartment of yours unless you get busted by Internal Revenue or Consumer Affairs. I know *I* don't have the guts.

But—

But your point's well taken. The Queen could disappear anytime. *If* she wants to. Does she want to? You're the one dickin' her. Why don't you ask her?

You know how she is.

Don't worry about her then, the pedophile said, and suddenly Tyler began to feel Smooth's replies leading him on *toward* something, good or bad he couldn't tell yet, like the long thick line of San Francisco lights in the foggy blue night as he came over the Golden Gate Bridge from Sausalito. Whatever you and I know, she knows better.

So you're not worried at all?

Did your envious ears hear what I said or not? Everybody worries in his own way, Henry.

Well, that's a beautiful Hungarian proverb, but let me ask you something, said Tyler, swallowing hard and staring into Dan Smooth's eyes, because in his profession he sometimes encountered what he called "dead-on reads," meaning people who were absolutely unassailably lying: people whose eyes flicked away or people who blinked too often, or people who answered every single question when the questions dealt with fifteen seconds out of somebody's day six months before. Smooth was lying about something, or at the very least withholding something. Tyler leaned forward, raised his voice, and said: Dan, is there anything about this whole situation that you know and the Queen doesn't?

Cross my heart, *no,* said Smooth, his eyes moving away.

Is there anything you know about Domino that I ought to know?

Sometimes people just don't want to *talk* to you, now, do they, Henry? Smooth chuckled. It's like pulling teeth, isn't it?

Don't forget whom you're talking to. I can check up on you. I can get your *tax return* for Christ's sake.

What are you going to do, Henry? Put me through the polygraph? Now there's a guy down the street who does that. We cross paths. My understanding is you can pop a couple of valium and you can just cruise right through it.

It's something about Domino, isn't it?

That Domino, she's a crack monster. She—

Oh, fuck it, said Tyler.

Henry, I'm sorry. Domino's balling your brother.

· BOOK XXVI ·

Celia

•

You will be saved from the loose woman, from the adventuress with her smooth words . . . for her house sinks down to death, and her paths to the shades . . .

PROVERBS 2.16–18

•

| 384 |

In the winter night they reached OAK HILLS, whose letters were tricked out in spurious gold on the wall. Steel gates slid apart. John eased the car down the glistening black
circle studded with streetlamps whose Christmas lights had been formed into alien coil-
springs of luminosity. This "gated community," no community at all, but rather a monument to the rich's justified fear of the poor, was actually, like the subatomic spaces
between electrons, empty and cold. A manhole cover was shining. John drove slowly between grey houses whose black roofs loomed. Occasionally a string of lights blinked idiotically in some window (pathetically, I should say, pathetic as the mobile swinging in
the upper window of the police station's Juvenile Divison at Sixteenth and Mission. Can
you believe what the mobile said? I swear that it said LOVE!), but most of the time John
and Celia could see no electrons at all because the householders, rich, lonely old empty-
nesters, had flown to Phoenix, Lubbock or Salem to inflict themselves on their children
and bribe their grandchildren with presents.

My cousin lived here for two years, and she stayed with us, Celia said vaguely.

All right, said John. Where do we park? The friggin' driveway's full.

John?

What?

Did you hear what I said?

Oh, so it's going to be one of those nights. What's your brother's name again? I like to
know a name when I see a face.

Donald. And my sister is Leslie, but she won't be there. I've told you about Donald so
many times . . .

Yeah, that's right. Lock the back door on your side.

Do you even care about my cousin?

What's her name?

Ashley.

Point her out when we go in.

John, weren't you listening? I told you that Ashley wasn't going to be here.

Well, then it isn't relevant information, Ceel. You forgot the bottle of wine. It's right
there on the back seat.

They still own me for another three years, Celia's father was saying. I'm expecting that
they'll kick me out right before they'd be obligated to honor my pension, but then at
least they'll have to give me some kind of retirement package because it's an involuntary
separation.

Oh, don't worry, Dad, said Celia, longhaired, in white slacks. I'm sure you're going to
go the full distance.

How much vacation did you say you had? John asked Celia's brother.

Six weeks.

Interesting.

Are you interested? the brother said challengingly.

Very interested, said John. I have four weeks, but I never get to take it.

I heard that Sis completely arranges her vacation time around you, and that's why we hardly ever get to see her. Is that true?

Why don't you ask her? was John's curt reply.

John, this wine looks extremely expensive, Celia's mother said. Are you sure we're worth it?

Positive, said John.

I don't think I've ever seen this brand. Where does it come from? Is it French?

Well, there's the label. Do you see it? It's in French, so—

John, don't!

Don't what, Ceel? Your mother asked me a question, and I not only answered her, I proved my case. What's wrong with that? Are you going to tell me I was patronizing?

John, there's something I've always wondered, interposed Celia's mother. People talk about good wine and bad wine. But I've always wondered how you can tell the difference, if you don't go by price alone.

Two things to look for, John explained. First of all, the wine needs to taste like fruit. It can taste dry or even bitter, but that fruit taste has to be there.

He's kind of a know-it-all, Donald said into his father's ear.

And secondly, it has to have a steady aftertaste that stays on your palate.

He kind of talks like a fruity television commercial.

Oh, I see, said Mrs. Keane. Well, I always wondered, and now I know.

Tell John about your new TV, Donald, said Celia.

What? Why should I?

Because he's interested, silly.

Is he really?

Very interested, said John.

A little shyly, Donald said: Well, John, I have direct TV at my place.

How big is your screen? asked John.

Fifty-four inches, said Donald. The screen here is only forty-eight inches. But watch this.

He squeezed a button on his parents' remote control, and an action movie appeared on the screen, with a winking blinking menu embedded in the protagonist's head. A person was hurting another person until blood came.

If you scroll down, Donald explained, you can hear the special effects on the ceiling speakers—*but no one is being quiet,* he concluded with a sudden glare.

And what do you do with your six weeks of vacation? John asked.

What do you mean, what do I *do* with it? It's my vacation. I don't have to do anything. And by the way, about your and Celia's vacation, I just wanted to know. I was actually just trying to make conversation, John. No need to get huffy.

John's not huffy, Celia interposed. That's just how he is.

Correct, said John, crossing his legs. That's just my nature.

You think they're going to terminate me? said Celia's father anxiously.

Oh, Daddy, sighed Celia.

The back office prides itself on being a separate company. And they hold all the aces. If they terminated me, you think your legal eagle boyfriend could help me sue?

Sure, said John cheerfully. Pro bono.

How many people have you sued?

Thousands. They're all dead now.

Celia's mother, whose nervousness had already been aroused by the exchanges between John and Donald, tried to think of something to say and finally blurted: Are you still in your mourning period, John? I always thought it was good manners if the mourning period lasted a year.

Well, let's see now, he said, raising his eyebrows. How long has it been since my wife killed herself? That's what you're asking me, right? I mean, why put too fine a point on it?

Please, John, whispered Celia, her eyes watering. Mama didn't mean any harm.

Oh, well, forget it, John began, and if someone had rushed to dilute the silence he might have truly been able to let the topic pass, but since Donald was so evidently distempered by his bluntness, and since Celia's parents, their countenances well sculpted but slightly timeworn, like the Elgin Marbles, hung on his words like vampires, he knew that if he did not speak he would choke with sadness, humiliation and rage, so he burst out, staring them all down: June twenty-seventh. Is that what you were all fishing for?

John, I'm so sorry. I—

She was a great gal, you know, terrific gal. But I'll tell you something, Mrs. Keane (and here a horrid smile crossed his lips. Celia was tongue-tied with dread.). She couldn't keep house as well as Celia here. Would you believe that?

John—

Your daughter sure knows how to clean. I'll say that much for her. She knows what's important to me. I'll give you an example. She was the one who hit on that Blue Wave cleanser. That took the stains right off. Well, most of the stains. I still had to get the bathtub refinished. They say blood and protein's the worst. And today is December twenty-first. So that makes a hundred and seventy-seven days, or six months, depending on how you count—how do you count a month, Mrs. Keane? Do you use the lunar month of twenty-eight days or the variable calendar month? Since June has thirty days and July has thirty-one days, was July twenty-seventh the one month anniversary of her death or not? Donald, my man, a penny for *your* friggin' thoughts.

John, I'm *so* sorry, said Celia's mother.

Now, what we need to determine, he went on, raising his voice, is whether Emily Post and the other mavens of etiquette actually permit me to be here whooping it up with you *fine* people on this—should we call it a *fine* evening? —or whether it would be more befitting for me to sit in a bar somewhere in the Tenderloin, the way my grungy brother would—

That's a district of San Francisco, Celia explained brightly, clenching her fists.

The Tenderloin? said Celia's father. Doesn't he mean the bad area?

. . . Drinking myself into a stupor until next June twenty-seventh, or would June twenty-sixth be good enough? If there's no leap year I guess then we could wrap it up. The *mourning* period, I mean, John shouted.

(Celia would not forget the sight in that bathtub, not ever. Nor would she forget the refinishing man who'd arrived two days later and lounged in the doorway saying to John: That bathtub's gonna be as smooth as a baby's ass, Mr. Tyler. Don't you worry about that. I take pride in my work.

(All right, fine, said John. Just make sure you mask it off. I'm a clean freak.

(What happened in this bathtub, anyway? said the refinishing man. It don't really look so bad.

(My wife died in it, said John. Just make sure you mask it off, all right?)

Donald said: For Christ's sake, John, we get the picture.

Oh, you do? Good. Then let's talk about something more pleasant. Mutual funds, for instance. Do you have a Keough IRA, Donald?

I don't even know what I have. When I started working for the company last year they told me something about stock options, but . . .

Wrong answer, said John. I want you to tell me yes or no.

Celia laid a hand on his shoulder, but he shook her off. He went on and on. He talked about stocks and bonds. Only Celia's father was interested, but Celia's father was *extremely* interested.

| 385 |

Easy to put John in a bad light, to perceive in him a desire to torment! But, if we set aside his undeniable territorialism regarding his inner life, his mastiff's instinct of self-defense even to growling and barking, we're left with a sincere, almost ingenuous enthusiast of market forces, an almost convivial do-gooder, who enjoyed shepherding his fellow creatures towards security and riches. (Come tax time, Donald's life is *not* going to be pretty, he said.) Mr. Keane's anxiety about the future might have been tiresome to the family; to John, it was natural, prudent, appropriate. John would help him if he could. Passionate believer in self-help and mutual aid, unsurpassed justifier of insurance, accumulation and other end goals, he remained in his own peculiar way as kind to human beings as he was to his mother's dog. It was natural that in due course he would advise Domino, who always wondered where the money was in her life. (He easily withstands comparison with his fraternal antipode, one Henry Tyler, whose twenty-thousand-dollar investigative access bond with the Department of Motor Vehicles John had paid half of, out of duty to that same Henry Tyler who when walking down Jones Street, enjoying in equal measure clouds over Ellis Street and fire escape shadows on that classy watering hole the Cinnabar, was approached by a man who said: Yo, brother, can I bum a quarter? I ain't gonna lie to you. It's for a beer. —You can smoke crack with it for all I care, said Tyler, fishing for a promise-keeper. Sure I'll give you a quarter.) John wanted the best for everyone, even for the impudent Donald. Did his pity contain contempt? To be sure, John loved dignity. But his hardness was less a means of intimidation, or even of expression of any sort, than an inescapable constituent of his being.

I recall the afternoon at the office when Mr. Singer grinned, sneered and shrugged at the same time, back-tilting his massive bald head. —You're certainly all business, John, he said. If it weren't for the fact that the clients seem to like you so much, I'd have to consider you—well, almost abrasive—

If they like me, it must be because I'm all business, replied John. After all, we bill them for my time. They don't want to pay me to talk baseball. I had a lawyer once who—

But, you know, sometimes talking a little baseball puts a person at ease. Sometimes you can get them to open up . . .

You mean, like a girl on the first date, said John.

Now, you see, said Mr. Singer with a tiresomely professorial air, you can say that to me, and it's really quite funny. But if I were to say that to Joy, or, God forbid, to Ellen, why I could be sued for sexual harassment. Creating an unsuitable working environment, they'd call it. I'm sure you know what not to say to the client . . .

That's why I keep it all business.

Maybe you're right, John. Maybe you're right. God knows, it's easier to get castrated than you think.

And if John had failed to keep it all business that night at Celia's house, it was because that very day an untoward discovery had caught him up. Celia's allergies to mold had impelled him to have his carpet steam-cleaned. It was one of those half-rare Saturdays when he did not need to be reading briefs or visiting the tall, windowed huddle of downtown, so while Celia, who was an excellent cook, went home and made peach ice cream, meanwhile adding to her latest list the following items:

```
call Jeffrey
return video
draft exclusion to Merino policy
call John—dinner on Monday or not?
delete Sandy from system
create agenda document
database A-2
```

John began moving furniture up against the wall, rather enjoying the work. The bed was on casters. When John rolled it aside, he discovered among the inevitable accruement of dust, lint, a penny, and several of Irene and Celia's hairs, black and brown together, mixed together in the dirt, a sheet of Irene's blue notepaper, which he recognized as instantaneously as he did the handwriting of Irene's which rippled so evenly across it. Longing then to rid himself of all such memory-capabilities fluttering like voracious moths amidst the already moth-eaten curtains of self which hung inside his airless skull, John sat down on the bed with a dully submissive look upon his face, weakened by the immensity of his anger and anguish. His first impulse was to tear up the letter without reading it, but he mastered this desire, believing (though he could not have said so) that communications from the dead are sacred, that they must be accepted with trembling awe. He was afraid. But he also hoped. His wife's suicide would never, could never, be entirely explicable to him, but he understood it well enough to interpret it as a reproach. Had Irene been less desperate on her last day, or perhaps less vindictive, she could have left him with an explanation or a few lines of tactful self-blame, so that John could try more successfully to persuade himself of his own righteousness in the matter. After all, what had she to gain by torturing him after her death—unless, indeed, that motive was the wellspring of her act? This question haunted John. And there had been no message whatsoever. The two policemen who came to take his statement told him that in San Francisco only about one out of every four people who killed themselves left a note; he mustn't feel bad about that aspect of the case, they said. But of course he wondered whether he'd been too lenient with her, or not lenient enough, or simply negligent; and if his hostility later fastened upon his brother, one reason was that Irene had herself been negligent in allowing that hostility no proven act or assertion of hers to cling to. Work, time, Celia, self-discipline, and above all the logic of hopelessness had combined to dull the ache. Now it throbbed so fearfully that for a moment he could almost believe—he *had* to believe—that she who would never rise again now stood before him, calming him and helping him. She would speak to him. She would explain. Sitting there on the stripped bed, he brushed the dust off that blue page and began to read—only to cry out when he saw that it was not addressed to him:

Dear Henry,

I rarely write people, the occasional letter yes, I have written a few, but not enough really. I feel bad that I haven't written more letters in my life. The idea of writing to people strikes me as very pleasant. I write them and think not to send them. Someday I will come across this and wonder why I didn't send it.

No, I will send this one, if only to write you—when you thought I wouldn't. What did you think?

Did you think I would?

Will you write back . . .?

I was feeling pretty unhappy that day at the Korean restaurant. It made me feel better being with you. Thank you for holding my hand.

I feel so strange writing to you. But first letters are usually difficult. No matter what, they sound forced.

It's good that I wrote it, though. I wanted to write you. And I have.

I'll say goodbye now. And goodnight.

IRENE

He was still sitting there half an hour later when the phone rang. He sat listening as on the answering machine Celia's voice asked over and over where he was; they were supposed to leave for OAK HILLS in forty-five minutes . . .

| 386 |

Did something happen to upset you today? Celia asked.

Oh, Brady wants some stupid clause about protecting himself from market saturation. I thought we'd be done months ago. That's like me wanting a clause in a friggin' marriage contract to protect myself from unhappiness . . .

| 387 |

Tell me what I should do, said Irene, playing one of John's computer games.

The Queen or the King? asked John, and he stroked her face.

| 388 |

The plan is to expand *internationally,* was what Brady had actually said in a rambling, tedious message on John's voicemail. (Wherever John went, he had to call his private line at the office for voicemail, check his answering machine at home, read his electronic mail, then return telephone calls in a breezy voice, after which he hung up, and swore, then with an addict's eagerness called new numbers in order to leave contingency messages or, more likely, to get caught up in conversations he didn't care about so that he fidgeted, tapped his foot and silently implored his watchdial until he could hang up once more.) Brady went on: We gotta capitalize on our opportunities, son We gotta launch Feminine Circus outlets in Amsterdam and Tokyo. The American market may get saturated faster than we think, or there may be local legal repercussions, and in fact, John, I want, no, I *demand,* some quick-release option allowing me to pull out at or just before we reach that point . . .

John hadn't moved the bed yet. Irene remained temporarily deniable. He sat down on the leather couch and called Brady. Lighting a cigar, he said: You seem to think I'm a stockbroker or something. I'm just your contract lawyer.

All right, son, Brady said vaguely; John could tell that he was "with someone," as they say, that his message had not been about anything anyhow except making sure that his hired help remained on the ball. John knew Brady's type very very well.

Now, did we talk about executive compensation, John?

Yes we did. Several times.

Good. I want you to structure executive compensation to make it performance-based, because that way we can say screw you to the revenue code. Get the hint? And I presume you know how to get us a full tax deduction for non-qualified stock options . . .

That means that nobody actually gets the use of the income when the option is first granted, John said, stubbing out his cigar, which he had not once placed in his mouth.

That's right, Brady was saying.

Then you'll get your deduction for *ordinary* income above the market value . . .

Yeah, yeah. —Brady cleared his throat. —We've added two new members to the senior management team, John. So they'll be needing to sign off on all this paperwork.

Fine with me, said John. If it takes up more of my time, that's just more of your money. Was there anything else?

Yeah. You heard how to titillate an oscelot?

Oh, brother, said John.

Oscillate her tit a lot. This little girl here in the room just told me . . .

All right, Mr. Brady. You have a good weekend, said John, hanging up.

Sometimes I think that guy's a clod, he said to Celia.

| 389 |

A week before her suicide, John had attempted for the last time to make love to Irene.

As he laid his hand on her naked shoulder, she began murmuring sadly in her sleep. He reached up under her nightgown. Usually she wore clean white cotton underpants to bed, but tonight she was wearing nothing. Stroking her thick, hot pubic hair, John felt the vibrations of desire. His fingers began probing and searching.

Ouch, said Irene, wide-eyed. You're hurting me.

John believed that he had actually been very gentle, but he removed his hand and placed it on her breast instead.

My nipples are sore, Irene told him. Can't you see how big and swollen my breasts are? This pregnancy really hurts me. I feel awful all the time. I don't like to be touched.

All right, said John, slipping an arm around her so that they could simply go back to sleep.

You're hurting my neck, Irene said. Please take your arm away.

He lay on his back all night, desiring his wife and wondering why that was so—probably because he couldn't have her, he decided. At dawn, not long before the alarm was due to go off, he found himself touching Irene again. She opened her eyes wearily when he pulled her legs apart.

You're so selfish, she said. You only think of yourself.

John, attempting to suppress his pain and rage, rolled onto his wife, pulling her thighs wider apart and entering her. The lips of her womb were wet and loose, not the other way which they so often had been, and he had almost convinced himself that she might actually be feeling pleasure when she grimacingly closed her eyes, but after his second or third thrust she said: Would you please hurry up? I really hate this.

John lost his erection. Staring into his wife's face, he knew that he could do nothing. It seemed to him that he had been forlornly wandering across the desert of her loathing for an immeasurably long time. After the shock of the repulsion, and then the sadness and anger of being rejected, he began to feel himself to be falling or departing, in much the same way as when, walking east on California Street your feeling is mainly one of *awayness* until, reaching Gough Street, you find yourself looking down into a deep bowl of building-rows whose far side begins the pale, windowed towers of the financial district, on the horizon of which a flag bares itself to the ruminant clouds. And so John rolled silently off Irene, so bitterly sad that his knees were weak. He could barely walk away. He didn't hate her, nor was he angry anymore; but now that he knew that she would never want to be alone with him, that she had nothing to say to him when she had so much to say to someone else, the remainder of his life became a long dark trap filled with stale darkness, like some ghoul's tunnel from one coffin to another. He was not the ghoul, but the thing in the grave for the ghoul to eat. She was not the ghoul, either. She was no monster. It was only their marriage that was monstrous.

I suppose I should get up and take a shower, he thought.

Well, go ahead, Irene said coarsely. What's wrong now? If you want to fuck me, then fuck me.

Oh, forget it, said John. By the way, I may be back late tonight.

You mean after all that you're just going to leave me like this? Irene said. You mean you don't want to make love?

Well, *you* obviously don't want to, so forget it, John said.

He got up and turned on the shower.

That's not fair, Irene said. I deserve to use the shower first. I have to wash myself off now that you . . .

No, said John, shaking with fury. I'm using the shower first.

He entered the shower and closed the frosted window-door behind him.

You're so selfish, Irene repeated, sitting down naked on the toilet. Then John lowered his head into the stream of hot water, and became blessedly deaf.

| 390 |

Hurry up, Domino was saying. I don't have all morning. I'm tired. You already used up your fifty dollars' worth.

Grunting anxiously, the old man rode her up and down, his flaccid penis hardly even touching her.

All right, Domino said. That's it. I have to go now.

The old man burst into tears.

You're disgusting, Domino said. You have no consideration. You think I enjoy getting sucked and fucked by every stranger? You men are all the same. Now get off me.

The old man obeyed, blubbering.

You know what? said Domino, pulling up her panties. You're really manipulative. Crying like that is what a little kid does. You're a grownup, mister. You had your chance. I did what I was supposed to do. It's not my fault that you're too old and worthless to get it up, so don't come crying to me. That won't cut any ice.

She took her bra off the chair and hooked it back on.

Or do you enjoy getting humiliated? she asked the old man sternly. Is that what this is all about?

The old man hung his head.

Why, you stupid *shit!* laughed Domino. That's what it is! You're just a pussy slave! Say it! Say, *I'm a pussy slave.*

I'm a pussy slave, the old man muttered, his head down.

I suppose you want me to piss in your mouth, but you know what? I don't feel like it, laughed the blonde. You don't even deserve to be my toilet. Get down on your hands and knees.

Eagerly, the old man obeyed.

All right. Now say it. Say *I'm a dog.*

I'm . . . I'm . . .

Hurry up, asshole. I don't have all day.

The old man groaned and whispered, then suddenly screamed with an eagle's triumph as his semen shot out upon the dusty floor.

Domino slapped his shoulder, not unkindly. —Congratulations, sport. Now do I get a tip?

| 391 |

Celia with her toes together leaned enthusiastically over the kitchen counter, saying: Oh, this is *divine*, Mrs. Singer.

Call me Iris, please, urged her hostess.

Iris, you're such a good cook, Celia said.

There's something about adding nutmeg, said Mrs. Singer.

And what a charming china set you have, said Roland's wife, Amanda, who'd seen the china set many times before.

I don't know, disagreed Mrs. Rapp. There's something about adding dishes. After a certain point, you don't really need any more.

The dishes I use the most are my red, white and blue dishes, Celia said hastily.

I suppose I should put the guacamole in the refrigerator, said Amanda. It's been sitting out so long. Iris, if you leave the seeds in, will that really keep it from turning brown?

That's what I'm told.

Iris, you know the *most interesting* things.

Well, I figure if I can clean the floor, I can organize the food.

I use my dollar-ninety-nine dishes because they're so light, said Mrs. Rapp, who was well known for her stinginess, which she preferred to consider frugality.

Observing how the corners of Mrs. Singer's mouth had begun to tremble at this renewed attack, Celia said: Let me cut the cake, Iris.

This dessert is an example to all of us, said Amanda, who had a reputation for venial flattery. It's just so damn *tempting*.

Oh, my God, Iris. That looks *wonderful,* said Mrs. Rapp, suddenly worrying that the other ladies might have considered her rude. You added a touch of chocolate?

Just cocoa. Cocoa *powder,* you now, not the other kind—

Should we bring the silverware over here? said Celia.

In this household, Irene had once tried to carry everyone's scraped, licked plates out to the kitchen, but she had forgotten one, which Mrs. Singer, who loved to punish youthfulness, had added to her armload with a brightly malicious smile like sunlight coming in through glass bricks in a Tenderloin bar. Celia experienced no such difficulties. Was she less youthful? Perhaps (she was certainly too jaded already to be impressed by Berkeley's espresso cafes, whose little round tables were blond wood or black Italian laminate), but the other thing was that Mrs. Singer considered Celia to be exactly suited to John. The episode of Irene of course had been a terrible tragedy. Mrs. Singer would have liked to ask John how he was coping, but did not dare. Gazing into his face at dinner, she'd searched with intense curiosity (like a Tenderloin motorist studying the effect of streetlights upon dark miniskirts) for any traces of grief, but could find nothing exceptional. But then, John was famously unreadable. (Yeah, but it's not even a question of making a decision when something global happens, he was saying. Then all anyone can do is react. —Mr. Rapp nodded bored and uncomprehending agreement.) As for Irene, beneath her pliancy (she gave with every push, just like the green doors of Jonell's Bar swinging back and forth) a certain resistance to the whole universe had become all too obvious. Celia, whom Mrs. Singer was sure that John had carefully chosen, seemed more appropriate: Stick a pin into her, and you'd see her bleed. Only the two Tyler brothers had ever seen Irene's bloody tears. No matter how cruelly Mrs. Singer had slighted the little Korean girl—which she invariably did out of John's sight—she failed to accomplish any effect except a trembling rigidity which she mistakenly believed to be anger rather than humiliated pain. (You don't cook John a decent dinner, do you? said Irene's sister Pammy. —What do you mean? —You always serve him frozen food. If I were John, I'd dump you. —Irene kept quiet. That was Irene, silent, outwardly submissive. She never forgot a grudge.) That was why Mrs. Singer preferred Celia, who was unable to pretend that she had not been hurt. Expressiveness in others enriched Mrs. Singer's confidence in her own interpretations, possibly because a certain fear that she had not accomplished anything in life left her all the more desirous of discovering easy clues to less consequential questions.

Should I put the chocolate sauce in the microwave? said Amanda.

Yes, please, said Mrs. Singer. A minute and forty-five seconds should be about right. Celia, would you tell my husband that he may now open the champagne? And see if John needs anything. I'm very fond of John.

Celia blushed.

How's John's mother? I understand she's very ill now.

Yes, she is. The doctor said to be prepared for the worst.

Oh, I'm so sorry. I'll have to be sure to say something to John.

You know what, Iris? said Celia. I think it might upset John to talk about it. He's very close to his mother.

Everybody knows that, honey, Mrs. Rapp butted in. I don't know *anything*, and even I know that.

Celia went into the dining room, only to find that Mr. Singer had already opened the champagne.

I never break a promise, Brady was saying to John. Why, thirty-one years ago today I was dead drunk and I promised the barkeep I'd go file for a small business license. Well, the next day when I told him I'd done it, he couldn't believe it. But I always keep a promise, see. And by the same token, if you ever lie to me, even once, then it's all over except the crying.

(That man is so *colorful*, Mrs. Rapp said.)

John? said Celia.

Her companion looked up irritably.

Do you want a big piece of cake or a small piece?

Oh, forget it, said John. I'm trying to keep my weight down.

Iris made it, Celia said in a gently monitory tone. You should really have a little bit.

Oh, balls to that, laughed Mr. Singer. If you don't want it, don't eat it.

I'll take a big piece then, said John.

And what about Feminine Circus stock? Mr. Singer was saying like some blank old slot machine player.

Not a high-yield investment, said John. It really doesn't suit my temperament.

I *love* you, kid! laughed Brady, descending into John's face like a dog waddling with its nose down, sniffing for rotten meat. —You'll stand up to anybody! You'll even bite the hand that feeds you. I just got a few more small investors who—

The trouble with small investors is that they're finicky, John said coolly. They'll just say screw you and pull out in an instant.

Isn't that a mixed metaphor, John? said Mr. Singer. Do you pull out when you're making love with Celia over there, or do you finish the job?

You're talking about an oxymoron, not a mixed metaphor, said John in his glory.

Celia made a face and went back to the kitchen.

Everything's fine, she reported. The champagne's already opened.

Oh, who cares about them? said Mrs. Rapp. Those men just sit there and talk. If it wasn't for us, they'd starve to death.

| 392 |

But what precisely is it all about? said Mrs. Rapp.

Entertainment, ma'am, said Brady.

And do you—I mean, do they . . . ?

It's the wild west in there, ma'am. It's every man for himself. And you know what? They seem to like it.

Believing that the conversation was in no danger of becoming genuine, that Mrs. Rapp did not really desire to know, nor Brady to tell, what his establishment actually did, John had convulsed his numb face into an expression of almost malignant boredom, when Mrs. Rapp leaned forward and remarked: They say it's a wicked thing you're doing.

Linda! cried her husband in dismay.

The look of amiability upon Brady's face coarsened, and he said: Ma'am, business is business. I'm not here to justify myself. In fact, ma'am, if I may be so crass, I *bought* you this fine supper which you and Iris prepared. I'm a *client;* I'm keeping you in pocket change, and I don't ask what legal tricks young John here pulled or whether you yank your cleaning lady's hair whenever she misses a cobweb. Ma'am, I run a whorehouse franchise, which according to others' views may or may not be wicked, but at least I'm no hypocrite. At least I—

That's enough, Mr. Rapp interrupted, slamming his fork down on his plate. —Linda, you were indiscreet, and, Jonas, you're getting rude. Isn't it too bad that we—

Too *bad?* laughed Brady. What do I care about *too bad* now the ink is dry? I'll tell you something. Out of all you people, you know the only one I respect? The only one of you I care a rat's ass about is your boy John here. He's the only one of you who's got the guts to come out and say that everyone's shit stinks.

John burst out laughing. And Celia in the kitchen doorway, simultaneously horrified and amused, began to flush almost pleasurably. As much as she loathed Brady, she could not but be proud that he had singled out John above all others.

| 393 |

Were this a Japanese novel, our plot would be enriched by all kinds of family complications: How can lovelorn Younger Sister persuade Eldest Brother-in-Law to endorse her marriage? What to do about Middle Sister, who should have married first? And if this were an eastern European novel from the Cold War era, the searchlight of political tyranny would unfailingly cast each character into superhuman relief, so that Vyshpensky-Buda's fling with Olga might be elevated into the noblest of struggles. Set in Antarctica, this novel might conceivably scrape by without any human characters whatsoever, and I could pad out chapter after chapter with descriptions of the most delicious icebergs. But here in California we must make do with human beings, who comprise as strange a breed as the mumbling cab drivers of Philadelphia. Moreover, those human beings form, deform and dissolve their attachments more or less unmediated by those family and political difficulties which make any success all the more fulfilling: eating pomegrantes might not be half so pleasant, if it weren't so much trouble to pick out the seeds. For just this reason, there were times when Celia could not refrain from wishing that some unknown force, not necessarily God, would intervene to join her to John, or to completely sunder them. She was now thirty-two years old; she had been John's girlfriend, first illicitly, then licitly, ever since she was twenty-nine, and she thought it hardly too much to expect that the uncertainty be concluded by now. Was John simply not serious about her, or did he hold her in active contempt, or did Celia herself fail to muster a certain enthusiasm? She felt as if she were going through mummified forms, helplessly, obtusely. She tried to blame her weariness on the bladder infection which had been annoying her for ten days now. Like a sick, bored child at home with a box of crayons, lying in bed making colorfully wasteful scrawls, Celia composed her latest list:

```
order coffee set from Damask
birthday present for Donald
create job description notebook
make John commit on birth control
give John ultimatum: weekend getaway or not?
draft memo to Grace
thank you to Iris
process fax from Heidi
change return address for Heidi in database
```

She had chosen John originally because she believed she could get nobody else. An affair with a married man, resentful and apprehensive though that left her, at least had the virtue of aiming low enough to avoid certain sorts of disappointment. How could a man who was never there, who planned to have children with another woman, and who most likely would get old with that other woman, then die in her arms, shatter Celia's life? How could she trust him in the first place? He could always break off the affair, to be sure, and indeed there was so high a probability of this happening that Celia refused to let herself stand more than an inch or two in his shadow. He could lie to her, and get or even keep a second mistress. He could be cruel, and had been. Oh, there were so many nasty things that John could do! But he was nothing to her except a generic male medicine for female loneliness. He'd given Irene a diamond, and he gave Celia the glass bauble of temporary companionship. At least she need not feel that she owed him very much.

And then Irene had taken her own life. Celia's arrangement became quite different. In so many situations which we pretend merely to endure, the lightning-flash of sudden change will often reveal to us our own desperate involvement and investment. Celia loved John, or had come to love him, she knew not how or when. She had wandered entirely into his shadow. She trusted him no more than before, but the hope which Irene's permanent absence now gave her proved that John possessed the power to disappoint her after all, that she'd fallen into his keeping.

John could hardly be called gentle, but he did own what gentle natures often lack: namely, the power of steadiness. When he made a promise to Celia, he generally kept it. What if she could render him trustworthy after all? Could she persuade him to promise to be hers less precariously? She was anxious; she wanted children; her previous boyfriends had never been particularly kind, perhaps on account of some particular quality of hers; and so the fact that John was not kind, either, became less of a liability than it might have been for another woman. And in fact he was capable of kindness in his offhand, self-protective way. Call Celia loyal or call her lazy, the truth is that she couldn't bear to look for anyone else.

| 394 |

Your father would like this mug, John said.

Excuse me, said Celia, but how do you know what mug my father would like? He's a specific *person*. He likes specific *things*. He's actually very difficult to shop for.

Whatever, said John, handing the mug to the salesgirl. We'll take this, please.

The infuriating thing was that John was right. Celia's father loved the mug. John often had the talent of knowing others' tastes. He thought that he always had it. Actually, it operated most reliably with people he barely knew. Celia, Irene and Henry had all found his gifts to them to be disappointingly impersonal.

| 395 |

Let's get him this dictionary set, Celia said enthusiastically.

No, said John. I don't want any nephew of mine to turn into an egghead.

| 396 |

John came out of the elevator with a new black-and-gold necktie and his hand in his pocket. The white shirt he wore made the marble columns of the elevator bank look yellow. Rapp and Singer would not arrive for another hour. John had no desire for that emptiest of titles, *The Earliest,* and anyhow he wasn't that; he simply had too much to do to waste his time sleeping. Moreover, it had become apparent from certain haggard words which Celia had let drop the previous night that the power struggle between them was about to resume. John had never gone so far as to assert that thanks to Irene's suicide he was entitled to a vacation from what Californians loved to call "a serious relationship"; there was something so hopeless and helpless about Celia, and yet at the same time he could not bring himself to reject her, and he simply fucked her and went out to dinner with her, determined not to indulge anymore than he was compelled to in that sad vice called thinking. This could last only so long, as he was the first to admit. Once her anxiety had risen beyond a certain threshold, Celia would put a stop to their affair, which had outlived Irene only to exchange sordidness for dreariness.

Good morning, Joy, he said.

The secretary waved. Sitting by the phone, impatient, laughing, so amused by her interlocutor's stupidity, she continued: No, no, no, no. I don't want to do that. Wait. Wait. Wow. —Joy leaned forward very abruptly, stabbing with her finger. She loved to interrupt people to make them look at something. —But if I say it's six-thirty, will I have to drive around the city with people? No, no. It always happens that I've been lucky and have been the last person to be picked up. But you already know. Oh, you *don't* know. All right, all right, all right.

Smiling, she put the phone down and tapped John on his knee.

Let me guess, said John. Vacation.

How did you know?

Because if that were a work-related phone call, you'd get fired.

Joy wrinkled her nose and said: John, why are you always so mean?

Look, said John. You were talking like a client, not like an employee. That's not mean; it's obvious. You were talking the way Brady talks to me.

He does? He doesn't respect you?

I'm actually quite busy now, Joy. What was it that you wanted?

Oh, forget it, said the girl sadly. I—I only . . .

John sighed and looked at his watch. —You know, Joy, your slip is showing. And another thing. Red is not your color. People would treat you better if you stopped wearing red. Now what was it?

Just go away, John, would you?

Although his manner remained the same, John had begun to feel uneasy. His psychic machinery busily transformed impatience into guilt. He neither believed that he had done anything wrong; nor did he recognize his own proclivity for reducing himself to vulnerability. Like most human beings, he categorized others as elect, worthless or menacing. Joy by virtue of her subordinate relation and what he perceived as her mediocrity could never be one of the elect. When he thought of her at all, it was as a marginally useful cipher. But a sense that he might have gone too far now urged him to reassign Joy, however temporarily, to the menacing category. He felt obliged to placate her. And so he said: Let me buy you a drink this evening, Joy. How about five-thirty? But I only have half an hour.

Just then Roland came by, very agitated, and said: They'll see what they can do to us, mark my words.

Who's being fired? said John, forgetting all about Joy.

Did you hear? Over at Synergetics, everybody who hired Ellen's being fired. They fired Rich, and then they fired Mark, and then they fired Jackie Grazier . . . And so, let me get this straight. They never called you?

No, said John. But I got a call on my voicemail this morning.

Did you mean it? said Joy.

What? John said. Oh, sure. What did I say, five-fifteen? No, it's going to have to be five-thirty. I can't make it a second before then. Roland, tell me about it later. Grazier deserved whatever he got. Okay, now I need to put the Ibarra file to bed . . .

He had promised to call Celia at six. But as the drinks flowed, Joy was grabbing his knee again so happily and John, who ordinarily was square, smooth, clean and quiet like the lobby of one of those bank towers on California Street, found himself enjoying not Joy herself but his powers of attraction over her.

They were in the Tenderloin, fifteen minutes from the office by cab, at a downscale place Joy had heard about called the Wonderbar. Joy said that it was hip or cool or one of those words that she used, but all John cared to note about it was that two barstools down from them, a man was talking to himself. —Goddamnit, the man said. I can't wash off that Mark of Cain. Fuck me fuck me God.

Sir, said Loreena the barmaid, would you please keep your voice down?

Fuck me fuck me God.

Sir, said Loreena, you're having a schizophrenic episode. Tell those little green men in your head to take the night off.

John grimaced.

So do you think that the Polk Street look's starting to invade the Tenderloin? said Joy quickly.

What do you mean?

I don't know, I just . . . Look at that woman. Don't you think she's beautiful?

She's not my type, said John.

That's Chocolate, laughed Loreena, leaning over the bar, hungry for tips. She's a prostitute, honey. Disposable babies is what she makes. She gives them all away. In four years she's had four. Or is it eight? Can you believe it? I think somebody ought to take a shotgun to her.

So where was your vacation again? said John.

Cancun, said Joy. But my boyfriend just dropped me. Now I have nobody to go with. And I paid for the tickets and everything. So I was just thinking I'd meet somebody and, you know, try to have some fun.

Can I get you another round? said Loreena.

Okay, Joy said quickly. John frowned and looked at his watch.

Having already gone shopping where Mason Street was shinily striped with cable car tracks, Celia now lay on the sofa, waiting for John's promised telephone call, in each unrequited minute seeing further evidence that his regard for her was dying, but nonetheless or perhaps consequently needing him so acutely that her hand crawled to the back of the lefthand kitchen drawer where she had stashed a half-pack of cigarettes on the third and last occasion that she had quit, just in case there might be some emergency which justified nicotine. She freely admitted that she was what they called "an addictive personality." But that didn't shame or worry her, because she had observed, or perhaps merely convinced herself, that every person she had ever gotten to know was possessed by at least one need whose divine purpose it was to counter virtue. Celia was often bored or angry when she was with John, and sometimes jealous, but, with occasional bitter exceptions, these feelings comforted her rather than otherwise. Her grandfather, before they took his license away, used to drive with his seat belt off, because the shrill concern for him expressed by the car alarm "kept him company," as he put it. Celia for her part needed something to shout out the silence of herself, of the apprehensiveness of her lonesome incompletion, of the life she sometimes thought worse than death (because she had no familiarity with death). It often seemed to her that she was as sievelike, punched through, as the skyscrapers of the financial district with its thousands of dark square windows honeycombing them so that they bled from these wounds, or sweated from these pores, perpetually losing their essence. They towered, wearisomely existing, hollowed out, living like a coral reef inhabited by pale office organisms. —Where were her cigarettes? There, behind the worn-out can opener, the packing tape, the book of now underpowered twenty-cent stamps, the instruction manual for her food processor. The cigarettes weren't even crushed. (She thought she heard the click of the answering machine, but it was nothing.) Now for her lighter—oh, she'd been a good girl; she'd thrown it out. Matches for the stove. Close cover before proceeding any further. The cigarette smoke became happiness as soon as she breathed. She lay down on the sofa, with an ashtray in easy reach on the floor, clicked the remote control, and waited for the television to speak to her.

It kept me out of jail, kept me out of trouble, said a cute kid in a red uniform, peering sincerely into Celia's face. He was a television manifestation. —No one's encouraging me to accept chastity, he said. No one's pressuring me. I'm just doing it because it's the right thing to do. I just want to thank everybody.

A long cylinder of ash trembled at the end of Celia's cigarette.

The phone rang.

Hello, I'd like to speak with Miss Celia Caro, said an uncertain girl, obviously a telephone solicitor just starting out. I'd like to tell you a little about our new—

I'm waiting for a really important phone call, Celia said. And I'm really tired of people trying to sell me things over the phone.

Is this Miss Celia Caro?

Yes, it is, said Celia, gritting her teeth.

Dope-sucking, home-poisoning, home-wrecking sex machines are being manufactured even as we speak, the television said.

Well, Miss Caro, if I could, I'd like to just briefly tell you—

I said I'm really not interested, and I have a really important phone call that I'm waiting for.

Could I call back at another time?

Please don't, Celia said. I mean, I hate to be rude, but I'm just really really tired of—

The solicitor hung up on her.

We have to increase visible security in the streets, the TV was saying. We need a security guard at every corner. And above all we need to teach those young girls the street smart techniques to avoid being targeted. We got the fire marshal on our side.

Well, thank you, Mr. Lovinson, replied the TV. We've just been speaking with Mr. Manuel Lovinson of the controversial new Network Against Public Vice, known to most of us as "Brady's Boys." And tonight we have Mr. Brady himself to answer a few questions.

The TV went on talking to itself. Celia grunted, got up, went to the kitchen, brought matches and the rest of the pack, just as she had known she would do. Then she reached for her little yellow pad and wrote:

```
mask face
complete taxes
med. shelf for kitchen $69
all things in boxes
adopt kitten?
cancel account
```

The phone rang. Celia was sure that it wasn't John.

Hello, I'd like to speak with Miss Celia Caro, said the same uncertain telephone salesgirl, and this time Celia hung up on her.

She lit another cigarette.

The phone rang.

Hello? she said wearily.

Guess who? said John.

Hey, babe! cried Celia, trying to be happy.

You want me to come over?

Where are you?

I'll be downstairs in ten minutes, he said, hanging up.

In eight minutes the buzzer rang. She muted the television.

He looked tired and harrassed. He took his coat off and she hung it up for him. She went to the kitchen and poured them each a glass of wine, then gave him his and sat down on the sofa. He came and sat beside her.

Smoking again, he said, looking at the ashtray.

Celia said nothing, but her lips tightened bitterly. Lonely or not, this was hardly what she took pleasure in, to wait half the evening for this half-stranger to come and nag her.

So, she said. How's work?

Oh, Rapp's being a sonofabitch, and Singer's making retirement noises. I'm sick of both of them, he said, raising the glass to his lips. His hand trembled.

How about with you? he said.

I've got two projects that I'm working on, and Sunday I've got a corporate brunch, she said. Today I was really jammin', like they say. On top of everything else I had to get some some last minut e-mail out to a client in Thailand, and then I went to see this woman whom I'm helping with data entry and when I got back home, just after I'd heated up a big plate of food, the data entry woman called and—

She saw that as usual he was not listening.

You want to go see that crime documentary tomorrow night? she said, clenching the glass.

What do I want to see that movie for? laughed John. That movie's all about reality. It's depressing. I'm more interested in trying to get away from reality.

Celia nodded miserably.

It's like reading *The Diary of Anne Frank,* he went on, rubbing it in. It's a really good book, they say, a great book. That's just why I don't want to read it. Not even the unexpurgated edition where she's talking about her period or something.

Did your mother make you read it? asked Celia with sudden understanding.

Leave my mother out of this.

He gulped the rest of his wine.

She picked up the remote control and was just about to turn on the television with the volume up loud when he said in an almost terrified voice: Celia . . .

She looked at him. Her heart began to pound again.

Celia, he said, I need you, Celia.

With a sense of sad and cruel triumph, she understood that at this moment—and probably for this moment only—she had license to torment him as much as she pleased. Just as one can tell when men in neckties and shiny shoes stop in front of monuments and reach into shoulderbags that they will pull out cameras which operate with a quiet and elegant click, so Celia recognized John's purpose, and the mechanisms of it, and the rules for operating those mechanisms. She was not a vindictive woman, but she had met more pleasant men than John in her life, and it infuriated her that through some chemical accident she loved him. She knew all too well that he did not love her and never would, that he could not love anyone (with the exception of his mother), that he had made Irene miserable—but, that being said, he was as well disposed toward her as he could be.

Smiling, she un-muted the television.

Celia, did you hear what I said?

She increased the volume by two iterations.

Celia, he said.

This is grotesque, she replied happily.

| 397 |

He drummed his fingers and muttered: *Klexter, klokan, kladd, kludd, kligrapp* . . .

What's that? said Celia.

Oh, I don't know. Just a kind of jingle. A friend of mine—well, actually, one of my clients—is always saying it, and now it's stuck in my head.

| 398 |

He had not lied. At that moment he'd truly needed Celia. Why? Because he'd come very close to being unfaithful to her with Joy. He was guilty, so he needed her to forgive him. Whenever he looked at Joy's sad dog eyes after that, he thought about the Wonderbar.

The next time he went to the Wonderbar, he went without Joy. That was when he met Domino.

| 399 |

The blonde, studying John with as much attention as she usually paid to her crack pipe, saw a suit, a perfect necktie, a haircut and well-shined shoes. Through the avarice of courtship shining more brightly than the lemon-yellow socks of the Korean barmaid at Jonell's she began to sense something familiar, yet displaced, like the upside-down reflections of bottles on a Tenderloin bar's mirrored ceiling, glowing transparent multicolored stalactites. She sensed his brother Henry.

Don't get me wrong, she said in a trembling voice. I have a legitimate job. I work nine to five downtown.

John, who until then had never thought otherwise, gazed at her in a surprise which also reflected amazement at his own presence in this place. What was he doing? He had so many obligations at the office, and then Celia . . .

You need lime in that, he said. Loreena! Bring Domino some lime.

Why, you're a real gentleman, said the blonde.

My oh my, Loreena muttered. Aren't we hoity-toity around here.

Shut the *fuck* up! screamed Domino, and John looked on in astonishment.

It made no sense, his being here. Since he was here, he might as well stay for another twenty minutes, but how was it all explicable? The blonde attracted him; he didn't know why. Just as a lawyer's briefcase is almost by definition too small for all his paperwork, so John's narrow strip of active mentality could not contain more than a few of his longings. It would be better if after today he never returned to the Wonderbar. He sat grinning and relaxed, only his fingers unconsciously fooling with each other.

Are you married? she whispered.

My wife died.

Are you in a relationship?

Yes, John said.

You're a hetaerist, aren't you? said Domino. That's one word I'll never forget. You don't know what that means, do you, scum? It means *one who thinks that women are common property.*

Are you trying to impress me? People who recite words don't impress me. Anyone can do that.

She slapped him hard on the cheek and, strangely, this stinging sensation felt delightful.

This is so strange, he muttered, entirely disoriented.

It was just some basic flatbacking as far as Domino was concerned. Within half an hour she'd lured him into a twelve-dollar trick pad on Ellis Street and had drawn him down on top of her crying: Come *on*, come *on!* —She was trying to figure out how to steal his wallet. He for his part was mesmerized by her scars and bruises like Coptic crosses, especially by the long white eye-shaped bullet scar. As he caressed the blonde's long, stockinged body, he felt himself carried farther and farther away from everything familiar, like a little child lost at sundown. Instead of the smell of the Tenderloin, about him rose an incongruous movie theater smell of stale popcorn and breath; silhouettes, illuminated around the edges, ran into place during the previews, while a blood-red sun rose upon the big screen. It was all the blonde's magic.

When you pay, it's a whole different thing, she explained. The man fantasizes because he's paying the money. He's *paying* for the feeling that he's getting power.

John gazed at her, fascinated. Perhaps there was an element of helplessness in his fascination, but it would not be too much to say that never before in his entire life had he felt so thrillingly engrossed and enmeshed, like a lost tourist, unable to speak Japanese, wandering through the swarming Shinjuku district of Tokyo. Of course work, hobbies and other licit and illicit love affairs had called forth his best harmonizing instinct; everything within a given contract, session, year or world which was supposed to match up, did, because John set out to make matters so, and the proceedings, calculations, and downright artistry which achieved that result filled him with pleasure, to be sure. But Domino was no model airplane whose thousand plastic parts he carefully and at times tediously sanded, glued and painted until she was all put together, accomplished; rather, she was something superior and exterior to himself, which seized hold of him and dragged him into a delicious blindness.

So pay me, she said, sliding her warm hand up his leg. Then you can come play inside my cage.

Domino seized him, her arms as remorseless as the huge white stripes horizontal and vertical of downtown skyscrapers in the rain when the pavement is as grey as rain. She closed her arms around him.

So you see, all of you have different experiences in this cage, Domino whispered, gaping her long thighs apart.

Oh, whatever, said John.

Are you paying attention to what I said, asshole? Because if you're not I might just have to slap you again.

John shuddered with pleasure.

You need somebody like me, he said to her.

You're pretty fuckin' opinionated, said the blonde.

John Tyler is a unique animal, said John complacently. John Tyler likes to speak his mind.

Tyler? Are you Henry Tyler's brother?

Oh, this is *all* I need, said John, losing his erection. Has Hank been porking you, too?

Hell, no. He porks Maj.

Who's that?

Just some skanky little nigger bitch. All right, John, now let's cut to the chase, because I don't have all night. You wanna fuck me or not?

Fine, said John. But first I want to know whether Hank—

He's the kind who goes through the garbage, gets a handwritten scrap of paper with someone's phone number on it, calls up and say I'm a friend of so-and-so. He's a real sleaze. We've already wasted enough brain cells on him. So. You gotta pay me a hundred dollars up front, she said, watching him with a menacingly greedy smile.

Silently, John removed a crisp hundred dollar bill from his wallet and gave it to her. Unable to believe in her luck, the blonde kept thinking: I've got to get into the sonofabitch's pocket. I've got to. I've just go to.

Okay, John, you can get undressed, but you have to hurry up. You got a condom on you? Otherwise I'm gonna have to charge you five more dollars.

Grinning, John pulled a condom out of his wallet and slapped it down in the bed. Then he began to unbuckle his trousers.

You have to know this, Domino said steadily. If I hurt you, don't ever hit me back. John bit his lip and nodded.

Domino smirked for a moment. Then she slapped his face until his ears rang.

I'm the *Queen,* she said. Say it.

You're the Queen.

That's right, you dumb fuck. Say it again.

You're the Queen.

Again.

You're the Queen.

That'll work. Am I the Queen?

Yeah . . .

That's right. And you know something? If I don't fuck you better than anyone else, how can I be your Queen? said Domino very reasonably. Now put me to the test.

Pulling her urine-stinking panties down around her left ankle, she rolled the condom onto John's penis most expertly, opened her legs, and lay there looking at her watch.

Hurry up, she said. I told you I don't have all night.

Eagerly John entered her. She kept slapping his face as he thrust. He climaxed almost instantly.

All right, lover boy, she said, resigned to not snagging his wallet this time. You came, so get out.

John studied his mirror image carefully to make sure that Domino had left no marks. All the very long narrow dark doorways now seemed to him to take on the shapes of slinking women.

| 400 |

About a week after these events, Celia presented him with a gift, although it was not his birthday or any holiday. —I just wanted to, she said with an unreadable smile. John was silent. But when he opened the box and saw within it the octagonal silvery pen with its knurling just above the tapering cone from which the point grew, and the counterpoint knurling on the other side of the pen just above the clip; when he saw how the light shone on its uppermost facet so that the metal became a warm white mirror; when, above all, he closed his hand about the instrument and lifted it out of its long black box, enjoying the feel and weight of solid stainless steel, he felt a sensation of pleasure so powerful as almost to convert the expression of his face into dreaminess. He kept turning the pen round and round in his fingers, watching the band of mirror-brightness altering against the darker smoothness of the pen's seven other faces; and his joy in the ownership, that is, of the lifelong, unlimited control, of this beautiful thing, compelled him to draw a long slow spiral on the sheet of paper, with the ink-track unrolling beneath his hand, miraculously even and dark. This was his own power which he'd brought forth from the box. Rotating the pen between his fingers once again, he perceived that where the cap was fitted against the body, the corner of each facet-edge had been cut away in V-shaped notches which lined up just so between the two pieces to form diamond shapes.

What Celia did not know was that the affair with Domino was likewise something to be removed from a box of secret ownership to be admired, treasured.

| 401 |

She walked by herself through the glowing green jewel of Union Square. Then she let herself be drawn to the long glowing rows of jewel-pews at the Shreve Company, whose marble-pillared interior enhanced the ambiance of a church. She closed her eyes, pretending that John had bought her an emerald ring. She wanted a Hawaiian honeymoon. How were the beaches there? she'd asked her friend Heidi, who went often with her rich lesbian lover. Heidi said that the big island was much, much nicer than Maui. Heidi said that the eastern coast of the island was almost unbelievable. Celia already had three brochures hidden away—no need to show them to John just yet. In fact, when she imagined her ring and her honeymoon, it did not seem to matter very much whether John were even there. That was how she protected herself against any foreseeable disappointment. She did not feel restless anymore. When she thought of Irene, it was with utter indifference; that woman couldn't hurt her anymore. And John with his difficulties and failures seemed so safely immune from any harm that Celia *or* Irene could do, like one of those immense stone figures in front of the Pacific Stock Exchange, that she almost felt that she could treat him any way she liked.

On Geary and Mason, a businessman in radiantly blue sunglasses wheeled two suitcases behind him; maybe he'd just come from the airport. Celia wandered on. Her lunch hour had almost ended.

Gracie's American Brasserie was serving roasted lavender chicken with garlic mashed potatoes. The grilled portabella mushroom *au poivre* was adequate, John had said. Last time he'd taken her there, she'd tried it, but couldn't remember how it tasted. He had ordered the ginger-glazed baby back ribs with the two-cabbage cole slaw.

| 402 |

The tall man was standing outside the Wonderbar when John approached, because Sapphire had not yet been insulted and so the debacle with Heavyset had not yet occurred.
—Got any questions? he said.

Nope, said John, a little intimidated, a little soft from office life as he fully admitted, but determined not to show it.

Nice shoes you got, said the tall man.

Thanks, said John, pushing past him.

'Scuse me, said the tall man, but you lookin' for someone or just lookin'?

Some people don't have time to just look, John told him scornfully. Some people don't have time to answer a lot of nosy questions.

Then you lookin' for somebody, huh?

Shrugging, John entered the bar. Domino wasn't there yet. He sat on a scarred old barstool and ordered a gin and tonic.

I *know* who you're looking for, Loreena said archly.

Congratulations, John said.

Last night she and I got a little drunk. In this business it happens.

John had not yet formulated a reply when the tall man came in and sat beside him. Loreena said: Heavyset won't like your being in here. He's due any minute. You'd better get out.

Fuck Heavyset, said the tall man. He's the only guy I know got eighty-sixed from his own bar.

You know what? said Loreena.

What, bitch?

You got eighty-sixed from this bar, too, Justin, and you just called me a bitch, and if you care to feast your eyes you'll see I'm holding this baseball bat and I'm going to bring it down on your head if you don't *git.*

Gimme a drink, the tall man whined. John looked away.

I'm going to call the police, said Loreena.

Someday somebody gonna take you down, bitch, said the tall man. — He turned to John. —You gonna buy me a drink?

Don't feel obligated, honey, Loreena said. He's not dangerous. I've got him under control. Justin, get out and stop bothering my customers.

Had Loreena not implied that the tall man might be making John nervous, John would have let him be eighty-sixed. But he was very sensitive to issues of courage. Indeed, his willingness to face up to and sometimes to escalate unpleasant situations had contributed to his effectiveness as a lawyer. Whenever he and Celia went to the Mission for lunch on those sunny weekends, they worried a little that the meter maid might punish John's daringly illegal parking jobs on Lexington or another such alley, in front of some slate-blue or white old Victorian house, John parallel parking perfectly on the first try, then opening the door for Celia, ready to protect her from the Chicano gangsters with crossed-dagger or teardrop tattoos who lounged on the sidewalk; and for much the same reasons the tall man hawked drugs in hotel hallways instead of on the street; yet both of them took their chances if they thought that would get them somewhere fast. And so adventurous John said to the tall man: If I buy you a beer, will you apologize to Loreena and go sit over there so I can think?

Sure, boss, said the tall man with a white grin. Us plantation darkies like nothin' better than 'pologizin'. Hey, bitch, sorry I called you a bitch.

Oh, fuck off, said Loreena. Why do I even bother.

I'm sorry, the tall man whined with sarcastic obsequiousness. I really need a drink. If I be good, will y'all let me be a house slave?

Shut up, John said.

If I shut up will you buy me a drink?

I'll call the police, said Loreena. Both men saw she didn't mean it.

The tall man moved two stools down and said: Loreena, I'll have me a tequila sunrise.

Fine, said John.

Thank you, said the tall man while Loreena mixed and poured. Now lemme tell you something.

I thought the deal was that you wouldn't tell me anything, said John. Just for once, can't you shut your fat mouth? I don't give a damn about you. Period. Okay?

You lookin' for pussy, mister?

Oh, please, said Loreena, amused in spite of herself.

The tall man leaned back in his stool with a lordly air and said: Me, I'd rather jerk off than scratch the open sore between some bitch's legs. If I can't bring her somewhere, go out with her, show her off, it's not worth it. Say, why don't you take me out to lunch?

I've got some private business with a friend, said John as curtly as he could.

That'll be four-fifty, sweetie, said Loreena. John gave her a five.

What kind of business? said the tall man.

Private business.

Say, white boy—

Hey! shrilled Loreena. You say one word to my customers and you're *out* of here! They're good people.

Right on! Right on, right on! an old drunk shouted.

Say, I'd sure like to know what your private business is. You gonna deliver him a couple of keys?*

Something like that. Now shut up or I'll throw this drink in your face.

The tall man rose, opened his mouth wide, and uttered a cawing, sneering laugh which showed his epiglottis and all his teeth. Then he advanced on John, who leaped to his feet.

Gentlemen, *gentlemen!* cried Loreena, rushing between them with the baseball bat upraised. The tall man stalked back to his seat.

You know what? said John. This man is threatening me. Either you get him out of here or I'm going out. This is no way to run a business.

Loreena picked up the phone. —This time I mean it, Justin. Get out.

Cursing, the tall man swilled his drink. He spat one ice cube on the floor and went out crunching another between his teeth.

The sights you see when you don't have a gun! laughed Loreena. John refused to look at her.

He sat there waiting for Domino for ten more minutes. Then he left also.

| 403 |

Back again, said Loreena.

Yeah, said John, clearing his throat.

She just went out on a date. She'll be back in fifteen minutes, I'd say, or an hour at the absolute latest.

Fine.

I hope you mean to take good care of her. She's a keeper.

John said nothing.

Oh, we love her, Loreena went on. We take care of her. We leave her alone. She's still beautiful.

Hey, Domino loves me! shouted the drunk two barstools away.

---

*Kilos (of marijuana).

What the fuck, another man sneered. Domino kicks your ass.

Another round, Bentley? Loreena asked the sneerer. That whitehaired gentleman nodded and leaned back with a happy smile on his face because now that Louis Armstrong was singing on the jukebox and Loreena would serve him, he was momentarily King.

A black woman whom John did not know was Bernadette vomited on the floor. — Sorry, Loreena, she said. 'Cause I drank that Tom Collins on top of my pills I'm almost ready to pass out . . .

John drank two beers. Then through the swinging double doors came Domino.

| 404 |

Domino raised the candle (dark crimson because dark wax burns hotter) and told the john to be quiet. Looking him up and down, she smiled, then abruptly tilted the candle so that a molten ball of wax fell glowingly out. The john screamed.

Oh, do shut up, said Domino. It's not that bad.

The man shut up.

Roll over on your stomach, said Domino. Head to the right. Close your eyes.

The box opened. Then she lovingly stroked the john's back and bottom. She placed her palm on his buttock, then patted it, then spanked it. Then suddenly he felt a stinging blow. —What was it? A hairbrush, a paddle, a cord? —Another thud— harder, then harder. Another. One on his back which made him grunt. He knew that Domino was happy then, although he couldn't see her (he wasn't allowed to).

She said: How are you feeling?

Okay.

Do you want more?

Up to you.

Ask me for more.

Please give me more.

Thud, thud, slap in the flesh.

Do you want more?

Up to you, John repeated. The more tightly he closed his eyes, the more vividly he saw Celia's face.

Ask me for more.

Please give me more, he groaned out.

Thud, thud, slap in the flesh. The pain pooled all over him like the merging streams of hot wax on his belly, like a trail of crimson blood. The john looked into her happy exalted face as the wax came down, and he looked again later when she peeled the congealed wax off his pubic hair. After a while he began to feel the sting all over. Timidly, he squeezed her naked thigh to share the pain with her. She told him to leave her alone.

When they were finished, he tipped her. Domino grinned and slapped him on the back. —You're a real sport, honey, she said.

Where are you staying?

Oh, with this old black man, Domino lied heartily. Every night he gets drunk and violent. Every day he has prostitutes coming over, which offends me. He's no damn good.

You want me to break his legs? said John, thrilled with his own boldness.

Oh, he's not that bad. Okay, I gotta go. Anytime you need me, just whistle four times.

| 405 |

What did John want, but success? His vocation, although to most of us it seems as stale and tortuous as some medieval allegory, offered slow, strenuous accomplishments. Other souls preferred what gets disparagingly called "instant gratification"—that is, happiness sufficiently present to count on, like the joy crouching inside a perfect crystal of crack cocaine lying in the palm of a whore's hand, ready to be combusted into pleasure all for her. It is related of Saint Ignatius that when his Jesuits spoke of tomorrow or next year, he'd cry in astonishment: What? You can be certain that God will allow you to live so long? —This too is the crack whore's philosophy, and the strategem of the vultures who sent Tyler the form letter which advised: The CASH you NEED is in your CAR. Tap into your autmobile equity TODAY. BORROW and REPAY! Introductory rate: 6.25%. Tyler wanted cash; of course he did. And Irene—ah, what did Irene want? Maybe I'll start swimming, Mom, she'd said to Mrs. Tyler, who shook her head as she replied: Irene, honey, you shouldn't take up swimming unless you have the kind of hair that you can do up yourself. —But Irene wanted freedom. She wanted not to be told what to do. —As for Dan Smooth, he envisoned Paradise as a hot Italian beach with long jetties and a breakwater, a hotel room with metal blinds halfway up a hill of olive trees, vineyard-terraces twisting on and on. Smooth needed this for his stage set, but center stage was the place where cobalt blue ocean expressed itself in a frothy white line, then became an olive-brown kingdom of wet sand. There the young children squatted and built their sandcastles. Hexagonal beach umbrellas, striped like candy, cooled candied, taffyed flesh which lived and quivered on the sand. Here his eye could freely hunt among the dimpled thighs of old age; youth had a certain color—how could he describe it? He'd never stop revering it. Pubescent breasts and prepubescent breasts and the slender ribcages of children, these comprised his spiritual food. A little pinkish-brown girl, too young for breast-buds, too young not to be naked-chested, licked an ice cream cone. Now she was playing with the bottom of her bathing trunks. Smooth, nostrils flaring, withstood the craving to lean forward in his beach chair. He waited. Suddenly the child pulled her bathing trunks midway down her thighs—right there amidst the beach-umbrellaed crowd! —displaying her creamy bikini zone, and as she turned toward him, evidently perceiving his gaze, he glimpsed her long narrow mound, as white as new photographic paper, and the slit-lips in the middle, so soft and white like slices of mushrooms in a perfect salad. Meanwhile a matchstick-legged boy fiddled with the back pockets of his swimsuit.

And Domino, what did she want? She resembled a purring cat in heat rubbing up against a human being, circling, mewing, hoping for the impossible.

| 406 |

Check it out! cried Chocolate with a wink.

Check *what* out? said John wearily.

Check it out, check it out, check it out! You blowjobbin' it or what?

Not with you. I'm looking for Domino.

Oh, that bitch! She'll give you venereal warts. I guarantee it. But I'm clean. I'm *Chocolate* clean. I'm the Queen. I can suck a baseball bat through thirty-five feet of garden hose.

Where is she?

Where you from?

None of your business. Where is she?

Well, la-di-*da*. If you won't tell me that, at least tell me where you were born. I'm into astrology.

Sacramento.

Sac's real different. San Francisco and Oakland, they're real party towns, huh? In Sacramento, when they do party, they get violent. I don't like violence so much. Leave that to the younger generation. I always say—

Where is she?

In there. Asshole.

Domino sat listlessly at the Wonderbar reading a science fiction novel. Her hair was greying and she had bruises on her thighs.

What's up? said John.

Oh, just killing time.

It's already dead.

Excuse me? Are you making fun of me?

Oh, for God's sake, said John in disgust.

In the doorway old Tenderloin George was crying out: Shoeshine? Wanna shine?

Don't give him anything, said Domino angrily. He always comes when I'm trying to pick up dates and he sits on the fire hydrant and plays with himself. He's a pervert.

Give me a smile, baby, John said.

My face is crooked, Domino replied in a low voice. I always smile crooked, because two years ago some fourteen-year-old kids jumped me and hit me in the mouth with a two-by-four and broke my teeth and I didn't get any of them reset right because I . . . oh, fuck it. Hey, mister, why don't you buy me a car?

I'm not mister. I'm John.

I want a Land Rover. Forty-five grand's the invoice price.

Invoice prices are not exactly what they pay for the car, John said learnedly.

Oh, fuck off.

Look, Domino. I know dealers. I can get you a much better price than that.

How much better?

Maybe thirty-two. I'm looking for a new car myself. The E class you can't buy any more cheaply, because it's really hot.

So. You're going to give me thirty-two grand for a Land Rover or not? I don't have time to fuck around.

That's a piece of shit car anyway. You'll have to change everything.

Are you married?

You already asked me that.

So sue me. Are you?

Not anymore.

Oh, so she left you, huh? Serves you right, you tightass prick. You wanna get married again? You wanna marry me, John?

Marrying you would be like buying a cheap Mercedes, John said. You're buying a name, so why buy at all when you're just buying some generic heap of shit right off the assembly line?

You're too fuckin' much, the blonde laughed. I like you. You're honest. You're hard-boiled. Know who you remind me of?

Clark Gable.

Shit. You remind me of Henry.

What?

You gonna buy me a car?

What about me reminds you of Hank?

It's gotta happen for me, John, Domino whispered. It's just got to. I need a car to get away and to—oh, fuck, I feel sick. I gotta puke . . .

| 407 |

You're sure friendly with that guy, said the tall man sarcastically.

Are you accusing me of being a hypocrite?

Dom, I don't give a goddamn what you are. But he insulted me. Someday I'm gonna break his whitebread ass.

Being nice with the customers like that is just good business, the blonde said defensively. It's not false. It's just exhausting.

And yet, strange to say, Domino kept seeing John, and not merely for money. She said there was a difference between being used and using (although all her other customers would have been amazed that there was any such distinction between themselves and John).

Sometimes he paged her, and she called him back. His voice sounded quite tender on the phone. She wondered if he were holding his dick in his hand.

Let's say that Domino actually did care for John in a way. (She thought him realistic.) That didn't matter. He could neither predict nor control her. His predicament sickened him even though he knew that he didn't love her in the least; the fascination she cast on him might well have been the result less of her own person or soul than of her actions. No one had ever before slapped John in that vicious yet teasing way which he found to be so desperately erotic. The blonde's regular customers did not return to her solely to be gaffled and humiliated; she had about her at times a playful quality which allowed them to feel, however briefly, that they were her playmates, carefree like rich vacationers, because they could laugh when she laughed as she pissed on their faces. Tyler saw only the sadness and frailty in her; John saw the dominatrix. Being dominated by her, he could not hope to understand her more than a worshiper understands his God. She was fitful, terrible, dangerous. John was afraid of her. His work would soon begin to suffer if he weren't careful. Celia would suspect something. —Actually, Celia did not, because his guilt drove him to be kinder and tenderer than ever before, so that she smiled upon him with an innocent joy which increased his guilt almost to the point of agony. But John could compartmentalize, as they say of organization men; he went on with everything just as before, and it certainly never struck him that the blonde might be approaching her own sea-change.

She wanted to be loved—how she wanted that! And she could never believe it when someone loved her. The Queen had loved her genuinely, but her affection hurt almost as much as cruelty, because since no possible attestation could ever suffice, Domino suspected and sometimes rejected the Queen's caresses, which must someday turn out to be mocking, expedient, sadistic. Her heart ached with anxiety that the Queen might be speaking against her. One night at this time she dreamed that she and Henry Tyler stood facing each other across an open grave, and she was drunk and cried out: I know now she loved me. I can believe that, 'cause she's gone. And I—

She wanted love. And she *believed* that she wanted status, but would she have really been any happier had she metamorphosed into one of those high-class women who while away afternoons and evenings in vast hotel lobbies whose recessed ceiling-bulbs make up dully regular constellations far outdazzled by the brass handles of the sliding doors through which money just might come walking, with its hands in the pockets of its silk suit?

She trusted Dan Smooth because he was her ruthless friend whose interests coincided with hers, and because his patronizing ways allowed her to convince herself that she'd "seen through him" to the mockery, which was not so very bad and thus did not alienate her. She herself, however, never reasoned any of this out.

I have a secret, she said to him.

No secrets from your old Uncle Dan! laughed the pedophile, wagging his fingers as if she'd been naughty. You have *designs,* you see. You have buried treasures, and I don't just mean your hot little—

Oh, cut it out, said Domino. My secret is that I'm topping* Henry Tyler's brother, and he's a stinking rich lawyer connected to that Brady man who runs the vigs . . .

Ah, very good! And what's your plan? You can cause Brady some headaches, or you can betray our Queen, or both, or neither. Or maybe you can find out from John if Henry really screwed Irene, and somehow use that to make Maj drop him. If this were a novel, I'd scream *here comes the suspense!* But somehow it doesn't feel too suspenseful. I suppose I know you too well . . .

Look. I'm not a bad person. I'm not ungrateful. I just need a chance to better myself, and if you can't understand that, then go fuck yourself.

Smooth grinned. He loved the blonde. He'd seen her cry silently at romantic movies, her lower lip trembling as she wiped her eyes with her forefinger; then she sat straight up with her jaw clenched, obviously hoping that no one had seen. At disaster movies she wrung her hands, her mouth wide open while the movie heroine wept over her dead lover.

| 408 |

May I tell him who's calling, please? said the receptionist.

Oh, he knows me, said Tyler, with a wink at the Queen. She gazed back sadly.

Sir, you'll have to give me your name and the place you're calling from, said the receptionist. Otherwise I can't put you through.

Tell him it's his brother, Tyler said wearily.

And where are you calling from?

Could you please tell him that his brother is on the line?

And your name, sir?

---

*A top is an S & M dominant. A bottom is a submissive.

Henry, said Tyler, defeated.

Just a moment.

He leaned against the wall, waiting. The Queen stroked his cheek.

Sir, he says to tell you that he's busy right now. Is there any message?

He was silent for a moment, smelling the humiliation which soiled him like vomit.

—Tell him I'll call again later, he said.

He hung up slowly.

No go, huh? said the Queen.

No go.

Don't be sad, baby. It's gonna take some time. That's all.

He said: It's the same as when I visit Irene at the cemetery. I know that I can never ever reach her, not ever again.

Gun up now. C'mere. C'mere. He'll phone you tonight. I know it.

| 409 |

You want me to talk to him? said Smooth. The Queen told me—

Oh, forget it. After all, he's my own brother.

They stood and waited.

You see, Henry, we both believe her. We both take her on faith.

Yeah.

She said tonight, so—

But I still don't get quite what you're doing here.

Maj wants you to try harder with me, Henry. Maj wants us to be *bosom buddies*.

Yeah, well, go be bosom buddies with Domino. Sometimes you're just so much work . . .

You mean when you're depressed.

Yeah.

You mean when you're horny for Coreen.

Irene.

Got your goat, didn't I? Ha, ha! Works every time! You know there's no *malice* in me, don't you, Henry? You know I'm not all *evil* and *envious* like you.

Oh, leave me alone.

Nice million-dollar white man place you got here.

Don't you ever do anything but play with people?

But this isn't about playing, Henry. This is really quite serious, you see. This is about saving our Queen. Because if your brother can convince Brady to lay off, for Domino's sake—

I told you it won't work.

How do you know that?

Because I know John and I know Brady, all right?

Then let *me* try. Put me on the line when it rings. I mean, what the *heck*. You don't care what *John* thinks, now, do you, Henry?

Tyler clenched his fists.

I've got you coming and going, don't I? Just the same way Domino's got your brother. I've got you by the *balls*. And you know what, Henry? I'm one of those perverts who sometimes likes to *squeeze* . . .

Even Maj said it wouldn't work.

No she did *not*. She said we could try if we liked. I think it makes her happy, that we're trying to save her . . .

Good, said Tyler abruptly.

You mind if I get personal? Smooth whispered. You mind if I tell you about my niece?

You already told me.

I'll tell you how it was.

You already told me how it was.

Since we have time to kill, I'll tell you how it was, said Smooth. You know how those Asians love giving really nice fruit for presents? Go over to your Chinese friend's house for dinner, and for dessert there'll be lots of perfect pears—you know, high quality, the succulent kind.

Yeah, I know.

Well, of *course* you know, Henry. You were *with* an Asian girl. Your brother's girl.

Oh, go to hell.

And sometimes they have these little tangerines. You peel the skin off, and then there are juicy little wedges—well, segments I suppose you'd call them. And this girl, when I pulled her little underpants down . . .

The phone rang.

| 410 |

So you're dirtying this part of my life, too, said John. Tell me something. Have you fucked her? *Have you fucked her?*

Who? sneered Tyler. Domino—or Irene?

Sitting near him on the kitchen floor, Dan Smooth contorted himself in a thousand silent grimaces of laughter, wriggling and twitching, shivering and twitching, rolling his eyes and bulging out his cheeks, so that Tyler, repulsed and terrified, was reminded once again that *he was Dan Smooth* with his illictness and his defiance. He was treating John the way that Smooth always treated him, the way he loathed to be treated.

I'm sorry, John, he said into the telephone. No, I never slept with Domino. And I won't. I'm her friend, John, that's all. And, you know, she's to be pitied because—

How dare you say that to me? shouted John.

I think she wants to be a part of your world. She wishes that she could be your kind of person, and dress like you, eat like you, live like you. I mean, I don't know what your relationship is, but—

What do you want?

Has Domino ever told you about our little family down here?

Oh, so you finally found a family for yourself, did you? Old Hank got religion. As for your own—

Brady's Boys are putting Domino at risk, John. And they're threatening a very good woman who's helped Domino a lot and who—

A *whore*, you mean, said John. A filthy whore.

That's right.

Oh, I see it now. And you're plugging this whore and you know better than to ask me for any favors, so you—

She's been good to Domino, John.

She's good to her. Does she fuck her? Is this some—

Do you really want to know?

Fine. So you want me to call up Brady and say exactly what?

(This is all so *dreary!* whispered Dan Smooth in delight. Tyler felt unspeakably nauseated.)

I don't know what you should say. Brady's pretty hard to appeal to, as I recall. But if you . . .

I could set Domino up. I'd be happy to give her a start. Anytime she wants to get out of that sleazy world of yours I can—

John, she *can't.* She won't. That's what she is. That's—

Don't you dare tell me who she is.

She—

I said don't you dare tell me who she is. Anyhow, continued John with his usual shrewdness, you don't care about helping Domino, do you? You want to take the heat off that filthy whore you're plugging.

Let me ask you something. How do you feel about a man who on the one hand hires you to write contracts for his whorehouse and on the other—

So you're saying he's a hypocrite. Well, what about you? *You* know what I mean, Hank. Jonas Brady is an amazing man. Jonas Brady is maybe even a great man, and I *will not* have you—

Seeing Smooth making frantic backpedalling signals there on the kitchen floor, Tyler swallowed his bile and said: Can I ask you to think about it? Talk to Domino—

Don't tell us what to talk about.

Well, will you please at least think about it?

John hung up.

| 411 |

That was when Tyler called himself aside and explained to himself what his self admitted—namely, that Irene and John's marriage had never been as hellish as he for his own convenience had pretended. He remembered one Fourth of July in San Francisco when housetops flickered in and out of fog as if on lightning-fire, and then the occasional green and blue flower of fireworks blossomed over the city, then cast down seeds and embers into the white darkness while Irene lay under a blanket on the sofa next to her husband, watching romantic thriller-videos which accompanied themselves with soft piano music, and she slowly got paler and sleepier until her eyes closed and her long pale fingers gripped the cushion while John frowned at the video, half-bored but unwilling to turn it off before he'd learned how the story turned out—and maybe, just maybe, he'd wished to avoid disturbing his dreaming wife. Fireworks pounded like Tyler's heart.

| 412 |

Mr. Rapp, smiling piratically gold-toothed, licked his upper lip with an almost indescribably delicate motion of his tapering tongue.

Gibbon's always good for one-liners, said Mr. Rapp. I read him every night before I go to sleep. Gibbon's been on my night-table for thirty years. I *love* that man. I've never finished his book, and I never will. John, how often do you read Gibbon?

Corruption is the most infallible symptom of constitutional liberty, John quoted sourly. He added: I hate Gibbon.

Too good! shrieked Mr. Rapp in high glee. John can quote Gibbon. Do it again, John, please!

Does this have anything to do with my job, Mr. Rapp? If it doesn't, I'd rather not quote Gibbon. The guy was an egghead. My mother force-fed him to me.

John, I'd like to ask you something, said Mr. Rapp, and this does have something to do with your job. John, are you listening?

I'm right here, Mr. Rapp.

John, the question I want to ask you is this: *Are you an egghead?*

You asked me that once before.

And what did you say?

That I was your performing animal.

Oh yes. That was really quite naughty of you, John—almost cruel. Well, I'll ask it in a different way. Are you yourself, in spite of all your boorish precautions, actually, deep down, a *soulful fellow?* Do you actually *know things?* Are you hiding your light under a bushel-basket, John?

Having a soul is not what you pay me for, Mr. Rapp. Excuse me, but I need to get back to that immigration brief.

Do you have a soul or not, John?

Mr. Rapp, you yourself know that this kind of talk is not appropriate in the work-place, even if it's your workplace. Sure I have a soul. Sure I'm an egghead. Now may I please get back to work?

Singer! cried Mr. Rapp, ringing the other senior partner's buzzer. John's finally admitted that he's an egghead!

Then lower his salary, said Mr. Singer's bored voice. Or else raise it.

Mr. Rapp was looking at John with an expression which somehow reminded him of something which Irene had once been saying in a low, earnest plaintive voice, in it already the knowledge that she would not be able to convince John of whatever it was, her hand flittering sadly through the air. He couldn't remember the details. Irene was looking at him. He gritted his teeth.

| 413 |

The bay was very calm and almost indigo that weekend, with the occasional steep white triangle of a sail between Coit Tower and the islands. John and Domino could see the Marin headlands more distinctly than usual; the water became milky near those far shores, ringing them with the haze of adulation.

You told me you know Hank, said John.

You mean Henry? That *sonofabitch!* chuckled Domino. So you and Henry really truly came out of the same hole? I mean, you have such class, and that scumbag—

John laughed delightedly, then was ashamed. He hated Hank, but still, Hank was his brother. It was fitting and good that Domino had derogated Hank—this time. But she shouldn't do it too often. That privilege must be reserved for John.

He said: He tells me that the heat's really on you down there.

Down where? drawled the blonde, widening her eyes with pretended innocence as she pulled John's hand between her legs.

Look, he said. If there's some friend you care about who's being—

You mean Maj? Stinking old Maj? That's Henry's new hole. So *that's* why he's come crying to you. I'm saying it's a dog eat dog world. (Oh, sorry, I forgot your wife was Korean. They eat dogs, don't they?) Let Maj cut her own goddamned cake, you hear what I'm saying?

Fine. So you don't care. Well, that makes it easy.

Domino was bitterly sad and ashamed of the words she had just uttered. But it felt so unnatural, so positively *dangerous,* for her to admit that she cared about any other human being! And she could not forget how Maj had georgia'd her right before the entire family, using that subhuman little dildo of hers, Sapphire—although she also had to admit that that had been the best orgasm she'd ever had. She didn't hold a grudge, but . . . but Maj had *humiliated* her! Moreover, as soon as John had finished with her, she would be transformed back again into just another pale woman checking her makeup in the side mirror of somebody's parked car, shivering, desperate to follow any stranger into excrement-smeared alleys. She scowled, and a tear rolled down her cheek.

What's the problem now? said John, who hated crying women.

Nothing. Forget it, said the blonde, knowing that there was still time to step back across the moral divide, knowing likewise that she was incapable of so doing.

She knew that her omission was no crime against Maj. John had offered not to save everyone in the royal family, but only to protect Domino herself and perhaps Maj. She knew Maj well enough to be sure that she would never leave the others, for after all she had nowhere to be sent to; she already was and always would be saved. Maj was her mother, her only love, her dear—rotten old nigger Maj!

Let's talk about you and me, baby, she said.

| 414 |

Have *we* the right to accuse Domino of failing her Queen? Peter denied Christ three times before cockcrow, and still got to be gatekeeper of Heaven. Canaanites, who must live incomparably harsher lives—for *His* self-sacrifice lasted only a few thirsty bloody hours, while theirs runs forever—surely ought to be exempt from moral crucifixion for similar acts. Moreover, she did *not* betray her Queen through any positive act, and she was no weaker in her heart than the tall man, say, or Chocolate, or Strawberry . . .

| 415 |

Smooth tried to talk with the blonde about the matter, but she swore up and down that she'd made John speak to Brady himself. —John's just a prick, she said. I can twist any man's prick around my little finger; I don't care how hard it is. But what Bady's going to do about it, I have no fuckin' idea. That's not my department, okay?

Smooth didn't believe her. He knew her too well.

Daytimes I work at Costco now, she said wearily to John. That pays my expenses. But in the night times I have to do this, to pay Maj's expenses. She's no good. I don't even want to talk about it or I'm going to cry.

That night the Queen gazed into Domino's heart, which was as filled with colors as the reflections of many strip clubs' neon signs in a single fresh puddle on new black asphalt, and the Queen said: I love you, Dom.

I love you, *too!* shrieked Domino, sticking her tongue in the Queen's ear.

| 416 |

Maj?

What?

I learned something about Henry.

From who?

His brother.

And?

It's something bad.

Dom, forget it. Don't be a snitch. You know I love Henry.

| 417 |

At an office party, John heard a woman say: I want to divest. I want somebody to buy us. Then we can relax. Our stock hasn't gone public yet, but soon it will.

John thought: You sound like one of the Capp Street girls.

| 418 |

There is nothing quite like putting on a clean, well-starched dress shirt to make a man feel good. John stood frowning pleasantly at his reflection in the patchily steamed bathroom mirror, wondering whether or not to shave again, while Celia adjusted his tie for him. —Let her do it, he thought to himself. I can do it better, but it makes her happy. (Besides, he liked her tender hands against his throat.)

They were going to the opera. John had never entirely made up his mind whether dress circle were the best value, all things being weighed in proportion, but this year he'd chosen the very same tier. Irene had never liked opera. She'd gone uncomplainingly throughout their short marriage—in part, he supposed, to be dutiful, in part to show off her clothes. Celia, on the other hand, loved opera—or else she loved John, which practically speaking was the same thing. They sat side by side high up in the steep rows of brass-number-plated red velvet seats, gazing down on the golden curtain in the gilded arch. Leonine reliefs yawned upon the wall. The other operagoers filed in, spectacles in hand or on their noses, covering their mouths, crying: Nice to *see* you! —which meant: Nice for you to see me! —People kept boiling up from the hidden corridors. Bemusedly, Celia gazed down on their bald heads and grey heads, with the occasional lush young crown of hair to set the others off. Here came Mr. Rapp in a very dark navy blazer; he raised his nose and craned about until he spotted John, whose responsive wave half-resembled the Roman salute. (Why did I feel like going to sleep? Mr. Rapp would afterward query himself. I think it must be the dinner. And I didn't like the way . . . —You didn't like what? his wife said. —Well, I'm not sure it affected me.) Beaming ushers read tickets and pointed. Celia herself looked as stunning as any of the Asian girls who in lowcut black dresses were accompanied by alert, cleancut husbands with binoculars.

John had his lightweight Zeisses, which he hardly ever used, his eyesight being as good as any test pilot's, but it gave him pleasure to let Celia look through them. She would actually have preferred the less practical but more ornate opera glasses which accompanied the skinny old ladies in pearl necklaces; they raised them high to peer at the redecorated ceiling, whose illuminated rosettes crawled reflected in the lenses like upside-down images of daisy-heads in a pond.

When do you think they'll ease your workload? Celia was saying.

When Singer has a stroke, said John impatiently. Can we talk about something else?

The gong struck for the first, then the second time. It became dark. Celia gazed down into the orchestra pit's lights and shining horns. At least she always knew where she stood with John. She gripped John's hand, her head on his shoulder.

| 419 |

Between them there lay many a conversation from Irene's epoch, a time in which Celia had simultaneously suffered greater misery (or allowed herself a greater consciousness of the same old misery) and also been able to command more respect from John, because he and she both knew that as a married man he was wronging two women, and therefore had better restrain his curtness. That long ago night when Tyler after taking Irene out for dinner at Kabuki Cho had chanced upon his brother holding Celia's hand, John had been saying: Are you tired?

No, Celia sighed. Just depressed. I feel so awful.

Do you want to sleep? John said, bringing his face aggressively close to hers, as if she might run away.

I want to sleep with you, Celia said dully. And you want to sleep with me. Or maybe you don't want to sleep with me.

I want to sleep with you, John said wearily. But we can't tonight.

We can't ever. Never ever.

That's not true, he said, his mouth tightening.

It feels like never ever.

I understand, John said, wondering: Is this worth it? How much of this crap will I have to put up with?

I don't think you do know how I feel, said Celia. I do believe you think you know.

Well, that's a start, said John.

Would it make any difference if I threw a tantrum? she rasped, revelling in her pain and his anger. And would Irene—

Let's leave Irene out of this, John exploded.

Celia lowered her face, and her long hair occluded it, clinging to her tear-sodden cheeks. John took her hand.

It was at that moment that Tyler had driven by.

Now that Irene had removed herself from a position which had necessarily obstructed Celia's aspirations, Celia found herself proportionally closer to John, but only in the sense that she had fallen into his orbit, becoming Irene's successor planetoid. Casting his harsh radiance upon her, he remained on his own cosmic trajectory while she whirled helplessly round him. (As for Tyler, he was a lonely comet who scorched himself as he rushed far away from John and Celia's solar system. Emerging from the Chinatown evening with the gold pores of skyscrapers oozing moist light on the edge of the financial district, he drove past Tokai Bank on Sacramento Street, crossing the decorative grillwork in the dull orange door-light of another house of Mammon, and plumbed the tired old bricks and clean desolation of commercial night until he'd reached Bush Street. No John. No Brady. The bright and open demarcation of Market Street lay ahead. He crossed it, and returned to the Mission district where he felt more like himself.) Meanwhile, Celia's question hung in space, written in letters of stardust: What was the right thing? The only way to know was for her to envision John's behavior should she draw still closer to him, or should she leave him. And because she did not have a great deal of faith in herself, both of these hypothetical images buzzed and wavered blurrily before her.

| 420 |

And even now she's costing me, John had said to her that morning. There's a greens fee, just like at the golf course. They have to keep mowing the grass over her bones, I guess, and there's no friggin' deductible for dead people on my insurance . . .

Did you love her so very much? said Celia. Please tell me what you're feeling for once.

Oh, I don't know, he sighed. Sometimes I get so angry. Irene had her points . . .

Celia, who would have trusted John much less had he always sung the dead woman's praises, nevertheless felt a truth-seeking impulse powerful enough to overcome her fear of becoming dislikeable. She said: Who do you love more right now—Irene or me?

You, he said without any hesitation.

Well, that's the right answer, anyway. What made you marry her?

She was a very good wife in so many ways, he said. She was loving, or tried to be; she did things my way; she was pretty . . .

| 421 |

During the overture John's attention drifted, as it always did. For no particular reason he found himself remembering a hot outdoor Vietnamese wedding in San Jose, the vows stuttered and inaudible. Two Vietnamese violinists in gangster sunglasses uncertainly played, while the soloist wiped sweat from her wide brown forehead and sang "Ave Maria" so sweetly that it brought a lump to his throat. The bride, faintly reading a poem about love, wept. Yellowjackets settled on people's sweating shoulders, and hot dry grass stood all around. Whose wedding had that been? For a long time he couldn't recall. Had Irene been there? Yes, and she was out of sorts. Why, that had been Irene's best friend's wedding! He remembered it now . . . Irene had been a bridesmaid. She'd looked so beautiful that John had been very proud of her.

Celia squeezed his hand. And then suddenly, with a nauseating feeling of dread, he found himself thinking of Domino.

| 422 |

At the intermission, those spectators who didn't need to relieve themselves sat stretching or reading their programs or gazing at each other through their spectacles.

Well, what did you think? said Celia, stretching her ankles (her mirror-black shoes melting light like butter).

It's fine, said John. At least they gave us decent seats. I hate being too close to the aisle. Once when I brought Mom here they tried to pull that one on me. I made quite a scene, I'll tell you.

Do you think it's good? Celia said hesitantly.

What do you mean, do I think it's good? It's Puccini, that's all.

John.

What?

John, she said, taking a deep breath, um, John, you would never lie to me about anything important, would you?

And John turned red, shamed almost to the point of vomiting, seeing before his eyes his crooked, grungy brother Hank, who lied through his teeth and who at this very moment was probably lurching down some Tenderloin alleyway muttering: Irene, irridium, lady, palladium, *ladium* . . .

Oh, you're mad, whispered Celia, entirely misconstruing his complexion. John, I made you mad. Oh, John, I'm so, so sorry.

John, unable for the moment to speak, scarcely able to breathe, longed to *get the thing done,* but what thing it was he couldn't have said—make a confession to Celia, break off with her, break off with Domino . . . He was afraid of both women as he had never been afraid of Irene.

John, Celia was saying. Please forget what I said, John.

The lights dimmed until the red carpet and the dark suits of the orchestra members were lost. The conductor came striding out, as the audience applauded and Celia gazed apprehensively at the side of John's rigid face. And John, almost panic-stricken, longed to rush down to the Wonderbar to see Domino. He knew that it would be absurd to see her without a reason. He *must* want to break it off, he *must* . . . Surely that was what his heart-thud meant.

| 423 |

Now all the well-dressed people had gone inside, and only newspapers twitched on the long steps. A gentle old man in a suit stood at the summit of the red carpet, while a partridge-plump photographer, also in a suit, took his portrait. The opera had long since begun, and at first Tyler thought that he could faintly hear it—a soprano, no overture—but then he saw a shopping bag man, a fat man, a sad dirty man, a homeless man who was sitting there with his suitcase opened, and within the suitcase an old gramaphone was playing for his sadness. Was it battery powered? Now Tyler could hear the sob-like scratches in the woman's song. She died, and then the homeless one began to play another record. This time a man's voice was singing: *Beautiful woman, my desire.*

They don't know how to train 'em anymore, the homeless man said. Beverly Sills, now, she was the last one who was really trained to sing.

Now Tyler saw that the phonograph was crank-operated. —It's kind of fun, the man said.

Then it was midnight, and John and Celia were driving home. (Bowing his head and grimacing, his tie flying ahead of his chest, Mr. Rapp descended the steps.) John made a quip, and Celia pretended to be amused, although beneath her bright smile lurked an almost terrifying hostility. A black boy was getting handcuffed in a doorway, the back of his submissive neck shaved and sad. He stared into the wall, so that no one would see the shame upon his face.

| 424 |

Night. The clock had just disgorged that extra hour which it had swallowed in the spring. So now it got dark much earlier. Roland came running out of the office tower, his black shoes gleaming with goldness from all the riches of window-light that fell upon them, and followed the crosswalk between white lines, then ran into his wife's car. On John's floor the lights were very bright. Tyler was cold. A number 15 bus went by, displaying its cargo of standees as if it were a mobile aquarium. A man swung a square briefcase, leather-padded, which emitted palely poisonous gleams from its brass fittings. The man stepped into the street, and the gleams vanished.

Hello, Domino, said Tyler.

Look, said the blonde. I've got to go make money. Let's move things along.

Same to you, darling. Where's the Queen?

Downstairs. She's interrogating again. Does that make you scared? You wanna get interrogated?

By you? With which mouth?

Laughing, she threw a mock punch at him and shouted: I *love* you, you old misogynist!

A misogynist is somebody who's really good at eating pussy, right?

Oh, get lost. Always talking about pussy. You know what you and your brother have in common? You're pussy-whipped pussy *addicts*.

So how *is* John these days?

Still hates you—ha-ha-ha! Hey, did you hear the one about the hooker with a glass eye? This one's really rich. I forget who told it to me. Okay, so, there's this hooker with a glass eye, see, and the john comes up to her and says he doesn't have enough money to stick her, so *she* says: Never mind, honey, I'll keep an *eye* out for you any time! Ha, ha, ha! Ain't that rich? I heard that one in jail, from some girl named—oh, what the *fuck's* her name?

Yeah, that's a good one, all right.

And guess what else John said? I think John is really well connected.

Well, sure he is. He's connected to you.

You pervert! He says, the whole entire Tenderloin's gonna be *sterilized*. And then they're gonna do Capp Street. And then it'll all be over.

How does that make you feel?

Scared, she said frankly.

And what can he do about it?

With a choking, coughing laugh she said: I'm still bargaining for that. I . . . Anyhow, Maj keeps insisting it's the end, so why even—

Well, at least we don't have to repent of our sins, because we're Canaanites. And John has his good side. I'm sure he'll take care of you. And, you know, you and John have a lot in common, too. You're both in business; you both like to get straight to the point . . .

| 425 |

But to what extent would John *really* take care of her? Having never slept with any Canaanites before, he had expected his affair with Domino to be easy and pleasant. (Henry Tyler had begun beclouded by a similar illusion regarding the false Irene.) The seduction of Celia had proceeded smoothly, just as soft round lights go on like excited robot breasts over those elevators in banks; and likewise the courtship of the true Irene— or so it all seemed in his recollection. But finding out how bitter and anxious Domino was made *him* anxious. Sour tyrant, rapacious thief, unwashed liar, she ruled him so rigorously that whenever he was away from her, as when he drove beneath blue clouds up the rainy hill to Washington Street, the degree of his submission amazed him, troubling his steadfastness toward all that he had previously believed.

She insisted, for instance, that John make love to her three or four times every night they were together. When he didn't or couldn't, she'd fly into a rage. And the sex also had to occur in a very particular and laborious way involving manual, oral and penile stimulation. But then she could assert the frequency of their intercourse as proof that she withheld nothing from him, that he was using her solely for his own pleasure.

That'll work, she always said when he paid her, but somehow it never did.

From time to time, either wearied of her own imprecations or else (what was more likely) caught up in bitter brooding, she'd fall silent, so that for a moment or two his eyes could close. But just as he was about to be swallowed by sleep's narrow gorge, terror would strike a shocking blow upon his breastbone: —sometimes it was her actual touch, grasping and pinching and slapping to prevent his escape into unconsciousness; sometimes it was strange words; often it was simply a presence which suddenly invaded him; his eyes would fly open; he'd emit a strangled groan, and see her still sitting at the foot of the bed, gazing at the wall, her long, greying hair flowing down her back. He waited for her to turn around and commence upon him again.

| 426 |

Now you've pissed away an opportunity, Domino, and I don't *like* that, Smooth was saying. An opportunity, you see, to save our Queen.

God save the Queen.

I'll talk with him myself.

Whatever.

Does he turn you on?

Excuse me?

Does he make your pussy wet? Does his presence kind of *loosen up* your insides?

I'll give you fifteen minutes in there and that's it. My business is my business.

Oh, so you're worried I might steal him away?

Smooth, John's not going to give you the time of day.

Hmm, the pedophile said. If I tell him what color your insides are, maybe I'll get his interest.

Fuck you.

You don't like me, do you? Smooth whined. I've done you so many favors, I've put in good words for you, and now it comes out that you have a heart of brass.

I don't have time, the blonde contemptuously replied, and she went her ass-wiggling, heel-clacking way down Jones Street.

Smooth entered the Wonderbar, where John was sitting, anxiously and morosely staring at his watch. —Hi there, he said. I'm a friend of a friend. May I buy you a beer?

A friend of *which* friend? said John.

Let's spell it backward, John, because that's more *fun.* Spelled backward, her name is *Onimod.* I'll bet that's in the Bible somewhere, don't you think? If not, maybe it's one of those monsters in the Book of Mormon, which is one of my favorite books because some Mormons are *polygamous.*

What do you want?

I'm here to help you out. Well, actually I'm here to help Domino out, but isn't that sort of the same thing? I mean, you're in love, so I understand.

I've met insects like you before, said John. What's your name, fellow? I like to know the name of the fellow who's bothering me.

Strangely enough, Smooth, ordinarily more invincible in his defiance than Henry Tyler himself, felt daunted by John's abrasive confidence. Perhaps he should have stuck to his subject, although I myself, as a believer in the Queen and her prophecies, remain sure that his actions would have come to nothing in any event. Instead, Smooth made the mistake of trying in the face of this strong current of hostile contempt to swim at an angle, as it were, but because he was a little drunk and because he was limited and damaged like anybody else, the only topic of small talk he could conceive of just then was *children,* a category which his obsessions had long polished into the same *fascinating legitimacy* as Celia's mind had done with *stoneware dishes.* Sincerely seeking to entertain John, in order to ingratiate himself and then buy the favor of the Queen's safety, Smooth began to relate a tale he'd heard not long since when he and Tyler were at the Inn Justice bar on Bryant Street, drinking with a quasi-colleague from the public defender's office. The public defender said: So this one cop goes into a massage parlor in the Tenderloin, and he fancies a prostitute, I forget whether the chick was Laotian or Thai or Vietnamese; anyhow, he snatched her right out of there. This is kidnapping, right? This is no five- or ten-year case. This is a *life* case. All right. So he drags her out, actually starts doing her in front of some tourists, then thinks better of it and drags her somewhere else, then makes her orally copulate him. Now here comes the interesting part. The evidence, well—you'll like this, Smooth—there was semen all over the place, because I guess she didn't want to swallow, so she, well, anyhow, they found the guy's semen on her. Did a DNA match. It was definitely his. Now here comes the cha-cha-cha. Guy said for his defense: No way in the world I'm gonna make anybody in the world orally copulate me, because my father used to force me to watch my sister orally copulate *him* when I was a kid! And the sister, who's also a cop, takes her place on the witness stand and confirms it. This is like, well, it's talk show justice! The cop did get convicted, but he only got six years. If it had been one of *our* clients . . . Kind of a unique defense, don't you think? — Smooth chortled and chortled, thinking about the cop's defense made absurd by the semen itself but rendered somehow amazingly believable by the sister's tears; and he was trying to explain this to John, who cut him short, saying: You sure know how to be a sleazy asshole. I'll say that much for you. I don't care whether you're a friend of Domino's or not. Get out of here. —And he balled up his fists, which even the tall man had never done to Smooth, and Smooth left the Wonderbar in apprehensive haste, he couldn't have said exactly why . . .

| 427 |

It was Saturday evening. The worst of the traffic had already drained from the financial district, rendering John's driving pleasurable as he descended the hill at Bush and Grant with Celia in the passenger seat, her shoulder belt and lap belt both safely in-clicked, and John felt richer and more luxurious than silk because they were about to try Camponegro's Grill, whose pesto-lobster gnocchi came highly recommended by both Rapps and both Singers; and to John the expectation of excellent food in a refined atmosphere, no matter to what degree reality might compromise that expectation, always spellbound him into celebratory thoughts and sensations. The next two hours would probably be the pinnacle of his weekend (he couldn't speak for Celia, of course). Upon them both beamed the yellow sun-star on the blue of the Triton Hotel sign.

Then his heart slammed so nauseatingly that it almost burst. On the corner, in a silver miniskirt, stood Domino, grinning at all the passing cars.

Don't let her see me, he prayed.

But she saw, and her gaze was like light coming through many upturned silvery shot-glasses.

Hey! she yelled. *Hey, John!*

The light would not change.

The blonde came striding menacingly toward the car as if she were about to pound on the windshield with her nightmare claws, and Celia sat there gaping. She was almost upon them now, smiling crazy and evil like a monster who would never forgive him for being her prey. Suddenly John realized that he had always known that it would end like this, with his being exposed and humiliated in front of Celia as he sat paralyzed just as in one of his nightmares of Irene's avenging specter.

The light changed.

John, you fucker! screamed Domino, thumping on the side of the car with her fist as he pulled away.

She knows you, Celia said quietly.

For God's sake. Just let me—

You're all pale and sweaty, John. Tell me what this is about.

I—oh, balls.

John. Who is she, John?

She's . . .

Is she a hooker, John? She looks like a hooker.

Yes she is.

How did she know your name? Have you been sleeping with hookers?

John gripped the steering wheel very tightly, his face red.

What's her name, John?

I don't know her real name. Her street name's Domino.

Domino. I see. And you've been having sex with her.

I did sleep with her, Ceel. But that was before I met you.

How many times?

Knowing that if he pretended he'd had intercourse with Domino only once, the fact that Domino knew his name would strike Celia as very peculiar, to say the least, John thought very rapidly and said: A number of times. Several times. I don't remember how many.

And you say you did this before you were with me?

Yes, that's what I said.

When was the last time? Were you already cheating on Irene with this Domino before you started having an affair with me? You never told me anything about Domino before.

I never wanted to think about it.

So when was the last time?

Three years ago, he muttered.

And you started seeing me two and a half years ago, but you never told me about Domino until now. Is there anybody else you're not telling me about?

Look, can we just—

Is there?

No.

So. You're now telling me that you had sex several times with this Domino, but it happened three years ago and then you never saw her again. And yet she remembers you by sight. How can you explain that?

I paid her a lot of money, said John, thinking fast.

Now, that's possible, said Celia in the same cool tone, but he could tell that he had finally said something plausible and that she wished to believe him. —John, did you always use a condom with her?

Always, said John truthfully.

And you're not seeing her now?

No.

You swear to me?

I swear.

Celia sighed and stroked his hand on the steering wheel. —I believe you. I'm sorry.

John bit his lip. This hurt the worst of all—that he had just betrayed Celia again with his lies, and been believed.

| 428 |

God, her eyes! he muttered.

| 429 |

John?

What?

I want to ask you something.

What?

About Domino.

What about her? he said in an exasperated voice. He foresaw many, many questions, like a line of tweedy smokers' elbows upon some long walnut bar.

Was she . . .

Was she *what?*

Did she do anything I don't do?

I'll tell you something, Ceel. My brother Hank doesn't have very progressive views about women, you know. And one time he said to me: *They're all pink on the inside.*

That's disgusting.

Yeah.

No, I mean it. That's really disgusting. That offends me.

Well, to be honest with you, I had a feeling as soon as you raised the subject of Domino that you were angling to get offended.

You're so uncaring sometimes.

I admit it. But be honest, Ceel. Isn't it convenient sometimes to be with somebody who doesn't care?

As he said this, of course, he was thinking about Irene. Like most of us, he loved to generalize. He'd been married to a Korean woman, so he believed he understood the Korean character: the utter unthinking self-sacrifice for the family, the stoic attitude which drove them to immense lengths; combined with a secret resentment, even hostility, toward the object of that self-sacrifice; and an indifference bordering on arrogance toward anyone outside the bloodline. Had someone told him that not all Koreans were exactly this way, John would have shrugged. Ultimately, he didn't care that much if he reified and oversimplified on his own time. The idea of analyzing Irene herself would have caused him such pain as to be out of the question.

Does your brother care? Celia was inquiring in an angry voice. About anything? I mean, to say something like that, it—well, I'd think he must be a very angry person, or . . .

He's angry at me, I guess.

Why?

Because I got Irene and he didn't. Of course, now that I think about it, if I had to say who got her, I mean really *got* her—

Okay, but is it only about Irene?

I thought we were talking about Domino.

That's one of your tricks.

What do you mean, my *tricks?*

I think that you kind of push people away and kind of keep yourself safe through the way you—

Oh, so we're not talking about Domino or Hank. We're really talking about me. I'm just going to shut up until I know what we're really talking about here. Maybe you'll change the subject on me again . . .

Does he have something against your life?

Do *you?*

John!

Oh, fine. Whatever. He thinks I've sold out and turned corporate and plastic or something like that. He inherited the artistic temperament from Mom, except he's not refined like her. He thinks it's artistic just to sit around spending money you don't have and pissing your life away.

Is it really selling out if you really start thinking about the world instead of only thinking about yourself? I mean, you're out there in the business world. You're providing a service—

Who are you trying to defend me from, little Ceel? he said with an ironic smile. We're on the same side, for Christ's friggin' sake.

John, you *know* my deepest fear is being abandoned.

Now what the hell does that have to do with anything? Hank's not here and if I can have my way he'll never be. Anyway, could we talk about something else?

I think that either he's afraid or he doesn't want to hurt your feelings or he knows you want closure or . . . He's so wounded, I don't know.

Thank you for the consultation, Dr. Freud. You never even met the sonofabitch—

What on earth do you mean? I've met him twice—once at that party at Lowensohn's, and then that night when—

Yeah, when he was stalking us. You remember? We were kissing, and then suddenly he was shining his headlights on us . . .

I don't know what he's about. He seems so . . . Maybe he just—maybe he's looking for the real thing.

What real thing? There is no real thing.

I just want the real thing. I just want somebody who loves me and talks to me and wants to be with me.

Well, you have that, and how *real* does it feel? Jesus Christ.

Well, if you don't want to talk about that can we talk about Domino for a minute?

I am so *sick* of this conversation! John screamed.

You know what? I don't care.

I can see that. I'm going home.

John.

What?

If you walk out of here right now, don't ever come back.

The television said: Of course fertility difficulties are so common these days. Consult your fertility specialist. Next: Rose from Pleasanton.

Oh, so it's going to be one of *those* nights, said John.

I just—I just wanted to know . . . about Domino—

Yes?

I wish I could meet her. I want to ask her—I want to know, I . . . I feel it every time I'm confronted with pornography and prostitution. Because she's a woman, too, and yet I'm so far away from what she is. I can't understand that part in a woman that is able to happily give her body and *sell* her body. There's something about her that I don't understand, like how she could so happily without any issues just get into brokering sex for men.

You're repeating yourself.

Would you feel more attracted to me if you could just buy sex with me and then not have to talk with me?

That has *nothing* to do with anything!

But, you know, John, I don't want to be a prostitute like Domino. Or this insect Queen the television keeps talking about. I don't want to do what she does.

Good career move. Are you almost finished?

I guess the reason why I don't want to do it is because *I don't want to give men what they want.* Because men already seem to get what they want—

So now I'm the enemy because I'm male, huh? That's just another version of *they're all pink on the inside.* Should I be offended now? But you know what? I'm not. What you're saying is so godamned *stupid,* so far *beneath me,* that *I refuse to get friggin' offended!*

I guess if I saw Domino, continued Celia in a dreamy voice, you know what I'd tell her? I'd say, I can't relate. I just can't.

| 430 |

After slowly sinking her teeth into his tongue, she said: This is *me* you're feeling. Me doing it to you. Me hurting you to show that you're mine. You're so pretty when you're in pain.

John thought to himself: I will never forget these words.

When she finally spat into his mouth, he drank it eagerly, sobbing and trembling. He awaited her pleasure, in exactly the same way that the Chinese prostitute Yellow Bird bowed her naked legs out while clicking her white high heels together, anxiously gripping her own throat with both hands while gazing into each man's face with the expression of a beaten child. John paid to be beaten and Yellow Bird did not. What did that make each of them?

Domino's mons was furry, broad and generous like the refreshing green mound of park on Gough and Sacramento with its wall of bushes, its palm trees, stairs and clouds, the rollercoaster drop of streets below, the financial district far away.

| 431 |

You bastard, said Domino.

Look, said John. I'm busy. I feel—I don't know how I feel about you, but I feel something. I've got to do my job right now.

That won't work, said Domino. You can't do that to me. Part of you belongs to me now.

No it doesn't.

Part of every man belongs to me, and I'm going to get my due. Do you understand?

John shuddered, momentarily unable even to speak.

She was weeping so hard that the bed shook, and then she was struggling so that he had to hold her down with all his weight, which afforded him an almost sexual feeling of riding her like a horse; all night, she kept sobbing: I'm no good. Finally she'd run down her batteries and lay there heavy and dead. Then he too collapsed. He slept. The sound of little bells woke him, and his heart vomited up dread. She was in the other bed squirming, and her anklets were tinkling. The hot dawn was already upon them like a nuclear bomb. He could not call out. After an hour she came and lay beside him, and he seized her hand and tucked it under her to imprison her to him, but quietly she slipped away. She was packing her little backpack. She came back a third time and kissed him, then got up and walked out the door.

Now I want to do the bad thing, she said. I can do anything, John. I can heal suffering. I can cause suffering. I can fuck Jesus. I can cook; I can make money. I can do this, too. Whatever I promise, I do. I promise I'm going to go away and never see you again.

John was silent. He could not forget how when Domino was sitting on him and then she began to smile and her eyes cruelly narrowed, he almost couldn't bear the joyous excitement.

She glared into his eyes until, hypnotized and paralyzed, he fell back into strangling dreams. When he awoke she was sitting in a chair snoring. He got up and put his hand on her shoulder.

Can't you see I'm just waking up? she muttered. Stupid dick-sucking sonofabitch.

| 432 |

And a sliver of garlic, concluded the waiter with a genial smile.

There's no egg in it? asked Celia anxiously.

Exactly, ma'am.

I love these olives, John, don't you?

Not bad, said John.

This appetizer doesn't taste like crab, does it? It tastes like really garlicky calimari.

There goes the Wine Train, said John, pointing out the window. I wonder if Mom would enjoy that. I don't think she would.

You're so good to your mother, John.

Well, somebody has to be, he said, regarding her through the tall green carafe of sodium-free sparkling water. The lemon half on ice at the bottom of his bloody mary glass resembled a triumphantly unbroken egg yolk.

I'm sorry, Celia said.

Sorry for what?

I don't know. Sorry I'm not better to your mother, I guess.

She likes you fine, Ceel.

But you're disappointed in me, aren't you?

What's all this about?

I'm sorry. I said I'm sorry. I'm sorry I keep bringing my thoughts back to you. The way you are. The way your brother is. The way I am. How can I spend another damned minute here?

So you're in another of your moods.

I can feel that darkness inside me coming on. Maybe it has something to do with Domino. And you don't care.

What do you mean, I don't care? Aren't I paying out good money right now to do exactly what you wanted to do, eating your lunch in the restaurant you picked, being driven up here in my goddamned car? Doesn't that count for anything?

So you bought me for the weekend. You—

Cut to the chase. What do you want?

I don't know. This is what I always come back to. That's all I seem to do in life, she went on in her breathless whining tone, just one thing after another, because life just won't let me have someone to love instead.

Oh, horseshit, said John.

Someone to look at every day, she mumbled, sloshing wine out of her glass as she tremblingly raised it to her lips. Someone to muss my hair . . .

Well, he said wearily, here I am. You want me to muss your hair or will you complain about your permanent?

They never stay. You won't stay. Your brother buys sex and I masturbate. At least your brother's not alone when he—

Oh, so it's "they" now. Who are the *they* I'm a part of? Men? Jerks? Jesus Christ.

And the peach-crayfish fettucine for the lady, the waiter said. How were your appetizers?

Adequate, said John. The spring rolls were a little stale. Well, maybe they were just dried out. The lady would like more lemon.

I'm so often afraid, she whispered. I need a new thought, or a new interest, or something . . . With all the information out there, you'd think I'd be able to give the world one new thought—

So read the encyclopedia, Celia. Develop your goddamned mind.

I know you don't know the answer. If you knew, I would have known it, too, and I would have already done something about it. If you knew, everyone else would know, too, because you're not so smart, she muttered, her lower lip trembling spitefully.

Fine, said John. So I'm not the answer. Well, I've had enough of this for the afternoon. I want to be in love so bad, Celia whispered to herself. I want to be loved so bad.

You sit there and get snookered. I'm going to read the paper.

John? John!

What is it now, Ceel?

John, I want a baby.

Listen to you. With your mood swings, what kind of mother would you be?

Didn't you ever feel excited when you . . .

When I what?

Didn't you put your hand on Irene's tummy, just to feel . . . ?

The baby never moved inside her, John said. Irene never reached that stage.

| 433 |

John's erection reminded Celia of the cigarette upslanted between Domino's fingers. She wanted to shout at him, but instead she started crying as he sat there, and at length she said through her tears: I know I have a pattern. I'm aware of it, thank you very much.

Well? said John.

Celia wanted to say: You're just making me feel worse. Will you please shut up? —Instead, she cried harder.

John softened. He could be very kind with weak and broken creatures.

I feel bad that I feel this way, she whispered. I feel defeated and insecure as a result of all this. I'm back at the beginning again. At least when I'm at the office I'm something. They actually look up to me, John—

Exactly, John said. I totally understand you there.

Well, here I am. I'm in your hotel room that you paid for and so I'm not anything. I'm just Celia.

You are that, he said.

I wonder where all these fears come from. I remember when I was in high school, I was such a good swimmer, but I was afraid to be a lifeguard. I don't know why.

She dreamed that she went out of the hotel, and from the window where a man in a suit who had just made love with her remained there protruded a big green gun. She began to run. She was getting away with it. She ran and ran. Then she began to wonder how she would get home, and how she would know when she was home, because she was very lost now. She remembered something about the North Star and hoped that she would be able to figure it all out. She came to the top of the hill, and saw an army of the enemy, all men, playing a ball game involving half-remembered toys from her childhood. She ran on, hoping they wouldn't see her. She was going downhill now. She was at the edge of a cliff.

But her dream was (by conventional logic, at least) in error, because John never slept with Domino again.

· BOOK XXVII ·

Geary Street

•

By faith Enoch was translated that he should not see death; and he was not found, because God translated him . . .

Hebrews 11.5

•

| 434 |

Is it fair to accept on faith the dogma that each and every soul who dwells in San Francisco is perfectly represented by one of that city's streets? Celia's street would be Union Street because that was where all the expensive merchandise incubated by night in the wombs of exclusive shops, growing in beauty as in price until the moment when Celia happened to walk by the window display so that each new thing could be seen by her, then loved, then ceremonially packaged. Tyler's street would not be Turk Street—oh, no, he was not yet pure enough to abase himself as successfully as that; he couldn't lick up the spittle of others (excepting only his Queen). Perhaps he could become Eddy or Ellis Street—or, better yet, some brief grey alley lost somewhere south of Market. —And John? Here there's but one answer, and in keeping with John it's truly a magnificent one: Geary Street.

| 435 |

Of all the multitudinous arteries of San Francisco, Geary Street is perhaps the most important of the overlooked. —Yes, the overlooked—what a fine category! Failing private detectives with their envious ears, self-pitying child molesters who want to "explain" themselves to every stranger at every bar, customerless prostitutes, lawyers who haven't yet made full partner, and I myself, described in the introduction to the Japanese translation of one of my novels as "a minor writer"—oh, sting! —and you yourself, reader, who suffer from this world's deficient appreciation of your qualities—and for that matter all of us living creatures, for up to now we've been rudely overlooked by death— which reminds me of the dead, for they get overlooked not only by us but also by each other . . . In short, *overlooked* signifies everyone except lucky Cain, who flees from one wilderness to the next, pursued by recognition of his immortal Mark.

I admit that Geary Street cannot boast Cain's flair. And yet in its length and in the proliferation of its speeding corpuscles it ranks almost as mighty as Market Street, which bisects the city into a pair of angled grids, as if San Francisco were a sheet of graph paper diagonally folded, then torn, with the lower triangle, the scrap South of Market, getting magically rotated a hundred and thirty-five degrees before being rejoined. Geary Street likewise is kin to Van Ness Avenue, which offers love-seekers a convenient route of travel from the Tenderloin to Capp Street. Nor should we omit to mention the fraternal relations between Geary and Gough, Franklin and Fell, all three of which the devotees of Freeway 101 employ with scarcely a thought, but what will do they when the inevitable earthquake reduces those serviceways to twisted segments of disconnection?

But enough name-dropping. Market Street can go promote itself for all I care.

The tale of Geary Street is the tale of life itself, which begins, as did the first prehistoric unicellular organisms, at the ocean. In that very first block somewhere in the mists of Forty-Eighth Avenue, which almost touches the low sea-horizon and the wet silver-tan sand of Ocean Beach, Geary Street, here known to meter maids as Geary Boulevard, as indeed it will remain all the way to Van Ness, already foreshadows the business character of its adulthood, for it promises wideness, smoothness and above all *accessibility*, in sober defiance of the maniacal laughter of that convulsing female automaton at the Musée Mechanique on the lower terrace of the Cliff House, where tourists come to gaze upon white-dunged Seal Rock, enter the camera obscura, and afterward buy overpriced hot dogs. Resolutely rejecting these follies, and above all refusing to acknowledge the insanely laughing robot as its mother, Geary Street faces east and grows workmanlike into existence. At this stage, the infant pavement carries with it only dimunitive pastel-painted cube-houses for its toys. Hedges and flowers adorn these properties, some of which actually stand alone, lawn to lawn, unlike the promiscuous blocks of wall-kissing flats which make up so much of San Francisco. Every now and then one can glimpse the tea-smoke forest ribbon of Golden Gate park below and to the right, with the outer Sunset district gently rising into the fog beyond, like some pearlescently obsolete circuit-board studded with pale cubical transistors and resistors. Were we in the Sunset, Geary Street itself and the Richmond district it passes through would look the same way, the Richmond and the Sunset being almost mirror images of one another. (What would the Sunset's Geary Street be? Judah, maybe, or Taraval.) But already, striving to outdistance the repose of these seaside beginnings, where planktonic destinies allow for nothing but flotation and cool grey submission, Geary Street strains to carry and to convey, to facilitate, to make business happen, to *go between*. At Fortieth Avenue, in the spirit of corporate mergers, it swallows up Point Lobos Avenue; and as early as Thirty-Eighth Avenue I've seen the first panhandler, wrapped in silver fog, listlessly overlooking grey pavement, hoping for nickels, dimes and quarters to congeal out of grey and silver air. He is the *genius loci* or tutelary deity of Geary Street. He is Business.

By Thirty-Sixth Avenue the houses have begun to crowd and to swell, like muscular apprentice construction workers old enough to bleed in wars but too young to vote, old enough to lift the heaviest buckets of paint and bags of sheet rock but too young to sit guarding the coffeepot; and so they hustle, trying to get what they can as time advances down Geary Street's blue-grey ribbon, and the number 38 Geary bus, the most frequent in the city, I believe, except perhaps the 30 Stockton, roars beeping in and out of fog. A few homes, the so-called multiplexes constructed in the 1950s and 1960s, still resemble squarish concretions of mist, but as they move farther from the greenish hazy sea they begin to dry off and get down to brass tacks. Each one wants to be voted Most Likely To Succeed. Each one wants to receive a loyalty certificate. Each one wants to get rich. What to do, then, but *work*? And at Twenty-Sixth Avenue, demarcated by the teardrop domes, more yellow than gold, of the Orthodox church, whose saints gaze out across the thoroughfare, blessing transport, commerce and journeying, the business world properly begins, and Geary Street comes into full strength. In this Russian zone, the restaurants and video parlors like as not proclaim themselves in Cyrillic—more so now at the end of the twentieth century than in the days of the USSR, when Little Russia was mainly comprised of ageing aristocrats and counterrevolutionaries. Now post-Soviets can come and sell pizzas, which is why the character of this thoroughfare is precisely characterlessness. Long before we've reached the Moscow and Tbilsi Bakery, banks and Irish pubs have rushed in, and one never knows whether to expect the Wirth Brothers pastry shop or an income tax service, because Geary Street, nomadically epitomized by Geary Shoe Repair, owns such a plainly utiliarian personality—Jack-of-all-Trades Street, we ought to call it. We can bully ourselves into pretending that Geary is something special, but it eschews preciousness; if only lava were to seal it off for five centuries, anthropologists would love it. Shunning Haight Street's narcissism, Clement Street's dreaminess, Geary Street expresses pure functionality, like a well-made Indian arrowhead. And Little Russia? As long gone as the ocean! At Sixteenth Avenue, that outpost of expensive grandeur, the Russian Renaissance Restaurant, where I used to transform money into lemon-flavored vodka in the cause of unrequited love, fails to hold the line laid down by the Orthodox saints: it's all motleyness now, pied and commercially nondescript in the convenient manner of freeways, although at Fifteenth the two wide ribbons of opposing traffic get purified by the fragrance of fresh bagels, and somewhere around there I remember Shenson's Kosher style deli, whose proudly pregnant Russian-looking countergirl makes Reuben sandwiches, stuffed cabbages, and other treats. May she and her baby remain always overlooked by death.

After Little Russia comes Little Korea with its Hangul newspapers, its excitable, clannish grocerywomen, and above all its temples of grilled meat where for a price one can offer up to heaven the greasy incense of barbeque-smoke, faithfully attended by many small round dishes of pickles. Do I write too much about food? Geary Street knows that everybody needs to eat, just as everybody sooner or later needs an undertaker's services, and, as I recall, there's a funeral parlor right here. Geary Street, practical and grey, solves all your necessities! And what's Geary Street's necessity? Why, to strain continually eastward, toward the greenery of Union Square and the jewelry shops beyond, none of which it can yet imagine. Ask an entrepeneur what his maximum profit will be, and he can't tell you, because he's refrained from limiting himself; on his own forehead he's inscribed the mark of infinity. Geary Street knows only that there's no returning to the ocean. So it must vibrate straight ahead, toward the steadily increasing murmur and din of downtown, which is at least partially of its own making. And Little Korea, was it ever anything but the brainchild of Geary Street's brother-in-law, who worked for the Chamber of Commerce? Don't ask me. Which of its Korean restaurants is the best? Don't ask Geary Street. Geary Street has other worries. And now Little Korea lies behind us.

In the Richmond district on a spring Sunday afternoon after many rainy nights, the pale houses shine, with every shadow seemingly painted on. A garage door slowly, magically rolls upward. Sunlight extends its tongue inside. Nothing moves. A sparrow chirps. Clouds hang upended in the sky; the nearly tamed forests of Golden Gate Park peer over the stores and apartments of Geary Street; the morning brightens. A young Asian couple slowly walk down the sidewalk, reading newspapers as they go. But Geary Street hurries past them; Geary Street does not have time for spring.

Perhaps you'll get the idea from all this that Geary Street is the soul of nothing but practicality. While that would almost be true, I ought to mention Eighth Avenue, where the middle-aged street vaguely remembers its ocean infancy, the mnemonic being the Star of the Sea Catholic church (I forgot to mention the kindred Lighthouse Lighting and Lamp Repairs a few blocks back), but that's mere dutifulness, like a grown man's grimacing smile when his maiden aunt tells him how cute he was in diapers; for by Seventh Avenue, Geary Street has reverted to type, insisting that water was not meant to lie foolishly in oceans, but to be *used,* which is why from beneath the used car lot's gleaming numbered windshields and shiny hoods there trickles a braided river of soap-blotched water like a molten leopard, thereby underlining another of Geary Street's important principles: Business ought to be clean.

Davis Realty, the Dragon Restaurant, the car wash and the gas station—thus the heterogenously mundane sweeps on, and by Fourth Avenue many proprietorships have become outlets, chains, warehouses, copy services, banks, dental offices, storage lockers. Swelling and bustling, Geary Street propels itself into the next level of mercantile prosperity, getting but not spending.* At Stanyan Street, which itself imust be considered another of the most important of the unimportant streets, not only as a traffic artery, but also as a demarcation between "the streets" and "the avenues"—here too end the Richmond and Sunset Districts, with Golden Gate Park concluding between them—Geary Street widens, rushing into even more incontrovertible *ordinariness*, which it proclaims more aptly than ever by means of Commercial Street.

As a prize for this redoubled speed and salesmanship, Geary Street gets its first tunnel at Emerson, where it *brightly and shallowly* dives, so that no bad sorts can lurk there. Geary prefers the higher class of operators who pay taxes and whose wares are returnable, subject to fine print boilerplate on various warranties; and so it quickly expels us from that tunnel of shining yellow tiles, conveying us to Lyon Street, where we gain our first dissectionist's view of the white spinal columns of the financial district, that paradisiacal goal of the street, heaven of boutiques, department stores and jewelers. Of course, all that's still as far away as the imaginary countries painted on the backdrops of the Opera House, but Geary Street has heard rumors from a passing 38 Geary bus that someday, after many city blocks, generations and improvisations, it will find at the summit of its old age a gem laid down for the taking—namely, Union Square, immense emerald set in the stonework and brickwork and pavement of San Francisco—and emeralds, like all precious things, possess the ability to render us first shyly self-conscious, then, as the infection of overpowering greenness strikes us, rolling down on our heads like cabbage balls from a Chinatown produce truck, burying us beneath its stacks of green bean bundles, we numbly doubt our own existences, seeking ourselves amist the shining labyrinths of green eternities. Why on earth instead of real emeralds do I go on describing Chinatown's produce shops, harbors for nomadic Chevvy trucks full of wooden crates of celery? Why mention an earringed Chinese girl, her arms full of broccoli, coming down the gangplank? Because Geary Street, longing though it certainly does for emerald fulfillment—why, even the baser joys of jade would do! —cannot really believe that it is entitled to anything that fine. In green pears and apples, in the fresh chlorophyll of plants, in greengrocers' stocks it can believe, for the vocations of its shopkeepers who toil patiently on its westernmost reaches provide them. Every day, Geary Street turns vegetables into dollars and sense. It can rely on their greenness. But soon it must shake off its provincial rudeness, for it will intersect Van Ness Avenue not too many blocks hence, and beyond Van Ness lies downtown itself. Yes, Union Square will crown Geary Street's career, but can it wear such a tremendous emerald without blushing? It wants to; then it will have finally arrived. But can so broad and bluff and workaday a street pull it off? And so Geary Street retreats into dull meditations on broccoli.

Lusting all the more and nonetheless for the pale beauty of that distant cluster of towers surrounded by parkland, Bay and sky, Geary Street, which is as endless as the 38

---

*And there's a good side to this, for (much to its credit) Geary Street remains immune to the sterile *noblesse* of the hedges and the fountain at Leavenworth and Green.

Geary bus itself with the long black accordion-bellows between segments so that it can go around corners, now exerts itself to the fullest, contorting itself, rolling round and round past parks and murals and the occasional grafitti'd fence at Divisadero, Scott, and Steiner. At Webster it dips down through Japantown, then up again in respectful advance of Sushiland. Japantown will be as brief a diversion as Little Korea and Little Russia. Geary Street is in a lascivious hurry for riches now, its wide grey ribbon, adorned by dashed white lines and rectangular patches of blackish-grey or whitish grey asphalt, making haste to approach that angelic venue of old age—

. . . But it never can, never will, at least not in its present incarnation, because at Laguna and Gough fatality sets in, and suddenly Geary Street, renamed Starr King, shunts rightward past the Montessori House and Universalist Center, and the motorist who, trusting Geary Street for all these blocks, crosses Van Ness, abruptly finds himself on *O'Farrell Street* as he enters the Tenderloin . . .

How could this calamity have happened? Because Geary Street, which parallels him one block to the left, has become one-way, the *other* way. Continuity is impossible. Geary Street will indeed stretch all the way to the heart of the financial district; the prophecy will be fulfilled; but only that most worthless of human beings, the pedestrian, can get there that way. All is vanity.

Thus, at least, runs the explanation dictated to me by my Lutheran forbears. Hubris and graspingness must be punished. Midas's touch is a curse.

And yet nobody else thinks so. Whenever I take a little drive down Geary Street to buy apple juice or condoms, I realize that the street has become more smug than ever. I don't see any wriggles of shame in its pavement! And so I ask myself: What if the revocation of its bidirectionality were not a chastisement at all, but an *arrangement* in which it connived? What could be more important to such a street than two-way access itself?

The crux: Could Geary Street have consented to its own maiming in order to avoid being defiled by the Tenderloin? O'Farrell Street runs right through that district, and is accordingly hooker-studded, greased by the excrement of lost addicts, stamped on by pimps, leaned on by crack dealers with the serenely downcast faces of Kabuki string-players who sit cross-legged on royal cloth; whereas Geary Street almost escapes from the Tenderloin, or at worst uneasily grazes it, anxious to achieve the fancy brasserie on Geary and Mason, attended by the cylindrical pillar which showcases a smallbreasted young blonde whose face and crotch are supposed to sell bluejeans. This is the kind of prostitution which Geary Street prefers. Just as it converts emeralds to broccoli, so, too, dimly seeking to emulate the Orthodox saints whose paths it crossed back on Twenty-Sixth Avenue, it slimes reality over with its native sea-fog, until all relations between human beings have been blurred into orthodox respectability.

· BOOK XXVIII ·

John

•

If I speak with the tongues of men and of angels, but have not love, I am become sounding brass, or a clanging cymbal.

I CORINTHIANS 13.1

•

Sacramento is River City, they say, out of logic as long and gentle as the sweep of the American River. What they are actually doing (and by "they" I mean the Chamber of Commerce) is casting about for a slogan to make Sacramento's ghastly conformity seem somehow *different*—to them it wouldn't matter whether Sacramento were Mountain City, Ocean City, Oil City, Balloon City, Army City, Love City, Emerald City, or the veriest necropolis—the gimmick's the thing, good citizens! —But I'm not being fair. To impute to my City Fathers this much cynicism is necessarily to suppose them capable of seeing through their own inventions, and I have no reason to think that these warm-hearted merchants didn't look around them most pridefully once they'd transformed Sacramento into River City, that they didn't say: By golly! What a beautiful pair of rivers we have here! —even the ones whose bid for necropolisdom had been downvoted, buried in the graveyard of uncommercial ideas. And they'd have meant it; I'd stake my last share of AllCo shopping mall stock! If I were only a higher being, I'd be watching them on television, applauding their sincerity. At least I can do that much for John. Miss Deborah Treisman, who allowed some pages of this novel in *Grand Street,* and rejected others from *The New Yorker,* asserted that John was a mere caricature, like the so-called "postcard view" from Russian Hill of pale buildings and accidental trees clothing the steep, fog-colored slopes of the city. Deborah, I'm absent-minded, I admit; I make mistakes. What if, resting jovially upon my labors, like the capitalist compradores who now sit on the deck of the Virgin Sturgeon restaurant, toasting their newborn River City, what if I'd forgotten to bring *anybody* to life? The Queen's but a figment, mouthpiece of my pompous symbology, her whores only grimy cardboard props dripping with the semen of the vulgar; Irene similarly assumes a merely erotic aspect; Henry Tyler remains limited to being Henry Tyler, which is to say, a grey nothingness. But *John,* now—oh, but *John!* How can he be a caricature, when I can't get rid of him?

A masculine Christian name, that of John the Baptist and John the Evangelist, explains my Oxford English Dictionary; hence, from early ME. times one of the commonest in England. Also used as a representative proper name for a footman, butler, waiter, messenger, or the like. John's also a priest; he's John-a-dogs the dog-whipper (a very unlikely occupation for *this* John, who loves Mugsy); he's John-of-all-trades, which might well be true; in my slang dictionary he's a dried fish and a policeman; on the San Francisco streets he's a customer of prostitutes. John, in short, is Everyman. Deny him life, and we'd be compelled by all statutes of consistency to reduce the Evangelist first to torpor, then to the veriest non-existence.

John himself, I am sure, would plead the real and essential nature of his own being, without disfiguring himself with the least tic or twitch of affectation. And whatever he says, he means. In a word, John was born with the gift of *sincerity.*

Thus the conception of River City, hanging in the air like a rainbow mist, engaged John's sincerity. Our Sacramento boy had swum, waded, waterski'd, rafted, fished, and frogged all around town. He believed in the riverine nature of his home town and even thought he understood it. John daydreamed less than most, but sometimes when he was tired or when Mr. Singer exasperated him, he let his mind rise higher than the Transamerica Pyramid, then higher still, the fish-blue fog of San Francisco gradually getting as white as the paint on the fuselage of a brand-new airplane, then blue beyond the clouds' white fur, and even before Captain John has activated the FASTEN SEAT-BELTS sign the eyes of lordly passengers already begin to be beguiled by farmland checkerboards—surprising how many farms are still left, squatting on their squares of green and brown! Now to the south one can see the wide silver shining of the wet Delta. In spring the fields are so lushly green as to approach turquoise. Summer quickly comes to blast them. —Ladies and gentlemen, in preparation for landing, please raise your innermost barriers and insure that your souls are securely stowed beneath your feet and that your mindlessness is in *full, upright, LOCKED position;* welcome to Sacramento, where, low to the ground, it's all so sad and dull.

But to John it was not dull, and he refused to believe in the sadness.

Maybe it wasn't sad. John's Sacramento nostalgia proceeded with the abnormal smoothness of the riverbank's curve—so many rivers! Or were they just a couple of rivers doubling? Amidst bright fields those darkly tree-lined, dishwater-colored rivers offered strange light. To Henry Tyler, needless to say, the rivers meant less than those river-trees, which resembled the hair on the Queen's armpits.

It was the middle of March. John knew so well that the fresh Christmas-colored leaves of riverberry bushes were now sweating in the sun of Sacramento, the smell of dead fish ascending from blue mud-banks, the damps of spring not yet burned away by the summer's golden anger. Wasn't it right about this time last year that Irene had told him she was pregnant?

You want to look in on Mom this weekend and then drive back through the Delta?

I want to have a torrid time, Celia said with what she hoped to be a sensual pout. Will it be torrid?

Come on, said John impatiently. Tell me yes or no.

Maybe, said Celia, licking her lips.

Laughing, John looked at his watch, accepting her complaisance in advance. When can you leave? he asked.

On Friday? Six o'clock.

Four, said John, drumming his fingers.

Oh, four-thirty, I guess. But that means I . . . What should I bring?

The hell with that. Just throw a few clothes in a suitcase and go. But you'll need a nice dress to cheer up Mom. Well, you'll be in your work clothes. You can wear that burgundy blazer I bought you. And we'll take Mom out to dinner if she's well enough and then maybe we'll spend the night in Rio Vista or Walnut Grove. Or maybe we'll just get an early start on Saturday. Mom needs company, you know, and I ought to mow the lawn. You can take Mom grocery shopping. And then we'll head for the Delta. You'll love it. You'll absolutely love it. It's like another world down there, Celia, it's . . .

It's what?

Oh, forget it, said John, remembering from his boyhood the funny old bartender at Al the Wop's bar in Locke, and the gas station attendant at Walnut Grove like an emperor, commanding each motorists to slow, to advance, to halt. He wanted Celia to be surprised, to discover all these wonders for herself.

You're smiling, said Celia. What are you thinking about?

You'll see when we get to Locke. In Locke they all remember me. One time Homer Fessendon and Charlie Wong and Sam Smith and I drove down there and stapled Monopoly money to the ceiling of China Mike's. Even Hank was there. And Ronnie the barkeep . . . oh, it's all too funny. You'll see.

So your mother's—

Well, it's not good. She's not comfortable. —John glared at his watch. —They were supposed to give her medicine two hours ago. If they didn't, they'll hear about it from me.

Having more than a half-memory of the purple and white wisteria flowers in his mother's back yard in April, and likewise remembering the strangely intense perfume of her jasmine hedge, John found himself driving to Saramento in that season when, letting more luminescence into life, we set all our clocks and watches back an hour—an hour less sleep, to be sure, but John read in his Sunday *Examiner-Chronicle* that people used to sleep nine hours and now slept only seven—not that they didn't complain, not that the traffic experts and economists didn't bemoan the costs—more accidents, lower productivity—but the point was that *it could be done.* John got by quite well on six and a half hours of sleep—not as remarkable as the achievement of my friend Lara Lorson in Washington, D.C., who lives on four—but John wouldn't have complained because he hated complainers. In that late spring season, John got by on even less sleep than that, because it was almost June twenty-seventh when for the rest of his life John would wake up from fearful nightmares of Irene, who'd reincarnated herself either as some dangerous animal or as a skeleton or a bleeding corpse, chasing him with intent to devour him, gnawing her way through fences, killing all his protectors, and even though John knew that it was a dream, a stupid dream, he could never awake to shake away the taint of horror that he inhaled with every stifling breath; every June twenty-seventh he'd awake feeling exhausted and anxious, his eyes locking in on the clock radio to find out whether Irene was still alive or whether 9:37 A.M., the time he'd found her in the bathroom, had already come; in fact he always awoke miserably early on June twenty-seventh, at 6:30 or before, compelled to lie half-paralyzed in his bed, watching the crawl of the second hand, and the absurdly glacial moment of the minute hand, until Irene had died again, releasing him into an abyss of loathing and self-loathing so that he could begin his weary day. The day after the Brady contracts for the Dallas franchise of Feminine Circus were drawn up to everyone's satisfaction, John threw on bluejeans and his favorite polo shirt, setting out with the half-acquiescent Celia, whose desire to belong to him and be taken care of (or, as she liked to think of it, to be used) enhanced her availability.

It's all very well for Mom to think she can take care of herself, John was saying. But she's getting old. No one wants to get old, I guess. And . . .

Celia stared at him in amazement. She had scarcely ever heard him be so introspective.

And Hank of course is always hanging around, said John, checking his watch and the speedometer at the same time. —He says he's helping her but really he's just freeloading, eating up her groceries.

Should we stop at the supermarket?

I already made up a list.

I—

She's afraid to die, Celia. But I asked her, Mom, do you believe in Heaven? and she blinked her eyes yes. Thank God she can talk again now. And I said, well, Mom, that's where you're going. It's going to be better than it is for you here.

And do you think she agrees?

Who the hell knows? said John. Poor Mom.

And do you believe it?

Believe what?

What you just said.

Look, Celia. Let's leave me out of this.

I'm sorry.

And you know another thing that gripes me? The way those nurses dress. Can't you remember when all the nurses dressed in white, with those starched white caps and the class pin on the cap just so? And now they come in dressed like—I dunno, dressed *crazy*. And they talk on the phone to their boyfriends; they don't turn Mom often enough; now she's getting bedsores . . .

They turned onto R Street, and John said: Oh, shit. Fucking Hank is here.

Why do you worry so much about meeting him?

Look, said John. What seems like nothing to you is not nothing to me. Enough said.

Tyler was just getting into his car. John drove past the driveway and waited on the other side of the street with the windows up. When Tyler, not seeing him, continued to take his time, John leaned viciously on the horn. Tyler stiffened. Spying John's car at last, he ostentatiously turned his back and got into the driver's seat.

He looks really sad and bitter, Celia said.

Can we drop that subject? said John.

Finally Tyler's car started, and he backed out of the driveway, farting smoke. —He needs a smog check, John muttered. I wonder if he . . . —Slowly Tyler drove past them, heading toward the freeway.

All right, great, laughed John. That asshole's gone.

He pulled up into the driveway. Celia got out glumly as he strode to the front door and rang the bell.

Mrs. Tyler embraced him and said: Did you say hello to Henry?

The snails are eating up your magnolia bushes, Mom, said John. He plucked them off where they clung like hard brown fruit, and crushed them under his heel.

They said it was going to be a bad year for slugs and snails, said Mrs. Tyler.

They're not kidding. Oh, my God, they're all over the place. They're eating you out of house and home, Mom.

It's terrible, Mrs. Tyler said.

We're going to have to do something about this, John said grimly, spreading white snail-poisoning powder, bending and stretching. Celia, who was allergic, leaned against the car.

Look at this, Ceel! Up here! No wonder these leaves look like hell.

Imagine how many more there must be at night, said his mother in her now customary trembling voice.

A very scary thought, Mom.

They drove to the farmers' market under the freeway and Celia mixed in among smiling old Japanese men who were slowly picking through flashing and rolling tangerines while a tiny Asian girl sat on the concrete plucking off stems. Celia bought two pounds of the fruit, and a pound of Fuji apples from the boys in caps and sweatshirts, while John commanded two pounds of live clams to be clicked into a plastic bag because his mother loved clams, and then for himself and Celia he bought a huge-eyed goldeneyed American mackerel. —Okay! shouted a Japanese in a yellow rubber apron. Buffalo fish! Seeben tweeny five! —No, thanks, said John.—Oh, yes! cried the oyster salesman. These are *very* fresh. —Forget it, said John. —Right here! Best asparagus in town! Five dollars! Taste the difference! —Fine, said John. Ceel, give him five dollars.

They had already passed the so-called executive airport and the Sky Riders Motel. Soon they would enter the shining muck of ricefields.

Sunglasses, said John.

Celia reached in the glove compartment as her lover, going thirty-five in a twenty-five-mile-an-hour zone, rolled down the window.

All the pear blossoms will be gone by now anyway, he warned.

How do you know?

Because they don't last forever, idiot.

To Celia herself, to whom John's open exuberance gave hopes that matters might finally be decided between them one way or another, this journey smelled strange and wild, and she began to feel almost afraid. John resembled her in his soul. She understood that now. He had immense expectations. In her own life, most expectations had been disappointed, but she refused to give them up; she'd rather be bitter than cynical. She could not really understand why this drive was so important to John, and she knew that if she questioned him too much his exultation would simply vanish into anxious vindictiveness like fog-devoured Ocean Beach in San Francisco, where homebody Irene had once sat with folded legs before the television, reading an article about a woman who had a liposuction.

What kind of hedge is that? she asked ingratiatingly.

I have no idea, John laughingly shrugged. Generic hedge.

And so they entered fog, and sun-yellow mustard fields, then tall wet grass and the water tower, after which Sacramento lay behind them and they were in Freeport where the wide, bright flat world of the Delta commenced. To John, the Delta was the loveliest place in the world, whose loveliness was compounded by other people's failures of appreciation. He needed no protection from any bad thoughts there, because it was a heavenly maze whose exit passageways were themselves deliciously langorous and misleading, like Celia's endless lists; and John for his part epitomized the Delta by its crown jewel, Grand Island, which was surrounded by low river-channels and which offered roads like Moebius strips: easy to follow one all the way around and end up somewhere else; easy likewise to turn off a road and go away and away and away and end up where you started . . . John had had a dream the night before about being here. (Celia for her part dreamed that she was in bed with a strange man in a grey suit who was very worried about something. The man climbed on top of her and began to fuck her, but when he was finished, blue stuff like some strange new toothpaste came out of him.) John dreamed that he was opening a jewel box filled with rubies, and that Celia had played with the precious stones as a happy child would play with beach pebbles, and then behind the rubies, in the bottom of the box, lay a plate glass window through which the entire Delta was inexplicably passing. —There's Cliff's Marina, John said in the dream. See the sign that says LIVE CRAYFISH? —Uh huh, said Celia, playing with her rubies. (I just want to sit on the beach and stare, or maybe read and dream and then swim

in warm water somewhere, she had confided to him that night before they fell alseep.)
The wide silvery river was very still. Birds and fog hung about them as their dream-
window flashed along the levee top, showing them orchards, brown spring fields, and
the occasional palm tree. When John awoke, he realized that the magic panorama must
have taken place in March or early April at the latest, when the hot blasts of present time
had not yet withered anything. Apples and pears promised themselves through blossoms
as white as the now sunny river, and they'd already come into Hood, elevation twenty-
three feet above sea level, whose attractions included HOME MILK and Skittles's bar.
A fat dog was lying on his side by the drugstore. Wet muck under the flowering orchards
reflected the blossoms. After Hood came Courtland and then flowering orchard-tops by
the trestle bridge, then a yellow steel drawbridge attended by river-smell; after that came
Galt, and finally Locke, whose elevation was thirteen. John woke up smiling.

Now the dream was over and decayed back to moldy shadowhood, for it was mid-
May and the Delta was getting hot, with double rows of trees presiding over the browning grass whose golden and silver seedheads would continue to accrete their jewels of life
until the sudden day of spending came, that day yet as unimaginable as any day of
bustling urban life in the Delta. Passing the sign for LIVE CRAYFISH, John floored
it, honking at a farm rig which might have slowed him down. He almost wished that
they had come the other way so that Celia could hear the bells clanging on Walnut
Grove's steel-decked drawbridge now splitting itself and rising away from the river-
sparkle, but soon enough she would. He was getting so excited now about showing his
younger self off to Celia that memories from nowhere buzzed him like little white cropduster planes.

It's beautiful, she said.

There's nothing beautiful about it, he said happily. It's just suburban, that's all.

The Sacramento River was wide and pale and sparkling along the levee. On the other
side stretched long furrow-etched fields, and vineyards whose stakes offered multiple
vanishing points as the car rushed along. A speedboat whined up the river, and John
smiled, remembering how he had shaken off his virginity in a speedboat. He switched
on the radio, which announced a rollover on Interstate-5, nobody killed. —Lots of stupid drivers out there, he sighed, switching it off in a restless, almost anxious motion. The
reflective orchard puddles in John's dream were now yellow and rubbery-looking with
algae.

See, there are no pear blossoms, he said triumphantly. I'm telling you, they're gone.
They've all fallen off.

And what kind of tree is that?

You know, you ask me these things, and it's frustrating, because I don't know anything
about trees.

Passing through Courtland, John raised his arm like a maestro so that Celia would
pay attention to the bells and the humming as the yellow bridge slowly parted company
from itself, the bright halves straining at the sky's sunny wind and citrus smell, and finally a solitary high-masted vessel passed through, sails furled, and then the drawbridge
redescended for the sake of the queue of cars.

This is doing *so* well, that white azalea, John said.

She cleared her throat.

Ceel, you think Mom is okay?

Well, I . . . I guess. She seems to be, the girl said, anxious or sleepy (in fact she was thinking that Mrs. Tyler looked very poorly, and she knew that if John were to ask her whether she believed that his mother would soon die she would truthfully answer: I can't bear the idea of it), and then they passed the orchard where John had once made love with a girl named Mary, a girl from one of these hot still Delta towns; there'd been emerald grass beneath, no puddles the way there were in spring, and he remembered sparkles on the cool blue river like the drops of sweat on Mary's forehead; and as he drove on, Celia gazing tolerantly upon Courtland's pale white and grey buildings, upon the tiny pillared courthouse, upon big-tired farm vehicles rolling down the levee road, John found himself longing to make love with Celia right now, perhaps beneath this palm tree whose leaves were loose, glossy, dark like an excited lover's hairy labia; but he extricated himself from his desire by convincing himself rightly or wrongly that such lovemaking would be an act of violation and exploitation, using Celia in Mary's place as he had used her to be Irene (strangely enough, he didn't think of Domino, either because her image would have scalded him or because she was so unique as to be a placeholder for nobody else before or since in his life). John remembered swimming past the Levee Cafe with little blonde Isleton girls who wore baseball caps in the water; he must have been very young then. And then he'd met Allie, the one to whom he'd husked his virginity in the speedboat, and then he'd found Mary, whose skin and soul were both as white as a new houseboat on the Sacramento River. Celia cleared her throat, allergically or anxiously, he couldn't tell. Driving past Queen Anne's lace so tall and white, John longed for Mary frivolously and desperately. He'd met her in China Mike's bar in Locke. Her cunt had reminded him of soft-cut brown and golden fields. Did he comprehend that this Mary who touched him now wasn't even Mary anymore, and that Mary had never been *his* memory, that all he felt now was a carnal ghost like one of the shadows which sometimes came down upon his brother like flesh in a black miniskirt walking, flesh in black high heels, flesh and a black purse, flesh and long red hair or black hair or the face of a sister-in-law or a Queen, meaningless flesh, to which all flesh is susceptible, because pleasure hides death? He tried to think of Celia, who left him cold, and of Irene, who left him cold, and then Celia smiled and touched his wrist very lightly with her long sensitive fingers and he was overwhelmed by love and guilt.

Ceel? he said, a little awkwardly.

What?

Do you feel like making love?

Celia looked away. —I think sex is wonderful when I feel safe and loved.

So you don't feel safe? he said, trying to be angry, but unable to because the bitter taste of guilt remained in his mouth.

I—

Oh, forget it, he said. The pear groves were now an indistinct mass of life. Rich orchards looked up at the leveee, merging and blurring.

Uh, John, listen, I—

I don't know, he sighed. Maybe I'm getting too stressed out over nothing. You think I'm a jerk, don't you?

Then Celia was stroking his neck and saying: Yes, honey, yes I want to make love with you . . . —and John smiled in happy triumph.

And so in a wet mustard-yellow sunny fog they came to Locke with its smell of river-rot and old wood, its chamomile flowers, its dark damp plankwork spanning the gap from the weedy levee to the two-storey houses, some boarded up, some leaning, some with laundry hanging and dogs sleeping. The same sensations inspired in his brother by ageing prostitutes slowly going bust were felt by John in this weedgrown old Chinese town whose bleached ideograms hung like crushed moths in the blackened windows. They parked across from the marina and John led her down River Road past the Joe Shoong Chinese school whose walls were pale yellow and grey, their ideograms the color of teahouse smoke.

Lovely, said Celia.

You see? said John, waving his hand.

Ancient dolls grimaced at her from a dark window, and at Locke China Imports there were heart-shaped old doilies. Silver clouds weighed down white clouds. Birds and silent gnats were everywhere.

John took her to the Dai Loy Museum and paid a dollar for each of them so that beneath the leaking skylight he could show her how the giant, red-and-white-dot-studded dice used to be shaken for illegal gambling games of *pai ngow.* —You see all those white money chips on the tables? he said. Just think what it would have been like to win!

Did you ever gamble? Celia asked, amused by his excitement.

Well, one time Hank and I . . .

His voice trailed off. There was a cold and moldy smell. He pointed to a row of mahjong pieces laid out on a long black box. Sticks of ivory, black with ideograms and wheels and flowers, seemed to offer Celia some gnomic key to her "situation," but she didn't really believe in fortune-telling and anyway John was explaining something to her regarding the rich indigo blueprint of Locke in the old days with its numbered squares of fields.

She stared down at a dry-rotted old butterfly harp.

Now we're going to China Mike's to meet Ronnie, John said. That's the whole point of this trip—for you to meet Ronnie.

They sat at the bar beneath the faded notice which read: WARNING: DRINK-ING BEER, WINE OR OTHER ALCOHOLIC BEVERAGES CAN CAUSE SEXUAL AROUSAL AND MAY RESULT IN PREGNANCY. He showed her the three baseball caps on the antlers of the stags' heads, the dollar bills on the ceiling. He longed to order beers and greasy fries on the worn bar which glowed unevenly like the river; a second river, a glowing uneven river of copper, ran where the bar joined the floor.

Look, said John, grinning. There's Ronnie himself. He's a real character. Ronnie's kind of my hero in a way. I remember the time I—

That would be yours, Ronnie was saying to another customer.

Smiling, John waited for Ronnie to notice him.

You're perfect, Ronnie said to an old Chinese lady.

Celia had begun to feel anxious. John was drumming his fingers.

Almost got you with the bloody mary! Ronnie shouted to a tattooed Brady's Boy.

Ronnie! John called out at last. Hey, Ronnie!

Who the fuck are you? said Ronnie.

John turned white. Horrified, Celia tried to speak. Ronnie glared viciously into her eyes and said: Shut up, bitch! Or do *you* wanna make the same mistake?

· BOOK XXIX ·

Space Invaders

●

But the Light, since he possessed a great power, knew the abasement of the Darkness and his disorder, namely that the root was not straight. But the crookedness of the Darkness was lack of perception, namely the illusion that there is no one above him.

Gnostic Scriptures, *The Paraphrase of Shem,* VII, 1, 10–15 (date unknown)

●

| 437 |

At the beginning of the new year there were floods in the farmland around Sacramento and dozens of homes went underwater to the eaves. —Those poor people, said Mrs. Tyler, shaking her head. —On the seventeenth Tyler was driving in to San Francisco and the flats just west of the river gleamed silver with mist and water, above which the railroad embankment shrugged its endless shoulder. White pickup trucks dazzled him with their unearthliness. Then above a long narrow green field a green billboard said MENTHOL. Inside garages and greenhouses, stale incandescent yellow glowed like sunlight through worn seashells. The road quivered under him as he sped most pleasantly alongside the divider-hedge.

It was a very cold January night at Leidesdorff and Commercial, where the triangular sign said A CULTURED SALAD. A man in livery passed, and his shadow stained the clean, empty street-wall which was otherwise hemorrhaging light. He half expected to see John, simply because this part of town was John's kingdom. Granting the childishness of his conceptions did not dispell them. John did not appear. He felt disappointment and relief. Inside Boudin Sourdough, upended chairs went on and on like a chain of mahogany vertebrae.

On Washington Street he entered a very brightly lit Chinese ginseng place and had a cup of tea for fifty cents. On the topmost glass shelf lay some human-shaped roots for three hundred dollars a pound, but when he explained that he only wanted to eat some to get strong, the man recommended broken pieces like wood-chips. He bought five dollars' worth and the man's daughter put them in a little plastic bag for him. Then he went out, that good dirt taste of ginseng in his mouth, a strange feeling of excitement in his heart as he gazed upon the ruby-scaled snake of night-traffic, the families holding each others' hands, the wide-striding loners with their paper bags.

New Year's Day! A new orbit, new lies, new juries empaneled! The Queen had given him permission to go to Los Angeles; she said that it would do him good. She said that someday maybe he could love the whole world as much as he loved Irene. He asked her whether she knew that he loved her more than he loved Irene, and she said: I don't care about that. I know you love me. —From his car he saw Irene's relatives kneeling on plastic bags around the wet grave, scissoring away grass-tufts from the headstone, scrubbing with window ammonia, uncovering the flower-holder from the sod and filling it with water before they lowered the carefully trimmed carnations in. Now they were upraising their golden-foredged Korean hymnals, and they began to sing with closed eyes, the kids merely earnest, the older relations dabbing at their eyes. He wondered if they would prostrate themselves like the family two graves down, the mother in a sky-blue robe, the pigtailed daughter's dress, snow-white, with bright red, blue, yellow and green stripes, the father in black—that family actually touched their heads to earth, but Irene had not been old enough to gain much ancestral seniority before she died. Besides, that other family appeared to be Chinese; their necromantic rites might be different.

By now maybe she would have been serving giant won tons with a baby tied to her back with a blue sash—but she was moving farther and farther away from that as it was, her rotten bones partially demineralized.

He stood on Sacramento Street, lonely and helpless, chewing his chunks of ginseng.

It was at that moment that time began to come undone for him, as if the Beasts of Light and the Beasts of Darkness were eating each other; and he truly believed that the Queen's reign must close. A moment later, it seemed, he was harvesting the honey from days long past when Irene still lived; and a moment after that it was already a foggy Easter Sunday and he found himself trapped in a fair on Union Street, almost every float being an ad for some business. Peruvian musicians, in rain-bowed national or pseudo-national dress, sweetly, liquidly piped, so that once again he remembered that hot day in Union Square last July, just after Irene's suicide. Mostly he remained preoccupied with continuing to display his futile love and loyalty for his Queen. He had memorized her like a poem and now he could recite her; perhaps his mother's books and all the hours he'd spent browsing at City Lights had done that much for him. He freely acknowledged, of course, that she was but the local solution to a universal equation. Other citizens solved each other's philosophical and erotic problems in coffeeshops without any reference to her; and a bald man smiled, wrinkling his head all the way to the crown. A brown girl tossed her head, sulkish. It began to rain, and when he tore the already sodden parking ticket off his windshield and drove down Filbert Street, tiny drops appeared between him and the world, like the ominous spheres of the old "Space Invaders" game which John had been crazy about in law school. John had killed those electronic aliens very well. When they'd been children there'd been a fallen log in the river, and John had walked on it, keeping his balance, instructing his brother: If you don't think about it, you won't fall. —That would be a perfect epitaph for John, thought Tyler malevolently, crushing the space invader raindrops with his windshield wipers.

BOOK XXX

Little Baby Birds

•

Buddha does not always appear as a Buddha. Sometimes He appears as an incarnation of evil, sometimes as a woman, a god, a king, or a statesman; sometimes He appears in a brothel or a gambling house.

The Teaching of Buddha

•

| 438 |

You feel like takin' a ride with me? said Lily's new trick, whose gaze was as hot as the ribbons of sunlight in the Tenderloin street-canyons.

If I'm pretty for you then that validates me up to Heaven, wept Lily. I could get drunk on validation. Last week I was dopesick and so I got drunk on cough medicine—oh, so drunk!

Are you drunk now? the trick asked.

No no no no *no,* trilled Lily, whose arms were streaked with the long red slit-scars of cut-open abscesses.

Where are you from? asked the trick, who was now driving her down Valencia Street past the Slanted Door where John sometimes came at lunchtime for the Vietnamese chicken salad.

I come from an ugly place, said Lily. I hope you don't come from hell because I—I—

We're almost there now, said the trick.

They passed the Mission district police station whose welcoming doorway said JU-VENILE DIVISION (Lily had been there many times), and at Twenty-First just past Val 21 where John, seeing many trendy diners, had irritably insisted to Celia, who'd wanted to go home and lie down: This is a hot spot. I'm going to have a look! the trick turned left, crossing Mission, then Capp Street where Strawberry was working, then South Van Ness where Domino, blonde and dazzling, stood facing traffic with her hands in her hair, and then everything got darker and emptier.

I wish I was the prettiest and best, said Lily. Maybe I'm one of the top girls, but on account of a lot of financial stuff am I so down, so down to earth. Not to say I'm past the bloom. You know how Beatrice always has that expression on her face and how Domino always has that expression on her face? They think I've gone psycho. It's frozen on my face. But what makes me simmer down just slightly, and then I go back to normal, is my Queen. She always hugs me or kisses me or gives me a suck, and then I want to give her a suck to make her feel good and show her that I love her. I don't have a minor psychosis. I'm a neurotic fuck but I don't have any psychosis. I'm on a hit list, but I don't have any psychosis. I am so dumb, so dumb, I am the stupidest person in the world and it really pays off. Some people really like to fuck with me because some people just like to fuck hoes.

Okay, said the trick. We just have to turn in this alley here . . .

| 439 |

Lily's dead, may she rest in peace, said Beatrice. They found her stabbed seventeen times in her throat. Our Mama she told me one of her titties got cut off . . .

Lily? laughed Domino, who was flying on crystal meth and could not bear to come down. She had already risen almost as high as the sky. Who was Lily to ballast her with sadness? —Don't worry about her, laughed Domino. She's not worth worrying about. Once I went on a date with Lily and her date, and my date didn't have enough money, so fuckin' Lily paid for both of them to get in—

That was so very nice of her, said Beatrice.

It was really stupid. Lily made about five bucks and I made twenty-five, she sneered.

But, Domino, Lily she is—

I'll tell you a good one about her, the blonde scuttered on, hating to think about death because one day death might get her, too. She's so desperate she smokes packets of sweet-and-sour sauce that she steals from that Chinese restaurant near the Thor Hotel . . . What scum!

She's *dead*, Domino. Mama saw her.

You saw some other slut by the same name. Lily's too stupid to die. She's always telling us she's stupid. She *admits* it. And if she did croak, who the fuck cares? Get out of my light, Bea—you stink! When's the last time you took a bath?

But later, when the meth wore off, Domino came into the Queen's presence where she could no longer escape or deny her sisters' tear-shining faces even though the Queen stood very straight, upraising her chin with her hands clasped behind her back as if she were some old Nubian figurine whose arms had been broken off by centuries or vandals. Then, expressing what others considered mere mercuriality but which was really an almost holy empathy with her surroundings, Domino also cried. (Even Tyler would be infected by this surprising outbreak of sadness, which he certainly would not have felt had he simply never happened to see Lily again. This taught him the vanity and egotism of grief, which so often comprises nothing except childish rebellion against the closing off of possibilities.)

We got to give the bitch a funeral, said Chocolate. That was one messed up bitch, but that was our bitch. That was our *sister*.

Where is she? said Domino.

Cops took her someplace, maybe to Dr. Jasper's office. You know who Dr. Jasper is?

Yeah, I know.

I think maybe her Mama was still alive . . .

I hate this life, Domino said. I hate my life.

What the fuck's *your* life got to do with this? This is somebody else's tragedy here. This ain't your tragedy.

The Queen gestured impatiently, and all fell silent.

Can we see her again, Mama? asked Beatrice.

Never mind about that, the Queen said. Close your eyes tight and you'll see her.

Sapphire, touching the Queen's face wide-eyed, finally understood that something might be amiss and began to whimper fearfully. All the whores saw how the Queen's arms trembled as she embraced the idiot girl. Domino began to sob loudly then. —Let's not allow those fuckers to take her away, Maj! she shouted. Let's go get Lily and—

Never mind, Dom, the Queen whispered. Gonna have a nice little going-away party for her, I promise . . .

Bernadette got excited and said: Can we take the night off like we did when Sunflower passed away?

'Course we can, child.

Is she gonna be with Sunflower now, Mama?

Yeah, she is, Bea, oh yes. You're my angel. Someday you gonna be up there with 'em, too. You're my sweetheart. You're my dear little girl.

In just the same way that Chocolate always stood hand on hip with a bewildered look whenever she needed to return to the sexual disease clinic even though she'd already been there so many times, Domino now fretted and puzzled over what was, after all, not such a surprising event—who can count all the street-whores who've been murdered, for God's sake?

I knew you bitches couldn't be trusted, she muttered. You're all running away from me . . .

Allrightie, Dom, all right, said the Queen. C'mere.

What about me? said Chocolate. Me an' Lily, we was *this* close. So why the fuck can Dom go first? It's not right.

That's not your line, sneered Domino from the safety of the Queen's arms. That's Strawberry's line.

All right now, the Queen said.

Holding Domino almost fiercely while Sapphire clung to her knees, she composed herself, then raised her hand reassuringly as they filed before her, and she touched them one by one. Later they gashed themselves with the edges of their bottlecap charms.

| 440 |

Who's gonna kick in for Lily's funeral? said the Queen. How 'bout you, Beatrice?

All right, said Beatrice without enthusiasm, maybe I can go out an' do a B.J. or somethin' and kick in five dollars . . .

Strawberry?

Why do we have to help that fuckin' *bitch?* She's scandalous. She snitched on me one time—

Strawberry, shut the fuck up when the Queen's talkin', warned the tall man.

I am, I am!

Talk about snitches! You're all fuckin' snitches!

Well, Strawberry?

Gimme a few hours, Maj. I'll try an' get five dollars. That bitch is gonna owe me in Heaven.

Bernadette?

Oh, come on, Maj, I got the shakes; I gotta get well . . .

If you got the shakes then *use* 'em. Go *shake* some ass and make some money. That's the way to get well, child. Domino?

This is not going to work with me, the blonde said coolly.

An' you was just cryin'! tittered Chocolate.

Shut up! *Shut up!* You're the one who abandoned me that time on South Van Ness. How *dare* you even—Maj, make her . . .

How much you gonna put in, Dom?

I told you. Zip. Squat. Fuck, that's all Lily ever did, was zip and squat. I say good riddance.

Dom, I don't like your attitude.

Oh, leave me alone for once, Maj. You're always picking on me. Lily's nothing to me, so why the hell do I have to break bread?

'Cause she's your *sister*.

I don't care; she never—

The Queen rose. —Hey, ho, shake it down; break some bread, you little cocksucker fuckin' bitchmama shitass, she said tonelessly.

| 441 |

Where are you from? the trick said.

Africa, said the small black woman. How 'bout you?

From here.

Well, what brought you here?

My wife got a job here, said the trick.

And where's your wife now?

At home.

Oh, so she's at home, but you're out and about, huh? chuckled the Queen. What was you fixin' to do?

You feel like takin' a ride with me?

Sure. Sure we can have some fun.

She got into the car.

How far is it you be wantin' to take me? she asked.

About two miles, he said. He was a balding, bigheaded man, whose white moustache curved down, and whose heavy eyes expressed a crazy sadness and vulnerability, like some bestubbled pouting child.

Allrightie now, the Queen said. What's your plan? Or you just playin' with me like I was a little bird?

I want to—I, uh . . .

It's okay, mister. Nobody have to be shy around me. I know what you want. You want me to make wee-wee on your face?

How did you guess that? said the bigheaded man, agitated.

Well, sweetie, I guess I just know sometimes. I can do that. That's no problem if I can drink a beer or something first, to make some water for you . . .

I want to ask you something, the trick said.

Shoot, said the Queen.

What did you like to do when you were little?

Oh, playin.' I just used to play an' play. Playin' with the boys.

We're almost there now, the bigheaded man said. We just have to turn in this alley here . . .

Now, how much was you fixin' to spend?

Twenty dollars.

If you pay me forty I'll give you *lots and lots* of wee-wee, sang the Queen in her lullaby voice.

Uh—okay . . . the trick whispered.

They pulled into the dark alley and he switched off the motor and unzipped his pants. His penis was tall and thin like the antenna on the left rear of a police car. The Queen smiled at him. He took her little hand and wrapped it around his glans. Then, with the habitual motion of the bearded shopping cart man who always checks every pay phone for forgotten change he reached under the floormat and came up with a knife.

She gazed at him with sad brown eyes. She'd known it all along. —That's him, Maj, Strawberry had whispered. That's the one that hurt Lily.

Are you sure?

Cross my heart.

Did you see them together?

No, but Justin said—

Never mind, child. Queen can see the light of truth. Queen can look inside everything. That's him. Can't you see that shinin' slime come oozin' from his heart?

No, Maj, I—

All right then, Strawberry. You run along and take care of Sapphire while I deal with him.

That was why she'd gotten in the big man's car.

Now just what was you fixin' to do with that blade? she said. You fixin' to get fierce with me?

The bigheaded man glared into her face, raising the knife high above her upturned throat. But the Queen breathed upon him, and he was still. As wide-eyed as hordes of goldfish in a tank in some Chinatown aquarium store whose proprietor's happy radio blared into the street, he sat choking, turning purple, and the knife fell out of his hand.

You think you can put a hook in my jaw? laughed the Queen. You think I'm gonna beg and plead to you? You think I'll just be your bitch? You gonna put me on a leash an' bargain over me with pimps an' chop me into little bites? You think a woman is just a thing to use and hurt even if she don't wanna be hurt? You think you can lay hands on me? You think you can stand up to me?

The bigheaded man fell back against the door, chewing on his moustache. A big bubble formed and burst between his lips.

Havin' a little heart attack, the Queen explained. Gonna be three or four days before they find you. Meter maid's gonna be sliding her tickets down and down on your windshield, and all the time you'll be in here rottin.'

He coughed. His eyes bulged with pleading pain. His sweaty face turned white.

If you'd been good, I could've made it feel good. Don't feel too good now, huh? You goin' straight to hell now. I know that for a fact.

The Queen slid her hand into his pocket and worked his hot fat wallet out. She said to him: This money's gonna go straight to Lily. You know who Lily is? You even know that? She's that poor girl that just tried to bring you happiness, that little girl that you hurt . . .

All right, heart, said the Queen as she opened the passenger side door. Wicked old heart, you can stop an' go to sleep now. An' all that blood in there, you can dry up an' turn to dirt.

Thought he could put a hook in my jaw, she muttered to herself as she walked away. Thought he could play with me like I was a little baby bird . . .

· BOOK XXXI ·

Filial Duties

•

Hear the words of the Lord, O nations . . .
"He who scattered Israel will gather him, and keep him as a shepherd keeps his flock."

JEREMIAH 31.10

•

It's going to be a decent open casket funeral with flowers, John said. And a top-quality casket, too. That's the least we can do for Mom.

Tyler looked at him.

And you're going to wear a real suit for once, I hope, John went on. Assuming you want to attend. Assuming you're willing to do that much for Mom.

And will there be a brass band, with all the brass painted black? Tyler said. I'm sure Mom's going to hear every note.

Don't you irritate me one more time, you asshole, John told him. I'm trying to deal with you now for Mom's sake. It's not because I like you. You're dead to me, Hank. Irene and Mom will always be alive in my heart, but you're nothing but a goddamned corpse.

What can I say to that? replied Tyler, swallowing. You're so convinced you've been wronged—

I'm not even talking about that. I'm not even *thinking* about that (a self-evident contradiction, thought Tyler). I'm just talking about the fact that you make me sick. Now, I'm making all the arrangements. Are you going to participate or not?

Participating means what, if you made all the arrangements? —Oh, I get it. It means paying.

I'm doing you a favor, Hank, believe it or not. You know you'd screw the arrangements up. Your idea of a funeral would be a travesty. You'd cut corners. You know that with me on top of it, it's going to be done right.

Tyler was stunned to hear in his brother's voice a tenor almost of pleading. Pity gushed through his blood vessels and dissolved the hard stone of rage in his chest.

(You feel totally passive in a way, Dan Smith had once told him. Totally open.

(But Smooth had been talking about popping amyl nitrate.)

I understand, he said.

Do you mean that, Hank?

I know you'll do the right thing for Mom.

Okay. At least you'll do that much.

Yeah.

At least there's a corner of you that's not completely—

Yeah, yeah, *yeah.*

Tell me one thing, though. Did you ever love Mom? Did you care about her?

Look, said Tyler in a shaking voice, I'll try to cooperate with you if you can just keep from getting abrasive. Can we make a deal, John? Can we lower the crap level for the three days?

So I'm abusive, John said. I know that's exactly the catchword. I could say that about Dad and go cry my heart out at some abandoned children's group. You could say that about Dad, too, but you'd rather say it about me. But who slammed whose fingers in the car door? And, more importantly, who screwed who over?

All right, John, I give up. Go have your own goddamned funeral.

Naturally. The asshole walks out on his responsibilities once again.

All right, Tyler sighed, how much will it cost?

This was the kind of question that his brother could process well. The reply came quickly: five thousand for the casket, two thousand for a classy embalming job (he'd found a really good place, the best in Sacramento), six thousand for the plot, seven hundred fifty or thereabouts for the flowers, two thousand for the service. John had it all written down, in two columns. He'd employed the octagonal silver pen which Celia had given him.

I get it. So that's thirteen grand plus eight plus two, so twenty-three grand, right?

Very good, said John. You can add. I already knew you and my wife could *multiply.* Get it?

All right, so my half will be around twelve, I figure . . .

What's the matter? Too rich for your blood, Hank? You going to come crying to me for another loan?

And I guess I'll finally get to chat with Celia again, he said, determined to be polite to the very end. That was his only plan now. John doubtless had other plans.

Aha, returned his brother with accustomed mirthlessness. You want to chat with Celia. Well, why should I be surprised? Just don't expect me to leave you alone with her.

Would you please cut it out?

Fine. I apologize. You're innocent. So how's the spying business?

Slow, said Tyler, drinking thick bitter coffee which slowly dissolved the ache in the back of his head, like an archival wash patiently clearing a yellow fixer stain from a photograph.

When was the last time you actually talked to Mom?

About a week before she . . .

I was there, Hank. She asked for you.

I was—

Yeah, where were you? Out fucking around?

I—

In the Tenderloin?

Capp Street.

For Mom's sake, I tried to reach you all day. She kept asking for you, so I kept calling and calling.

I—

I kept calling, but your answering machine was off. Technical difficulties, I guess, laughed John. And Mom kept asking me where you were. And she loved you so much, but you were busy cavorting with whores, you goddamned asshole.

Yeah, something like that.

And the phone rang and rang, but *you* weren't fucking there! You were out spreading AIDS!

I don't have AIDS, John.

Whatever. Don't you want to know what Mom said about you?

I guess I don't.

Then you never will. I swear before God right now, Hank, that I will never, *ever* tell you what Mom said.

Get a grip, John, please.

Listen to that! Bastard tells me to get a grip! And meanwhile he—

How's Domino, John?

His brother's face altered, and Tyler could not resist a sense of triumph.

| 443 |

So how much pain did she feel? he asked.

Oh, not much. She was having her chest pains, and then about five minutes later she—

John began sobbing.

Tyler sat across the table gazing at him, wanting to put an arm around his shoulder, knowing that if he did then John would punch him. He inquired of himself what the Queen would do, and knew the answer: Comfort John. Slowly his head drooped down toward the floor.

| 444 |

Dan Smooth put him in touch with an undertaker named Mort Robinson who was willing to talk.

My brother wants an open casket funeral for our mother, he said. Is that reasonable? I'd like to save some—

Oh, they're almost always open caskets. Just yesterday I did one closed casket. The family didn't want to see her, because she was old. It was the first in a long time.

But just what is the point? I figure an hour after the funeral she'll be in the ground anyway, so—

The point is *art,* Henry. A good embalming job is a pearl without price. When I first started thirty-two years ago, if somebody fell out of an airplane, you had to make 'em look pretty or they thought you were a lousy funeral director. When I started, they wouldn't let you use gloves for the autopsy. They used to lock up the gloves to save money. Everything had to be done the hard way. And now they try to take shortcuts such as closed casket funerals where they don't have to do anything except roll the corpse into the box. In my way of thinking, that's not art. But lemme tell you something. It's all a crock of shit. When my time comes, run me through the garbage disposal, man. Henry, you know how many times I've had a stiff sit up and thank me for a job well done? I'll bet you can count the times.

I figure it's going to be around twenty-five grand.

So you're going lavish. Your brother has a reputation for that. I remember his high school graduation. Well, Henry, take it from one who knows: It's all vanity. Let your brother throw his money down the hole. This industry is nothing but a guilt trip. Don't swallow it. Don't think you're doing your mother any favors. Who are you using?

Lewis.

Oh, him. Little glitzy, but he does a good job. Listen, Henry, I can call him up and get him to switch that mahogany job for a plain pine box. He's using mahogany, isn't he?

Yeah, I—

See, I *knew* he was the type! Switch it, man. Nobody'll ever know. It can be done after the viewing. The burial will look just the same. Save you at least three grand right there. And . . .

Let me think about it.

So you're going to stick with the program. Hey, I respect that. Who am I to come between a guy and his mother?

| 445 |

For some time now Tyler's debts had been rising, but this sudden new expense, for which he really should have prepared and for which he had laid away nothing whatsoever, in part on account of his unwillingness to acknowledge to himself the seriousness of his mother's condition, in part simply because his obsession with the Queen *requires* him to neglect everything else, looked fair to trip him up. Last year he'd resigned from the Department of Motor Vehicles database in order to regain possession of his twenty thousand dollar bond, but somehow that money didn't go as far as he'd expected. Now he couldn't search the DMV records directly anymore, unless he wanted to take a chance and employ somebody else's password. If they ever busted him when he did that, he'd be sunk. The previous August, in between desperate stabs at loving the false Irene, he'd taken a hot grim Sacramento freeway drive to the credit counselor's office, weaving between long white trucks filled with tomatoes. As he watched, a tomato blew off and smashed on the asphalt, and then his right front wheel went over it—a bad omen. He felt nauseous. Broken glass sparkled loathsomely in the yellow grass. The American River was low and brown. (Decades ago, he and John had gone to the riverbank to see a meteor shower, but there was too much ambient light, so in disappointment Tyler had focused his binoculars upon the canted half-moon and actually saw a crater, as well as the tan continent of serenity which clung to that clean white sea of light which bled white beauty into the darkness, like a menstruating goddess.) Green lawns and long low offices with their grass lawns assaulted him. He turned in, and the shadow of a bird passed over the black parking lot.

It was lunchtime. The office, immense, air conditioned, bright and carpeted, lay almost empty. He had an appointment. The receptionist led him to his assigned place in front of the L-shaped desk with the two computers.

His credit counselor wore an eggshaped stone in her wedding ring. She was very well kept. She grimaced. She said: I'm not an attorney. I recommend you consult an attorney.

Dandy, said Tyler. Why didn't I think of that?

And this is just a copy, the well kept woman said. You just sign right here. And here. And also here on page three.

| 446 |

Celia, suddenly anxious that she might not yet possess the perfectly appropriate dress to wear at Mrs. Tyler's funeral, and encouraged in this nervousness by John, who believed it impossible for anybody to take too many pains at the impending ceremony, drove with the two brothers down to I Street in order after obtaining the appropriate parking validation to join the big-buttocked matrons at Macy's stalking down bargains, lonely old ladies inspecting tag after tag, letting the fabric drift through their fingers; hearty old shopping women with two Macy's bags already in each hand, still wandering and gathering, while from ceiling speakers so-called "easy listening" music fell like a mist of insecticide, not quite drowning out the real music of cash registers. A crisp indigo skirt hung in the PETITES section like a pinioned butterfly; that would have looked very pretty on Irene (who'd been fascinated by shoes and who knew every relative's waist size). An Asian mother wheeled her little boy in a stroller, looking for something secret and specific. A saleswoman in high heels clattered rapidly back to PETITES, returning an escaped dress to prison. Women mulled through the sales racks in meditative pairs, slowly nodding and considering. Sometimes they looked up, gazing vaguely toward a nonexistent horizon. This was the kind of place in which, like an elf-queen's cave, one spent a moment and lost a life. By some cheerfully hypocritical caprice, the addictions that it sold were all legal; thus they lacked the thrill of real need and predaciousness. Macy's smelled better than the Tenderloin, and people didn't hurt each other in its chrome-trunked forests of sweaters and checked pants-skirts; Tyler used to rebel against it all, as if he were some Communist, but now he was contented enough to sit in one of the overstuffed armchairs because he wasn't struggling anymore; he had no hope of working free. This place had belonged to Irene's world, so how could he have anything against it? Where could he go anyhow?

| 447 |

Two necktied men swung open the double glass doors as John, Celia and Tyler entered the funeral parlor. —Aw, horseshit, Tyler muttered.

They kept the lights burning all day in there, to mimic a vigil atmosphere.

John, is my tie on straight? Tyler whispered. I haven't worn one in so long, I—

Let me adjust it for you, said Celia with a friendly smile. He felt her cool fingers on his neck.

It's all right now, she said.

Thanks, Tyler said. Which room is it? I—

Hank, you were just *in* this room yesterday, John said. Are you going to screw up now and wander into the wrong room?

Henry, do you want me to run and get you a drink of water? asked Celia. Are you okay?

No, I—

Hank's fine, laughed John. It's just an act he puts on to get the girls. Here's Mom.

Mom never wore lipstick, said Tyler.

Yeah, well, it's not so bad on her. What do you think, Ceel?

She looks very . . . well, I don't know. I feel a little uncomfortable. I—

Hank, where did you get that ratty necktie? That looks like one of my high school castoffs.

I think it is.

Did I ever tell you about Gaspard's? That's the place for ties. If I'd known you were going to wear that piece of shit necktie, I would have—oh, hell. So that's Mom.

Tyler stared at his mother's corpse in silence.

I remember that dress, Celia said faintly.

Of course you do, John said. That was her favorite dress.

She looks so thin, Tyler said.

That's because you haven't *seen* her in a long time, John instantly replied in a needling voice.

Henry, why don't you sit down for a minute, Celia said.

I'm fine, Tyler said.

He's actually eating up all your attention, John explained. Hank's a bit like a vampire. Well, that's not exactly the right comparison at a time like this, but . . .

But you get the gist, Tyler said to Celia, who said nothing.

| 448 |

When he saw how happy John was to get a bargain on the casket, Tyler felt him to be *innocent;* he felt that he himself had fallen so far below him, into hellish guilt. He thought John infinitely better than himself. John thought the same.

| 449 |

John rolled the wine around in his mouth and made a face.

It's okay, sir?

If this were a cabernet I'd send it back.

He's a schmuck, said John to everyone (a category comprising Celia, his brother, some of the neighbors—his mother's best friends Mr. and Mrs. King were on vacation in Santa Barbara—and an aunt they hardly knew). I've had this waiter for two years and he never improves.

Celia cleared her throat. —I feel a little tickling feeling, she said.

How's the wine, Hank? said John.

Good, thanks.

Well, that was a beautiful, beautiful funeral, Mrs. Simms said. You brothers certainly went all out.

It was the least we could do for Mom, John said.

And, Henry, it was such a pleasure to see you doing your part.

Thank you, Mrs. Simms.

You looked so nice in that suit. Did John loan it to you?

No, it was a rental, except for the tie, which I, uh—

That's the sort of man I like, said Mr. Simms. Pays his own way. No obligations.

And the casket was beautiful, said the old aunt. Was it mahogany?

Tyler nodded with his mouth full, hastily swallowed, and prepared to explain, but by then John was already saying: Celia and I looked at every damned casket they had in stock. When we saw the mahogany, we knew it was just right for Mom.

And she was smiling almost, said Mrs. Simms. Well, well. And what's going to happen to the house?

Hank and I were about to talk about that, said John, and Tyler's heart sank. He cleared his throat and was swallowing a mouthful of half-chewed asparagus, trying to think of some polite way to change the subject when John slipped his arm around Mrs. Simms, leaned toward her as her husband and Celia looked complacently on, and said: Now tell me the latest with your daughter. —Then Tyler remembered: Oh, yes. Mrs. Simms has a daughter.

She still doesn't want to work. She wants us to keep doing everything.

Well, what are you gonna do? John chuckled. Maybe she'll change her mind.

She listens to that Satanic music in her headphones. That really bothers me.

Well, her *friend* does, Mr. Simms interjected. We don't know about Fiona. Maybe Fiona listens when we're not around. How would we ever know?

I read that Satanism is the biggest problem in America today, said Celia. Of course I never—

It really bothers me, Mrs. Simms repeated. Actually it makes me quite upset to talk about it. Could we please talk about something else?

Have you tried one of those reprogrammers? the elderly aunt put in. Apparently they can kidnap your child and readjust her to get her back in tune with reality. They do a lot of work with cults.

It really bothers me, said Mrs. Simms. I need to see the dessert list now. This place has the best desserts.

Look, Hank, said John. Why don't you let me buy you some shares of Tostex? It's a revenue builder.

In Tyler's heart a feeling had begun to unfurl itself until it was as big, tall and ugly as Sacramento's new courthouse. Sooner or later, he always got that feeling from his brother. It resembled his sensations upon entering the Wonderbar early on a rainy week-day afternoon and seeing the sadfaced unhealthy regulars already there, the jukebox silent, the place dark and ghastly, and no one wearing even the excuse of exhaustion, the day not having yet advanced sufficiently to be dismissed, merely wasted and dismissed like life itself, passing without desperation, passing, just passing, until cirrhosis, accident, stroke, cancer, suicide, homicide or heart attack.

The other thing is that you've got to improve your cash flow. What I want is for you to take Mom's house.

Well, John, that's very—

I mean, it needs a lot of work to maintain it, but at least you could live there rent-free until you grew up and made something of your life.

Oh, fuck off, Tyler said.

Mrs. Simms gasped.

Or if you sold it off, well, of course you'd get socked with capital gains, but you might as well take what you can get. I mean, how often do gift horses come begging in your life, Hank?

Oh, every once in a while, but they usually give me V.D.

Unbelievable, said Mr. Simms.

Cut the clowning around and face facts. You're a nobody and you're going downhill fast. You've got to try to reverse the slide. It's a bit late, but you can still make something of yourself. Just write off the first forty years and forget 'em. Just—

I don't want the house.

So you don't want the house.

When the time comes to clean it, or sell it, or whatever, I'll come up if you need my support. I can do unskilled work—

I don't need your support. Mom needed your support. But that's something I guess you never—

This is so *unpleasant,* said Celia.

The will's going to get probated in this case, John informed him. So . . .

Tyler continued to be silent.

You know what? You know what the difference is between you and me? I may be a pain in the ass sometimes. I may be meticulous or demanding. But at least I *feel* something. At least I act. I know you think I pick on you. You're much more polite than I am in conversation. But I refuse to get mad at myself. You may be more polite but you're the exploiter in all this. You just sit there on your fat duff and—

Mr. Simms cleared his throat and said: I know that at stressful times like this, feelings within families, sometimes run high, but—

Yeah, you're right, Tyler said wearily. Of course, even that you can't accept. I can see your face. You think I'm just trying to avoid conflict.

Should we order more wine? asked Celia.

What are you *about*, Hank? That's just what Singer always asks me. And—

And what *are* you about, Mr. Noble Principles? How do you answer him? I know! I just bet I know! You say, *leave me out of this!*

John laughed a merry, ringing laugh and struck Tyler on the back. —You've got me pegged, he said in high good humor.

How do I feel about this? Tyler asked himself. Why, how terrible! I must be damned! I feel nothing. It's just as he says: I *am* nothing! But how can that be? Didn't my Queen promise me I bore the Mark of Cain? Maybe it's *he* who's nothing. But compared to me he *is* noble. At least he never . . .

Look, said John. When all's said and done, I don't want you ending up as some homeless bum, okay?

I don't figure it will come to that, said Tyler palely.

I don't believe we're wanted here, said Mrs. Simms. This is such an extraordinarily *personal* conversation.

You hang out with homeless people, don't you? I mean, those crack whores, those tramps . . .

In John's eyes, Tyler thought he saw an appeal: *Don't say anything about Domino in front of Celia. Please.*

(Smooth white shirts and soft black trousers, shiny black shoes—that was how Domino thought of John. She gave him good marks for money, cleanliness, and deportment. But now he was trying to run away from her. It was only natural that she would refuse to let him go. And he had gone.)

Yeah, some of them are a bit transient, he said.

The homeless guys that get forced into that lifestyle, I don't really have a beef with them, his brother announced. The ones that choose it really piss me off.

Something in the pomposity, in the sheer chutzpah of this man's assertion, why, it reminds me of Domino, Tyler realized. He clenched his fists and said: How's Brady?

Fine. I hear you parted on bad terms.

Well, he laid me off.

He fired you.

This is the atmosphere I always come back to, Celia told Mr. and Mrs. Simms with an ugly smile. —They say you can't escape your background, so this must be my background.

I had no idea it would be like this, said Mrs. Simms.

John, he *laid me off*. We had an agreement, and—

I'd like to see a copy of that agreement.

Now who's spying and snooping?

I want to help you, Hank, John pleaded.

Oh, you're the better man, Tyler said. You'll do fine. You don't lie to people the way I do. You make good money. You wear nice neckties. You take care of yourself and others . . .

Do you want me to forgive you or not?

What kind of forgiveness would it be, if it were up to me? Anyway, it's too late.

How do you know what too late is?

You want to know about too late? Fine. I figure that since this is May, Irene was already five months pregnant this time last year, Tyler said defiantly.

| 450 |

He shook John's hand goodbye. Celia wouldn't look at him. He'd already dropped by the funeral parlor with his cashier's check. It pleased him to feel that he owed John and his mother nothing now. He would make his own way, or not. He almost felt sorry for John, because it would have made John so happy to help him. Let John help Celia. He did not sleep in his mother's house. John and Celia were there. In his motel there was a Bible in the bedside drawer, and he opened it to Genesis and read: *Abraham journeyed toward the territory of the Negeb, and dwelt between Kadesh and Shur; and he sojourned in Gerar.* Outside, he heard a train go clinking musically by. The place-names, ancient and strange, clattered in his mind like boxcars. He thought upon his doings, and was satisfied with what he had done.

Early next morning, anxious to escape from his mother's grave, he packed his suitcase, guzzled two styrofoam cups of coffee in the lobby, checked out and drove toward the freeway, wondering whether he ought to visit Irene's grave in Los Angeles, but somehow that seemed of no importance. His mother was gone, Irene was gone; soon the Queen would be gone. *They shall die of deadly diseases,* the motel Bible had said. *They shall not be lamented, nor shall they be buried; they shall be as dung on the surface of the ground.* He rejected this. John had invited him to breakfast. He and Celia were almost certainly still sleeping in each other's arms. Tyler had made up his mind that the best policy would be to make Celia hate him, and to accomplish this in an unostentatious manner which would give John no grounds for suspicion. It was not that he thought himself in danger of propositioning her; he would much have preferred to win a new friend. But any such friendship would damage the pattern of his brother's tranquility. Best to be gone, unlamented, where he could lie upon his Queen's breast like dung.

Now he was approaching Loaves and Fishes on Sixteenth Street where the bleak-packed stones on the dirt comprised a pavement which plateaued up above the overpass by the railroad tracks which ran dully perfect beneath the clouds, and a longhaired girl wheeled her bicycle, whose basket was full of clothes, her husband or boyfriend in camouflage stopping, reaching under the fence for his bottle of beer. Tyler felt restless. His energies could settle on no firm object now that he had given up Irene's grave. He longed to eavesdrop on this couple, or photograph them, or merely go steal mail from anybody's mailbox. Displeased with these yearnings, he parked, locked all four doors, and walked through the underpass tunnel, in which somebody had painted the words **WHITE POWER**. Where was he going? Between Kadesh and Shur. Slowly he retraced his steps. Before he knew it, he had walked all the way to the river where it had just rained and the anise was already shoulder high and there were purple blossoms everywhere. The water trembled with blue stains between cloud-reflections. Bending down, he picked up a little plastic liquor bottle frosted by stale crack smoke.

An old panhandler stood holding an illegible message like one of the lost Gnostic Scriptures or Dead Sea Scrolls. He glared at Tyler and said: Repent.

Repent what?

Everything, brother.

I already do.

Then you're saved. Move on, so others can see the message.

Tyler shrugged. He moved on. Then, having considered, he returned to the panhandler and said: You know what? I don't repent of absolutely everything. There's a dead woman I love, and I also love my Queen. I don't repent of either of those loves. So what do you say to that, hey?

So you're damned. Move aside.

What about my mother? She just died.

Did she repent?

I wasn't there.

Then why ask me? Move on.

You know what, *brother?* I'm your enemy. I bear the Mark.

I love my enemies, because Jesus told me to. Move on.

Where do you want me to move to?

Hell.

I get it, sniggered Tyler, and he wandered off, rolling his eyes.

| 451 |

It was a Sunday warmly fogged over. He wanted to be home even though he wasn't sure whether home meant being with the Queen or something else. Actually, he dreaded seeing the Queen. The uneasy disorganization of her hive had begun to affect him, and the loving guidance he'd previously received from her now seemed unreasonable to demand; he was selfish; she must be tired; for her sake he wanted to go away but feared that such an act would likewise be a kind of betrayal. Suddenly he remembered how late one winter afternoon, it must have been in December, he had met her amidst the immense brick and concrete buildings south of Market, some of whose roofs bore smokestacks like giant cigarettes, or metallic whirling onions for ventilation; at sunset those cubes all had pulled down as snug, heavy, thick, and safe as a good girl's underpants those steel accordions graffiti'd with signs and signatures resembling snarled wires—pulled down snug, yes, thereby sealing off those loading docks which on whores were known as cunts. Against the steel-shuttered face of a shop whose owner had gone to bed hours since, she who was his Queen was waiting in a long pale coatdress which came almost down to her sneakers, and she was almost smiling, with light weeping from her eyes. That was the last time he had seen her happy. (She always laced her breasts tight against her chest.)

Just as the Queen's long insectlike eyelashes upcurved whenever she nodded off, so Tyler and his car ascended into dreaminess. Wasn't this cityscape made up of trivialities? Sometimes it was foggier than today, and the Bay Bridge's silver girders stood alone in whiteness in much the same way that at noon Capp Street was always so wide and white, the walls of its little houses like naptime sheets. Sometimes the weather was clear, and then the city offered itself so beautifully to his gaze, although of course what one saw of it from the Bay Bridge was only John's San Francisco, perhaps Brady's, not his; he didn't belong among the financial district's computer punchcard facades whose coldness and sharpness the fog had pasteled into utopia. He drove nearer. San Francisco's streets were inlaid with little white apartment squares. The window-pitted faces of those skyscrapers smiled on him, almost close enough to be caressed. Passing the Harbor Terminal, he descended into the zone of billboards, riddled with an anxiety which almost made his teeth chatter. There were too many secrets inside him which might fall out with a loud rattling noise, all his fear and shame corroding off rusty metal parts of his insides, so that they might clank and give him away. He had to move on tiptoe all the time. Sooner or later he'd trip up.

He exited at the freeway at Bryant Street near the Hall of Justice where at that moment a black man in orange sat beside the chest-starred bailiff, both gazing in parallel at the huddle around the judge, and the smiling, bustling, waxy-faced public defender prepared to be Christ. Tyler meanwhile drove to Land's End, accompanied by the coarse buzzing of a small plane over the Bay, a fishing boat not quite on the horizon, the faint smell of pines as couples sneaker-crunched the sandy path. The day became gloomy, the sky as white as Chocolate's best tricking sweater. When he got out of the car, a stupid little bulldog with a pink bandana tied around its throat gazed at him.

Some Brady's Boys with their shirts off were sitting in a circle on the beach with their arms across each other's shoulders. A man was reading from the Book of Ezra: *Of the sons of Nebo: Je-i'el, Mattithi'ah, Zabad, Zebi'na, Jaddai, Jo'el, and Benai'ah. All these had married foreign women, and they put them away with their children.* Amen.

Yeah, yeah. My God is a jealous God, Tyler sighed to himself.

| 452 |

He went to Green Apple Books on Clement Street, opened the Buddhist Scriptures, and read: *Things do not come and do not go, neither do they appear and disappear; therefore, one does not get things or lose things.*

This stunned him. He thought it one of the most amazing things that he had ever read. Thinking about his mother's death and the Queen's impending disappearance, he felt comforted.

But then he read: *. . . the mind that creates its surroundings is never free from memories, fears or laments, not only in the past but the present and the future, because they have arisen out of ignorance and greed.*

Irene swooped into consciousness, and he rejected this teaching. He rejected everything. He refused to accept that there was nothing more than ignorance and greed to his love. Granted, he was selfish, delusional, desperate; so must his love be. But he *honored* Irene. He would go on honoring her to the last, even more now, perhaps, that he could not have her.

Things do not come and do not go. Now in his anger he denied that also. He was a Canaanite, proud of his own pain. Irene was his pain. She had come. She would never go. He would carry her decomposing corpse on his back, fleeing God's righteousness down the ages.

| 453 |

Just after the inbound L Taraval line leaves Taraval for Ulloa, its tracks curve in, along with other ingathered routes and ways, right before the Philosophers Club offers its green neon shot glass to the foggy night, gapes West Portal, whose arched palate hovers above the tooth-pillars which separate outbound and inbound lines. The gullet of that mouth goes on and on, all the way downtown to Embarcadero, where one can transfer to the beast's intestines, the Bay Area Rapid Transit, and continue on under the Bay itself to Berkeley, Richmond, Hayward or Walnut Creek. West Portal's long dark grooves echo with faraway voices and useless travels.

Tyler stood beside the tall man, watching a strangely crowded streetcar enter the tunnel, heading away from the sea.

Looks like everybody had the same idea, he said.

The tall man looked at him. —You mean to get out of this fucking city?

Tyler shrugged.

See, this is California, with all the beautiful pictures, and all the beautiful women, and all the rotten attitudes.

You've got that right, Justin.

Better believe I do.

Now hop in my faggoty car and I'll drive you to my million dollar white man place.

Soon the tall man was drinking beers with him in the kitchen and calling him *brother.* Tyler said: Thanks, Justin. My mother just died.

The phone rang twice, stilled itself, then rang again. The tall man answered. He said to Tyler: She'll see you now.

| 454 |

Dreams sought him out like hands touching Sapphire's hands which she flutteringly pushed away. The Queen woke him up in the middle of the night, whispering: Do you love me? Are you disappointed in me? and he hugged her and they went back to sleep.

He heard the tall man stealing pills and vials from his medicine cabinet. He lay with his Queen, his dear little Queen who was sleeping now with her neck bent back and her eyes rolled whitely up in her head and her hair fluffing darkly down and back.

| 455 |

He dreamed that she had vanished and that he had searched for her everywhere. His brother was lecturing him, shouting: You're a private detective who doesn't want to know the truth. You *know* where she is.

No, said Tyler, feeling his face going pale.

Why don't you go to Feminine Circus, you asshole? They probably have her stuffed and plasticized . . .

No, no, no! he screamed. And the Mark on his forehead glowed as bright as the yellow sign for the Cinnabar with the inverted white blue-bordered trapezoid of Jonell's beyond and then Bamboo Pizza's white crest, and finally the yellow zone of Pho Hoa Hung which had once been Pho Xe Lua and beyond which crack-flames and malice shot down into darkness and sometimes whizzed up to Hyde Street, then went left past the 222

Club all the way to Turk Street where they expended themselves in misery, disappointment and drunkenness.

| 456 |

Okay, baby, it's okay, the Queen was whispering, and he fell asleep again, comforted by her rich chocolatey smell.

| 457 |

The phone rang. —Yeah, it said. This here's a fella lookin' for an asset search. I got the judgment.

All right, answered Tyler. It was eight in the morning. The Queen snored softly in the crook of his arm.

You think you can find him?

Well, your guy had *one* chance to hide his assets, Tyler said with a chuckle. But I have an *infinite* number of chances to find 'em. Who do you think is going to win?

Amen. How much will it cost me?

Minimum of five hundred. I don't charge anything more unless I find something. Do you have his social security number?

Well, gosh, now, Mr. Tyler, I—

If you don't have his social, I have to charge extra to get that. Not only do I have to access some expensive databases, I also have to run a check to make sure that you're legit. If you actually have a judgment against this guy you should have his social.

Well, the judgment hasn't quite come through yet.

I see. Do you know anything else about him?

Well, I don't know how much money he has squirreled away, but this is his partner. His former partner I should say. I thought he was family, but he robbed me blind.

I get the picture.

Mr. Tyler?

Yeah.

This *is* Mr. Tyler?

Yeah.

I can't rest until I get this guy.

There may not be enough money to pay off your judgment, sir, Tyler warned him. We'll have to charge you five hundred dollars no matter what, just to kind of grease the wheels.

(Grease the wheels, laughed the tall man in the living room. That's rich.)

I don't care about that, Mr. Tyler. I want justice.

What's your name, sir?

Bill Bullock. I treated him like a brother, Mr. Tyler, and he—

And your ex-partner lives here in the city?

I don't rightly know.

So you really can't tell me anything else about him? I suppose I could run a couple of traces . . .

Well, what's your advice? Before I pay anybody, I need to know what I'm getting. It's harder to *trust* these days.

I would never spend more than ten percent of what I might collect. You want to go ahead?

Five hundred, huh? What the hell.

What's his name?

James R. Chong.

Lemme do some ultimate weapons research here. Lemme see if he's on the California Criminal Index. You want to come by in an hour? No, make that two hours. Bring your retainer.

What, you mean pay in advance?

That's what *she* said, Tyler laughed jeeringly.

Henry and his faggoty come-on bullshit, joshed the tall man in an affectionate voice. It sounded as if he were stealing Tyler's cassette tapes.

You mean you can't just invoice me? I mean, I, uh—

Well, think about it, said Tyler, hanging up on that potential client, who never called again. Stretching out his arm very carefully in order not to disturb the sleeping Queen, he captured the envelope, just yesterday received, which announced that it contained an important notice, and inside, just in case he'd forgotten that announcement, the blue-bordered flier began in flaming red letters:

IMPORTANT NOTICE!!!

and continued (employing typographical variations far more impressive than the monotonously chiseled words of the Los Angeles sign he now knew so well which said COMPARE FOREST LAWN'S MORTUARY PRICES): You may already qualify for this **Debt Consolidation Loan** *UP TO* $200,000!!! *PAY OFF YOUR BILLS—PLUS!* (At New Year's, the green slope of graves had been strewn with Christmas flowers beneath the white statue.)

Letting envelope and letter drop out of his hands, he rolled back and began kissing the Queen's lips.

| 458 |

He went to Macy's and stood looking out at Union Square while Irene tried on dresses and she said: Come into the dressing room with me, baby and help me with the straps, so he went in and the saleslady came after him very fast and said: Excuse me sir but men are not allowed in the women's dressing area and he said: Why? —That's our policy, she said. —He stared at her. He said: My Queen needs me in there. —She said: Sir, you're going to have to leave the store.

| 459 |

I don't wanna do this anymore, said the tormented Queen. I'm so tired.

Of me?

No, baby. Of everything.

Where will you go?

Where I came from.

Who are you? he said. Where do you come from?

She continued silent, and he said: How old are you?

Well, pretty goddamned old. So now you don't love me?

I figure I'll always love you, he said. I just want to know you better. I really want to know everything about you, because after you're gone it'll be harder for me to understand everything if I don't, you know, uh—

I'm yours, Henry. You believe that?

No.

Okay. You're mine. How's that sound?

Plausible.

Well, then that's who I am. I'm the one you belong to.

Are you my God?

Kneel down.

He knelt.

People like you an' me, baby, we don't have no God. But sure. If you had a God, I could be your God, if you want. What the hell. I can do magic. I can love an' kill an' protect. I can hear your heart sighin' an' I can answer your heart . . .

I don't get it. Please just give me something to keep in my soul.

That's all you people from here ever say, just *gimme gimme gimme* . . .

You know I love you. You know I believe in you. I just—

Allrightie. Look me in the eyes. Now, where I come from, and where I'm going, and where *you're* going, there's a big wide red desert of dried blood that chokes you when you breathe, an' a big yellow sun made of burning, dried-up piss that stinks so bad you can't hardly think, an' there's winged demons with whips an' that's all there is. All a body can do is run. But when you got the Mark like I gave you, they can't do you no harm. They just move you along like the cops kickin' us off Capp Street for two or three weeks, 'cause we got that gift. An' you can wander around an' try an' find some shade, but *there ain't no shade.*

Will I find Irene when I go there?

All that dried blood, that's from her.

I thought you said she was in Heaven.

Henry, she was, but you kept thinkin' about her too much.

Will I find you?

If you love me, you'll find me. If you don't find me, it's 'cause you breathed in too much of Irene's blood an' forgot me. But I'm not jealous of Irene. I'll always wait for you. Just don't let your mind go.

What about Lily and Sunflower? he asked in a strangely childlike voice.

They're burnin' up in that yellow sun, tryin' to help us, givin' us light.

And where's my mother?

She's in Heaven. You can't see her no more.

But if I think about her really hard like I did about Irene, then—

You won't. You know why?

I—

Last time I'll ever ask you, baby. Try an' answer. It'll do you good. Henry, child, *did you make love with Irene?*

I—don't you believe I'll be thinking about you, Africa?

Sure.

Don't you believe you're my darling?

That's my line, not yours, said the Queen with a hoarse and gentle laugh.

And can I ask you about Domino? I kind of figure that she—

No. I told you enough.

Just tell me about Sapphire then. You told us that after you were gone then Sapphire would be you—

Yeah, baby. Lots of pieces of me in different places.

| 460 |

Tightly gripping his skull between her knees, she urinated into his mouth and he hallucinated with ecstasy because for him as for Sapphire the womb of worshipful craving could still conceive; the power of the Queen's secretions had never dwindled, only withheld itself from the others for their own good, to prepare them to feed themselves; the mother had weaned her children. Later, Tyler's irony gland, which itself uncontrollably excreted upon and tainted so much of his reality, discharged chemicals in his bloodstream which incited his brain to remember one long dim afternoon years ago in the Inn Justice when his buddy Daro at the public defender's office had bought him a shot of Glenlivet and told him the tale of a defendant he'd had to meet in the lockup whom all the other uglies and miserables had reverentially avoided before because the man kept smearing excrement on his own head, then eating it. Revolted, Daro had pronounced the man insane, but one wise old walrus at the office had aphorized: *Never call a man crazy unless he eats somebody else's shit!* And indeed it had transpired that this defendant, whose crime Tyler could no longer recollect, had been shamming. And yet Tyler himself, who might not have been crazy, was already craving to eat his Queen's excrement. Why? She endowed Tyler with herself and all the good things which God allowed her to give him because he was truly hers and faithfully went in to her without scruple or quibble or malice, so she would not wean him before she must with her absence, and every fleck of her spittle seasoned his happiness more richly than the best cocaine or heroin. And so once again we turn to the notion of chemical happiness. —In my job I meet all kinds of people, and I don't like most of them, Loreena the barmaid once said. If I drink enough, I don't feel anything. —And whenever Tyler drank two or three cups of coffee his perceptions improved and focused so that he could see every hair on a passing woman's head; and this temporary superiority over his accustomed listless dullness not only pleased him but also gave him hope. Was he somewhere else? Was he escaping anything? He would have denied it. He saw every character of every advertisement—didn't that mean he was more in the world than before? Wasn't he living more densely, resisting death?

| 461 |

Tyler was standing in the doorway talking with the false Irene, whom the Queen had asked him to put up at his apartment for one week and who had already been the subject of three warning telephone calls from his landlord, when a man he had never before seen approached. —Watch it, said the false Irene out of the side of her mouth. You're gonna take the fall for something or else you're gonna . . . —The man had been leaning up against a lamppost for half a minute, watching him. As he came near, Tyler casually brought his clipboard down at an angle between them, keeping the man out of the doorway. —What can I do for you? he said in a neutral grey voice.

Can I talk to you in private?

The false Irene, who could barely hobble ten steps anymore but who could still shoot up heroin as deftly as a Kabuki dancer rotates his pretty wrist, thereby causing his gilded fan to flash like a fish in sunlight, stood there beside her brother, her protector whom she now desired to protect, glaring and listening.

About what? Tyler said.

Can I hire you for half an hour?

We don't do half an hour jobs, said Tyler, keeping the clipboard between them.

Can you recommend somebody?

Try Wessels on Stockton. He might do half-hours.

Well, really what I wanted to do was put you back on Mr. Brady's payroll. You know, help you out, cut a little deal . . .

Go on inside, Consuelo, he said to the false Irene. I'm right behind you.

He locked the man out and took Irene upstairs. She stuck her fishy-rotten tongue in his mouth. Gently he patted her between her shoulderblades, thinking: I participate in this not out of lust or disloyalty to my Queen, but out of duty. This is my religion now.

You got ten dollars on you? said Irene.

· BOOK XXXII ·

The Fall of Canaan

•

Happiness follows sorrow, sorrow follows happiness, but when one no longer discriminates between happiness and sorrow, a good deed and a bad deed, one is able to realize freedom.

The Teaching of Buddha

•

Who's got a radio? said Harry. Okay, let's have 'em on the desk. What number you got?
Fourteen.
Fifteen.
Twenty-one.
Nineteen.
Outside, a car alarm was honking and honking
Come on, boys. Radios, radios!
Three. We're gonna double up with Exercise.
Twenty.
Okay, said Harry, tell the slapper it's time.
What the fuck you talking like that to me for? said the slapper, his face empurpled.
You think I don't know what time it is? You think I'm working for Mr. Brady and I don't
know what time it is?
Yeah, yeah, yeah, said Harry, to humor him. And you can lead us to the whores, right?
Told ya I don't hang out with them anymore, the slapper said. I just know 'em.
Harry yawned. —Big day. Queen's day.
That cunt, said the slapper. Trying to start shit with Mr. Brady . . .
On Harry's desk, an alarm clock began to buzz.
Let's pull everybody inside, please, called the slapper. (Majestic as a New York cop, he
wore sunglasses, storm-blue duds and a wide orange belt. Spread-legged, he towered like
a statue.) Everybody inside. Mannie! Mannie! Everybody inside.
They came inside, and the slapper sang out: Hey! Lockdown! Can't you show some
respect? Mr. Brady's about to speak!
Okay, said bowling-pin-shaped Brady with his hands in his pockets, strolling slowly,
his suspenders tight. Let's listen up. I'm only going through the breakdown once, so
when you hear your group number, listen for your name. Here we go. Group Apple:
Chu, Darrah, Davis, Glovinski, Goebel, Haji, Hall, Hameed, Hamidi . . .
The slapper kicked Harry's desk and cried: Chuckles! Chuckles! Hey, you, fat boy!
Dude, *Brady's* talkin'! Gotta pay attention!
Out front, a bunch of Brady's Boys in the media brigade were signing the cast of a
Puerto Rican in a wheel chair.
You have Mannie's group going out with the press, Brady was saying: Don't show 'em
anything they really don't want to see. On Turk Street at five-minute intervals we have
groups Apple, Bacon, Cabbage and Doughnut, with the usual squad leaders. Doughnut
will record. Shazib, I want you to baby that microphone. Don't swing it around, don't
whack some lowlife's skull with it; you got other tools for that. Show 'em how you respect Allah, how the Queen of the Whores stinks in your nostrils. Got that? Halliday,

you be ready with batteries and tapes and whatever the fuck Shazib needs. All right. Apple, Bacon and Cabbage, when history starts to go down, give Doughnut Group plenty of room. We have to document what we do. It protects us in court and it helps with our fundraising. All you apes understand that? Good. And no one had better lie to me. The slapper's going to take charge of the new group and break 'em in. Slapper, keep 'em tight tonight; keep 'em alert. Now, on Ellis Street at five-minute intervals we have groups Exercise, Frantic, Gallop and Hunk. Hunk will be recording. Porterfield, you know your stuff now with the video camera? You gonna take the lens cap off this time? Good. And we have Group Ice on Market Street and Hyde, posted as reserves. Be ready to block their rabbit hole on Capp Street, too. Keep your engines running. Harry, I'm pulling you to run the command post tonight. Everybody got that? You call command, you don't say C.P., you say Harry. Why make it easy on the enemy? And before you go out, make sure you let Harry know what radios you have on your patrols. Questions? No questions? All right. Chuckles, front and center. Situation report.

I don't think they'll try to fight back or burn us or rush our HQ, Chuckles said. They was all drunk or cranked up last time I looked.

And when was that, Chuckles?

'Bout half an hour ago, Mr. Brady.

Well, they're tricky bitches and vicious sons of bitches. Be ready for anything, boys. And do what you have to do. Don't start anything, but do what you've been sent out to do, and if they get in your faces, you get in their faces. Questions?

Uh, Mr. Brady . . .

What is it, Porterfield?

If they get serious with us, how bad can we hurt 'em?

Don't worry about a thing. It'll take a quarter of an hour for the police to come. Anyway, we're just doing what the police don't have the guts to do. We're gonna shut the bitch down.

Shut 'er down!

Nuke the bitch!

Out, out, out! Let's *go,* crazies!

| 463 |

Look at those Brady's Boys! a woman called happily.

I haven't seen them for a while, her husband said.

Like a green serpent, the column flanked the theater crowds. Young and fast, it offered to the public a constellation of solemn, wide-eyed expressions, reminiscent of Marines.

Brady's Boys! a girl cried.

People came up and shook their hands.

An old black lady came up to the head of the column and said: I pray for Mr. Brady.

Thank you, dear.

Have a good night, ma'am, another vigilante said.

Oh, you Brady's Boys are so *polite.*

I *love* it, man! the vig shouted.

Ten-*shun!* a man on the sidewalk sneered.

The Brady's Boys looked him up and down, saying nothing.

Just before the tunnel, George, the black shoeshine man, basking on his throne, raised his palm in an Indian salute.

| 464 |

Gimme more bump, begged Strawberry. I swear I'm gonna pay you . . .

Oh, you don't have to do that, said the trick with a patronizing smile.

That's just the type I am, Strawberry replied, feeling very proud of her rectitude even though she and the trick both knew that she would never pay him. —Hey, where you goin'?

She stood cleaning the pipe and then slowly uplifted it like a monstrance and breathed blue flame while the TV's blueness whirled with hubcaps, dogs and falling cereal.

I said where you goin'?

I don't talk much, said the trick, already at the door. He flipped the switch, and the bare bulb on the hotel ceiling flickered on, sizzling and glaring uneasily.

Dim the light! the whore cried in a panic. She rushed to the window, peering around the curtain as if she were waiting for something.

What for?

I'm tweaking. I'm naked. Dim the light.

Hey, this is my room, lady. I paid for it. I don't wanna be in the darkness.

Come on. Dim it.

Grimacing, he turned it down. He was a well-built and steelyhearted man in his fifties or very late forties. She thought that she'd seen him somewhere. But of course her memory illuminated all comers as evenly as the dun-colored light deep in pedestrian underpasses.

You're making me nervous, he said to her. Are you setting me up?

I'm just tweaking, that's all.

In the hall, when he opened the door, a black face, woeful and baleful, wanted and needed and promised something. On the TV, a four-wheel drive rushed to the edge of a cliff. He stared gloomily outward for awhile, then closed the door again and doublelocked it, employing both the lock that functioned and the lock that didn't.

What's your name?

Strawberry.

Hey, Strawberry, you know what I want you to do?

Shhhh! she whispered in a panic. Don't say my name.

Slow footsteps crept in the hall outside. Then they stopped outside the door.

Is it locked? she whispered in terror.

The door burst open, and two Brady's Boys came in. —Good work, they said to the trick. The boss is waiting.

All right. See you, Strawberry.

Before the wide-eyed girl could even begin screaming, one of the men clapped a hand over her mouth and shoved her down onto the bed so that the other man, having locked the door again (which she saw only too clearly now that her supposed trick had only pretended to lock), could sit down on her stomach with his full weight so that she could scarcely breathe. They kept her there for a good five minutes while she desperately squirmed, unable to utter even the most muted sounds, and the stink of her fear-sweat was occluded by the smell of the cigarettes which the two men sat placidly smoking.

Cool, the man who was leaning on her mouth finally said. —Now, are you ready to listen? Nod your head if you're ready.

Frantically, she nodded.

Just think of all the time she's stolen from your life, the man said. Know who I mean? You can move your head yes or no.

Strawberry shook her head.

I'm referring to your so-called Queen. I'm not saying you should be bitter, but this is your chance to get even. Now, Strawberry, what we need is a *location.* An *up to date* location. If you tell us, I think you'll feel a great sense of relief.

Oh, cut to the chase, would you? the other vig said. This little tart probably can't even sign her own name. *Can* you, bitch? *Can* you, bitch?

He slammed the heel of his hand into her left breast while the other man clamped his palm even more tightly down over her mouth so that her shriek could not come out.

Maybe you can tell we're serious, the first vig said. We're here to find out where the Queen is. Now, if I take my hand off your mouth for a minute, will you be a good girl and answer me or will we have to hurt you a little bit? Shake your head yes or no. Yes means you'll be a good girl.

Strawberry nodded very very quickly.

| 465 |

One down, one down! laughed the Brady's Boys.

The breast-slammer's cell phone rang, and he answered, listened, and said: He says he's issued by John Deere but he doesn't know the policy number. Yeah, that's right. The guy says don't touch me, I says who ya talking to? No, we got one here. We chalked up another one. Don't worry. We always get there before the cops.

| 466 |

That was the future; that was July. Right now it was June twenty-seventh, one year to the day since Irene's death. Tyler sat in the Wonderbar all day, drunk and paralyzed. Then it was June twenty-eighth. Then it was June twenty-ninth.

Crack smoke didn't taste bitter and clean to him anymore. It tasted bitter and dirty. Of course maybe he wasn't getting the good stuff.

At the Cinnabar, the shouting and bullying of the television made him sick. It stank of cigarette smoke in there, and nausea unballed itself within his stomach, extending curious tendrils to probe him. —You gotta pick one, the television commanded. That's how it works here.

He remembered how when Irene and his mother were putting on their coats to go meet John for a movie (he had needed to stay by the phone for an infidelity job) and when his mother was in the bathroom he asked what they were going to see and Irene told him and he said: Hey, haven't you seen it before? and she said: Yes, but please don't tell anybody because I want to make her happy.

He remembered seeing her in a corner of the kitchen table later that night, stroking the dog's furry ears and trying to explain something to his mother, who gazed at her in a deeply searching and skeptical manner, and he wanted to shout: Leave her alone! Don't you know how good she is?

He dwelled among the whitish mist and ice-plants at Ocean Beach, one of several silhouettes in beach fog. Fleeing south, a solitary jogger in a yellow sweatshirt vanished like a yellow sunset, and then Tyler was left alone to stare at the lovely white foam of greyish waves. Fog rode the foam and the waves. He gazed at the silhouettes of fishermen.

He sat drinking amidst the ruins of the Sutro Baths, which once must have been like an ocean greenhouse with a view of Seal Rock, and ranks of young women in black one-piece bathing suits, everything clean for the people's aristocracy (so at least it appears in the old photographs). Now the baths are roofless. Rebar protrudes from their concrete honeycombs, which do not remain quite ornate enough to be stately or "pretty" like Roman ruins.

His apartment reeked. The false Irene kept pissing on the carpet, and two nights before the Queen had defecated in his mouth; he'd washed the sheets, but he couldn't get rid of the smell, which was now also Irene's smell. His Mark of Cain was becoming more literally evident night by night, and his home resembled a cast-off snakeskin. (On the television, Brady was laughing: Nine Hydras in every realm.) Irene sometimes tried to thank him and even to love him, for which he ought to have been grateful because she was his sister, but he did not much want to talk.

Have you ever had the feeling that something isn't on the level? Smooth had said. Well, of course you do—every time you look in the mirror.

Knock it off, said Tyler.

But seriously.

Oh, probably when I come across something like a staged accident. All the sudden, nothing adds up, and so somebody must be bullshitting. You just get to know people. You go back to the attorney and say, hey look, this client's lying to you.

Tyler looked in the mirror and said: I'm nothing. I'm a phony. I want to be something real like her. Help me, please. Help me, help me. I'll give up everything.

It now seemed to him that Smooth was correct, and his love for Irene had never been genuine, that had she been alive, unmarried and interested in him, he would not even necessarily have been drawn to her, although at the same time he was capable of doubting that supposition, for his heart lunged toward her in odd surges like a compass needle in a magnetic storm—what if it had all been one of those impermanent distractions falsely dignified as "escapes"? The terrible thing was that here had been no escape then or now. Love meant nothing, solved nothing, being but a garment of hypocrisy or desperation thrown over naked solitude. He awoke anxious. Did life have no purpose? Or had he merely failed to discover that purpose? What if he never found it, or, worse yet, learned it too late, as he lay dying?

Hoping for work, he went out to the beach while Irene snored and drooled. An hour later he ascended the carpeted stairs and approached his answering machine, knowing that the round red eye would not wink at him, shocked to hear himself muttering aloud: Please, please, please. —No one had called. —He said to himself: *It's not gonna happen. It's not gonna happen.* —He said it like a mantra. He was trying to convince himself not to expect anything ever again. He wanted to die. He wanted to be dead. *It's not gonna happen.* He fell down onto his bed without even taking his shoes off, and he wept. He dreamed that he was with Irene. When he awoke, his eyes were swollen, aching and wet.

He masturbated, imagining that his tongue was inside Irene's cunt and that he was giving her happiness.

Suddenly it occurred to him that he might not have gazed carefully enough at the red light on his answering machine. What if the battery were weak? He went and studied it again, but it was dark. He pushed the replay just in case, and heard silence, followed by a fatuous beep.

He drove to the Tenderloin, taking what John would have referred to as the scenic route on that hot day when Chinatown smelled like barbequed pork, urine and fresh oranges: He drove past the Sam Wong Hotel, then turned into the shade of Bow Bow Cocktails and the Hop Yick Meat Market. In a window, tongs moved barbequed duck legs. Then came a produce market, proudly showing off its cherries which resembled iridescent pink eyeballs. He turned down Powell Street in the direction of Pine, with the deep valley of the Tenderloin lying ahead. Celia bought faux jewelry somewhere around here. Then his way went down and down and down. Traversing the northern border of the Tenderloin, he followed Geary Street west, as if he were searching for the Queen as in the old days. Geary and Taylor was Walgreens and news, cafes and delis. Then it became harder at the Hob Nob bar, but Wing Fat Travel and Tomiko's Beauty Saloon reminded him that the Tenderloin was much softer than it used to be even five years earlier, let alone fifteen. So it went, right to Polk Street, where Sophia Spa and Adult Video reminded him of the existence of nude celebrities. Down that cold grey slope of Polk Street was a motor lodge outside which the tall man stood bloody-eyed and smelly, trying to sell *Street News* to tourists. Tyler waved to him and then drove aimlessly for hours. He was killing time to avoid killing himself. —One of the moves we make at Eight-Fifty Bryant, another weary public defender had told him year ago, is what we call a convenience move. If you're already serving life for one crime, why waste everyone's time and money trying the guy on another charge? Shuffle some papers. If the other verdict is overturned, then you can always bring the guy up for trial. —But Tyler was shuffling his own papers now, driving uselessly round and round and round. As night fell he was rolling up Columbus where he saw a long restaurant with many people at many tables all sitting behind glass; he perceived a woman's bluejeaned buttocks and blonde hair at a bank machine, then cars cold and fishy in the night, all framed by a string of lights. A red Chinese sign dwelled upon a white wall. Then he drove to the wharf, in downsloping smooth silence. The bright boiled-crab red neon sign of the Safeway directed him onward toward a multi-tier parking garage which was open and lit like those "pretty" Roman ruins. It was foggy in Cow Hollow, and foggy going down Gough Street. When he crossed Jackson, a yellow light winked at him like a friend, and so he let himself coast back into the Tenderloin again.

On Geary and Jones, the Nazareth Hotel, he was happy to learn, was NOW RENTING. Chocolate was strutting up Eddy Street in a jet black raincoat, swishing a riding crop made of a broken-off car antenna.

See that bitch? she said, strung out on an unknown drug, pointing at nothing. I did twelve months on account of that bitch 'cause some white lady said I looked like her. Can't she see? I dunno. She drinks too many sodas.

Is that right, said Tyler.

You think I'm out to lunch, don't you? You think I'm crazy like Mary. You know, you have your females and you have your *deep thought* females. I'm just different. I wanna climb trees and help build the treehouse.

I get it.

Henry, can you lend me five dollars? I need to fix so bad I'm gonna puke. Just five, Henry. Just this once.

What did the Queen say?

I'm afraid to ask her.

Why's that?

'Cause I done asked her too many times awready.

Where is she now?

You wanna date her?

Sure.

Why not me, Henry? I got a pussy, too. Maj'll never find out. You can pay me twenty an' I'll give you a nice flatback. I give real good head. I bet I can give better head than Maj. Please.

You love her, Chocolate?

More than anybody in the world, definitely including you. But love is love an' business is *business.*

At least you're honest, he laughed, giving her four ones, which was all the cash he had left.

You don't love her as much as you used to, the whore accused. All the time your lips be mumblin' *Irene, Irene.*

Cut it out.

Hey. I'm getting fifty bucks a shot from that guy over there. If you gimme thirty I'll give you better than I give him.

All right, Chocolate, he said, not really listening. I've got to find Maj now.

She's sleepin', Henry. Half a black down, inside that junked car.

Nudging him, she pulled down her shorts to show him her blackish, raw-scratched crotch.

Thanks, he said, walking on. She slowly and disconsolately followed. Tonight or tomorrow would be the end, he believed. *Why has the LORD pronounced all this great evil against us? What is our iniquity? . . . Because your fathers have forsaken me, says the LORD, and have gone after other gods.* His face was as dark grey as the Tenderloin streets at night with the pale, slotted cliffs shimmering above them, the darkness lit up with whores' brassieres which shone like globs of glowworms. He tasted tears in his mouth.

Justin, what's happening? he said.

Just kickin' back with our Queen, the tall man said, leaning wearily with his hands in the pockets of his bright new bluejeans. Just stealin' some nightshade.

Ah, said Tyler wisely, picking his teeth. Does your leg hurt?

It *goddamn* hurts. You packin'?

Not tonight.

That's what *she* said.

Why, you old *misogynist!*

No, I do not know where Domino is at. Why ain't you packin'?

I sold my gun, Tyler explained. Needed to pay some expenses.

Then you be a worthless mother. Some gangstas popped a cap at me, but they missed. I wanna track 'em down, ex 'em out . . .

That's life in our set, muttered Chocolate sarcastically.

You talkin' smack to me, girl? I said, you givin' me static?

Oh, brother, said Tyler. Where's Maj?

Why? Wanna turn her out? Wanna pimp her out?

Something like that, he sighed.

She's takin' Sapphire to the emergency room, Chocolate said. Comin' back pretty soon, maybe about one two three hours . . .

What's wrong?

Just one of her fits. She bit her tongue pretty bad, that's all . . . And I been feelin' poorly, too. I had a fever of a hundred an' four degrees an' they wanted to call the emergency room but I said what the hell 'cause if I kick the bucket so fuckin' what. Know what I mean? An' now I feel so dizzy an' I got no place to stay. I gotta make ten dollars so I can . . .

Around the corner Domino was saying: And if we continue to let her, we'll never make an honest buck.

That's right, that's right, said Bernadette.

Making a buck out of us is *her* program, said Domino, strolling into sight.

Christ, Domino, where would you be without her? Tyler cried out, utterly dejected in his soul. At that moment the whole crew of them seemed to him to be as beasts, ferocious and incapable of love or gratitude.

Without *whom?* returned Domino pertly.

You know your relative pronouns at least. I like that . . . he muttered.

Oh, leave her alone, said Bernadette. She just got georgia'd by two black men. She's in pain. She's agitated.

And what's their blackness got to do with it is what I want to know, Chocolate said. What's the difference what color their cocks were if they made her do the G? You're all the same. Deep down, you all think black folks is just niggers.

Did you get hurt bad, Domino? he said, sorry for the blonde but still almost insufferably weary.

What's it to you? You're not here to see me anyway. You're here to eat out Maj's pussy. Why would you care?

My car's parked by the Wonderbar, he said. You want a ride to the hospital?

Thank you, the blonde said. I know you mean well. It's too late. Everything's too late.

Tyler narrowed his eyes and asked: Are you bleeding?

Oh, fuck off.

Your whole face is swollen. But wait a second, Dom. Those are old bruises.

She stepped beneath a streetlight so that he could see her better, muttering: No, uh, I—

Look at you! he cried, shocked. You've got a black eye and a split lip. And your tooth . . . Those aren't from today, either. What happened to you?

Stuff, said the blonde wearily.

You okay? he asked again and again.

Who do you think you are, the Queen? You're not my mother. You're just a prick like everybody else.

Irritated and hurt, Tyler walked away, peering into the obsidian darknesses of parked cars. The tall man smirked.

Chocolate was pouring out a line of detergent at the back door of the Wonderbar when he got back. Literacy is a disease, she mumbled

You want a ride? Tyler said.

She never answered. She was getting cracked up and paranoid.

Finally he had to leave. —Thanks for the ride, she said bitterly.

| 467 |

What had happened was this. Have you ever seen one of those antique jigsaw puzzles whose pieces are held together by a springloaded frame? Depress a lever, and everything flies apart. The royal family was a family no longer, and its members associated merely out of vestigial habit. They had every practical reason to continue honoring their kinship; but such sensible behavior as that would hardly be human.

The first outright cleavage had been precipitated (one could almost say perpetrated) by insects. Just as when, peering beneath the twin freeway bridges at Mission and Duboce into the grimy shade, you can spy Mission Street palmy and picturesque beyond, so when the tall man steel-shuttered his eyelids and went to sleep his perceptions carried him past his grief into strangely happy dreams. But when he awoke he was already scratching. His ankles wore chains of whitish bites which his fingernails quickly turned red. He went about his business that day and tried not to think about it, but at night he couldn't sleep, and in the morning the desperately itching welts were on his buttocks and elbows and behind his knees. Again he went about his business, scratching. His sisters were clamoring for their medicine, but all he did was cop a dime bag for Strawberry. Surely the Queen took note of his discomfort, but she said nothing. In the old days one pass of her magic hands across his body would have relieved his misery entirely. The next day the welts reached his wrists, which he scratched until they bled, and then they began to blossom on his belly below the navel. He entered the Rolley's supermarket on Geary Street and approached the pharmacist's counter. Beside him stood one other customer, an old Chinese, who was being unenthusiastically waited on by a bored white girl. Behind the glass Justin could see two other pharmacy employees drinking coffee. Finally a Filipino-looking lady came out and asked him what he wanted.

I got scabies, the tall man said. See them red bumps on my hands? I have 'em all over my body now. They be gettin' worse and they itch like hell. I want you to sell me some Mites-Off cream.

Have you tried anything else? the woman said.

Slabbered that calamine lotion on 'em, which didn't do no good.

You'll have to see a doctor, the woman said. Calamine is the strongest thing we can sell you over the counter. Maybe you have a virus.

Look, lady, I'm *aware* what scabies is, said Justin. Know who you're talkin' to? You're talkin' to the scabies *expert*.

I'm sorry, the woman said. Mites-Off is by prescription only. You'll have to go to the doctor first.

I go to some doctor they gonna make me wait a couple of days and pay 'em sixty dollars, said the tall man, trying to keep his temper. I *know* you can find some way round that.

There's a free clinic on Eddy Street, the woman said, looking him up and down. Why don't you go there? The wait's only half an hour.

You see that snail slime down there? said Justin. You want to really fuck with somebody, you take 'em and make 'em lick it.

The woman turned her back on him and returned behind the glass to her colleagues.

The tall man could see the Mites-Off bottle behind the counter and he almost could have reached it, but then the Chinese would have opened his mouth in amazement, and the other pharmacist would have called Security and he would have been caught before he could run very far. The tall man departed, scratching.

He had been to the free clinic several times before. It was always closed. He stalked over there and it was closed again.

He scored three dime bags for the girls, scratching. Without him what would those sad bitches do?

Down under O'Farrell and Leavenworth's walls which were so white and sunny under the cloudless sky he met by prearrangement his sisters who came heel-clacking by: Chocolate, Strawberry and Domino. (The false Irene was sitting in a doorway sniffling. He wasn't about to support that bitch.) First he saw them silhouetted like the shoulders of beer bottles in a bar cooler whose windowpane was white with condensation. They stopped. They smiled at him, and he scratched himself in a rage.

You lookin' like a *fierce* O.G. full of stories, Chocolate tried to compliment him. Strawberry fired off a jealous glare at her, and he grinned a little, scratching.

What you got for me? he said shortly, scanning the cars for vigs. You get me some fresh money, bitch?

Why you talkin' that way to me, Justin? I be your trueblue homegirl.

Quit playin' them games, Choc. You know who his homegirl is. Leave my man alone.

Only Domino still hadn't said anything. She stared into the tall man's eyes, licking her lips with that chemical craving which he knew so well and which stupid-ass johns so often mistook for sexual desire. At Strawberry's interjection she grimaced, then began looking up and down the street out of habit as she combed her hair.

Strawberry, you be lookin' a *mess*. What the fuck's wrong with you?

Oh, I, uh, I need to make some money. Hey, you seen Maj? I wanted to ask her—

No, I ain't seen her. Just get on with it.

He sat down regally upon the topmost step of a dark doorway, and his love and fellatrice rushed up to him, kissing his knees as he slipped the balloon into her hand. —Now go do your thing, he said, scratching. Show some willpower. Go *maintain* yourself. Next.

Chocolate flew upstairs for her own private audience, whispering: Justin, you lookin' so *good* to me . . . and the way she said *good* made the tall man's penis harder than superclass rock cocaine, but he replied: Don't you feel even a little bit ashamed, to be cockstealin' from your own sister? Ain't *you* a snaky skanky bitch! Now, gimme gimme. I paid out good money for that dime bag.

Please, Justin, jus' carry me one more time. I feel so sick. I don't feel right. I *swear* I'm gonna make it up to you. Swear I'll do *anything*.

Don't make no difference. If you tell you do anything you gonna do anything *regardless*. 'Cause I be your *connection,* bitch. You so scandalous. Now break bread.

Maj said—

Don't make no difference.

Last came Domino, who, knowing the score, crawled up to him with a ten dollar bill in her hand. He always gave her quality stuff, and she for her part, although he'd offended and threatened her many times, never tried to deceive him anymore. The tall man liked Domino at that moment. She paid her way. She never disrespected him. If she weren't such a royally *vicious* pain-in-the-ass bitch, he might have taken her on. Strawberry for her part had become a pretty spiritless bitch. Sooner or later he'd have to fight somebody over her, and he didn't know that she was worth it. Why should he always have to keep her protected? Domino might be a psychotic old broad, but at least she kept herself together whenever trouble came. Still, he pitied Strawberry, who for all her faults was loyal. Wishing to avoid further trouble between her and Domino, and flattering himself that he could have Strawberry, Domino, and Chocolate, too, in any combination and at any time of the day or night, he smiled patronizingly into the blonde's face, making certain that she understood what a favor he was doing her, and then he said: You got sense. More sense than a whole lot of niggers I know.

Domino flushed with pleasure. —Hey, Justin, thanks.

He slipped the balloon into her bra. —No charge, he said.

Justin, daddy, I really really appreciate this.

You owe me. Once I get my solid gold Cadillac you better wash my windshield with you pussy. Now let's fade out of here.

Then it was sunset in the Mission district, with the Altamont Hotel, newly painted yellow, contributing as best it could to the luminescence of the evening whose grey sky glowed like a puddle of irridescent steel—gorgeous light, summer light. Chocolate was still on Eddy Street trying to peddle her tail. The false Irene lay in an alley off Sixth Street, retching in withdrawal sickness, praying for Tyler to come. The Queen sat in what used to be Lily's room at the Lola Hotel on Leavenworth Street, teaching Sapphire how to tie her shoelaces, listening to the crazy whore's stories, singing hymns with Beatrice, whose optimistically twinkling vaginal work had paid for the room and whose breasts now dangled, and last but not least passing out pinches of pure angel dust from a cardboard box which many many whores had grafitti'd for her. The crazy whore turned off the light, asking Beatrice: *Is that your most favorite?* and all the women knelt around their Queen who rose and stood naked, shining for them like a lamp. As for the tall man, he was feeling good because Strawberry had copped a prescription for his Mites-Off and then earned the Mites-Off, too, with a quick ass fuck in the back seat of a stretch limousine full of drunken Japanese businessmen on their way to the airport. Her sodomist's colleagues had photographed the act many many times with their whizzing little Japanese cameras; Strawberry got a hundred dollars, which could have bought her a full gram and a quarter of pure China white. They let her off way down by Daly City where it was chilly and foggy; Strawberry stood hugging herself behind a eucalyptus tree, wondering how she would get back home as meanwhile blood and sperm trickled slowly out of her anus. Although Tyler lived not far away and had once offered to give her a ride whenever she needed it, she had no change to telephone him, saw no phone booth, and had forgotten his number. So she flagged down a taxi which was coming back from the airport. The driver refused to turn the meter on. He said to her: I believe in the Bible. Your time's going to come. —At Sixteenth and Mission he charged her fifty-two dollars for what should have been a twenty-five-dollar ride. Strawberry didn't care. She was so happy to be able to help her man that she flew into the Walgreens not even caring about the reddish-brown stain on the back of her dress, oh, that dress, that once-white emblem of a bride—Cain's bride. They awarded her that Brady-shaped bottle of salvation, and without a prescription, either! The tall man stripped down inside his sleeping bag, which Strawberry had stolen for him weeks earlier from a German tourist, scratched, uncapped his joy, scratched again, rubbed himself from neck to ankles with the bitter white salvation which Strawberry had purchased, then proceeded to the laundromat and washed all his clothes except his coat, under which he was naked. For good measure he dressed himself in brand-new hand-me-downs which obedient Chocolate had obtained for him at San Francisco General Hospital, and now he was sitting tremendously at his ease in a room at the Crown Hotel, a hot dark stuffy room with television, a *safe* room which Strawberry had rented with the remainder of her sodomy fee.

I think you ought to stop scratching, Strawberry said. You might get an infection.

Listen, bitch. My business is my business.

Domino said: Strawberry, you're still bleeding. You need to change that toilet paper.

It's okay, you know, just a little bit sore. That always happens down there when I, uh—

How much did he give you?

Fifty dollars, Strawberry lied, knowing that Domino and Justin would both despise her if they knew that she had allowed the taxi driver to gaffle her like that.

Shit, the tall man said.

Shit what?

Why we all doin' this? We could move on. We could be gettin' what's ours.

I know this guy who runs a meth lab, Strawberry said brightly, and he, uh, he really likes me. So maybe we could, uh—

We can't let some goddamned trick be our boss, know what I'm sayin'? 'Cause that go against our *pride*.

The two women nodded, downcast, afraid of a rage from nowhere.

Tell you a story, the tall man said, as Strawberry lit her crack pipe. You wanna hear a story?

Always, Strawberry said, laying her hand gently on his.

The tall man was feeling majestic and wise. He believed that within his head and heart and soul was gathered a hoard of hard, gleaming jewels which it would cost him nothing to pass around. His eyes scuttled rapidly across their faces. He longed for admiration.

He said: All right, so once upon a time there was this homeless guy walkin' down the streets with a bike, walkin', walkin' . . .

Suddenly he realized that he was not at all certain what would happen in this story. He could not remember where the homeless man and the bicycle had come from. Had the homeless man been himself? He had hustled and lied for so long that he scarcely knew anymore what was true about himself. —Gimme a hit off that, bitch, he said to buy himself time to think. He took a long, sweet toot, feeling alert and happy as the two women gazed at him with puzzled attention.

Listen up, he said. I ain't talkin' just for the hell of it. You know what makes me feel so sad? I . . . Well, you got to understand this was a *nice* old Schwinn Varsity bike from maybe 1960 or 1970 that was maybe somethin' rusty but it ran good. I'm telling you it ran like a dream. Took that guy everywhere. And as long as it stayed rusty and crappy it was safe and he was OK but he loved it so much that one day he painted it and then it got stolen, brother. It got ripped off. You hear what I'm telling you?

Yeah, so you lost your bike, sneered Domino, scratching her ear. Hey Strawberry, give me a hit off that.

Don't make no difference if it was me or if it was not me, the tall man said. The thing is that it *happened*.

So what's the point? Let's move things along. Hey, Strawberry, I said I could use a hit.

Domino, I got everything I own in this plastic bag, and this plastic bag's almost empty, and I'm tired.

So you're not going to give me a hit. Is that what you're saying?

Fuck your whinin' ways, Dom. Don't talk shit. I'm tryin' to tell you somethin' . . .

I'm all ears, said the blonde, her self-protective words and thoughts resembling concertina wire rolled loosely around barbed wire above high concrete walls. —You're telling me we're supposed to hide what we've got and dress like junkyard dogs, right?

I'm tellin' you, beware of golden aspirations. You already got the easy life, bitch, so—

So you're afraid to aim higher than crappy old Maj. Well, fine. Why should I give a shit about you? But—

'Scuse me, said Strawberry to Domino, and the tall man actually permitted her to interrupt him because he still for the life of him could not remember the punchline of his own story, and he was ashamed.

What? You finally going to let me have one teeny-weeny hit from your precious pipe? Just tell me what hoops I have to jump through.

Strawberry shook her head until her hair whirled. —You actually owe *me* a rock, hon.

I goddamned well *do not!*

From before you was in the joint. Remember? You shorted me that time with the fat trick, you know, that old white guy with the bad breath . . .

Do *not* insult me with your bullshit anymore, you fungus-encrusted old cunt!

At this, the tall man, smiling grimly, clapped his palms echoingly together so that the whole world almost collapsed like a beer can ground under someone's heel, and he said to the blonde: Yeah, bitch, don't get smart with *my* bitch. You *heard* what she said.

Well, lordy lordy day, as Maj would say. Ain't he in a grand mood? Did your *bitch* let you cornhole her today, or is that just for fifty-dollar Japanese johns? Is that why she's so uppity? They call her Strawberry because of her big red ugly nose . . .

The tall man punched her straight in the face. To Domino it was as if she were sitting on a stool in the Wonderbar and then suddenly came the earsplitting slam of dice on the counter as a cheater shouted: *I'm clean, I'm clean! I just paid you!* Only the shock of it assaulted her at first. There was no pain yet. But she went down and stayed down for a long time. Then the pain arrived—she knew that part so well because pain was and always would be her offering to the Canaanite idols—and then the shame, rage and sick sadness of the assault began to settle weirdly down upon her shoulders like a crowd of fruit bats coming home, and she felt more alone than she had ever felt since she'd joined her Queen. That night at the Lola Hotel when the Queen had georgia'd her—that was what it had been; rape is rape no matter how many orgasms the rapist chokes down your throat—had commenced the withering of her affection for the Queen; and yet she still loved Maj more than anyone else and had trusted her by trusting the tall man and her other sisters, even Chocolate, from whom she had expected the first backstab to originate. And now with this one punch the tall man had forced her to don once again the scarlet mantle of the outcast. Now she must make her own way over the hard flat plain of grief, across which irrelevant caravans pass into winter. She felt appalled.

Slowly, warily, she rose to her feet, breathing heavily, with blood trickling from her mouth. She spat a bloody tooth into her hand.

I s'pose you'll go to Maj with this, the tall man sneered. Go ahead, bitch. Do your worst. I know I broke the rules.

Domino laughed in his face. —There are no rules now.

Don't bet on that. There's rules about snitches, know what I'm sayin'? Strawberry, step back from this dangerous bitch. We gonna make her fade now. This be *our* room.

Domino stood fixedly. Her face of course was expressionless, but they could both see the throat working. Domino had always been very pale anyhow. In those last months of the Queen's reign she seemed worse. Strawberry suddenly found herself imagining that the blonde had kept her aborted baby and was suckling it. For some reason she wanted to gaze upon Domino's snowy chest. The blonde's pallid face had gone paler still with hatred, then paler yet again in contrast with her greying hair, and her eyes gleamed so that she seemed almost like a vampire. Her pale face became paler still against her hair. Strawberry's heart pounded with fear.

The blonde walked downstairs, passed through the heavy grating that stood between her and the night, and posted herself at Eighteenth and Capp, wiggling her hips at the slow-eyed cars, grinning crookedly into the glare of headlights, her face covered with blood. All night her teeth rattled like glass ampoules rolled together in a drug pusher's palm.

| 468 |

I'm sorry for my part in our misunderstanding, Strawberry said when Domino was emerging from a strange man's bedroom. —I hope that you are for yours . . . —for of course it had all been Domino's fault.

Not really, said Domino with a dry laugh.

Well, I like you and respect you and want to get on with you, but if it's not going to work out then maybe I should steer clear, no hard feelings . . .

Well, I'm a muller. I'll have to mull it over, said Domino, walking away.

| 469 |

That bitch is scandalous, said Strawberry. I hate that bitch.

Why, what she done to you now?

What *hasn't* she done?

You make it sound like it goes way back, Chocolate replied cautiously. Like a citizen of a totalitarian country, she knew better than to launch any criticisms, however supposedly secret, of those who had the power to hurt her—which in no way implied that she might not under certain very controlled circumstances acquiesce in the complaints of others. Unable to forget that she had wronged the blonde, she feared her accordingly—even more now after her lapse on Mission Street not so many months before when she'd screamed at Domino and threatened her—and Domino had forbearingly *not* cut her with that naked razorblade.

We was in the joint together, an' she snitched on me when I drank my homegirl's methadone. You ever tried that shit?

I don't like them downers, said Chocolate.

Fuckin' A, girl, it's better than heroin. Lasts longer, too. Makes me feel so good and dreamy, I can hardly tell you. And my homegirl loved me. Her name was Denise. Shit, she was one good bitch. She let me drink her methadone 'cause she loved me. And that bitch Domino snitched on me. And now she snitched again to the Queen, when Justin took up some business with her, just protecting me from her bad vibes.

Now, *that* I can believe!

She was *threatening* me, Choc! And then she snitched me off . . .

(Of course none of this was true, although Strawberry believed it—or rather, she believed in its future likelihood, and so rounded a half-probability up into a certainty. It was Strawberry herself who would snitch to the Brady's Boys only two nights later.)

With all respect, that's a strange one for me to get my head around, girl. Domino, now, she's hard and mean, but I ain't never seen her snitch.

Well, I'm tellin' you, Choc, that's what she did.

You sure?

Yeah.

And you tole the Queen?

Shit, what the fuck's the point of dragging in Maj for? She'd only take Domino's side anyways. Domino's her little blonde pet. Besides, she *snitched* to Maj, which puts me in the wrong . . .

You swear she snitched on you?

I swear it, said Strawberry with a trembling voice.

Chocolate cleared her throat, then insinuated: Why don't you give her the snitch mark? Where I come from, that's what we do. I promise not to tell . . .

Mm hm, said Strawberry noncommitally, unwilling to admit that she didn't know what a snitch mark was, but Chocolate, perceiving her blankness, rushed proudly to fill the breach in her knowledge, thus: What you do, see, is take a straight razor, and you cut her real slow and deep from her mouth to her ear, so everytime for the rest of her worthless life she gotta look in the mirror, or in some stranger's eyes lookin' at *her*, she gotta see the connection between snoopin' and snitchin', an' hopefully she'll learn to *shut the fuck up* about another girl's business.

I see, Strawberry said palely, afraid to take this wrongful and irrevocable step.

Then the Brady's Boys had caught her.

| 470 |

Bitch! Bitch! Bitch! Come on out here and fight, bitch! You stole my trick, you lowdown stinking bitch! I'd commit suicide before I passed up my revenge on you, bitch! Bitch! Bitch! Bitch! You fuckin' bitch! You put every nigger dick in the Tenderloin in your mouth, bitch!

Then Domino, drunk, coked up and methed up, finally came staggering furiously out of the Overflo bar to rebut these words of Strawberry's, and she was pounding the sidewalk with somebody's padded crutch. —You stole my wedding ring, fucker! she screamed. You ruined my life! And the Queen's gonna . . . Queen's gonna . . .

But then Strawberry lunged, snatched the crutch, and smashed it down onto Domino's head. Domino started screeching like a vampire into whose heart a stake is being pounded, and Strawberry dragged her down to the sidewalk, beating her and choking her. The pimps came from across the street and stood around watching the fight. Strawberry raised the crutch and walloped Domino's forehead again. Finally the tall man strode out of the bar and wrenched the crutch out of his sweetheart's hands. —Knock it off, bitches, he said. Queen's not gonna like this.

In her rage, Strawberry tried to lay hands on him, but he threw her off, kicked her away from Domino, and said: Don't you ever hand me like that, you stinkin' ho.

Actually he was delighted. Strawberry had shown heart. She was his mean, ruthless street bitch.

Domino leaped up from the sidewalk, weeping with rage and humiliation. Her head was bleeding, but it didn't look serious. She ran at Strawberry, but the tall man interposed himself with an almost kindly impersonality, walling her off from further self-mischief. —Leave her be, Domino, he said. Domino! *Domino!*

The girl struggled in his crushing arms.

Listen to me, Domino, said the tall man, his eyelids sinking down like twilight warehouse gratings. —Quit your foolishness. You been beat and you know it. Just let it go an' I'll keep her off you. Queen's rules.

Then they all saw the Queen standing there with her hands on her hips, shaking her head and weeping as she had wept over them so many times before, but this time it meant nothing to them; she was only an old woman crying.

| 471 |

And those two niggers that georgia'd Domino, I know where they both is at, said Chocolate.

The sun glanced blindingly off a white-painted driveway gate on Folsom Street as Tyler walked past, and struck his cheek. He wondered what species the pretty trees garlanded with fernleaves at heads and hips might be.

I only told 'em about South Van Ness, I swear, Strawberry said. She was crying. —Justin? Justin? I was so so scared.

We be holdin' it down for our Queen, said Chocolate out of habit. And Justin got him a shark killer. You know what I mean? Shoot one shotgun shell from a tube . . .

I wanna get high, whined Strawberry. I want some liquid juice.

You better stop causin' us static, said the tall man. Henry, you packin'?

Sure.

You told me you sold your gun.

That's right. And just now I told you what you wanted to hear.

Reality will get you, the old acidhead Californians liked to say; reality will obtrude itself. If you're in a cattle car bound for Auschwitz, you can't wish your destiny away. —I grant that fully, said Tyler to himself, but isn't it also true that after reality has done its worst I cease to exist, which means that reality ceases to exist? So if I want to wish upon a star or a Queen, all I need do is steel myself against the worst possible pain. —This had been his attitude until the Queen had spoken of Sunflower's pain, and then he'd begun to wonder whether steeling himself might be wrong and even unworthy; shouldn't he let the pain in, feel it, be destroyed by it, and thereby get his blessed ending? Like a woman's dress on a hanger under a whirling fan, sleeves patiently gesticulating in the breeze, endlessly touching and stroking the limp form they came from, so his thoughts moved, but not really to any purpose, like a naked woman's fidgeting legs, the flesh so perfectly and unconsciously obeying impulses which the mind probably wasn't even aware that it had; if the woman lived to get old, her legs would ache and fight her even if she stirred them in a necessary and deliberate cause; reality would have gotten them then.

Okay now, the Queen whispered. This is it. Now I gotta visit with everybody in private, give everyone a chance to remember an' to cry.

(You think *I'm* crying? sneered Domino.)

The Queen said: Strawberry, you remember when the black-and-white almost picked us up an' we pretended to be fighting?

An' you slapped me in the face, Maj, an' I called you a bitch! Remember that? You're the one I love so much an' I called you a bitch!

'Course I do, sweetie, laughed the Queen, butterfly-tapping her so lightly on the shoulder.

If the vigs come in here then we gotta run back out again. Maj, I'm so sorry . . .

You didn't tell 'em nothin'. Don't worry you head, child. Vigs wanna find me, they gonna find me. An' they forced you. An' I have so many places to go, let 'em scour South Van Ness high an' low . . .

This, uh, Maj, is this goodbye? I don't see any vigs.

'Course not, Strawberry. This ain't no goodbye. I'll always be here.

Next came the blonde, so hate-strong and hate-strung like a careful sinister violin and so hate-cheerful, sounding elegant chords of hatred, and she said: You *promised* me, Maj. You said nobody would ever rape me again. And these two niggers . . .

Domino. *Domino.*

What? wept the blonde.

You're lying. I'll never tattle on you, honey, but Queen knows when you're tellin' the truth or not. Nobody georgiaed you this time.

Domino whispered: I don't trust anyone but you. But I never snitched . . .

The Queen said: You didn't wanna be marked. Let go now, Domino. Let go.

Am I marked now, Maj?

Yes, baby, you bear my Mark. So don't worry. You were my good little girl. I love you so much. Run along now.

Domino dug her fingernails tightly into her lower lip. She sat down in a dark doorway and whispered: I'm all in. I'm cashing in on these motherfuckers.

As for Beatrice, she merely hung her head and remembered faded sky-blue houses. Her Mama had not died yet. Her Mama went next door and asked: Are the Marias at home? The little girls reached up and clung to the railing kicking and smiling. They were the Marias. Beatrice had always wanted to be a Maria likewise, because then she would have owned the Virgin's name.

I think I'll take a little walk now, said the Queen, but Beatrice cried: Don't go out there, Maj—please!

You know, I was fixing to go out for a minute, said the Queen. I was calling to see if Sapphire needed some help.

What the *fuck* you talkin' about, Maj? said the tall man. Sapphire she standin' right there . . .

And now Sapphire began to dance before her Queen, kneeling with the scraps of her torn dress flaring out on either side of her like petals of a flower. She bowed her pallid face almost to the floor and rotated a greasy piece of streetstained cardboard so gracefully like a fan.

Look! said Kitty. Here comes Mr. Smooth!

It was indeed old pedophile Dan in his green Prowler, circling the block and waving. Finally he parked in an alley. —Get out of here! he cried. The vigs are coming!

Danny, said the Queen, would you kindly take Sapphire for a little ride? I'll be speakin' with you.

Biting his lip, Smooth nodded. He took Sapphire by the hand. The retarded girl didn't cry.

Okay, guys, cried Rodrigo to the other Brady's Boys. Watch me, guys.

Chill out, everybody, whispered the Queen. Better do a ghost. Come on. Move. Get out of here.

And where was Henry Tyler? Why, he wasn't there! He was—where was he? He missed the end. Was he drunk, sad or just scared? It's said that he was on Harrison Street kissing the false Irene.

| 472 |

On Powell Street, the big guy leaned against the phone booth talking, his cigarette smoking into space. That was Brady. The hot stale machine wind of the subway came up from the grating and kissed him. —If it goes up above what we can handle, we call the cops, he was saying. But you can't get contractors to do anything these days. So I think we'd better try to handle it. The whole Kloncilium backs me on that.

After this, we're going back, right? said a fat Brady's Boy. I can't take this no more. I got asthma, you know.

Here's the cops, said Rodrigo. Afternoon, officer.

Howdy, said a policeman. Where are you folks headed?

We've tracked the Queen to the Royal Motel right now, officer. We're going to see if we can make a citizens' arrest.

Well, well, the Royal Motel, mused the cop. We've had killings there over trick pads and dope. We call it the Homicide Hilton. Ninety percent of that is black stuff. Don't quote me on that. So you're gonna try to sweep her in, huh?

Well, we plan for a full Brady Search whenever Mr. Brady gives the go-ahead, explained the slapper, who was always considerate of Brady's words and breath. —The night before, we decide where we want to go. In the morning, well, we get up, go outside, and see what's there. Personally, I'm in the Empowerment Group. Our job is to go out and take the street girls away from the pimps, to *empower* 'em, you see.

Oh, dial down your bullshit extruder, the cop said.

Excuse me, officer? Excuse me! This is Mr. Brady's righthand man you're talking to! Officer, I'm a *professional*.

Yeah, yeah. Well, good luck, boys. Hope you bring her in. She's got a couple outstanding warrants.

On Mission and Seventeenth by the graffiti **SAD KING HEROIN** a Mexican kid was puking something as translucent as Asian rice noodles while his mother tranquilly held his hand. The Brady's Boys filed past.

Hey, put me through to a Hydra, would you? Brady was shouting on his cell phone. Or gimme a Kleagle if you want; I just need somebody to bounce ideas off of.

Two sad, pimpled, miniskirted women showed thigh in a doorway. One said: That Domino, some days she'll act as smooth as a bumblebee. But other days she's just an asshole. I'm takin' it to the Queen. I tole the Queen . . .

Look, baby, you ain't tellin' the Queen *nothin'*, said the other. You think the Queen got any trust left in you? Like that time you was rippin' us all off, holdin' out . . .

Oh, shit, said the first woman. Oh, shit. Here come them fuckin' vigs. Go tell the Queen!

You tell the Queen. You're the one that keeps goin' on about takin' it to the Queen. I need to get well. I need to make money. I tole you already, I sez . . .

You think Maj is in trouble?

Ain't no trouble she can't get out of, yawned the other woman. Man, I feel sleepy. An' I'm sick. An' my crabs be itchin'.

| 473 |

The vigs grabbed the crazy whore, who cried out: 'Cause I'm completely innocent. I just like to get my rock really fast and get away from you. Everybody says it's only because of my confidence that the police don't see me move oh so fast.

Slapper, should we let her go?

Yeah, bust her loose.

Get out and never come back! Keep going! *Keep going!*

See, this one's a crackhead, a vig said to the starry-eyed reporter. You can tell from the reaction you get when you watch 'em. Now we'll get up and move, an' she'll—

You want me down on the sidewalk or you want me up here? said the crazy whore. I know how to spread my legs. My pussy is worth a million electrical dollars.

| 474 |

I hear you call the shots around here, said the slapper.

Not me, said Justin. Queen does that.

Aw, don't give me your *shit*. You're a shot-caller, right?

That's right.

And I'm the slapper. Now what happens when a slapper meets a shot-caller?

The Queen appeared with the noise of a cat leaping down from the wall, a soft rapid double-bounce.

| 475 |

It ain't hot today, but it sure does feel hot, said the Queen.

She stood with somebody's unbuttoned flowerprint dress thrown around her nakedness like a robe, with her arms crossed over her breasts and the edges of the fabric falling away from each other just below so that her slightly protruding belly showed with light glowing from her navel as from a stained glass window and her crotch-moss clamped up tightly underneath and then the softness of her varicose thighs peculiarly soft and vulnerable as she stood so unmoving with her head thrown a little back and her frizzed hair slicked down across her skull and her eyes so huge and bitter far beyond suspicion and so sad.

Okay, you guys, said Rodrigo. We're gonna catch this Queen of the Scumbags now. That's her over there. I have a positive ID from Mr. Brady. Post me, boys. Let's go, you guys!

My cousins and aunts and them, they used to call us you guys, said the Queen. My sister and I, we'd always say: We're not guys!

Shut up, bitch!

I just blended in, said the Queen in a dreamy voice, but they told me that I sounded a little proper.

| 476 |

We read in the Book of Nirgal how in the epoch after Moses, when the Chosen People swept into Canaan, slaughtering all whose foreheads bore the mark of Cain, they presently reached an unknown vermillion land of purple shrubs and broad low W-shaped gullies. And they prayed that they would succeed in throwing down all the idols and enslaving the idol-worshippers, and their prayer was heard by the great God. Then a dark man sixty cubits high came toward them, striding across the dirt as red as Mars, and whenever he put down his heel the ground shook. And the man called out: My Queen bids me ask who you are, and of which tribe you come, and for what reason you enter her domains. —But the Chosen People were not afraid, and without replying to him, their great captains gave the signal, so that multitudes of archers shot him full of arrows, and he died. Then the Chosen People came on across the yellow grass, watching for lurkers beneath the dark grey-green shrubs. But there was no one. Now presently they breached a wall hewn of great blocks of marble chiseled with inscriptions in an unknown language, and saw the old pale yellow arches of the Queen's city, incised with roses and sheaves in abundance, but the city was ruined and silent. Their great captains were greatly troubled, for they could feel the breath of the enemy on their necks. They descended sunken stairs and discovered only cool dry cisterns. (Later, anthropologists would find red shards with scribbly black decorations like pubic hair, and a plump-teated mother-goddess figure fashioned out of clay.) The sand was overgrown with flowers, and beneath it wormed many dark tunnels and galleries, but never did they find inhabitants or treasure. And they knew not what to do. So again they prayed to their God. And God said: I have commanded you to be great, and therefore to usher in the jackals to howl in this place. But the heart is not yet dead. You must ravish the heart. — Then God went away. So the great captains conferred, and one among them who was wise besought them to search for the temple of the idols. Then in the center of the silent city they saw a high place with a brass door, and they broke the door down. Listening, they heard no sound. The darkness was as rich and moist as the inside of a winebarrel. Their great captains called for torches. Then searching in a dark-roofed labyrinth of timegraven arches and columns upon which the Canaanites had carved flowers and snakes, grapes and thistles, they found a wet stone passage which they called the Throat. Descending this, and shielding their torches as best they could from the cold dripping water, they found swallow-caves in the rock, as if carved out with spoons, and the swallows flew affrightedly about their heads. The swallows had no eyes, and the eggs in their nests were written on in the same unknown language. And the Chosen People were afraid, but their great captains called upon them to remain pure in their wrath, and hearken to their God. So they went on, and beneath their feet the rock burst open, and there ran a skinny brown stream. On the walls of the Throat their enemies had painted reddish faces then figures in blue-ocher outlines, and finally a blue female silhouette outlined in red ocher with a penis added. And the great captains cried out that this man-woman was unpleasing to God, and so they scratched it away. The roof was blackened with charcoal handprints, which they considered to be a mockery of their God, but they could not obliterate them, so they left them. So they descended the Throat, and as they went down, so fell a new fear upon them, because they saw marks of high water on the greyish-plated reddish walls. But their great captains exhorted them on, until at last they reached a cavern surmounted by a stone dais upon which had been painted many insect-legged figures within yellowish-white concentric circles, and upon this dais there stood an altar, and upon this altar there sat an Ethiopian woman weeping. And when they asked her why she wept, she would not answer. (Domino later swore to Bernadette, who was the only person she ever talked to about that night, and even Bernadette only heard her open her lips on the subject one time, one sad and early time before that fierce woman had entirely imprisoned herself within her new plaster mask of queenly dignity, that upon being taken away the Queen had swept the air with a raking, despairing gesture, then turned to her captors and said: I trusted these people. I had nobody else. And I still don't. —But Bernadette had been there, too, and all she heard was the Brady's Boys asking her yes or no questions; the Queen answered very quietly yes or no.) Then the great captains bade the archers nock their arrows, and they came forward with their trumpets, but one captain who pitied the woman held up his hand, and he strode to her and asked who she was. And still she did not answer. Then he asked her: Are you the Queen of this city? And the Ethiopian woman replied: *I am.* Then the captain said: Who is your God? And the Ethiopian woman said: *Love.* And the captain said: Who is your father? And she said: *Cain.* Then the captain turned away from her, and told the other captains what she had said, laying an accusation against her. And they judged and determined that she was a Canaanite harlot, fit only for death. And according to their customs, and according to the wisdom of the God who had led them to Canaan, to this city in Canaan, and down the very Throat of Canaan, they blared their trumpets and then the archers shot a hundred arrows into her breast. And as she died she cried out: *I am Love.* When she no longer spoke or moved, then they cut her into many pieces with their swords, as her iniquity deserved, and left her lying in her own blood for the vermin to eat. Then they returned the way they had come, and when they came back into the temple with the brass door they pulled it all down out of loyalty to their God, so that none could ever find the entrance to the Throat again. And the number of that multitude which came into that city was seven hundred thousand. And they took possession of that place, and lifted their faces most gladly to Heaven.

| 477 |

Actually, there was a woman I ran into last night, Mr. Cortez was saying on the phone when the tall man walked in. Mr. Cortez would soon go home to his wife and six children, with San Francisco shining white below him on the J Church streetcar line, and palms and clouds accompanying him all the way to dinner. The tall man folded his arms. Mr. Cortez winked and raised the peace sign, continuing: Her husband employed a guy and the guy didn't work out, so they got into a little scuffle and both got taken to jail and she was really distraught and tearing her hair out. —Well, buddy. I have to go. There's a client.

He replaced the headpiece's hard strange double breasts in the cradle, stood up smiling, and cried: *Justin,* my man! How's life?

Passing, said the tall man. Did Lily ever pay you off?

Yes, she settled her account if that's what you mean. Case closed. How's she doing?

Dead.

Dead? Well, uh, I—so who's in the clutches of 850 Bryant today? Domino? No. Let me guess. Strawberry?

Beatrice.

Beatrice D. Lorenzo, as I recollect, said the bail bondsman, delighted with himself. Let me call Room 201. Just Beatrice, huh?

And the Queen.

The Queen! cried Mr. Cortez in amazement. She's *never* gotten touched!

Tell me about it, said the tall man.

A cop carrying an envelope, his pistol loose against his hip, wandered slowly up to his doubleparked black-and-white, waving to the meter maid who would long since have ticketed anyone of another occupation. Then he looked over at the tall man and the bondsman, cheerily calling: Hey, Mr. Cortez, what's up?

Peace, brother, said Mr. Cortez.

Look, guy, said the tall man. We got a serious situation here.

What's her real name?

Africa.

Africa what?

Just Africa. Maybe Africa Johnston. Just Africa, I s'pose.

Mr. Cortez made a telephone call, shaking his head.—They have Beatrice, he said. But the Queen, well, they don't know anything about her.

| 478 |

And all that night the ripples of desperation widened with the Queen's girls scattering in the rain, long naked legs in high heels rushing or slowly gliding into the rain; and Tyler sat in the driver's seat hopelessly trying to figure out what to do next as rain descended his windshield so that the parking garage sign slowly vanished under the white ovals.

· BOOK XXXIII ·

Kitty's Soliloquy

•

If you do not presently meet the standard, now is the time to take action.

"Getting Ready for the Physical Ability Test" (San Francisco police recruitment pamphlet), 1998

•

I remember somewhere in the Bible it says that *dead flies make the perfumer's ointment give off an evil odor.* I memorized that 'cause that just about sums it up. An' it also says: *He who digs a pit will fall in it.* Makes me so depressed. Makes me wanna kill myself. I've been fallin' so long it's like I can't never see the sun, maybe 'cause I do my work at night time, but maybe that's bullshit since I can also remember too much light that I be tryin' to hide from like a bug. At least that lady I bought the sofa from, back when I still had a house, when I got evicted I got my money back, 'cause I went to her house an' stole it, just for my own self-respect. Now I don't got shit. I look like a fool. Know what end I shoot for? All ends, honey. Front an' back an' up an' down. I know I got more at stake. I may act poor but I was born rich. God will make diamonds fall from Heaven. Do I believe that? I don't even know. I'm tryin' to act like a big shot but I'm just a sole survivor. I don't wanna have to do anything crappy like pick up a nigger. But I do. What the fuck. My own grandmother was a nigger. I got nigger blood. Here I am, stuck with obstacles. Oh, I had riches. I had fruit inside me. I guess I was seven months along an' then this drunk fucker tried to play with me. I wasn't really his, but he didn't accept that, so my baby died. Is that why I'm driven to drink? Why shouldn't I be? I got receipts; I'm legal; I'm a certified washup. Sometimes I do what I gotta do but I ain't no street woman. I do it 'cause I wanna find a gentleman to save me, an' they know it. But they get on my damn nerves. Always want me to give 'em hits. I work hard for my medicine. I need it as much as they do. Everytime I go over to them for friendship, I have to fuck up my cunt an' smoke up my money just for them. I got one john, I was living with him an' his girlfriend. But I always had to fuck them both, day an' night, just to get a little weed. He always wants me to party with him an' her, suck on his . . . I don't like that. All of them, they always want me suckin' on his dick. An' his girlfriend, even though I eat her stinkin' pussy she gets jealous. After the fact, she wants to argue with me. An' I say, look, honey, I'm just a toy. I got no plan of my own. I'm just a rapeseed tryin' to grow any old way. I'm just a tumbleweed, rollin' an' rollin' through the desert, tryin' to get away, but there ain't no away. This is drivin' me crazy. I be wantin' to kick back an' relax, find my patch of shade, enjoy gettin' high all by my lonesome. But most times I can't. I try to get friends. They tell me come by, I come by with my own cunt, ready to work. I do it 'cause they drive me crazy an' I give up. They don't care, an' they always be stoppin' me, in between me an' my pleasure. They say: Someone's at the door. It's like someone's come to hunt me down. But ain't never nobody there. It's just their way to kick me out, when they done come already on my face or between my tits or in my ass or on my belly or in my sweet little cunt that works so hard for me an' gets so tired. An' most times I can't never even wash, because just when I want to wash off their jizz or piss or whatever, they say: Kitty, someone's at the door. They kick me out. That's why I got no friends I can trust. They all smoke. They all freaky-dealin' with me an' with each other. Me now, I just wanna relax. Why do we always got to have that freaky thing goin'? I'm serious. I want to get the fuck out of here. But Heaven won't take me an' I'm not sure Hell is any better than here.

I remember when we lived in L.A., I used to be with a man that used to scare all the men in the streets. They called him the six o'clock man, 'cause by six o'clock he'd always have been in at least one fight. Oh, he used to beat me so bad. Thanks to him I even got shot in the back. Some drive-by shooting was goin' on because everybody wanted to ex* him; he was so hated. It was on the freeway, an' then this gangstermobile pulled up an' fired one gunshot into our car. It hit me down under my shoulderblades. I started feelin'—oh, how can I even tell you? I don't wanna discuss it. Well, I passed out. My six o'clock man wouldn't let me go to the hospital 'cause he said that was *snitching*. So I laid on my tummy for about two weeks an' then I . . . Sometimes it still hurts. That was about three years back. An' one night he put a Mark on me so if I run away he could always find me an' catch me. See it here, on my forehead? It's invisible in the wrong light, but it says I'm his. It says that I'm just his kitty, an' he can sell me or punish me or kick me out. When he got behind, he traded me so he could catch up. He traded me to a nigger that every day woke me up by spittin' in my face an' yellin': *Hey, white trash!* I was too scared of him even to scream. But one morning when he had drunk himself to sleep I ran out. I always knew I was gonna do it. But by night time my Mark was burnin' red on my forehead like a whole city on fire, an' it felt like a big ironworks or something like that where it gets so hot that metal turns red like blood an' burns you so bad you can't even live. An' so the six o'clock man found me easy. All he had to do was look out the window. I was like some fire runnin' an' runnin'. I thought I was gonna die. His face was like darkness eatin' me. But there was a sweep just then, an' for once the cops helped me. So I got away from him. An' I went out an' *worked* my little cunt 'till I had enough to run run *run*, an' I came up here, all the time prayin' to God because I believe in Him. Believe in God, baby, 'cause he keeps us pure an' he keeps us safe. (No, I don't go to church but I believe.)

Well, I'm sellin' my candy right in the Tenderloin, an' one night this ho on Taylor Street she tells me about the Queen. Is it the truth or is it a lie? I know I would go to find out, so I go to where I see this big flock of girls standin' under the streetlight, an' I look an' I look an' I can't hardly believe it 'cause I see no pimps. An Chocolate here, she says to me, am I happy? I tell her: You wanna hear about me an' *happy?* Huh. Last time I was happy I can't even remember. Ain't that a shame, she says. An' I say, that's a shame. Well, bein' introduced to Maj, that was the happiest time I can . . . I guess the way I'm built, I just need to feel the power helpin' me. In Narcotics Anonymous they say trust your higher power. We seen with our own eyes that Maj is *Queen*. Our Queen is our higher power. An' she is also just my fun friend. Just a fun-loving friendly person that loves me an' cares for me. You know what? You very rarely find people that is *deep inside their own heart*. There's nobody else.

Yes, I did have a boyfriend. 'Bout a month ago I got rid of him. He was no good for me, same like all of 'em here. Maybe I dream of some man sometimes, not a nigger but a decent black man. I'm attracted to black men. (Actually, I haven't dreamt in I don't

*Execute.

know how long, 'cause I haven't slept in a while.) But why should anybody be attracted back to me? I don't feel that special. 'Cause now my Queen's gone. I don't want 'em to look at me. Even when I be out there on streets in a skimpy dress an' no underwear just for my business an' their cars slow down to give me the once over, I wanna cry out *Why do they keep lookin' at me like that?* Then I know. It's not my booty they wanna be lickin' with their eyes. It's that they see my Mark burnin' an' flamin' so they can't miss it even if they want to. That's why sometimes even women drivers slow down to look me over from my head to my toes. I want to say I'm sorry. Everybody's just thinkin' we're fucked up. Well, they're right. I can only say I—I—I'm enticed by your acknowledgements.

| 480 |

The entire time that Kitty was talking, she kept pulling condoms out from between her breasts, and milking herself unconsciously.

· BOOK XXXIV ·

Dan Smooth

·

. . . and whoever does not fall down and worship shall immediately
be cast into a burning fiery furnace.

Daniel 3.6

·

Past the buzzer, a revelation: Authority, in an ecstasy of sanctimonious prayer, would until the end of time keep busy destroying monsters. Tyler saw phony-wood desks, an industrial tape dispenser; staplers, and staple-removers everywhere. A vending machine's front comprised a rectangular glass eye. Everywhere he looked, some poster or other explained how sad and tricky this world was: PARENTING IS DIFFICULT—TO HELP YOU COPE, TALK ABOUT IT. No wonder so many parents made mistakes, then.

That's a nice poster, said Tyler to the secretary.

Sir, I'm actually quite busy this morning, the secretary said, adjusting her headset (that microphone should be closer to your mouth, Tyler wanted to explain).

Why, what a *coincidence!* cried Tyler heartily. So am I!

Well, then, said the secretary, how about if you do your job and I'll just do mine.

Your job must be difficult, too, said Tyler, pointing to the poster.

Excuse me? the woman said.

Can I help you cope, baby? You feel like crying on my shoulder?

My, aren't we hostile today, the secretary said. I hope you get busted big time.

On her desk, a buzzer rang.

All right, Mr. Tyler, she said. You can go in now.

With or without Vaseline? Tyler wondered aloud.

You're disgusting, said the secretary. If you have any kids I hope we take them away forever.

No sweat, said Tyler. You and I can always make some more. I know how to do it. I'm an abuser from way back.

In the next room, tables and chairs were set up as if for a family conference. There were two baby seats. A pair of handcuffs hung from a pipe. There was a big white plastic crate of toys: trucks, a plastic bowling ball, miscellaneous government-issue snuggly things with flame-retardent stickers. Here, perhaps, the uncomprehending children were peeled away from their abusive parents.

Today the FBI was comprised of a man and a woman in business suits. They were very charming. Tyler could see that they knew how to deal with the public.

Dan Smooth sat facing them across the table, his fingers open like those of a small child playing patty-cake.

Tyler said: Are you okay, Dan?

I've had better days, but these FBI turds aren't going to break me. I appreciate your coming by, Henry, I really do. The reason I'm late, well, I'm not actually late . . .

So what's going on? said Tyler to the FBI agents.

Would you like some coffee, Mr. Tyler? the woman said.

No thanks. What kind of trouble is Dan in?

Three guesses, laughed Smooth greyly.

Just as when during a special session with Domino the living drops fall slowly from the candle, making a sizzling noise when they hit, then in warm silence spreading into the man's flesh, the warmth becoming painful and tender, so the various burning stimuli which Tyler had already encountered in this place began to make his stomach ache. The ambiance of the situation, which many people would have called "serious," preoccupied him more than he would have liked. Disposed, as always, to meet disrespect with defiance, he nonetheless decided that for the sake of expediency (that is, of a happy ending), he would accept some degree of degradation, like the Queen's girls, who gave head to unwashed men and were always telling each other to be careful. This is not to say that he regretted his rudeness to the secretary, especially since her words had been uncalled for; in this deeper sanctum of officialdom, however, rank domination would probably have to be swallowed, in order to avoid a force-feeding.

Well, strictly speaking, Mr. Tyler, you're not really a part of the actual investigation process, the FBI woman said.

Imagine that, said Tyler. Nice blouse you have on.

In other words, Mr. Tyler, we're going to need some time alone with Mr. Smooth, for his own protection and ours.

Dan, you want me to stay or go?

Do what they want, his friend said dully. I've been through this so many times before. They always get their way . . .

Dan, are you okay?

You're going to have to leave now, Mr. Tyler, the woman said. You're welcome to take a seat in our waiting room if you'd like.

Count me in, said Tyler. That sure is the prettiest little waiting room I ever did see.

And, Mr. Tyler, I'd appreciate it if you let Sheila work. You seem to have made her upset.

Are you going to shoot me? said Tyler. I only regret that I have but one life to give for my country.

The FBI stood waiting for him to go, so he said: Dan, if you need me, call me.

The FBI man laughed and said: If you hear any screaming, come running in.

Tyler went back to the room of posters, winked at the tense, rigid secretary, and sat down as close to the door as he could. The secretary didn't take her eyes off him. The FBI woman closed the door. Tyler watched the minute hand on the clock, smacking his lips as loudly and vulgarly as he could to irritate the secretary. He farted. —Terribly sorry, he said to the secretary. It's a disease that all of us child molesters have. —The minute hand on the clock went round and round.

After a long time, the FBI man came out and said to Tyler confidentially while sharpening a pencil: This guy's got nothing to worry about. There's nothing to implicate him, not even remotely. He's wasted his money on a lawyer. He's not the suspect.

Well, that'll make him happy to hear, Tyler replied.

The FBI man, who was old and somehow very affable-looking, went back into the room with the toys and handcuffs, but this time failed to close the door all the way. Tyler could hear much better now.

Well, basically what we're trying to determine is what you think Henry Tyler was trying to do with these color photographs, said the FBI woman so sweetly.

Oh, so now you're investigating him, too? came Smooth's voice.

The affable FBI man said: He's got a lot of stuff that shows girls dancing and stuff. We're not concerned with that. But some of the stuff is very graphic: Nudes, genitals and stuff like that. And we generally find that photographers take pictures of what they like to look at.

In all the pictures—about sixty of them—the light was shining in the crotch, and it's very exposed, the FBI woman said.

Do you know this young girl? the FBI man said.

That's Sapphire, said Smooth. She's a retarded prostitute.

Is she a minor?

If she were, that would be a felony section 311.3, now, wouldn't it? replied Smooth with a shadow of his accustomed superiority. You see, I know California law as well as Numbers and Deuteronomy. But guess what? She's *twenty-something*—hee, hee! And her vagina's actually kind of—

So you're saying that she isn't a minor.

Can't you tell from the flesh tones? It's actually somewhat *interesting* if you look at that enlarged area there . . .

And what about this copper device?

I think it hides orgasms easier, and meets changes better, Dan Smooth whispered.

Now this *Queen*, this Africa female, I understand that she compelled Sapphire to engage in nonconsensual sex acts with—

You're being tautological, you see. Compelled and nonconsensual refer to the same concept.

We're not in grammar school anymore, Mr. Smooth. Although I do understand you have a penchant for grammar schools. Now, this Africa—or should I call her the Queen?

And the Queen honored and nourished us with her love, Smooth muttered.

So it went. They were very reasonable, and explained to Smooth their personal interest.

The nice old guy came out and permitted Tyler to *rethink* things a little, to warn him that when Dan Smooth fell, Tyler should be careful that he didn't drag him down, too.

So you're investigating me too, huh? said Tyler.

Not at this time, Henry, the FBI man said. You really have nothing to worry about. These photographs we're referring to were actually confiscated from Mr. Smooth's residence on Q Street in Sacramento. I understand you were a frequent visitor?

Yeah, I know where the toilet is, said Tyler.

Well, we don't want to upset Mr. Smooth all at once, so for politeness's sake we're just asking him about the photographs as if they were yours. There's a lot of felony count stuff here. Full frontal crotch shots of young children. I'm talking underage females, and some underage males. It's really quite distressing, Henry.

Yeah, I'll say, said Tyler. You think all those kids are virgins? Are there any wet split beaver shots of the young girls where you can get a good look at the maidenhead? I think that would be important evidence.

The FBI man shot him a nauseated look and walked away.

Meanwhile, in the other room, behind the half closed door, Tyler could hear the FBI woman saying to Dan Smooth very nicely: Well, from examining the files in your computer, it seems to me that you and Tyler were pretty, well, intertwined. I mean he wrote your resume.

Henry has always been a big help, said Smooth hoarsely.

Tweed men entered from the street, signing IN and OUT on the bulletin board.

Tyler heard the woman clear her throat, and then she said: And your activities with the fifty-two children on this list, you deny that you had carnal—

Listen, came Smooth's voice, heartbreakingly honest in its anger, so unlike its usual patronizing oiliness. —You insult me.

We're all adults in this room, Mr. Smooth, unlike the kids on this list. They'll never get over what was done to them. But *you're* old enough to stay calm and cooperate, don't you think?

I—

Is there anyone at all in law enforcement who can vouch for you about this?

Third Precinct. They know me there.

I bet they do, the FBI woman sneered. Don't you ever have nightmares about the faces of those poor, poor kids?

No matter what you think, I don't hurt anybody and I never have. You should be aware that I cracked the Kaylin Kohler case . . .

Mr. Smooth, the information we have suggests classic sexual exploitation on a multiple level, and, besides, you're already a registered sex offender.

Don't you realize that anybody who's a registered sex offender already bears the Mark of Cain? You can't go after us or you'll be punished sevenfold. Aren't you ashamed, to go against Jehovah?

Mr. Smooth, we're not really interested in your religious views. What we're interested in is whether you engaged in repeated acts of sexual conduct with children under the age of eighteen and with children under the age of fourteen.

I want to tell you something. You can't always say I've been a useful citizen. But I'm a good excuse to people who need to hurt themselves, and to witch-burners like you who—

Did you go meet with this young girl Sapphire in April? the FBI woman was saying, as Tyler sat there and the FBI man gazed lovingly into Tyler's eyes

I don't know, Smooth said.

Did your Queen procure underage minors for illicit sexual activity?

I don't know.

Well, why don't you try to remember, Mr. Smooth, the woman said. You really ought to try to cooperate with the investigation.

Why?

Because we have you dead to rights on penal code section 261.5, that's unlawful sexual intercourse with persons under eighteen; and section 269, which is *aggravated* sexual assault of these children; and section 288, lewd and lascivious acts with minors including many, *many* counts of oral copulation and sodomy; and section 288.5, continuous sexual abuse of children; and section 289, penetration of genital or anal openings by foreign objects.

If you have me dead to rights, why don't you arrest me?

The investigation is continuing, Mr. Smooth.

Call me Uncle Dan. Call me Daddy. Call me—

How about if I just call you scum?

You know, ma'am, I'm always joshing my friend Henry in the waiting room about his envious ears. But you have envious *eyes*. I saw how your face lit up when you looked at those crotch shots. I saw how you got so happy right then, because you *wanted* to think the worst of me and now you could. You can't do without me—

Excuse me just a minute, Henry, the FBI man said, entering the waiting room, with the door gaping behind him. Over his shoulder he said: Mr. Smooth, when you walk out the door today, if we never see you again and you never see us again, you'll be a happy man. Just tell us what these felony count child pornography photographs were doing in your house on Q Street.

I don't know, Smooth said.

Did Henry Tyler take those pictures?

I don't know.

Did Queen Africa take those pictures?

I don't know.

The FBI man strolled back into the interrogation room, brought his face close to Smooth's, and said: Let's refresh our memory.

About what?

Well, what about this big grey box of Henry Tyler's? See, all I'm saying is, tell the truth and be honest with us, and it'll work out. Our only job is to seek the truth.

I don't know.

You're being consistently evasive to protect somebody's interest.

Because I've sworn to protect my Queen.

And where is she?

I don't know.

And what does she have to do with the big grey box?

I don't know.

As long as everyone's being so vague, we have to make certain assumptions. So where does Tyler do his color work?

Come on, Dan, the FBI woman interjected, and her laugh was as loud and inhuman as a trolleycar bell, I think you know. You've known him for years. He wrote your letters for you. You didn't write that garbage.

Smooth was silent.

As busy as a hen in a blender, said the FBI woman brightly. Tyler wrote that, Dan. *As busy as a chicken in a blender.*

The affable FBI man came out and said to Tyler: Any child that's been up to Dan Smooth's house on Q Street is in danger of having been molested. Henry, I would never lose that thought.

Who else came over to your house on Q Street, Dan? the FBI woman was saying. Do you know anything about that?

She led Dan Smooth out. Smooth was red and sweating. The FBI man shook Tyler's hand. When he saw Smooth's sad and terrified face, Tyler wanted to kill those two tormentors.

| 482 |

You got time to come with me? Tyler said.

You a cop? said the used-up woman.

Not me, he sighed. Not me.

How far do you live?

Just past Harrison Street.

They started walking, and she said bitterly: Well, I guess you're going to take me to the paddy wagon, right?

You don't trust me much, do you? said Tyler.

I don't even trust myself.

Well, I'll take that as a compliment.

Why is that a compliment?

Because if I admitted that it wasn't a compliment, then I might get hurt feelings, said Tyler with a wink.

The woman laughed. Then she said: So, if I was to just turn around and run right now, I guess you'd come after me with the sirens, right?

That's right. What flavor of handcuffs do you want, strawberry or banana?

When Tyler was much, much younger and had first begun to meet street prostitutes, he'd mistaken for a miraculous capacity to instantly size men up, determining whether they were muff-divers, harmless old impotents, serial killers, rich men with deeper wallets than they let on, or undercover cops, what was actually circumstantial *compulsion* to render quick judgments: Here he is in the bus zone, with his window rolled down, and he wants me to get in the car and date him. I have five seconds to make up my mind. Some prostitutes, granted, did have built in bullshit detectors, like an old cop Tyler once knew who had looked him in the eye and instantly known he was lying. Tyler had only been fifteen or sixteen then. He'd been trying to impress the cop by saying he knew some street criminals he didn't know. The cop's eyes had flicked out some awful ray of instantaneous truth, and Tyler turned red. Then the cop turned away wearily. Nothing had been said. Domino was that intuitively excellent at times. But most of her colleagues just guessed fast, risking, risking, sometimes falling into chance's jaws.

The whore cleared her throat. —We turn here, you said?

That's right, sweetheart. Paddy wagon's just around the corner.

He unlocked the front door and said: Pretty big paddy wagon, huh?

Hey, I remember you. Ain't you the old Queen's boyfriend?

I was. How's the new Queen working out?

Oh, I ain't supposed to talk about that stuff. I mean, it's not cool. New Queen's not the same as the old Queen. With the new Queen a girl could get in serious trouble.

That means it's Domino, right?

You ain't stupid. Now, whatcha wanna do? You wanna date me or what? If you want me to take care of you, you gotta pay me five bucks extra, 'cause five bucks is the Queen's percent. You come home without the Queen's percent, honey, you better not come home.

He locked the door behind them, and she started to take off her clothes.

You miss your Queen? he said.

Now there's a mine-field of a question, the whore said. I told you already we have a Queen . . .

You miss the Queen? The real Queen.

Even if I was to say nothing, you'd probably snitch to the Queen and get me in black with her. I don't wanna be in black with the Queen. Don't think I don't know you. You're just another of those suck-up guys. When the Queen spits in our mouths, we swallow 'cause that's our job. When she spits in your mouth, you like it. You're a pervert. Now where's my money?

So since I'm going to snitch on you even if you keep quiet, you might as well tell me what you think, sweetheart. Here's twenty and five for Domino. Do you miss your Queen or not?

And if I did? What the fuck good would that do? And another thing the Queen said, she said we have to call the old queen just plain Africa now, 'cause that's her name and she's not Queen no more. And nobody's supposed to say Domino like you did. That's a serious offense. I'm warning you. You gotta be careful. If she hears a girl say Domino, she'll take her and—and . . .

And what?

I'm not gonna talk about it. I saw it one time. I don't want to think about it.

How's Strawberry doing?

I haven't seen her.

How about Beatrice?

She's fine. Bea's cool. Bea can get along with anybody.

And Justin?

Justin's turned mean. Please please *please* don't tell anyone I said that . . . But I still have my magic charm. It's like a car antenna that Bernadette stole because she's my friend, and then the Queen took it and made love to it so it's alive from Maj. And I keep it hidden with my Mark of Cain. And Justin he knows . . .

And Sapphire?

Oh, she lets Sapphire hang around. That girl's out of Protective Services now, 'cause she's not a minor. Anyways, Sapphire can't do no harm . . .

Listen. If I find the Queen, you have any message for her?

The woman burst into tears. —Tell her I love her. Tell her she's my Mama and please come back . . .

And I want you to tell Sapphire—

Oh, what time is it? I got a regular waiting for me. I love you, baby. Okay, I wanna go take care of that guy.

He let her out and stood watching as she fled. It was dark across the roofs of Harrison and Folsom Streets with yellow residential lights glowing unhealthily all around. Then he went to bed. In the morning he was not quite lonely because he had the sunny company of rusty fences.

| 483 |

After that, all the whores he met were sullen and suspicious. —Whatcha up to? they might say. You datin'? but if he asked: You wanna come to my place? they'd say: No, you have to come to *my* place. —That Queen, they'd say, she just a black widow spidah. — He saw one of them across the street from the pay phone at Seventeenth and South Van Ness and watched her approach him; she looked familiar; but when he greeted her she just walked on. At Capp Street there were none; at Mission Street there were half a dozen, but they all stood within protective knots of men who watched for enemies.

You lookin'? a man said to him. You lookin'?

Nope, said Tyler. Just lookin.'

Late at night it was now, almost midnight, and enough alcohol lived inside him now to give his step a slight roll as he passed under the rhythmically thudding cars at the steel bridge at South Van Ness, and the used car lot, fissured like a mongoloid's tongue, was so blue beneath the streetlights like the inner world of a detergent commercial; and a radio quietly talked to itself. Not a soul was anywhere in that world except the sleeping-bagged homeless pupae in the most discreet nests that they could find, and, of course, people in cars; at the red light, a grimacing woman rested her map on the steering wheel two steps from him, the light on in her station wagon; she was determined not to exist for him, and equally determined to keep him from existing for her—well, fair enough. Blue pulses came from a TV in a window.

| 484 |

He wandered past the Hall of Justice where at that moment a judge was saying: Your swap surrender day would be October seventh. You have a warrantless search condition. There is a two hundred dollar fine to the indemnity fund. Based on your ability to pay, there's a forty dollar probation fee . . . and Tyler crossed the street, entering the office of Mr. Cortez the bail bondsman.

What can I do for you, brother? asked Cortez with a knowing look.

My name's Henry Tyler. I'm looking for a black lady named Africa Johnston whom I think you might have bailed—

Say, aren't you the private detective?

Yeah.

I knew I'd heard of you. Who was it now? I think maybe Mike Hernandez in Vice dropped your name one time. Well, you know, Henry, with the market contraction right now we're all going through some hard times. I wish I could use you. Most of the time we don't have to hire a detective, because the family will lose their money, so they want to track the guy down.

Narrowing his eyes, Tyler said: You don't quite get it, Mr. Cortez. Nobody's hiring me. I'm just looking for her because I—

Well, it's a free country, so I wish you good sport in your looking, laughed Mr. Cortez. I really can't help you. Peace, brother.

| 485 |

In search of that priceless jewel of sources, the neighborhood snitch, he revisited the abandoned warehouse in Oakland where the Queen's outcasts used to sleep, shoot up, hide and dream. It was August eighth, the day before Irene's birthday. In the parking lot with the black cloth on his head, peering through the ground glass of his view camera, Ken the street photographer was saying to a whore so sincerely: You're beautiful. That's beautiful. —Tyler crawled under the dogeared flap of sheetmetal and found mounds of yellowed newspapers which dated back to the time that Deng Xiao Ping had still been alive, but which seemed to be wet with fresh spittle or some other substance. These burrows were all ringed round by concrete blocks. In the Queen's day there'd been mattresses. —*Anybody home?* he called desolately. There had never been any signal to announce oneself to the Queen because her eyes and ears would have already done the announcing long before any visitor could have spied her out, but, remembering Domino's call sign, he kicked the wall four times. He waited. Then he scraped one of the concrete blocks along the floor as loudly as he could. Nobody answered; nobody lived there anymore except for an ancient black lady he'd never seen before who whispered: 'Member I kept sayin' there was somebody there? I miss the place, creeps and all.

| 486 |

But Beatrice with her smell of soap and cigarette smoke saw him one evening when it was already late enough for the fat red stripes on the back doors of ambulances to turn a cold purplish-black in the darkness, much less vivid than the purple lips of Beatrice who now rushed over, simultaneously lisping and croaking in her half-harsh, half-babyish voice: Henry, I come *running, running!* She had lost weight.

Hello, baby, he said.

Can I be your wife?

Sure you can, Bea.

Am I your wife? You said I'm your wife, so give me money!

Yeah, sure, Bea. Business isn't so great for these days, but I can scrape together a couple of bucks . . .

Thank you, Henry. Now I know I'm your wife. You gotta always give your wife money. And that money you gave me before, I lost it at the bus 'cause somebody took my purse, so I couldn't buy my baby his operation. You know, his *tripas*, his guts, they doan stay in his insides, so I got to go to the hospital, and get a ticket for way in line, maybe one-two, three-four hours so they can fix my baby. But he's too far anyway; he's way down in Mexico. I won't never go back down there. Too far from my Mama. My Mama is my Queen. My other Mama said, Doan let him play outside 'cause he's not strong, and maybe his *tripas* gonna get dirty. —But she's dead like Irene, so I guess she didn't really say that but I wish she was here to tell me what to do and how to live. She was a good Mama, just like my Queen. I always respect her so much. He's a good baby, too, name Christian, just like you and me when we were babies, always playing, always good, like even you, even me. And my Queen says . . .

You never told me about your baby.

He's a bastard.

Is his father one of your customers?

One night four men robbed me and cut me and beat me up, and then all night fuck me, fuck me, fuck me, and that's how I got this bastard.

Is he a nice kid?

I doan know, said Beatrice with a cheery shrug.

They went to the Imperial Motel where she started to go down on him and he said: No, I don't need it! but she snarled, bent his fingers back until they hurt, and did her job.

Thank you, he said wearily.

Thanks for nothing.

She opened her legs like the low spread-out buildings of Mexicali. Realizing that she actually wanted it, he went down on her. She reeked of excrement. When her orgasm came, tears exploded from her eyes.

Seconds afterward, her every word high-contrast and blatant like Mexican signs urgent red on yellow, like Mexicali grapes green and black shining in the sun, she told him that she was alone, that she'd fled from Domino and the others, that all her dreams told her that the Queen was dead.

| 487 |

Two decades before, when Tyler was just learning his trade, a wise old private eye had explained: Here's the way you get information. Drugs. If you're trying to get somebody's rap sheet, well, people who need quick cash have always been for hire, whether it's the phone company or whether it's somebody who has access to computers or what. In other words, I don't have access to rap sheets but I know people who do. We don't jack each other on that stuff. It's just like Mobil and Shell. We need each other, and we can't all have everything. I know a guy who has access to unlisted numbers . . .

Tyler possessed his own list of such people. He called every one of them, and could hardly believe that these were the same "sources" who'd been so grandly infallible in years before.

| 488 |

Tightly gripping his heavy and reliable old telephone, made back in the monopoly days when such devices were rented, not owned, he called Mike Hernandez in Vice, who had first brought him knowledge of Dan Smooth so long ago. Usually he got that detective's answering machine, but this time he reached the man himself, who jovially said: *Yeah?* as shouts of office glee rang out in the background—some party, some practical joke; maybe it was April Fool's Day . . .

Mike, it's—

Henry, old chum! How's the life? You ever find that Queen of the Whores you were bugging me about last year? I figure she's probably related by incest to the Loch Ness Monster . . .

That kind of rings a bell, said Tyler.

Listen, what can I do for you? Things are kind of in chaos around here, so I—

Wondered if you guys had picked up a Miss Africa Johnston.

What's her social?

No social.

What do you mean, no social?

I took her prints, but even the FBI couldn't find a match.

Then she must not be a U.S. citizen.

She's a—

One of your whores?

Yeah, said Tyler, narrowing his eyes.

Look, buddy. I've been in Vice for fourteen years. If she's been in the business, she has to have been busted. Now misdeameanors drop off the record, for the most part, within ten years. That's the paperwork Reduction Act. But I'm sure if she's *in the life,* as they say, then she must have committed some felonies. She's the one you were looking for last year, right?

Yeah, but I found her. She exists. She—

Okay. Then you lost her. Listen, buddy, gotta go, but let's have a drink sometime. Happy trails, eh?

| 489 |

He tried the National Death Index, current up to three months before, and by then it had been four months, and she wasn't there, not on that computer-web version, at least. (Irene was there.) Well, why *should* the Queen be there? He called the San Francisco Department of Health but they didn't have any death certificate, either. (They had one for Lily.)

| 490 |

Well? the tall man had said.

All right, Tyler had said. (She had been missing for less than twenty-four hours back then.)—So if she's arrested on the street, she'll be brought in and booked, and they'll keep one copy of that booking in the jail and send another copy to the state and another copy to the FBI. I guess we'd better not go to the FBI, so that leaves the state and the jail. Now, Mr. Cortez checked out Eight-Fifty Bryant and found nothing, so we'll go to the state. You have any quarters? Lemme make a few phone calls . . .

You don't even have any quarters? Man, you are solid horseshit.

Well, we're billing a hundred and fifty, two hundred grand a year, but usually they don't pay in quarters, Justin. Still, if you have the patience it's kind of good. In other word, you're doing twelve—

Will you stop babbling like a fucking crackhead bitch?

Ordinarily they pay in million dollar bills, laughed Tyler. He left the tall man and broke a five on a shot of whiskey at Jonell's bar. He got three dollars back. One he used for a tip, and the barmaid brightened. When he asked her to transform the other two bills into quarters, she smilingly obliged. He tried to smile back, but couldn't.

What's wrong? she said.

Oh, just a minor emergency, he chuckled, showing his stained teeth. He went back into the darkness near the men's restroom where the pay phone was and began calling various minions of the state of California, confident of imminent success.

Later, when he stepped back onto the street, the tall man was gone and three drunken Brady's Boys laughed at Tyler, shouting: *God save the Queen!* His car was in the towing yard, so he took the bus home and stayed up all night trying to do an extended trace . . .

| 491 |

The Queen of the Tenderloin is really three people put into one person who's the illegitimate son of the Queen of England, explained the crazy whore, whose eye-blinks were more numerous even than late afternoon Tenderloin pigeons. In the thirties she was a teenager and then a movie star. In the forties she married the Duke of Windsor by mistake. But when she was aspiring to be a movie star she abandoned seven children. My grandmother is one of those children. That's why I'm dyslexic with a not very well formed thyroid gland connected to my urine by electricity. And the name of the Queen, the one and only true Queen, is and always has been Domino. You know why? Well, first of all, the strongest woman of all is a male that's stuck in a female's body. Then there's the second sort of men who just dress as women, just to snoop around and see what men do to women. Isn't that lucky for them? But Domino's the first kind. She has a penis. She rapes me. She's my Queen.

| 492 |

The Hotel Liverpool on Turk Street had been taken over by Romanians since the last time he'd stayed there, which had been a good six or seven years ago. Tired burly middle-aged men worked in Reception and mopped the floors. When he saw somebody mopping the floors he was impressed. Upstairs, of course, the same old carpet lingered on, fuzzed, linted, worn and grimed, with pale stain-islands of urine and beer and toothpaste. Thirty-five by the day, one forty-five by the week. His room was spacious. On its blue walls some creative tenant with a felt tip marker had portrayed whores in fishnet bras and fishnet stockings, and then all around the lintel marched well-rendered ants and spiders. There was an attached bathroom with a tub and toilet; on its walls one of the middle-aged men had too frugally attempted to whitewash away those magnificent insect studies, but as only one coat of paint had been employed the great spiders still lurked, more cunning and sinister now than ever, because they seemed to be hiding themselves in ambush.

He opened the window to let the smell out. The room quickly filled with flies.

It wasn't a bad place, though. The lock on the door was solid, and the dresser had all its drawers.

He went out to search for the Queen, street by street. The Tenderloin was nothing but a blighted, darkened, stained place in his heart. Shadows oozed beneath the signs of the Oriental massage clubs. Returning in the darkness, he learned where the entomological inspiration on the wall had come from, for upon that sea of mildew called "carpet" sailed a goodly fleet of cockroaches.

Seven o'clock, eight o'clock, night. His throat was raw; maybe he was crying in his sleep. Night, then night. (When the crazy whore finally believed and accepted that the Queen had been taken, she cried: *No hope for my electricity!* then threw herself headfirst out of a fourth-storey window.) Early in the morning his sleep was ended by the cheeps of a backing truck almost drowned out by rain, while somewhere nearby the new Queen was butt-fucking the other girls with dildoes. He parted the grimy curtain and saw that the streetlamp still burned; at that instant a pale seagull occluded that fierce yellow globe and then flew on up Mason Street. His eyes watered and he sneezed. A fly crawled on his hand. On the street, a man shouted. A pigeon uttered its liquid purring from some nearby window-ledge. Two leaners stood under the awning of the Greek food place because it was not yet seven-thirty and so the Greeks didn't know or care that their home island was being used by non-payers. He listened to the rain. The sidewalk sweepers were all wearing yellow raincoats. The streetlamp was the same color. He had a sore throat.

His mind fled down long halls made longer and spookier by the peephole's lens. He yearned for the lamp's warm shadows.

It rained all day. Finally he flicked the switch and watched the lamp's groping wings of light and shadow upon the wall's sad blue sky.

That night Red was loudly singing: *Baby, baby, oh-h-h-h-h, bay-bee* in the street-garbage. Someone had smeared an immense brownish-red turd across the sidewalk where Red pranced.

Halloween dawned rainy. He feared Halloween because it was the day of the dead.

Now that his Queen was gone, she wouldn't be able to protect him anymore from Irene's ghost. He found a Gideon's Bible, but it spoke to him artificially, like Irene's drab voice on the telephone toward the end, her sad voice which told him nothing; which was why for her, because she had never really let him into her heart, he'd begun to cultivate dislike, even hatred, thinking to kill his love and make the sadness go away, the result being that he ached for her when he thought of her, and whenever he saw her was cold to her (as was she to him) and he longed to get away from her; his wish being gratified, he then immediately despaired once again. By seven o'clock the bearded old panhandlers with top hats and cane were already leaning or squatting under papered-up windows, sharing cigarettes, rubbing their eyes, too hung over to sing. In the hallway a new tenant, longterm most likely from all the trouble he was going to, had been banging and creaking already for over an hour, trying bullheadedly to fortify his door with screw-eyes and padlocks.

Just before eight the sun came out. The tops of the grubby old brick buildings looked almost handsome in that new light. Somebody was vacuuming. A black-and-white eased softly round the corner, stalking criminals and undesirables. A man crept across the sidewalk, his face and cigarette angled straight down.

On Mission and Fifteenth he saw Beatrice with a little bag of bananas, and she greeted him gladly, so he put his arm around her and asked where she was off to. She said: In Mexico my people teach me how to feed the dead ones who we love. Now I want to do that for Mama my Queen.

What do they do?

They make like a little house and fill it with fruits and *mole* and stuff for the dead people. You have to go in the window.

Where are you going to do that?

In the tunnel, you know, by South Van Ness.

I get it.

Because I believe.

You believe that the dead people come?

Maybe I doan know if I believe or if I doan. My Mom does, my first Mama, but she passed away. There are signs that tell you that the dead people arose. Like the animals are nervous, or a little bug running like around for the food. They say the bug is the dead person coming back for his stuff. If you eat before the dead, you get a stomach-ache.

And then *noon* and *sunny* and *cool* were the labels for this moment of Tyler's life. The smell of piss and dirt from the pigeon-trees in front of the bus terminal were almost garden-fresh; piss-rain even if from drunks and unclean persons had brought out the good smell of soil even in that abused earth studded by cigarette butts. Downtown's cubescape coolly shadowed the emboldened Halloween ghouls already creeping out from under the tombstones which roof the collective unconscious—let's be psychoanalytical! The woman at the Greyhound desk was witch-garbed. Two Brady's Boys came as themselves, standing shinyshoed, the senior partner telling the other: You don't wanna cover the same pattern. You have a sector. We're working P Sector today. —But Tyler hardly ever saw Brady's Boys anymore. Having accomplished their mission, they'd dwindled away. (He thought about burglarizing their headquarters to search their files, but by the time he'd gotten his courage or recklessness to full steam the office had closed.) The film guy downstairs at Adolph Gasser's had come as a robot comprised of silver-painted cardboard boxes, his circuit-board heart upon his breast. Up First Street came a woman dressed as a cow, with an immense pink rubber udder suspended from her crotch, the many nipples thrashing like keys upon a jailor's belt.

A thin black boy in goggling sunglasses clung to a fire hydrant in the style of a praying mantis.

As he stared at the hydrant, Tyler felt himself begin to succumb to a terrible sense of filth and death because he had passed through here for too long; that was all anyone could do in that world, pass through: stay, and it ate you; go, and you were gone; and while you were there your alternatives were the stale and stuffy stench inside or the smell of piss outside—actually, it wasn't that bad; he was forgetting the Vietnamese restaurants, the sheer beauty of the night women decked out for maximum sexual recognition; in other species that was most often the role of the male—but he could not deny that whenever he came out of one of those hotels he felt as if he just escaped being stifled, or as if he could practically unpeel from his face, like the gauze curtains in some bar which half-toned the passers-by into quasi-silhouettes, a film of congealed malice and despair; and whenever he went back inside, it was worse. Still, he had bars. Who could fail to value the Cinnabar's late afternoon goldenness, its warmth like the inside of a whiskey bottle? —And I don't mind being unable to explain it, said the television; would you call this a miracle? —Outside, rotten bananas, gorgeously black and yellow like some scrambled tiger, lay on top of the pay phone.

| 493 |

The Queen was gone, but the world did not end. The Tenderloin half opened one eye, smelled itself, scratched itself, and went back to sleep. (I'm the last to go to sleep and the first to get up, bragged a sad vig; he was almost the last of the Brady's Boys.) Time will not stop. Living in the past is as illegal as possessing a fellow citizen's rap sheet. Once upon a time, the Tenderloin used to be the Barbary Coast with its Chinese opium dens, which now have gone, obliterated in the great fire after the quake of 1906, and now the Tenderloin, too, with its danger and its hard, vibrant blackness has begun to slip away. Japanese high-life hotels and jazz clubs punctuate the streets. And Capp Street without the Queen, that was like some old Roman amphitheater revivified by the shouts and laughs of little Arab schoolgirls. Time-blasted columns rise everywhere around them, and, like the thistles and flowers, the girls don't care. They form in a circle and dance around their teacher to cassette music played loud on a ghetto blaster, singing Arab disco songs. San Francisco without the Queen forgot the Queen. She'd been an interesting chapter, to be sure, as unforgettable *while she lasted* as the sensations of unlucky johns who sat clutching their balls, clipboards on their knees as they waited for the pain to pause so that they could complete their health questionnaires. —Wait a minute, said the lady behind the glass. Her muffled voice called the petitioners back and back. Children cried in the corner, playing with plastic toys which stank of anger. A little boy screamed. Domino was there too. She experienced a fiery feeling whenever she made urine. She pushed her blonde hair up, wrinkled her forehead and scowled at the baby. She was thinking about some money which she'd heard was hidden under a certain old man's mattress. She wondered whether she could get him to stand up beside the bed so that he wouldn't notice while her hand explored the boxsprings. Of course she could hold him close to her and give him a good suck to distract him while she . . . Meanwhile Chocolate smiled and swirled her high heels, her eyes getting bigger and more frightened by the moment. Chocolate was wearing a black rayon windbreaker which she believed made her look glamorous. It stank of the streets. She got up when her name was called, slung her purse over her shoulder, brushed her hair back with one hand, stuck out her chin and approached the appointment window where a plastic bottle and a key attached to a theftproof plastic block were waiting for her. She took these items to the women's toilet, which she unlocked with the key, then entered. Groaning with pain, she pissed into the plastic bottle. Then came the doctor, then the prescription, and three days later she'd forgotten all about it.

| 494 |

His uninvited guest, the FBI man, sat down in the chair once occupied by Irene during that ill-fated chicken dinner so long ago now when John had advised him to find another girlfriend and Irene had remained so sad and silent. Tyler could scarcely prevent his face from splitting open with rage, to see another person sitting in her chair. It seemed like desecration to think of Irene in front of this intruder, so he tried to think about something else. Into his mind came an image of the genital-less child on the family sculptural column of the Pacific Stock Exchange. The hypocrisy of that rendering charged him with a salutary Canaanite bloodlust; he longed to sink his teeth into the FBI man's throat.

They gazed out the window at the fog for a while, and then the FBI man said: May I ask you something?

Shoot, chuckled Tyler. Or is that the wrong thing to say to a G-man?

What do you honestly think of Dan Smooth?

I honestly think that he has sacrificed himself and others for something beyond human comprehension. You can put that in your case report.

Let's keep this on the level, the FBI man said. You want to worship snakes or hug a tree, you can do that on your own time. I don't have a problem with that. This is a free country. But come down to earth for a minute, Henry. Let's talk about Dan Smooth. First of all, anything to do with kids will get to me. I just love kids.

So does Dan Smooth bugger little kids? Is that what you're asking me?

Well, does he, Henry?

I wish you the best of luck in your investigation.

Just answer me this. Do you like him? Do you approve of him?

Not particularly. There. I answered you honestly.

This guy is in trouble, Henry. You know that. Felonies up the kazebo.

Is that dorsal or ventral to the blazzazza?

All you have to do is cooperate.

Said the spider to the fly. Hey, I hear the Bureau is so behind the times today, still back in the 1950s and 1960s that they use three-by-five index cards. Is that just a rumor?

You're a private detective, Henry, said the FBI man. In a very loose sense, you could be said to be part of this justice system of ours. Now, Henry, this is a case about *justice*. This is good against evil, Henry. Which side do you stand on?

As long as we have professionals on both sides, drawled Tyler, this great justice system of ours will be in good shape.

| 495 |

Tyler refused to cooperate with the FBI partly because after that first interrogation flanked by the posters which warned PARENTING IS DIFFICULT the memory of Dan Smooth's face sat heavy on his chest. No matter what Smooth had done, he would not betray him. Perhaps Smooth's semicontrovertible arguments that as it was he had already betrayed Irene, the Queen, his mother *and* John swayed his unconsciousness's deliberations in the direction of silence, which after all defined the ethos of the entire royal family.

| 496 |

Biting his lip, he telephoned Detective Hernandez again.

Yo, buddy, what's up? Any luck with that broad you were checking out?

Still looking, said Tyler. I had something else I wanted to ask you about. You remember that Dan Smooth guy you turned me onto that time?

Oh, *hey,* Danny Smooth! Do I remember? Do frogs catch flies? Hoo, boy, is that old lech in a heap of trouble! Kind of sorry to see him go down in a way, because he did help us out a few times, but them's the breaks. You can't be messin' around with twelve-year-old nookie.

Well, Mike, I was wondering if there's anything we can do for the guy. You know, he—

Henry, my very good chum, listen up. Dan Smooth *knew* what he was doing and he *deserves* whatever he's going to get. He's seen it coming for years. I know, because he told me. You know what I think? A guy can get away with things and keep getting away with things for so long, and then one day some insignificant little episode wraps around his ankle, and then he can't get away with a damned thing more, because he's *done, kaput.* Know what I'm saying? Dan Smooth is at that stage, Henry, and there is *nothing* that you or I or anybody can do except maybe grease the drop he's gonna fall through after the hangman puts the noose around his goddamn stinkin' child molestin' neck . . .

| 497 |

What sort of proof do you want? he gently asked the telephone.

What do you mean? the woman said. Just *proof.*

In a hit-and-run homicide, is a fingerprint on a car enough to prove guilt beyond a reasonable doubt? I mean, for a probation revocation hearing, yes, but . . .

Mr. Tyler, I really don't understand.

All right. Do you want eight-by-ten glossies of the two of them having intercourse, or will it be enough for me to call you up and tell you that I saw them going into such-and-such a motel together for one hour in the middle of the afternoon?

I—

Do you want to know or don't you want to know? I'm not trying to bully you, ma'am. This is what I say to all my clients.

I . . . I guess if you tell me you saw them together in a hotel, that would—I mean, I . . .

I understand. What you never want to do in a situation like this is to go halfway. Better either to resolve to trust your husband absolutely, or else you gotta go for the nitty-gritty. It's so hard to know anything, I mean *really* know anything. There's always another explanation if you want to believe it enough. Let's say you see the two of them humping under the covers; maybe you can convince yourself he's helping her find her car keys—

Mr. Tyler, do you really have to be so graphic?

Sure I do. Lemme give you another example. Let's say you're in love with somebody who maybe doesn't even exist and you—and you—oh, forget it.

Are you okay? the woman whispered. I thought this was about my problem but somehow it's starting to feel like it's about you, I mean, I . . .

Because *you can't ever know anything.* What if the woman you love doesn't even have a social security number or fingerprints? Then how can you believe anything? So maybe you want those eight-by-ten glossies so that years from now if you ever regret divorcing him and your mind starts trying to be kind you can take 'em out of the drawer and see how *ugly* they look together and then you'll believe, yeah, this was *real; this happened.*

I see.

What's your religion?

I'm a Catholic.

Then you do see. Because don't all those crosses and relics and holy pictures help you believe? Don't they make it all real?

I feel like we're kind of going on a tangent here, Mr. Tyler.

All right. Well, let me just say one more thing. The reason that Jesus worked miracles was *to provide material proof* that what He was saying was true. If you feel bad when you get those photos, just remember that proof is a miracle. It's a spiritual thing. Because it's so goddamned hard to get proof of anything, and even with proof I sometimes . . .

Mr. Tyler?

Yeah?

Is there anything I can do to help you?

I'm sorry. I know I was going off on tangents like you said. Chalk it up to professional enthusiasm. Tell you what. I feel embarrassed now. How about if I follow your husband and the other woman for nothing? I mean, I . . .

| 498 |

Lifting his head, he could just see above the wooden railing the rival lecterns whose black nameplates read respectively DEFENDANT and PLAINTIFF.

Henry Tyler, said the voice of judgment.

Here.

V. T. & R. Credit, Incorporated, said judgment.

Represented, came the hearty, remorseless voice of his enemy, whom he'd never met until now. He and his enemy were sitting alone together in the front row, inches from that forehead-high railing whose sign commanded NO GUM, FOOD OR DRINKS IN COURT. His enemy was a pale, somewhat flabby young man in a blue blazer. Perceiving Tyler's inspection, his enemy rewarded him with a sincere and indeed rather sweet smile whose only odious quality, if any, would have been its self-confidence. Tyler could not help liking him. His enemy's colleagues, the agents who'd haunted and infested Tyler's telephone for months now, who'd nagged, then warned, then threatened, and finally, in a stunning abrogation of their personalized ill will, offered to negotiate for pennies on the dollar, just so they could close Tyler's case, these ghosts had never meant any more to him than entities which must be kept off; they shamed him and he dreaded them, for which cause he'd been rude to them, faithful to his cardinal axiom that one's only choice lies between belligerence and cravenness. Now all that lay buried deeper than Irene's bones. He loved his enemy. He longed to turn the other cheek.

We do have stipulated judgment forms that you will be required to fill out, said the official voice.

The previous case had finished now. A businessman had come in rolling an immense flat tire, Exhibit T. A cop had held the courtroom door open as he came. The door closed; the cop stood scratching his thigh beneath the holster. Now the tire was gone; likewise the businessman with his anger, his shame, his sweaty armpits and tire-grimed hands. —Judgment suspended, ruled the court.

And Tyler himself, he hung suspended above his own future, just as he had throughout that instant longer and more barren than infinity when he had watched his twitching fingers begin, in utter disobedience to his will, to strain toward Irene's thigh for the very first time; just as he had when, learning from his mother that Irene was dead, he'd resolved to be faithful to her forever; just as he had when the tall man had led him down that dark and dripping tunnel to the Queen and he had allowed himself to believe in her, giving up his gun and kneeling to receive her saliva; just as he had when she'd offered him the false Irene to love and he'd accepted; just as he had when he'd known that he could not love the false Irene anymore; just as he had when he'd accepted the Mark of Cain as his own emblem of damnation and integrity forever; just as he had when the Queen had offered him her soul, her magic, her heart and her cunt; just as he had when he'd realized that she was doomed; just as he had when she'd left this earth and he'd searched ever more unavailingly; just as he had when Dan Smooth had turned to him in need; just as he had when Irene's ghost rushed back into his arms to love and hate and smother him; just as he had when, understanding that the Queen, Sunflower and Sapphire were all holy by virtue of being degraded unto the very death, he'd resolved likewise to go in the highest, lowest direction he could, determined at the eleventh hour to make something of himself, to become "authentic" or honest or purified or more like one of those three prostitutes, no matter what it cost him; and now the next thing was about to occur. He knew that it was a trivial thing, but still it was the next thing.

He did not feel present anywhere anymore. Did this constitute a failure spiritual or otherwise? Sapphire had been present only in the most unearthly way. Sunflower had died sleepy and confused. Only the Queen had continued ever aware.

He did not understand what he should do now. He needed his Queen—oh, how he needed her! If only he'd thought to ask her more questions, or—

Summoned, Tyler and his creditor approached their respective lecterns. Tyler felt shabby. Erect, his creditor proved more resplendent yet from the waist down—wool slacks, shiny shoes. *He* required no Mark!

And suddenly I get served with these papers, Tyler explained, hardly listening to himself. So I actually got so upset that I just stopped payment. You know how it is, your honor.

Knees apart, his creditor nodded sympathetically, gazing into Tyler's eyes. Tyler admired him more and more.

So, uh, the way I see it, your collections people violated the law, Tyler concluded. For an instant he felt awed by his own righteousness, but then his creditor's shining eyes made him sleepy, submissive, ready to settle on any terms.

His new friend said: Mr. Tyler, we can either request a continuance to find out what they promised on the phone, or we can resolve this matter right now . . .

Tyler discovered a sign which read: DO NOT ARGUE, QUESTION OR IN-TERRUPT EACH OTHER. When his turn came round again, he tried to respect the sign, and said: Look, I don't want to be a jerk or anything. Just tell me what you think we should do.

If you want to compromise with me, replied his friend in a tone of the utmost kindness. I can certainly take a down payment. Meanwhile, what I'm gonna do is request a continuance. But my question is, we called you several times and—

Well, I don't know about the several times, Tyler lied, hanging his head.

Mr. Tyler, you're not to interrupt.

Sorry, Your Honor, I just . . .

Yeah, Mr. Tyler, I understand, his friend told him sympathetically. But all you had to do was call us. V. T. & R. is always just a phone call away. Anyway, that's history. Here's the balance you owe, and I'm gonna . . .

Tyler stopped listening. He longed for the moment when all the muffled underwater voices would cease, and his creditor would sit down next to him again in the front row, drooping his wrists between his thighs, gazing lovingly into space. Or maybe they'd meet in the corridor and go out afterward for a drink at the Wonderbar. His creditor wanted to help him; his creditor would save him—

| 499 |

Past the body-piercing shop Haight Street begins to steepen, and at Baker commences the plateau called Upper Haight, with Buena Vista Park a slanted wall of green on the left, bearing its loungers, panhandlers, sleepers, tourists, map-readers, and bus-watchers; here it was on an afternoon of sweetness infused with the perfectly pitched almost painful bugling of bus brakes and the smell of just-cut grass that Tyler, paying homage to a compulsion he could not control, went into the bead store and bought some pewter and bone beads. An hour swirled by like the new Queen slowly unwinding the chain from her wrist as the latest bitch in trouble knelt, not daring to gaze upon her tattooed glitter-frescoes. He sat on the grass and strung unhappiness on a piece of silver wire.

A boy with long blond hair and eyes whose lids resembled Tyler's tattered leather wallet sat beside him and said: Where are you staying?

Capp Street.

Oh. *Oh.*

And what are *you* about? sighed Tyler, stringing beads.

Meeting *you!* —and with this the boy thrust out his hand and left it hanging weirdly in midair until Tyler took it. It felt like white bread soaked in milk.

I like how your hand feels, said the boy yearningly.

Well, glad you enjoyed it, said Tyler. You have anything to tell me before I go?

You're going? You're going?

Yep.

Where?

To pick up some prostitutes.

Boys or girls?

Girls.

Girls! said the boy, stunned.

See you, said Tyler, but the boy didn't answer.

Nodding at the blonde stubble-headed girl whose skull was tattooed or dyed with sky-blue stars, at the cat-quick skinny runaways who giggled and then suddenly spilled out shrill obscenities like blowfishes puffing themselves menacingly against some threat; bowing to black girls whose dreadlocks were chased in gold—not as many tie-dyed people as ten or twenty years ago; the thing now seemed to be short hair and T-shirts— Tyler strolled, playing with his beads.

At Shrader Street he noticed two Brady's Boys excitedly pacing, one saying to the other: See that guy in the trenchcoat? He's a pickpocket. He used to work for the Queen. Let's bust his ass! —Sutro Tower's red and white backbone rose headlessly above the Victorian houses, its hollow vertebrae blue with sky. At the end of Haight Street, Golden Gate Park drew its green line against the evil world. More people stationed themselves on the grass than he remembered, cigarette smoke rising at a slow slant between coughing and spitting heads and greasy little backpacks and ball caps pointed backward. They shared cartons of french fries. Sometimes a man would stride across the grass, his shirt opened to the tanned or tainted flesh, and another shirt tied around his waist, and pigeons would flock around his head. In a year or so, just as Strawberry had prophesied on that day when the tall man came home from the hospital, our local government would build a fence here to keep them out. A boy in a cap, a hooded sweatshirt and tall rubber rainboots which came up to his knees struggled in the hot sun, dragging his pack behind him; sighing, he threw it down and lay on it. A girl dressed in blue denim from head to toe wandered past him, sipping from a paper cup.

Why don't you sleep in the park? said the hooded boy to the girl.

Tried that once but it's too cold.

It's not so bad. Anyone can do it.

Tyler listened, strangely excited and encouraged, he didn't know why.

It's a secret, the boy went on. The manager he don't know I sleep here.

What time does he get there?

Eight o'clock. I hear the first bus, and then the second bus, and then I know I gotta be awake and out of here.

On a bench, three Brady's Boys were looking at a tourist map, one of them laughingly reciting: There's *scum* on the streets! We got right on our side! —But the second Brady's Boy, who was older, sadly shook his head and said: It's called rapport, guys. You don't want treat 'em like crap. You wanna *develop* 'em.

Sighing, Tyler clattered his beads.

| 500 |

The pink form said in English and Spanish:

— NOTICE TO DEFENDANT—
YOU ARE BEING SUED BY PLAINTIFF

To protect your rights, you must appear in court on the trial date shown . . .

Let's see, there was his small claims case number: 97SC08089 . . .

It was some bank in South Dakota this time. His other credit card company used them.

DEFAULT ON A REVOLVING CHARGE ACCOUNT DATED 22/20/93

A. _x__I have asked defendant to pay this money but it has not been paid.

Maybe I'll challenge the venue, he muttered to himself. Bastards.

Oh, the hell with it. I'll just default.

For a moment, he imagined himself in court, looking into his debtor's eyes. Then he said to himself: Hell, I don't care what they think.

One of the first indications that a person is becoming an addict is that he loses interest in others. A love-addict masks this symptom by virtue of the addiction itself, which *is* others.

He still had his computer, on whose monitor sailed a pretty screen saver depicting the outer planets. Accessing Webscape Crawler, he grimaced at the familiar connecting noise and ran a nationwide credit check on himself.

Oh, fuck, he said. This really is not too good.

Hardened in his defiance, like any sinner destined for hell, which must be as hot as the Greyhound station in Marysville on a July day, Tyler had long since walled his pallid heart away from embarrassment, so that when Irene was still alive he'd tortured her with endless declarations of that submission which really is not submission at all since it insists on being accepted; he'd yielded himself to what he believed was Irene, but in reality was nothing but his own terrible passion which drove him day after day to telephone Irene and leave such messages as: Irene, I wanted to tell you how happy I was to hear your voice on the answering machine last night because you know that I love you so much; I'm passionate about you, Irene; Irene, I wish I could be the ground you walked on. Irene, I'm yours. I belong to you. —Did he know or care that John could call in from work at any time and by pressing two keys of the touchtone phone play back every recorded message? Once when he and John and Irene were all staying at Mrs. Tyler's house in Sacramento, Irene and John had gone home a day early due to a crisis at John's office, and the lovesick man stayed on with his mother, then left a message for Irene (who was out buying oranges, halibut and long green beans in Chinatown) that he had slept last night between the sheets she'd slept in and on her pillow found two long, beautiful strands of her black hair which he would keep forever; he felt happy uttering these words for the record, or at any rate relieved; but as soon as he'd hung up, sadness welled up through his chest, flooding and drowning his heart, rising into his throat so that he almost choked and then burst out of his eyes in very painful tears; rising still higher, it flooded his skull, sinking into his brain to make him almost drunk; he stared at the telephone, licking his lips, craving to take the receiver into his hand and dial Irene's number again (it hadn't even been five minutes). He didn't call her for the rest of the day. That night at seven and then at eight and at nine he glanced at the phone but it did not ring. When he went to bed he brought the telephone close, just in case, but she never called. The next day he was so sad and anxious he felt almost crazy. He wanted to dial her but said aloud: Don't you have any shame?

(Oh, he was entirely capable of shame. One windy afternoon when John, Irene, Tyler, the dog and Mrs. Tyler drove across the Golden Gate Bridge for a stroll on Stinson Beach, Irene had walked alone, looking squat and disheveled as she sand-trudged with her head down, her hair messed up, her legs braced apart, a bulky sweater further widening her; and John was chatting quite cheerfully with his mother while Tyler tried to be good but never quite succeeded in dragging himself into the breeze-snatched conversation (which had to be shouted, almost, against the sea-roar), so he gradually allowed air currents to guide him closer to the dark wet sand-edge and found Irene beside him. He stroked her hair. She neither smiled, nor spoke, nor moved away. For a good quarter-hour they walked side by side, he feeling dull and almost angry at Irene, who possibly felt the same; on the way back, uphill through the windy dunes, John had dropped behind to throw sticks into the ocean for the dog, and Mrs. Tyler gasped to Irene: I'm not so young anymore; you're so strong; and she grasped her daughter-in-law's shoulder. — Oh, come on, said Irene, shrugging her off, and marched ahead alone. Tyler hung his head, humiliated by Irene's rudeness to his mother.)

His hand lifted the receiver; he overruled his hand. At six that evening the tension within him locked him almost breathless, so he dialled Irene's number and got a busy signal. He felt a sickening illicit thrill, as if he had heard her micturating behind a closed door. She was *there* at that moment. (No matter that it might have been John.) Irene was talking to someone. Could it be Jesus? Had she been just then guaranteed a ticket to Heaven? Slightly eased, he was able to resist phoning her for another two hours. At 8:01, he called and Irene answered. She said that she was busy. She was very nice to him. She chatted with him for nearly fifteen minutes, after the third or fourth of which he felt his desperation begin to ebb. For the remaining ten minutes he felt amazed and thankful to be his old self. Irene had saved him. He told her this, at which she laughed lightly and said: I never knew I was so powerful! —He babbled: Now I know how my heroin junkie friends feel when they fix. They call it getting well. You're my drug, Irene. You're my best, best drug. —That was how he spoke to her. She laughed and seemed to like it (although really she might have felt uncomfortable; she might have even hated him). She said it always calmed her to talk to him. That night he won a victory against himself: he insisted that he need not tell her anymore that he loved her. If he had, she would merely have woodenly replied *thank you.* He left the conversation gracefully, feeling not exactly happy, but immensely relieved. Five or ten minutes after he was alone again, with the darkness outside, the tension began to return. He almost panicked. It was a sickness. He remembered how when he'd been learning to swim, aged eight or nine, they'd told him to tread water and he was all right until suddenly the water didn't hold him up anymore and he was going under, drowning, not knowing why. Now with Irene he was terrified by what was happening to him. Above all he was terrified of his own evil.

The next day he called her answering machine and said: Irene, last night I had a fever and a sore throat and I, uh, I dreamed that I was sucking your breasts, which were full of very hot, sweet, thick, whitish-yellow, sweet milk that glowed in the dark and tasted like vanilla. In my dream, your milk soothed my throat. I woke up and my sore throat was better.

He hesitated, then went smoothly on: The other news is that I can either come in on Friday and take you out for lunch, or I can wait until Saturday and meet you at any time you wish. Please call me and let me know.

Irene did not return that call.

The next day he called her answering machine and said: Irene, please forgive me. I'm sorry. I'll try to control my feelings better. I'll try not to call you every day anymore. I won't call you unless you call me. I'm just calling now because I didn't hear from you about lunch. If you feel uncomfortable around me now, I won't bother you anymore, I swear, Irene. Just let me know your plans. I'm sorry I've been so stupid. I haven't felt like this since I was sixteen. I feel so idiotic and angry at myself and so miserable. I don't know why this had to happen. Don't stop being my friend.

Irene had not returned that call, either.

| 501 |

There was a Cambodian girl he knew who looked a little like Irene.

He put his hand on her thigh. All day she let him hold her hand; she'd held his hand back; she'd snuggled up into his arms. He began to stroke her thigh. He stroked her hair.

You like to touch my hair? she said.

Your hair is so soft, he said.

(She had to stay home to care for her parents. Her sister she didn't trust so much.)

Now his hand was right between her legs, and he was rubbing her mons veneris which he could feel through the polyester slacks which were getting damp there. Imperceptibly she opened her thighs a little more. He stroked, and they never looked at one another.

You like to touch that? she finally said.

So much, he said.

She put her hand on his hand and drew her fingers across his as he masturbated her. A moment later she moaned. That animal happiness of hers thrilled him.

But then she said: It's making me nervous.

Sometimes he called her on the phone to give her compliments. As soon as he had hung up, he felt sad and miserable inside. Once he called her back five minutes again and she seemed just as happy to talk to him as ever. He felt happy, too. Then the conversation ended, and he hung up and felt miserable again.

| 502 |

Speak when spoken to, you little *bitch,* chuckled Domino, slapping Sapphire across the face.

Doan hit back! whispered Beatrice, for whom running away had not worked out.

| 503 |

Mr. Brady? said Tyler.

How the fuck did you get my number? This is an unlisted number. This is a *business* number.

Unfortunately, it was in a new CD-ROM product that just arrived today, said Tyler.

Wait a second, said Brady. Do I know you?

Do you know me, boss, or do you just believe that you know me, or do you believe that I believe that you believe that I know you?

Henry fucking Tyler! boomed Brady in high delight. This San Francisco voice reminded him that he had fond memories of the Ritz Carlton Hotel, of the bells from Grace Cathedral mingling with the trolleycar bells. —Well, how the blazes *are* you, old son?

Can't complain, Mr. Brady. And you?

I personally am doing quite well, said Brady. This Feminine Circus thing, well, everyone just loves it. Feminine Circus is going places, son.

Well, how about that, said Tyler.

We ran a lot of marketing experiments, said Brady. We tested the product within an inch of tolerance. And you know what, Henry?

What? said Tyler.

The goddamned product held up.

Well, I'll be, said Tyler.

Cut to the chase now, said Brady. What do you need?

Where's the Queen, Mr. Brady?

Which Queen? laughed Brady. Don't tell me that even you ended up falling for that horseshit you snookered me with . . .

That's a mixed metaphor, boss. Well, no. I guess it could just be an odd one.

I don't have time to screw around, said Brady.

Okay, boss, but I do. So where's the Queen?

What do you really want? Brady said wearily.

I want the Queen back. I want my Queen.

You're a nutcase, Brady growled. Falling for some skanky little black bitch who never even existed. It's not going to happen, Henry. Take a hint. You're nuts. You're in dreamland. Now, let me ask you something. Are you just a nut, or are you going to make yourself a dangerous nut?

I'll say just one word more, Tyler said. *Please.*

This is embarrassing, said Brady. Now, Henry, I'm sorry for you, but I'm going to have to let you go now . . .

| 504 |

Toward the end of November he dated Beatrice again. (Outside, two kinky-looking, fat-buttocked cops were helping a weeping woman into an ambulance, the one at her elbow, leading her up the ramp; nobody was in any hurry so any other passengers must have died.) He asked about the Queen. Beatrice whispered that she was too afraid to revisit that subject, but Strawberry was up in Sacramento now, and Sacramento was far enough away from Domino and Brady that Strawberry might feel safe . . .

But she didn't. When he finally tracked her down, she wasn't hooking downtown or in Oak Park anymore; she was doing three months in Rio Consumnes for parole violation. Her real name was Naomi Luisa Ehernberger. Inmates whose last names began with any letter between A and M inclusive were allowed visitors on Saturday mornings, provided that their behavior had been apathetic or assiduous. He drove down from Sacramento in Dan Smooth's car at seven on a bright cool leafy Saturday morning with scarcely any traffic to hinder him. He took Route 99 south to the exit for Elk Grove Boulevard and then pulled into the first service station he saw and got directions to the prison. The cop at the door sent him back to the car twice, the first time because he'd dared to show up with his wallet in his pocket, and the second time because there were too many keys on his keyring. These contraband items having been rendered inoffensive, the cop at the door slowly read his visiting application slip twice, disparaged his penmanship, and motioned him into the hallway where after waiting in a line of quiet patient people he met a second cop who scrutinized his application slip and sent him upstairs where after showing the application slip and his driver's license to an old desk cop who stamped his hand **WDF** for Women's Detention Facility he had the pleasure of settling into one of the many white plastic chairs which faced the television's advertisements for wonderful cars with almost no money down and easy hazy future obligations; he stayed there for about half an hour, until they called for all persons whose hands had been stamped **WDF** to line up. He followed his peers across the parking lot past the high fence with the sign MALE PRISONER INTAKE to the Women's Detention Facility upon the ivied walls of whose exercise yard another sign read NOTICE: IT IS UNLAWFUL TO COMMUNICATE WITH INMATES IN THIS FACILITY. Inside the cafeteria where he was going to meet Strawberry, another sign prohibited the inmates from attempting communication with the food servers, and Strawberry would tell him in that place the women weren't suposed to talk to each other, either. They had ten or fifteen minutes to eat, four to a table, and the administration didn't want any fights. Tyler showed his application slip to a pretty deputy behind glass, then went to the bathroom because the deputy had just announced that anybody who needed to use the toilet during the visit would not be allowed to come back. A hale, whitehaired old man stood straining over the toilet. Tyler heard three or four staccato drops of liquid splash into the bowl. —Weren't hardly worth it, laughed the man with a wink, leaving the toilet to Tyler, who after a more volumetrically successful urination returned to the waiting hall to discover that beside the panoramic window-view of steel seats and telephones a door had been opened permitting egress to the cafeteria into which uncertain women in yellow or red institutional shirts were now advancing, each searching for her visitor. Later, when Tyler met Chocolate at the Wonderbar and told her where he'd been, she asked what color shirt Strawberry was wearing, and when he said yellow, Chocolate looked sad and said: She's in the bad place. Poor thing. —Camelia Dorm, he said. —That's the worst, Chocolate said. That's the fishbowl place where they don't trust you. Screws watching you everywhere.

(That was almost the last time he saw Chocolate. He saw her once more a month later in lacy black, limping eagerly after the tall man who, pushing a stolen shopping cart heaped with stolen women's clothes, scarcely glanced at her. A car slowed, and the tall man said to the driver: You lookin'? —Naw, just lookin', said the driver, and sped off. The tall man cursed. Tyler was too heartsick even to call out. He watched them vanish down Sixteenth Street.)

At the prison the other visitors were embracing their women, and when he saw Strawberry approaching him, tanned, overweight, tense and glum, he thought that she would embrace him, too, the way she always did at the Queen's or in the Wonderbar, so he was actually stupid enough to have begun to outstretch his arms to her when he saw that she had another visitor, an old regular who sometimes entertained her down in Stockton, a half-toothless ex-con who loved Strawberry and had taken the risk of coming here— luckily, they hadn't checked his record this morning; otherwise, he'd have been busted. —Strawberry flew into his arms, gazing apprehensively at Tyler.

Hi, Henry, she said tonelessly.

Seeing that she feared the ex-con's jealousy, Tyler shook the man's hand and talked exclusively to him for a moment or two, then said: Well, listen, if you two need some privacy maybe I'll just sit over at this other table for a bit. Take your time.

Just five minutes, said the ex-con, very friendly now that Tyler had put him first.

Tyler sat gazing at nothing for fifteen minutes until Strawberry called him over.

How's everything? he said.

Fine.

Beatrice says to tell you she loves you.

Strawberry shrugged.

Dan Smooth's in trouble.

So what?

Are they treating you okay?

Fine.

How many girls in your dorm?

Fifty-nine. Five toilets. We get up at four in the morning for breakfast and sometimes there's a long line for the toilet, but otherwise it ain't bad.

Look, you're kind of my family, so I . . . You got any friends in here?

I just keep to myself, Strawberry said. She sat anxiously gazing at the ex-con, so Tyler turned to him and for five minutes the two men spoke of beer and whiskey and Delta towns. Tyler asked the ex-con if he ever got into San Francisco much and the ex-con said he didn't. Tyler told him to come to the Wonderbar and he'd buy him a drink.

Well, I don't go drinking that much on my own anymore, the ex-con said. When Strawberry's there I kind of keep in line. Otherwise I seem to get myself in trouble.

Yeah, I understand, said Tyler. Well, you're a lucky man to have Strawberry to look after you.

Strawberry hung her head.

Strawberry, he said, I need to know something. There's a lady I'm looking for—a lady I love. I think you know who she is.

Don't, said Strawberry, weeping. Please don't.

A guard came over to their table and said: Calm yourself down now. You don't want to go upsetting everybody else.

Just tell me this, Tyler said. Can I keep looking? Is there any hope?

Do you have any idea what would happen to me if Domino heard that we had this conversation?

Well, said Tyler to the ex-con, I'm sure that you and Strawberry have a lot to talk about, so I'll be on my way. Strawberry, I'll put ten dollars in your account.

Good to know you, said the ex-con, accepting Tyler's hand.

The Queen used to say I always kept a dirty clod of dirt in my mouth, Strawberry laughed desperately.

You miss her, too, don't you?

She was so good to Sapphire. I used to cut out curtains from paper and glue them into little cardboard boxes to make dollhouses for Sapphire but she never played with 'em 'cause she . . .

Wasn't she good to you, too? he bullied her. Wasn't she good to all of us?

You were leaving, the ex-con said. I already shook your hand.

Tyler went out. —I want a Queen with number eighteen trisomy syndrome, he muttered with a laugh. Or a hyperactive microcephalic girl . . .

| 505 |

At eight-thirty the next morning it was sunny and cool, and while somebody with a long-handled swab washed the windows of Pancho Villa's until they were as sparkling mirrors, a black man and a Chicana woman argued on the far side of the street. Tyler had seen the woman working on South Van Ness a couple of nights ago. The man had a stick. First they launched at one another the small arms fire of curses, gradually more highly charged. —Don't you threaten me or I'll tell the Queen, you S.O.B., the woman snarled, raising her arms, at which the man got her in a chokehold and started dragging her away by her neck, shaking her as a hunting dog does some still struggling duck. Joyously he shouted: *There is no Queen anymore, you ignorant bitch!* The old lady beside Tyler shook her head, enjoying every minute of it. When Tyler was younger he had once tried to break up a similar scene in which the man pulled a knife on the woman, but at his approach the woman had thrown one arm around the man, shaken her fist, and told him to mind his own fucking business, while the one with the knife chuckled and sneered. Now Tyler was more like the woman on the sidewalk who was enjoying herself so much, the formulaic head-shakings merely an easy sacrifice on the altar of that enjoyment, the only distinction (and, in the long view of things, not a very important one) being that he didn't enjoy watching it at all. In short, he didn't get involved.

The man glanced across the street, saw Tyler, and winked. He yelled: No rub wit' the Capp Street hoes!

What'd he say, what'd he say? whispered the old lady beside him in fascination.

Well, ma'am, explained Tyler, I think he was telling me not to use condoms if I have sex with the prostitutes on Capp Street. Or else he might have been suggesting that he doesn't believe I use condoms when I have sex with the prostitutes on Capp Street. Those are the two possibilities that occur to me. Which one do you think is right?

The man came over to them and the lady's face slammed shut and Tyler said howdy.

Why you standing on the corner like that? the man said to him. You make me nervous. If you stand on the corner you might get popped.

That's okay, said Tyler. My name's Mr. Popcorn.

The black man laughed and walked away, muttering over his shoulder: You stupid honky sonofabitch.

| 506 |

Since that first descent into the royal tunnel now so long ago, Tyler's wounds, trivial though perhaps they were, had never stopped bleeding; in everything he did, he left behind a dark and sticky spoor of sadness which predators could follow. Brady smelled it from the first. That was why he sent Tyler a videocassette meant to humiliate him. Having had no news of the Queen for so long, Tyler took the black plastic cartridge in his hand with helpless dread. After the football game on television cut off, superseded by the now rewound footage, static sizzled with blue harshness on the screen, and then abruptly the tunnel appeared again, or one like it. A procession was approaching. There they were, all the street whores he'd once known, proceeding down a dark passage, each with a bridle in her mouth—a detail which Brady's slapper, who enjoyed the classics, had gotten out of Herodotus. Brady had dressed the Queen as a slave, in rags and chains. She had a black eye, and her front teeth were knocked out. It was probably all faked, just virtual reality, one of Brady's nasty jokes. The camera zoomed in. Now he could see that the whores were being required to balance turds on their heads. Most of them were crying. The Queen wasn't allowed to speak anymore, so she couldn't comfort them—Brady had threatened to cut her tongue out if she did—and the turd had been placed on the back of her head so that she had to bow her face to keep it from falling. Her eyelids were like cigarette-burned curtains trying to keep out the light.

| 507 |

I keep thinking that she's somewhere and needs our help, he said, but I don't even know where to look. It's all so hopeless. Just for a second I'll believe that she's alive and is waiting for us to get her out, and then I'll come to my senses and . . .

Oh, shut up, said Smooth. Nice view, huh?

A lady was pushing her infant in a stroller. Tyler couldn't tell whether the baby was a boy or a girl. But to Smooth it didn't matter.

Sacramento's in my blood now, Smooth said. I like this house. I like Q Street. Do you like Q Street?

(Sacramento may be dull but it is centrally located, they say, because westward lies San Francisco only an hour and a half away, unless traffic is terrible; eastward lies skiing and waterskiing at Lake Tahoe; northeastward and southeastward we can also quickly strike the "gold country"—Tyler for his part well remembered a boyhood visit to the Empire Mine whose main shaft slanted down infinitely, buttressed and skeletonized with barrel-ribs, stays, rusty corsets fabricated according to the envisonings of long-dead engineers. Silver droplets of yesterday's rain leaked through the soil and then transected that endless square shaft, wriggling on a beam of its cold lights. The boy smelled dirt, gravel and old metal. This was earth. This was where he must go.)

I said, do you like Q Street? You know what the FBI calls this house? They call it *the Q Street compound.*

I hope that makes you feel important.

Don't be a goody-goody, Henry, said Smooth, whose words remained as always long and slow and unstoppable like a string of cylindrical wine cars on some old train. —Fill up that glass of yours. I love living in Sacramento. But I don't want to die here. I'd rather die in San Francisco. It sounds more *sinful,* don't you think?

But is there any chance that the Queen, uh—

That's a perfect thought. That thought is as fresh as a young boy's anus.

Smooth, I—

You had your chance and you didn't use it, I'm sorry to say. You could have taken her somewhere if you'd really cared, but you know what, Henry? Your envious ears got in the way. You never loved her. You only loved Irene. And for once I'm not trying to be cruel; I'm just speaking the truth.

Would you *stop it?*

You want my help again, don't you? Hey, you want me to be a bloodhound on the trail of the Queen's abductors? Buddy, I'm a private eye from way back! Send me into any men's room and I'll sniff the urinal to get their traces. Are they *fresh* traces? I'll wonder aloud . . . Let me see. —Somebody drank a lot of coffee recently, I'll say to you. It's got a real strong odor to it. How would those wine connoisseurs put it? Well, a strong Java nose, let's say, not light and fruity at all, nothing fancy—he's not one of your espresso men—moving on to a bold finish in the low register with overtones of beer and something meaty, maybe roast beef, maybe a hamburger. And you'll say thank you, case *closed.* You'll say—

Oh, shut up, you twisted sonofabitch.

She's *gone,* Henry. Get it? We *know* that. From her *prophecies.* Was she ever wrong? Never.

And what did she say?

But that's bullshit, Dan, just to give up on someone because—

Then don't give up. You're the private detective. You know how to find lost people. Or at least you *should* know, Sherlock.

Knowing that if he did not patiently persist and bear the other man's insults, still another hope would be closed—remembering likewise the Queen's fantastic notions on the virtue of undeserved suffering—he controlled his despairing rage and said: What about Domino?

What about her?

She's got to know something.

Look, Henry. Domino's as much a victim in all this as anyone. I don't care how evil you think she is.

But it doesn't add up. She—

That avenue is closed, Henry. It's closed even to me. Domino and I have an agreement not to see each other anymore. It's too painful for both of us.

Now what's *that* supposed to mean? Were you in on it, too?

Paranoia will get you everywhere.

I'm going to talk to Domino.

That's better. It's better to be confronted with your failures at every turn. You'll see. Tell me what she smells like these days . . .

Why?

Why what?

Why don't you care about Africa?

I'll bet you just wish you had the guts to punch me, don't you? But you're afraid you might lose *information*.

Tyler, feeling almost unbearably disgraced and humiliated, burst out: Whatever you and I talk about, and it's been this way every goddamned time, I always have the feeling that it's *useless* . . .

As it is. And you know why? Because you're useless. You remember when I told you that I could see from your mouth that you like to go down on women? Well, now let's talk about your *teeth,* Henry, your lying, grinning teeth. You lie through your teeth, you know that? If you ever said anything straight and honest it would choke you coming out of your crooked soul. —And Smooth, fixing his blinking, bleary eyes on him as best he could, brought his face closer and closer until Tyler was trapped in the stench of his breath and cried out: Now you're just goading me again—for nothing. And you always tell me I don't like you, and you do everything you can to make that true.

At least I got you off the topic of the Queen, so grin and bear it. But you're avoiding the issue, because in addition to your envious ears and your lying teeth you have a coward's heart. Have another shot, said Smooth, refilling his own glass first. —There's ice in the freezer. I *accuse* you, Henry Tyler. I accuse you of letting down everyone you ever loved or had a tie to, of failing the Queen, betraying your brother, seducing and torturing your sister-in-law, neglecting your mother, rejecting Domino—oh, I could go on and on. The one thing I'll say for you is that you've run your little business into the ground; that shows some integrity. You see, Henry, if I could get you angry then you wouldn't be sad about other trifling points. Isn't that how it works? Or are you a man like me who can be angry and sad at the same time?

And whom didn't *you* let down, Dan?

Oh, almost nobody. You, Domino and the Queen, I suppose. I like to believe I never let you down, Henry. So don't start kvetching and asserting that I'm letting you down now. All this has a higher purpose.

I don't get it. I mean, I—

Know what those FBI turds told me? Let's say you have your dick up some eight-year-old boy's ass and it slips out. You know, accidents happen. And so you put it back in and . . . Well, that's an additional felony count right there, even though you hadn't even finished. Can you get *that?*

Dan, when you talk that way you're just smearing yourself with filth. It's as if you—

So I'm letting you down.

It has nothing to do with letting me down. I'm trying to tell you not to—

And you think, and the FBI thinks, and everybody except the Queen thinks that I let those kids down. Well, did I?

Can we just for one minute make this about the Queen and not about you and me?

Isn't this a religious experience, Henry? Can't you see God in my shit? And you know what makes you so dishonest? God's speaking now, so you'd better listen. I'm telling you loud and clear, boy, that the reason you've let everyone down is because you can only love completely what you don't have.

Tyler was silent.

You had her! You had her and she loved you!

I had whom?

Why didn't you kill yourself? Then you could have been with Irene, at least. Maybe if you hurry up and do it you can still catch up with the Queen before she turns into fog—

Don't think I haven't thought about it, Tyler muttered.

You'll never do it. She told you to travel, so you'll travel. I'll do it long before you. You know as little as I do, said Tyler, how all this will end.

| 508 |

Through interviews with former friends, associates and intimates, [CEN-SORED] learned of numerous allegations that Smooth had had sexual relations with boys and girls younger than 16 years of age, including oral, vaginal and rectal penetration. These allegations would later arise in the Bureau's affidavit in support of the search and arrest warrants.

| 509 |

He wandered into the public defender's office on Seventh Street and waited behind the counter, staring at the wall inset with a window made of pigeonholes, some empty, some overstuffed with swollen folders. —What's it on for tomorrow? Your case I mean, the receptionist was saying to a sad defendant. —Department Eighteen, the defendant said. —All right then. —The defendant cleared his throat. —You don't have a message for me, do you? he asked so sadly. —No sir. And what can I do for *you,* sir?

I'm looking for a lady named Africa Johnston, Tyler said wearily. I was wondering if she . . . Oh, forget it.

| 510 |

He knew that the ringleaders of Domino's crew didn't go to the Wonderbar anymore after what had happened between the old Queen and Heavyset (oh, so you saw that tall nigger called Justin? the owner remarked to Tyler one afternoon. On account of what he did to me, there's a warrant out for his arrest! and Tyler felt almost shocked at the vicious self-satisfaction which shone from Heavyset's face), but one day he spied Domino, dressed from head to toe in glittering silver, drinking alone at the bar at the Naked Eye on Mason Street, on her face a strange, haughtily dreamy expression, as if she were so far lost now that she could barely find her way back to herself; while in the padded lounge-nooks behind her sat three or four of her prostitutes, solemn and anxious.

Well, she said drily.

How's everything, Dom?

The streets belong to me, the blonde said pompously. She sighed and said: Only thing is, I don't want 'em.

Well, what *do* you want?

Good pussy, drawled the blonde, and the other whores clapped their hands over their mouths and laughed.

Domino, he said, please, do you know where the Qu—I mean, where Africa is?

Fuck, that's just her trick name, said Domino. How can I keep track of some other bitch's trick names?

I love her. I'm looking for her. That's all.

Yeah, well what do I care about your love? What good's it do me?

If I got some money together would you—

A grand'll work, laughed Domino (and the other whores giggled and whispered: Did you hear what she said to Henry?). Until then I don't want you talking to me. I don't want you even coming around.

If I'm going to scrape up a grand for you, I need some proof that what you'll tell me is worthwhile.

I don't give a fuck for proof! the blonde snarled. I don't care if you come back or not.

You must have altered your money-loving ways then, he said. Or maybe you just don't know anything.

Look, she said. I used to like you okay. You always treated me like an equal. Henry, listen to me. That bitch is dead. And I don't want you ever, ever to mention her in front of me again. And I don't want to ever see your face again. I can't stand to even look at you. I . . .

Then she slammed her face into her hands and sat there, rocking and trembling, until he was safely gone.

| 511 |

In the upper Tenderloin, before the Aloha Spa (Oriental Massage & Sauna), with its painted green palm trees on yellow, he asked two cute black whores from Oakland: You know Africa?

Darkskinned? Oh, her! Used to be the Queen. Yeah, yeah!

She got killed?

She got killed.

Are you sure?

You mind standing away from the door? one of the whores said.

You mind standing a little closer to the door? Tyler said politely.

He half expected to get screamed at or punched, but the whore, whose sarcasm detector had a dead battery, obligingly moved closer to the door. He then felt impelled to honor his end of the bargain.

Yeah, the other whore said. That Maj you be talkin' about, she got offed by a runaway car. You know, a hit-and-run. I saw the blood in the street . . .

Uh-*uh,* the first whore said. She got some kinda growth tumor in her eye and it formed into cancer. I saw it for myself.

| 512 |

When you take a street whore into your car, you actually carry two passengers—a woman and her addiction.

Excuse me, but I don't really know you, the whore said. I don't like your face. You make me nervous.

Well, I don't know whether to take that as a compliment or not, Tyler said.

It ain't no compliment, the whore said. You got an evil face. You look like an axe murderer.

All right, then, it's not a compliment, he said. Where do we go from here? You want to get out of the car? I can let you off here.

In this rain? the whore said. I'm soaked and you want me to go back into the rain? Can't you see how wet my pants are? And I swear I ain't pissed my pants; it's the rain.

It happens sometimes, said Tyler.

How much you gonna gimme?

Nothing. I'm doing the Queen a favor, is all. You just got of jail and I'm driving you home to her. That is, if you want to go home.

Ain't no Queen no more. Don't you know that?

I don't believe it. Anyway, Domino's the new Queen, didn't you hear?

Oh, *her,* the whore sneered.

Who told you the Queen's dead?

Everybody knows it.

Has anyone seen her dead?

Of course not, 'cause they burned her body. They *destroyed the evidence.* That's what they always do.

So no one you know has actually seen her dead, Tyler pursued.

I think you ought to give me some money because it's my first time, the whore said.

Your first time what?

My first time with you.

So that's what you think, is it?

Yes it is.

Well, you can think whatever you want, said Tyler. He'd given up trying to ask her anything.

I'm tellin' you, I'm *broke,* the girl said.

By now the car stank of her, the smell of unwashed flesh, dirty socks, excrement and wet clothes.

So you want me to drive you to Capp Street or not? he said.

You wanna drive me up to Market Street first so I can get me some french fries and a burger? I'm *hungry.*

I don't have time right now, sweetheart, he said. But I'll take you to Domino if you want.

You won't buy me a burger? It won't take but five seconds. We can go through the drive-through lane. Turn here. I said take a right here. You missed it. What's your fucking problem? Now go back and make that turn. I tole you I'm hungry.

Tyler, glancing for a moment into her scared and angry eyes, understood that she had been recently raped.

| 513 |

That was about the time that he gave up trying to make his car payments. It was the anniversary of his mother's death. He continued to make inquiries about the Queen, even though the weary silences and insistent avowals of others conspired to uproot the last feebly growing shoots of his hopes. Everybody acted as though he were forcing the issue. He thought to himself: Why shouldn't it be forced? I'm just disappointed that Smooth is too much of a mess to follow this through . . . —He was already two months late on his rent, and just as the heads of old locomotives sometimes resemble praying mantis heads or the beaked helmets of robot angels, so his landlord's face came in his dreams to assume a strangely metallic appearance because Tyler was afraid of him and hated himself, hence deserved to be a mantis's prey and he could not hide from fate the way that John and Celia could when they attended foggy windy Sundays of street fairs less festive than commercial: booths selling, or trying to sell, robot T-shirts, custom-made wine corks, earrings which resembled fishing lures, elaborate bongs with carven faces inset with colored glass . . . But he was still chasing, still hunting. He showed everyone photographs of his Queen.

| 514 |

He saw the tall man one Sunday morning in Berkeley when he was buying a ticket to be sped underneath the Bay to San Francisco. Sliding in three successive bills for a $2.45 fare to Sixteenth and Mission, Tyler clicked on the downward-pointing blue arrow to reduce the value of his investment by five-cent increments. When the coins came clattering back out, the tall man approached him with a murky gaze and said: You got twenny-five cents?

Sure, Justin, said Tyler. Why the hell not?

He gave the tall man a quarter.

Where's the Queen, Justin?

What's the use?

I visited Strawberry up in Rio Consumnes.

What's the difference?

Where you headed? said Tyler then in a conversational way.

I can't say, said the tall man. No place good.

Well, I hope your return trip is better.

It won't be, said the tall man.

All right, said Tyler, wearily narrowing his eyes. I get it.

I can't handle it, the tall man said. I still be thinkin' about it. Now beat it. I don't wanna never talk with you no more.

Tyler waved sunnily and went through the turnstile. When he turned, he saw the tall man mouthing and re-mouthing the words *Just twenny-five cents more* while turning away from the ticket machine, into which of course he had delivered no coins, and he began to walk upstairs. He saw Tyler looking at him and said with what might have been ironic servility: Hey, thanks, bro. Gonna get me a forty double up . . .

Tyler went downstairs to the tracks, angry and saddened.

| 515 |

You never call me or talk to me, an arch teenage voice was saying on Dan Smooth's answering machine. I gave up on you *long* ago.

The FBI tracked the originating telephone number and extended the investigation.

| 516 |

[CENSORED] It is clear that Smooth sexually abused minor males and females at the Q Street compound, in addition to having consensual sexual relations with several adult females (misdemeanor counts of prostitution). A number of Smooth's former friends provided affidavits detailing these sexual relations, including the sexual abuse involving [CENSORED]. [CENSORED], an employee of the Children's Protective Services Agency, provided the Bureau with a cassette tape of an interview she conducted with a child named Sapph [CENSORED] who repeatedly visited the Q Street compound. This child detailed an incident of sexual abuse involving three counts of oral copulation with a minor and [CENSORED]. This child testified about her experience at the [CENSORED]. Also, during conversation between an informant and Henry Tyler during the week of December 21, Tyler admitted that he knew of Smooth's sexual abuse of this minor female. The Bureau's behavioral expert [CENSORED], in a December 2 memoranda to the Bureau, opined that "Smooth may continue to make sexual use of any minor male or female children whom he can lure into the compound."

| 517 |

That's very very interesting, he muttered, switching on his computer. That's where the death records would be kept . . .

He stared at the screen for a very long time without doing a search. Then he switched the computer off.

| 518 |

Tyler was at the Wonderbar getting drunk. All the barmaids he knew had gotten fired. There weren't any girls inside.

Have you seen my little streetbird? asked old Jack, clutching at Tyler's shoulder despairingly.

Which one is she again?

You know her. She's the most beautiful one of all—you know, the one who . . .

The old drunk in the cowboy hat interrupted them, shouting: Hey! Hey! Hey! until everyone looked up. —I was in this little old bar in the Ozarks and this gal six foot seven named Sal, she taught me how to jitterbug. Hey! Pay attention! I seen bar fights. I *seen* 'em. I seen everything.

Yeah, I get it, Tyler said to Jack. But what does she look like?

Some days she says she's eighty-five percent Sioux Indian and fifteen percent black. Other days she's fifty percent Indian and fifty percent Irish. I say she's fifty percent liar. But I don't care. She's my streetbird.

I'm trying to find somebody myself just now. I really don't have all day. You mean Strawberry? I know where she is. You mean Domino?

Strawberry? said Jack in confusion (and ordinarily Jack, that piercing-eyed yet half-blind old ex-welder who sucked his wrinkled cheeks in against his skull whenever he looked a man up and down, was as quick to generalize as the Cantino map of 1502, which, showing parrots on Brazilian coast, named that entire country the Land of Parrots). Well, I don't rightly . . . Strawberry! Yeah. That's her. But to me, you know, she's just my little streetbird. You should see her when she's flying high—Henry, you know what I mean—and then she's happy and beautiful it just breaks my heart. There are times when I'd give her everything, and I *have*. Yes I have. And that girl doesn't give a damn for me. Well, none of 'em care anyhow. You know that. Don't you know that? They'll just say whatever to get all they can out of you. They're so ruthless—why, they'd set you up to be killed if it would benefit 'em for five minutes. Goddamned whores. But I don't care. I don't care, and now I can't find her.

Strawberry's in jail, said Tyler. I've got to go.

Strawberry? What do you mean Strawberry? Now her name comes back to me. It was Lily! You've got to help me, Henry, because Lily's the one I love. Lily's my—

Lily's dead, said Tyler. But what's the difference? You can't even remember her god-damned name.

And he went out. They'd impounded his car. He must have parked incorrectly or something. He had a headache. He inhaled the smoke of burning trash cans and of his dead and burning Queen.

| 519 |

He called the district attorney's office where after several wearisome recorded pushbutton choices he finally had the option of speaking to a real live operator, which meant that he was treated to a fifteen-second blast of classical music, followed by the voice of a firm but pleasant woman saying: *That extension does not answer. Please try again later. Goodbye!* —He tried again later, three times. Then he tried the criminal investigation number. Nobody there had ever heard of any Africa Johnston.

| 520 |

The Cambodian girl who provisionally resembled Irene, the one whose mons he'd rubbed through the polyester, sent him a letter which ran:

TO: HENRY ! ! !

 I got you letter on 02-23-97, that is very nice of you letter, and I am very thank you to hear all those words from your heart.

 I hope I see you again as a good friend and I feel so sorry that I can't give you any love more than a good friend.

Thank you

SOEUN

 He kept that letter for a long time. Then he tore it into strips which issued from his opening fingers into separate trash cans, because he was afraid of being unfaithful to the Queen or Irene . . .

 Later that day he was on Kearney Street and saw John and his colleagues all in a football huddle, deciding where to go for drinks. As he passed them, they stared at him with the bright round goldish eyes of pigeons.

 We've got fifteen PEMEX engineers working on the project, he heard John say.

 Tyler's face turned crimson. He waved to John without looking and hurried off, walking and walking until he'd come all the way down to Sixteenth across from the Roxie Theater, practically in the doorway of Ti Couz which was too loud or too busy for John except on weekends when John liked to feel free. Tyler watched cloud-cream glowing down on the slate-blue sky of twilight, lamps already shining in a row halfway up the height of each street-block's dwelling-crystal. Now the clouds were going yellow. People rushed to dinner, cars peered troll-eyed ahead, and buses, almost friendly in shape, rolled up and down before him. A huge group of tourists received birth from a Dodge van and gathered in front of Ti Couz, reading the menu aloud.

 The next morning John telephoned him.

 Yeah, he said.

 How's business? John said.

 Fine.

 Don't bullshit me.

 You're wrong. You're trying to force the issue, John, and everybody's always saying *I'm* forcing the issue but—

 How are you doing, Hank?

 All right, he said, his heart aching, remembering not Irene at all, strangely enough, but the Queen standing before the mirror with her arms raised, affixing the pink plastic curling set that Beatrice had gotten her, her armpits full of darkness.

 Bullshit, said John.

 How about you, John? How's Celia? How's business?

 Listen, Hank, his brother said. What do you need to get your life together?

 Oh, hell, said Tyler. I, uh—

 I'm not asking this for you, John continued in a shriller voice. I don't give a damn about you. But I promised Mom before she died. I'm doing it for Mom.

 All right, great. You've done your duty to Mom. Now let her bones and my bones and Irene's bones rest in peace, said Tyler, slamming down the receiver savagely.

| 521 |

My slaves know what to do when they're in there, don't they? drawled Domino.

The reaching arms in the cage, the stroking Queen, the strange squeals and squeaking in parallel with the black dildo that stank, still gave off an insect hive impression. A woman muttered: Well, it stinks because you haven't . . . —Yes, she was talking about the Queen's long black shiny dildo in that cage filled with women playing with each other. Beatrice with quick and fearful side-smiles told the Queen she loved her.

Snapping her whip in the air, Domino chuckled, I'm not just going to break the *sound* barrier, I'm going to break the *skin* barrier.

A shaved head began gliding up the Queen's thighs.

Let me just pet you, Domino purred. You're such a gentle little thing. You're so . . . That *hurts,* the girl said.

Speak when spoken to, Domino chuckled, slapping her across the face.

Walking slowly around her little cherubs, her little girls (who included a whore as wide as Australia), her little toys—how nicely they played for her! —she admired rosy arms and legs in the cage, tongues and laughs, swollen labia. They'd all forgotten the old Queen, she was sure. (But I am starting to feel better about myself, she mumbled. I don't think about myself as much as I used to.) And, indeed, it would be surpassingly easy for us to forget the old Domino as well—which is to say, the young Domino, the runaway. Go back fifteen years and see her barefoot and dirty. The pale unsmiling face kept blinking, lost, the blonde hair tarnished, as she sat there in the American Embassy in Mexico City, cradling a dirty blanket about her. The tall boy in the white shirt, grimacing, took a pen out of his pocket. —First you tell me one name, then another, he said. Is there anyone else?

Please let me think, she whispered. Please. Leave me alone and let me think.

Oh, so there *is* another father? said the clerk.

Mr., uh, Northway. Please. This time it's for real. He's my real father. His name's Mr. Northway and I know he lives on Northway Lane . . .

Oh, so now you want me to call Mr. Northway on Northway Lane. No, I won't call him. I've had it. It's too much.

Yeah, I'm Northway, Tyler would have said, butting his way into the conversation. I'll take custody of my daughter right now. Come on, honey, I'm taking you home.

Hey, who the fuck are you? slurred the girl in semiconscious alarm.

You can call me Dad, Tyler would have said, grabbing her hand and pulling her out before she shredded his cover story any further.

They got in the elevator and she said: You gonna hurt me?

No, Domino, Tyler sighed. No, probably not.

They went out. The guard gave them back their passports, and they passed through the tall steel gate.

You wanna french me? said the girl vaguely.

Sure, said Tyler, popping an antacid. I know French. *Ne pencher pas au dehors* means don't pinch the whores.

But none of that happened; nobody came along to rescue Domino until the old Queen did and by then it was already too late.

And so, kneeling outside the door and mewing like mice, they welcomed their long-thighed new Queen coming out from the closet to whip their tattooed flesh with black movements and gritting teeth while their friends kept singing and giggling and kissing each other, laughing in the cage, Queen Domino now leaning on the cage, black-clothed with her black eyes peeling blue-black jewels away from their souls, positioning shining leather girls in each other's arms, terrifying them with her stranger's teeth, wide open lips, applying jewel-like bruises down their tattooed backs, hugging them, shaking breasts, playing, rubbing the triple-pink lips, pinching and licking buttocks, devouring alike the wise and the lovely heads, the shadowed eyes, Strawberry's heels clicking on the floor, Bernadette's fat heart-shaped buttocks (she could have been any old varicose slut with sneakers and a slave's upturned eyes). A whore knelt, cage-shadows on her flesh, praying to the Queen's apples . . .

I reach into that little place right inside of me, Domino said to them. I feel everything. I am everything. I'm your Queen.

She slowly sank her fingernails into Strawberry's nipple until the woman screamed. She drank the cool feel of Bernadette's navel.

We're playing with each other, she whispered, because we're reaching inside . . .

Terrified, Chocolate cleared her throat.

I've always been a showgirl, Domino murmured to them all. Every time you walk on-stage, every time you do a lap, every time you rise some man, that's about bravery. Then he has to *cough the fuck up*—not necessary money, but something. And so do you. If I can sit here and spread my legs for money and not know any of these people, can you take off your bras? Can you let me stick my dildoes up you? Can you suck me? I guess that would depend on what you wanted, wouldn't it? But I'm telling what what I want— oh, you *sluts,* you *cunts,* you *fucking whores!*

And she was happy, coasting the long curves of back and pussy, until Bernadette started lifting her hands and going *a-a-a-a-a-a-aaaaaah*—

Oh, she's going into one of her convulsions, said Domino, bored. Forget it! The rit-ual's ruined.

Domino's reign was supposed to go on forever. But one night when she was walking across the freeway in her dazzling silver hotpants, a car swerved toward her. With a started cry, Domino raised her hand to her mouth, then began to back away just as the car struck her. That was months later, long after she'd been established and other amus-ing things had happened. (She was real cranky, Chocolate later recalled. I was, like, I didn't wanna be on the other side from that bitch.)

| 522 |

On the anniversary of Irene's death the false Irene was out selling pussy on Eighteenth and Capp when a gentleman picked her up, a nice old gentleman she knew named Brady, who paid well for a quick no-nonsense suck. She'd just been beaten up by two tall black men, and told him so. He grinned a little and said: Why don't you girls stick to-gether more and protect each other?

We used to do it like that, she said, but the girls have changed. They're usin' too much. You just can't trust another girl no more.

| 523 |

As for Beatrice, she finally went back to Mexico where she wore pink cotton dresses and walked slowly in the heat, swaying from side to side.

| 524 |

Here in America we aren't willing to treat each other as human beings anymore, Smooth was saying, standing in the air-conditioned darkness with a cigarette flame shooting like escaping treasure from his lips.

Tell me about it, said Tyler.

And you know what? When I cross this burning earth—hey, asshole, are you listening to me? I said: *When I cross this burning earth . . .*

You're drunk, Dan. Don't call me an asshole.

You're the one who's going to cross the earth. Your Mark is shining tonight.

I'm not going anywhere, Tyler muttered.

You're going to get you an education, boy. Remember what the Queen said?

The Wonderbar was louder and noisier now that Loreena had gotten fired. In the corner beside Tyler, a drunk resembled a Brady's Boy snoozing at headquarters, chin on hand, in an armchair by the wall of recycling cartons.

So what if I'm drunk? Are your ears getting envious, Henry? Don't interrupt me. I needed to tell you how irritatingly commonplace it's now become to hear such stupidities as: *Speaking as a woman, I find this piece of pornography offensive.*

You don't like women much, do you, Dan?

You know I like twats! And that sister-in-law of yours, I—

Go to hell, Dan.

I never felt that women understood me. When I was in my twenties I used to . . . I . . .

What would the Queen have done? Tyler asked himself. And then he knew. He put his hand on Smooth's shoulder. He said: I'm listening.

He'd already kept Smooth company for two hours in the Mother Lode, whose tinsel purple and green resembled seaweed. Even though it was Friday, the disco ball had remained still. They'd sat among the easy transvestites and the hard transvestites drinking their beers, made-up men's made-up faces expressionless beneath the powder as their bloody-red lips made O's and they crossed their big thighs in their shimmery miniskirts. There was one genetic female in the place, an uneasy soul who seemed to be realizing only gradually that she was the sole representative of her gender. Meanwhile, Smooth's utterances grew charged with enthusiastic and increasingly incoherent bitterness. Tyler was torn between boredom and pity.

They're funding the attack, said Smooth, shaking off his hand. I'm sure Brady's in on it. So it's very very duplicitous what they're doing. Do you even care? Justin cares. Our Queen would have cared, but she's in the same place as your sister-in-law.

Tyler bit his lip.

Your fucking sister-in-law. That dead rotten fucking sister-in-law bitch. That cunt. That whore. That *she.* What does she have to *speak as a woman* for?

Yeah, yeah, yeah, said Tyler, scratching his face.

She's saying: If you disagree with me, you're disagreeing with half the human race. And I'd wager that she knows half the human race no better than I do. It's a cowardly and dishonest attempt at *intimidation,* is what it is. And I find it very sad that such words pit one group against another when right now we all need to help each other because we're all under attack, and if you don't agree, you can just go *eat your dead sister-in-law's twat . . .*

Are you okay, Dan?

What the fuck do you mean, am I okay? I'm under investigation and this jerk asks me if I—if I . . .

Let me drive you home, Dan.

Aren't we being schoolboyish? And you expect me to go on feeding you with my divine wisdom—my, I'd never have thought it! And those FBI turds . . . There's *nothing* that's okay the way it is.

All right, Dan. Here we go. Door's wide open.

And the Queen—

Lean on me for a minute there.

And you and your envious ears—

Lean back so I can put your seat belt on, Dan.

The Queen, Henry.

Yeah, the Queen.

Do you read the Scriptures?

You must have asked me that a hundred times.

I think she made it easier to make changes, to like experiment, try and be somebody better. And now I . . . Although I can't believe it, either. I'm on your side, Henry, but she's truly gone. I love you, Henry. I want myrrh and aloes to wrap up inside her shroud. I want to lay her in a new tomb and wait for her to rise. I want to believe in fucking miracles. Isn't that rich? As if that asshole up in the clouds would ever give anybody with the mark of Cain a break!

You're wrong there, Dan. He put the mark of Cain on us to save us, and you know it. He said: *If anyone slays Cain, vengeance shall fall upon him sevenfold.*

I don't give a shit. I need miracles, Smooth wept.

I know, said Tyler, seeing with his soul's eye the Queen's soul leaping tall and slender and stiff into a smoky yellow sky.

And I know what that brother of yours would say. He'd say, *Let's keep the Queen out of this.* But that won't do any good, Henry, because you're going to have to live without Irene and without the Queen for the rest of your whole goddamned *life.* You're going to have to live with *yourself,* Henry, you poor sad bastard. I feel so sorry for you, I just pity your stinking guts . . .

All right, Dan. Here we go. Now, when we get to your house, I'm going to need your key so I can let you in. Do you know where your housekeys are?

They're in Irene's twat, Henry. They're jammed up your victim's cunt. She died because she hated you. You wouldn't leave her alone and she was so desperate to get away from you that she—

Tyler switched on the radio.

| 525 |

On August ninth, which was Irene's birthday, two black girls approached the counter giggling and whispering, and the righthand one, who was very pretty and dark and full-breasted, said to the man: Excuse me, but are you helping anybody?

Nope, the man said. The sign beside him said: ALL SALES FINAL.

Where the long glass counter started was at the partition that said LOAN DEPT., behind which, attended by a dozen safes, a nighthawk of an old woman sat watching the world with jaundiced eyes.

Beneath that stretch of counter, harmonicas large and small slept on blue felt, some of them cheap, made in China, and a few grand Hohners as silver as the barrel of a Colt Python, cold mirror-silver chased with floral swirls as folkishly stylish as the designs on the immense silver belt buckles sometimes seen in Mexico.

Can you play them harmonicas? asked the girl shyly.

The man folded his arms. —Nope, he said.

How come this little one's only twenty dollars and this big one's a hundred and seventy-three dollars?

Well, the man replied, that's like asking the difference between a Cadillac Fleetwood and a Cadillac Whatchamacallit.

Oh, said the girl.

She looked at the harmonicas for a while, then said: Why's this big one a hundred and seventy-three dollars and this little one's two hundred dollars?

I can't rightly say, the man answered.

The wall behind the counter was hung with banjos and guitars, some black-lacquered. After those, just behind the man, rifles and shotguns leaned barrel up in a long row like prison bars. Within the region of glass case which touched the man's belly were the pistols and revolvers, beautiful, black, silver and grim.

Can I hold one of those? pleaded the girl laughingly.

Nope, said the man.

I have I.D.

Let's see it, then.

I'm nineteen.

Then you're not old enough.

Please?

Nope.

I'm not going to buy it, I promise. I just want to look.

If you can't buy it, what's the use of looking? the man said, pleased with his own logic.

I just want to know what it feels like to hold a gun, the girl whispered with lowered eyes.

Her friend screeched mirthfully: Don't you let her, mister!

Nope, said the man calmly.

The two girls fled. When they were safely outside the store, the pleader turned around and outstretched her tongue.

Can I see that Browning there? said Dan Smooth. What is it, a Buck Mark?

Nope. That's a Browning Challenger III.

Ah, so it is, said Smooth, flicking his driver's license down onto the glass counter. The man took it between two fingers and studied it with all the weary thoroughness of an immigration agent inspecting passports. Then he unlocked the counter and took out the dark, gleaming thing with its walnut grips.

Beautiful, said Smooth. But I might not have the *guts,* you see.

Oh, yeah, said the man. That's almost new.

How much?

Three twenty-nine.

Uh huh, said Smooth wisely, setting the gun down. At once, the man secreted it under glass again.

Those homeless people still living in the tunnels around the corner? he asked.

Nope.

I see, said Smooth, looking the man in the face. And why's that?

Why do you want to know?

Business reasons, Smooth explained.

There's nothing, the man said. Just the *traces* of 'em. Just the traces of people having been there.

(Down the counter, an 1898 silver dollar caught Smooth's glance.)

We've been around fifty years, the man volunteered unexpectedly. Them homeless, they've been around fifty thousand years.

Shame on you, said Smooth with a wink. I've told you a million times not to exaggerate.

The man smiled politely.

Of course you never saw a small black woman named Africa in one of those tunnels, Smooth said. Of course you never went inside . . .

Nope.

How much for that Ruger? said Smooth.

You can have it for four hundred. It's a 1945 original.

I didn't know they had Rugers in 1945.

Nope, said the man.

Well, said Smooth, raising his left eyebrow. Then why not three hundred?

Nope.

He took out his wallet. —Here's two seventy-five for the Browning.

Three hundred.

Nope! screamed Smooth gleefully.

| 526 |

Tyler set off the metal detector. —If you do that three times I'll have to arrest you, joked the deputy. Now go stand over there.

All right, said Tyler. Once you arrested me, I guess I wouldn't set it off anymore, would I?

Striding across the new granite flagstones, he arrived at the computer printout and looked up the name, XREF, floor, cell, and pod number. There was no release date. At considerable taxpayer expense they'd installed an aquarium and sandblasted the rock wall with kitschy foliage.

Beaming lawyers turned their backs to the public who had to wait. There were two lines, one for the public and one for the lawyers. The line for the lawyers moved. The one for the public didn't.

Another lawyer appeared.

The old lady ahead of Tyler said: I've been waiting for my entire lunch hour to see my daughter. I'll probably have to leave soon. Can you hold my place while I feed the parking meter?

Sure can, ma'am.

I'm going to be late for work. Excuse me. Thank you, sir.

She hobbled out. When she returned five minutes later, the public line had not moved an inch, and another lawyer with a big fat grin had stepped into the fast line.

Look what just walked in, the old lady said. There goes another fifteen minutes.

Half an hour later another lawyer walked in, and the old lady said: Screw this! and walked out.

An hour later, Tyler had reached the head of the line.

What is it? said the policeman behind glass.

I'm here to see Daniel Clement Smooth, please, said Tyler. This is his reference number, his floor, his cell, and his pod number.

Oh, today's his court date, said the cop. No visits allowed today. Come back again another day.

| 527 |

Tyler called his friend Buddy Lopez at the public defender's office. Perhaps Lopez wasn't quite his friend after all, for it took him awhile to place Tyler. Finally he said: Okay, I get it. Yeah. You're the one who . . . Hey, didn't I help you out on the Louise Nugent case?

No, lied Tyler, I kind of figure I helped *you* out.

You did? What did you do for me?

I got you the tape that proved that Louise was hit over the head *before* she slit that guy's throat.

And how did you do that?

No offense, chum, said Tyler, but if your memory's really that bad, you're going to forget it all before the next time I call you. So let's just say I told you and you already forgot. How does that grab you?

Why, you impudent sonofabitch. What do you want?

You familiar with the Dan Smooth case?

What about it? That asshole doesn't need a public defender. He's got a house. He's got *assets*. Let him liquidate his assets and hire an attorney. Scuttlebutt is, they have him dead in the water. Crimes against children and all that. That's gonna be one helluva case. Pretty juicy details if you ask me. Hey, you know what I heard? In that compound of his on Q Street, they found three dildoes covered with blood. They're doing the DNA tests now. And you wanna hear the kicker? *These dildoes are tiny, man.* They had to've been used on kids. *Little* kids.

Who knows? said Tyler. Maybe Smooth was into consensual S & M with midgets. Innocent until proven guilty, right?

You're quite the party pooper, said Lopez.

Yeah, there's a sourpuss like me at every Roman circus. How much time do you figure he'll do?

Well, with time, everyone relaxes. Even a case with a lot of news coverage just becomes another matter in court with the passage of time. If you know the process, Henry, first comes the initial public outcry. The D.A. can beat his chest and demand the death penalty, and when the case gets settled, it could be for something mild the newspapers might be appalled at. And this ain't no death penalty case, so . . .

Five years?

Maybe twenty, if he's lucky. Multiple cases. Multiple victims. For something like this, maybe the statute of limitations will *never* run out.

| 528 |

Dan Smooth lay dreaming that he was watching his niece make a sand castle. She said: It's got to be dark inside, 'cuz the King hates the sun.

Why is that? said Smooth, resting a hand on the child's buttock.

I dunno. The name of this castle is Virgin Castle—no, Mayflower Castle. The name of the King is King James. That's my daddy.

Ah, Smooth said. Do go on.

And this rock is Mommy and this stick is you and this stick is me. We're the royal family. And now it's snowing, and a big monster—a *BIG* monster—is going to kill everybody. First he kills Daddy, then Mommy, then the Queen, then you, then me. Now I want to make everybody alive again, but the sand castle's too messy. Let's make up another game.

· BOOK XXXV ·

Coffee Camp

●

And I will heap evils upon them; I will spend my arrows upon them; they shall be wasted with hunger, and devoured with burning heat and poisonous pestilence; and I will send the teeth of beasts against them, with venom of crawling things of the dust.

DEUTERONOMY 32.23-24

●

It was just before ten o'clock when Tyler got into Dan Smooth's car. The keychain with the pink plastic heart on it hung between his fingers. He plucked the silver-colored key from its trembling amidst copper keys large and small (more copper-mass here than the Queen's magic charm), guided it into the angled ignition slit, slowly began turning it until the seatbelt alarm sounded and the windshield wipers began their eager idiotic arcs, rotated it farther until the motor sang, turned off the windshield wipers, clicked his lap belt buckle into the receptacle by his hip, which silenced the alarm, idled the motor for another ten seconds of conscientiousness, then shifted into reverse and backed out of Dan Smooth's driveway far more slowly than he could have walked. Q Street lay traffic-less. He stopped, shifted into drive, alone inside this latest unconscious partner, and headed northwest through midtown. The cassette in Dan Smooth's tape deck clicked like a shy child clearing its throat, reached its silent limit, and passed successfully through the ritual of reversal. Then a Bulgarian women's choir began to sing sweet dirges. Half-listening, Tyler found himself already halfway across the trestle bridge, which was reflected in the river as it would have been in the fingerprinted mirror of an old Tenderloin pay phone whose metal-scaled cord had been wrenched out and twisted into an infinity sign: almost a hundred miles from the Tenderloin, he'd lost himself, found himself, lost himself, found himself now passing the sign which neither encouraged nor discouraged him from entering Yolo County. —Don't you forget old Dan Smooth, the very same had said to him once, and he wouldn't, not ever, although remembering was as lonely as Ocean Beach at night. —Connie, check that pink case note, Dr. Jasper had said. Can you read it to me? —*Two glasses of liquid were found by deceased near his feet*, replied dutiful Connie, pulling off the sheet. —Dan Smooth's eyes were open, dark and fixed, not unlike the glass spheres in a trophy deer's head. No more sly sidewise glances from him! Smooth gazed straight up at the ceiling, or maybe at heaven, where he doubtless would have charmed all the prepubescent angels. —Dr. Jasper stepped on the pedal of the dictaphone, picked up his scapel, and said to the world: The head is symmetrical and shows no trauma period. —Tyler, grimacing, stood with his hands folded behind his back. He hadn't tied the green scrub gown on tightly enough.

Why are you *here*, exactly? said Connie.

I ask myself that every day, said Tyler. I hope I figure it out before they bring me to Dr. Jasper here.

Well, you only have a one in four chance of ending up in this room, said Connie. More than six thousand deaths every year get signed off elsewhere in the county.

I'm not from this county anyway, said Tyler. I mean, I was, but not now.

Could you step to one side, please? asked Connie.

Where are you from? said Tyler.

Moldavia, said Connie.

Oh, how is it over there?

Fine, said Connie.

And how is it over here?

All right.

Well, I guess we've covered all the bases, said Tyler. If it's all right over here, then why don't you want me to end up here?

I really don't care, to be honest, Connie said. You can step back closer now if you want.

Nicely done, he said.

Sorry it smells in here, said Connie. The next one over there is a little bit decomposed.

Something to look forward to. Are you near the Black Sea?

Sort of.

Echoing Connie's first unanswerable question, Dr. Jasper slashed Dan Smooth open from each shoulder to the chest, and then down to the base of the belly, in an immense, bloodless letter Y. The skin and fat was a good finger's breadth thick. Steadily Dr. Jasper peeled and skinned away that human hide, announcing to his invisible audience: The exterior genitalia is male comma circumcised period. There is a one-and-one-fourth- by three-and-five-eighths-inch scar.

They had brought Irene to this room which smelled like the Hotel Liverpool, which is to say like garbage, she not falling into the ranks of the six thousand who'd died un-suspicious deaths. Perhaps she'd lain naked and cut open on this very table: one chance in six. But the fat beneath Irene's skin and inside her breasts would have been yellow-ish—white, most likely, not bright orange as was Dan Smooth's. (And the Queen, had they brought her here, too, or was she still alive somewhere?) Inner color was no mys-tery. It all depended on blood content, Dr. Jasper would later explain.

Then the knife went grating across the rib cage, and Connie was pressing the whirling blade of a stainless steel saw across the top of Dan Smooth's head, her bloody gloves slowly whitening with bone dust.

The river now behind him, the new county a *tabula rasa* of free opportunity, he bore right, the white round bulk of a storage tank glowing in the night like Dan Smooth's skull. Another right, and he was parking in the lot above the launching slip. Quietly he walked down to the water, listening to the crickets. His father had courted his mother here. On the other shore, an ugly red light hung in the sky, brighter and steadier than any star—the eye of some radio tower, he supposed. He didn't remember it, although doubtless it had unwinkingly overseen every river night for years. The pale cube of a houseboat was not quite as still as that, and its moonlit reflection even less so, continu-ally decaying and renewing itself. The night was beautiful and smelled of water.

An impure mixture of emotions polluted his chest. He admitted that he had always turned away from Smooth, in death as in life, that he had been disgusted by the man and in equal measure afraid of him, that his omnivorous needs had nonetheless most cheer-fully taken everything which Smooth, who had done him only but good, had ever of-fered him; in sum, that Smooth's death afforded him not only a car, but relief. Yet, having confessed (if only to the river and to himself) his selfishness, which had gone be-yond exploitation almost to cruelty, he now with unfocused surprise discovered within himself a sincere grief, too, which stank within his soul like one of Dr. Jasper's partially decayed patients—no doubt because it was tainted with the greenish bile of guilt. First his life had been full of Irene; then briefly the false Irene had accomodated his despair, afterwards, of course, the Queen had had him. He felt that only now was he coming to possess himself. —But how had he done wrong? —By worshiping only his own desires, came the answer. —But that was one reason why I loved them all, he protested, to *help* them! —a fact undeniably true—but what had he ever done for Smooth, who'd wanted to be his friend? From the prostitutes he'd taken only the worst maxims, the ways of giving not himself, but his mere shell, like that gorgeous scarlet and yellow mantle of flesh which Dr. Jasper had undone with his scapel and thrown open across Smooth's shoulders. Hadn't the ancient Athenians, the rich ones, gotten interred in cloaks of scarlet? That came back to him, maybe from Plutarch . . . John would know for sure. It had been so long since Tyler had done anything worthwhile, even reading, which was not worthwhile in and of itself but could dispose one to worthwhile acts. And for a moment, but only a moment, he felt that he had awakened from a long and flabby sleep. But he didn't want to wake up anymore. —My days are late and wasted, he thought to himself. Better to float back into the river-night. The Queen had been awake; perhaps Smooth had been, too, between or behind repulsive dreams. (The Queen done offed him, said a Polk Street runaway, a scrawny little blond boy, in unshakeable and malicious ignorance.) Had Irene killed herself out of knowledge or out of dreamy fear of knowledge? Tyler, however, wanted to live life selfish and unaware like everyone else he knew—but none of his desires and pretensions were licit. After all, this had been precisely the situation of Dan Smooth.

I must remember, he said to himself distractedly, that he helped me, never did me any harm . . .

A sudden, incoherent anxiety lurked at his ear, as meaningless as his tears.

So only the Queen had been awake, then. So awake, and hence so tired! For a moment he could almost hear her rich, hoarse, lilting voice.

The skyscrapers of Sacramento, such as they were, rose white and stubby above the dark trestle bridge over which he had just driven, which made a tolerable frontier between the moon-clouds and the long thin water-fingers of orange light. Entering the wooded darkness alongside the river, he began to walk toward the bridge, loaded pistol in the pocket of his big, baggy jacket, and suddenly saw a silhouette, stocky and hunched, which stood upon the riverbank, never turning round, although it must have heard his footsteps. The cool air was growing cold.

He walked on, and the tramp rose up behind him and said: What're you doin' down here? Fishin'?

Walking, he said. How about you?

Just spendin' the day out, the tramp said.

He and John had caught some perch here when they were boys, so he said to the tramp: Any perch here?

Nope, said the tramp, walking away.

Ahead, between the trees, he saw a pale light, but when he got to that spot, thinking to see a homeless camp, he found nothing there.

A train whistle, rich with sadness of the longing rather than the despairing kind, drew him on until he stood beneath the bridge, almost blind to the moving of the darkness, which rumbled and squeaked westward; but at strange intervals he'd be granted the sight of vertical light-bars marching by. This train was as endless as darkness—solid it was, heavy, groaning, hissing; while beyond and below its empty purposefulness the river bled and bled from severed fingers of light, and another man stood silhouetted on the shore-sand, gazing down at a lantern, while two silhouettes went fishing. The rump of the last freight car dragged behind it a chain of silence. Foliage reappeared through the trestle's hollow segments, and the signal rang mutely like a desk-bell at a bank or hotel lobby, while at that moment a real bell began to toll across the river. Tyler looked at his watch, but couldn't read the dial.

Cause of death colon compression of the neck vessels period, said Dr. Jasper. Severe emphysema comma heart disease comma unrelated to direct cause of death period. No changes consistent with . . . —as meanwhile Connie lifted off the top quarter of Smooth's skull, withdrew a syringeful of clear cerebospinal fluid, then with crooked scissors pulled away at the stubbornly crackling meninges. Dr. Jasper, lifting his foot from the dictaphone pedal, swigged from a cup of coffee (which he held in a bloody latex glove) and said: Okay, we still have the neck to take out . . .

Golden ripples infused the black river, finger-whirls of gods; round lights clustered on the far bank like the leaves of the tree of heaven.

Tyler ascended the smooth-worn embankment, stepped onto the bridge, and began to walk out toward the water, pale dirty darkness far underfoot, while ahead the gleaming tracks, soberly precious, met across the river in four lines of shining silver. Dan Smooth, the Queen, and the two Irenes true and false were all in the place where parallel lines meet. Now the darkness bled and trembled into a silhouette—as unexpected and forced a differentiation as that suffered by the heart-shaped chunk of fatty ribs which Dr. Jasper had crunched out of Dan Smooth's chest; this darkness ought to have been granted the right to remain itself, but from its flesh, without reference to the shining, burning ribs behind, nonetheless came that silhouette, approaching almost silent, a stranger, a black man with a bedroll who uttered a low, shy greeting, a murmur, and did not stop. Then darkness asserted its rights after all: The man became darkness again. Darkness smiled. Tyler stood alone on the bridge, gazing downriver at the pale yellow glowing phallus which rose from the drawbridge to the south . . .

| 530 |

He had planned to drive down to L.A. one more time to visit Irene's grave, but opening the glove compartment to look for the registration, he saw a note in Smooth's handwriting which read: *Henry—Please give the car to Domino.*

Tyler clenched his teeth. Then he drove to San Francisco. He parked on Capp Street between Seventeenth and Eighteenth, got out, and locked up, striding along with the car keys jingling in his hand. Nobody on Capp Street, so he went to South Van Ness and by a lucky chance saw Strawberry.

It's the black Dodge right around the corner there, he said. Give it to Domino. From Dan Smooth.

She stared at him.

Happy fuckin' New Year, he said.

What are you talking about?

You don't remember me either, huh? he muttered with a sad grin. I guess I can leave word at the parking garage, too. Does she still use that place for her mail drop?

He dropped the keys in her hand and started to walk away, but when he looked back she was still staring at him with eyes like marbles.

It's for *Domino,* he said. You got that, sweetheart?

A flash of terror illuminated her understanding, and she began to piss.

Lift up your skirt or it'll be bad for business, he said. Oh, hell.

| 531 |

It was almost chilly on Haight Street. Two fat cops slowly trudged past Villain's. Nobody sat in front of the Goodwill store. In a glitter-shop's window he saw an old silver-painted wooden crown which reminded him of his Queen. His feet hurt. The sidewalk smelled like meat and urine. On the wall of Cala Foods someone had written: **TONIGHT'S A BLAST, TOMORROW YOU'RE HOMELESS.**

It was then that he realized he was homeless, too.

| 532 |

And so his way led to the yellow-orange freight cars of the Union Pacific, land-ships of freedom, thrilling the lonely souls who rode them from broken promises to promises not yet broken, ferrying the dead souls from one sunset to another, carrying the fearful and the hopeful out of law's imminence. Long low warehouses hunkered in the Sacramento twilight. A man lay upon a loading dock, his head pillowed on his bed roll and his boots dangling into space. Tyler heard booming sounds coming from the direction of the ru-ined mill. A man in a red wool cap walked toward the sunset, holding a Bible near his eyes. Four or five years ago one homeless camp had gotten religion and erected a great cross in the trees, but the new Christ who was going to launch the cult got cancer and died. The long curvy train tracks led to that rotten monument to a dead belief. The smell of creosote annointed him with labor's seriousness. He knelt and picked up a heavy crooked old spike gone red and yellow with rust. Then he let it fall out of his hand and clang against the steel. His right leg moved, and then his left. With a blanket rolled be-neath his arm, he approached the sad self-absorbed hum of generators, passed beneath the conveyor bridge of the Blue Diamond almond factory, and left the hum behind, heading toward the American River, with long trains sleeping beside him. He walked for a long time, but the trains' length kept pace with him. On one freight car someone had drawn the ace of spades. Then on his left a train loaded with cargo from or for Portland, Oregon, came rapidly, smoking and silhouetted, the heavy cars clattering ear-ringingly, the emptier ones merely clicking. Far ahead, the locomotive reached the trestle bridge and began to slow down. From the doorway of a reddish-brown boxcar leaped a long bedroll, followed by a man who landed softly in the gravel on his knees and outstretched hands, a shirtless man in his late prime whose muscular chest and arms screamed with tattoos. He powerfully rose, slung the bedroll over his shoulder, and began to lope with immense sureness toward another train.

Pardon me, called Tyler.

The man stopped and faced him, alert, unafraid.

What's the quickest way out of here? said Tyler.

See that track over there? the man said. That goes north.

Any chance of getting locked in?

Take a loose pin and stick it in the boxcar door. I've got to head my way now.

The man was gone.

Tyler stood looking after him with admiration. The man had known who he was and what he was about. He was travelling but not searching. Tyler longed to be like him.

Half-heartedly following the track that the man had pointed out, he finally found himself at the skeleton-roofed silver trestle bridge which invited him into the evening river-smell. A tagger who went by the monicker "T.F." had painted said initials on every strut, and someone else had x'd them out with equal painstakingness, but the black x's had run and faded after many rainstorms, while T.F.'s blue initials lived triumphantly on. A swastika grinned its crooked grin. Beneath his feet, the river was low and still and silver, bisected by the reflections of cloud trails. Bored, weary, lacking self-surprise, Tyler withdrew his keychain, which clasped the outer and inner keys to his former apartment in San Francisco, his old office key, a key whose provenance he'd forgotten, and the front and back door keys to his mother's house, let them all roll out of his hand and watched them spread apart in the air like a fist opening, every key glittering white, loose upon the chain, dwindling until they met the water with a ridiculous little splash. The sun began to balefully glow, like the eyes of someone with a lethal secret; but its rays had not yet come to their summer strength, and so the air continued to get cool. A duck quacked, almost in an undertone. The bridge led him on and on. Tyler would not be riding any freight trains today; he was already considerably beyond the place that the tattooed man had pointed out to him.

Halfway across the river, a diamond-shaped concrete platform, graffiti'd with stars, grids and more swastikas, looked out on the water. A man with a long, long beard was sitting on it. The man gazed into Tyler's eyes and said: I'm lost.

I know the feeling, said Tyler, walking on. Gnats and mosquitoes boiled about his arms.

He came to the far side, and clambered down beneath the bridge where the air was heavy and chilly and a fanged face had been painted on the concrete. He heard a crackling noise. A man came out of the weeds hitching up his trousers and said to Tyler: You fishing?

That describes it pretty well.

Where's your rod?

Hidden away, said Tyler.

Oh, I love them German browns, said the man. They're not native fish, but they offer a helluva lot of fight. I go after 'em with anchovies or even rebels. Sometimes I pan for gold.

Uh huh, said Tyler. So you're looking, too.

Are you a Christian? asked the man.

Only Jesus knows the answer to that, Tyler replied.

Yep, said the man. You can be walking down the road, pickin' your nose, and it's still okay to call on Jesus because He loves you; He *hears* you. You can just say, Jesus, I don't need nothin' but I love you.

Is Jesus in all the waste places? Tyler asked.

Friend, Jesus is everywhere.

Even where Cain's hiding?

No question of it. That old murdering Cain he can't run no more.

And how about the Land of Canaan?

I ain't never been there, said the man. But Jesus has. He's everywhere.

And how about the idols? Tyler went on in a grating tone which startled even himself.

—How about them, huh? And how about the Whore of Babylon? How about the Queen of the Whores? Has Jesus taken them all over, too?

There's always two voices whispering in every man's head, the fisherman said. One's Jesus's voice. And the other—well, friend, you know who the other is. Which voice is whispering in your head right now, bro?

The Queen. And Dan Smooth. And sometimes Irene—

Friend, I'm going to pray over you right now. In just a minute. You have a cigarette?

Where's the best place to sleep around here? said Tyler.

Just go up that path there and you'll see plenty of hollows where those bushes are. They look impossible to get into, but if you lay down in there, you'll find lots of good canopy so no rain can be botherin' your head. Just lay down there and give some thought to Jesus.

Thanks, said Tyler. He felt a tightness in the back of his head, bone pressing urgently through along the arc where Dr. Jasper's circular saw had gone to take out Dan Smooth's brain. The orange sky's image slowly dulled in the river.

Well? the man said.

Well what?

You gonna listen to Jesus?

Can't get away from Jesus, that's for sure, Tyler bitterly replied. Old Jesus has certainly won the victory.

Your words give me joy, friend, the man said. You know why? I used to have a family. Now I'm divorced. I'm an ex-con; I'm an ex-felon. All I have now is Jesus.

Yeah, I know you do, said Tyler.

You got a cigarette?

I only smoke rock.

You might be able to score something down the river there, where that smoke's coming up through the trees . . .

All right. Good to meet you, said Tyler, heading on into moist darkness scented with anise. The crickets sang. His mother had hated crickets. He remembered once coming home—it must have been in around 1970—and when they pulled into the driveway his mother screamed because the porch was black with crickets. She stayed in the car until he got a broom from the garage and swept then all away . . .

| 533 |

We call this place Coffee Camp because whenever you come by, we'll give you coffee if we have it. If we don't, we'll boil some leaves, or dead cats, or whatever.

Oh, shut up, said Dragonfly. To Tyler he said: That's just Donald talking.

I'm Donald, said Donald. What's your name?

Henry, said Tyler. Pleased to meet you.

At Coffee Camp, at least you won't go thirsty! cried Donald with black-toothed enthusiasm. You want me to boil some leaves or something?

Shut up, Donald, said Dragonfly.

That's all right, Tyler said, seeing by their firelight a toilet paper roll on a stump, two bumpy foam mattresses, a lovingly potted weed not yet dead, some blankets, a half-full pack of cigarettes lying on the sand.

He's retarded, Dragonfly explained. He's a moron. I kind of look after him. His

Mama gave birth to him in an outhouse. By the time they dug him out of the shithole, he was half suffocated. They say it affected his brain.

How often do you guys actually serve coffee around here? said Tyler, suddenly wanting some.

Never. When we get coffee—which isn't very often—we drink it right up. Why? You have some? Donald would sure be tickled.

Don't believe I do.

You won't go thirsty, Donald repeated.

Sounds like a regular Java palace around here.

No, stranger, said Donald. It's not Java Camp. It's only Coffee Camp.

They sat in silence for a while. Just above Tyler's head, the moon bulged and burned through the foliage. From across that river so beautifully cool with wrinkles of night came the greensmoke-smell of a campfire which resembled a quivering yellow diamond. Somewhere near or far, a flashlight swung at ankle height, swung through the crackling bushes. He heard a dog's bark. Then the moon burst through the bushes, and the world was bright.

My name's Dragonfly, said Dragonfly. You looking for a place to camp? Not that I'm meaning to meddle or nothing.

Yeah, in fact I am.

You can sleep under that tree if you want.

All right.

Hey, Dragonfly, said Donald. What's his name again?

My name's Henry, said Tyler.

Henry, can I tell you something?

Sure, Donald. You go right ahead.

I just wanted to tell you that whenever we make coffee here at Coffee Camp, it feels just like Sunday. When the coffee starts to boil, Henry, well, I—I feel like I'm in church. I wanted to tell you that.

Thanks for letting me know, said Tyler, unrolling his blanket.

That's all he talks about, Dragonfly explained. And you know the pisser? He don't even like the taste of coffee!

Across the river, he could hear his fellow souls breaking branches for their fire, with a noise like exploding firecrackers.

What's your name again? said Donald.

Cain, said Tyler. Don't you see the mark on my forehead? Now, Donald, I want you to listen to me. I'm running away, and I don't want to talk to anybody anymore. Now let me sleep.

| 534 |

When he awoke the next morning, an hour or so after dawn, it was already as hot as black, creosoted railroad gravel on a Sacramento summer's day—windy over the green water, the steel bridge walkway trembling under his tread. It might have been the third anniversary of Irene's suicide, but he was less than entirely certain; perhaps he was finished with dates. He saw a crew of homeless men sitting under a tree with their dog. He nodded, but they stared him down. Coming to the cagelike maze between railroad cars, he found no signs of any impending departure from Coffee Camp. His prospects remained unchanged, at least until he ended up on Dr. Jasper's table, and he was hot and sweating. To further his education he swung himself up into the chest-high cave of an open railroad car, inside which a treasury of initials and dates had been scribbled, marked and carved upon hurtfully hot metal walls. The car was hollow and vast. He felt like a single grain of salt in an empty shaker. The question he had to decide consisted of two parts. The first was: Should I live or die? The second was: *How* should I live or die? He found himself unable to conclude anything. Seeking to flee the glary illumination thus cast upon his freedom, he boarded a passing memory-train, revisiting first his brother's late wife, who admitted to being afraid of so many things; when she was young, Irene used to wear her hair in a bun until a neighborhood boy told her that if she did that, spiders could nest inside and in the night time they'd crawl down and eat her eyes. —I used to have all these ideas, she'd said to Tyler once—at which John, gazing good-humoredly up from his laptop, snickered: As if ideas would do *you* any good! —But Irene had been riding her own train. John would not be able to derail her self-sorrow so easily. —I used to want to accomplish all these things, but I never did anything, she went on. And now I know I'm never going to do anything. I'm just going to have a pro-tected, boring life. Sometimes I feel disappointed, but I have to remember that God is protecting me from a lot of bad things. —Uh huh, Tyler had said, pitying her so well that for a moment his own life took on almost a royal luster: hidden (or not) in *everyone's* mind, he'd become sure then, were the same two fears: fear of the unknown bad things, and fear that one's known good things might be even worse than those. No one was free, he said to himself; but today as he sat in the boxcar by Coffee Camp, this truism, which sometimes soothed him into a beneficent smugness, merely increased his restless terror.

In his pocket he had sixty-two dollars—more than most people at Coffee Camp pos-sessed, perhaps, but once it was gone it was gone. Thus fear of the unknown. What he ought to do was lie low on a piece of cardboard and stretch his money out, but he couldn't: fear of the known. The Queen, Smooth, his mother, and the two Irenes haunted him. —Well, that's a natural part of getting older, he thought. Other people die first, and then their ghosts perch on your shoulders, like the cargo of steel rods on that open boxcar . . .

Resolving to wander among the hollows until he found someone who could give him good advice (for his mind felt as empty and echoey as the car he sat in), he let himself down, and, hurriedly recrossing the bridge, reclaimed his blanket from Donald and Dragonfly's camp. Neither of those two was anywhere in sight, so he wandered down the dirt road which ran through the weeds until he saw a bush shake. Squatting and bend-ing, a human being emerged, rear end first, from a thicket, calling warning to his girl-friend still in the cave. Straightening and turning round, the man approached Tyler through the waist-high hissing grass.

What do you want? the man said threateningly. You trying to spy on us?

That's just what my brother used to ask me, Tyler answered, turning his back on the man and beginning to walk away. But the man flew after him and seized him by the shoulder, digging in with long sharp fingernails. Wordlessly, Tyler swung round and punched his face. The man went down, sinking in the grass.

If you know what's good for you, you'll leave me alone, Tyler addressed him. I don't take kindly to being grabbed from behind.

The grass didn't answer.

Do you hear? Tyler said.

The grass still didn't answer.

Just like John . . . he sighed again, and continued his search for a good adviser, turning off the road into higher grass which sometimes flattened into cardboard-paved hollows. It was early May, but already some blackberries were ripe. Hearing a tree's creaking chuckle, he whirled round, but did not discover the man he had punched—nor, indeed, anyone. He followed a narrow trail which led him to a shopping cart filled with water jugs, a mattress whose blankets were thrown back, purses hanging on a tree branch, an open watercolor set. Nobody. The trail led him out of the trees, onto a field of immense girdered power towers, so he followed it back to a junction and chose another path which went beneath a fringe of dead branches to a very dark hollow, a weedy niche of pollen-fuzzed cardboard sheets hidden among the trees and plant-stalks. The trail dipped deeper, and brought him to a huge fire, beside which a squint-eyed and shirtless man who smelled like woodsmoke stood holding a can of beer. —What's up, bro? the shirtless man said warily.

Tyler had a bad feeling about the man and the place, probably on account of the other man who had grabbed him. It seemed to him that he was among ogres. So he merely said: Will this trail take me on through to the river?

Right on through, said the shirtless man, watching him carefully. Tyler now saw that the man's left hand gripped the hilt of a long hunting knife which hung in a sheath at his belt.

Is this all Coffee Camp? Tyler asked, sweeping his hand about.

I never heard of no Coffee Camp.

Last night I was staying with Donald and Dragonfly. That's all they talked about.

Never heard of them, either.

Thanks for your time, sir, said Tyler as courteously as he could, sauntering up the trail, which now began to climb steeply up again toward the river. He ducked around a hollow tree studded with an immense burl like some fibroid tumor, and arrived on the ridge.

A woman was singing. He listened, swallowing. Her song reminded him of the sadness which scaled his heart, like the islands of rust on a boxcar's thickly crusted and peeling paint.

He walked toward the song. In the blackberry brambles on the river bluff, he saw a black woman on a blanket, singing about her own Jesus as she gazed across the turquoise river at Sacramento. He listened. The song was wild and loving. He stood there until she had finished.

I feel good listening to you, he said.

No need to shine about it, the woman said, smiling at him. You got a good angel.

My angel is dead, he replied.

Maybe she is, but she's still lovin' you and helpin' you.

A train sang far away, calling to the sand, the dusty weeds, the purple flower-clusters, the tarps under trees, uttering its longings to the voices rising like smoke from those deep hollows.

Do you hear that? the black woman said. That's your angel callin' you. She's tellin' you to come to her. You can't stay around Coffee Camp no more. Coffee Camp's just a waitin' kind of place. You got to go to your angel.

My angel's name is Africa.

I know it, the black woman said. Now go hop one of them trains. Do it now.

I don't know how, he said.

You're gonna love it, honey.

Tyler sighed. —Well, maybe I ought to stay here and not find her, instead of going far away and not finding her. I honestly think she's dead.

You're not old yet, the black woman said sternly. Go on! Africa's crying for you!

So what do *you* like the best about hopping freight trains?

The noise. That rattling noise. And the way they have tracks everywhere. I remember when I was a little girl and saw my first train I got so excited. I asked my Mama: *What's that?* And remember what I told you: Tracks go 'most anywhere. Tracks even go to glory, maybe. Everytime I hop on one of them trains I think maybe this one will bring me to glory. I'm the Hundred Thousand Dollar Boxcar Queen!

| 535 |

He found an abandoned campsite, lay down on his face, and slowly chewed a mouthful of dirt because he knew that he would never stay a Canaanite if he didn't degrade and martyrize himself like a whore telling her customer to use whatever hole he wanted. It made him sick. He wished that he had eaten dirt from Irene's grave. Rolling onto a rotten sheet of cardboard which smelled like urine and unwashed feet, he fell asleep and all day dreamed gloomy dreams of his Queen. Later he suspected that he might have dreamed of Sapphire, too, but he wasn't sure. He awoke heavy and sluggish. The thought that he had wasted another day of his life, instead of riding a boxcar in obedience to the black woman's word, pained and shamed him. He wanted to go seek her out this very moment and beg her forgiveness. Struggling to his feet, he observed local conditions: a high full moon above the weeds of Coffee Camp, anise smell after a hundred-degree day. Silhouettes of moths visited the looming anise stalks.

He went to the place where he'd seen the black woman, but in the darkness vaguely made out what seemed to be the silhouette of two figures sleeping in each other's arms. He walked quietly away.

A tall silhouette wavered on the bridge. It was Water Woman, whom Tyler would never get to know. Beyond her sat a circle of men with their backpacks and growling dog. They uttered quiet deep laughs, gazing at the sky. A barefoot man with his shoes in his hands led his dog across the bridge. Tyler listened to the clicking of the dog's paws.

And now memories came down like horses, neighing against the gates of his mind. He remembered how he had once been alone with Irene in her car, driving across the Bay Bridge, and he patted her thigh. He could not help himself. She went on driving.

He stroked Irene's hair. His hand was between her legs.

You like that? she said.

Yes, darling, he said thickly.

He was stroking her cunt now.

You like to touch that? she said, gazing at him without expression.

Very much.

She went on driving. (No, that wasn't Irene, it was the Cambodian girl—what was *her* name?

He remembered Irene's eyes, Irene's dark, made-up eyes, almost sickeningly beautiful, certainly hurtfully so, while fireworks pounded like his heart.

He remembered the Queen's dark, scarred little face. He remembered going fishing with John up near Placerville when he was a boy. He remembered the moving stream of heads in Chinatown, heads like boulders in a stream.

Suddenly he felt that his position in the world was absolutely intolerable. He could not remain at Coffee Camp for another instant. He could scarcely bear to remain himself.

A new campfire, which appeared to be just above the shoreline, swelled into hemisphericality like a rising second moon. Twin fires made a tunnel of light beneath a tree.

Now he realized that he had left his blanket somewhere, but he could not for the life of him recall the place—probably Donald and Dragonfly's camp, but he felt an inexplicable revulsion against going there . . .

From under the other bridge, the railroad bridge, women's husky voices and radio music ascended through the grating. Over the river, the pale full moon left a trail of shimmering greenish wrinkles. A train blared in the night, its utterance hollowing and decreasing in pitch, like metallic fluid being poured out of an immense metal jug.

I missed my train again, he thought to himself in agony.

He walked across the railroad bridge, leaving Coffee Camp, he hoped forever.

| 536 |

A steamy hissing from the almond factory accompanied him on his journey into darkness. He entered the train tunnel and heard a spooky laugh, and then footfalls running echoingly away. The twin track-ribbons were dull grey, leading him deeper into the trap. A crunch of broken glass around the railroad pillars exemplified the brittleness of the night.

| 537 |

A man stood in the center of the tunnel, barring his way. Tyler said to the man: I'm hungry.

Silently, the man reached inside his jacket and pulled out a dirty crust of bread. He broke off a hunk and put it into Tyler's hand.

Thank you, brother, said Tyler.

The man laughed. His laugh echoed. He stepped aside, and Tyler went on.

At sunrise he was walking between two very long trains whose boxcars blanketed most of the world with immense shadow-blocks interrupted by narrow ribbons of light.

| 538 |

I'm hungry, Tyler said to a man.

The man said: My name is Peter. What's your name?

Henry.

Come in, Henry, said the man, and I'll give you the most nourishing food there is.

He led Tyler into a room where there was nothing but a table, two chairs and a Bible.

I wouldn't mind a glass of water, Tyler said.

First things first, said Peter. Have you been saved?

Depends on whom you talk to. Would you have anything to eat?

The essence of Christ is *forgiveness,* Peter said. Christianity is the only religion which forgives. I can testify to that, because God has forgiven me. When Jesus forgives us, he buries our sins so deep and so far that we remember them but we feel no *pain*. I'm saying that to you *personally*, Henry.

I guess you are, said Tyler, shifting in his chair. I mean, I appreciate that.

The Bible does not leave any room for speculation, Peter went on earnestly, and Tyler nodded with a glum face and said: I wish it did.

Any questions so far? asked Peter.

What's your position on Catholics? asked Tyler, just to say something.

We've got a wonderful woman, a Catholic woman, on our board of directors. She received Christ as her Lord but she still lives within the Catholic church.

Suddenly Tyler rose to his feet and said: I have something to say to Jesus.

Peter cocked his head, a little disconcerted. —And what might that be?

Tyler took a deep breath. He gazed upward at the bare light bulb. Then he shouted: *Let my people go!*

| 539 |

On the concrete embankment, chin-bone of the night, an immense whitish menacing face winked its painted eye.

| 540 |

I'm hungry, he said.

Then get a job, the woman said.

| 541 |

I can boil some leaves for you if you want, said Donald. I'd be happy to do it. Because this is Coffee Camp.

Little white speedboats and jet-skis played upon the river, sometimes wiping out and making big waves. He heard the laughter of the unhomeless. Fat oiled legs clenched small boats.

I need to get out of here, he said.

Dragonfly likes to say that, too, said Donald. What did you say your name was?

A pair of knees and a cap passed along the riverbank, enthroning themselves upon a sofa statioined amidst concrete. Donald's voice was as brassy as a train horn. It was early afternoon. Gazing around, Tyler seemed to see a beer bottle in the crotch of every tree. He listened to the ringing clinking of the signal on the trestle bridge, and despaired.

| 542 |

You have to be careful, Jose said. Sometimes it go fast and sometimes it go slow. When it go fast, dem wheel can chop off your arm or leg just like that. Can kill you. Dat's why I ride my bike. I ride my bike down to San Diego no problem.

How long does that take?

One or two week. Sometimes one or two month. I don't care. My wife is dead. Nobody to hurry up for no more . . .

You must meet bad people from time to time, said Tyler.

Laughing grimly, Jose flashed a serrated kitchen knife and said: Die is OK. But I tell them, cut de throat is a bad way to die. You cut your finger with a knife by mistake, and you feel that pain right away for fifteen minute. I think just see the knife, start the pain. And when I cut your throat, you got mebbe two long, long minutes, man . . .

| 543 |

Here's how I know where to git off, Riley the tramp explained. I git on in Roseville shit-faced drunk, and when that wine wears off, I know I'm in Reno.

Uh huh, said Tyler.

Jist do zackly like I tole you. An' be sure you jump off before you get to the yard.

Even if it's moving?

Well, no. You wanna lose a leg? Wait till it *stops*. Dead *stops*.

| 544 |

Slipping onto a boxcar, he waited for hours, but it never moved.

| 545 |

Then finally came the night when the yellow eyes of the train's face came boring along the embankment so that the trestle burst into radiant light; and from among the squatting backpackers silhouetted at trackside Tyler ran, seized the first ladder of a boxcar, not the dangerous second one, and pulled himself up, threw himself in, and clackety-clacked triumphant into the darkness.

| 546 |

Trains and trains and trains: he wanted to ride them all! Long blue cloud-lines shot across the salmon-colored sky, stretching on like railroad tracks. Riley the tramp, hunched and grizzled, would be proud of him yet. See Tyler at seven on a June evening with the Sierras faint and bleached-blue on the horizon, at his ease in an open boxcar which was creeping into the yard at Roseville, probably seen but ignored by the benign and brawny driver whose arm he could see hanging out of the locomotive window. The train slowed. He threw his bedroll out and leaped, not wanting to meet any yard bulls because he'd been warned that Roseville was a hot yard, but his precautions were about as availing as superstitions because everything was already very open and exposed there among the slow trains. Long black cylinder cars of liquefied petroleum gas moved slowly forward and back, their rusty wheels turning slowly enough for him to count the revolutions. He wanted to climb between the cars so that he could get to the edge of the yard and run, but didn't dare. Suddenly there came a tremendous slamming boom, and the cars stopped, then eased backward again, creaking. The whole horizon was train. When the cars were still, he rushed between them, arriving just in time to hide behind an oak tree before the bull in the blue uniform came motor-scootering by . . .

Thanks to the benevolence of the city council, the Home Start shelter disallowed sin-

gle men from sleeping there, so a drunk warned, and Tyler had neither means nor inclination to bring a whore along to be his wife, so he trudged directly to the park and
napped uneasily until dawn, attacked by mosquitoes from the river. With relief he returned to the edge of the yard, an inch on the legal side of the NO TRESPASSING
sign, watching the trains. Immense shadow-blocks craned across the embankment, carving up his world. —Jist wait in the shade, Riley the tramp had advised him. Wait by the
liquor store. —That was easy, because right now it was all shade. Under the Crystal
Dairy trucks lay old clothes and empty sardine tins; his predecessors had taken their
shade where they could find it. Blue-overalled trackmen rollstepped in the distance,
speaking into walkie-talkies. Everybody said that trainhopping was more likely to get
punished now that Union Pacific had bought Southern Pacific.

A freight train lay still and ready, with three locomotives on it. That meant it was going somewhere. Looking both ways, he spied no spies, and ran to the open boxcar. He
threw himself in, insured his life with the spikenail, crawled into the back, and met a
migrant worker who smiled at him gravely. He offered the man a drink of water. The
man smiled, and gave him a fresh ripe peach.

The boxcar jerked. The train began to move.

| 547 |

Well, looky here, laughed the railroad dick. All right, fellas. You might as well come out
now.

His heart overwhelmed him with booming echoes as of dark boxcars.

Come back here now, said the railroad dick.

The train slid away, leaving him and the Mexican alone on the gravel with the railroad dick. It was almost night. At the back of the receding train blinked a red eye. That
was FREDdy, the Fucking Rear End Device. A tramp had said that it was called that because it had stolen three railwaymen's jobs. FREDdy flashed triumphantly in the twilight. Two more parasites, two more evildoers had fallen into the hands of the righteous.

You first, said the railroad dick. What's your name?

Tyler, said Tyler.

What's *your* excuse?

I'm homeless.

Yeah, you could pass for homeless. That's against the law. Don't get upwind of me. I
could cite you. I should cite you. Now get out.

Thanks, said Tyler, as sincerely as he could. He started walking away.

Now you, said the railroad dick to the Mexican. We don't call you wetbacks no more.
Call you *scratchbacks* from duckin' under the border fence. Call you *gravelknees.* Is that
right? Hey, fella, are you a scratchback?

The Mexican smiled and nodded three times quickly.

Okay. That's the spirit. Now beat it, and don't let me catch you riding my train again.

When Tyler and the Mexican were out of sight, the railroad dick radioed the locomotive and told the driver that his two unwanted pasengers were gone.

What were they this time? asked the driver, bored.

Usual. One drunk and one Spic.

Used to be just them hobos, the driver ruminated. Pleasant people. Sometimes you just gotta throw rocks at 'em. And them migrant workers, them scratchbacks. But now I keep seeing the gangs. They use my train for transportation. They got guns. What am I supposed to do against a gun?

Carry a gun, laughed the railroad dick.

| 548 |

Well, see, those people are kinda leery, unless you have the look, the tattooed man said.

So you're saying I don't have it, said Tyler. Ain't that a shame.

That's what I'm saying. Now, that Mexican there, he has it, but who cares? He's just a Mexican. As for you, they gotta be careful. Maybe somebody could justify how you look, but they don't trust you.

Who doesn't trust me, partner? You?

The Mexican waved and began to walk away. Tyler waved back, a little sadly.

What are you about? asked the tattooed man.

Riding the rails, I guess, said Tyler. How come I need to justify my existence to you?

The tattooed man smiled weakly and resentfully, his gaze like some cold yellow light at the end of a long trestle bridge, and Tyler sighed.

All right, he said.

What are you about? asked the tattooed man again, standing in his way like a sentinel in some ancient myth.

Looking for somebody I know I'll never find, said Tyler. Getting away from people who know me.

Amen to that, said the tattooed man; and Tyler felt that he had answered correctly and could move on. —So which way goes east? he said.

As far as how to go, said the tattooed man, carefuly spying him out, they got certain routes. There's certain places they got to catch you, but normally they let you do it. I more or less quit doing it after my last stretch in jail. I don't really enjoy dogging it that much. Where you from?

Sacramento.

Oh. Well, what're you gonna do? You got to run it somewhere else. Sac's just got that evil feel to it. Just feels too negative to me.

Tell me about it. I was born there.

The tattooed man laughed, his eyes yellow like empty plastic cigarette lighters on railroad gravel.

So where was you an' that Mexican when you got busted?

Boxcar, said Tyler.

Normally, the boxcar's the lousiest ride you can get. I can see you need advice. Now, the ones that know, they're lookin' for the grainers, those T-48s or whatever. There are holes in the back. You just pop right in like a prairie dog. And you got water? You don't want to go without a bunch of water.

Yeah, I have water, said Tyler. And when that runs out, I can just marry somebody and drink her spit.

Ooh, said the tattooed man with a sort of sinister gentleness.

So which track runs east?

Normally, see, some people are hooked up with the people in the yard. There's certain tracks set up already. So if I want to go to Salt Lake, these here are the tracks I can get on. You got another track there that's gonna wind north. Let's say you want to go to Washington . . .

And suddenly Tyler felt an exultation that he hadn't been able to own for so long now, a breezy thrill of freedom even as he stood there sweating with the evening sun burning his arms. He could go anywhere. He had nothing to guard and defend except his own body. He had fallen, but he had landed. Now he was happy and safe.

The tattooed man read his eyes and said: There's *something* about trainhoppers, anyway. All of us are transients on this earth. I'm a Buddhist. This is just taking it to the next level.

And you feel free? Tyler couldn't help asking.

My whole concept is, what's out there and rolls my way I have a right to. Like if I go into a supermarket and can walk out with a can of tomato soup in my pocket and they don't catch me, I have a right to it. See what I'm sayin'? Because they're bilking the world anyway. And when I steal from them, nobody gets hurt.

Well, I guess I'll be heading my way, Tyler said. Thank you.

I been wanting to ride the rails myself, the tattooed man suddenly volunteered. I just can't decide which direction to go . . .

Behind the man's wistfulness, behind his softspoken charm, Tyler had begun to sense a crocodile's soul, intelligent and vicious, perhaps even lethal—held in check right now mainly by the inertia of this exceedingly hot day (certainly over a hundred degrees). If a cloud were to pass over the sun, so that the tattooed man's reptilian blood could cool sufficiently to refresh his torpid brain, then Tyler might be in danger. This was only intuition, and very possibly wrong, like the intuition of so many street-whores who had been sure at first that Tyler was a cop; nonethless, he was afraid of the tattooed man.

I'll walk up with you, the tattooed man said with an insidious grin.

Why, thank you, said Tyler, his heart pounding.

This used to be the Greyhound bus station, right here where it says GOLF, the tattooed man was saying. I know where I'd catch out if I was riding. See that track there, with all those grainers? That's where I'd catch out.

All right, said Tyler plodding steadily toward the sleeping train.

Watch out for the heat, laughed the tattooed man lazily, although *they* must be sweatin' it more than ever, I mean those *cops*.

Okay. See you when I look at you, said Tyler.

And watch out for the Sidetrack types. You remember Sidetrack? He rode the rails and he befriended trainhoppers like you, and then in the night he slit their throats. Ha, ha, ha!

I hope he enjoyed it, said Tyler wearily, looking for the perfect grainer to crawl into, one where the hole would be too small for him and the tattooed man together.

Shit, he got caught right here, in this fuckin' town. The fuckin' S.P. bulls said he told them he was just cleanin' up the lowlifes, the ripoff artists.

You a friend of his? asked Tyler.

No, but I know a woman who used to know him. You want to meet her?

No, I think I'll take this bus, said Tyler, clambering up up the ladder of a grainer whose oval womb, as he could see, was choked with juice bottles, wine bottles and crumpled newspapers. This train had been thoroughly hopped. Now he was high above the world. Safe and lofty, he waved to the tattooed man.

Hey, I'm kind of broke, said the tattooed man. You mind helping me out?

Here's a buck, said Tyler, letting the paper note flutter down.

That'll work, said the tattooed man. Well, watch out, or somebody just might get you.

Thanks for the warning, Sidetrack, replied Tyler with a harsh and ugly laugh . . .

| 549 |

It took a good three hours before the train began to slam and thud, and another hour or so before it went anywhere. When he finally felt the clittery-clatter in his bones, Tyler stuck his head out of the hole and saw in the hole of the facing car the head of an ancient black man. He waved, and the black man smiled at him.

Somewhere in the desert before Salt Lake, the train stopped for an hour, and he woke up and looked out. The black man looked back at him.

Where you bound, sonny? said the black man.

Bound for heaven, sir, said Tyler.

Just remember, child, you're only stealin' a ride. Nothin' else. Don't you harm anything on them cars. Don't take nothin'. The railroad is good to us. It gives us our freedom. Don't you take advantage of that.

All right. Kind of a nice ride up here, don't you think?

The black man smiled. It was the smile of one who knew. He said to Tyler: If you ain't seen America on a boxcar, you ain't seen America.

| 550 |

Striding into Coffee Camp like a conqueror, he found at afternoon's end the black woman, the Hundred Thousand Dollar Boxcar Queen, who had herself, as she said, just emerged from the long, long place between two trains where rectangular worlds of boxcar-shadow were separated by narrow bright zones of sunlight on the gravel, and she didn't remember him. Midges crawled like flecks of living gold in the sun-barred air between vine covered trees. The sandy space where he'd slept at Donald and Dragonfly's camp a month ago was already bursting with poison oak. Mosquitoes bit him silently. Above the black woman's Jesus-singing, strange half-shadowed lattices of trumpet vines greenly glowed in the dusk. He could smell smoke and roasting hot dogs.

I still feel good listening to you, he said.

Who the fuck are you? she said.

The one you told to go ride the trains to find my angel.

And you done it, she said, softening. I can see you done it.

He grinned, filled with pride.

And you found your lovin' angel, she said.

Actually, I'm getting pretty sure I'll never see her again. But if I keep looking, it gives me something to do.

So you didn't find her? That why you come back to Coffee Camp, with your tail between your legs? Maybe you just don't *believe*.

Maybe I never did, he said sadly.

But she *helped* you, the black woman insisted, her sentences thrilling him like Union Pacific locomotives riding backward, ringing their bells. —You *rode* them trains when you thought you couldn't do it. That's good for you. That train wind baptizes all your sorrow away. Even just come and go, come and go, those trains takin' you somewhere. Takin' you to *freedom.*

You feel like taking a walk with me, Hundred Thousand Dollar Boxcar Queen?

Honey, I'm not your queen and I'm not your angel but if you want to take a walk with me I'll gladly welcome you home. Just a minute. Just a minute. Let my hide my stash in this hollow tree . . .

On the concrete under the bridge, someone had painted a giant purple heart. He took her hand in his and touched it to the heart. She kissed him. Just then a yellow and red Union Pacific train flickered overhead, and night came and sun and colors were lost. He heard a woman's screaming laugh.

That night the black woman was sleeping in another's arms. His soul began to swing back to loneliness, like the bridge between Sacramento and West Sacramento pivoting on its cylindrical concrete base, turning counterclockwise to rejoin its own metal flesh, swinging like a door, its shadow following it upon the water, slow and slow; then suddenly no lacuna anymore; the rails now went all the way from West Sac to Old Sac; and a metal piece dropped and a white box hummed. The bridge swung again, adjusted again, until the raised rails dropped with a slam. Now anyone could walk like Jesus over the sunny green water.

He wandered through midtown and reached that bridge one day; then he crossed it, standing where he'd stood on that night now months ago when he'd come in Dan Smooth's car; and looking down and to the side, he perceived three who sat beneath the bridge with their hats on—a woman between two men, bleary-eyed railroad tramps swinging their arms at their sides. The Hundred Thousand Dollar Boxcar Queen was the woman. She began to unzip one man's fly and the man grunted, his breath full of beer.

Not jealous, not sick at heart, not even empty, he slept in the bushes on the West Sacramento side that night, in an abandoned camp with plenty of pieces of cardboard. He smelled bad, and he had holes in his shirt. He wanted to bathe in the river, but it was too cold. The next morning he returned to the greasy ledge where the three had been, and found the black woman's dress, slick and silky to his touch, probably rayon, with a dozen cigarette butts beside it, and above its collar, empty air. A drunk lay above him, cackling. Pawn of providence, the drunk threw down in place of the black woman's missing head a woman's wadded-up panties which were now stiff and dusty and the color of mud; and this sad ball duly landed on the ledge just above the collar of that blue dress which he remembered from yesterday. Then the drunk staggered down beside him and pissed on everything. Tyler walked on, continuing beneath the belly of that strange half-living armature for tramps and trains, the river lashing and sizzling against the embankment below. Overhead came the rumbling roar as the train crossed the river.

| 551 |

He learned how to scoop out for himself a hollow along the riverbank laid down with cardboard and jugs, and sometimes even with a couple of coats. Nine in the morning, and he could already tell that the day was going to be as hot as Mexicali, everyone sweating and lurking in the shade. A guy in a white sombrero and grey coveralls hitched up his belt. Hiding the railroad spike underneath his shirt, Tyler went to the shelter, got his ticket, played poker for cigarettes with an old goner named Red, stood in line for two hours, and got lunch.

You have to deal with the total man, preached Reverend Bobby as they all ate. —Part of our Christianity has to deal with puttin' food on a mon's table. History has taught us that the church has sometimes gone overboard, like in the Inquisition days, and we have to strive for balance.

In one ear and out the other! a man muttered, furtively, like a first-grader warned by the teacher not to talk.

After lunch, Tyler went to Reverend Bobby and asked: Where did evil come from? *Satan,* mon.

Did Satan invent the Mark of Cain?

Those questions aren't for the likes of you, said Reverend Bobby. You have your own problems to deal with. Don't worry about technicalities.

Somebody said I have the Mark of Cain on my forehead, Reverend. I was wondering if you could see anything right here . . .

Good Lord, mon, that's just a mosquito bite you've been scratchin'. That's just—

Reverend, do I bear the Mark of Cain or not?

Do you believe you deserve to bear it?

Yes.

Then you bear it. Have you ever been baptized?

When I was christened.

That doesn't count. You have to be baptized anew. What's your name?

Henry.

Henry, are you prepared to receive the sacrament of holy baptism today?

I don't know, Tyler said. I guess I'm still trying to figure out what I ought to be.

| 552 |

A man was sitting beside a culvert, reading his Bible by lantern light whose brightness stained his hands and knees and forehead. Every moment or two, the man swept mosquitoes away from his face. Crickets sang around him, and moths visited his lantern in its harshly lit patch of sand. Far away, a boxcar door slammed. A dog was barking in the darkness. Above him, where the gulley ended, stretched a lightless field whose laborers had at twilight resembled blurred bushes. He was reading in the Book of Chronicles about the reign of the unclean Queen Athaliah, who was overwhelmed in the end by the soldiers, captains and trumpets of righteousness; and she tore her clothes and cried treason. Then Jehoiada the priest made a channel like a long train track between his rows of captains, and he commanded: *Bring her out between the ranks; anyone who follows her is to be slain with the sword.* And he who read knew then that he should have followed his Queen and died with her; and so he wept. And the captains dragged her to the Horse Gate, which was a safely unholy place, and executed her there. *Then all the people did go to the House of Baal, and razed it. Baal's altars and images they rent in pieces; and they slew Mattan the priest of Baal before the altars.* He crushed the mosquitoes on his face, so far from her whom he had loved, distant even from Coffee Camp where upon the river which beneath the moon was as a pale blue stone the struts of the reflected bridge formed a rake's teeth, which combed and devoured everything as Jehoiada the priest had done. Righteousness, malignant and sure of itself, rose up against the sky.

He stood up. A barely discernible figure was approaching on the white road. Suddenly he believed that his Queen had once passed here, and he knelt to kiss the road.

A light blossomed inside a bush, and he saw two tramps, sitting unspeaking. Dogs barked. The approaching figure, which he could now see was that of a woman with a water-jug in her hand, muttered wearily: Shut up! Shut the fuck up! —And, strangely, the dogs stopped.

That gal got the power, one of the tramps said wisely.

The woman passed and was lost. Tyler said to the tramp: What's the secret of power? What do you know?

You don't got the right to know, the tramp said. Not yet.

You don't know me.

When you got the right to know, you'll know. Then you don't got to ask. You want to know about power? Wait till you feel a cop's boot in your face . . .

Were you ever at Coffee Camp? Tyler asked him conversationally. That's the place, you know, where sometimes the river smells like oranges.

Yeah, yeah, you come out of California, the tramp said. You got it easy. Your kind throw their *bike* up on them boxcars. We call you rubber tramps. That's why you don't know about power yet. When you know, you ain't gonna like it. You got to travel more. And I don't just mean on earth. Look up there at them stars. More stars than skeeter-bugs. Look at that expanse up there where it's all windy and fresh. What's occurred to me, friend, is *enormous changes over the expanse of time.* I can't even really express it. But I know what I feel.

So you know about good power, too, said Tyler. That's what I want to learn about. I already know about bad power, maybe as much or more than you.

What are you talking to me for then? You ought to be talking to them stars. Then stars will tell you everything.

Thank you, friend, said Tyler.

He went back down into his hollow, where the mosquitoes were now not quite so greedy, and read his Bible. Then he closed the lantern-valve and looked up at the stars, longing to be alone and away from lurking humanity, from the crouchers and the sleepers, alone with ducks, crickets and stars.

Points of light came down the gulley, moving like fireflies, and he wanted to believe that it was the stars talking to him. But the lights rushed and jerked too much. Gruff voices swore, and then he heard a man pissing in the sand. On the road, he heard the clatter of a shopping cart.

| 553 |

The next morning the two tramps were snoring under their bush, dead drunk, and another old fellow, unshaven and lean, but with neatly slicked back hair and wearing new clothes and fine hiking boots (the reason he looked so good, as it turned out, was that he'd just gotten out of detox), sat up against a tree reading a thriller.

You heard about FREDdy? he said to Tyler.

Yeah, I heard.

You heard how that goddamned machine took away three good men's jobs. Now on the whole train they only have two men, the engineer and the conductor or whatever the hell he's called. Well, sometimes they have an inspector, too, but he lies low so he can catch you. Eventually they'll get rid of all the humans. They'll have just computers and lasers.

I'm surprised they don't have a sensor on every boxcar, Tyler said. That way they could bust us all, no sweat.

They tried that. Had the heat-seeking kind. But when them wheels get hot, they get so hot, why, them sensors get confused. Had to rip 'em all out.

Uh huh, said Tyler, not quite believing it, sipping from his water bag.

How long you been catching out, son?

Just a couple of months. How about you?

The very first time I ever hopped a train, I must have been about ten years old. That was back in Missouri. That's why my handle's Missouri. My kid brother and I, we jumped on, right by the crick that ran near our house, and we rode about three miles and then walked back, just to try it. Man, we was scared!

Does your brother still ride the rails?

I ain't seen him in about ten years. I ain't seen my two sisters in fourteen years. But I seen my other brother recently. He's collecting SSI, just like me. He's a paranoid schizophrenic. I see him whenever I go home. I go home about every two years, whenever I lose my birth certificate.

Your folks still alive?

I never knew my father. My mother died years ago. *The hospital killed her,* Missouri suddenly snarled, and gazed at Tyler expectantly, waiting to be asked to tell the whole sad story, but Tyler didn't feel like it.

I don't suppose you've seen a small thin black woman, he began hopelessly, about forty-five years old, who—

Missouri looked him over scornfully. —If you got to have more than one person in order to survive, you don't belong out here.

And you've been alone your entire life, said Tyler in a tone of almost nasty defiance.

Oh, I lasted almost six months with one partner once, said Missouri. He went into one detox place and said he'd be back in ten minutes, but after three hours he never come out so I took off.

Maybe they wouldn't let him out.

Maybe, said Missouri. But I'll tell you a better one. I know one guy up there in Oregon. He woke up there in a boxcar and found everything gone: his food, his duffel bag, his wallet, his knife, his money—not to mention his partner of twelve years. He expected that, so he didn't mind too much, but what really pissed him off was that his partner even stole his dog. Now that's *low.*

Yeah, that is, Tyler agreed. So where are you headed today?

Oh, north. Generally north. Well, I've gone as far back as Cleveland by freight. I know how to do it. From Indiana, everywhere east is great because the cities are so close together you just need to go a few miles to escape the cops and jump the state line, but out here you got three or four hundred miles between towns, so you gotta hop a freight; you gotta be an expert so that they don't get you.

Tyler rubbed his chin. —Who's after you?

You heard about that Tent City down there in Arizona? That's where they take all the homeless people and put 'em like in a prison camp. I don't want to go there. Salt Lake's building one, too. Everywhere you go now, they're out to get you.

I think God's been closing in since the get-go, Tyler said. I think pretty soon we're not going to have anyplace left to run.

You're one of them religious nuts, said Missouri complacently. I live and let live myself. But if you think prayin' for me's gonna do any good, why, then, you just send up a prayer for old Missouri. I ain't never turned down anything free, even something I can't see.

Have you run into a small thin black woman who—?

You already asked me that, sonny. I'm not interested. Hey, you got any tobacco on you?

You already asked *me* that, said Tyler.

No, I didn't.

All right, so you didn't. I was just checking on you.

On the embankment, the locomotives of the long, long train shrieked brassily past, and then the train began to slow.

Which way's this one going? asked Tyler.

Check the first two numbers on the lead car. Didn't you even know that? If they're even, it's going east or west. If they're odd, it's north or south, just like the highway. This one's going north.

The train was going much more slowly now, and Tyler saw the square mouth of an open boxcar coming toward him. He slid his pack over his shoulder and got ready to jump into it.

They got a change off in Phoenix, Missouri said. Then it gets a local. They got a nice mission there in Phoenix where you can eat decent.

I'm not much into decency anymore, said Tyler.

Hey, you got any tobacco on you?

You never asked me that.

I hate boxcars, Missouri said. You got all this metal here that gets hot in the sun. Round about four or five in the afternoon, you get cooked.

Well, I like the view from a boxcar, said Tyler.

I always try to catch a grainer with an air compressor, Missouri said, trailing after him. But really I'm too old for this.

The train stopped. Tyler threw himself up onto his boxcar.

Can't get inside them car carriers anymore, Missouri went on, looking up at him, in no hurry to board. —Used to be paradise. They put a couple gallons of gas in every tank, so on a cold night you could hop right in, turn on the heater and the radio, and later on tear the speakers out, rip off the cassette decks and sell everything . . . Where's your spike?

Without waiting for an answer, he snatched up one of his own and pounded it into the groove beside the boxcar door, so that Tyler would not be lethally trapped by any sudden lurch.

Thank you, Tyler said.

I seen some Mexicans, the old man said, I seen how they died in a boxcar. They pounded their hands bloody, trying to get out, but nobody heard. Sun cooked 'em to death.

A loud hiss almost woke up the two sleeping tramps.

Getting ready to move, Missouri shouted. Or maybe he's just testing his brakes . . .

You'd better grab your grainer, said Tyler, and the older man started and scurried down the track.

The brakes hissed again. Then the train began to move. His heart thrilled with joy.

| 554 |

He was somewhere in northern California again. The hot strip of daylight, sand, gravel, trees, wires and skies unwound, anonymously strange. Every now and then he could glimpse a striped signal bar and a line of automobiles waiting for his train to finish occluding them. He felt a sense of borrowed power, that the train could interrupt so many people. It was only mid morning, but the temperature felt like it might breach a hundred. His skin was hot and sweaty. He dwelled inside the humming rattling roar of trainness. The train began to accelerate, and with dreamlike surprise he saw Sacramento: midtown, a signal tower, a brief ring of tunnel-darkness, graffiti; here stretched the yard he'd walked through on that first night; they were making up a long train at perpendiculars to him on the embankment behind; the train rattled in his teeth. Edging closer to the boxcar door, he gazed deliciously out as he flashed across the bridge with the river so lovely below and a guy on the bank fishing and then he was rushing through Coffee Camp; two cyclists waved from the pedestrian bridge—a whiff of steaming anise, and then Coffee Camp was gone . . .

Heat rose from the rails. He sped across dusty streets and gravel embankments, followed only by wires, going maybe forty miles an hour now, way too fast to jump. A smoldering burnt heat dried his nostrils every time he breathed.

Now the train really started going, flashing and flickering past man-shaped wicker-wire power towers, shaking him from side to side as if he were a single pea in a collander. It rushed him past a country road where he saw more backed-up traffic. He wondered if anyone could see him. The vibration massaged him within the base of his skull and in his back which was pressed against the dusty boxcar wall, and above all in his teeth like a speedball rush; and he understood the orgasms of the Hundred Thousand Dollar Boxcar Queen. Roaring and shaking past a long cornfield, he imagined fucking her right there on the floor of the boxcar with the vibration dissolving them into each other. He thought of his own dead Queen but no longer believed in her.

For hours, the parallelogram of sunlight in the open door kept swaying and pulsing, like his own brightly blank mind. He drank from his bag of water, which was still cool. A cropduster plane followed him, jetting what looked like flour which tumbled with slow gorgeousness. The train was slowing. He came to the doorway and gazed upon bright golden grass and fields of strange, blackened crops. On an impulse, having no idea where he was, he threw his backpack into space and then himself made the leap, falling exultantly to earth.

| 555 |

It was very hot. The flesh-rags of a dead cat lay stiff and flat in a ditch, reeking of mucilage. He walked for miles. Finally he came to a town, his lips cracking, and heard the blessed sound of a sprinkler. Across the road, behind a picket fence, a little blonde girl stood in the center of a green, green lawn, playing in the water. He waved, and she waved back. He was happy.

He walked on and on, looking for a store where he could buy a cold soda. Finally he stopped at a crossroads and drank from his water bag. The water was hotter than spit from having pressed up against his back.

Far away, he heard the whistle of a train. His soul glowed like a crackhead's after that first hit of rock, and he began to run.

| 556 |

Look at that crazy tramp, a man at a gas station said. Look at him running. A hundred and five degrees. Maybe we'll be lucky. Maybe we can watch him croak.

| 557 |

There was no train. He found a hobo's abandoned camp, where sheets of cardboard made good resting and wooden planks spanned rocks and stumps to form benches, with castoff trousers tucked underneath. He took it over, picked blackberries, and slept. In the morning he was getting low on water when his train came . . .

| 558 |

Now, those two guys under the bridge, they're good people, the old hobo said.

Groovy, said Tyler.

The whole deal is, we put one man over there to watch the gear, and another man here to collect from the citizens. I'm explainin' all this for your own good, so you'd better be listening.

Tyler smiled sarcastically.

Now, you know what this is? said the old hobo.

A bedroll.

Wrong. It's a prop. The more props you have, the more money you can make. The more shit you have hangin' off, the more scratch you have. Get a bag on a stick like an oldtime bindlestiff. Get a hat. Put patches in your pants. You dig?

Tyler hesitated, sighed, and whispered: Props are for magic. Props keep me close to my Queen.

For by now he had a talisman, in the manner of his departed Queen, or for that matter like any whore brooding lovingly over her crack pipe. Just as the man called Sneakers, who begged on Steiner and Haight, bore beneath his baggy jacket in the nest made by the unzipped fly of his pants a plastic cup wedged in so secretly that it was as an organ of his body—this was his change-organ, his dime-collector; all he'd gotten that day was pennies, he said, and he always lied—so Tyler learned to attach himself to a rusty railroad spike. He never forgot what both old Missouri and that superhuman trainhopper at Coffee Camp had told him: If the boxcar doors closed on you in the desert and the train sat for a week, you were sunk. Wedge it into the track, and you owned salvation. Then you couldn't pull it out; you had to get another spike for next time; better just to carry a spare, which he'd never use because it was his good luck charm to comfort him as he sat with legs dangling, looking out at the tracks when he was certain of being unseen, listening to night-creaks and cracks and hissings, while the whole world rumbled like a boxcar door slamming shut. So many of the homeless men he met on the road owned knives, which gave them peace of mind instead of actual safety because they had to be concealed, and often not under clothes but deep inside duffel bags—how could they save anyone when quickly assailing death came? But let something become part of you, and you feel better—which is all that matters; you have to die anyway.

You got to snap out of it, son, said the old hobo, about whom there was something slow and kind which reminded him of the Queen. You got to wake up. Otherwise somebody's gonna lift everything you have or even shank you in your fuckin' sleep. You think it ain't happened? You think you got a guardian angel? Oh, Jesus. I'm wasting my time.

All right, said Tyler.

I'm turning off my generosity.

Okay, said Tyler.

Then he was ashamed, and said: Listen, I'm sorry. I appreciate the advice. I was just dreaming about someone I love.

Forget it, the hobo said. They're all just *citizens*. You got to keep your pride, or God's gonna nail you.

Oh, I have my pride, all right.

You may have your pride, but you're in a fuckin' slump.

Tyler, understanding finally that the old hobo was trying desperately to reach out to him, said: Is it a friend you're wanting? My name's Henry. And I'm happy to be your friend.

He put out his hand.

Texas Pete, said the old hobo, shaking it. You know, uh, Henry, I was in Spokane last fall and this guy named John I was tryin' to be partners with stole my frickin' gear. He's just a flat-out thief. His name's John Hayden. He's out in Seattle someplace suckin' off someone else. He always expected me to buy the beer.

Sure, I'll be partners with you if you want, said Tyler. I'll buy drinks when I get money, and I'll look after your bedroll.

Oh, they won't go after this, Texas Pete said, kicking the bedroll, but they may go after my backpack.

The thing I need to tell you, Pete, is that I'm looking for a skinny little black gal named Africa. She may be dead, but I have to check every lead.

You're better off with me, Henry. Forget the bitch. I'll be there for you. I know how to be what you need. And we'll ride the rails from A to Z. We'll never come back here. We'll never stay anywhere, until we get all the way to the sun.

Dan Smooth had read aloud from the Apocryphon of John how Cain, "whom generations of men call the sun," was the sixth son of the lion-faced dragon Yaltabaoth. Did he believe it? Too late to ask. Was Cain the sun? Did Texas Pete have the Mark of Cain? Everything was all twisted up.

When we get to the sun, what do you want to do there? he asked.

Shit, fella, we gonna burn up! cackled Texas Pete, and then Tyler knew that they were brothers, lost and getting more lost, and he was happy.

But in the nighttime, when Texas Pete tried to unzip his fly, Tyler knew he had to get away. He ran and ran until he was all the way up in Butte, Montana, by the Christian mission in sight of the rusty railroad tracks. The preacher earbanged him and then gave him soggy twice-warmed casserole. He went out. In an open shop, a welder's spark resembled the gloomy greyish sky malignantly magnified. The tawny ruin of the Berkeley open pit mine spread out behind and above everything. He gazed at sagebrush, crushed cans and bottles on the tracks where the brown Santa Fe and the blue Montana Rail Link cars were parked, bearing sad graffiti from years ago. He read it all; he wandered cuts, embankments, and other rusty tracks, but never saw anything more Queenish than the signature of Chuck from 1958.

| 559 |

He went north to Havre on the High Line; then west to Cut Bank where the Burlington Northern railroad bull who cited him crowed: This area is patrolled real heavy. You drifters ain't got a chance. We even got a K-9 unit out here. Sniffin' dogs. You hear me, bum? You ain't got a chance! —When they kicked him off the yard, a security car drove very slowly at his heels. He turned back one last time to admire the beautiful orange locomotive with its blackish-green stripes, but then the security car honked its horn. He was hungry. That night, praying to his Queen, who always helped him, he hopped a long string of grainer cars and then a man came on a motor scooter, shining a light into every orifice. By some miracle or illusion or perseverance on the part of the hunted, the motor man didn't see him, or else saw but pitied or did not care. No dogs barked. So he rode west and south again, in just the same way that half of the old bridge in West Sacramento could swing clockwise with remorseless rusty elegance, obliging as a whore's thighs; and then a white paddleboat might toil into the gap as the bridge continued its now needless swing, silver rail ending sharply at the green river . . . His instinct now was not to seek stale clues, but only to elude all authority and recognition because his Mark of Cain now glowed inside his reeking clothes so that he continued ever more rapidly to go and on without knowing where he was going, knowing only that this crisis could not endure much longer; soon he'd adjust or break. Lucky enough to pass through Glacier International Park without getting parked for days on a snowy siding, he crouched shivering for a long cold night of swaying and rushing before he could set foot on the earth again, by which time he was in the BN yard in Spokane. Another train, a better train, was already building up steam. Gazing coldly through steel spectacles, the engineer, blue-clad, leaned forward so that one shoulder twisted, and the song of the locomotive increased in pitch. Tyler sprinted across the gravel of the freight yard and leaped inside a boxcar's darkness, sliding forward on his belly to read the words **CHICAGO'S MOST WANTED** and **TURD BIRD**. Crumpled scraps of clothing lay trampled into the gravel like the grisly souvenirs of Cambodian killing fields. They began to crawl behind him as the boxcar shuddered. He would find the Queen of the great eternal angels, or else he would find Irene. Wasn't he gaining power over everything? On the wall was written **JESUS IS LORD**, so he quickly scratched below those curse-words the infinity-sign of the Mark of Cain. He passed empty plastic water bottles, then a bleached cow or deer skull buried in the embankment, an oily sheet of squashed coveralls, crinkled snakes of bleached used toilet paper, and a crumpled flattened goose with a little fat still on the bones, sharp pebbles resembling silver—anthracite, perhaps. The train trembled and began to gain velocity. Leaning out, he could see the blue-denim'd arm of the engineer shaking cigarette ash out the window of the first locomotive. And now it seemed that he was doing precisely as he wished, proceeding from the smoking mountains to the snowy mountains, and he was not afraid. For he had begun to know the trains now, to understand how to touch the rivet-scales and rust on their metal skin. Sweet forgetfulness was blooming in his mind, like a summer's path at Coffee Camp half overgrown with goldenflowered thistles.

But sometimes he still had Irene, for instance washing the dishes from a multicourse

Korean meal she'd cooked in her mother's house while the relatives sat around the table eating melon slices and sugarcoated sunflower seeds, trying to decide some recalcitrant teenager's future, the cousin sitting tired from helping his parents all day, watching Korean television news about high school violence and auto accidents. The cousin had realized that all grls were hysterical. —I'm just not a good female handler, he said mournfully to his sister, who was getting ready for her week-long basketball tournament. The uncles, the tired old grocery store owners and dry cleaners, almost ready for retirement, cracked peanuts while the baby crawled upstairs, reaching for the dog while everybody laughed . . .

| 560 |

He remembered all the times he'd phoned and phoned but she never called back, the time above all when the three of them met for dinner and she'd never said a word to him, nor he to her. John prattled on. Irene answered, upholding her part of the conversation in a perfectly acceptable way, although Tyler, listening, thought that she seemed far less submissive than usual; her "I thinks" and "maybes" had been stricken out, so that she now spoke with the blunt authority of Koreans among equals; in fact, he sensed almost a contentious edge to her voice, a pulsing anger beneath the translucently banal membrane of her words. She was wearing a white sweater. Later, he'd remember its weave very well. Irene's long inky hair occasionally entered his vision. He kept his gaze on her shoulder (she was sitting across from him); he couldn't bear to look into her face. — What's wrong? said John. Are you sick? —I'm OK, he said, looking into John's face; at the same moment, Irene leaned forward, coming accidentally into view, so that he saw her grimace. Her pale face was so beautiful that he actually thought for a moment that he was going insane. He staggered to his feet and went to the men's room, standing for a long time with his face in the sink, the cold water playing over his neck. He dried himself on his shirttails and went back. Amidst his terrifying love for Irene there now flowered a swift hatred, strengthening by the second; she could have at least greeted him when they met, or asked him how he was. He was bleeding inside from her cruelty. And then he reminded himself that he'd been the evil one, and should be grateful to her for not telling on him to John. The hatred disappeared. (John was saying something to him. He felt very lightheaded. He said: I'm sorry. My mind went blank.) He said to himself: Well, I can always go pick up a whore, and indeed, just that day on Ellis Street he'd met a stinking girl who lived in the Lincoln Hotel and who had begged him for money for epilepsy medicine, a favor he'd granted her; she'd said God bless you and kissed him with her reeking herpid lips; she'd said: If you ever need a woman, if you ever want somebody like me . . . and he didn't want her but the fact that someone, at least, was willing to take him, made the pain recede. He tried to concentrate on the stinking woman with the herpid lips while they sat there in the restaurant. It took forever for the bill to come. He could feel Irene's hatred now. There was no mistaking it. She despised him. She had avoided him and would go on doing so. She never wanted to see him again. He had sinned against her. She'd never forgive him. There was nothing he could do. After it was finally over, he and John punched each other's shoulders half-heartedly, telling each other to be good, and then he looked up into the doorway where Irene, already turning away, but forcing herself to accomplish this one gesture for the sake of elementary politeness, fluttered her hand in a listless, resentful wave.

| 561 |

He went to San Francisco, and all the shelters he knew about were full. On Irene's birthday he had to sleep in the street, in an alley south of Market. Two other men were already there, both of them black, and he asked them to help him. He was looking for a slender little black woman, maybe in overalls and suspenders.

Oh, it's not so bad, one of them said. Lots of pussy around here. Trash can pussy, I call it.

That's nice.

What's your name?

Henry.

Henry, you a sharin' type?

Sure.

Good. 'Cause if pussy come my way, if I got it, I share it.

Her name was Africa. And her shot-caller was a tall man named Justin. She . . .

Probably skipped all the way to Spokane by now, bro. Forget her. Keep your eye on reality. In this place we all gotta watch each other's backs.

What's your name?

Marcus.

So, Marcus, you telling me we have a few bad people around here?

When I first laid down on the streets, every night I wondered would I wake up alive. It goes farther back in your mind as the years go by, but it's still there. I've had guns pulled on me, machetes pulled on me. But I used to teach martial arts, thanks to God's grace. That man with the gun, I tripped him, slammed him into the wall. His buddy ran off. The store owner across the streets called the cops, and I'm glad to say the guy got five years in jail straight off . . .

Tyler sighed.

Don't sweat it, bro, said the other man. Marcus always dwells on the bad side. Actually the best thing is the easiness, so to speak. You can leave your stuff, take a shower. A thief comes by, next guy will get him.

Does that mean you trust me? he asked in surprise.

Sure, we're apprehensive about everyone at first, Henry. Don't take it personal. But nobody gonna try to coerce you. Trust is building. We give you the rope to hang yourself.

A little more rope is all I need, he muttered, turning his face away from the garbage can.

| 562 |

He wanted to embrace life more and more. While his new brothers still snored, he buried his head in the garbage can, smelling John's odor, the strong, sweaty scent he remembered so well from their boyhood. At John and Irene's he'd once opened the laundry can with its dead frog smell. There's been Irene's panties with the precious golden dot of dried urine; he'd never forget that. Before the tramps woke, he reached deep into the hot, wet, stinking garbage with both hands and shoveled it over his face, feeling closer than ever to his adorable Queen.

| 563 |

The easiest course would have been to forget all about the Capp Street girls, but the next morning he walked down there in his heel-flapping shoes to satisfy himself one more time that nobody knew anything about the Queen, and his absurd hopes were burning like cigarette-ends in an ashtray. First he walked slowly past the fences and zigzag grill-work of Valencia Street where now a man stood holding a greasy cardboard sign which read HOMELESS—PLEASE HELP ME and where long ago Tyler used to meet the false Irene, who'd always stuck her abscessed tongue in his mouth, then mumbled: Hey, can you gimme five dollars? Just five. Or ten would be okay, 'cause then I could really really truly get well for a couple hours . . . —and her diseased body had been red and white just like one of these tacqueria-fronts. Here he was, gaping at a row of white-painted grilles between Fourteenth and Fifteenth, with the low whitish skyscrapers of the inner Mission District to remind him that things might well endure for a time. He hesitated, however, to wander far from his obligations. Perhaps he had never belonged here. He yearned to be safely back at Coffee Camp, or, better still, on a boxcar on a long, long train hitched to at least three or four locomotives so that he knew he was going somewhere far away because that was how you did an extended trace. But he ought to take advantage of his stay in San Francisco to get information for the details description sheet he now kept inside his cranium. At Capp and Seventeenth, the very intellectual-looking black prostitute who wore spectacles at first refused to even return his greeting since by his appearance and odor he probably possesed insufficient financial means to fulfill her expectations of life, but when he humbled himself, when he implored her, when asked after the old Queen, whom she'd never met, she relented a little and said: I don't know about that. But Strawberry used to know her. Strawberry passed away. I found her, and it was pretty icky. The cops came and the EMT came and I told 'em to please cover her face but they couldn't do anything till the coroner came.

(I feel a little nervous, Strawberry had said to the two men as they held the door for her, but you gotta do what you gotta do.)

And suddenly Tyler turned away in a revulsion of frustration and rage against that sinister world he used to know well. He couldn't believe that the concrete hereabouts even held the impressions of his Queen's darling footprints. He longed now for light and space, where his exalted Queen might perhaps be flying overhead.

| 564 |

Daringly he breached the eastern border of the Tenderloin (which the Queen's girls always used to call *the other side of the mountain)* and came into the financial district, John's kingdom, where the phony welcomingness of light fixtures in galleries, the groanings of cable cars, the promenading tourists, the slamming of car doors as passengers in a hurry ran away from stalled traffic, their high heels emphatically clicking, infected him with vindictive shame. Everybody literally turned up his nose at Henry Tyler! Just as booted feet sometimes twitch uselessly, scratching one another's unscratchable itch, so he scratched together *Queen* and *Irene* in his head, and experienced only the same old disaster. He approached the old lady whose fur collar was twice the size of her head, and she departed him in disgust, as did the young black girl who was trying to be cool but who was obviously embarrassed by her own ghetto blaster. Another cable car passed by, the driver jazzily jangling his bell.

I just wanna show you this place, a father was explaining to his two sons, one of whom cast scared eyes on Tyler. The cable car's bell jingled, its festiveness as brassy and fake as the bright warm diamonds of lamplight across the street.

Tyler thought to himself: I should really have it out with John. I should really . . .

| 565 |

On one of the columns of the Pacific Stock Exchange, a bas-relief girl with granite hair turned her head against the snow, diagonally bisected by shadow while with a superhuman lack of awkwardness she gazed across the street at the floral nipples and lion-heads which studded the facade of the eleven-storey building occupied in part by Radio Shack; around the corner (Pine and Sansome) rose a stubby brick building of about the same height overtopped by an immense white tower whose flag streamed in the cold sky, shrunk by distance to the slenderness of ribbon, a scarlet ribbon. Just as the skyscraper overshadowed the granite woman, so she in turn dwarfed the kiosk a mere twenty feet high on one of whose curving sides a sultry, Italian-looking model with rouged and parted lips gazed straight at the steps, all the more fiery by contrast with her icy-blue halter-top above which the necessary hint of cleavage began; the advertisement (for what, lurking Tyler couldn't see) had frozen her in the act of cocking her hip, which had a black leather belt-pouch slung on it. Perhaps the granite woman was actually looking down at her; that must have been the reason her turned head was pressed so uncomfortably against the stone she was made of. The model, however, did not seem to perceive her elder sister. Flushed and ready, she gazed vaguely into space. Amidst the river of human beings now approaching on Sansome Street came John in a pinstripe shirt. He barely made it up to the model's knees, which of course remained hopelessly far beneath the soles of the granite woman's feet. Then Celia in her sunglasses and high heels came hurrying up the sidewalk, holding an iced latte. Neither of them looked up at the Queen of Mammon. They clasped arms around each other's shoulders. John needed her to try on a new pair of shoes. After they departed, a swarthy pigeon landed and kissed the specks of filth at the granite woman's feet.

Four o'clock, and the downtown streets were stricken with a bad case of the shadows as John's colleague and rival, Roland, bought a newspaper and stood on the corner with his bulging attache case, waiting for his wife to pick him up and drive him to Sutter and Kearney. (John for his part used to like to have Irene drive up California Street when she was chauffeuring him home from the office. The Pacific Bank's golden letters passed on his left, then the obsidian tower of Great Western Bank, and at Montgomery the trolleytrack-grooved street shot up into the sun where a summit of flags and domes awaited him.) Advancing on him, Roland saw a black man in a black skull cap who was licking a cigarette, his sign saying HELP IF YOU CHOOSE. Roland looked away.

Tyler remained. A rich man approached. Tyler extended his hand.

Let's see if I have more than three cents, sighed Mr. Rapp, dropping three shiny copper pennies into the panhandler's palm. —Let's see. Yup. You caught me at a good time. Here's a quarter.

Thank you, bro, said the panhandler gravely, and Mr. Rapp felt strangely pleased that he was someone's brother. The top of his head gleamed in the autumn sun as he crossed Grant Street, swinging his briefcase of Italian leather.

| 566 |

Tyler wanted to go to City Lights. He believed that he could remember every book he'd ever seen there. When Allen Ginsberg died, in April 1997, Tyler had paged through a glorious monograph on Soviet photography, compiled by Margarita Tupitsyo, he was pretty sure. He always used to drive there back in those days, penetrating the Broadway tunnel, which was yellow, tiled, curvy and sometimes empty; its light-strings had reminded him of the vertebrae of a dead snake. The Queen had done her business in that tunnel sometimes. One he'd picked her up there and given her a ride someplace in his car, maybe to one of those cafes just north of City Lights where the capuccinos in their snow-white cups were not just foamy but full-bodied, the foam itself stiff and striped, gilded and brown, like crème brûlée. He remembered the smell of cigarettes and the sound of Italian speech. But no; that hadn't been the Queen he'd been with there, but the false Irene. And since the false Irene had been involved, maybe it actually hadn't been very much fun. Where had he driven the Queen? It couldn't have been to City Lights; he'd never seen her reading any book except the Bible. It had always been difficult to find a parking place around City Lights. At least he didn't have that problem anymore. He started to walk up Columbus Avenue but by the time he got to City Lights he realized that he was too ashamed of his own stench to go inside.

| 567 |

Joining the long line of human beings in sweaters, coats, caps and boots who waited for a meal at Glide Memorial, he remembered very well how many times he'd driven by them in the old days when he had a car and a job and was following some unfaithful banker through the Tenderloin or was going to meet Irene. He remembered that dinner with Irene so long ago now at the Kabuki Cho restaurant with its sashimi dashboard clocks. —Please don't tell any of this to John, she'd said. —The man in the yellow **GLIDE STAFF** windbreaker ignored everyone until four, when he suddenly began taking meal tickets, chatting on a walkie-talkie while the first bunch went through. Majestically, he held up his hand to halt the line. Tyler was still far away, about two-thirds of the way down. He felt very hungry. The staff man was pawing through a trash can with one gloved hand. Then he yawned and turned away from the homeless ones, gazing up at skyscrapers and signs with a disdain entirely befitting the representative of a despotic theocracy. Tyler shifted his aching feet and blew on his hands. A cigarette stub in a scowling mouth shot past. He remembered one day when the Queen in her black high-heeled boots was dancing to the radio while the tall man sat with his head in his hands.

Now the man in yellow was accepting the second batch of tickets. They moved quickly and happily past him, heading for the entrance beneath the blue awning. One unauthorized being tried to creep in, but the man in yellow extended a long black gloved finger and he tumbled back to his place. Everyone halted at the next silent command, waiting with their hands on their hips or folded behind their backs or hidden in their pockets. Tyler felt very tired now.

The Queen walked by swinging her purse and singing. No, it wasn't she; it wasn't she.

| 568 |

One more time and *one* more time he strolled the Tenderloin and actually found Strawberry, who wasn't dead at all. He remembered her out in front of the Wonderbar, her eyes wild and glassy as she leaned against the door. Now her hair was greyer, that was all. Maybe nobody ever died. Maybe he'd find Irene, or his dearest and most adorable little Queen, the Queen of his love, the keeper of his spirit, his tender Queen.

Don't you remember me? he said.

What the fuck? Oh, yeah. You're the Queen's trick. About time Maj got up off her ass and used it for something . . . Oh, that's right. Maj is gone. It's Domino now . . .

Strawberry, you've got something in your hair.

Well, why don't you touch me? You afraid to touch me? Whatcha afraid for? I fuck everybody.

Okay, honey, he said. See, it's chewing gum.

Honey, I hate to say this but you got some miles on your tires. Well, what the heck. You look like a nice date. Probably only do it for a couple of minutes . . .

Thanks.

Well, so what's the story? said Strawberry. You want some company or what?

Uh . . .

Then her manner became as tight as the pussy of the skeletal whore whose face, like Beatrice's, had been destroyed in an automobile accident, and she said to him: No hard feelings, Henry, but I need to make a little money out here. You mind moving away from me?

| 569 |

It was foggy in John's neighborhood, with a white-chocolate fog that at ten o'clock in the morning persisted like a hangover. He strolled up to the front door, read on the nameplate the words J & I TYLER and found no courage, or perhaps simply no inclination, to ring the bell. Slowly he turned the corner. Half an hour later he was sitting in one of the coffee shops which had metastasized all over Union Street; and he sat among the backpacked, baseball-capped persons of leisure who, heads still glistening from the shower, read the newspaper: the President had declared tobacco an addictive drug. The FBI had found traces of explosive in a piece of the jet which had fallen into the sea. A woman of unknown name and address had been found dead on Capp Street. New cars were available for NO GIMMICKS—NO HASSLES.

The two women at the adjoining table glared at him, wrinkling their noses and fanning the air. Enraged, humiliated, he tried to stare them down. He'd truly had no ill intentions! But that didn't matter. He lived, so he stank. Presently the manager came and said: Sir, I'm sorry, but you'll have to leave. You're disturbing the other patrons.

Tyler leaned toward his enemies and whispered: My body's made of white sugar. That's why I don't take showers. C'mon, sweethearts, can I take a bath in your cookie jar?

| 570 |

He hopped a freight to Coffee Camp and then went to Loaves and Fishes to get his blue ticket for a free lunch. Then he got seconds. Drunks were sneering and scratching themselves beneath the arms. Nobody had heard of the Queen. No one knew the Hundred Thousand Dollar Boxcar Queen. He picked little grapes like blue ballbearings which left his sweaty fingers purple-black almost like railroad grime. Sitting high above the river on a log so rotten that he could scratch the word IRENE into it with his fingernail, he wondered whether this final most extended trace of his private eye career might not prove to be more than the waste that John would have thought it, because even if he could never find the Queen again, if he could at least prove her perpetual nonexistence then he would at least have destroyed one more lie in this world. He feared nothing now except a death of extended physical pain. He felt stronger and more honest than he'd ever been. Maybe he'd finally gotten to the point of living life with a flaming joy like a yellow California Northern train sliding through the yellow hills, not afraid of any risk (because anyway, no matter what you do, death will find you out), just doing whatever he wanted to do and hoping for the best. —Look at that bum, said the trackman. Yep, he thinks he's a hundred-car train! —Naw, he's just goin' to south Sacramento, laughed the engineer. Just switchin'. —The engineer was wrong. Tyler hopped a freight to Bakersfield, and another to Barstow via Los Angeles. Then he kept going, his train blowing sadness along the horizon in a lovely roaring wind which must be blowing white ripples upstream back at Coffee Camp which had become his home as much as the false Irene had once become the dead Irene. Soon it would be autumn there. The grass would be getting yellow, and spiny leaves would blow down his neck; there'd be star thistles in charge of the world, but not now because he was traveling southward into summer on a train as silvery as the river seen between grape leaves. Lonely, lost, hot and thirsty, he hoboed on his way increasingly free from preconceived intentions. He was freer every day. He needed nothing except water and a few excuses. Mosquitoes crawled under his hatbrim and on his sweaty cheeks. A slam, then a deeply reverberating squeak sent him farther outward into the world, as the huge, shiny wheel-disks slowly began rotating, their shining rims ready to hew off his leg if he were careless. On his boxcar someone had written in blue paint: **TO LIVE ALONE IS TO DIE ALIVE**. Sometimes he slept near unmoving trains, still trains, striped pale and grey in the darkness. In the morning he always shook his shoes out in case scorpions had crawled inside. Before he knew it, he was almost in Mexico . . .

| 571 |

We're about to get a burst of high winds, Waldo said, looking at his watch. He wore nothing but shoes, underpants and a baseball cap. —Over there, he said, that just *looks* like a burned-out bus, but that's actually my command post, where I watch for all the marauders. All the electronic things we can't talk about, the things that go whirly-whirly and that talk to you, those are the things that are there.

Tyler had been through this patch of desert six months ago, so he remembered the vans, the broken down truck, the missile nosecone, the mattresses and sofas all monumental against the flatness like some dry Mexican necropolis of flowers and spindly gravestones, their neighbors being pyrites and granite and sedimentery rock. Waldo definitely possessed more couches and shoes and everything now. Especially he owned more vehicular hulks. Soon the Park Service would be bound to notice, and then Waldo would lose everything. Waldo, who was autistic, sweet, longhaired, gray bearded, skinny and old, would then wilt and maybe even die. On the other hand, maybe Waldo would just die right here before anything else happened. He'd been burglarized a week ago. He would be as easy to kill as Irene's child.

The sun heated a broken sink and a rusty cylindrical tank all the way to hurtfulness. Waldo said: When it gets around a hundred twenty-five or so, when it gets iffy, you got to follow the shade around, cancel any patrols that are necessary. Take special options, with doughnuts and flying saucers in radiators, and drink lots of ice water, and no unnecessary movement.

Waldo splashed ice water over himself. He did not offer Tyler any. He never offered any guest a drink cold or otherwise. That was his way. He was not selfish, only different.

Where do you get that ice from? asked Tyler.

I get those who have transpo or whatever, Waldo said. I put up signs and signals, and they keep watch on me.

Then that frail, gentle man turned away, gazing toward the Salton Sea, which was not visible from here, his thought-radiations perhaps travelling as far as Bombay Beach, which would appear less deserted than it actually was once night came—a few streetlights came on, and two or three trailer- or house-lights shone on every block, struggling with electric automatism against the smell of the Salton Sea and all the dry, broken things. Or who knew? Maybe Waldo's thoughts were already all the way to Mars.

Waldo, Tyler asked him earnestly, recalling what the wise tramp had said, have you ever learned anything from the stars?

Oh, we beam in. We maintain transmission.

Who's we?

Oh, yeah, we got a badger out there. He's a wild one, but we get along fine even though base regs say absolutely no pets or furry critters.

Well, I want to screen out everything but pure transmissions, Tyler said. Can you make me a bullshit detector?

Let's take this concept here, Waldo replied thoughtfully, raising a propeller from the dirt. I use it to track wind speed against time factor. This is all multi-purpose. This might be the building block. Got all kinds of fans, he added with satisfaction. If it's ugly, paint it. If it doesn't work, make it spin.

Well, Tyler asked, can I buy it from you? There's too much bullshit in this world. I need to know where it is.

Couldn't sell it myself, said Waldo. It's one of the project groups. One of the off-budget type groups.

And I'd like an anti-loneliness device, said Tyler.

Waldo spun a propeller, thinking deeply. —Well, it sounds simple but that's actually as deep and wide as an aircraft carrier.

How much would it cost me?

I'd probably give you a variety of options, and then you can dial in. I'm rated for microprocessors and basic machine language.

Here's five dollars, said Tyler. Maybe you could give me a prototype next time I come through.

Waldo took the money and stared at it. Then he put it in his shirt pocket. Flies crawled on the underside of his cap.

Could I see your command post?

Yeah, all right, said Waldo, hopping on his bicycle and slowly pedaling, brown like a Missouri Pacific boxcar and almost naked, with a load of bottled juice in his saddle-baskets. Tyler walked behind, overseen by the low blue mountains with their tan ridge of boulders, and then the hot wind rattling sheet metal against the van with boarded up windows. That most infallible of all guardians, the nosecone, never blinked.

On the edge of a low wash lay a dead bus whose windows were blacked out by more boards, in regulation style, and whose skin had been painted a sort of crude camouflage. —It's been here the longest time, Waldo boasted, but you don't see it. Now this just looks like a trailer, but this is actually a deployment of the Marine Corps group. Any re-cono pod in strange places, we monitor that. We see what drug deals and what activities he's committing and where he's fencing his goods.

On the inside of the rusty door was handwritten: **EMERGENCY FIRE EXIT**. On the walls: **TRUE LOVE** and **DANGER—RESTRICTED**.

Waldo explained: We threw out the useless love-sex books and replaced 'em with technical books you can use, books on electronic circuits and how-to books . . .

The interior of the van was almost cool. On the counter lay a packet of breakfast pow-der, circuit boards, rusty gears, a meat thermometer, and alertness aid tablets. On the floor was a cooler full of ice.

This is part of our conceptual dream group where we lay down the hardware like our gear rotor, said Waldo. We cover the whole range.

He raised a kaleidoscope and said: This is called our cold fusion power. Aim it right at this reflector; that thing'll give you an eye burn.

On the counter Tyler saw a palm-sized metal disk which Waldo had painted beauti-fully green, white and flesh-pink, all pastel-blended. —What is it? he said.

They got some good drugs, they think they're gonna fly that. That used to be one of our saucers, a remotely powered three-man toroidal anti-magnetic jewel lift system. They developed that back in the early 40s and 50s, during the Philadelphia Experiment. Me, I don't believe in none of that stuff. I believe in the theoretical technology.

All right, said Tyler. If you have the technology to do that, and even make me an anti-loneliness device, maybe you can help me with a project that will make the anti-loneliness device obsolete. See, I want to find my Queen even though it's no use because she's dead.

Lots of queens out there.

I mean the Queen of the Whores.

Well, said Waldo, hitching up his underpants, so what you're requisitioning is a way to help you track a whore type critter. Well, we can build kites for faggots and all them critters, but it's just an image that'll dance around; it's just a piece of plastic. Well, it works really well if you want to piss off your old lady . . .

| 572 |

In Niland, California, which as the crow flies was not very far from where Waldo lived, but if a man walked straight it would be a pretty hot and lethal march, there was a cafe whose long wood-veneer counter had been worn into dark brown spots in front of each stool. Stuffed fish, birds and deer-heads hung on the walls from the long gone days be-fore the Salton Sea turned poison. The proprieter, who was eighty-eight years old, said: It's a shame, though, what they've done to the Salton Sea. Hurts the whole Imperial Val-ley. Probably cost us a hundred and fifty thousand a year in sales.

Tyler nodded wearily, drinking his root beer float, and the waitress came and added more root beer for free. The glass was huge and there was about a quarter-pint of vanilla ice cream in there, so cold and good that for the first time since the sun had come out he felt that he could think.

When I come here in 1956, this was winter tomato country, the proprieter was saying. In '65 they took the duty off at the border. Then we couldn't compete against the Mexican tomatoes. That just killed our tomato growers.

Tyler said: Did you ever see a skinny little black woman named Africa? I expect she's long dead now.

Doesn't ring a bell, the proprieter said. But there's so many transients at Slab City up the road, just about a three-mile piece . . .

You look pretty hard up, the waitress whispered. Don't worry about that float. I'll charge it to me.

Thanks, he said.

What's that? said the proprieter, cupping his ear.

Oh, shut up, the waitress said. She turned back to Tyler and said to him: You gonna stay at Slab City? she said.

That depends, ma'am, he said.

(The proprieter, deaf and bored, had gone back to reading his newspaper.)

My parents brought me out there from when I was in fourth grade until I was fourteen years old and got a boyfriend and could get away from it, she said.

Doesn't sound as if you enjoyed it too much.

In the winter you'd wake up with frozen feet. In the summer those slabs would be scorching. And scorpions and ants and everything. Strange, strange people. I hated every minute of it.

On the refrigerator case, near the row of decals of a longtime Ducks Unlimited donor, hung a handwritten sign in English and Spanish which read: **I WOULD LIKE TO BUY A BOX OF FLAME GRAPES.**

Boy, it's slow, the waitress said. The day goes so slow when you just sit. You want a refill?

That would be mighty kind, he said. He hunched himself smaller, hoping that he did not stink too much.

Tyler went into the men's room and filled up his water bag. The advertisement on the vending machine for adult novelties read: IF SHE IS A MOANER THIS WILL MAKE HER A SCREAMER. IF SHE IS A SCREAMER THIS WILL GET YOU ARRESTED. When the waitress wasn't looking, he paid for his root beer float, left a tip and went out. He still had twenty-two dollars in his pocket.

In the vast gravel lot, a painted sign said: SALVATION MOUNTAIN 3 MI.

He turned down that road and started walking away from Niland, where this store was closed and that store was boarded up and the Mexican restaurant closed at two in the afternoon, and every now and then one saw a notice to buy a great business opportunity—not that Niland didn't still have some life left: just ask the old café proprieter and the waitress, who were still hanging on . . . It was now nine in the morning and very hot. A train oozed slowly by, bearing immense blue Hanjin crates. He wondered what might be inside. Whatever it was, it must not be for him. Swallowing dust, he walked on, knowing that somewhere near the horizon his destiny might be dryly slithering down the wide paths and roads of Slab City. Not a single car passed him on his trudge. The Salton Sea stewed and stank unseen at his back. Ahead lay the dusty-blue Chocolate Mountains; and after a weary two miles or so he began to see Salvation Mountain gleaming whitely like a bunch of melted candle-wax. The landscape in which it stood (in company with its tamarisk tree and its two trucks which said REPENT) could have been Hebrew, but the mountain itself resembled an aquatic amusement park, because its bulk of desert dirt had been painted in white and blue streaks to resemble water. The mountain itself, with all its colored slogans bulging like breasts, was composed of dirt, hay bales, and colored latex paint which felt smooth and cool under his hand. On the mountain's chest, a scarlet heart, tricked out in white adobe letters, said to him: JESUS, I'M A SINNER. COME UPON MY BODY AND INTO MY HEART. He ascended to the summit-cross, and in place of inspiration discovered more dogged artifice, where a long dry ridge marked the watermark of a lake which had vanished four centuries before, and hay bales and paint cans were discreetly laid, ready for the next good work. Irene would have loved it here. She'd been a good Christian girl. That was why Tyler respected the preacher's mad sincerity. He had started building back in 1984, but after three years the Mountain collapsed, so he started all over again. Tyler stood there for a while, alone on the hot flat sand below Salvation Mountain except for one cicada which produced the only sound. He thought: If only I could build a mountain for her, or a . . . —But he could not decide what he wanted to build.

| 573 |

Past Salvation Mountain the road went on toward the Chocolate Range, but before it had gone very far there was another sign which said SLAB CITY—WELCOME. Turning right, he entered a grid of dirt streets, desert scrub in between. Past the rusty red bus you had to go deeper into that maze of wide empty roads in the low brush, with trailers lurking between on the half-broken low concrete flatforms, trailers with tarps, singles with mailboxes, until you came to a trailer with a sticker that said AWOL, and on the slab beside it, under a tree-shaded tarp, an old man sat at a manual typewriter which didn't work, thinking about composing a letter. His white poodle lay beside him, guarding the cartridge box and other gear against death as the old man explained to Tyler:

Now the left side over there, they call that Poverty Flat. On the right, that's called High Rent Area. Actually, the names are reversed, just to keep people amused. In the High Rent Area, people live kind of hand to mouth.

We got a club in here called the Slab City Singles. I founded it fifteen years ago and I've been coming every year for fourteen years, ever since I lost my wife. But Slab City itself has been around much longer than that. Back in World War II, General Patton had these kind of camps all over the desert. After they moved out, the Navy moved in and then the Marines took over. That slab over there, that was a hospital. Then they shut the whole thing down and sold it. My slab, that was the officers' latrine. And this lot here, that's the parade ground.

(One of the old man's thermometers said 105° and the other said 120°.)

We still don't have too many rules, the old man said. With all that nice shade and everything, I can't stop others from moving in. Anyone can drive in and park. This is America. That guy over there, he's dying to move in.

Tyler inquired: Have you seen a skinny little black lady named Africa? I wanted to live and die with her.

They don't allow a man and a woman not married to live in the same rig, but we talked it over and decided to let 'em. And we got eight of 'em now, married couples, and we set up an auxilliary.

I get it, said Tyler.

This little gal and I, we play trionomoes, said the old man. This little gal here, she weighs only sixty-five pounds. And she used to drive a big truck! he said proudly.

Well, the little gal said (she was tattooed with the word MOTHER), I'd rather be where it's cooler. I'd rather be in Oakdale where I come from. I used to have a home. I had to buy this trailer because of my health. I've been here for four years. I'm stuck here this summer because my motor home needs work and I can't afford it.

Clearing his throat, Tyler said: Or have you seen a pregnant Korean lady named Irene?

| 574 |

The tracked and trodden sand on either side of the trestle bridge at Coffee Camp might not have been so different from the sand of Slab City, but in Slab City there was more sand and less of everything else, long wide dazzling avenues of sand down which no one passed, so that he recalled a typical oddball comment uttered by Waldo, who'd heard of Slab City even through his ringing autism, though he'd never been there, and said to Tyler: They don't move around in the daytime, man. Just like vampires. —Already the white shimmer of Salvation Mountain like cake icing or wax running down the ridge lay out of sight because Salvation Mountain was actually not very high and at Slab City the hot sandy plain had begun a downward slope which steepened a little near the canal's edge where Slab City gave way to the Drops, or as some called it, the outback, where the true squatters lived. The place felt wild and strange to him.

Past the cross by an immense flat slab, past the perimeter of tires laid down upon the sand in a long strange black line of symbolic menace, he swung round one camp's snarling dogs, and at the next camp under some shade-trees he met an angry man.

How long have you been out here? said Tyler.

Shoot, said the angry man in disgust. We're havin' a hell of a time out here, on account of some bad people. I was attacked by two persons with clubs, and I defended myself with a baseball bat. They attempted to murder me. One woman out there, she instigated the whole thing. They knocked me unconscious. They beat my head in. I get up, defend myself, police show up, and my attackers tell the police I'm just some drunken maniac. The D.A. takes their side of it. And then the bureaucrats take us down. Since it never goes to trial, I never get my say. They make me come down to court, and then they keep changing the court dates. Once I spent the whole day in court so they could tell me in thirty seconds to come back on another day, and while I was there I had to keep my dog chained up out here all day, and because he wasn't used to being chained up, he strangled to death. I feel I'm beat down.

I'm his only source of income, his mother said. I get my widow's pension. It's hard for me to maintain. I promised I'd help him out for four or five months. And every time we go to court, I have to worry about gasoline, gasoline. The trip to court and back costs about fifteen dollars.

Where is all them court papers, Mom? said the angry man.

He spread them out on the hood of one of his dead cars and began to reread them obsessively. Then he looked up at Tyler and said: My plan was to be out of here before the summer hit.

How long have you been here? said Tyler.

Last time we went to court in the truck, his mother said. An officer pulled us over for a cracked windshield and Idaho plates. So they slapped that fine on top of that.

It's like they're keepin' us broke, the angry man said.

How did you end up here? said Tyler.

Well, we came here originally around Thanksgiving, the old mother said. We left twice. Somebody told me about Slab City, and there are some good things about this place, but I hope we get out of here before it gets too hot. I'm afraid this heat will kill me. Put a wet towel on me, is the only thing that will keep me cool. And then this happens, with those people trying to murder my son.

What made you pick the Drops over the slabs? asked Tyler.

Privacy, the man said. And on the slabs, it's hard to find any trees to live under. Them snowbirds are already in the good spots.

Hey, said Tyler urgently. Have you seen a little black gal who, uh—

By the mother's trailer lurked a skinny woman who watched Tyler with a sort of weary gingerliness. Finally, as the angry man returned to his court papers, Tyler strolled over to her and asked her how she was.

The skinny girl looked shyly down. —What we're doin' is mopin' around. I used to have an apple ranch . . .

How long's it been for you? he said.

I been here about fourteen months now. My boyfriend brought me here but then he took off on me. He'd already got us kicked out of the place we'd stayed in town, this condemned apartment run by a black con artist. When my boyfriend took off, he ripped off the best of my food stamps, ninety goddamn dollars' worth.

Yeah, they keep on kickin' you in the teeth when you're down, the angry man said, anxious to resume talking about himself. He showed Tyler a nunchuck that his would-be murderers had left—two pieces of steel pipe connected by a chain.

Well, said Tyler to the skinny woman, how about you? Have you ever met a black woman named Africa who—

She shook her head. —I don't guess I got any enemies.

I just hope you can get things together, the angry man's mother said to her very gently.

Tyler cleared his throat and said: If I gave you five dollars could you tell me if you ever saw Africa?

Pretty much out here there's no economy, said the angry man. I buy junk cars and sell parts. I want a good pickup, just a good pickup. I used to be a mechanic, but ain't no work around here anyway. I'm in a pit of lions, armed with a flyswatter.

My best friend died in my arms, the skinny woman went on in a whisper. My boyfriend shot her in the back in our house, right through the back door. I carried her off next door and she wanted me to hold her. I still have some bad dreams . . .

And then what happened? said Tyler.

They went to shoot my boyfriend, I think, and the gun misfired and then they arrested him.

Things happen all the same though, the angry man's mother said wisely.

I have a headache, said the skinny woman.

What's for dinner? said the angry man to himself. Got some hamburger, I think. Don't know how the cheese will hold up. Soon it'll be cooler.

Well, said Tyler starting to feel oppressed, maybe I'll move on. What are you folks going to do now?

Relax during the night, the angry man said. Enjoy the coolness and get the labor stuff done. I'm tryin' to get this swamp cooler to work . . .

Tyler peeled off his last twenty and gave it to the mother. —Maybe this'll buy you enough gas to get your son to court and back.

The angry man looked at him with big owl eyes and said: *I* could sure use some help, too.

Tyler sighed.

The angry man sat there for a while and then said hopelessly: Guess I'll go into Mom's trailer and try to swat off all the flies.

| 575 |

As for Tyler, he continued on his extended trace. Ten minutes' footwork further out into the Drops he met a thin, bespectacled, beatific man with scraggly long hair who walked steadily in the hundred and fifteen degree heat, swinging his black-greased hands, his bare torso tanned almost to negritude.

Everybody's friendly out here, he said. Everybody works together. Even when the snowbirds come in, we are not like a big city. We don't get involved in other people's business. I leave my place unlocked. And if you don't cause trouble, you don't get trouble. You don't have to worry about someone come up the road behind you and shoot . . .

Tyler nodded.

I been workin', the man said. I do mechanic work. Sometimes the guys at the shop invite me inside where it's cool, but I always say no. You get into air conditioning and then when you come out you gonna have a heat stroke. Anybody could be walkin' out here and it could hit you all at once.

Yeah, it feels pretty warm, said Tyler.

Name's Clyde.

Henry.

You find you a spot out here, you can make it. But if you don't got tough skin, you ain't gonna make it. I been here seven years.

You must get lots of thinking done around here, said Tyler.

Yep. I think about my past, and about my dead wife and about how to make a nickel; I'm always hustlin' . . .

I think pretty about much the same, Tyler admitted.

Clyde gave him a loving gaze. I can see that you do, he said.

I'm looking for someone, Tyler began hopelessly, a black lady, well, a small, slender black gal who . . .

I hope you find her, said Clyde.

You think she could be living here?

You got some women that live by theirselves, and one black guy, but no black gals that I know of.

How about past the Drops?

You can go nine miles down that road and then it cuts off to the right and then it goes on to Calpatria, but half a mile down from here the people stop. There's not over seventy of us, including Slab city and all the kids . . .

And what about the other way?

Drop Eleven is the last, said Clyde, sincerely sorry for him, and at that moment Tyler felt that the man's kindness was as immense as the scarlet heart on the white breast of Salvation Mountain.

What's her name? said Clyde. The name of the gal you're tryin' to find.

Oh, he mumbled, Africa was her name, but she . . . Maybe now the Hundred Thousand Dollar Boxcar Queen would be good enough, because Africa must be dead.

Well, why don't you sleep on it, said Clyde. If you was to ask your homeless, what does it take to get what you need, I bet they'll all answer, an argument and a wait. But here, I could go to anyplace here and get me a ride, food and a cold drink. And it's not so hard to get you a nickel or two. We haul scrap iron to get by.

Now the hot trees and trailers glowed in the sand as the sun began to set. A tire stood on end, now jet black like its own shadow, everything private and set back in the trees. A few silhouettes crept silently out on the sand. He knew that when morning came, scorching and dry, there'd be nobody.

Later he sat out by Salvation Mountain, with the Milky Way spread out as rich as a stain upon the sky; and stars, stars, stars! Salvation Mountain was like a groundsloth, a hunkered down elephant or maybe a snail barely poking its head out of its shell, all whitish and jigsawed in the night.

| 576 |

A train, dark against the darkness, barely discernible, comprised a mere shifting of the night which hissed and clicked to itself.

| 577 |

He drifted through Coffee Camp one night in midsummer and there were no campfires, the river silver and still, with the trestle bridge's reflection floating on it like a fallen ladder, barely trembling, as if disturbed a little by the faint harsh voices. Across the river, a spear of city light exposed an immense bat which then vanished back into its element. The next day he walked up and down the river, but the Hundred Thousand Dollar Boxcar Queen was long gone. He was getting so bored with disappearances.

| 578 |

I bear the Mark of Cain, he said wearily to the next missionary.

You do not, the missionary replied. You are a white man. You are no Negro. I quote to you from Brigham Young, the second prophet of my church: *Cain slew his brother, and the Lord put a mark on him, which is a flat nose and black skin.*

My Queen was black, said Tyler. Therefore, so am I.

You can't be Negro just by wishing it, man!

Oh, yes I can.

| 579 |

Up above the freeway where the razor-wire was, they'd cut a hole in the fence with their wirecutters. The railroad or the city had patched that one up, so they'd cut another hole. That was how life worked.

Got change for a five? a woman said.

Nope, said Tyler. Where are you headed?

I don't answer any questions, the woman snarled. That rule comes from *moi*.

Oh, well, then I won't answer any questions, either, said Tyler. How's that for a deal?

The woman whispered into her boyfriend's ear, who said to Tyler: I oughta gut you.

A deal's a deal, said Tyler serenely.

The couple glared at him. Then they moved down the fence to meet their crack pusher out of earshot.

Tyler sat under the lone shade tree until mid-morning, when he was joined by a black man puffed up with balloon tricks. He could tie a balloon like a pretzel, bite off a piece of it, and somehow insert the piece into the balloon without popping anything. Then he put a cigarette lighter in his mouth, and before Tyler knew it, the cigarette lighter was inside the balloon, too! The result was called a pregnant giraffe. When the black man started to hit him up for money, Tyler ducked through the hole and clambered up the embankment, discovering a long lost hobo camp containing a rusty tin can of ashes, a frying pan with no handle, now filled with leaves, a piece of angle-iron which had served as a griddle, dirty paper plates, a plastic spoon, a scrap of cardboard which had probably been used for hitchhiking since it said **TRINITY,** a filthy pair of pants, and many bottle-caps, to say nothing of used condoms baked and hardened to the semblance of bottle caps, everything beaten into the gravel by some seemingly irrevocable process. Far down below, near the Salvation Army, he heard sirens. Trains shuttled back and forth. He gazed at the segmented grey horizon of gravel cars and grainers, with the ruined Globe Mill in the background, and he longed to get out of this world, just to go.

He heard the crackheads smashing bottles and screeching.

Far away, a figure crossed the shimmering gravel and broken glass with what seemed to be incredible slowness, finally reached the hole in the fence, and kept on moving. Tyler waited. His new companion was a drunk in possession of many tattoos and two little puppies. The man had a kindly, laughing face. Tyler liked him right away.

Drink? said the drunk, passing him a half-drunk quart of beer.

Thanks, said Tyler. He drank. The beer tasted cool and good.

My name's Tyler, he said.

George, said the drunk. He took the beer back, gulped it down to nothing, and said: I'm not doin' shit without my morning wakeup.

I get it, said Tyler.

You catching out?

Yep.

You're gonna need lots of water. And fruit . . .

I've got two gallons.

For two or three days, if you're careful, you can parley that into nothing.

Where are you from, George?

I grew up on a dairy farm and got sick of it. I don't know how many tits passed through my hands.

A yellow locomotive flashed between the grainer cars and paused at their head. Tyler rose, ready to make his leap, but just then the yard bulls came in their white car. He sat back down again next to George. The hot morning shimmered above the gravel like a swarm of midges.

Not half bad, laughed George, up here on top of the world . . .

He felt that George was a good and sincere person, tranquil, beneficent, maybe even enlightened far beyond the false Irene—a drunken Buddha. He smiled.

The sun beat down upon their necks and shoulders and knees. It was not yet ten. He studied the cars: Golden West, Cotton King, Union Pacific, Southern Pacific. The yard bulls drove back and forth, their pale car standing out against the dark freight cars whose pale grafittit was comprised either of exaggeratedly outlined capital letters or else of hooky loopy scrawls. A concrete barrier read: **STINKY BOBBY "97"**.

George most regally pointed and said: You don't wanna ride no flatbed. Them motherfuckers gonna bounce you right off.

Railroad men in white helmets came carrying shovels, marching wearily across the sky. The railroad bulls whizzed near.

Oh, he's picking up his cell phone, said George. We'd better duck back through that fence.

The balloon magician being long gone, George and Tyler shared undisputed possession of their shade tree, waiting for the bulls to go away.

See, if it has two locomotives like that, or three, you're gonna have a good run, said George. That car's goin' somewhere. Get on that car.

When the coast is clear, said Tyler.

A skinny bald man in a grey pickup drove right up to the hole in the fence and said: I'm looking for Seed. Skinny blonde girl who ran away from me. Man, am I fuckin' pissed!

I'm looking for Africa myself, said Tyler. But if I see any blondes, I'll send them your way.

Yeah, right. As if they'd come!

The bald man laughed grimly, put the pickup in reverse, and drove off.

Now across the embankment came a man in a loud shirt, holding a paper sack of beer. In the most lordly and self-satisfied way, he ambled up onto the coupling between two grainer cars and leaped on down. Just then George jumped up and yelled to the man: Get off them fuckin' tracks! Police!

Then Tyler knew that GOD NEVER FAILS, as is written on Salvation Mountain.

| 580 |

Well, well, who do we have here on my railroad? the cop said, grinning.

George, Tyler, and the man in the Hawaiian shirt all loudly laughed.

Right, smirked the cop. Get your hands out of your pcokets, all of you. Put 'em where I can see 'em. Now all of you line up in front of me.

You have on the loudest shirt I ever saw, said the cop. My wife wouldn't let me be caught dead wearing a shirt like that. I have grounds to bust you just for wearing that shirt.

The man in the Hawaiian shirt was quick to laugh at this joke.

Now what about you? said the cop to Tyler. Did you snitch on anybody?

No, officer, said Tyler.

Did you snitch on me, partner? he said to George.

George was silent.

Who snitched me off? said the cop. I have good hearing. I know one of you two did it. That's against the law, folks. Who was it?

George hunched and grinned and said: Guilty.

What? smiled the cop, grinning like a shark, spreading squeaky clean terror. Tyler could almost see him as the high school football bully he might have recently been, kicking people to make his friends laugh, confident, always on the winning side.

So you snitched me off, teased the cop merrily. As long as you snitch me off and don't tell on your buddies, you're legal, right? Or did I get it wrong, you scum?

They all laughed hilariously.

The cop paced up and down.

What's in the backpack? said the cop to Tyler.

Food and water, officer.

Any canned food?

Yes, officer.

Well, why don't you try eating a can of sardines in front of me so that I can bust it across your face? the cop jested.

Tyler managed a smile.

And you, snitch, said the cop to George. Nice tattoos. What joint were you in?

San Quentin and Soledad, officer, said George ingratiatingly.

Hands on your head, snitch. You in the loud shirt, you ever been arrested?

Yes, officer.

For what?

Drunk and disorderly.

All right. I'm going to arrest you again. You were on the tracks. Or maybe I'll just cite you. It all depends on my mood. As for you, snitch, I told you snitching off a cop is an offense—and he rattled off the number of the criminal code. —I sound just like a Bible, don't I?

Sounds good to me, officer, everyone hastily agreed.

Now the cop caressed his pistol, which for some reason made Tyler think of old Missouri the Hobo talking about a weapon he'd seen once in his Nam days, called Puff the Magic Dragon: *They could put a 40-millimeter round every couple of inches in the space of a fuckin' football field in two minutes!* —Tyler kept as still and quiet as he could.

All right, said the cop to Tyler. Get out of here. You other two, come on down to the car.

| 581 |

He returned to Coffee Camp at sunset, the river now molten gold and bearing the cool black reflection-shadows of bridge-pilings and trees, like tarnish or a char. He didn't know anybody and didn't want to. He hid himself under a bush and slept . . .

| 582 |

It's not too late, the next preacher said.

Tyler grinned. He said: In my line of work—

Your line of *work!* That's a good one, you dirty old bum!

. . . You try to establish what the relationship is with the person. If there's any connection at all, you figure that's biased. If it's something like a police officer that happens by the scene, you don't question it. If it's a union guy, let's see, a UPS driver sees a UPS guy get hurt, well, they're both Teamsters, get it? It's kind of like kissing cousins. You have to figure somebody like that's biased. It's like when Paul writes in 2 Corinthians 6.14, *Do not be mismated with unbelievers.* Unbelievers, they're like non-union guys, see. They're undercutting the Teamsters. Or when the guy that wrote Genesis kept putting down Cain. How did *he* know that Cain bumped off Abel? It says they were alone, so that scribbler wasn't there. Now, I grant that in a civil case the preponderance of the evidence is enough, but we're talking about *damnation* here! That's a criminal case. Talk about preaching to the converted! That's why no private detective can accept the Bible. It reeks of conflict of interest.

The preacher said: I pity you.

Tyler said: So do I.

He hopped a string of grainer cars which, slow and solemn, like Irene brushing back her hair, bore him away.

| 583 |

For my soul is full of troubles, runs the Book of Psalms, *and my life draws near to Sheol.** Domino could say that—oh, she certainly could, for it was quite a job keeping other street-whores under her thumb—and so could John in his office, and so could the bail bondsman who'd misplaced some cash, to say nothing of the reporter for the alternative newspaper in Sacramento who could not get any more advances on his paycheck; and the same complaint might plausibly have been uttered in the slow exhausted gravel-speech of the Wheelchair Men, or in faster parlance by members of the newspaper-fascinated coffee-house crew on Valencia Street: the rain-wetted, cigar-smoking old poet, the thoughtful leather-vested women who licked chocolate-covered spoons to the dreamiest possible music while they gazed across the street at the word HEALTH which formed part of an arch upon a miraculously shining window; hemmed in by the hissing of rain and the sucking sounds of raincoat-sleeves, they polished their troubles to a sheen as of wet window-glass—boyfriend troubles and girlfriend troubles, troubles of money, troubles of pain; how could you say that the woes of the elite were not just as cruel as Domino's? What hurts hurts. —Make me look happy, rentable Strawberry said to the artist. I'm always sad, so draw a smile on my face. Please? —And John progressed likewise toward Sheol, angry and sad even though his stocks had split twice; and Irene, leaving behind a diamond wedding ring, killed herself to become mistress of the dirt. *All the kings of the nations lie in glory, each in his own tomb, but you are cast out, away from your sepulchre like a loathed untimely birth.*[†] It is the occupation of politicians to deny this ubiquity, nay, universality of corroded hearts, to discount the barren laboriousness of all paths. Reduce corporate taxes, they say, or redistribute the wealth of the parasitic class to the desperate class, and then all who matter can cross the Jordan together and enter into

---

* Psalm 88:3.
† Isaiah 14:18–19.

a new land of happiness whose prior inhabitants will dissolve into sea-colored ghosts of dust. Pain may be divided, but no Euclid or Leibniz has yet proven that it can be subtracted. Thus Tyler's do-nothing's logic, which led him from Coffee Camp to the quiet of two tents on the riverbank, then onto the rails, to Roseville, Olivehurst, Portland, Barstow, Victorville (burning tracks, brown Santa Fe cars, blue and yellow cars), to Waldo's desert and Slab City and the Drops; then finally beneath the white pillars of the Miami freeway to the opened hydrant from which homeless nestlings drank—both drink and drinkers eternally approachable like a whore or like God, unnatural spring which flowed down the sidewalk just as the grapevines of rejoicing creep across the vineyard. Water of drunkenness, water of tears, water of coffee-making and handwashing, water that carries away the taint of sweat and excrement down to Sheol, where someday all of us must lie, at one with our filth at last; water of death, poured kindly out to wash and purify the body of his dead Queen, scrubbing the lines and calluses of her hardworking hands before the wailers set her deep into the ground, beyond reach of vigilantes, johns, whores, cares and destruction—she *was* destroyed, had vanished from the land—water which joins us all, slain and slayers, entering us through our organs of speech, departing from us as poison; water is grateful to the troubled; water quenches the anguish of Irene or Domino: the jackal and the rose must both have water. My Queen is no more! he said to himself, wandering, remnant of himself, from San Francisco to Los Angeles to New Orleans, and then by stages of walking, freight-hopping and hitchhiking to Tampa and finally Miami where beneath the white freeway pillars the hydrant flowed.

On account of that now perpetual fountain's likeness to a whore and to God, the city fathers, so called, kept resolving between intervals of other desolate business to shut it down, but the mayor of the white outcasts had replied without affected defiance to their sentries and messengers the squad car men that if they sealed off the hydrant, his constituency would have to take their water where they could find it—a fact of nature which the officers recognized and relayed back to the city fathers as such: Vagabonds, goldbricks, self-destroyers, sojourners, fugitives, crooks, whores, panhandlers, fruit loops and banana boats need to drink, too! Why not make it easy on all three sides—namely, on the leaders, on the led like John, Irene, Tyler himself, and the coffeehouse and Coffee Camp people, and on those who drank from fire hydrants? That was how the white mayor told the story, but whether the city fathers had ever (to use a tired civic metaphor) played ball or even been apprised of the hydrant's continual flow, to say nothing of the homeless mayor's very existence, the mayor had no basis for saying, although his foundationlessness in no wise impeded his orations, he being almost as greedy of reputed omniscience as he was of cash, which was why he charged every toll he could whenever a new constituent wandered under the freeway pillars to his Caucasian island, whose boards of different colors and sizes had been nailed up under (predominantly) mayoral control to make walls of rough cubes enflanking a line of laundry, an American flag hanging out to dry; and above that island the stretched-elastic sounds of wind and blind traffic comprised the chorus to the mayor's endless act. The freeway was so high above him that the palm trees which God had permitted in the long thin rectangles of light were as blades of grass; from far away there was only the freeway, beneath which lurked a handful of tiny square silhouettes: the mayor's box-houses. The mayor kept a little pistol up his ass, so everybody said; at least he kept it somewhere inside his bluejeans, ready to reify his authority as needed. Let's say that a new couple, good and white, showed up beneath the freeway, admitting that they might stay for more than a night or two: the mayor was willing to rent them a plywood shanty for fifty dollars a month, television hookup included because he knew how to drain images most reliably and illegally from among the cables which buzzed overhead among the roaring cars. The mayor did not pull out his pistol then. He explained that if you were accepted into the community you'd be protected. The main rule was the American rule: to respect the property of others. The mayor gave you two chances. The first time you were caught stealing, out came the pistol as needed; then everybody beat you up, you made restitution, and it blew over. The second time, they pulled down your house and you were never allowed back. But obey the social contract, act a white islander's part, and you had friends. The niggers on *their* far too adjacent island were too much like animals to be represented by any mayor, the mayor said. Over there it was the law of the jungle for jungle bunnies. Now, some niggers were all right, and then they were worthy of being called black people. If a black man or a black woman was proved by repeated fair dealing to be such, why, that person was welcome to live on the white island because we weren't racists. That mattress on the island's edge, for instance, was Stanley's. Stanley was the mayor's best friend. Anita was another worthy black lady who lived with her white man in a palatial packing crate for which they paid the mayor the unofficial rate of thirty dollars a month. Down by the portable toilet, whose shit and used toilet paper now reached to shoulder height, lived Ellen. Ellen was a slut (explained the mayor to visiting Chamber of Commerce dignitaries), a black nigger slut, but she gave good head, so he let her stay. Sometimes she shorted on her rent when her customers went on vacation or whatever it was that they did, but the white mayor was willing to work with her; he had *heart,* you see. And Ellen obeyed the other rules. In her two years on the island, she had never stolen from anybody. What was more, she lived both tranquilly and literally in the shadow of the toilet. Not every white woman would have been satisfied to breathe that stench! Her religiousness was of the quiet kind. The mayor didn't go for religion much himself. Sometimes the Catholic relief volunteers showed up with food and clothes for those who prayed, so he'd pray along, but with his fingers crossed, so to speak; he was thinking of giving up that luxurious hypocrisy since rents, haircuts and protection were actually bringing in so much money that he was getting rich. He didn't need the christlike bastards! Now, if somebody wanted to swallow their crap, he had nothing against it. It was a free country, an *American* country. If Ellen could bear to live there breathing in the smell of rotten turds all day and all night, why, she could scarf up Jesus, too, for all he cared. Near the river was the island where the Spics lived—Nicaraguans, Cubans, Haitians, Mexicans, the whole lot—and most of them were religious. Ellen sometimes went over to sing hymns with them. That was no skin off the mayor's nose.

The palm sapling in the middle of the sidewalk, figment of an oasis, appeared to be doing well. Soiled underpants and plastic bags lay scattered in the weeds.

I have been all over the U.S., the mayor said to Stanley. I have never seen white people get the respect we deserve. But we need a few blacks. Some blacks, they're an extra set of eyes.

And I'm your eyes, huh? said Stanley, amused. Charles, you're more full of shit than that shithouse next to Ellen's place.

Stanley, you're a goddamned black nigger.

That's the best kind. Gimme a swig of that beer.

You disgust me, you fucking low-life nigger, said the mayor. Here. Take the whole can. You think I want to drink out of any can you've nigger-lipped?

Come the black revolution, Mr. Mayor, you know what we're gonna do to you?

Spraypaint me black so I can keep being mayor. How's that? Then I'm going to raise the rent on all my white people and give you your kickback, you fucking nigger. How's that?

All right, said Stanley. Now you listen. From now on, every time you call me nigger, you got to give me a beer. Is that fair or is that square?

The mayor belched and rubbed his head.

Hey, said Stanley. I'm talking to you, Charles. I mean it. Are you my friend or not?

My head hurts, said the mayor.

What do you always got to be calling me nigger for? I don't go out of my way to insult you. Most of the time I don't pay you any mind, but today for some reason you're getting to me, so would you lay off?

I'm sorry, Stan, said the mayor. Case closed. Now *you* lay off. I've got a bad headache.

They sat there for a while drinking and breathing in smog, and then the mayor said: Hey, Stan.

What?

Did anyone ever tell you that you're a goddamned ugly stupid monkeybrained black black nigger?

Stanley stood up and tried to punch the mayor in the face but the mayor blocked it and shot a hard brawny punch into Stanley's chest which knocked him down onto the concrete. Stanley lay there groaning.

Jesus, Stan, said the mayor, I'm sorry. I didn't mean to hit so hard. You okay?

I hit my head, said Stanley. I'm gonna have a lump the size of a robin's egg. What did you have to keep calling me names for?

Listen, Stanley, I'm sorry. I mean it. I was an asshole.

I'm not so young, you know, Stanley said.

All right, the mayor said. Please let me help you up.

Charles, I want you to know something, Stanley said. People been calling me nigger when I was still inside my Mama's ass. I really don't like it. I want you to listen to me, Charles. If you call me nigger one more time today, I'm not gonna say nothing, but when I get a chance I'm gonna hit you over the head or stab you. Tomorrow I don't say nothing about. Tomorrow nobody can hold you to, you ornery old cracker fool.

You're bleeding on the back of your head, the mayor told him. I'm going to bandage you up.

Did you hear what I said, Charles?

I heard, and I've already told you twice that I'm sorry, which I wouldn't say to anybody else. You know I have a short fuse.

Oh, fuck it, said Stanley, getting to his feet. I'm the one with the bleeding head and he's the one with the short fuse.

The mayor looked around to see if anybody was listening, but the place was empty except for one drunk who, attended by the friendly goggling faces of parking meters, snored in a lair of cardboard plates and newspaper sheets draped over ridges of garbage, with his shoes off and his stinking stockinged feet inside an old lampshade. The mayor wasn't worried abut him. His other constituents were sleeping, screwing, shitting, whoring, scoring, snorting, shooting or most likely panhandling. The mayor himself never left camp. That was why he was the mayor. He ran security.

It must have been three o'clock now, because the blue truck with the white cross on it pulled up to the brown-skinned island.

Oh, shit, the mayor said, treasuring this distraction. —Our guys go out and they work all day and they're tired, and then those Spics set up the loudspeaker in Spanish. Guys in the holy circle getting saved.

My head hurts worse than yours, said Stanley. Gimme another beer.

I only have but one more.

Give it to me, Charles.

The mayor turned red and clenched his teeth. Then he slammed the beer down on the arm of Stanley's chair.

Why, thank you, Mr. Mayor. You're gonna make a nice cocktail waitress someday. Beer could be colder, though.

The mayor rose and stalked away, swearing.

A dirty man whose beard was almost as long and ragged as his backpack came slowly ambling toward the white island. Stanley sat watching him regally, a beer in his hand. The man came closer. Now the man could see the shelters, some of wood, some of cardboard roofed with plastic. The mayor's house was roofed with an American flag.

The mayor came hurrying back from the toilet. He looked the stranger up and down. He said: You a cop? You a cop?

Nope, said the stranger.

A woman stuck her head out of her cardboard box and perorated: Hey, the police's attitude toward the homeless sucks. They catch your ID to check on warrants and they don't return it. I'm monogamous, but I'm homeless so I must be a whore or a crack addict . . .

So sue me, said the stranger. I said I'm not a cop.

Nobody bothers anybody down here, the woman went on eagerly, because this is the *white* end. We used to live in the black end. We got robbed three times a day. Anything they think might be useful to trade or sell, they gotta take. And Charles over there, he's the mayor. He's the one that saved us from the blacks.

When the woman's head first appeared, the mayor had wondered whether she might have heard his argument with Stanley, and he was afraid, but her comments appeased his scuttling eyes, so that he smiled.

You look familiar, the stranger said to her. You know Dan Smooth?

Oh, him? said the woman. He raped my daughter an' only gimme forty bucks . . .

To no one in particular the stranger said: You mind if I set my bedroll here for a night or two?

Where are you from? said the mayor.

California.

If you want bare ground, that's free, said the mayor. If you want a house, you'll have to pay me rent.

How about a house with a yard and a white picket fence? said the stranger.

Are you trying to pull my chain? said the mayor. Stanley! Hey, Stanley! Security!

I'll just take the yard, the stranger said. I'll just spread out my roll right there. Any thieves in these parts?

Watch out for those niggers over there, said the mayor. But this guy's all right. This guy's my buddy. This is Stanley.

What's your name, man? said Stanley.

Henry. Henry Tyler.

Not just any black can move in here, Henry, continued the mayor with relish. We had problems when we first went here, so we came out with baseball bats.

Pleased to meet you, Henry, said Stanley.

Tyler shook his hand.

These people in this little area are the only ones I asociate with, the mayor explained. And I advise you to do the same. As soon as you cross that street there, they'll come after you. Just addicts over there, Henry. Anything they can do, they will do.

Okay, said Tyler. What are the rules here?

Now, everybody here, they're all fixing to follow either Plan A or Plan B, said Stanley, looking Tyler up and down with shrewd eyes. Which one is it for you?

I don't know what you're talking about, said Tyler wearily.

Plan A or Plan B. You can either go to jail, turn your life around and get back to what you need, or you can stay here. What's your goal, Hank? What's your aspiration?

Plan P, said Tyler. I could use some pussy. You people have a problem with that?

Stanley said: Mr. Mayor, I think we got another jerk. It's a good thing you called me. I'm gonna be *watching* this one.

Why? said Tyler. Is getting a piece of ass against your rules? You still haven't told me your rules.

A tiny bluish TV shone far away, illegally hooked into the grid. Ellen was bent over the fire hydrant, filling a jug and goose-stepping like a chicken, mumbling beneath the gracious palm trees that bordered the island.

You stayin' out of trouble, Henry? said the mayor.

Yeah, I'm on a good ticket.

No bullshit, but you just need to respect everybody else. I don't care what else you do or where you come from.

I know what he gonna do, said Stanley, giggling idiotically. He gonna get me a place. Gonna get me a piece of the rock.

The mayor whirled round. —Stan, did you just snort something? You told me you weren't going to use no more. You were trying to keep clean. I thought you were going to do it. Oh, you stupid fucking nigger.

Nigger this and nigger that, Stanley chuckled, his pupils huge.

Goddamn. When could you have done that? I thought I was watching you every second. Now what's going to become of you? Don't you remember that seizure you had, Stan?

Stanley put his arm around the mayor's neck. He whispered in his ear: I wanna get out of here, man. So bad.

All right, Stan. Sit down, boy. Sit down and sleep it off. Yeah, I still have that tongue depressor here. Look how you chewed it last time when you seized up. I don't know why I love you, you worthless nigger.

The woman's head continued to suspend itself from her box's doorway, the hanging twitching blanket covering the rest of her.

Tell Stan to get a job, Mr. Mayor, she called laughingly.

Oh, Celeste, you know better than that, the mayor said, getting on his soapbox. Americans can't get a motherfuckin' job these days. When we try, they ask us: You speak Spanish? The Spics rule. An' you know what the Jews say? They say: *Take care of your own.*

Tyler unrolled his sleeping bag onto the concrete, enjoying the woman's eyes upon him.

Celeste emerged from her box, armed with mirror sunglasses, almost blonde, trying to look good, checking herself in a dagger-shard of mirror which she kept in her ripped and greasy purse. —You know what kind of job I like best? she whispered in Tyler's ear.

He smiled at her long cat-face trying to look good, her lipsticked face, her hair shining feebly in the wind, and said: Let me see. Oh, I know. A blow job.

You wanna blow job? I can see you got a big dick.

No, I'm married to Queen Africa.

Oh, well that's cool. I didn't really want to do the blow job. What I wanted was the money.

Can I go inside with you and we'll talk about it?

I got my girlfriend in there. Lemme see if it's cool with her. I think she's probably passed out or something . . .

Celeste scampered back inside, wiggling her rear at him, and then rushed out again and said: Okay, come on, come on, come on, she's cool with it. What you got for me?

Nice place you have here, said Tyler as soon as he was in the humid stinking darkness. He heard the girlfriend's unsteady snoring.

Celeste groped for his penis. He put his arm around her and stroked her hair.

You didn't come in here for head or for pussy, did you?

Nope.

Are you one of them right-wing virgins?

Nope.

I like the Bible a lot, Celeste said shyly. I started out reading the New Testament, reading about Jesus. The thing is, I forget the chapter and the scripture and the verse, but I know it says: *No man cometh to the Father except through Me.* It doesn't really matter which church I go to, 'cause I pray to Him twenty-four hours a day, seven days a week. But don't tell the mayor that. He's an atheist.

Okay. I won't tell him.

So, the woman said then, using the word with Germanic finality. What the fuck do you want?

Did you ever hear tell of the Queen of the Whores?

That's just a stupid old story, like the King of the Road . . .

No it isn't, he said. And maybe the King of the Road is out there somewhere, too. You never can tell. But this one, she's my Queen. I love her and I'm married to her and she's in trouble so I want to help her. First I need to find her.

Oh, baloney, said Celeste.

Look, you have a mayor, don't you?

Yeah, he calls himself that.

All right, so why can't I have my Queen?

What's her name then?

I already told you she's Queen Africa.

So she's a nigger. Then what did you come to me for? Why don't you live on that nigger island over there?

She lost something magic and I'm trying to get it back for her, which I guess is another way of saying that I lost *her*.

What did she lose then?

A sapphire.

I'll put the word out. You have something to make it worth my while?

Well, he said thoughtfully, I could give you five, but if I do that I might as well try out that pussy of yours.

Deal.

When he came out, the mayor said to him: See? Nobody touched your backpack.

Thank you, said Tyler.

We never had a victim in this lot, the mayor said. We call it the American place. Nobody can build here except your black and white Americans. That one over there, you have your Hispanics, and whatever you have over there, we have better over here. We might get into it against each other, but we don't kill each other like they do.

I get it, said Tyler wearily.

He could see how it had to be. —At Coffee Camp, or even at Slab City, anyone who wanted to could have his bushy privacy; humanity hid away from itself; but under the freeway people couldn't get away from each other like that; they had to deal with each other, to be citizens.

It was almost evening now. The panhandlers were coming home. Stanley lay reading on a knitted quilt on a piece of foam rubber on a cement divider in the parking lot, next to his coffee can on its two bricks which smoked and smudged to keep the mosquitoes away, and the man beside him, tattooed, naked except for a pair of underpants, sweaty, went and crouched in his box of plywood and tarps, brick bricks on top to keep it dry; and the yellow lights glowed in the tiers beyond the great pillar—the brownskinned island and the white and black islands of separateness.

The Cubans on the brownskinned island knew something about magic, Celeste had said. —And you think she's sane? said Stanley in disgust when Tyler told him. —And yet I did hear the same story, Henry. I don't go over there much. Everybody says they sacrifice stray cats and dogs on Thursdays. Maybe it's true and maybe it isn't.

What day is it today?

Monday. No, maybe it's Saturday. I don't know what the fuck day it is, guy. Now lemme read!

Okay, said Tyler, stretching and yawning and wandering across this dismal concrete place, past the box in which Celeste and her girlfriend Pat were loudly making love, and he came to the Cuban island.

The first Cuban he met said: I a good man. I never been in prison. Immigration don't wanna give me my residence. Four months I wait for my permit, two and one-half year . . . I leave my work because I don't like it anymore. Then my possibility is finished.

What kind of work was it? yawned Tyler, narrowing his eyes with boredom. Hey, have you seen a small, black-skinned—

In the field, some illegal job pick the fruit, you know. They pay me for one hour one dollar. By the river there is a lot of job they give you, but now with Haiti people come here, not so many job. A lot of people you see here no have the job. Many people here have paper but the problem is they have no job. Some mission come here with food. I think that's the Baptist church. Right now I have the part-time work for the fields. I been here only one month. Before I was in my sister apartment and she change the apartment and they change their regulation so I can no stay with her no more. My sister is cry . . .

Do those other people bug you?

The white people, they always say the stupid thing about us, so we watch them. And the black people, three people have the knife cut them bad, but the people here is no knife like that. No knife, but no water, no medicine. And sometimes if you look for jobs the police arrest you.

The man pointed, and Tyler saw a police car rolling slowly and silently by.

I want a magic blue stone, Tyler said. You have any friends who can help me?

Magic for what?

For my Queen.

You a faggot? I no like faggot job.

No, she's a woman.

Holy Mother! And somebody annoy her for you?

Yeah, said Tyler.

Okay, I ask my friends about this blue stone. You look for me tomorrow? My name Manuel.

I'm Henry.

Good night.

Good night.

The city wants to cut our water off, the mayor was saying when Tyler came back to the white island. A hundred seventy-five thousand a year it's costing the city taxpayers.

Oh, get out of my face, muttered Celeste.

Stanley was away, his quilt stretched out on the foam rubber pad, his science fiction book from the library opened and face-down.

Lying down, Tyler soon felt Celeste's caressing hand on his neck. —You wanna come sleep with me and Pat tonight? she said.

Sure, baby, he said. I'll come in an hour or so, all right?

That'd be really cool, she said. I like you. —She smelled of sweat and shit.

Tyler slept. Sometimes he heard the voices of ghosts, but their wails quickly become as incomprehensible and tedious as the whistling you hear when you let the air out of someone's tires. When he awoke, the Catholics had arrived at the whiteskinned island, some of whose members were now in a circle holding hands and praying; and the mayor was sitting in his armchair in the parking lot. It was almost dark. The mayor was passing a can of beer back and forth with Stanley. A white dog circled about, with bumps in his head. The bumps were ticks. —Yeah, he's a street dog, Stanley muttered whenever he noticed. The dog was his.

So how you feeling, Stan? said the mayor.

I didn't seize, did I?

Not this time.

You know how it is, Stanley said. It's a day to day process. You get frustrated until you reach the breaking point, and then you go out and do something stupid.

I know, the mayor said.

First you lose your job, then you lose your wife, and then you're here, Stanley said. And then you're safe. Not much else can happen to you, except death or prison.

If I'm so safe, how come I feel so punk?

Because you're coming down off your stupid chemical shit, said the mayor. Ellen gave me some more beer. Help yourself.

The mayor, yawning, went to the hydrant to rub soap into his greying chest hairs while Ellen passed by with her bucket, and Stanley rubbed the back of his head and squished ticks on his dog. Tyler carried his gear into Pat and Celeste's box. Inside, he felt a touch. The other woman said: What are you gonna do to me and Celeste tonight?

He said: Well, first I'm going to put my hand between your legs and make you come. I'll suck your tits, too, if you want. Then I'm going to suck Celeste's tits and put my dick inside her. And I'll do whatever else you want me to do to you.

Will you kiss me? Pat said.

Kiss me, too, said Celeste.

He heard the resolute hissing of somebody's Coleman lantern outside.

Have you eaten? said Celeste.

No, he said.

You want some crackers? That's all we got.

I'll kiss you both, he said sleepily.

Celeste stuck her tongue in his mouth. He stroked her matted hair, thinking of the false Irene. He tried not to think about the dead Irene.

He slept well with his arms around the two women, and dreamed of nothing that he could remember. In the morning he crawled out to get water and found himself now already an enfranchised dweller among the rows of plywood houses, all built a little differently, in one a long narrow slit as if for an archer and in another a real picture-window; and from the opposing island he saw a pair of eye-whites in a black man's face watching him with cautious neutrality. He would have to go over there today and ask about the Queen's sapphire. Smoke rose from improvised stoves. A black man, naked to the waist, hefted his water jug and sat down with it on the milk crate which constituted the stoop of his house.

Ellen got arrested on a bench warrant last night, the mayor said.

Is her house going to be safe? Tyler asked.

There's a lot of violence but we don't have it here, said the mayor. This is white America right here.

Oh, shut up, said Stanley.

Celeste crawled out of that cardboard coffin yawning. —You want some crackers, honey? she said. As far as today, we don't go hungry. The public's been real nice to us. You want me to panhandle for you? You're so nice. I'd do anything for you.

Looks like you got yourself a live wife, said Stanley. More expensive than the dead kind.

Celeste sat down on the curb beside Tyler and took his hand.

How's Pat doing? he said.

Still snoring away! she chuckled. That girl must have been sleep-deprived all her life.

Hey, Charley, said Stanley. I mean, Mr. Mayor, you demon. You still got that little twenty-two up your ass?

So what if I do? said the mayor. That's my business.

The only thing to do about violence is take away all the guns, man. I truly believe that.

Well, try and take my gun and you're going to be one very dead nigger, said the mayor. Violence cannot be solved. You have to solve that one when you're very young.

I was shot by a police officer when I was fourteen and then I robbed twenty-two banks, Stanley said.

Oh, so you don't like guns because somebody shot you for doing wrong, said the mayor. My heart bleeds!

Hey, Stanley, stuff your baloney, said Celeste with a cheery laugh. You never robbed no twenty-two banks! Maybe you took a quarter out of a pay phone one time with a piece of wire . . .

I did so rob banks! cried Stanley, hurt.

Celeste kissed Tyler's ear and said quietly: Pat and I both love you, you know. Why don't you forget about your Queen and stay with us? You'll never have to lift a finger. We'll do everything for you. We'll panhandle for you day and night. We just want to have a decent man around the house.

Inside his chest, Tyler felt a sad warm feeling. He squeezed her hand without saying anything.

The first two houses in this parking lot went up on New Year's, 'ninety-three, the mayor was saying. And we have one rule here, Henry. If you steal, we beat you up and take your house down. That's the second time. Now, the first time . . .

Yeah, you told me yesterday, Mr. Mayor. I'll be good, said Tyler.

They call me the Mayor. I'm always here.

But, getting back to violence, said Stanley, I watched a man get shot in the head four times, right around here. That was back in 'ninety-four. And I thought to myself, I thought . . .

What are you thinking, Henry? said Celeste.

I'm not thinking much, he said. I'm dead inside.

Why? What happened to you?

Well, I loved my brother's wife and she killed herself. Then I loved somebody just for having the same name she did, and that didn't work too well. Then I loved my Queen, and she died. And my mother died, and I lost my job and my car and my house.

My house got run over by a taxicab seven months after I moved in, Celeste said. That taxi came right through the wall and it went through the other wall. Can you believe it? And that's how I ended up here. But I have to make the best out of it.

How much does the mayor charge you?

No, that's my box. Mine and Pat's. We used to live in a big wooden house, but the rent for that home was fifty a month, and twenty-five per person with electricity, and I thought: Who needs this rat race? You know what I'm saying, Henry? Look at that box of ours. It may be cardboard, but it's free. And it cannot be stolen.

Tyler gripped her hand.

Pat likes you, Celeste said pleadingly. And she never likes *anybody*. She *loves* you.

I like her and I love you, he said.

Why do you love me?

Because we have the same sadness, I guess. Because neither of us will ever find what we're looking for.

And you don't love Pat?

Well, I don't know her that well.

Take a walk with me, Henry?

Sure.

Hand in hand, they followed those heavy white double freeway pillars which could go anywhere, even into the brown canal water at the edge of the Hispanic island where a woman pulled a bucket up and carried it back into the world, into the faint smell of excrement.

What we had here once, said Celeste, there's a big house with a pipe where we can hook us up. That's what the mayor always talks about. So the county comes up and rips it down. Then they want to cut the water in the fire hydrant. The mayor's right. Pretty soon we're all going to have to move.

Tyler waited.

You're not going to stay with me and Pat, are you?

I don't know, honey, he said. I just met you yesterday.

I mean, stay for good.

You might have fallen as far as you can fall, he said. You're maintaining, like the addicts say. I have a feeling I'm going to keep falling and falling, he said.

Well, would anything *make* you stay? Like, if you found that sapphire, or if you got convinced that it could never be found?

I don't know, he said again.

Oh, cut the baloney, Henry. I want to know what's going on inside your mind.

Does Pat beat you?

She hit me once. How did you know? She promised she'd never do it again.

And has she?

No. Yes. Twice. But I love her, so it's okay. And I know she loves me.

So you do follow the Bible, he said. Doesn't it say that we're supposed to love our cross?

What are you trying to tell me, Henry? I'm not stupid.

I love my cross, too.

So when you said you loved me and Pat, was that just bullshit?

No. But my Queen was the Queen of the Whores. I lived with her. I could feel myself changing. Now I'm like one of her girls, he said. Love comes pretty easy to me now, maybe too easy. Maybe it comes pretty easy to you, too.

So you love her more than me. Well, that's only natural. I love Pat more than you. Why's that such a problem?

Maybe what you call love is just the feeling of needing to be loved, and maybe what I call love is just—I don't know what it is anymore.

I don't need you! she cried fiercely. *I just love you!*

And why do you love me? said Tyler, walking beside her with his hands in his pockets. The concrete made his feet hurt.

Celeste looked as if she were about to cry. But instead she made herself smile and said: Why do I love you? I told you right when I met you that I could see you had a big dick.

| 584 |

Tyler hopped a freight train—or, I should say, a series of freight trains—to get himself back to Sacramento because he might be able to collect his Supplemental Security Income benefits; and in Indianapolis he met on the rails none other than Missouri the hobo, who, being once again fresh out from detox, was filled with eloquent words for Tyler, whom he did not quite remember.

Oh, I ain't been able to get nothing, the old man whined. That's why this country

spits on its vets. The hippies were right back in the sixties. I tried to get a mental instability when I got out of Nam, but they just gave me what I call a drunk check. And I
only got that for about seven or eight years. Now they go and cut me off. But I showed
them. I blew my last SSI check in Reno playing slots . . . And then the Vietnamese, they
get a billion dollars. I never met a decent Vietnamese. The only ones I met, they're out
there hustlin' and sellin' their mothers and their sisters. Dealin' drugs.

Tyler rubbed his eyes, longing for a drink.

I can't stand authority and I can't stand the government, Missouri went on. I got a
basic commonsense philosphy: *Anything the government is for, I'm against.*

Sounds like a good political platform to me, said Tyler. Say, Missouri, would you happen to have a dollar on you? I could use a cold drink.

Oh, no you don't, Missouri said. Don't you go and hit me up, too. I'm always getting
robbed and rolled, especially by the cops. They hate doin' anything with druggies, because them types got guns. But I'm a drunk, and drunks is easy pickings. There's no such
thing as an honest cop. You think about it. They go to a restaurant, so they get a free coffee. That's graft, is what it is. The cops didn't pay for it. That's insurance. Restaurant
knows if they don't give way, cops just might not show up when they get robbed.

Forget it, said Tyler. By the way, have you run across a small, slender black—

And I'll tell you something else, kid, said Missouri. There ain't such a thing as a decent wetback, just as there ain't such a thing as a decent cop.

All right, Missouri. I'll file that away under W. I'm going to crawl inside this grainer
and sleep.

Hey, where you headed? asked the old man.

What's the difference? laughed Tyler. Long as I'm rolling, I'm rolling.

I heard that.

Maybe Sacramento. Is Loaves and Fishes still open?

That place? They never give you nothing. Why, the food's only half cooked. And they
tried to take control of my entire SSI check, back when I had SSI. Why, if I'd allowed
them push me around that way, I wouldn't even have had tobacco! But I always have tobacco, 'cause I buy a month ahead of time.

Okay, Missouri, said Tyler. I feel rotten. I need to sleep. You taking this train?

Damn right I am . . . You got any tobacco?

See you in the yard in Omaha . . .

And he crawled into the back of his grainer and refused to stick his head out, even
though Missouri whined and pleaded.

| 585 |

When he got back to his former home eight days later, thirsty and stinking, Coffee
Camp looked crowded, so he wandered through midtown and downtown, which didn't
seem to have grown, and crossed the I Street bridge to West Sacramento where it was
cool by the river and the long swirly pillars of light slanted through the water. This was
the last place he'd ever seen the Hundred Thousand Dollar Boxcar Queen. The water-
smell of the dark black night flowed around the windy bridge where Tyler stood gazing
at downtown. One skyscraper resembled a perfume bottle full of light. A long time ago,
when he'd been a teenager in high school, he'd walked along this catwalk holding a girl's

hand. Here at the midpoint where it was bright they'd kissed. He looked down through the grating at water-darkness.

Two men with a dog were coming down the bridge. The dog's paws clicked upon the grating. One of the men said to Tyler: You want some doses?

Africa's my drug, he replied.

The men walked on, with ugly sneering laughs.

He thought to himself: Is there no place anymore, not one, not the smallest darkest hiding place for me?

| 586 |

He longed to know whether he had failed or whether he was already there. Had he continued steadfast enough? Was the Queen proud of him? Most important of all, was he becoming a better person, or had he merely laid himself waste?

He knew what John would saty. And Dan Smooth would not have praised him, ever. But in his living dream, when slumberous Africa comforted him in her arms, and Irene opened her womb to him, the world's shadow-figures amused him only, unable to touch him either for good or harm. In a sense, he lived now like Buddha himself—or Cain, wandering, free of all attatchments except his own adorable charms. And so . . . And so . . .

But why did he feel so radically isolated from *her,* the only one of the two he really loved, the one who . . .

The two men came back. They set their dog on him.

| 587 |

Once upon a time there lived a man named Henry Tyler whose enemy was Jesus. This may seem peculiar, since that Name's purity remains as white as the naked-scratched steel on railroad tracks; besides, Jesus loves and is loved by losers-of-everything, in whose ranks Tyler had long since been enrolled, but because he was a Canaanite, which is to say idol-worshiper and lover of an overthrown goddess, he held Jesus blameable for his loss, no matter that the Israelites, not Jesus, were the ones who swarmed down upon Canaan—no matter that the Canaanites held their own even in Jesus's own time; no matter that Jesus healed a Canaanite woman's daughter of some demoniacal sickness (not, however, without first feeding her a helping of scorn). Down on the gravel, looking at the railroad spikes which had worked themselves into varying degrees of looseness on those long rusty double journey-blades, Tyler wanted to run away from Jesus, but wherever he went, he saw Jesus's name chalked up on walls and trestle-bridges. For him, **JESUS** equalled DEATH. Whenever Jesus was signified to him, he said: Oh, please, don't let it be true. —Whom was he begging? Not Jesus, for certain. Did he believe in God? The vanished Queen of Darkness couldn't help him. He believed in her—and maybe only in her. He knew that she couldn't help him, and so when he whispered or muttered *please don't* he was entreating only as a child does, hopeless and fearful, but still thinking that some miracle may come, if only the need becomes desperate enough or can be expressed movingly enough. We stop being children when we stop believing that we can move the immovable or ride all trains grey, green, brown and blue. A week after my latest AIDS test, with another week to go before learning whether the verdict is doom or the usual qualified anxiety, I wake up with a sore throat, aching and feverish. Wouldn't it be too much of a coincidence, if it were really AIDS? It must be the flu. But of course, waiting for life or death never stops being stressful, and stress lowers resistance, so that the AIDS virus which already lurks in my blood now laughingly proclaims its existence. And Irene is pregnant. What if she and the baby were doomed, too? I can't eat anything. I can't sleep. I can't wake up; I know I'm not awake because how could this horror be so real? Oh, please, don't let it be true. I want to die because I'm afraid to live, but unfortunately I'm also afraid to die. Who will help me? The people who live are the ones I've injured. How can I go to them? And Jesus? That quickwitted, intolerant, impatient, sarcastic disputant, who told a bereaved man: *Leave the dead to bury the dead,* who scourged the moneychangers in the temple, who quizzed and commanded those he met, who refused to see his own mother because he had no mother anymore, no earthly family, no kin at all except those who believed as he did, how can I face him? I'm not quite dead, but I want to bury myself. I don't want to be flogged out of my sordid niche; I don't dare to be questioned or answered. Please love me; help me. I love without doctrine. Can't you? I've loved righteous and evildoing women alike. I feel sick and afraid, and my throat hurts. Oh, Jesus, come to my aid. Help me. Help me. But I'm afraid of your help. I'm afraid that you might gaze into my eyes and then burst out like Domino: *Why am I so ashamed of your life?* I don't dare to examine my life anymore. Don't examine me. Maybe I didn't wash myself clean enough for you. I'm so ashamed. Don't seek to know me. I cannot ever be unknowable like you in your majestic incomprehensibility; I am all too knowable; I have grimy secrets to hide. I am human. I am wicked. I am a bad boy. Now my father, who is DEATH, comes to punish me. He comes as stately as a train rolling rustily over a rust-brown river. Jesus, I know you could persuade him not to drag me away this time. I know you could defend me from him. But I dare not appeal to you, because self-revelation is worse than death. I'd rather die miserably alone; I'll shoot myself in a tall field of grass; I'll go to the edge of town on one of these cloudy or rainy purple days which mark the last season of my life, and with my pistol in a paper bag I'll walk until I can't see the highway anymore. I'll lie down in the mud. Quickly now, before I get cold! I'm already shivering. Raise the heavy gun. My hands shake. I'm cold; I waited too long. The grass hisses over my head. Now I'm wet to the skin. I've lived too long. I'm breaking promises even at the very end. I lie on my back in a muddy puddle. I bring the gun down against my forehead. I will escape revelation. I will sneak sordidly out of life because I haven't the courage to see or be my own shame.

But Henry Tyler was not that kind of coward. The smoldering red sun of judgment already hung over his left shoulder. He had faced it; he had participated in his trial and heard the sentence. He'd eaten his portion of scorn. Now Jesus inscribed seductions before him everywhere; why didn't Tyler want to be reconciled? But Tyler did not want to. He was too proud. He wanted to be *honorably* damned. Oh, please, don't let it be true. But if it's true, then don't ever presume to believe you can extort my full soul as the price for rendering it untrue. A piece of my soul I'll sell you, by all means; like other prostitutes I've been amputating meaty hunks of myself for all comers ever since the Vice Squad shut Eden down. I can be numb; I can lose most of myself, but inside my spinal column lives a shy sad caddisworm who's not for sale.

The three eyes of a locomotive came glaring down the track. Tyler wanted to run away from Jesus. But instead of escape he met only the stale diesel breath and diesel wind of a train which wasn't going to stop, the engineer high up in his sunshine-hued loco-motive peering out the window, and then the train rumbled past with double- and triple-tiered loads of cars bound for Stockton or Los Angeles.

Beside him on the gravel sat a middle-aged hobo whose sad-hound eyes watched the train vanish, then blinked, watered, blinked again with bloodshot patience.

Where are you bound? said Tyler.

I finally just quit worrying about all that crap, all those things to do, said the hobo. I don't even care anymore whether I get on a train or not.

Tyler said: I want to go someplace far away from Jesus.

The hobo pointed in the direction of the faintly whistling train. He said: It's sixty-four miles to Gold Run. I been there. It's six hundred and ninety miles to Terminus, Utah . . .

Trusting in him, struggling to see some hidden lesson in what he'd already seen, Tyler saw how the tracks tapered and curved into a vanishing point—a point beyond God, yet much nearer than Terminus. Indeed, the vanishing point did not look very far away. Might it not be possible that faith could get him there?

That was south. He turned and gazed north, in the direction that the train had come. Long before the horizon, conveniently marked for him by the developer Benvenuti's so-called Renaissance building and by the pallid, blue-windowed library high-rise, he saw another vanishing point.

He went behind a bush, so that the hobo couldn't see him, and kneeling down on the tarry gravel he prayed to the Queen: I know you're dead, so you're too far away and too busy to come back to me, but please can't you send me an angel to show me how to get to the vanishing point?

Then he stood up. He had faith. His knees hurt from the gravel. His shoulders ached from carrying a duffel bag full of heavy ripe fruit, a blanket and clothes, and most of all, *water* (sixty-four pounds per cubic foot) across bridges and freeway overpasses in the hot sun. He walked around the bush and found a girl sleeping on his bedroll. It was his dead sister-in-law. He took off his coat and quietly draped it over her legs.

She ain't moved none while you were gone, said the hobo. She just been catchin' up on her shuteye. She sure is a purty little peach.

Yes she is, said Tyler.

I used to be married one time, the hobo said. But then I died.

Is everybody dead around here? said Tyler.

I don't know about you, said the hobo.

Well, how would I know?

Do you cast a shadder? said the hobo. They say that's the most reliable test. Stand up an' walk around. Well, heaven's all clouded over. Can't really tell. I ain't cast no shadder ever since I got good and dead and buried.

They're phasing out this yard, Tyler said. I used to see so many trains here. Now it's going to be new houses, and where that trestle bridge is down there, that's going to be a mall.

That's why we're here, the hobo said. We all been phased out. 'Course I don't know about you.

You already said that.

Well, look. You got a mirror, son? Breathe on the mirror. If it don't turn misty, then you're dead. It's that simple.

Now why would I have a mirror? asked Tyler reasonably. Do I look like the type who shaves? I gave up shaving when I became homeless.

All right. See if you can hold your breath forever. Just stop breathing. If you can do that, you know you're dead.

You don't know what you're talking about, said Tyler in disgust. You're telling me you're dead, but you've been sitting here breathing all this time. What's more, brother, you have wicked bad breath.

I do? said the hobo in amazement. I guess I ain't brushed my teeth in a week or two. My wife used to nag me about that, but I don't hold it against her. Out of all the woman I've known, she was the one who . . . You know, her mind . . .

You talk as if *she's* the one who's dead.

She might as well be. Don't you know that the dead grieve for the living? Don't you know *nothin'*?

From the coupling between two tanker cars a young man appeared, leaping down onto the tracks. Tyler waved. The young man swerved toward them, coming rapidly, alertly along the splintered, splitting ties whose stamped dates proclaimed them to be less than fifteen years old. How quickly everything goes! Strips had rusted off the verde-grising rails. The hobo looked him over, then cracked open a hip flask of Wild Turkey in a paper bag and gulped. Tyler watched the young man stony-eyed, not sure yet whether he was friend or foe. He was still far away, but now they could hear the young man's rapid footsteps on the gravel. Irene's eyelids trembled open. Tyler ran to her and held her hand. —It's okay, honey, he said. Don't be afraid.

Irene smiled and gripped his fingers tight. Her dark, made-up eyes were sickeningly beautiful. He felt as intimate with her as with his Queen, with whom he had shared so much pain.

Anyone been bothering you? said the young man.

So far, so good, said Tyler. What've you been up to?

Just checking out some pieces, the young man said.

Over the same coupling now emerged a black-uniformed railroad bull, with another bull coming briskly around from the rear of that string of cars. —Hold it! they called.

The young man lowered his head and began to walk away.

Stop right there! called the first railroad bull.

The young man ran.

The railroad bulls chased him but couldn't catch him. So they gave up and came slowly gravel-crunching back to Tyler, the hobo and Irene.

Did he say anything to you? said the first bull.

Just asked if anybody were bothering us, said Tyler.

And what did you say?

I said nope, said Tyler.

He must've been doing something wrong, to be running away like that, the bull said smugly.

You got that right, officer, Tyler said.

What do you mean? cried Irene. Is it wrong to run away from a man with a gun?

Nobody said anyting.

Well, said the first bull, upon whose silver badge the sun sparkled with an ominous splendor, what are *you* all doing here?

We love trains, said Tyler. We're train buffs, officer. We're just trying to figure them all out.

What do you mean, figure them out?

Well, like you see that car over there? That says Burlington Northern. And right next to it, there's a Southern Pacific car. And it's so strange to think that two railroad cars from so far apart would end up coupled like that. It's almost like magic. In fact, it's almost divine. I for one never could have predicted it. I mean, can you explain how that could have happened?

Explanations aren't exactly my job, said the bull with a sly smile.

You see what I mean? said Tyler enthusiastically. And then there's the matter of that train that just blew through here without stopping. It was loaded full of brand new automobiles! And we wondered where it was going. I was thinking maybe Stockton or maybe Los Angeles. But both of those places already have so much traffic that they almost don't need any more cars. So it's quite a mystery. There's so much to think about.

So you're saying you're train buffs, said the railroad bull.

I guess you could call us that. Train enthusiasts.

We'll need to see your identification now, said the first bull.

Tyler took out his driver's license, and the second bull took it and began writing up a report.

You're homeless, right? said the first bull to the old hobo.

Homeless, well, I don't know about that, officer. I got my own little plot of ground.

Where are you from?

Georgia, originally. But I been out here in California for about thirty some-odd years.

You have any ID?

Well, I have this food bank card but it's expired.

The second bull took the card, studied it, and announced: This card is *expired.*

Yeah, that's what I said, the hobo replied. I'm expired. I done expired four years ago now. And this fellow here, we needed you to figure out if he casts a shadder or what.

He's drunk, said the second bull.

The first bull, spying around wisely, saw the paper bag with the bottle of Wild Turkey in it. —Whose is this? he said.

Tyler and Irene kept quiet. After a long silence the hobo said: It ain't mine.

Sure looks pretty fresh, said the bull. And the cap is off. —Expertly he kicked it over, and every drop sank down into the gravel. The hobo licked his lips more sadly than ever. And the railroad bull smiled.

How about you, miss? said the railroad bull to Irene. You live with him?

We're just friends, said Tyler quickly, not wanting to implicate Irene in his own filthiness. Do you have any ID, honey?

Irene stood up and took her billfold out from under Tyler's coat. She opened it. Tyler suddenly began to get a sinking feeling in his chest, confirmed by the whistle and glimmer of an oncoming locomotive. Irene withdrew her California driver's license and gave it to Tyler, who passed it over to the second bull.

This ID card is expired also, the bull said.

Well, sonny, now you know, the hobo said to Tyler. The gummint test is more reliable than mirrors and shadders. 'Cordin' to the gummint test, you ain't dead. She and I, we flunked the test. But the gummint said you're still alive. You still gotta pay taxes to the gummint.

Pardon me, officer, said Tyler. I was wondering if my ID was expired.

Nope, said the railroad bull.

All right then, said Tyler to Irene. I was pretending about you, but you're—

Please please don't say it, said Irene. I'm not here for that. It hurts me to hear that said.

The locomotive screamed loudly. The train roared and clanked through the yard while everyone waited patiently. Tyler counted cars until he was nauseated. He never saw a single open doorway. The train trembled angrily, perspiring diesel-fumes. Then it was gone.

Don't they ever stop here anymore? he asked the bulls.

Why don't you ask your friend there, chuckled the bull who'd kicked over the hobo's Wild Turkey.

In silence, the other bull handed back everyone's identification cards.

We're going to have to ask you to move on, said the first bull. Technically, you know, you shouldn't be on Union Pacific property.

I understand, officer. How about just letting us watch the next train go by? said Tyler.

All right, the bull said. But you'll have to move up to the right of those power poles. That way you'll be off railroad property.

All right, said Tyler. Thank you, officer.

Thank you, officer, said the hobo obsequiously.

Irene, glaring nobly at the two bulls, gathered up her belongings in silence.

Now what? she said when they reached the power poles.

What are you asking me for, sweetheart? I thought you were supposed to be telling me what to do.

Oh, that's rich, the hobo said. You're such an idiot. You don't even know if you're dead or alive.

Knock it off, said Tyler. If you're so enlightened, how come you can't stop being an alcoholic even after you're dead?

Irene smiled sadly.

After a long time, the long, wheeled wall of waiting boxcars across the track suddenly clanked. Then hissing screams of steam were uttered. The engineer was testing the breaks. In a moment, the train would depart. Anxiously the three sojourners looked both ways, and found the railroad bulls gone or at least out of sight. Tyler and Irene ran across the gravel-clattering open space, knowing that the engineer could see them and hoping that he did not care. Just in time they threw themselves up into the sunstruck interior of a boxcar: yellowed old paint with brown scratches and black rust-islands all indescribably beautiful like taffy with caramelized sugar. As for the hobo, he first rabbited himself into a grainer car, then changed his mind and leaped into Tyler and Irene's almost perambulating cave. —I still move pretty good, he chuckled. I ain't got no complaints. — Tyler sat beside Irene on his bedroll, with his arm around her waist.

The train began to move. The whole world paraded past! And Tyler realized that this was the ultimate extended trace.

Look! said the hobo raptly, raising his arm in a Roman salute. The new courthouse! —He had civic pride.

When she was alive, Irene, who thanks to a dangerously well hidden addiction to unrealistic expectations had never known much happiness anyhow, excepting the anticipatory kind, had developed a stomach ulcer in her first half-year of marriage—fitting emblem of that marriage: painful, bloody wound. She vomited blood in secret. She didn't want to tell John. She pitied herself, seeking out Tyler's pity in an oblique manner obscured by layers of affection. And he'd obliged; he'd pitied her and worried about her.

I love you so much, she said then.

I love you, too, he said. You have to go to the doctor or you'll croak.

Maybe that would be the best solution.

But where would I be? he cried out.

I love you so much, she said.

And where *would* Tyler have been? Why, right here! And right here was not so bad . . . The ceiling was corroded beach-white and sky-blue around the edges, metal semblance of some tropical heaven. And yet Irene's expressionlessness as she stared out the open door stirred up in him an unpleasant thrill of eeriness, which rapidly sank to dreariness, as if he had hopped a freight train which was surely going all the way to Elko but which after crossing the river then backed up, turned, and went west across the I Street bridge to end in some dead switching yard in West Sacramento where, after having been slammed back and forth for a long time, he suddenly felt deadness: his locomotives had abandoned him; he was to be left amidst gravel and mosquitoes all night and maybe all the next day or even all week; his water would last two days, so he'd better come out, put his bedroll on his back, and start walking to God knows where, maybe to the Land of Nod. Irene did not care for him at all.

I love you so much, he said experimentally.

What's the use of loving a dead person? she bitterly replied.

I don't see what *use* has to do with anything.

How do you feel now, Henry?

I feel—well, tortured and confused, but I know that my unhappiness isn't yours.

Irene was silent.

Well, he said finally, do you still love me?

I don't remember. You didn't call me back to love you. You just prayed that I'd come and be your angel.

That's rich, the hobo said. You're both just a couple of chumps.

They reached Coffee Camp and crossed the American River, then backed up near Loaves and Fishes, and the old mill towered grimly out the open door. Tyler and Irene passed rusty wire, sunlight, bowing trees, the stylized outline of a woman white on a grey siding. Irene wanted to lean out to see everything, but he gripped her arm, he said because that was how you did things when you were pulling a surveillance job, but really because he did not want her to fly away.

A glossy black locomotive bore toward them. It said TRUCKEE. The paint shone and glistened with a mirror finish, reflecting golden blobs of sunlight. Then came the long mahogany passenger cars. Irene gasped with pleasure. Through one of the windows Tyler glimpsed playing cards laid out by a sherry decanter.

Did you see that? cried the hobo. That was a blast from the past. That train sure don't cast no shadder.

What do you care? said Tyler. You're a blast from the past yourself.

The tarnished pigeonholes of an old mail car rattled by, gaping its many lips of canvas mail sacks.

My Daddy told me they used to dump a mailbag every five seconds an' sort it out, the hobo said.

Oh, come on, said Irene.

No, darlin', I swear it. My Daddy didn't never lie to me.

Irene smiled. —I know what's on that mailcar, Henry, she said.

What's that? Tyler said.

All the letters I never sent you, and all the letters you wrote me that I never answered.

Maybe you're right, he said, and just then an envelope blew out the window and into the open boxcar where Irene, laughing, snatched it up and opened it. It said: *Irene, please. I want to live inside your heart, to know you, care for you, and sleep within your arms. I want to drink your spit. I want to make you happy. I think about you every day.* —Irene giggled and showed it to the hobo, who said: I don't give a fuck. —Tyler was red with humiliation and rage.

Oh, are you angry? said Irene. I'm sorry. I forgot that people who aren't dead yet still have secrets to hide.

Just forget it, he muttered.

Henry?

What?

Will you really forget it? I'm sorry if I hurt your feelings. You're just so funny sometimes. Oh, look!

The dining car was going by, showing off bone china and sterling silver for Irene.

A fire-red caboose made Irene smile happily, and then the train was gone.

We all shoulda caught that train, the hobo said. Train like that only comes along every hundred years. That's the train bound straight for Jesus and his angels.

Glad I missed it, then, said Tyler. I don't know about you.

Where were all the passengers? said Irene.

How should I know? You're the angel. You're supposed to have all the answers.

That was a nasty thing to say.

I'm sorry, Irene. I didn't mean it that way.

Another strange train rushed past. First he could see the cow-catcher of the locomotive with its vertical ribs like teeth, the great number 1 inscribed on a circular window and also on a metal breast—was this the fabled Governor Stanford train back from the days when X Street was still walled with trees? He narrowed his eyes, frowning at the smoking-car, which resembled a mummy's sarcophagus, all golden, golden, inset with nested beads, webs, zigzags and narrow figures in fields of burnished gold-leaf within blue and red boxes.

Irene said: I told you there's no use loving a dead person.

Was there any use loving you when you were alive?

Sometimes you're so mean. Maybe I was mean, too. Do you want me to go? I could just go right now. Maybe that's what I should do. Is that what you want?

No, said Tyler.

I'm going to go anyway. We're all going to go now. We're almost there. Listen, Henry. You need to think really hard now. There's an answer, I promise. But it has to come from you. If you figure it out now, you'll be saved.

Can you give me a hint?

There's no time for hints, Henry! Look, there it is! I'll tell you this much—it has to do with love . . .

Then they were in sight of the vanishing point where train tracks became metal rivers veined by the shadows of cottonwood trees just as women's breasts are veined so richly by blood vessels in infrared photography.

Loving you?

What did I tell you about loving a dead person? That's all you talk about. Oh, Henry, if you end up being damned I'm going to cry.

Loving Jesus? he said wearily. I *refuse* to do that. He killed my Queen . . .

Henry, Jesus isn't what you think. He doesn't hate you. He's not against you. But—

You know what, Irene? I don't like this guessing game. If what you say is accurate, which means that you know but won't tell me, then you don't love me.

You truly believe that, Henry? That means you don't trust me. That means you don't love me . . . Oh, and now it's too late.

At the exact vanishing point, a fish leaped. Then Irene, the hobo and the train all vanished, and Tyler drowned in sadness.

| 588 |

Time went by, a good long time, and of course he never found the Queen or either of the two Irenes. By then he wasn't even really trying. In that strange half-season when winter has been outgrown but spring continues grey and bleak we find him standing under the freeway on Alaskan Way South, leaning against a concrete pillar with his hands in his pockets, his skull a reliquary of broken golden beads and tarnished copper thoughts as he looked out at the long grey strata of sky, land and sea in Puget Sound. He was cold and wet, his wool hat wet; he had ten dollars in his pocket, so he wandered up to a sporting goods store to buy another hat but the clerk, Middle Eastern and excitable, shouted: *Get out, bum!* —That night it rained heavily, almost overpowering the groans and farts of the other men in the shelter, and the next morning it was sunny, windy and cold. He sat on the granite perimeter of a garden strip which abutted the Federal Office Building on Marion and Western, and gazed up beyond the gently swinging traffic lights at the long tight rope of concrete which bisected the world, and a black prostitute in bright white jeans drifted by, smoking a cigarette, peering down at the sidewalk in hopes of miraculous treasure.

Sunlight suddenly struck the concrete ribbon, and transformed the rare people bestriding it into angels. Now it was very sunny and bright throughout the whole world, and Tyler with his wool cap and grubby little duffel bag rose up to become part of the sun.

The sun dazzled the pavement between a bowlegged panhandler's thighs. Tyler nodded. The man nodded back. He was as old as a Northern Electric train from 1914.

How ya doin'? said Tyler.

Bad, said the other, as Tyler had expected. That was what they always said.

Well, why's *that?* cried Tyler in cheery amazement.

Don't feel too good.

Uh huh.

You got any cigs?

I don't smoke.

Any change?

Lemme see, said Tyler, his fingers ostentatiously snailing through his pockets. What's the cheapest place to stay around here?

The cheapest or the *cheapest?*

The *cheapest.*

Pioneer Square.

Tyler went there. That night there was another storm. Seattle's skyscrapers wriggled and swayed in the rain like hollowed out tree trunks eaten by phosphorescent worms.

He awoke with the taste of Irene's cunt in his mouth.

Merry Christmas, a man said, slipping a twenty-dollar bill into Tyler's cup.

Is it Christmas already? he said. That's Christ's day. I can't accept that money, sir. I'm a Canaanite. Well, what the hell. I guess I can use it. I never did have principles.

Merry Christmas, the man said again, insistently.

You're welcome, said Tyler.

The man sighed and walked away. Then Tyler felt sad and guilty, and decided to catch out to Sacramento to become however peripheral a part of one of those superdark foggy blue nights when the light inside was as bright as lemon peels in drinks and all the whores were singing along with the jukebox as if they were opera stars, and the whores caressed each other, rubbed each other's necks, and talked about getting the hell out of here, know what I'm saying? and the light outside was Tyler's light, the rainy streetlight radiance of Canaanites and sad lean men the color of cigarette smoke. So he departed Seattle's long sagging alleys whose dumpsters sparkled with fresh rain, black puddles in its blackness and the smell of piss. Sensing that the Celestial Vice Cop was tailing him with intent to reduce him into a thinly shrieking ghost like Irene or a silent ghost like his eternally adored Queen, all the way to Roseville he boxcar-flew like one of the many sick lost seagulls one sees in inland places, squeaking feebly in the creosote wind of the Union Pacific yard as the grass bowed and chittered, and he breathed locomotive-clouds as he hid from bulls and preachers behind barbed wire. Over by the auction yard he found a syringe stuck in a crack in a telephone pole, but left it because it was some other wanderer's treasure. He came to a little grey man who hunched rapidly along between the tracks. When Tyler asked where the vanishing point was, the man said he'd never heard of it. When Tyler asked him where to camp, he said he had no idea. He asked about Irene and the Queen, and the man would not reply. So Tyler thanked the man, who said nothing. An instant later, the man had completely disappeared. Later, when the Reno bound freight began to move, Tyler saw him poke his head out of the back of a grainer car. Tyler himself went west. Thunder crawled over the tracks, pounding him with light and icy drops. He jumped off the train in the yard just south of Coffee Camp which was now sodden and almost deserted, only one hardy speed freak couple living in a dome tent, the others all gone to shelters; the river was flooding; the paths were underwater . . .

Sometimes he speculated that the Queen and Irene were actually one—that is to say, a double-sided incarnation of Something Else—but on a certain cold and tule-fogged morning he awoke still clinging to his Queen and shouted: *I hate Irene!* and felt eased of half his pustulent love. So he shouted it again and again. Unripened raspberries sometimes wilted on the vine, the leaves riotous red like an alcoholic's cheeks. *I hate Irene! I hate Irene! I hate Irene! I hate Irene!* On the fifth anniversary of Irene's suicide he hopped a train all the way down to Los Angeles to try to find her grave but Forest Lawn now held so many new dead people that he wasn't sure where it was, and as he tramped around in his dirty clothes and boots trying to find it a security car pulled up, and two guards politely drove him out. (After they had dropped him a good distance away, one guard said to the other: God, that guy stinks worse than any stiff!) As long as he could, he stared back over his shoulder at the columned pseudoclassical white palace that said FOREST LAWN. *I hate Irene!* Then he kept going down toward San Bernardino, everything bluish grey below him, the mountains like swirls of smoke. There were bands of pressure in his head. The mountains gradually became clearer, and his headache went away. But Irene had blackjacked him, and his head would never be right again. Fifty-odd miles out from Palm Springs he took refuge in a huge freight yard which paralleled the freeway, its grainers and boxcars forming a new horizon with smoggy mountains behind the Burlington Northern. But soon he was hot and out of water. He began to walk down the hot black ribbon of track which lanced on into the desert past the whirling windmills, and by sunset, his throat swelling up with thirst, was standing beneath a big yellow billboard that said HELP US CATCH KILLERS, the desert foaming and boiling with creosote bush and rabbitbrush and sand as pale as steamed milk dolloped on coffee. The heat took his thoughts away from Irene with her vague smile and her bright trivialities. His neck steamed and his brain boiled. Sweat ran from his eyes like tears. He inhaled the hot dry air, moving carefully. A cicada chattered like some distant generator. Then he saw a Mexican lying in the sand. He turned the man over and said: How are you doing? —Not too good, said the Mexican. Too hot. I got sun poison . . . —Yeah, me, too, Tyler laughed. I figure we both got that years ago. —but then darkness fell down on them to save them, and a long cool train came hollering by to carry them all the way to Indio where before dawn they were drinking their fill from the restroom of a gas station. He never saw the Mexican again. *I hate Irene!* he shouted. Then everything became white and bright, like coming up out of the ocean into the light—so much light!

He went to visit Waldo, but authority had banished the autistic man, leaving his hulks and his nosecone useless in the sand. —In Phoenix you know what they done awhile back? another hobo said to him. Passed an ordnance that garbage is city property. So if you gotta eat, if you open a dumpster, they can bust you for stealing.

He went to Slab City. The angry man and his mother were still there. —Once you get here, it's hard to get back out, the angry man said. It's like a hole. —The shy woman was out collecting cans. *I hate Irene!*

So many of us are sure we'll always be wherever we are; but Tyler knew better because he traveled a little more than Irene. And in his life Tyler had not had very good luck in finding and keeping people. *I hate Irene!* So one day he blew in to Miami, wanting to see if Celeste still lived under the freeway, because she had said to him: I hate all those women that get a new husband every week. The guys here respect me like a sister, because I don't do that. But Ellen has a new husband every week. And worse yet, her kids have a new Daddy every week. When her baby cries, she blows crack smoke in its mouth until he gets quiet. Sometimes I want to take a bullwhip to her! —Celeste had wanted to be unchanging, and he had wanted to believe her, so he imagined that nothing would change, but of course Freewayville was gone. The city fathers had razed it and then fenced it. Their justice was as cruel and useless as that painted water on Salvation Mountain.

A couple of miles northeast of the freeway, almost within sight of a homeless shelter, the mayor's black friend Stanley and some other men were lying on mattresses on the sidewalk.

City cut that fire hydrant off, Stanley said. Then they moved us out and up to that shelter. So we were allowed to stay there only two months. Now we don't know what to do. I guess everybody figured they'd help us get a job. Only by the time we got to that shelter there weren't no jobs. So here we are, out on the Slab. We call this place the Slab, Henry.

Those words of Stanley's detonated a terrifying flash of comprehension within Tyler's brain. The Slab and Slab City were both equivalent places with equivalent names: they both derived from the slabs on which Dr. Jasper performed his autopsies.

You ever find that broad you was lookin' for? asked Stanley.

I never did.

How long you keep lookin' for her?

Oh, what's the difference, Tyler muttered. I hate Irene anyway. And the Queen, I can hardly remember her as she really was. I don't *believe.* I don't love. I'm just lost. How long's it been for you, Stan?

Since what?

Since everything went bad.

I been homeless since 1987, so it's been exactly ten years now. It comes from using crack cocaine. And it sucks out here. Too much fightin'.

Well, let's see, it's been three years for me now, Tyler said.

Congratulations, sucker. Where you been?

Fell asleep on a grainer car last year and woke up in Dubuque.

Aw, Henry, you was always the wise-ass.

Stanley, he said, sitting himself comfortably down, are we ever going to get out of this?

Out of what? To do what and go where, for what reason?

Look. You remember what you thought the first night you slept out in the street?

Stanley laughed bitterly. —That I wouldn't be out there too long. And now look at me. I'm all scarred from gettin' in these fights. Happens every time I get drunk. When I drink, I win some, I lose some. Don't matter one way or the other. Last fight, some fool took my crack stem and wouldn't give it back. But crack's still good to me . . . And now I'm finally gettin' to like being homeless. Best thing is, people gimme money sometimes for nothin' . . .

He yawned, stretched, rolled over so that he was lying on his suitcase. —I went up to North Carolina to work, he said. Spent three months cutting cabbages for $4.75 an hour. It was too much work for me. I swiped this knife here, which I use for self-defense.

You'd better sharpen that blade, Stan. Hey, what happened to the mayor?

Who?

Charles. That white guy.

Him, laughed Stanley. We got rid of him. Showed him he couldn't hack it.

Where is he now?

He might still be in jail. Weapons charges, plus assault on an officer, plus battery. I think he had a death wish. He's an arrogant, arrogant asshole. If your personality don't fit his stereotype of somebody supposed to be how he wants you, then you just can't get along with him.

And Celeste?

She left town, Henry. There was some trouble over her.

What kind of trouble?

You sure you want to hear about it?

Shoot.

Well, this guy named Ivan—I don't think you met him—she let him shack up with her after you left. Her girlfriend Pat had just died of cirrhosis, and she was pretty lonely. You shouldn't hold it against her, Henry, the shacking up, I mean, 'cause you didn't stay with her . . .

No complaints on my end. Go on.

And this asshole named Lightning Bug had the hots for her, too. So one night when Ivan got sleepin' right here on the Slab, about two mattresses down from me, Lightning Bug got him a gas can and poured gas on Ivan and burned him up. So Ivan woke up runnin' around with fire on him like a stunt man. You shoulda seen him, Henry. It was just like the movies. Well, he screamed and screamed, just like a fuckin' human torch. Then the firemen come and give him morphine. Lightning Bug got no right to do that. If he got some disagreement with Ivan, he coulda broke his leg with a pipe or somethin' . . .

Well, I see where Lightning Bug got his name,

Firebug more like!

So what happened to him?

We hopin' he get life, Stanley said, and Tyler suddenly realized how, ghetto style, he sometimes left out inessential verbs now, as if any extra effort were too much. —Before the man come, Stanley went on, Lightning Bug run away, but then he come into the shelter where we eatin' an everyone started shoutin' right there at the dinner table: *Murderer, murderer!* He of course said he didn't know that Ivan had died. Well, Henry, I lay right here *watchin'* it! I couldn't put his flames out! It took about ten minutes for him to burn up! Well, they arrested the bastard. When Celeste heard about it, she cried a long time. Then she left town. She mentioned your name more than once. I dunno if she was going to look for you or what . . .

Tyler said nothing. He remembered how Celeste had said to him: I was like holding in there for the past couple of years, but then I guess I got tired. I had to let go. And then I ended up here. I could feel myself going, but I was just so tired I didn't care anymore . . .

He thought to himself: And *now* how tired must she be? *I hate Irene!*

Hey, guy, said another black man. What's your name?

Tyler, said Tyler. Everybody calls me Henry. How's the food down here?

Not bad. Pretty decent cooking at that shelter. A little bit of red tape before and after is all.

What the hell, said Tyler.

I been on the Slab here about a year, the other black man went on. I was under that freeway, too, but I never met you. But it's good to remember old times, ain't it, bro?

Sure, said Tyler dully.

I remember *unity,* the man said. But it was segregated type unity. It was all about those cliques, man. And when they closed us down, it was all political. They came in early one morning with paddy wagons and got us all out, drove us to the shelter. They let us take what we could carry. Then they burned down the shacks. By noon everything was gone. A lot of people, you know, if you bring 'em straight up off the street like that, they gonna rebel. Ellen was there at the time. She rebelled. They dragged her off screaming.

The man couldn't stop talking about it. He had to tell the story again. —They told us to vacate, he said. They held us up on trespassing charges. Couldn't go back. They let us take some of our stuff, our blankets . . .

How were you feeling? Tyler asked, wanting to understand.

Empty inside. Angry, 'cause I didn't understand why. We're not harmin' anyone; we're not burglarizin' . . .

Tyler nodded, sitting there on the sidewalk.

I didn't go to jail, said the black man, strangely desperate to continue his story. Went to an abandoned building on Ninth and Fourth. The city would come in and roust us out for a day on misdemeanor charges, then back we'd go. We called it the round robin.

All right, brothers, Tyler suddenly cried, filled with the same meaningless but searing urgency which had rushed him out of Coffee Camp and which sometimes drew him back to Coffee Camp, which had locked him into being the Queen's slave and into loving Irene and hating Irene and fucking the false Irene and making love to Celeste, *so what's to live for?*

Moneyman! they replied laughing, and Stanley explained: When Moneyman come around, he come in his station wagon. Everybody be here, he get a handout from Moneyman. Moneyman hand out the dollar bills like candy, then he go.

Tyler looked at him. —How's the habit, Stanley?

When you set a time to stop, to stop smokin' crack, to get up off the Slab, then you settin' yourself up for a relapse. Recognize the Power that's greater than you, Henry. Trust Him. That's the only thing you can count on.

Tyler watched as he counted his quarters, stood up painfully, and went off to buy crack.

| 589 |

He awoke with the taste of Irene's cunt in his mouth. *I hate Irene! I hate Irene! I hate Irene! I hate Irene! I hate Irene! I hate Irene! I hate Irene!*

| 590 |

I like the slow, nice, quiet life, Waldo had said. No adventures, no drama. It is the last spot on earth.—And he'd spread his hands, there in his underwear.

· BOOK XXXVI ·

The Royal Family

•

And the Lord put a mark on Cain, lest any who came upon him
should kill him.

GENESIS 4.15

•

Hal Lipset died, said Celia.

What's that? John irritably returned, checking international exchange. The Thai baht, the Korean won and the Malaysian ringgit were still low. Already foreseeing the day months ahead when the *Chronicle* would read **Stocks Lose 207 Points on Asian Jitters**, he decided to devolatilize, which is to say coagulate, certain investments.

You know, that guy that bugged the martini olive.

Uh huh. And whatever Greenspan does is going to hurt. I can see that coming. Good thing your mutual fund is—

John, are you listening?

Oh, him, said John, bored. Back in 1965, right? Just a demo for the Senate. A life of twenty minutes and a range of twenty feet. I'm going to be home late tonight. Rapp's at his wit's end with that stupid Pannel file, so I have to clean up his mess—

How do you remember all that stuff? said Celia in astonishment.

What stuff? That's my *job*. Some people have to *work*.

No, I mean like all that stuff about Lipset's olive.

Mom brought me up well, I guess. Which reminds me. We need to shoot up to Sacramento to clean the headstone of Mom's grave.

What about Irene's grave?

What about it? Are you jealous?

Yes.

John laughed. Connoisseur of restaurants, he preferred to memorialize Irene not only with the occasional angry and fugitive visit to Forest Lawn, but also with a drive to Western Avenue for a long lunch at Cho Sun Galbi, which had been Irene's favorite establishment when she still lived at home. The gleaming aluminum plates and equally gleaming fume-hoods in the middle of the plasticized granite tables gave him a sense of satisfaction. He missed Koreatown a little. It gave him a sense almost of gaiety to imagine bringing Irene's successor, Celia, to Cho Sun Galbi where, admiring the mellow beer-colored shadow of his drinking glass, he'd offer her kimchee as red as blood, and allow her to help herself from small white porcelain bowls of bean sprouts, sugar-dried fish. Laughing, talking loud, he'd regain his pleasures. Irene with her suicide had poisoned this place; so be it. Celia would impart new associations. Afterwards, in some pleasant hotel room, he'd get to enjoy Celia's white legs like chopsticks flashing in a bowl of red kimchee.

John?

What is it now, Ceel?

John, how come you don't like people to know you're smart?

Oh, for God's sake. Just for once, can't we leave me out of this? One goddamned time.

That's all I ask . . . Fidelity made me five hundred dollars last week, but I think I'm going to lose it. You need to get your financial shit together, too, kiddo. How many times do I need to keep telling you? My goddamned broker's just sitting on his fat ass. I call him my broker because he's making me broke. Ripping me off, driving me straight to the poorhouse . . .

John?

Yeah, I *know* my tie's not straight. I'm sick of this tie anyway . . .

John, do you ever worry about your brother?

John slammed the newspaper down. —And just what does Hank have to do with anything?

I don't know. I guess that bugged martini olive reminded me of him.

Look, said John. He's my brother that I don't talk about. Period. Okay?

Do you think he knows how to bug olives?

Now you're trying to goad me, John said.

Maybe he's got this whole apartment bugged and he's listening to us right now.

Wouldn't put it past him, John laughed. Except that he's probably sleeping it off in some doorway. I can't believe that piece of work is my blood relative.

John?

What? I've got to go.

John, I'm pregnant.

From me or from a bugged olive?

You know, John, I had a talk with Irene once. Before she died.

Well, when else would it have been? Unless you believe in ouijah boards.

And she told me you said the same thing to her. She said you never trusted her. But you were in the wrong, John. She was always faithful to you. And you really shouldn't say such hurtful things—

Oh, balls, said John. Whose side are you on—mine or Irene's? Well, congratulations. What's it going to be, marriage or an abortion? Let me know, but not right now, because I have to go. Can you straighten this tie for me?

Did you just propose to me, John?

Whatever. All right, so you won't straighten my tie. I'm going. Make sure you double-lock when you go to work . . .

Let's get married, John.

All *right* already. Twist the knife! Do we have to go on and on about it? No, cinch up the knot. Is it still crooked right here? Oh, Jesus, I'm late. I'm really late. You and your bugged olives . . .

| 592 |

They honeymooned in Hawaii, and then on a blue-grey Sunday John wanted to fly to Las Vegas to wrap up some Feminine Circus business with Brady (who in prison would resemble some old grey tree shooting up like the skeleton of a fabled pike, leaning each year farther against empty air). In the stretch limo which Brady had sent, the tulip-shaped glasses gleamed like rubies behind the long long windows, and the crystal decanters in their mirror-backed cases wore gold. John grinned and laid his hand on the back of his wife's wrist.

Celia was in the bathroom, having just begun her first marital quarrel, during which she'd sighed: I guess I'm just saying that I think there's room for you to open your arms to more people than just yourself, and John, who'd heard it all before, was sitting on the bed removing his suits and her dresses from the garment bag when the phone rang. — What's up? he said.

Brady, said the telephone.

Afternoon, Mr. Brady, said John. What's the good word?

Say, Johnny boy—you mind if I call you Johnny?

Had anyone else been so presumptuous. John would have been filled with wrath. As it was, he was thrilled.

Downstairs, John and Brady shook hands. Brady was explaining: We want to make sure we always give the customer what he wants, where, when and how he wants it, at a low price and with no complications afterward. No complications may be the most important thing. That requires tact, foresight, and above all *innovation* on our part.

When he said that, he smiled with self-adulation over his latest acquisition, a hairless wrinked dwarf lady who whispered: Donald Duck! Donald Duck! and the men who went in to her had to pretend to be Donald Duck to make her happy.

Celia stood trailing her fingers along one of the railings which ran along one side of the administration room at Feminine Circus so that spectators such as herself could look down into all the various worlds, each of them as stuffy as a museum. To me, Feminine Circus was much the same as the SuperSaverStore where Irene used to go through heaps of cheap clothes for toddlers, trying to pick out Christmas presents for her cousins and her sister's boy while John very slowly smelled a genuine cedarwood shoetree. (Tyler, hiding behind a chin-high mountain of Date Flakes, watched Irene picking out childrens' books.) But to Celia this comparison would have rung entirely false. When she was thoroughly bored, she escaped into an echoing expectoration of dollar coins. Her own secret wish in playing the slots was always to get rid of this heavy burden of quarters which God had given her: when they came clattering out after she pushed the **CASH CREDIT** button, she felt pleased, even victorious; but once she'd gathered them into her fist she wondered what to do with them. In her pocket they made an uncomfortable bulge which resembled an erection. In the big plastic cup they weighed her down. When the machine ate them back again ("like a dog goggling his vomit," says some medieval tract on apostasy), she felt relief.

No, the house percentages are really quite small, Brady was explaining to her husband. For instance, if everyone in the world were to give me five minutes out of his life, I could live almost forever, and don't tell me any of those people would miss that time.

Retreating to the hotel room, Celia got underneath the bedcovers, turned on the television's remote control, and wrote:

```
protocol update
prep memo to Heidi
make John promise to do dishes 3 x/week
make calendar for Ellen
update for Jeff
floaters to cover breaks
order cannister mailers
adopt puppy?
dining room set
```

I'm a slick girl, the TV said. You wanna get slick with me? Get *Slick.* Now available in pharmacies near you. Federal restrictions may apply.

Celia's mind wandered. She pretended that she and John were hiking up Coyote Peak to see Napa Valley with its multi-greened corrugations of vineyard, and it was cool and windy with blue and turquoise shadows on the facing mountains, as if the newlyweds had entered one of the buccolic scenes on the labels of Calistoga mineral water. A tiny woodpecker drummed for them, accompanied by the buzz of a little plane. It no longer embarrassed her to be spinning fantasies. Sometimes clutched by insomnia, Celia had long since grown accustomed to imagining herself to sleep. She felt very secure to be married, and the inevitable disappointment after the wedding ceremony was best dealt with by careful planning for their future together, and, whenever that temporarily failed, by mental movies of her own devising.

She and John were supposed to meet Brady for lunch, but just as they arrived, Brady's cell phone rang and Brady began a long conversation by saying: Those girls usually come by the pair, but maybe I can get you one on open stock.

He put down the phone for a moment to lift his wineglass, and Celia heard the client say: Well, I like this shape here.

Winking at Celia, Brady picked up the phone and said: These can be shipped. They're very high quality.

Finally he hung up. Tapping his finger against his glass, he said to John: You know, they say a good glass is important when you drink good wine. You see the parallel?

Excuse me, Mr. Brady, said Celia, clearing her throat. These girls you're talking about are all virtual, right? I mean, nobody gets hurt, right?

Yeah, yeah, yeah, the man said boredly. These girls come in all versions.

Gazing upward, Celia discovered chandeliers like flowers, crystal beehives, and transparent glass spiderwebs.

Actually, Brady said to her, we'll give your husband a very special price. And listen, John. I can give you the same price for the next five years. Celia, after lunch I need to borow your husband for a minute. I guarantee I'll return him in better shape than I found him. Perfect balance.

Celia stared miserably at the tablecloth.

Come and see this one, John, Brady was saying. It is *gorgeous.* You'll see the hipbones. They're extremely elegant pieces. And extremely strong. And extremely elastic.

I guess it all goes together, Celia said dully.

From his shirt pocket, Brady removed the transparent cast or likeness of a human nipple as astoundingly beautiful as the crystal stopper of a thousand dollar glass decanter. The thing was a dodecahedron each of whose faces sent the light back in a different shade of blueness.

No, John, said Celia. You don't need another one.

Brady laughed. —I'll bet you two aren't the first pair who've come to blows in a place like this. And in a dispute like this, the wife always wins. Know how I know, John? Because you *brought* your wife. It's not about you and any of these so-called pieces. It's about you and her.

Celia was silent, so Brady patted her arm and said: You should give a Christmas present to your husband.

He's already very spoiled.

So spoil him a little more.

Do whatever you want, John. I don't feel so well. I'm going to lie down . . .

The air conditioning was as cold as a cretin's hand.

| 593 |

You have been summoned, Domino said pompously, lolling back on her purple-sequined wrists. All the girls, come and kneel around the Queen . . . Where's my ash-tray?

Here, ma'am. Yes, ma'am.

Oh, brother, said John. This is lame.

Beatrice, I want you right now to go get the bitch. You are not in any trouble. Just go an' get her.

That's not Beatrice, John said to himself.

The Queen lay very still, lolling around on her swollen, abscessed legs, scratching at the purple sequins.

Now, *Chocolate!* she laughed. Chocolate, you little *bitch!* Come here. Siddown. On your butt.

The other girl was hanging her head in the corner with her hand held out and her other hand on her thighs.

That's not Chocolate either, John realized.

I just brushed my hair, Domino was saying, smashing a beer bottle on the stage. Y'all are *crazy.* I want you to beat the bitch up. Take this, little motherfucker, and beat her up! I'm not playing. Awright. Now this is what we're gonna do.

The whores were sitting in the corner at stage left, pouting and quickly wiping their lips before their cigarettes.

An' every guilty woman, I want their pussies sewn shut, Domino mumbled. An' all the men—*everyone*—I want them all brought to me. —You know who you are? You're the first to have your pussy sewn shut. Do you want your teeth knocked out, too? How'd you like it if I took this cigarette and put it right out between your eyes? Oh, didn't it hurt enough for you to scream? Well, let's try it again, you little *slut.* Get out of my sight. Don't drink that beer. It's got that tramp's lipstick all over it. Come 'ere, Sapphire little one. I'm gonna give you one chance.

The little one quickly put the Queen's shoes on, and Justin tied them.

The Queen's belly was sagging.

You'll never be number one shotgun under me, she said. You'll never be a shot-caller anymore.

The tall man was smiling vaguely under the long matted hair as he started taking the collar off, holding the chain, and the lady-in-waiting bowing double . . .

Sapphire tried to cling to her ankle. —Let go of me, said the Queen.

That's not Justin, said John. That's not Sapphire.

(He was right. Domino had sold the real Sapphire to Brady long ago for five hundred dollars cash. Sapphire had lasted for months. She'd been one of Brady's star money-makers.)

I want you to beat this bitch into oblivion, Domino was saying. Someone in the audience gasped, and she quickly said: Don't worry, baby. It's all virtual.

Somebody booed her. Pretending not to hear, she said to the ersatz Justin: I want you to bring her back when she has one breath left. Just *one* breath.

This is pathetic, John thought. This is embarrassing. This is Feminine Circus.

When he and Celia got back to San Francisco, he went straight to the Wonderbar and almost shyly asked the barmaid, whom he didn't recognize, how business was, at which she froze in suspicion and fear, saying: We got no business here! and shouted something in Spanish, at which the solitary whore, fat, old and miniskirted, sent a hateful glance John's way and went out. John never saw Domino again.

| SOURCES |

All Biblical citations are from *The New Oxford Annotated Bible with the Apocrypha,* expanded edition (rev. standard), ed. Herbert G. May and Bruce M. Metzger (New York: Oxford University Press, 1973), although I have sometimes archaized certain passages.

BOOK I:–THE REDUCTION METHOD
Bacon epigraph—Sir Francis Bacon, *Advancement of Learning, Novum Organum, New Atlantis* (Chicago: Encyclopaedia Britannica, Inc., Great Books of the Western World, vol. 30), p. 107 (*Novum Organum* [1620], Book I, paragraph VI).

BOOK II:–IRENE
Dostoyevsky epigraph—Fyodor Dostoyevsky, *The Idiot,* trans. Constance Garnett (New York: Bantam, 1981 repr. of 1958 ed.; orig. Russian ed. 1869), p. 299.
Extract from *Irène's Cunt*—Lous Aragon, *Irène's Cunt,* trans. Alexis Lykiard (London: Velvet Books / Creation Books, 1996), p. 65.

BOOK III:–VISITS AND VISITATIONS
Police manual epigraph—Wayne W. Bennett and Kären M. Hess, *Criminal Investigation,* 3rd ed. (San Francisco: West Publishing Co., 1991), p. 298.
"Light and darkness, life and death . . ." —James M. Robinson, gen. ed., *The Nag Hammadi Library in English,* 3rd. rev. ed., trans. and introduced by the members of the Coptic Gnostic Library Project of the Institute for Antiquity and Christianity, Claremont, California (San Francisco: HarperSanFrancisco, 1990), p. 142 (The Gospel of Philip, II, 3, 14–20).

BOOK IV:–BILLABLE HOURS
Sulfuric acid epigraph—H. Clark Metcalfe, John E. Williams, Joseph F. Castka, *Modern Chemistry* (New York: Holt, Rinehart and Winston, 1970), p. 258.

BOOK V:–THE MARK OF CAIN
Gnostic Scriptures epigraph—Robinson, p. 249 (Dialogue of the Savior).
Darwin on *Formica (Polyerges) rufescens*—Charles Darwin, *The Origin of Species by Means of Natural Selection* and *The Descent of Man and Selection in Relation to Sex* (Chicago: Encyclopaedia Britannica, Inc., Great Books of the Western World, no. 49, 1952), p. 2125 (*Origin*).

BOOK VI:–LADIES OF THE QUEEN
Psistratus and Athena epigraph—[attributed to Aristotle or one of his students], *The Athenian Constitution,* trans. P.J. Rhodes (New York: Penguin, 1984), pp. 56–57.

BOOK VIII:–SUNFLOWER
Romantic reaction epigraph—Antonio Gramsci, *Selections from the Prison Notebooks,* ed. & trans. Quentin Hoare and Goeffrey Nowell Smith (New York: International Publishers, 1981), p. 296.

BOOK X:–AN ESSAY ON BAIL
Bail for rape, kidnapping, etc.—Misdemeanor-Felony Bail Schedule in the Municipal Court of the City and County of San Francisco, State of California (effective date: August 15, 1997).

Extracts from and references to the California penal code—*West's California Codes,* 1997 Compact Edition (Saint Paul, Minn.: West Publishing Co., 1997), p. 70 (ch. 3, sec. 207).

Memorandum from the public defender's office re: police reports and perjury—Memo to all deputies, from Grace Suarez, Office of the Public Defender, Research Unit, dated 16 July 1991, re: *McLaughlin v. Riverside # 6: Assembling the Class Action.*

BOOK XI:–"EASIER THAN YOU MIGHT EVER DREAM" (CONTINUED)

Witches' curse epigraph—Pierre de Lancre (d. 1630), quoted in Kurt Seligmann, *Magic, Supernaturalism and Religion* (New York: Pantheon Books, 1948), p. 180 ("The Witch").

BOOK XIII:–"BUSINESS COMES FIRST"

Midas epigraph—Nathaniel Hawthorne, *Tales and Sketches* (New York: Library of America, 1982), p. 1199 ("The Golden Touch," in *A Wonder-Book for Girls and Boys, 1851).*

BOOK XVI:–THE QUEEN OF LAS VEGAS

Gnostic Scriptures epigraph—Robinson, p. 138 (*The Gospel of Thomas,* V, 5, II, 2, 114.20–25).

BOOK XVII:–BUYING THEIR DREAM HOUSE

Epigraph on circumcision—Mary Jane Sherfey, M.D., *The Nature and Evolution of Female Sexuality* (New York: Vintage, 1973), p. 87.

BOOK XIX:–A MEDITATION ON THE STOCK MARKET

Gnostic Scriptures epigraph—Robinson, p. 284 (*The Apocalypse of Adam,* V, 5, 15–20).

BOOK XXIII:–JUSTIN

Book of Mormon epigraph—*The Book of Mormon: An Account Written by the Hand of Mormon Upon Plates Taken from the Plates of Nephi,* trans. Joseph Smith, Jun. (Salt Lake City, Utah: The Church of Jesus Christ of Latter-day Saints, 1986 corr. ed; "first English edition published in 1830"), p. 383 (Hel. 6.27).

BOOK XXV:–THE TRUTH

Buddha epigraph—*The Teaching of Buddha* (Tokyo: Bukkyo Dendo Kyokai [Buddhist Promoting Foundation], 127th rev. ed., 1980), p. 108 ("Dharma," ch. 2, "The Theory of Mind-only and the Real State of Things," pt. III, "Real State of Things").

BOOK XXX:–LITTLE BABY BIRDS

Buddha epigraph—*The Teaching of Buddha,* p. 66 ("Buddha," ch. 3, "The Form of Buddha and His Virtues," pt. III, "Buddha's Virtue").

BOOK XXXI:–FILIAL DUTIES

Bible extract on Abraham: Genesis 20.1

Bible extract on the unburied dead: Jeremiah 16.4

Buddha extract: "Things do not come and go . . ."—*The Teaching of Buddha,* p. 106 ("Dharma," ch. 2, "The Theory of Mind-only and the Real State of Things," pt. II, "The Theory of Mind-Only").

Buddha extract: ". . . the mind that creates its surroundings . . ."—*The Teaching of Buddha,* p. 98 (loc. cit.)

BOOK XXXII:–THE FALL OF CANAAN

Buddha epigraph—*The Teaching of Buddha*, p. 376 ("The Way of Practice," ch. 2, "The Way of Practical Attainment," pt. IV, "Sacred Aphorisms").

Bible extract: "Why has the Lord pronounced all this great evil against us?"—Jeremiah 16.10–11.

BOOK XXXIV:–DAN SMOOTH

Gnostic Scriptures epigraph—Robinson, p. 342 (The Paraphrase of Shem, VII, 1, 10–15).

| ACKNOWLEDGMENTS |

I want to thank the following people and institutions for their assistance in this project:

Noah Richler of BBC Radio paid for the auditions of several Tenderloin whore-queens and tall men. At the San Francisco Public Defender's office, Ron Albers, Matt Gonzalez, Daro Inouye (who makes a cameo appearance as a friend of my entirely imaginary Henry Tyler) kindly answered many questions about bail and other legal-ethical matters. So did Al Graf and Geri Compana of Al Graf Bail Bonds in San Francisco and Roger Adair of Ace Bail Bonds in Sacramento. I would also like to thank the supervisory deputy D.A. in Sacramento, Albert Locher, for his time and trouble. Chuck Pfister in San Francisco and John Walsh and David McBride in Sacramento taught me a few fundamentals of private investigative procedure and gave me loads of local color.

Laurie Berkman, Debbie Trevellini, Jeanine Bray, an anonymous employee of Planned Parenthood (all of San Francisco), Shauna Heckert of the Feminist Women's Health Center (Sacramento), Regina Lorenzo and her friend Bill (New York City), and other women who wish to be unnamed gave me useful information on abortion clinics.

Ruth Ellis and her colleague Teddy at the Sacramento Room of the Sacramento Public Library allowed me to see some old photographs of the Sacramento region which added to the train context.

Mr. Jacob Dickinson of Los Angeles discussed chip design and security as it related to the RoboGraphix chapter.

Paul Wilner at the *San Francisco Examiner* got me access to the chief medical examiner's office, whose staff I would like to thank. Most of the notes I took there wound up in my long essay on violence, *Rising Up and Rising Down,* of which Paul published a smidgeon (not to mention the Geary Street and financial district chapters of this book). However, more than enough descriptions remained to be inlaid into the tale of Dan Smooth's demise. Dr. Jasper, Connie, and the autopsy doctor do not represent any particular real-life individuals.

Jonathon Keats of *San Francisco Magazine* was kind enough to publish a small excerpt from the beginning of this novel. He also encouraged, then rejected, the "Essay on Bail."

Jean Stein and Deborah Treisman, both then of *Grand Street,* published other snippets of this novel and sent me delicious cold cash. My thanks and friendship will always go to those two most nurturing Muses.

Vanessa Renwick protected, comforted and cherished me when a certain street prostitute and I were treated in a degrading fashion.

Against his better judgment, Paul Slovak at Viking permitted me to refrain from cutting the book by one-third. Paul, I want to thank you for having stood by me for so long.

(As for me, I was a good boy, too. Since I refused the page cut, I took a royalty cut instead.)

Mike Pulley and Lizzy Gray rode freight trains with me (Lizzy's maiden voyage took her all the way from Sacramento to West Sacramento. Mike's took him as far as Marysville before the heat got to him.) Mike got me access to the new Sacramento coroner's facility, which proved good for a few of Dan Smooth's finer moments. He also drove me around and kept me while I took note on various Sacramento and San Francisco street scenes. Mr. Kent Lacin listened patiently to my half-baked theories on Buddhism and drug addiction. William Linne discussed Gnostic Scriptures with me in and out of various Tenderloin bars. My old friend Ben Pax has chatted with me about Christian spiritual issues many times over the years. Some of our conversations meandered into the text, or at least stained it. Mr. Chuck Stevens and I met several nice Tenderloin prostitutes together. Mr. David Golden kept me cheerful company on a few nighttime Tenderloin strolls, and allowed me to use his car in place of a photographic tripod. Heaven the barmaid deserves a book of her own. Peter at City Lights bookstore has done me many kindnesses.

Larry McCaffrey and his wife and Sinda McCaffrey introduced me to the Imperial Valley and in particular to Slab City, a place of some interest to Henry Tyler. I just may write another novel set there.

Most of all, I would like to thank the San Francisco and Sacramento street prostitutes whom I have gotten to know over the years. Without them I never could have imagined "the life."